THE MAMMOTH BOOK OF
BEST NEW
SCIENCE FICTION

Also available

The Mammoth Book of 20th Century Science Fiction
The Mammoth Book of Best New Horror 16
The Mammoth Book of Celebrity Murder
The Mammoth Book of Celtic Myths and Legends
The Mammoth Book of Chess
The Mammoth Book of Comic Fantasy
The Mammoth Book of Comic Quotes
The Mammoth Book of Egyptian Whodunnits
The Mammoth Book of Extreme Science Fiction
The Mammoth Book of Famous Trials
The Mammoth Book of Great Detective Stories
The Mammoth Book of Great Inventions
The Mammoth Book of Haunted House Stories
The Mammoth Book of Historical Whodunnits
The Mammoth Book of Illustrated True Crime
The Mammoth Book of IQ Puzzles
The Mammoth Book of How It Happened: Ancient Egypt
The Mammoth Book of How It Happened: Ancient Rome
The Mammoth Book of How It Happened: Battles
The Mammoth Book of How It Happened: Trafalgar
The Mammoth Book of How It Happened: WWI
The Mammoth Book of How It Happened: WW II
The Mammoth Book of Jacobean Whodunnits
The Mammoth Book of Jokes
The Mammoth Book of Kakuro, Worduko and Super Sudoku
The Mammoth Book of King Arthur
The Mammoth Book of Maneaters
The Mammoth Book of Mountain Disasters
The Mammoth Book of New Terror
The Mammoth Book of New Jules Verne Adventures
The Mammoth Book of On The Edge
The Mammoth Book of On the Road
The Mammoth Book of Pirates
The Mammoth Book of Private Eye Stories
The Mammoth Book of Roaring Twenties Whodunnits
The Mammoth Book of Roman Whodunnits
The Mammoth Book of Secret Codes and Cryptograms
The Mammoth Book of Seriously Comic Fantasy
The Mammoth Book of Sex, Drugs & Rock 'n' Roll
The Mammoth Book of Short Spy Novels
The Mammoth Book of Sorcerers' Tales
The Mammoth Book of Space Exploration and Disasters
The Mammoth Book of SAS & Special Forces
The Mammoth Book of Special Operations
The Mammoth Book of Shipwrecks & Sea Disasters
The Mammoth Book of Sudoku
The Mammoth Book of Travel in Dangerous Places
The Mammoth Book of True Crime
The Mammoth Book of True War Stories
The Mammoth Book of Unsolved Crimes
The Mammoth Book of Vampires
The Mammoth Book of Vintage Whodunnits
The Mammoth Book of Wild Journeys
The Mammoth Book of Women's Fantasies
The Mammoth Book of Women Who Kill
The Mammoth Book of the World's Greatest Chess Games
The Mammoth Encyclopedia of Unsolved Mysteries

THE MAMMOTH BOOK OF BEST NEW SCIENCE FICTION

19th Annual Collection

Edited by
GARDNER DOZOIS

ROBINSON
London

Constable & Robinson Ltd
3 The Lanchesters
162 Fulham Palace Road
London W6 9ER
www.constablerobinson.com

First published in the USA by St Martin's Press 2006

First published in the UK by Robinson,
an imprint of Constable & Robinson Ltd 2006

A copy of the British Library Cataloguing in
Publication Data is available from the British Library

ISBN-13: 978-1-84529-423-6
ISBN-10: 1-84529-423-8

Printed and bound in the EU

1 3 5 7 9 10 8 6 4 2

CONTENTS

Acknowledgments	ix
Summation: 2005	xi
THE LITTLE GODDESS Ian McDonald	1
THE CALORIE MAN Paolo Bacigalupi	36
BEYOND THE AQUILA RIFT Alastair Reynolds	61
SECOND PERSON, PRESENT TENSE Daryl Gregory	88
THE CANADIAN WHO CAME ALMOST ALL THE WAY BACK FROM THE STARS Jay Lake and Ruth Nestvold	106
TRICERATOPS SUMMER Michael Swanwick	125
CAMOUFLAGE Robert Reed	136
A CASE OF CONSILIENCE Ken MacLeod	185
THE BLEMMYE'S STRATEGEM Bruce Sterling	195
AMBA William Sanders	222
SEARCH ENGINE Mary Rosenblum	248
PICCADILLY CIRCUS Chris Beckett	264
IN THE QUAKE ZONE David Gerrold	280
LA MALCONTENTA Liz Williams	359
THE CHILDREN OF TIME Stephen Baxter	366
LITTLE FACES Vonda N. McIntyre	379
COMBER Gene Wolfe	407
AUDUBON IN ATLANTIS Harry Turtledove	415
DEUS EX HOMINE Hannu Rajaniemi	457
THE GREAT CARUSO Steven Popkes	469
SOFTLY SPOKE THE GABBLEDUCK Neal Asher	484
ZIMA BLUE Alastair Reynolds	503
PLANET OF THE AMAZON WOMEN David Moles	521
THE CLOCKWORK ATOM BOMB Dominic Green	545
GOLD MOUNTAIN Chris Roberson	561
THE FULCRUM Gwyneth Jones	576
MAYFLY Peter Watts and Derryl Murphy	602
TWO DREAMS ON TRAINS Elizabeth Bear	615
ANGEL OF LIGHT Joe Haldeman	622
BURN James Patrick Kelly	629
Honourable Mentions: 2005	711

ACKNOWLEDGMENTS

The editor would like to thank the following people for their help and support: Susan Casper, Ellen Datlow, Gordon Van Gelder, Peter Crowther, Nicolas Gevers, David Pringle, Andy Cox, Jeste de Vries, Susan Marie Groppi, Karen Meisner, Jed Hartman, Andrew Wilson, Damien Broderick, Marty Halpern, Gary Turner, Chris Roberson, Ellen Asher, Andy Wheeler, Lou Anders, James A. Owen, Eileen Gunn, Mike Resnick, Cory Doctorow, Robert E. Howe, Darrell Schweitzer, Richard Freeburn, Patrick Swenson, Bridget McKenna, Marti McKenna, Jay Lake, Deborah Layne, Edward J. McFadden, Sheila Williams, Brian Bieniowski, Trevor Quachri, Jayme Lynn Blaschke, Lou Antonelli, Ruth Nestvold, Benjamin Rosenbaum, Joe Haldeman, Alastair Reynolds, Michael Swanwick, Ken MacLeod, Peter F. Hamilton, Stephen Baxter, Bruce Sterling, Kim Stanley Robinson, Paul McAuley, Gregory Benford, Vandana Singh, Ron Hahn, David Hartwell, Warren Lapin, Shawna McCarthy, Kelly Link, Gavin Grant, Gordon Linzner, Kathryn Wilham, Matthew Bey, Diane L. Walton, Gerard Houarner, David Chang, Steve Wilson, Dr. Henry Gee, Christopher Rowe, Gwenda Bond, Alan DeNiro, John Klima, Mark Rudolph, Eric M. Heideman, John O'Neill, Ian Nichols, Sally Beasley, Stuart Barrow, Roelf Goudriaan, John Kenny, William Rupp, Jason B. Sizemore, Sean Wallace, David Lee Summers, Steve Mohn, Holly Phillips, Peter Watts, Susan McGregor, Diane C. Watson, Vaughne Lee Hansen, Rich Horston, Mark R. Kelly, Mark Watson, Tim Pratt, Jonathan Strahan, and special thanks to my own editor, Marc Resnick.

Thanks are also due to Charles N. Brown, whose magazine *Locus* (Locus Publications, P.O. Box 13305, Oakland, CA 94661. $56 for a one-year subscription [twelve issues] via second class; credit card orders call 510 339-9198) was used as an invaluable reference source throughout the Summation; *Locus Online* (www.locusmag.com); edited by Mark R. Kelly, has also become a key reference source.

Thanks are also due to Ian Randal Strock and Warren Lapine of *Science Fiction Chronicle* (DNA Publications, Inc., P.O. Box 2988, Radford, VA 24143-2988. $45 for a one-year/twelve-issue subscription via second class), which was also used as a reference source throughout.

SUMMATION: 2005

It was a fairly quiet and stable year for the science fiction publishing world, with the only big changes (most of them negative, alas) coming in the struggling short fiction market. None of the long-established SF lines were lost, and there were no huge mergers of the sort that can have disastrous consequences for the publishing houses being absorbed. In 2004, we saw five new SF imprints and five young adult fantasy or SF imprints launched. While we seem to be over that growth spurt for the moment (no new imprints launched in 2005), most of the new imprints started in 2004 seem to have had successful initial seasons. Prometheus Books's new SF/fantasy imprint, Pyr, published fourteen books, and Phobos Books's new Phobos Impact imprint published four.

Once again, to the regret of some, SF didn't die – in fact, it seems to be doing pretty well. Many titles sold substantial numbers (although, admittedly, few of them sold well enough to get anywhere near the top of the fantasy food chain occupied by blockbusters such as J. K. Rowling's *Harry Potter and the Half-Blood Prince* and George R. R. Martin's *A Feast of Crows*), and though the field didn't expand again this year, as it had in 2004, it didn't significantly contract, either. Most of the changes in the publishing scene were relatively minor: Fitzhenry & Whiteside purchased Red Deer Press, which includes the Robert J. Sawyer Books SF imprint; Meisha Merlin went through an internal reorganization and switched distributors, as did ibooks (which seems to have survived both the tragic death of founder Byron Preiss and the departure early in 2006 of editor in chief Howard Zimmerman, who is starting his own book packaging company, Z File Inc.), and Bloomsbury acquired Walker. Jeff VanderMeer's Ministry of Whimsy Press closed down after several years.

There were major shakeups at Del Rey at the beginning of 2005, which have some industry insiders worried about the status of Del Rey as a distinctive imprint at Random House: Publishing director Anthony Ziccardi left for a job as deputy director at Pocket Books; editor Chris Schluep moved to Ballantine; senior editor Steve Saffel was fired, as was publicist Colleen Lindsay; Shelly Shapiro announced she would be stepping down as editorial director in order to begin working as an editor-at-large from home; and Scott Shannon joined Random House as vice president and deputy publisher of Del Rey, moving from Pocket Books, where he had been vice president and associate publisher. Earlier in 2005, Jim Minz had moved to Del Rey from Tor. In other editorial news, Juliet Ulman was promoted to senior editor at Bantam Spectra, Cindy Hwang has been promoted to executive editor at Penguin, Michelle Frey was promoted to executive editor at Knopf and Crown, and Jean Feiwel has been named senior vice president and publisher of a new children's unit at Holtzbrinck.

The future that's been predicted by cyberoptimists for years now, where computer technology brings about sweeping changes in the way that books get published and in the nature of books themselves, crept a bit closer to reality. Major publishers such as Random House, HarperCollins, and Holtzbrinck are investigating ways to provide their backlists and new books in a variety of electronic formats, hoping to avoid the problems that the music industry ran into with on-line music piracy. The e-book may not be quite as dead as many have thought. (See also the story about the "Amazon Shorts" program, below.)

The big story in the short fiction market this year, unfortunately negative, was the cancellation of the electronic magazines *SCI FICTION* and *The Infinite Matrix* (see below for more on this). Even as new magazines rush into publication, the traditional print magazines continue to struggle with declining circulation.

Asimov's Science Fiction registered a dismaying 23 percent loss in overall circulation in 2005, with subscriptions dropping from 23,933 to 18,050, and newsstand sales dropping from 3,936 to 3,397; sell-through dropped from 34 percent to 29 percent. Sheila Williams completed her first year as new Asimov's editor this year. *Analog Science Fiction & Fact* registered an 8.2 percent loss in overall circulation in 2005, much less than last year's 18 percent drop, losing 3,899 in subscriptions, with subscriptions dropping from 27,816 to 25,933, while newsstand sales dropped from 5,456 to 4,614; sell-through dropped from 50 percent to 30 percent. *The Magazine of Fantasy & Science Fiction*, although still lower in overall circulation than *Asimov's* and *Analog*, was at least able to put the brakes on a swiftly dropping circulation this year in a way that the other magazines have not been able to do (as Charles Brown of *Locus* says, "Flat is the new up!"), registering only a 1 percent drop in overall circulation, with subscriptions dropping from 15,033 to 14,918, while newsstand sales declined from 3,886 to 3,822; sell-through actually *increased*, from 40 percent to 44 percent. Circulation figures for 2005 are not yet available for *Realms of Fantasy*, but their 2004 figures show them registering a 2.7 percent loss in overall circulation from 2003, with subscriptions dropping from 18,337 to 17,191, but newsstand sales rising from 8,995 to 9,398, the second year in a row of gains in newsstand sales; sell-through also increased, from 14 percent to 20 percent.

Interzone, which had seemed just about down for the count only a couple of years ago, returned to full vigor in 2005 under new editor Andy Cox, who completed his first full year, publishing six issues, including *Interzone*'s two hundredth issue. The quality of the fiction has been high, including work from both old *Interzone* regulars such as Dominic Green and new *Interzone* stalwarts such as Jason Stoddard. The magazine switched to high gloss full-color partway through the year (from stapled to perfect-bound), making it a more handsome magazine than it's been at any time in its long lifetime.

Amazing published two issues and then announced early in 2005 that it was going "on hiatus," for reasons that weren't entirely clear. Nothing has subsequently been heard from them, and I suspect, knowing the history of the magazine market, that this is probably the last we'll see of *Amazing* in this particular incarnation.

The British *Postscripts*, edited by Peter Crowther with an assist by Nicholas Gevers, one of two high-end magazines that debuted in 2004, solidly established itself throughout 2005 as a thoroughly professional magazine in every way except circulation. In fact, it published several of the year's best stories in several different genres – it features a mix of science fiction, fantasy, slipstream, horror, mystery, and even some mainstream fiction – by writers such as Alastair Reynolds, Gene Wolfe, Chris Roberson, Joe Hill, Stephen Baxter, Eric Brown, Jack Dann, Adam Roberts, and others. I consider it to be the most promising new magazine of the twenty-first century to date. *Argosy*, the other high-end launch of 2004 (and the one, in fact, that drew most of the buzz at the time), now being edited by publisher James Owen after several changes in editorial personnel. It spent most of the last two years struggling with distribution problems with the chain bookstores and managed only one issue this year, early in 2005; two more are promised for next year. Let's hope that Owen can work through their difficulties and get this magazine back on its feet.

While the traditional professional magazines struggled, new magazines optimistically threw themselves into the fray (most of them are discussed in the semiprozine section below). One that also promises to operate on a high professional level is *Subterranean*, edited by Subterranean Press editor William Schafer, a mixed SF/horror magazine stuffed with big names such as Harlan Ellison, Robert Silverberg, George R. R. Martin, Joe R. Landsdale, Jack McDevitt, and Caitlin R. Kiernan. Since I didn't actually see them until pretty late in the year, I'm going to hold consideration of stuff from *Subterranean* over for next year's book, but this could well become a very important market in years to come.

Another market operating on a professional level launched this year, a cross between a magazine and an anthology, *InterNova, the Magazine of International Science Fiction*, edited by Ronald M. Hahn, Olaf G. Hilscher, and Michael K. Iwoleit. This publication performs the very valuable service of bringing stories by SF writers from all over the world to the English-speaking market. The first issue featured good work by Vandana Singh, Eric Brown, Aleksandar Ziljak, Lino Aldani, and others.

SF stories continued to pop up in unlikely places this year, including a series of short-shorts by many of the field's big-name authors in nearly every issue of the science magazine *Nature*, and a series of shorts by authors such as Joe Haldeman, Charles Stross, Gregory Benford, Paul Di Filippo, and others appearing in the newly launched Australian science magazine *Cosmos*. Amazon.com also launched a program called "Amazon Shorts," where you can purchase individual stories over the Internet. There were stories available in several different genres, including excellent SF stories by Michael Swanwick, Mary Rosenblum, Allen Steele, Walter Jon Williams, James Morrow, Terry Bisson, Lucius Shepard, and others. SF even penetrated into the usually impregnable bastion of *The Best American Short Stories* this year, the latest issue of which featured several stories that had originally been published in the genre.

It wasn't an entirely downbeat year in the magazine market (Interzone pulled itself back from the brink of extinction, *Realms of Fantasy* went up in newsstand sales, *F&SF* at least didn't continue to slide at the rate that it had been sliding, even if it didn't go up), but it's hard to be too optimistic in the face of these circulation figures either. These magazines shouldn't be counted out yet; one of their advantages, especially for the more-or-less digest-sized titles, is that they're cheap to produce, meaning you don't need to sell a lot of them in order to make a profit – still, you have to sell some of them, and the fact that circulation is continuing to slide, especially with *Asimov's* and *Analog*, is worrisome. Fiction magazines face a large number of problems in today's newsstand market (there really isn't any place for them, since they don't really fit into any of the established display niches), and there may be only a few years left to rebuild circulation for most of the professional SF magazines, if they're going to survive.

If they don't survive, my fear is that we'll end up more or less where the horror genre ended up after the collapse of the Big Horror Boom of the '80s: a lot of stories being published in semiprozines and in electronic magazines, but no decent-paying *professional* markets left, so it not only becomes harder for readers to find stories (there no longer being a central source that everybody knows they should check), it becomes harder for writers to make any kind of money by writing them. The reader savvy enough to know where to look for stories may not even notice any difference. There'll still be plenty of SF stories out there to be read, but it makes things even harder for the *writers*, in an area where many of them already write short fiction against their own economic best interests – which may eventually discourage some writers from even bothering to try.

That's why I'm urging everybody who reads these words, if you like there being a lot of short SF and fantasy out there where it can be easily found, to take the time to *subscribe* to one of the genre magazines. It's never been easier to subscribe to most of the genre magazines since you can now do it electronically on-line with the click of a few buttons, without even a trip to the mailbox. In the Internet age, you can also subscribe from overseas just as easily as you can from the United States, something formerly difficult-to-impossible. Internet sites such as *Fictionwise* (www.fictionwise.com), sell electronic downloadable versions of many of the magazines to be read on your PDA or home computer, something becoming increasingly popular with the computer-savvy set. Therefore, I'm going to list the URLs for those magazines that have Web sites: *Asimov's* site is at www.asimovs.com. *Analog's* site is at www.analogsf.com. *The Magazine of Fantasy & Science Fiction's* site is at www.sfsite.com/fsf. *Interzone* can be subscribed to on-line at www.ttapress.com/onlinestore1.html. *Postscripts* can be subscribed to on-line at www.pspublishing.co.uk/postscripts.asp. *Subterranean* can be subscribed to on-line at www.subterraneanpress.com. *InterNova, the Magazine of International Science Fiction*, can be subscribed to at www.inter.nova-sf.de.

And here are the subscription addresses for more traditional mail subscriptions for the professional magazines.

The Magazine of Fantasy & Science Fiction, Spilogale, Inc., P.O. Box 3447, Hoboken, NJ 07030, annual subscription – $44.89 in U.S.; *Asimov's Science Fiction*, Dell Magazines, 6 Prowitt Street, Norwalk, CT 06855 – $43.90 for annual subscription in U.S.; *Analog Science Fiction and Fact*, Dell Magazines, 6 Prowitt Street, Norwalk, CT 06855 – $43.90 for annual subscription in U.S.; *Postscripts*, PS Publishing, Hamilton House, 4 Park Avenue, Harrogate HG2 9BQ, England, UK, published quarterly, £30 to £50 outside the UK; *Interzone*, TTA Press, 5 Martins Lane, Witcham, Ely, Cambs CB6 2LB, England, UK, $36 for a six-issue subscription, make checks payable to "TTA Press"; *Argosy Magazine*, Coppervale International, P.O. Box 1421, Taylor, AZ, 85939, $49.95 for a six-issue subscription; *Realms of Fantasy*, Sovereign Media Co. Inc., P.O. Box 1623, Williamsport, PA 17703, $16.95 for an annual subscription in the U.S.; *Subterranean*, Subterranean Press, P.O. Box 190106, Burton, MI 48519, four-issue subscription (U.S.), $22, four-issue subscription (int'l), $36.

Subscribe now, however you do it, if you want to help ensure the survival of the print SF/fantasy magazines as we know them.

Let's now turn to the Internet scene, which is always a place of rapid change. That was especially true this year, and not always for the better. The most downbeat story in the whole short fiction market this year, in fact, on-line or off, was the death of Ellen Datlow's *SCI FICTION* (www.scifi.com/scifiction), which was killed by shortsighted corporate bean counters at The Sci Fi Channel after six years of stellar performance. Under Datlow's editorship, *SCI FICTION* had become the most important and universally recognized place on the Internet to reliably find SF, fantasy, and horror of high professional quality, and its loss is a blow to the entire genre. Although it's not much consolation, at least it went out on a high note, publishing good stories this year by Vonda N. McIntyre, Howard Waldrop, Jay Lake and Ruth Nestvold, Lucius Shepard, A. M. Dellamonica, Elizabeth Hand, Elizabeth Bear, Jeffrey Ford, Bruce McAllister, and others. Eileen Gunn's *The Infinite Matrix* (www.infinitematrix.net) also threw in the towel after a couple of years of trying to make bricks without straw once their funding dried up, although they still managed to publish a lot of interesting material during the year, including an excellent story by Cory Doctorow; stories by Robert Sheckley, Rudy Rucker, Nisi Shawl, and others; regular columns by Howard Waldrop and David Langford, and even a whole novel by Richard Kadrey.

With these leaders gone, the question in the on-line market now becomes, is there any other Internet fiction site that will be able to step up to the plate and take *SCI FICTION*'s place as the site to look at first when you want to find good SF and fantasy on-line? If so, my money's on *Strange Horizons* (www.strangehorizons.com), which still publishes too much slipstream, fantasy, and soft horror for my taste, but which also published some of the year's best SF stories this year by David Moles, Liz Williams, and Elizabeth Bear, as well as good stuff in various genres by Theodora Goss, Jason Stoddard, Anil Menon, Marguerite Reed, and others. Another candidate might be new electronic magazine *Aeon*, available for download through subscription (see their Web site at www.aeonmagazine.com for subscription information), which published good stuff this year by Joe Hill, Howard V. Hendrix, Carrie Richerson, Jay Lake, and others. *Oceans of the Mind*, also available by electronic subscription (see their Web site at www.trantorpublications.com/oceans.htm for subscription information), bucks the trend dominant elsewhere on-line by publishing mostly core science fiction, which is a welcome change in a market where the default position seems to be to publish slipstream and horror instead. The fiction here seemed somewhat weaker than it has been in other years, but they still managed to do worthwhile fiction by John Alfred Taylor, David Drake, Ryck Neube, Cherith Baldry, and others. A big factor in this market next year may be two flashy new electronic magazines, *Orson Scott Card's Intergalactic Medicine Show* (www.intergalacticmedicineshow.com), edited by Card, which debuted late in the year, and is available for download through subscription, and *Jim Baen's Universe* (subtitled *A Three-Ring Circus of Science Fiction, Fantasy, and Fact*), edited by Eric Flint (www.baensuniverse.com), which will start up in early 2006, and also will be available for download through subscription; see their respective Web sites for subscription information.

There are also lots of sites that feature mostly slipstream, literary surrealism, and soft horror, there's some good reading to be found on these sites, although only very occasionally anything that comes even close to core SF. One such site, *Lenox Avenue*, died this year as well, but there are still plenty of them. Among the best are *Revolution SF* (www.revolutionsf.com), *Fortean Bureau – A Magazine of Speculative Fiction* (www.forteanbureau.com), *Abyss and Apex: A Magazine of Speculative Fiction* (www.abyssandapex.com); *Ideomancer Speculative Fiction* (www.ideomancer.com); *Futurismic* (www.futurismic.com/fiction/index.html) and *Bewildering Stories* (www.bewilderingstories.com).

There's also a lot of good *reprint* SF and fantasy stories to be found out there on the Internet. Sites where reprint stories can be accessed for free include the British *Infinity Plus* (www.infinityplus.co.uk), which has a wide selection of good quality reprint stories, in addition to biographical and bibliographical information, book reviews, interviews, and critical essays. *Strange Horizons*, *SCI FICTION*, and *The Infinite Matrix*; (*SCI FICTION* in particular, while it stays up, anyway) has a substantial archive of "classic reprints." Most of the sites that are associated with existent print magazines, such as *Asimov's*, *Analog*, and *The Magazine of Fantasy & Science Fiction*, also have extensive archives of material, both fiction and nonfiction, previously published by the print versions of the magazines, and some of them regularly run teaser excerpts from stories coming up in forthcoming issues.

If you're willing to pay a small fee, though, an even greater range of reprint stories becomes available. Perhaps the best such site is *Fictionwise* (www.fictionwise.com), where you can buy downloadable e-books and stories to read on your PDA or home computer. In addition to individual stories, you can also buy "fiction bundles" here, which amount to electronic collections; as well as a selection of novels in several different genres. You can also subscribe to downloadable versions of several of the SF magazines here, in a number of different formats. A similar site is *ElectricStory* (www.electricstory.com), where, in addition to the downloadable stuff (both stories and novels) you can buy, you can also access for free movie reviews by Lucius Shepard, articles by Howard Waldrop, and other critical material. Access for a small fee to both original and reprint SF stories is also offered by *Alexandria Digital Literature* (http://alexlit.com).

There are other reasons to go Web-surfing, though, other than finding fiction to read. There are many general interest sites that publish lots of interviews, critical articles, reviews, and genre-oriented news of various kinds. The site I check most frequently, nearly every day, and perhaps the most valuable genre-oriented site on the entire Internet, is *Locus Online* (www.locusmag.com), the on-line version of the newsmagazine *Locus*. Not only is this often the first place in the genre to find fast-breaking news, you can also access an incredible amount of information, including book reviews, critical lists, obituary lists, links to reviews and essays appearing outside the genre, and links to extensive database archives such as the Locus Index to Science Fiction and the Locus Index to Science Fiction Awards. Other essential sites include: *Science Fiction Weekly* (www.scifi.com/sfw), more media-and-gaming oriented than

Locus Online, but still featuring news and book reviews, as well as regular columns by John Clute, Michael Cassutt, and Wil McCarthy; *Tangent Online* (www.tangentonline.com), one of the few places on the Internet to access a lot of short fiction reviews; *Best SF* (www.bestsf.net), another great review site, and one of the other few places that makes any attempt to regularly review short fiction venues; *SFRevu* (www.sfsite.com/sfrevu), a review site that specializes in media and novel reviews; the *SF Site* (www.sfsite.com), which not only features an extensive selection of reviews of books, games, and magazines, interviews, critical retrospective articles, letters, and so forth, plus a huge archive of past reviews, but also serves as host site for the Web pages of *The Magazine of Fantasy & Science Fiction* and *Interzone*; SFF NET (www.sff.net), which features dozens of home pages and "newsgroups" for SF writers, plus sites for genre-oriented "live chats"; the *Science Fiction Writers of America* page (www.sfwa.org), where news, obituaries, award information, and recommended reading lists can be accessed; *Audible* (www.audible.com) and *Beyond 2000* (www.beyond2000.com), where SF-oriented radio plays can be accessed; *The Internet Review of Science Fiction* (www.irosf.com), which features both short fiction reviews and novel reviews, as well as critical articles; and *Lost Pages* (http://lostpages.net), which features some fiction as well as the critical stuff. Multiple Hugo winner David Langford's on-line version of his funny and iconoclastic fanzine Ansible is available at http://news.ansible.co.uk, and *Speculations* (www.speculations.com) a long-running site that dispenses writing advice, and writing-oriented news and gossip (although to access most of it, you'll have to subscribe to the site).

If you can't find a site, Google for it; things change *fast* in the Internet world.

It was another chaotic year in the semiprozine market, with promising new magazines being born even as others seemed to be struggling.

Warren Lapine's DNA Publications suffered another year of being unable to meet its announced publication schedules, with the exception of the newszine *Chronicle* (formerly *Science Fiction Chronicle*); the DNA group also lost two of its magazines, *Weird Tales* and the speculative poetry magazine *Mythic Delirium*. *Absolute Magnitude, the Magazine of Science Fiction Adventures and Fantastic, Stories of the Imagination* managed only one issue apiece this year; *Weird Tales*, which had been the most reliably published of the DNA fiction magazines, and which also managed only one issue this year, was sold to Wildside Press, and will become a bimonthly publication under the editorship of George H. Scithers, Darrell Schweitzer, and Wildside's editor John Betancourt. Wildside also published one issue this year of *H. P. Lovecraft's Magazine of Horror* (which seems a bit redundant with *Weird Tales* added to the stable), and launched a slick new fantasy magazine, called, appropriately enough, *Fantasy Magazine*, edited by

Sean Wallace. The premier issue featured strong work by Jeff Ford, Tim Pratt, Eugie Foster, and others.

Once again, I saw no issues this year of *Century*, *Orb*, *Altair*, *Terra Incognita*, *Spectrum SF*, *Jupiter*, or *Artemis Magazine: Science and Fiction for a Space-Faring Society*, and I'm beginning to think these magazines should be considered dead. There were supposedly three issues of *Neo-Opsis* this year, but I didn't see them.

There were no issues of *Eidolon* in magazine format, but apparently there's going to be an *Eidolon* anthology in 2006. I also didn't see any issue of the other Australian semiprozine, *Aurealis*. I saw two issues of the Irish fiction semiprozine *Albedo One* this year, one of *Tales of the Unanticipated*, two of the sword and sorcery magazine *Black Gate*, one of newcomer *Fictitious Force*, and one of the long-running *Space and Time*.

There's a whole block now of similar "slipstreamish" fiction semiprozines that produce a lot of enjoyable fiction every year, although you'll rarely (if ever) find any core science fiction there (and only occasionally genre fantasy). *Lady Churchill's Rosebud Wristlet*, the first of these and still the flagship of the slipstream movement, published three issues this year, and featured good work by Bruce McAllister, Eric Schaller, Richard Parks, John Waters, and others. *Electric Velocipede* also published three issues, and good work by Mark W. Tiedemann, Liz Williams, and others. *Flytrap* (which was particularly strong this year, with stories by Theodora Goss, Jeff Ford, Jay Lake, and Sonya Taaffe). *Say . . .* and *Full Unit Hookup: A Magazine of Exceptional Literature* managed one issue apiece. *Talebones: The Magazine of Science Fiction and Dark Fantasy*, had two issues, with good stuff by Ken Scholes and James Van Pelt; and the Alternate History magazine *Paradox* managed two as well.

Turning now to the more vigorous of the fiction semiprozines, at least judging by how well they meet their production schedules. There were six issues of the Australian magazine *Andromeda Spaceways Inflight Magazine*; the scheduled four issues of the long-running Canadian magazine *On Spec*; three issues of a new fantasy magazine edited by David Lee Summers, the former editor of *Hadrosaur Tales*, called *Tales of the Talisman*; and the scheduled four issues of a new magazine called *Apex Science Fiction and Horror Digest*. The leading British semiprozine, *The Third Alternative*, which usually keeps to schedule, published only two issues this year, but editor Andy Cox should be cut some slack, as he was also busy shepherding sister magazine *Interzone* through its first full year under his editorship. (*The Third Alternative*, which is going to concentrate more on horror now that *Interzone* is there to absorb the occasional SF story they used to run, is going to change its name to *Black Static* in 2006. Maybe not the best idea in the world, since they'll lose all the reputation they'd built up as *The Third Alternative*, and maybe confuse some readers as well, but they didn't ask me; we'll see how it goes.) *Andromeda Spaceways Inflight Magazine* is very uneven in tone and quality from issue to issue – not surprising, as the magazine is edited by someone different every time – one of a group of rotating editors. This has never seemed like a good idea to me, as it makes it hard for a magazine to develop a distinctive editorial "voice" or personality. The best stuff from *Andromeda Spaceways* this year included stories by Stephen Dedman, Lou Antonellia, and Sandra McDonald. I continue to find most of the stuff in *On Spec* to be rather gray, although the covers were great, as usual. The best stuff there included stories by Leah Bobet, Jack Skillingstead, and E. Thomas. Nothing in *Apex Science Fiction and Horror Digest* is as yet running at a high professional level, but the magazine deserves encouragement simply for meeting its production schedule, not at all an easy thing to do, and there's always room for improvement.

I don't follow the horror semiprozine market anymore; as far as I can tell from a cursory look, the current horror magazines at the moment seem to include *Cemetery Dance*, *Black Static*, *Weird Tales*, and *H. P. Lovecraft's Magazine of Horror*, with horror also to be found in *Talebones*, *Subterranean*, *Postscripts*, *The Magazine of Fantasy & Science Fiction*, *Apex Science Fiction and Horror Digest*, and probably other places as well.

The critical magazine market has been whittled away, and now there are really only three of them left. As always, if you can only afford one magazine in this category, then the one to get is *Locus: The Magazine of the Science Fiction and Fantasy Field*, edited by multiple Hugo winner Charles N. Brown, which remains, as it has for years, an indispensable source of information, news, and reviews for anyone interested in the science fiction field. *Chronicle* (formerly *Science Fiction Chronicle*), although not quite so vital as *Locus*, is also full of interesting information, and actually supplements it quite well; editor John Douglas was replaced by Ian Randall Strock, but the magazine has managed to stay on a reliable schedule after a couple of shaky years when it was missing issues. David G. Hartwell's *The New York Review of Science Fiction*, perhaps the most reliably published magazine in the entire semiprozine field, having kept to its schedule like clockwork now for more than a decade, is more eclectic than the straight newsmagazines, publishing in-depth critical essays on a variety of academic and pop-culture subjects relating to science fiction now, as well as reading lists, letters, memoirs, and japes of various sorts.

And that's really about all there is left. Everything above this level are heavy professional journals, probably more for the academic reader than the average citizen.

Locus, The Magazine of the Science Fiction & Fantasy Field, Locus Publications, Inc., P.O. Box 13305, Oakland, CA 94661 – $60.00 for a one-year, first-class subscription, twelve issues; ***The New York Review of Science Fiction,*** Dragon Press, P.O. Box 78, Pleasantville, NY, 10570 –

$36.00 per year, make checks payable to "Dragon Press", twelve issues; *Black Static*, TTA Press, 5 Martins Lane, Witcham, Ely, Cambs. CB6 2LB, England, UK – $36.00 for a six-issue subscription, checks made payable to "TTA Press"; *Talebones, a Magazine of Science Fiction & Dark Fantasy*, 5203 Quincy Ave SE, Auburn, WA 98092 – $20.00 for four issues; *On Spec, the Canadian Magazine of the Fantastic*, P.O. Box 4727, Edmonton, AB, Canada T6E 5G6 – $22.00 for a one-year (four-issue) subscription; *Neo-Opsis Science Fiction Magazine*, 4129 Carey Rd., Victoria, BC, V8Z 4G5 – $24.00 Canadian for a four-issue subscription; Albedo, Albedo One Productions, 2 Post Road, Lusk, Co., Dublin, Ireland – $32.00 for a four-issue airmail subscription, make checks payable to "Albedo One"; *Absolute Magnitude, the Magazine of Science Fiction Adventures, Fantastic, Stories of the Imagination, Dreams of Decadence, Chronicle* – all available from DNA Publications, P.O. Box 2988, Radford, VA 24142-2988 – all available for $16 for a one-year subscription, although you can get a group subscription to four DNA fiction magazines for $60 a year; with *Chronicle* $45 a year (12 issues), all checks payable to "D.N.A. Publications"; *Tales of the Unanticipated*, P.O. Box 8036, Lake Street Station, Minneapolis, MN 55408 – $28 for a four-issue subscription (three or four years' worth) in the U.S.A, $31 in Canada, $34 overseas; *Artemis Magazine: Science and Fiction for a Space-Faring Society*, LRC Publications, 1380 E. 17th St., Suite 201, Brooklyn, NY 11230-6011 – $15 for a four-issue subscription, checks payable to LRC Publications; *Lady Churchill's Rosebud Wristlet*, Small Beer Press, 176 Prospect Avenue, Northampton, MA 01060 – $16.00 for four issues; *Say . . .*, The Fortress of Worlds, P.O. Box 1304, Lexington, KY 40588-1304 – $10.00 for two issues in the U.S. and Canada; *Full Unit Hookup: A Magazine of Exceptional Literature*, Conical Hats Press, 622 West Cottom Avenue, New Albany, IN 47150-5011 – $12.00 for a three-issue subscription; *Flytrap*, Tropism Press, P.O. Box 13322, Berkeley, CA 94712-4222 – $16 for four issues, checks to Heather Shaw; *Electric Velocipede*, Spilt Milk Press, P.O. Box 663, Franklin Park, NJ 08823 – http://www.electricvelocipede.com; $15 for a four-issue subscription; *Andromeda Spaceways Inflight Magazine*, P.O. Box 127, Belmont, Western Australia, 6984 – www.andromedaspaceways.com; $35.00 for a one-year subscription; *Tales of the Talisman*, Hadrosaur Productions, P.O. Box 2194, Mesilla Park, NM 88047-2194 – $24.00 for a four-issue subscription; *Space and Time, the Magazine of Fantasy, Horror, and Science Fiction*, Space and Time, 138 West 70th Street (4B), New York, NY 10023-4468 – $10.00 for a one-year (two-issue) subscription; *Black Gate*, New Epoch Press, 815 Oak Street, St. Charles, IL 60174 – $29.95 for a one-year (four-issue) subscription; *Paradox*, Paradox Publications, P.O. Box 22897, Brooklyn, New York 11202-2897 – $15.00 for a one-year (four-issue) subscription, *Cemetery Dance*, CD Publications, 123-B Industry Lane, Unit #7, Forest Hill, MD 21050 – $27.00 for six issues;

Fantasy Magazine, Wildside Press, Sean Wallace, 9710 Traville Gateway Drive, #234, Rockville, MD 20850 – annual subscription (four issues) $20 in the U.S., $25 Canada and overseas; *Weird Tales*, Wildside Press, 9710 Traville Gateway Drive, #234, Rockville, MD 20850 – annual subscription (four issues) $24 in the U.S., *H. P. Lovecraft's Magazine of Horror*, Wildside Press, 9710 Traville Gateway Drive, #234, Rockville, MD 20850 – annual subscription (four issues) $19.95 in the U.S.A.; *Fictitious Force*, Jonathan Laden, 1024 Hollywood Avenue, Silver Spring, MD 20904 – $16 for four issues; *Apex Science Fiction and Horror Digest*, Apex Publications, 4629 Riverman Way, Lexington, KY 40515 – $18.00 for a one-year, four-issue subscription.

There was no clearly dominant original anthology this year, in either SF or fantasy, although there were several pretty-good-overall anthologies that featured a few major stories apiece.

The front runners for the title of best original SF anthology of the year, although none of them could claim a clear-cut victory, were probably Constellations (DAW), edited by Peter Crowther, *Down These Dark Spaceways* (SFBC), edited by Mike Resnick, and *Nova Scotia: New Scottish Speculative Fiction* (Crescent); edited by Neil Williamson and Andrew J. Wilson. *Constellations* contained more weak stories than Crowther's other recent anthologies, *Moon Shots* and *Mars Probes*, and featured too many fantasy stories for my taste – but it also included some of the year's best SF stories, by Alastair Reynolds, Gwyneth Jones, and Paul McAuley, other good SF stories by Stephen Baxter, Eric Brown, and others, as well as quirky fantasy/slipstream stuff by Ian McDonald and Adam Roberts, and at least one straight mainstream story. *Down These Dark Spaceways*, an SF Book Club original, proved remarkably solid in spite of what seemed an unpromising premise (the hackneyed old "hard-boiled detective stories recast as SF" motif). It featured two of the year's best novellas, by David Gerrold and Robert Reed, as well as good work by Jack McDevitt, Resnick himself, and others. *Nova Scotia; New Scottish Speculative Fiction* is, as the title indicates, a "regional" anthology, with the usual quirks and contradictions of same (with some people selected as "Scottish authors" on very dubious grounds). Unlike many recent anthologies of this type, most of the stories here do have a strong regional flavor (sometimes too much so; one story is written in such a heavy dialect as to be nearly incomprehensible) but at least the anthology collects some first-rate stories, the best being by total newcomer Hannu Rajaniemi (who manages the remarkable feat of out-Strossing Charles Stross with his very first story) and relative veteran Ken MacLeod (with a clever reply to James Blish's famous "A Case of Conscience"). Also included is a first-rate fantasy by Jane Yolen, intriguing SF/fantasy hybrids by Charles Stross and A. J. McIntosh, and good work by Jack Deighton, John Grant, Neil Williamson, and others.

Another regional anthology, *Tesseracts Nine: New Canadian Speculative Fiction* (Edge), edited by Nalo Hopkinson and Geoff Ryman, may have a claim on the title of follow-up candidate for best original SF anthology – it's uneven in quality, with a fair amount of weak work, but it does feature an excellent story by Peter Watts and Darryl Murphy, plus good stuff by Jerome Stueart, Candas Jane Dorsey, Elisabeth Vonarburg, Pat Forde, and others. Other candidates were *Cosmic Tales: Adventures in Far Futures* (Baen), edited by T. K. F. Weisskopf, and *Gateways* (DAW), edited by Martin H. Greenberg. Both of these tended to be solid rather than exceptional, but they did feature a decent amount of good-quality work, and so were a good bet for your money. Of the two, *Cosmic Tales: Adventures in Far Futures* shades *Gateways* by a hair, in my opinion, even though most of the stories in the Weisskopf anthology don't really fit my definition of "far future" stories. There's enjoyable work by Paul Chafe, James P. Hogan, Mark L. Van Name, and others in *Cosmic Tales*, and enjoyable work by Gregory Benford, Kristine Kathryn Rusch, Irene Radford, and others in *Gateways*, along with one of Robert Scheckley's last stories. A step or two below these are *I, Alien* (DAW) edited by Mike Resnick, and *Women of War* (DAW), edited by Tanya Huff and Alexander Potter – entertaining but mostly minor stuff, probably worth your money in entertainment value at their relatively low mass-market prices. Yet another regional anthology, *Future Washington* (WSFA Press); edited by Ernest Lilley, was somewhat disappointing overall, especially since the strongest story here (by a considerable margin), Cory Doctorow's "Human Readable," had only the most tenuous of connections to Washington itself. The book's also somewhat disappointing in its bleak uniformity of tone, with story after story showing future Washington destroyed, drowned, in flames, ravaged by terrorists, torn by riots, Balkanized by civil war, and so on. Apparently dredging up any sort of optimism about the nation's future is beyond the abilities of most SF writers at the moment, although an upbeat or even utopian story or two would have made for a welcome variation of tone.

There was an Alternate Worlds anthology this year, *Alternate Generals III* (Baen), edited by Harry Turtledove. Although not as strong as Turtledove's *The First Heroes: New Tales of the Bronze Age*, from last year, and less freewheeling (*First Heroes* pushed the edge of the envelope for Alternate History stories in several respects), the more-conventional *Alternate Generals III* does feature some worthwhile stuff. The best stories here are by William Sanders and Lee Allred, but there's also good work by Mike Resnick, Judith Tarr, A. M. Dellamonica, the late Chris Bunch, and others. (It may be overpriced as a hardcover, though – I would have thought it would sell better as a mass-market paperback.) There were two "tribute" anthologies, honoring dead authors by encouraging other authors to produce work influenced by their style and concerns, or set in fictional worlds they'd created: *The*

Enchanter Completed (Baen), edited by Harry Turtledove, honoring L. Sprague de Camp, and *Hal's World* (Wildside), edited by Shane Tourtellotte, honoring Hal Clement. The better of the two is the Turtledove, which features light but entertaining work by Michael F. Flynn, David Drake, Judith Tarr, Turtledove himself, and what may be Poul Anderson's last published story. It saddens me a bit, though, that almost all the authors here have picked De Camp's fantasy worlds to play in, mostly ignoring his science fictional ones – a new tale or two of the *Viagens Interplanetarias* would have been welcomed, at least by me. Most of the new fiction in *Hal's World* is rather weak, although the nonfiction tributes and memoirs are often quite interesting.

The trend toward "retro-pulp" anthologies, typified by last year's *All Star Zeppelin Adventure Stories* and *McSweeney's Enchanted Chamber of Astonishing Stories*, continued this year with *Adventure, Volume 1* (MonkeyBrainBooks), edited by Chris Roberson. Blurbed as "the all-genre, all-adventure pulp anthology for the new millennia!!," this unpretentious and easygoing anthology accomplishes exactly what it sets out to do. There's nothing of award caliber here, but many of the stories – spread across several different genres: SF, fantasy, horror, historical, mystery – are among the year's most enjoyable and fun to read, including stories by Kage Baker, Mike Resnick, John Meaney, Mark Finn, Neal Asher, Michael Kurland, Matthew Rossi, Roberson himself, and others. (Oddly, the stories here that don't work are the ones that are the most self-consciously "retro-pulp," crudely satirizing old pulp forms in a heavy-handed "Boy's Own Adventure" style – fortunately, there're only a couple of these.) A cross between a "retro-pulp" anthology and a tribute anthology is *The Mammoth Book of New Jules Verne Adventures* (Carroll & Graf), edited by Mike Ashley and Eric Brown. More tightly focused and specialized than *Adventure*, concentrated as it is on stories inspired by the work of one author, it suffers from the same weakness, in that the most unsuccessful stories descend into arch parody rather than admiring homage. Nevertheless, there is good work here by Stephen Baxter, Liz Williams, Adam Roberts, Brian Stableford, Eric Brown, Peter Crowther, and others. Jules Verne also showed up in Eric Brown's chapbook novella *The Extraordinary Voyage of Jules Verne* (PS Publishing) – a busy year for a dead guy. Another curious cross, this time between a "retro-pulp" anthology and a Young Adult anthology, and *easily* winning the competition for the longest title of the year (if not the decade), was *Noisy Outlaws, Unfriendly Blobs, and Some Other Things That Aren't As Scary, Maybe, Depending on How You Feel About Lost Lands, Stray Cellphones, Creatures from the Sky, Parents Who Disappear in Peru, a Man Named Lars Farf, and One Other Story We Couldn't Quite Finish, So Maybe You Could Help Us Out* (McSweeney's), edited by Lemony Snicket; the best work here is by Neil Gaiman and Kelly Link, but there is also likeable work by Nick Hornby and Jonathan Safran Foer.

There seemed to be fewer slipstream/fabulist/New Weird/whatever anthologies this year than there'd been the previous few years. Practically the only ones I saw were all from the same publisher: *Polyphony 5* (Wheatland), edited by Deborah Layne and Jay Lake, *TEL: Stories* (Wheatland), edited by Jay Lake, and The Nine Muses (Wheatland), edited by Forrest Aguirre and Deborah Layne. *Polyphony 5* seemed weaker overall than previous volumes of *Polyphony* had been, although there was still good work here by Richard Wadholm, Theodora Goss, Jeff VanderMeer, Sally Carteret, M. K. Hobson, Alexander Lamb, Leslie What, and others. The enigmatically titled *TEL: Stories* seemed for the most part more self-consciously self-indulgent than successful in producing viable "experiments" in "extremes of style and vision." Of course, as a veteran of last century's New Wave Wars, reading this book was an exercise in déjà vu, with many of the "experiments" virtually indistinguishable from ones you could have found in any number of books or magazines back in the '60s, which perhaps explains the leaden feeling of ennui that gradually stole over me as I read it. (As someone said, "One thing that never changes – the avant-garde.") Best story here, by a considerable margin, is Gregory Feeley's "Fancy Bread," although there's also interesting work by Carrie Vaughn, Tim Pratt, Anil Menon, Dean Wesley Smith, and others. *The Nine Muses* seemed rather dry and abstract, with none of the stories coming near being as interesting as the introductory essay by Elizabeth Hand. The best thing here is probably by Ursula Pflug.

There weren't quite as many good novellas in individual chapbook form this year as last, but there were a few. The best was probably *Burn*, by James Patrick Kelly, from Tachyon, but PS Publishing brought out the previously mentioned *The Extraordinary Voyage of Jules Verne*, as well as *The Cosmology of the Wider World*, by Jeff Ford and *Fishin' with Grandma Matchie*, by Steven Erikson. Temporary Culture brought out *Arabian Wine* by Gregory Feeley; Subterranean Press brought out *Inside Job*, by Connie Willis and *The Life of Riley*, by Alex C. Irvine. Telos brought out *Approaching Omega* by Eric Brown, and the Aqueduct Press brought out *The Red Rose Rages* (Bleeding), by L. Timmel Duchamp and *Alien Bootlegger*, by Rebecca Ore.

As usual, novice work by beginning writers, some of whom may later turn out to be important talents, was featured in *L. Ron Hubbard Presents Writers of the Future Volume XXI* (Bridge); edited by Algis Budrys.

In the odd but meaningless coincidence department, there were two stories this year about ornithologists searching in unknown territory for bird species thought to be extinct ("Audubon in Atlantis," by Harry Turtledove and "The Last Akialoa," by Alan Dean Foster); and two stories about firefighters battling blazes set by terrorists ("Burn," by James Patrick Kelly and "Point of Origin," by Catharine Wells).

It was a moderately weak year for original fantasy anthologies. The

best of the year, with little real competition, was undoubtedly another
Book Club original, *The Fair Folk* (SFBC), edited by Marvin Kaye,
which featured good stories by Tanith Lee, Patricia A. McKillip, Kim
Newman, Jane Yolen, Midori Snyder, and others. There was also an
original anthology devoted to sword and sorcery stories this year, *Lords
of Swords* (Pitch Black Books), edited by Daniel E. Blackston. Most of
the other original fantasy anthologies this year were pleasant but minor,
including *Renaissance Faire* (DAW); edited by Andre Norton and Jean
Rabe; *Magic Tails* (DAW), a cat anthology (what else?) edited by Martin
H. Greenberg and Janet Pack, and *Maiden, Matron and Crone* (DAW),
edited by Kerrie Hughes and Martin H. Greenberg. There were several
good YA fantasy anthologies this year, including *Young Warriors*
(Random House), edited by Tamora Pierce and Josepha Sherman, and
Fantastic Companions (Fitzhenry & Whiteside); edited by Julie E.
Czerneda, and even a new Best of the Year series dedicated to YA stuff,
The Year's Best Fantasy for Teens (Tor); edited by Jane Yolen and
Patrick Nielsen Hayden.

I only saw one cross-genre anthology this year, *Winter Moon* (Luna),
a romance/fantasy cross containing stories by Mercedes Lackey, Tanith
Lee, and C. E. Murphy. There were several shared-world anthologies, in
both SF and fantasy, including *The Man-Kzin Wars XI* (Baen), edited by
Larry Niven; *Crossroads and Other Tales of Valdemar* (DAW), by
Mercedes Lackey; and *Bedlam's Edge* (Baen), edited by Mercedes
Lackey and Rosemary Edghill. *Kong Unbound* (Pocket); edited by Karen
Haber, is made up mostly of pop-culture articles about "You Know
Who," but does contain one good story by Howard Waldrop.

I don't follow horror closely anymore, but there, as far as I could tell,
the prominent original anthologies of the year included *Outsiders:
Twenty-two All-New Stories From the Edge* (Roc); edited by Nancy
Holder and Nancy Kilpatrick, and *Dark Delicacies: Original Stories of
the Macabre from Today's Greatest Horror Writers* (Carroll & Graf),
edited by Del Howison and Jeff Gelb. Other original horror anthologies
included *All Hell Breaking Loose* (DAW), edited by Martin H.
Greenberg, and *In the Shadow of Evil* (DAW); edited by Martin H.
Greenberg and John Helfers.

Finding individual pricings for all of the items from small presses
mentioned in the Summation has become too time-intensive, and since
several of the same small presses publish anthologies, novels, *and* short-
story collections, it seems silly to repeat addresses for them in section
after section. Therefore, I'm going to attempt to list here, in one place, all
the addresses for small presses that have books mentioned here or there
in the Summation, whether from the anthologies section, the novel
section, or the short-story collection section, and, where known, their
Web site addresses. That should make it easy enough for the reader to
look up the individual price of any book mentioned that isn't from a
regular trade publisher. Such books are less likely to be found in your

average bookstore, or even in a chain superstore, and so will probably have to be mail-ordered. Addresses: **PS Publishing**, Grosvener House, 1 New Road, Hornsea, West Yorkshire, HU18 1PG, England, UK, www.pspublishing.co.uk; **Golden Gryphon Press**, 3002 Perkins Road, Urbana, IL 61802, www.goldengryphon.com; **NESFA Press**, P.O. Box 809, Framinghan, MA 01701-0809, www.nesfa.org; **Subterranean Press**, P.O. Box 190106, Burton, MI 48519, www.subterraneanpress.com; **Old Earth Books**, P.O. Box 19951, Baltimore, MD 21211-0951, www.oldearthbooks.com; **Tachyon Press**, 1459 18th St. #139, San Francisco, CA 94107, www.tachyonpublications.com; **Night Shade Books**, 1470 NW Saltzman Road, Portland, OR 97229, www.nightshadebooks.com; **Five Star Books**, 295 Kennedy Memorial Drive, Waterville, ME 04901, www.galegroup.com/fivestar; **Wheatland Press**, P.O. Box 1818, Wilsonville, OR 97070, www. wheatlandpress.com; **Small Beer Press**, 176 Prospect Ave., Northampton, MA 01060, www.smallbeerpress.com; **Crescent Books**, Mercat Press Ltd., 10 Coates Crescent, Edinburgh, Scotland EH3 7AL, www.crescentfiction.com; **Wildside Press/Cosmos Books/Borgo Press**, P.O. Box 301, Holicong, PA 18928-0301, www.wildsidepress.com; **Thunder's Mouth**, 245 West 17th St., 11th Flr., New York, NY 10011-5300, www.thundersmouth.com; **Edge Science Fiction and Fantasy Publishing, Inc. and Tesseract Books, Ltd.**, P.O. Box 1714, Calgary, Alberta, T2P 2L7, Canada, www.edgewebsite.com; **Aio Publishing**, P.O. Box 30788, Charleston, SC 29417; **Rose Press**, 22 West End Land, Pinner, Middlesex, HA5 1AQ, England, UK, therosepress@groups.msn.com; **Aqueduct Press**, P.O. Box 95787, Seattle, WA 98145-2787, www.aqueductpress.com; **WSFA Press**, Washington Science Fiction Association, Inc., 10404 43rd Avenue, Beltsville, MD 20705; **Phobos Books**, 200 Park Avenue South, New York, NY 10003, www.phobosweb.com; **Fairwood Press**, 5203 Quincy Ave. SE, Auburn, WA 98092, www.fairwoodpress.com; **BenBella Books**, 6440 N. Central Expressway, Suite 508, Dallas, TX 75206, www.benbellabooks.com; **Red Deer Press/Robert J. Sawyer Books**, 813 MacKimmie Library Tower, 2500 University Drive NW, Calgary, Alberta, Canada T2N 1N4; **Darkside Press**, 13320 27th Ave. NE, Seattle, WA 98125, www.darksidepress.com; **Haffner Press**, 5005 Crooks Rd., Suite 35, Royal Oak, MI 48073-1239, www.haffnerpress.com; **Meshia Merlin**, P.O. Box 7, Decatur, GA 30031, www.meishamerlin.com; **North Atlantic Press**, P.O. Box 12327, Berkeley, CA, 94701; **Prime**, P.O. Box 36503, Canton, OH, 44735, www.primebooks.net; **Fairwood Press**, 5203 Quincy Ave SE, Auburn, WA 98092, www.fairwoodpress.com; **MonkeyBrain Books**, 11204 Crossland Drive, Austin, TX 78726, www.monkeybrainbooks.com; **Altair Australia**, www.altair-australia.com; **Seven Stories Press**, 140 Watts St., New York, NY 10017, www.sevenstories.com; **Telos Publishing**, www.telos.co.uk; **Pitch Black Books**, www.pitchblackbooks.com; **University of Nebraska Press/Bison**

Books, 1111 Lincoln Mall, Lincoln, NE 68588-0630; **Wesleyan University Press**, University Press of New England, Order Dept., 37 Lafayette St., Lebanon NH 03766-1405, www.wesleyan.edu/wespress; **Overlook Press**, www.overlookpress.com; **Temporary Culture**, P.O. Box 43072, Upper Montclair, NJ 07043-0072; **Centipede Press**, 2565 Toller Court, Lakewood, CO 80214, www.millipedepress. com/centipede_press.html; **Beccon Publishing**, Roger Beccon, 75 Rosslyn Avenue, Harold Wood, Essex RM3 ORG, England, UK.

2005 seemed like another pretty good year for novels; total numbers declined slightly, yes, but only after four previous years of record increases, and there were still far more novels published than any one reader is going to be able to read unless they made a full-time job of doing nothing else.

According to the newsmagazine *Locus*, there were 2,516 books "of interest to the SF field," both original and reprint (but not counting "media tie-in novels," gaming novels, novelizations of genre movies, print-on-demand novels, or novels offered as downloads on the Internet) published in 2005, down 1 percent from 2,550 titles in 2004. (To put these figures in some historical perspective, for the benefit of those who will leap in screaming "SF is dying!" at the mention of a 1 percent loss, there were 2,158 books published in 2001, and only 1,927 books as recently as 2000.) Original books were up by 4 percent to 1,469 from last year's total of 1,417, a new record. Reprint books were down by 8 percent, to 1,047 from last year's total of 1,133, after several years of increases. The number of new SF novels was up by 2 percent to 258 as opposed to last year's 253. The number of new fantasy novels was up by 6 percent to 414 as opposed to last year's 389, a new high. Horror was up by a whopping 23 percent, rising to 212 titles as opposed to last year's 172 (in 2002, the total for horror was only 112, so I guess this market has largely recovered from the Big Horror Bust of the late '90s).

Busy with all the reading I have to do at shorter lengths, I didn't have time to read many novels myself this year, so, as usual, I'll limit myself to mentioning those novels that received a lot of attention and acclaim in 2004:

Accelerando (Ace), by Charles Stross; *Olympos* (Eos) by Dan Simmons; *Old Twentieth* (Ace), by Joe Haldeman; *The Well of Stars* (Tor), by Robert Reed; *Transcendent* (Del Rey), by Stephen Baxter; *Pushing Ice* (Ace), by Alastair Reynolds; *Fifty Degrees Below* (Bantam Spectra), by Kim Stanley Robinson; *Anansi Boys* (Morrow), by Neil Gaiman; *A Feast for Crows* (Bantam Spectra), by George R. R. Martin; *Buried Deep* (Roc), by Kristine Kathryn Rusch; *Learning the World* (Tor), by Ken MacLeod; *A Princess of Roumania* (Tor), by Paul Park; *Shadow of the Giant* (Orbit), by Orson Scott Card; *Seeker* (Ace), by Jack McDevitt; *Mind's Eye* (Simon & Schuster UK), by Paul McAuley; *Band* of *Gypsys* (Gollancz), by Gwyneth Jones; *The House of Storms* (Ace), by Ian R. MacLeod; *Sunstorm* (Del Rey), by Arthur C. Clarke and Stephen Baxter; *Lady of Mazes* (Tor), by Karl Schroeder; *Brass Man* (Tor), by Neal Asher; *Destroyer* (DAW), by C. J. Cherryh; *The Rosetta Codex* (Orbit), by Richard Paul Russo; *The Seven Hills* (Ace), John Maddox Roberts; *Resolution* (Pyr), by John Meaney; *Godplayers* (Thunder's Mouth), by Damien Broderick; *The Hidden Family* (Tor), by Charles Stross; *The Narrows* (Del Rey), by Alexander C. Irvine; *Orphans of Chaos* (Tor), by John C. Wright; *The Hallowed Hunt* (Eos), by Lois McMaster Bujold; *9 Tail Fox* (Gollancz), by Jon Courtenay Grimwood; *The Sunborn* (Warner Aspect), by Gregory Benford; *To Crush the Moon* (Bantam Spectra), by Wil McCarthy; *The World Before* (Eos), by Karen Traviss; *Mammoth* (Ace), by John Varley; *Glass Soup* (Tor), by Jonathan Carroll; *Snake Agent* (Night Shade), by Liz Williams; *The Carpet Makers* (Tor), by Andreas Eschbach; *Living Next Door to the God of Love* (Bantam Spectra), by Justina Robson; *Mists of Everness* (Tor), by John C. Wright; *Double Vision* (Orbit), by Tricia Sullivan; *Spin* (Tor), by Robert Charles Wilson; *The Mysteries* (Bantam), by Lisa Tuttle; *Woken Furies* (Del Rey), by Richard K. Morgan; *Fledgling* (Seven Stories), by Octavia E. Butler; *Od Magic* (Ace), by Patricia A. McKillip; and *Thud!* (HarperCollins), by Terry Pratchett.

The first novel that drew the most attention this year was probably *Counting Heads* (Tor), by David Marusek, although if you go by the Locus convention of considering it one novel split into three parts, then *Hammered/Scardown/Worldwired* (Bantam Spectra), by Elizabeth Bear got a lot of reviews, as did *Rocket Science* (Fairwood), by Jay Lake. Other good first novels this year included *Bear Daughter* (Ace), by Judith Berman; *The Prodigal Troll* (Pyr), by Charles Coleman Finlay; *Old Man's War* (Tor), by John Scalzi; *Here, There and Everywhere* (Pyr), by Chris Roberson; *The Strange Adventures of Rangergirl* (Bantam Spectra), by Tim Pratt; *Singer of Souls* (Tor), by Adam Stemple; *Melusine* (Ace), by Sarah Monette; *Vellum* (Del Rey), by Hal Duncan; *Magic or Madness* (Razorbill), by Justine Larbalestier; *Spotted Lily* (Prime), by Anna Tambour; *Fly by Night* (HarperCollins), by Frances Hardinge; *Zahrah the Windseeker* (Houghton Miffllin), by Nnedi Okorafor-Mbachu; and *Poison Study* (Luna), by Maria V. Snyder.

As usual, there were some hard-to-classify novels out on the edge of genre this year, including books by mainstream authors who were dipping their toes into genre to one degree or another, as well as associational novels by genre authors. These included: *Lord Byron's Novel: The Evening Land* (Morrow), by John Crowley; *Someone Comes to Town, Someone Leaves Town* (Tor), by Cory Doctorow; *Quantico* (HarperCollinsUK), by Greg Bear; *The Girl in the Glass* (Harper/Dark Alley), by Jeffrey Ford; *The Amphora Project* (Grove), by William Kotzwinkle; *Zanesville* (Villard), by Kris Saknussemm; *The War at Troy* (HarperCollins UK), by Lindsay Clarke; and *The Necessary Beggar*

(Tor), by Susan Palwick. Small presses also published a fair number of novels this year, including one of the year's best, *The Summer Isles* (Aio Publishing), by Ian R. MacLeod, as well as *Alanya to Alanya* (Aqueduct), by L. Timmel Duchamp; *The Engine of Recall* (Robert J. Sawyer Books), by Karl Schroeder; and *Lint* (Thunder's Mouth), by Steve Aylett.

My subjective opinion, based on reviews and "buzz," is that this year was a bit weaker overall for novels than last year, but that there were still more good novels published in 2005 than any one person is ever likely to be able to find time to read. There was a good deal of fantasy and hard-to-categorize genre-mixing stuff on the lists, but also quite a lot of novels that were unmistakably center-core SF, including the Stross, the Haldeman, the Baxter, Rusch, the Robinson, the Marusek, the Bears, the Asher, the Clarke & Baxter, the Reynolds, the MacLeod, the Simmons, and a bunch of others.

Tor clearly had a good year, as did Ace. New SF line Pyr did well in its first year. And now that small presses such as Night Shade, Aqueduct, and Thunder's Mouth are getting into publishing novels in addition to the big commercial houses, there's more out there to choose from than ever.

The last few years have also been the best time in decades to pick up reissued editions of formerly long-out-of-print novels, and that remained true in 2005 as well. There's such a flood of titles coming back into print these days, from both small presses and regular trade publishers (to say nothing of Print On Demand books from places such as Wildside Press, and the availability of out-of-print books as electronic downloads on Internet sources such as Fictionwise, and through reprints issued by The Science Fiction Book Club) that it's become difficult to produce an exhaustive list of such titles. I'll just list some of the more prominent reprints that caught my eye this year: ibooks reissued: *Triplanetary*, by E. E. Smith, *Emphyrio*, by Jack Vance, *Blood Music*, by Greg Bear; *Against the Fall of Night*, by Arthur C. Clarke; *The Gate of Worlds*, by Robert Silverberg; and *Strangers*, by Gardner Dozois; Eos reissued: *Beauty*, by Robin McKinley; Bantam Spectra reissued: *A Game of Thrones*, by George R. R. Martin; Ace reissued: *Podkayne of Mars*, by Robert A. Heinlein and *Silverlock*, by John Myers Myers; Pocket reissued: *Have Space Suit, Will Travel, Starman Jones, Tunnel in the Sky*, and *Citizen of the Galaxy* all by Robert A. Heinlein; BenBella Books reissued: *Soothsayer*, by Mike Resnick; Tor reissued: *Flying in Place*, by Susan Palwick and *The Prestige*, by Christopher Priest; Tor Teen reissued: *The Borribles*, by Michael de Larrabeiti; Orb reissued: *When Gravity Fails*, by George Alec Effinger; Pyr reissued: *Star of Gypsies*, by Robert Silverberg; Vintage reissued: *Dr. Futurity and The Crack in Space*, by Philip K. Dick; Warner Aspect reissued: *Furious Gulf and Sailing Bright Eternity*, by Gregory Benford; Wesleyan University Press reissued: *The Two of Them and We Who Are About To . . .* , by Joanna Russ;

HarperCollins reissued: *Alas, Babylon,* by Pat Frank; Penguin Classics reissued; *The War of the Worlds* and *The Time Machine,* by H. G. Wells; Overlook Press reissued: *Non-Stop,* by Brian W. Aldiss and *Bug Jack Barron,* by Norman Spinrad; Small Beer Press reissued: *Mockingbird,* by Sean Stewart; The University of Nebraska Press/Bison Books reissued: *At Winter's End,* by Robert Silverberg; Gollancz reissued: two mainstream novels by Philip K. Dick, *In Milton Lumky Territory* and *Mary and the Giant*; Thunder's Mouth Press reissued: *Master of Time and Space,* by Rudy Rucker; Simon & Schuster reissued: *Empire of the Sun,* by J. G. Ballard; Cold Spring Press reissued: *Lud-in-the-Mist,* by Hope Mirrlees.

There were a lot of omnibus collections of reissued novels this year, including some that mixed novels with short stories by the same author. They included: *Cities in Flight* (Overlook Press), three famous novels by James Blish; *Deathworld* (BenBella Books), three equally famous novels plus some related material by Harry Harrison; *Imperium* (Baen), three novels plus some short stories in the same sequence by Keith Laumer; *Viriconium* (Bantam Spectra), three novels plus one collection in the "Viriconium" series, by M. John Harrison; *A Logic Named Joe* (Baen), three novels and three short stories by Murry Leinster; and *Stark and the Star Kings* (Haffner Press), five novels plus a new novelette with shared settings and characters by Edmond Hamilton and Leigh Brackett, writing either solo or in collaboration. Plus many omnibuses of novels – and many individual novels – are reissued each year by The Science Fiction Book Club, too many to individually list here.

Get 'em now, while you have the chance. If the present wave of reprints ends, they might not be available again for years.

Susanna Clarke's *Jonathan Strange & Mr. Norrell* did win the Hugo last year, as I predicted, but Gene Wolfe's *The Knight* lost the Nebula to Lois McMasters Bujold's *Paladin of Souls,* so my record as a prophet is uneven. I don't think I'm even going to try to call the major awards this year, as I don't see any clear favorites, or any bestsellers of the stature of Clarke's book. The critical favorite was probably Charles Stross's *Accelerando,* and if you put a gun to my head and forced me to guess, I'd predict that as the Hugo winner. I rarely have any feeling for what's going to win the Nebula anymore, and I doubt that this year will be different.

This was another good year for short-story collections, although perhaps not quite as strong as last year. The year's best collections included: *The Cuckoo's Boys* (Golden Gryphon), by Robert Reed; *The Children of the Company* (Tor), by Kage Baker; *Heart of Whitenesse* (Subterranean), by Howard Waldrop; *Greetings and Other Stories* (Tachyon), by Terry Bisson; *Numbers Don't Lie* (Tachyon), by Terry Bisson; *Mothers and Other Monsters* (Small Beer Press) by Maureen F. McHugh; *Starwater Strains: New Science Fiction Stories* (Tor), by Gene Wolfe; *Magic for*

Beginners (Small Beer Press), by Kelly Link; *The Fiction Factory* (Golden Gryphon), by Jack Dann, et al.; *Little Machines* (PS Publishing), by Paul McAuley; *Eternity and Other Stories* (Thunder's Mouth), by Lucius Shepard; *The Gist Hutner and Other Stories* (Night Shade), by Matthew Hughes; *Attack of the Jazz Giants and Other Stories* (Golden Gryphon), by Gregory Frost; *Bloodchild and Other Stories Second Edition* (Seven Stories Press), by Octavia E. Butler; *The Emperor of Gondwanaland and Other Stories* (Thunder's Mouth), by Paul Di Filippo; *Ordinary People* (Aqueduct), by Eleanor Arnason; and *George Alec Effinger Live! From Planet Earth* (Golden Gryphon) by George Alec Effinger. There were also a number of big career-spanning retrospective collections: *Years in the Making: The Time-Travel Stories of L. Sprague de Camp* (NESFA Press) by L. Sprague de Camp; *Platinum Pohl* (Tor), by Frederik Pohl; *Tales* (Library of America), by H. P. Lovecraft; *The Man Who Lost the Sea: Volume X: The Complete Stories of Theodore Sturgeon* (North Atlantic) by Theodore Sturgeon; *Two-Handed Engine: The Selected Stories of Henry Kuttner and C. L. Moore* (Centipede), by Henry Kuttner and C. L. Moore; *A Sound of Thunder* (HarperPerennial), by Ray Bradbury; *Sea-Kings of Mars and Otherworldly Stories* (Gollancz), by Leigh Brackett; *The Night Land and Other Perilous Romances* (Night Shade), by William Hope Hodgson; *Adrift on Haunted Seas* (Cold Springs), by William Hope Hodgson; *The Masque of Manana* (NESFA Press), by Robert Sheckley; *Once upon a Time (She Said)* (NESFA Press), by Jane Yolen; *The Collected Clark Ashton Smith, Volume 1* (Night Shade Books), by Clark Ashton Smith; *Homecalling and Other Stories: The Complete Solo Short SF of Judith Merril* (NESFA Press), by Judith Merril; and *Eternity Lost: The Collected Stories of Clifford D. Simak* (Darkside Press), by Clifford D. Simak.

Other good collections this year included: *Cultural Breaks* (Tachyon), by Brian W. Aldiss; *The Periodic Table of Science Fiction* (PS Publishing), by Michael Swanwick; *The Last of the O-Forms* (Fairwood Press), by James Van Pelt; *Wild Things* (Subterranean), by Charles Coleman Finlay; *Strange Itineraries* (Tachyon), by Tim Powers; *Looking for Jake and Other Stories* (Del Rey), by China Mieville; *20th Century Ghosts* (PS Publishing), by Joe Hill; *Across the Wall: A Tale of the Abhorsen and Other Stories* (Eos), by Garth Nix; *To Charles Fort, with Love* (Subterranean), by Caitliln R. Kiernan; *I Live with You* (Tachyon), by Carol Emshwiller; *The Fall of Tartarus* (Gollancz), by Eric Brown; *In the Palace of Repose* (Prime), by Holly Phillips; *Ships in the Night* (Altair Australia), by Jack McDevitt; *A Tour Guide to Utopia* (MirrorDanse), by Lucy Sussex; *Harrowing the Dragon* (Ace), by Patricia A. McKillip; *Wasps at the Speed of Sound* (Prime), by Derryl Murphy; *Catastrophies, Chaos & Convolutions* (Baen), by James P. Hogan; *Gunning for the Buddha* (Prime), by Michael Jasper; *Dogs of Truth* (Tor), by Kit Reed; *Singing Innocence and Experience* (Wildside), by Sonya Taaffe; and *Gravity Wells* (Eos), by James Alan Gardner.

Reissued collections this year included: *Her Smoke Rose Up Forever* (Tachyon), by James Tiptree, Jr.; *The Last Defender of Camelot* (ibooks), by Roger Zelazny, *Expanded Universe* (Baen), by Robert A. Heinlein, and *R Is for Rocket* (PS Publishing) and *S Is for Space* (PS Publishing), by Ray Bradbury.

And, as usual, "electronic collections" continue to be available for downloading on-line as well, at sites such as *Fictionwise* and *ElectricStory*.

As has been true for a long time now, the bulk of collections released this year were done by small-press publishers such as Golden Gryphon, Tachyon, NESFA, Subterranean, Night Shade, and Small Beer. The regular trade publishers such as Tor, Baen, and Eos continue to do a few collections a year – but for the most part, if you want collections, you have to go to the small presses. Since the advent of on-line bookselling, this has become easier, and many small-presses now have Web sites that you can order from (do a Google search on the name of the press), and you can even find titles from some of the more prominent small presses on the shelves of specialty SF bookstores or the larger chain stores. But in some cases, you'll still have to go to mail-order to get what you want. It can be worth the time and trouble, though, especially for material you can't get anywhere else.

It was another fairly good year in the reprint anthology market; in addition to the usual "Best of the Year" and award anthologies, there were some big retrospective anthologies and some strong stand-alones giving you good value for your money. This year there were *ten* "Best of the Year" anthologies available, including a specialized regional anthology and one devoted to fiction for teenagers. Science fiction was covered by six anthologies: the one you are holding in your hand, *The Year's Best Science Fiction* series from St. Martin's, now up to its twenty-third annual collection; the *Year's Best SF* series (Eos), edited by David G. Hartwell and Kathryn Cramer, now up to its tenth annual volume; *Science Fiction: The Best of 2004* (ibooks), edited by Jonathan Strahan and Karen Haber; *Best Short Novels 2005* (Science Fiction Book Club), edited by Johanthan Strahan; plus the SF halves of two anthologies split between SF and fantasy, *The Year's Best Australian Science Fiction and Fantasy: Volume 1* (MirrorDanse), edited by Bill Congreve and Michelle Marquardt, and *The Year's Best Science Fiction and Fantasy for Teens* (Tor), edited by Jane Yolen and Patrick Nielsen Hayden. There were two "Best of the Year" anthologies covering horror: the latest edition in the British series *The Mammoth Book of Best New Horror (*Carroll & Graf), edited by Stephen Jones and now up to its sixteenth edition; and the Ellen Datlow half of a huge volume covering both horror and fantasy, *The Year's Best Fantasy and Horror* (St. Martin's Press) – this year up to its eighteenth annual collection, edited by Ellen Datlow and Kelly Link and Gavin Grant. Fantasy was covered by five anthologies: by the Kelly Link and Gavin Grant half of the Datlow/Link & Grant anthology; by *Year's Best Fantasy 5* (Eos), edited by David G. Hartwell and Katherine Cramer; by *Fantasy: The Best of 2004* (ibooks), edited by Jonathan Strahan and Karen Harber, and by the fantasy halves of the Congreve/Marquardt and Yolen/Hayden anthologies. The most recent Nebula Awards anthology is *Nebula Awards Showcase 2005* (Roc), edited by Jack Dann.

There were a number of good retrospective SF anthologies, including *Fourth Planet from the Sun: Tales of Mars from The Magazine of Fantasy and Science Fiction* (Thunder's Mouth), edited by Gordon Van Gelder, which featured stories by Roger Zelazny, John Varley, Leigh Brackett, Philip K. Dick, and others; *The Best Time Travel Stories of the 20th Century* (Del Rey), edited by Harry Turtledove and Martin H. Greenberg, which featured stories by L. Sprague de Camp, Poul Anderson, Robert Silverberg, Joe Haldeman, Theodore Sturgeon, and others; *The Tiptree Award Anthology 2* (Tachyon), edited by Karen Joy Fowler, Pat Murphy, Debbie Notkin, and Jeffrey D. Smith, which featured stories by Ursula K. Le Guin, Eileen Gunn, Leslie What, Gwyneth Jones, L. Timmel Duchamp, and others; and *The World Turned Upside Down* (Baen), edited by David Drake, Jim Baen, and Eric Flint, which featured stories by Fritz Leiber, John W. Campbell, Jr., Leigh Brackett, Arthur C. Clarke, and others. Noted without comment is a similar big retrospective anthology, *The Best of the Best: 20 Years of the Year's Best Science Fiction* (St. Martin's), edited by Gardner Dozois.

Also noted without comment are: *Galileo's Children* (Pyr), edited by Gardner Dozois, and *Beyond Singularity* (Ace) and *Robots* (Ace), edited by Jack Dann and Gardner Dozois.

Just about the only reprint fantasy anthologies I saw were both big solid collections of classic fantasy stories: *The Mammoth Book of New Comic Fantasy* (Carroll & Graf), edited by Mike Ashley – which was a good value if you like comic fantasy, featuring reprint stories by the likes of Neil Gaiman, Esther M. Friesner, Paul Di Filippo, and others (and a few originals, including stories by Tom Holt and Adam Roberts); and *Seekers of Dreams: Masterpieces of Fantasy* (Cold Springs Press), edited by Douglas A. Anderson, another mixed reprint (mostly) and original anthology. The only reprint horror anthology I saw was *H. P. Lovecraft's Favorite Weird Tales* (Cold Springs Press), edited by Douglas A. Anderson, but at least it was an intriguing idea for an anthology, and featured some rarely-seen material.

It seemed like 2005 was a decent if not exceptional year in the SF-and-fantasy-oriented nonfiction and reference book field. Reference books included: *Historical Dictionary of Fantasy Literature* (Scarecrow Press), by Brian Slableford, a companion volume to last year's *Historical Dictionary of Science Fiction Literature; The Greenwood Encyclopedia of Science Fiction and Fantasy: Themes, Works, and Wonders*

(Greenwood), edited by Gary Westfahl; *Supernatural Literature of the World: An Encyclopedia* (Greenwood), edited by S. T. Joshi and Stefan Dziemiqnowicz *Fantasy Literature for Children and Young Adults: Fifth Edition* (Libraries Unlimited), by Ruth Nadelman Lynn; *Horror: Another 100 Best Books* (Carroll & Graf), edited by Stephen Jones and Kim Newman; and *Latin American Science Fiction Writers: An A-to-Z Guide* (Greenwood), edited by Darrell B. Lockhart.

Sometimes the line between "reference books" and "critical studies" is a hard one to draw, and some may argue that some of those above belong in one category rather than the other. Somewhat arbitrarily I'm going to categorize the books that follow as critical studies, although many of them can be used as reference books as well: *Anatomy of Wonder: A Critical Guide to Science Fiction, 5th Edition* (Libraries Unlimited), by Neil Barron; *Transformations: The Story of the Science Fiction Magazine from 1950 to 1970* (Liverpool), by Mike Ashley; *Science Fiction* (Polilty), by Roger Luckhurst; *The Science in Science Fiction* (BenBella Books), by Robert Bly; *Archaeologies of the Future: The Desire Called Utopia and Other Science Fictions* (Verso) by Frederic Jameson; and Speculations on *Speculation: Theories of Science Fiction* (Scarecrow Press), edited by James Gunn and Matthew Candelaria.

There were critical studies of specific authors, including *Ursula K. Le Guin: Beyond Genre* (Routledge), by Mike Cadden, *Diana Wynne Jones: Children's Literature and the Fantastic Tradition* (Routledge), by Farah Mendlesohn, *Parietal Games: Critical Writings by and on M. John Harrison* (Science Fiction Foundation), edited by Mark Bould and Michelle Reid, *Christopher Priest: The Interaction* (Science Fiction Foundation), edited by Andrew M. Butler; and an update of *A Master of Adventure: The Worlds of Edgar Rice Burroughs* (Bison Books), by Richard A. Lupoff. Books of essays by specific authors, included: *A Reverie for Mister Ray* (PS Publishing), by Michael Bishop; *Bradbury Speaks: Too Soon From the Cave, Too Far From the Stars* (HarperCollins), by Ray Bradbury; *The SEX Column and Other Misprints* (Cosmos), by David Langford; *The Lifebox, The Seashell, and the Soul* (Thunder's Mouth), by Rudy Rucker; *Soundings: Reviews 1992–1996* (Beccon), by Gary K. Wolfe; On SF (University of Michigan Press), by Thomas M. Disch; and *The Disappointment Artist and Other Essays* (Doubleday), by Jonathan Lethem. There were biographies of authors, including *Wish You Were Here: The Official Biography of Douglas Adams* (Ballantine), by Nick Webb and The Bradbury *Chronicles: the Life of Ray Bradbury* (William Morrow), by Sam Weller; an autobiography, the updated version of *Wonder's Child: My Life in Science Fiction* (BenBella Books), by Jack Williamson, and a book-length autobiographical sketch of one author's nervous breakdown, *Nervous System: Or, Losing My Mind in Literature* (Raincoast Books), by Jan Lars Jensen. There were how-to-write books, including *Storyteller: Writing Lessons and More from 27 Years of the Clarion Writers' Workshop*

(Small Beer Pres), by Kate Wilhelm; *Writing the Other* (Aqueduct), by Nisi Shawl and Cynthia Ward; and *About Writing* (Wesleyan University Press), by Samuel R. Delany. Books of interviews with authors included, *Conversations with Isaac Asimov* (University Press of Mississippi), by Carl Howard Freedman; *J. G. Ballard: Conversations* (ReSearch), edited by V. Vale; and *Voices of Vision* (Bison Books), by Jayme Lynn Blaschke; and even a book of quotations drawn from SF stories, *Science Fiction Quotations* (Yale), edited by Gary Westfahl.

For media fans, there was a book of acerbic but often hilarious movie reviews, *Weapons of Mass Seduction* (Wheatland), by Lucius Shepard; an anthology of critical essays about a cancelled TV show, *Finding Serenity: Anti-Heroes, Lost Shepards, and Space Hookers* in Joss Whedon's *Firefly* (BenBella Books), edited by Jane Espenson; and two anthologies of critical essays about "You-Know-Who," the big hairy fella, *Kong Unbound: The Cultural Impact, Pop Myths, and Scientific Plausibility of a Cinematic Legend* (Pocket), edited by Karen Haber, and *King Kong Is Back!: An Unauthorized Look at One Humongous Ape!* (BenBella Books), edited by David Brin and Leah Wilson (if you're only going to get one Kong book this year, make it the Haber, which not only has the more interesting and entertaining essays of the two, but throws in a good story by Howard Waldrop as well). There was also an art book of paintings of King Kong by Joe DeVito; see below for more information.

It seemed like a fairly weak year in the art book field. The best bet for your money was probably the latest edition in a Best of the Year–like retrospective of the year in fantastic art, *Spectrum 12: The Best in Contemporary Fantastic Art* (Underwood Books), by Cathy Fenner and Arnie Fenner. There were also a number of retrospective overviews of the work of individual artists, including: *Imago* (Heavy Metal), by Jim Burns; *Daydreaming: The Art of Slawek Wojtowicz* (xlibris), by Slawek Wojtowicz; *Through Prehensile Eyes: Seeing the Art of Robert Williams* (Last Gasp), by Robert Williams; *Welcome to My Worlds: The Art of Rob Alexander* (Paper Tiger), by Rob Alexander; *Revelations: The Art of Max Bertolini* (Paper Tiger), by Max Bertolini; *Arts Unknown: The Life and Art of Lee Brown Cove* (Nonstop), compiled by Luis Ortiz; and *Visions of Heaven and Hell* (Rizzoli), a collection of drawings by well-known horror writer Clive Barker, who also has a considerable reputation as a graphic artist.

More specific projects include *Worlds: A Mission of Discovery* (Design Studio Press), by Alec Gillis, which takes us mock-documentary style through a landing on an alien planet; *Kong: King of Skull Island* (DH Press), by Joe DeVito and Brad Strickland, with John Michlig, which takes us on a visual tour around the famous monster's home; and *The Stardragons* (Paper Tiger), by Bob Eggleton and John Grant, which takes us into Deep Space. George R. R. Martin fans will want *The Art of George R. R. Martin's a Song of Ice and Fire* (Fantasy Flight Games), edited by Brian Wood.

Turning to more general genre-related nonfiction books of interest, there were several futurology books this year that took a shot at forecasting the unexpected twists and turns the next few decades may take, including *Shaping Things* (MIT Press), by Bruce Sterling, a "manifesto for the future of design" and an exploration of how the design of everyday objects will transform society; *Nano Future: What's Next for Nanotechnology* (Prometheus Books), by J. Storrs Hall, and *The Singularity Is Near: When Humans Transcend Biology* (Viking), by Ray Kurzweil. There's also an update of Wil McCarthy's similar book from 2003, *Hacking Matter*, available for download at McCarthy's site, www.wilmccarthy.com. A cautionary note, warning that our society may already be in the midst of making the same kind of mistakes that have destroyed advanced civilizations throughout history is struck by *Collapse: How Societies Choose to Fail or Succeed* (Viking), by Jared Diamond. These books vary on how radical a future they predict for the coming decades – Sterling's is the most plausible-sounding, Kurzweil's is wild-eyed and extreme enough that it's tempting to picture him walking through Times Square wearing a sign-board that reads "The Singularity Is Near!" On the other hand, it's worth remembering that the most outrageous and far-out of the social satires of '50s writers like Pohl and Kornbluth now look pretty much like everyday mundane reality here in the 'oughts – so who knows?

It's harder to come up with a genre-related justification for mentioning *Life in the Undergrowth* (BBC Books), by David Attenborough, except that, like the best science fiction, it gives us a fascinating look at worlds we'd otherwise never see, even if those worlds are in the grass beneath our feet rather than in outer space – the lifeways, survival tactics, and mating rituals of the creatures who inhabit that grass-roots world, in fact, are far stranger, more surprising, and more intricate than those attributed to most of SF's aliens. It's probably even harder to come up with a rationalization for mentioning *Greek Fire, Poison Arrows & Scorpion Bombs: Biological and Chemical Warfare in the Ancient World* (Overlook Duckworth), by Adrienne Mayor, except that many SF/fantasy readers are also interested in the ancient world, or at least in the reflection of it used in many fantasy novels. This book does an excellent job of demonstrating that the ancient world was much more complex and contradictory than it's usually portrayed as being by writers of pseudo-medieval fantasy. No reason at all to mention a paperback reprint of *The Meadowlands: Wilderness Adventures on the Edge of a City* (Anchor Books) and *Rats: Observations on the History & Habitat of the City's Most Unwanted Inhabitants* (Bloomsbury), both by Robert Sullivan, except for that one above about showing us worlds that we'd otherwise never see and, in fact, wouldn't even know were there – but it's my book, and I'm going to mention them anyway.

It was a busy year for genre films – there were a lot of them made, and a number of them made a lot of money. (According to the Box Office Mojo site, of the ten movies that grossed the most money worldwide in 2005, eight were genre films; out of the top twenty moneymaking films, thirteen were genre movies.) Some of them were even worth watching.

The big moneymaker of the year, and certainly the top-grossing film for science fiction, was *Star Wars: Episode III: The Revenge of the Sith*, which managed to be more action-packed and straightforward than most of the current run of *Star Wars* films, although since it was still loaded with the plot logic holes, stiff acting, and the bad dialog characteristic of this series of late, it's hard to call it an artistic success – "better than the last two movies" is about the best you could get even most *Star Wars* fans to say. (The classical arc of the rise and fall of Darth Vader actually has a lot of potential mythological resonance, as Lucas knows perfectly well, and if they'd gotten a good actor to play Anakin Skywalker/Darth Vader, rather than the almost comically wooden Hayden Christensen, had given him some better psychological motivation, and had written some good dialog for him, his story might actually have been quite powerful; as it was, though, most of that potential was lost.) This theoretically brings the *Star Wars* storyline to a close, since even Lucas is now admitting that he's probably never going to actually make the other three movies originally projected back in 1976. There's no way this cash cow is not going to continue to be milked, though, and there's already talk about forthcoming *Star Wars*–related television series (and, of course, *Star Wars* books and computer games will continue to appear, as is also true with *Star Trek*, even after the death of that franchise on both the big or the little screen).

The year's other big moneymaker in science fiction was Steven Spielberg's remake of *The War of the Worlds*. The movie was fast-paced and suspenseful, and, being a Spielberg movie (Spielberg is always good at the visuals), there are some wonderful images in it – it is almost worth watching the whole movie just for the image of the flaming train racing through the countryside. That being said, I regretted the fact that Spielberg somehow managed to skew the movie into being yet another Spielberg "small child in jeopardy (Dakota Fanning sure does *scream* a lot in this film)/self-centered-immature-father-in-a-dysfunctional-family-learns-to-value-his-children-over-himself" movie rather than really focusing on the disaster that's overcoming humanity at large. This was a frustrating movie for me, since in some ways it's more faithful to H. G. Wells's novel than the previous Hollywood version was – and yet at the same time gave me the feeling that in spite of all that faithfulness to the text, Spielberg had somehow ended up missing the point of the novel altogether. It made bucketloads of money, though, even if not quite as much as *Revenge of the Sith*.

Below this point, most of the year's other SF films were failures to one degree or another, at least at the box office. *The Hitchhiker's Guide to the Galaxy* was slick and flashy, with impressive special effects, but somehow forgot to be *funny*. The best version of this by far remains the original BBC radio version, which is even preferable to Douglas Adams's original book in some ways. *The Island* had a "surprise" twist that most experienced genre fans figured out from the coming attractions, and little else to recommend it – even a lot of car chases and explosions couldn't keep this one afloat. That was true of several movies this year, including *Aeon Flux*; the "killer robot airplane runs amok" movie *Stealth* (which had lots of explosions in it); and even *Doom*, a movie "adapted" from a popular video game that was practically *nothing* but guys shooting things with very big guns – perhaps an indication that the "all you need are car chases, gun battles, and big explosions" school of moviemaking is finally losing its charm. In spite of less violent and more imaginative special effects, the "family" movie *Zathura* failed at the box office, too, as did a better movie, by far the best of this bunch, and one of the best SF movies of the year, *Serenity*.

Based on Joss Whedon's failed TV series "Firefly," which also couldn't manage to find an audience, *Serenity* is actually a pretty good piece of entertainment – fast-paced, action-packed, and shot through with Whedon's trademark wry wit. Why didn't it work at the box office, then? Perhaps the cross of Western and space movie was just too jarring for most people, too odd a taste. Perhaps, in spite of many ingenious SF touches (such as having the characters occasionally speaking Chinese to each other), it was too *blatantly* a cowboy show "translated" into SF, recycling plots and situations familiar from a thousand old Westerns. Or perhaps it was the fact that the underlying assumptions here just don't make a lot of sense (you use a *spaceship* to transport seven or eight cows across space to *another planet*, as they do in one of the *Firefly* episodes, and, in spite of the vast amounts of energy this would take, this is somehow a financially worthwhile proposition?), that put people off – although this is hardly the first genre show to be based on underlying assumptions that don't really bear scrutiny. Whatever the reason, this is the second time that *Firefly/Serenity* has failed to find an audience, and may be the last shot it gets – although Whedon is reportedly hoping that the sales of the movie on DVD will be good enough to generate interest in another television series. (This seems dubious to me – but who knows?)

Most of the year's other top-selling films were fantasy movies – although that category wasn't without its failures, either. The top-grossing fantasy movie was also one of the best, at least among the live-action films: *Harry Potter and the Goblet of Fire*. I myself didn't think this was quite as stylishly directed as last year's *Harry Potter and the Prisoner of Azkaban*, still the best of the series in my opinion, but if the picaresque plot occasionally bogged down, as it did (I thought that three magical contests were at least one too many, and possibly two too many), it was a pretty decent job of handling the material all in all, and there probably were few who left the theater feeling that they didn't get their money's worth of entertainment. *King Kong* was also pretty successful, both critically and at the box office, though not quite at the *Lord of the Rings*–level of ticket sales they apparently were hoping for, perhaps because word of mouth rapidly spread that it needed editing. Almost everybody, critics and ordinary viewers alike, agreed that it needed cutting, although opinion varied whether it needed twenty minutes, a half an hour, or even a full hour's worth of footage chopped out. *The Chronicles of Narnia: The Lion, the Witch, and the Wardrobe* was also moderately successful, although perhaps not as big a smash as the producers had hoped. It struck me as *Lord of the Rings*–lite myself, but then, I never much liked the original book itself, which had too much undisguised Christian propaganda for my taste. *Charlie and the Chocolate Factory* also did moderately well in ticket sales, but I disliked that even more; the old Gene Wilder version, *Willy Wonka and the Chocolate Factory*, was hardly my favorite movie either, but Tim Burton's *Charlie* struck me as inferior to it in almost every respect (even the songs were worse!), and especially in the portrayal of Willy Wonka – I usually like Johnny Depp, but the broad imitation of Michael Jackson he does throughout here as Willy Wonka made my skin crawl and added a pederastic subtext that the movie really didn't need.

Below this point, we're back in bomb-out territory again, as far as live-action fantasy movies are concerned. The movie version of the old TV series *Bewitched* was a box-office disaster, and perhaps the most critically savaged movie of the year. (Its competition for that title might be another old TV series made into a movie, *The Honeymooners*, but it's out of our purview here, not being a fantasy, just bad.) *The Brothers Grimm* was also a box-office bomb, territory director Terry Gilliam has visited before, but even the most fanatical Terry Gilliam fans, who usually sing his praises no matter how few tickets were sold, can't seem to find a lot positive to say about this one. *Son of the Mask*, an ill-advised sequel to *The Mask* in which the family dog is gifted with the powers of a god, also (dare I say it? Oh, what the hell) dogged-out.

Animated fantasy movies also had their ups and downs. The box-office champ undoubtedly was *Madagascar*, the most successful critically were *Wallace and Gromit: The Curse of the Were-Rabbit* and *Tim Burton's Corpse Bride* (which I liked a lot better than *Charlie and the Chocolate Factory*). As is usual with films by Japanese master Hayao Miyazaki, *Howl's Moving Castle* seemed to slip through town without anybody taking much notice of it, but although it's not quite as good as his masterpiece *Spirited Away*, it is stuffed with wonderful and magical things, like all Miyazaki films, and is well worth making the effort to track down. *Chicken Little* did okay, although not as well as some recent Pixar movies have done, which is probably what they were shooting for. *Robots* and *Hoodwinked* did less well.

In the field of comic-book movies, *Batman Begins* was a commercial and critical success, ranking up there with *Spider-Man* and *The X-Men*; and *The Fantastic Four* was a jaw-dropping disaster, ranking up there with, unfortunately, *The Hulk* – it'll probably end up making a decent amount of money, especially with overseas and DVD sales thrown in, but it was an extremely bad movie regardless, a disappointment for all those comics fans who had a right to expect better for one of the comics world's most famous and beloved franchises. *The Adventures of Sharkboy and Lavagirl in 3D*, sort of *Spy Kids*–lite, tanked, as did *Sky High*, sort of *The Incredibles*–lite.

Kingdom of Heaven was another expensive box-office disappointment in the sword and sandal movie field. They haven't had a big success in this area since *Gladiator*, and you have to wonder how many more shots they're going to get. *Kingdom of Heaven* actually wasn't a bad movie, certainly better than *Alexander the Great* and *Troy*, even though it tromped down a bit hard on the "Author's Message" pedal, and should have starred costar Liam Neeson instead of the wispy Orlando Bloom (as a blacksmith, yet! Have you ever *seen* a blacksmith? They have arms wider around than Orlando's entire body!), who lacked the *gravitas* for the part.

Horror movies? Yes, there were horror movies – *Constantine. The Fog, Underworld: Evolution House of Wax* – but I didn't see any of them. For what it's worth, I've heard that *Constantine* was a commercial failure (Whoa, dude!), and apparently *Underworld: Evolution* is not.

Coming up next year: little I'm looking forward to. There'll be a new X-Men movie, and an attempt to establish some other comic-book franchises.

The winds of change seem to be blowing coldly through the movie industry, as DVD sales become more important than first-run box office as overall ticket sales for the industry continue to fall year after year as ticket prices continue to rise. Oddly, no Hollywood genius has figured this equation out yet, even though with the turnover between a film in first-run release and that same movie being available for sale or rental on DVD now down to three months or less, and the costs of taking a family of five to a movie creeping inexorably toward sixty bucks. Few families bother to go to the movies anymore unless it's for a Big Screen Spectacular like *Lord of the Rings* or *Harry Potter* that won't look as good on the home screen. "The hell with it, we'll wait for the DVD to come out" is something heard more and often these days for all but the most big ticket of events. With movies now readily available on your iPod and even your cell phone, to say nothing of DVDs of those movies delivered right into your house via Netflix and pay-on-demand cable and satellite systems, the urge just to stay at home and not bother to go out, even to a video-rental store, *let alone* to a movie theater, must grow more widespread all the time. Some producers are experimenting with releasing movies to theaters and to DVD *at the same time*, a move that some say will doom the movie industry and some say will save it, reaching the eighty percent of the potential audience who never go to the theater at all. Although probably some art-house and specialty theaters will survive, and big-screen IMAX theaters are doing increasingly well with Big Ticket releases like *Harry Potter* movies, it may be that the days of the cineplex are numbered.

Turning to SF and fantasy television shows, most of this year was just the fallout from last year's sudden explosion of unexpected mega-hit genre shows, from *Lost* and *Desperate Housewives* (although this is really a genre show only by courtesy, in spite of the conceit that it's being narrated by a ghost) to *Medium*, which in turn spawned a trio of "alien invasion" SF shows – *Surface*, *Invasion*, and *Threshold* – and a few more "I see and/or fight dead people" shows such as *The Ghost Whisperer*, *The Night Stalker*, and *Supernatural*. This year was spent shaking down from all that, with shows enjoying one degree or another of success, and few new contenders being added to the race.

The once-potent ratings blockbuster *Joan of Arcadia* died after network suits fixed it to death. *The Night Stalker* went through town as fast as green corn through the hired man. *Andromeda* breathed its last, and I believe that *The Dead Zone* is gone as well. *The Ghost Whisperer* and *Supernatural* seem to have established themselves as fairly solid series. Of the alien-invasion trio, *Threshold* has died, but *Invasion* and *Surface* seem to be doing okay enough to stay on the air, for the moment, anyway (although the ultimate fate of *Surface* may still be in doubt), although neither is a ratings monster. *Invasion* seems to be the one that's the most popular with the critics, and it may be getting some advantage from holdover audiences from *Lost*, which airs just before it. Veteran shows *Smallville* and *Charmed*, which looked likely to be canceled all last year, got picked up for new seasons after all, and, as both seem to be doing better this year, will probably be picked up for another new season (moving *Smallville* to another night and away from head-to-head competition with *Lost* seems to have helped).

Lost and *Desperate Housewives* both continue to be *very* popular and successful shows, with *Lost* winning the Golden Globe for Best Drama and *Desperate Housewives* winning the Golden Globe for Best Comedy. Some critics are muttering about a "sophomore slump" for *Desperate Housewives*, and some *Lost* fans seem to find the solutions to enigmas such as what's in the Hatch and what the monster looks like less evocative than the mysteries themselves had been – a problem that this series is always going to have, I fear.

Now that *Star Trek: Enterprise*, *Firefly*, *Farscape*, *Babylon 5*, and *Andromeda* have sunk, vanishing into hyperspace with nary a ripple left behind, the special-effects-heavy hardcore SF show is left in the hands of the "Stargate" franchise – *Stargate SG-1* and *Stargate Atlantis* – and in those of popular new contender *Battlestar Galactica*. All seem to be doing well. It was hard to even get me to watch *Battlestar Galactica*, since I loathed the old Lorne Green series so much, but I must admit that they've done a good job with the remake, which is much darker and more concerned with psychological motivations and *realpolitik* than the ham-handed Battlestar Galactica of old. It's very reminiscent in tone of Babylon Five in fact, and seeming to do nearly as well with the critics. Of course, although shows like *Babylon Five* and *Farscape* were *successes d'estime*, they never succeeded in pulling in large-enough audiences to keep them on the air, and it'll be interesting to see if *Battlestar Galactica* can pull that off where they could not.

In spite of the huge success of *Lost*, and the lesser but not entirely trivial success of *Invasion, Surface, Battlestar Galactica*, and the *Stargate* shows, few new science fiction shows seem to be on the drawing boards for next season. Guess it's a lot cheaper to produce *Medium/Ghost Whisperer*–type shows instead. Or even cheaper, the ever-reliable reality shows. (Feh.)

The 63rd World Science Fiction Convention, Interaction, was held in Glasgow, Scotland, from August 4–8, 2005, and drew an estimated attendance of 4,321. The 2005 Hugo Awards, presented at Interaction, were: Best Novel, *Jonathan Strange & Mr. Norrell*, by Susanna Clarke; Best Novella, "The Concrete Jungle," by Charles Stross; Best Novelette, "The Faery Handbag," by Kelly Link; Best Short Story, "Travels with My Cats," by Mike Resnick; Best Related Book, *The Cambridge Companion to Science Fiction*, edited by Edward James and Farah Mendlesohn; Best Professional Editor, Ellen Datlow; Best Professional Artist, Jim Burns; Best Dramatic Presentation (short form), *Battlestar Galactica*, "33"; Best Dramatic Presentation (long form) *The Incredibles*; Best Semiprozine, *Ansible*, edited by David Langford; Best Fanzine, *Plokta*; Best Fan Writer, David Langford; Best Fan Artist, Sue Mason; Best Web site, *SCI FICTION*; plus the John W. Campbell Award for Best New Writer to Elizabeth Bear.

The 2004 Nebula Awards, presented at a banquet at the Bismark Hotel in Chicago, Illinois, on April 30, 2005, were: Best Novel, *Paladin of Souls*, by Lois McMaster Bujold; Best Novella, "The Green Leopard Plague," by Walter Jon Williams; Best Novelette, "Basement Magic," by Ellen Klages; Best Short Story, "Coming to Terms," by Eileen Gunn; Best Script, *The Lord of the Rings: The Return of the King*, by Fran Walsh, Philippa Boyens, and Peter Jackson; plus the Grand Master Award to Anne McCaffrey.

The 2005 World Fantasy Awards, presented at the Fourteenth Annual World Fantasy Convention in Madison, Wisconsin, on November 6, 2005, were: Best Novel, *Jonathan Strange & Mr. Norrell*, by Susanna Clarke; Best Novella, "The Growlimb," by Michael Shea; Best Short Fiction, "Singing My Sister Down," by Margo Lanagan; Best Collection, *Black Juice*, by Margo Lanagan; Best Anthology, *Acquainted with the Night*, edited by Barbara and Christopher Roden and *Dark Matter:*

Reading the Bones, edited by Sheree R. Thomas (tie); Best Artist, John Picacio; Special Award (Professional), to S. T. Joshi, for scholarship; Special Award (Non-Professional), to Robert Morgan, for *Sarob Press*, plus Life Achievement Awards to Tom Doherty and Carol Emshwiller.

The 2005 Bram Stoker Awards, presented by the Horror Writers of America during a banquet at the Hilton Burbank Hotel in Burbank, California, on June 25, 2005, were: Best Novel, *In the Night Room*, by Peter Straub; Best First Novel, *Covenant*, by John Everson and *Stained*, by Lee Thomas (tie); Best Long Fiction, *The Turtle Boy*, by Kealan-Patrick Burke; Best Short Fiction, "Nimitseahpah," by Nancy Etchemendy; Best Collection, *Fearful Symmetries*, by Thomas F. Monteleone; Best Anthology, *The Year's Best Fantasy and Horror: Seventeenth Annual Collection*, edited by Ellen Datlow, Kelly Link, and Gavin Grant; Nonfiction, *Hellnotes*, edited by Judi Rohrig; Best Illustrated Narrative, *Heaven's Devils*, by Jai Nitz; Best Screenplay, *Eternal Sunshine of the Spotless Mind*, by Charlie Kaufman, Michel Gondry, and Pierre Bismuth and *Shaun of the Dead*, by Simon Pegg and Edgar Wright (tie); Best Work for Younger Readers, *Abarat: Days of Magic, Nights of War*, by Clive Barker and *Oddest Yet*, by Steve Burt (tie); Best Poetry Collection, *The Women at the Funeral*, by Corinne De Winter; Best Alternative Forms, *The Devil's Wine*, by Tom Piccirilli; plus the Lifetime Achievement Award to Michael Moorcock.

The 2004 John W. Campbell Memorial Award was won by *Market Forces*, by Richard Morgan.

The 2004 Theodore Sturgeon Memorial Award for Best Short Story was won by "Sergeant Chip," by Bradley Denton.

The 2004 Philip K. Dick Memorial Award went to *Life*, by Gwyneth Jones.

The 2004 Arthur C. Clarke award was won by *Iron Council*, by China Mieville.

The 2004 James Tiptree, Jr. Memorial Award was won by *Camouflage*, by Joe Haldeman and *Troll: A Love Story*, by Johanna Sinisalo (tie).

The Cordwainer Smith Rediscovery Award, awarded at Readercon, went to Leigh Brackett.

Dead in 2005 or early 2006 were: **ROBERT SHECKLEY**, 77, one of SF's foremost humorists and satirists, author of *The Status Civilization*, *Journey Beyond Tomorrow*, and *Mindswap*, as well as hundreds of short stories, including the famous "The Seventh Victim, which was filmed as *The Tenth Victim*; **CHARLES L. HARNESS**, 90, veteran author whose most famous stories were probably "The Rose" and "The New Reality," author as well of many other novels and stories, including *The Ring of Ritornel* and *The Catalyst*; **KENNETH BULMER**, 84, veteran British author, author of dozens of novels, perhaps best known for the "Dray Prescott" series written as "Alan Burt Akers"; **MICHAEL G. CONEY**, 73, SF writer, author of *Mirror Image*, *The Hero of Downways*, *Brontemek*, and many others; **J. N. WILLIAMSON**, horror writer and editor of the long-running horror anthology series *Masques*, winner of the Lifetime Achievement Award from the Horror Writers of America; **CHRIS BUNCH**, 62, SF writer, author of *Shadow Warrior*, *Star Risk*, *Last Legion*, and others; **WARREN NORWOOD**, 59, SF writer, author of *The Planet of Flowers* and *The Windhover Tapes*, among others; **JOSEF NESVADBA**, 79, leading Czech SF writer, **CHRISTIAN ANTON MAYER**, 83, German SF writer who wrote as "Carl Amery"; **DENIS LINDBOHM**, 78, Swedish author; **VLADIMIR VOLKOFF**, 72, French SF writer; **DAN TSALKA**, 69, Israeli SF writer; **PIERRE BURTON**, 84, Canadian author; **WILLO DAVIS ROBERTS**, 79, Young Adult and fantasy writer; **ELIZABETH CHATER**, 94, romance writer and occasional SF author; **BRUCE B. CASSIDAY**, 84, veteran author and editor; **MAGDALENA MOUJAN OTANO**, 79, Argentine author; **JEFF SLATEN**, 49, SF writer; **EVAN HUNTER**, 78, who wrote under both that name and as "Ed McBain" – under which name he wrote the "87th Precinct" novels – was one of the mainstays of the mystery genre, and who also wrote a few SF novels such as *Tomorrow's World* and *Rocket to Luna*; **JOHN FOWLES**, 79, well-known author of novels such as *The French Lieutenant's Woman* and *The Magus*, who also wrote books such as *A Maggot*, which incorporated some genre elements; **SAUL BELLOW**, 89, prominent author and Nobel laureate whose *Mr. Sammler's Planet* had mild genre elements; **BYRON PREISS**, 52, prominent book packager and editor whose companies included *Byron Preiss Visual Publications* and *ibooks*; **HOWARD DEVORE**, fan and fannish scholar, best known for producing, with Donald Franson, the reference book *A History of the Hugo, Nebula*, and *World Fantasy Awards*; **DANIEL RICHE**, 56, French editor and anthologist; **JOHN BROSNAN**, 58, author, critic, and fan; **SAMUEL H. POST**, 81, SF editor and father of SF writer Jonathan Vos Post; **KEITH PARKINSON**, 47, well-known fantasy artist, winner of two Cheslea Awards; **BERNIE ZUBER**, 72, artist and fan; **GERALD POLLINGER**, 79, prominent literary agent; **DAN HOOKER**, 54, literary agent; **SCOTT WINNETT**, 42, former *Locus* editorial assistant and reviewer; **BILL BOWERS**, 62, well-known Cincinnati-area fan and fanzine editor; **ROBERT WISE**, 86, famous movie director, best known to the genre as director of such movies as *The Day the Earth Stood Still* and *The Andromeda Strain*; **JAMES DOOHAN**, 85, actor, best known for his role as Scotty on the original *Star Trek* TV show, although he also wrote a few genre-related novels; **BOB DENVER**, 70, actor, best known for his role as Gilligan on the semi-fantasy TV show (it certainly had nothing to do with reality) *Gilligan's Island*, although I remember him better as Maynard G. Krebbs from *The Many Loves of Dobie Gillis*; UFO researcher **PHILIP**

J. KLASS, 86 (not to be confused with the Phil Klass who writes as William Tenn); **NOREEN SHAW**, widow of SF editor Larry Shaw and coeditor with him of the Hugo-nominated fanzine Axe; **TAMMY VANCE**, 43, daughter-in-law of SF writer Jack Vance; **HAROLD WOOSTER**, 86, father of SF critic Martin Morse Wooster; **ERMYN HECK**, mother of SF critic and novelist Peter Heck; and **JUDITH LOUISE KOHN**, 63, sister of SF writer Susan Casper.

THE LITTLE GODDESS

Ian McDonald

British author Ian McDonald is an ambitious and daring writer with a wide range and an impressive amount of talent. His first story was published in 1982, and since then he has appeared with some frequency in *Interzone*, *Asimov's Science Fiction*, *New Worlds*, *Zenith*, *Other Edens*, *Amazing*, and elsewhere. He was nominated for the John W. Campbell Award in 1985, and in 1989 he won the Locus "Best First Novel" Award for his novel *Desolation Road*. He won the Philip K. Dick Award in 1992 for his novel *King of Morning, Queen of Day*. His other books include the novels *Out on Blue Six* and *Hearts, Hands and Voices*, *Terminal Cafe*, *Sacrifice of Fools*, *Evolution's Shore*, *Kirinya*, a chapbook novella, *Tendeleo's Story*, *Ares Express*, and *Cyberabad*, as well as two collections of his short fiction, *Empire Dreams* and *Speaking in Tongues*. His most recent novel, *River of Gods*, was a finalist for both the Hugo Award and the Arthur C. Clarke award in 2005. Coming up is another novel, *Brazil*. His stories have appeared in our Eighth through Tenth, Fourteenth through Sixteenth, and Nineteenth and Twentieth Annual Collections. Born in Manchester, England, in 1960, McDonald has spent most of his life in Northern Ireland, and now lives and works in Belfast. He has a Web site at www.lysator.liu.se/~unicorn/mcdonald/.

In the brilliant story that follows, he plunges us into a future India of dazzling complexity and cultural diversity, where the highest of high-tech exists side by side with the most ancient of ancient ways, and unbelievable wealth cheek by jowl with utter poverty, for the compelling and fascinating story of what it feels like to become a god . . . and then have to find your way in an indifferent world on the *other* side of divinity.

I REMEMBER THE NIGHT I became a goddess.

The men collected me from the hotel at sunset. I was light-headed with hunger, for the child-assessors said I must not eat on the day of the test.

I had been up since dawn; the washing and dressing and making up were a long and tiring business. My parents bathed my feet in the bidet. We had never seen such a thing before and that seemed the natural use for it. None of us had ever stayed in a hotel. We thought it most grand, though I see now that it was a budget tourist chain. I remember the smell of onions cooking in *ghee* as I came down in the elevator. It smelled like the best food in the world.

I know the men must have been priests but I cannot remember if they wore formal dress. My mother cried in the lobby; my father's mouth was pulled in and he held his eyes wide, in that way that grown-ups do when they want to cry but cannot let tears be seen. There were two other girls for the test staying in the same hotel. I did not know them; they were from other villages where the *devi* could live. Their parents wept unashamedly. I could not understand it; their daughters might be goddesses.

On the street, rickshaw drivers and pedestrians hooted and waved at us with our red robes and third eyes on our foreheads. The *devi*, the *devi* look! Best of all fortune! The other girls held on tight to the men's hands. I lifted my skirts and stepped into the car with the darkened windows.

They took us to the Hanumandhoka. Police and machines kept the people out of the Durbar Square. I remember staring long at the machines, with their legs like steel chickens' and naked blades in their hands. The King's Own fighting machines. Then I saw the temple and its great roofs sweeping up and up and up into the red sunset and I thought for one instant the upturned eaves were bleeding.

The room was long and dim and stuffily warm. Low evening light shone in dusty rays through cracks and slits in the carved wood; so bright it almost burned. Outside you could hear the traffic and the bustle of tourists. The walls seemed thin but at the same time kilometers thick. Durbar Square was a world away. The room smelled of brassy metal. I did not recognize it then but I know it now as the smell of blood. Beneath the blood was another smell, of time piled thick as dust. One of the two women who would be my guardians if I passed the test told me the temple was five hundred years old. She was a short, round woman with a face that always seemed to be smiling, but when you looked closely you saw it was not. She made us sit on the floor on red cushions while the men brought the rest of the girls. Some of them were crying already. When there were ten of us the two women left and the door was closed. We sat for a long time in the heat of the long room. Some of the girls fidgeted and chattered but I gave all my attention to the wall carvings and soon I was lost. It has always been easy for me to lose myself; in Shakya I could disappear for hours in the movement of clouds across the mountain, in the ripple of the grey river far below, and the flap of the prayer banner in the wind. My parents saw it as a sign of my inborn divinity, one of the thirty-two that mark those girls in whom the goddess may dwell.

In the failing light I read the story of Jayaprakash Malla playing dice

with the *devi* Taleju Bhawani who came to him in the shape of a red
snake and left with the vow that she would only return to the Kings of
Kathmandu as a virgin girl of low caste, to spite their haughtiness. I
could not read its end in the darkness, but I did not need to. I was its
end, or one of the other nine low-caste girls in the god-house of the *devi*.

Then the doors burst open wide and firecrackers exploded and
through the rattle and smoke red demons leaped into the hall. Behind
them men in crimson beat pans and clappers and bells. At once two of
the girls began to cry and the two women came and took them away.
But I knew the monsters were just silly men. In masks. These were not
even close to demons. I have seen demons, after the rain clouds when
the light comes low down the valley and all the mountains leap up as
one. Stone demons, kilometers high. I have heard their voices, and their
breath does not smell like onions. The silly men danced close to me,
shaking their red manes and red tongues, but I could see their eyes
behind the painted holes and they were afraid of me.

Then the door banged open again with another crash of fireworks
and more men came through the smoke. They carried baskets draped
with red sheets. They set them in front of us and whipped away the
coverings. Buffalo heads, so freshly struck off the blood was bright and
glossy. Eyes rolled up, lolling tongues still warm, noses still wet. And
the flies, swarming around the severed neck. A man pushed a basket
towards me on my cushion as if it were a dish of holy food. The crashing
and beating outside rose to a roar, so loud and metallic it hurt. The girl
from my own Shakya village started to wail; the cry spread to another
and then another, then a fourth. The other woman, the tall pinched one
with a skin like an old purse, came in to take them out, carefully lifting
her gown so as not to trail it in the blood. The dancers whirled around
like flames and the kneeling man lifted the buffalo head from the basket.
He held it up in my face, eye to eye, but all I thought was that it must
weigh a lot; his muscles stood out like vines, his arm shook. The flies
looked like black jewels. Then there was a clap from outside and the
men set down the heads and covered them up with their cloths and they
left with the silly demon men whirling and leaping around them.

There was one other girl left on her cushion now. I did not know her.
She was of a Vajryana family from Niwar down the valley. We sat a
long time, wanting to talk but not knowing if silence was part of the
trial. Then the door opened a third time and two men led a white goat
into the *devi* hall. They brought it right between me and the Niwari girl.
I saw its wicked, slotted eye roll. One held the goat's tether, the other
took a big ceremonial *kukri* from a leather sheath. He blessed it and
with one fast strong stroke sent the goat's head leaping from its body.

I almost laughed, for the goat looked so funny, its body not knowing
where its head was, the head looking around for the body and then the
body realizing that it had no head and going down with a kick, and why
was the Niwari girl screaming, couldn't she see how funny it was, or
was she screaming because I saw the joke and she was jealous of that?
Whatever her reason, smiling woman and weathered woman came and

took her very gently away and the two men went down on their knees in the spreading blood and kissed the wooden floor. They lifted away the two parts of the goat. I wished they hadn't done that. I would have liked someone with me in the big wooden hall. But I was on my own in the heat and the dark and then, over the traffic, I heard the deep-voiced bells of Kathmandu start to swing and ring. For the last time the doors opened and there were the women, in the light.

"Why have you left me all alone?" I cried. "What have I done wrong?"

"How could you do anything wrong, goddess?" said the old, wrinkled woman who, with her colleague, would become my mother and father and teacher and sister. "Now come along with us and hurry. The King is waiting."

Smiling Kumarima and Tall Kumarima (as I would now have to think of them) took a hand each and led me, skipping, from the great looming Hanuman temple. A road of white silk had been laid from the foot of the temple steps to a wooden palace close by. The people had been let into the square and they pressed on either side of the processional way, held back by the police and the King's robots. The machines held burning torches in their grasping hands. Fire glinted from their killing blades. There was great silence in the dark square.

"Your home, goddess," said Smiling Kumarima, bending low to whisper in my ear. "Walk the silk, *devi*. Do not stray off it. I have your hand, you will be safe with me."

I walked between my Kumarimas, humming a pop tune I had heard on the radio at the hotel. When I looked back I saw that I had left two lines of bloody footprints.

You have no caste, no village, no home. This palace is your home, and who would wish for any other? We have made it lovely for you, for you will only leave it six times a year. Everything you need is here within these walls.

You have no mother or father. How can a goddess have parents? Nor have you brothers and sisters. The King is your brother, the kingdom your sister. The priests who attend on you, they are nothing. We your Kumarimas are less than nothing. Dust, dirt, a tool. You may say anything and we must obey it.

As we have said, you will leave the palace only six times a year. You will be carried in a palanquin. Oh, it is a beautiful thing, carved wood and silk. Outside this palace you shall not touch the ground. The moment you touch the ground, you cease to be divine.

You will wear red, with your hair in a topknot and your toe- and fingernails painted. You will carry the red *tilak* of Siva on your forehead. We will help you with your preparations until they become second nature.

You will speak only within the confines of your palace, and little even then. Silence becomes the Kumari. You will not smile or show any emotion.

You will not bleed. Not a scrape, not a scratch. The power is in the blood and when the blood leaves, the *devi* leaves. On the day of your first blood, even one single drop, we will tell the priest and he will inform the King that the goddess has left. You will no longer be divine and you will leave this palace and return to your family. You will not bleed.

You have no name. You are Taleju, you are Kumari. You are the goddess.

These instructions my two Kumarimas whispered to me as we walked between kneeling priests to the King in his plumed crown of diamonds and emeralds and pearls. The King *namasted* and we sat side by side on lion thrones and the long hall throbbed to the bells and drums of Durbar Square. I remember thinking that a King must bow to me but there are rules even for goddesses.

Smiling Kumarima and Tall Kumarima. I draw Tall Kumarima in my memory first, for it is right to give pre-eminence to age. She was almost as tall as a Westerner and thin as a stick in a drought. At first I was scared of her. Then I heard her voice and could never be scared again; her voice was kind as a singing bird. When she spoke you felt you now knew everything. Tall Kumarima lived in a small apartment above a tourist shop on the edge of Durbar Square. From her window she could see my Kumari Ghar, among the stepped towers of the *dhokas*. Her husband had died of lung cancer from pollution and cheap Indian cigarettes. Her two tall sons were grown and married with children of their own, older than me. In that time she had mothered five Kumari *Devis* before me.

Next I remember Smiling Kumarima. She was short and round and had breathing problems for which she used inhalers, blue and brown. I would hear the snake hiss of them on days when Durbar Square was golden with smog. She lived out in the new suburbs up on the western hills, a long journey even by the royal car at her service. Her children were twelve, ten, nine, and seven. She was jolly and treated me like her fifth baby, the young favorite, but I felt even then that, like the demon-dancing-men, she was scared of me. Oh, it was the highest honor any woman could hope for, to be the mother of the goddess – so to speak – though you wouldn't think it to hear her neighbors in the unit, *shutting yourself away in that dreadful wooden box, and all the blood, medieval, medieval*, but they couldn't understand. Somebody had to keep the king safe against those who would turn us into another India, or worse, China; someone had to preserve the old ways of the divine kingdom. I understood early that difference between them. Smiling Kumarima was my mother out of duty. Tall Kumarima from love.

I never learned their true names. Their rhythms and cycles of shifts waxed and waned through the days and nights like the faces of the moon. Smiling Kumarima once found me looking up through the lattice of a *jali* screen at the fat moon on a rare night when the sky was clear and healthy and shouted me away, *don't be looking at that thing, it will call the blood out of you, little devi, and you will be the devi no more.*

Within the wooden walls and iron rules of my Kumari Ghar, years become indistinguishable, indistinct. I think now I was five when I became Taleju Devi. The year, I believe, was 2034. But some memories break the surface, like flowers through snow.

Monsoon rain on the steep-sloped roofs, water rushing and gurgling through the gutters, and the shutter that every year blew loose and rattled in the wind. We had monsoons, then. Thunder demons in the mountains around the city, my room flash lit with lightning. Tall Kumarima came to see if I needed singing to sleep but I was not afraid. A goddess cannot fear a storm.

The day I went walking in the little garden, when Smiling Kumarima let out a cry and fell at my feet on the grass and the words to tell her to get up, not to worship me were on my lips when she held, between thumb and forefinger, twisting and writhing and trying to find a place for its mouth to seize: a green leech.

The morning Tall Kumarima came to tell me people had asked me to show myself. At first I had thought it wonderful that people would want to come and look at me on my little *jharoka* balcony in my clothes and paint and jewels. Now I found it tiresome; all those round eyes and gaping mouths. It was a week after my tenth birthday. I remember Tall Kumarima smiled but tried not to let me see. She took me to the *jharoka* to wave to the people in the court and I saw a hundred Chinese faces upturned to me, then the high, excited voices. I waited and waited but two tourists would not go away. They were an ordinary couple, dark local faces, country clothes.

"Why are they keeping us waiting?" I asked.

"Wave to them," Tall Kumarima urged. "That is all they want." The woman saw my lifted hand first. She went weak and grabbed her husband by the arm. The man bent to her, then looked up at me. I read many emotions on that face; shock, confusion, recognition, revulsion, wonder, hope. Fear. I waved and the man tugged at his wife, *look, look up*. I remember that against all the laws, I smiled. The woman burst into tears. The man made to call out but Tall Kumarima hastened me away.

"Who were those funny people?" I asked. "They were both wearing very white shoes."

"Your mother and father," Tall Kumarima said. As she led me down the Durga corridor with the usual order not to brush my free hand along the wooden walls for fear of splinters, I felt her grip tremble.

That night I dreamed the dream of my life, that is not a dream but one of my earliest experiences, knocking and knocking and knocking at the door of my remembering. This was a memory I would not admit in daylight, so it must come by night, to the secret door.

I am in the cage over a ravine. A river runs far below, milky with mud and silt, foaming cream over the boulders and slabs sheared from the mountainsides. The cable spans the river from my home to the summer grazing and I sit in the wire cage used to carry the goats across the river. At my back is the main road, always loud with trucks, the prayer banners and Kinley bottled water sign of my family's roadside teahouse.

My cage still sways from my uncle's last kick. I see him, arms and legs wrapped around the wire, grinning his gap-toothed grin. His face is summer-burned brown, his hands cracked and stained from the trucks he services. Oil engrained in the creases. He wrinkles up his nose at me and unhooks a leg to kick my cage forward on its pulley-wheel. Pulley sways cable sways mountains, sky and river sway but I am safe in my little goat-cage. I have been kicked across this ravine many times. My uncle inches forward. Thus we cross the river, by kicks and inches.

I never see what strikes him – some thing of the brain perhaps, like the sickness Lowlanders get when they go up to the high country. But the next I look my uncle is clinging to the wire by his right arm and leg. His left arm and leg hang down, shaking like a cow with its throat cut, shaking the wire and my little cage. I am three years old and I think this is funny, a trick my uncle is doing just for me, so I shake back, bouncing my cage, bouncing my uncle up and down, up and down. Half his body will not obey him and he tries to move forward by sliding his leg along, like *this*, jerk his hand forward *quick* so he never loses grip of the wire, and all the while bouncing up and down, up and down. Now my uncle tries to shout but his words are noise and slobber because half his face is paralyzed. Now I see his fingers lose their grip on the wire. Now I see him spin round and his hooked leg come free. Now he falls away, half his body reaching, half his mouth screaming. I see him fall, I see him bounce from the rocks and cartwheel, a thing I have always wished I could do. I see him go into the river and the brown water swallow him.

My older brother came out with a hook and a line and hauled me in. When my parents found I was not shrieking, not a sob or a tear or even a pout, that was when they knew I was destined to become the goddess. I was smiling in my wire cage.

I remember best the festivals, for it was only then that I left the Kumari Ghar. Dasain, at the end of summer, was the greatest. For eight days the city ran red. On the final night I lay awake listening to the voices in the square flow together into one roar, the way I imagined the sea would sound, the voices of the men gambling for the luck of Lakshmi, *devi* of wealth. My father and uncles had gambled on the last night of Dasam. I remember I came down and demanded to know what all the laughing was about and they turned away from their cards and really laughed. I had not thought there could be so many coins in the world as there were on that table but it was nothing compared to Kathmandu on the eighth of Dasain. Smiling Kumarima told me it took some of the priests all year to earn back what they lost. Then came the ninth day, the great day and I sailed out from my palace for the city to worship me.

I traveled on a litter carried by forty men strapped to bamboo poles as thick as my body. They went gingerly, testing every step, for the streets were slippery. Surrounded by gods and priests and *saddhus* mad with holiness, I rode on my golden throne. Closer to me than any were my Kumarimas, my two Mothers, so splendid and ornate in their red robes and headdresses and make-up they did not look like humans at all. But Tall Kumarima's voice and Smiling Kumarima's smile assured me as I rode with Hanuman and Taleju through the cheering and the music and the banners bright against the blue sky and the smell I now recognized from the night I became a goddess, the smell of blood.

That Dasain the city received me as never before. The roar of the night of Lakshmi continued into the day. As Taleju *Devi* I was not supposed to notice anything as low as humans but out of the corners of my painted eyes I could see beyond the security robots stepping in time with my bearers, and the streets radiating out from the *stupa* of Chhetrapati were solid with bodies. They threw jets and gushes of water from plastic bottles up into the air, glittering, breaking into little rainbows, raining down on them, soaking them, but they did not care. Their faces were crazy with devotion.

Tall Kumarima saw my puzzlement and bent to whisper.

"They do *puja* for the rain. The monsoon has failed a second time, *devi*."

As I spoke, Smiling Kumarima fanned me so no one would see my lips move. "We don't like the rain," I said firmly.

"A goddess cannot do only what she likes," Tall Kumarima said. "It is a serious matter. The people have no water. The rivers are running dry."

I thought of the river that ran far down deep below the house where I was born, the water creamy and gushing and flecked with yellow foam. I saw it swallow my uncle and could not imagine it ever becoming thin, weak, hungry.

"So why do they throw water then?" I asked.

"So the *devi* will give them more," Smiling Kumarima explained. But I could not see the sense in that even for goddesses and I frowned, trying to understand how humans were and so I was looking right at him when he came at me.

He had city-pale skin and hair parted on the left that flopped as he dived out of the crowd. He moved his fists to the collar of his diagonally striped shirt and people surged away from him. I saw him hook his thumbs into two loops of black string. I saw his mouth open in a great cry. Then the machine swooped and I saw a flash of silver. The young man's head flew up into the air. His mouth and eyes went round: from a cry to an oh! The King's Own machine had sheathed its blade, like a boy folding a knife, before the body, like that funny goat in the Hanumandhoka, realized it was dead and fell to the ground. The crowd screamed and tried to get away from the headless thing. My bearers rocked, swayed, uncertain where to go, what to do. For a moment I thought they might drop me.

Smiling Kumarima let out little shrieks of horror, "Oh! Oh! Oh!" My face was spotted with blood.

"It's not hers," Tall Kumarima shouted. "It's not hers!" She moistened a handkerchief with a lick of saliva. She was gently wiping the young man's blood from my face when the Royal security in their dark suits and glasses arrived, beating through the crowd. They lifted me, stepped over the body and carried me to the waiting car.

"You smudged my make-up," I said to the Royal guard as the car swept away. Worshippers barely made it out of our way in the narrow alleys.

Tall Kumarima came to my room that night. The air was loud with helicopters, quartering the city for the plotters. Helicopters, and machines like the King's Own robots, that could fly and look down on Kathmandu with the eyes of a hawk. She sat on my bed and laid a little transparent blue box on the red and gold embroidered coverlet. In it were two pale pills.

"To help you sleep."

I shook my head. Tall Kumarima folded the blue box into the sleeve of her robe.

"Who was he?"

"A fundamentalist. A *karsevak*. A foolish, sad young man."

"A Hindu, but he wanted to hurt us."

"That is the madness of it, *devi*. He and his kind think our kingdom has grown too western, too far from its roots and religious truths."

"And he attacks us, the Taleju *Devi*. He would have blown up his own goddess, but the machine took his head. That is almost as strange as people throwing water to the rain."

Tall Kumarima bowed her head. She reached inside the sash of her robe and took out a second object which she set on my heavy cover with the same precise care as she had the sleeping pills. It was a light, fingerless glove, for the right hand; clinging to its back was a curl of plastic shaped like a very very tiny goat fetus.

"Do you know what this is?"

I nodded. Every devotee doing *puja* in the streets seemed to own one, right hands held up to snatch my image. A palmer.

"It sends messages into your head," I whispered.

"That is the least of what it can do, *devi*. Think of it like your *jharoka*, but this window opens onto the world beyond Durbar Square, beyond Kathmandu and Nepal. It is an aeai, an artificial intelligence, a thinking-thing, like the machines up there, but much cleverer than them. They are clever enough to fly and hunt and not much else, but this aeai can tell you anything you want to know. All you have to do is ask. And there are things you need to know, *devi*. You will not be Kumari forever. The day will come when you will leave your palace and go back to the world. I have seen them before you." She reached out to take my face between her hands, then drew back. "You are special, my *devi*, but the kind of special it takes to be Kumari means you will find it hard in the world. People will call it a sickness. Worse than that, even . . ."

She banished the emotion by gently fitting the fetus-shaped receiver behind my ear. I felt the plastic move against my skin, then Tall Kumarima slipped on the glove, waved her hand in a *mudra* and I heard her voice inside my head. Glowing words appeared in the air between us, words I had been painstakingly taught to read by Tall Kumarima.

Don't let anyone find it, her dancing hand said. *Tell no one, not even Smiling Kumarima. I know you call her that, but she would not understand. She would think it was unclean, a pollution. In some ways, she is not so different from that man who tried to harm you. Let this be our secret, just you and me.*

Soon after, Smiling Kumarima came to look in on me and check for fleas, but I pretended to be asleep. The glove and the fetus-thing were hidden under my pillow. I imagined them talking to me through the goose down and soft soft cotton, sending dreams while the helicopters and hunting robots wheeled in the night above me. When the latch on her door clicked too, I put on the glove and earhook and went looking for the lost rain. I found it one hundred and fifty kilometers up, through the eye of a weather aeai spinning over east India. I saw the monsoon, a coil of cloud like a cat's claw hooking up across the sea. There had been cats in the village; suspicious things lean on mice and barley. No cat was permitted in the Kumari Ghar. I looked down on my kingdom but I could not see a city or a palace or me down here at all. I saw mountains, white mountains ridged with grey and blue ice. I was goddess of this. And the heart went out of me, because it was nothing, a tiny crust of stone on top of that huge world that hung beneath it like the full teat of a cow, rich and heavy with people and their brilliant cities and their bright nations. India, where our gods and names were born.

Within three days the police had caught the plotters and it was raining. The clouds were low over Kathmandu. The color ran from the temples in Durbar Square but people beat tins and metal cups in the muddy streets calling praise on the Taleju *Devi.*

"What will happen to them?" I asked Tall Kumarima. "The bad men."

"They will likely be hanged," she said.

That autumn after the executions of the traitors the dissatisfaction finally poured on to the streets like sacrificial blood. Both sides claimed me: police and demonstrators. Others yet held me up as both the symbol of all that was good with our Kingdom and also everything wrong with it. Tall Kumarima tried to explain it to me but with my world mad and dangerous my attention was turned elsewhere, to the huge, old land to the south, spread out like a jeweled skirt. In such a time it was easy to be seduced by the terrifying depth of its history, by the gods and warriors who swept across it, empire after empire after empire. My kingdom had always been fierce and free but I met the men who liberated India from the Last Empire – men like gods – and saw that liberty broken up by rivalry and intrigue and corruption into feuding states; Awadh and Bharat, the United States of Bengal, Maratha, Karnataka.

Legendary names and places. Shining cities as old as history. There aeais haunted the crowded streets like *gandhavas.* There men outnumbered women four to one. There the old distinctions were abandoned and women married as far up and men as few steps down the tree of caste as they could. I became as enthralled by their leaders and parties and politics as any of their citizens by the aeai-generated soaps they loved so dearly. My spirit was down in India in that early, hard winter when the police and King's machines restored the old order to the city beyond Durbar Square. Unrest in earth and the three heavens. One day I woke to find snow in the wooden court; the roofs of the temple of Durbar Square heavy with it, like frowning, freezing old men. I knew now that the strange weather was not my doing but the result of huge, slow changes in the climate. Smiling Kumarima came to me in my *jharoka* as I watched flakes thick and soft as ash sift down from the white sky. She knelt before me, rubbed her hands together inside the cuffs of her wide sleeves. She suffered badly in the cold and damp.

"*Devi*, are you not one of my own children to me?"

I waggled my head, not wanting to say yes.

"*Devi*, have I ever, ever given you anything but my best?"

Like her counterpart a season before, she drew a plastic pillbox from her sleeve, set it on her palm. I sat back on my chair, afraid of it as I had never been afraid of anything Tall Kumarima offered me.

"I know how happy we are all here, but change must always happen. Change in the world, like this snow – unnatural, *devi*, not right – change in our city. And we are not immune to it in here, my flower. Change will come to you, *devi*. To you, to your body. You will become a woman. If I could, I would stop it happening to you, *devi*. But I can't. No one can. What I can offer is . . . a delay. A stay. Take these. They will slow down the changes. For years, hopefully. Then we can all be happy here together, *devi*." She looked up from her deferential half-bow, into my eyes. She smiled. "Have I ever wanted anything but the best for you?"

I held out my hand. Smiling Kumarima tipped the pills into my palm. I closed my fist and slipped from my carved throne. As I went to my room, I could hear Smiling Kumarima chanting prayers of thanksgiving to the goddesses in the carvings. I looked at the pills in my hand. Blue seemed such a wrong color. Then I filled my cup in my little washroom and washed them down, two gulps, down, down.

After that they came every day, two pills, blue as the Lord Krishna, appearing as miraculously on my bedside table. For some reason I never told Tall Kumarima, even when she commented on how fractious I was becoming, how strangely inattentive and absent-minded at ceremonies. I told her it was the *devis* in the walls, whispering to me. I knew enough of my specialness, that others have called my *disorder*, that that would be unquestioned. I was tired and lethargic that winter. My sense of smell grew keen to the least odor and the people in my courtyard with their stupid, beaming upturned faces infuriated me. I went for weeks without showing myself. The wooden corridors grew sharp and brassy with old blood. With the insight of demons, I can see now that my body was a chemical battlefield between my own hormones and Smiling Kumarima's puberty suppressants. It was a heavy, humid spring that year and I felt huge and bloated in the heat, a waddling bulb of fluids under my robes and waxy make-up. I started to drop the little blue pills down the commode. I had been Kumari for seven Dasains.

I had thought I would feel like I used to, but I did not. It was not unwell, like the pills had made me feel, it was sensitive, acutely conscious of my body. I would lie in my wooden bed and feel my legs growing longer. I became very very aware of my tiny nipples. The heat and humidity got worse, or so it seemed to me.

At any time I could have opened my palmer and asked it what was happening to me, but I didn't. I was scared that it might tell me it was the end of my divinity.

Tall Kumarima must have noticed that the hem of my gown no longer brushed the floorboards but it was Smiling Kumarima drew back in the corridor as we hurried towards the *darshan* hall, hesitated a moment, said, softly, smiling as always.

"How you're growing, *devi*. Are you still . . . ? No, forgive me, of course . . . Must be this warm weather we're having, makes children shoot up like weeds. My own are bursting out of everything they own, nothing will fit them."

The next morning as I was dressing a tap came on my door, like the scratch of a mouse or the click of an insect.

"*Devi?*"

No insect, no mouse. I froze, palmer in hand, earhook babbling the early morning news reports from Awadh and Bharat into my head.

"We are dressing."

"Yes, *devi*, that is why I would like to come in."

I just managed to peel off the palmer and stuff it under my mattress before the heavy door swung open on its pivot.

"We have been able to dress ourselves since we were six," I retorted.

"Yes, indeed," said Smiling Kumarima, smiling. "But some of the priests have mentioned to me a little laxness in the ritual dress."

I stood in my red and gold night-robe, stretched out my arms and turned, like one of the trance-dancers I saw in the streets from my litter. Smiling Kumarima sighed.

"*Devi*, you know as well as I . . ."

I pulled my gown up over my head and stood unclothed, daring her to look, to search my body for signs of womanhood.

"See?" I challenged.

"Yes," Smiling Kumarima said, "but what is that behind your ear?" She reached to pluck the hook. It was in my fist in a flick.

"Is that what I think it is?" Smiling Kumarima said, soft smiling bulk filling the space between the door and me. "Who gave you that?"

"It is ours," I declared in my most commanding voice but I was a naked twelve-year-old caught in wrongdoing and that commands less than dust.

"Give it to me."

I clenched my fist tighter.

"We are a goddess, you cannot command us."

"A goddess is as a goddess acts and right now, you are acting like a brat. Show me."

She was a mother, I was her child. My fingers unfolded. Smiling

Kumarima recoiled as if I held a poisonous snake. To her eyes of her faith, I did.

"Pollution," she said faintly. "Spoiled, all spoiled." Her voice rose. "I know who gave you this!" Before my fingers could snap shut, she snatched the coil of plastic from my palm. She threw the earhook to the floor as if it burned her. I saw the hem of her skirt raise, I saw the heel come down, but it was my world, my oracle, my window on the beautiful. I dived to rescue the tiny plastic fetus. I remember no pain, no shock, not even Smiling Kumarima's shriek of horror and fear as her heel came down, but I will always see the tip of my right index finger burst in a spray of red blood.

The *pallav* of my yellow sari flapped in the wind as I darted through the Delhi evening crush-hour. Beating the heel of his hand off his buzzer, the driver of the little wasp-colored *phatphat* cut in between a lumbering truck-train painted with gaudy gods and *apsaras* and a cream Government Maruti and pulled into the great chakra of traffic around Connaught Place. In Awadh you drive with your ears. The roar of horns and klaxons and cycle-rickshaw bells assailed from all sides at once. It rose before the dawn birds and only fell silent well after midnight. The driver skirted a *saddhu* walking through the traffic as calmly as if he were wading through the Holy Yamuna. His body was white with sacred ash, a mourning ghost, but his Siva trident burned blood red in the low sun. I had thought Kàthmandu dirty, but Delhi's golden light and incredible sunsets spoke of pollution beyond even that. Huddled in the rear seat of the autorickshaws with Deepti, I wore a smog mask and goggles to protect my delicate eye make-up. But the fold of my sari flapped over my shoulder in the evening wind and the little silver bells jingled.

There were six in our little fleet. We accelerated along the wide avenues of the British Raj, past the sprawling red buildings of old India, toward the glass spires of Awadh. Black kites circled the towers, scavengers, pickers of the dead. We turned beneath cool *neem* trees into the drive of a government bungalow. Burning torches lit us to the pillared porch. House staff in Rajput uniforms escorted us to the *shaadi* marquee.

Mamaji had arrived before any of us. She fluttered and fretted among her birds; a lick, a rub, a straightening, an admonition. "Stand up stand up, we'll have no slumping here. My girls will be the bonniest at this *shaadi*, hear me?" Shweta, her bony, mean-mouthed assistant, collected our smog-masks. "Now girls, palmers ready." We knew the drill with almost military smartness. Hand up, glove on, rings on, hook behind ear jewelry, decorously concealed by the fringed *dupattas* draped over our heads. "We are graced with Awadh's finest tonight. Crème de la crème." I barely blinked as the résumés rolled up my inner vision. "Right girls, from the left, first dozen, two minutes each then on to the next down the list. Quick smart!" Mamaji clapped her hands and we formed a line. A band struck a medley of musical numbers from *Town and Country*, the soap opera that was a national obsession in sophisticated Awadh. There we stood, twelve little wives-a-waiting while the Rajput servants hauled up the rear of the pavilion.

Applause broke around us like rain. A hundred men stood in a rough semi-circle, clapping enthusiastically, faces bright in the light from the carnival lanterns.

When I arrived in Awadh, the first thing I noticed was the people. People pushing people begging people talking people rushing past each other without a look or a word or an acknowledgement. I had thought Kathmandu held more people than a mind could imagine. I had not seen Old Delhi. The constant noise, the everyday callousness, the lack of any respect appalled me. You could vanish into that crowd of faces like a drop of rain into a tank. The second thing I noticed was that the faces were all men. It was indeed as my palmer had whispered to me. There were four men for every woman.

Fine men good men clever men rich men, men of ambition and career and property, men of power and prospects. Men with no hope of ever marrying within their own class and caste. Men with little prospect of marrying ever. *Shaadi* had once been the word for wedding festivities, the groom on his beautiful white horse, so noble, the bride shy and lovely behind her golden veil. Then it became a name for dating agencies: *lovely wheat-complexioned Agarwal, U.S.-university MBA, seeks same civil service-military for matrimonials*. Now it was a bride-parade, a marriage-market for lonely men with large dowries. Dowries that paid a hefty commission to the Lovely Girl *Shaadi* Agency.

The Lovely Girls lined up on the left side of the Silken Wall that ran the length of the bungalow garden. The first twelve men formed up on the right. They plumped and preened in their finery but I could see they were nervous. The partition was no more than a row of saris pinned to a line strung between plastic uprights, fluttering in the rising evening wind. A token of decorum. Purdah. They were not even silk.

Reshmi was first to walk and talk the Silken Wall. She was a Yadav country girl from Uttaranchal, big-handed and big-faced. A peasant's daughter. She could cook and sew and sing, do household accounts, manage both domestic aeais and human staff. Her first prospective was a weaselly man with a weak jaw in government whites and a Nehru cap. He had bad teeth. Never good. Any one of us could have told him he was wasting his *shaadi* fee, but they *namasted* to each other and stepped out, regulation three paces between them. At the end of the walk Reshmi would loop back to rejoin the tail of the line and meet her next prospective. On big *shaadis* like this my feet would bleed by the end of the night. Red footprints on the marble floors of Mamaji's courtyard *haveli*.

I stepped out with Ashok, a big globe of a thirty-two-year-old who wheezed a little as he rolled along. He was dressed in a voluminous white *kurta*, the fashion this season though he was fourth generation Punjabi. His grooming amounted to an uncontrollable beard and oily hair that smelled of too much Dapper Deepak pomade. Even before he *namasted* I knew it was his first *shaadi*. I could see his eyeballs move as he read my résumé, seeming to hover before him. I did not need to read his to know he was a *dataraja*, for he talked about nothing but himself and the brilliant things he was doing; the spec of some new protein processor array, the 'ware he was breeding, the aeais he was nurturing in his stables, his trips to Europe and the United States where everyone knew his name and great people were glad to welcome him.

"Of course, Awadh's never going to ratify the Hamilton Acts – no matter how close Shrivastava Minister is to President McAuley – but if it did, if we allow ourselves that tiny counterfactual – well, it's the end of the economy: Awadh is IT, there are more graduates in Mehrauli than there are in the whole of California. The Americans may go on about the mockery of a human soul, but they *need* our Level 2.8s – you know what that is? An aeai can pass as human 99 percent of the time – because everybody knows no one does quantum crypto like us, so I'm not worrying about having to close up the data-haven, and even if they do, well, there's always Bharat – I cannot see the Ranas bowing down to Washington, not when 25 percent of their forex comes out of licensing deals from *Town and Country* . . . and that's hundred percent aeai generated . . ."

He was a big affable clown of a man with wealth that would have bought my Palace in Durbar Square and every priest in it and I found myself praying to Taleju to save me from marrying such a bore. He stopped in mid-stride, so abruptly I almost tripped.

"You must keep walking," I hissed. "That is the rule."

"Wow," he said, standing stupid, eyes round in surprise. Couples piled up behind us. In my peripheral vision I could see Mamaji making urgent, threatening gestures. Get him *on*. "Oh wow. You're an ex-Kumari."

"Please, you are drawing attention to yourself." I would have tugged his arm, but that would have been an even more deadly error.

"What was it like, being a goddess?"

"I am just a woman now, like any other," I said. Ashok gave a soft harrumph, as if he had achieved a very small enlightenment, and walked on, hands clasped behind his back. He may have spoken to me once, twice before we reached the end of the Silk Wall and parted: I did not hear him, I did not hear the music, I did not even hear the eternal thunder of Delhi's traffic. The only sound in my head was the high-pitched sound between my eyes of needing to cry but knowing I could not. Fat, selfish, gabbling, Ashok had sent me back to the night I ceased to be a goddess.

Bare soles slapping the polished wood of the Kumari Ghar's corridors. Running feet, muted shouts growing ever more distant as I knelt, still unclothed for my Kumarima's inspection, looking at the blood drip from my smashed fingertip onto the painted wood floor. I remember no pain; rather, I looked at the pain from a separate place, as if the girl who felt it were another person. Far far away, Smiling

Kumarima stood, held in time, hands to mouth in horror and guilt. The voices faded and the bells of Durbar Square began to swing and toll, calling to their brothers across the city of Kathmandu until the valley rang from Bhaktapur to Trisuli Bazaar for the fall of the Kumari *Devi*.

In the space of a single night, I became human again. I was taken to the Hanumandhoka – walking this time like anyone else on the paving stones – where the priests said a final *puja*. I handed back my red robes and jewels and boxes of make-up, all neatly folded and piled. Tall Kumarima had got me human clothes. I think she had been keeping them for some time. The King did not come to say goodbye to me. I was no longer his sister. But his surgeons had put my finger back together well, though they warned that it would always feel a little numb and inflexible.

I left at dawn, while the street cleaners were washing down the stones of Durbar Square beneath the apricot sky, in a smooth-running Royal Mercedes with darkened windows. My Kumarimas made their farewells at the palace gate. Tall Kumarima hugged me briefly to her.

"Oh, there was so much more I needed to do. Well, it will have to suffice."

I felt her quivering against me, like a bird too tightly gripped in a hand. Smiling Kumarima could not look at me. I did not want her to.

As the car took me across the waking city I tried to understand how it felt to be human. I had been a goddess so long I could hardly remember feeling any other way, but it seemed so little different that I began to suspect that you are divine because people say you are. The road climbed through green suburbs, winding now, growing narrower, busy with brightly decorated buses and trucks. The houses grew leaner and meaner, to roadside hovels and *chai*-stalls and then we were out of the city – the first time since I had arrived seven years before. I pressed my hands and face to the glass and looked down on Kathmandu beneath its shroud of ochre smog. The car joined the long line of traffic along the narrow, rough road that clung to the valley side. Above me, mountains dotted with goatherd shelters and stone shrines flying tattered prayer banners. Below me, rushing cream-brown water. Nearly there. I wondered how far behind me on this road were those other government cars, carrying the priests sent to seek out little girls bearing the thirty-two signs of perfection. Then the car rounded the bend in the valley and I was home, Shakya, its truck halts and gas station, the shops and the temple of Padma Narteswara, the dusty trees with white rings painted around their trunks and between them the stone wall and arch where the steps led down through the terraces to my house, and in that stone-framed rectangle of sky, my parents, standing there side by side, pressing closely, shyly, against each other as I had last seen them lingering in the courtyard of the Kumari Ghar.

Mamaji was too respectable to show anything like outright anger, but she had ways of expressing her displeasure. The smallest crust of roti at dinner, the meanest scoop of *dhal*. New girls coming, make room make room – me to the highest, stuffiest room, furthest from the cool of the courtyard pool.

"He asked for my palmer address," I said.

"If I had a rupee for every palmer address," Mamaji said. "He was only interested in you as a novelty, dearie. Anthropology. He was never going to make a proposition. No, you can forget right about him."

But my banishment to the tower was a small punishment for it lifted me above the noise and fumes of the old city. If portions were cut, small loss: the food had been dreadful every day of the almost two years I had been at the *haveli*. Through the wooden lattice, beyond the water tanks and satellite dishes and kids playing rooftop cricket, I could see the ramparts of the Red Fort, the minarets and domes of the Jami Masjid and beyond them, the glittering glass and titanium spires of New Delhi. And higher than any of them, the flocks of pigeons from the *kabooter* lofts, clay pipes bound to their legs so they fluted and sang as they swirled over Chandni Chowk. And Mamaji's worldly wisdom made her a fool this time, for Ashok was surreptitiously messaging me, sometimes questions about when I was divine, mostly about himself and his great plans and ideas. His lilac-colored words, floating in my inner-vision against the intricate silhouettes of my *jali* screens, were bright pleasures in those high summer days. I discovered the delight of political argument; against Ashok's breezy optimism, I set my readings of the news channels. From the opinion columns it seemed inevitable to me that Awadh, in exchange for Favored Nation status from the United States of America, would ratify the Hamilton Acts and outlaw all aeais more intelligent than a langur monkey. I told none of our intercourse to Mamaji. She would have forbidden it, unless he made a proposal.

On an evening of pre-monsoon heat, when the boys were too tired even for cricket and the sky was an upturned brass bowl, Mamaji came to my turret on the top of the old merchant's *haveli*. Against propriety, the *jalis* were thrown open, my gauze curtains stirred in the swirls of heat rising from the alleys below.

"Still you are eating my bread." She prodded my *thali* with her foot. It was too hot for food, too hot for anything other than lying and waiting for the rain and the cool, if it came at all this year. I could hear the voices of the girls down in the courtyard as they kicked their legs in the pool. This day I would have loved to be sitting along the tiled edge with them but I was piercingly aware that I had lived in the *haveli* of the Lovely Girl *Shaadi* Agency longer than any of them. I did not want to be their Kumarima. And when the whispers along the cool marble corridors made them aware of my childhood, they would ask for small *pujas*, little miracles to help them find the right man. I no longer granted them, not because I feared that I had no power any more – that I never had – but that it went out from me and into them and that was why they got the bankers and television executives and Mercedes salesmen.

"I should have left you in that Nepalese sewer. Goddess! Hah! And me fooled into thinking you were a prize asset. Men! They may have share options and Chowpatty Beach apartments but deep down, they're as superstitious as any back-country *yadav*."

"I'm sorry, Mamaji," I said, turning my eyes away.

"Can you help it? You were only born perfect in thirty-two different ways. Now you listen, *cho chweet*. A man came to call on me."

Men always came calling, glancing up at the giggles and rustles of the Lovely Girls peeping through the *jalis* as he waited in the cool of the courtyard for Shweta to present him to Mamaji. Men with offers of marriage, men with prenuptial contracts, men with dowry down-payments. Men asking for special, private viewings. This man who had called on Mamaji had come for one of these.

"Fine young man, lovely young man, just twenty. Father's big in water. He has requested a private rendezvous, with you."

I was instantly suspicious, but I had learned among the Lovely Girls of Delhi, even more than among the priests and Kumarimas of Kathmandu, to let nothing show on my painted face.

"Me? Such an honor . . . and him only twenty . . . and a good family too, so well connected."

"He is a Brahmin."

"I know I am only a Shakya . . ."

"You don't understand. He is a *Brahmin*."

There was so much more I needed to do, Tall Kumarima had said as the royal car drove away from the carved wooden gates of the Kumari Ghar. One whisper through the window would have told me everything: the *curse of the Kumari*.

Shakya hid from me. People crossed the street to find things to look at and do. Old family friends nodded nervously before remembering important business they had to be about. The *chai-dhabas* gave me free tea so I would feel uncomfortable and leave. Truckers were my friends, bus-drivers and long-haulers pulled in at the biodiesel stations. They must have wondered who was this strange twelve-year-old girl, hanging around truck-halts. I do not doubt some of them thought more. Village by village, town by town the legend spread up and down the north road. Ex-Kumari.

Then the accidents started. A boy lost half his hand in the fan belt of a Nissan engine. A teenager drank bad *rakshi* and died of alcohol poisoning. A man slipped between two passing trucks and was crushed. The talk in the *chai-dhabas* and the repair shops was once again of my uncle who fell to his death while the little goddess-to-be bounced in her wire cradle laughing and laughing and laughing.

I stopped going out. As winter took hold over the head-country of the Kathmandu valley, whole weeks passed when I did not leave my room. Days slipped away watching sleet slash past my window, the prayer banners bent almost horizontal in the wind, the wire of the cableway bouncing. Beneath it, the furious, flooding river. In that season the voices of the demons spoke loud from the mountain, telling me the most hateful things about faithless Kumaris who betray the sacred heritage of their devi.

On the shortest day of the year the bride buyer came through Shakya. I heard a voice I did not recognize talking over the television that burbled away day and night in the main room. I opened the door just enough to admit a voice and gleam of firelight.

"I wouldn't take the money off you. You're wasting your time here in Nepal. Everyone knows the story, and even if they pretend they don't believe, they don't act that way."

I heard my father's voice but could not make out his words. The bride buyer said,

"What might work is down south, Bharat or Awadh. They're so desperate in Delhi they'll even take Untouchables. They're a queer lot, those Indians; some of them might even like the idea of marrying a goddess, like a status thing. But I can't take her, she's too young, they'll send her straight back at the border. They've got rules. In India, would you believe? Call me when she turns fourteen."

Two days after my fourteenth birthday, the bride buyer returned to Shakya and I left with him in his Japanese SUV. I did not like his company or trust his hands, so I slept or feigned sleep while he drove down into the lowlands of the Terai. When I woke I was well over the border into my childhood land of wonder. I had thought the bride-buyer would take me to ancient, holy Varanasi, the new capital of the Bharat's dazzling Rana dynasty, but the Awadhis, it seemed, were less in awe of Hindu superstitions. So we came to the vast, incoherent roaring sprawl of the two Delhis, like twin hemispheres of a brain, and to the Lovely Girl *Shaadi* Agency. Where the marriageable men were not so twenty-forties sophisticated, at least in the matter of *ex-devis*. Where the only ones above the curse of the Kumari were those held in even greater superstitious awe: the genetically engineered children known as Brahmins.

Wisdom was theirs, health was theirs, beauty and success and status assured and a wealth that could never be devalued or wasted or gambled away, for it was worked into every twist of their DNA. The Brahmin children of India's super-elite enjoyed long life – twice that of their parents – but at a price. They were indeed the twice-born, a caste above any other, so high as to be new Untouchables. A fitting partner for a former goddess: a new god.

Gas flares from the heavy industries of Tughluq lit the western horizon. From the top of the high tower I could read New Delhi's hidden geometries, the necklaces of light around Connaught Place, the grand glowing net of the dead Raj's monumental capital, the incoherent glow of the old city to the north. The penthouse at the top of the sweeping wing-curve of Narayan Tower was glass; glass walls, glass roof, beneath me, polished obsidian that reflected the night sky. I walked with stars at my head and feet. It was a room designed to awe and intimidate. It was nothing to one who had witnessed demons strike the heads from goats, who had walked on bloody silk to her own palace. It was nothing to one dressed, as the messenger had required, in the full panoply of the goddess. Red robe, red nails, red lips, red eye of Siva painted above my own black kohled eyes, fake-gold headdress hung with costume pearls, my fingers dripped gaudy rings from the cheap jewelry sellers of Kinari Bazaar, a light chain of real gold ran from my nose stud to my ear-ring; I was once again Kumari *Devi*. My demons rustled inside me.

Mamaji had drilled me as we scooted from old city to new. She had swathed me in a light voile *chador*, to protect my make-up she said; in truth, to conceal me from the eyes of the street. The girls had called blessings and prayers after me as the *phatphat* scuttled out of the *haveli*'s courtyard.

"You will say nothing. If he speaks to you, you duck your head like a good Hindu girl. If anything has to be said, I will say it. You may have been a goddess but he is a *Brahmin*. He could buy your pissy palace a dozen times over. Above all, do not let your eyes betray you. The eyes say nothing. They taught you that at least in that Kathmandu, didn't they? Now come on *cho chweet*, let's make a match."

The glass penthouse was lit only by city-glow and concealed lamps that gave off an uncomfortable blue light. Ved Prakash Narayan sat on a *musnud*, a slab of unadorned black marble. Its simplicity spoke of wealth and power beneath any ornate jewelry. My bare feet whispered on the star-filled glass. Blue light welled up as I approached the dais. Ved Prakash Narayan was dressed in a beautifully worked long *sherwani* coat and traditional tight *churidar* pajamas. He leaned forward into the light and it took every word of control Tall Kumarima had ever whispered to me to hold the gasp.

A ten-year-old boy sat on the throne of the Mughal Emperor.

Live twice as long, but age half as fast. The best deal Kolkata's genetic engineers could strike with four million years of human DNA. A child-husband for a once-child goddess. Except this was no child. In legal standing, experience, education, taste, and emotions, this was a twenty-year-old man, every way except the physical.

His feet did not touch the floor.

"Quite, quite extraordinary." His voice was a boy's. He slipped from his throne, walked around me, studying me as if I were an artifact in a museum. He was a head shorter than me. "Yes, this is indeed special. What is the settlement?"

Mamaji's voice from the door named a number. I obeyed my training and tried not to catch his eye as he stalked around me.

"Acceptable. My man will deliver the prenuptial before the end of the week. A goddess. My goddess."

Then I caught his eyes and I saw where all his missing years were. They were blue, alien blue, and colder than any of the lights of his tower-top palace.

These Brahmins *are worse than any of us when it comes to social climbing,* Ashok messaged me in my aerie atop the *shaadi haveli*, prison turned bridal boudoir. *Castes within castes within castes*. His words hung in the air over the hazy ramparts of the red fort before dissolving into the dashings of the musical pigeons. *Your children will be blessed.*

Until then I had not thought about the duties of a wife with a ten-year-old boy.

On a day of staggering heat I was wed to Ved Prakash Narayan in a climate-control bubble on the manicured green before Emperor Humayun's tomb. As on the night I was introduced, I was dressed as Kumari. My husband, veiled in gold, arrived perched on top of a white horse followed by a band and a dozen elephants with colored patterns worked on their trunks. Security robots patrolled the grounds as astrologers proclaimed favorable auspices and an old-type brahmin in his red cord blessed our union. Rose petals fluttered around me, the proud father and mother distributed gems from Hyderabad to their guests, my *shaadi* sisters wept with joy and loss, Mamaji sniffed back a tear and vile old Shweta went round hoarding the free and over-flowing food from the buffet. As we were applauded and played down the receiving line, I noticed all the other somber-faced ten-year-old boys with their beautiful, tall foreign wives. I reminded myself who was the child bride here. But none of them were goddesses.

I remember little of the grand *durbar* that followed except face after face after face, mouth after mouth after mouth opening, making noise, swallowing glass after glass after glass of French champagne. I did not drink for I do not have the taste for alcohol, though my young husband in his raja finery took it, and smoked big cigars too. As we got into the car – the *honeymoon* was another Western tradition we were adopting – I asked if anyone had remembered to inform my parents.

We flew to Mumbai on the company tilt-jet. I had never before flown in an aircraft. I pressed my hands, still hennaed with the patterns of my mehndi, on either side of the window as if to hold in every fleeting glimpse of Delhi falling away beneath me. It was every divine vision I had ever had looking down from my bed in the Kumari Ghar on to India. This was indeed the true vehicle of a goddess. But the demons whispered as we turned in the air over the towers of New Delhi, *you will be old and withered when he is still in his prime.*

When the limousine from the airport turned on to Marine Drive and I saw the Arabian Sea glinting in the city-light, I asked my husband to stop the car so I could look and wonder. I felt tears start in my eyes and thought, *the same water in it is in you.* But the demons would not let me be: *you are married to something that is not human.*

My *honeymoon* was wonder upon wonder: our penthouse apartment with the glass walls that opened on sunset over Chowpatty Beach. The new splendid outfits we wore as we drove along the boulevards, where stars and movie-gods smiled down and blessed us in the virtual sight of our palmers. Color, motion, noise, chatter; people and people and people. Behind it all, the wash and hush and smell of the alien sea.

Chambermaids prepared me for the wedding night. They worked with baths and balms, oils and massages, extending the now-fading henna tracery on my hands up my arms, over my small upright breasts, down the *manipuraka chakra* over my navel. They wove gold ornaments into my hair, slipped bracelets on my arms and rings on my fingers and toes, dusted and powdered my dark Nepali skin. They purified me with incense smoke and flower petals, they shrouded me in veils and silks as fine as rumors. They lengthened my lashes and kohled my eyes and shaped my nails to fine, painted points.

"What do I do? I've never even touched a man," I asked, but they *namasted* and slipped away without answer. But the older – the Tall Kumarima, as I thought of her – left a small soapstone box on my bridal divan. Inside were two white pills.

They were good. I should have expected no less. One moment I was standing nervous and fearful on the Turkestan carpet with a soft night air that smelled of the sea stirring the translucent curtains, the next visions of the Kama Sutra, beamed into my brain through my golden earhook, swirled up around me like the pigeons over Chandni Chowk. I looked at the patterns my *shaadi* sisters had painted on the palms of my hands and they danced and coiled from my skin. The smells and perfumes of my body were alive, suffocating. It was as if my skin had been peeled back and every nerve exposed. Even the touch of the barely moving night air was intolerable. Every car horn on Marine Drive was like molten silver dropped into my ear.

I was terribly afraid.

Then the double doors to the robing room opened and my husband entered. He was dressed as a Mughal grandee in a jeweled turban and a long-sleeved pleated red robe bowed out at the front in the manly act.

"My goddess," he said. Then he parted his robe and I saw what stood so proud.

The harness was of crimson leather intricately inlaid with fine mirror-work. It fastened around the waist and also over the shoulders, for extra security. The buckles were gold. I recall the details of the harness so clearly because I could not take more than one look at the thing it carried. Black. Massive as a horse's, but delicately upcurved. Ridged and studded. This all I remember before the room unfolded around me like the scented petals of a lotus and my senses blended as one and I was running through the apartments of the Taj Marine Hotel.

How had I ever imagined it could be different for a creature with the appetites and desires of an adult but the physical form of a ten-year-old boy?

Servants and dressers stared at me as I screamed incoherently, grabbing at wraps, shawls, anything to cover my shame. At some tremendous remove I remember my husband's voice calling *Goddess! My Goddess!* over and over.

"Schizophrenia is a terribly grating word," Ashok said. He twirled the stem of a red thornless rose between his fingers. "Old-school. It's disso-ciative disorder these days. Except there are no disorders, just adaptive behaviors. It was what you needed to cope with being a goddess. Dissociating. Disjuncting. Becoming you and other to stay sane."

Night in the gardens of the Dataraja Ashok. Water trickled in the stone canals of the *charbagh*. I could smell it, sweet and wet. A pressure curtain held the smog at bay; trees screened out Delhi's traffic. I could even see a few stars. We sat in an open *chhatri* pavilion, the marble still warm from the day. Set on silver *thalis* were medjool dates, *halva* – crisp with flies – folded paan. A security robot stepped into the lights from the Colonial bungalow, passed into shadow. But for it I might have been in the age of the rajas.

Time broken apart, whirring like *kabooter* wings. Dissociative behavior. Mechanisms for coping. Running along the palm-lined boulevards of Mumbai, shawls clutched around my wifely finery that made me feel more naked than bare skin. I ran without heed or direction. Taxis hooted, *phatphats* veered as I dashed across crowded streets. Even if I had had money for a *phatphat* – what need had the wife of a *Brahmin* for crude cash? – I did not know where to direct it. Yet that other, demonic self must have known, for I found myself on the vast marble concourse of a railway station, a sole mite of stillness among the tens of thousands of hastening travelers and beggars and vendors and staff. My shawls and throws clutched around me, I looked up at the dome of red Raj stone and it was a second skull, full of the awful realization of what I had done.

A runaway bride without even a *paisa* to her name, alone in Mumbai Chhatrapati Shivaji Terminus. A hundred trains leaving that minute for any destination but nowhere to go. People stared at me, half Nautch-courtesan, half Untouchable street-sleeper. In my shame, I remembered the hook behind my ear. *Ashok*, I wrote across the sandstone pillars and swirling ads. *Help me!*

"I don't want to be split, I don't want to be me and *other*, why can't I just be one?" I beat the heels of my hands off my forehead in frustration. "Make me well, make me right!" Shards of memory. The white-uniformed staff serving me hot *chai* in the first-class private compartment of the *shatabdi* express. The robots waiting at the platform with the antique covered palanquin, to bear me through the Delhi dawn traffic to the green watered geometries of Ashok's gardens. But behind them all was one enduring image, my uncle's white fist slipping on the bouncing cable and him falling, legs pedalling air, to the creamy waters of Shakya river. Even then, I had been split. Fear and shock. Laughter and smiles. How else could anyone survive being a goddess?

Goddess. My Goddess.

Ashok could not understand. "Would you cure a singer of his talent? There is no madness, only ways of adapting. Intelligence is evolution. Some would argue that I display symptoms of mild Asperger's syndrome."

"I don't know what that means."

He twirled the rose so hard the stem snapped.

"Have you thought about what you're going to do?"

I had thought of little else. The Narayans would not give up their dowry lightly. Mamaji would sweep me from her door. My village was closed to me.

"Maybe for a while, if you could . . ."

"It's not a good time . . . Who's going to have the ear of the Lok Sabha? A family building a dam that's going to guarantee their water supply for the next fifty years, or a software entrepreneur with a stable of Level 2.75 aeais that the United States government thinks are the sperm of Shaitan? Family values still count in Awadh. You should know."

I heard my voice say, like a very small girl, "Where can I go?"

The bride-buyer's stories of Kumaris whom no one would marry and could not go home again ended in the woman-cages of Varanasi and Kolkata. Chinese paid rupees by the roll for an ex-Goddess.

Ashok moistened his lips with his tongue.

"I have someone in Bharat, in Varanasi. Awadh and Bharat are seldom on speaking terms."

"Oh thank you, thank you . . ." I went down on my knees before Ashok, clutched his hands between my palms. He looked away. Despite the artificial cool of the *charbagh*, he was sweating freely.

"It's not a gift. It's . . . employment. A job."

"A job, that's good, I can do that; I'm a good worker, work away at anything I will; what is it? Doesn't matter, I can do it . . ."

"There are commodities need transported."

"What kind of commodities? Oh it doesn't matter, I can carry anything."

"Aeais." He rolled a *paan* from the silver dish. "I'm not going to wait around for Shrivastava's Krishna Cops to land in my garden with their excommunication ware."

"The Hamilton Acts," I ventured, though I did not know what they were, what most of Ashok's mumbles and rants meant.

"Word is, everything above level 2.5." Ashok chewed his lower lip. His eyes widened as the *paan* curled through his skull.

"Of course, I will do anything I can to help."

"I haven't told you how I need you to transport them. Absolutely safe, secure, where no Krishna Cop can ever find them." He touched his right forefinger to his Third Eye. "Self, and *other*."

I went to Kerala and had processors put into my skull. Two men did it on a converted bulk gas carrier moored outside territorial waters. They shaved my long lovely black hair, unhinged my skull and sent robots smaller than the tiniest spider spinning computers through my brain. Their position out beyond the Keralese fast patrol boats enabled them to carry out much secret surgery, mostly for the Western military. They gave me a bungalow and an Australian girl to watch over me while my sutures fused and hormone washes speed-grew my hair back.

Protein chips: only show on the highest resolution scans but no one'll look twice at you; no one'll look twice at another shaadi *girl down hunting for a husband.*

So I sat and stared at the sea for six weeks and thought about what it would be like to drown in the middle of it, alone and lost a thousand kilometers from the nearest hand that might seize yours. A thousand kilometers north in Delhi a man in an Indian suit shook hands with a man in an American suit and announced the Special Relationship that would make Ashok an outlaw.

You know what Krishna Cops are? They hunt aeais. They hunt the people who stable them, and the people who carry them. They don't care. They're not picky. But they won't catch you. They'll never catch you.

I listened to demons in the swash and run of the big sea on the shore. Demons I now knew were facets of my other self. But I was not afraid of them. In Hinduism, demons are merely the mirrors of the gods. As with men, so with gods; it is the winners who write the history. The universe would look no different had Ravana and his Rakshasas won their cosmic wars.

No one but you can carry them. No one but you has the neurological architecture. No one but you could endure another mind in there.

The Australian girl left small gifts outside my door: plastic bangles, jelly-shoes, rings, and hairslides. She stole them from the shops in town. I think they were her way of saying that she wanted to know me, but was afraid of what I had been, of what the things in my head would make me become. The last thing she stole was a beautiful sheer silk *dupatta* to cover my ragged hair when she took me to the airport. From beneath it I looked at the girls in business saris talking into their hands in the departure lounge and listened to the woman pilot announce the weather in Awadh. Then I looked out of the *phatphat* at the girls darting confidently through the Delhi traffic on their scooters and wondered why my life could not be like theirs.

"It's grown back well." Ashok knelt before me on my cushions in the *chhatri*. It was his sacred place, his temple. He raised his palmer-gloved hand and touched his forefinger to the *tilak* over my third eye. I could smell his breath. Onions, garlic, rancid *ghee*. "You may feel a little disoriented . . ."

I gasped. Senses blurred, fused, melted. I saw heard felt smelled tasted everything as one undifferentiated sensation, as gods and babies sense, wholly and purely. Sounds were colored, light had texture, smells-spoke and chimed. Then I saw myself surge up from my cushions and fall toward the hard white marble. I heard myself cry out. Ashok lunged toward me. Two Ashoks lunged toward me. But it was neither of those. I saw one Ashok, with two visions, inside my head. I could not make shape or sense out of my two seeings, I could not tell which was real, which was mine, which was me. Universes away I heard a voice say *help me*. I saw Ashok's houseboys lift me and take me to bed. The painted ceiling, patterned with vines and shoots and flowers, billowed above me like monsoon storm clouds, then blossomed into darkness.

In the heat of the night I woke stark, staring, every sense glowing. I knew the position and velocity of each insect in my airy room that smelled of biodiesel, dust, and patchouli. I was not alone. There was an other under the dome of my skull. Not an awareness, a consciousness; a sense of separateness, a manifestation of myself. An avatar. A demon.

"Who are you?" I whispered. My voice sounded loud and full of bells, like Durbar Square. It did not answer – it could not answer, it was not a sentience – but it took me out into the *charbagh* water garden. The stars, smudged by pollution, were a dome over me. The crescent moon lay on its back. I looked up and fell into it. *Chandra. Mangal. Budh. Guru. Shukra. Shani. Rahu. Ketu.* The planets were not points of fight, balls of stone and gas; they had names, characters, loves, hatreds. The twenty-seven *Nakshatars* spun around my head. I saw their shapes and natures, the patterns of connections that bound the stars into relationships and stories and dramas as human and complex as *Town and Country*. I saw the wheel of the *rashis*, the Great Houses, arc across sky, and the whole turning, engines within engines, endless wheels of influence and subtle communication, from the edge of the universe to the center of the earth I stood upon. Planets, stars, constellations; the story of every human life unfolded itself above me and I could read them all. Every word.

All night I played among the stars.

In the morning, over bed-tea, I asked Ashok, "What is it?"

"A rudimentary Level 2.6 A *janampatri* aeai, does astrology, runs the permutations. It thinks it lives out there, like some kind of space monkey. It's not very smart, really. Knows about horoscopes and that's it. Now get that down you and grab your stuff. You've a train to catch."

My reserved seat was in the women's *bogie* of the high-speed *shatabdi* express. Husbands booked their wives on to it to protect them from the attentions of the male passengers who assumed every female was single and available. The few career women chose it for the same reason. My fellow passenger across the table from me was a Muslim woman in a formal business shalwar. She regarded me with disdain as we raced across the Ganga plain at three hundred and fifty kilometers per hour. *Little simpering wife-thing.*

You would not be so quick to judge if you knew what we really were, I thought. *We can look into your life and tell you everything that has, is and will ever happen to you, mapped out in the* chakras *of the stars.* In that night among the constellations my demon and I had flowed into each other until there was no place where we could say aeai ended and I began.

I had thought holy Varanasi would sing to me like Kathmandu, a spiritual home, a city of nine million gods and one goddess, riding through the streets in a *phatphat*. What I saw was another Indian capital of another Indian state; glass towers and diamond domes and industry parks for the big world to notice, slums and bastis at their feet like sewage pigs. Streets began in this millennium and ended in one three before it. Traffic and hoardings and people people people but the diesel smoke leaking in around the edges of my smog mask carried a ghost of incense.

Ashok's Varanasi agent met me in the Jantar Mantar, the great solar observatory of Jai Singh; sundials and star spheres and shadow discs like modern sculpture. She was little older than me; dressed in a cling-silk top and jeans that hung so low from her hips I could see the valley of her buttocks. I disliked her at once but she touched her palmer-glove to my forehead in the shadows around Jai Singh's astrological instruments and I felt the stars go out of me. The sky died. I had been holy again and now I was just meat. Ashok's *girli* pressed a roll of rupees into my hand. I barely looked at it. I barely heard her instructions to get something to eat, get a *kafi*, get some decent clothes. I was bereft. I found myself trudging up the steep stone steps of the great Samrat not knowing where I was who I was what I was doing halfway up a massive sundial. Half a me. Then my third eye opened and I saw the river wide and blue before me. I saw the white sands of the eastern shore and the shelters and dung fires of the *sadhus* I saw the *ghats*, the stone river steps, curving away on either side further than the reach of my eyes. And I saw people. People washing and praying cleaning their clothes and offering *puja* and buying and selling and living and dying. People in boats and people kneeling, people waist deep in the river, people scooping up silver handfuls of water to pour over their heads. People casting handfuls of marigold flowers onto the stream people lighting little mango-leaf *diya* lamps and setting them afloat, people bringing their dead to dip them in the sacred water. I saw the pyres of the burning *ghat*, I smelled sandalwood, charring flesh, I heard the skull burst, releasing the soul. I had heard that sound before at the Royal burning *ghats* of Pashupatinath, when the King's Mother died. A soft crack, and free. It was a comforting sound. It made me think of home.

In that season I came many times to the city by the Ganga. Each time I was a different person. Accountants, counselors, machine-soldiers, *soapi* actors, database controllers: I was the goddess of a thousand skills. The day after I saw Awadhi Krishna Cops patrolling the platforms at Delhi station with their security robots and guns that could kill both humans and aeais, Ashok began to mix up my modes of transport. I flew, I trained, I chugged overnight on overcrowded country buses, I waited in chauffeured Mercedes in long lines of brightly decorated trucks at the Awadh–Bharat border. The trucks, like the crack of an exploding skull, reminded me of my kingdom. But at the end was always the rat-faced *girli* lifting her hand to my *tilak* and taking me apart again. In that season I was a fabric weaver, a tax consultant, a wedding planner, a *soapi* editor, an air traffic controller. She took all of them away.

And then the trip came when the Krishna Cops were waiting at the

Bharat end as well. By now I knew the politics of it as well as Ashok.
The Bharatis would never sign the Hamilton Acts – their multi-billion-
rupee entertainment industry depended on aeais – but neither did they
want to antagonize America. So, a compromise: all aeais over Level 2.8
banned, everything else licensed and Krishna Cops patrolling the
airports and railway stations. Like trying to hold back the Ganga with
your fingers.

I had spotted the courier on the flight. He was two rows in front of
me; young, wisp of a beard, Star-Asia youth fashion, all baggy and big.
Nervous nervous nervous, all the time checking his breast pocket,
checking checking checking. A small time *badmash*, a wannabe
dataraja with a couple of specialist 2.85s loaded onto a palmer. I could
not imagine how he had made it through Delhi airport security.

It was inevitable that the Varanasi Krishna Cops would spot him.
They closed on him as we lined up at passport control. He broke. He
ran. Women and children fled as he ran across the huge marble arrivals
hall, trying to get to the light, the huge glass wall and the doors and the
mad traffic beyond. His fists pounded at air. I heard the Krishna Cops'
staccato cries. I saw them unholster their weapons. Shrieks went up. I
kept my head down, shuffled forward. The immigration officer checked
my papers. Another *shaadi* bride on the hunt. I hurried through, turned
away toward the taxi ranks. Behind me I heard the arrivals hall fall so
shockingly silent it seemed to ring like a temple bell.

I was afraid then. When I returned to Delhi it was as if my fear had
flown before me. The city of *djinns* was the city of rumors. The
government had signed the Hamilton Act. Krishna Cops were sweeping
house to house. Palmer files were to be monitored. Children's aeai toys
were illegal. US marines were being airlifted in. Prime Minister
Shrivastava was about to announce the replacement of the rupee with
the dollar. A monsoon of fear and speculation and in the middle of it all
was Ashok.

"One final run, then I'm out. Can you do this for me? One final run?"

The bungalow was already half-emptied. The furniture was all
packed, only his processor cores remained. They were draped in
dustsheets, ghosts of the creatures that had lived there. The Krishna
Cops were welcome to them.

"We both go to Bharat?"

"No, that would be too dangerous. You go ahead, I'll follow when
it's safe." He hesitated. Tonight, even the traffic beyond the high walls
sounded different. "I need you to take more than the usual."

"How many?"

"Five."

He saw me shy back as he raised his hand to my forehead.

"Is it safe?"

"Five, and that's it done. For good."

"Is it safe?"

"It's a series of overlays, they'll share core code in common."

It was a long time since I had turned my vision inward to the jewels

Ashok had strung through my skull. Circuitry. A brain within a brain.
"Is it safe?"

I saw Ashok swallow, then bob his head: a Westerner's *yes*. I closed
my eyes. Seconds later I felt the warm, dry touch of his finger to my
inner eye.

We came to with the brass light of early morning shining through the
jali. We were aware we were deeply dehydrated. We were aware that we
were in need of slow-release carbohydrate. Our serotonin inhibitor
levels were low. The window arch through which the sun beamed was
a Mughal true arch. The protein circuits in my head were DPMA one-
eight-seven-nine slash omegas, under licence from BioScan of
Bangalore.

Everything we looked at gave off a rainbow of interpretations. I saw
the world with the strange manias of my new guests: medic, nutritionist,
architectural renderer, biochip designer, engineering aeai controlling a
host of repair-shop robots. Nasatya. Vaishvanara. Maya. Brihaspati.
Tvastri. My intimate demons. This was not *other*. This was *legion*. I
was a many-headed *devi*.

All that morning, all afternoon, I fought to make sense of a world that
was five worlds, five impressions. I fought. Fought to make us *me*.
Ashok fretted, tugging at his woolly beard, pacing, trying to watch
television, check his mails. At any instant Krishna Cop combat robots
could come dropping over his walls. Integration would come. It had to
come. I could not survive the clamor in my skull, a monsoon of interpretations. Sirens raced in the streets, far, near, far again. Every one of
them fired off a different reaction from my selves.

I found Ashok sitting amongst his shrouded processors, knees pulled
up to his chest, arms draped over them. He looked like a big, fat, soft
boy, his Mama's favorite.

Noradrenaline pallor mild hypoglycaemia, fatigue toxins, said
Nasatya.

Yin Systems bevabyte quantum storage arrays, said Brihaspati simultaneously.

I touched him on the shoulder. He jerked awake. It was full dark
outside, stifling: the monsoon was already sweeping up through the
United States of Bengal.

"We're ready," I said. "I'm ready."

Dark-scented hibiscus spilled over the porch where the Mercedes
waited.

"I'll see you in a week," he said. "In Varanasi."

"In Varanasi."

He took my shoulders in his hands and kissed me lightly, on the
cheek. I drew my *dupatta* over my head. Veiled, I was taken to the
United Provinces Night Sleeper Service. As I lay in the first class
compartment the aeais chattered away inside my head, surprised to
discover each other, reflections of reflections.

The *chowkidar* brought me bed-tea on a silver tray in the morning.
Dawn came up over Varanasi's sprawling slums and industrial parks.

My personalized news-service aeai told me that Lok Sabha would vote
on ratifying the Hamilton Accords at ten a.m. At twelve, Prime Minister
Shrivastava and the United States Ambassador would announce a Most
Favored Nation trade package with Awadh.

The train emptied onto the platform beneath the spun-diamond
canopy I knew so well. Every second passenger, it seemed, was a
smuggler. If I could spot them so easily, so could the Krishna Cops.
They lined the exit ramps, more than I had ever seen before. There were
uniforms behind them and robots behind the uniforms. The porter
carried my bag on his head; I used it to navigate the press of people
pouring off the night train. *Walk straight, as your Mamaji taught you.
Walk tall and proud, like you are walking the Silken Way with a rich
man.* I drew my *dupatta* over my head, for modesty. Then I saw the
crowd piling up at the ramp. The Krishna Cops were scanning every
passenger with palmers.

I could see the *badmashs* and smuggler-boys hanging back, moving to
the rear of the mill of bodies. But there was no escape there either.
Armed police backed by riot-control robots took up position at the end
of the platform. Shuffle by shuffle, the press of people pushed me
toward the Krishna Cops, waving their right hands like blessings over
the passengers. Those things could peel back my scalp and peer into my
skull. My red case bobbed ahead, guiding me to my cage.

Brihaspati showed me what they would do to the circuits in my head.
Help me! I prayed to my gods. And Maya, architect of the demons,
answered me. Its memories were my memories and it remembered
rendering an architectural simulation of this station long before robot
construction spiders started to spin their nano-diamond web. Two
visions of Varanasi station, superimposed. With one difference that
might save my life. Maya's showed me the inside of things. The inside
of the platform. The drain beneath the hatch between the rear of the
chai-booth and the roof support.

I pushed through the men to the small dead space at the rear. I
hesitated before I knelt beside the hatch. One surge of the crowd, one
trip, one fall, and I would be crushed. The hatch was jammed shut with
dirt. Nails broke, nails tore as I scrabbled it loose and heaved it up. The
smell that came up from the dark square was so foul I almost vomited.
I forced myself in, dropped a meter into shin-deep sludge. The rectangle
of light showed me my situation. I was mired in excrement. The tunnel
forced me to crawl but the end of it was promise, the end of it was a
semi-circle of daylight. I buried my hands in the soft sewage. This time
I did retch up my bed tea. I crept forward, trying not to choke. It was
vile beyond anything I had ever experienced. But not so vile as having
your skull opened and knives slice away slivers of your brain. I crawled
on my hands and knees under the tracks of Varanasi Station, to the
light, to the light, to the light, and out through the open conduit into the
cess lagoon where pigs and rag-pickers rooted in the shoals of drying
human manure.

I washed as clean as I could in the shriveled canal. *Dhobi*-wallahs beat laundry against stone slabs. I tried to ignore Nasatya's warnings about the hideous infections I might have picked up.

I was to meet Ashok's girl on the street of *gajras*. Children sat in doorways and open shop fronts threading marigolds onto needles. The work was too cheap even for robots. Blossoms spilled from bushels and plastic cases. My *phatphat*'s tires slipped on wet rose petals. We drove beneath a canopy of *gajra* garlands that hung from poles above the shop-fronts. Everywhere was the smell of dead, rotting flowers. The *phatphat* turned into a smaller, darker alley and into the back of a mob. The driver pressed his hand to the horn. The people reluctantly gave him way. The alcofuel engine whined. We crept forward. Open space, then a police jawan stepped forward to bar our way. He wore full combat armor. Brihaspati read the glints of data flickering across his visor: deployments, communications, an arrest warrant. I covered my head and lower face as the driver talked to him. What's going on? Some *badmash*. Some dataraja.

Down the street of *gajras*, uniformed police led by a plainclothes Krishna Cop burst open a door. Their guns were drawn. In the same breath, the shutters of the *jharoka* immediately above crashed up. A figure jumped up onto the wooden rail. Behind me, the crowd let out a vast roaring sigh. *There he is there the badmash oh look look it's a girl!*

From the folds of my *dupatta* I saw Ashok's *girli* teeter there an instant, then jump up and grab a washing line. It snapped and swung her ungently down through racks of marigold garlands into the street. She crouched a moment, saw the police, saw the crowd, saw me, then turned and ran. The *jawan* started toward her, but there was another quicker, deadlier. A woman screamed as the robot bounded from the rooftop into the alley. Chrome legs pistoned, its insect head bobbed, locked on. Marigold petals flew up around the fleeing girl but everyone knew she could not escape the killing thing. One step, two step, it was behind her. I saw her glance over her shoulder as the robot unsheathed its blade.

I knew what would happen next. I had seen it before, in the petal-strewn streets of Kathmandu, as I rode my litter among my gods and Kumarimas.

The blade flashed. A great cry from the crowd. The girl's head bounded down the alley. A great jet of blood. Sacrificial blood. The headless body took one step, two.

I slipped from the *phatphat* and stole away through the transfixed crowd.

I saw the completion of the story on a news channel at a *chai-dhaba* by the tank on Scindia *ghat*. The tourists, the faithful, the vendors and funeral parties were my camouflage. I sipped chai from a plastic cup and watched the small screen above the bar. The sound was low but I could understand well enough from the pictures. Delhi police break up a notorious aeai smuggling ring. In a gesture of Bharati-Awadhi friendship Varanasi Krishna cops make a series of arrests. The camera cut away before the robot struck. The final shot was of Ashok, pushed down into a Delhi police car in plastic handcuffs.

I went to sit on the lowest *ghat*. The river would still me, the river would guide me. It was of the same substance as me, divinity. Brown water swirled at my be-ringed toes. That water could wash away all earthly sin. On the far side of the holy river, tall chimneys poured yellow smoke into the sky. A tiny round-faced girl came up to me, offered me marigold *gajras* to buy. I waved her away. I saw again this river, these *ghats*, these temples and boats as I had when I lay in my wooden room in my palace in Durbar Square. I saw now the lie Tall Kumarima's palmer had fed me. I had thought India a jeweled skirt, laid out for me to wear. It was a bride-buyer with an envelope of rupees, it was walking the Silken Way until feet cracked and bled. It was a husband with the body of a child and the appetites of a man warped by his impotence. It was a savior who had always only wanted me for my sickness. It was a young girl's head rolling in a gutter.

Inside this still-girl's head, my demons were silent. They could see as well as I that that there would never be a home for us in Bharat, Awadh, Maratha, any nation of India.

North of Nayarangadh the road rose through wooded ridges, climbing steadily up to Mugling where it turned and clung to the side of the Trisuli's steep valley. It was my third bus in as many days. I had a routine now. Sit at the back, wrap my *dupatta* round me, look out the window. Keep my hand on my money. Say nothing.

I picked up the first bus outside Jaunpur. After emptying Ashok's account, I thought it best to leave Varanasi as inconspicuously as possible. I did not need Brihaspati to show me the hunter aeais howling after me. Of course they would have the air, rail, and bus stations covered. I rode out of the Holy City on an unlicensed taxi. The driver seemed pleased with the size of the tip. The second bus took me from Gorakhpur through the *dhal* fields and banana plantations to Nautanwa on the border. I had deliberately chosen small, out-of-the-way Nautanwa, but still I bowed my head and shuffled my feet as I came up to the Sikh emigration officer behind his tin counter. I held my breath. He waved me through without even a glance at my identity card.

I walked up the gentle slope and across the border. Had I been blind, I would have known at once when I crossed into my kingdom. The great roar that had followed me as close as my own skin fell silent so abruptly it seemed to echo. The traffic did not blare its way through all obstacles. It steered, it sought ways around pedestrians and sacred cows lolling in the middle of the road, chewing. People were polite in the bureau where I changed my Bharati rupees for Nepalese; did not press and push and try to sell me things I did not want in the shop where I bought a bag of greasy *samosas*; smiled shyly to me in the cheap hotel where I hired a room for the night. Did not demand demand demand.

I slept so deeply that it felt like a fall through endless white sheets that smelled of sky. In the morning the third bus came to take me up to Kathmandu.

The road was one vast train of trucks, winding in and out of the bluffs, looping back on itself, all the while climbing, climbing. The gears on the old bus whined. The engine strove. I loved that sound, of engines fighting gravity. It was the sound of my earliest recollection, before the child-assessors came up a road just like this to Shakya. Trains of trucks and buses in the night. I looked out at the roadside *dhabas*, the shrines of piled rocks, the tattered prayer banners bent in the wind, the cableways crossing the chocolate-creamy river far below, skinny kids kicking swaying cages across the high wires. So familiar, so alien to the demons that shared my skull.

The baby must have been crying for some time before the noise rose above the background hubbub of the bus. The mother was two rows ahead of me, she shushed and swung and soothed the tiny girl but the cries were becoming screams.

It was Nasatya who made me get out of my seat and go to her.

"Give her to me," I said and there must have been some tone of command from the medical aeai in my voice for she passed me the baby without a thought. I pulled back the sheet in which she was wrapped. The little girl's belly was painfully bloated, her limbs floppy and waxen.

"She's started getting colic when she eats," the mother said but before she could stop me I pulled away her diaper. The stench was abominable; the excrement bulky and pale.

"What are you feeding her?"

The woman held up a *roti* bread, chewed at the edges to soften it for baby. I pushed my fingers into the baby's mouth to force it open though Vaishvanara the nutritionist already knew what we would find. The tongue was blotched red, pimpled with tiny ulcers.

"Has this only started since you began giving her solid food?" I asked. The mother waggled her head in agreement. "This child has ceoliac disease," I pronounced. The woman put her hands to her face in horror, began to rock and wail. "Your child will be fine, you must just stop feeding her bread, anything made from any grain except rice. She cannot process the proteins in wheat and barley. Feed her rice, rice and vegetables and she will brighten up right away."

The entire bus was staring as I went back to my seat. The woman and her baby got off at Naubise. The child was still wailing, weak now from its rage, but the woman raised a *namaste* to me. A blessing. I had come to Nepal with no destination, no plan or hope, just a need to be back. But already an idea was forming.

Beyond Naubise the road climbed steadily, switching back and forth over the buttresses of the mountains that embraced Kathmandu. Evening was coming on. Looking back I could see the river of headlights snaking across the mountainside. Where the bus ground around another hairpin bend, I could see the same snake climb up ahead of me in red taillights. The bus labored up a long steep climb. I could hear, everyone could hear, the noise in the engine that should not have been there. Up we crawled to the high saddle where the watershed divided, right to the valley of Kathmandu, left to Pokhara and the High Himalaya. Slower, slower. We could all smell the burning insulation, hear the rattling.

It was not me who rushed to the driver and his mate. It was the demon Trivasti.

"Stop stop at once!" I cried. "Your alternator has seized! You will burn us up."

The driver pulled into the narrow draw, up against the raw rock. On the offside, trucks passed with millimeters to spare. We got the hood up. We could see the smoke wafting from the alternator. The men shook their heads and pulled out palmers. The passengers piled to the front of the bus to stare and talk.

"No no no, give me a wrench," I ordered.

The driver stared but I shook my outstretched hand, demanding. Perhaps he remembered the crying baby. Perhaps he was thinking about how long it would take a repair truck to come up from Kathmandu. Perhaps he was thinking about how good it would be to be home with his wife and children. He slapped the monkey wrench into my hand. In less than a minute I had the belt off and the alternator disconnected.

"Your bearings have seized," I said. "It's a persistent fault on pre-2030 models. A hundred meters more and you would have burned her out. You can drive her on the battery. There's enough in it to get you down to Kathmandu."

They stared at this little girl in an Indian sari, head covered but sleeves of her *choli* rolled up and fingers greasy with biolube.

The demon returned to his place and it was clear as the darkening sky what I would do now. The driver and his mate called out to me as I walked up beside the line of vehicles to the head of the pass. We ignored them. Passing drivers sounded their multiple, musical horns, offered lifts. I walked on. I could see the top now. It was not far to the place where the three roads divided. Back to India, down to the city, up to the mountains.

There was a *chai-dhaba* at the wide, oil-stained place where vehicles turned. It was bright with neon signs for American drinks and Bharati mineral water, like something fallen from the stars. A generator chugged. A television burbled familiar, soft Nepali news. The air smelled of hot *ghee* and biodiesel.

The owner did not know what to make of me, strange little girl in my Indian finery. Finally he said, "Fine night."

It was. Above the smogs and soots of the valley, the air was magically clear. I could see for a lifetime in any direction. To the west the sky held a little last light. The great peaks of Manaslu and Anapurna glowed mauve against the blue.

"It is," I said, "oh it is."

Traffic pushed slowly past, never ceasing on this high crossroads of the world. I stood in the neon flicker of the *dhaba*, looking long at the mountains and I thought, *I shall live there.* We shall live in a wooden house close to trees with running water cold from high snow. We shall have a fire and a television for company and prayer banners flying in the wind and in time people will stop being afraid and will come up the path to our door. There are many ways to be divine. There is the big divine, of ritual and magnificence and blood and terror. Ours shall be a little divinity, of small miracles and everyday wonders. Machines mended, programs woven, people healed, homes designed, minds and bodies fed. I shall be a little goddess. In time, the story of me will spread and people will come from all over; Nepalis and foreigners, travelers and hikers and monks. Maybe one day a man who is not afraid. That would be good. But if he does not come, that will be good also, for I shall never be alone, not with a houseful of demons.

Then I found I was running, with the surprised *chai-wallah* calling, "Hey! Hey! Hey!" after me, running down the side of the slow-moving line of traffic, banging on the doors, "Hi! Hi! Pokhara! Pokhara!" slipping and sliding over the rough gravel, toward the far, bright mountains.

THE CALORIE MAN

Paolo Bacigalupi

New writer Paolo Bacigalupi made his first sale in 1998 to *The Magazine of Fantasy & Science Fiction*. He took a break from the genre for several years and has returned in the new century with new sales to *F&SF* and *Asimov's*. He's had stories in our Twenty-first and Twenty-second Annual Collections. Bacigalupi lives with family in western Colorado, where he works for an environmental newspaper.

In the suspenseful story that follows, Bacigalupi takes us across an Earth that has been transformed almost beyond recognition by biological science and bitter economic necessity, on a perilous journey that, if successful, might transform the Earth yet *again*, in a very different way . . .

NO MAMMY, NO PAPPY, poor little bastard. Money? You give money?" The urchin turned a cartwheel and then a somersault in the street, stirring yellow dust around his nakedness.

Lalji paused to stare at the dirty blond child who had come to a halt at his feet. The attention seemed to encourage the urchin; the boy did another somersault. He smiled up at Lalji from his squat, calculating and eager, rivulets of sweat and mud streaking his face. "Money? You give money?"

Around them, the town was nearly silent in the afternoon heat. A few dungareed farmers led mulies toward the fields. Buildings, pressed from WeatherAll chips, slumped against their fellows like drunkards, rain-stained and sun-cracked, but, as their trade name implied, still sturdy. At the far end of the narrow street, the lush sprawl of SoyPRO and HiGro began, a waving rustling growth that rolled into the blue-sky distance. It was much as all the villages Lalji had seen as he traveled upriver, just another farming enclave paying its intellectual property dues and shipping calories down to New Orleans.

The boy crawled closer, smiling ingratiatingly, nodding his head like a snake hoping to strike. "Money? Money?"

Lalji put his hands in his pockets in case the beggar child had friends and turned his full attention on the boy. "And why should I give money to you?"

The boy stared up at him, stalled. His mouth opened, then closed.

Finally he looped back to an earlier, more familiar part of his script, "No mammy? No pappy?" but it was a query now, lacking conviction.

Lalji made a face of disgust and aimed a kick at the boy. The child scrambled aside, falling on his back in his desperation to dodge, and this pleased Lalji briefly. At least the boy was quick. He turned and started back up the street. Behind him, the urchin's wailing despair echoed. "Nooo maaaammy! Nooo paaaapy!" Lalji shook his head, irritated. The child might cry for money, but he failed to follow. No true beggar at all. An opportunist only – most likely the accidental creation of strangers who had visited the village and were open-fisted when it came to blond beggar children. AgriGen and Midwest Grower scientists and land factotums would be pleased to show ostentatious kindness to the villagers at the core of their empire.

Through a gap in the slumped hovels, Lalji caught another glimpse of the lush waves of SoyPRO and HiGro. The sheer sprawl of calories stimulated tingling fantasies of loading a barge and slipping it down through the locks to St. Louis or New Orleans and into the mouths of waiting megadonts. It was impossible, but the sight of those emerald fields was more than enough assurance that no child could beg with conviction here. Not surrounded by SoyPRO. Lalji shook his head again, disgusted, and squeezed down a footpath between two of the houses.

The acrid reek of WeatherAll's excreted oils clogged the dim alley. A pair of cheshires sheltering in the unused space scattered and molted ahead of him, disappearing into bright sunlight. Just beyond, a kinetic shop leaned against its beaten neighbors, adding the scents of dung and animal sweat to the stink of WeatherAll. Lalji leaned against the shop's plank door and shoved inside.

Shafts of sunlight pierced the sweet manure gloom with lazy gold beams. A pair of hand-painted posters scabbed to one wall, partly torn but still legible. One said: "Unstamped calories mean starving families. We check royalty receipts and IP stamps." A farmer and his brood stared hollow-eyed from beneath the scolding words. PurCal was the sponsor. The other poster was AgriGen's trademarked collage of kink-springs, green rows of SoyPRO under sunlight and smiling children along with the words "We Provide Energy for the World." Lalji studied the posters sourly.

"Back already?" The owner came in from the winding room, wiping his hands on his pants and kicking straw and mud off his boots. He eyed Lalji. "My springs didn't have enough stored. I had to feed the mulies extra, to make your joules."

Lalji shrugged, having expected the last-minute bargaining, so much like Shriram's that he couldn't muster the interest to look offended. "Yes? How much?"

The man squinted up at Lalji, then ducked his head, his body defensive. "F-Five hundred." His voice caught on the amount, as though gagging on the surprising greed scampering up his throat.

Lalji frowned and pulled his mustache. It was outrageous. The

calories hadn't even been transported. The village was awash with
energy. And despite the man's virtuous poster, it was doubtful that the
calories feeding his kinetic shop were equally upstanding. Not with
tempting green fields waving within meters of the shop. Shriram often
said that using stamped calories was like dumping money into a
methane composter.

Lalji tugged his mustache again, wondering how much to pay for the
joules without calling excessive attention to himself. Rich men must
have been all over the village to make the kinetic man so greedy. Calorie
executives, almost certainly. It would fit. The town was close to the
center. Perhaps even this village was engaged in growing the crown
jewels of AgriGen's energy monopolies. Still, not everyone who passed
through would be as rich as that. "Two hundred."

The kinetic man showed a relieved smile along with knotted yellow
teeth, his guilt apparently assuaged by Lalji's bargaining. "Four."

"Two. I can moor on the river and let my own winders do the same
work."

The man snorted. "It would take weeks."

Lalji shrugged. "I have time. Dump the joules back into your own
springs. I'll do the job myself."

"I've got family to feed. Three?"

"You live next to more calories than some rich families in St. Louis.
Two."

The man shook his head sourly but he led Lalji into the winding
room. The manure haze thickened. Big kinetic storage drums, twice as
tall as a man, sat in a darkened corner, mud and manure lapping around
their high-capacity precision kink-springs. Sunbeams poured between
open gaps in the roof where shingles had blown away. Dung motes
stirred lazily.

A half-dozen hyper-developed mulies crouched on their treadmills,
their rib cages billowing slowly, their flanks streaked with salt lines of
sweat residue from the labor of winding Lalji's boat springs. They blew
air through their nostrils, nervous at Lalji's sudden scent, and gathered
their squat legs under them. Muscles like boulders rippled under their
bony hides as they stood. They eyed Lalji with resentful near-intelli-
gence. One of them showed stubborn yellow teeth that matched its
owner's.

Lalji made a face of disgust. "Feed them."

"I already did."

"I can see their bones. If you want my money, feed them again."

The man scowled. "They aren't supposed to get fat, they're supposed
to wind your damn springs." But he dipped double handfuls of SoyPRO
into their feed canisters.

The mulies shoved their heads into the buckets, slobbering and
grunting with need. In its eagerness, one of them started briefly forward
on its treadmill, sending energy into the winding shop's depleted
storage springs before seeming to realize that its work was not
demanded and that it could eat without molestation.

"They aren't even designed to get fat," the kinetic man muttered.

Lalji smiled slightly as he counted through his wadded bluebills and handed over the money. The kinetic man unjacked Lalji's kink-springs from the winding treadmills and stacked them beside the slavering mulies. Lalji lifted a spring, grunting at its heft. Its mass was no different than when he had brought it to the winding shop, but now it fairly seemed to quiver with the mulies' stored labor.

"You want help with those?" The man didn't move. His eyes flicked toward the mulies' feed buckets, still calculating his chances of interrupting their meal.

Lalji took his time answering, watching as the mulies rooted for the last of their calories. "No." He hefted the spring again, getting a better grip. "My helpboy will come for the rest."

As he turned for the door, he heard the man dragging the feedbuckets away from the mulies and their grunts as they fought for their sustenance. Once again, Lalji regretted agreeing to the trip at all.

Shriram had been the one to broach the idea. They had been sitting under the awning of Lalji's porch in New Orleans, spitting betel nut juice into the alley gutters and watching the rain come down as they played chess. At the end of the alley, cycle rickshaws and bicycles slipped through the mid-morning gray, pulses of green and red and blue as they passed the alley's mouth draped under rain-glossed corn polymer ponchos.

The chess game was a tradition of many years, a ritual when Lalji was in town and Shriram had time away from his small kinetic company where he rewound people's home and boat springs. Theirs was a good friendship, and a fruitful one, when Lalji had unstamped calories that needed to disappear into the mouth of a hungry megadont.

Neither of them played chess well, and so their games often devolved into a series of trades made in dizzying succession, a cascade of destruction that left a board previously well-arrayed in a tantrum wreck, with both opponents blinking surprise, trying to calculate if the mangle had been worth the combat. It was after one of these tit-for-tat cleansings that Shriram had asked Lalji if he might go upriver. Beyond the southern states.

Lalji had shaken his head and spit bloody betel juice into the overflowing gutter. "No. Nothing is profitable so far up. Too many joules to get there. Better to let the calories float to me." He was surprised to discover that he still had his queen. He used it to take a pawn.

"And if the energy costs could be defrayed?"

Lalji laughed, waiting for Shriram to make his own move. "By who? AgriGen? The IP men? Only their boats go up and down so far." He frowned as he realized that his queen was now vulnerable to Shriram's remaining knight.

Shriram was silent. He didn't touch his pieces. Lalji looked up from the board and was surprised by Shriram's serious expression. Shriram said, "I would pay. Myself and others. There is a man who some of us would like to see come south. A very special man."

"Then why not bring him south on a paddle wheel? It is expensive to go up the river. How many gigajoules? I would have to change the boat's springs, and then what would the IP patrols ask? Where are you going, strange Indian man with your small boat and your so many springs? Going far? To what purpose?' " Lalji shook his head. "Let this man take a ferry, or ride a barge. Isn't this cheaper?" He waved at the game board. "It's your move. You should take my queen."

Shriram waggled his head thoughtfully from side to side but didn't make any move toward the chess game. "Cheaper, yes . . ."

"But?"

Shriram shrugged. "A swift, inconsequential boat would attract less attention."

"What sort of man is this?"

Shriram glanced around, suddenly furtive. Methane lamps burned like blue fairies behind the closed glass of the neighbors' droplet-spattered windows. Rain sheeted off their roofs, drumming wet into the empty alley. A cheshire was yowling for a mate somewhere in the wet, barely audible under the thrum of falling water.

"Is Creo inside?"

Lalji raised his eyebrows in surprise. "He has gone to his gymnasium. Why? Should it matter?"

Shriram shrugged and gave an embarrassed smile. "Some things are better kept between old friends. People with strong ties."

"Creo has been with me for years."

Shriram grunted noncommittally, glanced around again and leaned close, pitching his voice low, forcing Lalji to lean forward as well. "There is a man who the calorie companies would like very much to find." He tapped his balding head. "A very intelligent man. We want to help him."

Lalji sucked in his breath. "A generipper?"

Shriram avoided Lalji's eyes. "In a sense. A calorie man."

Lalji made a face of disgust. "Even better reason not to be involved. I don't traffic with those killers."

"No, no. Of course not. But still . . . you brought that huge sign down once, did you not? A few greased palms, so smooth, and you float into town and suddenly Lakshmi smiles on you, such a calorie bandit, and now with a name instead as a dealer of antiques. Such a wonderful misdirection."

Lalji shrugged. "I was lucky. I knew the man to help move it through the locks."

"So? Do it again."

"If the calorie companies are looking for him, it would be dangerous."

"But not impossible. The locks would be easy. Much easier than carrying unlicensed grains. Or even something as big as that sign. This would be a man. No sniffer dog would find him of interest. Place him in a barrel. It would be easy. And I would pay. All your joules, plus more."

Lalji sucked at his narcotic betel nut, spit red, spit red again, considering. "And what does a second-rate kinetic man like you think this calorie man will do? Generippers work for big fish, and you are such a small one."

Shriram grinned haplessly and gave a self-deprecating shrug. "You do not think Ganesha Kinetic could not some day be great? The next AgriGen, maybe?" and they had both laughed at the absurdity and Shriram dropped the subject.

An IP man was on duty with his dog, blocking Lalji's way as he returned to his boat lugging the kink-spring. The brute's hairs bristled as Lalji approached and it lunged against its leash, its blunt nose quivering to reach him. With effort, the IP man held the creature back. "I need to sniff you." His helmet lay on the grass, already discarded, but still he was sweating under the swaddling heat of his gray slash-resistant uniform and the heavy webbing of his spring gun and bandoliers.

Lalji held still. The dog growled, deep from its throat, and inched forward. It snuffled his clothing, bared hungry teeth, snuffled again, then its black ruff iridesced blue and it relaxed and wagged its stubby tail. It sat. A pink tongue lolled from between smiling teeth. Lalji smiled sourly back at the animal, glad that he wasn't smuggling calories and wouldn't have to go through the pantomimes of obeisance as the IP man demanded stamps and then tried to verify that the grain shipment had paid its royalties and licensing fees.

At the dog's change in color, the IP man relaxed somewhat, but still he studied Lalji's features carefully, hunting for recognition against memorized photographs. Lalji waited patiently, accustomed to the scrutiny. Many men tried to steal the honest profits of AgriGen and its peers, but to Lalji's knowledge, he was unknown to the protectors of intellectual property. He was an antiques dealer, handling the junk of the previous century, not a calorie bandit staring out from corporate photo books.

Finally, the IP man waved him past. Lalji nodded politely and made his way down the stairs to the river's low stage where his needleboat was moored. Out on the river, cumbrous grain barges wallowed past, riding low under their burdens.

Though there was a great deal of river traffic, it didn't compare with harvest time. Then the whole of the Mississippi would fill with calories pouring downstream, pulled from hundreds of towns like this one. Barges would clot the arterial flow of the river system from high on the Missouri, the Illinois, and the Ohio and the thousand smaller tributaries. Some of those calories would float only as far as St. Louis where they would be chewed by megadonts and churned into joules, but the rest, the vast majority, would float to New Orleans where the great calorie companies' clippers and dirigibles would be loaded with the precious grains. Then they would cross the Earth on tradewinds and sea, in time for the next season's planting, so that the world could go on eating.

Lalji watched the barges moving slowly past, wallowing and bloated with their wealth, then hefted his kink-spring and jumped aboard his needleboat.

Creo was lying on deck as Lalji had left him, his muscled body oiled and shining in the sun, a blond Arjuna waiting for glorious battle. His cornrows spread around his head in a halo, their tipped bits of bone lying like foretelling stones on the hot deck. He didn't open his eyes as Lalji jumped aboard. Lalji went and stood in Creo's sun, eclipsing his tan. Slowly, the young man opened his blue eyes.

"Get up." Lalji dropped the spring on Creo's rippled stomach.

Creo let out a whuff and wrapped his arms around the spring. He sat up easily and set it on the deck. "Rest of the springs wound?"

Lalji nodded. Creo took the spring and went down the boat's narrow stairs to the mechanical room. When he returned from fitting the spring into the gearings of the boat's power system, he said, "Your springs are shit, all of them. I don't know why you didn't bring bigger ones. We have to rewind, what, every twenty hours? You could have gotten all the way here on a couple of the big ones."

Lalji scowled at Creo and jerked his head toward the guard still standing at the top of the riverbank and looking down on them. He lowered his voice. "And then what would the MidWest Authority be saying as we are going upriver? All their IP men all over our boat, wondering where we are going so far? Boarding us and then wondering what we are doing with such big springs. Where have we gotten so many joules? Wondering what business we have so far upriver." He shook his head. "No, no. This is better. Small boat, small distance, who worries about Lalji and his stupid blond helpboy then? No one. No, this is better."

"You always were a cheap bastard."

Lalji glanced at Creo. "You are lucky it is not forty years ago. Then you would be paddling up this river by hand, instead of lying on your lazy back letting these fancy kink-springs do the work. Then we would be seeing you use those muscles of yours."

"If I was lucky, I would have been born during the Expansion and we'd still be using gasoline."

Lalji was about to retort but an IP boat slashed past them, ripping a deep wake. Creo lunged for their cache of spring guns. Lalji dove after him and slammed the cache shut. "They're not after us!"

Creo stared at Lalji, uncomprehending for a moment, then relaxed. He stepped away from the stored weapons. The IP boat continued upriver, half its displacement dedicated to massive precision kink-springs and the stored joules that gushed from their unlocking molecules. Its curling wake rocked the needleboat. Lalji steadied himself against the rail as the IP boat dwindled to a speck and disappeared between obstructing barge chains.

Creo scowled after the boat. "I could have taken them."

Lalji took a deep breath. "You would have gotten us killed." He glanced at the top of the riverbank to see if the IP man had noticed their panic. He wasn't even visible. Lalji silently gave thanks to Ganesha.

"I don't like all of them around," Creo complained. "They're like ants. Fourteen at the last lock. That one, up on the hill. Now these boats."

"It is the heart of calorie country. It is to be expected."

"You making a lot of money on this trip?"

"Why should you care?"

"Because you never used to take risks like this." Creo swept his arm, indicating the village, the cultivated fields, the muddy width of river gurgling past, and the massive barges clogging it. "No one comes this far upriver."

"I'm making enough money to pay you. That's all you should concern yourself with. Now go get the rest of the springs. When you think too much, your brain makes mush."

Creo shook his head doubtfully but jumped for the dock and headed up the steps to the kinetic shop. Lalji turned to face the river. He took a deep breath.

The IP boat had been a close call. Creo was too eager to fight. It was only with luck that they hadn't ended up as shredded meat from the IP men's spring guns. He shook his head tiredly, wondering if he had ever had as much reckless confidence as Creo. He didn't think so. Not even when he was a boy. Perhaps Shriram was right. Even if Creo was trustworthy, he was still dangerous.

A barge chain, loaded with TotalNutrient Wheat, slid past. The happy sheaves of its logo smiled across the river's muddy flow, promising "A Healthful Tomorrow" along with folates, B vitamins, and pork protein. Another IP boat slashed upriver, weaving amongst the barge traffic. Its complement of IP men studied him coldly as they went by. Lalji's skin crawled. Was it worth it? If he thought too much, his businessman's instinct – bred into him through thousands of years of caste practice – told him no. But still, there was Gita. When he balanced his debts each year on Diwali, how did he account for all he owed her? How did one pay off something that weighed heavier than all his profits, in all his lifetimes?

The NutriWheat wallowed past, witlessly inviting, and without answers.

"You wanted to know if there was something that would be worth your trip upriver."

Lalji and Shriram had been standing in the winding room of Ganesha Kinetic, watching a misplaced ton of SuperFlavor burn into joules. Shriram's paired megadonts labored against the winding spindles, ponderous and steady as they turned just-consumed calories into kinetic energy and wound the shop's main storage springs.

Priti and Bidi. The massive creatures barely resembled the elephants that had once provided their template DNA. Generippers had honed them to a perfect balance of musculature and hunger for a single purpose: to inhale calories and do terrible labors without complaint. The smell of them was overwhelming. Their trunks dragged the ground.

The animals were getting old, Lalji thought, and on the heels of that thought came another: he, too, was getting old. Every morning he found gray in his mustache. He plucked it, of course, but more gray hairs always sprouted. And now his joints ached in the mornings as well. Shriram's own head shone like polished teak. At some point, he'd turned bald. Fat and bald. Lalji wondered when they had turned into such old men.

Shriram repeated himself, and Lalji shook away his thoughts. "No, I am not interested in anything upriver. That is the calorie companies' province. I have accepted that when you scatter my ashes it will be on the Mississippi, and not the holy Ganges, but I am not so eager to find my next life that I wish my corpse to float down from Iowa."

Shriram twisted his hands nervously and glanced around. He lowered his voice, even though the steady groan of the spindles was more than enough to drown their sounds. "Please, friend, there are people . . . who want . . . to kill this man."

"And I should care?"

Shriram made placating motions with his hands. "He knows how to make calories. AgriGen wants him, badly. PurCal as well. He has rejected them and their kind. His mind is valuable. He needs someone trustworthy to bring him downriver. No friend of the IP men."

"And just because he is an enemy of AgriGen I should help him? Some former associate of the Des Moines clique? Some ex-calorie man with blood on his hands and you think he will help you make money?"

Shriram shook his head. "You make it sound as if this man is unclean."

"We are talking of generippers, yes? How much morality can he have?"

"A geneticist. Not a generipper. Geneticists gave us megadonts." He waved at Priti and Bidi. "Me, a livelihood."

Lalji turned on Shriram. "You take refuge in these semantics, now? You, who starved in Chennai when the Nippon genehack weevil came? When the soil turned to alcohol? Before U-Tex and HiGro and the rest all showed up so conveniently? You, who waited on the docks when the seeds came in, saw them come and then saw them sit behind their fences and guards, waiting for people with the money to buy? What traffic would I have with this sort of people? I would sooner spit on him, this calorie man. Let the PurCal devils have him, I say."

The town was as Shriram had described it. Cottonwoods and willows tangled the edges of the river and over them, the remains of the bridge, some of it still spanning the river in a hazy network of broken trusses and crumbling supports. Lalji and Creo stared up at the rusting construction, a web of steel and cable and concrete, slowly collapsing into the river.

"How much do you think the steel would bring?" Creo asked.

Lalji filled his cheek with a handful of PestResis sunflower seeds and started cracking them between his teeth. He spit the hulls into the river one by one. "Not much. Too much energy to tear it out, then to melt it." He shook his head and spat another hull. "A waste to make something like that with steel. Better to use Fast-Gen hardwoods, or WeatherAll."

"Not to cover that distance. It couldn't be done now. Not unless you were in Des Moines, maybe. I heard they burn coal there."

"And they have electric lights that go all night and computers as large as a house." Lalji waved his hand dismissively and turned to finish securing the needleboat. "Who needs such a bridge now? A waste. A ferry and a mulie would serve just as well." He jumped ashore and started climbing the crumbling steps that led up from the river. Creo followed.

At the top of the steep climb, a ruined suburb waited. Built to serve the cities on the far side of the river when commuting was common and petroleum cheap, it now sprawled in an advanced state of decay. A junk city built with junk materials, as transient as water, willingly abandoned when the expense of commuting grew too great.

"What the hell is this place?" Creo muttered.

Lalji smiled cynically. He jerked his head toward the green fields across the river, where SoyPRO and HiGro undulated to the horizon. "The very cradle of civilization, yes? AgriGen, Midwest Growers Group, PurCal, all of them have fields here."

"Yeah? That excite you?"

Lalji turned and studied a barge chain as it wallowed down the river below them, its mammoth size rendered small by the height. "If we could turn all their calories into traceless joules, we'd be wealthy men."

"Keep dreaming." Creo breathed deeply and stretched. His back cracked and he winced at the sound. "I get out of shape when I ride your boat this long. I should have stayed in New Orleans."

Lalji raised his eyebrows. "You're not happy to be making this touristic journey?" He pointed across the river. "Somewhere over there, perhaps in those very acres, AgriGen created SoyPRO. And everyone thought they were such wonderful people." He frowned. "And then the weevil came, and suddenly there was nothing else to eat."

Creo made a face. "I don't go for those conspiracy theories."

"You weren't even born when it happened." Lalji turned to lead Creo into the wrecked suburb. "But I remember. No such accident had ever happened before."

"Monocultures. They were vulnerable."

"Basmati was no monoculture!" Lalji waved his hand back toward the green fields. "SoyPRO is monoculture. PurCal is monoculture. Generippers make monoculture."

"Whatever you say, Lalji."

Lalji glanced at Creo, trying to tell if the young man was still arguing with him, but Creo was carefully studying the street wreckage and Lalji let the argument die. He began counting streets, following memorized directions.

The avenues were all ridiculously broad and identical, large enough to run a herd of megadonts. Twenty cycle-rickshaws could ride abreast easily, and yet the town had only been a support suburb. It boggled Lalji's mind to consider the scale of life before.

A gang of children watched them from the doorway of a collapsed house. Half its timbers had been removed, and the other half were splintered, rising from the foundation like carcass bones where siding flesh had been stripped away.

Creo showed the children his spring gun and they ran away. He scowled at their departing forms. "So what the hell are we picking up here? You got a lead on another antique?"

Lalji shrugged.

"Come on. I'm going to be hauling it in a couple minutes anyway. What's with the secrecy?"

Lalji glanced at Creo. "There's nothing for you to haul. 'It' is a man. We're looking for a man."

Creo made a sound of disbelief. Lalji didn't bother responding.

Eventually, they came to an intersection. At its center, an old signal light lay smashed. Around it, the pavement was broken through by grasses gone to seed. Dandelions stuck up their yellow heads. On the far side of the intersection, a tall brick building squatted, a ruin of a civil center, yet still standing, built with better materials than the housing it had served.

A cheshire bled across the weedy expanse. Creo tried to shoot it. Missed.

Lalji studied the brick building. "This is the place."

Creo grunted and shot at another cheshire shimmer.

Lalji went over and inspected the smashed signal light, idly curious to see if it might have value. It was rusted. He turned in a slow circle, studying the surroundings for anything at all that might be worth taking downriver. Some of the old Expansion's wreckage still had worthy artifacts. He'd found the Conoco sign in such a place, in a suburb soon to be swallowed by SoyPRO, perfectly intact, seemingly never mounted in the open air, never subjected to the angry mobs of the energy Contraction. He'd sold it to an AgriGen executive for more than an entire smuggled cargo of HiGro.

The AgriGen woman had laughed at the sign. She'd mounted it on her wall, surrounded by the lesser artifacts of the Expansion: plastic cups, computer monitors, photos of racing automobiles, brightly colored children's toys. She'd hung the sign on her wall and then stood back and murmured that at one point, it had been a powerful company . . . global, even.

Global.

She'd said the word with an almost sexual yearning as she stared up at the sign's ruddy polymers.

Global.

For a moment, Lalji had been smitten by her vision: a company that pulled energy from the remotest parts of the planet and sold it far away within weeks of extraction; a company with customers and investors on every continent, with executives who crossed time zones as casually as Lalji crossed the alley to visit Shriram.

The AgriGen woman had hung the sign on her wall like the head of a trophy megadont and in that moment, next to a representative of the most powerful energy company in the world, Lalji had felt a sudden sadness at how very diminished humanity had become.

Lalji shook away the memory and again turned slowly in the intersection, seeking signs of his passenger. More cheshires flitted amongst the ruins, their smoky shimmer shapes pulsing across the sunlight and passing into shadows. Creo pumped his spring gun and sprayed disks. A shimmer tumbled to stillness and became a matted pile of calico and blood.

Creo repumped his spring gun. "So where is this guy?"

"I think he will come. If not today, then tomorrow or the next." Lalji headed up the steps of the civil center and slipped between its shattered doors. Inside, it was nothing but dust and gloom and bird droppings. He found stairs and made his way upward until he found a broken window with a view. A gust of wind rattled the window pane and tugged his mustache. A pair of crows circled in the blue sky. Below, Creo pumped his spring gun and shot more cheshire shimmers. When he hit, angry yowls filtered up. Blood swatches spattered the weedy pavement as more animals fled.

In the distance, the suburb's periphery was already falling to agriculture. Its time was short. Soon the houses would be plowed under and a perfect blanket of SoyPRO would cover it. The suburb's history, as silly and transient as it had been, would be lost, churned under by the march of energy development. No loss, from the standpoint of value, but still, some part of Lalji cringed at the thought of time erased. He spent too much time trying to recall the India of his boyhood to take pleasure in the disappearance. He headed back down the dusty stairs to Creo.

"See anyone?"

Lalji shook his head. Creo grunted and shot at another cheshire, narrowly missing. He was good, but the nearly invisible animals were hard targets. Creo pumped his spring gun and fired again. "Can't believe how many cheshires there are."

"There is no one to exterminate them."

"I should collect the skins and take them back to New Orleans."

"Not on my boat."

Many of the shimmers were fleeing, finally understanding the quality of their enemy. Creo pumped again and aimed at a twist of light further down the street.

Lalji watched complacently. "You will never hit it."

"Watch." Creo aimed carefully.

A shadow fell across them. "Don't shoot."

Creo whipped his spring gun around.

Lalji waved a hand at Creo. "Wait! It's him!"

The new arrival was a skinny old man, bald except for a greasy fringe of gray and brown hair, his heavy jaw thick with gray stubble. Hemp sacking covered his body, dirty and torn, and his eyes had a sunken, knowing quality that unearthed in Lalji the memory of a long-ago sadhu, covered with ash and little else: the tangled hair, the disinterest in his clothing, the distance in the eyes that came from enlightenment. Lalji shook away the memory. This man was no holy man. Just a man, and a generipper, at that.

Creo resighted his spring gun on the distant cheshire. "Down south, I get a bluebill for every one I kill."

The old man said, "There are no bluebills for you to collect here."

"Yeah, but they're pests."

"It's not their fault we made them too perfectly." The man smiled hesitantly, as though testing a facial expression. "Please." He squatted down in front of Creo. "Don't shoot."

Lalji placed a hand on Creo's spring gun. "Let the cheshires be."

Creo scowled, but he let his gun's mechanism unwind with a sigh of releasing energy.

The calorie man said, "I am Charles Bowman." He looked at them expectantly, as though anticipating recognition. "I am ready. I can leave."

Gita was dead, of that Lalji was now sure.

At times, he had pretended that it might not be so. Pretended that she might have found a life, even after he had gone.

But she was dead, and he was sure of it.

It was one of his secret shames. One of the accretions to his life that clung to him like dog shit on his shoes and reduced himself in his own eyes: as when he had thrown a rock and hit a boy's head, unprovoked, to see if it was possible; or when he had dug seeds out of the dirt and eaten them one by one, too starved to share. And then there was Gita. Always Gita. That he had left her and gone instead to live close to the calories. That she had stood on the docks and waved as he set sail, when it was she who had paid his passage price.

He remembered chasing her when he was small, following the rustle of her salwar kameez as she dashed ahead of him, her black hair and black eyes and white, white teeth. He wondered if she had been as beautiful as he recalled. If her oiled black braid had truly gleamed the way he remembered when she sat with him in the dark and told him stories of Arjuna and Krishna and Ram and Hanuman. So much was lost. He wondered sometimes if he even remembered her face correctly, or if he had replaced it with an ancient poster of a Bollywood girl, one of the old ones that Shriram kept in the safe of his winding shop and guarded jealously from the influences of light and air.

For a long time he thought he would go back and find her. That he might feed her. That he would send money and food back to his blighted land that now existed only in his mind, in his dreams, and in half-awake hallucinations of deserts, red and black saris, of women in dust, and their black hands and silver bangles, and their hunger, so many of the last memories of hunger.

He had fantasized that he would smuggle Gita back across the shining sea, and bring her close to the accountants who calculated calorie burn quotas for the world. Close to the calories, as she had said, once so long ago. Close to the men who balanced price stability against margins of error and protectively managed energy markets against a flood of food. Close to those small gods with more power than Kali to destroy the world.

But she was dead by now, whether through starvation or disease, and he was sure of it.

And wasn't that why Shriram had come to him? Shriram who knew more of his history than any other. Shriram who had found him after he arrived in New Orleans, and known him for a fellow countryman: not just another Indian long settled in America, but one who still spoke the dialects of desert villages and who still remembered their country as it had existed before genehack weevil, leafcurl, and root rust. Shriram, who had shared a place on the floor while they both worked the winding sheds for calories and nothing else, and were grateful for it, as though they were nothing but genehacks themselves.

Of course Shriram had known what to say to send him upriver. Shriram had known how much he wished to balance the unbalanceable.

They followed Bowman down empty streets and up remnant alleys, winding through the pathetic collapse of termite-ridden wood, crumbling concrete foundations, and rusted rebar too useless to scavenge and too stubborn to erode. Finally, the old man squeezed them between the stripped hulks of a pair of rusted automobiles. On the far side, Lalji and Creo gasped.

Sunflowers waved over their heads. A jungle of broad squash leaves hugged their knees. Dry corn stalks rattled in the wind. Bowman looked back at their surprise, and his smile, so hesitant and testing at first, broadened with unrestrained pleasure. He laughed and waved them onward, floundering through a garden of flowers and weeds and produce, catching his torn hemp cloth on the dried stems of cabbage gone to seed and the cling of cantaloupe vines. Creo and Lalji picked their way through the tangle, wending around purple lengths of eggplants, red orb tomatoes, and dangling orange ornament chiles. Bees buzzed heavily between the sunflowers, burdened with saddlebags of pollen.

Lalji paused in the overgrowth and called after Bowman. "These plants. They are not engineered?"

Bowman paused and came thrashing back, wiping sweat and vegetal debris off his face, grinning. "Well, engineered, that is a matter of definition, but no, these are not owned by calorie companies. Some of them are even heirloom." He grinned again. "Or close enough."

"How do they survive?"

"Oh, that." He reached down and yanked up a tomato. "Nippon gene-hack weevils, or curl.lll.b, or perhaps cibiscosis bacterium, something like that?" He bit into the tomato and let the juice run down his gray bristled chin. "There isn't another heirloom planting within hundreds of miles. This is an island in an ocean of SoyPRO and HiGro. It makes a formidable barrier." He studied the garden thoughtfully, took another bite of tomato. "Now that you have come, of course, only a few of these plants will survive." He nodded at Lalji and Creo. "You will be carrying some infection or another and many of these rarities can only survive in isolation." He plucked another tomato and handed it to Lalji. "Try it."

Lalji studied its gleaming red skin. He bit into it and tasted sweetness and acid. Grinning, he offered it to Creo, who took a bite and made a face of disgust. "I'll stick with SoyPRO." He handed it back to Lalji, who finished it greedily.

Bowman smiled at Lalji's hunger. "You're old enough to remember, I think, what food used to be. You can take as much of this as you like, before we go. It will all die anyway." He turned and thrashed again through the garden overgrowth, shoving aside dry corn stalks with crackling authoritative sweeps of his arms.

Beyond the garden a house lay collapsed, leaning as though it had been toppled by a megadont, its walls rammed and buckled. The collapsed roof had an ungainly slant, and at one end, a pool of water lay cool and deep, rippled with water skippers. Scavenged gutter had been laid to sluice rainwater from the roof into the pond.

Bowman slipped around the pool's edge and disappeared down a series of crumbled cellar steps. By the time Lalji and Creo followed him down, he had wound a handlight and its dim bulb was spattering the cellar with illumination as its spring ran its course. He cranked the light again while he searched around, then struck a match and lit a lantern. The wick burned high on vegetable oil.

Lalji studied the cellar. It was sparse and damp. A pair of pallets lay on the broken concrete floor. A computer was tucked against a corner, its mahogany case and tiny screen gleaming, its treadle worn with use. An unruly kitchen was shoved against a wall with jars of grains arrayed on pantry shelves and bags of produce hanging from the ceiling to defend against rodents.

The man pointed to a sack on the ground. "There, my luggage."

"What about the computer?" Lalji asked.

Bowman frowned at the machine. "No. I don't need it."

"But it's valuable."

"What I need, I carry in my head. Everything in that machine came from me. My fat burned into knowledge. My calories pedaled into data analysis." He scowled. "Sometimes, I look at that computer and all I see is myself whittled away. I was a fat man once." He shook his head emphatically. "I won't miss it."

Lalji began to protest but Creo startled and whipped out his spring gun. "Someone else is here."

Lalji saw her even as Creo spoke: a girl squatting in the corner, hidden by shadow, a skinny, staring, freckled creature with stringy brown hair. Creo lowered his spring gun with a sigh.

Bowman beckoned. "Come out, Tazi. These are the men I told you about."

Lalji wondered how long she had been sitting in the cellar darkness, waiting. She had the look of a creature who had almost molded with the basement: her hair lank, her dark eyes nearly swallowed by their pupils. He turned on Bowman. "I thought there was only you."

Bowman's pleased smile faded. "Will you go back because of it?"

Lalji eyed the girl. Was she a lover? His child? A feral adoptee? He couldn't guess. The girl slipped her hand into the old man's. Bowman patted it reassuringly. Lalji shook his head. "She is too many. You, I have agreed to take. I prepared a way to carry you, to hide you from boarders and inspections. Her," he waved at the girl, "I did not agree to. It is risky to take someone like yourself, and now you wish to compound the danger with this girl? No." He shook his head emphatically. "It cannot be done."

"What difference does it make?" Bowman asked. "It costs you nothing. The current will carry us all. I have food enough for both of us." He went over to the pantry and started to pull down glass jars of beans, lentils, corn, and rice. "Look, here."

Lalji said, "We have more than enough food."

Bowman made a face. "SoyPRO, I suppose?"

"Nothing wrong with SoyPRO," Creo said.

The old man grinned and held up a jar of green beans floating in brine. "No. Of course not. But a man likes variety." He began filling his bag with more jars, letting them clink carefully. He caught Creo's snort of disgust and smiled, ingratiating suddenly. "For lean times, if nothing else." He dumped more jars of grains into the sack.

Lalji chopped the air with his hand. "Your food is not the issue. Your girl is the issue, and she is a risk!"

Bowman shook his head. "No risk. No one is looking for her. She can travel in the open, even."

"No. You must leave her. I will not take her."

The old man looked down at the girl, uncertain. She gazed back, extricated her hand from his. "I'm not afraid. I can live here still. Like before."

Bowman frowned, thinking. Finally, he shook his head. "No." He faced Lalji. "If she cannot go, then I cannot. She fed me when I worked. I deprived her of calories for my research when they should have gone to her. I owe her too much. I will not leave her to the wolves of this place." He placed his hands on her shoulders and placed her ahead of him, between himself and Lalji.

Creo made a face of disgust. "What difference does it make? Just bring her. We've got plenty of space."

Lalji shook his head. He and Bowman stared at one another across the cellar. Creo said, "What if he gives us the computer? We could call it payment."

Lalji shook his head stubbornly. "No. I do not care about the money. It is too dangerous to bring her."

Bowman laughed. "Then why come all this way if you are afraid? Half the calorie companies want to kill me and you talk about risk?"

Creo frowned. "What's he talking about?"

Bowman's eyebrows went up in surprise. "You haven't told your partner about me?"

Creo looked from Lalji to Bowman and back. "Lalji?"

Lalji took a deep breath, his eyes still locked on Bowman. "They say he can break the calorie monopolies. That he can pirate SoyPRO."

Creo boggled for a moment. "That's impossible!"

Bowman shrugged. "For you, perhaps. But for a knowledgeable man? Willing to dedicate his life to DNA helixes? More than possible. If one is willing to burn the calorie for such a project, to waste energy on statistics and genome analysis, to pedal a computer through millions upon millions of cycles. More than possible." He wrapped his arms around his skinny girl and held her to him. He smiled at Lalji. "So. Do we have any agreement?"

Creo shook his head, puzzling. "I thought you had a money plan, Lalji, but this . . ." He shook his head again. "I don't get it. How the hell do we make money off this?"

Lalji gave Creo a dirty look. Bowman smiled, patiently waiting Lalji stifled an urge to seize the lantern and throw it in his face, such a confident man, so sure of himself, so loyal . . .

He turned abruptly and headed for the stairs. "Bring the computer, Creo. If his girl makes any trouble, we dump them both in the river, and still keep his knowledge."

Lalji remembered his father pushing back his thali, pretending he was full when dal had barely stained the steel plate. He remembered his mother pressing an extra bite onto his own. He remembered Gita, watching, silent, and then all of them unfolding their legs and climbing off the family bed, bustling around the hovel, ostentatiously ignoring him as he consumed the extra portion. He remembered roti in his mouth, dry like ashes, and forcing himself to swallow anyway.

He remembered planting. Squatting with his father in desert heat, yellow dust all around them, burying seeds they had stored away, saved when they might have been eaten, kept when they might have made Gita fat and marriageable, his father smiling, saying, "These seeds will make hundreds of new seeds and then we will all eat well."

"How many seeds will they make?" Lalji had asked.

And his father had laughed and spread his arms fully wide, and seemed so large and great with his big white teeth and red and gold earrings and crinkling eyes as he cried, "Hundreds! Thousands if you pray!" And Lalji *had* prayed, to Ganesha and Lakshmi and Krishna and Rani Sati and Ram and Vishnu, to every god he could think of, joining the many villagers who did the same as he poured water from the well over tiny seeds and sat guard in the darkness against the possibility that the precious grains might be uprooted in the night and transported to some other farmer's field.

He sat every night while cold stars turned overhead, watching the seed rows, waiting, watering, praying, waiting through the days until his father finally shook his head and said it was no use. And yet still he had hoped, until at last he went out into the field and dug up the seeds one by one, and found them already decomposed, tiny corpses in his hand, rotted. As dead in his palm as the day he and his father had planted them.

He had crouched in the darkness and eaten the cold dead seeds, knowing he should share, and yet unable to master his hunger and carry them home. He wolfed them down alone, half-decayed and caked with dirt: his first true taste of PurCal.

In the light of early morning, Lalji bathed in the most sacred river of his adopted land. He immersed himself in the Mississippi's silty flow, cleansing the weight of sleep, making himself clean before his gods. He pulled himself back aboard, slick with water, his underwear dripping off his sagging bottom, his brown skin glistening, and toweled himself dry on the deck as he looked across the water to where the rising sun cast gold flecks on the river's rippled surface.

He finished drying himself and dressed in new clean clothes before going to his shrine. He lit incense in front of the gods, placed U-Tex and SoyPRO before the tiny carved idols of Krishna and his lute, benevolent Lakshmi, and elephant-headed Ganesha. He knelt in front of the idols, prostrated himself, and prayed.

They had floated south on the river's current, winding easily through bright fall days and watching as leaves changed and cool weather came on. Tranquil skies had arched overhead and mirrored on the river, turning the mud of the Mississippi's flow into shining blue, and they had followed that blue road south, riding the great arterial flow of the river as creeks and tributaries and the linked chains of barges all crowded in with them and gravity did the work of carrying them south.

He was grateful for their smooth movement downriver. The first of the locks were behind them, and having watched the sniffer dogs ignore Bowman's hiding place under the decking, Lalji was beginning to hope that the trip would be as easy as Shriram had claimed. Nonetheless, he prayed longer and harder each day as IP patrols shot past in their fast boats, and he placed extra SoyPRO before Ganesha's idol, desperately hoping that the Remover of Obstacles would continue to do so.

By the time he finished his morning devotions, the rest of the boat was stirring. Creo came below and wandered into the cramped galley. Bowman followed, complaining of SoyPRO, offering heirloom ingredients that Creo shook off with suspicion. On deck, Tazi sat at the edge of the boat with a fishing line tossed into the water, hoping to snare one of the massive lethargic LiveSalmon that occasionally bumped against the boat's keel in the warm murk of the river.

Lalji unmoored and took his place at the tiller. He unlocked the kink-springs and the boat whirred into the deeper current, stored joules dripping from its precision springs in a steady flow as molecules unlocked, one after another, reliable from the first kink to the last. He positioned the needleboat amongst the wallowing grain barges and locked the springs again, allowing the boat to drift.

Bowman and Creo came back up on deck as Creo was asking, ". . . you know how to grow SoyPRO?"

Bowman laughed and sat down beside Tazi. "What good would that do? The IP men would find the fields, ask for the licenses, and if none were provided, the fields would burn and burn and burn."

"So what good are you?"

Bowman smiled and posed a question instead. "SoyPRO – what is its most precious quality?"

"It's high calorie."

Bowman's braying laughter carried across the water. He tousled Tazi's hair and the pair of them exchanged amused glances. "You've seen too many billboards from AgriGen. 'Energy for the world' indeed, indeed. Oh, AgriGen and their ilk must love you very much. So malleable, so . . . tractable." He laughed again and shook his head. "No. Anyone can make high calorie plants. What else?"

Nettled, Creo said, "It resists the weevil."

Bowman's expression became sly. "Closer, yes. Difficult to make a plant that fights off the weevil, the leafcurl rust, the soil bacterium which chew through their roots . . . so many blights plague us now, so many beasts assail our plantings, but come now, what, best of all, do we like about SoyPRO? We of AgriGen who 'provide energy to the world'?" He waved at a chain of grain barges slathered with logos for SuperFlavor. "What makes SuperFlavor so perfect from a CEO's perspective?" He turned toward Lalji. "You know, Indian, don't you? Isn't it why you've come all this distance?"

Lalji stared back at him. When he spoke, his voice was hoarse. "It's sterile."

Bowman's eyes held Lalji's for a moment. His smile slipped. He ducked his head. "Yes. Indeed, indeed. A genetic dead-end. A one-way street. We now pay for a privilege that nature once provided willingly, for just a little labor." He looked up at Lalji. "I'm sorry. I should have thought. You would have felt our accountants' optimum demand estimates more than most."

Lalji shook his head. "You cannot apologize." He nodded at Creo. "Tell him the rest. Tell him what you can do. What I was told you can do."

"Some things are perhaps better left unsaid."

Lalji was undaunted. "Tell him. Tell me. Again."

Bowman shrugged. "If you trust him, then I must trust him as well, yes?" He turned to Creo. "Do you know cheshires?"

Creo made a noise of disgust. "They're pests."

"Ah, yes. A bluebill for every dead one. I forgot. But what makes our cheshires such pests?"

"They molt. They kill birds."

"And?" Bowman prodded.

Creo shrugged.

Bowman shook his head. "And to think it was for people like you that I wasted my life on research and my calories on computer cycles.

"You call cheshires a plague, and truly, they are. A few wealthy patrons, obsessed with Lewis Carroll, and suddenly they are everywhere, breeding with heirloom cats, killing birds, wailing in the night, but most importantly, their offspring, an astonishing ninety-two percent of the time, are cheshires themselves, pure, absolute. We create a new species in a heartbeat of evolutionary time, and our songbird populations disappear almost as quickly. A more perfect predator, but most importantly, one that spreads.

"With SoyPRO, or U-Tex, the calorie companies may patent the plants and use intellectual property police and sensitized dogs to sniff out their property, but even IP men can only inspect so many acres. Most importantly, the seeds are sterile, a locked box. Some may steal a little here and there, as you and Lalji do, but in the end, you are nothing but a small expense on a balance sheet fat with profit because no one except the calorie companies can grow the plants.

"But what would happen if we passed SoyPRO a different trait, stealthily, like a man climbing atop his best friend's wife?" He waved his arm to indicate the green fields that lapped at the edges of the river. "What if someone were to drop bastardizing pollens amongst these crown jewels that surround us? Before the calorie companies harvested and shipped the resulting seeds across the world in their mighty clipper fleets, before the licensed dealers delivered the patented crop seed to their customers. What sorts of seeds might they be delivering then?"

Bowman began ticking traits off with his fingers. "Resistant to weevil and leafcurl, yes. High calorie, yes, of course. Genetically distinct and therefore unpatentable?" He smiled briefly. "Perhaps. But best of all, fecund. Unbelievably fecund. Ripe, fat with breeding potential." He leaned forward. "Imagine it. Seeds distributed across the world by the very cuckolds who have always clutched them so tight, all of those seeds lusting to breed, lusting to produce their own fine offspring full of the same pollens that polluted the crown jewels in the first place." He clapped his hands. "Oh, what an infection that would be! And how it would spread!"

Creo stared, his expression contorting between horror and fascination. "You can do this?"

Bowman laughed and clapped his hands again. "I'm going to be the next Johnny Appleseed."

Lalji woke suddenly. Around him, the darkness of the river was nearly complete. A few windup LED beacons glowed on grain barges, powered by the flow of the current's drag against their ungainly bodies. Water lapped against the sides of the needleboat and the bank where they had tied up. Beside him on the deck the others lay bundled in blankets.

Why had he wakened? In the distance, a pair of village roosters were challenging one another across the darkness. A dog was barking, incensed by whatever hidden smells or sounds caused dogs to startle and defend their territory. Lalji closed his eyes and listened to the gentle undulation of the river, the sounds of the distant village. If he pressed his imagination, he could almost be lying in the early dawn of another village, far away, long ago dissolved.

Why was he awake? He opened his eyes again and sat up. He strained his eyes against the darkness. A shadow appeared on the river blackness, a subtle blot of movement.

Lalji shook Bowman awake, his hand over Bowman's mouth. "Hide!" he whispered.

Lights swept over them. Bowman's eyes widened. He fought off his blankets and scrambled for the hold. Lalji gathered Bowman's blankets with his own, trying to obscure the number of sleepers as more lights flashed brightly, sliding across the deck, pasting them like insects on a collection board.

Abandoning its pretense of stealth, the IP boat opened its springs and rushed in. It slammed against the needleboat, pinning it to the shoreline as men swarmed aboard. Three of them, and two dogs.

"Everyone stay calm! Keep your hands in sight!"

Handlight beams swept across the deck, dazzlingly bright. Creo and Tazi clawed out of their blankets and stood, surprised. The sniffer dogs growled and lunged against their leashes. Creo backed away from them, his hands held before him, defensive.

One of the IP men swept his handlight across them. "Who owns this boat?"

Lalji took a breath. "It's mine. This is my boat." The beam swung back and speared his eyes. He squinted into the light. "Have we done something wrong?"

The leader didn't answer. The other IP men fanned out, swinging their lights across the boat, marking the people on deck. Lalji realized that except for the leader, they were just boys, barely old enough to have mustaches and beards at all. Just peachfuzzed boys carrying spring guns and covered in armor that helped them swagger.

Two of them headed for the stairs with the dogs as a fourth jumped aboard from the secured IP boat. Handlight beams disappeared into the bowels of the needleboat, casting looming shadows from inside the stairway. Creo had somehow managed to end up backed against the needleboat's cache of spring guns. His hand rested casually beside the catches. Lalji stepped toward the captain, hoping to head off Creo's impulsiveness.

The captain swung his light on him. "What are you doing here?"

Lalji stopped and spread his hands helplessly. "Nothing."

"No?"

Lalji wondered if Bowman had managed to secure himself. "What I mean is that we only moored here to sleep."

"Why didn't you tie up at Willow Bend?"

"I'm not familiar with this part of the river. It was getting dark. I didn't want to be crushed by the barges." He wrung his hands. "I deal with antiques. We were looking in the old suburbs to the north. It's not illeg – " A shout from below interrupted him. Lalji closed his eyes regretfully. The Mississippi would be his burial river. He would never find his way to the Ganges.

The IP men came up dragging Bowman. "Look what we found! Trying to hide under the decking!"

Bowman tried to shake them off. "I don't know what you're talking about – "

"Shut up!" One of the boys shoved a club into Bowman's stomach. The old man doubled over. Tazi lunged toward them, but the captain corralled her and held her tightly as he flashed his light over Bowman's features. He gasped.

"Cuff him. We want him. Cover them!" Spring guns came up all around. The captain scowled at Lalji. "An antiques dealer. I almost believed you." To his men he said, "He's a generipper. From a long time ago. See if there's anything else on board. Any disks, any computers, any papers."

One of them said, "There's a treadle computer below."

"Get it."

In moments the computer was on deck. The captain surveyed his captives. "Cuff them all." One of the IP boys made Lalji kneel and started patting him down while a sniffer dog growled over them.

Bowman was saying, "I'm really very sorry. Perhaps you've made a mistake. Perhaps . . ."

Suddenly the captain shouted. The IP men's handlights swung toward the sound. Tazi was latched onto the captain's hand, biting him. He was shaking at her as though she were a dog, struggling with his other hand to get his spring gun free. For a brief moment everyone watched the scuffle between the girl and the much larger man. Someone – Lalji thought it was an IP man – laughed. Then Tazi was flung free and the captain had his gun out and there was a sharp hiss of disks. Handlights thudded on the deck and rolled, casting dizzy beams of light.

More disks hissed through the darkness. A rolling light beam showed the captain falling, crashing against Bowman's computer, silver disks embedded in his armor.

He and the computer slid backwards. Darkness again. A splash. The dogs howled, either released and attacking or else wounded. Lalji dove and lay prone on the decking as metal whirred past his head.

"Lalji!" It was Creo's voice. A gun skittered across the planking. Lalji scrambled toward the sound.

One of the handlight beams had stabilized. The captain was sitting up, black blood lines trailing from his jaw as he leveled his pistol at Tazi. Bowman lunged into the light, shielding the girl with his body. He curled as disks hit him.

Lalji's fingers bumped the spring gun. He clutched after it blindly. His hand closed on it. He jacked the pump, aimed toward bootfalls, and let the spring gun whir. The shadow of one of the IP men, the boys, was above him, falling, bleeding, already dead as he hit the decking.

Everything went silent.

Lalji waited. Nothing moved. He waited still, forcing himself to breathe quietly, straining his eyes against the shadows where the handlights didn't illuminate. Was he the only one alive?

One by one, the three remaining handlights ran out of juice. Darkness closed in. The IP boat bumped gently against the needleboat. A breeze rustled the willow banks, carrying the muddy reek of fish and grasses. Crickets chirped.

Lalji stood. Nothing. No movement. Slowly he limped across the deck. He'd twisted his leg somehow. He felt for one of the handlights, found it by its faint metallic gleam, and wound it. He played its flickering beam across the deck.

Creo. The big blond boy was dead, a disk caught in his throat. Blood pooled from where it had hit his artery. Not far away, Bowman was ribboned with disks. His blood ran everywhere. The computer was missing. Gone overboard. Lalji squatted beside the bodies, sighing. He pulled Creo's bloodied braids off his face. He had been fast. As fast as he had believed he was. Three armored IP men and the dogs as well. He sighed again.

Something whimpered. Lalji flicked his light toward the source, afraid of what he would find, but it was only the girl, seemingly unhurt, crawling to Bowman's body. She looked up into the glare of Lalji's light, then ignored him and crouched over Bowman. She sobbed, then stifled herself. Lalji locked the handlight's spring and let darkness fall over them.

He listened to the night sounds again, praying to Ganesha that there were no others out on the river. His eyes adjusted. The shadow of the grieving girl kneeling amongst lumped bodies resolved from the blackness. He shook his head. So many dead for such an idea. That such a man as Bowman might be of use. And now such a waste. He listened for signs others had been alerted but heard nothing. A single patrol, it seemed, uncoordinated with any others. Bad luck. That was all. One piece of bad luck breaking a string of good. Gods were fickle.

He limped to the needleboat's moorings and began untying. Unbidden, Tazi joined him, her small hands fumbling with the knots. He went to the tiller and unlocked the kink-springs. The boat jerked as the screws bit and they swept into the river darkness. He let the springs fly for an hour, wasting joules but anxious to make distance from the killing place, then searched the banks for an inlet and anchored. The darkness was nearly total.

After securing the boat, he searched for weights and tied them around the ankles of the IP men. He did the same with the dogs, then began shoving the bodies off the deck. The water swallowed them easily. It felt unclean to dump them so unceremoniously, but he had no intention of taking time to bury them. With luck, the men would bump along under water, picked at by fish until they disintegrated.

When the IP men were gone, he paused over Creo. So wonderfully quick. He pushed Creo overboard, wishing he could build a pyre for him.

Lalji began mopping the decks, sluicing away the remaining blood. The moon rose, bathing them in pale light. The girl sat beside the body of her chaperone. Eventually, Lalji could avoid her with his mopping no more. He knelt beside her. "You understand he must go into the river?"

The girl didn't respond. Lalji took it as assent. "If there is anything you wish to have of his, you should take it now." The girl shook her head. Lalji hesitantly let his hand rest on her shoulder. "It is no shame to be given to a river. An honor, even, to go to a river such as this."

He waited. Finally, she nodded. He stood and dragged the body to the edge of the boat. He tied it with weights and levered the legs over the lip. The old man slid out of his hands. The girl was silent, staring at where Bowman had disappeared into the water.

Lalji finished his mopping. In the morning he would have to mop again, and sand the stains, but for the time it would do. He began pulling in the anchors. A moment later, the girl was with him again, helping. Lalji settled himself at the tiller. Such a waste, he thought. Such a great waste.

Slowly, the current drew their needleboat into the deeper flows of the river. The girl came and knelt beside him. "Will they chase us?"

Lalji shrugged. "With luck? No. They will look for something larger than us to make so many of their men disappear. With just the two of us now, we will look like very small inconsequential fish to them. With luck."

She nodded, seeming to digest this information. "He saved me, you know. I should be dead now."

"I saw."

"Will you plant his seeds?"

"Without him to make them, there will be no one to plant them."

Tazi frowned. "But we've got so many." She stood and slipped down into the hold. When she returned, she lugged the sack of Bowman's food stores. She began pulling jars from the sack: rice and corn, soybeans and kernels of wheat.

"That's just food," Lalji protested.

Tazi shook her head stubbornly. "They're his Johnny Appleseeds. I wasn't supposed to tell you. He didn't trust you to take us all the way. To take me. But you could plant them, too, right?"

Lalji frowned and picked up a jar of corn. The kernels nestled tightly together, hundreds of them, each one unpatented, each one a genetic infection. He closed his eyes and in his mind he saw a field: row upon row of green rustling plants, and his father, laughing, with his arms spread wide as he shouted, "Hundreds! Thousands if you pray!"

Lalji hugged the jar to his chest, and slowly, he began to smile.

The needleboat continued downstream, a bit of flotsam in the Mississippi's current. Around it, the crowding shadow hulks of the grain barges loomed, all of them flowing south through the fertile heartland toward the gateway of New Orleans; all of them flowing steadily toward the vast wide world.

BEYOND THE AQUILA RIFT

Alastair Reynolds

Alastair Reynolds is a frequent contributor to *Interzone*, and has also sold to *Asimov's Science Fiction*, *Spectrum SF*, and elsewhere. His first novel, *Revelation Space*, was widely hailed as one of the major SF books of 2001; it was quickly followed by *Chasm City*, *Redemption Ark*, *Absolution Gap*, and *Century Rain*, all big books that were big sellers as well, establishing Reynolds as one of the best and most popular new SF writers to enter the field in many years. His other books include a novella collection, *Diamond Dogs*, *Turquoise Days*, and a new novel, *Pushing Ice*. A professional scientist with a Ph.D. in astronomy, Reynolds comes from Wales but lives in the Netherlands, where he works for the European Space Agency.

In the ingenious and suspenseful story that follows, he takes us on a voyage to places so far away that *almost* no one has ever gone there before – but where some surprises await at journey's end.

GRETA'S WITH ME *when I pull Suzy out of the surge tank.*

"Why her?" Greta asks.

"Because I want her out first." I say, wondering if Greta's jealous. I don't blame her: Suzy's beautiful, but she's also smart. There isn't a better syntax runner in Ashanti Industrial.

"What happened?" Suzy asks, when she's over the grogginess. "Did we make it back?"

I ask her to tell me the last thing she remembered.

"Customs," Suzy says. "Those pricks on Arkangel."

"And after that? Anything else? The runes? Do you remember casting them?"

"No," she says, then picks up something in my voice. The fact that I might not be telling the truth, or telling her all she needs to know. "Thom. I'll ask you again. Did we make it back?"

"Yeah," I say. "We made it back."

Suzy looks back at the starscape, airbrushed across her surge tank in luminous violet and yellow paint. She'd had it customised on Carillon. It was against regs: something about the paint clogging intake filters. Suzy didn't care. She told me it had cost her a week's pay, but it had been worth it to impose her own personality on the gray company architecture of the ship.

"Funny how I feel like I've been in that thing for months."

I shrug. "That's the way it feels sometimes."

"Then nothing went wrong?"

"Nothing at all."

Suzy looks at Greta. "Then who are you?" she asks.

Greta says nothing. She just looks at me expectantly. I start shaking, and realize I can't go through with this. Not yet.

"End it," I tell Greta.

Greta steps toward Suzy. Suzy reacts, but she isn't quick enough. Greta pulls something from her pocket and touches Suzy on the forearm. Suzy drops like a puppet, out cold. We put her back into the surge tank, plumb her back in and close the lid.

"She won't remember anything," Greta says. "The conversation never left her short term memory."

"I don't know if I can go through with this," I say.

Greta touches me with her other hand. "No one ever said this was going to be easy."

"I was just trying to ease her into it gently. I didn't want to tell her the truth right out."

"I know," Greta says. "You're a kind man, Thom." Then she kisses me.

I remembered Arkangel as well. That was about where it all started to go wrong. We just didn't know it then.

We missed our first take-off slot when customs found a discrepancy in our cargo waybill. It wasn't serious, but it took them a while to realize their mistake. By the time they did, we knew we were going to be sitting on the ground for another eight hours, while in-bound control processed a fleet of bulk carriers.

I told Suzy and Ray the news. Suzy took it pretty well, or about as well as Suzy ever took that kind of thing. I suggested she use the time to scour the docks for any hot syntax patches. Anything that might shave a day or two off our return trip.

"Company authorized?" she asked.

"I don't care," I said.

"What about Ray?" Suzy asked. "Is he going to sit here drinking tea while I work for my pay?"

I smiled. They had a bickering, love-hate thing going. "No, Ray can do something useful as well. He can take a look at the q-planes."

"Nothing wrong with those planes," Ray said.

I took off my old Ashanti Industrial bib cap, scratched my bald spot and turned to the jib man.

"Right. Then it won't take you long to check them over, will it?"

"Whatever, Skip."

The thing I liked about Ray was that he always knew when he'd lost an argument. He gathered his kit and went out to check over the planes. I watched him climb the jib ladder, tools hanging from his belt. Suzy got her facemask, long black coat and left, vanishing into the vapor haze of the docks, boot heels clicking into the distance long after she'd passed out of sight.

I left the *Blue Goose*, walking in the opposite direction to Suzy. Overhead, the bulk carriers slid in one after the other. You heard them long before you saw them. Mournful, cetacean moans cut down through the piss-yellow clouds over the port. When they emerged, you saw dark hulls scabbed and scarred by the blocky extrusions of syntax patterning, jibs and q-planes retracted for landing and under-carriage clutching down like talons. The carriers stopped over their allocated wells and lowered down on a scream of thrust. Docking gantries closed around them like grasping skeletal fingers. Cargo handling 'saurs plodded out of their holding pens, some of them autonomous, some of them still being ridden by trainers. There was a shocking silence as the engines cut, until the next carrier began to approach through the clouds.

I always like watching ships coming and going, even when they're holding my own ship on the ground. I couldn't read the syntax, but I knew these ships had come in all the way from the Rift. The Aquila Rift is about as far out as anyone ever goes. At median tunnel speeds, it's a year from the center of the Local Bubble.

I've been out that way once in my life. I've seen the view from the near side of the Rift, like a good tourist. It was about far enough for me.

When there was a lull in the landing pattern, I ducked into a bar and found an Aperture Authority booth that took Ashanti credit. I sat in the seat and recorded a thirty-second message to Katerina. I told her I was on my way back but that we were stuck on Arkangel for another few hours. I warned her that the delay might cascade through to our tunnel routing, depending on how busy things were at the Aperture Authority's end. Based on past experience, an eight-hour ground hold might become a two day hold at the surge point. I told her I'd be back, but she shouldn't worry if I was a few days late.

Outside a diplodocus slouched by with a freight container strapped between its legs.

I told Katerina I loved her and couldn't wait to get back home.

While I walked back to the *Blue Goose*, I thought of the message racing ahead of me. Transmitted at lightspeed up-system, then copied into the memory buffer of the next outgoing ship. Chances were, that particular ship wasn't headed to Barranquilla or anywhere near it. The Aperture Authority would have to relay the message from ship to ship until it reached its destination. I might even reach Barranquilla ahead of it, but in all my years of delays that had only happened once. The system worked all right.

Overhead, a white passenger liner had been slotted in between the bulk carriers. I lifted up my mask to get a better look at it. I got a hit of ozone, fuel, and dinosaur dung. That was Arkangel all right. You couldn't mistake it for any other place in the Bubble. There were four hundred worlds out there, up to a dozen surface ports on every planet, and none of them smelled bad in quite the same way.

"Thom?"

I followed the voice. It was Ray, standing by the dock.

"You finished checking those planes?" I asked.

Ray shook his head. "That's what I wanted to talk to you about. They were a little off-alignment, so – seeing as we're going to be sitting here for eight hours – I decided to run a full recalibration."

I nodded. "That was the idea. So what's the prob?"

"The *prob* is a slot just opened up. Tower says we can lift in thirty minutes."

I shrugged. "Then we'll lift."

"I haven't finished the recal. As it is, things are worse than before I started. Lifting now would not be a good idea."

"You know how the tower works," I said. "Miss two offered slots, you could be on the ground for days."

"No one wants to get back home sooner than I do," Ray said.

"So cheer up."

"She'll be rough in the tunnel. It won't be a smooth ride home."

I shrugged. "Do we care? We'll be asleep."

"Well, it's academic. We can't leave without Suzy."

I heard boot heels clicking toward us. Suzy came out of the fog, tugging her own mask aside.

"No joy with the rune monkeys," she said. "Nothing they were selling I hadn't seen a million times before. Fucking cowboys."

"It doesn't matter," I said. "We're leaving anyway."

Ray swore. I pretended I hadn't heard him.

I was always the last one into a surge tank. I never went under until I was sure we were about to get the green light. It gave me a chance to check things over. Things can always go wrong, no matter how good the crew.

The *Blue Goose* had come to a stop near the AA beacon which marked the surge point. There were a few other ships ahead of us in the queue, plus the usual swarm of AA service craft. Through an observation blister I was able to watch the larger ships depart one by one. Accelerating at maximum power, they seemed to streak toward a completely featureless part of the sky. Their jibs were spread wide, and the smooth lines of their hulls were gnarled and disfigured with the cryptic alien runes of the routing syntax. At twenty gees it was as if a huge invisible hand snatched them away into the distance. Ninety seconds later, there'd be a pale green flash from a thousand kilometers away.

I twisted around in the blister. There were the foreshortened symbols of our routing syntax. Each rune of the script was formed from a matrix of millions of hexagonal platelets. The platelets were on motors so they could be pushed in or out from the hull.

Ask the Aperture Authority and they'll tell you that the syntax is now fully understood. This is true, but only up to a point. After two centuries of study, human machines can now construct and interpret the syntax with an acceptably low failure rate. Given a desired destination, they can assemble a string of runes which will almost always be accepted by the aperture's own machinery. Furthermore, they can almost always guarantee that the desired routing is the one that the aperture machinery will provide.

In short, you usually get where you want to go.

Take a simple point-to-point transfer, like the Hauraki run. In that case there is no real disadvantage in using automatic syntax generators. But for longer trajectories – those that may involve six or seven transits between aperture hubs – machines lose the edge. They find a solution, but usually it isn't the optimum one. That's where syntax runners come in. People like Suzy have an intuitive grasp of syntax solutions. They dream in runes. When they see a poorly constructed script, they feel it like a toothache. It *affronts* them.

A good syntax runner can shave days off a route. For a company like Ashanti Industrial, that can make a lot of difference.

But I wasn't a syntax runner. I could tell when something had gone wrong with the platelets, but otherwise I had no choice. I had to trust that Suzy had done her job.

But I knew Suzy wouldn't screw things up.

I twisted around and looked back the other way. Now that we were in space, the q-planes had deployed. They were swung out from the hull on triple hundred-meter long jibs, like the arms of a grapple. I checked that they were locked in their fully extended positions and that the status lights were all in the green. The jibs were Ray's area. He'd been checking the alignment of the ski-shaped q-planes when I ordered him to close-up ship and prepare to lift. I couldn't see any visible indication that they were out of alignment, but then again it wouldn't take much to make our trip home bumpier than usual. But as I'd told Ray, who cared? The *Blue Goose* could take a little tunnel turbulence. It was built to.

I checked the surge point again. Only three ships ahead of us.

I went back to the surge tanks and checked that Suzy and Ray were all right. Ray's tank had been customized at the same time that Suzy had had hers done. It was full of images of what Suzy called the BVM: the Blessed Virgin Mary. The BVM was always in a spacesuit, carrying a little spacesuited Jesus. Their helmets were airbrushed gold halos. The artwork had a cheap, hasty look to it. I assumed Ray hadn't spent as much as Suzy.

Quickly I stripped down to my underclothes. I plumbed into my own unpainted surge tank and closed the lid. The buffering gel sloshed in. Within about twenty seconds I was already feeling drowsy. By the time traffic control gave us the green light, I'd be asleep.

I've done it a thousand times. There was no fear, no apprehension. Just a tiny flicker of regret.

I've never seen an aperture. Then again, very few people have.

Witnesses report a doughnut shaped lump of dark chondrite asteroid, about two kilometers across. The entire middle section has been cored out, with the inner part of the ring faced by the quixotic-matter machinery of the aperture itself. They say the q-matter machinery twinkles and moves all the while, like the ticking innards of a very complicated clock. But the monitoring systems of the Aperture Authority detect no movement at all.

It's alien technology. We have no idea how it works, or even who made it. Maybe, in hindsight, it's better not to be able to see it.

It's enough to dream, and then awake, and know that you're somewhere else.

Try a different approach, Greta says. Tell her the truth this time. Maybe she'll take it easier than you think.

"There's no way I can tell her the truth."

Greta leans one hip against the wall, one hand still in her pocket. "Then tell her something half way to it."

We unplumb Suzy and haul her out of the surge tank.

"Where are we?" she asks. Then to Greta: "Who are you?"

I wonder if some of the last conversation did make it out of Suzy's short-term memory after all.

"Greta works here," I say.

"Where's here?"

I remember what Greta told me. "A station in Schedar sector."

"That's not where we're meant to be, Thom."

I nod. "I know. There was a mistake. A routing error."

Suzy's already shaking her head. "There was nothing wrong . . ."

"I know. It wasn't your fault." I help her into her ship clothes. She's still shivering, her muscles reacting to movement after so much time in the tank. "The syntax was good."

"Then what?"

"The system made a mistake, not you."

"Schedar sector . . ." Suzy says. "That would put us about ten days off our schedule, wouldn't it?"

I try to remember what Greta said to me the first time. I ought to know this stuff off by heart, but Suzy's the routing expert, not me. "That sounds about right," I say.

But Suzy shakes her head. "Then we're not in Schedar sector."

I try to sound pleasantly surprised.

"We're not?"

"I've been in that tank for a lot longer than a few days, Thom. I

know. I can feel it in every fucking bone in my body. So where are we?"
I turn to Greta. I can't believe this is happening again.
"End it," I say.
Greta steps toward Suzy.

You know that "as soon as I awoke I knew everything was wrong" cliché? You've probably heard it a thousand times, in a thousand bars across the Bubble, wherever ship crews swap tall tales over flat company-subsidized beer. The trouble is that sometimes that's exactly the way it happens. I never felt good after a period in the surge tank. But the only time I had ever come around feeling anywhere near this bad was after that trip I took to the edge of the Bubble.

Mulling this, but knowing there was nothing I could do about it until I was out of the tank, it took me half an hour of painful work to free myself from the connections. Every muscle fiber in my body felt as though it had been shredded. Unfortunately, the sense of wrongness didn't end with the tank. The *Blue Goose* was much too quiet. We should have been heading away from the last exit aperture after our routing. But the distant, comforting rumble of the fusion engines wasn't there at all. That meant we were in free-fall.

Not good.

I floated out of the tank, grabbed a handhold and levered myself around to view the other two tanks. Ray's largest BVM stared back radiantly from the cowl of his tank. The bio indices were all in the green. Ray was still unconscious, but there was nothing wrong with him. Same story with Suzy. Some automated system had decided I was the only one who needed waking.

A few minutes later I had made my way to the same observation blister I'd used to check the ship before the surge. I pushed my head into the scuffed glass halfdome and looked around.

We'd arrived somewhere. The *Blue Goose* was sitting in a huge zero-gravity parking bay. The chamber was an elongated cylinder, hexagonal in cross-section. The walls were a smear of service machinery: squat modules, snaking umbilical lines, the retracted cradles of unused docking berths. Whichever way I looked I saw other ships locked onto cradles. Every make and class you could think of, every possible configuration of hull design compatible with aperture transitions. Service lights threw a warm golden glow on the scene. Now and then the whole chamber was bathed in the stuttering violet flicker of a cutting torch.

It was a repair facility.

I was just starting to mull on that when I saw something extend itself from the wall of the chamber. It was a telescopic docking tunnel, groping toward our ship. Through the windows in the side of the tunnel I saw figures floating, pulling themselves along hand over hand.

I sighed and started making my way to the airlock.

By the time I reached the lock they were already through the first stage of the cycle. Nothing wrong with that – there was no good reason to prevent foreign parties boarding a vessel – but it was just a tiny bit impolite. But perhaps they'd assumed we were all asleep.

The door slid open.

"You're awake," a man said. "Captain Thomas Gundlupet of the *Blue Goose*, isn't it?"

"Guess so," I said.

"Mind if we come in?"

There were about half a dozen of them, and they were already coming in. They all wore slightly timeworn ochre overalls, flashed with too many company sigils. My hackles rose. I really didn't like the way they were barging in.

"What's up?" I said. "Where are we?"

"Where do you think?" the man said. He had a face full of stubble, with bad yellow teeth. I was impressed with that. Having bad teeth took a lot of work these days. It was years since I'd seen anyone who had the same dedication to the art.

"I'm really hoping you're not going to tell me we're still stuck in Arkangel system," I said.

"No, you made it through the gate."

"And?"

"There was a screw-up. Routing error. You didn't pop out of the right aperture."

"Oh, Christ." I took off my bib cap. "It never rains. Something went wrong with the insertion, right?"

"Maybe. Maybe not. Who knows how these things happen? All we know is you aren't supposed to be here."

"Right. And where is 'here'?"

"Saumlaki Station. Schedar sector."

He said it as though he was already losing interest, as if this was a routine he went through several times a day.

He might have been losing interest. I wasn't.

I'd never heard of Saumlaki Station, but I'd certainly heard of Schedar sector. Schedar was a K supergiant out toward the edge of the Local Bubble. It defined one of the seventy-odd navigational sectors across the whole Bubble.

Did I mention the Bubble already?

You know how the Milky Way galaxy looks; you've seen it a thousand times, in paintings and computer simulations. A bright central bulge at the Galactic core, with lazily curved spiral arms flung out from that hub, each arm composed of hundreds of billions of stars, ranging from the dimmest, slow-burning dwarfs to the hottest supergiants teetering on the edge of supernova extinction.

Now zoom in on one arm of the Milky Way. There's the sun, orange-yellow, about two-thirds out from the center of the Galaxy. Lanes and folds of dust swaddle the sun out to distances of tens of thousands of light-years. Yet the sun itself is sitting right in the middle of a four-hundred-light-year-wide hole in the dust, a bubble in which the density is about a twentieth of its average value.

That's the Local Bubble. It's as if God blew a hole in the dust just for us.

Except, of course, it wasn't God. It was a supernova, about a million years ago.

Look further out, and there are more bubbles, their walls intersecting and merging, forming a vast froth-like structure tens of thousands of light years across. There are the structures of Loop I and Loop II and the Lindblad Ring. There are even super-dense knots where the dust is almost too thick to be seen through at all. Black cauls like the Taurus or RhoOphiuchi dark clouds or the Aquila Rift itself.

Lying outside the Local Bubble, the Rift is the furthest point in the galaxy we've ever traveled to. It's not a question of endurance or nerve. There simply isn't a way to get beyond it, at least not within the faster-than-light network of the aperture links. The rabbit-warren of possible routes just doesn't reach any further. Most destinations – including most of those on the *Blue Goose*'s itinerary – didn't even get you beyond the Local Bubble.

For us, it didn't matter. There's still a lot of commerce you can do within a hundred light-years of Earth. But Schedar was right on the periphery of the Bubble, where dust density began to ramp up to normal galactic levels, two hundred and twenty-eight light-years from Mother Earth.

Again: not good.

"I know this is a shock for you," another voice said. "But it's not as bad as you think it is."

I looked at the woman who had just spoken. Medium height, the kind of face they called "elfin," with slanted ash-gray eyes and a bob of shoulder-length chrome-white hair.

The face hurtingly familiar.

"It isn't?"

"I wouldn't say so, Thom." She smiled. "After all, it's given us the chance to catch up on old times, hasn't it?"

"Greta?" I asked, disbelievingly.

She nodded. "For my sins."

"My God. It is you, isn't it?"

"I wasn't sure you'd recognize me. Especially after all this time."

"You didn't have much trouble recognizing me."

"I didn't have to. The moment you popped out, we picked up your recovery transponder. Told us the name of your ship, who owned her, who was flying it, what you were carrying, where you were supposed to be headed. When I heard it was you, I made sure I was part of the reception team. But don't worry. It's not like you've changed all that much."

"Well, you haven't either," I said.

It wasn't quite true. But who honestly wants to hear that they look about ten years older than the last time you saw them, even if they still don't look all that bad with it? I thought about how she had looked naked, memories that I'd kept buried for a decade spooling into daylight. It shamed me that they were still so vivid, as if some furtive part of my subconscious had been secretly hoarding them through years of marriage and fidelity.

Greta half smiled. It was as if she knew exactly what I was thinking.

"You were never a good liar, Thom."

"Yeah. Guess I need some practice."

There was an awkward silence. Neither of us seemed to know what to say next. While we hesitated, the others floated around us, saying nothing.

"Well," I said. "Who'd have guessed we'd end up meeting like this?"

Greta nodded and offered the palms of her hands in a kind of apology.

"I'm just sorry we aren't meeting under better circumstances," she said. "But if it's any consolation, what happened wasn't at all your fault. We checked your syntax, and there wasn't a mistake. It's just that now and then the system throws a glitch."

"Funny how no one likes to talk about that very much," I said.

"Could have been worse, Thom. I remember what you used to tell me about space travel."

"Yeah? Which particular pearl of wisdom would that have been?"

"If you're in a position to moan about a situation, you've no right to be moaning."

"Christ. Did I actually say that?"

"Mm. And I bet you're regretting it now. But look, it really isn't that bad. You're only twenty days off schedule." Greta nodded toward the man who had the bad teeth. "Kolding says you'll only need a day of damage repair before you can move off again, and then another twenty, twenty-five days before you reach your destination, depending on routing patterns. That's less than six weeks. So you lose the bonus on this one. Big deal. You're all in one shape, and your ship only needs a little work. Why don't you just bite the bullet and sign the repair paperwork?"

"I'm not looking forward to another twenty days in the surge tank. There's something else, as well."

"Which is?"

I was about to tell her about Katerina, how she'd have been expecting me back already.

Instead I said: "I'm worried about the others. Suzy and Ray. They've got families expecting them. They'll be worried."

"I understand," Greta said. "Suzy and Ray. They're still asleep, aren't they? Still in their surge tanks?"

"Yes," I said, guardedly.

"Keep them that way until you're on your way." Greta smiled.

"There's no sense worrying them about their families, either. It's kinder."

"If you say so."

"Trust me on this one, Thom. This isn't the first time I've handled this kind of situation. Doubt it'll be the last, either."

I stayed in a hotel overnight, in another part of Saumlaki. The hotel was an echoing multilevel prefab structure, sunk deep into bedrock. It must have had a capacity for hundreds of guests, but at the moment only a handful of the rooms seemed to be occupied. I slept fitfully and got up early. In the atrium, I saw a bib-capped worker in rubber gloves removing diseased carp from a small ornamental pond. Watching him pick out the ailing metallic-orange fish, I had a flash of déjà vu. What was it about dismal hotels and dying carp?

Before breakfast – bleakly alert, even though I didn't really feel as if I'd had a good night's sleep – I visited Kolding and got a fresh update on the repair schedule.

"Two, three days," he said.

"It was a day last night."

Kolding shrugged. "You've got a problem with the service, find someone else to fix your ship."

Then he stuck his little finger into the corner of his mouth and began to dig between his teeth.

"Nice to see someone who really enjoys his work," I said.

I left Kolding before my mood worsened too much, making my way to a different part of the station.

Greta had suggested we meet for breakfast and catch up on old times. She was there when I arrived, sitting at a table in an "outdoor" terrace, under a red-and-white striped canopy, sipping orange juice. Above us was a dome several hundred meters wide, projecting a cloudless holographic sky. It had the hard, enameled blue of midsummer.

"How's the hotel?" she asked after I'd ordered a coffee from the waiter.

"Not bad. No one seems very keen on conversation, though. Is it me or does that place have all the cheery ambience of a sinking ocean liner?"

"It's just this place," Greta said. "Everyone who comes here is pissed off about it. Either they got transferred here and they're pissed off about that, or they ended up here by routing error and they're pissed off about that instead. Take your pick."

"No one's happy?"

"Only the ones who know they're getting out of here soon."

"Would that include you?"

"No," she said. "I'm more or less stuck here. But I'm OK about it. I guess I'm the exception that proves the rule."

The waiters were glass mannequins of a kind that had been fashionable in the core worlds about twenty years ago. One of them placed a croissant in front of me, then poured scalding black coffee into my cup.

"Well, it's good to see you," I said.

"You too, Thom." Greta finished her orange juice and then took a corner of my croissant for herself, without asking. "I heard you got married."

"Yes."

"Well? Aren't you going to tell me about her?"

I drank some of my coffee. "Her name's Katerina."

"Nice name."

"She works in the department of bioremediation on Kagawa."

"Kids?" Greta asked.

"Not yet. It wouldn't be easy, the amount of time we both spend away from home."

"Mm." She had a mouthful of croissant. "But one day you might think about it."

"Nothing's ruled out," I said. As flattered as I was that she was taking such an interest in me, the surgical precision of her questions left me slightly uncomfortable. There was no thrust and parry, no fishing for information. That kind of directness unnerved. But at least it allowed me to ask the same questions. "What about you, then?"

"Nothing very exciting. I got married a year or so after I last saw you. A man called Marcel."

"Marcel," I said, ruminatively, as if the name had cosmic significance. "Well, I'm happy for you. I take it he's here too?"

"No. Our work took us in different directions. We're still married, but . . ." Greta left the sentence hanging.

"It can't be easy," I said.

"If it was meant to work, we'd have found a way. Anyway, don't feel too sorry for either of us. We've both got our work. I wouldn't say I was any less happy than the last time we met."

"Well, that's good," I said.

Greta leaned over and touched my hand. Her fingernails were midnight black with a blue sheen.

"Look. This is really presumptuous of me. It's one thing asking to meet up for breakfast. It would have been rude not to. But how would you like to meet again later? It's really nice to eat here in the evening. They turn down the lights. The view through the dome is really something."

I looked up into that endless holographic sky.

"I thought it was faked."

"Oh, it is," she said. "But don't let that spoil it for you."

I settled in front of the camera and started speaking.

"Katerina," I said. "Hello. I hope you're all right. By now I hope someone from the company will have been in touch. If they haven't, I'm pretty sure you'll have made your own enquiries. I'm not sure what they told you, but I promise you that we're safe and sound and that we're coming home. I'm calling from somewhere called Saumlaki Station, a repair facility on the edge of Schedar sector. It's not much to look at: just a warren of tunnels and centrifuges dug into a pitch-black D-type asteroid, about half a light-year from the nearest star. The only reason it's here at all is because there happens to be an aperture next door. That's how we got here in the first place. Somehow or other *Blue Goose* took a wrong turn in the network, what they call a routing error. The Goose came in last night, local time, and I've been in a hotel since then. I didn't call last night because I was too tired and disoriented after coming out of the tank, and I didn't know how long we were going to be here. Seemed better to wait until morning, when we'd have a better idea of the damage to the ship. It's nothing serious – just a few bits and pieces buckled during the transit – but it means we're going to be here for another couple of days. Kolding – he's the repair chief – says three at the most. By the time we get back on course, however, we'll be about forty days behind schedule."

I paused, eyeing the incrementing cost indicator. Before I sat down in the booth, I always had an eloquent and economical speech queued up in my head, one that conveyed exactly what needed to be said, with the measure and grace of a soliloquy. But my mind always dried up as soon as I opened my mouth, and instead of an actor I ended up sounding like a small time thief, concocting some fumbling alibi in the presence of quick-witted interrogators.

I smiled awkwardly and continued: "It kills me to think this message is going to take so long to get to you. But if there's a silver lining, it's that I won't be far behind it. By the time you get this, I should be home in only a couple of days. So don't waste money replying to this, because by the time you get it I'll already have left Saumlaki Station. Just stay where you are, and I promise I'll be home soon."

That was it. There was nothing more I needed to say, other than: "I miss you." Delivered after a moment's pause, I meant it to sound emphatic. But when I replayed the recording it sounded more like an afterthought.

I could have recorded it again, but I doubted that I would have been any happier. Instead I just committed the existing message for transmission and wondered how long it would have to wait before going on its way. Since it seemed unlikely that there was a vast flow of commerce in and out of Saumlaki, our ship might be the first suitable outbound vessel.

I emerged from the booth. For some reason I felt guilty, as if I had been in some way neglectful. It took me a while before I realized what was playing on my mind. I'd told Katerina about Saumlaki Station. I'd even told her about Kolding and the damage to the *Blue Goose*. But I hadn't told her about Greta.

It's not working with Suzy.

She's too smart, too well-attuned to the physiological correlatives of surge tank immersion. I can give her all the reassurances in the world, but she knows she's been under too long for this to be anything other than a truly epic screw-up. She knows that we aren't just talking weeks or even months of delay here. Every nerve in her body is screaming that message into her skull.

"I had dreams," she says, when the grogginess fades.

"What kind?"

"Dreams that I kept waking. Dreams that you were pulling me out of the surge tank. You and someone else."

I do my best to smile. I'm alone, but Greta isn't far away. The hypodermic's in my pocket now.

"I always get bad dreams coming out of the tank," I say.

"These felt real. Your story kept changing, but you kept telling me we were somewhere . . . that we'd gone a little off course, but that it was nothing to worry about."

So much for Greta's reassurance that Suzy will remember nothing after our aborted efforts at waking her. Seems that her short-term memory isn't quite as fallible as we'd like.

"It's funny you should say that," I tell her. "Because, actually, we are a little off course."

She's sharper with every breath. Suzy was always the best of us at coming out of the tank.

"Tell me how far, Thom."

"Farther than I'd like."

She balls her fists. I can't tell if it's aggression, or some lingering neuromuscular effect of her time in the tank. "How far? Beyond the Bubble?"

"Beyond the Bubble, yes."

Her voice grows small and childlike.

"Tell me, Thom. Are we out beyond the Rift?"

I can hear the fear. I understand what she's going through. It's the nightmare that all ship crews live with, on every trip. That something will go wrong with the routing, something so severe that they'll end up on the very edge of the network. That they'll end up so far from home that getting back will take years, not months. And that, of course, years will have already passed, even before they begin the return trip.

That loved ones will be years older when they reach home.

If they're still there. If they still remember you, or want to remember. If they're still recognizable, or alive.

Beyond the Aquila Rift. It's shorthand for the trip no one ever hopes to make by accident. The one that will screw up the rest of your life, the one that creates the ghosts you see haunting the shadows of company bars across the whole Bubble. Men and women ripped out of time, cut adrift from families and lovers by an accident of an alien technology we use but barely comprehend.

"Yes," I say. "We're beyond the Rift."

Suzy screams, knitting her face into a mask of anger and denial. My hand is cold around the hypodermic. I consider using it.

A new repair estimate from Kolding. Five, six days.

This time I didn't even argue. I just shrugged and walked out, wondering how long it would be next time.

That evening I sat down at the same table where Greta and I had met over breakfast. The dining area had been well lit before, but now the only illumination came from the table lamps and the subdued lighting panels set into the paving. In the distance, a glass mannequin cycled from empty table to empty table, playing *Asturias* on a glass guitar. There were no other patrons dining tonight.

I didn't have long to wait for Greta.

"I'm sorry I'm late, Thom."

I turned to her as she approached the table. I liked the way she walked in the low gravity of the station, the way the subdued lighting traced the arc of her hips and waist. She eased into her seat and leaned toward me in the manner of a conspirator. The lamp on the table threw red shadows and gold highlights across her face. It took ten years off her age.

"You aren't late," I said. "And anyway, I had the view."

"It's an improvement, isn't it?"

"That wouldn't be saying much," I said with a smile. "But yes, it's definitely an improvement."

"I could sit out here all night and just look at it. In fact sometimes that's exactly what I do. Just me and a bottle of wine."

"I don't blame you."

Instead of the holographic blue, the dome was now full of stars. It was like no kind of view I'd ever seen from another station or ship. There were furious blue-white stars embedded in what looked like sheets of velvet. There were hard gold gems and soft red smears, like finger smears in pastel. There were streams and currents of fainter stars, like a myriad neon fish caught in a snapshot of frozen motion. There were vast billowing backdrops of red and green cloud, veined and flawed by filaments of cool black. There were bluffs and promontories of ochre dust, so rich in three-dimensional structure that they resembled an exuberant impasto of oil colors; contours light-years thick laid on with a trowel. Red or pink stars burned through the dust like lanterns. Orphaned worlds were caught erupting from the towers, little spermlike shapes trailing viscera of dust. Here and there I saw the tiny eyelike knots of birthing solar systems. There were pulsars, flashing on and off like navigation beacons, their differing rhythms seeming to set a stately tempo for the entire scene, like a deathly slow waltz. There seemed too much detail for one view, an overwhelming abundance of richness, and yet no matter which direction I looked, there was yet more to see, as if the dome sensed my attention and concentrated its efforts on the spot where my gaze was directed. For a moment I felt a lurching sense of dizziness, and – though I tried to stop it before I made a fool of myself – I found myself grasping the side of the table, as if to stop myself falling into the infinite depths of the view.

"Yes, it has that effect on people," Greta said.

"It's beautiful," I said.

"Do you mean beautiful, or terrifying?"

I realized I wasn't sure. "It's big," was all I could offer.

"Of course, it's faked," Greta said, her voice soft now that she was leaning closer. "The glass in the dome is smart. It exaggerates the brightness of the stars, so that the human eye registers the differences between them. Otherwise the colors aren't unrealistic. Everything else you see is also pretty accurate, if you accept that certain frequencies have been shifted into the visible band, and the scale of certain structures has been adjusted." She pointed out features for my edification. "That's the edge of the Taurus Dark Cloud, with the Pleiades just poking out. That's a filament of the Local Bubble. You see that open cluster?"

She waited for me to answer. "Yes," I said.

"That's the Hyades. Over there you've got Betelguese and Bellatrix."

"I'm impressed."

"You should be. It cost a lot of money." She leaned back a bit, so that the shadows dropped across her face again. "Are you all right, Thom? You seem a bit distracted."

I sighed.

"I just got another prognosis from your friend Kolding. That's enough to put a dent in anyone's day."

"I'm sorry about that."

"There's something else, too," I said. "Something that's been bothering me since I came out of the tank."

A mannequin came to take our order. I let Greta choose for me.

"You can talk to me, whatever it is," she said, when the mannequin had gone.

"It isn't easy."

"Something personal, then? Is it about Katerina?" She bit her tongue. "No, sorry. I shouldn't have said that."

"It's not about Katerina. Not exactly, anyway." But even as I said it, I knew that in a sense it was about Katerina, and how long it was going to be before we saw each other again.

"Go on, Thom."

"This is going to sound silly. But I wonder if everyone's being straight with me. It's not just Kolding. It's you as well. When I came out of that tank I felt the same way I felt when I'd been out to the Rift. Worse, if anything. I felt like I'd been in the tank for a long, long time."

"It feels that way sometimes."

"I know the difference, Greta. Trust me on this."

"So what are you saying?"

The problem was that I wasn't really sure. It was one thing to feel a vague sense of unease about how long I'd been in the tank. It was another to come out and accuse my host of lying. Especially when she had been so hospitable.

"Is there any reason you'd lie to me?"

"Come off it, Thom. What kind of a question is that?"

As soon as I had come out with it, it sounded absurd and offensive to me as well. I wished I could reverse time and start again, ignoring my misgivings.

"I'm sorry," I said. "Stupid. Just put it down to messed up biorhythms, or something."

She reached across the table and took my hand, as she had done at breakfast. This time she continued to hold it.

"You really feel wrong, don't you?"

"Kolding's games aren't helping, that's for sure." The waiter brought our wine, setting it down, the bottle chinking against his delicately articulated glass fingers. The mannequin poured two glasses and I sampled mine. "Maybe if I had someone else from my crew to bitch about it all with, I wouldn't feel so bad. I know you said we shouldn't wake Suzy and Ray, but that was before a one-day stopover turned into a week."

Greta shrugged. "If you want to wake them, no one's going to stop you. But don't think about ship business now. Let's not spoil a perfect evening."

I looked up at the stars. It was heightened, with the mad shimmering intensity of a Van Gogh nightscape.

It made one feel drunk and ecstatic just to look at it.

"What could possibly spoil it?" I asked.

What happened is that I drank too much wine and ended up sleeping with Greta. I'm not sure how much of a part the wine played in it for her. If her relationship with Marcel was in as much trouble as she'd made out, then obviously she had less to lose than I did. Yes, that made it all right, didn't it? She the seductress, her own marriage a wreck, me the hapless victim. I'd lapsed, yes, but it wasn't really my fault. I'd been alone, far from home, emotionally fragile, and she had exploited me. She had softened me up with a romantic meal, her trap already sprung.

Except all that was self-justifying bullshit, wasn't it? If my own marriage was in such great shape, why I had I failed to mention Greta when I called home? At the time, I'd justified that omission as an act of kindness toward my wife. Katerina didn't know that Greta and I had ever been a couple. But why worry Katerina by mentioning another woman, even if I pretended that we'd never met before?

Except – now – I could see that I'd failed to mention Greta for another reason entirely. Because in the back of my mind, even then, there had been the possibility that we might end up sleeping together.

I was already covering myself when I called Katerina. Already making sure there wouldn't be any awkward questions when I got

home. As if I not only knew what was going to happen but secretly
yearned for it.

The only problem was that Greta had something else in mind.

"Thom," Greta said, nudging me toward wakefulness. She was lying
naked next to me, leaning on one elbow, with the sheets crumpled down
around her hips. The light in her room turned her into an abstraction of
milky blue curves and deep violet shadows. With one black-nailed
finger she traced a line down my chest and said: "There's something you
need to know."

"What?" I asked.

"I lied. Kolding lied. We all lied."

I was too drowsy for her words to have much more than a vaguely
troubling effect. All I could say, again, was: "What?"

"You're not in Saumlaki Station. You're not in Schedar sector."

I started waking up properly. "Say that again."

"The routing error was more severe than you were led to believe. It
took you far beyond the Local Bubble."

I groped for anger, even resentment, but all I felt was a dizzying
sensation of falling. "How far out?"

"Further than you thought possible."

The next question was obvious.

"Beyond the Rift?"

"Yes," she said, with the faintest of smiles, as if humoring a game
whose rules and objectives she found ultimately demeaning. "Beyond
the Aquila Rift. A long, long way beyond it."

"I need to know, Greta."

She pushed herself from the bed, reached for a gown. "Then get
dressed. I'll show you."

I followed Greta in a daze.

She took me to the dome again. It was dark, just as it had been the
night before, with only the lamp-lit tables to act as beacons. I
supposed that the illumination throughout Saumlaki Station (or wherever this was) was at the whim of its occupants and didn't necessarily
have to follow any recognizable diurnal cycle. Nonetheless, it was still
unsettling to find it changed so arbitrarily. Even if Greta had the
authority to turn out the lights when she wanted to, didn't anyone
else object?

But I didn't see anyone else *to* object. There was no one else around;
only a glass mannequin standing to attention with a napkin over one
arm.

She sat us at a table. "Do you want a drink, Thom?"

"No, thanks. For some reason I'm not quite in the mood."

She touched my wrist. "Don't hate me for lying to you. It was done
out of kindness. I couldn't break the truth to you in one go."

Sharply I withdrew my hand. "Shouldn't I be the judge of that? So what is the truth, exactly?"

"It's not good, Thom."

"Tell me, then I'll decide."

I didn't see her do anything, but suddenly the dome was filled with stars again, just as it had been the night before.

The view lurched, zooming outwards. Stars flowed by from all sides, like white sleet. Nebulae ghosted past in spectral wisps. The sense of motion was so compelling that I found myself gripping the table, seized by vertigo.

"Easy, Thom," Greta whispered.

The view lurched, swerved, contracted. A solid wall of gas slammed past. Now, suddenly, I had the sense that we were outside something – that we had punched beyond some containing sphere, defined only in vague arcs and knots of curdled gas, where the interstellar gas density increased sharply.

Of course. It was obvious. We were beyond the Local Bubble.

And we were still receding. I watched the Bubble itself contract, becoming just one member in the larger froth of voids. Instead of individual stars, I saw only smudges and motes, aggregations of hundreds of thousands of suns. It was like pulling back from a close-up view of a forest. I could still see clearings, but the individual trees had vanished into an amorphous mass.

We kept pulling back. Then the expansion slowed and froze. I could still make out the Local Bubble, but only because I had been concentrating on it all the way out. Otherwise, there was nothing to distinguish it from the dozens of surrounding voids.

"Is that how far out we've come?" I asked.

Greta shook her head. "Let me show you something."

Again, she did nothing that I was aware of. But the Bubble I had been looking at was suddenly filled with a skein of red lines, like a child's scribble.

"Aperture connections," I said.

As shocked as I was by the fact that she had lied to me – and as fearful as I was about what the truth might hold – I couldn't turn off the professional part of me, the part that took pride in recognizing such things.

Greta nodded. "Those are the main commerce routes, the well-mapped connections between large colonies and major trading hubs. Now I'll add all mapped connections, including those that have only ever been traversed by accident."

The scribble did not change dramatically. It gained a few more wild loops and hairpins, including one that reached beyond the wall of the Bubble to touch the sunward end of the Aquila Rift. One or two other additions pierced the wall in different directions, but none of them reached as far as the Rift.

"Where are we?"

"We're at one end of one of those connections. You can't see it because it's pointing directly toward you." She smiled slightly. "I needed to establish the scale that we're dealing with. How wide is the Local Bubble, Thom? Four hundred light-years, give or take?"

My patience was wearing thin. But I was still curious.

"About right."

"And while I know that aperture travel times vary from point to point, with factors depending on network topology and syntax optimization, isn't it the case that the average speed is about one thousand times faster than light?"

"Give or take."

"So a journey from one side of the Bubble might take – what, half a year? Say five or six months? A year to the Aquila Rift?"

"You know that already, Greta. We both know it."

"All right. Then consider this." And the view contracted again, the Bubble dwindling, a succession of overlaying structures concealing it, darkness coming into view on either side, and then the familiar spiral swirl of the Milky Way galaxy looming large.

Hundreds of billions of stars, packed together into foaming white lanes of sea spume.

"This is the view," Greta said. "Enhanced of course, brightened and filtered for human consumption – but if you had eyes with near-perfect quantum efficiency, and if they happened to be about a meter wide, this is more or less what you'd see if you stepped outside the station."

"I don't believe you."

What I meant was I didn't want to believe her.

"Get used to it, Thom. You're a long way out. The station's orbiting a brown dwarf star in the Large Magellanic Cloud. You're one hundred and fifty thousand light-years from home."

"No," I said, my voice little more than a moan of abject, childlike denial.

"You felt as though you'd spent a long time in the tank. You were dead right. Subjective time? I don't know. Years, easily. Maybe a decade. But objective time – the time that passed back home – is a lot clearer. It took *Blue Goose* one hundred and fifty years to reach us. Even if you turned back now, you'd have been away for three hundred years, Thom."

"Katerina," I said, her name like an invocation.

"Katerina's dead," Greta told me. "She's already been dead a century."

How do you adjust to something like that? The answer is that you can't count on adjusting to it at all. Not everyone does. Greta told me that she had seen just about every possible reaction in the spectrum, and the one thing she had learned was that it was next to impossible to predict how a given individual would take the news. She had seen people adjust to the revelation with little more than a world-weary shrug, as if this were merely the latest in a line of galling surprises life had thrown at them, no worse in its way than illness or bereavement or any number of personal setbacks. She had seen others walk away and kill themselves half an hour later.

But the majority, she said, did eventually come to some kind of accommodation with the truth, however faltering and painful the process.

"Trust me, Thom," she said. "I know you now. I know you have the emotional strength to get through this. I know you can learn to live with it."

"Why didn't you tell me straight away, as soon as I came out of the tank?"

"Because I didn't know if you were going to be able to take it."

"You waited until after you knew I had a wife."

"No," Greta said. "I waited until after we'd made love. Because then I knew Katerina couldn't mean that much to you."

"Fuck you."

"Fuck me? Yes, you did. That's the point."

I wanted to strike out against her. But what I was angry at was not her insinuation but the cold-hearted truth of it. She was right, and I knew it. I just didn't want to deal with that, any more than I wanted to deal with the here and now.

I waited for the anger to subside.

"You say we're not the first?" I said.

"No. We were the first, I suppose – the ship I came in. Luckily it was well equipped. After the routing error, we had enough supplies to set up a self-sustaining station on the nearest rock. We knew there was no going back, but at least we could make some kind of life for ourselves here."

"And after that?"

"We had enough to do just keeping ourselves alive, the first few years. But then another ship came through the aperture. Damaged, drifting, much like *Blue Goose*. We hauled her in, warmed her crew, broke the news to them."

"How'd they take it?"

"About as well as you'd expect." Greta laughed hollowly to herself. "A couple of them went mad. Another killed herself. But at least a dozen of them are still here. In all honesty, it was good for us that another ship came through. Not just because they had supplies we could use, but because it helped us to help them. Took our minds off our own self-pity. It made us realize how far we'd come and how much help these newcomers needed to make the same transition. That wasn't the last ship, either. We've gone through the same process with eight or nine others, since then." Greta looked at me, her head cocked against her hand. "There's a thought for you, Thom."

"There is?"

She nodded. "It's difficult for you now, I know. And it'll be difficult for you for some time to come. But it can help to have someone else to care about. It can smooth the transition."

"Like who?" I asked.

"Like one of your other crew members," Greta said. "You could try waking one of them, now."

Greta's with me when I pull Suzy out of the surge tank.

"Why her?" Greta asks.

"Because I want her out first," I say, wondering if Greta's jealous. I don't blame her: Suzy's beautiful, but she's also smart. There isn't a better syntax runner in Ashanti Industrial.

"What happened?" Suzy asks, when's she over the grogginess. "Did we make it back?"

I ask her to tell me the last thing she remembered.

"Customs," Suzy says. "Those pricks on Arkangel."

"And after that? Anything else? The runes? Do you remember casting them?"

"No," she says, then picks up something in my voice. The fact that I might not be telling the truth, or telling her all she needs to know. "Thom. I'll ask you again. Did we make it back?"

A minute later we're putting Suzy back into the tank.

It hasn't worked first time. Maybe next try.

But it kept not working with Suzy. She was always cleverer and quicker than me; she always had been. As soon as she came out of the tank, she knew that we'd come a lot further than Schedar sector. She was always ahead of my lies and excuses.

"It was different when it happened to me," I told Greta, when we were lying next to each other again, days later, with Suzy still in the tank. "I had all the nagging doubts she has, I think. But as soon as I saw you standing there, I forgot all about that stuff."

Greta nodded. Her hair fell across her face in dishevelled, sleep-matted curtains. She had a strand of it between her lips.

"It helped, seeing a friendly face?"

"Took my mind off the problem, that's for sure."

"You'll get there in the end," she said. "Anyway, from Suzy's point of view, aren't you a friendly face as well?"

"Maybe," I said. "But she'd been expecting me. You were the last person in the world I expected to see standing there."

Greta touched her knuckle against the side of my face. Her smooth skin slid against stubble. "It's getting easier for you, isn't it?"

"I don't know," I said.

"You're a strong man, Thom. I knew you'd come through this."

"I haven't come through it yet," I said. I felt like a tightrope walker halfway across Niagara Falls. It was a miracle I'd made it as far as I had. But that didn't mean I was home and dry.

Still, Greta was right. There was hope. I'd felt no crushing spasms of grief over Katerina's death, or enforced absence, or however you wanted to put it. All I felt was a bittersweet regret, the way one might feel about a broken heirloom or long-lost pet. I felt no animosity toward Katerina, and I was sorry that I would never see her again. But I was sorry about not seeing a lot of things. Maybe it would become worse in the days ahead. Maybe I was just postponing a breakdown.

I didn't think so.

In the meantime, I continued trying to find a way to deal with Suzy. She had become a puzzle that I couldn't leave unsolved. I could have just woken her up and let her deal with the news as best as she could, but this seemed cruel and unsatisfactory. Greta had broken it to me gently, giving me the time to settle into my new surroundings and take that necessary step away from Katerina. When she finally broke the news, as shocking as it was, it didn't shatter me. I'd already been primed for it, the sting taken out of the surprise. Sleeping with Greta obviously helped. I couldn't offer Suzy the same solace, but I was sure that there was a way for us to coax Suzy to the same state of near-acceptance..

Time after time we woke her and tried a different approach. Greta said there was a window of a few minutes before the events she was experiencing began to transfer into long-term memory. If we knocked her out, the buffer of memories in short term storage was wiped before it ever crossed the hippocampus into long-term recall. Within that window, we could wake her up as many times as we liked, trying endless permutations of the revival scenario.

At least that was what Greta told me.

"We can't keep doing this indefinitely," I said.

"Why not?"

"Isn't she going to remember *something*?"

Greta shrugged. "Maybe. But I doubt that she'll attach any significance to those memories. Haven't you ever had vague feelings of déjà vu coming out of the surge tank?"

"Sometimes," I admitted.

"Then don't sweat about it. She'll be all right. I promise you."

"Perhaps we should just keep her awake, after all."

"That will be cruel."

"It's cruel to keep waking her up and shutting her down, like a toy doll."

There was a catch in her voice when she answered me.

"Keep at it, Thom. I'm sure you're close to finding a way in the end. It's helping you, focusing on Suzy. I always knew it would."

I started to say something, but Greta pressed a finger to my lips.

Greta was right about Suzy. The challenge helped me, taking my mind off my own predicament. I remembered what Greta had said about dealing with other crews in the same situation, before *Blue Goose* put in. Clearly she had learned many psychological tricks: gambits and shortcuts to assist the transition to mental well-being. I felt slight resentment at being manipulated so effectively. But at the same time I couldn't deny that worrying about another human being had helped me with my own adjustment. When, days later, I stepped back from the immediate problem of Suzy, I realized that something was different. I didn't feel far from home. I felt, in an odd way, privileged. I'd come further than almost anyone in history. I was still alive, and there were still people around to provide love and partnership and a web of social relations. Not just Greta, but all the other unlucky souls who had ended up at the station.

If anything, there appeared more of them than when I had first arrived. The corridors – sparsely populated at first – were increasingly busy, and when we ate under the dome – under the Milky Way – we were not the only diners. I studied their lamp-lit faces, comforted by their vague familiarity, wondering what kinds of stories they had to tell, where they'd come from home, who they had left behind, how they had adjusted to life here. There was time enough to get to know them all. And the place would never become boring, for at any time – as Greta had intimated – we could always expect another lost ship to drop through the aperture. Tragedy for the crew, but fresh challengers, fresh faces, fresh news from home, for us.

All in all, it wasn't really so bad.

Then it clicked.

It was the man cleaning out the fish that did it, in the lobby of the hotel. It wasn't just the familiarity of the process, but the man himself.

I'd seen him before. Another pond full of diseased carp. Another hotel.

Then I remembered Kolding's bad teeth, and recalled how they'd reminded me of another man I'd met long before. Except it wasn't another man at all. Different name, different context, but everything else the same. And when I looked at the other diners, really looked at them, there was no one I couldn't swear I hadn't seen before. No single face that hit me with the force of utter unfamiliarity.

Which left Greta.

I said to her, over wine, under the Milky Way: "Nothing here is real, is it?"

She looked at me with infinite sadness and shook her head.

"What about Suzy?" I asked her.

"Suzy's dead. Ray is dead. They died in their surge tanks."

"How? Why them, and not me?"

"Something about particles of paint blocking intake filters. Not enough to make a difference over short distances, but enough to kill them on the trip out here."

I think some part of me had always suspected. It felt less like shock than brutal disappointment.

"But Suzy seemed so real," I said. "Even the way she had doubts about how long she'd been in the tank . . . even the way she remembered previous attempts to wake her."

The glass mannequin approached our table. Greta waved him away.

"I made her convincing, the way she would have acted."

"You *made* her?"

"You're not really awake, Thom. You're being fed data. This entire station is being simulated."

I sipped my wine. I expected it to taste suddenly thin and synthetic, but it still tasted like pretty good wine.

"Then I'm dead as well?"

"No. You're alive. Still in your surge tank. But I haven't brought you to full consciousness yet."

"All right. The truth this time. I can take it. How much is real? Does the station exist? Are we really as far out as you said?"

"Yes," she said. "The station exists, just as I said it does. It just looks . . . different. And it is in the Large Magellanic Cloud, and it is orbiting a brown dwarf star."

"Can you show me the station as it is?"

"I could. But I don't think you're ready for it. I think you'd find it difficult to adjust."

I couldn't help laughing. "Even after what I've already adjusted to?"

"You've only made half the journey, Thom."

"But you made it."

"I did, Thom. But for me it was different." Greta smiled. "For me, everything was different."

Then she made the light show change again. None of the other diners appeared to notice as we began to zoom in toward the Milky Way, crashing toward the spiral, ramming through shoals of outlying stars and gas clouds. The familiar landscape of the Local Bubble loomed large.

The image froze, the Bubble one among many such structures.

Again it filled with the violent red scribble of the aperture network. But now the network wasn't the only one. It was merely one ball of red yarn among many, spaced out across tens of thousands of light-years. None of the scribbles touched each other, yet – in the way they were shaped, in the way they almost abutted against each other – it was possible to imagine that they had once been connected. They were like the shapes of continents on a world with tectonic drift.

"It used to span the galaxy," Greta said. "Then something happened. Something catastrophic, which I still don't understand. A shattering, into vastly smaller domains. Typically a few hundred light-years across."

"Who made it?"

"I don't know. No one knows. They probably aren't around any more. Maybe that was why it shattered, out of neglect."

"But we found it," I said. "The part of it near us still worked."

"All the disconnected elements still function," Greta said. "You can't cross from domain to domain, but otherwise the apertures work as they were designed. Barring, of course, the occasional routing error."

"All right," I said. "If you can't cross from domain to domain, how did *Blue Goose* get this far out? We've come a lot further than a few hundred light-years."

"You're right. But then such a long-distance connection might have been engineered differently from the others. It appears that the links to the Magellanic Clouds were more resilient. When the domains shattered from each other, the connections reaching beyond the galaxy remained intact."

"In which case you *can* cross from domain to domain," I said. "But you have to come all the way out here first."

"The trouble is, not many want to continue the journey at this point. No one comes here deliberately, Thom."

"I still don't get it. What does it matter to me if there are other domains? Those regions of the galaxy are thousands of light-years from Earth, and without the apertures we'd have no way of reaching them. They don't matter. There's no one there to use them."

Greta's smile was coquettish, knowing.

"What makes you so certain?"

"Because if there were, wouldn't there be alien ships popping out of the aperture here? You've told me *Blue Goose* wasn't the first through. But our domain – the one in the Local Bubble – must be outnumbered hundreds to one by all the others. If there are alien cultures out there, each stumbling on their own local domain, why haven't any of them ever come through the aperture, the way we did?"

Again that smile. But this time it chilled my blood.

"What makes you think they haven't, Thom?"

I reached out and took her hand, the way she had taken mine. I took it without force, without malice, but with the assurance that this time I really, sincerely meant what I was about to say.

Her fingers tightened around mine.

"Show me," I said. "I want to see things as they really are. Not just the station. You as well."

Because by then I'd realized. Greta hadn't just lied to me about Suzy and Ray. She'd lied to me about the *Blue Goose* as well. Because we were not the latest human ship to come through.

We were the first.

"You want to see it?" she asked.

"Yes. All of it."

"You won't like it."

"I'll be the judge of that."

"All right, Thom. But understand this. I've been here before. I've done this a million times. I care for all the lost souls. And I know how it works. You won't be able to take the raw reality of what's happened to you. You'll shrivel away from it. You'll go mad, unless I substitute a calming fiction, a happy ending."

"Why tell me that now?"

"Because you don't have to see it. You can stop now, where you are, with an idea of the truth. An inkling. But you don't have to open your eyes."

"Do it," I said.

Greta shrugged. She poured herself another measure of wine, then made sure my own glass was charged.

"You asked for it," she said.

We were still holding hands, two lovers sharing an intimacy. Then everything changed.

It was just a flash, just a glimpse. Like the view of an unfamiliar room if you turn the lights on for an instant. Shapes and forms, relationships between things. I saw caverns, wormed-out and linked, and things moving through those caverns, bustling along with the frantic industry of moles or termites. The things were seldom alike, even in the most superficial sense. Some moved via propulsive waves of multiple clawed limbs. Some wriggled, smooth plaques of carapace grinding against the glassy rock of the tunnels.

The things moved between caves in which lay the hulks of ships, almost all too strange to describe.

And somewhere distant, somewhere near the heart of the rock, in a matriarchal chamber all of its own, something drummed out messages to its companions and helpers, stiffly articulated antlerlike forelimbs beating against stretched tympana of finely veined skin, something that had been waiting here for eternities, something that wanted nothing more than to care for the souls of the lost.

Katerina's with Suzy when they pull me out of the surge tank.

It's bad – one of the worst revivals I've ever gone through. I feel as if every vein in my body has been filled with finely powdered glass. For a moment, a long moment, even the idea of breathing seems insurmountably difficult, too hard, too painful even to contemplate.

But it passes, as it always passes.

After a while I can not only breathe, I can move and talk.

"Where . . ."

"Easy, Skip," Suzy says. She leans over the tank and starts unplugging me. I can't help but smile. Suzy's smart – there isn't a better syntax runner in Ashanti Industrial – but she's also beautiful. It's like being nursed by an angel.

I wonder if Katerina's jealous.

"Where are we?" I try again. "Feels like I was in that thing for an eternity. Did something go wrong?"

"Minor routing error," Suzy says. "We took some damage and they decided to wake me first. But don't sweat about it. At least we're in one piece."

Routing errors. You hear about them, but you hope they're never going to happen to you.

"What kind of delay?"

"Forty days. Sorry, Thom. Bang goes our bonus."

In anger, I hammer the side of the surge tank. But Katerina steps toward me and places a calming hand on my shoulder.

"It's all right," she says. "You're home and dry. That's all that matters."

I look at her and for a moment remember someone else, someone I haven't thought about in years. I almost remember her name, and then the moment passes.

I nod. "Home and dry."

SECOND PERSON, PRESENT TENSE

Daryl Gregory

Here new writer Daryl Gregory, who has made sales to *The Magazine of Fantasy & Science Fiction*, *Amazing*, and *Asimov's*, tells a moving – and ultimately rather unsettling – story of memory, identity, and loss, with implications that will haunt you long after you turn the last page.

> If you think, "I breathe," the "I" is extra. There is no you to say "I." What we call "I" is just a swinging door which moves when we inhale or when we exhale.
>
> – *Shun Ryu Suzuki*

> I used to think the brain was the most important organ in the body, until I realized who was telling me that.
>
> – *Emo Phillips*

WHEN I ENTER THE OFFICE, Dr. S is leaning against the desk, talking earnestly to the dead girl's parents. He isn't happy, but when he looks up he puts on a smile for me. "And here she is," he says, like a game show host revealing the grand prize. The people in the chairs turn, and Dr. Subramaniam gives me a private, encouraging wink.

The father stands first, a blotchy, square-faced man with a tight belly he carries like a basketball. As in our previous visits, he is almost frowning, struggling to match his face to his emotions. The mother, though, has already been crying, and her face is wide open: joy, fear, hope, relief. It's way over the top.

"Oh, Therese," she says. "Are you ready to come home?"

Their daughter was named Therese. She died of an overdose almost two years ago, and since then Mitch and Alice Klass have visited this hospital dozens of times, looking for her. They desperately want me to be their daughter, and so in their heads I already am.

My hand is still on the door handle. "Do I have a choice?" On paper I'm only seventeen years old. I have no money, no credit cards, no job, no car. I own only a handful of clothes. And Robierto, the burliest orderly on the ward, is in the hallway behind me, blocking my escape.

Therese's mother seems to stop breathing for a moment. She's a slim, narrow-boned woman who seems tall until she stands next to anyone. Mitch raises a hand to her shoulder, then drops it.

As usual, whenever Alice and Mitch come to visit, I feel like I've walked into the middle of a soap opera and no one's given me my lines. I look directly at Dr. S, and his face is frozen into that professional smile. Several times over the past year he's convinced them to let me stay longer, but they're not listening anymore. They're my legal guardians, and they have Other Plans. Dr. S looks away from me, rubs the side of his nose.

"That's what I thought," I say.

The father scowls. The mother bursts into fresh tears, and she cries all the way out of the building. Dr. Subramaniam watches from the entrance as we drive away, his hands in his pockets. I've never been so angry with him in my life – all two years of it.

The name of the drug is Zen, or Zombie, or just Z. Thanks to Dr. S I have a pretty good idea of how it killed Therese.

"Flick your eyes to the left," he told me one afternoon. "Now glance to the right. Did you see the room blur as your eyes moved?" He waited until I did it again. "No blur. No one sees it."

This is the kind of thing that gets brain doctors hot and bothered. Not only could no one see the blur, their brains edited it out completely. Skipped over it – left view, then right view, with nothing between – then fiddled with the person's time sense so that it didn't even *seem* missing.

The scientists figured out that the brain was editing out shit all the time. They wired up patients and told them to lift one of their fingers, move it any time they wanted. Each time, the brain started the signal traveling toward the finger up to 120 milliseconds before the patient consciously decided to move it. Dr. S said you could see the brain warming up right *before* the patient consciously thought, *now*.

This is weird, but it gets weirder the longer you think about it. And I've been thinking about this a lot.

The conscious mind – the "I" that's thinking, hey, I'm thirsty, I'll reach for that cold cup of water – hasn't really decided anything. The signal to start moving your hand has already traveled halfway down your arm by the time you even realize you are thirsty. *Thought* is an afterthought. By the way, the brain says, we've decided to move your arm, so please have the thought to move it.

The gap is normally 120 milliseconds, max. Zen extends this minutes. Hours.

If you run into somebody who's on Zen, you won't notice much. The person's brain is still making decisions, and the body still follows orders. You can talk to the them, and they can talk to you. You can tell each other jokes, go out for hamburgers, do homework, have sex.

But the person isn't conscious. There is no "I" there. You might as well be talking to a computer. And two people on Zen – "you" and "I" – are just puppets talking to puppets.

It's a little girl's room strewn with teenager. Stuffed animals crowd the shelves and window sills, shoulder to shoulder with stacks of Christian rock CDs and hair brushes and bottles of nail polish. Pin-ups from *Teen People* are taped to the wall, next to a bulletin board dripping with soccer ribbons and rec league gymnastics medals going back to second grade. Above the desk, a plaque titled "I Promise . . ." exhorting Christian youth to abstain from premarital sex. And everywhere taped and pinned to the walls, the photos: Therese at Bible camp, Therese on the balance beam, Therese with her arms around her youth group friends. Every morning she could open her eyes to a thousand reminders of who she was, who she'd been, who she was supposed to become.

I pick up the big stuffed panda that occupies the place of pride on the bed. It looks older than me, and the fur on the face is worn down to the batting. The button eyes hang by white thread – they've been re-sewn, maybe more than once.

Therese's father sets down the pitifully small bag that contains everything I've taken from the hospital: toiletries, a couple of changes of clothes, and five of Dr. S's books. "I guess old Boo Bear was waiting for you," he says.

"Boo W. Bear."

"Yes, Boo W!" It pleases him that I know this. As if it proves anything. "You know, your mother dusted this room every week. She never doubted that you'd come back."

I have never been here, and *she* is not coming back, but already I'm tired of correcting pronouns. "Well, that was nice," I say.

"She's had a tough time of it. She knew people were talking, probably holding her responsible – both of us, really. And she was worried about them saying things about you. She couldn't stand them thinking that you were a wild girl."

"Them?"

He blinks. "The Church."

Ah. *The Church*. The term carried so many feelings and connotations for Therese that months ago I stopped trying to sort them out. The Church was the red-brick building of the Davenport Church of Christ, shafts of dusty light through rows of tall, glazed windows shaped like gravestones. The Church was God and the Holy Ghost (but not Jesus – he was personal, separate somehow). Mostly, though, it was the congregation, dozens and dozens of people who'd known her since before she was born. They loved her, they watched out for her, and they evaluated her every step. It was like having a hundred overprotective parents.

I almost laugh. "The Church thinks Therese was wild?"

He scowls, but whether because I've insulted the Church or because I keep referring to his daughter by name, I'm not sure. "Of course not. It's just that you caused a lot of worry." His voice has assumed a sober tone that's probably never failed to unnerve his daughter. "You know, the Church prayed for you every week."

"They did?" I do know Therese well enough to be sure this would have mortified her. She was a pray-er, not a pray-ee.

Therese's father watches my face for the bloom of shame, maybe a few tears. From contrition it should have been one small step to confession. It's hard for me to take any of this seriously.

I sit down on the bed and sink deep into the mattress. This is not going to work. The double bed takes up most of the room, with only a few feet of open space around it. Where am I going to meditate?

"Well," Therese's father says. His voice has softened. Maybe he thinks he's won. "You probably want to get changed," he says.

He goes to the door but doesn't leave. I stand by the window, but I can feel him there, waiting. Finally the oddness of this makes me turn around.

He's staring at the floor, a hand behind his neck. Therese might have been able to intuit his mood, but it's beyond me.

"We want to help you, Therese. But there's so many things we just don't understand. Who gave you the drugs, why you went off with that boy, why you would – " His hand moves, a stifled gesture that could be anger, or just frustration. "It's just . . . hard."

"I know," I say. "Me too."

He shuts the door when he leaves, and I push the panda to the floor and flop onto my back in relief. Poor Mr. Klass. He just wants to know if his daughter fell from grace, or was pushed.

When I want to freak myself out, "I" think about "me" thinking about having an "I." The only thing stupider than puppets talking to puppets is a puppet talking to itself.

Dr. S says that nobody knows what the mind is, or how the brain generates it, and nobody *really* knows about consciousness. We talked almost every day while I was in the hospital, and after he saw that I was interested in this stuff – how could I *not* be? – he gave me books and we'd talk about brains and how they cook up thoughts and make decisions.

"How do I explain this?" he always starts. And then he tries out the metaphors he's working on for his book. My favorite is the Parliament, the Page, and the Queen.

"The brain isn't one thing, of course," he told me. "It's millions of firing cells, and those resolve into hundreds of active sites, and so it is with the mind. There are dozens of nodes in the mind, each one trying to out-shout the others. For any decision, the mind erupts with noise, and that triggers . . . how do I explain this . . . Have you ever seen the

British Parliament on C-SPAN?" Of course I had: in a hospital, TV is a constant companion. "These members of the mind's parliament, they're all shouting in chemicals and electrical charges, until enough of the voices are shouting in unison. Ding! That's a 'thought,' a 'decision.' The Parliament immediately sends a signal to the body to act on the decision, and at the same time it tells the Page to take the news – "

"Wait, who's the Page?"

He waves his hand. "That's not important right now." (Weeks later, in a different discussion, Dr. S will explain that the Page isn't one thing, but a cascade of neural events in the temporal area of the limbic system that meshes the neural map of the new thought with the existing neural map – but by then I know that "neural map" is just another metaphor for another deeply complex thing or process, and that I'll never get to the bottom of this. Dr. S said not to worry about it, that *nobody* gets to the bottom of it.) "The Page takes the news of the decision to the Queen."

"All right then, who's the Queen? Consciousness?"

"Exactly right! The self itself."

He beamed at me, his attentive student. Talking about this stuff gets Dr. S going like nothing else, but he's oblivious to the way I let the neck of my scrubs fall open when I stretch out on the couch. If only I could have tucked the two hemispheres of my brain into a lace bra.

"The Page," he said, "delivers its message to Her Majesty, telling her what the Parliament has decided. The Queen doesn't need to know about all the other arguments that went on, all the other possibilities that were thrown out. She simply needs to know what to announce to her subjects. The Queen tells the parts of the body to act on the decision."

"Wait, I thought the Parliament had already sent out the signal. You said before that you can see the brain warming up before the self even knows about it."

"That's the joke. The Queen announces the decision, and she thinks that her subjects are obeying her commands, but in reality, they have already been told what to do. They're already reaching for their glasses of water."

I pad down to the kitchen in bare feet, wearing Therese's sweatpants and a T-shirt. The shirt is a little tight; Therese, champion dieter and Olympic-level purger, was a bit smaller than me.

Alice is at the table, already dressed, a book open in front of her. "Well, you slept in this morning," she says brightly. Her face is made up, her hair sprayed into place. The coffee cup next to the book is empty. She's been waiting for hours.

I look around for a clock, and find one over the door. It's only nine. At the hospital I slept in later than that all the time. "I'm starved," I say. There's a refrigerator, a stove, and dozens of cabinets.

I've never made my own breakfast. Or any lunch or dinner, for that matter. For my entire life, my meals have been served on cafeteria trays. "Do you have scrambled eggs?"

She blinks. "Eggs? You don't – " She abruptly stands. "Sure. Sit down, Therese, and I'll make you some."

"Just call me 'Terry,' okay?"

Alice stops, thinks about saying something – I can almost hear the clank of cogs and ratchets – until she abruptly strides to the cabinet, crouches, and pulls out a non-stick pan.

I take a guess on which cabinet holds the coffee mugs, guess right, and take the last inch of coffee from the pot. "Don't you have to go to work?" I say. Alice does something at a restaurant supply company; Therese has always been hazy on the details.

"I've taken a leave," she says. She cracks an egg against the edge of the pan, does something subtle with the shells as the yolk squeezes out and plops into the pan, and folds the shell halves into each other. All with one hand.

"Why?"

She smiles tightly. "We couldn't just abandon you after getting you home. I thought we might need some time together. During this adjustment period."

"So when do I have to see this therapist? Whatsisname." My executioner.

"Her. Dr. Mehldau's in Baltimore, so we'll drive there tomorrow." This is their big plan. Dr. Subramaniam couldn't bring back Therese, so they're running to anyone who says they can. "You know, she's had a lot of success with people in your situation. That's her book." She nods at the table.

"So? Dr. Subramaniam is writing one too." I pick up the book. *The Road Home: Finding the Lost Children of Zen.* "What if I don't go along with this?"

She says nothing, chopping at the eggs. I'll be eighteen in four months. Dr. S said that it will become a lot harder for them to hold me then. This ticking clock sounds constantly in my head, and I'm sure it's loud enough for Alice and Mitch to hear it too.

"Let's just try Dr. Mehldau first."

"First? What then?" She doesn't answer. I flash on an image of me tied down to the bed, a priest making a cross over my twisting body. It's a fantasy, not a Therese memory – I can tell the difference. Besides, if this had already happened to Therese, it wouldn't have been a priest.

"Okay then," I say. "What if I just run away?"

"If you turn into a fish," she says lightly, "then I will turn into a fisherman and fish for you."

"What?" I'm laughing. I haven't heard Alice speak in anything but straightforward, earnest sentences.

Alice's smile is sad. "You don't remember?"

"Oh, yeah." The memory clicks. "*Runaway Bunny.* Did she like that?"

Dr. S's book is about me. Well, Zen O.D.-ers in general, but there are only a couple thousand of us. Z's not a hugely popular drug, in the U.S. or anywhere else. It's not a hallucinogen. It's not a euphoric or a depressant. You don't speed, mellow out, or even get high in the normal sense. It's hard to see what the attraction is. Frankly, I have trouble seeing it.

Dr. S says that most drugs aren't about making you feel better, they're about not feeling anything at all. They're about numbness, escape. And Zen is a kind of arty, designer escape hatch. Zen disables the Page, locks him in his room, so that he can't make his deliveries to the Queen. There's no update to the neural map, and the Queen stops hearing what Parliament is up to. With no orders to bark, she goes silent. It's that silence that people like Therese craved.

But the real attraction – again, for people like Therese – is the overdose. Swallow way too much Zen and the Page can't get out for weeks. When he finally gets out, he can't remember the way back to the Queen's castle. The whole process of updating the self that's been going on for years is suddenly derailed. The silent Queen can't be found.

The Page, poor guy, does the only thing he can. He goes out and delivers the proclamations to the first girl he sees.

The Queen is dead. Long live the Queen.

"Hi, Terry. I'm Dr. Mehldau." She's a stubby woman with a pleasant round face, and short dark hair shot with gray. She offers me her hand. Her fingers are cool and thin.

"You called me Terry."

"I was told that you prefer to go by that. Do you want me to call you something else?"

"No . . . I just expected you to make me say my name is 'Therese' over and over."

She laughs and sits down in a red leather chair that looks soft but sturdy. "I don't think that would be very helpful, do you? I can't make you do anything you don't want to do, Terry."

"So I'm free to go."

"Can't stop you. But I do have to report back to your parents on how we're doing."

My parents.

She shrugs. "It's my job. Why don't you have a seat and we can talk about why you're here."

The chair opposite her is cloth, not leather, but it's still nicer than anything in Dr. Subramaniam's office. The entire office is nicer than Dr. S's office. Daffodil walls in white trim, big windows glowing behind white cloth shades, tropically colored paintings.

I don't sit down.

"Your job is to turn me into Mitch and Alice's daughter. I'm not going to do that. So any time we spend talking is just bullshit."

"Terry, no one can turn you into something you're not."

"Well then we're done here." I walk across the room – though "stroll" is what I'm shooting for – and pick up an African-looking wooden doll from the bookshelf. The shelves are decorated with enough books to look serious, but there are long open spaces for arty arrangements of candlesticks and Japanese fans and plaques that advertise awards and appreciations. Dr. S's bookshelves are for holding books, and books stacked on books. Dr. Mehldau's bookshelves are for selling the idea of Dr. Mehldau.

"So what are you, a psychiatrist or a psychologist or what?" I've met all kinds in the hospital. The psychiatrists are MDs like Dr. S and can give you drugs. I haven't figured out what the psychologists are good for.

"Neither," she says. "I'm a counselor."

"So what's the 'doctor' for?"

"Education." Her voice didn't change, but I get the impression that the question's annoyed her. This makes me strangely happy.

"Okay, Dr. Counselor, what are you supposed to counsel me about? I'm not crazy. I know who Therese was, I know what she did, I know that she used to walk around in my body." I put the doll back in its spot next to a glass cube that could be a paperweight. "But I'm not her. This is my body, and I'm not going to kill myself just so Alice and Mitch can have their baby girl back."

"Terry, no one's asking you to kill yourself. Nobody can even make you into who you were before."

"Yeah? Then what are they paying you for, then?"

"Let me try to explain. Please, sit down. Please."

I look around for a clock and finally spot one on a high shelf. I mentally set the timer to five minutes and sit opposite her, hands on my knees. "Shoot."

"Your parents asked me to talk to you because I've helped other people in your situation, people who've overdosed on Z."

"Help them what? Pretend to be something they're not?"

"I help them take back what they *are*. Your experience of the world tells you that Therese was some other person. No one's denying that. But you're in a situation where biologically and legally, you're Therese Klass. Do you have plans for dealing with that?"

As a matter of fact I do, and it involves getting the hell out as soon as possible. "I'll deal with it," I say.

"What about Alice and Mitch?"

I shrug. "What about them?"

"They're still your parents, and you're still their child. The overdose convinced you that you're a new person, but that hasn't changed who they are. They're still responsible for you, and they still care for you."

"Not much I can do about that."

"You're right. It's a fact of your life. You have two people who love you, and you're going to be with each other for the rest of your lives. You're going to have to figure out how to relate to each other. Zen may have burned the bridge between you and your past life, but you can build that bridge again."

"Doc, I don't *want* to build that bridge. Look, Alice and Mitch seem like nice people, but if I was looking for parents, I'd pick someone else."

Dr. Mehldau smiles. "None of us get to choose our parents, Terry."

I'm not in the mood to laugh. I nod toward the clock. "This is a waste of time."

She leans forward. I think she's going to try to touch me, but she doesn't. "Terry, you're not going to disappear if we talk about what happened to you. You'll still be here. The only difference is that you'll reclaim those memories as your own. You can get your old life back *and* choose your new life."

Sure, it's that easy. I get to sell my soul and keep it too.

I can't remember my first weeks in the hospital, though Dr. S says I was awake. At some point I realized that time was passing, or rather, that there was a me who was passing through time. *I* had lasagna for dinner yesterday, *I* am having meat loaf today. *I* am this girl in a bed. I think I realized this and forgot it several times before I could hold onto it.

Every day was mentally exhausting, because everything was so relentlessly new. I stared at the TV remote for a half hour, the name for it on the tip of my tongue, and it wasn't until the nurse picked it up and turned on the TV for me that I thought: *Remote.* And then sometimes, this was followed by a raft of other ideas: *TV. Channel. Gameshow.*

People were worse. They called me by a strange name, and they expected things of me. But to me, every visitor, from the night shift nurse to the janitor to Alice and Mitch Klass, seemed equally important – which is to say, not important at all.

Except for Dr. S. He was there from the beginning, and so he was familiar before I met him. He belonged to me like my own body.

But everything else about the world – the names, the details, the *facts* – had to be hauled into the sunlight, one by one. My brain was like an attic, chock full of old and interesting things jumbled together in no order at all.

I only gradually understood that somebody must have owned this house before me. And then I realized the house was haunted.

After the Sunday service, I'm caught in a stream of people. They lean across the pews to hug Alice and Mitch, then me. They pat my back, squeeze my arms, kiss my cheeks. I know from brief dips into Therese's memories that many of these people are as emotionally close as aunts or uncles. And any of them, if Therese were ever in trouble, would take her in, feed her, and give her a bed to sleep in.

This is all very nice, but the constant petting has me ready to scream.

All I want to do is get back home and take off this dress. I had no choice but to wear one of Therese's girly-girl extravaganzas. Her closet was full of them, and I finally found one that fits, if not comfortably. She loved these dresses, though. They were her floral print flak jackets. Who could doubt the purity of a girl in a high-necked Laura Ashley?

We gradually make our way to the vestibule, then to the sidewalk and the parking lot, under assault the entire way. I stop trying to match their faces to anything in Therese's memories.

At our car, a group of teenagers take turns on me, the girls hugging me tight, the boys leaning into me with half hugs: shoulders together, pelvises apart. One of the girls, freckled, with soft red curls falling past her shoulders, hangs back for awhile, then abruptly clutches me and whispers into my ear, "I'm so glad you're okay, Miss T." Her tone is intense, like she's passing a secret message.

A man moves through the crowd, arms open, smiling broadly. He's in his late twenties or early thirties, his hair cut in a choppy gelled style that's ten years too young for him. He's wearing pressed khakis, a blue Oxford rolled up at the forearms, a checked tie loosened at the throat.

He smothers me in a hug, his cologne like another set of arms. He's easy to find in Therese's memories: This is Jared, the Youth Pastor. He was the most spiritually vibrant person Therese knew, and the object of her crush.

"It's so good to have you back, Therese," he says. His cheek is pressed to mine. "We've missed you."

A few months before her overdose, the youth group was coming back from a weekend-long retreat in the church's converted school bus. Late into the trip, near midnight, Jared sat next to her, and she fell asleep leaning against him, inhaling that same cologne.

"I bet you have," I say. "Watch the hands, *Jared*."

His smile doesn't waver, his hands are still on my shoulders. "I'm sorry?"

"Oh please, you heard me."

He drops his hands, and looks questioningly at my father. He can do sincerity pretty well. "I don't understand, Therese, but if – "

I give him a look that makes him back up a step. At some point later in the trip Therese awoke with Jared still next to her, slumped in the seat, eyes closed and mouth open. His arm was resting between her thighs, a thumb against her knee. She was wearing shorts, and his flesh on hers was hot. His forearm was inches from her warm crotch.

Therese believed that he was asleep.

She believed, too, that it was the rumbling of the school bus that shifted Jared's arm into contact with the crease of her shorts. Therese froze, flushed with arousal and embarrassment.

"Try to work it out. Jared." I get in the car.

The big question I can help answer, Dr. S said, is why there is consciousness. Or, going back to my favorite metaphor, if the Parliament is making all the decisions, why have a Queen at all?

He's got theories, of course. He thinks the Queen is all about story-telling. The brain needs a story that gives all these decisions a sense of purpose, a sense of continuity, so it can remember them and use them in future decisions. The brain can't keep track of the trillions of possible *other* decisions it could have made every moment; it needs one decision, and it needs a who, and a why. The brain lays down the memories, and the consciousness stamps them with identity: *I* did this, *I* did that. Those memories become the official record, the precedents that the Parliament uses to help make future decisions.

"The Queen, you see, is a figurehead," Dr. S said. "She represents the kingdom, but she isn't the kingdom itself, or even in control of it."

"I don't feel like a figurehead," I said.

Dr. S laughed. "Me neither. Nobody does."

Dr. Mehldau's therapy involves occasional joint sessions with Alice and Mitch, reading aloud from Therese's old diaries, and home movies. Today's video features a pre-teen Therese dressed in sheets, surrounded by kids in bathrobes, staring fixedly at a doll in a manger.

Dr. Mehldau asks me what Therese was thinking then. Was she enjoying playing Mary? Did she like being on stage?

"How would I know?"

"Then imagine it. What do you *think* Therese is thinking here?"

She tells me to do that a lot. Imagine what she's thinking. Just pretend. Put yourself in her shoes. In her book she calls this "reclaiming." She makes up a lot of her own terms, then defines them however she wants, without research to back her up. Compared to the neurology texts Dr. S lent me, Dr. Mehldau's little book is an Archie comic with footnotes.

"You know what, Therese was a good Christian girl, so she probably loved it."

"Are you sure?"

The wise men come on stage, three younger boys. They plop down their gifts and their lines, and the look on Therese's face is wary. Her line is coming up.

Therese was petrified of screwing up. Everybody would be staring at her. I can almost see the congregation in the dark behind the lights. Alice and Mitch are out there, and they're waiting for every line. My chest tightens, and I realize I'm holding my breath.

Dr. Mehldau's eyes on mine are studiously neutral.

"You know what?" I have no idea what I'm going to say next. I'm stalling for time. I shift my weight in the big beige chair and move a leg underneath me. "The thing I like about Buddhism is Buddhists understand that they've been screwed by a whole string of previous selves. I had nothing to do with the decisions Therese made, the good or bad karma she'd acquired."

This is a riff I've been thinking about in Therese's big girly bedroom. "See, Therese was a Christian, so she probably thought by overdosing that she'd be born again, all her sins forgiven. It's the perfect drug for her: suicide without the corpse."

"Was she thinking about suicide that night?"

"*I don't know.* I could spend a couple weeks mining through Therese's memories, but frankly, I'm not interested. Whatever she was thinking, she wasn't born again. I'm here, and I'm still saddled with her baggage. I am Therese's donkey. I'm a karma donkey."

Dr. Mehldau nods. "Dr. Subramaniam is Buddhist, isn't he?"

"Yeah, but what's . . . ?" It clicks. I roll my eyes. Dr. S and I talked about transference, and I know that my crush on him was par for the course. And it's true that I spend a lot of time – still – thinking about fucking the man. But that doesn't mean I'm wrong. "This is not about that," I say. "I've been thinking about this on my own."

She doesn't fight me on that. "Wouldn't a Buddhist say that you and Therese share the same soul? Self's an illusion. So there's no rider in charge, no donkey. There's just *you.*"

"Just forget it," I say.

"Let's follow this, Terry. Don't you feel you have a responsibility to your old self? Your old self's parents, your old friends? Maybe there's karma you *owe.*"

"And who are you responsible to, Doctor? Who's your patient? Therese, or me?"

She says nothing for a moment, then: "I'm responsible to you."

You.

You swallow, surprised that the pills taste like cinnamon. The effect of the drug is intermittent at first. You realize that you're in the backseat of a car, the cell phone in your hand, your friends laughing around you. You're talking to your mother. If you concentrate, you can remember answering the phone, and telling her which friend's house you're staying at tonight. Before you can say goodbye, you're stepping out of the car. The car is parked, your phone is away – and you remember saying goodnight to your mother and riding for a half hour before finding this parking garage. Joelly tosses her red curls and tugs you toward the stairwell: *Come on, Miss T!*

Then you look up and realize that you're on the sidewalk outside an all-ages club, and you're holding a ten dollar bill, ready to hand it to the bouncer. The music thunders every time the door swings open. You turn to Joelly and –

You're in someone else's car. On the Interstate. The driver is a boy you met hours ago, his name is Rush but you haven't asked if that's his first name or his last. In the club you leaned into each other and talked loud over the music about parents and food and the difference between the taste of a fresh cigarette in your mouth and the smell of stale smoke. But then you realize that there's a cigarette in your mouth, you took it from Rush's pack yourself, and you don't like cigarettes. Do you like it now? You don't know. Should you take it out, or keep smoking? You scour your memories, but can discover no reason why you decided to light the cigarette, no reason why you got into the car with this boy.

You start to tell yourself a story: he must be a trustworthy person, or you wouldn't have gotten into the car. You took that one cigarette because the boy's feelings would have been hurt.

You're not feeling like yourself tonight. And you like it. You take another drag off the cigarette. You think back over the past few hours, and marvel at everything you've done, all without that constant weight of self-reflection: worry, anticipation, instant regret. Without the inner voice constantly critiquing you.

Now the boy is wearing nothing but boxer shorts, and he's reaching up to a shelf to get a box of cereal, and his back is beautiful. There is hazy light outside the small kitchen window. He pours Froot Loops into a bowl for you, and he laughs, though quietly because his mother is asleep in the next room. He looks at your face and frowns. He asks you what's the matter. You look down, and you're fully dressed. You think back, and realize that you've been in this boy's apartment for hours. You made out in his bedroom, and the boy took off his clothes, and you kissed his chest and ran your hands along his legs. You let him put his hand under your shirt and cup your breasts, but you didn't go any further. Why didn't you have sex? Did he not interest you? No – you were wet. You were excited. Did you feel guilty? Did you feel ashamed?

What were you thinking?

When you get home there will be hell to pay. Your parents will be furious, and worse, they will pray for you. The entire church will pray for you. Everyone will *know*. And no one will ever look at you the same again.

Now there's a cinnamon taste in your mouth, and you're sitting in the boy's car again, outside a convenience store. It's afternoon. Your cell phone is ringing. You turn off the cell phone and put it back in your purse. You swallow, and your throat is dry. That boy – Rush – is buying you another bottle of water. What was it you swallowed? Oh, yes. You think back, and remember putting all those little pills in your mouth. Why did you take so many? Why did you take another one at all? Oh, yes.

Voices drift up from the kitchen. It's before 6 a.m., and I just want to pee and get back to sleep, but then I realize they're talking about me.

"She doesn't even *walk* the same. The way she holds herself, the way she talks . . ."

"It's all those books Dr. Subramaniam gave her. She's up past one every night. Therese never read like that, not *science.*"

"No, it's not just the words, it's how she *sounds*. That low voice . . ." She sobs. "Oh hon, I didn't know it would be this way. It's like she's right, it's like it isn't her at all."

He doesn't say anything. Alice's crying grows louder, subsides. The clink of dishes in the sink. I step back, and Mitch speaks again.

"Maybe we should try the camp," he says.

"No, no, no! Not yet. Dr. Mehldau says she's making progress. We've got to – "

"Of course she's going to say that."

"You said you'd try this, you said you'd give this a chance." The anger cuts through the weeping, and Mitch mumbles something apologetic. I creep back to my bedroom, but I still have to pee, so I make a lot of noise going back out. Alice comes to the bottom of the stairs. "Are you all right, honey?"

I keep my face sleepy and walk into the bathroom. I shut the door and sit down on the toilet in the dark.

What fucking camp?

"Let's try again," Dr. Mehldau said. "Something pleasant and vivid."

I'm having trouble concentrating. The brochure is like a bomb in my pocket. It wasn't hard to find, once I decided to look for it. I want to ask Dr. Mehldau about the camp, but I know that once I bring it into the open, I'll trigger a showdown between the doctor and the Klasses, with me in the middle.

"Keep your eyes closed," she says. "Think about Therese's tenth birthday. In her diary, she wrote that was the best birthday she'd ever had. Do you remember SeaWorld?"

"Vaguely." I could see dolphins jumping – two at a time, three at a time. It had been sunny and hot. With every session it was getting easier for me to pop into Therese's memories. Her life was on DVD, and I had the remote.

"Do you remember getting wet at the Namu and Shamu show?"

I laughed. "I think so." I could see the metal benches, the glass wall just in front of me, the huge shapes in the blue-green water. "They had the whales flip their big tail fins. We got drenched."

"Can you picture who was there with you? Where are your parents?"

There was a girl, my age, I can't remember her name. The sheets of water were coming down on us and we were screaming and laughing. Afterward my parents toweled us off. They must have been sitting up high, out of the splash zone. Alice looked much younger: happier, and a little heavier. She was wider at the hips. This was before she started dieting and exercising, when she was Mom-sized.

My eyes pop open. "Oh God."

"Are you okay?"

"I'm fine – it was just . . . like you said. Vivid." That image of a younger Alice still burns. For the first time I realize how sad she is now.

"I'd like a joint session next time," I say.

"Really? All right. I'll talk to Alice and Mitch. Is there anything in particular you want to talk about?"

"Yeah. We need to talk about Therese."

Dr. S says everybody wants to know if the original neural map, the old Queen, can come back. Once the map to the map is lost, can you find it again? And if you do, then what happens to the new neural map, the new Queen?

"Now, a good Buddhist would tell you that this question is unimportant. After all, the cycle of existence is not just between lives. Samsara is every moment. The self continuously dies and recreates itself."

"Are you a good Buddhist?" I asked him.

He smiled. "Only on Sunday mornings."

"You go to church?"

"I golf."

There's a knock and I open my eyes. Alice steps into my room, a stack of folded laundry in her arms. "Oh!"

I've rearranged the room, pushing the bed into the corner to give me a few square feet of free space on the floor.

Her face goes through a few changes. "I don't suppose you're praying."

"No."

She sighs, but it's a mock-sigh. "I didn't think so." She moves around me sets the laundry on the bed. She picks up the book there, *Entering the Stream*. "Dr. Subramaniam gave you this?"

She's looking at the passage I've highlighted. *But loving kindness – maitri – toward ourselves doesn't mean getting rid of anything. The point is not to try to change ourselves. Meditation practice isn't about trying to throw ourselves away and become something better. It's about befriending who we already are.*

"Well." She sets the book down, careful to leave it open to the same page. "That sounds a bit like Dr. Mehldau."

I laugh. "Yeah, it does. Did she tell you I wanted you and Mitch to be at the next session?"

"We'll be there." She works around the room, picking up t-shirts and underwear. I stand up to get out of the way. Somehow she manages to straighten up as she moves – righting books that had fallen over, setting Boo W. Bear back to his place on the bed, sweeping an empty chip bag into the garbage can – so that as she collects my dirty laundry she's cleaning the entire room, like the Cat in the Hat's cleaner-upper machine.

"Alice, in the last session I remembered being at Sea World, but there was a girl next to me. Next to Therese."

"Sea World? Oh, that was the Hammel girl, Marcy. They took you to Ohio with them on their vacation that year."

"Who did?"

"The Hammels. You were gone all week. All you wanted for your birthday was spending money for the trip."

"You weren't there?"

She picks up the jeans I left at the foot of the bed. "We always meant to go to Sea World, but your father and I never got out there."

"This is our last session," I say.

Alice, Mitch, Dr. Mehldau: I have their complete attention.

The doctor, of course, is the first to recover. "It sounds like you've got something you want to tell us."

"*Oh* yeah."

Alice seems frozen, holding herself in check. Mitch rubs the back of his neck, suddenly intent on the carpet.

"I'm not going along with this anymore." I make a vague gesture. "Everything: the memory exercises, all this imagining of what Therese felt. I finally figured it out. It doesn't matter to you if I'm Therese or not. You just want me to think I'm her. I'm not going along with the manipulation anymore."

Mitch shakes his head. "Honey, you took a *drug*." He glances at me, looks back at his feet. "If you took LSD and saw God, that doesn't mean you really saw God. Nobody's trying to manipulate you, we're trying to *undo* the manipulation."

"That's bullshit, Mitch. You all keep acting like I'm schizophrenic, that I don't know what's real or not. Well, part of the problem is that the longer I talk to Dr. Mehldau here, the more fucked up I am."

Alice gasps.

Dr. Mehldau puts out a hand to soothe her, but her eyes are on me. "Terry, what your father's trying to say is that even though you feel like a new person, there's a *you* that existed before the drug. That exists now."

"Yeah? You know all those O.D.-ers in your book who say they've 'reclaimed' themselves? Maybe they only feel like their old selves."

"It's *possible*," she says. "But I don't think they're fooling themselves. They've come to accept the parts of themselves they've lost, the family members they've left behind. They're people like you." She regards me with that standard-issue look of concern that doctors pick up with their diplomas. "Do you really want to feel like an orphan the rest of your life?"

"What?" From out of nowhere, tears well in my eyes. I cough to clear my throat, and the tears keep coming, until I smear them off on my arm. I feel like I've been sucker punched. "Hey, look Alice, just like you," I say.

"It's normal," Dr. Mehldau says. "When you woke up in the hospital, you felt completely alone. You felt like a brand new person, no family, no friends. And you're still just starting down this road. In a lot of ways you're not even two years old."

"*Damn* you're good," I say. "I didn't even see that one coming."

"Please, don't leave. Let's – "

"Don't worry, I'm not leaving yet." I'm at the door, pulling my backpack from the peg by the door. I dig into the pocket, and pull out the brochure. "You know about this?"

Alice speaks for the first time. "Oh honey, no . . ."

Dr. Mehldau takes it from me, frowning. On the front is a nicely posed picture of a smiling teenage boy hugging relieved parents. She looks at Alice and Mitch. "Are you considering this?"

"It's their big stick, Dr. Mehldau. If you can't come through for them, or I bail out, *boom*. You know what goes on there?"

She opens the pages, looking at pictures of the cabins, the obstacle course, the big lodge where kids just like me engage in "intense group sessions with trained counselors" where they can "recover their true identities." She shakes her head. "Their approach is different than mine . . ."

"I don't know, doc. Their *approach* sounds an awful lot like 'reclaiming.' I got to hand it to you, you had me going for awhile. Those visualization exercises? I was getting so good that I could even visualize stuff that never happened. I bet you could visualize me right into Therese's head."

I turn to Alice and Mitch. "You've got a decision to make. Dr. Mehldau's program is a bust. So are you sending me off to brain-washing camp or not?"

Mitch has his arm around his wife. Alice, amazingly, is dry-eyed. Her eyes are wide, and she's staring at me like a stranger.

It rains the entire trip back from Baltimore, and it's still raining when we pull up to the house. Alice and I run to the porch step, illuminated by the glare of headlights. Mitch waits until Alice unlocks the door and we move inside, and then pulls away.

"Does he do that a lot?" I ask.

"He likes to drive when he's upset."

"Oh." Alice goes through the house, turning on lights. I follow her into the kitchen.

"Don't worry, he'll be all right." She opens the refrigerator door and crouches down. "He just doesn't know what to do with you."

"He wants to put me in the camp, then."

"Oh, not that. He just never had a daughter who talked back to him before." She carries a Tupperware cake holder to the table. "I made carrot cake. Can you get down the plates?"

She's such a small woman. Face to face, she comes up only to my chin. The hair on the top of her head is thin, made thinner by the rain, and her scalp is pink.

"I'm not Therese. I never will be Therese."

"Oh, I know," she says, half sighing. And she does know it; I can see it in her face. "It's just that you look so much like her."

I laugh. "I can dye my hair. Maybe get a nose job."

"It wouldn't work, I'd still recognize you." She pops the lid and sets it aside. The cake is a wheel with icing that looks half an inch thick. Miniature candy carrots line the edge.

"Wow, you made that before we left? Why?"

Alice shrugs, and cuts into it. She turns the knife on its side and uses the blade to lever a huge triangular wedge onto my plate. "I thought we might need it, one way or another."

She places the plate in front of me, and touches me lightly on the arm.

"I know you want to move out. I know you may never want to come back."

"It's not that I – "

"We're not going to stop you. But wherever you go, you'll still be my daughter, whether you like it or not. You don't get to decide who loves you."

"Alice . . ."

"Shhh. Eat your cake."

THE CANADIAN WHO CAME ALMOST ALL THE WAY BACK FROM THE STARS

Jay Lake and Ruth Nestvold

Highly prolific new writer Jay Lake seems to have appeared nearly everywhere with short work in the last couple of years, including *Asimov's SCI FICTION, Interzone, Strange Horizons, The Third Alternative, Aeon, Postscripts, Electric Velocipede,* and many other markets. He's produced enough short fiction to have already released four collections, even though his career is only a few years old: *Greetings from Lake Wu, Green Grow the Rushes-Oh, American Sorrows,* and *Dogs in the Moonlight.* He's the coeditor, with Deborah Layne, of the prestigious *Polyphony* anthology series, and has also edited the anthologies *All-Star Zeppelin Adventure Stories,* with David Moles, and *TEL: Stories.* He won the John W. Campbell Award for Best New Writer in 2004. His most recent book is his first novel, *Rocket Science.*

New writer Ruth Nestvold is a graduate of Clarion West whose stories have appeared in *Asimov's, SCI FICTION, Strange Horizons, Realms of Fantasy, Andromeda Spaceways Inflight Magazine, Futurismic, Fantastic Companions,* and elsewhere. A former professor of English, she now runs a small software localization business in Stuttgart, Germany.

Here they join forces to give us a surprising story that's about exactly what it *says* that it's about.

K ELLY MACINNES WAS PRETTY, prettier than I had expected. She had that sort of husky blond beauty I associated with the upper Midwest. Or in her case, the Canadian prairie.

Together we stared out across Emerald Lake, one of those small mountain lakes jeweling western North America, framed by a vista of Douglas firs, longleaf pines, and granite peaks clawing their way into the echoing summer sky. Midway out on the lake, the water gathered into a visible depression, as if a huge weight had settled on it. The dimple was about forty feet in diameter and ten feet deep, perfectly flat at the bottom, with steeply angled sides like a giant inverted bottle cap. It had appeared five days after Nick MacInnes had mysteriously called home three months ago – years after he was presumed dead.

At which point Nick's widow had promptly dropped everything and come here to Yoho National Park in darkest British Columbia. "It looks unnatural." It was a dumb thing to say, but I didn't have much to offer. I was an intruder after all, a U.S. agent come to investigate phone call and dimple – and Mrs. MacInnes.

"It is unnatural," she replied. "A couple of weeks after it appeared, every fish in the lake had beached or moved downstream."

I could imagine the rot. Such a stench seemed impossible in this mountain paradise. The air had the sharp tang of snow on pines, the flinty odor of wet rock, the absolute purity of the Canadian Rockies.

But there was a lot that was impossible going on here. I had seen the satellite tracking reports – NORAD, NASA, ESA, even some Chinese data. The dimple had appeared, fish had died – *something* had happened – but there was no evidence of re-entry, no evidence of any precipitating event whatsoever. Only the hole in the lake in front of me.

And a phone call that couldn't have happened, from a dead man lost in interstellar space.

"You say your husband told you to come here." They'd all asked her the questions before: the RCMP, the Special Branch, the FBI, several U.N. High Commissions. Kelly MacInnes had met her husband in college, where they both studied astrophysics, but her name had never been on any of his papers or patents. They asked her the questions anyway.

And now it was my turn, on behalf of the NSA. We still didn't know what had happened out there in that lake, but we wanted to make sure no one else knew either. The first step had been to clear out the park – except for Kelly MacInnes. My job wasn't as much to drag information out of her as it was to make sure it didn't get to anyone else first if she was moved to start talking.

She stared out at the hole in the water, the unfilled grave of her absent husband. "He's not dead."

I nodded. "I've read the transcripts – it's clear to me you believe that." *Or at least you claim you do.* "But, Mrs. MacInnes, there is no evidence your husband survived his rather spectacular departure from earth six years ago."

She hugged her plaid flannel jacket closer, her gaze drifting up to the sky. Despite the sun, the air was crisp. "The trip was supposed to take less than a week. Then six years after he left, he called and told me to meet him here. Just after 2:30 a.m. on April seventeenth, the center of the lake collapsed into that hole. That's what I know, Mr. Diedrich."

I followed her stare toward the summer sky. Somewhere behind that perfect blue shell was an explanation for what happened to Nicholas MacInnes.

Too bad the sky wasn't talking today.

Barnard's Star is slightly less than six light-years from Sol. A red dwarf, it is interesting only for its convenient position in the interstellar neighborhood and the fact that it is moving noticeably faster than any of our other stellar neighbors. Until Nick MacInnes decided to go there six years ago.

Four years prior to his launch, he'd published a paper in the *Canadian Journal of Aerospace Engineering and Technology Applications*, "Proposal for a Cost-Effective Method of Superluminal Travel." CJAETA was about one step above vanity publishing, and the article was soon well on its way to the dustbin of history.

Recently, I had seen to it that all copies of Volume XXXVI, Issue 9, had been destroyed, along with computer files, Web sites, mirror sites, tape backups, printer plates, CD-ROMs, library microfiche archives, and everything else we could think of. Because one fine spring day, Nick MacInnes, sometime mobile communications billionaire, made a space shot from a privately built and previously unknown launch site on the prairie east of Calgary, found his way into orbit on top of surplus Russian missile hardware, and did something that crashed a significant portion of the world's electronic infrastructure. At which point, he disappeared in a rainbow-colored flash visible across an entire hemisphere of the planet.

It soon became known that he was carrying four surplus Russian M-2 nuclear warheads. "For the bomb-pumped lasers," the Ph.Ds assisting MacInnes said, as if the rest of the world were worrying excessively over trivialities.

When I returned to Emerald Lake three months later to check on Kelly MacInnes and security at the park, the Canadian Air Force and NASA were back. The CAF had flown a Lockheed Orion P-3C AIP over the lake back in late April and through most of May.

Now, in October, NASA and the Canadian Space Agency had stuck some added instrumentation on it. They gave up on towed sonar after losing two rigs in the trees along the shoreline. Recon satellites had performed various kinds of imaging and discovered a significant gravitational anomaly at the bottom of Emerald Lake. Or maybe they hadn't. The dimple in the lake surface was caused by the stress of the anomaly. Or maybe not.

There wasn't a ferrous body in the lake, but a significant mass concentration rested on the bottom, absorbing radar and creating weird thermal gradients. Wild theories were thrown around concerning polymerization of water, stress on molecular bonds, microscopic black holes, time singularities, and so on. There was some hard data about a heat rise in the center of the dimple, a heat rise that declined in temperature during the first three weeks of observation before leveling out about nine degrees centigrade above historical ambient surface temperature.

Curiously, remote sensing indicated ice at the bottom of the lake in the area of the dimple. Cameras and instrument packages sent down didn't add much to the picture – the mascon was big, it was inert, and it distorted the lake's temperature profile.

But then the search for additional meaningful data was complicated by the one incontrovertible thing discovered besides the heat rise: radioactive contamination. Everyone working at the lake was being exposed to radionuclides equivalent to three hundred rem a year, sixty times the permitted exposure level for workers in the United States. Well into cancer-causing territory, especially leukemia, but not enough to give you an immediate case of the pink pukes or make your hair fall out.

When I heard, I sought out the CSA project manager in charge of the current phase of the investigation, Ray Vittori. I was no physicist, but I'd been a technology spook for years. This stank. "How in holy hell could you not have noticed this before?"

Vittori shook his head. "It wasn't here before, Diedrich. Simple."

I crossed my arms. Behind me, I thought I could feel Kelly MacInnes smile, but I didn't bother to turn around to see if I was right. She mistrusted government institutions, including her own, but she loathed the United States government.

As it was, we couldn't justify trucking the required diving equipment, mini-subs, and underwater instrumentation high into the Canadian Rockies to find out more about the dimple. So much data had already been collected that it would take years to analyze it in the first place. And the anomaly didn't seem to be going anywhere anytime soon. The radiation levels just complicated whatever case I might have made for increased allocation of intelligence assets.

The Orion went back to hunting subs in the maritime provinces. The think tanks went back to thinking somewhere else. Some cameras and sensors remained, wired in around the lakeshore, shooting telemetry back to my agency in Maryland. Other than that, only the satellites still provided us with information, along with the occasional research team willing to sign their souls away in indemnity clauses. A barebones contingent continued to secure the perimeters of the park, all volunteer agents at exorbitant pay for assurances that they wouldn't seek damages if they ever showed signs of sickness that could be attributed to radiation.

By the time the first snow fell, I was left alone to observe the astonishing natural beauty of Yoho National Park and the equally attractive Mrs. Kelly MacInnes. Just me, after all the attention and the hardware went away, with a dosimeter, a sixteen-foot bass boat, and lots of time.

We ate corned beef hash and canned peaches in the echoing stillness of the lodge's dining hall. The worst of winter was past, but it was damned cold anyway, and we wore down jackets everywhere – and extra layers when we dared to go outside.

"At least he picked a national park," I said, looking around the empty lodge. My visits to Emerald Lake had been getting longer and longer over the winter. The agency kept me largely free, since it was hard to get anyone else to come up here with the threat of contamination. Not to mention the godawful remoteness.

And then there was Kelly. Nick knew what he was about, choosing this woman with the loyalty of a lioness. Though at times I rather imagined it was she who had done the choosing.

She smiled. "Quiet place, facilities nearby, eh, Mr. Diedrich?"

"I was thinking more in terms of access control. Difficult to secure and patrol private land."

Her big laugh rang out louder than was natural in the empty spaces of the lodge. "Do you see anyone trying to violate your vaunted security in this godforsaken place?"

I grimaced. A psychiatrist would probably have a field day with me – NSA spook falls for married woman who laughs at him.

But what a magnificent laugh it was.

I lowered my forkful of peach. "Why are you still here in this godforsaken place?" Kelly still had plenty of money – Nick's misadventures in orbit had barely depleted his fortunes, even after the staggering fines assessed against his estate for sundry air traffic and orbital protocol violations. She could have checked on the dimple then headed for Tahiti.

She cocked her head. "I could ask the same question, with more justification. I'm waiting for my husband, making sure you lot don't muck up his chances of returning. Keeping my eye on the dimple. What are you waiting for, Mr. Diedrich? Why do you keep coming back?"

I couldn't give her a true answer, not one that she would accept.

The melting of the snow was like a revelation.

Patches of green appeared in the unremitting white of the landscape just as the first anniversary of Nick MacInnes's telephone call from the stars approached.

In celebration of one or the other, Kelly and I hiked out to the lake to inspect the dimple. All winter long, it hadn't frozen over, despite the blankets of snow on all sides, despite the fact that other lakes in the region were solid sheets of ice.

The dimple still appeared much as it had the first day I had seen it, even with the snow on the north side of the lake – wide, unnatural, a mystery to be solved.

And the key stood next to me.

"In some ways I'm waiting for the same thing as you, you know," I said finally.

She was silent for a long time. I knew she understood me – during the time we had spent together over the last winter, we had developed that odd pattern of shortcuts and silences that many married couples use to communicate. I just barely remembered it from my own failed marriage.

She nodded out at the dimple. "You were born in the United States?"

Non sequitur. We had advanced to those as well. But I still didn't know where she was going with this. "Yes."

"You've been on the winning team all your life. You don't have a clue what it's like to be Canadian, having the world's biggest brother next door." A hare hopped into our line of vision. I watched it make tracks in the snow left in the sun's shadow.

"The United States," Kelly continued, not looking at me. "The 'we did it first' country. You build the space shuttle, we build a robot arm. Canada makes another contribution to progress."

She seemed to expect a serious answer. I didn't give it to her.

"And now your government keeps sending you here to babysit me. Because the hard men with the bright lights didn't learn anything."

"No one is forcing me."

She gave me a look that asked me whom I thought I was kidding, one eyebrow raised and her wide lips somewhere close to a smile. "No, but I know why you're here. You hate it, the whole world hates it, but especially you Yanks. You hate that a Canadian went to the stars first, without you."

She was partly right.

But only partly.

Kelly was a hard nut to crack, laughter or no laughter. It wasn't until we'd been alone together regularly for almost a year before she started calling me by my first name.

Even though I had been waiting for it for what seemed forever, I almost didn't notice. We were out on the lake in the park's Ranger Cherokee to take some measurements of our own of the surface temperature near the dimple, cross-checking the instruments. My Geiger counter kept acting up – the third one the agency had sent me – but there was nothing wrong with our old-fashioned thermometers.

I had no interest in taking the boat into the middle. The drop to the flat surface of the dimple was about ten feet and looked vaguely like a ring of waterfalls.

"I'm keeping at least five boat lengths away," I said. "We'll circle."

Kelly trailed the thermometer on a length of fishing line. "Fine with me, Bruce."

I was so busy navigating the rim of the dimple, the fact that she had called me "Bruce" didn't immediately register. When it did, it was like a kick to the gut, and I jerked the tiller toward the edge.

I corrected immediately, and Kelly looked up. "Temperature holding steady here. What about you?"

"I'm fine."

The pines whistled with the mountain wind; even in July, it was chilly up here. As I drove the boat, I watched a hawk work the thermals off toward the granite massif that sheltered the headwaters of the Kicking Horse River. There was something seriously wrong with me if Kelly's use of my first name felt as intimate as a kiss.

It was about time I called my boss, Marge Williams, and returned to Maryland again for a while.

Somehow, I didn't have much success fleeing Emerald Lake. The next time I came back, I came back for good. The ostensible excuse was Marge's gentle insistence – the government still wanted whatever information Kelly MacInnes could provide badly enough to make it a permanent assignment. The potential value of what Nick had done, even with its fatal flaws, outweighed any cost of my time and effort.

But the real reason was Kelly. NSA couldn't force me, given the radiation risk – and they didn't have to.

I returned in October. To my surprise, she was waiting at the park landing zone as the helicopter came in.

"What took you so long!" she shouted out over the whirring of the blades as I hopped down from the cabin. "We've had no less than seven dimple-fans succeed in breaching security since you left."

"Seven! Guess I better get back on the job." Of course I had already been informed about the handful of trespassers who weren't bright enough to be scared off by radioactive fallout – Marge had used them as a further argument to get me to return. For the good of the project, of course. And Kelly's safety. That and a huge bonus I could put aside to finance my medical bills if I ended up with cancer in a decade or two.

It all seemed worth it with Kelly glad to see me. Perhaps it was just the basic human need for companionship, but I was happy to delude myself into thinking it was more.

By our third year at Emerald Lake, it began to appear that the world had forgotten us. Over the winter, attempts to breach park security had dwindled to nothing, and even with the arrival of spring and the second anniversary of the appearance of the dimple, there had been less than half a dozen. Of course, I still spoke with headquarters nearly every week. We also had occasional contact with maintenance personnel and an RCMP trooper by the name of Sergeant Perry who actually came by on horseback when the weather was good and sometimes brought us old newspapers. I went back to Maryland regularly for my quarterly mission reviews and radiation assessments, and we were connected with the outside world through the Internet, but for the most part we were alone.

Me, Kelly, and the dimple.

She looked at that damn dimple every day as if Nick MacInnes was going to come walking out of it and embrace her. I just looked at it.

And so we hadn't become lovers. To me she was a widow, but Kelly thought of herself as a wife.

An extremely loyal wife.

We got along well enough, had even become friends of sorts. That is if you disregarded the fact that I dreamed about the scent of her every night.

It was a warm day in late August when I finally asked the question. "So, why are we still here?"

Kelly and I sat in front of the lodge on a little pebbled strip of land too modest to call a beach. The dimple punctuated the lake in front of us, and the mountains loomed high in the sky around it. For a change it was warm enough that I didn't have to wear a jacket.

"Why are *you* still here?"

I shrugged. "You're my job." You and Nick, I thought, but I tried to say his name as little as possible. "According to my boss, they don't have anything else for me."

She placed her left hand on my right forearm, a rare moment of physical contact between us. "Oh, surely there's more for you to do than wait by a lake. You Americans, you always have some mess to go fix. Or make."

I didn't move a muscle, afraid to dislodge her touch. "I wouldn't have to be here all the time just to oversee the security of the site. Your husband achieved something no one ever did before him, and there are a lot of people who want to know what he didn't tell us." *What you're not telling us.* "Marge sent me here to find out why you're still keeping such a sharp eye on the dimple."

Kelly smiled, one eyebrow arched. "Marge?"

"Sure. Not everyone is as afraid of first names as you are."

She moved her hand away. Me and my big mouth. My arm still tingled where her fingers had been.

"Actually," she said, "I'm waiting for another message from him."

I couldn't help laughing. "Another phone call?"

She grinned. "No, no. Nick promised to set a sign in the heavens."

Despite her grin, I had the strange feeling that she was serious.

After the snows melted the next spring, Kelly started bugging me to go into the center of the dimple with her, a squint of worry around her eyes. The thing had never frozen over, even as the ice crusted around the edges. A heavy snow could cover it for a day or so, before the snow blanket sagged into the warm water beneath. The dimple was there like a great blind eye in the water, staring at the sky, trapping us in its unseeing gaze.

I studied the curious phenomenon that had become such an everyday part of life. "How do you propose we get back out if we go down in there?"

Kelly gazed at me speculatively. "How good a swimmer are you, Bruce?"

I shook my head. "No, no way."

She gave me her wide smile. I could almost believe I had imagined the worry – but only almost. "If we had a long enough rope with us, you could belay the boat back for sure. You're strong. I bet you're a good swimmer."

"I was all-New England in prep school," I admitted. "But I'm still not going to do it."

"Why not?"

Oh, Christ, Kelly. "One, I don't want to drown in those damned waterfalls. Two, I don't want to put my body near that thermal gradient without a boat between me and it. The overflight data suggested ice layers down there, at the reverse end of the heat rise. That's why we have cameras and instrument packages."

"Sometimes there's nothing like a first-hand look."

"No."

"You're already exposing yourself to constant radiation," she pointed out, flirting and pleading at the same time. I hadn't thought her capable of either. "Why worry about a simple mascon?"

This time I said it out loud. "Christ, Kelly."

She let loose a lovely peal of laughter and took my elbow. "Besides, it's not like you have anything else to do this summer."

When Kelly realized I wasn't going to get into that water for her anytime soon, she decided we needed to build a "dimple observatory." We spent several days hauling lumber from the park's maintenance shed to a beautiful old rock maple right up by the water with just the right spread of branches. Kelly's big laugh echoed between the trees and the mountains more often than I had ever heard it as we messed with ropes and nails, building our tree fort.

I had thought I was lost in love before, but I hadn't known how charming, how fun she could be.

Our Mountie showed up while we were up there hammering away. He regarded us seriously for a moment from his big bay mare, like a critical parent.

Kelly took the nail out of her mouth and called down to him. "Come on, Sergeant Perry. Don't you want to work on a tree fort again?"

He cracked a smile and gave us a few hours of his time. I finally thanked him for his help when I noticed him watching his dosimeter more carefully than he was watching the hammer in his hand.

One night Kelly and I were grilling hot dogs over a campfire next to our "observatory" when she gave me *that look* again. "Bruce, won't you at least take me out to the surface of the dimple? I want to see it for myself."

"Christ, Kelly." I pulled my dog out of the fire and tried to brush off some of the burned spots. What the hell. I'd already signed up for cancer for her sake, had been throwing away red-lined dosimeters for a while. "Sure."

She tackled me with a squeal that made it all worthwhile.
I hoped.

"How deep can you dive?"

I looked up from the gear I was stowing in the Ranger Cherokee. I hadn't done any diving in years. "Now wait a minute – "

"If you're going into the water anyway, you could also see if you could get down to the mascon."

I straightened, shaking my head. "The anomaly is in thirty meters of water. I don't think I can hold my breath more than ninety seconds. That's not enough."

"So we tie a fifteen meter rope to your ankle, drop you over with something heavy to take you down fast, and you push a pole down the rest of the way."

I laughed. "And do what? Tap?"

She smiled her real smile. "You come back up, tell me what you saw, what it felt like. What's down there."

"You were planning on asking me this all along, weren't you?"

Her smile took on a guilty cast. "Well, yes."

I sighed. How much did it matter now? There wasn't much I could do to compete with her rich, dead genius husband. At least I could do this for her.

I wired the butt of an ancient oak post to the end of a twenty-foot aspen pole, then made a wrist loop at the other end of the pole out of an old bootlace. I would jump headfirst out of the bass boat clutching an old wheel rim to weigh me down and follow the pole toward the bottom. First I smeared my body with a mixture of Vaseline and mud – we didn't have enough of the petroleum jelly around the lodge to use it straight up, but I was worried about the cold.

"We're nuts," I said. Kelly drove the boat straight for the dimple. Our long line trailed behind us toward the nearest shore, some two hundred feet distant, ready for my belaying act.

Kelly looked happier than she had since I first met her. "Nick's down there."

"I'm not knocking on any doors." I already had mud in some very uncomfortable places.

Her smile was like the sunrise. "Just see what you see."

What I saw was what Nick MacInnes had seen in her. What I wondered was what she had seen in him: the record suggested he had been a monomaniacal nutcase who happened to have gotten it right.

The Ranger Cherokee slid down into the dimple, and my stomach did a sharp flop – the world's shortest log-flume ride. Kelly cut the trolling motor, and the boat circled loosely in the base of the dimple, a forty-foot wide bowl. The ten-foot walls of water around us were incredibly disconcerting, a violation of every sense and sensibility. It didn't help that our trailing line strained *upward*, vanishing into those angled waterfalls.

We tipped the stripped aspen pole overboard. The oak block pulled it straight down until it was stopped by the bootlace loop I'd slipped over a cleat, rocking our little boat. I stared down at the rippling black water beneath which lay the mascon.

"Don't think too hard," said Kelly. "You won't do it."

I checked the knot of the lifeline on my ankle. I was only doing it for her, and she was doing it for her husband – she was right, I'd better not think too hard. "Count to thirty, then start pulling up, as fast as you can." I slipped my hand through the loop on the gunwale cleat, pulled the pole free with the tether around my wrist, and fell in headfirst, clutching the wheel rim to my chest.

The water wasn't any colder than I expected, but it pushed up my nose in a way that seemed stronger, sharper than reasonable. Venting a little air from my lips, I released the wheel rim; I was getting enough downward pull from the weighted aspen pole.

My ears throbbed with mild pain. The breathing panic started, but I ignored it, letting the pole drag me down past the visible light.

The water got cooler as I sank. I wondered how deep I was, wondered if Kelly had tossed my line over, sending me off to meet her husband. My ankle jerked up short, and I almost lost my grip on the pole, but the bootlace loop around my wrist held.

I bobbed head down for a moment, the pole pulling me down, the rope holding me back. I worked my hands to get a firmer grip on the pole. With my eyes open, there was a vague greenish quality to the darkness. The water pressure on my body was like a giant fist slowly closing.

That was when I realized my fingers were cold, way too cold. I brought my free hand up in front of my face, but there wasn't enough light to see it. I touched my fingers to my lips – ice scum. I knew what the reports had said, but still . . . water froze from the *top*, not the *bottom*.

Then the pole jumped in my hands. The downward pull was gone, the pole floating slowly upward. What had happened to the weight? My chest tightened with anoxia and fear. The water felt much colder. Where the hell was Kelly? I tried to turn my body, but with the pole in the way, I started to get trapped in the rope.

My ankle jerked.

Kelly.

Thank God.

I held the pole while she tugged the rope from somewhere inside the blue sky far above. I followed my heart toward the bright air.

Kelly wrapped me in two blankets when I rolled into the boat, and I shivered in their scratchy depths. I didn't have the strength to swim to shore yet.

She examined the aspen pole. "Looks like it snapped off."

I shook my head. Now that I wasn't panicking, it was easier to figure out what might have happened to the pole. "No applied pressure – I would have felt that."

Kelly pointed the broken end toward me. The end looked more like it had been blown off. Would my hand have done the same, under the pressure of the rapidly expanding ice?

Kelly came to the same conclusion at about the same time. "Cold," she said, her voice strangely satisfied. "The aspen shattered from the cold."

"What's so great about cold?" The cold could have killed me. I was feeling groggy from the dive, chilled in the half-hearted sun of the Canadian Rockies.

Her smile flashed. "Very slow entropic progression, that's what's so great about cold."

Very slow entropic progression. I'd never heard her talk like that before.

The following winter, we were enjoying a comfortable afternoon in front of the lodge fireplace when we heard shots. We looked at each other in shock for a moment before we jumped up, pulled on our Gore-Tex snowpants and parkas, and headed out for the snowmobile.

Less than a mile from the lodge, we found Sergeant Perry's body in the snow, his skis sticking up at an odd angle, his blood spattering the pristine white of the landscape.

Kelly stifled a sob, then bent to close his eyes. I had to stop myself from reaching to comfort her, so I scanned the woods for signs of movement instead. Nothing.

I called Maryland. There wasn't much point in seeking cover – if the shooter was still out there, we were in their sights.

"Perhaps it was a hunting accident?" Marge said over the static-filled connection.

"A hunting accident?" Islamists, Chinese, environmentalists – I could think of a lot more likely explanations than that. "Marge, no one should be able get past our security for there to *be* a hunting accident. You need to initiate an outside investigation."

Kelly knelt in the snow next to the body, tears streaming down her face. We hadn't known the Mountie well, but he had been one of the few people we'd had any contact with in the last four-plus years.

On the other end of the line, Marge sighed. "You're right, this needs to be looked into. I'll take care of it, Bruce."

"Thanks."

An NSA helicopter flew in to collect the body and take Perry back to wherever he had come from. Kelly and I watched it wing away again, and to my surprise, her arm slid around my waist.

I had the odd thought that I wished I could die right then, standing in the snow like one half of a couple with Kelly MacInnes.

The dimple was definitely changing. During the summer following Sergeant Perry's mysterious death – which NSA had failed to clear up – it had grown visibly wider and shallower. Even with our crude measurements, the heat rise was becoming noticeably greater. Radiation levels remained stable, however the dosimeters and my Geiger counter were consistent.

I suggested calling in surveillance aircraft from the agency once more, but Kelly would have none of it. "What good are they? That could have been one of us out in the snow – and no record of a breach in security according to your precious Marge!"

She was right, of course. I had taken to carrying a pistol, something I'd never done before – I no longer trusted my agency's ability to keep us safe. But that didn't have anything to do with whatever was happening in the lake. "Their equipment could still give us valuable data on the dimple."

"And how do we know whether we can even trust their data?"

I wasn't happy with how Marge had handled the security breach either, but I still thought Kelly was overreacting. "What if I ask for the CAF Orion again?"

Kelly shook her head. "No. Not if they're sent by your NSA."

Damn me if I didn't let her talk me out of it.

She couldn't talk university research teams out of coming, though. Suddenly, interest in the dimple revived, and we were no longer as alone as we had been. It seemed like they were everywhere, bitching about agency controls on their equipment, about the mosquitoes, about how we wouldn't let them use the restrooms in the lodge. But we still didn't allow the journalists clamoring for a permit into the park.

Kelly eyed the researchers suspiciously, as if they were going to take her dimple away from her or something. She sat in the tree fort and watched Emerald Lake with a simple pair of binoculars, jealous of anyone else who went near it. I joined her sometimes, but the more the lake changed, the more she left me. I didn't need that reminder of how far away she was again after what had seemed so close.

She was spending the day in the "dimple observatory" as usual when I brought her sandwiches one late autumn afternoon. We had the park to ourselves again for a change, for what little it was worth. The leaves of the maple around her were brilliant with shades of orange and red and yellow, but Kelly only had eyes for that damn dimple.

"Look at the way it's steaming," she said, hardly glancing at me as she took a peanut butter and jelly. "Things are getting even warmer down there."

"Hm." I stared across the water, at the steam rising above the lake. It wasn't that hot, but there was enough temperature differential with the air to build miniature fog banks that rolled down inside the dimple and occasionally crept out. The first snow had not yet fallen, but the days were near freezing now. "You expecting anything?"

"Entropic progression is speeding up," she said instead of answering my question. "Coming up on the sixth anniversary of Nick's return."

Perhaps it was an answer.

By the time the snow started melting again in late March, the dimple was so wide and shallow it spilled onto the shores of Emerald Lake and it was developing a noticeable bulge in the middle. The water was quite warm.

The research teams had mostly disappeared over the winter. Alone again, Kelly and I had settled into a routine a lot like an old marriage – subdued acrimony, half-secrets, and mutual celibacy – so I was surprised when she came looking for me in my room in the lodge one day, with that huge smile I hadn't seen in a year.

I fell in love all over again.

"Bruce, can you help me with something?"

I tossed aside the tablet computer with the report I was writing. "Sure."

She led me down to the tree fort. In front of the trunk stood a big plastic shipping crate with rusted catches. I had never seen it before, although I recognized the chain saw and the plastic gas can next to it. There was fresh dirt clinging to the crate.

"What's this?"

"Something I buried a long time ago," Kelly said. "When I first got here."

Almost six years in the middle of nowhere together, and she starts pulling crates out of the ground? Entropic progression, my ass.

She was undoing the latches of the crate. "I need to get this up to the observatory. Do you think we can construct some kind of pulley system?"

"Okay. But what is it?"

"See for yourself," she said, throwing open the top. As I watched, she drew out a nice Celestron G-8 Schmidt-Cassegrain telescope.

"What are we waiting for?" It was cold as hell in the tree fort in the middle of the night, and Emerald Lake sounded like it was bubbling in the dark.

"April 8, 2:30 a.m." Kelly trained the flashlight on her watch. "Which is in about twenty minutes."

I stared up at the stars. "He told you something in that phone call, didn't he?"

Her nod was little more than a shifting shadow. "There was more of a mission profile than we admitted."

I didn't miss the *we*. "You were part of it all along."

Kelly turned away from the Celestron, trained on Ophiuchus, low in the southern sky this time of year. "We had contingency plans."

Mission or no mission, she was finally showing me the core of her, the part she had kept hidden all these years. "So tell me."

She sighed, one hand trailing down the barrel of the telescope. "Obviously, we couldn't test his drive in advance. Nick was pretty sure he'd get a simultaneous translation to Barnard's Star, but he couldn't predict when he'd come out. One analysis said he'd just show up, the other that he had to wait out a lightspeed lag in a state of reduced entropy. Nothing's for free in nature, right? When he didn't come back right away, I knew he was waiting out the lag."

Assuming he hadn't just croaked out there in the depths of space in the violent spray of energy with which his homebuilt starship had departed. I shook my head. "How did he make the phone call from Barnard's Star?"

She laughed, her real laugh. And then I understood – the thing out there in the lake, the dimple, the mascon – that wasn't just a symbol of a man, someone I could compete with. No, that was her dream, the dream she shared with Nick MacInnes.

"The same paired-quantum effects that allow the drive to function can be used to open an electromagnetic channel," she lectured me. "We tested that here on earth. Once he got to Barnard's, Nick used a satellite phone with a virtual antenna that could hit the orbital network he'd built years earlier in our telecomm days. It totally blows Einsteinian simultaneity."

It dawned on me how ridiculous it was that a man went to the stars and called home on a cell phone. "You can say that again."

"It's how I knew we got the math right." In the dark, a ghost of a smile. "He didn't blow up when he got there. He called, promised to come home." Kelly leaned over, handing me what appeared to be a fat manila envelope. "Here."

"What is it?"

"Schematics, mission profile, the data about the cost-effective drive none of you believed in. Just in case things don't work out."

Things don't work out? What things? Her very slow entropic progression, presumably. I squeezed the envelope, checking the thickness of the paper, then slipped it inside my shirt. "Why me? Why now? I'm the enemy."

She put her face back against the eyepiece of the telescope. "Yeah, you are the enemy. You and all your government kind. But I also know you're an honorable guy. I've been hanging out here all these years to keep someone like you from messing things up. But you turned out okay, Bruce."

I swallowed. That was more than she had ever given me before.

She went on. "You're also a survivor. If it turns out we're wrong about something important, you'll get the data to the Canadian people for us."

I had questions, dozens, hundreds of questions about the documents in the envelope, but the warm, rotten reek from the lake bothered me too much to ask them. The Canadian Rockies in April are not supposed to smell like a Louisiana summer. After years of just sitting around, it was all coming together, too fast.

"Ophiuchus. You're looking for Barnard's Star. It's about six light years, right?"

"Five point nine seven," she said without moving her head. She had her telescope where she wanted it and was staring intently. "Five years and three hundred and fifty-five days. Plus a few hours."

Emerald Lake was definitely bubbling now, like a pot on to boil. "Which is now, right?"

"Five minutes, give or take a slight margin of error."

"And you expect . . ."

Her smile gleamed at me briefly in the darkness before she turned her face back to the eyepiece. "A sign set in the heavens."

I suddenly remembered the bomb-pumped lasers. Below us, Emerald Lake was in full boil. Literally. The reeking steam was the mud bottom being cooked.

"Christ," I whispered. "You're watching for the laser light. He set off the Russian nukes, then hit his drive and came home."

"Got it. You Americans aren't all dumb after all. He'll be home a few seconds after we see the laser light."

I finally understood the slowly growing heat rise in the lake – it was energy leakage from whatever that mascon really was, some very exotic bloc of matter, a giant quark, something. Nick had been back for the last six years, wrapped in an indeterminate envelope of arrested entropy, sitting out reality in his lightspeed lag. Traveling through space and time, waiting for the equations to balance out and spit him out.

Kelly's husband was down in the bottom of the lake – literally waiting for his time to come.

The lake bottom. "He came out in hard vacuum, somewhere near Barnard's Star, right?"

"Yeah . . . cometary orbit . . ." She wasn't really listening.

"Why not come back to vacuum here?"

"Reentry," she said absently. "Added an entire layer of complexity and design requirements. Throw weight for the launch, all kinds of issues. We figured on translating straight home."

Right smack in the middle of a much, much higher density of matter than the single hydrogen atom per cubic centimeter he would have encountered out in deep space. The burst of his arrival at Barnard's would have been nothing but a light show. Back here, though . . . I was no physicist, but even I could imagine the energy gradient coming together when his wave front finally collapsed out there in the lake.

"Kelly," I said, my voice as calm as I could make it. "Nick's ship is exploding. It's been exploding for six years, very, very, very slowly – that's what the dimple has been. In three minutes, it's going to explode in real time."

"He didn't bring the nukes back." Kelly's voice was dreamy. "The ship was set to ditch them before reengaging the drive. Just in case he couldn't set them off."

"Nukes or no nukes, something is blowing up. We have to go, now."

I reviewed the escape routes, paths to higher ground versus how far we could get in my Ford Explorer parked up by the lodge. "I said no nukes," Kelly replied absently, still peering through the Celestron.

"To hell with the nukes. He's carrying too much potential energy out there, without a hard vacuum to bleed it off into!"

Agonized, I could hear the smile in her voice. "The math worked. He got there, he'll get back. I have to be here to meet him."

She had a scientist's faith in the numbers, damn her – and a lover's faith in the future. "For Christ's sake, no matter what the numbers tell you, Nick's ship is blowing up. Emerald Lake will be coming down around our heads." Was there such a thing as a quantum explosion?

"No. We modeled everything. We knew if he got there, he'd get back, and – Hey! Barnard's Star is getting brighter! I can see Nick's lasers!"

"Kelly, come on!" I broke my cardinal rule for dealing with her and tried to force the issue. Grabbing her arm, I pulled her away from the telescope, but she whirled on me. Her fist connected with my jaw.

"I'm not leaving, Bruce. You're afraid, *you* run."

And to my shame, I did. The instinct for survival won out, and I found myself scrambling down the ladder and running up the incline away from the lake and the disaster I was almost sure was about to occur. I decided against taking the extra time to find the Ford and get it started and just kept running uphill, for all the seconds left to me, leaving the woman I loved behind with her telescope and her dimple and her long-lost husband.

And then the lake exploded.

I groaned myself awake in a puddle of mud, wondering how long I had been lying there. What had once been Emerald Lake was awash with light, and I heard the chattering of a helicopter in the distance.

I had gotten far enough away. I was alive.

And Kelly almost certainly was not.

About a quarter mile away, I saw the remains of the lodge, splintered timbers rising above a sea of mud, a nightmare landscape of shadows and destruction glowing in a spotlight from above. With all that radioactive lake bottom blown everywhere, this place was a real hot zone now.

I pushed myself up, every joint screaming in protest. Coughing water out of my sinuses, or maybe blood, I turned to head back in the direction of the shore.

A pale glow in front of me turned out to be Marge, finding her way through the debris with a red-filtered flashlight. She was wearing street clothes – a knee-length skirt, for the love of God, out here. "Glad to see you survived, Bruce."

And right behind her was Ray Vittori, the project manager from the Canadian Space Agency – who had told us about the radioactivity coming from the dimple in the first place.

And Vittori was in shirtsleeves, despite all the blown mud. God damn was I an idiot. So much for the radionuclides. No wonder my Geiger counters never worked right – they'd had to rig them up back at the agency. Hell, even *I* could think of three or four ways to fake a dosimeter.

"Nice to see you again, Agent Diedrich," Vittori said. "Although the circumstances could certainly be better."

I just stared at him.

He held out his hand, but it wasn't for a shake. It was palm up, expecting something. "I'll take those documents now."

"What – ?"

Marge smiled, teeth gleaming pink in the flashlit darkness as she lit a cigarette. "Microphones, Bruce. You should know better."

Yeah, I did know better. Passive surveillance was cheap. They could have wired the entire Canadian Rockies for sound during the time I'd been hanging around here.

I looked from Marge to Vittori. Kelly had said I should give the documents to the Canadian people, but I didn't think this was what she had in mind.

"There never was any radioactive fallout." My voice sounded as dead as I felt.

Vittori shook his head. "No."

"But why?"

He shrugged, finally lowering his expectant hand. "We already had all the data we were going to get from the dimple, Diedrich. All that was left was the woman."

The woman.

Kelly MacInnes, a laughing woman who had lived and died for a dream and a long-lost husband.

"Oh, God," I said, remembering someone else who was dead.

"Sergeant Perry – ?"

Marge's expression hardened, and she took another drag on her cigarette. "Died in a hunting accident, Bruce. Headed the wrong way, you might say."

Hunting accident. Perry had been ready to say too much. I turned to her with the same question I'd asked Vittori: "Why?"

"There are plenty of people on both sides of the border who will do a lot for a working star drive."

For Nick MacInnes's plans, which we had all rejected twelve years ago. The Canadian who had made it almost all the way home from the stars.

With a sigh, I sat down on a shattered log, cruddy and mossy from the lake. Wedged behind it, I noticed a plastic gas container, the top still on.

"Can I bum a cigarette from you, Marge?"

"You quit years ago." Her voice was impatient.

"I need one now." I hugged myself, cold and wet in the dark April night. The envelope crinkled under my shirt, the one accurate record of MacInnes's cost-effective method of superluminal travel.

Marge held a lit cigarette out to me. I took it. "Thanks."

"Now smoke it and let's get going. There are some very important people waiting for you in Washington."

She turned to Vittori, whispering something I couldn't hear. Cigarette clenched between my lips, I twisted around and unscrewed the cap, pouring the liquid on the ground.

It didn't smell right – muddy lake water. The container must have cracked from the force of the blast. I threw my cigarette into it. The butt fizzled and went out.

"You ready?" Marge asked.

I nodded. Pulling the envelope out of my shirt, I handed it over to the Canadian.

Some Canadian. I couldn't fool myself into thinking that it was what Kelly had wanted.

As we walked toward the helicopter, I realized I could no longer remember the sound of her laugh.

TRICERATOPS SUMMER

Michael Swanwick

Michael Swanwick made his debut in 1980, and, in the twenty-five years that have followed, has established himself as one of SF's most prolific and consistently excellent writers at short lengths, as well as one of the premier novelists of his generation. He has won the Theodore Sturgeon Award and the *Asimov's* Readers Award poll. In 1991, his novel *Stations of the Tide* won him a Nebula Award as well, and in 1995 he won the World Fantasy Award for his story "Radio Waves." He's won the Hugo Award four times between 1999 and 2003, for his stories "The Very Pulse of the Machine," "Scherzo with Tyrannosaur," "The Dog Said Bow-Wow," and "Slow Life." His other books include the novels *In the Drift*, *Vacuum Flowers*, *The Iron Dragon's Daughter* (which was a finalist for the World Fantasy Award and the Arthur C. Clarke Award, a rare distinction!), *Jack Faust*, and, most recently, *Bones of the Earth*, as well as a novella-length book, *Griffin's Egg*. His short fiction has been assembled in *Gravity's Angels*, *A Geography of Unknown Lands*, *Slow Dancing Through Time* (a collection of his collaborative short work with other writers); *Moon Dogs*, *Puck Aleshire's Abecedary*, *Tales of Old Earth*, *Cigar-Box Faust and Other Miniatures*, and *Michael Swanwick's Field Guide to the Mesozoic Megafauna*. He's also published a collection of critical articles, *The Postmodern Archipelago*, and a book-length interview, *Being Gardner Dozois*. His most recent book is a new collection, *The Periodic Table of SF*, and he is at work on a new novel. He's had stories in our Second, Third, Fourth, Sixth, Seventh, Tenth, and Thirteenth through Twenty-first Annual Collections. Swanwick lives in Philadelphia with his wife, Marianne Porter. He has a Web site at www.michaelswanwick.com.

Here's a poignant and lyrical reaffirmation of the idea that sometimes it matters more how you spend your time than how much time you have to spend . . .

THE DINOSAURS LOOKED all wobbly in the summer heat shimmering up from the pavement. There were about thirty of them, a small herd of what appeared to be *Triceratops*. They were crossing the road – don't ask me why – so I downshifted and brought the truck to a halt, and waited.

Waited and watched.

They were interesting creatures, and surprisingly graceful for all their bulk. They picked their way delicately across the road, looking neither to the right nor the left. I was pretty sure I'd correctly identified them by now – they had those three horns on their faces. I used to be a kid. I'd owned the plastic models.

My next-door neighbor, Gretta, who was sitting in the cab next to me with her eyes closed, said, "Why aren't we moving?"

"Dinosaurs in the road," I said.

She opened her eyes.

"Son of a bitch," she said.

Then, before I could stop her, she leaned over and honked the horn, three times. Loud.

As one, every *Triceratops* in the herd froze in its tracks, and swung its head around to face the truck.

I practically fell over laughing.

"What's so goddamn funny?" Gretta wanted to know. But I could only point and shake my head helplessly, tears of laughter rolling down my cheeks.

It was the frills. They were beyond garish. They were as bright as any circus poster, with red whorls and yellow slashes and electric orange diamonds – too many shapes and colors to catalog, and each one different. They looked like Chinese kites! Like butterflies with six-foot wingspans! Like Las Vegas on acid! And then, under those carnival-bright displays, the most stupid faces imaginable, blinking and gaping like brain-damaged cows. Oh, they were funny, all right, but if you couldn't see that at a glance, you never were going to.

Gretta was getting fairly steamed. She climbed down out of the cab and slammed the door behind her. At the sound, a couple of the Triceratops pissed themselves with excitement, and the lot shied away a step or two. Then they began huddling a little closer, to see what would happen next.

Gretta hastily climbed back into the cab. "What are those bastards up to now?" she demanded irritably. She seemed to blame me for their behavior. Not that she could say so, considering she was in my truck and her BMW was still in the garage in South Burlington.

"They're curious," I said. "Just stand still. Don't move or make any noise, and after a bit they'll lose interest and wander off."

"How do you know? You ever see anything like them before?"

"No," I admitted. "But I worked on a dairy farm when I was a young fella, thirty-forty years ago, and the behavior seems similar."

In fact, the Triceratops were already getting bored and starting to wander off again when a battered old Hyundai pulled wildly up beside us, and a skinny young man with the worst-combed hair I'd seen in a long time jumped out. They decided to stay and watch.

The young man came running over to us, arms waving. I leaned out the window. "What's the problem, son?"

He was pretty upset. "There's been an accident – an *incident*, I mean. At the Institute." He was talking about the Institute for Advanced Physics, which was not all that far from here. It was government-funded and affiliated in some way I'd never been able to get straight with the University of Vermont. "The verge stabilizers failed and the meson-field inverted and vectorized. The congruence factors went to infinity and . . ." He seized control of himself. "You're not supposed to see *any* of this."

"These things are yours, then?" I said. "So you'd know. They're Triceratops, right?"

"*Triceratops horridus*," he said distractedly. I felt unreasonably pleased with myself. "For the most part. There might be a couple other species of *Triceratops* mixed in there as well. They're like ducks in that regard. They're not fussy about what company they keep."

Gretta shot out her wrist and glanced meaningfully at her watch. Like everything else she owned, it was expensive. She worked for a firm in Essex Junction that did systems analysis for companies that were considering downsizing. Her job was to find out exactly what everybody did and then tell the CEO who could be safely cut. "I'm losing money," she grumbled.

I ignored her.

"Listen," the kid said. "You've got to keep quiet about this. We can't afford to have it get out. It has to be kept a secret."

"A secret?" On the far side of the herd, three cars had drawn up and stopped. Their passengers were standing in the road, gawking. A Ford Taurus pulled up behind us, and its driver rolled down his window for a better look. "You're planning to keep a herd of dinosaurs secret? There must be dozens of these things."

"Hundreds," he said despairingly. "They were migrating. The herd broke up after it came through. This is only a fragment of it."

"Then I don't see how you're going to keep this a secret. I mean, just look at them. They're practically the size of tanks. People are bound to notice."

"My God, my God."

Somebody on the other side had a camera out and was taking pictures. I didn't point this out to the young man.

Gretta had been getting more and more impatient as the conversation proceeded. Now she climbed down out of the truck and said, "I can't afford to waste any more time here. I've got work to do."

"Well, so do I, Gretta."

She snorted derisively. "Ripping out toilets, and nailing up sheet rock! Already, I've lost more money than you earn in a week."

She stuck out her hand at the young man. "Give me your car keys."

Dazed, the kid obeyed. Gretta climbed down, got in the Hyundai, and wheeled it around. "I'll have somebody return this to the Institute later today."

Then she was gone, off to find another route around the herd.

She should have waited, because a minute later the beasts decided to leave, and in no time at all were nowhere to be seen. They'd be easy enough to find, though. They pretty much trampled everything flat in their wake.

The kid shook himself, as if coming out of a trance. "Hey," he said. "She took my *car*."

"Climb into the cab," I said. "There's a bar a ways up the road. I think you need a drink."

He said his name was Everett McCoughlan, and he clutched his glass like he would fall off the face of the Earth if he were to let go. It took a couple of whiskeys to get the full story out of him. Then I sat silent for a long time. I don't mind admitting that what he'd said made me feel a little funny. "How long?" I asked at last.

"Ten weeks, maybe three months, tops. No more."

I took a long swig of my soda water. (I've never been much of a drinker. Also, it was pretty early in the morning.) Then I told Everett that I'd be right back.

I went out to the truck, and dug the cell phone out of the glove compartment.

First I called home. Delia had already left for the bridal shop, and they didn't like her getting personal calls at work, so I left a message saying that I loved her. Then I called Green Mountain Books. It wasn't open yet, but Randy likes to come in early and he picked up the phone when he heard my voice on the machine. I asked him if he had anything on *Triceratops*. He said to hold on a minute, and then said yes, he had one copy of *The Horned Dinosaurs* by Peter Dodson. I told him I'd pick it up next time I was in town.

Then I went back in the bar. Everett had just ordered a third whiskey, but I pried it out of his hand. "You've had enough of that," I said. "Go home, take a nap. Maybe putter around in the garden."

"I don't have my car," he pointed out.

"Where do you live? I'll take you home."

"Anyway, I'm supposed to be at work. I didn't log out. And technically I'm still on probation."

"What difference does that make," I asked, "now?"

Everett had an apartment in Winooski at the Woolen Mill, so I guess the Institute paid him good money. Either that or he wasn't very smart how he spent it. After I dropped him off, I called a couple contractors I knew and arranged for them to take over what jobs I was already committed to. Then I called the *Free Press* to cancel my regular ad, and all my customers to explain I was having scheduling problems and had to subcontract their jobs. Only old Mrs. Bremmer gave me any trouble over that, and even she came around after I said that in any case I wouldn't be able to get around to her Jacuzzi until sometime late July.

Finally, I went to the bank and arranged for a second mortgage on my house.

It took me a while to convince Art Letourneau I was serious. I'd been doing business with him for a long while, and he knew how I felt about debt. Also, I was pretty evasive about what I wanted the money for. He was half-suspicious I was having some kind of late onset midlife crisis. But the deed was in my name and property values were booming locally, so in the end the deal went through.

On the way home, I stopped at a jewelry store and at the florist's.

Delia's eyes widened when she saw the flowers, and then narrowed at the size of the stone on the ring. She didn't look at all the way I'd thought she would. "This better be good," she said.

So I sat down at the kitchen table and told her the whole story. When I was done, Delia was silent for a long while, just as I'd been. Then she said, "How much time do we have?"

"Three months if we're lucky. Ten weeks in any case, Everett said."

"You believe him?"

"He seemed pretty sure of himself."

If there's one thing I am, it's a good judge of character, and Delia knew it. When Gretta moved into the rehabbed barn next door, I'd said right from the start she was going to be a difficult neighbor. And that was before she'd smothered the grass on her property under three different colors of mulch, and then complained about me keeping my pickup parked in the driveway, out in plain sight.

Delia thought seriously for a few minutes, frowning in that way she has when she's concentrating, and then she smiled. It was a wan little thing, but a smile nonetheless. "Well, I've always wished we could afford a real first-class vacation."

I was glad to hear her say so, because that was exactly the direction my own thought had been trending in. And happier than that when she flung out her arms and whooped, "I'm going to *Disney*world!"

"Hell," I said. "We've got enough money to go to Disneyworld, Disneyland, *and* Eurodisney, one after the other. I think there's one in Japan, too."

We were both laughing at this point, and then she dragged me up out of the chair, and the two of us were dancing around and round the kitchen, still a little spooked under it all, but mostly being as giddy and happy as kids.

We were going to sleep in the next morning, but old habits die hard and anyway, Delia felt she owed it to the bridal shop to give them a week's notice. So, after she'd left, I went out to see if I could find where the *Triceratops* had gone.

Only to discover Everett standing by the side of the road with his thumb out.

I pulled over. "Couldn't get somebody at the Institute to drive your car home?" I asked when we were underway again.

"It never got there," he said gloomily. "That woman who was with you the other day drove it into a ditch. Stripped the clutch and bent the frame out of shape. She said she wouldn't have had the accident if my dinosaurs hadn't gotten her upset. Then she hung up on me. I just started at this job. I don't have the savings to buy a new car."

"Lease one instead," I said. "Put it on your credit card and pay the minimum for the next two or three months."

"I hadn't thought of that."

We drove on for a while and then I asked, "How'd she manage to get in touch with you?" She'd driven off before he mentioned his name.

"She called the Institute and asked for the guy with the bad hair. They gave her my home phone number."

The parking lot for the Institute for Advanced Physics had a card system, so I let Everett off by the side of the road. "Thanks for not telling anybody," he said as he climbed out. "About . . . you know."

"It seemed wisest not to."

He started away and then turned back suddenly and asked, "Is my hair really that bad?"

"Nothing that a barber couldn't fix," I said.

I'd driven to the Institute by the main highway. Returning, I went by back ways, through farmland. When I came to where I'd seen the *Triceratops*, I thought for an instant there'd been an accident, there were so many vehicles by the side of the road. But it turned out they were mostly gawkers and television crews. So apparently the herd hadn't gone far. There were cameras up and down the road and lots of good looking young women standing in front of them with wireless microphones.

I pulled over to take a look. One *Triceratops* had come right up to the fence and was browsing on some tall weeds there. It didn't seem to have any fear of human beings, possibly because in its day mammals never got much bigger than badgers. I walked up and stroked its back, which was hard and pebbly and warm. It was the warmth that got to me. It made the experience real.

A newswoman came over with her cameraman in tow. "You certainly look happy," she said.

"Well, I always wanted to meet a real live dinosaur." I turned to face her, but I kept one hand on the critter's frill. "They're something to see, I'll tell you. Dumb as mud but lots more fun to look at."

She asked me a few questions, and I answered them as best I could. Then, after she did her wrap, she got out a notebook and took down my name and asked me what I did. I told her I was a contractor but that I used to work on a dairy farm. She seemed to like that.

I watched for a while more, and then drove over to Burlington to pick up my book. The store wasn't open yet, but Randy let me in when I knocked. "You bastard," he said after he'd locked the door behind me. "Do you have any idea how much I could have sold this for? I had a foreigner," by which I understood him to mean somebody from New York State or possibly New Hampshire, "offer me two hundred dollars for it. And I could have got more if I'd had something to dicker with!"

"I'm obliged," I said, and paid him in paper bills. He waved off the tax but kept the nickel. "Have you gone out to see 'em yet?"

"Are you nuts? There's thousands of people coming into the state to look at those things. It's going to be a madhouse out there."

"I thought the roads seemed crowded. But it wasn't as bad as all of that."

"It's early still. You just wait."

Randy was right. By evening the roads were so congested that Delia was an hour late getting home. I had a casserole in the oven and the book open on the kitchen table when she staggered in. "The males have longer, more elevated horns, where the females have shorter, more forward-directed horns," I told her. "Also, the males are bigger than the females, but the females outnumber the males by a ratio of two to one."

I leaned back in my chair with a smile. "Two to one. Imagine that."

Delia hit me. "Let me see that thing."

I handed her the book. It kind of reminded me of when we were new-married, and used to go out bird-watching. Before things got so busy. Then Delia's friend Martha called and said to turn on Channel 3 quick. We did, and there I was saying, "dumb as mud."

"So you're a cattle farmer now?" Delia said, when the spot was over.

"That's not what I told her. She got it mixed up. Hey, look what I got." I'd been to three separate travel agents that afternoon. Now I spread out the brochures: Paris, Dubai, Rome, Australia, Rio de Janeiro, Marrakech. Even Disneyworld. I'd grabbed everything that looked interesting. "Take your pick, we can be there tomorrow."

Delia looked embarrassed.

"What?" I said.

"You know that June is our busy season. All those young brides. Francesca begged me to stay on through the end of the month."

"But – "

"It's not that long," she said.

For a couple of days it was like Woodstock, the Super Bowl, and the World Series all rolled into one – the Interstates came to a standstill, and it was worth your life to actually have to go somewhere. Then the governor called in the National Guard, and they cordoned off Chittenden County so you had to show your ID to get in or out. The *Triceratops* had scattered into little groups by then. Then a dozen or two were captured and shipped out of state to zoos where they could be more easily seen. So things returned to normal, almost.

I was painting the trim on the house that next Saturday when Everett drove up in a beat-up old clunker. "I like your new haircut," I said. "Looks good. You here to see the trikes?"

"Trikes?"

"That's what they're calling your dinos. *Triceratops* is too long for common use. We got a colony of eight or nine hanging around the neighborhood." There were woods out back of the house and beyond them a little marsh. They liked to browse the margins of the wood and wallow in the mud.

"No, uh . . . I came to find out the name of that woman you were with. The one who took my car."

"Gretta Houck, you mean?"

"I guess. I've been thinking it over, and I think she really ought to pay for the repairs. I mean, right's right."

"I noticed you decided against leasing."

"It felt dishonest. This car's cheap. But it's not very good. One door is wired shut with a coat hanger."

Delia came out of the house with the picnic basket then and I introduced them. "Ev's looking for Gretta," I said.

"Well, your timing couldn't be better," Delia said. "We were just about to go out trike-watching with her. You can join us."

"Oh, I can't – "

"Don't give it a second thought. There's plenty of food." Then, to me, "I'll go fetch Gretta while you clean up."

So that's how we found ourselves following the little trail through the woods and out to the meadow on the bluff above the Tylers' farm. The trikes slept in the field there. They'd torn up the crops pretty bad. But the state was covering damages, so the Tylers didn't seem to mind. It made me wonder if the governor knew what we know. If he'd been talking with the folks at the Institute.

I spread out the blanket, and Delia got out cold cuts, deviled eggs, lemonade, all the usual stuff. I'd brought along two pairs of binoculars, which I handed out to our guests. Gretta had been pretty surly so far, which made me wonder how Delia'd browbeat her into coming along. But now she said, "Oh, look! They've got babies!"

There were three little ones, only a few feet long. Two of them were mock-fighting, head-butting and tumbling over and over each other. The third just sat in the sun, blinking. They were all as cute as the dickens, with their tiny little nubs of horns and their great big eyes.

The other trikes were wandering around, pulling up bushes and such and eating them. Except for one that stood near the babies, looking big and grumpy and protective. "Is that the mother?" Gretta asked.

"That one's male," Everett said. "You can tell by the horns." He launched into an explanation, which I didn't listen to, having read the book.

On the way back to the house, Gretta grumbled, "I suppose you want the number for my insurance company."

"I guess," Everett said.

They disappeared into her house for maybe twenty minutes and then Everett got into his clunker and drove away. Afterwards, I said to Delia, "I thought the whole point of the picnic was you and I were going to finally work out where we were going on vacation." She hadn't even brought along the travel books I'd bought her.

"I think they like each other."

"Is that what this was about? You know, you've done some damn fool things in your time – "

"Like what?" Delia said indignantly. "When have I ever done anything that was less than wisdom incarnate?"

"Well . . . you married me."

"Oh, that." She put her arms around me. "That was just the exception that proves the rule."

So, what with one thing and the other, the summer drifted by. Delia took to luring the *Triceratops* closer and closer to the house with cabbages and bunches of celery and such. Cabbages were their favorite. It got so that we were feeding the trikes off the back porch in the evenings. They'd come clomping up around sunset, hoping for cabbages but willing to settle for pretty much anything.

It ruined the yard, but so what? Delia was a little upset when they got into her garden, but I spent a day putting up a good strong fence around it, and she replanted. She made manure tea by mixing their dung with water, and its effect on the plants was bracing. The roses blossomed like never before, and in August the tomatoes came up spectacular.

I mentioned this to Dave Jenkins down at the home-and-garden and he looked thoughtful. "I believe there's a market for that," he said. "I'll buy as much of their manure as you can haul over here."

"Sorry," I told him, "I'm on vacation."

Still, I couldn't get Delia to commit to a destination. Not that I quit trying I was telling her about the Atlantis Hotel on Paradise Island one evening when suddenly she said, "Well, look at this."

I stopped reading about swimming with dolphins and the fake undersea ruined city, and joined her at the door. There was Everett's car – the new one that Gretta's insurance had paid for – parked out front of her house. There was only one light on, in the kitchen. Then that one went out, too.

We figured those two had worked through their differences.

An hour later, though, we heard doors slamming, and the screech of Everett's car pulling out too fast. Then somebody was banging on our screen door. It was Gretta. When Delia let her in, she burst out into tears, which surprised me. I wouldn't have pegged Everett as that kind of guy.

I made some coffee while Delia guided her into a kitchen chair, got her some tissues, and soothed her down enough that she could tell us why she'd thrown Everett out of her house. It wasn't anything he'd done apparently, but something he'd said.

"Do you know what he *told* me?" she sobbed.

"I think I do," Delia said.

"About timelike – "

" – loops. Yes, dear."

Gretta looked stricken. "You too? Why didn't you tell me? Why didn't you tell everybody?"

"I considered it," I said. "Only then I thought, what would folks do if they knew their actions no longer mattered? Most would behave decently enough. But a few would do some pretty bad things, I'd think. I didn't want to be responsible for that."

She was silent for a while.

"Explain to me again about timelike loops," she said at last. "Ev tried, but by then I was too upset to listen."

"Well, I'm not so sure myself. But the way he explained it to me, they're going to fix the problem by going back to the moment before the rupture occurred and preventing it from ever happening in the first place. When that happens, everything from the moment of rupture to the moment when they go back to apply the patch separates from the trunk timeline. It just sort of drifts away, and dissolves into nothingness – never was, never will be."

"And what becomes of us?"

"We just go back to whatever we were doing when the accident happened. None the worse for wear."

"But without memories."

"How can you remember something that never happened?"

"So Ev and I – "

"No, dear," Delia said gently.

"How much time do we have?"

"With a little luck, we have the rest of the summer," Delia said. "The question is, how do you want to spend it?"

"What does it matter," Gretta said bitterly. "If it's all going to end?"

"Everything ends eventually. But after all is said and done, it's what we do in the meantime that matters, isn't it?"

The conversation went on for a while more. But that was the gist of it.

Eventually, Gretta got out her cell and called Everett. She had him on speed dial, I noticed. In her most corporate voice, she said, "Get your ass over here," and snapped the phone shut without waiting for a response.

She didn't say another word until Everett's car pulled up in front of her place. Then she went out and confronted him. He put his hands on his hips. She grabbed him and kissed him. Then she took him by the hand and led him back into the house.

They didn't bother to turn on the lights.

I stared at the silent house for a little bit. Then I realized that Delia wasn't with me anymore, so I went looking for her.

She was out on the back porch. "Look," she whispered.

There was a full moon and by its light we could see the *Triceratops* settling down to sleep in our backyard. Delia had managed to lure them all the way in at last. Their skin was all silvery in the moonlight; you couldn't make out the patterns on their frills. The big trikes formed a kind of circle around the little ones. One by one, they closed their eyes and fell asleep.

Believe it or not, the big bull male snored.

It came to me then that we didn't have much time left. One morning soon we'd wake up and it would be the end of spring and everything would be exactly as it was before the dinosaurs came. "We never did get to Paris or London or Rome or Marrakech," I said sadly. "Or even Disney World."

Without taking her eyes off the sleeping trikes, Delia put an arm around my waist. "Why are you so fixated on going places?" she asked. "We had a nice time here, didn't we?"

"I just wanted to make you happy."

"Oh, you idiot. You did that decades ago."

So there we stood, in the late summer of our lives. Out of nowhere, we'd been given a vacation from our ordinary lives, and now it was almost over. A pessimist would have said that we were just waiting for oblivion. But Delia and I didn't see it that way. Life is strange. Sometimes it's hard, and other times it's painful enough to break your heart. But sometimes it's grotesque and beautiful. Sometimes it fills you with wonder, like a *Triceratops* sleeping in the moonlight.

CAMOUFLAGE

Robert Reed

Robert Reed sold his first story in 1986 and quickly established himself as a frequent contributor to *The Magazine of Fantasy & Science Fiction* and *Asimov's Science Fiction* as well as to *Science Fiction Age, Universe, New Destinies, Tomorrow, Synergy, Starlight,* and elsewhere. Reed may be one of the most prolific of today's young writers, particularly at short fiction lengths, seriously rivaled for that position only by authors such as Stephen Baxter and Brian Stableford. And – like Baxter and Stableford – he manages to keep up a very high standard of quality *while* being prolific, something that is not at all easy to do. Reed stories such as "Sister Alice," "Brother Perfect," "Decency," "Savior," "The Remoras," "Chrysalis," "Whiptail," "The Utility Man," "Marrow," "Birth Day," "Blind," "The Toad of Heaven," "Stride," "The Shape of Everything," "Guest of Honor," "Waging Good," and "Killing the Morrow," among at least a half dozen others equally as strong, count as among some of the best short work produced by anyone in the eighties and nineties. Many of his best stories were assembled in his first collection, *The Dragons of Springplace*. Nor is he nonprolific as a novelist, having turned out ten novels since the end of the eighties, including *The Leeshore, The Hormone Jungle, Black Milk, The Remarkables, Down the Bright Way, Beyond the Veil of Stars, An Exaltation of Larks, Beneath the Gated Sky, Marrow,* and *Sister Alice*. His most recent books are a chapbook novella, Mere, a new collection, *The Cuckoo's Boys,* and a new novel, *The Well of Stars*. Reed lives with his family in Lincoln, Nebraska.

Here he unravels a deadly murder mystery, set on a spaceship bigger than worlds.

I

THE HUMAN MALE had lived on the avenue for some thirty-two years. Neighbors generally regarded him as being a solitary creature, short-tempered on occasion, but never rude without cause. His dark wit was locally famous, and a withering intelligence was rumored to hide behind the brown-black eyes. Those with an appreciation of human beauty claimed that he was not particularly handsome, his face a touch asymmetrical, the skin rough and fleshy, while his thick mahogany-brown hair looked as if it was cut with a knife and his own strong hands. Yet that homeliness made him intriguing to some human females, judging by the idle chatter. He wasn't large for a human, but most considered him substantially built. Perhaps it was the way he walked, his back erect and shoulders squared while his face tilted slightly forwards, as if looking down from a great height. Some guessed he had been born on a high-gravity world, since the oldest habits never died. Or maybe this wasn't his true body, and his soul still hungered for the days when he was a giant. Endless speculations were woven about the man's past. He had a name, and everybody knew it. He had a biography, thorough and easily observed in the public records. But there were at least a dozen alternate versions of his past and left-behind troubles. He was a failed poet, or a dangerously successful poet, or a refugee who had escaped some political mess – unless he was some species of criminal, of course. One certainty was his financial security; but where his money came from was a subject of considerable debate. Inherited, some claimed. Others voted for gambling winnings or lucrative investments on now-distant colony worlds. Whatever the story, the man had the luxury of filling his days doing very little, and during his years on this obscure avenue, he had helped his neighbors with unsolicited gifts of money and sometimes more impressive flavors of aid.

Thirty-two years was not a long time. Not for the creatures that routinely traveled between the stars. Most of the ship's passengers and all of its crew were ageless souls, durable and disease-free, with enhanced minds possessing a stability and depth of memory ready to endure a million years of comfortable existence. Which was why three decades was little different than an afternoon, and why for another century or twenty, locals would still refer to their neighbor as the newcomer.

Such was life onboard the Great Ship.

There were millions of avenues like this one. Some were short enough to walk in a day, while others stretched for thousands of uninterrupted kilometers. Many avenues remained empty, dark and cold as when humans first discovered the Great Ship. But some had been awakened, made habitable to human owners or the oddest alien passengers. Whoever built the ship – presumably an ancient, long-extinct species – it had been designed to serve as home for a wide array of organisms. That much was obvious. And there was no other starship like the Great Ship: larger than most worlds and durable enough to survive eons between the galaxies, and to almost every eye, lovely.

The wealthiest citizens from thousands of worlds had surrendered fortunes for the pleasure of riding inside this fabulous machine, embarking on a half-million-year voyage to circumnavigate the galaxy.

Even the poorest passenger living in the tiniest of quarters looked on the majesty of his grand home and felt singularly blessed.

This particular avenue was almost a hundred kilometers long and barely two hundred meters across. And it was tilted. Wastewater made a shallow river that sang its way across a floor of sugar-and-pepper granite. For fifty thousand years, the river had flowed without interruption, etching out a shallow channel. Locals had built bridges at the likely places, and along the banks they erected tubs and pots filled with soils that mimicked countless worlds, giving roots and sessile feet happy places to stand. A large pot rested outside the man's front door – a vessel made of ceramic foam trimmed with polished brass and covering nearly a tenth of a hectare. When the man first arrived, he poisoned the old jungle and planted another. But he wasn't much of a gardener, apparently. The new foliage hadn't prospered, weed species and odd volunteers emerging from the ruins.

Along the pot's edge stood a ragged patch of Ilano vibra – an alien flower famous for its wild haunting songs. "I should cut that weed out of there," he would tell neighbors. "I pretty much hate the racket it's making." Yet he didn't kill them or tear out the little voice boxes. And after a decade or two of hearing his complaints, his neighbors began to understand that he secretly enjoyed their complicated, utterly alien melodies.

Most of his neighbors were sentient, fully mobile machines. Early in the voyage, a charitable foundation dedicated to finding homes and livelihoods for freed mechanical slaves leased the avenue. But over the millennia, organic species had cut their own apartments into the walls, including a janusian couple downstream, and upstream, an extended family of harum-scarums.

The human was a loner, but by no means was he a hermit.

True solitude was the easiest trick to manage. There were billions of passengers onboard, but the great bulk of the ship was full of hollow places and great caves, seas of water and ammonia and methane, as well as moon-sized tanks filled with liquid hydrogen. Most locations were empty. Wilderness was everywhere, cheap and inviting. Indeed, a brief journey by cap-car could take the man to any of six wild places – alien environments and hidden sewage conduits and a maze-like cavern that was rumored to never have been mapped. That was one advantage: At all times, he had more than one escape route. Another advantage was his neighbors. Machines were always bright in easy ways, fountains of information if you knew how to employ them, but indifferent to the subtleties of organic life, if not out and out blind.

Long ago, Pamir had lived as a hermit. That was only sensible at the time. Ship captains rarely abandoned their posts, particularly a captain of his rank and great promise.

He brought his fall upon himself, with the help of an alien.

An alien who happened to be his lover, too.

The creature was a Gaian and a refugee, and Pamir broke several rules, helping find her sanctuary deep inside the ship. But another Gaian came searching for her, and in the end, both of those very odd creatures were nearly dead. The ship was never at risk, but a significant facility was destroyed, and after making things as right as possible, Pamir vanished into the general population, waiting for the proverbial coast to clear.

Thousands of years had brought tiny changes to his status. By most accounts, the Master Captain had stopped searching for him. Two or three or four possible escapes from the ship had been recorded, each placing him on a different colony world. Or he had died in some ugly fashion. The best story put him inside a frigid little cavern. Smugglers had killed his body and sealed it into a tomb of glass, and after centuries without food or air, the body had stopped trying to heal itself. Pamir was a blind brain trapped inside a frozen carcass, and the smugglers were eventually captured and interrogated by the best in that narrow field. According to coerced testimonies, they confessed to killing the infamous captain, though the precise location of their crime was not known and would never be found.

Pamir spent another few thousand years wandering, changing homes and remaking his face and name. He had worn nearly seventy identities, each elaborate enough to be believed, yet dull enough to escape notice. For good reasons, he found it helpful to wear an air of mystery, letting neighbors invent any odd story to explain the gaps in his biography. Whatever they dreamed up, it fell far from the truth. Machines and men couldn't imagine the turns and odd blessings of his life. Yet despite all of that, Pamir remained a good captain. A sense of obligation forced him to watch after the passengers and ship. He might live on the run for the next two hundred millennia, but he would always be committed to this great machine and its precious, nearly countless inhabitants.

Now and again, he did large favors.

Like with the harum-scarums living next door. They were a bipedal species – giants by every measure – adorned with armored plates and spine-encrusted elbows and an arrogance earned by millions of years of wandering among the stars. But this particular family was politically weak, and that was a bad way to be among harum-scarums. They had troubles with an old Mother-of-fathers, and when Pamir saw what was happening, he interceded. Over the course of six months, by means both subtle and decisive, he put an end to the feud. The Mother-of-father came to her enemies' home, walking backwards as a sign of total submission; and with a plaintive voice, she begged for death, or at the very least, a forgetting of her crimes.

No one saw Pamir's hand in this business. If they had, he would have laughed it off, and moments later, he would have vanished, throwing himself into another identity in a distant avenue.

Large deeds always demanded a complete change of life.

A fresh face.

A slightly rebuilt body.

And another forgettable name.

That was how Pamir lived. And he had come to believe that it wasn't a particularly bad way to live. Fate or some other woman-deity had given him this wondrous excuse to be alert at all times, to accept nothing as it first appeared, helping those who deserved to be helped, and when the time came, remaking himself all over again.

And that time always came . . .

II

"Hello, my friend."

"Hello to you."

"And how are you this evening, my very good friend?"

Pamir was sitting beside the huge ceramic pot, listening to his Ilano vibra. Then with a dry smirk, he mentioned, "I need to void my bowels."

The machine laughed a little too enthusiastically. Its home was half a kilometer up the avenue, sharing an apartment with twenty other legally sentient AIs who had escaped together from the same long-ago world. The rubber face and bright glass eyes worked themselves into a beaming smile, while a happy voice declared, "I am learning. You cannot shock me so easily with this organic dirty talk." Then he said, "My friend," again, before using the fictitious name.

Pamir nodded, shrugged.

"It is a fine evening, is it not?"

"The best ever," he deadpanned.

Evening along this avenue was a question of the clock. The machines used the twenty-four-hour ship-cycle, but with six hours of total darkness sandwiched between eighteen hours of brilliant, undiluted light. That same minimal aesthetics had kept remodeling to a minimum. The avenue walls were raw granite, save for the little places where organic tenants had applied wood or tile facades. The ceiling was a slick arch made of medium-grade hyperfiber – a mirror-colored material wearing a thin coat of grime and lubricating oils and other residues. The lights were original, as old as the ship and laid out in the thin dazzling bands running lengthwise along the ceiling. Evening brought no softening of brilliance or reddening of color. Evening was a precise moment, and when night came . . . in another few minutes, Pamir realized . . . there would be three warning flashes, and then a perfect smothering blackness.

The machine continued to smile at him, meaning something by it. Cobalt-blue eyes were glowing, watching the human sit with the singing weeds.

"You want something," Pamir guessed.

"Much or little. How can one objectively measure one's wishes?"

"What do you want with me? Much, or little?"

"Very little."

"Define your terms," Pamir growled.

"There is a woman."

Pamir said nothing, waiting now.

"A human woman, as it happens." The face grinned, an honest delight leaking out of a mind no bigger than a fleck of sand. "She has hired me for a service. And the service is to arrange an introduction with you."

Pamir said, "An introduction," with a flat, unaffected voice. And through a string of secret nexuses, he brought his security systems up to full alert.

"She wishes to meet you."

"Why?"

"Because she finds you fascinating, of course."

"Am I?"

"Oh, yes. Everyone here believes you are most intriguing." The flexible face spread wide as the mouth grinned, never-used white teeth shining in the last light. "But then again, we are an easily fascinated lot. What is the meaning of existence? What is the purpose of death? Where does slavery end and helplessness begin? And what kind of man lives down the path from my front door? I know his name, and I know nothing."

"Who's this woman?" Pamir snapped.

The machine refused to answer him directly. "I explained to her what I knew about you. What I positively knew, and what I could surmise. And while I was speaking, it occurred to me that after all of these nanoseconds of close proximity, you and I remain strangers."

The surrounding landscape was unremarkable. Scans told Pamir that every face was known, and the nexus traffic was utterly ordinary, and when he extended his search, nothing was worth the smallest concern. Which made him uneasy. Every long look should find something suspicious.

"The woman admires you."

"Does she?"

"Without question." The false body was narrow and quite tall, dressed in a simple cream-colored robe. Four spidery arms emerged from under the folds of fabric, extending and then collapsing across the illusionary chest. "Human emotions are not my strength. But from what she says and what she does not say, I believe she has desired you for a very long time."

The Ilano vibra were falling silent now.

Night was moments away.

"All right," Pamir said. He stood, boots planting themselves on the hard pale granite. "No offense meant here. But why the hell would she hire you?"

"She is a shy lady," the machine offered. And then he laughed, deeply amused by his own joke. "No, no. She is not at all shy. In fact, she is a very important soul. Perhaps this is why she demands an intermediary."

"Important how?"

"In all ways," his neighbor professed. Then with a genuine envy, he added, "You should feel honored by her attentions."

A second array of security sensors was waiting. Pamir had never used them, and they were so deeply hidden no one could have noticed their presence. But they needed critical seconds to emerge from their slumber, and another half-second to calibrate and link together. And then, just as the first of three warning flashes rippled along the mirrored ceiling, what should have been obvious finally showed itself to him.

"You're not just my neighbor," he told the rubber face.

A second flash passed overhead. Then he saw the shielded cap-car hovering nearby, a platoon of soldiers nestled in its belly.

"Who else stands in that body?" Pamir barked.

"I shall show you," the machine replied. Then two of the arms fell away, and the other two reached up, a violent jerk peeling back the rubber mask and the grit-sized brain, plus the elaborate shielding. A face lay behind the face. It was narrow, and in a fashion lovely, and it was austere, and it was allowing itself a knife-like smile as a new voice said to this mysterious man:

"Invite me inside your home."

"Why should I?" he countered, expecting some kind of murderous threat.

But instead of threatening, Miocene said simply, "Because I would like your help. In a small matter that must remain – I will warn you – our little secret."

III

Leading an army of captains was the Master Captain, and next in command was her loyal and infamous First Chair. Miocene was the second most powerful creature in this spectacular realm. She was tough and brutal, conniving and cold. And of all the impossible crap to happen, this was the worst. Pamir watched his guest peel away the last of her elaborate disguise. The AI was propped outside, set into a diagnostic mode. The soldiers remained hidden by the new darkness and their old tricks. It was just the two of them inside the apartment, which made no sense. If Miocene knew who he was, she would have simply told her soldiers to catch him and abuse him and then drag him to the ship's brig.

So she didn't know who he was.

Maybe.

The First Chair had a sharp face and black hair allowed to go a little white, and her body was tall and lanky and ageless and absolutely poised. She wore a simple uniform, mirrored in the fashion of all captains and decorated with a minimum of epaulets. For a long moment, she stared into the depths of Pamir's home. Watching for something? No, just having a conversation through a nexus. Then she closed off every link with the outer world, and turning toward her host, she used his present name.

Pamir nodded.

She used his last name.

Again, he nodded.

And then with a question mark riding the end of it, she offered a third name.

He said, "Maybe."

"It was or wasn't you?"

"Maybe," he said again.

She seemed amused. And then, there was nothing funny about any of this. The smile tightened, the mouth nearly vanishing. "I could look farther back in time," she allowed. "Perhaps I could dig up the moment when you left your original identity behind."

"Be my guest."

"I am your guest, so you are safe." She was taller than Pamir by a long measure – an artifact of his disguise. She moved closer to the wayward captain, remarking, "Your origins don't interest me."

"Well then," he began.

And with a wink, he added, "So is it true, madam? Are you really in love with me?"

She laughed abruptly, harshly. Stepping away from him, she again regarded the apartment, this time studying its furnishings and little decorations. He had a modest home – a single room barely a hundred meters deep and twenty wide, the walls paneled with living wood and the ceiling showing the ruddy evening sky of a random world. With a calm voice, she announced, "I adore your talents, whoever you are."

"My talents?"

"With the aliens."

He said nothing.

"That mess with the harum-scarums . . . you found an elegant solution to a difficult problem. You couldn't know it at the time, but you helped the ship and my Master, and by consequence, you've earned my thanks."

"What do you wish from me tonight, madam?"

"Tonight? Nothing. But tomorrow – early in the morning, I would hope – you will please apply your talents to a small matter. A relatively simple business, we can hope. Are you familiar with the J'Jal?"

Pamir held tight to his expression, his stance. Yet he couldn't help but feel a hard kick to his heart, a well-trained paranoia screaming, "Run! Now!"

"I have some experience with that species," he allowed. "Yes, madam."

"I am glad to hear it," said Miocene.

As a fugitive, Pamir had lived among the J'Jal on two separate occasions. Obviously, the First Chair knew much more about his past. The pressing question was if she knew only about his life five faces ago, or if she had seen back sixty-three faces – perilously close to the day when he permanently removed his captain's uniform.

She knew his real identity, or she didn't.

Pamir strangled his paranoia and put on a wide grin, shoulders managing a shrug while a calm voice inquired, "And why should I do this errand for you?"

Miocene had a cold way of smirking. "My request isn't reason enough?"

He held his mouth closed.

"Your neighbors didn't ask for your aid. Yet you gave it willingly, if rather secretly." She seemed angry but not entirely surprised. Behind those black eyes, calculations were being made, and then with a pragmatic tone, she informed him, "I will not investigate your past."

"Because you already have," he countered.

"To a point," she allowed. "Maybe a little farther than I first implied. But I won't use my considerable resources any more. If you help me."

"No," he replied.

She seemed to flinch.

"I don't know you," he lied. "But madam, according to your reputation, you are a bitch's bitch."

In any given century, how many times did the First Chair hear an insult delivered to her face? Yet the tall woman absorbed the blow with poise, and then she mentioned a figure of money. "In an open account, and at your disposal," she continued. "Use the funds as you wish, and when you've finished, use some or all of the remaining wealth to vanish again. And do a better job of it this time, you should hope."

She was offering a tidy fortune.

But why would the second most powerful entity on the ship dangle such a prize before him? Pamir considered triggering hidden machines. He went as far as activating a tiny nexus, using it to bring a battery of weapons into play. With a thought, he could temporarily kill Miocene. Then he would slip out of the apartment through one of three hidden routes, and with luck, escape the pursuing soldiers. And within a day, or two at most, he would be living a new existence in some other little avenue . . . or better, living alone in one of the very solitary places where he had stockpiled supplies . . .

Once again, Miocene confessed, "This is a confidential matter."

In other words, this was not official business for the First Chair.

"More to the point," she continued, "you won't help me as much as you will come to the aid of another soul."

Pamir deactivated the weapons, for the moment.

"Who deserves my help?" he inquired.

"There is a young male you should meet," Miocene replied. "A J'Jal man, of course."

"I'm helping him?"

"I would think not," she replied with a snort.

Then through a private nexus, she fed an address to Pamir. It was in the Fall Away district – a popular home for many species, including the J'Jal.

"The alien is waiting for you at his home," she continued.

Then with her cold smirk, she added, "At this moment, he is lying on the floor of his backmost room, and he happens to be very much dead."

IV

Every portion of the Great Ship had at least one bloodless designation left behind by the initial surveys, while the inhabited places wore one or twenty more names, poetic or blunt, simple or fabulously contrived. In most cases, the typical passenger remembered none of those labels. Every avenue and cavern and little sea was remarkable in its own right, but under that crush of novelty, few were unique enough to be famous.

Fall Away was an exception.

For reasons known only to them, the ship's builders had fashioned a tube from mirrored hyperfiber and cold basalt – the great shaft beginning not far beneath the heavy armor of the ship's bow and dropping for thousands of perfectly vertical kilometers. Myriad avenues funneled down to Fall Away. Ages ago, the ship's engineers etched roads and paths in the cylinder's surface, affording views to the curious. The ship's crew built homes perched on the endless brink, and they were followed by a wide array of passengers. Millions now lived along its spectacular length. Millions more pretended to live there. There were more famous places onboard the Great Ship, and several were arguably more beautiful. But no other address afforded residents an easier snobbery. "My home is on Fall Away," they would boast. "Come enjoy my view, if you have a free month or an empty year."

Pamir ignored the view. And when he was sure nobody was watching, he slipped inside the J'Jal's apartment.

The Milky Way wasn't the largest galaxy, but it was most definitely fertile. Experts routinely guessed that three hundred million worlds had evolved their own intelligent, technologically adept life. Within that great burst of natural invention, certain patterns were obvious. Half a dozen metabolic systems were favored. The mass and composition of a home world often shoved evolution down the same inevitable pathways. Humanoids were common; human beings happened to be a young example of an ancient pattern. Harum-scarums were another, as were the Glory and the Aabacks, the Mnotis and the Striders.

But even the most inexpert inorganic eye could tell those species apart. Each humanoid arose on a different life-tree. Some were giants, others quite tiny. Some were built for enormous worlds, while others were frail little wisps. Thick pelts of fur were possible, or bright masses of downy feathers. Even among the naked mock-primates, there was an enormous range when it came to hands and faces. Elaborate bones shouted, "I am nothing like a human." While the flesh itself was full of golden blood and DNA that proved its alienness.

And then, there were the J'Jal.

They had a human walk and a very human face, particularly in the normally green eyes. They were diurnal creatures. Hunter-gatherers from a world much like the Earth, they had roamed an open savanna for millions of years, using stone implements carved with hands that at first glance, and sometimes with a second glance, looked entirely human.

But the similarities reached even deeper. The J'Jal heart beat inside a spongy double-lung, and every breath pressed against a cage of rubbery white ribs, while the ancestral blood was a salty ruddy mix of iron inside a protein similar to hemoglobin. In fact, most of their proteins had a telltale resemblance to human types, as did great portions of their original DNA.

A mutation-by-mutation convergence was a preposterous explanation.

Ten million times more likely was a common origin. The Earth and J'Jal must have once been neighbors. Ages ago, one world evolved a simple, durable microbial life. A cometary impact splashed a piece of living crust into space, and with a trillion sleeping passengers safely entombed, the wreckage drifted free of the solar system. After a few light-years of cold oblivion, the crude ark slammed into a new world's atmosphere, and at least one microbe survived, happily eating every native pre-life ensemble of hydrocarbons before conquering its new realm.

Such things often happened in the galaxy's early times. At least half a dozen other worlds shared biochemistries with the Earth. But only the J'Jal world took such a similar evolutionary pathway.

In effect, the J'Jal were distant cousins.

And for many reasons, they were poor cousins, too.

Pamir stood over the body, examining its position and condition. Spider-legged machines did the same. Reaching inside the corpse with sound and soft bursts of X-rays, the machinery arrived at a rigorous conclusion they kept to themselves. With his own eyes and instincts, their owner wished to do his best, thank you.

It could have been a human male lying dead on the floor.

The corpse was naked, on his back, legs together and his arms thrown up over his head with hands open and every finger extended. His flesh was a soft brown. His hair was short and bluish-black. The J'Jal didn't have natural beards. But the hair on the body could have been human – a thin carpet on the nippled chest that thickened around the groin.

In death, his genitals had shriveled back into the body.

No mark was visible, and Pamir guessed that if he rolled the body over, there wouldn't be a wound on the backside either. But the man was utterly dead. Sure of it, he knelt down low, gazing at the decidedly human face, flinching just a little when the narrow mouth opened and a shallow breath was drawn into the dead man's lungs.

Quietly, Pamir laughed at himself.

The machines stood still, waiting for encouragement.

"The brain's gone," he offered, using his left hand to touch the forehead, feeling the faint warmth of a hibernating metabolism. "A shaped plasma bolt, something like that. Ate through the skull and cooked his soul."

The machines rocked back and forth on long legs.

"It's slag, I bet. The brain is. And some of the body got torched too. Sure." He rose now, looking about the bedroom with a careful gaze.

A set of clothes stood nearby, waiting to dress their owner.

Pamir disabled the clothes and laid them on the ground beside the corpse. "He lost ten or twelve kilos of flesh and bone," he decided. "And he's about ten centimeters shorter than he used to be."

Death was a difficult trick to achieve with immortals. And even in this circumstance, with the brain reduced to ruined bioceramics and mindless glass, the body had persisted with life. The surviving flesh had healed itself, within limits. Emergency genetics had been unleashed, reweaving the original face and scalp and a full torso that couldn't have seemed more lifelike. But when the genes had finished, no mind was found to interface with the rejuvenated body. So the J'Jal corpse fell into a stasis, and if no one had entered this apartment, it would have remained where it was, sipping at the increasingly stale air, its lazy metabolism eating its own flesh until it was a skeleton and shriveled organs and a gaunt, deeply mummified face.

He had been a handsome man, Pamir could see.

Regardless of the species, it was an elegant, tidy face.

"What do you see?" he finally asked.

The machines spoke, in words and raw data. Pamir listened, and then he stopped listening. Again, he thought about Miocene, asking himself why the First Chair would give one little shit about this very obscure man.

"Who is he?" asked Pamir, not for the first time.

A nexus was triggered. The latest, most thorough biography was delivered. The J'Jal had been born onboard the ship, his parents wealthy enough to afford the luxury of propagation. His family's money was made on a harum-scarum world, which explained his name. Sele'ium – a play on the harum-scarum convention of naming yourself after the elements. And as these things went, Sele'ium was just a youngster, barely five hundred years old, with a life story that couldn't seem more ordinary.

Pamir stared at the corpse, unsure what good it did.

Then he forced himself to walk around the apartment. It wasn't much larger than his home, but with a pricey view making it twenty times more expensive. The furnishings could have belonged to either species. The color schemes were equally ordinary. There were a few hundred books on display – a distinctly J'Jal touch – and Pamir had a machine read each volume from cover to cover. Then he led his helpers to every corner and closet, to new rooms and back to the same old rooms again, and he inventoried every surface and each

object, including a sampling of dust. But there was little dust, so the
dead man was either exceptionally neat, or somebody had carefully
swept away every trace of their own presence, including bits of dried
skin and careless hairs.

"Now what?"

He was asking himself that question, but the machines replied, "We
do not know what is next, sir."

Again, Pamir stood over the breathing corpse.

"I'm not seeing something," he complained.

A look came over him, and he laughed at himself. Quietly. Briefly.
Then he requested a small medical probe, and the probe was inserted,
and through it he delivered a teasing charge.

The dead penis pulled itself out of the body.

"Huh," Pamir exclaimed.

Then he turned away, saying, "All right," while shaking his head.
"We're going to search again, this place and the poor shit's life. Mote by
mote and day by day, if we have to."

V

Built in the upper reaches of Fall Away, overlooking the permanent
clouds of the Little-Lot, the facility was an expansive collection of natural
caverns and minimal tunnels. Strictly speaking, the Faith of the Many
Joinings wasn't a church or holy place, though it was wrapped securely
around an ancient faith. Nor was it a commercial house, though money
and barter items were often given to its resident staff. And it wasn't a
brothel, as far as the ship's codes were concerned. Nothing sexual
happened within its walls, and no one involved in its mysteries gave his or
her body for anything as crass as income. Most passengers didn't even
realize that a place such as this existed. Among those who did, most
regarded it as an elaborate and very strange meetinghouse – like-minded
souls passed through its massive wooden door to make friends, and when
possible, fall in love. But for the purposes of taxes and law, the captains
had decided on a much less romantic designation: The facility was an
exceptionally rare thing to which an ancient human word applied.

It was a library.

On the Great Ship, normal knowledge was preserved inside laser files
and superconducting baths. Access might be restricted, but every word
and captured image was within reach of buried nexuses. Libraries were
an exception. What the books held was often unavailable anywhere
else, making them precious, and that's why they offered a kind of
privacy difficult to match, as well as an almost religious holiness to the
followers of the Faith.

"May I help you, sir?"

Pamir was standing before a set of tall shelves, arms crossed and his
face wearing a tight, furious expression. "Who are you?" he asked, not
bothering to look at the speaker.

"My name is Leon'rd."

"I've talked to others already," Pamir allowed.

"I know, sir."

"They came at me, one by one. But they weren't important enough." He turned, staring at the newcomer. "Leon'rd," he grunted. "Are you important enough to help me?"

"I hope so, sir. I do."

The J'Jal man was perhaps a little taller than Pamir. He was wearing a purplish-black robe and long blue hair secured in back as a simple horsetail. His eyes were indistinguishable from a human's green eyes. His skin was a pinkish brown. As the J'Jal preferred, his feet were bare. They could be human feet, plantigrade and narrow, with five toes and a similar architecture of bones, the long arches growing taller when the nervous toes curled up. With a slight bow, the alien remarked, "I am the ranking librarian, sir. I have been at this post for ten millennia and eighty-eight years. Sir."

Pamir had adapted his face and clothing. What the J'Jal saw was a security officer dressed in casual garb. A badge clung to his sleeve, and every roster search identified him as a man with honors and a certain clout. But his disguise reached deeper. The crossed arms flexed for a moment, hinting at lingering tensions. His new face tightened until the eyes were squinting, affecting a cop's challenging stare; and through the pinched mouth, he said, "I'm looking for somebody."

To his credit, the librarian barely flinched.

"My wife," Pamir said. "I want to know where she is."

"No."

"Pardon me?"

"I know what you desire, but I cannot comply."

As they faced each other, a giant figure stepped into the room. The harum-scarum noticed the two males facing off, and with an embarrassment rare for the species, she carefully backed out of sight.

The librarian spoke to his colleagues, using a nexus.

Every door to this chamber was quietly closed and securely locked.

"Listen," Pamir said.

Then he said nothing else.

After a few moments, the J'Jal said, "Our charter is clear. The law is defined. We offer our patrons privacy and opportunity, in that order. Without official clearance, sir, you may not enter this facility to obtain facts or insights of any type."

"I'm looking for my wife," he repeated.

"And I can appreciate your – "

"Quiet," Pamir growled, his arms unfolding, the right hand holding a small, illegal plasma torch. With a flourish, he aimed at his helpless target, and he said one last time, "I am looking for my wife."

"Don't," the librarian begged.

The weapon was pointed at the bound volumes. The smallest burst would vaporize untold pages.

"No," Leon'rd moaned, desperately trying to alert the room's weapon suppression systems. But none was responding.

Again, he said, "No."

"I love her," Pamir claimed.

"I understand."

"Do you understand love?"

Leon'rd seemed offended. "Of course I understand – "

"Or does it have to be something ugly and sick before you can appreciate, even a little bit, what it means to be in love."

The J'Jal refused to speak.

"She's vanished," Pamir muttered.

"And you think she has been here?"

"At least once, yes."

The librarian was swiftly searching for a useful strategy. A general alarm was sounding, but the doors he had locked for good reasons suddenly refused to unlock. His staff and every other helping hand might as well have been on the far side of the ship. And if the gun discharged, it would take critical seconds to fill the room with enough nitrogen to stop the fire and enough narcotics to shove a furious human to the floor.

Leon'rd had no choice. "Perhaps I can help you, yes."

Pamir showed a thin, unpleasant grin. "That's the attitude."

"If you told me your wife's name – "

"She wouldn't use it," he warned.

"Or show me a holo of her, perhaps."

The angry husband shook his head. "She's changed her appearance. At least once, maybe more times."

"Of course."

"And her gender, maybe."

The librarian absorbed that complication. He had no intention of giving this stranger what he wanted, but if they could just draw this ugly business out for long enough . . . until a platoon of security troops could swoop in and take back their colleague . . .

"Here," said Pamir, feeding him a minimal file.

"What is this?"

"Her boyfriend, from what I understand."

Leon'rd stared at the image and the attached biography. The soft green eyes had barely read the name when they grew huge – a meaningful J'Jal expression – and with a sigh much like a human sigh, he admitted, "I know this man."

"Did you?"

Slowly, the implication of those words was absorbed.

"What do you mean? Is something wrong?"

"Yeah, my wife is missing. And this murdered piece of shit is the only one who can help me find her. Besides you, that is."

Leon'rd asked for proof of the man's death.

"Proof?" Pamir laughed. "Maybe I should call my boss and tell her that I found a deceased J'Jal, and you and I can let the law do its important and loud and very public work?"

A moment later, with a silent command, the librarian put an end to the general alert. There was no problem here, he lied; and with the slightest bow, he asked, "May I trust you to keep this matter confidential, sir?"

"Do I look trustworthy?"

The J'Jal bristled but said nothing. Then he stared at shelves at the far end of the room, walking a straight line that took him to a slender volume that he withdrew and opened, elegant fingers beginning to flip through the thin plastic pages.

With a bully's abruptness, Pamir grabbed the prize. The cover was a soft wood stained blue to identify its subject as being a relative novice. The pages were plastic, thin but dense, with a running account of the dead man's progress. Over the course of the last century, the librarians had met with Sele'ium on numerous occasions, and they had recorded his uneven progress with this very difficult faith. Audio transcripts drawn from a private journal let him speak again, explaining his mind to himself and every interested party. "My species is corrupt and tiny," Sele'ium had confessed with a remarkably human voice. "Every species is tiny and foul, and only together, joined in a perfect union, can we create a worthy society – a universe genuinely united."

A few pages held holos – stark, honest images of religious devotion that most of the galaxy would look upon as abominations. Pamir barely lingered on any picture. He had a clear guess about what he was looking for, and it helped that only one of the J'Jal's wives was human.

The final pages were key. Pamir stared at the last image. Then with a low snort and a disgusted shake of the head, he announced, "This must be her."

"But it isn't," said the librarian.

"No, it's got to be," he persisted. "A man should be able to recognize his own wife. Shouldn't he?"

Leon'rd showed the barest of grins. "No. I know this woman rather well, and she is not – "

"Where's her book?" Pamir snapped.

"No," the librarian said. "Believe me, this is not somebody you know."

"Prove it."

Silence.

"What's her name?"

Leon'rd straightened, working hard to seem brave.

Then Pamir placed the plasma torch against a random shelf, allowing the tip of the barrel to heat up to where smoke rose as the red wood binding of a true believer began to smolder.

The woman's journal was stored in a different room, far deeper inside the library. Leon'rd called for it to be brought to them, and then he stood close while Pamir went through the pages, committing much of it to a memory nexus. At one point, he said, "If you'd let me just borrow these things."

The J'Jal face flushed, and a tight hateful voice replied, "If you tried to take them, you would have to kill me."

Pamir showed him a wink.

"A word for the not-so-wise?" he said. "If I were you, I wouldn't give my enemies any easy ideas."

VI

How could one species prosper, growing in reach and wealth as well as in numbers, while a second species, blessed with the same strengths, exists for a hundred times longer and still doesn't matter to the galaxy?

Scholars and bigots had deliberated that question for ages.

The J'Jal evolved on a lush warm world, blue seas wrapped around green continents, the ground fat with metal ores and hydrocarbons, and a massive moon riding across the sky, helping keep the axis tilted just enough to invite mild seasons. Perhaps that wealth had been a bad thing. Born on a poorer world, humans had evolved to live in tiny, adaptable bands of twenty or so – everyone related to everyone, by blood or by marriage. But the early J'Jals moved in troops of a hundred or more which meant a society wrapped around a more tolerant politics. Harmony was a given. Conflicts were resolved quietly, if possible; nothing was more precious to the troop than its own venerable peace. And with natural life spans reaching three centuries, change was a slow, fitful business brought on by consensus, or when absolutely necessary, by surrendering your will to the elders.

But quirks of nature are only one explanation for the future. Many great species had developed patiently. Some of the most famous, like the Ritkers and harum-scarums, were still tradition-bound creatures. Even humans had that sorry capacity: The wisdom of dead Greeks and lost Hebrews was followed long after their words had value. But the J'Jal were much more passionate about ancestors and their left-behind thoughts. For them, the past was a treasure, and their early civilizations were hide-bound and enduring machines that would remember every wrong turn and every quiet success.

After a couple hundred thousand years of flint and iron, humans stepped into space, while it took the J'Jal millions of years to contrive reasons for that kind of adventure.

That was a murderous bit of bad fortune.

The J'Jal solar system had metal-rich worlds and watery moons, and its neighbor suns were mature G-class stars where intelligence arose many times. While the J'Jal sat at home, happily memorizing the speeches of old queens, three different alien species colonized their outer worlds – ignoring galactic law and ancient conventions in the process.

Unknown to the J'Jal, great wars were being waged in their sky.

The eventual winner was a tiny creature accustomed to light gravity and the most exotic technologies. The K'Mal were cybernetic and quick-lived, subject to fads and whims and sudden convulsive changes of government. By the time the J'Jal launched their first rocket, the

K'Mal outnumbered them in their own solar system. Millions of years later, that moment in history still brought shame. The J'Jal rocket rose into a low orbit, triggering a K'Mal fleet to lift from bases on the moon's hidden face. The rocket was destroyed, and suddenly the J'Jal went from being the masters of Paradise to an obscure creature locked on the surface of one little world.

Wars were fought, and won.

Peaces held, and collapsed, and the new wars ended badly.

True slavery didn't exist for the losers, even in the worst stretches of the long Blackness. And the K'Mal weren't wicked tyrants or unthinking administrators. But a gradual decay stole away the wealth of the J'Jal world. Birthrates plunged. Citizens emigrated, forced to work in bad circumstances for a variety of alien species. Those left home lived on an increasingly poisonous landscape, operating the deep mantle mines and the enormous railguns that spat the bones of their world into someone else's space.

While humans were happily hamstringing mammoths on the plains of Asia, the J'Jal were a beaten species scattered thinly across a hundred worlds. Other species would have lost their culture, and where they survived, they might have split into dozens of distinct and utterly obscure species. But the J'Jal proved capable in one extraordinary endeavor: Against every abuse, they managed to hold tight to their shared past, beautiful and otherwise; and in small ways, and then in slow large ways, they adapted to their far flung existence.

VII

"You'll be helping another soul."

Miocene had promised that much and said little else. She knew the dead J'Jal would point him to the library, and she had to know that he was bright enough to realize it was the human woman who mattered. Why the First Chair cared about the life of an apparently unremarkable passenger, Pamir couldn't guess. Or rather, he could guess too easily, drawing up long lists of motivations, each entry reasonable, and most if not all of them ridiculously wrong.

The human was named Sorrel, and it had been Sorrel since she was born two centuries ago. Unless she was older than that, and her biography was a masterful collection of inspired lies.

Like most of the library's patrons, she made her home on Fall Away. Yet even among that wealthy company, she was blessed. Not one but two trust funds kept her economy well fed. Her rich father had emigrated to a colony world before she was born, leaving his local assets in her name. While the mother – a decorated member of the diplomatic corps – had died on the ill-fated Hakkaleen mission. In essence, Sorrel was an orphan. But by most signs, she didn't suffer too badly. For the next several decades, she had appeared happy and unremarkable, wealthy and untroubled, and nothing Pamir found said otherwise.

What was the old harum-scarum saying?

"Nothing is as massive as the universe, but nothing is half as large as a sentient, imaginative mind."

Some time ago, the young woman began to change.

Like many young adults, Sorrel took an early vow of celibacy. With a million years of life stretching before her, why hurry into sex and love, disappointment and heartbreak? She had human friends, but because of her mother's diplomatic roots, she knew quite a few aliens too. For several years, her closest companions were a janusian couple – double organisms where the male was a parasite rooted in his spouse's back. Then her circle of alien friends widened . . . which seemed perfectly normal. Pamir searched the archives of forgotten security eyes and amateur documentaries, finding glimpses of luncheons and shopping adventures in the company of other species. Oxygen breathers; the traditional human allies. Then came the luxury cruise across a string of little oceans spread through the interior of the Great Ship – a brief voyage accomplished in the midst of the circumnavigation of the Milky Way – and near the end of that tame adventure, while drifting on a dim cold smooth-as-skin methane sea, she took her first lover.

He was a J'Jal, as it happened.

Pamir saw enough on the security eyes to fill in the blanks.

Cre'llan was a spectacularly wealthy individual, and ancient, and in a Faith that cherished its privacy, he flaunted his membership and his beliefs. Elaborate surgeries had reshaped his penis to its proper form. Everyone involved in the Many Joinings endured similar cosmetic work; a uniform code applied to both genders, and where no gender existed, one was invented for them. During his long life, Cre'llan had married hundreds if not thousands of aliens, and then on that chill night he managed to seduce a young virginal human.

After the cruise, Sorrel tried to return to her old life. But three days later she visited the library, and within the week, she underwent her own physical reconfigurations.

Pamir had seen glimpses of the surgery in her journal – autodocs and J'Jal overseers hovering around a lanky pale body. And when he closed his eyes now, concentrating on the buried data reserve, he could slowly and carefully flip his way through the other pages of that elaborate but still incomplete record.

After a year as a novice, Sorrel purchased a bare rectangle of stone and hyperfiber some fifty kilometers directly beneath the library. The apartment she built was deep and elaborate, full of luxurious rooms as well as expansive chambers that could be configured to meet the needs of almost any biology. But while every environmental system was the best available, sometimes those fancy machines didn't interact well with one another, and with the right touch, they were very easy to sabotage.

"Is it a serious problem, sir?"

"Not for me," Pamir allowed. "Not for you, I'd guess. But if you depend on peroxides, like the Ooloops do, then the air is going to taste sour. And after a few breaths, you'll probably lose consciousness."

"I understand," the apartment offered.

Pamir was standing in the service hallway, wearing his normal rough face as well as the durable jersey and stiff back of a life-long technician. "I'll need to wander, if I'm going to find your trouble. Which is probably an eager filter, or a failed link of code, or a leak, or who knows what."

"Do whatever is necessary," the soft male voice replied.

"And thanks for this opportunity," Pamir added. "I appreciate new business."

"Of course, sir. And thank you."

The apartment's usual repair firm was temporarily closed due to a bureaucratic war with the Office of Environments. A search of available candidates had steered the AI towards the best candidate. Pamir was releasing a swarm of busy drones that vanished inside the walls, and he continued walking down the hallway, pausing at a tiny locked door. "What's past here?"

"A living chamber."

"For a human?"

"Yes, sir."

Pamir stepped back. "I don't need to bother anyone."

"No one will be." The lock and seal broke. "My lady demands that her home be ready for any and all visitors. Your work is a priority."

Pamir nodded, stepping through the narrow slot.

His first thought was that captains didn't live half as well as this. The room was enormous yet somehow intimate, carpeted with living furs, art treasures standing about waiting to be admired, chairs available for any kind of body, and as an added feature, at least fifty elaborate games laid out on long boards, the pieces playing against each other until there was a winner, after which they would play again. Even the air tasted of wealth, scrubbed and filtered, perfumed and pheromoned. And in that perfect atmosphere, the only sound was the quiet precise and distant singing of a certain alien flower.

Llano vibra.

Pamir looked at monitors and spoke through nexuses, and he did absolutely nothing of substance. What he wanted to accomplish was already done. By a handful of means, the apartment was now invested with hidden ears and eyes. Everything else was for his senses and to lend him more credibility.

A tall diamond wall stood on the far side of the enormous bedroom, and beyond, five hectares of patio hung over the open air. A grove of highly bred Ilano vibra was rooted in a patio pot, its music passing through a single open door. The young woman was sitting nearby, doing nothing. Pamir looked at Sorrel for a moment, and then she lifted her head to glance in his general direction. He tried to decide what he was seeing. She was clothed but barefoot. She was strikingly lovely, but in an odd fashion that he couldn't quite name. Her pale skin had a genuine glow, a capacity to swallow up the ambient light and cast it back into the world in a softer form. Her hair was silver-white and thick, with the tips suddenly turning to black. She had a smooth girlish face and a tiny nose and blue-white eyes pulled close together, and her mouth was broad and elegant and exceptionally sad.

It was the sadness that made her striking, Pamir decided.

Then he found himself near the door, staring at her, realizing that nothing was simple about her sadness or his reactions.

Sorrel glanced at him a second time.

A moment later, the apartment inquired, "Is the lady a point of technical interest, sir?"

"Sure." Pamir laughed and stepped back from the diamond wall.

"Have you found the problem? She wishes to know."

"Two problems, and yes. They're being fixed now."

"Very well. Thank you."

Pamir meant to mention his fee. Tradesmen always talked money. But there came a sound – the soft musical whine of a rope deploying – that quickly fell away into silence.

The apartment stopped speaking to him.

"What – ?" Pamir began. Then he turned and looked outside again. The woman wasn't alone anymore. A second figure had appeared, dressed like a rock climber and running across the patio towards Sorrel. He was a human or J'Jal, and apparently male. From where Pamir stood, he couldn't tell much more. But he could see the urgency in the intruder's step and a right hand that was holding what could be a weapon, and an instant later, Pamir was running too, leaping through the open door as the stranger closed on the woman.

Sorrel stared at the newcomer.

"I don't recognize his face," the apartment warned her, shouting now. "My lady – !"

The inertia vanished from her body. Sorrel leapt up and took two steps backwards before deciding to stand and fight. It was her best hope, Pamir agreed. She lifted her arms and lowered them again. She was poised if a little blank in the face, as if she was surrendering her survival to a set of deeply buried instincts.

The stranger reached for her neck with his left hand.

With a swift clean motion, she grabbed the open hand and twisted the wrist back. But the running body picked her off her feet, and both of them fell to the polished opal floor of the patio.

The man's right hand held a knife.

With a single plunge, the stranger pushed the blade into her chest, aiming for the heart. He was working with an odd precision, or perhaps by feel. He was trying to accomplish something very specific, and when she struggled, he would strike her face with the back of his free hand.

The blade dove deeper.

A small, satisfied moan leaked out of him, as if success was near, and then Pamir drove his boot into the smiling mouth.

The stranger was human, and furious.

He climbed to his feet, fending off the next three blows, and then he reached back and pulled out a small railgun that he halfway aimed, letting loose a dozen flecks of supersonic iron.

Pamir dropped, hit in the shoulder and arm.

The injured woman lay between them, bleeding and pained. The hilt of the knife stood up out of her chest, a portion of the hyperfiber blade reflecting the brilliant red of the blood.

With his good arm, Pamir grabbed the hilt and tugged.

There was a soft clatter as a Darmion crystal spilled out of her body along with the blade. This was what the thief wanted. He saw the glittering shape and couldn't resist the urge to grab at the prize. A small fortune was within reach, but then his own knife was driven clear through his forearm, and he screamed in pain and rage.

Pamir cut him twice again.

The little railgun rose up and fired once, twice, and then twice more.

Pamir's body was dying, but he still had the focus and strength to lift the man – a bullish fellow with short limbs and an infinite supply of blood, it seemed. Pamir kept slashing and pushing, and somewhere the railgun was dropped and left behind, and now the man struck him with a fist and his elbows and then tried to use his knee. Pamir grabbed the knee as it rose, borrowing its momentum as well as the last of his own strength to shove the thief against a railing of simple oak, and with a last grunt, flung him over the edge.

Only Pamir was standing there now.

Really, it was a beautiful view. With his chest ripped open and a thousand emergency genes telling his body to rest, he gazed out into the open expanse of Fall Away. Thirty kilometers across and lit by a multitude of solar-bright lights, it was a glory of engineering, and perhaps, a masterpiece of art. The countless avenues that fed into Fall Away often brought water and other liquids, and the captains' engineers had devised a system of airborne rivers – diamond tubes that carried the fluids down in a tangle of spirals and rings, little lakes gathering in pools held aloft by invisible means. And always, there were flyers moving in the air – organic and not, alive and not – and there was the deep musical buzz of a million joyous voices, and there were forests of epiphytes clinging to the wall, and there was a wet wind that hadn't ceased in sixty thousand years, and Pamir forgot why he was standing here. What was this place? Turning around, he discovered a beautiful woman with a gruesome wound in her chest telling him to sit, please. Sit. Sir, she said, please, please, you need to rest.

VIII

The Faith of the Many Joinings.

Where it arose first was a subject of some contention. Several widely scattered solar systems were viable candidates, but no single expert held the definitive evidence. Nor could one prophet or pervert take credit for this quasi-religious belief. But what some of the J'Jal believed was that every sentient soul had the same value. Bodies were facades, and metabolisms were mere details, and social systems varied in the same way that individual lives varied, according to choice and whim and a deniable sense of right. What mattered were the souls within all of these odd packages. What a wise soul wished to do was to befriend entities from different histories, and when possible, fall in love with them, linking their spirits together through the ancient pleasures of the flesh.

There was no single prophet, and the Faith had no birthplace. Which was a problem for the true believers. How could such an intricate, odd faith arise simultaneously in such widely scattered places? But what was a flaw might be a blessing, too. Plainly, divine gears were turning the universe, and this unity was just further evidence of how right and perfect their beliefs had to be. Unless the Faith was the natural outgrowth of the J'Jal's own nature: A social species is thrown across the sky, and every home belongs to more powerful species, and the entire game of becoming lovers to the greater ones is as inevitable and unremarkable as standing on their own two bare feet.

Pamir held to that ordinary opinion.

He glanced at his own bare feet for a moment, sighed and then examined his arm and shoulder and chest. The wounds had healed to where nothing was visible. Unscarred flesh had spread over the holes, while the organs inside him were quickly pulling themselves back into perfect condition. He was fit enough to sit up, but he didn't. Instead, he lay on the soft chaise set on the open-air patio, listening to the Ilano vibra. He was alone, the diamond wall to the bedroom turned black. For a moment, he thought about things that were obvious, and then he played with the subtle possibilities that sprang up from what was obvious.

The thief – a registered felon with a long history of this exact kind of work – had fallen for several kilometers before a routine security patrol noticed him, plucking him out of the sky before he could spoil anybody else's day.

The unlucky man was under arrest and would probably serve a century or two for his latest crime.

"This stinks," Pamir muttered.

"Sir?" said the apartment. "Is there a problem? Might I help?"

Pamir considered, and said, "No."

He sat up and said, "Clothes," and his technician's uniform pulled itself around him. Its fabric had healed, if not quite so thoroughly as his own body. He examined what could be a fleck of dried blood, and after a moment, he said, "Boots?"

"Under your seat, sir."

Pamir was giving his feet to his boots when she walked out through the bedroom door.

"I have to thank you," Sorrel remarked. She was tall and elegant in a shopworn way, wearing a long gray robe and no shoes. In the face, she looked pretty but sorrowful, and up close, that sadness was a deep thing reaching well past today. "For everything you did, thank you."

A marathon of tears had left her eyes red and puffy.

He stared, and she stared back. For a moment, it was as if she saw nothing. Then Sorrel seemed to grow aware of his interest, and with a shiver, she told him, "Stay as long as you wish. My home will feed you and if you want, you can take anything that interests you. As a memento . . ."

"Where's the crystal?" he interrupted.

She touched herself between her breasts. The Darmion was back home, resting beside her enduring heart. According to half a dozen species, the crystal gave its possessor a keen love of life and endless joy – a bit of mystic noise refuted by the depressed woman who was wearing it.

"I don't want your little rock," he muttered.

She didn't seem relieved or amused. With a nod, she said, "Thank you," one last time, planning to end this here.

"You need a better security net," Pamir remarked.

"Perhaps so," she admitted, without much interest.

"What's your name?"

She said, "Sorrel," and then the rest of it. Human names were long and complex and unwieldy. But she said it all, and then she looked at him in a new fashion. "What do I call you?"

He used his most recent identity.

"Are you any good with security systems?" Sorrel inquired.

"Better than most."

She nodded.

"You want me to upgrade yours?"

That amused her somehow. A little smile broke across the milky face, and for a moment, the bright pink tip of her tongue pointed at him. Then she shook her head, saying, "No, not for me," as if he should have realized as much. "I have a good friend . . . a dear old friend . . . who has some rather heavy fears . . ."

"Can he pay?"

"I will pay. Tell him it's my gift."

"So who's this worried fellow?"

She said, "Gallium," in an alien language.

Genuinely surprised, Pamir asked, "What the hell is a harum-scarum doing, admitting he's scared?"

Sorrel nodded appreciatively.

"He admits nothing," she added. Then again, she smiled . . . a warmer expression, this time. Fetching and sweet, even wonderful, and for Pamir, that expression seemed to last long after he walked out of the apartment and on to his next job.

IX

The harum-scarum was nearly three meters tall, massive and thickly armored, loud and yet oddly serene at the same time, passionate about his endless bravery and completely transparent when he told his lies. His home was close to Fall Away, tucked high inside one of the minor avenues. He was standing behind his final door – a slab of hyperfiber-braced diamond – and with a distinctly human gesture, he waved off the uninvited visitor. "I do not need any favors," he claimed, speaking through his breathing mouth. "I am as secure as anyone and twelve times more competent than you when it comes to defending myself." Then with a blatant rudeness, he allowed his eating mouth to deliver a long wet belch.

"Funny," said Pamir. "A woman wishes to buy my services, and you are Gallium, her dear old friend. Is that correct?"

"What is the woman's name?"

"Why? Didn't you hear me the first time?"

"Sorrel, you claimed." He pretended to concentrate, and then with a little too much certainty said, "I do not know this ape-woman."

"Is that so?" Pamir shook his head. "She knows you."

"She is mistaken."

"So then how did you know she was human? Since I hadn't quite mentioned that yet."

The question won a blustery look from the big black eyes. "What are you implying to me, little ape-man?"

Pamir laughed at him. "Why? Can't you figure it out for yourself?"

"Are you insulting me?"

"Sure."

That won a deep silence.

With a fist only a little larger than one of the alien's knuckles, Pamir wrapped on the diamond door. "I'm insulting you and your ancestors. There. By the ship's codes and your own painful customs, you are now free to step out here, in the open, and beat me until I am dead for a full week."

The giant shook with fury, and nothing happened. One mouth expanded, gulping down deep long breaths, while the other mouth puckered into a tiny dimple – a harum-scarum on the brink of a pure vengeful rage. But Gallium forced himself to do nothing, and when the anger finally began to diminish, he gave an inaudible signal, causing the outer two doors to drop and seal tight.

Pamir looked left and then right. The narrow avenue was well-lit and empty, and by every appearance, it was safe.

Yet the creature had been terrified.

One more time, he paged his way through Sorrel's journal. Among those husbands were two harum-scarums. No useful name had been mentioned in the journal, but it was obvious which of them was Gallium. Lying about his fear was in character for the species. But how could a confirmed practitioner of this singular faith deny that he had even met the woman?

Pamir needed to find the other husbands.

A hundred different routes lay before him. But as harum-scarums liked to say, "The shortest line stretches between points that touch."

Gallium's security system was ordinary, and it was porous, and with thousands of years of experience in these matters, it took Pamir less than a day to subvert codes and walk through the front doors.

"Who is with me?" a voice cried out from the farthest room.

In J'Jal, curiously.

Then, "Who's there?" in human.

And finally, as an afterthought, the alien screamed, "You are in my realm, and unwelcome." In his own tongue, he promised, "I will forgive you, if you run away at this moment."

"Sorrel won't let me run," Pamir replied.

The last room was a minor fortress buttressed with slabs of high-grade hyperfiber and bristling with weapons, legal and otherwise. A pair of rail-guns followed Pamir's head, ready to batter his mind if not quite kill it. Tightness built in his throat, but he managed to keep the fear out of his voice. "Is this where you live now? In a little room at the bottom of an ugly home?"

"You like to insult," the harum-scarum observed.

"It passes my time," he replied.

From behind the hyperfiber, Gallium said, "I see an illegal weapon."

"Good. Since I'm carrying one."

"If you try to harm me, I will kill you. And I will destroy your mind, and you will be no more."

"Understood," Pamir said.

Then he sat – a gesture of submission on almost every world. He sat on the quasi-crystal tiling on the floor of the bright hallway, glancing at the portraits on the nearby walls. Harum-scarums from past ages stood in defiant poses. Ancestors, presumably. Honorable men and women who could look at their cowering descendant with nothing but a fierce contempt.

After a few moments, Pamir said, "I'm pulling my weapon into plain view."

"Throw it beside my door."

The plasma gun earned a respectful silence. It slid across the floor and clattered to a stop, and then a mechanical arm unfolded, slapping a hyperfiber bowl over it, and then covering the bowl an explosive charge set to obliterate the first hand that tried to free the gun within.

The hyperfiber door lifted.

Gallium halfway filled the room beyond. He was standing in the middle of a closet jammed with supplies, staring at Pamir, the armored plates of his body flexing, exposing their sharp edges.

"You must very much need this work," he observed.

"Except I'm not doing my work," Pamir replied. "Frankly, I've sort of lost interest in the project."

Confused, the harum-scarum stood taller. "Then why have you gone to such enormous trouble?"

"What you need," Pamir mentioned, "is a small, well-charged plasma gun. That makes a superior weapon."

"They are illegal and hard to come by," argued Gallium.

"Your rail-guns are criminal, too." Just like with the front doors, there was a final door made of diamond reinforced with a meshwork of hyperfiber. "But I bet you appreciate what the shaped plasma can do to a living mind."

Silence.

"Funny," Pamir continued. "Not that long ago, I found a corpse that ran into that exact kind of tool."

The alien's back couldn't straighten anymore, and the armor plates were flexing as much as possible. With a quiet voice – an almost begging voice – Gallium asked the human, "Who was the corpse?"

"Sele'ium."

Again, silence.

"Who else has died that way?" Pamir asked. It was a guess, but not much of one. When no answer was offered, he added, "You've never been this frightened. In your long, ample life, you have never imagined that fear could eat at you this way. Am I right?"

Now the back began to collapse.

A miserable little voice said, "It just worsens."

"Why?"

The harum-scarum dipped his head for a moment.

"Why does the fear get worse and worse?"

"Seven of us now."

"Seven?"

"Lost." A human despair rode with that single word. "Eight, if you are telling the truth about the J'Jal."

"What eight?" Pamir asked.

Gallium refused to say.

"I know who you are," he continued. "Eight of Sorrel's husbands, and you. Is that right?"

"Her past husbands," the alien corrected.

"What about current lovers – ?"

"There are none."

"No?"

"She is celibate," the giant said with a deep longing. Then he dropped his gaze, adding, "When we started to die, she gave us up. Physically, and legally as well."

Gallium missed his human wife. It showed in his stance and voice and how the great hand trembled, reaching up to touch the cool pane of diamond while he added, "She is trying to save us. But she doesn't know how – "

A sudden ball of coherent plasma struck the pane just then. No larger than a human heart, it dissolved the diamond and the hand, and the grieving face, and everything that lay beyond those dark lonely eyes.

X

Pamir saw nothing but the flash, and then came a concussive blast that threw him off his feet. For an instant, he lay motionless. A cloud of atomized carbon and flesh filled the cramped hallway. He listened and heard nothing. At least for the next few moments, he was completely deaf. Keeping low, he rolled until a wall blocked his way. Then he started to breathe, scalding his lungs, and he held his breath, remaining absolutely still, waiting for a second blast to shove past.

Nothing happened.

With his mouth to the floor, Pamir managed a hot but breathable sip of air. The cloud was thinning. His hearing was returning, accompanied by a tireless high-pitched hum. A figure swam into view, tall and menacing – a harum-scarum, presumably one of the dead man's honored ancestors. He remembered that the hallway was littered with the portraits. Pamir saw a second figure, and then a third. He was trying to recall how many images there had been . . . because he could see a fourth figure now, and that seemed like one too many . . .

The plasma gun fired again. But it hadn't had time enough to build a killing charge, and the fantastic energies were wasted in a light show and a burst of blistering wind.

Again the air filled with dirt and gore.

Pamir leaped up and retreated.

Gallium was a nearly headless corpse, enormous even when mangled and stretched out on his back. The little room was made tinier with him on the floor. When their owner died, the rail-guns had dropped into their diagnostic mode, and waking them would take minutes, or days. The diamond door was shredded and useless. When the cloud fell away again, in another few moments, Pamir would be exposed and probably killed.

Like Gallium, he first used the J'Jal language.

"Hello," he called out.

The outer door was open and still intact, but its simple trigger was useless to him. It was sensitive only to pressure from a familiar hand. Staring out into the hallway, he shouted, "Hello," once again.

In the distance, a shape began to resolve itself.

"I am dead," he continued. "You have me trapped here, my friend." Nothing.

"Do what you wish, but before you cook me, I would love to know what this is about."

The shape seemed to drift one way, then back again.

Pamir jerked one of the dead arms off the floor. Then he started to position it, laying the broad palm against the wall, close to the door's trigger. But that was the easy part of this, he realized.

"You're a clever soul," he offered. "Allow a human to open the way for you. I outsmart the harum-scarum's defenses, and then you can claim both of us."

How much time before another recharge?

A few seconds, he guessed.

The corpse suddenly flinched and the arm dropped with a massive thunk.

"Shit," Pamir muttered.

On a high shelf was a plate, small but dense as metal. He took hold of it, made a few practice flings with his wrist, and then once again called out, "I wish you would tell me what this is about. Because I haven't got a clue."

Nothing.

In human, Pamir said, "Who the hell are you?"

The cloud was clearing again, revealing the outlines of a biped standing down the hallway, maybe ten meters from him.

Kneeling, Pamir again grabbed the dead arm. Emergency genes and muscle memory began to fight against him, the strength of a giant forcing him to grunt as he pushed the hand to where it was set beside the trigger. Then he threw all of his weight on the hand, forcing it to stay in place. For a moment, he panted. Then he grabbed the heavy plate with his left hand, and with a gasping voice, he said, "One last chance to explain."

The biped was beginning to aim.

"Bye-bye, then."

Pamir flipped the plate, aiming at a target barely three meters away. And in the same instant, he let the dead hand fall onto the trigger. A slab of hyperfiber slid from the ceiling, and the final door was shut. It could withstand two or three blasts from a plasma gun, but eventually it would be gnawed away. Which was why he flipped the plate onto the floor where it skipped and rolled, clipping the edge of the shaped charge of explosives that capped his own gun.

There was a sudden sharp thunder.

The door was left jammed shut by the blast. Pamir spent the next twenty minutes using a dead hand and every override to lift the door far enough to crawl underneath. But a perfectly symmetrical blast had left his own weapon where it lay, untouched beneath a bowl of mirror-bright hyperfiber.

His enemy would have been blown back up the hallway.

Killed briefly, or maybe just scared away.

Pamir lingered for a few minutes, searching the dead man's home for clues that refused to be found, and then he slipped back out into the public avenue – still vacant and safe to the eye, but possessing a palpable menace that he could now feel for himself.

XI

A ninety-second tube ride placed him beside Sorrel's front door. The apartment addressed him by the only name it knew, observing, "You are injured, sir." Performing its own rapid examination, a distinct alarm entered into an otherwise officious voice. "Do you know how badly you are injured, sir?"

"I've got a fair guess," Pamir allowed, an assortment of shrapnel still buried inside his leg and belly, giving him a rolling limp. "Where's the lady?"

"Where you left her, sir. On the patio."

Everyone was terrified, it seemed, except for her. But why should she worry? Sorrel had only been knifed by a quick-and-dirty thief, which on the scale of crimes was practically nothing.

"Have her come to her bedroom."

"Sir?"

"I'm not talking to her in the open. Tell her."

"What about her friend – ?"

"Another husband is dead."

Silence.

"Will you tell her – ?" Pamir began.

"She is already on her way, sir. As you have requested." Then after a pause, the apartment suggested, "About Gallium, please . . . I think you should deliver that sorry news . . ."

He told it.

She was dressed now in slacks and a silk blouse made by the communal spiders of the Kolochon district, and her bare feet wore black rings on every toe, and while she sat on one of the dozens of self-shaping chairs, listening to his recount of the last brutal hour, her expression managed to grow even more sad as well as increasingly detached. Sorrel made no sound, but always there was a sense that she was about to speak. The sorry and pained and very pretty face would betray a new thought, or the pale eyes would recognize something meaningful. But the mouth never quite made noise. When she finally uttered a few words, Pamir nearly forgot to listen.

"Who are you?"

Did he hear the question correctly?

Again, she asked, "Who are you?" Then she leaned forward, the blouse dipping in front. "You aren't like any environmental technician I've known, and I don't think you're a security specialist either."

"No?"

"You wouldn't have survived the fight, if you were just a fix-it man." She almost laughed, a little dimple showing high on the left cheek. "And even if you had lived, you would still be running now."

"I just want you to point me in the safest direction," he replied.

She didn't respond, watching him for what seemed like an age. Then sitting back in the deep wide chair, she asked, "Who pays you?"

"You do."

"That's not what I mean."

"But I'm not pushing too hard for my wages," he offered.

"You won't tell me who?"

"Confess a few things to me first," he replied.

She had long hands, graceful and quick. For a little while, the hands danced in her lap, and when they finally settled, she asked, "What can I tell you?"

"Everything you know about your dead husbands, and about those who just happen to be alive still." Pamir leaned forward, adding, "In particular, I want to hear about your first husband. And if you can, explain why the Faith of the Many Joinings seemed like such a reasonable idea."

XII

She had seen him earlier on the voyage and spoken with him on occasion – a tall and slender and distinguished J'Jal man with a fondness for human clothes, particularly red woolen suits and elaborately knotted white silk ties. Cre'llan seemed handsome, although not exceptionally so. He was obviously bright and engaging. Once, when their boat was exploring the luddite islands in the middle of the Gone-A-Long Sea, he asked if he might join her, sitting on the long chaise lounge beside hers. For the next little while – an hour, or perhaps the entire day – they chatted amiably about the most ordinary of things. There was gossip to share, mostly about their fellow passengers and the boat's tiny crew. There were several attempts to list the oceans that they had crossed to date, ranking them according to beauty and then history and finally by their inhabitants. Which was the most intriguing port? Which was the most ordinary? What aliens had each met for the first time? What were their first impressions? Second impressions? And if they had to live for the next thousand years in one of these little places, which would they choose?

Sorrel would have eventually forgotten the day. But a week later, she agreed to a side trip to explore Greenland.

"Do you know the island?"

"Not at all," Pamir lied.

"I never made sense of that name," Sorrel admitted, eyes narrowing as if to reexamine the entire question. "Except for some fringes of moss and the like, the climate is pure glacial. The island has to be cold, I was told. It has to do with the upwellings in the ocean and the sea's general health. Anyway, there is a warm current upwind from it, which brings the moisture, and the atmosphere is a hundred kilometers tall and braced with demon-doors. The snows are endless and fabulous, and you can't sail across the Gone-A-Long Sea without visiting Greenland once. At least that's what my friends told me."

"Was Cre'llan in your group?"

"No." Somehow that amused her. She gave a little laugh, adding, "Everybody was human, except for the guide, who was an AI with a human-facsimile body."

Pamir nodded.

"We power-skied up onto the ice during an incredibly hard snowfall. But then our guide turned to us, mentioning that it was a clear day, as they went. And we should be thankful we could see so much."

At most, they could see twenty meters in any direction. She was with a good friend – a child of the Great Ship like Sorrel, but a thousand years older. Sorrel had known the woman her entire life. They had shared endless conversations and gone to the same fine parties, and their shopping adventures had stretched on for weeks at a time. They always traveled together. And in their combined lives, nothing with real substance had occurred to either of them.

The glacier was thick and swiftly built up by the waves of falling snow. Sorrel and her companion skied away from the rest of the group, scaling a tall ridge that placed them nearly a kilometer above the invisible sea. Then the snow began to fall harder – fat wet flakes joining into snowballs that plunged from the white sky. They were skiing close together, linked by a smart-rope. Sorrel happened to be in the lead. What happened next, she couldn't say. Her first guess, and still her best guess, was that her friend thought of a little joke to play. She disabled the rope and untied herself, and where the ridge widened, she attempted to slip ahead of Sorrel, probably to scare her when she was most vulnerable.

Where the friend fell was a bit of a mystery.

Later, coming to the end of the ridge, Sorrel saw that she was alone. But she naturally assumed her companion had grown tired and gone back to rejoin the others. There wasn't cause for worry, and she didn't like worry, and so Sorrel didn't give it another thought.

But the other tourists hadn't seen her missing friend, either.

A search was launched. But the heavy snowfall turned into what can only be described as an endless avalanche from the sky. In the next hour, the glacier rose by twenty meters. By the time rescue crews could set to work, it was obvious that the missing passenger had stumbled into one of the vast crevices, and her body was dead, and without knowing her location, the only reasonable course would be to wait for the ice to push to the sea and watch for her battered remains.

In theory, a human brain could withstand that kind of abuse.

But the AI guide didn't believe in theory. "What nobody tells you is that this fucking island was once an industrial site. Why do you think the engineers covered it up? To hide their wreckage, of course. Experimental hyperfibers, mostly. Very sharp and sloppy, and the island was built with their trash, and if you put enough pressure on even the best bioceramic head, it will crack. Shatter. Pop, and die, and come out into the sea as a few handfuls of fancy sand."

Her friend was dead.

Sorrel never liked the woman more than anyone else or felt any bond unique just to the two of them. But the loss was heavy and persistent, and for the next several weeks, she thought about little else.

Meanwhile, their voyage through the Great Ship reached a new sea.

One night, while surrounded by a flat gray expanse of methane, Sorrel happened upon the J'Jal man wearing his red jacket and red slacks, and the fancy white tie beneath his nearly human face. He smiled at her, his expression genuine with either species. Then quietly, he asked, "Is something wrong?"

Nobody in her own group had noticed her pain. Unlike her, they were convinced that their friend would soon enough return from the oblivion.

Sorrel sat with the J'Jal. And for a very long while, they didn't speak. She found herself staring at his bare feet, thinking about the fragility of life. Then with a dry low voice, she admitted, "I'm scared."

"Is that so?" Cre'llan said.

"You know, at any moment, without warning, the Great Ship could collide with something enormous. At a third the speed of light, we might strike a sunless world or a small black hole, and billions would die inside this next instant."

"That may be true," her companion purred. "But I have invested my considerable faith in the talents of our captains."

"I haven't," she countered.

"No?"

"My point here . . ." She hesitated, shivering for reasons other than the cold. "My point is that I have lived for a few years, and I can't remember ever grabbing life by the throat. Do you know what I mean?"

"Very well," he claimed.

His long toes curled and then relaxed again.

"Why don't you wear shoes?" she finally asked.

And with the softest possible touch, Cre'llan laid his hand on hers. "I am an alien, Sorrel." He spoke while smiling, quietly telling her, "And it would mean so much to me if you could somehow, in your soul, forget what I am."

"We were lovers before the night was finished," she admitted. A fond look passed into a self-deprecating chuckle. "I thought all J'Jal men were shaped like he was. But they aren't, he explained. And that's when I learned about the Faith of the Many Joinings."

Pamir nodded, waiting for more.

"They did eventually find my lost friend, you know." A wise sorry laugh came out of her. "A few years later, a patrol working along the edge of the glacier kicked up some dead bones and then the skull with her mind inside. Intact." Sorrel sat back in her chair, breasts moving under the blouse. "She was reconstituted and back inside her old life within the month, and do you know what? In the decades since, I haven't spoken to my old friend more than three times.

"Funny, isn't it?"

"The Faith," Pamir prompted.

She seemed to expect the subject. With a slow shrug of the shoulders, Sorrel observed, "Whoever you are, you weren't born into comfort and wealth. That shows, I think. You've had to fight in your life . . . probably through much of your life . . . for things that any fool knows are important. While someone like me – less than a fool by a long way – walks through paradise without ever asking herself, 'What matters?' "

"The Faith," he repeated.

"Think of the challenge," she said. Staring through him, she asked, "Can you imagine how very difficult it is to be involved – romantically and emotionally linked – with another species?"

"It disgusts me," he lied.

"It disgusts a lot of us," she replied. For an instant, she wore a doubting gaze, perhaps wondering if he was telling the truth about his feelings. Then she let the doubt fall aside. "I wasn't exceptionally horrified by the idea of sex outside my species," she admitted. "Which is why I wasn't all that interested either. Somewhere in the indifferent middle, I was. But when I learned about this obscure J'Jal belief . . . how an assortment of like-minded souls had gathered, taking the first critical steps in what might well be the logical evolution of life in our universe . . ."

Her voice drifted away.

"How many husbands did you take?"

She acted surprised. "Why? Don't you know?"

Pamir let her stare at him.

Finally, she said, "Eleven."

"You are Joined to all of them."

"Until a few years ago, yes." The eyes shrank, and with the tears, they brightened. "The first death looked like a random murder. Horrible, but imaginable. But the second killing was followed a few months later by a third. The same weapon was used in each tragedy, with the same general manner of execution . . ." Her voice trailed away, the mouth left open and empty. One long hand wiped at the tears, accomplishing little but pushing moisture across the sharp cheeks. "Since the dead belonged to different species, and since the members of the Faith . . . my husbands and myself . . . are sworn to secrecy – "

"Nobody noticed the pattern," Pamir interrupted.

"Oh, I think they saw what was happening," she muttered. "After the fifth or sixth death, security people made inquiries at the library. But no one there could admit anything. And then the killings slowed, and the investigation went away. No one was offered protection, and my name was never mentioned. At least that's what I assume, since nobody was sent to interview me." Then with a quiet, angry voice, Sorrel added, "After they linked the murders to the library, they didn't care what happened."

"How do you know that?"

She stared at Pamir, regarding him as if he were a perfect idiot.

"What? Did the authorities assume this was some ugly internal business among the Joined?"

"Maybe," she said. "Or maybe they received orders telling them to stop searching."

"Who gave the orders?"

She looked at a point above his head and carefully said, "No."

"Who wouldn't want these killings stopped?"

"I don't . . ." she began. Then she shook her head, adding, "I can't. Ask all you want, but I won't tell you anything else."

He asked, "Do you consider yourself in danger?"

She sighed. "Hardly."

"Why not?"

She said nothing.

"Two husbands are left alive," Pamir reminded her.

A suspicious expression played over him. Then she admitted, "I'm guessing you know which two."

"There's the Glory." Glories were birdlike creatures, roughly human-shaped but covered with a bright and lovely plumage. "One of your more recent husbands, isn't he?"

Sorrel nodded, and then admitted, "Except he died last year. On the opposite side of the Great Ship, alone. The body was discovered only yesterday."

Pamir flinched, saying, "My condolences."

"Yes. Thank you."

"And your first lover?"

"Yes."

"The J'Jal in the red suit."

"Cre'llan, yes. I know who you mean."

"The last man standing," he mentioned.

That earned a withering stare from a pained cold face. "I don't marry lightly. And I don't care what you're thinking."

Pamir stood and walked up beside her, and with his own stare, he assured, "You don't know what I'm thinking. Because I sure as hell don't know what I've got in my own soggy head."

She dipped her eyes.

"The J'Jal," he said. "I can track him down for myself, or you can make the introductions."

"It isn't Cre'llan," she whispered.

"Then come with me," Pamir replied. "Come and look him in the eye and ask for yourself."

XIII

As a species, the J'Jal were neither wealthy nor powerful, but among them were a few individuals of enormous age who had prospered in a gradual, relentless fashion. On distant worlds, they had served as cautious traders and inconspicuous landowners and sometimes as the bearers of alien technologies; and while they would always be aliens on those places, they had adapted well enough to feel as if they were home. And then the Great Ship had arrived. Their young and arrogant human cousins promised to carry them across the galaxy – for a fee. The boldest of these wealthy J'Jal left a hundred worlds behind, spending fortunes for the honor of gathering together again. They had no world of their own, yet some hoped to eventually discover some new planet reminiscent of their cradle world – an empty world they could claim for their own. Other J'Jals believed that the Earth and its humans were the logical, even poetic goal for their species – a place where they might blend into the ranks of their highly successful relatives.

"But neither solution gives me any particular pleasure," said the gentleman wearing red. With a nearly human voice, he admitted, "The boundaries between the species are a lie and impermanent, and I hope for a radically different future."

According to his official biography, Cre'llan was approximately the same age as *Homo sapiens*.

"What's your chosen future?" Pamir inquired.

The smile was bright and a little cold. "My new friend," the J'Jal said. "I think you already have made a fair assessment of what I wish for. And more to the point, I think you couldn't care less about whatever dream or utopia I just happen to entertain."

"I have some guesses," Pamir agreed. "And you're right, I don't give a shit about your idea of paradise."

Sorrel sat beside her ancient husband, holding his hand fondly. Divorced or not, she missed his company. They looked like lovers waiting for a holo portrait to be taken. Quietly, she warned Cre'llan, "He suspects you, darling."

"Of course he does."

"But I told him . . . I explained . . . you can't be responsible for any of this . . ."

"Which is the truth," the J'Jal replied, his smile turning into a grim little sneer. "Why would I murder anyone? How could it possibly serve my needs?"

The J'Jal's home was near the bottom of Fall Away, and it was enormous. This single room covered nearly a square kilometer, carpeted with green woods broken up with quick little streams, the ceiling so high that a dozen tame star-rocs could circle above and never brush wings. But all of that grandeur and wealth was dwarfed by the outside view: The braided rivers that ran down the middle of Fall Away had been set free some fifty kilometers above their heads, every diamond tube ending at the same point, their contents exploding out under extraordinary pressure. A flow equal to ten Amazons roared past Cre'llan's home, water and ammonia mixing with a spectacular array of chemical wastes and dying phytoplankton. Aggressive compounds battered their heads together and reacted, bleeding colors in the process. Shapes appeared inside the wild foam, and vanished again. A creative eye could see every face that he had ever met, and he could spend days watching for the faces that he had worn during his own long, strange life.

The window only seemed to be a window. In reality, Pamir was staring at a sheet of high-grade hyperfiber, thick and very nearly impervious to any force nature could throw at it. The view was a projection, a convincing trick. Nodding, he admitted, "You must feel remarkably safe, I would think."

"I sleep quite well," Cre'llan replied.

"Most of the time, I can help people with their security matters. But not you." Pamir was entirely honest, remarking, "I don't think the Master Captain has as much security in place. That hyperfiber. The AI watchdogs. Those blood-and-meat hounds that sniffed our butts on the way in." He showed a wide smile, and then mentioned, "If I'm not mistaken, you'd never have to leave this one room. For the next ten thousand years, you could sit where you're sitting today and eat what falls off these trees, and no one would have to touch you."

"If that was what I wished, yes."

"But he is not the killer," Sorrel muttered.

Then she stood and stepped away from the ancient creature, her hand grudgingly releasing his grip. She approached Pamir, kneeling before him. Suddenly she looked very young, serious and determined. "I know this man," she implored. "You have no idea what you're suggesting, if you think that he could hurt anyone . . . for any reason . . ."

"I once lived as a J'Jal," Pamir allowed.

Sorrel leaned away from him, taken by surprise.

"I dyed my hair blue and tinkered with these bones, and I even doctored my genetics, far enough to pass half-assed scans." Pamir gave no specifics, but he understood he was telling too much. Nonetheless, he didn't feel as if he had any choice. "I even kept a J'Jal lover. For a while, I did. But then she saw through my disguise, and I had to steal away in the middle of the night."

The other two watched him now, bewildered and deeply curious.

"Anyway," he continued. "During my stay with the J'Jal, a certain young woman came of age. She was very desirable. Extraordinarily beautiful, and her family was one of the wealthiest onboard the ship. Before that year was finished, the woman had acquired three devoted husbands. But someone else fell in love with her, and he didn't want to share. One of the new husbands was killed. After that, the other husbands went to the public hall and divorced her. They never spoke to the girl again. She was left unattached, and alone. What rational soul would risk her love under those circumstances?" Pamir shook his head while studying Cre'llan. "As I said, I slipped away in the night. And then several decades later, an elder J'Jal proposed to the widow. She was lonely, and he was not a bad man. Not wealthy, but powerful and ancient, and in some measure, wise. So she accepted his offer, and when nothing tragic happened to her new husband, not only did everyone understand who had ordered the killing. They accepted it, too. In pure J'Jal fashion."

With a flat, untroubled voice, Cre'llan said, "My soul has never been thought of as jealous."

"But I'm now accusing you of jealousy," Pamir countered.

Silence.

"Conflicts over females is ordinary business for some species," he continued. "Monopolizing a valuable mate can be a good evolutionary strategy, for the J'Jal as well as others, too. And tens of millions of years of civilization hasn't changed what you are, or what you can be."

Cre'llan snorted, declaring, "That old barbarism is something I would never embrace."

"Agreed."

The green gaze narrowed. "Excuse me, sir. I don't think I understand. What exactly are you accusing me of?"

"This is a beautiful, enormous fortress," Pamir continued. "And as you claim, you're not a jealous creature. But did you invite these other husbands to live with you? Did you offer even one of them your shelter and all of this expensive security?"

Sorrel glanced at the J'Jal, her breath catching for an instant.

"You didn't offer," Pamir continued, "because of a very reasonable fear: What if one of your houseguests wanted Sorrel for himself?"

An old tension rippled between the lovers.

"Every other husband was a suspect, in your mind. With those two harum-scarums being the most obvious candidates." He looked at Sorrel again. "Gallium would be his favorite – a relatively poor entity born into a biology of posturing and violence. His species is famous for stealing mates. Both sexes do it, every day. But now Gallium is dead, which leaves your husband with no one to worry about, it seems."

"But I am not the killer," Cre'llan repeated.

"Oh, I agree," Pamir said. "You are innocent, yes."

The statement seemed to anger both of them. Sorrel spoke first, asking, "When did you come to that conclusion?"

"Once I learned who your husbands were," Pamir replied. "Pretty much instantly." Then he sat forward in his chair, staring out at the churning waters. "No, Cre'llan isn't the murderer."

"You understand my nature?" the J'Jal asked.

"Maybe, but that doesn't particularly matter." Pamir laughed. "No," he said. "You're too smart and far too old to attempt this sort of bullshit with a human woman. Talk all you want about every species being one and the same. But the hard sharp damning fact is that human beings are not J'Jal. Very few of us, under even the most difficult circumstances, are going to look past the fact that their spouse is a brutal killer."

Cre'llan gave a little nod, the barest smile showing.

Sorrel stood, nervous hands clenching into fists. She looked vulnerable and sweet and very sorry. The beginnings of recognition showed in the blue-white eyes, and she started to stare at the J'Jal, catching herself now and forcing her eyes to drop.

"And something else was obvious," Pamir mentioned. "Pretty much from the beginning, I should think."

With a dry little voice, Cre'llan asked, "What was obvious?"

"From the beginning," Pamir repeated.

"What do you mean?" Sorrel asked.

"Okay," Pamir said, watching her face and the nervous fists. "Let's suppose that I'm killing your husbands. I want my rivals dead, and I want a reasonable chance of surviving to the end. Of course, I would start with Cre'llan. Since he enjoys the most security . . . better than everyone else combined, probably . . . I would hit him before he could smell any danger . . ."

That earned a cold silence.

Pamir shook his head. "The killer wants the husbands out of your life. From the start, I think he knew exactly what was required. The other ten husbands had to be murdered, since they loved you deeply and you seemed to love them. But this J'Jal . . . well, he's a different conundrum entirely, I'm guessing . . ."

Cre'llan appeared interested but distant. When he breathed, it was after a long breathless pause, and he sounded a little weak when he said, "I don't know what you are talking about."

"You told me," Pamir said to Sorrel.

"What did I – ?"

"How you met him during the cruise. And what happened to you and your good friend just before you went to bed with this alien man – "

"I don't understand," she muttered.

Cre'llan snapped, "Be quiet."

Pamir felt a pleasant nervousness in his belly. "Cre'llan wanted you, I'm guessing. He wanted you badly. You were a wealthy, unattached human woman – the J'Jal adore our species – and you would bring him a fair amount of status. But to seduce you . . . well, he needed help. Which is why he paid your friend to vanish on the ice in Greenland, faking her own death . . .

"He wanted to expose you emotionally, with a dose of mortality – "

"Stop that," she told him.

Cre'llan said, "Idiot," and little more.

"The AI guide was right," Pamir told her. "The chances of a mind surviving the weight of that ice and the grinding against the hyperfiber shards . . . well, I found it remarkable to learn that your good friend was found alive.

"So I made a few inquiries.

"I can show you, if you wish. A trail of camouflaged funds leads from your friend back to a company formed just hours before her death. The mysterious company made a single transfer of funds, declared bankruptcy and then dissolved. Your friend was the recipient. She was reborn as a very wealthy soul, and the principal stockholder in that short-lived company happened to have been someone with whom your first lover and husband does quite a lot of business."

Sorrel sat motionless. Her mouth closed and opened, in slow motion, and then it began to close again. Her legs tried to find the strength to carry her away, but she looked about for another moment or two, finding no door or hatchway to slip through in the next little while. She was caught, trapped by things awful and true. And then, just as Pamir thought that she would crack into pieces, the young woman surprised him.

Calmly, she told Cre'llan, "I divorce you."

"Darling – ?" he began.

"Forever," she said. And then she pulled from a pocket what seemed like an ordinary knife. Which it was. A sapphire blade no longer than her hand was unfolded, and it took her ten seconds to cut the Darmion crystal out of her chest – ripped free for the second time in as many days – and then before she collapsed, she flung the gory gift at the stunned and sorry face.

XIV

Pamir explained what had happened as he carried her into her apartment. Then he set her on a great round bed, pillows offering themselves to her head while a small autodoc spider-walked its way across the pale blue sheets, studying her half-healed wound, then with more penetrating eyes, carefully examining the rest of her body.

Quietly, the apartment offered, "I have never known her to be this way."

In his long life, Pamir had rarely seen any person as depressed, as forlorn. Sorrel was pale and motionless, lying on her back, and even with her eyes open, something in her gaze was profoundly blind. She saw nothing, heard nothing. She was like a person flung off the topmost portion of Fall Away, tumbling out of control, gusts of wind occasionally slamming her against the hard walls, battering a soul that couldn't feel the abuse anymore.

"I am worried," the apartment confessed.

"Reasonable," Pamir replied.

"It must be a horrid thing, losing everyone who loves you."

"But someone still loves her," he countered. Then he paused, thinking hard about everything again.

"Tell me," he said. "What is your species-strain?"

"Is that important?"

"Probably not," said Pamir.

The AI described its pedigree, in brief.

"What's your lot number?"

"I do not see how that matters."

"Never mind," he said, walking away from their patient. "I already know enough as it is."

Pamir ate a small meal and drank some sweet alien nectar that left him feeling a little sloppy. When the head cleared, he slept for a minute or an hour, and then he returned to the bedroom and the giant bed. Sorrel was where he had left her. Her eyes were closed now, empty hands across her belly, rising and falling and rising with a slow steady rhythm that he couldn't stop watching.

"Thank you."

The voice didn't seem to belong to anyone. The young woman's mouth happened to be open, but it didn't sound like the voice he expected. It was sturdy and calm, the old sadness wiped away. It was a quiet polite and rather sweet voice that told him, "Thank you," and then added, "For everything, sir."

The eyes hadn't opened.

She had heard Pamir approach, or felt his presence.

He sat on the bed beside her, and after a long moment said, "You know. You'd be entitled to consider me – whoever I am – as being your main suspect. I could have killed the husbands. And I certainly put an end to you and Cre'llan."

"It isn't you."

"Because you have another suspect in mind. Isn't that it?"

She said nothing.

"Who do you believe is responsible?" he pressed.

Finally, the eyes pulled open, slowly, and they blinked twice, tears pooling but never quite reaching the point where they would flow.

"My father," she said.

"He killed your husbands?"

"Obviously."

"He's light-years behind us now."

Silence.

Pamir nodded, and after a moment, he asked, "What do you know about your father?"

"Quite a lot," she claimed.

"But you've never seen him," he reminded her.

"I have studied him." She shook her head and closed her eyes again. "I've examined his biography as well as I can, and I think I know him pretty well."

"He isn't here, Sorrel."

"No?"

"He emigrated before you were even born."

"That's what my mother told me, yes."

"What else?" Pamir leaned closer, adding, "What did she tell you about the man . . . ?"

"He is strong and self-assured. That he knows what is right and best. And he loves me very much, but he couldn't stay with me." Sorrel chewed on her lip for a moment. "He couldn't stay here, but my father has agents and ways, and I would never be without him. Mother promised me."

Pamir just nodded.

"My father doesn't approve of the Faith."

"I can believe that," he said.

"My mother admitted, once or twice . . . that she loved him very much, but he doesn't have a diplomat's ease with aliens. And his heart can be hard, and he has a capacity to do awful things, if he sees the need . . ."

"No," Pamir whispered.

The pale blue eyes opened. "What do you mean?"

"Your father didn't do any of this," he promised. Then he thought again, saying, "Well, maybe a piece of it."

"What do you mean – ?"

Pamir set his hand on top of her mouth, lightly. Then as he began to pull his hand back, she took hold of his wrist and forearm, easing the palm back down against lips that pulled apart, teeth giving him a tiny swift bite.

A J'Jal gesture, that was.

He bent down and kissed the open eyes.

Sorrel told him, "You shouldn't."

"Probably not."

"If the murderer knows you are with me – "

He placed two fingers deep into her mouth, J'Jal fashion. And she sucked on them, not trying to speak now, eyes almost smiling as Pamir calmly and smoothly slid into bed beside her.

XV

One of the plunging rivers pulled close to the wall, revealing what it carried. Inside the diamond tube was a school of finned creatures, not pseudofish nor pseudowhales, but instead a collection of teardrop-shaped machines that probably fused hydrogen in their hearts, producing the necessary power to hold their bodies steady inside a current that looked relentless, rapid and chaotic, turbulent and exceptionally unappealing.

Pamir watched the swimming machines for a moment, deciding that this was rather how he had lived for ages now.

With a shrug and a soft laugh, he continued the long walk up the path, moving past a collection of modest apartments. The library was just a few meters farther along – a tiny portal carved into the smooth black basaltic wall. Its significance was so well hidden that a thousand sightseers passed this point every day, perhaps pausing at the edge of the precipice to look down, but more likely continuing on their walk, searching richer views. Pamir turned his eyes toward the closed doorway, pretending a mild curiosity. Then he stood beside the simple wall that bordered the outer edge of the trail, hands on the chill stone, eyes gazing down at the dreamy shape of the Little-Lot.

The massive cloud was the color of butter and nearly as dense. A trillion trillion microbes thrived inside its aerogel matrix, supporting an ecosystem that would never touch a solid surface.

The library door swung open – J'Jal wood riding on creaky iron hinges.

Pamir opened a nexus and triggered an old, nearly forgotten captain's channel. Then he turned towards the creaking sound and smiled. Sorrel was emerging from the library, dressed in a novice's blue robe and blinking against the sudden glare. The massive door fell shut again, and quietly, she said to him, "All right."

Pamir held a finger to his closed mouth.

She stepped closer and through a nexus told him, "I did what you told me."

"Show it."

She produced the slender blue book.

"Put it on the ground here."

This was her personal journal – the only volume she was allowed to remove from the library. She set it in front of her sandaled feet, and then asked, "Was I noticed, do you think?"

"I promise. You were seen."

"And do we just wait now?"

He shook his head. "No, no. I'm far too impatient for that kind of game."

The plasma gun was barely awake when he fired it, turning plastic pages and the wood binding into a thin cloud of superheated ash.

Sorrel put her arms around herself, squeezing hard.

"Now we wait," he advised.

Not for the first time, she admitted, "I don't understand. Still. Who do you think is responsible?"

Again, the heavy door swung open.

Without looking, Pamir called out, "Hello, Leon'rd."

The J'Jal librarian wore the same purplish-black robe and blue ponytail, and his expression hadn't changed in the last few days – a bilious outrage focused on those who would injure his helpless dependents. He stared at the ruins of the book, and then he glared at the two humans, focusing on the male face until a vague recognition tickled.

"Do I know you?" he began.

Pamir was wearing the same face he had worn for the last thirty-two years. A trace of a smile was showing, except around the dark eyes. Quietly, fiercely, he said, "I found my wife, and thanks for the help."

Leon'rd stared at Sorrel, his face working its way through a tangle of wild emotions. "Your wife?" he sputtered.

Then he tipped his head, saying, "No, she is not."

"You know that?" Pamir asked.

The J'Jal didn't respond.

"What do you know, Leon'rd?"

For an instant, Leon'rd glanced back across a shoulder – not at the library door but at the nearby apartments. The man was at his limits. He seemed frail and tentative, hands pressing at the front of his robe while the long toes curled under his bare feet. Everything was apparent. Transparent. Obvious. And into this near-panic, Pamir said, "I know what you did."

"No," the J'Jal replied, without confidence.

"You learned something," Pamir continued. "You are a determined scholar and a talented student of other species, and some years ago, by design or by dumb luck, you unraveled something. Something that was supposed to be a deep, impenetrable secret."

"No."

"A secret about my wife," he said.

Sorrel blinked, asking, "What is it?"

Pamir laughed harshly. "Tell her," he advised.

The blood had drained out of Leon'rd's face.

"No, I agree," Pamir continued. "Let's keep this between you and me, shall we? Because she doesn't have any idea, either – "

"About what?" the woman cried out.

"She is not your wife," the librarian snapped.

"The hell she isn't." He laughed. "Check the public records. Two hours ago, in a civil ceremony overseen by two Hyree monks, we were made woman and male-implement in a legally binding manner – "

"What do you know about me?" Sorrel pressed.

Pamir ignored her. Staring at the J'Jal, he said, "But somebody else knows what we do. Doesn't he? Because you told him. In passing, you said a few words. Perhaps. Unless of course you were the one who devised this simple, brutal plan, and he is simply your accomplice."

"No!" Leon'rd screamed. "I did not dream anything."

"I might believe you." Pamir glanced at Sorrel, showing a tiny wink. "When I showed him an image of one of your dead husbands, his reaction wasn't quite right. I saw surprise, but the J'Jal eyes betrayed a little bit of pleasure, too. Or relief, was it? Leon'rd? Were you genuinely thrilled to believe that Sele'ium was dead and out of your proverbial hair?"

The librarian looked pale and cold, arms clasped tight against his shivering body. Again, he glanced at the nearby apartments. His mouth opened and then pulled itself closed, and then Pamir said, "Death."

"What did you say?" Leon'rd asked.

"There are countless wonderful and inventive ways to fake your own death," Pamir allowed. "But one of my favorites is to clone your body and cook an empty, soulless brain, and then stuff that brain inside that living body, mimicking a very specific kind of demise."

"Sele'ium?" said Sorrel.

"What I think." Pamir was guessing, but none of the leaps were long or unlikely. "I think your previous husband was a shrewd young man. He grew up in a family that had lived among the harum-scarums. That's where his lineage came from, wasn't it, Leon'rd? So it was perfectly natural, even inevitable, that he could entertain thoughts about killing the competition, including his own identity . . ."

"Tell me what you know," Sorrel begged.

"Almost nothing," Pamir assured. "Leon'rd is the one who is carrying all the dark secrets on his back. Ask him."

The J'Jal covered his face with his hands. "Go away," he whimpered.

"Was Sele'ium a good friend of yours and you were trying to help? Or did he bribe you for this useful information?" Pamir nodded, adding, "Whatever happened, you pointed him toward Sorrel, and you must have explained, 'She is perhaps the most desirable mate on the Great Ship – ' "

A sizzling blue bolt of plasma struck his face, melting it and obliterating everything beyond.

The headless body wobbled for a moment and then slumped and

dropped slowly, settling against the black wall, and Leon'rd leaped backwards, while Sorrel stood over the remains of her newest husband, her expression tight but calm – like the face of a sailor who has already ridden through countless storms.

XVI

Sele'ium looked like a pedestrian wandering past, his gaze distracted and his manner a little nervous. He seemed embarrassed by the drama that he had happened upon. He looked human. The cold blond hair and purplish-black skin were common on high-UV worlds, while the brown eyes were as ordinary as could be. He wore sandals and trousers and a loose-fitting shirt, and he stared at the destroyed body, seeing precisely what he expected to see. Then he glanced at Sorrel, and with a mixture of warmth and pure menace, he said, "You do not know . . . you cannot . . . how much I love you . . ."

She recoiled in horror.

He started to speak again, to explain himself.

"Get away!" she snapped. "Leave me alone!"

His reaction was to shake his head with his mouth open – a J'Jal refusal – and then he calmly informed her, "I am an exceptionally patient individual."

Which wrung a laugh out of her, bitter and thin.

"Not today, no," he conceded. "And not for a thousand years, perhaps. But I will approach you with a new face and name – every so often, I will come to you – and there will be an hour and a certain heart-beat when you come to understand that we belong to one another – "

The corpse kicked at the empty air.

Sele'ium glanced at what he had done, mildly perturbed by the distraction. Then slowly, he realized that the corpse was shrinking, as if it were a balloon slowly losing its breath. How odd. He stared at the mysterious phenomenon, not quite able to piece together what should have been obvious. The headless ruin twitched hard and then harder, one shrinking leg flinging high. And then from blackened wound rose a puff of blue smoke, and with it, the stink of burnt rubber and cooked hydraulics.

With his left hand, Sele'ium yanked the plasma gun from inside his shirt – a commercial model meant to be used as a tool, but with its safeties cut away – and he turned in a quick circle, searching for a valid target.

"What is it?" Leon'rd called out.

"Do you see him – ?"

"Who?"

The young J'Jal was more puzzled than worried. He refused to let himself panic, his mind quickly ticking off the possible answers, settling on what would be easiest and best.

In the open air, of course.

"Just leave us," Leon'rd begged. "I will not stand by any longer!"

Sele'ium threw five little bolts into the basalt wall, punching out holes and making a rain of white-hot magma.

Somewhere below, a voice howled.

Sorrel ran to the wall and looked down, and Sele'ium crept beside her, the gun in both hands, its reactor pumping energies into a tiny chamber, readying a blast that would obliterate everything in its path.

He started to peer over, and then thought better of it.

One hand released the weapon and the arm wrapped around Sorrel's waist, and when she flung her elbow into his midsection, he bent low. He grunted and cursed softly and then told her, "No."

With his full weight, he drove the woman against the smooth black wall, and together, his face on her left shoulder, they bent and peered over the edge.

Pamir grabbed the plasma gun, yanking hard.

And Sorrel made herself jump.

Those two motions combined to lift her and Sele'ium off the path, over the edge and plummeting down. Pamir's gecko-grip was ripped loose from the basalt, and he was falling with them, one hand on the gun, clinging desperately, while the other arm began to swing, throwing its fist into the killer's belly and ribs. Within moments, they were falling as fast as possible. A damp singing wind blew past them, and the wall was a black smear to one side, and the rest of Fall Away was enormous and distant and almost changeless. The airborne rivers and a thousand flying machines were out of reach and useless. The three of them fell and fell, and sometimes a voice would pass through the roaring wind – a spectator standing on the path, remarking in alarm, "Who were they?" Three bodies, clinging and kicking. Sele'ium punished Pamir with his own free hand, and then he let himself be pulled closer, and with a mouth that wasn't more than a few days old, he bit down on a wrist, hard, trying to force the stranger to release his hold on the plasma gun.

Pamir cried out and let go.

But as Sele'ium aimed at his face, for his soul, Pamir slammed at the man's forearm and pushed it backwards again, and he put a hard knee into the elbow, and a weapon that didn't have safeties released its stored energies, a thin blinding beam that coalesced inside the dying man's head, his brain turning to light and ash, a supersonic crack leaving the others temporarily deafened.

Pamir kicked the corpse away and clung to Sorrel, and she held tight to him, and after another few minutes, as they plunged toward the yellow depths of a living, thriving cloud, he shouted into her better ear, explaining a thing or two.

XVII

Again, it was nearly nightfall.

Once again, Pamir sat outside his apartment, listening to the wild songs of the Ilano vibra. Nothing looked out of the ordinary. Neighbors strolled past or ran past or flew by on gossamer wings. The janusian couple paused long enough to ask where he had been these last days, and Pamir said a few murky words about taking care of family troubles. The harum-scarum family was outside their apartment, gathered around a cooking pit, eating a living passion ox in celebration of another day successfully crossed. A collection of machines stopped to ask about the facsimile that they had built for Pamir, as a favor. Did it serve its intended role? "Oh, sure," he said with a nod. "Everybody was pretty much fooled, at least until the joke was finished."

"Was there laughter?" asked one machine.

"Constant, breathless laughter," Pamir swore. And then he said nothing else about it.

A single figure was approaching. He had been watching her for the last kilometer, and as the machines wandered away, he used three different means to study her gait and face and manner. Then he considered his options, and he decided to remain sitting where he was, his back against the huge ceramic pot and his legs stretched out before him, one bare foot crossed over the other.

She stopped a few steps short, watching him but saying nothing.

"You're thinking," Pamir told her. "Throw me into the brig, or throw me off the ship entirely. That's what you're thinking now."

"But we had an agreement," Miocene countered. "You were supposed to help somebody, and you have, and you most definitely have earned your payment as well as my thanks."

"Yeah," he said, "but I know you. And you're asking yourself, 'Why not get rid of him and be done with it?' "

The First Chair was wearing a passenger's clothes and a face slightly disguised, eyes blue and the matching hair curled into countless tight knots, the cheeks and mouth widened but nothing about the present smile any warmer than any other smile that had ever come from this hard, hard creature.

"You know me," she muttered.

A moment later, she asked, "Will you tell me who you are?"

"Don't you know yet?"

She shook her head, and with a hint of genuine honesty, she admitted, "Nor do I particularly care, one way or the other."

Pamir grinned and leaned back a little more.

"I suppose I could place you in custody," Miocene continued. "But a man with your skills and obvious luck . . . well, you probably have twelve different ways to escape from our detention centers. And if I sent you falling onto a colony world or an alien world . . . I suppose in another thousand years or so, you would find your way back again, like a dog or an ugly habit."

"Fair points," he admitted.

Then with a serious, warm voice, he asked, "How is Sorrel?"

"That young woman? As I understand it, she has put her apartment up for sale, and she has already moved away. I'm not sure where – "

"Bullshit," he interrupted.

Miocene grinned, just for a moment. "Perhaps I do have an idea or two. About who you might be . . ."

"She knows now."

The woman's face seemed to narrow, and the eyes grew larger and less secure. "Knows what?" she managed.

"Who her father is," said Pamir. "Her true father, I mean."

"One man's conjecture," the First Chair reminded him. Then with a dismissive shake of the head, she added, "A young woman in a gullible moment might believe you. But she won't find any corroboration, not for the next thousand years . . . and eventually, she will have to believe what she has always believed . . ."

"Maybe."

Miocene shrugged. "It's hardly your concern now. Is it?"

"Perhaps it isn't," he allowed. Then as the overhead lights flickered for the first time, he sat up straighter. "The thief was your idea, wasn't he? The one who came to steal away the Darmion crystal?"

"And why would I arrange such a thing?"

"What happened afterwards was exactly what you were hoping for," he said. "An apparently random crime leaves Sorrel trusting me, and the two of us emotionally linked to each other."

With a narrow grin, Miocene admitted, "But I was wrong in one way."

"Were you?"

"I assumed that the killer, whoever he was, would likely put an end to you. Exposing himself in the process, of course."

A second ripple of darkness passed along the avenue. Pamir showed her a stern face, and quietly, he said, "Madam First Chair. You have always been a remarkable and wondrously awful bitch."

"I didn't know it was Sele'ium," she admitted.

"And you didn't know why he was killing the husbands, either." Pamir stood up now, slowly. "Because the old librarian, Leon'rd, pieced together who Sorrel was. He told Sele'ium what he had learned, and he mentioned that Sorrel's father was a woman, and as it happens, that woman is the second most important person onboard the Great Ship."

"There are some flaws in the public records, yes." She nodded, adding, "These are problems that I'm taking care of now."

"Good," he said.

Miocene narrowed her gaze. "And yes, I am a difficult soul. The bitch queen, and so on. But what I do in my life is enormous and very complicated, and for a multitude of good reasons, it is best if my daughter remains apart from my life and from me."

"Maybe so," he allowed.

"Look at these last few days. Do you need more reasons than this?" she asked. Then she took a step closer, adding, "But you are wrong, in one critical matter. Whoever you are."

"Wrong where?"

"You assume I wanted you to be killed, and that's wrong. It was a possibility and a risk. But as a good captain, I had to consider the possibility and make contingency plans, just in case." She took another little step, saying, "No, what all of this has been . . . in addition to everything else that it seems to have been . . . is what I have to call an audition."

"An audition?" Pamir muttered, genuinely puzzled.

"You seem to be a master at disappearing," Miocene admitted. Then she took one last step, and in a whisper, she said, "There may come a day when I cannot protect my daughter anymore, and she'll need to vanish in some profound and eternal fashion . . ."

A third ripple of darkness came, followed by the full seamless black of night.

"That's your task, if you wish to take it," she said, speaking into the darkness. "Whoever you happen to be . . . are you there, can you hear me . . . ?"

XVIII

Sorrel had been walking for weeks, crossing the Indigo Desert one step at a time. She traveled alone with her supplies in a floating pack tied to her waist. It was ten years later, or ten thousand. She had some trouble remembering how much time had passed, which was a good thing. She felt better in most ways, and the old pains had become familiar enough to be ignored. She was even happy, after a fashion. And while she strolled upon the fierce landscape of fire-blasted stone and purple succulents, she would sing, sometimes human songs and occasionally tunes that were much harder to manage and infinitely more beautiful.

One afternoon, she heard notes answering her notes.

Coming over the crest of a sharp ridge, she saw something utterly unexpected – a thick luxurious stand of irrigated Ilano vibra.

Louder now, the vegetation sang to her.

She started to approach.

In the midst of the foliage, a shape was sitting. A human shape, perhaps. Male, by the looks of it. Sitting with his back to her, his face totally obscured by the shaggy black hair. Yet he seemed rather familiar, for some reason. Familiar in the best ways, and Sorrel stepped faster now, and smiled, and with a parched voice, she tried to sing in time with the alien weed.

A CASE OF CONSILIENCE

Ken MacLeod

Ken MacLeod graduated with a B.S. in zoology from Glasgow University in 1976. Following research work in biomechanics at Brunel University, he worked as a computer analyst/programmer in Edinburgh. He's now a full-time writer, and widely considered to be one of the most exciting new SF writers to emerge in the nineties. His first two novels, *The Star Fraction* and *The Stone Canal*, each won the Prometheus Award. His other books include the novels *The Sky Road*, *The Cassini Division*, *Cosmonaut Keep*, *Dark Light*, *Engine City*, and *Newton's Wake*, plus a novella chapbook, *The Human Front*. His work has appeared in our Nineteenth Annual Collection. His most recent book is a novel, *Learning the World*. Coming up is the collection *Strange Lizards* from *Another Galaxy*. He lives in West Lothian, Scotland, with his wife and children.

In the sly story that follows, he shows us that sometimes the much-anticipated and desired first contact with aliens might not turn out exactly the way you *expected* it to . . .

W HEN YOU SAY IT'S Providence that brought you here," said Qasim, "what I hear are two things: it's bad luck, and it's not your fault."

The Rev. Donald MacIntyre, M.A. (Div.), Ph.D., put down his beer can and nodded.

"That's how it sometimes feels," he said. "Easy for you to say, of course."

Qasim snorted. "Easy for anybody! Even a Muslim would have less difficulty here. Let alone a Buddhist or Hindu."

"Do tell," said Donald. "No, what's really galling is that there are millions of *Christians* who would take all this in their stride. Anglicans. Liberals. Catholics. Mormons, for all I know. And my brethren in the, ah, narrower denominations could come up with a dozen different rationalizations before breakfast, all of them heretical did they but know it – which they don't, thank the Lord and their rigid little minds, so their lapses are no doubt forgiven through their sheer ignorance. So it's given to me to wrestle with. Thus a work of Providence. I think."

"I still don't understand what your problem is, compared to these other Christians."

Donald sighed. "It's a bit hard to explain," he said. "Let's put it this way. You were brought up not to believe in God, but I expect you had quite strong views about the God you didn't believe in. Am I right?"

Qasim nodded. "Of course. Allah was always . . ." He shrugged. "Part of the background. The default."

"Exactly. Now, how did you feel when you first learned about what Christians believe about the Son of God?"

"It was a long time ago," said Qasim. "I was about eight or nine. In school in Kirkuk. One of my classmates told me, in the course of . . . well, I am sorry to say in the course of a fight. I shall pass over the details. Enough to say I was quite shocked. It seemed preposterous and offensive. And then I laughed at myself!"

"I can laugh at myself too," said Donald. "But I feel the same way as you did – in my case at the suggestion that the Son was not unique, that He took on other forms, and so forth. I can hardly even say such things. I literally shudder. But I can't accept, either, that He has no meaning beyond Earth. So what are we to make of rational beings who are not men, and who may be sinners?"

"Perhaps they are left outside," said Qasim. "Like most people are, if I understand your doctrines."

Donald flinched. "That's not what they say, and in any case, such a question is not for me to decide. I'm perplexed."

He leaned back in the seat and stared gloomily at the empty can, and then at the amused, sympathetic eyes of the friendly scoffer to whom he had found he could open up more than to the believers on the Station.

Qasim stood up. "Well, thank God I'm an atheist, that's all I can say."

He had said it often enough.

"God and Bush," said Donald. This taunt, too, was not on its first outing. Attributing to the late ex-President the escalating decades-long cascade of unintended consequences that had annexed Iraq to the EU and Iran to China was probably unfair, but less so than blaming it on God. Qasim raised a mocking index finger in response.

"God and Bush! And what are you having, Donald?"

"Can of Export."

"Narrow it down, padre. They're all export here."

"Aren't we all," said Donald. "Tennent's, then. And a shot of single malt on the side, if you don't mind. Whatever's going."

As Qasim made his way through the crowd to the bar, Donald reflected that his friend was likely no more off-duty than he was. A chaplain and an intelligence officer could both relax in identical olive T-shirts and chinos, but vigilance and habit were less readily shrugged off than dress-codes. The Kurdish colonel still now and again called his service the *mukhabarat*. It was one of his running gags, along with the one about

electronics and electrodes. And the one about extra-terrestrial intelligence. And the one about . . . yes, for running gags Qasim was your man.

As I am for gloomy reflections, Donald thought. Sadness, *tristia*, had
been one of the original seven deadly sins. Which probably meant every
Scottish Presbyterian went straight to hell, or at least to a very damp
purgatory, if the Catholics were right. If the Catholics were right! After
three hundred and seventeen days in the Extra-Terrestrial Contact
Station, this was among the least heretical of the thoughts Donald
MacIntyre was willing to countenance.

Qasim came back with the passing cure, and lasting bane, of the
Scottish sin; and with what might have been a more dependably
cheering mood-lifter: a gripe about his own problems. Problems which,
as Donald listened to them, seemed more and more to resemble his own.

"How am I supposed to tell if an underground fungoid a hundred
metres across that communicates by chemical gradients is feeding us
false information? Or if an operating system written by an ET AI is a
trojan? Brussels still expects files on all of them, when we don't even
know how many civs we're dealing with. Bloody hell, Donald, pardon
my English, there's one of the buggers we only suspect is out there
because everyone comes back from its alleged home planet with weird
dreams." Qasim cocked a black eyebrow. "Maybe I shouldn't be telling
you that one."

"I've heard about the dreams," said Donald. "In a different context."
He sighed. "It's a bit hard to explain to some people that I don't take
confession."

"Confessions are not to be relied upon," Qasim said, looking
somewhere else. "Anyway . . . what I would have to confess, myself, is
that the Etcetera Station is a bit out of its depth. We are applying
concepts outside their context."

"Now *that*," said Donald with some bitterness, "is a suspicion I do
my best to resist."

It was one the Church had always resisted, a temptation dangled in
different forms down the ages. As soon as the faith had settled on its
view of one challenge, another had come along. In the Carpenter's
workshop there were many clue-sticks, and the whacks had seldom
ceased for long. In the beginning, right there in the Letters, you could
see the struggle against heresies spawned by Greek metaphysics and
Roman mysticism. Barely had the books snapped shut on Arius when
Rome had crashed. Then the Muslim invasions. The split between the
Eastern and Western churches, Christendom cloven on a lemma. Then
the discovery of the New World, and a new understanding of the
scope and grip of the great, ancient religions of the Old. The
Reformation. The racialist heresy. The age of the Earth. Biblical criti-
cism. Darwin. The twentieth century had brought the expanding
universe, the gene, the unconscious – how quaint the controversies
over these now seemed! Genetic engineering, human-animal chimerae,
artificial intelligence: in Donald's own lifetime he'd seen Synods,
Assemblies and Curia debate them and come to a Christian near-

consensus acceptable to all but the lunatic – no, he must be charitable – the fundamentalist fringe.

And then, once more, just when the dust had settled, along had come – predictable as a planet, unpredicted like a comet – another orb in God's great orrery of education, or shell in the Adversary's arsenal of error-mongery, the greatest challenge of all – alien intelligent life. It was not one that had been altogether unexpected. Scholastics had debated the plurality of worlds. The Anglican C. S. Lewis had considered it in science fiction; the agnostic Blish had treated it with a literally Jesuitical subtlety. The Christian poet Alice Meynell had speculated on alien gospels; the godless ranter MacDiarmid had hymned the Innumerable Christ. In the controversies over the new great discovery, all these literary precedents had been resurrected and dissected. They pained Donald to the quick. Well-intended, pious, sincere in their seeking they might be; or sceptical and satirical; it mattered not: they were all mockeries. There had been only one Incarnation; only one sufficient sacrifice. If the Reformation had meant anything at all, it meant that. To his ancestors Donald might have seemed heinously pliant in far too much, but like them he was not to be moved from the rock. In the matter of theological science fiction he preferred the honest warning of the secular humanist Harrison. *Tell it not in Gath, publish it not in the streets of Ashkelon . . .*

Donald left the messroom after his next round and walked to his quarters. The corridor's topology was as weird as anything on the Etc Station. A human-built space habitat parked inside an alien-built wormhole nexus could hardly be otherwise. The station's spin didn't dislodge the wormhole mouths, which remained attached to the same points on the outside of the hull. As a side-effect, the corridor's concave curve felt and looked convex. At the near ends of stubby branch corridors, small groups of scientists and technicians toiled on their night-shift tasks. At the far ends, a few metres away, thick glass plates with embedded airlocks looked out on to planetary surfaces and sub-surfaces, ocean depths, tropospheric layers, habitat interiors, virtual reality interfaces, and apparently vacant spaces backdropped with distant starfields. About the last, it was an open question whether the putatively present alien minds were invisible inhabitants of the adjacent vacuum, or more disturbingly, some vast process going on in and among the stars themselves. The number of portals was uncountable. There were never more than about five hundred, but the total changed with every count. As the station had been designed and built with exactly three hundred interface corridors, this variability was not comfortable to contemplate. But that the station's structure itself had somehow become imbricated with the space-time tangle outside it had become an accepted – if not precisely an acknowledged – fact. It received a back-handed recognition in the station's nickname: the Etcetra Station.

Use of that monicker, like much else, was censored out of messages home. The Station was an EU military outpost, and little more than its existence, out beyond the orbit of Neptune, had been revealed. Donald MacIntyre, in his second year of military service as a conscript chaplain, had been as surprised to find himself here as his new parishioners were to discover his affiliation. His number had come up in the random allocation of clergy from the list of religions recognized by the EU Act of Toleration – the one that had banned Scientology, the Unification Church, the Wahabi sect and, by some drafting or translation error, Unitarian Universalism – but to a minister of the Church of Scotland, there could in all conscience be no such thing as chance.

He had been sent here for a purpose.

"The man in black thinks he's on a mission from God," said Qasim.

"What?" Major Bernstein looked up from her interface, blinking.

"Here." Qasim tapped the desktop, transferring a file from his finger.

"What's this?"

"His private notes."

The major frowned. She didn't like Qasim. She didn't like spying on the troops. She didn't care who knew it. Qasim knew all this. So did Brussels. She didn't know that.

"What are your grounds?" she asked.

"He spoke a little wildly in the mess last night."

"Heaven help us all, in that case," said the Major.

Qasim said nothing.

"All right." Bernstein tabbed through the notes, skimming to the first passage Qasim had highlighted.

"'Worst first,'" she read out. "'The undetectable entities. No coherent communication. (Worst case: try exorcism???!) Next: colonial organisms. Mycoidal. Translations speculative. Molecular grammar. Query their concept of personhood. Also of responsibility. If this can be established: rational nature. Fallen nature. If they have a moral code that they do not live up to? Any existing religious concepts? Next: discrete animalia. Opposite danger here: anthropomorphism. (Cf. Dominican AI mission fiasco.) Conclusion: use mycoids as test case to establish consilience.'" She blinked the script away, and stared at Qasim. "Well? What's the harm in that?"

"He's been hanging around the team working on the mycoids. If you read on, you'll find he intends to preach Christianity to them."

"To the scientists?"

"To the mycoids."

"Oh!" Major Bernstein laughed. It was a sound that began and ended abruptly, like a fall of broken glass, and felt as cutting. "If he can get any message through to them, he'll be doing better than the scientists. And unless you, my overzealous *mukhabaratchik*, can find any evidence that Dr MacIntyre is sowing religious division in the ranks, practising rituals involving animal cruelty or non-consensual sexual acts, preaching

Market Maoism or New Republicanism or otherwise aiding and
abetting the Chinks or the Yanks, I warn you most seriously to not
waste your time or mine. Do I make myself quite clear?"

"Entirely, ma'am."

"Dismissed."

I do not what I wish I did.

It was a lot to read into a sequence of successive concentrations of
different organic molecules. In the raw transcript it went like this:

Titration	Translation
Indication-marker	THIS
Impulse-summation	MYCOID
Action (general)	DOES
Negation-marker	NOT
Impulse-direction	ACT
Affirmation-marker	[AS] INTENDED [BY]
Impulse-summation	[THIS] MYCOID
Repulsion-marker	[AND THIS] DISGUST[S]
Impulse-summation	[THIS] MYCOID

Donald looked at the print-out and trembled. It was hard not to see it
as the first evidence of an alien that knew sin. He well realized, of
course, that it could just as well mean something as innocent as *I
couldn't help but puke*. But the temptation, if it was a temptation, to
read it as an instance of the spirit warring against the flesh – well,
against the slime – was almost irresistible. Donald couldn't help but
regard it as a case of consilience, and as no coincidence.

"Is there any way we can respond to this?"

Trepper, the mycoid project team leader, shook his head. "It's very
difficult to reproduce the gradients. For us, it's as if . . . Look, suppose a
tree could understand human speech. It tries to respond by growing
some twigs and branches so that they rub against each other just so, in
the wind. And all we hear are some funny scratching and creaking
sounds."

Trees in the wind. Donald gazed past the tables and equipment of the
corridor's field lab to the portal that opened on to the mycoids' planet.
The view showed a few standing trees, and a lot of fallen logs. The
mycoids did something to force the trees' growth and weaken their
structure, giving the vast underground mycoid colonies plenty of rotting
cellulose to feed on. Far in the distance, across a plain of coppery grass,
rose a copse of quite different trees, tall and stately with tapered bulges
from the roots to halfway up the trunks. Vane-like projections of stiff
leaves sprouted from their sides. Bare branches bristled at their tops.
These were the Niven Pines, able to synthesize and store megalitres of
volatile and flammable hydrocarbons. At every lightning storm one or
other of these trees – the spark carried by some kind of liquid lightning

conductor to a drip of fuel-sap at its foot – would roar into flame and rise skyward. Some of them would make it to orbit. No doubt they bore mycoid travellers, but what these clammy astronauts did in space, and whether this improbable arboreal rocketry was the result of natural selection, or of conscious genetic manipulation by the mycoids – or indeed some other alien – was as yet unclear.

In any case, it had been enough to bring the mycoids a place at the table of whatever Galactic Club had set up the wormhole nexus. Perhaps they too had found a wormhole nexus on the edge of their solar system. Perhaps they too had puzzled over the alien intelligences it connected them to. If so, they showed little sign of having learned much. They pulsed their electrophoretically controlled molecular gradients into the soil near the Station's portal, but much of it – even assuming the translations were correct – was about strictly parochial matters. It was as if they weren't interested in communicating with the humans.

Donald determined to make them interested. Besides his pastoral duties – social as well as spiritual – he had an allotted time for scholarship and study, and he devoted that time to the work of the mycoid research team. He did not explain his purpose to the scientists. If the mycoids were sinners, he had an obligation to offer them the chance of salvation. He had no obligation to offer the scientists the temptation to scoff.

Time passed.

The airlock door slammed. Donald stepped through the portal and on to the surface. He walked forward along an already-beaten track across the floor of the copse. Here and there, mushroom-like structures poked up through the spongy, bluish moss and black leaf-litter. The bulges of their inch-wide caps had a watery transparency that irresistibly suggested that they were the lenses of eyes. No one had as yet dared to pluck a fungus to find out.

A glistening patch of damp mud lay a couple of hundred metres from the station. It occupied a space between the perimeters of two of the underground mycoids, and had become a preferred site for mycolinguistic research. Rainbow ripples of chemical communication between the two sprawling circular beings below stained its surface at regular intervals. Occasional rainstorms washed away the gradients, but they always seeped out again.

Donald stepped up to the edge of the mud and set up the apparatus that the team had devised for a non-intrusive examination of the mycoids' messages: a wide-angle combined digital field microscope and spectroscope. About two metres long, its support frame straddled the patch, above which its camera slowly tracked along. Treading carefully, he planted one trestle, then the other on the far side of the patch, then walked back and laid the tracking rail across them both. He switched on the power pack and the camera began its slow traverse.

There was a small experiment he had been given to perform. It had been done many times before, to no effect. Perhaps this variant would be different. He reached in to his thigh pocket and pulled out a plastic-covered gel disc, about five centimetres across, made from synthesized copies of local mucopolysaccharides. The concentric circles of molecular concentrations that covered it spelled out – the team had hoped – the message: *We wish to communicate. Please respond.*

Donald peeled off the bottom cover and, one knee on a rock and one hand on a fallen log, leaned out over the multicoloured mud and laid the gel disc down on a bare dark patch near the middle. He withdrew his hand, peeling back the top cover as he did so, and settled back on his haunches. He stuffed the crumpled wrappings in his pocket and reached in deeper for a second disc: one he'd covertly prepared himself, with a different message.

Resisting the impulse to look over his shoulder, he repeated the operation and stood up.

A voice sounded in his helmet: "Got you!"

Qasim stood a few metres away, glaring at him.

"I beg your pardon," said Donald. "I've done nothing wrong."

"You've placed an unauthorized message on the mud," said Qasim.

"What if I have?" said Donald. "It can do no harm."

"That's not for you to judge," said Qasim.

"Nor for you either!"

"It is," said Qasim. "We don't want anything . . . ideological or controversial to affect our contact." He looked around. "Come on, Donald, be a sensible chap. There's still time to pick the thing up again. No harm done and no more will be said."

It had been like this, Donald thought, ever since the East India Company: commercial and military interests using and then restricting missionaries.

"I will not do that," he said. "I'll go back with you, but I won't destroy the message."

"Then I'll have to do it," said Qasim. "Please step aside."

Donald stayed where he was. Qasim stepped forward and caught his shoulder. "I'm sorry," he said.

Donald pulled away, and took an involuntary step back. One foot came down in the mud and kept on going down. His leg went in up to the knee. Flailing, he toppled on his back across the tracking rail. The rail cracked in two under the blow from his oxygen tanks. He landed with a huge splash. Both pieces of the rail sank out of sight at once. Donald himself lay, knees crooked, his visor barely above the surface.

"Quicksand," said Qasim, his voice cutting across the alarmed babble from the watching science team. "Don't try to stand or struggle, it'll just make things worse. Lie back with your arms out and stay there. I'll get a rope."

"Okay," said Donald. He peered up through his smeared visor. "Don't be long."

Qasim waved. "Back in seconds, Donald. Hang in there."

The science team talked Donald through the next minute, as Qasim ran for the portal, stepped into the airlock, and grabbed the rope that had already been placed there.

"Okay, Donald, he's just – "

The voice stopped. Static hiss filled the speaker. Donald waited.

"Can anyone hear me?"

No reply.

Five more minutes passed. Nobody was coming. He would have to get himself out. There was no need to panic. He had five hours's worth of air supply, and no interruption to the portals had ever lasted more than an hour.

Donald swept his arms through the mud to his side, raised them above the mud, flung them out again, and repeated this laborious backstroke many times, until his helmet rested on solid ground. It had taken him half an hour to move a couple of metres. He rested for a few minutes, gasping, then reached behind him and scrabbled for something to hold. Digging his fingers into the soil, kicking now with his feet – still deep in the mud – he began to lever himself up and heave his shoulders out of the bog. He got as much as the upper quarter of his body out when the ground turned to liquid under his elbows. His head fell back, and around it the mud splashed again. He made another effort at swimming along the top of the mud on his back. His arms met less resistance. Around him the sludge turned to slurry. Water welled up, and large bubbles of gas popped all across the widening quagmire.

He began to sink. He swung his arms, kicked his legs hard, and the increasingly liquid mass closed over his visor. Writhing, panicking now, he sank into utter darkness. His feet touched bottom. His hands, stretched above his head, were now well below the surface. He leaned forward with an immense effort and tried to place one foot in front of the other. If he had to, he would walk out of this. Barely had he completed a step when he found the resistance of the wet soil increase. It set almost solid around him. He was stuck.

Donald took some slow, deep breaths. Less than an hour had passed. Fifty minutes. Fifty-five. At any moment his rescuers would come for him.

They didn't. For four more hours he stood there in the dark. As each hour passed he realized with increasing certainty that the portal had not reopened. He wondered, almost idly, if that had anything to do with his own intrusion into the bog. He wondered, with some anguish, whether his illicit message had been destroyed, unread, as he fell in on top of it.

The anguish passed. What had happened to the message, and what happened to him, was in a quite ultimate sense not his problem. The parable of the sower was as clear as the great commission itself. He had been in the path of duty. He had proclaimed, to the best of his ability, the truth. This was what he had been sent to do. No guarantee had been given that he would be successful. He would not be the first, nor the last, missionary whose mission was to all human reckoning futile. The thought saddened him, but did not disturb him. In that sense, if none other, his feet were on a rock.

He prayed, he shouted, he thought, he wept, he prayed again, and he died.

At last! The aliens had sent a communications package! After almost a year of low-bandwidth disturbances of the air and the electromagnetic spectrum, from which little sense could be extracted, and many days of dropping tiny messages of blurry resolution and trivial import, they had finally, *finally* sent something one could get one's filaments into!

The mycoid sent long tendrils around the package, infiltrating its pores and cracks. It synthesized acids that worked their way through any weak points in its fabric. Within hours it had penetrated the wrapping and begun a riotous, joyous exploration of the vast library of information within. The mycoid had in its own genetic library billions of years of accumulated experience in absorbing information from organisms of every kind: plant or animal, mycoid or bacterium. It could relate the structure of a central nervous system to any semantic or semiotic content it had associated with the organism. It probed cavities, investigated long transportation tubes, traced networks of neurons and found its way to the approximately globular sub-package where the information was most rich. It dissolved here, embalmed there, dissected and investigated everywhere. In an inner wrapping it found a small object made from multiple mats of cellulose fibre, each layer impregnated with carbon-based markings. The mycoid stored these codes with the rest. Seasons and years passed. A complete transcription of the alien package, of its neural structures and genetic codes, was eventually read off.

Then the work of translation and interpretation, shared out across all the mycoids of the continent, began.

It took a long time, but the mycoids had all the time in the world. They had no more need – for the moment – to communicate with the aliens, now that they had this vast resource of information. They, or their ancestors, had done this many times before, under many suns.

They understood the alien, and they understood the strange story that had shaped so many of the connections in its nervous system. They interpreted the carbon marks on the cellulose mats. In their own vast minds they reconstructed the scenes of alien life, as they had done with everything that fell their way, from the grass and the insects to the trees. They had what a human might have called a vivid imagination. They had, after all, little else.

Some of them found the story to be:

Affirmation-marker	GOOD
Information-marker	NEWS

Spores spread it to the space-going trees, and thence to the wormhole network, and thence to countless worlds.

Not quite all the seeds fell on stony ground.

THE BLEMMYE'S STRATEGEM

Bruce Sterling

Bruce Sterling sold his first story in 1976 and is one of the most powerful and innovative new talents to enter SF in the past few decades. By the end of the eighties, he had established himself with a series of stories set in his exotic "Shaper/Mechanist" future, with novels such as the complex and Stapeldonian *Schismatrix* and the well-received *Islands in the Net* (as well as with his editing of the influential anthology *Mirrorshades: The Cyberpunk Anthology* and the infamous critical magazine Cheap Truth). Sterling was perhaps the prime driving force behind the revolutionary "Cyberpunk" movement in science fiction, as well as one of the best new hard science writers to enter the field in some time. His other books include a critically acclaimed nonfiction study of the First Amendment issues in the world of computer networking, *The Hacker Crackdown: Law and Disorder on the Electronic Frontier*; the novels *The Artificial Kid, Involution Ocean, Heavy Weather, Holy Fire, Distraction*, and *Zeitgeist*; a novel in collaboration with William Gibson, *The Difference Engine*; an omnibus collection *Schismatrix Plus* (containing the novel *Schismatrix* as well as most of his Shaper/Mechanist stories); and the landmark collections *Crystal Express, Globalhead*, and *A Good Old-Fashioned Future*. His most recent books include a nonfiction study of the future, *Tomorrow Now: Envisioning the Next Fifty Years*, and a new novel, *The Zenith Angle*. Coming up is a new collection, *Visionary in Residence*. His story "Bicycle Repairman" earned him a long-overdue Hugo Award in 1997, and he won another Hugo in 1997 for his story "Taklamakan." His stories have appeared in our First through Eighth, Eleventh, Fourteenth, Sixteenth, and Twentieth Annual Collections.

Here he takes us back to the time of the Crusades, to demonstrate that political agents can never be quite sure who's pulling their strings – or what purpose they're pulling them *for*.

A MESSENGER FLEW ABOVE the alleys of Tyre, skirting the torn green heads of the tallest palm trees. With a flutter of wings, it settled high on a stony ledge. The pigeon was quickly seized by a maiden within the tower. She gratefully kissed the bird's sleek gray head.

Sir Roger of Edessa, the maiden's lover, roamed the Holy Land on his knight errantry. Thanks to the maiden herself, Sir Roger possessed one precious cage of homing pigeons. Roger's words winged it to her, straight to her tender hands, soaring over every obstacle in a Holy Land aflame. The birds flapped over drum-pounding, horn-blaring Seljuk marauders, and evil mamelukes with faces masked in chainmail. They flitted over Ismaili fedayeen bent on murder and utterly careless of life.

An entire, busy network of messenger pigeons moved over the unknowing populace. These birds carried news through Jerusalem, Damascus, Cairo, and Beirut. They flitted over cavaliers from every cranny of Christendom, armed pilgrims who were starving, sweating, flea-bitten, and consumed with poxes. Birds laden with script flew over sunburned, axe-wielding Vikings. Over fanatical Templars and cruel, black-clad Teutonic Knights, baking like armored lobsters in the blazing sun. Over a scum of Greek peltasts and a scrim of Italian condottiere.

With trembling, ink-stained fingers, the maiden untied the tidy scroll from the bird's pink leg. There was a pounding ache within her bosom. Would it be another poem? She often swooned on reading Roger's poems.

No. This bird had not come from Roger of Edessa. She had been cruelly misled by her own false hopes. The messenger bird was just another tiresome commercial bird. It carried nothing but a sordid rush of text.

"Salt. Ivory. Tortoiseshell. Saffron. Rice. Frankincense. Iron. Copper. Tin. Lead. Coral. Topaz. Storax. Glass. Realgar. Antimony. Gold. Silver. Honey. Spikenard. Costus. Agate. Carnelian. Lycium. Cotton. Silk. Mallow. Pepper. Malabathrum. Pearls. Diamonds. Rubies. Sapphires."

Every good in this extensive list was followed by its price.

The girl locked the pigeon into its labeled wooden cage, along with dozens of other birds, her fellow captives within the gloomy tower. Using cuttlefish ink and a razor-trimmed feather, the girl copied the message into an enormous dusty ledger. If she ever failed in her duty to record, oh the woe she would receive at the hands of the Mother Superior. Bread and water. Endless kneeling, many rosaries.

The pigeon clerk rubbed at her watery eyes, harshly afflicted by fine print and bad lighting. She returned to lean her silken elbows on the cool, freckled stone, to contemplate the sparkling Mediterranean and a black swarm of profiteering Italian galleys. Perhaps Sir Roger of Edessa was dead. Poor Roger had been slain by a cruel Moslem champion, or else he was dead of some plague. Roger would never write a poem to her again. At the age of seventeen, she was abandoned to her desolate fate.

How likely all this seemed. Her doom was so total and utter. If Roger failed to rescue her from this miserable life tending pigeons, she would be forced to take unwelcome vows . . . She would have to join the Little Sisters of the Hospitallers below the tower of birds, in that ever-swelling crowd of the Holy Land's black widows, another loveless wretch of a girl amid that pitiful host of husbandless crones and fatherless orphans, all of them bottled up behind tall, rocky walls, hopelessly trapped without any lands or dowries . . . The pale brides of Christ, moody and distracted, waiting in itchy torment for some fatal pagan horde of dark-eyed Moslem fiends to conquer Tyre and ravage their fortress of chastity . . .

Another bird appeared in flight. The maiden's heart rose to beat in her throat. This was a strong bird, a swift one. When he arrived, his legs were clasped by two delicate bands of gold. His feathers smelled of incense.

The writing, though very tiny, was the most beautiful the girl had ever seen. The ink was blood-red, and it glittered.

Dearest Hudegar
With the tip of my brush I give you the honey of good news
Our Silent Master has summoned us both
So prepare yourself quickly
For I hasten to you with a caravan of many strong men to take you
   to his Paradise
                              (signed) The Old Man of the Mountain

The maiden began to weep, for her name was not Hudegar. She had never heard of any woman named Hudegar.

Whether Christian or Moslem, hamlets in the Holy Land were always much the same: a huddle of dusty cottages around a well, a mill, and an oven. The Abbess Hildegart rode demurely into the plundered village, escorted by the heavily armed caravan of the Grand Assassin.

This hapless little village had been crushed with particular gusto. Vengeful marauders had hacked down the olive groves, set fire to the vineyard, and poisoned the well. Since they were still close to Tyre, the strongest city yet held by the reeling Crusader forces, Hildegart rather suspected the work of Hospitallers.

This conclusion disturbed her. Hildegart herself had founded the Hospitaller Order. She had created and financed a hospital corps in order to heal the sick, to run a chain of inns, and to give peace, comfort, and money-changing services to the endless sun-dazed hordes of holy European pilgrims.

Hildegart's idea had been a clever one, and was much appreciated by her patron, the Silent Master. However, some seventy years had passed since this invention of hers, and Hildegart had been forced to see her brilliant scheme degenerating. Somehow the Hospitaller corps, this kindly order of medical monks, had transformed itself into the most violent, fanatical soldiery in the Crusader forces. It seemed that their skills in healing injured flesh and bone also gave them a special advantage in chopping men apart. Even the Templars were scared of the Hospitallers, and the Templars frightened Assassins so badly that the Assassins often paid them for protection.

Some of the barns in the smashed village were still defensible. Sinan, the Old Man of the Mountain and the Ayatollah of Assassins, ordered his caravan to put up for the night. The caravan men made camp, buried several abandoned corpses, set up sentries, and struggled to water the horses with the tainted murk from the well.

The Abbess and the Assassin settled down behind their armed sentries, to eat and chat. Hildegart and Sinan had known each other for much longer than most people would ever live. Despite the fact that they both labored loyally for the Silent Master, their personal relations were rather strained. There had been times in her long, long life when Hildegart had felt rather safe and happy with Sinan. Sinan was an ageless Moslem wizard and therefore evil incarnate, but Sinan had once sheltered her from men even more dangerous than himself.

Those pleasant years of their history, unfortunately, were long behind both of them. At the age of one hundred seventeen, Sinan could not possibly protect Hildegart from any man more dangerous than himself, for Sinan the Assassin had become the most dangerous man in the world. The number of Crusaders who had fallen to his depredations was beyond all reckoning, though Hildegart shrewdly estimated it at somewhere over four thousand.

Underlit by red flames from his dainty iron camp stove, Sinan ate his roasted kabobs and said little. He offered her a warm, dark, gazelle-eyed look. Hildegart stirred uneasily in her dark riding cloak, hood, and wimple. Although Sinan was very intelligent and had learned a great deal about inflicting terror, Sinan's heart never changed much with the passing decades. He was always the same. Sinan was simple, direct, and devout in his habits, and he prayed five times every day, which (by Hildegart's reckoning) would likely make some two hundred thousand acts of prayer, every one of them involving a fervent hope that Crusaders would perish and burn in Hell.

Hildegart warmed one chilly hand at the iron brazier. Nearby, the homing pigeons cooed in their portable cribs. The poor pigeons were cold and unhappy, even more anxious to return to Tyre than she was. Perhaps they sensed that Sinan's mercenaries longed to pluck and eat them. "Sinan, where did you find this horrible band of cutthroats?"

"I bought them for us, my dear," Sinan told her politely. "These men are Khwarizmian Turks from the mountains far beyond Samarkand. They are quite lost here in Palestine, without any land or loyalties. Therefore they are of use to me, and to our Silent Master, and to his purposes."

"Do you trust these bandy-legged fiends?"

"No, I don't trust them at all. But they speak only an obscure dialect, and unlike you and me, they are not People of the Book. So they cannot ever reveal what they may see of our Silent Master. Besides, the Khwarizmian Turks were cheap to purchase. They flee a great terror, you see. They flee the Great Khan of the Mongols."

Hildegart considered these gnomic remarks. Sinan wasn't lying. Sinan never lied to her; he was just grotesquely persistent in his pagan delusions. "Sinan, do I need to know more about terrible Great Khan?"

"Better not to contemplate such things, my pearl of wisdom. Let's play a game of chess."

"Not this time, no."

"Why be coy? I'll spot you an elephant rook!"

"My markets for Chinese silk have been very disturbed these past ten years. Is this so-called Great Khan the source of my commercial difficulty?"

Sinan munched thoughtfully at his skewer of peppered mutton. Her remarks had irritated him. Brave men killed and died at Sinan's word, and yet she, Hildegart, was far richer than he was. Hildegart was the richest woman in the world. As the founder, accountant, banker, and chief moneylender of the Hospitaller order, Hildegart found her greatest joy in life managing international markets. She placed her money into goods and cities where it would create more money, and then she counted that money with great and precise care, and she placed it again. Hildegart had been doing this for decades, persistently and secretly, through a network of nameless agents in cities from Spain to India, a network linked by swift birds and entirely unsuspected by mankind.

Sinan knew how all this counting and placing of money was done, but as an Ayatollah of Assassins, he considered it boring and ignoble labor. That was why he was always sending her messenger birds and begging her for loans of cash.

"Dear, kind, sweet Hudegar," the Assassin said coaxingly.

Hildegart blushed. "No one calls me Hudegar. Except for you, they all died ages ago."

"Dear Hudegar, how could I ever forget my sweet pet name for you?"

"That was a slave girl's name."

"We're all the slaves of God, my precious! Even our Silent Master." Sinan yanked the metal skewer from his strong white teeth. "Are you too proud to obey his summons now, blessed Mother Superior? Are you tired of your long life, now that your Christian Franks are finally chased back into the sea by the warriors of righteousness?"

"I'm here with you, aren't I?" said Hildegart, avoiding his eyes. "I could be tending the wounded and doing my accounts. Why did you write to me in French? The whole convent's chattering about your mysterious bird and its message. You know how women talk when they've been cloistered."

"You never answer me when I write to you in Arabic," Sinan complained. He mopped at his fine black beard with a square of pink Chinese silk. "I write to you constantly! You know the cost of shipping these homing pigeons! Their flesh is more precious than amber!" The

Assassin waved away the thickening smoke from the coals of his cookstove.

Hildegart lit the sesame oil at the spout of a small brass lamp. "I do write to you, dear Sinan, with important financial news, but in return, you write to me of nothing but your evil boasting and your military mayhem."

"I'm composing our history there!" Sinan protested. "I am putting my heart's blood into those verses, woman! You of all women should appreciate that effort!"

"Oh, very well then." Hildegart switched to Arabic, a language she knew fluently, thanks to her years as a captive concubine.

" 'With the prodigies of my pen I express the marvel of the fall of Jerusalem,' " she quoted at him. " 'I fill the towers of the Zodiac with stars, and the caskets with my pearls of insight. I spread the joyful news far and wide, bringing perfume to Persia and conversation to Samarkand. The sweetness of holy victory surpasses candied fruits and cane sugar.' "

"How clever you are, Hudegar! Those were my finest verses, too." Sinan's dark, arching brows knotted hopefully. "That's some pretty grand stuff there, isn't it?"

"You shouldn't try to be a poet, Sinan. Let's face it, you are an alchemist."

"But I've learned everything there is to know about chemistry and machinery," Sinan protested. "Those fields of learning are ignoble and boring. Poetry and literature, by contrast, are fields of inexhaustible knowledge! Yes, I admit it, I do lack native talent for poesy – for when I began writing, my history was just a dry recital of factual events! But I have finally found my true voice as a poet, for I have mastered the challenge of narrating great deeds on the battlefield!"

Hildegart's temper rose. "Am I supposed to praise you for that? I had investments in Jerusalem, you silly block of wood! My best sugar presses were there – my favorite cotton dyes . . . and you can bet I'll tell the Blemmye all about those severe commercial losses!"

"You may quote me even further, and recite to him how Christian Jerusalem fell to the Moslems in flames and screams," said Sinan tautly. "Tell him that every tribe of Frank will be chased back into the ocean! Eighty-nine long years since these unbathed wretches staggered in from Turkey to steal our lands, looking like so many disinterred corpses! But at last, broken with righteous fire and sword, the occupiers flee the armies of Jihad like whipped dogs. Never to return! I have lived through all of that humiliation, Hudegar. I was forced to witness every sorrowful day of my people's long affliction. At last, in this glorious day of supreme justice, I will see the backs of those alien invaders. Do you know what I just heard Saladin say?"

Hildegart ate another salted olive. She had been born in Germany and had never gotten over how delicious olives were. "All right. What did he say?"

"Saladin will *build ships and sail after the retreating Christians to*

Europe." Sinan drew an amazed breath. "Can you imagine the stern qualities of that great soldier, who would trust to the perils of the open ocean to avenge our insulted faith? That's the greatest tribute to knightly bravery that I can imagine!"

"Why do you even bother with lowborn scum like Saladin? Saladin is a Kurd and a Shi'ite."

"Oh, no. Saladin is the chosen of God. He used the wealth of Egypt to conquer Syria. He used the wealth of Syria to conquer Mesopotamia. The wealth of Mesopotamia will finally liberate Palestine. Saladin will die with exhausted armies and an empty treasury. Saladin is very thin, and he suffers from bellyaches, but thanks to him, Palestine will be ours again. Those outlaw Crusader states of Christian Outremer will cease to be. That is the divine truth of history and yes, I will bear witness to divine truth. I must bear witness, you know. Such things are required of a scholar."

Hildegart sighed, at a loss for words. Hildegart knew so many words, reams and reams of words. She knew low German, French, Arabic, much Turkish, some Greek. Proper history was written in Latin, of course. Having successfully memorized the Old and New Testaments at the age of fourteen, Hildegart could manage rather well in Latin, but she had given up her own attempts to write any kind of history during the reign of Baldwin the Leper.

The Crusader King of Jerusalem had a loathsome Middle Eastern disease, and Hildegart found herself chronicling Baldwin's incessant defeats in a stale, stilted language that smelled of death. "King Baldwin the Leper suffered this crushing setback, King Baldwin the Leper failed at that diplomatic initiative . . ." The Leper seemed to mean well, and yet he was so stupid . . . One stormy morning Hildegart had pulled years of secret records from her hidden cabinets and burned every one of them. It felt so good to destroy such weary knowledge that she had sung and danced.

Sinan gazed on her hopefully. "Can't you say just a bit more about my glamorous poetic efforts, Hudegar?"

"You are improving," she allowed. "I rather liked that line about the candied fruits. Those jongleurs of Eleanor of Aquitaine, they never write verse half so luscious as you do."

Sinan beamed on her for a moment, and returned to gnawing his mutton. However, he was quick to sense a left-handed compliment. "That Frankish queen, she prefers the love poems made by vagrants for women. All Frankish ladies enjoy such poems. I myself can write very sweetly about women and love. But I would never show those poems of mine to anyone, because they are too deeply felt."

"No doubt."

Sinan narrowed his eyes. "I can remember every woman who ever passed through my hands. By name and by face!"

"All of them? Could that be possible?"

"Oh come now, I never married more than four at a time! I can remember all of my wives very vividly. I shall prove it to you now, my doubting one! My very first wife was the widow of my older brother; she was Fatima, the eldest, with the two sons, my nephews. Fatima was dutiful and good. Then there was the Persian girl that the Sultan gave me: she was Bishar. She had crossed eyes, but such pretty legs. When my fortunes prospered, I bought the Greek girl Phoebe to cook for my other two."

Hildegart shifted uneasily.

"Then there was you, Hudegar the Frankish girl, my gift from the Silent Master. What splendid flesh you had. Hair like wheat and cheeks like apples. How you thrived in my courtyard and my library. You wanted kisses more than the other three combined. We had three daughters and the small son who died nameless." Sinan sighed from the depth of his heart. "Those are all such songs of loss and sorrow, my sweet songs of all my dear wives."

Hildegart's early years had been tangled and difficult. She had left Germany as a teenaged nun in the massive train of Peter the Hermit, a tumbling migration of thousands of the wildly inspired, in the People's Crusade. They walked down the Rhine, they trudged down the Danube, they stumbled starving across Hungary, Byzantium, and the Balkans, asking at every town and village if the place might perhaps be Jerusalem.

The People's Crusade killed most of its participants, but a crusade was the only sure way that Hildegart, who was the humble daughter of a falconer, could guarantee the remission of her sins. Hildegart marched from April to October of 1096. She was raped, starved, survived typhus, and arrived pregnant on an obscure hilltop in Turkey. There every man in her dwindling band was riddled with Seljuk arrows by the troops of Kilij Arslan.

Hildegart was purchased by a Turkish speculator, who took her infant for his own purposes, and then sold her to the aging Sultan of Mosul. The Sultan visited her once for form's sake, then left her to her own devices within his harem. The Mosul harem was a quiet, solemn place, very much like the convent she had left in Germany, except for the silks, the dancing, and the eunuchs. There Hildegart learned to speak Turkish and Arabic, to play a lute, to embroider, and to successfully manage the considerable administrative overhead involved in running the palace baths.

After the Sultan's murder, she was manumitted and conveyed to a Jewish merchant, by whom she had a son.

The Jew taught her accounting, using a new system of numeration he had learned from colleagues in India. He and the son then vanished on an overly daring business expedition into Christian-held Antioch. Hildegart was sold to meet his business debts. Given her skills and accomplishments, though, she was quickly purchased by a foreign diplomat.

This diplomat traveled extensively through Islam, together with his train of servants, in a slow pilgrimage from court to court. It was a rewarding life, in its way. Moslem courts competed in their lavish hospitality for distinguished foreigners. Foreign merchants and envoys, who lacked local clan ties, often made the most honest and efficient court officials. The Blemmye profited by this.

Literate scholars of the Islamic courts had of course heard tell of the exotic Blemmyae people. The Blemmyae were men from the land of Prester John, the men whose heads grew beneath their shoulders.

The Blemmye had no head; he was acephalous. Across his broad, barren shoulders grew a series of horny plates. Where a man might have paps, the Blemmye had two round black eyes, and he had a large, snorting nose in his chest. Where a navel might have been was his mouth. The Blemmye's mouth was a round, lipless, speechless hole, white and pink and ridged inside, and cinching tight like a bag. The Blemmye's feet, always neatly kept in soft leather Turkish boots, were quite toeless. He had beautiful hands, however, and his dangling, muscular arms were as round and solid as the trunks of trees.

The Blemmye, although he could not speak aloud, was widely known for his courteous behavior, his peaceable demeanor, and his generous gifts. In the troubled and turbulent Damascene court, the Blemmye was accepted without much demur.

The Blemmye was generally unhappy with the quality of his servants. They lacked the keen intelligence to meet his exacting requirements. Hildegart was a rare find for him, and she rose rapidly in her Silent Master's estimation.

The Blemmye wrote an excellent Arabic, but he wrote it in the same way he read books: entire pages at once, in one single comprehensive glance. So rather than beginning at the top of a page and writing from right to left, as any Arab scholar would, the Blemmye dashed and dotted his black markings across the paper, seemingly at random. Then he would wait, with unblinking eyes, to see if enough ink had arrived for his reader's comprehension.

If not, then he would dabble in more ink, but the trial annoyed him.

Hildegart had a particular gift for piecing out the Blemmye's fragmentary dabblings. For Hildegart, Arabic was also a foreign language, but she memorized long texts with ease, and she was exceedingly clever with numbers. Despite her master's tonguelessness, she also understood his moods, mostly through his snorts and his nervous, hand-wringing gestures. The Blemmye became reliant on her services, and he rewarded her well.

When his business called him far from Damascus, the Blemmye conveyed Hildegart to the care of his chief agent within the Syrian court, an Iraqi alchemist and engineer. Rashid al-din Sinan made his living from "Naphth," a flaming war-product that oozed blackly from the reedy marshes of his native Tigris.

Like most alchemists, Sinan had extensive interests in hermetic theology, as well as civil engineering, calligraphy, rhetoric, diplomacy, and the herbarium. As a canny and gifted courtier, living on his wits, Sinan was quick to serve any diplomat who could pay for his provisions with small but perfect diamonds, as the Blemmye did. Sinan gracefully accepted Hildegart as his new concubine, and taught her the abacus and the tally-stick.

The Blemmye, being a diplomat, was deeply involved in international trade. He tirelessly sought out various rare oils, mineral salts, glasses, saltpeter, sulfur, potash, alchemical acids, and limes. He would trade in other goods to obtain the substances he prized, but his means were always subordinated to those same ends.

The Blemmye's personal needs were rather modest. However, he lavished many gifts on his mistress. The Blemmye was pitifully jealous of this female Blemmye. He kept her in such deep, secluded purdah that she was never glimpsed by anyone.

Hildegart and Sinan became the Blemmye's most trusted servants. He gave them his alchemical philters to drink, so that their flesh would not age in the mortal way of men and women. Many years of energetic action transpired, led by the pressing needs of their Silent Master. As wizard and mother abbess, Sinan and Hildegart grew in age and cunning, wealth and scholarship. Trade routes and caravans conveyed the Blemmye's goods and agents from the far reaches of Moslem Spain as far as the Spice Islands.

When Crusader ships appeared in the Holy Land, and linked the Moslem world with the distant commercial cities of the Atlantic and the Baltic, the Blemmye was greatly pleased.

Eventually, Sinan and Hildegart were forced to part, for their uncanny agelessness had aroused suspicion in Damascus. Sinan removed himself to a cult headquarters in Alamut, where he pursued the mystic doctrines and tactics of the Ismaili Assassins. Hildegart migrated to the Crusader cities of Outremer, where she married a wise and all-accepting Maronite. She had three more children by this union.

Time ended that marriage as it had all her other such relations. Eventually, Hildegart found that she had tired of men and children, of their roughness and their importunities. She resumed the veil as the female Abbess of a convent stronghold in Tyre. She became the wealthy commander of a crowd of cloistered nuns, busy women with highly lucrative skills at weaving, adorning, and marketing Eastern fabrics.

The Abbess Hildegart was the busiest person that she knew. Even in times of war, she received many informations from the farthest rims of the world, and she knew the price and location of the rarest of earthly goods. Yet there was a hollowness in her life, a roiling feeling that dark events were unfolding, events beyond any mastery.

Assuming that all her children had somehow lived – and that her children had children, and that they had lived as well – and that those grandchildren, remorseless as the calendar, had further peopled the Earth – Hildegart's abacus showed her as a silent Mother Superior to a growing horde of over three hundred people. They were Christians, Jews, Moslems, a vast and ever-ramifying human family, united in nothing but their ignorance of her own endlessly spreading life.

The Dead Sea was as unpleasant as its name. Cursed Sodom was to the south, suicidal Masada to the middle, and a bloodstained River Jordan to the north. The lake gave pitch and bitumen, and mounds of gray, tainted salt. Birds that bathed in its water died and were crusted with minerals.

Arid limestone hills and caves on the Dead Sea shores had gone undisturbed for centuries.

Within this barren wilderness, the Blemmye had settled himself. Of late, the Silent Master, once so restless in his worldly quests for goods and services, moved little from his secretive Paradise, dug within the Dead Sea's barren hills. Sometimes, especially helpful merchants from Hildegart's pigeon network would be taken there, or Assassins would be briefed there on one last self-sacrificing mission. It was in the Blemmye's Paradise that Sinan and Hildegart drank the delicious elixirs that lengthened their lives. There were gardens there, and stores of rare minerals. The Blemmye's hidden palace also held an arsenal. It concealed the many sinister weapons that Sinan had built.

No skill in military engineering was concealed from the cunning master of Assassins. Sinan knew well the mechanical secrets of the jarkh, the zanbarak, the qaws al-ziyar, and even the fearsome manjaniq, a death-machine men called "The Long-Haired Bride." With the Blemmye's aid and counsel, Sinan had built sinister crossbows with thick twisted skeins of silk and horsehair, capable of firing great iron beams, granite stones, red-hot bricks, and sealed clay bombs that splattered alchemical flames. Spewing, shrieking rockets from China were not beyond Sinan's war skills, nor was the Byzantine boiler that spewed ever-burning Greek Fire. Though difficult to move and conceal, these massive weapons of destruction were frighteningly potent. In cunning hands, they had shaped the fates of many a quarrelsome emirate. They had even hastened the fall of Jerusalem.

In his restless travels, the Blemmye had collected many rare herbs for the exquisite pergolas of his Paradise. He carefully collected the powder from within their flowers, and strained and boiled their saps for his marvelous elixirs. The Blemmye had forges and workshops full of curious instruments of metal and glass. He had struggled for years to breed superior camels for his far-ranging caravans. He had created a unique race of peculiar beasts, with hairless, scaly hides and spotted necks like cameleopards.

The choicest feature of the Blemmye's Paradise was its enormous bath. Sinan led his caravan men in a loud prayer of thanksgiving for their safe arrival. He commended their souls to his God, then he ushered the dusty, thirsting warriors within the marbled precincts.

Pure water gushed there from many great brass nozzles. The men eagerly doffed their chain-mail armor and their filthy gear. They laughed and sang, splashing their tattooed limbs in the sweet, cleansing waters. Delicate fumes of incense made their spirits soar to the heavens.

Very gently, their spirits left their bodies.

The freshly washed dead were carried away on handcarts by the

Blemmye's house servants. These servants were eunuchs, and rendered tongueless.

Through her long and frugal habit, Hildegart carefully sorted through the effects of the dead men. The Moslem and Christian women who haunted the battlefields of the Holy Land, comforting the wounded and burying the slain, generally derived more wealth from dead men than they ever did from their live protectors. Female camp followers of various faiths often encountered one another in the newly strewn fields of male corpses. They would bargain by gesture and swap the dead men's clothes, trinkets, holy medals, knives, and bludgeons.

Sinan sought her out as Hildegart neatly arranged the dead men's dusty riding boots. He was unhappy. "The Silent One has written his commands for us," he told her. He frowned over his freshly inked instructions. "The eunuchs are to throw the bodies of the men into the mine shaft, as usual. But then we are to put the caravan's horses into the bath as well. All of them!" The Assassin gazed at her moodily. "There would seem to be scarcely anyone here. I see none of his gardeners, I see no secretaries . . . The Master is badly understaffed. Scutwork of this kind is unworthy of the two of us. I don't understand this."

Hildegart was shocked. "It was well worth doing to rid ourselves of those evil foreign Turks, but we can't possibly stable horses in that beautiful marble bath."

"Stable them? My dear, we are to kill the horses and throw them down into the mine. That's what the Master has written for us here. See if there's not some mistake, eh? You were always so good at interpreting."

Hildegart closely examined the spattered parchment. The Blemmye's queer handwriting was unmistakable, and his Arabic had improved with the years. "These orders are just as you say, but they make no sense. Without pack-horses, how am I to return to Tyre, and you to Alamut?"

Sinan looked at her in fear. "What are you telling me? Do you dare to question the Silent Master's orders?"

"No, you're the man," she told him quickly. "You should question his orders."

Hildegart had not had an audience with the Blemmye in some eight years. Their only communication was through couriers, or much more commonly, through the messenger birds.

In earlier days, when his writings had been harder to interpret, Hildegart had almost been a body servant to the Blemmye. She had fetched his ink, brought him his grapes, bread, and honey, and even seen him off to his strange, shrouded bed. Then she had left him to dwell in his Paradise, and she had lived for many years many leagues away from him. As long as they were still writing to each other, however, he never complained about missing her.

The Blemmye gave her his old, knowing look. His eyes, round, black, and wise, spread in his chest a hand's span apart. The Blemmye wore baggy trousers of flowered blue silk, beautiful leather boots, and of course no headgear. He sat cross-legged on a velvet cushion on the floor of his office, with his Indian inks, his wax seals, his accounting books, and his elaborate plans and parchments. The Blemmye's enormous arms had gone thinner with the years, and his speckled hide looked pale. His hands, once so deft and tireless, seemed to tremble uncontrollably.

"The Master must be ill," hissed Hildegart to Sinan. The two of them whispered together, for they were almost certain that the Blemmye could not hear or understand a whispered voice. The Blemmye did have ears, or fleshy excrescences anyway, but their Silent Master never responded to speech, even in the languages that he could read and write.

"I will formally declaim the splendid rhetoric that befits our lordly Master, while you will write to him at my dictation," Sinan ordered.

Hildegart obediently seated herself on a small tasseled carpet.

Sinan bowed low, placing his hand on his heart. He touched his fingertips to lips and forehead. "A most respectful greetings, dread Lord! May Allah keep you in your customary wisdom, health, and strength! The hearts of your servants overflow with joy over too long an absence from your august presence!"

"How are you doing, dear old Blemmye?" Hildegart wrote briskly. She shoved the parchment forward.

The Blemmye plucked up the parchment and eyed it. Then he bent over, and his wrist slung ink in a fury.

"My heart has been shattered / the eternal darkness between the worlds closes in / my nights burn unbroken by sleep I bleed slowly / from within / I have no strength to greet the dawn / for my endless days are spent in sighing grief and vain regrets / the Light of All My Life has perished / I will never hear from her again / never never never again / will I read her sweet words of knowledge understanding and consolation / henceforth I walk in darkness / for my days of alien exile wind to their fatal climax."

Hildegart held up the message and a smear of ink ran down it like a black tear.

The two of them had never had the least idea that the Blemmye's wife had come to harm. The Blemmye guarded her so jealously that such a thing scarcely seemed possible.

But the mistress of their Silent Master, though very female, was not a Blemmye at all. She was not even a woman.

The Blemmye led them to the harem where he had hidden her.

This excavation had been the Blemmye's first great project. He had bought many slaves to bore and dig deep shafts into the soft Dead Sea limestone. The slaves often died in despair from the senseless work, perishing from the heat, the lack of fresh water, and the heavy, miasmic salt air.

But then, at Hildegart's counseling, the hapless slaves were freed and dismissed. Instead of using harsh whips and chains, the Blemmye simply tossed a few small diamonds into the rubble at the bottom of the pit.

Word soon spread of a secret diamond mine. Strong men from far and wide arrived secretly in many eager gangs. Without orders, pay, or any words of persuasion, they imported their own tools into the wasteland.

Then the miners fought recklessly and even stabbed each other for the privilege of expanding the Blemmye's diggings. Miraculous tons of limestone were quarried, enough rock to provide firm foundations for every structure in the Blemmye's Paradise. The miners wept with delight at the discovery of every precious stone.

When no more diamonds appeared, the miners soon wearied of their sport. The secret mine was abandoned and swiftly forgotten.

Within this cavernous dugout, then, was where the Blemmye had hidden his darling.

The Silent Master removed a counterweighted sheet of glass and iron. From the black gulf, an eye-watering, hellish stink of lime and sulfur wafted forth.

Strapping two panes of glass to his enormous face, the Blemmye inhaled sharply through his great trumpet of a nose. Then he rushed headlong into the stinking gloom.

Hildegart urged Sinan to retreat from the gush of foul miasma, but the Assassin resisted her urgings. "I always wondered what our Master did with all that brimstone. This is astonishing."

"The Blemmye loves a creature from Hell," said Hildegart, crossing herself.

"Well, if this is Hell, then we ourselves built it, my dear." Sinan shrouded his eyes and peered within the acid murk. "I see so many bones in there. I must go in there, you know, I must bear witness and write of all this . . . Why don't you come along with me?"

"Are you joking? A mine is no place for a woman!"

"Of course it is, my dear! You simply must come down into Hell with me. You're the only aide memoire available, and besides, you know that I rely on your judgment."

When Hildegart stiffly refused him, Sinan shrugged at her womanly fears and rushed forward into the gassy murk. Hildegart wept for him, and began to pray – praying for her own sake, because Sinan's salvation was entirely beyond retrieval.

At the fifth bead of her rosary, the brave Assassin reappeared, half-leading his stricken Master. They were tugging and heaving together at a great, white, armored plate, a bone-colored thing like a gigantic shard of pottery.

This broken armor, with a few tangled limbs and bits of dry gut, that was all that was left of the Blemmye's Lady. She had been something like a great, boiled, stinking crab. Something like a barb-tailed desert scorpion, living under a rock.

In her silent life, cloistered deep within the smoking, stony earth, the

Blemmye's Lady had fed well, and grown into a size so vast and bony and monstrous that she could no longer fit through the narrow cave mouth. Sinan and the Blemmye were barely able to tug her skeletal remnants into daylight.

The Blemmye pawed at a hidden trigger, and the great iron door swung shut behind him with a hollow boom. He wheezed and coughed, and snorted loudly through his dripping nose.

Sinan, who had breathed less deeply of the hellish fumes, was the first to recover. He spat, and wiped his streaming eyes, then gestured to Hildegart for pen and ink.

Then Sinan sat atop a limestone boulder. He ignored her questions with a shake of his turbaned head, and fervently scribbled his notes.

Hildegart followed the laboring Blemmye as he tugged at his bony, rattling burden. The Silent Master trembled like a dying ox as he hauled the big skidding carcass. His sturdy leather boots had been lacerated, as if chopped by picks and hatchets.

Ignoring his wounds, the Blemmye dragged the riddled corpse of his beloved, yard by painful yard, down the slope toward the Dead Sea. The empty carapace was full of broken holes. The she-demon had been pecked to pieces from within.

Hildegart had never seen the Blemmye hurt. But she had seen enough wounded men to know the look of mortal despair, even on a face as strange as his.

The Blemmye collapsed in anguish at the rim of the sullen salt lake.

Hildegart smoothed the empty sand before him with her sandaled foot. Then she wrote to him with a long brass pin from the clasp of her cloak. "Master, let us return to your Paradise. There I will tend to your wounds."

The Blemmye plucked a small table knife from his belt and scratched rapidly in the sand. "My fate is of no more consequence / I care only for my darling's children / though born in this unhappy place / they are scions of a great and noble people."

"Master, let us write of this together in some much better place."

The Blemmye brushed away her words with the palm of his hand. "I have touched my poor beloved for the last time in my life / How pitifully rare were our meetings / We sent each other word through the black gulfs and seas amid the stars / to understand one sentence was the patient work of years / her people and mine were mortal enemies / And yet she trusted me / She chose to become mine / She fled with me in exile to this distant unknown land / Now she has left me to face our dark fate alone / It was always her dear way to give her life for others / Alas my sweet correspondent has finally perished of her generosity."

The Blemmye tugged in fitful despair at his lacerated boots.

Resignedly, Hildegart knelt and pulled the torn boots from her Master's feet. His wounds were talon slashes, fearsome animal bites. She pulled the cotton wimple from her head and tore it into strips.

"I promised her that I would guard her children / sheltering them as I always sheltered her / That foolish vow has broken my spirit / I will fail her in my promise, for I cannot live without her / Her goodness and her greatness of spirit / She was so wise, and knew so many things / Great marvels I could never have guessed, known, or dreamed of / What a strange soul she had, and how she loved me / What wondrous things we shared together from our different worlds / Oh, how she could write!"

Sinan arrived. The Assassin's eyes were reddened with the fumes, but he had composed himself.

"What have you been doing?" Hildegart demanded, as she worked to bind the Blemmye's bleeding, toeless feet.

"Listen to this feat of verse!" Sinan declared. He lifted his parchment, cleared his throat, and began to recite. " 'With my own eyes, I witnessed the corpses of the massacred! Lacerated and disjointed, with heads cracked open and throats split; spines broken, necks shattered; noses mutilated, hair colored with blood! Their tender lips were shriveled, their skulls cracked and pierced; their feet were slashed and fingers sliced away and scattered; their ribs staved in and smashed. With their life's last breath exhaled, their very ghosts were crushed, and they lay like dead stones among stones!' "

Hildegart's bloodied fingers faltered on the knot of her rough bandage. The sun beat against her bared head. Her ears roared. Her vision faded.

When she came to, Sinan was tenderly sponging her face with water from his canteen. "You swooned," he told her.

"Yes," she said faintly, "yes, that overcame me."

"Of course it would," he agreed, eyes shining, "for those wondrous verses possessed me in one divine rush! As if my very pen had learned to speak the truth!"

"Is that what you saw in Hell?" she said.

"Oh no," he told her, "that was what I witnessed in the siege of Jerusalem. I was never able to describe that experience before, but just now, I was very inspired." Sinan shrugged. "Inside that ugly mine, there is not much to see. There is dark acrid smoke there, many chewed bones. The imps within, they screeched and rustled everywhere, like bats and lizards. And that infernal stench . . ." Sinan looked sidelong at the Blemmye's wounded shins. "See how the little devils attacked him, as he walked through the thick of them, to fetch out their dam."

Though the Blemmye did not understand Sinan's words, the tone of the Assassin's voice seemed to stir him. He sat up, his black eyes filmy and grievous. He took up his knife again, and carved fresh letters into the sand. "Now we will take the precious corpse of my beloved / and sink her to her last rest in this strange sea she loved so much. / This quiet lake was the kindest place to her of any in your world."

Sinan put his verses away, and pulled at one whitened limb of the Blemmye's ruined lover. The bony armor rocked and tilted like a pecked and broken Roc's egg. The wounded Blemmye stood on his bleeding feet, lifting and shoving at the wall of bone with all his failing strength. The two of them splashed waist-deep into the evil water.

As the skeleton sank into the shallows, there was a sudden stirring and skittering. From a bent corner of the shell, shaking itself like a wet bird, came a small and quite horrible young demon. It had claws, and a stinging tail, and a circlet of eyes like a spider. It hopped and chirped and screeched.

Sinan wisely froze in place, like a man confronting a leopard. But the Blemmye could not keep his composure. He snorted aloud and fled splashing toward the shore.

The small demon rushed after the Blemmye as if born to the chase. It quickly felled him to the salty shore. At once, it began to feed on him.

Sinan armed himself with the closest weapon at hand: he tore a bony flipper from the mother's corpse. He waded ashore in a rush, and swung this bone like a mace across the heaving back of the imp. Its armor was as tough as any crab's, though, and the heavy blow only enraged it. The little demon turned on the Assassin with awful speed, and likely would have killed a fighter less experienced. Sinan, though, was wise enough to outfox the young devil. He dodged its feral lunges, striking down and cracking the vulnerable joints in its twitching, bony limbs. When the monster faltered, foaming and hissing, he closed on it with a short, curved dagger from within his robe.

Sinan rose at last from the young beast's corpse, his robes ripped and his arm bloodied. He hid his blade away again, then dragged the dead monster to the salt shore. There he heaved it with a shudder of loathing into the still water beside its mother.

Hildegart knelt beside the panting Blemmye. His wounds had multiplied.

The Blemmye blinked, faint with anguish. His strength was fading visibly, yet he still had something left to write. He scraped at the sand with a trembling fingertip. "Take me to my Paradise and bind my wounds / See to it that I live / I shall reveal to you great wonders and secrets / beyond the comprehension of your prophets."

Sinan took Hildegart by the arm.

"I'm no longer much concerned about our horses, my dear," he told her. He knelt and smoothed out their Master's writing. A spatter of his own blood fell on the sand beside the Blemmye's oozings.

"That ugly monster has hurt you, my brave hero!"

"Do you know how many times this poor old body of mine has known a wound?" Sinan's left arm had been badly scored by the creature's lashing tail. He gritted his teeth as she tied off his arm with a scarf. "What a joy that battle was, my darling. I have never killed anything that I wanted to kill so much."

The Blemmye propped his headless body on one elbow. He beckoned at them feebly. Hildegart felt a moment of sheer hatred for him, for his weakness, for his foolish yieldings to the temptations of darkness. "What it is that the Blemmye wants to write of now, these 'great secrets' that he promises us?"

"It will be much the same as it was before," Sinan said with disgust. "That mystical raving about the Sun being only a star."

Hildegart shivered. "I always hated that!"

"The world is very, very old, he'll insist on that nonsense, as well. Come, let us help him, my dear. We shall have to patch the Master up, for there is no one else fit to do it."

"Thousands of years," Hildegart quoted, unmoving where she stood. "Then, thousands of thousands of years. And thousands, of thousands, of thousands. Then thirteen and a half of those units. Those are the years since the birth of the universe."

"How is it you can remember all that? Your skills at numeration are beyond compare!" Sinan trembled suddenly from head to foot, in an after-combat mix of rage, fear, and weariness. "My dear, please give me counsel, in your wisdom: Did his huge numbers ever make any sense to you? Any kind of sense at all?"

"No," she told him.

The Assassin looked wearily at the fainting Blemmye. He lowered his voice. "Well, I can fully trust your counsel in this matter, can't I? Tell me that you are quite sure about all that."

Hildegart felt a rush of affection for him. She recognized that look of sincere, weighty puzzlement on his face; he'd often looked like that in the days when they had played chess together, whiling away pleasant evenings as lord and concubine. It was Sinan who had taught her chess; Sinan had taught Hildegart the very existence of chess. Chess was a wonderful game, with the crippled Shah, and the swift Vizier, and all their valiant knights, stern fortresses, and crushing elephants. When she began to defeat him at chess, he only laughed and praised her cleverness; he seemed to enjoy their game all the more.

"My dear, brave Sinan, I can promise you: God Himself doesn't need such infinities, not even for His angels to dance on the heads of pins." Hildegart felt light-headed without her wimple, and she ran her hands self-consciously across her braids. "Why does he think that numbers are some kind of reward for us? What's wrong with gold and diamonds?"

Sinan shrugged again, favoring his wounded arm. "I think his grief has turned his mind. We must haul him away from his darling now. We must put him to bed, if we can. No man can be trusted at the brink of his lover's grave."

Hildegart gazed with loathing at the demonic skeleton. The dense salt water still bore the she-monster up, but her porous wreck was drowning, like a boat hull riddled with holes. A dark suspicion rose within Hildegart's heart. Then a cold fear came. "Sinan, wait one moment longer. Listen to me now. What number of evil imps were bred inside that great incubus of his?"

Sinan's eyes narrowed. "I would guess at least a hundred. I knew that by the horrid noise."

"Do you remember the story of the Sultan's chessboard, Sinan? That story about the great sums." This was one of Sinan's Arabic tales: the story of a foolish sultan's promise to a cheating courtier. Just one grain of wheat on the first square of the chessboard, but two grains of wheat on the second, and then four on the third, and then eight, sixteen, thirty-two. A granary-leveling inferno of numbers.

Sinan's face hardened. "Oh yes. I do remember that story. And now I begin to understand."

"I learned that story from you," she said.

"My clever darling, I well remember how we shared that tale – and I also know the size of that mine within the earth! Ha-ha! So that's why he needs to feed those devils with the flesh of my precious pack horses! When those vile creatures breed in there, then how many will there be, eh? There will be hundreds, upon hundreds, piled upon hundreds!"

"What will they do to us?" she said.

"What else can they do? They will spill out into our sacred homeland! Breeding in their endless numbers, they will spread as far as any bird can fly!"

She threw her arms around him. He was a man of such quick under-standing.

Sinan spoke in a hoarse whisper. "So, darling, thanks to your woman's intuition, we have found out his wicked scheme! Our course is very clear now, is it not? Are we both agreed on what we must do?"

"What do you mean?"

"Well, I must assassinate him."

"What, now?"

Sinan released her, his face resolutely murderous. "Yes, of course now! To successfully kill a great lord, one must fall on him like a thunderbolt from a clear sky. The coup de grâce always works best when least expected. So you will feign to help him to his feet. Then, without a word of warning, I will bury my steel blade between his ribs."

Hildegart blinked and wiped grains of salty sand from her cloak. "Does the Blemmye *have* ribs, Sinan?"

Sinan stroked his beard. "You're right, my dear; I hadn't quite thought that through."

But as they conspired together, the Blemmye himself rose from the bloodstained sand. He tottered and staggered into the stinging salts of the dead lake. His darling had failed to sink entirely from sight.

Half-swimming, their master shoved and heaved at the bony ridges and spars that broke the surface. The waters of the Dead Sea were very buoyant by nature, but the Blemmye had no head to keep above the water. He ignored their shouts and cries of warning.

There he sank, tangled in the heavy bones of his beloved. Minutes later, his drowned corpse bobbed to the surface like a cork.

After the death of the Silent Master, life in the Holy Land took a swift turn for the worse. First, exotic goods vanished from the markets. Then trade faltered. Ordered records went unkept. Currencies gyrated in price. Crops were ravaged and villages sacked, caravans raided and ships sunk. Men no longer traded goods, or learned from one another;

they were resolved upon massacre. Defeat after wave of defeat scourged the dwindling Christian forces. Relentlessly harassed, the Crusaders lurked and starved within their stone forts, or else clung fitfully to offshore ships and islands, begging reinforcements that were loath to come.

Sinan's Moslem raiders were the first to occupy the Blemmye's Paradise. Sinan had vaguely meant to do something useful with the place. The Assassin was a fiendish wizard whose very touch meant death, and his troops feared him greatly. But armies were low on discipline when loot was near. Soon they were breaking the plumbing, burning the libraries, and scraping at semi-precious stones with the blades of their knives.

Hildegart's own Crusader forces had arrived late at the orgy, but they were making up for lost time. The Christians had flung themselves on the Blemmye's oasis like wolves. They were looting everything portable, and burning all the rest.

Six guards dragged Hildegart into Sinan's great black battle tent. They threw her to the tassled carpet.

The pains of battlefield command had told on the alchemist. Sinan's face was lined, and he was thinner. But with Hildegart as his captive, he brightened at once. He lifted her to her feet, drew his scimitar, and gallantly sawed the hemp ropes from her wrists. "How astonishing life can be!" he said. "How did you reach me amid all this turmoil?"

"My lord, I am entirely yours; I am your hostage. Sir Roger of Edessa offers me to you as the guarantee of the good behavior of his forces." Hildegart sighed after this little set speech.

Sinan seemed skeptical. "How unseemly are these times at the end of history! Your paladin Roger offers me a Christian holy woman for a hostage? A woman is supposed to be a pleasant gift between commanders! Who is this 'Roger of Edessa'? He requires some lessons in knightly courtesy."

Hildegart rubbed her chafed wrists. Her weary heart overflowed toward the Assassin in gushing confidence. "Sinan, I had to choose Roger of Edessa to command this expedition. Roger is young, he is bold, he despises death, and he had nothing better to do with himself but to venture forth and kill demonic monsters . . ."

Sinan nodded. "Yes, I understand such men perfectly."

"I myself forced Sir Roger to appoint me as your hostage."

"I still must wonder at his lack of gallantry."

"Oh, it's all a very difficult story, very. The truth is, Roger of Edessa gave me to you as a hostage because he hates me. You see, Sir Roger dearly loves my granddaughter. This granddaughter of mine is a very foolish, empty-headed girl, who, despite her fine education, also despises me bitterly. When I saw the grip that their unchaste passion had on the two of them, I parted them at once. I kept her safe in a tower in Tyre with my message birds . . . Roger is a wandering adventurer, a freelance whose family fief was lost years ago. I had a much more prosperous match in mind for this young girl. However, even bread and water could not break her of her stupid habit of loving him . . . It is her hand in marriage that Roger seeks above all, and for her silly kisses he is willing to face hell itself . . . Do I tire you with all this prattling, Sinan?"

"Oh no, no, you never tire me," Sinan said loyally. He sat with a weary groan, and absently patted a plump velvet cushion on the carpet. "Please do go on with your exotic Christian romance! Your personal troubles are always fascinating!"

"Sinan, I know I am just a foolish woman and also a cloistered nun, but do grant me some credit. I, a mere nun, have raised an army for you. I armed all these wicked men, I fed them, I clothed them, I brought them here for you to kill those demons with . . . I did the very best I could."

"That was a very fine achievement, sweet little Hudegar."

"I am just so tired and desperate these days. Since the dark word spread of our Silent Master's death, all my agents have fallen to quarreling. The birds no longer fly, Sinan, the birds go neglected and they perish. And when the poor birds do arrive, they bear me the most awful news: theft, embezzlement, bankruptcies, every kind of corruption . . . All the crops are burned around Tyre and Acre, Saladin's fearsome raiders are everywhere in the Holy Land . . . There is famine, there is pestilence . . . The clouds take the shapes of serpents, and cows bring forth monsters . . . I am at my wits' end."

Sinan clapped his hands, and demanded the customary hostage cloak and hostage hat. Hildegart donned the official garments gratefully. Then Hildegart accepted a cool lime sherbet. Her morale was improving, since her Assassin was so kindly and dependable.

"Dearest Sinan, I must further inform you about this ugly band I have recruited for your daring siege of Hell. They are all Christians fresh off the boat, and therefore very gullible. They are Englishmen – well, not English – they are Normans, for the English are their slaves. These are lion-hearted soldiers, and lion-gutted, and lion-toothed, with a lion's appetites. I promised them much loot, or rather, I made Sir Roger promise them all that."

"Good. These savages of yours sound rather promising. Do you trust them?"

"Oh no, certainly not. But the English had to leave Tyre for the holy war anyway, for the Tyrians would not suffer them to stay inside the port. These English are a strange, extremely violent people. They are drunken, foul, rampaging, their French is like no French I ever heard . . ." Hildegart put down her glass sherbet bowl and began to sniffle. "Sinan, you don't know what it's been like for me, dealing with these dirty brutes. The decay of courtesy today, the many gross, impious insults I have suffered lately . . . They are nothing at all like yourself, a gentleman and true scholar."

Despite all difficulty, Hildegart arranged a formal parley between Sinan and Sir Roger of Edessa. Like most of the fighters dying in the Holy Land, Roger of Edessa was a native. Roger's grandfather had been French, his grandmother Turkish, his father German and his mother a

Greek Orthodox native of Antioch. His home country, Edessa, had long since fallen in flames.

Sir Roger of Edessa was a Turcopole, the child of Moslem-Christian unions. Roger wore a checkered surcoat from Italy, and French plate armor, and a Persian peaked cavalry helmet with an Arabian peacock plume. Sir Roger's blue eyes were full of lucid poetic despair, for he had no land to call his own. Wherever he went in the Holy Land, some blood relation was dying. The Turcopoles, the Holy Land's only true natives, were never considered a people to be trusted by anyone; they fought for any creed with indifference, and were killed by all with similar glee. Roger, though only twenty, had been fighting and killing since the age of twelve.

With Hildegart to interpret for him, Sir Roger and his boldest Englishmen inspected their new Moslem allies. Sinan's best efforts had raised a bare two hundred warriors to combat the fiends. Somewhere over the smoldering horizon, the mighty Saladin was rousing the Moslem faithful to fight yet another final, conclusive, epic battle with the latest wave of Western invaders. Therefore, heroic Moslem warriors willing to fight and kill demons were rather thin on the ground.

Word had also spread widely of the uniformly lethal fate of Sinan's suicide martyr assassins. Nevertheless, Sinan's occult reputation had garnered together a troop of dedicated fanatics. He had a bodyguard of Ismailis from a heretical madrassa. He had a sprinkling of Fatimid Egyptian infantry and their Nubians, and some cynical Damascenes to man his siege machines. These large destructive weapons, Sinan hoped, were his keys to a quick victory.

Roger examined the uncanny siege weapons with profound respect. The copper kettle-bellies of the Greek Fire machines spoke eloquently of their sticky, flaming mayhem. Much fine cedar of Lebanon had been sacrificed for the massive beams of the catapults.

Roger had been educated by Templars. He had traveled as far as Paris in their constant efforts to raise money for the wars. He was incurably proud of his elegant French. "Your Excellency, my pious troops are naturally eager to attack and kill these wicked cave monsters. But we do wonder at the expense."

Hildegart translated for Sinan. Although the wily Assassin could read French, he had never excelled at speaking it.

"My son, you are dealing with the Old Man of the Mountain here." Sinan passed Roger a potent handful of diamonds. "You and your fine boys may keep these few baubles. Inspire your troops thus. When the very last of these foul creatures is exterminated within that diamond mine, then we shall make a full inventory of their legendary horde of jewels."

Roger displayed this booty to his two top lieutenants. The first was a sunburned English sea captain with vast mustaches, who looked rather uneasy stuck on horseback. The second was a large crop-headed Norman rascal, shorn of both his ears. The two freebooters skeptically crunched the jewels between their teeth. When the diamonds failed to burst like glass, they spat them out into their flat-topped kettle-helmets. Then they shared a grin.

Sinan's Assassin spies had been keeping close watch over the cave. The small war council rode there together to reconnoiter the battle terrain. Hildegart was alarmed by the sinister changes that had taken place on the site. The mighty door of glass and iron had been riddled with pecked holes. Fresh bones strewed the ground, along with the corpse-pale, shed outer husks of dozens of crabs. All the vegetation was gnawed and stripped, and the dusty earth itself was chewed up, as if by the hooves of stampeding cattle.

Using their pennoned lances, Roger's two lieutenants prodded at a cast-off husk of pinkish armor. Roger thoughtfully rolled a diamond through his mailed fingertips. "O Lord High Emir Commander, this place is indeed just as you told us: a very mouth of Hell! What is our battle plan?"

"We will force the evil creatures into the open with gouts of fire. Then I place great confidence in your Christian knights who charge in heavy armor." Sinan was suave. "I have seen their shock tactics crush resistance in a twinkling. Especially from peasants on foot."

"My English knights will likely be sober enough to charge by tomorrow," Roger agreed. "Is our help required in moving all those heavy arbalests? I had some small acquaintance with those in Jerusalem."

"My Damascene engineers will acquit themselves to our general satisfaction," said Sinan. He turned his fine Arabian stallion. The party cantered from the cave.

"There is also the matter of our battle signals, Your Excellency," Roger persisted gamely. "Your minions prefer kettledrums, while my men use flags and trumpets . . ."

"Young commander, such a problem is easily resolved. Would you care to join me for this battle on the back of my elephant? With those flags, horns, drums . . . and our translator, of course."

Hildegart was so startled that she almost fell from her mare. "You have an elephant, Sinan?"

The Assassin caught the reins of her restive horse in his skilled hand. "My tender hostage, I brought you an elephant for the sake of your own safety. I hope you are not afraid to witness battle from atop my great beast?"

She met his eyes steadily. "Trusting in your wise care, I fear nothing, dread Prince!"

"How good you are."

Sinan's war elephant was the strangest creature to answer the call of his birds. The gray and wrinkled pachyderm had tramped some impossible distance, from the very shores of Hindustan maybe, arriving thirsty and lean at the Dead Sea, with his great padded feet wrapped in shabby, saltworn leather. The elephant had many battle scars on the vast bulging walls of his hide, and a man-killing glare in his tiny red eyes. His ivory tusks were carefully grooved for the insertion of sharp sword blades. He wore thick quilted cotton armor, enough for a dozen tents. His towering sandalwood howdah had a brass-inlaid crossbow, pulled back by two stout whirring cranks, and with forty huge barbed bolts of Delhi steel, each one fit to pierce three men clean through. His Master was a very terror of the Earth.

Hildegart gazed up at the vast beast and back to Sinan with heartfelt admiration. How had the Assassin managed such a magnificent gesture?

On the next day, Sinan made her some formal gifts: an ivory-handled dagger, a helmet with a visor and veil to hide her beardless face, padded underarmor, and a horseman's long tunic of mail. It would simply not do for the common troops to see a woman taking to the battlefield. However, Sinan required her counsel, her language skills, and a written witness to events. Clad in the armor and helmet, she would pass as his boyish esquire.

The dense links of greased mail crunched and rustled on Hildegart's arms. The armor was so heavy that she could scarcely climb the folding ladder to the elephant's gleaming howdah. Once up, she settled heavily into place amid dense red horsehair cushions, towering over the battlefield giddily, feeling less like a woman than an airborne block of oak.

The battle opened with glorious bursts of colored flames. Sinan's sweating engineers kept up a steady pace, pumping gout after gout of alchemical fire down the black throat of Hell.

A half-dozen imps appeared at once at the cave mouth. As creatures inured to sulfur, they seemed less than impressed by the spurts of Greek Fire. The beasts had grown larger now, and were at least the size of goats.

At the sight of their uncanny capering, the cavalry horses snorted and stamped below their mailed and armored masters. A few cowards fled in shock at the first sight of such unnatural monsters, but their manhood was loudly taunted by their fellows. They soon returned shamefaced to their ranks.

A drum pounded, a horn blasted, and a withering fire of crossbow bolts sleeted across the dancing crabs. In moments every one had been skewered, hopping, gushing pale ichor, and querulously plucking bolts from their pierced limbs. The men all cheered in delight. Watching through the slits in her visor, Hildegart realized that the imps had no idea that weapons could strike from a distance. They had never seen such a thing done.

Sinan's stores of Greek Fire were soon exhausted. He then ordered his catapults into action. Skilled Damascenes with great iron levers twisted the horsehide skeins until the cedar uprights groaned. Then, with concussive thuds, the machines flung great pottery jars of jellied Naphth deep into the hole. Sullen booms echoed within.

Suddenly there was a foul, crawling clot of the demons, an antlike swarm of them, vomiting forth in pain, with carapaces wreathed in dancing flames.

The creatures milled forth in an unruly burning mob. The fearless

Ismaili Assassins, seeking sure reward in the afterlife, screamed the name of God and flung themselves into the midst of the enemy, blades flailing. The bold martyrs swiftly died, cruelly torn by lashing tails and pincers. At the sight of this sacrifice and its fell response, every man in the army roared with the rage for vengeance.

A queer stench wafted from the monsters' burning flesh, a reek that even the horses seemed to hate.

Trumpets blew. The English knights couched their lances, stood in their stirrups, and rode in shield to shield. The crabs billowed from the shock, with a bursting of their gore and a splintering of lances. The knights, slashing and chopping with their sabers, fell back and regrouped. Their infantry rushed forth to support them, finishing off the wounded monsters with great overhand chops of their long-handled axes.

A column of black smoke began to block the sky. Then a great, choking, roiling tide of the demons burst from their filthy hole. They had been poisoned somehow, and were spewing thin phlegm from the gills on their undersides. There were hundreds of them. They leapt over everything in their path, filled with such frantic energy that they almost seemed to fly.

In moments the little army was overrun, surrounded. The Damascenes died screaming at their siege machinery. Horses panicked and fell as lunging, stinging monsters bit through their knees. Stout lines of spear-carrying infantry buckled and collapsed.

But there was no retreat. Not one man left the battlefield. Even those who died, fell on the loathsome enemy with their last breath.

Men died in clumps, lashed, torn, shredded. At the howdah's rear, Sir Roger pounded a drumskin and shouted his unheard orders. The elephant, ripped and slashed by things no taller than his knees, was stung into madness. With a shattering screech from his curling sinuous nose, he charged with great stiff-legged earthshaking strides into the thickest of the enemy. As the towering beast lurched in his fury, Sinan kept up a cool fire from the howdah's crossbow. His fatal yard-long bolts pierced demons through, pinning them to the earth.

A knot of angry demons swarmed up the elephant as if it were a moving mountain. The evil creatures seethed right up the elephant's armored sides.

Hildegart, quailing within her heavy helmet and mail, heard them crawling and scrabbling on the roof of the howdah as Roger and Sinan, hand to hand, lashed out around them with long bared blades.

Claws caught within the steel links of her chain mail and yanked her from the howdah. Along with the demons seizing her, she tumbled in a kicking, scrambling mass from the plunging elephant. They crashed and tumbled through a beleaguered cluster of Egyptians on horseback.

Hildegart lay stunned and winded as more and more of the foul creatures swarmed toward the great beast, their pick-like legs scrabbling over her. Chopped almost in half by the elephant's steel-bearing tusks, a demon came flying and crashed across her. It lay on her dying, and among its many twitching legs, its broken gills wheezed forth a pale pink froth.

Hildegart lay still as death, knowing that many survived battles that way. She was utterly terrified, flat on her back amid a flowing tide of jittering, chattering monsters, men's dying screams, curses, the clash of their steel. Yet there was almost a tender peace in such stillness . . . for she wanted for nothing. She only wished that she were somehow still in the howdah, together with dear Sinan, to wrap her arms around him one last time, to shield his body from his fate, even at the cost of her own life . . .

Suddenly, as often happened in battles, there was a weird lull. She saw the blue sky and a rising billow of poisoned smoke. Then the elephant came screaming and trampling over her, blinded, bleeding, staggering to its death. Its great foot fell and rose swiftly. It stamped her flat, and broke her body.

Coldness crept around her heart. She prayed in silence.

After some vague time she opened her eyes to see Sinan's torn and bloodied face inside his dented helmet.

"The day is ours," he told her. "We have killed all of them, save a very few that fled into the mine. Few of us survive – but none of them can be suffered to live. I have sworn a holy oath that they shall not trouble the next generation. My last two Assassins and I are walking into hell to settle them forever. We shall march into the very midst of them, laden with our very best bombs. That is a strategy that cannot fail."

"I must take notes for our glorious history," she murmured. "You must write the verses for me. I long to read them so!"

The Assassin eased the helmet from her braided hair, and carefully arranged her limbs. Hildegart could not feel her own numbed legs, but she felt him lift her mailcoat to probe her crushed flesh. "Your back is broken, precious." With no more word than that – for the coup de grâce always worked best without warning – she felt a sharp, exciting pang through her ribs. Her Assassin had stabbed her.

He kissed her brow. "No gentleman would write one word about our history! All that sweetness was our secret, it was just for you and me."

The tattered pigeon carried an urgent message:

"My Darling: At the evil shores of a dead sea, I have survived a siege of such blood and hellish fire that I pray that no survivor ever writes of it. My command was ravaged. All who came to this land to serve God have died for Him, and even the imps of Satan have perished, leaving nothing but cold ashes and bones. My heart now tells me: you and I will never know a moment's happiness as man and woman unless we flee this dreadful Holy Land. We must seek some shelter far beyond the Gates of Hercules, or far beyond the Spice Islands, if there is any difference. We must find a place so distant no one will ever guess our origins. There I swear that I will cleave to you, and you only, until the day I die.

"Trust me and prepare yourself at once, my beloved, for I am coming to take you from your tower and finally make you mine. I am riding to you as fast as any horse will carry me. Together we will vanish from all ken, so that no man or woman will ever know what became of us."

The laden pigeon left the stone sill of the window. She fluttered to the floor, and pecked at the useless husks of a few strewn seeds. The pigeon found no water. Every door hung broken from every empty cage. The tower was abandoned, a prey to the sighing wind.

AMBA

William Saunders

William Sanders makes his home in Tahlequah, Oklahoma, but his formative years were spent in the hill country of western Arkansas. He appeared on the SF scene in the early eighties with a couple of Alternate History comedies, *Journey to Fusang* (a finalist for the John W. Campbell Award) and *The Wild Blue and the Gray*. Sanders then turned to mystery and suspense, producing a number of critically acclaimed titles. He credits his old friend Roger Zelazny with persuading him to return to SF, this time via the short story form. His stories have appeared in Asimov's *Science Fiction, The Magazine of Fantasy & Science Fiction*, and numerous anthologies, earning himself a well-deserved reputation as one of the best short-fiction writers of the last decade, and winning two Sidewise Awards for Best Alternate History story. He has also returned to novel writing, with books such as *The Ballad of Billy Badass and the Rose of Turkestan* and *The Bernadette Operation*, a new SF novel, *J.*, and a mystery novel, *Smoke*. Some of his acclaimed short stories have been collected in *Are We Having Fun Yet?: American Indian Fantasy Stories*. His most recent book is a historical study, *Conquest: Hernando de Soto and the Indians, 1539–1543*, and a new collection, *Is It Now Yet?* (Most of his books, including reissues of his earlier novels, are available from Wildside Press or on Amazon.com.)

Here he takes us to a ruined – and all too probable – future Earth for a powerful story of people trying to cope as things go from bad to worse . . .

THE CLIENT LOOKED at his watch and then at Logan, raising an eyebrow. Logan nodded and spread his hands palm-down in what he hoped was a reassuring gesture. The client shook his head and went back to staring at the clearing below. His face was not happy.

Rather than let his own expression show, Logan turned his head and looked toward the other end of the blind, where Yura, the mixed-blood tracker, sat cross-legged with his old bolt-action Mosin rifle across his lap. Yura gave Logan a ragged steel-capped grin and after a moment Logan grinned back.

When he could trust his face again he turned back to look out the blind window. The sun was high now; yellow light angled down through the trees and dappled the ground. The early morning wind had died down and there was no sound except for the snuffling and shuffling of the half-grown pig tethered on the far side of the clearing.

The client was doing something with his camera. It was quite an expensive-looking camera; Logan didn't recognize the make. Now he was checking his damned watch again. Expensive watch, too. Definitely an upscale client. His name was Steen and he was an asshole.

Actually, Logan told himself without much conviction, Steen wasn't too bad, certainly not as bad as some of the other clients they'd had. He had a superior attitude, but then most of them did. But he was impatient, and that made him a real pain in the ass to have around, especially on a blind sit. All right, it was a little cramped inside the camouflaged tree blind, and you had to keep as still as possible; but all that had been explained to him in advance and if he had a problem with any of it he should have stayed back in Novosibirsk watching wildlife documentaries on television.

They'd been sitting there all morning, now, and maybe Steen thought that was too long. But hell, that was no time at all when you were waiting for a tiger, even on a baited site within the regular territory of a known individual.

Steen's shoulders lifted and fell in what was probably a silent sigh. At least he knew how to be quiet, you had to give him that much. Not like that silly son of a bitch last year, down in the Bikin valley, who made enough noise to scare off everything between Khabarovsk and Vladivostok and then demanded a refund because he hadn't gotten to –

Logan felt a sudden touch on his shoulder. He looked around and saw Yura crouching beside him, holding up a hand. The lips moved beneath the gray-streaked mustache, forming a silent word: *"Amba."*

Logan looked out the blind window, following Yura's pointing finger, but he saw nothing. Heard nothing, either, nothing at all now; the pig had stopped rooting around and was standing absolutely still, facing in the same direction Yura was pointing.

Steen was peering out the window, too, wide-eyed and clutching his camera. He glanced at Logan, who nodded.

And then there it was, padding out into the sunlit clearing in all its great burnt-orange magnificence.

Out of the corner of his eye, Logan saw Steen clap a hand over his mouth, no doubt to stifle a gasp. He didn't blame him; a male Amur tiger, walking free and untamed on his home turf, was a sight to take the breath of any man. As many times as he'd been through this, his own throat still went thick with awe for the first seconds.

The pig took an altogether different view. It began squealing and lunging desperately against its tether, its little terrified eyes fixed on the tiger, which had stopped now to look it over.

The client had his camera up to his face now, pressing the button repeatedly, his face flushed with excitement. Logan wondered if he realized just how lucky he was. This was one hell of a big tiger, the biggest in fact that Logan had ever seen outside a zoo. He guessed it would go as much as seven or eight hundred pounds and pretty close to a dozen feet from nose to tip of tail, though it was hard to be sure about the last now that the tail was rhythmically slashing from side to side as the tiger studied the pig.

If Steen was any good at all with that camera he ought to be getting some fine pictures. A bar of sunlight was falling on the tiger's back, raising glowing highlights on the heavy fur that was browner and more subdued than the flame-orange of a Bengal, the stripes less prominent, somehow making the beast look even bigger.

The tiger took a couple of hesitant, almost mincing steps, the enormous paws making no sound on the leaf mold. It might be the biggest cat in the world, but it was still a cat and it knew something wasn't quite right about this. It couldn't smell the three men hidden nearby, thanks to the mysterious herbal mixture with which Yura had dusted the blind, but it knew that pigs didn't normally show up out in the middle of the woods, tethered to trees.

On the other hand, it was hungry.

It paused, the tail moving faster, and crouched slightly. The massive shoulder muscles bunched and bulged as it readied itself to jump –

Steen sneezed.

It wasn't all that much of a sneeze, really not much more than a snort, and Steen managed to muffle most of it with his hand. But it was more than enough. The tiger spun around, ears coming up, and looked toward the direction of the sound – for an instant Logan had the feeling that the great terrible eyes were looking straight into his – and then it was streaking across the clearing like a brush fire, heading back the way it had come. A moment later it was gone.

Behind him Logan heard Yura mutter, "*Govno*."

"I'm sorry," Steen said stupidly. "I don't know why – "

"Sure." Logan shrugged. He heaved himself up off the little bench and half-stood, half-crouched in the low-roofed space. "Well, at least you got some pictures, didn't you?"

"I think so." Steen did something to his camera and a little square lit up on the back, showing a tiny colored picture. "Yes." He looked up at Logan, who was moving toward the curtained doorway at the rear of the blind. "Are we leaving now? Can't we wait, see if it comes back?"

"He won't," Logan said. "His kind got hunted almost to extinction, not all that long ago. He knows there are humans around. He's not going to risk it just for a pork dinner. Hell, you saw him. He hasn't been starving."

"Another one, perhaps – "

"No. Tigers are loners and they demand a hell of a lot of territory. A big male like that, he'll have easily fifty, a hundred square miles staked out. Maybe more."

They were speaking English; for some reason it was what Steen seemed to prefer, though his Russian was as good as Logan's.

"Now understand," Logan went on, "you've paid for a day's trip. If you want to stay and watch, you might get to see something else. Wolves for sure, soon as they hear that pig squealing. Maybe even a bear, though that's not likely. But you already saw a couple of bears, day before yesterday, and you said you'd seen wolves before."

"Yes. They are very common around Novosibirsk." Steen sighed. "I suppose you're right. May as well go back."

"All right, then." Logan started down the ladder and paused. The pig was still screaming. "Yura," he said tiredly in Russian, "for God's sake, shoot the damned pig."

A little while later they were walking down a narrow trail through the woods, back the way they had come early that morning. Logan brought up the rear, with Steen in front of him and Yura leading the way, the old Mosin cradled in his arms. Steen said, "I suppose he's got the safety on?"

Yura grunted. "Is not safe," he said in thickly accented but clear English, not looking around. "Is gun."

The back of Steen's neck flushed slightly. "Sorry," he said, "Really, I'm glad one of us is armed. With that animal out there somewhere."

Logan suppressed a snort. In fact he was far from sure that Yura would shoot a tiger, even an attacking one. To the Udege and the other Tungus tribes, Amba was a powerful and sacred spirit, almost a god, to be revered and under no circumstances to be harmed.

On the other hand, Yura was half Russian – unless you believed his story about his grandfather having been a Krim Tatar political prisoner who escaped from a gulag and took refuge in a remote Nanai village – and there was never any telling which side would prove dominant. Logan had always suspected it would come down to whether the tiger was attacking Yura or someone else.

The gun was mainly for another sort of protection. This was a region where people got up to things: dealers in drugs and stolen goods, animal poachers, army deserters, Chinese and Korean illegals and the people who transported them. You never knew what you might run into out in the back country; tigers were the least of the dangers.

The trail climbed up the side of a low but steep ridge covered with dense second-growth forest. The day was chilly, even with the sun up, and there were still a few small remnant patches of snow here and there under the trees, but even so Logan had to unzip his jacket halfway up the climb and he could feel the sweat starting under his shirt. At the top he called a rest break and he and Steen sat down on a log. Yura went over and leaned against a tree and took out his belt knife and began cleaning the blade on some leaves; despite Logan's order he'd cut the pig's throat rather than waste a valuable cartridge.

Steen looked at Logan. "You're American," he said, not making it a question. "If I may ask, how is it you come to be in this country?"

"I used to be in charge of security for a joint Russian-American pipeline company, up in Siberia."

"This was back before the warmup began?"

No, just before it got bad enough for people to finally admit it was happening. "Yes," Logan said.

"And you haven't been home since?"

"Home," Logan said, his voice coming out a little harsher than he intended, "for me, is a place called Galveston, Texas. It's been underwater for a couple of years now."

"Ah." Steen nodded. "I know how it is. Like you, I have nothing to go back to."

No shit, Logan thought, with a name like Steen. Dutch, or maybe Belgian; and what with the flooding, and the cold that had turned all of northwest Europe into an icebox after the melting polar ice deflected the Gulf Stream, the Low Countries weren't doing so well these days.

Steen would be one of the ones who'd gotten out in time, and who'd had the smarts and the resources and the luck – it would have taken all three – to get in on the Siberian boom as it was starting, before the stream of Western refugees became a flood and the Russians started slamming doors. And he must have been very successful at whatever he did; look at him now, already able to take himself a rich man's holiday in the Far East. Not to mention having the connections to get the required permits for this little adventure.

Logan stood up. "Come on," he said. "We need to get going."

The trail dropped down the other side of the ridge, wound along beside a little stream, and came out on an old and disused logging road, its rutted surface already overgrown with weeds and brush. A relic from the bad old days, when outlaw logging outfits ran wild in the country south of the Amur and east of the Ussuri, clearcutting vast areas of supposedly protected forest with no more than token interference from the paid-off authorities, shipping the lumber out to the ever-hungry Chinese and Japanese markets.

It had been a hell of a thing, and yet, in the end, it hadn't made any real difference. The old taiga forest, that had survived so much for so many thousands of years, hadn't been able to handle the rising temperatures; the warmup had killed it off even faster and more comprehensively than the clearcutters had done.

But by then the markets had collapsed, along with the economies of the market countries; and the loggers had moved north to Siberia with its vast forests and its ravenous demand for lumber for the mushrooming new towns. Left alone, the clearcut areas had begun to cover themselves again, beginning with dense ground-hugging brush and then ambitious young saplings.

Which, to the deer population, had meant a jackpot of fresh, easily accessible browse; and pretty soon the deer were multiplying all over the place, to the delight of the tigers and bears and wolves that had been having a pretty thin time of it over the last couple of decades.

On the road there was enough room for Logan and Steen to walk side by side, though Yura continued to stride on ahead. Steen was quiet for a long time, and Logan had begun to hope he was going to stay that way; but then finally he spoke again:

"It was not much."

Startled, Logan said, "What?"

"It was not much," Steen repeated. "You must admit it was not much. A minute only. Not even a minute."

Logan got it then. Christ, he thought, he's been working himself up to this for better than three miles.

He said carefully, "Mr. Steen, you contracted with us to take you around this area and give you a chance to see and photograph wildlife. You'll recall the contract doesn't guarantee that you'll see a tiger. Only that we'll make our best effort to show you one. Which we did, and this morning you did see one."

Steen's face had taken on a stubborn, sullen look. "Legally you are correct," he said. "But still it doesn't seem right. For all I am paying you, it was not much."

"Mr. Steen," Logan said patiently, "you don't seem to know how lucky you've been. Some of our clients spend as much as a week, sitting in a blind every day, before they see a tiger. Some never do."

Steen was shaking his head. "Look," Logan said, "if you think you didn't see enough this morning, if you'd like to try again, we can set you up for another try. Add it onto your original package, shouldn't cost you too much more."

Steen stared at Logan. "I will think about it," he said finally. "Perhaps. Still I don't think I should have to pay more, but perhaps. I will come to the office in the morning and let you know."

"Fine," Logan said. "I'm sure we can work out something reasonable."

Thinking: you son of a bitch. You smug rich son of a bitch with your Goddamned fancy camera that someone needs to shove up your ass and your Goddamned fancy watch after it. But he shoved his hands into his jacket pockets and kept walking, holding it in. The customer is always right.

A couple of hours later they came out onto a broad clear area at the top of a hill, where a short stocky man stood beside a big Mi-2 helicopter. He had a Kalashnikov rifle slung over his back.

"Logan," he called, and raised a hand. "*Zdrast'ye.*"

"Misha," Logan said. "Anything happening?"

"Nothing here. Just waiting for you, freezing my ass. Where is all this great warming I hear about?"

"Bullshit. Ten years ago, this time of year, you really would have been freezing your ass out here. You'd have been up to it in snow."

"Don't mind me, I'm just bitching," Misha said in English, and then, switching back to Russian, "How did it go? Did he get his tiger?"

Logan nodded, watching Steen climbing aboard the helicopter. Yura was standing nearby, having a lengthy pee against a tree. "So soon?" Misha said. "Bozhe moi, that was quick."

"Too quick." Steen was inside now and Logan didn't think he could hear them but he didn't really care anymore. He told Misha what had happened. "Don't laugh," he added quickly, seeing Steen watching them out a cabin window. "He's not very happy just now. Doesn't feel he got his money's worth."

"*Shto za chort?* What did he expect, tigers in a chorus line singing show tunes?" He glanced around. "What happened to the pig?"

"I had Yura kill it. Too much trouble dragging it all the way back here, and I couldn't very well leave the poor bastard tied there waiting for the wolves."

"Too bad. We could have taken it to Katya's, got her to roast it for us."

He unslung the Kalashnikov and handed it to Logan. "Take charge of this thing, please, and I'll see if I can get this old Mil to carry us home one more time."

"So," Misha said, "you think it was the same one? The big one, from last fall?"

"I think so," Logan said, pouring himself another drink. "Of course there's no way to know for sure, but the location's right and I can't imagine two males that big working that near to each other's territory."

It was late evening and they were sitting at a table in Katya's place in Khabarovsk. The room was crowded and noisy and the air was dense with tobacco smoke, but they had a place back in a corner away from the worst of it. There was a liter of vodka on the table between them. Or rather there was a bottle that had once contained a liter of vodka, its contents now substantially reduced.

"In fact," Logan went on, "it's hard for me to imagine two males that big, period. If it's not the same one, if they're all getting that big, then I'm going to start charging more for screwing around with them."

Misha said, "This is good for us, you know. If we know we can find a big fine-looking cat like that, we'll get some business."

He scowled suddenly. "If some bastard doesn't shoot him. A skin that big would bring real money."

"The market's just about dried up," Logan said. "The Chinese have too many problems of their own to have much interest in pretty furs – drought and dust storms, half the country trying to turn into Mongolia – and the rich old men who thought extract of tiger dick would help them get it up again are too busy trying to hang onto what they've got. Or get out."

"All this is true." Misha nodded, his eyes slightly owlish; he had had quite a few by now. "But you know there are still those who have what it takes to get what they want. There always will be, in China or Russia or anywhere else." He grinned crookedly. "And a good thing for us, *da*?"

Logan took a drink and made a grimace of agreement. Misha was right; their most lucrative line of business depended on certain people being able to get what they wanted. Between the restrictions on aviation – Russia might be one of the few countries actually benefiting from atmospheric warming, but enough was enough – and those on travel within what was supposed to be a protected wilderness area, it was theoretically all but impossible to charter a private flight into the Sikhote-Alin country. There were, however, certain obviously necessary exceptions.

Logan said, "Come now, Misha. You know perfectly well all our clients are fully accredited scientific persons on essential scientific missions. It says so in their papers."

"*Konyechno*. I had forgotten. Ah, Russia, Russia." Misha drained his own glass and poured himself another one. "All those years we were poor, so we became corrupt. Now we are the richest country in the world, but the corruption remains. What is that English idiom? 'Force of hobbit.' "

"Habit."

"Oh, yes. Why do I always – "

He stopped, looking up at the man who was walking toward their table. "Govno. Look who comes."

Yevgeny Lavrushin, tall and skinny and beaky of nose, worked his way through the crowd, the tails of his long leather coat flapping about his denim-clad legs. He stopped beside their table and stuck out a hand toward Logan. "Say hey," he said. "Logan, my man. What's happening?"

He spoke English with a curious mixed accent, more Brooklyn than Russian. He had driven a cab in New York for a dozen years before the United States, in its rising mood of xenophobia, decided to terminate nearly all green cards. Now he lived here in Khabarovsk and ran a small fleet of trucks, doing just enough legitimate hauling to cover for his real enterprises. He was reputed to have mafia connections, but probably nothing very heavy.

Logan ignored the hand. "Yevgeny," he said in no particular tone. "Something on your mind?"

"What the hell," Yevgeny said. "You gonna ask me to sit down?"

"No," Logan said. "What did you want?"

Yevgeny glanced theatrically around and then leaned forward and put his hands on the table. "Got a business proposition for you," he said in a lowered voice. "Serious money – "

"No," Logan said again, and then, more sharply as Yevgeny started to speak, "No, Goddamn it. *Nyet*. Whatever it is, we're not interested."

"Besides," Misha said in Russian, "since when do your usual customers travel by air? Did they get tired of being crammed like herring into the backs of your trucks?"

Yevgeny's coat collar jerked upward on his neck. "Christ, don't talk that shit . . ." He glanced around again. "Look, it's not Chinks, okay? Well, yeah, in a way it is, but – "

"Yevgeny," Logan said, "it's been a hell of a long day. Go away."

"Hey, I can dig it. I'm gone." He started to move away and then turned back, to lean over the table again. "One other thing. You guys know where there's some big tigers, right? If you ever need to make some quick money, I know where you can get a hell of a good price for a clean skin – "

Logan started to stand up. "Okay, okay." Yevgeny held up both hands and began backing away. "Be cool, man. If you change your mind, you know where to find me."

"Yeah," Logan muttered as he disappeared into the crowd. "Just start turning over rocks . . . hand me the bottle, Misha, I need another one now."

"Wonder what he wanted," Misha mused. "As far as I know, his main business is running Chinese illegals. You suppose he's branched out into drugs or something?"

"Doesn't matter." Logan finished pouring and looked around for the cap to the vodka bottle. "I don't even want to know . . . well, this has to be my last one. Have to deal with Steen tomorrow," he said, screwing the cap down tightly, "and I definitely don't want to do that with a hangover."

But Steen didn't show up the following morning.

"He hasn't been here," Lida Shaposhnikova told Logan when he came in. "I came in early, about eight-thirty, so I could have his account ready, and he never showed up."

Logan checked his watch. "It's not even ten yet. He probably slept late or something. We'll wait."

The office occupied the front room of a run-down little frame house on the outskirts of Khabarovsk, not far from the airport. The office staff consisted entirely of Lida. The back rooms were mostly full of outdoor gear and supplies – camping kit, camouflage fabric for blinds, night-vision equipment, and so on – and various mysterious components with which Misha somehow managed to keep the old helicopter flying. The kitchen was still a kitchen. Logan went back and poured himself a cup of coffee and took it to his desk and sat down to wait, while Lida returned to whatever she was doing on her computer.

But a couple of hours later, with noon approaching and still no sign of Steen, Logan said, "Maybe you should give him a call. Ask him when he's planning to come."

He got up and walked out onto the front porch for a bit of fresh air. When he went back inside, Lida said, "I phoned his hotel. He checked out this morning at nine."

"Shit. You better call – "

"I already did." Lida leaned back in her chair and looked at him with dark oblong eyes, a legacy from her Korean grandmother. "He left on the morning flight to Novosibirsk."

"Son of a bitch," Logan said in English.

"So it would seem," Lida said in the same language.

"Well." Logan rubbed his chin. "Well, go ahead and figure up his bill and charge him. You've already got his credit card number, from when he paid his deposit."

Lida nodded and turned to the computer. A few minutes later she muttered something under her breath and began tapping keys rapidly, as the front door opened and Misha came in.

"*Sukin syn,*" he said when Logan told him what was going on. "He's run out on us?"

"It's all right," Logan said. He nodded toward the front desk, where Lida was now talking to someone on the phone. "We'll just charge it to his credit – "

"No we won't." Lida put down the phone and turned around. "The credit card's no good. He's canceled it."

"He can do that?" Misha said. "Just like that?"

"He did it yesterday," Lida said. "He paid his bill at the hotel with a check."

Everyone said bad words in several languages. Misha said, "He can't get away with that, can he?"

"Legally, no. In the real world – " Logan shrugged heavily. "He's got to be connected. You know how hard it is to do anything to someone who's connected. We can try, but I don't think much of our chances."

"At the very best," Lida said, "it's going to take a long time. Which we don't have." She waved a hand at the computer. "I've been looking at the numbers. They're not good."

"Got some more costs coming up, too," Misha put in. "We're overdue on our fuel bill at the airport, and the inspector wants to know why he hasn't gotten his annual present yet. I was just coming to tell you."

"Hell." Logan felt like kicking something. Or someone. "I was counting on that money to get us off the hook. Well, I'll just have to get busy and find us another job."

There was a short silence. Logan and Misha looked at each other.

Misha said, "We could – "

"No we couldn't," Logan said.

But of course they were going to.

Yevgeny said, "Like I tried to tell you before, it's not Chinks. I mean, it's Chinamen, but it's not your regular coolies coming north looking for work and a square meal. These are high-class Chinamen, you know? Some kind of suits. The kind you don't just cram into the back of a truck behind a load of potatoes."

"Sounds political," Logan said. "No way in hell, if it is."

"No, no, nothing like that. This is – " Yevgeny hunched his bony shoulders. "I'll be straight with you guys, I don't really know *what* the fuck it's all about, but it can't be political. The people who want it done, that's just not their thing."

Which meant mafia, which meant Yevgeny was blowing a certain amount of smoke, because in Russia nowadays the concepts of mafia and political were not separable. This was starting to feel even worse.

Misha said, "I'll tell you right now, I'm not flying into Chinese airspace. Money's no good to a man with a heat-seeking missile up his ass."

"That's okay. See, there's this island in the river – "

"The Ussuri?" Logan said skeptically. The Ussuri islands were military and heavily fortified; there had been some border incidents with the Chinese.

"No, man, the Amur. Way to hell west of here, I'll show you on the map, they gave me the coordinates and everything. It's just a little island, not much more than a big sandbar. On the Russian side of the channel, but nobody gives a shit either way, there's nothing much around there, not even any real roads."

His fingers made diagrams on the tabletop. "You guys set down there, there'll be a boat from the Chinese side. Five Chinamen get out, you pick them up and you're outta there. You drop them off at this point on the main highway, out in the middle of nowhere. There'll be some people waiting."

"Sounds like they've got this all worked out," Logan said. "So why do they need us? I'd expect people like that to have their own aircraft."

"They did. They had this chopper lined up for the job, only the pilot made some kind of mistake on the way here and spread himself all over this field near Blagoveshchensk. So they got hold of me and asked could I line up somebody local."

"Yevgeny," Logan said, "if this goes wrong you better hope I don't make it back, because I'm going to be looking for you."

"If this goes wrong, you won't be the only one. These people," Yevgeny said very seriously, "they're not people you want to fuck with. Know what I'm saying?"

Lida said, "I wish I knew what you're getting mixed up in. Or perhaps I don't. It doesn't matter. You're not going to tell me, are you?"

"Mhmph," Logan replied, or sounds to that effect. His face was partly buried in his pillow. He was about half asleep and trying to do something about the other half if only Lida would quit talking.

"I talk with Katya, you know," she went on. "We've known each other for years. She's seen you with Yevgeny Lavrushin."

Logan rolled onto his back, looking up into the darkness of the bedroom. "It's nothing. Just a quick little flying job."

"Of course. A quick little flying job for which you will be paid enough to get the company out of debt. You can't help being a fool," she said, "but I wish you wouldn't take me for one."

She moved closer and put out a hand to stroke his chest. "Look at us. You need me more than you love me. I love you more than I need you. Somehow it works out," she said. "I'm not complaining. Only don't lie to me."

There was nothing to say to that.

"So," she said, "at least tell me when this is to happen."

"Tomorrow night. Wha – " he said as her hand moved lower.

"Then I'd better get some use out of you," she said, "before you get yourself killed or imprisoned."

"Lida," he protested, "I'm really tired."

She slid a long smooth leg over him and moved it slowly up and down his body. "No you're not. Maybe you think you are, but you're not. Not yet. See there," she said, rising up, straddling him, fitting herself to him, "you're not tired at all."

Logan's watch said it was almost one in the morning. He shivered slightly as a chilly breeze came in off the river.

Not too many years ago, at this time of year, the river would have carried big floes of ice from the spring thaw; but now there was only the smooth dark water sliding past in the dim light of a low crescent moon, and, away beyond that, a dark smudge that was the distant China shore.

The island was about half a mile long and maybe fifty or sixty feet across. As Yevgeny had said, it wasn't much more than a big sandbar. The upstream end was littered with brush and washed-up dead trees, but the other end was clear and open and flat in the middle, with plenty of room for the Mil.

He dropped his hand to the butt of the Kalashnikov and hefted it slightly, easing the pressure of the sling against his shoulder. Beside him, Misha squatted on the sand, his face grotesquely masked by bulky night goggles. "Nothing yet," Misha said.

"It's not quite time."

"I know. I just don't like this waiting."

Logan knew what was eating Misha. He hadn't wanted to shut down the Mil's engines; he'd wanted to be ready to take off fast if anything went wrong. But it wouldn't have done any good; as Logan had already pointed out, with those twin Isotov turbines idling they'd never hear a border patrol unit approaching until it was too late to run for it, and, after all, where would they run to?

Somewhere on the Russian side of the river a wolf howled, and was joined by others. Standing in the shadows nearby, Yura said something in a language that wasn't Russian, and chuckled softly.

"Wolves all over the place these days," Misha said. "More than I've ever seen before. I wonder what they're eating. I know, the deer population is up, but I wouldn't think that would be enough."

"It's been enough for the tigers," Logan pointed out.

"True . . . speaking of tigers," Misha said, "I've been thinking.

Maybe we ought to start giving that big male some special attention, you know? Take a pig or a sheep or something down there every now and then, get him used to visiting that clearing. A tiger that size, he's money in the bank for us if we can count on him showing up for the clients."

"Hm. Not a bad idea."

"Have Yura put out some of his secret tiger bait powder." Misha dropped his voice. "You think that stuff really works?"

"Who knows?" Logan wished Misha would shut up but he realized he was talking from nerves. "Could be."

"Those tribesmen know things," Misha said. "Once I saw – "

He stopped. "Something happening over there." He reached up and made a small adjustment to the night goggles. "Can't really see anything," Misha added. "Something that could be a vehicle, with some people moving around. Can't even be sure how many."

A small red light flashed briefly on the far shore, twice. Logan took the little flashlight from his jacket pocket and pointed it and flicked the switch three times in quick succession.

Misha said, "Shto za chort? Oh, all right, they're carrying something down to the river. Maybe a boat."

Logan wished he'd brought a pair of goggles for himself. Or a night scope. He listened but there was no sound but the night breeze and the barely audible susurrus of the current along the sandy shore. Even the wolves had gone quiet.

"Right, it's a boat," Misha said. "Coming this way."

Logan slipped the Kalashnikov's sling off his shoulder, hearing a soft flunk as Yura slid a round into the chamber of his rifle.

Misha stood up and slipped off the goggles. "I better go get the Mil warmed up."

A few minutes later Logan saw it, a low black shape moving toward the island. There was still no sound. Electric motor, he guessed. As it neared the bank he saw that two men stood in the bow holding some sort of guns. He reached for the Kalashnikov's safety lever, but then they both slung their guns across their backs and jumped out into the shallows and began pulling the big inflatable up onto the sand.

Several dark figures stood up in the boat and began moving rather awkwardly toward the bow, where the two men gave them a hand climbing down. When the fifth one was ashore the two gunmen pushed the boat back free of the shore and climbed back aboard while the passengers walked slowly across the sand to where Logan stood.

The first one stopped in front of Logan. He was tall and thin and bespectacled, wearing a light-colored topcoat hanging open over a dark suit. In his left hand he carried a medium-sized travel bag.

"Good evening," he said in accented Russian. "I am Doctor Fong – "

"I don't want to know who you are," Logan told him. "I don't want to know anything I don't need to know. You're in charge of this group?"

"I suppose. In a sense – "

"Good. Get your people on board." Logan jerked the Kalashnikov's muzzle in the direction of the helicopter, which was already emitting a high, whistling whine, the long rotor blades starting to swing.

The tall man nodded and turned and looked back at the boat and said something in Chinese. The boat began to move backward. The tall man spoke again and the others moved quickly to follow him toward the Mil, lugging their bags and bundles.

"Let's go," Logan told Yura. "*Davai poshli.*"

Off down the river the wolves were howling again.

The road was a dark streak in the moonlight, running roughly eastwest, across open plain and through dense patches of forest. There was no traffic in sight, nor had Logan expected any. This had been one of the last stretches of the Trans-Siberian Highway to be completed, but the pavement was already deteriorating, having been badly done to begin with and rarely maintained since; very few people cared to drive its ruinously potholed surface at night.

"Should be right along here," Logan said, studying the map Yevgeny had given them. "That's the third bridge after the village, isn't it?"

Beside him, Misha glanced out the side window at the ground flickering past beneath. "I think so."

"Better get lower, then."

Misha nodded and eased down on the collective. As the Mil settled gently toward the road Logan felt around the darkened cockpit and found the bag with the night goggles. The next part should be straightforward, but with people like this you couldn't assume anything.

Misha leveled off a little above treetop level. "If there's one thing I hate worse than flying at night," he grumbled, "it's flying low at night . . . isn't that something up ahead?"

Logan started to put on the night goggles. As he was slipping them over his head a set of headlights flashed twice down on the highway, maybe a quarter of a mile away.

"That should be them," he told Misha. "Make a low pass, though, and let's have a look."

Misha brought the helicopter down even closer to the road, slowing to the speed of a cautiously driven car, while Logan wrestled the window open and stuck his head out. The slipstream caught the bulky goggles and tried to jerk his head around, but he fought the pressure and a few seconds later he saw the car, parked in the middle of the road, facing east. He caught a glimpse of dark upright shapes standing nearby, and then it all disappeared from view as the Mil fluttered on up the road.

"Well?" Misha said.

Logan started to tell him it was all right, to come around and go back and land; but then something broke surface in his mind and he said, "No, wait. Circle around and come back up the road the same way. Take it slow so I can get a better look."

Misha kicked gently at the pedals and eased the cyclic over, feeding in power and climbing slightly to clear a stand of trees. *"Shto eto?"*

"I'm not sure yet." Something hadn't looked right, something about the scene down on the road that didn't add up, but Logan couldn't get a handle on it yet. Maybe it was just his imagination.

They swung around in a big circle and came clattering back up the road. Again the double headlight flash, this time slower and longer. "Slow, now," Logan said, pulling the goggles down again and leaning out the window. "All right . . . that's it, go on."

He pulled off the goggles and closed his eyes, trying to project the scene like a photograph inside his head: the dark shape of a medium-sized car in the middle of the road, flanked by a couple of human figures. Another man – or woman – standing over by the right side of the road.

"Shit," Logan said, and opened his eyes and turned around and looked back between the seats. "Hey. You. Doctor Fong."

"Yes?" The tall Chinese leaned forward. "Something is wrong?"

"These people you're meeting," Logan said. "They know how many of you there are?"

"Oh, yes." Reddish light from the instrument panel glinted off glasses lenses as Fong nodded vigorously. "They know our names and . . . everything, really. This is certain."

"What's happening?" Misha wanted to know.

"Three men in sight, back there," Logan said, turning back around. "At least one more in the car, operating the headlights. Five men expected."

"So?"

"So that's not a very big car to hold nine men. You could do it, but it would be a circus act. Which raises some questions."

"Huh." Misha digested this. "What do you think?"

"I think we better find out more." He thought for a moment. "All right, here's how we'll do it. Set her down right up here, past that rise, just long enough for me to get out. Then circle around a little bit, like you're confused, you know? Make some noise to cover me while I move in and have a look."

He tapped the comm unit in the pocket on his left jacket sleeve. "I'll give you a call if it's all right to land. If I send just a single long beep, come in as if you're going to land and then hit the landing lights."

"Got it," Misha said. "Taking Yura?"

"Of course. Right, then." Logan undid the seat harness and levered himself out of the right seat. As he clambered back into the passenger compartment, Doctor Fong said, "Please, what is the matter?"

"I don't know yet." Logan worked his way between the close-spaced seats to the rear of the cabin, where Yura sat next to the door. "Don't worry," he said over his shoulder, hoping Fong couldn't see him getting out the Kalashnikov. "It's probably nothing."

Misha brought the Mil down and held it in a low hover, its wheels a few feet above the pavement, long enough for Logan and Yura to jump out. As Logan's boots hit the cracked asphalt he flexed his knees to absorb the impact and almost immediately heard the rotor pitch change as Misha pulled up on the collective to lift out of there.

Yura came up beside him and Logan made a quick hand signal. Yura nodded and ran soundlessly across the road and disappeared into the shadows beneath the trees on the right side. Logan walked back along the road until he reached the top of the little rise and then moved off the pavement to the left.

The cover was poor on that side, the trees thin and scattered, with patches of brush that made it hard to move quietly. Logan guessed it was about a mile back to where the car was parked. Moving slowly and carefully, holding the Kalashnikov high across his chest, he worked his way along parallel to the road. The night goggles were pushed up on his forehead; they were too clumsy for this sort of thing, and anyway he could see all right now. The moon was higher and the clouds had blown away, and his eyes had adjusted to the weak light.

The Mil came back overhead, turbines blaring and rotor blades clop-clopping, heading back down the road. It swung suddenly off to one side, turned back and crossed the road, did a brief high hover above the trees, and then began zigzagging irregularly along above the highway. Logan grinned to himself; whoever was waiting down the road must be getting pretty baffled by now. Not to mention pissed off.

He thought he must be getting close, and he was about to move over by the road to check; but then here came the Mil again, coming back up the road maybe twenty feet up, and suddenly there was a bright light shining through the trees, closer than he'd expected, as the car headlights flashed again.

He stopped and stood very still. As the sound of the helicopter faded on up the road behind him, he heard a man's voice say quite distinctly, "Ah, yob tvoiu mat'."

He waited until the Mil began to circle back, so its noise would cover any sounds that he made. A few quick steps and he stood beside the road, pressed up against an inadequate pine. He slipped the night goggles down over his eyes and leaned cautiously out, feeling his sphincter pucker.

There they were, just as he remembered: the two men standing on either side of the car, and another one over by the far side of the road. All three of them, he saw now, were holding weapons: some sort of rifles or carbines, he couldn't make out any details.

He pushed the goggles back up, slung the Kalashnikov over his shoulder, and took the comm unit from his pocket and switched it on and pressed a single key. He held it down for a count of five, switched the unit off, slipped it back into his pocket, and unslung the Kalashnikov again.

The Mil came racketing up the road once more, slowing down as the headlights flashed again. Logan stepped out from behind the tree and began moving quickly along next to the road, not trying to be stealthy; by now these bastards wouldn't be paying attention to anything but the helicopter with the impossible pilot.

It was moving now at bicycle speed, and then even slower. When it was no more than twenty feet in front of the parked car it stopped in a low hover. Logan stopped, too, and pushed the Kalashnikov's fire selector to full automatic as Misha hit the landing lights.

The sudden glare threw the scene into harsh contrast, like a black-and-white photograph. One of the men beside the car threw a forearm over his face. Someone cursed.

Logan raised the Kalashnikov and took a deep breath. "Everyone stand still!" he shouted over the rotor noise. "Put down the weapons!"

For a second he thought it was going to work. The men on the road froze in place, like so many window dummies. Logan had just enough time to wonder what the hell he was going to do with them, and then it all came apart.

The man over on the far side of the road started to turn, very fast, the gun in his hands coming up and around. There was a deafening blang and he jerked slightly, dropped his rifle, and fell to the pavement.

While the sound of Yura's rifle was still rattling off through the trees the two men by the car made their play, moving simultaneously and with purposeful speed. The nearer one took a long step to one side and whirled around, dropping into a crouch, while the other dived to the ground and started to roll toward the cover of the car.

Logan got the farther one in mid-roll and then swung the Kalashnikov toward the remaining one. A red eye winked at him and something popped through the bushes, not very close; the gunman had to be shooting blind, his eyes still trying to catch up to the sudden changes in the light. Backlit by the landing lights, he was an easy-meat target; Logan cut him down with a three-shot burst to the chest.

The car door opened and someone stepped out. Yura's old rifle boomed again from the trees across the road. Four down.

Logan walked slowly toward the car, the Kalashnikov ready. A man lay beside the open door, a machine pistol in one hand. Logan looked in and checked the interior of the car.

He took the comm unit out and flicked it on again. "All right, Misha," he said. "You can set her down now."

He walked over to the body of the last man he had killed and studied the weapon that lay beside the body. A Dragunov sniper rifle, fitted with what looked like a night scope. Definitely some professional talent, whoever they were.

He went back and sat down on the hood of the car, for want of any better place, while Misha set the helicopter down. He noticed with disgust that his hands were starting to tremble slightly.

Yura came up, his rifle over his shoulder and what looked like a Kalashnikov in one hand. "Sorry I was so slow on that last one," he said. He raised the Kalashnikov and gestured with his free hand at the body on the far side of the road. "This is what he had."

"Then for God's sake get rid of it." Remembering, Logan cleared the chamber of his own rifle and slung it over his back. For the first time in a long time he wished he hadn't quit smoking.

The Mil's rotor blades were slowing, the turbine whine dropping to idle. A couple of minutes later Misha came walking toward the car. "Bozhe moi," he said, staring. "What – ?"

"Reception committee," Logan said. "Had a nice little ambush set up. At least that's how it looks."

Misha was looking around dazedly. "You're sure?"

"About the ambush, not entirely. It's possible they were going to let the passengers disembark and wait for us to leave before killing them. Hell," Logan said, "just look at the kind of firepower they were carrying. I don't think it was because they were afraid of wolves."

Yura was going over the car. "Couple of shovels in the trunk," he reported. "Some wire, some tape."

"See?" Logan turned his head and spat; his mouth felt very dry. "They weren't planning on taking anyone anywhere. Not any farther than a short walk in the woods."

The Chinese men were getting out of the helicopter now, stopping in front of the nose and staring at the car and the bodies. Misha cursed. "I told them to stay inside – "

"It's all right," Logan said. "Doesn't matter now."

Doctor Fong appeared, walking toward them. He didn't look happy, Logan thought, but he didn't look all that surprised either.

Logan said, "I don't suppose you have any idea what this was all about?"

Fong stopped beside the car and looked around. "Perhaps," he said. "I – let me think."

"Don't think too long," Logan said. "We've got to get out of here."

"Yes." He looked at Logan. "Do you speak English?"

"After a fashion."

"Aha." Fong's mouth quirked in a brief half-smile. "An American. Good. My English is much better than my Russian."

He pushed his glasses up on his nose with the tip of a slender finger. They weren't slipping; Logan guessed it was a nervous habit. He made a gesture that took in the car and the bodies. "Can we perhaps move away from . . . ?"

"Sure." Logan slid off the car and walked with Fong over to the side of the road. "I just need to know," he said, "what kind of trouble this is about. If you guys are anything political – "

"Oh, no." Fong stopped and turned to face him. "No, we're not, as you put it, political at all. Merely a group of harmless scientists."

"Some pretty heavy people trying to stop you," Logan said. "Someone must not think you're so harmless."

"Yes, well . . ." Fong looked off into the darkness under the trees and then back at Logan. "You saved our lives just now," he said in a different tone. "This is a debt we can hardly repay, but there's something I can give you in return. Some information."

"Scientific information?"

"Yes." If Fong noticed the sarcasm he didn't show it. He pushed his glasses up again. "It's the warming."

It took a moment for Logan to realize what he was talking about. The adrenalin edge had worn off; he felt tired and old.

"It's still getting warmer," Fong said. "I'm sure you already knew that, it's hardly a secret. But – " He paused, his forehead wrinkling. "The curve," he said. "I couldn't remember the word . . . the curve is different from what has been thought."

His forefinger drew an upward-sweeping curve in the air. "The warming is about to accelerate. It's going to start getting warmer at an increasing rate, and – I'm not sure how to say this – the rate of increase will itself increase."

"It's going to get warmer faster?"

Fong nodded. "Oh, you won't notice any real change for some time to come. Perhaps as much as two to five years, no one really knows as yet . . . but then," the fingertip began to rise more steeply, "the change will be very rapid indeed."

"You mean – "

"Wait, that's not all. The other part," Fong said, "is that it's likely to go on longer than anyone thought. The assumption has been that the process has all but run its course, that a ceiling will soon be reached. It's not clear, now, just where the ceiling is. Or even if there is one, in any practical sense."

Logan's ears registered the words, but his fatigue-dulled brain was having trouble keeping up. "It's going to keep getting warmer," he said, "it's going to do it faster and faster, and it's going to get a hell of a lot warmer than it is now. That's what you're saying?"

"Even so."

"But that's going to mean . . . Christ." Logan shook his head, starting to see it. "Christ," he said again helplessly, stupidly. "Oh, Christ."

"You might well call on him, if you believe in him," Fong said. "If I believed in any gods I would call on them, too. Things are going to be very, very bad."

"As if they weren't bad enough already."

"Yes indeed. I don't know how long you've been in this part of the world, but I'm sure you've heard at least some of the news from other regions."

"Pretty bad in China, I hear."

"You have no idea. Believe me, it is much, much worse than anything you can have heard. The government keeps very strict control over the flow of information. Even inside China, it's not always possible to know what's happening in the next province."

Fong put out a hand and touched the rough bark of the nearest pine. "You live in one of the few remaining places that have been relatively unharmed by the global catastrophe. A quiet, pleasant backwater of a large country grown suddenly prosperous – but all that is about to end."

He gave a soft short laugh with absolutely no amusement in it. "You think the Russian Federation has a problem with desperate Chinese coming across the border now? Just wait, my friend. Already the level of desperation in my country is almost at the critical point. When people realize that things are getting even worse, they will begin to move and it will take more than border posts and patrols, and even rivers, to stop them."

Logan started to speak, but his throat didn't seem to be working so well.

"Your American journalists and historians," Fong added, "used to write about the Chinese military using 'human wave' attacks. This frontier is going to see a human tsunami."

Logan said, "You're talking war, aren't you?"

"Of one kind or another." Fong fingered his glasses. "I really am not qualified to speculate in that area. All I'm telling you is that this is about to become a very bad place to live."

"Thanks for the warning."

"As I say, you saved our lives. In my case, you probably saved me from worse." Fong turned and looked back at the scene in the middle of the road, where the other Chinese were still milling around the car and the bodies. "I suspect they meant to question me. That would not have been pleasant."

Logan said, "So what was all this about? Since when is the mafia interested in a bunch of physicists or climatologists or whatever you are?"

"What?" Fong looked startled. He pushed his glasses up again and then he smiled. "Oh, I see. You misunderstand. None of us is that sort of scientist. No, our field is chemistry. Pharmaceutical chemistry," he said. "Which is of interest to . . . certain parties."

Logan nodded. It didn't take a genius to figure that one out.

"The information I just gave you," Fong went on, "has nothing to do with my own work. I got it from my elder brother, who was one of the team that made the breakthrough. He told me all about it, showed me the figures – it's not really difficult, anyone with a background in the physical sciences could understand it – just before they took him away."

"Took him away? What for? Oh," Logan said. "This is something the Chinese government wants to keep the lid on."

"That is a way to put it."

"And that's why you decided to get the hell out?"

"Not really. We've been working on this for some time. We had already made contact with the, ah, relevant persons. But I admit the news acted as a powerful incentive."

"And this business here tonight?"

Fong shrugged. "The so-called Russian mafia is no more than a loose confederacy of factions and local organizations. I would assume someone got wind of the plan and, for whatever reason, decided to stop us. Possibly rivals of the ones who were going to employ us. But that's only a guess."

He made a face. "I am not happy about being involved with people like this, but I would have done anything to get out of China. And I can't imagine myself as an underpaid illegal laborer on some construction project along the Lena or the Yenesei."

Logan nodded again. "Okay, well, we'd better get moving. What do you guys want to do? We can't very well take you back to Khabarovsk with us, but – "

"Oh, we'll be all right. The car appears to be undamaged – that really was remarkable shooting – and one of my colleagues is a very expert driver. We have contacts we can call on," Fong said, "telephone numbers, a safe address in Belogorsk."

Logan noticed that a couple of the Chinese men were examining the dead men's weapons, handling them in quite a knowledgeable way. Some scientists. He wondered what the rest of the story was. Never know, of course. What the hell.

"So you may as well be going." Fong put out a hand. "Thank you again."

Logan took it. "Don't mention it," he said. "A satisfied customer is our best advertisement."

"So," Misha said, "you think it's true?"

"Right now," Logan said, "I don't know what the hell I think about anything."

By now they were about three quarters of the way back to Khabarovsk. The moon was well up in the sky and the Trans-Siberian Highway was clearly visible below the Mil's nose. Perfect conditions for IFR navigation: I Follow Roads. Back in the cabin, Yura was sound asleep.

"He could have been making the whole thing up," Misha said. "But why?"

"People don't necessarily need a reason to lie. But," Logan said, "considering the situation, I don't know why he'd want to waste time standing around feeding me a line."

"Those people," Misha said, centuries of prejudice in his voice. "Who can tell?"

"Well, if Fong was right, there's going to be a hell of a lot of those people coming north in another couple of years – maybe sooner – and then it's going to get nasty around here. Even if Fong's story was ninety percent bullshit," Logan said, "we're still looking at big trouble. Those poor bastards have got to be pretty close to the edge already, from all I've heard. If things get even a little bit worse – " He turned and looked at Misha. "I think we don't want to be here when it happens."

Misha sighed heavily. "All right, I see what you mean."

In the distance the lights of Khabarovsk had begun to appear. Logan looked at the fuel gauges. They'd cut it a little close tonight; they wouldn't be running on fumes by the time they got home, but they'd certainly be into the reserve.

Misha said, "Where are you going to go, then?"

"Hell, I don't know." Logan rubbed his eyes, wishing they'd brought along a Thermos of coffee. "Back up north, maybe."

"Ever think of going back to America?"

"Not really. Actually I'm not even sure they'd let me back in. I've lived outside the country almost twenty years now, and anything over five automatically gets you on the National Security Risk list. Anyway," Logan said, "things have gone to hell in the States, and not just from the weather and the flooding. It's been crazy back there for a long time. Even before I left."

Misha said, "Canada, then?"

"Canada's harder than this country to get into, these days. Especially for people from the States. Alaska, now," Logan said thoughtfully, "that might be a possibility. They say the secessionists are paying good money for mercenaries. But I'm getting a little old for that."

"You weren't too old tonight." He could just make out the pale flash of Misha's grin in the darkness. "Man, I'd forgotten how good you are."

"Bullshit. No, I think it's Siberia again, if I decide to pull out. I know some people from the old days, we've kept in touch. You want to come along? Always work for a good pilot."

"Maybe. I'll think about it. We had some pretty good times in Siberia in the old days, didn't we? And now it wouldn't be so damned cold."

Khabarovsk was coming into view now, a sprawl of yellow lights stretching north from the river. Moonlight glinted softly off the surface of the Amur, limning the cluster of islands at the confluence with the Ussuri.

"Going to take Lida with you?" Misha asked.

"I don't know." Logan hadn't thought about it. "Maybe. If she wants to come. Why not?"

He sat upright in his seat and stretched as best he could in the confined space. "You understand," he said, "I haven't made up my mind yet. I'm not going to do anything until I've had time to think this over."

He stared ahead at the lights of Khabarovsk. "Right now I've got more urgent matters to take care of. Starting with a long private talk with Yevgeny."

But next day everything got crazy and there was no time to think about Yevgeny or the Chinese or anything else. A perfectly legitimate scientific expedition, some sort of geological survey team, called up from Komsomolsk in urgent need of transportation services, their pilot having gotten drunk and disappeared for parts unknown with their aircraft.

And so, for the next couple of weeks, life was almost unbearably hectic, though profitable. Logan was too preoccupied to pay much attention to anything but the most immediate concerns; he barely listened when Yura came in to say that he was taking off for a few days to check out something he'd heard about.

But at last the job was finished and life began to return to a less lunatic pace; and it was then, just as Logan was starting to think once again about old and new business, that Yura showed up at the office saying he'd found something Logan ought to see.

"You come," he said. "I have to show you."

There was something in his face that forestalled arguments or objections. Logan said, "Will we need the Mil?"

Yura nodded. Logan said, "All right. Let's go find Misha."

"Well," Misha said in a strangled voice, "now we know what the wolves have been eating."

Logan didn't reply. He was having too much trouble holding the contents of his stomach down.

"Bears too," Yura said, and pointed at the nearest body with the toe of his boot. "See? Teeth marks too big for wolves."

There were, Logan guessed, between fifteen and twenty bodies lying about the clearing. It was difficult to be sure because some had been dragged over into the edge of the forest and most had been at least partly dismembered.

"Tigers, some places," Yura added. "Not this one, though."

"How many?" Logan managed to get out. "Places, I mean."

"Don't know. Eleven so far, that I found. Probably more. I quit looking." Yura's face wrinkled into a grimace of disgust. "Some places, lots worse than this. Been there too long, you know? Gone rotten, bad smell – "

"Yes, yes," Logan said hastily, feeling his insides lurch again. "I'll take your word for it."

The smell was bad enough here, though the bodies didn't appear to be badly decomposed yet. At least it was still too early in the year for the insects to be out in strength. In a few more weeks – he pushed the picture out of his mind. Or tried to.

"And these places," Misha said, "they're just scattered around the area?"

Yura nodded. "Mostly just off old logging roads, like here. Always about the same number of Chinese."

Logan wondered how he could tell. The bodies he could see were just barely recognizable as human.

"They came up the logging road," Yura said, pointing. "One truck, not very big, don't know what kind. Stopped by those trees and everyone got out. They all walked down the trail to right over there. Chinese all lined up, facing that way, and knelt down. Four men stood a little way behind them and shot them in the back. Kalashnikovs." He held up a discolored cartridge case. "Probably shooting full automatic. Some of the Chinese tried to run. One almost made it to the woods before they got him."

Misha was looking skeptical; probably he wondered if Yura could really tell all that just by looking at the signs on the ground. Logan didn't. He'd seen Yura at work enough times in the past.

"Did it the same way every place," Yura added.

"Same truck too?"

"Couldn't tell for sure. A couple of places, I think so."

"Poor bastards," Misha said. "Packed in the back of a truck, getting slammed around on a dirt road, probably half starved – they'd be dizzy and weak, confused, easy to push around. Tell them to line up and kneel down, they wouldn't give you any trouble."

"One place," Yura said, "looked like some of the Chinese tried to fight back. Didn't do them any good."

"Your people," Logan said, "they knew about this?"

"Someone knew something. Stories going around, that's how I heard. Not many villages left around here," Yura said. "Most of the people moved out back when they started the logging. Or the loggers drove them out."

"Any idea how long it's been going on?"

"From what I heard, from the way the bodies looked at a couple of places," Yura said, "maybe a year."

Logan and Misha looked at each other.

"I think," Logan said, "there's someone we should go see."

"Chinks?" Yevgeny Lavrushin said incredulously. "This is about fucking Chinks?"

He rubbed the back of his hand against the raw spot on his face, where Yura had peeled the duct tape off his mouth. He did it clumsily; his wrists were still taped together.

Beside him in the back seat of the car, Logan said, "Not entirely. We were already planning to have a talk with you."

"Hey," Yevgeny said, "I don't blame you guys for being pissed off, I'd be pissed off, too. I swear I didn't know it was going to get fucked up like that."

His voice was higher than usual and his words came out very fast. There was a rank smell of fear-sweat coming off him, so strong Logan was tempted to open a window despite the chill of the early-morning air.

"There's a *lot* of people pissed off about what happened," he said. "Some pretty *heavy* people. If they thought I had anything to do with what went down that night, I wouldn't be alive right now talking to you guys. Trust me."

"Trust you?" Misha said over his shoulder. "The way those Chinese did?"

"Oh, shit. What's the big deal? Look," Yevgeny said, "you gotta understand how it works. Used to be you could bring in as many Chinks as you could haul and nobody cared, it's a big country and the big shots were glad of the cheap labor and the cops were cool as long as they got their cut."

Misha swerved the old Toyota to miss a pothole. Yevgeny lost his balance and toppled against Yura, who cursed and shoved him away. "God *damn*," Yevgeny cried. "Come on, you guys, can't you at least take this tape off?

"No," Logan said. "You were saying?"

"Huh? Oh, right. See, everything's tightened up now. You can still bring in a few now and then, like those suits you guys picked up. But if I started running Chinks in any kind of numbers," Yevgeny said, "enough to make a profit, man, the shit would come down on me like you wouldn't believe. A bunch of them get caught, they talk, it's my ass."

"So you take their money," Logan said, "and you load them into the truck and take them out into the woods and shoot them."

"For Chrissake," Yevgeny said. His voice had taken on an aggrieved, impatient note; his facial expression was that of a man trying to explain something so obvious that it shouldn't need explaining. "They're *Chinks*!"

"They're human beings," Misha said.

"The fuck they are. A Chink ain't a man. Anyway," Yevgeny said, looking at Logan, "like you never killed anybody? I heard what you did up in Yakutsk – "

His voice died away. "Sorry," he said almost in a whisper.

Logan looked out the windows. "Almost to the airport," he said. "Now you're not going to give us any trouble, are you, Yevgeny? You're going to go along with us without any noise or fuss, right? Yura, show him."

Yura reached out with one hand and turned Yevgeny's head to face him. With the other hand he held up his big belt knife, grinning.

"Okay, okay. Sure." Yevgeny's face was paler than ever. "No problem . . . hey, where are we going?"

"You'll see," Logan told him. "It's a surprise."

Going up the logging road, watching Yevgeny lurching along ahead of him, Logan considered that maybe they should have let him put on a jacket or something. He'd come to the door of his apartment, in answer to their knock, wearing only a grubby sweat suit that he'd evidently been sleeping in; and they'd let him put on his shoes, but by the time anyone thought about a coat they'd already taped his wrists and it was too difficult to get one onto him.

Now he was shivering in the cold breeze that blew across the ridge; and Logan didn't really care about that, but he was getting tired of listening to Yevgeny complaining about it. Well, it wouldn't be much longer.

Up ahead, Misha turned off the overgrown road and up the trail toward the crest of the ridge. "That way," Logan said to Yevgeny.

"Shit," Yevgeny whined. "What's all this about? I'm telling you guys, if you found some stiffs or something out here, it's got nothing to do with me. I never operated anywhere near here. I never even *been* anywhere near here."

"Shut up," Logan said, prodding him with the muzzle of the Kalashnikov. "Just follow Misha and shut up."

It was a long slow climb up the ridge and then down the other side. Yevgeny was incredibly clumsy on the trail; he stumbled frequently and fell down several times. At least he had stopped talking, except for occasional curses.

When they finally reached the little clearing he leaned against a tree and groaned. "Jesus," he said. "You guys do this all the time? What are you, crazy?"

Logan looked at him and past him, studying the tree. It wasn't the one he'd had in mind, but it would do just fine. He turned and nodded to the others.

"So," Yevgeny said, "are you gonna tell me now – hey, what the fuuuu – "

His voice rose in a yelp as Logan and Yura moved up alongside him and grabbed him from either side, slamming him back hard against the trunk of the tree. Misha moved in quickly with the roll of duct tape.

"Hey. Hey, what, why – " Yevgeny was fairly gobbling with terror now. "Come on, now – "

"*Harasho*," Misha said, stepping back. "Look at that. Neat, huh?"

Logan walked around the tree, examining the bonds. "Outstanding," he said. "Very professional job."

Misha held up the rest of the roll of tape. "Want me to tape his mouth again?"

Yevgeny was now making a dolorous wordless sound, a kind of drawn-out moan. Logan started to tell Misha to go ahead and gag him, but then he changed his mind and shook his head.

Yura had already disappeared up the narrow game trail on the far side of the clearing. Now he came back, carrying a small cloth bag from which he sprinkled a thick greenish-brown powder along the ground. When he reached the tree where Yevgeny hung in his tape bonds he pulled the mouth of the bag wide open and threw the rest of the contents over Yevgeny's face and body.

"Now you smell good," he told Yevgeny.

Yevgeny had begun to blubber, "Oh God, oh Jesus," first in English and then in Russian, again and again. Logan didn't think he was praying, but who knew?

"All right," Logan said, "let's go."

They made better time going back over the ridge, without Yevgeny to slow them down. They were halfway down the other side when they heard it: a deep, coughing, basso roar, coming from somewhere behind them.

They stopped and looked at each other. Yura said, "*Amba* sounds hungry."

They moved on down the trail, hurrying a little now. Just as they reached the logging road they heard the roar again, and then a high piercing scream that went on and on.

SEARCH ENGINE

Mary Rosenblum

One of the most popular and prolific of the new writers of
the nineties, Mary Rosenblum made her first sale, to
Asimov's Science Fiction, in 1990, and has since become one
of its most frequent contributors, with almost thirty sales
there to her credit. She has also sold to *The Magazine of
Fantasy & Science Fiction, Science Fiction Age, Pulphouse,
New Legends*, and elsewhere.

Rosenblum produced some of the most colorful, exciting,
and emotionally powerful stories of the nineties, earning her
a large and devoted following of readers. Her linked series of
"Drylands" stories have proved to be one of *Asimov's* most
popular series, but she has also published memorable stories
such as "The Stone Garden," "Synthesis," "Flight,"
"California Dreamer," "Casting at Pegasus," "Entrada,"
"Rat," "The Centaur Garden," "Skin Deep," "Songs the
Sirens Sing," and many, many others. Her novella "Gas
Fish" won the *Asimov's* Readers Award in 1996, and was a
finalist for that year's Nebula Award. Her first novel, *The
Drylands*, appeared in 1993 to wide critical acclaim,
winning the prestigious Compton Crook Award for Best
First Novel. That was followed in short order by her second
novel, *Chimera*, and her third, *The Stone Garden*. Her first
short story collection, *Synthesis and Other Virtual Realities*,
was widely hailed by critics as one of the best collections of
1996. Her most recent books are a trilogy of mystery novels
written under the name Mary Freeman, and coming up is a
new science fiction novel, *Horizons*. A graduate of Clarion
West, Mary Rosenblum lives in Portland, Oregon.

Much ink has been spilled in recent years worrying about
the erosion of privacy caused by computers, but as the
disquieting story that follows indicates, hold on – you ain't
seen *nothing* yet!

A MAN'S EYELIDS TWITCHED as the tiny skull and crossbones icon
flashed across his retinal screen. Uh-oh. He blinked away the
image and scowled at the office door. The feds. "Sit tight and pay

attention," he said to the new kid sitting in the chair beside the desk.

"What's up?" New Kid leaned forward. But the door was already opening, the soft whisper as it slid aside a reassurance that this was a high-end operation, that your money was being spent wisely. The real-life, physical office, the expensive woolen carpet and real wood furniture echoed that reassurance. No sleazy, virtual private eye here . . . you were at the top of the ladder in a hard office.

Not that the suit cared. He took off his shades, slipped 'em into the pocket of his very well made business tunic and fixed icy gray eyes on Aman's face. If he didn't like what he saw, he was too well trained to let it show. "Mr. Boutros." The suit didn't offer his hand, sat down immediately in the chair across from the desk. Cast New Kid a single pointed glance. Jimi. Aman remembered his name at last. Raul's latest, given to him to baby-sit and maybe even train.

"My assistant." Aman put finality in the tone. New Kid stays. He kept his body language relaxed and alpha, waited out the suit's evaluation of his options. Inclined his head at the suit's very slight nod. He had won that round. You won when you could. "How may I help you?"

The suit pulled a small leather case from inside his tunic, slipped a tiny data disk from it. Without a word, Aman extended a port. Clients did not store their files on the net. Not if they were paying Search Engine's fees. The disk clicked into place and Aman's desktop lit up. A man's head and shoulders appeared in the holofield, turning slowly. Medium-dark, about twenty, mixed Euro/African and Hispanic genes, Aman noted. About the same phenotype as New Kid – Jimi – a history of war, rape, and pillage made flesh. The runner's scalp gleamed naked, implanted with fiberlight gang-sign. Aman read it and sighed, thinking of his fight with Avi over his fiberlights. Tattoo your political incorrectness on your body for the cops, son. Just in case they don't notice you on their own. Stupid move, Avi. That hadn't been the final argument, but it had been damn close. Several data-file icons floated at the bottom of the field. Food preferences, clothing, personal services, sex. Aman nodded because the feds knew what he needed and it would all be here. "Urgency?" he asked.

"High." The suit kept his eyes on the runner's light-scribed profile.

Aman nodded. Jimi was getting tense. He didn't even have to look at him – the kid was radiating. Aman touched the icon bubbles, opening the various files, hoping Jimi would keep his mouth shut. Frowning, because you never wanted the client to think it was going to be easy, he scanned the rough summary of the runner's buying habits. Bingo. He put his credit where his politics were. Not a problem, this one. He was going to stand up and wave to get their attention. "Four days," he said. Start high and bargain. "Plus or minus ten percent."

"Twenty-four hours." The suit's lips barely moved.

Interesting. Why this urgency? Aman shook his head. No kinky sex habits, no drugs, so they'd have to depend on clothes and food. Legal-trade data files took longer. "Three point five," he finally said. "With a failure-exemption clause."

They settled on forty-eight hours with no failure-exemption. "Ten percent bonus if you get him in less." The suit stood. For a moment he looked carefully and thoroughly at Jimi. Storing his image in the bioware overlay his kind had been enhanced with? If he ran into Jimi on the street a hundred years from now he'd remember him. Jimi had damn well better hope it didn't matter.

"They really want this guy." Jimi waited for the green light to come on over the door, telling them that the suit hadn't left anything behind that might listen. "The runner's wearing Gaiist sign."

No kidding. Aman knew that scrawl by heart.

"What did he do?"

"How the hell should I know?" Aman touched one of the file icons, closing his eyes as his own bioware downloaded and displayed on his retina. That had been the final argument with Avi.

"Oh, so we just do what we're told, I get it." Jimi leaned back, propped a boot up on the corner of the desktop. "Say yessir, no questions asked, huh? Who cares about the reason, as long as there's money?"

"He's government." Aman blinked the display away, ignored Jimi's boot. Why in the name of everyone's gods had Raul hired this wet-from-birth child? Well, he knew *why*. Aman eyed the kid's slender, androgynous build. His boss had a thing for the African/Hispanic phenotype. Once, he'd kept it out of the business. Aman suppressed a sigh, wondering if the kid had figured it out yet. Why Raul had hired him. "How much of the data-dredging that you do is legal?" He watched Jimi think about that. "You think we're that good, huh? That nobody ever busts us? There is always a price, kid, especially for success."

Jimi took his foot off the desktop. "The whole crackdown on the Gaiists is just crap. A bread-and-circus move because the North American Alliance . . ."

Aman held up a hand. "Good thing you don't write it on *your* head in light," he said mildly. "Just don't talk politics with Raul."

Jimi flushed. "So how come you let him back you down from four days? An Xuyen is already backed up with the Ferrogers search."

"We won't need Xuyen." Aman nodded at the icons. "Our runner is organic. Vegan. Artisan craft only, in clothes and personal items. You could find him all by yourself in about four hours."

"But if he's buying farm-raised and hand-made?" Jimi frowned. "No universal tags on those."

Aman promised himself a talk with Raul, but it probably wouldn't change anything. Not until he got tired of this one, anyway. "Get real." He got up and crossed to the small nondescript desktop at the back of the office, camouflaged by an expensive Japanese shoji screen. This was the real workspace. Everything else was stage-prop, meant to impress clients. "You sell stuff without a u-tag and you suddenly find you can't get a license, or your E. coli count is too high for an organic permit, or your handspinning operation might possibly be a front for drug smugglers." He laughed. "Everything has a u-tag in it." Which wasn't quite true, but knowledge was power. Jimi didn't have any claim on power yet. Not for free.

"Okay." Jimi shrugged. "I'll see if I can beat your four hours. Start with sex?"

"He's not a buyer. I'll do it."

"How come?" Jimi bristled. "Isn't it too easy for you? If even *I* can do it?"

Aman hesitated, because he wasn't really sure himself. "I just am." He sat down at his workdesk as Jimi stomped out. Brought up his secure field and transferred the files to it. The runner got his sex for free or not at all, so no point in searching that. Food was next on the immediacy list. Aman opened his personal searchware and fed the runner's ID chipprint into it. He wasn't wearing his ID chip any more, or the suit wouldn't have showed up here. Nobody had figured out yet how to make a birth-implanted ID chip really permanent. Although they kept trying. Aman's AI stretched its thousand thousand fingers into the datasphere and started hitting all the retail data pools. Illegal, of course, and retail purchase data was money in the bank, so it was well protected, but if you were willing to pay, you could buy from the people who were better than the people who created the protection. Search Engine, Inc. was willing to pay.

Sure enough, forsale.data had the kid's profile. They were the biggest. Most of the retailers fed directly to them. Aman pulled the runner's raw consumables data. Forsale profiled, but his AI synthesized a profile to fit the specific operation. Aman waited the thirty seconds while his AI digested the raw dates, amounts, prices of every consumable item the runner had purchased from the first credit he spent at a store to the day he paid to have a back-alley cutter remove his ID chip. Every orange, every stick of gum, every bottle of beer carried an RNA signature and every purchase went into the file that had opened the day the runner was born and the personal ID chip implanted.

The AI finished. The runner was his son's age. Mid-twenties. He looked younger. Testament to the powers of his vegetarian and organic diet? Aman smiled sourly. Avi would appreciate that. That had been an early fight and a continuing excuse when his son needed one. Aman scanned the grocery profile. It had amazed him, when he first got into this field, how much food reflected each person's life and philosophy. As a child, the runner had eaten a "typical" North American diet with a short list of personal specifics that Aman skipped. He had become a Gaiist at nineteen. The break was clear in the profile, with the sudden and dramatic shift of purchases from animal proteins to fish and then vegetable proteins only. Alcohol purchases flatlined, although marijuana products tripled, as did wild-harvest hallucinogenic mushrooms. As he expected, the illegal drug purchase history revealed little. The random nature of his purchases suggested that he bought the drugs for someone else or a party event rather than for regular personal consumption. No long-term addictive pattern.

A brief, steady purchase rate of an illegal psychotropic, coupled with an increase in food purchase volume suggested a lover or live-in friend with an addiction problem, however. The sudden drop-off suggested a break up. Or a death. The food purchases declined in parallel. On a whim, because he had time to spare, Aman had his AI correlate the drop off of the drug purchases to the newsmedia database for Northwestern North America, the region where the drug purchases were made. Bingo. A twenty-year-old woman had died within eighteen hours of the last drug purchase. His lover? Dead from an overdose? Aman's eyes narrowed. The cause of death was listed as heart failure, but his AI had flagged it.

"Continue." He waited out the seconds of his AI's contemplation.

Insufficient data, it murmured in its androgynous voice. *Continue?* Aman hesitated because searches like this cost money, and the connection was weak, if there at all. "Continue." No real reason, but he had learned long ago to follow his hunches.

He was the last one out of the office, as usual. The receptionist said good night to him as he crossed the plush reception area, her smile as fresh as it had been just after dawn this morning. As the door locked behind him, she turned off. Real furniture and rugs meant money and position. Real people meant security risks. The night watchman – another holographic metaphor – wished him good night as he crossed the small lobby. Koi swam in the holographic pond surrounded by blooming orchids. Huge vases of flowers – lilies today – graced small tables against the wall. The display company had even included scent with the holos. The fragrance of lilies followed Aman out onto the street. He took a pedal taxi home, grateful that for once, the small wiry woman on the seat wasn't interested in conversation as she leaned on the handlebars and pumped them through the evening crush in the streets.

He couldn't get the suit out of his head tonight. Jimi was right. The Gaiists were harmless, back-to-the-land types. The feds wanted this kid for something other than his politics, although that might be the media reason. Absently, Aman watched the woman's muscular back as she pumped them past street vendors hawking food, toys, and legal drugs, awash in a river of strolling, eating, buying people. He didn't ask "why" much any more. Sweat slicked the driver's tawny skin like oil. Maybe it was because the runner was the same age as Avi and a Gaiist as well. Aman reached over to tap the bell and before the silvery chime had died, the driver had swerved to the curb. She flashed him a grin at the tip as he thumbprinted her reader, then she sped off into the flow of taxis and scooters that clogged the street.

Aman ducked into the little grocery on his block, enjoying the relief of its nearly empty aisles this time of night. He grabbed a plastic basket from the stack by the door and started down the aisles. *You opened the last orange juice today*, the store's major-domo spoke to him in a soft, maternal voice as he strode past the freezer cases. True. The store's major-domo had scanned his ID chip as he entered, then uplinked to smartshopper.net, the inventory control company he subscribed to. It had searched his personal inventory file to see if he needed orange juice and the major-domo had reminded him. He tossed a pouch of frozen juice into his basket. The price displayed on the basket handle, a running total that grew slowly as he added a couple of frozen dinners and a packaged salad. *The Willamette Vineyard's Pinot Gris is on sale this week.* The major-domo here at the wine aisle used a rich, male voice. *Three dollars off.* That was his favorite white. He bought a bottle, and made his way to the checkout gate to thumbprint the total waiting for him on the screen.

"Don't we make it easy?"

Aman looked to up find Jimi lounging at the end of the checkout kiosks.

"You following me?" Aman loaded his groceries into a plastic bag. "Or is this a genuine coincidence?"

"I live about a block from your apartment." Jimi shrugged. "I always shop here." He hefted his own plastic bag. "Buy you a drink?"

"Sure," Aman said, to atone for not bothering to know where the newbie lived. They sat down at one of the sidewalk tables next to the grocery, an island of stillness in the flowing river of humanity.

"The usual?" the table asked politely. They both said yes, and Aman wondered what Jimi's usual was. And realized Jimi was already drunk. His eyes glittered and a thin film of sweat gleamed on his face.

Not usual behavior. He'd looked over the intoxicant profiles himself when they were considering applicants. Aman sat back as a petite woman set a glass of stout in front of him and a mango margarita in front of Jimi. Aman sipped creamy foam and bitter beer, watched Jimi down a third of his drink in one long swallow. "What's troubling you?"

"You profile all the time?" Jimi set the glass down a little too hard. Orange slurry sloshed over the side, crystals of salt sliding down the curved bowl of the oversized glass. "Does it ever get to you?"

"Does what get to me?"

"That suit owned you." Jimi stared at him. "That's what you told me."

"They just think they do." Aman kept his expression neutral as he sipped more beer. "Think of it as a trade."

"They're gonna crucify that guy, right? Or whack him. No fuss, no muss."

"The government doesn't assassinate people," Aman said mildly.

"Like hell. Not in public, that's for sure."

Well, the indication had been there in Jimi's profile. He had been reading the fringe e-zines for a long time, and had belonged to a couple of political action groups that were on the "yellow" list from the government . . . not quite in the red zone, but close. But the best profilers came from the fringe. You learned early to evaluate people well, when you had to worry about betrayal.

"I guess I just thought I was working for the good guys, you know? Some asshole crook, a bad dealer, maybe the jerks who dump their kids on the public. But this . . ." He emptied his glass. "Another." He banged the glass down on the table.

You have exceeded the legal limit for operating machinery, the table informed him in a sweet, motherly voice. *I will call you a cab if you wish. Just let me know.* A moment later, the server set his fresh margarita down in front of him and whisked away his empty.

"Privacy, what a joke." Jimi stared at his drink, words slurring just a bit. "I bet there's a record of my dumps in some data-base or other."

"Maybe how many times you flush."

"Ha-ha." Jimi looked at him blearily, the booze hitting him hard and fast now. "When d'you stop asking why? Huh? Or did you ever ask?"

"Come on." Aman stood up. "I'll walk you home. You're going to fall down."

"I'm not that drunk," Jimi said, but he stood up. Aman caught him as he swayed. "Guess I am." Jimi laughed loudly enough to make heads turn. "Guess I should get used to it, huh? Like you."

"Let's go." Aman moved him, not all that gently. "Tell me where we're going."

"We?"

"Just give me your damn address."

Jimi recited the number, sulky and childlike again, stumbling and lurching in spite of Aman's steadying arm. It was one of the cheap and trendy loft towers that had sprouted as the neighborhood got popular. Jimi was only on the sixth floor, not high enough for a pricey view. Not on his salary. The door unlocked and lights glowed as the unit scanned Jimi's chip and let them in. Music came on, a retro-punk nostalgia band that Aman recognized. A cat padded over and eyed them greenly, its golden fur just a bit ratty. It was real, Aman realized with a start. Jimi had paid a hefty fee to keep a flesh-and-blood animal in the unit.

"I got to throw up," Jimi mumbled, his eyes wide. They made it to the tiny bathroom . . . barely. Afterward, Aman put him to bed on the pull-out couch that served as bed in the single loft room. Jimi passed out as soon as he hit the pillow. Aman left a wastebasket beside the couch and a big glass of water with a couple of old-fashioned aspirin on the low table beside it. The cat stalked him, glaring accusingly, so he rummaged in the cupboards of the tiny kitchenette, found cat food pouches, and emptied one onto a plate. Set it on the floor. The cat stalked over, its tail in the air.

It would be in the database, that Jimi owned a cat. And tonight's bender would be added to his intoxicant profile, the purchase of the margaritas tallied neatly, flagged because this wasn't usual behavior. If his productivity started to fall off, Raul would look at that profile first. He'd find tonight's drunk.

"Hey."

Aman paused at the door, looked back. Jimi had pushed himself up on one elbow, eyes blurry with booze.

"Thanks . . . fr feeding him. I'm not . . . a drunk. But you know that, right?"

"Yeah," Aman said. "I know that."

"I knew him. Today. Daren. We were friends. Kids together, y'know? Were you ever a kid? Suit's gonna kill him. You c'd tell." Tears leaked from the corners of his eyes. "How come? You didn't even ask. You didn't even ask me if I knew him."

Damn. He'd never even thought of looking for a connection there. "I'm sorry, Jimi," Aman said gently. But Jimi had passed out again, head hanging over the edge of the sofa. Aman sighed and retraced his steps, settling the kid on the cushions again. Bad break for the kid. He stared down at Jimi's unconscious sprawl on the couch-bed. *Why?* Didn't matter. The suit wouldn't have told them the truth. But Jimi was right. He should have asked. He thought about today's profile of the runner, that break where he had changed what he ate, what he wore, what he spent his money on. You could see the break. What motivated it . . . that you could only guess at.

What would Avi's profile look like?

No way to know. Avi's break had been a back cutter.

Aman closed the door and listened to the unit lock it behind him.

He carried his groceries the few scant blocks to his own modest condo tower. No music came on with the lights. No cat, just Danish furniture and an antique Afghani carpet knotted by the childhood fingers of women who were long dead now. He put the food away, stuck a meal in the microwave, and thought about pouring himself another beer. But the stout he'd drunk with Jimi buzzed in his blood like street-grade amphetamine. He smiled crookedly, thinking of his grandfather, a devout man of Islam, and his lectures about the demon's blood, alcohol. It felt like demon's blood tonight. The microwave chimed. Aman set the steaming tray on the counter to cool, sat down cross-legged on the faded wool patterns of crimson and blue, and blinked his bioware open.

His AI had been working on the profile. It presented him with five options. Aman settled down to review the runner's profile first. It wasn't all a matter of data. You could buy a search AI, and if that was all there was to it, Search Engine Inc. wouldn't be in business. Intuition mattered – the ability to look beyond the numbers and sense the person behind them. Aman ran through the purchases, the candy bars, the vid downloads for the lonely times, the gifts that evoked the misty presence of the girlfriend, the hope of love expressed in single, cloned roses, in Belgian chocolate, and tickets in pairs. They came and went, three of them for sure. He worried about his weight, or maybe just his muscles for a while, buying gym time and special foods.

Someone died. Aman noted the payments for flowers, the crematorium, a spike in alcohol purchases for about three months. And then . . . the break. Curious, Aman opened another file from the download the suit had given him, read the stats. Daren had been a contract birth – the new way for men to have children. Mom had left for

a career as an engineer on one of the orbital platforms. Nanny, private
school. The flowers had been for Dad, dead at 54 from a brain
aneurysm.

He had joined the Gaiists after his father had died.

Unlike Avi, who hadn't waited.

Aman looked again at the five profiles the AI had presented. All
featured organic, wild harvest, natural fiber purchasing profiles. Three
were still local. One had recently arrived in Montreal, another in the
Confederacy of South America, in the state of Brazil. Aman scanned the
data. That one. He selected one of the local trio. The purchases
clustered northeast of the city in an area that had been upscale suburb
once, was a squalid cash-worker settlement now. He was walking.
Couldn't use mass transit without a chip and didn't have access to a
vehicle, clearly. Naïve. Aman let his breath out slowly. Frightened. A
little kid with his head under the sofa cushions, thinking he was
invisible that way. He wondered sometimes if he could find Avi. It
would be a challenge. His son knew how he worked. He knew how to
really hide.

Aman had never looked.

On a whim, he called up the AI's flag from his earlier search. It had
flagged the woman who had died, who had probably been a live-in
friend or lover. This time, the AI presented him with clustered drug
overdose deaths during the past five years. A glowing question mark
tagged the data, crimson, which meant a continuation would take him
into secure and unauthorized data. Pursue it? He almost said no. "All
right, Jimi." He touched the blood-colored question mark. "Continue."
It vanished. Searching secure government data files was going to cost.
He hoped he could come up with a reason for Raul, if he caught it.

His legs wanted to cramp when Aman finally blinked out of his
bioware and got stiffly to his feet. The AI hadn't yet finished its search
of the DEA data files. The meal tray on the counter was cold and it was
well past midnight. He stuck the tray in the tiny fridge and threw
himself down on the low couch. Like Jimi, but not drunk on margaritas.

In the morning, he messaged Raul that he wasn't feeling well and asked
if he should come in. As expected, Raul told him no way, go get a screen
before you come back. You could count on Raul with his paranoia
about bioterrorism.

It wasn't entirely a lie. He wasn't feeling well. *Well* covered a lot of
turf. The AI had nothing for him on the overdose cluster it had flagged
and that bothered him. There wasn't a lot of security that could stop it.
He emailed Jimi, telling him to work on the Sauza search on his own
and attaching a couple of non-secure files that would give him
something he could handle in what would surely be a fuzzy and
hungover state of mind. He found the clothes he needed at the back of
his closet, an old, worn tunic-shirt and a grease-stained pair of jeans. He
put on a pair of scuffed and worn out boots he'd found in a city recycle

center years ago, then caught a ped-cab to the light rail and took the northeast run. He paid cash to the wary driver and used it to buy a one-way entry to the light rail. Not that cash hid his movements. He smiled grimly as he found a seat. His ped-cab and light rail use had been recorded by citizen.net, the data company favored by most transportation systems. It would just take someone a few minutes longer to find out where he had gone today.

City ran out abruptly in the Belt, a no-mans-land of abandoned warehouses and the sagging shells of houses inhabited by squatters, the chipless bilge of society. Small patches of cultivation suggested an order to the squalid chaos. As the train rocketed above the sagging roofs and scrubby brush that had taken over, he caught a brief snapshot glimpse of a round-faced girl peering up at him from beneath a towering fountain of rose canes thick with bright pink blossoms. Her shift, surprisingly clean and bright, matched the color of the roses perfectly and she waved suddenly and wildly as the train whisked Aman past. He craned his neck to see her, but the curve of the track hid her instantly.

At his stop, he stepped out with a scant handful of passengers, women mostly and a couple of men, returning from a night of cleaning or doing custom handwork for the upscale clothiers. None of them looked at him as they plodded across the bare and dirty concrete of the platform, but a sense of observation prickled the back of his neck.

Why would anyone be following him? But Aman loitered to examine the melon slices and early apples hawked by a couple of bored boys at the end of the platform. He haggled a bit, then spun around and walked quickly away – which earned him some inventive epithets from the taller of the boys. No sign of a shadow. Aman shrugged and decided on nerves. His AI's lack of follow-up data bothered him more with every passing minute. The rising sun already burned the back of his neck as he stepped off the platform and into the street.

The houses here were old, roofs sagging or covered with cheap plastic siding, textured to look like wood and lapped to shed rain. It was more prosperous than the no-man's-land belt around the city center, but not by much. Vegetables grew in most of the tiny yards, downspouts fed hand-dug cisterns and small, semi-legal stands offered vegetables, home-made fruit drinks, snacks, and various services – much like the street vendors on his block, but out here, the customers came to the vendors and not the other way around.

He paused at a clean-looking stand built in what had been a parking strip, and bought a glass of vegetable juice, made in front of his eyes in an antique blender. The woman washed the vegetables in a bucket of muddy water before she chopped them into the blender, but he smelled chlorine as he leaned casually on the counter. Safe enough. His vaccinations were up to date, so he took the glass without hesitation and drank the spicy, basil-flavored stuff. He didn't like basil particularly, but the smiled at her. "Has Daren been by today?" He hazarded the runner's real name on the wild chance that he was too naïve to have used a fake. "He was supposed to meet me here. Bet he overslept."

Her face relaxed a bit, her smile more genuine. "Of course." She shrugged, relaxing. "Doesn't he always? I usually see him later on. Like noon." And she laughed a familiar and comfortable "we're all friends" laughter.

He was using his real name. Aman sipped some more of the juice, wanting to shake his head. Little kid with his head under the friendly sofa cushions. A figure emerged from a small, square block of a house nearly invisible beneath a huge tangle of kiwi and kudzu vines and headed their way, walking briskly, his hand-woven, natural-dyed tunic as noticeable as a bright balloon on this street. Loose drawstring pants woven of some tan fiber and the string of carved beads around his neck might as well have been a neon arrow pointing. "Ha, there he is," Aman said, and the woman's glance and smile confirmed his guess. Aman waited until the runner's eyes were starting to sweep his way, then stepped quickly forward. "Daren, it's been forever." He threw his arms around the kid, hugging him like a long-lost brother, doing a quick cheek-kiss that allowed him to hiss into the shocked kid's ear, *"Act like we're old friends and maybe the feds won't get you. Don't blow this."*

The kid stiffened, panic tensing all his muscles, fear sweat sour in Aman's nostrils. For a few seconds, the kid thought it over. Then his muscles relaxed all at once, so much so that Aman's hands tightened instinctively on his arms. He started to tremble.

"Come on. Let's take a walk," Aman said. "I'm not here to bust you."

"Let me get some juice . . ."

"No." Aman's thumb dug into the nerve plexus in his shoulder and the kid gasped. "Walk." He twisted the kid around and propelled him down the street, away from the little juice kiosk, his body language suggesting two old friends out strolling, his arm companionably over the kid's shoulder, hiding the kid's tension with his own body, thumb exerting just enough pressure on the nerve to remind the kid to behave. "You are leaving a trail a blind infant could follow," he said conversationally, felt the kid's jerk of reaction.

"I'm not chipped." Angry bravado tone.

"You don't need to be chipped. That just slows the search down a few hours. You went straight from the hack-doc to here, walked through the Belt because you couldn't take the rail, you buy juice at this stand every day, and you bought those pants two blocks up the street, from the lady who sells clothes out of her living room. Want me to tell you what you had for dinner last night, too?"

"Oh, Goddess," he breathed.

"Spare me." Aman sighed. "Why do they want you? You blow something up? Plant a virus?"

"Not us. Not the Gaiists." He jerked free of Aman's grip with surprising strength, fists clenched. "That's all a lie. I don't know why they want me. Yeah, they're claiming bioterrorism, but I didn't do it. There wasn't any virus released where they said it happened. How can they do that? Just make something up?" His voice had gone shrill.

"They have to have proof and they don't have any proof. Because it didn't happen."

He sounded so much like Avi that Aman had to look away. "They just made it all up, huh?" He made his voice harsh, unbelieving.

"I . . . guess." The kid looked down, his lip trembling. "Yeah, it sounds crazy, huh? I just don't get *why*. Why *me*? I don't even do protests. I just . . . try to save what's left to save."

"Tell me about your girlfriend."

"Who?" He blinked at Aman, his eyes wet with tears.

"The one who died."

"Oh. Reyna." He looked down, his expression instantly sad. "She really wanted to kick 'em. The drugs. I tried to help her. She just . . . she just had so much fear inside. I guess . . . the drugs were the only thing that really helped the fear. I . . . I really tried."

"So she killed herself?"

"Oh, no." Daren looked up at him, shocked. "She didn't want to die. She just didn't want to be afraid. She did the usual hit that morning. I guess . . . the guy she bought from – he called himself Skinjack – I guess he didn't cut the stuff right. She ODed. I . . . went looking for him." Daren flushed. "I told myself I was going to beat him up. I guess . . . maybe I wanted to kill him. Because she was getting better. She would have made it." He drew a shaky breath. "He just disappeared. The son of a bitch. I kept looking for him but . . . he was just gone. Maybe he ODed, too," he added bitterly. "I sure hope so."

All of a sudden, it clicked into place. The whole picture.

Why.

They had reached an empty lot. Someone was growing grapes in it and as they reached the end of the rows, sudden movement in the shadows caught Aman's eye. Too late. He was so busy sorting it all out, he'd stopped paying attention. The figure stepped out of the leaf shadows, a small, ugly gun in his hand.

"I was right." Jimi's eyes glittered. "Didn't think I was smart enough to track you, huh? I'm stupid, I know, but not that stupid."

"Actually, I thought you'd be too hung over." Aman spread his hands carefully. "I think we're on the same side here, and I think we need to get out of here *now*."

"Shut up," Jimi said evenly, stepping closer, icy with threat. "Just shut *up*."

"Jimi?" Daren pushed forward, confused. "Goddess, I haven't seen you . . . what are you doing?"

"He found you," Jimi said between his teeth. "For the feds. You're not hiding very well, Daren, you idiot. Everything you buy has a damn tag on it. He looked up your buying habits and picked you out of the crowd, just like that. He laughed about how easy it was. You were too easy for him to even give the job to a newbie like me." Jimi's eyes burned into the kid's. "You got to . . ."

Aman shifted his weight infinitesimally, made a tiny, quick move with his left hand, just enough to catch Jimi's eye. Jimi swung right, eyes tracking, gun muzzle following his eyes. Aman grabbed Jimi's gun hand with his right hand, twisted, heard a snap. With a cry Jimi let go of the gun and Aman snatched it from the air, just as Daren tackled him, grabbing for the weapon. The hissing snap of a gas-powered gunshot ripped the air. Again. Aman tensed, everything happening in slow motion now. No pain. Why no pain? Hot wetness spattered his face and Jimi sprawled backward into the grape leaves, arms and legs jerking. Aman rolled, shrugging Daren off as if he weighed nothing, seeing the suit now, three meters away, aiming at Daren.

Aman fired. It was a wild shot, a crazy shot, the kind you did in sim-training sessions and knew you'd never pull off for real.

The suit went down.

Aman tried to scramble to his feet, but things weren't working right. After a while, Daren hauled him the rest of the way up. White ringed his eyes and he looked ready to pass out from shock.

"He's dead. Jimi. And the other guy." He clung to Aman, as if Aman was supporting him and not the other way around. "Goddess, you're bleeding."

"Enough with Goddess already." Aman watched red drops fall from his fingertips. His left arm was numb, but that wouldn't last.

"Why? What in the . . . what the *hell* is going on here?" His fingers dug into Aman's arm.

"Thank you." Hell was about right. "We need to get out of here. Do you know the neighborhood?"

"Yes. Sort of. This way." Daren started through the grapes, his arm around Aman. "I'm supposed to meet . . . a ride. This afternoon. A ride to . . ." He gave Aman a sideways, worried look. "Another place."

"You're gonna have to learn some things . . ." Aman had to catch his breath. "Or you're gonna bring the suits right after you." After that he stopped talking. The numbness was wearing off. Once, years and years ago, he had worked as private security, licensed for lethal force, paying his way through school. A burglar shot him one night.

It hurt worse than he remembered, like white-hot spears digging into his shoulder and side with every step. He disconnected himself from his body after a while, let it deal with the pain. He wondered about Jimi's cat. Who would take care of it? Raul would be pissed, he thought dreamily. Not about Jimi. Raul had no trouble finding Jimis in the world. But Aman was a lot better than Raul. Better even than An Xuyen, although Xuyen didn't think so. Raul would be pissed.

He blinked back to the world of hot afternoon and found himself sitting in dim light, his back against something solid.

"Man, you were out on your feet." The kid squatted beside him, streaked with sweat, drying blood, and gray dust, his face gaunt with exhaustion and fear. Daren, not Jimi. Jimi was dead.

"I don't have any first aid stuff, but it doesn't look like you're bleeding too much anymore. Water?" He handed Aman a plastic bottle. "It's okay. It's from a clean spring."

Aman didn't really care, would have drunk from a puddle. The ruins of an old house surrounded them. The front had fallen – or been torn – completely off, but a thick curtain of kudzu vine shrouded the space. Old campfire scars blackened the rotting wooden floor. The Belt, he figured. Edge of it, anyway.

"What happened?" Daren's voice trembled. "Why did he shoot Jimi? Who was he? Who are *you*?"

The water helped. "What sent you to get hacked?" Aman asked.

"Someone searched my apartment." The kid looked away. "I found . . . a bug in my car. I'm . . . good at finding those. I . . . told some of my . . . friends . . . and they said go invisible. It didn't matter if I'd done anything or not. They were right." His voice trembled. "I'd never do what they said I did."

"They know you didn't do anything." Aman closed his eyes and leaned back against the broken plasterboard of the ruined wall. Pain thudded through his shoulder with every beat of his heart. "It's the guy who killed your girlfriend."

"Why? I never hurt him. I never even found him . . ."

"You looked for him," Aman mumbled. "That scared 'em."

The kid's blank silence forced his eyes open.

"I'm guessing the local government is running a little . . . drug eradication program by eliminating the market," he said heavily. Explaining to a child. "They cut a deal with the street connections and probably handed them a shipment of . . . altered . . . stuff to put into the pipeline. Sudden big drop in users."

"Poisoned?" Daren whispered. "On purpose?"

"Nasty, huh? Election coming up. Numbers count. And who looks twice at an OD in a confirmed user?" Aman kept seeing Jimi's childlike curl on the couch, the cat regarding him patiently. Couldn't make it go away. "Maybe they thought you had proof. Maybe they figured you'd guess and tell your . . . friends. They might make it public." He started to shrug . . . sucked in a quick breath. Mistake. Waited for the world to steady again. "I should have guessed . . . the suit would know about Jimi. Would be tailing him." That was why the long look in the office. Memory impression so the suit could spot him in a crowd. "I figured it out just too late." His fault, Jimi's death. "How soon are your people going to pick you up?"

"Soon. I think." The kid was staring at the ground, looked up suddenly. "How come you came after me? To arrest me?"

"Listen." Aman pushed himself straighter, gritted his teeth until the pain eased a bit. "I told you you're leaving a trail like a neon sign. You listen hard. You got to think about what you buy . . . food, clothes, toothpaste, okay?" He stared into the kid's uncomprehending face, willing him to get it. "It's all tagged, even if they say it's not. Don't doubt it. I'm telling you truth here, okay?"

The kid closed his mouth, nodded.

"You don't buy exactly the opposite – that's a trail we can follow, too – but you buy random. Maybe vegan stuff this time, maybe a pair of

synth-leather pants off the rack at a big chain next purchase. Something
you'd never spend cash on. Not even before you become a Gaiist, got it?
You think about what you really want to buy. The food. The clothes.
The snacks, toys, services. And you only buy them every fifth purchase,
then every fourth, then every seventh. Got it? Random. You do that,
buy stuff you don't want, randomly, and without a chip, you won't
make a clear track. You'll be so far down on the profile that the searcher
won't take you seriously.

"I've been buying in the Belt," the kid protested.

"Doesn't matter." He had explained why to Jimi. Couldn't do it
again. Didn't have the strength. Let his eyes droop closed.

"Hey." The kid's voice came to him from a long way away. "I got to
know. How come you came after me? To tell me how to hide from you?
You really want me to believe that?"

"I don't care if you do or not." Aman struggled to open his eyes,
stared into the blurry green light filtering through the kudzu curtain.
"I'm . . . not sure how come I followed you." Maybe because he hadn't
asked why and Jimi had. Maybe because Avi had been right and the job
had changed him after all.

"But why? You a closet Gaiist?"

Aman wanted to laugh at that, but he didn't. It would hurt too much.

Voices filtered through nightmares full of teeth. People talking. No
more green light, so it must be almost dark. Or maybe he was dying.
Hard to tell. Footsteps scuffed and the kid's face swam into view, Jimi's
at first, morphing into the other kid . . . Daren. He tried to say the name
but his mouth was too dry.

"We're gonna drop you at an emergency clinic." Daren leaned close,
his eyes anxious. "But . . . well, I thought maybe . . . you want to go with
us? I mean . . . they're going to find out you killed that fed guy, right?
You'll go to prison."

Yes, they would find out. But he knew how it worked. They'd hold
the evidence and the case open. No reason to risk pointing some
investigative reporter toward the little dope deal they'd been covering
up. They'd have expectations, and he'd meet them, and Jimi's death
would turn out to have been another nasty little killing in the Belt. He
could adopt Jimi's cat. No harm done. Just between us.

"I'll come with you," he croaked. "You could use some help with
your invisibility. And I have the track to the proof you need . . . about
that drug deal. Make the election interesting." Wasn't pleading. Not
that. Trade.

"You can't come chipped." A woman looked over Daren's shoulder,
Hispanic, ice cold, with an air that said she was in charge. "And we got
to go *now*."

"I know." At least the chip was in his good shoulder.

She did it, using a tiny laser scalpel with a deft sureness that suggested
med school or even an MD. And it hurt, but not a lot compared to the

glowing coals of pain in his left arm and then they were loading him into the back of a vehicle and it was fully dark outside.

He was invisible. Right now. He no longer existed in the electronic reality of the city. If he made it back to his apartment, it wouldn't let him in. The corner store wouldn't take his card or even cash. He felt naked. No, he felt as if he no longer existed. Death wasn't as complete as this. Wondered if Avi had felt like that at first. I probably could have found him, he thought. If I'd had the guts to try.

"I'm glad you're coming with us." Daren sat beside him as the truck or whatever it was rocked and bucked over broken pavement toward the nearest clear street. "Lea says you probably won't die."

"I'm thrilled."

"Maybe we can use the drug stuff to influence the election, get someone honest elected."

He was as bad as Jimi, Aman thought. But . . . why not hope?

"You'll like the head of our order," Daren said thoughtfully. "He's not a whole lot older than me, but he's great. Really brilliant and he cares about every person in the order. *She* really matters to him . . . the Earth, I mean. Avi will really welcome you."

Avi.

Aman closed his eyes.

"Hey, you okay?" Daren had him by the shoulders. "Don't die now, not after all this." He sounded panicky.

"I won't," Aman whispered. He managed a tiny laugh that didn't hurt too bad.

Maybe it hadn't been the final fight after all.

Could almost make him believe in Avi's Goddess. Almost.

"Your head of the order sucks at hiding," he whispered. And fainted.

PICCADILLY CIRCUS

Chris Beckett

British writer Chris Beckett is a frequent contributor to Interzone, and has made several sales to *Asimov's Science Fiction*. His first novel, *The Holy Machine*, is available from Wildside Press. A former social worker, he's now a university lecturer living in Cambridge, England.

Here he shows us that quite a bit more than just beauty can be in the eye of the beholder . . .

CLARISSA FALL IS HEADING for central London to see the lights, bumping along the potholed roads at five miles an hour in her electric invalid car, oblivious to the honking horns, the cars queuing behind her, the angry shouts . . . How many times has she been warned? How many times has she been humiliated? But she must see the lights.

"When I was a little girl there were still physical lights in Piccadilly Circus," she's telling everyone she can. "I remember my father taking me. They were the most wonderful thing I'd ever seen."

She'd always been odd. There was that business when she cut holes in the wildlife fence to let the animals into the city. There were those young consensual tear-aways she used to insist on bringing home. But things really started getting bad when her husband Terence died, leaving her alone in that big old house by the perimeter, that big fake chateau with its empty fountains and those icy lights that lit it up at night like Dracula's castle. I suppose it was loneliness, though god knows when Terence was alive he and Clarissa never seemed to do anything but fight.

"I am two hundred years old, you know," she kept saying now. "I am the very last physical human being in London."

Neither of these were true, of course, but she was certainly very old and it was certainly the case that she could go for days and even weeks without seeing another physical person. There really weren't many of us left by now and most of us had congregated for mutual support in a couple of clusters in the South London suburbs. No one lived within five miles of Clarissa's phoney chateau on the northern perimeter and no one was much inclined to go and see her. She'd always been histrionic and self-obsessed, and now she was downright crazy. What's more – and most of us found this *particularly* unforgivable – she drew unwelcome attention onto us physicals, both from the consensuals, who already dislike us and call us 'outsiders' and 'spooks,' and from the hidden authorities in the Hub.

Her trouble was that she didn't really feel at home in either world, physical or consensual. The stiff arthritic dignity of the physicals repelled her. She thought us stuffy and smug and she despised our assumption that our own experience was uniquely authentic and true.

"Would you rather the world itself ended than admit the possibility that there may be other kinds of life apart from ours?" she once demanded.

But really, although she always insisted to us that it wasn't so, she was equally disgusted by the superficiality of the consensuals, their uncritical willingness to accept as real whatever the Hub chose to serve up, their lack of curiosity, their wilful ignorance of where they came from or what they really were. While she might criticise us physicals, she never seriously considered the possibility of giving up her own physical being and joining the consensuals with their constructed virtual bodies. And this meant that she would still always be an Outsider to them.

She may have felt at home with no one but she became a nuisance to *everyone* – physical and consensual – as a result of her forays into the city. At first she went on foot. Then, when she became too frail, she got hold of that little invalid car, a vehicle which the consensuals of North London would soon come to know and hate. Bumping slowly along the crumbling physical roads she would switch off her Field implant so as not to be deceived by the smooth virtual surface, but this meant that she couldn't see or hear the consensual traffic going by either. She could see only the empty buildings and the cracked and pockmarked surface of the empty road. Consensual drivers just had to cope as best they could with her wanderings back and forth.

When she parked her car, though, she always turned her implant on again. This of course instantly transformed empty ruined physical London into the lively metropolis that was the Urban Consensual Field, a virtual city in imitation of London as it once was, superimposed by the Hub over what London had become. Clarissa could still just remember those old days: the crowds, the fumes, the lights, the noise, the hectic life of a city in which, bizarrely, it still seemed feasible for millions of physical human beings to casually consume what they wanted of the physical world's resources, and casually discard what they didn't. And she craved that bustle and that life, she craved it desperately.

We all had Field implants, of course. They were a necessity for dealing with a civilisation that had become, whether we liked it or not, primarily digital. Spliced into our nervous system, they allowed consensual constructs to be superimposed over our perceptions of the material world, so that we could see the same world that the consensuals saw, hear what they heard and, to a limited degree, touch what they touched. The rest of us invariably took the position that we didn't like having to deal with the consensual world, but it was sometimes a necessary evil. But for Clarissa it was different. When she switched on her implant it wasn't a matter of practical necessity for her, it was more like injecting heroin into an artery. All at once there were people all around her, there was life, there were shop windows and market stalls piled high with colourful merchandise, and the dizzying suddenness of it was like the hit of a powerful drug.

But this drug wasn't the Field, it was the moment of crossing over. After that first moment the experience never lived up to its initial promise, for however hard Clarissa tried, the consensual world shut her out. And she did try. She spent hours in the consensual city outside shops and in parks and on street corners making rather pathetic efforts to engage people in conversation, but most people avoided her and some made no secret of their contempt. It was true that a few kind souls suppressed their revulsion at her age and her physicality and briefly allowed her the illusion that she had made a friend, but it was only out of kindness. Even apart from being an Outsider she really wasn't good company. She talked too much; she didn't listen; and, what was worse, however much she might criticise her fellow Outsiders for our existential snobbery, she herself was as much of a snob as any of us and a lot less inhibited about it. She could never resist pointing out to consensuals the shallow and illusory nature of their existence: "You're so *very* nice dear. It's such a pity that you're not really here."

Usually she found herself alone in a kind of lacuna, with people moving aside to pass her by at a safe distance. And in these situations she would often become distressed and start to rant and shout: "You're not real you know! You're just bits of nervous tissue plugged into a computer! You're far away from here and the computer is sending you pictures of the real London with all this consensual nonsense superimposed on top of it!"

Terence used to talk like that a lot when he was alive, as haughty old physicals tended to do, but in those days Clarissa always used to criticise him for it: "Who's to say our world is more real than theirs?" I remember her demanding of him at one of the physical community's periodic gatherings.

The two of them on opposite sides of a large dining table laden with silver and cut glass. Terence declined to answer. Everyone in the room was willing Clarissa to shut up and let them return to their customary state of numbness. "Come on Terence, who's to say?" she insisted. "At least consensuals engage with life and with one another." She glared up and down the table. "And what do you think would be left of us if we stripped away everything that had come from outside ourselves, everything that other people had made? We'd be naked. We'd be gibbering imbeciles. Think about it. Even when we talk to ourselves inside our own heads, we use words that other people gave us."

But that was then. Now it seemed that Terence had been speaking all along on behalf of a side of Clarissa's own self.

"Don't look at me like that!" she'd scold the consensuals when they pointed and laughed at her, "You sold your true bodies for the illusion of youth and plenty, but I am real!"

Sometimes, in the middle of one of these rants, she would defiantly turn off her Field implant, making the people and the traffic disappear from her view, houses become empty shells again and all the shop windows with their cheerful displays turn back into hollow caves: "I can't even see you, you know!" she shouted, knowing that the consensuals could nevertheless still see her, for sensors across the city pick up the sights and sounds and textures of everything physical and this becomes the matrix within which the consensual city is built. They had no choice but to see her. "I'm in the real world and I can't see you at all. *That's* how unreal you are. I can turn you off with a flick of a switch."

But though she might like telling the consensuals they didn't really exist, their opinion mattered to her desperately and she couldn't resist turning the implant on again to see what impact she was having. (I've never known anyone who turned an implant on and off as often as Clarissa did.) Almost invariably they would all be carefully ignoring her.

It was in these moments, when she had thrown a tantrum and discovered that no one was impressed, that things could get out of control. Once, a month or so before her trip to Piccadilly Circus, she found she could get no one to pay attention to her in the streets outside Walthamstow underground station. Rather than admit defeat, she insisted instead on going right down the stairs, arthritic and unsteady as she was, and waiting on the Southbound platform for a train. The platform emptied around her as the consensuals crowded up to the other end.

And then when the train came in, she promptly tried to step onto it. Of course she fell straight through onto the track, it being a virtual train, part of the Field, which couldn't bear physical weight, only the notional weight of consensual projections. She broke a small bone in her ankle. It hurt a great deal and she began to hobble up and down wailing for someone to help her up. The rules under which the Field operated meant that the train could not move off with her there. Yet she herself was breaking those rules. To the consternation of the passengers she appeared to them to be wading waist deep through the solid floor of the train, looking up at their averted faces accusingly and haranguing them for their lack of compassion: "Isn't there a single soul left in London prepared to help an old woman? Have you all lost your hearts as well as your bodies?"

Broken bones – and physical injuries in general – were completely outside their experience, so they would have had some excuse for not empathising with her plight, but actually they would have *liked* to help her, if not out of pure altruism, then out of self-interest. For she was holding up the train – not to mention the other trains behind it – and distressing everyone. Consensuals, unless they are destitute, are

uniformly beautiful and, although they die at last, they don't age in the
way we do. Spit never flies from their mouth. Snot never runs from their
noses. Their make-up doesn't run or smear. It must have been truly
horrific to see this dreadful wrinkled smeary creature wading up and
down among them with its head at knee-height, like some kind of
goblin out of a fairy tale. But what could they do? They could no more
lift Clarissa back onto the platform with their consensual hands and
arms, than the train could hold her up with its consensual floor.

So someone called the Hub, and the Hub put the word out to us in the
physical community that one of our people was in difficulties and did
we want to deal with it or should Agents be sent in? Phone calls went to
and fro. The physicals of London are like the members of some old
dysfunctional family who have seen right through each other's limited
charms, know every one of each other's dreary frailties, but who are
somehow chained together in misery.

"Bloody Clarissa. Have you heard?"

"Clarissa's up to her tricks again."

"Obviously we can't let Agents in. The real people have to deal with
their own."

"Bloody Clarissa. How dare she put us in this position?"

In the end I was delegated to go up there with Richard Howard to
sort it out. We travelled right across London and, since of course we
couldn't use the virtual escalators, climbed slowly and stiffly as Clarissa
had done, down the deep concrete staircase into the station. Clarissa
was still stuck on the track. She had turned off her implant again, partly
out of defiance, partly to avoid being overwhelmed by the agitated
consensuals around her. But as a result she had lost the lights that the
Field superimposed on the deserted and unlit physical station. For the
last hour she had been stumbling around crying and wailing in pitch
darkness with nothing for company except rats, and no sound at all
except the drip, drip of water from somewhere down the southbound
tunnel.

Richard and I had our implants switched on so as to be able to see
what we were doing, and so had to endure the cold gaze of consensuals.
They sat in the train watching as we clumsily extracted Clarissa from
the floor; they stood on the platform watching as we dusted her down;
they craned round on the virtual escalators to watch us half-carry her
up the concrete steps.

"Look at those spooks!" someone in the street said, quite loudly, as
Richard and I helped Clarissa into Richard's truck. "Look at the ugly
faces on them! Haven't they got any self-respect?"

And there was a general hum of agreement. As a rule consensuals are
scared of us Outsiders and our uncanny powers over the physical world.
(Richard in particular is an object of awe, with his immense height, his
great mane of white hair, and his tendency to walk contemptuously
through virtual walls.) But we couldn't have looked very scary just then:
two breathless old men, flushed and sweaty, helping a batty old woman
with an injured foot into an ancient truck.

"Don't forget my car!" wailed Clarissa.

Somehow we manhandled her invalid car into the back of the truck. God knows why we agreed to take it. We would have been within our rights to say it was too heavy and left it behind. But Clarissa was powerful in some ways. She always had been. However much you might resent it, however much you told yourself that there is no reason at all to comply, it was hard not to do what she asked.

"Don't expect us to bale you out like this again," Richard told her as he bandaged her foot up back at her house. "Next time it'll be Agents."

None of us is sure what Agents really are, except that they are the servants of the Hub in the physical world. They have no visible faces. Their smooth heads and bodies are covered all over with a costume or skin in a special shade of blue which isn't picked up by the Field sensors, and is therefore invisible to consensuals. Some of us think they are simply robots of some kind, but others maintain that they are a new kind of physical human being, bred and raised apart from us for the Hub's own purposes. But, whatever they are, we fear them almost as much as do the consensuals, who only know of them by rumour and can only infer their presence from secondary clues.

"I couldn't have borne that," Clarissa murmured, "not Agents coming for me down there in the dark."

"Well it's your choice," Richard told her. "You get yourself in a fix like that again, and that's all the help you'll get."

He had been married to her once, before the days of Terence. Absurd as it now seemed, they had once, briefly, been lovers, enchanted by the sheer fact of one another's presence in the world. And even now, absurdly, Clarissa attempted to defuse his anger by flirting with him.

"I know I've been a silly girl, Richard dearest, but I promise I won't do it again."

I'm thinking about what I wrote earlier:

"The rest of us took the position," I said, "that we didn't like having to deal with the consensual world, but it was sometimes a necessary evil . . ."

I'm imagining Clarissa reading that and snorting with derision.

"Would you prefer it then if there was just us and no consensual world at all?"

Actually that very thing is looking increasingly on the cards.

When the consensual cities were first established as a way of withdrawing human beings from an environment which they were about to destroy, it was decided that these virtual cities would be congruent with the old physical ones. There were three reasons for this. Firstly many people could only be persuaded to accept consensual status on the basis that they would still have access to what they still thought of then as the 'real world.' Secondly, it was thought important to allow consensuals to continue to be able to interact with those of us who bought an exemption from the dephysicalisation process, by paying the enormous levy and by allowing ourselves to be sterilised. (In those days, after all, physicals and consensuals might be brother and sister, father and son, schoolmates, life-long friends . . .) And thirdly it was because the processing capacity of the Hub, though huge, was finite and a consensual world based on the physical one was less heavy on the Hub's resources than a purely invented one.

All three of those considerations have largely ceased to apply. The Hub has grown bigger, the physicals and the consensuals have grown apart and the consensuals have long since lost any sense of the physical world as being the 'real' one. So it would now be politically and technically possible for the Hub to decouple the physical city from the consensual one. In some ways this would be much easier than maintaining the status quo with its costly network of sensors.

But I suppose, if I am honest, that when I contemplate the possibility of waking up to a London where the implants no longer work, the consensuals can no longer be encountered and we are left on our own among the ruins, then I don't welcome it. In fact what I experience is a sense of dread, abandonment, isolation. I suppose I simply rationalise this feeling by saying that we need the consensuals for practical reasons, that their presence is a necessary evil.

I think Clarissa's promise held for all of two days before she was off in her car again. Within a week she was back in Walthamstow, though she avoided the station and didn't make any scenes. Before the end of the month, she was charging up the battery for a major trip, right into the centre of London. And then she was off again in earnest, bumping and bouncing grimly along the road and stubbornly refusing to think about how far her battery would take her.

As ever she drove with her implant switched off. She saw empty houses, abandoned petrol stations, an empty road, badly damaged by years of frost. But once in a while she stopped for that hit she so constantly craved, that momentary burst of comfort and reassurance that came from switching on her implant and seeing a living city emerging from the silent ruins.

"I'm going down to Piccadilly Circus," she told the people outside a row of shops in Stoke Newington. "They used to take me there when I was a little girl, to look at the coloured lights."

The shoppers all turned away.

"I used to love those lights," she told a man outside a betting shop in Islington, "the way they rippled and flowed. All that electricity! All that lovely colour!"

"Why don't you go home, spook?" the betting man muttered as he hurried off.

"I expect they still have lights like that now, don't they?" she asked a young woman in King's Cross, "Not *real* ones obviously, but ones for you people to see?"

"Oh yes," said the young woman, whose name was Lily, "they're lovely lights in Piccadilly Circus, but they're *quite* real you know. They're not physical or nothing like that."

Lily was not very bright and was happy to be friendly with anyone. She had a simple round very low res face that was quite flat and looked like something from a cartoon strip. Consensuals could choose their own appearance and be as pretty and as interesting and as high resolution as their bank balances would allow, but some consensuals couldn't afford much in the way of looks – and Lily was very obviously poor. Her eyes were dots, her skin a completely uniform pink, her clothes mere slabs of colour and her smile a simple upward curve of the single line that was her mouth.

"I'm pretty sure they're not physical anyway," she said, in her tinny little low res voice. And then she realised she had been rude and the smile abruptly inverted itself into a downward curve of regret. "Oh dear. I didn't mean to say there was something wrong with being – you know – physical. That came out all wrong."

"Oh don't worry. I get that all the time. And you're the first friendly person I've met since I left home."

Clarissa had opened a flask of coffee and, still sitting in her little car, she poured herself a small cup. It was mid-October, a fresh autumn day getting on towards evening, and she was beginning to feel the cold.

"My father took me to see the lights in Piccadilly Circus when I was a little girl. Apparently when we got there I asked him where the clowns and tigers were. 'And where are the pretty ladies in tights?' I wanted to know. He said it wasn't that kind of circus: 'Circus just means a circle for the cars to go round.' I don't remember that conversation myself, but I do remember standing there with the beautiful electric lights all round me and realising that I didn't care about the tigers and the pretty ladies. Colours are so magical when you are a child. I looked one way and then the other, but I wanted to see it all at once, so in the end I decided to spin round and round on the spot."

She lifted the coffee cup to her lips and took a sip.

"I'm Lily," Lily said helpfully, staring wonderingly at the intricate wrinkles all over Clarissa's hands, and at the brown liver-spots on them, and the way they trembled all the time so that coffee kept sloshing out down the sides of the cup. If Lily's low res looks were short on detail. Clarissa seemed to possess detail in reckless abandon. And yet – and this was the part that puzzled Lily – it was to no apparent decorative purpose. That look must have cost a fortune, Lily thought, but why would anyone choose to look like *that*?

"I'm Clarissa, my dear. I'm Clarissa Fall," said the old lady grandly, finishing her coffee and shaking the drips out of the cup before screwing it back onto the top of the flask.

"Do you know the way?" Lily ventured. "Do you know the way to Piccadilly Circus?"

"*I* should think so," Clarissa snorted. "I'm over two hundred years old and I've lived in London since I was born. I'm the last physical person left in London, you know." She looked at her watch. She craved company and attention and yet when she actually had it, she was always curiously impatient and off-hand.

"Oh. Two hundred," repeated Lily humbly. "That's quite old. Only otherwise I was going to suggest I could come and show you the way . . ."

"Yes, do come by all means," said Clarissa magnanimously.

The laws of the physical universe prevented physical people from riding on virtual vehicles, but there was nothing in the rules of the Field to prevent virtual people from riding a physical car. The only difficulty was that the invalid car was only designed for one, so Lily had to ride at the back on the little rack intended to carry bags of shopping.

"I don't mind," said Lily, who couldn't afford dignity. "It's not that far."

"I'll have to turn my implant off, I'm afraid," Clarissa told her, "so I can see the bumps on the road. You won't be able to talk to me until we're there."

"I don't mind," said Lily gamely. She had no idea what Clarissa meant, but she had long since accepted that life was largely incomprehensible.

Clarissa turned the key to start the car. As she did so she noticed the meter that showed the remaining charge in the battery. When she set out, the needle had pointed to FULLY CHARGED, but now it was on the edge of the red area marked WARNING! VERY LOW! She allowed herself for a single moment to see the trouble she was in – and to feel fear – and then she pushed it firmly from her conscious mind.

Clarissa drove slowly down Tottenham Court Road. The shop buildings were dark and empty, their windows blank, or sometimes broken and full of dead leaves. The roads were bare and strewn with rubble. Apart from the whine of her electric car and the click of stones thrown up by its rubber wheels, there was utter silence.

But Lily saw windows full of goods for sale, cars and buses all around them, and people everywhere.

"Nearly there!" she called out cheerfully, still not fully grasping that Clarissa with her implant inactivated couldn't hear her or sense her presence in any way. Then she gave a little shriek as Clarissa nonchalantly swerved across the road directly into the path of oncoming traffic and carried on down the wrong side of the road, magnificently indifferent to honking horns and shouts of indignation.

"She's physical," Lily called out by way of explanation from her perch on the back of Clarissa's little car. "She's just physical."

Half-way along Shaftesbury Avenue, the battery gave out and the car died.

And now Clarissa *was* scared. It was getting towards evening; it was turning very cold; and she was an elderly woman with an injured foot in the middle of a ruined city. She had nowhere to stay, nothing to eat or drink, and no means of getting home.

But Clarissa was good at pushing things out of her mind.

"It's not far," she muttered, referring not to the fake chateau, her distant home, but to Piccadilly Circus which still lay ahead. Piccadilly Circus offered no warmth, no nourishment, no resolution at all of her difficulties, but all of that was beside the point. "I'll just have to walk," she said. "It's absurd to come this far and not get to see it."

She dismounted from her car and began, painfully, to limp the last couple of hundred metres, but then she remembered Lily and stopped.

"I'M GOING TO WALK THE LAST BIT!" she bellowed back, assuming correctly that Lily was trailing behind her, but erroneously that Lily's invisibility made her deaf. "I Can't SEE YOU because MY IMPLANT'S TURNED OFF and I don't want to turn it on again until I get there, or it will SPOIL THE EFFECT."

She had it all planned out. She would not turn on her implant until she was right in the middle of the Circus.

"YOU'RE VERY WELCOME TO COME ALONG THOUGH!" she shouted, as if she personally controlled access to the public streets.

She hobbled forward a few steps along the silent ruined avenue (while in the other London, cars swerved around her, pedestrians turned and stared and Lily patiently plodded behind her as if the two of them were Good King Wenceslas and his faithful page).

"I'll tell you what though," Clarissa said, pausing again. Her face was screwed up with the pain of her injured foot, but her tone was nonchalant. "If you felt like calling the council and asking them to get hold of someone physical to come and help me out, I would be grateful . . . Only my dratted car has QUITE RUN OUT OF POWER you see, so it's not going to be able to get me back."

"I don't have any money," said Lily. "Is it an emergency do you think? Shall I call the emergency number?"

But of course Clarissa couldn't hear her.

It was getting dark as she limped into Piccadilly Circus. The buildings were inert slabs of masonry, all those thousands of coloured light bulbs on the old advertising signs were cold and still and the statue of Eros was more like the angel of death on a mausoleum than the god of physical love.

Some gusts of rain came blowing down Regent Street. Clarissa's lips and fingers were blue with cold and her whole body was trembling. (Lily was amazed: she had never seen such a thing, for consensuals are never cold.) Clarissa was in great pain too – the broken bone in her ankle had slipped out of place and felt like a blade being twisted in her flesh – and she was tired and hungry and thirsty. Too late she realised she had left her flask of coffee behind in her abandoned car.

"You're a fool, Clarissa Fall," she told herself. "You don't look after yourself. One of these days you'll just keel over and the rats will come and eat you up. And it will be your own stupid fault." Then she remembered her low res companion. "ARE YOU STILL THERE LILY?" she bellowed. "Did you make that CALL FOR ME? I'm just going to get across to the statue there and then I'll turn my implant on and WE CAN TALK."

She hobbled to the base of Eros and then reached up to the implant switch behind her ear. The colour, the electricity, the teeming life of a great city at night came flooding instantly into the desolate scene. There were people everywhere, and cars with shining headlamps and glowing tail-lights, and black taxis and red double-decker buses full of passengers, lit upstairs and down with a cheery yellow glow. But above all there were *the* lights, the wonderful electric streams of colour that made shining moving pictures and glittering logos and words that flowed across fields of pure colour in purple and red and green and yellow and blue and white.

"Ah!" cried Clarissa in rapture, "almost like when I was a little girl and the lights were real!"

"I told you they were lovely," Lily said, like a pet dog that will wait an hour, two hours, three hours for its mistress to glance in its direction, and still be no less grateful when the longed-for attention finally comes.

Clarissa turned, smiling, but the sight of Lily's cartoonish moon-face had an unexpected effect on her. She felt a stab of pity for Lily and at the same time revulsion. Her smile ceased to be real. Her pleasure vanished. She felt the bitter cold of the physical world pushing through, the needle-sharp physical pain nagging at her from her foot, the physical ache in her head that came from tiredness and dehydration.

Lily sensed her change of mood and the simple line that represented her mouth was just starting to curve downwards when Clarissa switched off her implant again. Lily vanished, along with lights, taxis, buses and crowds. It was very dark and quite silent and the buildings were dim shadows.

"The thing is, Lily," Clarissa announced to the empty darkness, "that you consensuals are all just like these lights. Just moving pictures made out of little dots. Just pictures of buses, pictures of cars, pictures of people, pictures of shop windows."

Deliberately turning away from where Lily had been, Clarissa turned the implant on again and watched the lights come back. But there was no thrill this time, no exhilarating shock, nothing to offset the cold and the pain. It was no different really to changing channels on a TV set, she thought bitterly, and straight away reached up to flick the implant off again. But now the switch, which was designed to be turned on and off a couple of times a day, finally broke under the strain of her constant tinkering with it and refused to stay in one position or the other. Clarissa's perceptual field now flickered randomly every few seconds from the consensual to the physical world and back again – and she couldn't make it stop. She stood helplessly and ineffectually fingering the switch for a short time, then gave up and sank down to the ground at the foot of the statue. What else was there to do?

"Did you call up the council, Li – " she began, and then the consensual world disappeared. "Oh dear. LILY, ARE YOU STILL THERE? . . . Oh you are, good. Did you call the council only I think I

ought to go home now . . . Lily? LILY! ARE THE COUNCIL
GETTING HELP? . . . Tell them I don't want Agents mind. Tell them to
get some physicals out. They'll be cross with me, but they'll come
anyway. I don't care what Richard said."

Actually, whether she liked it or not, Agents were coming, four of them,
from different directions, from different errands in different parts of
London. They were still some way off but they were on their way. The
Hub had sent them, having contacted Richard Howard and been told
by him that we physicals wouldn't come out again.
    Later Richard began to worry about what he'd done and called me.
"I know it seems harsh," he said, rather defensively, "but I do feel we've
got to keep out of this, don't you agree? Clarissa's got to learn that
when we say something we mean it, or she'll keep doing this stuff over
and over again. I mean she's in *Piccadilly Circus* for god's sake! Even
Clarissa must be perfectly well aware that she couldn't go into central
London and get back again in that silly little car of hers. She obviously
just assumed that we would come and fetch her. She just banked on it."
    I was as furious with Clarissa as he was. I had spent the afternoon
raking leaves and tidying up in my secluded little garden. I had just
eaten a small meal and taken a glass of port and was looking forward to
a quiet evening alone in the warm behind drawn curtains, making some
preparatory notes for Chapter 62 of my book *The Decline and Fall of
Reality*. (I had dealt in Chapters 60 and 61 with the advent of the
Internet and the mobile telephone and was just getting to what was to
be the great central set-piece of my whole account: the moment where
the human race is presented for the first time with incontrovertible
evidence that its own activity will destroy the planet, not in centuries or
even decades but in years, unless it can reduce its physical presence to a
fraction of its current levels.)
    "Bloody Clarissa! *Bloody bloody* Clarissa!"
    Why *should* I give up the treat of a quiet evening and a new chapter,
when she herself had deliberately engineered her own difficulties? I
absolutely dreaded going into the centre of London at any time, as
Clarissa surely knew, and yet here she was calmly assuming that I could
and should be dragged there whenever it suited her convenience. And
yet I knew I had to go to her.
    "I can't leave her to the Agents, though, Richard. I know she's a pain,
I know we're being used, but I can't just leave her."
    "Oh for goodness' sake, Tom, it'll teach her a lesson," Richard said,
hardening in his resolve now he had my own flabbiness of will to kick
against. "How will she ever learn if we don't stay firm now? It's really
for her own good. And anyway, the Agents can't be called off now. You
know what they're like."
    "Well if they're going to be there anyway, I'd better be there too," I
said. "They scare her silly. I'll drive up there now, so at least there's
someone on hand that she knows."

I went out into the cold and started up my car. I resented Clarissa bitterly. I absolutely dreaded a reprise of the dark feelings that trips into London invariably churned up in me, the shame, the embarrassment, the feeling of loss, the envy, the deep, deep grief that is like the grief of facing a former lover who belongs now to another and will never be yours again . . . I was exhausted by the very thought of the effort of it all, not to mention the discomfort and the cold.

When I got to Piccadilly Circus, Agents were just arriving, one emerging from Shaftesbury Avenue, one from Piccadilly and one each from the northern and southern branches of Regent Street. But, huddled up under the statue of Eros, Clarissa couldn't see them, for when she was in purely physical mode it was too dark and when she was in consensual mode they were invisible. Beside her squatted Lily with her consensual arm round Clarissa's physical shoulder. Sometimes Clarissa could see Lily and sometimes she couldn't, but either way she could get no warmth from the embrace, however much Lily might want to give it.

As my physical headlights swept across the physical space, the first thing Clarissa saw was two of the Agents looming out of the darkness and advancing towards her. It felt like some nightmare from her childhood, and she screamed. Then her implant switched on by itself and the lights and the buses and the crowds returned to screen them out. But that was even worse because she knew that behind this glossy facade the Agents were still really there, slowly advancing, though now unseen.

She screamed again.

"Keep away from me, you hear me! Just keep away."

"Don't be scared, Clarissa," said Lily. "I'm here for you."

But Lily didn't have a clue. She had never experienced cold. She had never known physical pain. She wasn't aware of the presence of the Agents. She had no inkling of the other world of silence and shadow that lay behind the bright lights of Piccadilly Circus.

I got out of my car. I had my own implant switched on and I picked my way gingerly over the ground between me and Clarissa, knowing only too well how easily nasty physical potholes can be concealed by the virtual road surface. I was doing my best to ignore the many consensual eyes watching me with disapproval and dislike and I was seething all the while with rage at self-obsessed Clarissa for putting me through all this yet again. How dare she drag me out here into the cold night? How dare she expose me to the illusion of the consensual city and to the disapproving gaze of the consensual people, when I all I ever wanted was to be at home behind my high hedges that I had cut into the shape of castle walls, behind my locked doors, behind my tightly drawn curtains, writing about reality.

"You know her do you?" a man asked me. "Well, you want to do something about her, mate. She's nuts. She's mental. She needs help"

I didn't respond. I had never known how to speak to these people, so manifestly unreal and yet so obviously alive. I both despised and envied them. How tawdry their constructed world was and how craven their meek acceptance of it. Yet how narrow and dull my own world was by comparison, my bleak garden, my clipped hedges, my book, my nightly glass of port, my weekly sally down the road to the Horse and Hounds, the Last Real Pub, to drink Real Beer with the diminishing band of decrepit and barren old men and woman who call themselves the Last Real People.

"She needs locking up more like," said a woman. "That's the same one that blocked the Northern Line last month with her carrying on. I saw her face in the paper."

I picked my way through the traffic.

"Alright Clarissa," I called coldly as I came up to her, "I'm here again for you. Muggins is here again as you no doubt expected he would be. I've come to fetch you home."

"Muggins? Who's that?" she quavered. She was afraid it was one of the Agents.

"It's just me, Clarissa. It's just Tom."

"It's who?" muttered Clarissa, straining to see me.

"He said Tom, dear," Lily told her.

Clarissa glanced sideways at the cartoon face with its little black dot eyes and its downward curved mouth. Then Lily vanished again, along with the whole Field, and Clarissa was back in the dark physical world. But the lights of my car were there now and, without the distraction of the Field, Clarissa could clearly see me approaching as well as the Agents around me, waiting to step in if I couldn't resolve things.

Awkwardly, wincing with pain, she rose to her feet.

"I just wanted to see the lights again, like they were when I was a child," she said stubbornly.

And then she began to spin round on the spot like children sometimes do in play, but very very slowly, shuffling round and round with her feet and grimacing all the while with pain. And as she revolved, the faulty switch on her implant continued to flicker on and off so that, for a few seconds the bright lights and the buses and the cars span around her, and then it was the turn of the darkness that was the source of her coldness and her pain, and it was the dim cold walls of the empty buildings that moved round her, lit only by the headlights of my car.

Lily appeared and disappeared. When she was there the Agents vanished. When she vanished, they appeared. The constant was me, who like Clarissa could both feel the physical cold, and see the consensual lights.

"Come on Clarrie," I said to her gently. "Come on Clarrie."

The old lady ignored me for a while, carrying on with her strange slow-motion spinning and singing a tuneless little song under her breath. People were craning round in cars and buses to look at us. Pedestrians were standing across the road and watching us as frankly as if this really *was* a Circus and we were there expressly to put on a show. Then abruptly Clarissa stopped spinning. She tottered with dizziness, but her eyes were blazing like the eyes of a cornered animal.

"Who are you?" she demanded. "Who exactly are you?"

It was odd because in that moment everything around me seemed to intensify: the sharpness of the cold night air in the physical world, the brilliance of the coloured lights in the consensual one, the strange collision of the two worlds that my Clarrie had single-handedly brought about . . . And I found that I didn't feel angry any more, didn't even mind that she'd brought me all this way.

I switched off the implant behind my ear, so that I could check up on what the Agents were doing. But they were still standing back and waiting for me to deal with things.

"It's me, Clarrie," I said to her. "It's Tom. Your little brother."

The Agent nearest me stiffened slightly and inclined its head towards me, as if I had half-reminded it of something.

"I reckon you've had enough adventure for one day, my dear," I told my sister, flicking my implant on again to shut the Agents out of my sight. "Enough for one day, don't you agree? Don't mind the Agents. I've brought the car for you. I've come to take you home."

She let me lead her to the car and help her inside. She was in a very bad state, trembling, bloodless, befuddled, her injured foot swollen to nearly twice its normal size. I was glad I had thought to bring a rug for her, and a flask of hot cocoa, and a bottle of brandy.

That strange moon-faced creature, Lily, a human soul inside a cartoon, followed us over and stood anxiously watching. "Is she alright?" she asked. "She's gone so strange. What is it that's the matter with her?"

"Yes, she'll be alright. She's just old and tired," I told her, shutting the passenger door and walking round the car to get in myself.

I flipped off my implant, cutting off Lily and the sights and sounds of Piccadilly Circus. In the dark dead space, the four Agents were silhouetted in the beam of my headlights. They had moved together and were standing in a row. I had the odd idea that they wished they could come with us, that they wished that someone would come to meet *them* with rugs and brandy and hot cocoa.

I got my sister comfortable and started up the car. I was going to drive like she always did without being able to see the consensual traffic. I didn't like doing it. I knew how arrogant it must seem to the consensuals and how much they must resent it – it was things like that, I knew, that gave us Outsiders a bad name – but I just couldn't risk a broken axle on the way home on top of everything else.

"Really we're no different when you come to think of it," said Clarrie after a while. Her implant was off and she looked out at abandoned streets as lonely as canyons on some lifeless planet in space. "*That's* the physical world out there, that's physical matter. But we're not like that, are we? We're patterns. We're just patterns rippling across the surface."

"Have a bit more brandy, Clarrie," I told her, "and then put the seat back and try to get some sleep. It's going to be some time before we get back."

She nodded and tugged the rug up around herself. Her implant switched itself on and she saw a taxi swerve to avoid us and heard the angry blast of its horn. Briefly the busy night life of the Consensual Field was all around her. Then it was gone.

"Just the same," she said sleepily. "Just like the lights in Piccadilly Circus."

IN THE QUAKE ZONE

David Gerrold

David Gerrold has been a hardworking and highly acclaimed professional in several different fields since the sixties. As a screenwriter, he produced the screenplay for one of the most famous of all of the episodes of the original *Star Trek*, "The Trouble with Tribbles." He later produced a book about the experience, *The Trouble with Tribbles*, as well as a study of the show, *The World of Star Trek*, and two *Star Trek* novels, *Encounter at Far Point* and *The Galactic Whirlpool*. He won both Hugo and Nebula Awards in 1995 for his story "The Martian Child." His many SF novels include the well-known *The Man Who Folded Himself*, as well as *When Harlie Was One*, *A Matter for Men*, *A Rage for Revenge*, *A Season for Slaughter*, *The Middle of Nowhere*, *The Voyage of the Star Wolf*, *Space Skimmer*, *Star Hunt*, *Yesterday's Children*, *A Covenant of Justice*, *A Day for Damnation*, *Blood and Fire*, *The Martian Child*, *Chess with a Dragon*, *Under the Eye of God*, *Jumping off the Planet*, *Bouncing off the Moon*, and *Leaping to the Stars*. His short fiction has been collected in *With a Finger in My I*. As editor, he has produced the anthologies *Protostars*, *Generation*, *Science Fiction Emphasis*, *Alternities*, and *Ascents of Wonder*. In addition to the *Star Trek* study, his nonfiction includes *Worlds of Wonder: How to Write Science Fiction and Fantasy*. His most recent books are a new novel, *Child of Earth*, and a new collection, *Alternate Gerrolds*.

In the intricate and subtle story that follows, where all is mutable and nothing is certain or solid or imperishable, he gives a whole new meaning to the expression *on shaky ground* . . .

THE DAY AFTER TIME collapsed, I had my shoes shined. They needed it.

I didn't know that time had collapsed, wouldn't find out for years, decades – and several months of subjective time. I just thought it was another local timequake.

Picked up a newspaper – *The Los Angeles Mirror*, with its brown-tinted front page – and settled into one of the high-backed, leather chairs in the Hollywood Boulevard alcove. There were copies of the *Herald*, the *Examiner*, and the *Times* here as well, but the *Mirror* had Pogo Possum on the funny pages. "Mighty fine shoes, sir," Roy said, and went right to work. He didn't know me yet. I snapped the paper open.

I didn't have to check the papers for the date, this was late fifties, I already knew from the cars on the boulevard, an ample selection of Detroit heavy-iron; the inevitable Chevys and Fords, a few Buicks and Oldsmobiles, the occasional ostentatious Cadillac, a few Mercurys, but also a nostalgic scattering of others, including DeSoto, Rambler, Packard, Oldsmobile, and Studebaker. Not a foreign car to be seen, just a bright M&M flow of chrome-lined monstrosities growling along, many of them two-toned. The newer models had nascent tailfins, the evocation of jet planes and rocketships, giddy metal evolution, the hallmark of a decade and an industrial dead end.

The Mirror and *The Examiner* both disappeared late '58, maybe early '59, if I remembered correctly, the result of a covert deal by the publishers. Said Mr. Chandler to Mr. Hearst, I'll shut down my morning paper if you'll shut down your afternoon. "Let us fold our papers and go."

A new Edsel cruised by – right, this was '58. But I could already smell it. The Hollywood day felt gritty. The smog was thick enough to taste. The Hollywood Warner's theater had another Cinerama travelogue – the third or fourth, I'd lost track. I was tempted; not a lot of air-conditioning in this time zone. A dark old theater, cooled by refrigeration, I could skip the sweltering zenith. But, no – I might not have enough time.

The papers reported that timefaults had opened up as far north as Porter Ranch, popping Desi and Lucy seven years back into the days of chocolate conveyer belts and Vitameatavegamin: as far east as Boyle Heights where ten years were lost and the diamond-bright DWP building disappeared from the downtown skyline, along with the world famous four-level freeway interchange; as far south as Watts, they only rattled off a couple years, but it set back the construction of Simon Rodilla's startling graceful towers; and all the way west to the Pacific Ocean. Several small boats and the Catalina Ferry had disappeared, but a sparkling new Coast Guard Cutter from 1963 had chugged into San Pedro. The big red Pacific Electric streetcars were still grinding out to the San Fernando Valley. I wondered if I'd have a chance to ride one before the aftershocks hit.

Caltech predicted several days of aftershocks and the mayor was advising folks to stay close to home if they could, to avoid further discontinuities. The Red Cross had set up shelters at several high schools for those whose homes had disappeared or were now occupied by previous or subsequent inhabitants.

Already the looters and collectors from tomorrow were flocking to the boulevard. Most of them were obvious, dressed in jeans and T-shirts,

but they gave themselves away by their stare-gathering unkempt haircuts and beards, their torn jeans and pornographic T-shirts. They'd be
stripping the racks at World Book and News, buying every copy they
could find of *Superman, Batman, Action,* and especially *Walt Disney's
Comics* with the work of legendary Carl Barks. And *MAD* magazine too;
the issues with the Freas covers were the most valuable. Later, they'd
move west, hitting Collector's Books and Records and Pickwick's as
well. The smart ones would have brought cash. The smartest ones would
have brought year-specific cash. The dumb ones would have credit cards
and checkbooks. Not a lot of places took credit cards yet, none of them
recognized Visa or MasterCard. And nobody took checks anymore; not
unless they were bank-dated; most of the stores had learned from
previous timequakes.

The Harris Agency – there was no Ted Harris, but he had an agency
– was just upstairs of the shoeshine stand; upstairs, turn left and back all
the way to the end of the hall, no name on the glass, no glass. The door
was solid pine, like a coffin-lid, and painted green for no reason anyone
could remember, except an old song, *"What's that happenin' behind
the green door . . . ?"* The only identification was a small card that said
BY APPOINTMENT ONLY. That wasn't true, but it stopped the casual
curiosity seekers. My key still worked, the locks wouldn't be changed
until 1972; there was no receptionist, the outer office was filled with
cardboard file boxes and stacks of unfiled folders. Two typists were
cataloging, they glanced up briefly. If I had a key, I belonged here.

Georgia was still an intern, working afternoons; she'd started when
she was a student at Hollywood High, half a mile west and a couple
blocks south. Now she was taking evening courses in business
management at Los Angeles City College, over on Vermont, a block
south of Santa Monica Boulevard. A few years from now, she'd be a
beautiful honey-blonde, but she didn't know that yet and I wasn't going
to risk a bad first impression by speaking out of turn. I pretended I
didn't know her. I didn't, not yet.

I brushed past, into the cubby we called a conference room. More old
paper and two old women. Pinched-faced and withered, they might
have been the losers in a Margaret Hamilton look-alike contest. Sooner
or later, one of them was probably going to demand, "Who killed my
sister? Was it you?!"

Opened my wallet, started to flash my card, but the dustier of the two
waved it off. "I recognize you. Wait. Sit." But I didn't recognize her. I
probably hadn't met her yet. Some younger iteration of her had known
an older iteration of me. I wondered how well. I wondered if I would
remember this meeting then. The other woman left the room without
saying a word. Just as well; some folks get uncomfortable around time-
ravelers. Not travelers – *ravelers*. The folks who tend the tangled webs.

I sat. A dark mahogany table, thick and heavy. A leather chair, left
over from the previous occupant of this office, someone who'd bellied
up early in the thirties. She disappeared into a back room, I heard the
scrape of a wooden footstool, the sound of boxes being moved on

shelves, a muffled curse, very unladylike. A moment later, she came back, dropped a sealed manila envelope on the table in front of me. I slid it over, turned it around, and scanned the notations. Contract signed in 1971, backshifted to '57. Contract due date 1967. It had only been sitting here a year, and the due date was still nine years away.

A noise. I looked up. She'd put a bottle on the table and a stubby glass. I turned the bottle. It said Glenfiddich. I didn't recognize the name. I gave her the eyebrow. She said, "My name's Margaret. Today's the day you acquire this taste. You'll thank me for it later. Take as much time as you need to read the folder, but leave it here. Here's a notepad if you need to copy out anything. That contract's not due for nine years, so the best you can do today is familiarize yourself, maybe do a little scouting. There's an aftershock due tomorrow morning, about 4:30 a.m.; go to West Hollywood and it'll bounce you closer to the due date. Oh, wait – one more thing." She disappeared again, this time I heard the sounds of keys jingling on a ring. A drawer opened, stuff was shuffled around, the drawer was closed. She came back with a cash box and an old-fashioned checkbook. "I can only give you three hundred in time-specific cash, but it'll still be good in '67. There's a bank around the corner, you've got two hours until it closes, I'll give you a check for another seven hundred. You can pick up more in '67. But be careful, your account doesn't get fat for awhile. How's your ID?"

In the past, my personal past, I'd renewed my driver's license as quickly as I could after every quake, but a DL expires after three years, a passport is good for ten. The lines at the Federal Building were usually worse than the DMV, especially in a broken time zone, but except for a gap of three years in the early '70s, I had valid passports from now until the mid-eighties.

"I'm good," I nodded. I signed my name and today's date to the next line on the outside of the envelope, then broke the wax seal. It was brittle; it had been sitting on the shelf for a year, waiting for today, and who knows how long before it got to this time zone. I didn't have a lot of curiosity, most of my cases were small-timers. The big stuff, the famous stuff, most of that went to the high-profile operations, the guys on Wilshire Boulevard, some downtown, some in Westwood. There was a lot of competition there – stop Sirhan from killing RFK, catch Manson before he and the family move into the Spahn movie ranch, apprehend the Hillside Stranglers, find out who killed the Black Dahlia, help O.J. find the killers of Ron and Nicole . . . and so on.

The thing about the high-profiles, those were easy cases. The victims were known, so were the perps. The big agencies had a pretty good idea of the movements of their targets long before the crimes occurred. But most of the laws had been written before time began unraveling and the justice system wasn't geared for prevention, only after-the-fact cleanup.

Then one hot night in an August that still hasn't happened. Charles "Tex" Watson gets out of the car up on Cielo Drive and someone puts a carbon-fiber crossbow bolt right through his neck, even before he gets the gun out of his jacket. The girls start shrieking and two more of them take bolts, one of them right through the sternum, Sexie Sadie gets one in the head. The third girl, the Kasabian kid, goes screaming down the hill, and some redheaded kid in a white Nash Rambler nearly runs her down, never knowing that the alternative was having his brains splashed across the front seat of his parents' car. I didn't do it, but I knew the contract, knew who'd paid for it. Approved the outcome.

That was the turning point. After that, the judicial system learned to accommodate itself to preventive warrants, and most of the worst perps will be safe in protective custody weeks or even months before they have a chance to commit their atrocities. The question of punishment becomes one of pre-rehabilitation – is it possible? When can we let these folks back out on the streets? If ever. Do we have the right to detain someone on the grounds that they represent potential harm to others, even if no crime has been committed? The ethical questions will be argued for three decades. I don't know yet how it resolves, only that an uneasy accommodation will finally be achieved – something to the effect that there are no second chances, it's too time-consuming, pun intended; a judicial review of the facts, a signed warrant, and no, they don't call it pre-punishment. It's terminal prevention.

Meanwhile, it's the big agencies that get the star cases – save Marilyn and Elvis, save James Dean and Buddy Holly, Natalie Wood, Sal Mineo, Mike Todd, Lenny Bruce, RFK and Jimmy Hoffa. Stop Ernest Hemingway from sucking the bullet out of his gun and keep Tennessee Williams from choking to death on a bottle cap. Save Mama Cass and Jimi Hendrix and Jim Morrison and Janis Joplin and John Lennon. And later on, Karina and Jo-Jo Ray. And Michael Zone. Kelly Breen. Some of those names don't mean anything yet, won't mean anything for years; the size of the up-front money says everything – but we don't get those cases. The last one we bid on was Ramon Novarro, beaten to death with his own dildo by a couple of hustler-boys, and we didn't get that job either; later on, after the Fatty Arbuckle thing, and that was a long reach back anyway, all of those cases went through the Hollywood Preservation Society, funded by the big studios who had investments to protect.

No, it's the *other* cases, the little ones, the unsolved ones that fall through the cracks – those are the ones that keep the little agencies going. Most families can't afford five or six figure retainers, so they come to the smaller agencies, pennies in hand, desperate for help. "My little girl disappeared in June of '61, we don't know what happened, nobody ever found a trace." "I want to stop the man who raped my sister." "My girlfriend had a baby. She says it's mine. Can you stop the conception?" "My boyfriend was shot next November, the police have no clue." "I was abused by my stepfather when I was a child. Can you keep my mom from ever meeting him?"

There were a lot of amateurs in this business – and more than a few do-it-yourselfers too. But most folks don't like to go zone-hopping; it's not a round-trip. You don't want to end up someplace where you have no home, no family, no job. Just the same, some people try. Sometimes people clean up their own messes, sometimes they make bigger ones. Some things are better left to the professionals.

The Harris Agency had three or six or nine operatives, depending on when you asked. But some of them were the same operative, inadvertently (or maybe deliberately) time-folded. Eakins was a funny duck, all three of him, all ages. The Harris Agency didn't advertise, didn't have a sign on the door, didn't even have a phone, not a listed one anyway; you heard about it from a friend of a friend. We took the jobs that people didn't want to talk about, and sometimes we handled them in ways that even we didn't talk about.

You knocked on the door and if you knocked the right way, they'd let you in. Georgia would sit you down in the cubby we called a conference room, and if she liked your look, she'd offer you coffee or tea. If she didn't trust you, it would be water from the cooler. Or nothing. She conducted her interviews like a surgeon removing bullet fragments, methodically extracting details and information so skillfully you never knew you'd been incised. Most cases, she wouldn't promise anything, she'd spend the rest of the day, maybe two or three days, writing up a report, sending an intern down to the Central Library or the *Times'* morgue to pull clippings. She'd pull pages out of phone directories, call over to the Wilcox station to get driver's license information (if available), and even scanned the personal ads in the *L.A. Free Press* a couple times. For the most part, a lot of what the outer office staff did was "clipping service" – pulling out data before, during, and after the events; the more complete the file, the easier the job. Working with Margaret, the jobs were usually easy. Usually, not always.

Georgia replaced Margaret in '61, right after Kennedy's election; Margaret retired to a date farm in Indio, as soon as she felt Georgia was ready; she'd managed the agency since '39, never missing a beat. She trained Georgia and she trained her well. The kid had been a good intern, the best, a quick-study; after graduation from Hollywood High, she stayed on full time while she picked up her degree at L.A.C.C. The work wasn't hard, but it was painstaking; Margaret had been disciplined, but Georgia was meticulous. She relished the challenge. Besides, the pay was good and the job was close enough to home that she could walk to work. And at the end of the day, she'd satisfied her spirit of adventure without mussing her hair.

The files demonstrated their differences in approach. Margaret never wrote anything she couldn't substantiate. She wasn't imaginative. But Georgia was and always added a page or two of advice and suggestions – her own feelings about the matter at hand. Margaret didn't disapprove. She'd learned to respect Georgia's intuition. I had too.

This envelope was thin, thinner than usual. Inside, there were notes from both, I recognized Margaret' crimped precise handwriting, Georgia's flowing hand. A disappearance. Jeremy Weiss. Skinny kid. Glasses. Dark curly hair. Dark eyes, round face, an unfinished look – not much sense yet what kind of adult he might be. A waiter, an accountant, an unsuccessful scriptwriter. Seventeen and a half. Good home. Good grades. No family problems. Disappears summer of '68, somewhere in West L.A. Not a runaway, the car was found parked on Melrose, near La Cienega. But no evidence of foul play either. Parents plaster the neighborhood with leaflets. Police ask the public for help. The synagogue posts a reward for information. Nothing. Case remains open and unsolved. No clues here. Nothing to go on. The file was a list of what we didn't know.

Two ways to proceed with this one – shadow the kid or intercept him. Shadowing is a bad risk. Sometimes, you're too late, the perp is too fast, and you end up a witness instead of a hero. Agents have been sued for negligence and malpractice, for not being fast enough or smart enough, for not stopping the murder. Interception is better. But that means keeping the vic from ever getting to his appointment in Samarra. And that means the perp never gets ID'd either.

The easiest interception is a flat tire or even an inconvenient fender-bender. That can delay a person anywhere from fifteen to forty-five minutes. That's usually enough to save a life. Most cases we get are events of opportunity. Take away the opportunity, the event doesn't happen – or it happens to someone else. That's the other problem with preventive interception. It doesn't always stop the bad luck, too often it just pushes it onto the next convenient opportunity. I don't like that.

Give me a case where the perp is known ahead of time, I can get a warrant. I don't have a problem taking down a known bad-boy. I don't have to be nice, I don't have to be neat. And there are times when I really don't want to be. But give me an unsolved case, it's like juggling hand grenades. Sometimes the victim is the real perp. It's messy. You can get hurt.

But this one – I listened for the internal alarm bells – they always go off when something smells wrong; this one felt different, I'm not sure why. I had a hunch, a feeling, an intuition, call it whatever – a sense that this case was merely a loose unraveled thread of something else. Something worse. Like the redheaded kid who didn't die on August 9 was merely a sidebar.

Think about it for a minute. Hollywood is full of manboys. They fall off the buses, naïve and desperate. They're easy targets for all kinds of opportunists. Old enough to drive, but not old enough to be street smart. They come for the promise of excitement. Ostensibly, it's the glamour of the boulevard, where the widescreen movies wrap around the audience; it's the bookstores rich with lore, shelves aching with volumes of forgotten years; it's the smoky jazz clubs and the fluorescent record stores and the gaudy lingerie displays; it's the little oddball places where you can find movie posters, scripts, leftover props, memorabilia, makeup, bits and pieces of costumery – they come in from all the surrounding suburbs, looking for the discarded fragments of excitement. Sometimes they're looking for friends, for other young men like themselves, sometimes they're unashamedly looking for sex. With hookers, with hustlers, with each other. With whoever. A few years from now, they'll be looking for dope.

But what they're really looking for is themselves. Because they're unformed, unfinished. And there's nobody to give them a clue because nobody has a clue anymore. Whatever the world used to be, it hasn't finished collapsing, and whatever is going to replace it, it hasn't finished slouching toward Bethlehem. So if they're coming down here to the boulevard to look for themselves, because this looks like the center, because this looks like where it's happening, they're looking in the wrong place; because nobody ever found themselves in Hollywood, no. Much more often, they lose whatever self they had to start with.

You can't save Marilyn and Elvis because they don't exist, they never existed – all that existed was a shitload of other people's dreams dumped on top of a couple of poor souls who'd had the misfortune to end up in front of a camera or a microphone. And you can't save anyone from that. Hollywood needs a warning label. Like that pack of cigarettes I saw up the line. "Caution, this crap will kill you."

Jeremy Weiss wasn't a runaway. He didn't fit the profile. And he didn't end up in a dumpster somewhere, his body was never found. He wasn't a hustler or a druggie. I doubted suicide. I figured he was probably destined for an unmarked grave somewhere up above Sunset Boulevard, maybe in the side of a hill, one of those offshoots of Laurel Canyon that wind around forever, until they finally turn into one-lane dirt scars. Someone he met, a casual pickup, I know where there's a party, or let's go to my place –

So yeah, I could probably save this kid from the Tuesday express, but that wouldn't necessarily stop him from lying down on the tracks again on Wednesday night. Or if not him, then maybe Steve from El Segundo or Jeffrey from Van Nuys. Most of the disappearances went unreported, unnoticed. Not this one, though.

Margaret sat down opposite me. She put a second glass on the table and poured herself a shot, poured one for me.

I knew Margaret only from her work – the files that Georgia had passed me, up the line. Margaret was compulsive; she annotated everything on every case, including newspaper clippings, police reports when she could get them, and occasionally witness interviews. Reading through a file, reading her notes, her advice, her suggestions, it was like having a six-foot invisible rabbit standing behind every moment.

But today was the first time I'd actually met Margaret, and I held my tongue, still gauging what to say. Should I thank her for the cases yet to solve? Did she want to know how these cases would play out? Would it affect her reports if she knew what leads were fruitless and which ones were pay dirt? Do we advance to Go or do we go directly to jail? The real question – should we put warnings into the files? Watch out for Perry, a harmless little pisher, but an expensive one; stay away from Chuck Hunt, the chronovore; don't go near Conway, the bigger thief; and especially watch out for Maizlish, the destroyer.

Should I ask – ?

"Don't talk," she said. "There's nothing you have to say that I need to hear. I've already heard it. I'll do the talking here because I have information that you need." She pushed the glass toward me.

I took a sniff. Not bad. Normally, I don't drink scotch. I prefer bourbon. But this was different, sharper, lighter. Okay, I can drink scotch.

"Something's happening," she said.

I waited for her to go on. There's this trick. Don't say anything. Just sit and wait. People can't stand silence. The longer you wait, the more unbearable it becomes. Pretty soon, they have to say something, just to break the silence. Leave an unanswered question in the air and wait, it'll get answered. Unless they're playing the same game. Except Margaret wasn't playing games.

She finished her scotch, neat, put the glass down, and stared across the table at me. "The perps are starting to figure it out." She let that sink in for a moment. "The timequakes. The perps are using public quake maps to avoid capture. Or to commit their crimes more carefully. Bouncing forward, back, sideways. They call it the undertime railway. LAPD has taken down the Manson clan three times now. Each time, earlier. Now they're talking about maybe legalizing preemptive abortion. Just stop them from being born. Nobody's sure yet. The judges are still arguing. The point is, you'll have to be careful. Especially with cases like this where we don't have any information. The perp always knows more about the crime than the investigator. The more the perp knows, the harder the job becomes. If the case gets any publicity, the perp gets dangerous.

"Here's the good news. Caltech has been mapping the timequakes. They've been putting down probes all over the county for thirty years now. We have their most recent chart. The one they didn't make public. It cost us some big bucks and a couple of blow jobs." She unrolled a scroll across the table – it looked like the paperback edition of the Torah, smaller but no less detailed. "It stretches from 1906 all the way to 2111, so far. All of the big quakes and aftershocks are noted, those are the public ones, the ones the perps know. But all of the littler ones are in here too." She tapped the scroll. "This is your advantage.

"Most people don't notice the little tremors, the unnoticeable ones. You know that feeling when you keep thinking it's Monday when it's really Sunday? That's a dayquake. Or when you've been driving for an hour and you can't remember the last ten miles? Or when you've been at work eight hours and you still have seven hours to go? Or when you're out clubbing and suddenly the evening's over before it's really started? Those are all tremors so small you don't even feel them, or if you do notice, you figure it's just you. But Caltech has them charted, has the epicenters noted, can tell you almost to the second how far forward or back each quake bounces. See the arrows? You can chart a time-trajectory from here to forever – well at least up to 2111, depending on which of the local trajectories you choose. They probably have even more complete charts uptime, but we can't get them yet. We expect Eakins to send back copies, but nothing's arrived yet, not this far back.

But it should have reached '67 by now. So as soon as you get there, come back to this office. I won't be here, I'm already retired in '67, but Georgia will have what you need. We start bringing her up to speed right after Kennedy's election.

"The point is, this timeline gives you more maneuverability. Protect it like it's gold. If a perp gets it, it'd be a disaster. That's why it's on proof paper. It goes black after twenty minutes' exposure to UV." She rolled it up, slid it into a tube, capped it, and passed it over to me. "Right. Get to the bank, get yourself some dinner, then get out to the quake zone. You've got a reservation at the Farmer's Daughter Motel. That puts you half a block from the epicenter. You can get a good night's sleep. Georgia will see you here in '67."

Picked up some comics at the Las Palmas newsstand and shoved them into my briefcase, I do a little collecting myself, on the fringes, mostly just for my retirement. But not only comics. Barbie dolls, G.I. Joe, Hot Wheels cars, Pez boxes, stuff like that. And I'm saving up for a trip back to '38, I hope to pick up some IBM stock.

The Farmer's Daughter is better than it sounds. On Fairfax, walking distance from Farmer's Market. Of course, it isn't the Farmer's Daughter yet, but it will be in '67.

I check in, check the room, check the bed, think about a hooker, I have the number of an escort service, they'll be in business for another year or so; but it's not a good idea. There might be a foreshock. Almost certainly, there will be a foreshock. Not fair to the girl.

So I content myself with a nightcap in the bar. It's almost deserted. Just the bartender and me. His name is Hank. I ask him what time he gets off, he thinks I'm hitting on him, he gives me a big friendly grin, but I say, no thanks. Close up and go home. Timequake tonight, an after-shock. He shrugs. He's already been caught in two quakes. He won't even keep a cat now. Everything important, he keeps in a bag by the door. Just like me.

Not a lot of out-of-towners visit L.A. anymore; they don't want to risk the possibility of time-disruption, finding themselves a year or ten away from their families. But some folks deliberately come to L.A., hoping to ride a quake back so they can prevent some terrible event in their lives. Some succeed, some don't. Others have meticulous lists of sporting events and charts of stock fluctuations; they expect to get rich with their knowledge. Some do, some don't.

I fall asleep in front of the TV, watching Jack Paar on *The Tonight Show*. I wake up and it's the last week of April '67. The smog is the same, the cars are smaller and more teenage; on the plus side, the skirts are a lot shorter. But my old brown suit is out of style. And my car is visibly obsolete – a '56 Chevy. Obvious evidence that I'm a wandering time-raveler.

Caught breakfast in the market, fresh fruit, not too expensive yet, then headed back up to the boulevard. Santa Monica Boulevard was now a tawdry circus of adult bookstores, XXX theaters, and massage parlors. The buildings all looked like garish whores.

Hollywood Boulevard was worse. The stink of incense was almost strong enough to cover the smog. Clothing had turned into costumes, with teens of both sexes wearing tight pants and garish shirts – not quite hippies yet, but almost. The first bell-bottom jeans were showing, the Flower Children were just starting to bloom. The summer of love was about to begin.

Several storefronts had signs for time-tours and maps of the quake-zones; probably a better business than maps to the homes of the stars. I noticed several familiar faces – a small herd of comic book collectors – heading toward the newsstand on Cahuenga; they were probably the first customers of the quake-maps.

Roy was still shining shoes, twelve years older, but just as slick and just as fast. "Shoes look good, Mr. Harris," he said, as I walked in. He called all of us Mr. Harris. Nobody ever corrected him. Maybe it was his way of keeping track. He knew who we were, but he never asked questions, and he never offered advice. He kept his own counsel. But sometimes, he steered the right people to the office and sometimes he turned other folks away. "What you lookin' for ain't up those stairs, mister." Every so often, Georgia would march downstairs and hand him an envelope. She never said why. I assumed that was something else she'd learned from Margaret.

The office had been redecorated; it felt more like Georgia now. All of the typewriters were IBM Selectrics. New lateral filing cabinets, a Xerox photocopier, even a fax machine. The cubby had been painted light blue with white trim and the stacks of boxes and files had disappeared, replaced by dark oak bookshelves. Most of the files had moved into the offices next door, which we'd leased in '61, when the accountant finally died. It'd be another few decades before we would have all that information on hard drives and optical discs. The same heavy mahogany table and leather chairs remained in the center of the room, but looking a lot more worn.

Georgia was expecting me. She tossed the same manila envelope on the table, brought in another bottle of Glenfiddich, two glasses, and a new pocket Torah. I passed her the old one, as well as the few collectible treasures I'd picked up in '58. She'd put them in storage for me.

"Lose the brown suit," she said. "I bought you a new one, dark gray. It's in the closet. Already tailored. Read the file, there's some new information." She reached for the bottle.

"Not this early, thanks." I was already signing the envelope. The file had been accessed only three times in the last twelve years. Margaret twice, Georgia once. But it was significantly thicker.

This time there was a bundle of newspaper clippings. Not about Jeremy Weiss, but about a dozen *others*. I checked the dates first. June of '67 to September of '74. Georgia had typed up a chart. At least thirteen young men had disappeared. Jeremy Weiss was the third. The third that we knew about. I wasn't surprised. I'd had a hunch there was more.

We weren't obligated to investigate the disappearances of the others;

Weiss was the only one we had a contract on. But if the disappearances were related . . . if they had a common author, then finding that author would not only save Weiss, but a dozen others as well. Preemptive action. But only if the disappearances were connected. We'd still have to monitor – *save* – Weiss. Just in case.

I read through the clippings, slowly, carefully. Three times. There was a depressing similarity. Georgia sent out for sandwiches. After lunch, she sat down next to me – she was wearing the Jasmine perfume again, or maybe still, or maybe for the first time – and walked me through the similarities she'd noticed. The youngest victim was fifteen, but big for his age; the oldest was twenty-three, but he looked eighteen.

Last item in the envelope was a map of West Los Angeles with a red X at the site of each vic's last known location; his apartment, his job, where his car was discovered, or the last person to see him alive. There were no X's north of Sunset, none south of Third. The farthest west was Doheny, the farthest east was just the other side of Vine Street. It was a pretty big target area, but at the same time fairly specific.

"I want you to notice something," she said. She pointed to the map, tracing an area outlined by a yellow highlighter. All of the red X's were inside, or very close to the border of the yellow defined region, except for the one east of Vine. "Look at this." She tapped the paper with her fingernail. "That's West Hollywood. Have you seen it?"

"Drove through it this morning."

"Ever hear of *Fanny Hill*?"

"Isn't that a park in Boston?"

"Not funny. Don't quit your day job. It's a book, by John Cleland. *Memoirs of a Woman of Pleasure*. It has redeeming social value. Now."

"Sorry, I'm not following."

"John Cleland was born in 1710. He worked for the East India Company, but he didn't make much money at it. He ended up in Fleet debtors' prison from 1748–1749. While there, he wrote or rewrote a book called *Fanny Hill*. It's written as a series of letters from Fanny to another woman, and it is generally considered the first work of pornography written in English, its literary impact derives from its elaborate sexual metaphor and euphemistic language."

"And this is important because . . . ?"

"Because last year – 1966 – the Supreme Court declared that it is not obscene." She didn't wait for me to look puzzled. "In 1957, in Roth versus the United States, the Supreme Court ruled that obscenity is not within the area of constitutionally protected freedom of speech or press, neither under the first amendment, nor under the due process clause of the fourteenth amendment. They sustained the conviction of a bookseller for selling and mailing an obscene book and obscene circulars and advertising.

"In 1966, in Cleland versus Massachusetts, the court revisited their earlier decision to clarify the definition of obscenity. Since the Roth ruling, for a work of literature to be declared obscene, a censor has to demonstrate that the work appeals to prurient interest, is patently offensive, and has no redeeming social value. It's that last one that's important, because it could not be demonstrated to the court that *Fanny Hill* has no redeeming social value. The case can be made that the book is an historical document, presenting an exaggerated and often satirical view of the mores of eighteenth-century London, just as the *Satyricon* by Petronius presents an exaggerated and satirical view of ancient Rome; so a very strong case can be made that pornography represents a singular insight into the morality of its time. Thus, it has redeeming social value. Therefore, it cannot be prosecuted as obscene."

"Redeeming social value . . ."

"Right."

"Since the *Fanny Hill* ruling, pornography has become an industry. If a publisher can claim redeeming social value, the work is legal. A book of erotic pictures with a couple quotes from Shakespeare. A sex film with a preface by a doctor – or an actor playing a doctor. It's a legal fan dance – you don't go to the fan dance to see the fan. The pornographers will be testing the limits of the law for years. The fans are going to get a lot smaller."

"Okay, so what does all this have to do with West Hollywood?"

"I'm getting to that. For the next decade, enforcement of obscenity laws will be left to local communities. There will be years of debate. Nothing will be clear or certain, because the definition of obscenity will be determined by local community standards. Until even that argument gets knocked down. At some point, the whole issue of redeeming social value becomes moot because it becomes unenforceable. How do you define it? And that'll be the end of antismut laws. But right now, today – it's all about local community standards."

"And West Hollywood is a local community . . . ?"

"It's an *unincorporated* community," Georgia said. "It's not part of Los Angeles. It's not a city. It's a big hole in the middle of the city. L.A.P.D. has no authority inside this yellow area. There's no police coverage. The only enforcement is the L.A. County Sheriff Department. So there's no community and there are no standards. It's the wild west."

"Mm," I said.

"Right," she agreed. "None of the city ordinances apply. Only the county ones. And the county is a lot less specific on pornography. So you get bookstores. And more. The county doesn't have specific zoning restrictions or statutes to regulate massage parlors, sex stores, and other adult-oriented businesses. The whole area is crawling with lowlifes and opportunists. Here – " She pulled out another map. This one showing a corridor of red X's stretching the length of Santa Monica Boulevard, with a scattered few on Melrose.

"What's this?"

"A survey of sex businesses in West Hollywood. Red for hetero, purple for homo, green for the bookstores. You get clusters. Here, all the way from La Brea to La Cienega, this used to be a quiet little neighborhood where seniors could sit in the sun at Plummer Park and play pinochle. Now, there are male hustlers in hot pants, posing at the bus stops.

"Take a drive around the neighborhood. You'll see things like massage parlors advertising specific attention to love muscle stiffness – Greek, French, and English massage. Or sex therapists who will help you work out your inhibitions with sex fantasy role-playing. Here, here, and here, these are gay bars, this is a bath house, so is this. This place sells costumes, chains, things made of leather – and realistic prostheses."

"Prostheses – ?" And then I got it. "Never mind."

"If you can imagine a sexual service, you'll find it here. This is the land of negotiable virtue. It's a sexual carnival, the fun zone, the zoo. This is the reservoir of licentiousness. This is where AIDS will start. You'll need to start carrying condoms. Anyway – " She stretched out the two maps side by side. "Notice the congruence? I'm going to make a guess – "

"These kids are horny?"

"And gay."

"Is that a hunch, or – ?"

She didn't answer immediately. "Okay, I might be wrong. But if I'm right, then the police will be useless to us. Ditto the sheriff's department. They don't care. Not here. They won't take this seriously. And we can't talk about this with any of the parents. And probably not even with the kids themselves. This is still the year of the closet . . . and will be until June of '69. Stonewall," she explained.

"I know about Stonewall. We bid on a contract to videotape it. The problem will be getting cameras onsite."

"Eakins is working on that. There's a thing called . . . never mind, I don't have time to explain it." She tapped the table. "Let's get back to this case. We've got six weeks until the first disappearance. This is as close as you can get by time-skipping. You'll have to live concurrently, but that'll be an advantage. You can familiarize yourself with the area, locate the victims, make yourself part of the landscape. Let your sideburns grow. We've found an apartment for you, heart of the district, corner of North Kings Road and Santa Monica, second floor. Here, wait a minute – " She stepped out of the room for a second, came back with a cardboard filebox, and a set of keys. "We bought you a new car too. You can't drive a '56 Chevy around '67 L.A. It attracts too much attention."

"But I like the Chevy – "

"We bought you a '67 Mustang convertible. You'll be invisible. There are a hundred thousand of these ponies in California already. It's in the parking lot behind. Give me the keys to the Chevy. We'll restore it and put it in storage. Another forty years, it'll be worth enough to buy a retirement condo. A high-priced apartment."

She popped the top off the box. In it were another dozen envelopes of varying thicknesses. "Everything we've got on the other disappearances. Including pictures of the vics. It's the first two you want to focus on."

I sorted through the reports. "Okay, so we have an approximate geographical area and a pretty specific age range. Is there anything else to connect these victims?"

"Look at the pictures. They're all twinks."

"Twinks?"

"Pretty boys."

"And based on that, you think they're gay?"

"I think we're dealing with a serial killer. Someone who preys on teenage boys. Yeah, I know – lots of kids go missing every year just in L.A. County. They hop on a bus, they go to Mexico or Canada, they go underground to avoid the draft. Or maybe they just move without leaving a forwarding address. But these thirteen don't fit that profile. The only connection is that there's no other connection. I don't know. But that's what it smells like to me." She finished her drink. Neat. Just like Margaret. "I think if we find out what happened to the first victim, we unravel the whole string."

I finished my drink, pushed my glass away, empty. Put my hand over it in response to her questioning glance. One shot was enough. If she was right, this was big. Very.

Took a breath, let it out loudly, stared across at her. "Georgia, you've been working these streets long enough to know every gum spot by brand name. I won't bet against you." I gathered the separate files. "I'll check them out." I thought for a moment. "How old am I now?"

Georgia didn't even blink. "According to our tracking, you're twenty-seven." She squinted. "With a little bit of work, we could probably make you look twenty-one or twenty-two. Put a little bleach in your hair, put you in a surfer shirt and shorts, you'll look like a summer-boy. What are you thinking? Bait?"

"Maybe. I'm thinking I might need to talk to some of these kids. The closer I am to the same age, the more likely I'll get honesty."

Something occurred to me. I turned the maps around and peered back and forth between them. Pulled the disappearance map closer.

"What are you looking for?"

"The dates. Which one of these was first?"

"This one, over here." She tapped the paper. The one east of Vine. "Why?"

"Just something I heard once about serial killers. Always look closest at the first vic. That's the one closest to home. That's more likely a crime of opportunity than premeditated. And sometimes that first vic and the perp – sometimes they know each other."

"You've never done a serial killer before," Georgia said.

"You're thinking about bringing in some help?"

"It might not be a bad idea."

Considered it. "Can't bring in L.A.P.D. They have no jurisdiction. And County isn't really set up for this."

"Bring in the Feds?"

I didn't like that idea either. "Not yet. We might embarrass ourselves. Let me do the groundwork first. I'll poke around for a few days, then we'll talk. See if you can get anything from uptime."

"I've already put a copy of the file in the long-safe. I'll add your notes next week. Then we'll look for a reply."

The long-safe was a kind of time capsule. It was a one-way box with a time-lock. You punch in a combination and a due date, a drawer opens and you put a manila envelope in. On the due date – ten or twenty or thirty years later – the drawer pops open, you take the file out and read it. Usually, the top page is a list of unanswered questions. Someone uptime does the research, looks up the answers, writes a report, puts it in another manila envelope, and hands it to a downtime courier – someone headed backwards, usually on a whole series of errands. The downtime courier rides the quakes until he or she reaches a point before the original memo was written. The courier delivers the envelope, and it goes into the long-safe, with a due date after the send date of the first file, the one with all the questions. This was one of the ways, not the only one, that we could ask the future for help with a case.

Sometimes we sent open-ended queries – what should we know about that we don't know yet to ask? Sometimes we got useful information, more often not. Uptime was sensitive about sending too much information back. Despite the various theories about the chronoplastic construction of the stress-field, there weren't a lot of folks who wanted to take chances. One theory had it that sending information downtime was one of the things that triggered time-quakes, because it disturbed the fault lines.

Maybe. I dunno. I'm not a theorist. I'm just a meat-and-potatoes guy. I roll up my sleeves and pick up the shovel. I prefer it that way. Let somebody else do the heavy thinking, I'll do the heavy lifting. It's a fair trade.

I didn't set out to be a time-raveler. It happened by accident. I was in the marines, got a promotion to sergeant, and re-upped for another two years. Spent eighteen months in Nam as an advisor, mostly in Saigon, but occasionally up-country and twice out into the Delta. The place was a fucking time bomb. Victor Charlie wanted to give me an early retirement, but I had other plans. Rotated stateside the first opportunity.

Got off the plane in San Francisco, caught a Greyhound south, curled up to sleep, and the San Andreas time-fault let loose. It was the first big timequake and I woke up three years later. 1969. Just in time to see Neil Armstrong bounce down the ladder. Both Dad and the dog were dead. I had no one left, no home to return to. Someone at the Red Cross Relocation Center took my information, made some phone calls, came back and asked me if I had made any career plans. Not really, why? Because there's someone you should talk to. Why? Because you have the right set of skills and no close family connections. What kind of work? Hard work. Challenging, sometimes dangerous, but the money's good, you can carry a gun, and at the end of the day you're a hero. Oh, that kind of work. Okay. Sure, I'll meet him. Good, go to this address, second floor, upstairs from the shoeshine stand. Your appointment is at three, don't be late. And that was it.

My first few months, Georgia kept me local, bouncing up and down the early '70s, doing mostly easy stuff like downtime courier service. She needed to know that I wouldn't go off the rails. The only thing the agency has to sell is trust. But I wasn't going anywhere. The agency was all I had – they were a serendipitous liftoff from the drop zone of '69, and you don't frag the pilot. A lieutenant maybe, but never a pilot – or a corpsman.

I'd thought about corpsman training early, even gone so far as to sit down with the sergeant. He just looked across the desk at me and shook his head. "There's more to it than stabbing morphine needles into screaming soldiers. You're better where you are." I didn't know how to take that, but I understood the first time mortar shells came dropping in around us and voices all around started screaming, "Medic! Medic!" I wouldn't have known which way to run. And I just wanted to keep my head down as low as possible until the whole damn business was over. It was only later, I got angry enough to start shooting back. But that was later.

After the courier bit became routine, Georgia started increasing my responsibilities. When you pass through '64, pick up mint-condition copies of these books and magazines. Pick up more if they're in good condition, but don't be greedy. Barbie dolls, assorted outfits (especially the specials), and Hot Wheels, always. Buy extras if they have them. Sometimes she just wanted me to go someplace and take pictures – of the street, the houses, the cars, the signs.

After a couple months, I told Georgia that the work didn't seem all that challenging. Georgia didn't blink. She told me that I had to learn the terrain, I had to get so comfortable with the shifting kaleidoscope of time that I couldn't be rattled. That's why the '60s and the '70s were such a good training ground. The nation went through six identifiable cultural transitions in the course of sixteen years. But even though the '50s were supposed to be a lot quieter, she didn't think so. They weren't all that safer, it was just a different kind of danger. Georgia said she wanted to keep me out of that decade as much as possible. "You've got tombstones in your eyes," she said. "You'll scare the shit out of them. And frightened people are dangerous. Especially the ones with power. Later, after you've mellowed, we'll send you back. We'll see."

After a bit, she started passing me some of the little jobs, the ones where clients bought themselves a bit of protection, or closure, or prevention.

For instance: "Here, this file just came up. Here's fifty dollars. Go to this address, give it to this person. Find a way to make it legit, tell him you're a location manager for Warner Brothers, you're shooting a pilot, some TV series, a cop show, lots of location work like *Dragnet*, you want to measure the apartment, photograph the view from the balcony, and here's a few bucks for your trouble." That one was easy. A struggling young writer with no food in the house, desperate and waiting to find out if he'd sold his first book, all he needed was another week – his future self was giving him a lifeline.

Another one: "The mail carrier delivers the mail to this address between 1 and 2 p.m. Nobody will be home before five. Open the mailbox and remove any letters with this return address. Do this every day for the next two weeks." A fraternity at USC. That one didn't make sense until a year later when that same fraternity was thrown off campus for a hazing scandal. Somebody didn't get the invitation to rush, didn't pledge, didn't get injured, and didn't have his college career stained.

And a third: "Tomorrow afternoon, this little boy's pet dog gets out an open window and wanders away from the house. Nobody's home until three. Pick up the dog before it gets to the avenue, come back at seven, knock on the door, and ask if they know who the dog belongs to, you found it the next block over." Right. No mystery there.

"Tuesday evening, Lankershim Boulevard, across the street from the El Portal Theater. There's a blue Ford Falcon. Somebody sideswipes it, sometime between 6:45 and 9:30. Get the license number, leave a note on the windshield."

After those, I started getting the weird jobs. Some of them made no sense, there was no rational explanation; but the client doesn't always give reasons. Our rule is that we only take oddball cases on the condition that no physical or personal harm is intended.

Here's one: "Take this copy of *Popular Mechanics*, thumb through it so it looks used. Tomorrow afternoon, 1:30, go out to Van Nuys, 5355 Van Nuys Boulevard, Bobs #7. Sit at the counter near the front, near the go-order window. Order a Big Boy hamburger and a Coke. Read the magazine while you eat. Fold it so the ad on page 56 is visible. Leave a dollar tip. Leave the magazine on the table."

And another: "Friday night, just after the bars close, stand in front of the door at this address, like you're waiting for a ride. That's all. Nothing will happen. You can leave at 2:30."

And one more: "Take this package. No, don't open it. At 4:25, catch the 86 bus at Highland. Get off at Victory and Laurel Canyon. Cross the street and wait for the return bus. Leave the package on the bench."

And the weirdest: "Here's a white T-shirt, blue jeans, and a red jacket; right, the James Dean look. You've got the face for it. Tomorrow afternoon, Studio City, corner of Ventura and Laurel Canyon. When this kid comes out of the drugstore, you stop her and say, 'When you are ready to learn, the universe will provide a teacher. Even when you are not ready to learn, the universe will provide a teacher.' Hand her this paper. It has a poem by Emily Dickinson. Don't answer questions. Go into the drugstore, go all the way to the back and out to the parking lot, turn right and duck around the corner of the building, she won't follow, but she mustn't see you again. Walk west till you get to the ice cream store. You can park your car behind it."

Finally, when Georgia was satisfied that I could follow orders, she gave me a tough one. "Do you trust me? Good. Go to this address and kneecap this son of a bitch."

"Kneecap?"

"Slang term. Shoot him in the kneecap. Both kneecaps. We want him in a wheelchair for the rest of his life. Oh, and rip the phone off the wall. Wear these gloves, wear these shoes – use this gun, here's ammunition, here's a silencer, put everything in this plastic trash bag, bring it all back here for disposal."

"You're kidding."

"We don't joke about things like this."

"Shoot him in the kneecaps – y'know, that's a tricky shot. Especially if he's moving."

"If you can't manage it – "

"I can manage it."

"Would you rather just kill him?"

Thought about it for two or three seconds. "What'd he do?"

"You don't like being hired muscle, do you?"

"I just need to know – "

"It's righteous," she said. "He's a rapist. He rapes little girls. The youngest is six. And then he kills them. He goes off the rails tomorrow. Cripple him tonight and you'll save three lives that we know of, probably more if he starts time-walking."

"Can I ask you a question? Who makes these decisions?"

She shook her head. "It's a need-to-know thing." Then she added, "Think of it this way. The perps choose it when they choose to be perps. We try to provide permanent solutions. This guy tonight – he's a dangerous asshole. Do your job and tomorrow, he'll just be an asshole." She shrugged. "Or a corpse. Either is part of the contract. Whatever's easiest for you. Or most enjoyable. Your call."

"I'm not a psychopath."

"That's too bad. We really do need one. For the big jobs."

I let that pass. "Do we have a preemptive warrant?"

Georgia shook her head. "That law hasn't been passed yet. But we can't wait. Here, ease your conscience. After you do him, drop this envelope out of the plastic bag, leave it on the floor."

"What's in it? Cash?"

"Clippings. About how he'll torture his victims. Leave it for the cops, they'll get it. Don't touch anything, don't leave prints."

There were other jobs like that. They never got any easier.

In real life, you don't shoot the gun out of the bad guy's hand. The bad guys don't drop the gun, say ouch, and reach for the sky – no, they shoot back. With everything they've got, with bullets and mortars and mines that take your best buddy's legs off. They just keep coming at you, spraying blood and fire, hammering explosions, hailstorms of dirt and flesh and bone. You have to keep your head down and your helmet tight and hope you have a chance to lay down a carpet of fire, burn them alive and screaming, just to buy those moments of empty dreadful silence while you wait to see if it starts up again. In real life, you beat them senseless just to slow them down. And if that doesn't slow them down, you kill them, you blow them away, you turn them into queasy red gobbets.

On TV, everything is neat. Real life is messy, ugly, scabrous, squalid, festering, putrid, and painful. In real life, the bad guys don't think they're bad, they think they're good guys too, just doing their stuff because that's the stuff that a man's gotta do; but in real life, there are no good guys, just guys, doing each other until everybody's done. And then maybe afterward, while you're picking up the pieces of your corporal or your radioman, you get a chance to sort it out. Maybe. And that's when it doesn't matter if anybody's a good guy, they're still dead.

Because in real life, there are no good guys. They don't exist and neither do you. That's the cold hard truth. You're not there, you're just another TV death, consumed like a TV dinner, until it's time to change the channel. You think you have a life? No. You're just the space where all this shit is happening. That cascade of experience – you don't own it, it owns you. You're the bug in the trap. The avalanche of time, the pummeling of a trillion quantum-instants, second after second, it pounds you down into the sand, and whatever you think you are, it's an illusion – you exist only as a timebinding hallucination of continuity. And after long enough, after you realize you can't endure anymore of this senseless pummeling – whether it's mortar shells or rifle bullets or cosmic zingers so tiny you don't know you've taken one in the heart until you get to the third paragraph – you just continue anyway. Waiting. Sooner or later, the snipers will get your range.

You don't survive, you just take it a day at a time, a moment at a time. You pick your steps carefully, always watching for the one that might go click. You look, you listen, and you never move fast – until you have to. And when you do, you take the other guy down first, and keep him down, and you don't worry about nice and you don't worry about pretty; the whole idea is to keep him from ever getting up again. So you do what you do so he can't do what he does. And once in a while, somebody tells you it was worth it, but you know better, because you're still carrying the ruck through the hot zone, not them. In real life, real life stinks.

So I took him down. Him and the next three. And I learned to drink Glenfiddich straight from the bottle.

Until one morning, Georgia dragged me out of bed, still covered in vomit and stink, rolled me into a tub and filled it with cold water. Grabbed me by the hair, dunked me until I screamed, and poured cold black stale coffee down my throat until I was swearing in English again. My head hammering like a V-8 with a broken rod, she dressed me, drove me to the gym and handed me over to Gunter, the personal trainer. After that, 7 a.m. every day. In the afternoon, language classes at the Berlitz. Monday evenings, firing range – hands-on experience with weapons from here to flintlocks. Tuesday, world history class. Wednesday, Miss Grace's Academy of Deportment, I'm not kidding. Thursday, meeting – friends of Bill W. Friday, movie night. With Georgia. Not a date – cultural acclimatization. Saturday, assigned research and dinner at Georgia's. Not a date – a full report on the week. Sunday . . . breakfast with Georgia.

She didn't save my life. She made it worth enduring. Especially when we started sleeping together. Not at her place, not at mine, she wouldn't have that. We went to one of those little cardboard motels out on Cahuenga, where it turns into Ventura, halfway between here and the San Fernando Valley. She needed danger and I needed sex. So we rumpled the sheets like a war zone for three months regular, every Saturday night – until the next timequake and I had to go to Sylmar and bounce forward three years, and even though I was up for it, even thinking maybe I should buy her a ring, she'd already moved on, and that was the end of it. That was the zinger right through the heart.

I found something else to do on Thursday nights and let myself have one glass of scotch every time I finished a dirty job. Sometimes the clean jobs too. It didn't help. And I told her why.

No, it wasn't her. It was that other thing. The good-guy thing. I didn't feel like one. Killing for peace is like fucking for chastity. It doesn't work.

She offered to buy out my contract, send me off somewhere to retire, I'd certainly earned it. But no – I don't know why I said no. Maybe it was because there was still work to do. Maybe it was because I still wanted to believe there was something to believe in. What the hell. It was better than sitting on my ass and poisoning my liver.

So I took the envelope and left the bottle. Maybe someday I'd figure it out, but for now, I wasn't looking anymore.

Picked up the first vic at his job, tailed him to his place. Brad Boyd. He lived in a courtyard apartment on Romaine, just east of Vine. In two and a half months, the bitchy neighbor who hates his dog and his motorcycle will be the last person to see him. She'll scream at him about the bike being on the walk, in everybody's way; then she'll push it over. He'll pick it up, get on it, turn it away from her so both exhaust pipes are pointing in her direction, and rev it as loud as he can, belching out huge clouds of oil-smelling smoke; then he'll roar away. 9:30 p.m. on a hot Thursday night in July. It's a blue Yamaha, two-stroke engine, 750 cc, a mid-sized bike; it'll never be found. Left this vic at home, watching TV. The blue glow is visible from the street.

Headed out to the valley and drove past the Van Nuys home of the Weiss kid. He still lives with his mother, his dad died a year ago; he's in his last year at San Fernando Valley State College in Northridge. His room is in the back of the house, I can't see any lights. But his car is in the driveway.

The fourth vic lives on Hyperion in the Silver Lake area, catches the bus downtown, where, he works for a bank. I ride the bus opposite him, sit where I'm not in his line of sight, and study him all the way to Hill Street. Randy something. Skinny little kid, very fair complexion, too pretty to be a boy; put a dress on him you can take him anywhere. They must have teased the hell out of him in school.

After that, I check the locations, the last known sightings. I'll start working on the other vics next week; I want to read the neighborhood first. Weiss's car will be found on Melrose Avenue, two-three blocks east of the promising lights of La Cienega. Carefully parked, locked up tight. He went someplace, he never came back. I park across the street. I lean back against the warm fender of the Mustang and study the street. At first glance, it seems innocent enough.

This forgotten little pocket of West Hollywood is a time zone unto itself, with most of its pieces left over from the twenties and thirties. In '67, Melrose is dotted with tacky little art galleries, interior decorators, and a scattering of furniture stores hoping to get trendy. It's a desolate avenue, even during the day.

At night, the street is dry and deserted, amber streetlights pockmark the gloom; a few blocks away, the bright bustle of life hurtles down La Cienega, but here emptiness, the buildings huddled dark and empty against themselves, waiting for the return of day and the illusion of life. Bits of neon shine from darkened storefronts. Occasional red-lit doorways hint at secret worlds.

Few cars cruise here, even fewer souls are seen on the sidewalks – only the occasional oasis of a sheltered restaurant, remaining open even after everyone else has fled; departing customers move quickly from bright doorways to the waiting safety of their automobiles, tuck a bill into the valet's hand, and whisper away into the night.

There's this thing they do in the movies, in a western, or a war picture, where someone says, "It's quiet, too quiet." Or: "Listen. Even the birds are silent." That's how they do it in the movies, but that's not how it works in the hot zone. In the zone, it's more like a little timequake. There's this sense, this feeling that you get – like the air doesn't taste quite right. And when you get that feeling, sometimes the little hairs on the back of your neck start tickling. You stop, you look around, you look for the reason why those little hairs are rising. Sometimes, it's just a shift in the wind and the way the grass ripples across the hillside, and as you watch the ripples, you realize that one of those ripples isn't like the others. And you wake up inside your own life in a way that makes the rest of the day feel like somnambulism.

Sometimes the feeling isn't anything at all. Sometimes the feeling is just too much coffee. But it's a real feeling and you learn to respect it anyway because you're out there in the hot and the guy who drew the pretty pictures on the chalkboard isn't. You hit the dirt – and the one time you hit the dirt and hear the round go past just over your head instead of through your gut – that one time makes up for all the times you hit the dirt and there's nothing overhead.

You learn to listen for the feeling. You never stop. Years later, even after the Delta has receded into time, you're still listening. You listen to the world like it's ticking off, counting down. You listen, not even knowing what you're listening for anymore.

Standing on Melrose, I got something. Not the same feeling, but a feeling. A sense there's something *else* here. Something that comes out, late at night. And good folks don't want to be here when it's up and about.

Get back in the car. Lean back and disappear into the shadows. Sit and wait, not for anything in particular. Just to see what comes out in the darkness. Picket duty. Eyes and ears open; mind catching forty. Watching. Reading the street.

The avenue has a vampiric life of its own. Every so often, motion. A manboy, sometimes two. Sometimes a girlboy. The children of the night climb out of their daytime coffins and drift singly through the shadows, flickering briefly into existence for a block or two, then disappearing just as ephemerally. It isn't immediately obvious what's happening here.

Finally, got out of the car and went for a walk. West, where Melrose angles in toward La Cienega. Where are the manboys going? Where are they coming from?

Ah.

Half a block east of the lights. A darkened art gallery with an unpaved parking lot. The lot is dark, unlit. At the back is a fenced-in covered patio. Discreet. Unobtrusive. Inconspicuous to the point of invisibility. You could drive by a thousand times and never notice, even if you were looking for it. It's furtive. Like Charlie. Things that hide are either frightened or stalking. Either way, dangerous.

Two-three teens standing in the lot, smoking, chatting. Only room for a few cars here. I fumble around in my pockets for a pack of cigarettes. I stopped smoking when Ed Murrow died, again when I left Da Nang, and a third time when I got off the plane in San Francisco; the third time it stuck; but it's still convenient to carry them. Pull one out of the pack, approach the girlboys, ask for a light, say thanks, nod, wait.

"You new?"

Shrug. "Back in town."

"Where were you?"

"Nam."

"Oh. I heard it's pretty bad."

"It is. And getting worse."

The boys have no real names. The tall thin one with straight black hair is "Mame." The shorter rounder one is "Peaches." The blond is "Snoopy."

"You got a name?"

"Solo."

"Napoleon?"

"Han."

"What'd you do in Nam?"

"Piloted a boat. Called The Maltese Falcon." Almost added, "Went upriver to kill a man named Kurtz." But I didn't. They wouldn't get it, not for twelve years anyway. I doubted any of them had ever read either Conrad or Chandler. Mame was more likely a Bette Davis fan than Humphrey Bogart. The other two . . . hard to tell. Shaun Cassidy probably.

"You goin' in?"

Took a puff on the cigarette. "In a minute." Hang back, listening. The girlboys are gossiping, overlapping dialogue, about someone named Jerry and his unrequited crush on someone else named Dave, except Dave has a lover. Jerry has a secret too. Honey, don't we all? Oh, guess what? Speaking of secrets, Dennis's real age is twenty-three, he's a chicken hawk, he's dating Marc. Marc? That's funny. Marc has the crabs, he got them from Lane. Lane? That sissy? Lane isn't even his real name. He's cheating on his sugar daddy, you know. Hey, have you met the new girl? With the southern accent? You mean, Miss Scarlett? More like Miss Thing. She's way over the top. She's just a sweet ole Georgia peach. I thought she said Alabama. Whatever. Do you believe her? Honey, I don't even believe me. She says she went in drag to her senior prom. In Alabama? Girl, I'll believe that when I hear it from Rock Hudson Jr.

Mame turns to me abruptly. "Getting an earful?"

Shrug again. "Doesn't mean anything to me. I don't know any of those people."

Satisfied, Mame turns back to the others. Did you hear about Duchess and Princess? I only know what you've told me. They were arrested – in drag – for stealing a car. Has anybody heard anything else? Not me. Have you ever seen them out of drag? No, have you? I have. Princess puts the ugh into ughly. Her and Duchess, it's Baby Jane and Blanche. I wonder who'll get their wardrobe. Honey, just one of Princess's gowns is big enough for all three of us. If we're friendly. I'm friendly, very friendly. Honey, get real. What are you and I going to do together – bump pussies, try on hats, and giggle?

Gossip is useful. It's a map of the social terrain. It tells you which way the energy is flowing. It tells you who's important. It's the quick way of tapping into the social gestalt. Find me three gossips and I can learn a community. Except this isn't a community. This is a fragmentary maelstrom of whirling bodies. A quantum environment, with particles flickering in and out of existence so fast they can only be detected by their wakes.

Eventually, I go in. There's no sign, but the place is called Gino's. Admission is fifty cents. The man at the door is forty-five, maybe fifty. This is Gino. He has curly black hair, a little too black. He dyes it. Okay, fifty plus. He looks Greek. He hands me a red ticket from a roll, the anonymous numbered kind they use at movie theaters. Good for one soda. He recites the rules. This is a club for eighteen and up. No drugs, no booze. If the white light goes on, it means the vice are here, stop dancing.

The outdoor patio is filled with jostling teens, all boys, some giggling, some serious. Several are standing close. Some make eye contact, others turn away, embarrassed. Others sit silently, sullenly, on heavy benches along the walls. Potting benches? Perhaps this used to be a nursery.

The patio connects to a second building, tucked neatly behind the art gallery. Invisible from the street. Perfect. Inside, it's darker than the patio. A quick survey reveals a bar, sandwiches, Cokes; in one corner a pool table, another a pinball machine. There's a jukebox playing a song by Diana Ross and the Supremes; several of the boys are singing falsetto-accompaniment. "Love Child." And an area for dancing. But no one's dancing. The same embarrassment in the high school gym.

A slower survey of the inhabitants – almost no one over the age of twenty-five. Most of the boys here are high school girls, even the ones of college age. A few pretend to be butch, others don't care. Every so often, two or three of them leave together. I listen for conversations. More gossip. Some of it desperate. Longings. Judgments. Hopes. And the usual chatter about classmates, teachers, schools, movies . . . and Shaun Cassidy.

Someone behind me says to someone else. "Let's go to the Stampede." "What's the Stampede?" "You've never been there? Come on." I follow them out. Discreetly.

The Stampede is on Santa Monica, near the corner of Fairfax. It's a beer bar. Inside, it's decorated to look like a western street. A shingled awning around the bar has a stuffed cougar. Black lights make white T-shirts glow. A young crowd, drinking age. All the way to the back, a small patio. The place is filled with manboys standing around, looking at each other and pretending that they're not standing around and looking at each other, imagining, wishing, dreaming. Some of them search my face, I nod dispassionately, then turn away. The jukebox plays "Light My Fire," Jim Morrison and The Doors. If Gino's is high school, then The Stampede is junior year at city college. The boys are a little more like boys here, but they still seem much too young.

I know what it is – they're unfinished. They don't know who they are. They haven't had to dive into the mud and shit and blood. They haven't had anyone shooting at them.

Two couples walk in the front door, the wives holding the husbands' arms possessively. Some of the queers exchange glances. Tourists. Visiting the zoo, the freak show. They've never seen real faggots before. Someone behind me whispers bitchily. "The husbands will be back next week. Without the fish. It's always that way."

A couple blocks west, there's another bar, The Rusty Nail. More of the same, maybe a rougher crowd, a little older. A couple blocks east, The Spike. East of that, a leather bar. Okay, I got it. Circus of Books stays open twenty-four hours – the adult section, pick up a copy of the Bob Damron guide book. This is what I need. I take it back to my apartment and make X's on the map. No surprises here. Georgia was right. Queer bars and bathhouses. Another cluster of congruency.

Draw the connecting lines. Traffic goes back and forth on Santa Monica Boulevard, occasionally down to Gino's on Melrose. Oh, and there's a place over here on Beverly, The Stud. Enter in the rear. Unintended irony. They hang bicycles and canoes and rocking chairs from the high ceiling. It's funky and faddish. Up on Sunset, the Sea Witch. Glass balls in nets, and a great view of the city lights. They allow dancing – furtively. On Santa Monica, a little west of La Cienega, hidden among the bright lights of the billboards, another hidden dance club. Everybody's testing the limits of enforcement.

For two weeks, I check out all the bars, all the clubs. But my first hunch is strongest. Gino's is the hunting ground. I can feel it. I don't need to listen for the little hairs.

As the nights warm up, something is awakening. A restlessness in the air. A feverish subculture of summer is readying itself. But this year, it's reckless. Next year, it'll be worse, self-destructive. The year after that, 1969, it'll implode on itself. But right now, this moment, it still hasn't realized itself yet.

It's the boomers, the baby boomers, all those children of war coming of age at the very same moment, their juices surging, their chaotic desires and wants and needs – the wildness unleashed, the rebels without a pause; the ones who think that college has made them educated, and the ones who resent them because they have to work for their daily bread – all of them, horny as hell, possessed with the sense of freedom that comes behind the wheel of a Mustang or a Camaro or a VW Beetle, liberally lubricated with cheap gasoline, marijuana and beer and raging hormones, out on the streets, looking for where it's happening.

It isn't happening anywhere, it's happening everywhere, and the noise and the stink pervades the night. The straight ones hit the Sunset Strip or the peppermint places on Ventura Boulevard. Or they cruise up and down Van Nuys Boulevard or Rosecrans Avenue, and especially Hollywood Boulevard. But the other ones – the quieter ones, the ones who didn't chase the girls, the music majors and the theater arts students, the shy boys and the wild boys – after all those years of longing, they're finally finding a place where they belong too, where there are others just like them. No, not just like them. But close enough. Here are others who will understand. Or not understand. There are so many different kinds, so many different ways of being queer. But at least, for a little while, in these furtive secret places, they won't have to pretend that they don't want what they want.

During the day, they'll rage about the unfairness of discrimination, about the ugliness of war – but at night, they all want to get laid. And that's what's surging here. The desolate lust of loneliness. It's a fevered subculture, a subset of the larger sickness that roils in the newspapers.

Our little vics – I pin their pictures to the wall and study them – they're cannon fodder. As innocent as the boy who stepped on the land mine, as unfinished as the new kid who took a bullet in the head from a jungle sniper on his first picket duty, as fresh and naïve as the one who got knifed by a Saigon whore. As stupid and trusting as the asshole who went out there because he thought it was his duty and came back with tombstones in his heart.

Finally pulled their pictures down and shoved them into a folder so I wouldn't have to look at their faces and the unanswered questions behind their eyes.

Didn't know much about queers. Didn't really want to. But I was starting to figure it out. Everything I knew was wrong.

Resumed surveillance of the vics. I had the first six now. Charting their habits, their patterns, their movements. Most of it was legwork. Confirmation of what I already knew. Thursday, vic number one shows up in the parking lot. Brad-boy. On his motorcycle. He rolls it right up behind Mame, playfully goosing her with the front wheel. Without even turning around, Mame wriggles her ass and says, "Wanna lose it?" Mame has a blond streak in her black hair now. The others are gushing over it. Brad grins, relaxes on the bike, eventually offers a ride to eager Lane, and roars off with him to catch the crabs.

A few nights later, Jeremy Weiss shows up at Gino's. Bingo. The connection. Georgia was right. Gay. Twinks. Horny.

Faded into shadow. Watched. He was smitten with a little blond twink who couldn't be bothered. Was this the Jerry that Mame was talking about? A crush on Dave who had a lover? Tailed him for the rest of the evening. He ended up at a featureless yellow building, a few blocks east. A very small sign on the door. You had to walk up close to read it. Y.M.A.C. Young Men's Athletic Club. Hmm. I had a feeling it was not a gymnasium. Observed for a while. Thinking.

I had three weeks left until the first vic disappeared. I was getting a good sense of the killing ground – this was the land of one-night stands. The perp didn't know the vics. He was hunting, just like everybody else, but hunting for a different kind of thrill. My guess, the vics didn't know him. They met him and disappeared. I wasn't going to find any other connectivity.

Had to think about this. How to ID the bastard. Mr. Death. That's what I was calling him now. How to stop him? Talked it over with Georgia. She made suggestions, most of them hands-on. But the way things work, the onsite agent is independent, has complete authority. Translation: It's your call.

Later. Past midnight.

Matt Vogel. Slightly built. Round face, round eyes, puppy eyes. Sweet-natured. In the parking lot at Gino's, sitting alone against the wall, between two cars, where no one can see him. Hands wrapped around his knees, head almost buried. Almost missed him. Stepped backward, took a second look. Yes, Matt. Just graduated from high school. Works as a busboy in a local coffee shop. Disappears in two months. Victim number two.

"What do you want?" He looks at me with wide eyes. Terrified.

"Are you all right?"

"What do you care?"

"You look like you're hurting."

"My parents found out. My dad threw me out of the house."

Couldn't think of anything to say. Scratched my neck. Finally. "How'd he find out?"

"He went through my underwear drawer."

"Found your magazines?"

He hesitates. "He found my panties. I like to wear panties. They feel softer. He ripped them all up."

"I knew a lieutenant who liked to wear panties. It's no big deal."

"Really?"

No, not really. But it was a game we played. Whenever anybody heard a horror story about anybody or anything, somebody always knew a lieutenant who did the same thing. Or worse. "Yeah, really. Listen, you can't stay here all night. Do you have a place to go?"

He shook his head. "I was waiting – to see if anyone I knew showed up – maybe I could crash with someone."

I noticed he didn't use the word "friend." That was the problem with this little war zone. Nobody made friends. I remembered foxholes and trenches where we clung to each other like brothers, like lovers, while the night exploded around us. But here, if two of these manboys clung to each other, it wasn't bombs that were exploding. I wondered if they had the same fear of dying alone – maybe even more so.

He'd given up waiting for Prince Charming. Mr. Right wasn't coming. And even Mr. Right Now hadn't shown up.

"Look, it's late. I live a couple blocks, close enough to walk." To his suspicious glance, I said, "You can sleep on the couch."

"No, it's all right. I can sleep at the tubs."

"The tubs?"

"Y-Mac. You been there?"

Shook my head.

"It's only two bucks. And I can shower in the morning before going to work. Scotty might even wash my clothes."

"You sure?"

"No."

At least, he's honest.

"Okay. As long as you have a place to go. It's not safe to hang out here – " And what if Mr. Death started early? But I didn't want to say that. Didn't want to scare the shit out of the kid.

"It's as safe here as anywhere – "

Something about the way he said it. "Somebody hurt you?"

"Sometimes people shout things as they drive by. Once, a couple of guys chased me for a block or so, then gave up and went back to their car."

Started to turn away, turned back. Didn't want to leave him alone. Damnit. "Look – you can come with me. I won't – I got meat loaf in the fridge. And ice cream. You want to talk, I'll listen. You don't want to talk, I won't bug you. You can crash for a couple of days, until you sort things out with your folks. All right?"

Matt thinks about it. He might look sweet and innocent, but he's learned how to be suspicious. That's how life works. First it beats you up, then it beats you down.

His posture is wary. "You sure?"

Oh hell, of course I'm not sure. And this is going to fuck up the timeline. Or is it? A thought occurs to me. An ugly thought. I don't like it, but maybe . . . bait? I dunno. But what the fuck, I can't leave him out here in a dirty parking lot. "Yeah, come on."

He levers himself to his feet, brushes off his jeans. "I wouldn't do this, but – "

"Yeah, I know."

" – I've seen you around. Gino says you're okay."

"Gino doesn't know me."

"You were in Vietnam." A statement, not a question. I should have realized. I'm not invisible here. Some of the gossip is about me.

"Yeah," I admit. I was in Nam. I point him toward the street. "My pad is that way."

"Did you see any – "

"More than I wanted to." My reply is a little too gruff. He falls silent. Why am I doing this? Why not? It's a chance to pry open the scab and look at the wound.

"I'm Matt."

"Yeah, I know."

"You got a name?"

"Oh, right. I'm . . . Mike."

"Mike? I thought your name was Hand. Hand Solo. But that's like a . . . a handle, isn't it. 'Cause everybody knows what a hand solo is, right?"

"Yeah. Right. It's a handle."

"Well. Glad to meet you, *Mike*."

We shake hands, there on the street. It changes the dynamic. Now we know each other. More than before anyway. Resume walking.

He's cute in a funny kind of way. If I liked boys, he'd be the kind of boy I liked. If this were the world I wanted to live in, he'd be my little brother. I'd make him hot chocolate. I'd read him bedtime stories and tuck him in at night. And I'd beat up anybody who made fun of him at school.

But this isn't that world – this is the world where men don't stand too close to men because . . . men don't do that.

"Mike?"

"Yeah?"

"Can I take a shower at your place?"

"Of course."

"Just enough to blow the stink off me."

"When did your dad throw you out?"

"Two days ago."

"You've been out here on the street two days?"

"Yeah."

"What a shit."

"No, he's all right."

"No, he isn't. Anyone who throws their kid out *isn't* all right."

Matt doesn't answer. He's torn between a misguided sense of loyalty and gratefulness that someone's trying to understand. He's afraid to disagree.

We reach the bottom of the stairs. I hesitate. Why am I doing this? In annoyance, I snap back. "Because that's the kind of person I am."

"Huh?" Matt looks at me curiously.

"Sorry. Arguing with myself. That's the answer that ends the argument."

"Oh." He follows me up the stairs.

He looks around the apartment, looks at the charts on the walls. I'm glad I pulled the pictures down. He would have freaked to have seen his yearbook picture here.

"Are you a cop?"

"No. I'm a – researcher."

"These look like something a detective would do. What are you researching?"

"Traffic patterns. It's – um, sociology. We're studying the gay community."

"Never heard it called that. 'Gay community.' "

"Well, no, it isn't much of one." Not yet, anyway. "But nobody's ever studied how it all works, and so – "

"You're not gay, are you?"

No easy answer to that. I don't even know myself. The night goes on forever here. Daytime is just an unpleasant interruption. "Look, I'm not anything right now. Okay?"

"Okay."

I feed him. We talk for a while. Nothing in particular. Mostly food. Cafeteria food. Restaurant food. Army food. Mess halls. C-rations. Fast food. Real food. Places we've been. Hawaii. Disneyland. San Francisco. Las Vegas. His family traveled more than mine. He's seen more of the surrounding countryside than me.

Eventually, we both realize it's late. He steps into the shower, I toss him a pair of pajamas, too big for him, but it's all I've got, and take his clothes downstairs to the laundry room. T-shirt, blue jeans, white gym socks, pink panties, soft nylon, a little bit of lace. So what.

He's a sweet kid. Too sweet really. Fuckit. He's entitled to a quirk. Who knows? Maybe he'll make lieutenant. When I come back up, he's already curled up on the couch.

The other bedroom is set up as an office. A wooden desk, an IBM Selectric typewriter, a chair, a lockable filing cabinet. I'll be up for a while, typing my notes for Georgia. God knows what she'll think of this. But I'll have his stuff into the dryer and laid out on a chair in less than an hour, long before I'm ready to collapse into my own bed.

Georgia taught me how to write a report. First list all the facts. Just what happened, nothing else. Don't add any opinions. The first few weeks, she'd hand me back my reports with all my opinions crossed out in thick red stripes. Pretty soon, I learned what was fact, what was story. After you've listed the facts, you don't need anything else. The facts speak for themselves. They tell you everything. So I learned to enjoy writing reports, the satisfying clickety-clickety-click of the typewriter keys, and the infuriated golf ball of the Selectric whirling back and forth across the page, leaving crisp insect-like impressions on the clean white paper. One page, two. Rarely more. But it always works. Typing calms me, helps me organize my thoughts.

Only thing is, if you don't have all the facts, if you don't have enough facts, if you don't have any facts, you stay stuck in the unknown. That's the problem.

Later, much later, as I'm staring at the dark ceiling, waiting for sleep to come, I listen for the sound of vampires on the street below. But most of them have found their partners and crept off to their coffins. So the war zone is silent. For now, anyway.

Somewhere, out there, Mr. Death is churning. And I still know nothing about him.

Sunday morning. I wake up late. Still tired. My back hurts. I smell coffee. Wearing only boxers, I pad into the kitchen. Matt is wearing my pajama tops. They're too big on him. He's obviously given up on the bottoms, too long, and they won't stay up. He looks like the little boy version of a Doris Day movie. He's cooking eggs with onions and potatoes. And toast with strawberry jam. And a fresh pot of coffee. It's almost like being married.

"Is this okay?" he asks uncertainly. "I thought – I mean, I wanted to do something to say thank you."

"You did good," I say, around a mouthful. "Very good. You can cook for me anytime." Why did I say that? "Oh, your clothes are on the chair by the door. I washed them last night."

"Yeah, I saw. Thanks. I have to go to work at noon." He hesitates. "Um, I'm going to try calling my dad today. Um. If it doesn't work out – you said something about – a couple days . . . ?"

"No problem. I'll leave a key under the mat. If I'm not here, just let yourself in."

"You trust me?"

"You're not a thief."

"How do you know?"

"I know." I added, "People who cook like this, don't steal."

He's silent for a moment. "My mom used to say I'd make someone a wonderful wife someday. My dad would get really pissed off."

"Well, hey, your dad doesn't get it."

Matt looks over at me, waiting for an explanation.

"It's simple. You take care of other people, they take care of you. The best thing you can do for someone else is cook for them, feed them, serve them a wonderful meal. That's how you tell someone that you – well, you know – that you care."

He blushes, covers it by looking at the clock. "I gotta get to work – " And he rushes to leave.

Sunday. There's no such thing as an afternoon off, but I cut myself some personal time anyway. Took a drive out to Burbank. Shouldn't have. Wasn't supposed to. It was part of the contract. Your old life is dead. Hands off. But I did it anyway. I owed it to them. No. I owed it to myself.

The place was pretty much as I remembered it. The tree in front was bigger, the house a little smaller, the paint a little more faded. I parked in front. Rang the bell and waited. Inside, Shotgun barked excitedly.

Behind the screen door, the front door opened. Like the house, he looked smaller. And like the house, a little more faded.

"Yes?" he squinted.

"Dad. It's me – Michael."

"Mickey?" He was already pushing open the screen door. Shotgun scrambled out. Even with his bad hip, that dog was still a force to be reckoned with. Dad fell into my arms, and Shotgun leapt at us both, with frenzied yowps of impatience. "Down you stupid son of a bitch, down!" That worked for half a second.

Dad held me at arm's length. "You look different. But how – ? They said you were lost in the timequake."

"I was. I am. I found my way back – it's a long story."

He hugged me again, and I felt his shoulders shaking. Sobbing? I held him tight. He felt frail. Then abruptly, he broke away, and turned toward the house. "Come on in. I'll make some tea. We'll talk. I think I have some coffee cake. You don't know how hard it's been without you. I haven't touched your room. It'll be good to have you back – "

I followed him in. "Um, Dad. I don't know how long I can stay. I have a job – "

"A job. That's good. What kind of a job?"

"I'm not really allowed to discuss it. It's that kind of a job."

"Oh. You're working for the government."

"I'm not really allowed to discuss it. I'm not even supposed to be here, but – "

"That's all right, I understand. We'll talk about other things. Come sit. Sit. You'll stay for dinner. It'll be like old times. I have spaghetti sauce in the freezer. Just the way you like it. No, it's no trouble at all. I still cook for two, even though it's just me and that old dog, too stubborn to die. Both of us."

I didn't tell him that wasn't true. I didn't tell him that he and that stubborn old dog would both be gone in a few short months. I rubbed my eyes, suddenly full of water. This was harder than I thought.

Somewhere between the spaghetti and the ice cream, Dad asked what had happened over there. I struggled inside, trying to figure out what to say, how to say it, realized it couldn't be explained, and simply finally shrugged and said, "It was . . . what it was." Dad knew me well enough to know that was all the answer he was going to get, and that was the end of that. The walls were comfortably up again.

Somewhere after the ice cream, I realized we didn't have all that much to talk about anymore. Not really. But that was okay. Just being able to watch him, just being able to skritch the dog behind the ears again, that was okay. That was enough. So I let him talk me into spending the night. My old bed felt familiar and different, both at the same time. I didn't sleep much. In the middle of the night, Shotgun oozed up onto the foot of the bed and sprawled out lazily, pushing me off to the side, grumpling his annoyance that I was taking up so much room; every so often, he farted his opinion of the spaghetti sauce, then after a while he began snoring, a wheezing-whistling noise. He was still snoring loudly when the first glow of morning seeped in the window.

Over breakfast, I told a lie. Told Dad I was on assignment. That part wasn't a lie. But I told him the assignment was somewhere east, I couldn't say exactly where, but I'd call him whenever I could. He pretended to understand.

"Dad," I said. "I just wanted you to know, you didn't lose me. Okay?"

"I know," he said. And he held me for a long time before finally releasing me with a clap on the shoulder. "You go get the bad guys," he said, something he'd said to me all my life – from the day he'd given me my first cowboy hat and cap pistol. Something he said again the day I got on the plane to Nam. You go get the bad guys.

"I will, Dad. I promise."

I kissed him. I hadn't kissed him since I was eight, but I kissed him now. Then I drove away quickly, feeling confused and embarrassed.

It was a drizzly day, mostly gray. Skipped the gym, filled the tank, drove around the city, locating the homes of the other seven victims. Two lived in the dorms at UCLA, Dykstra and Sproul. Didn't know if they knew each other. Maybe. One was a T.A. major, the other music. Another lived with a roommate (lover?) in a cheap apartment off of Melrose, almost walking distance from me, except in L.A., there's no such thing as "walking distance." If it's more than two doors down, you drive.

One lived way the hell out in Azusa. That was a long drive, even with the I-10 freeway. Another in the north end of the San Fernando Valley. All these soft boys, so lonely for a place to be accepted that they'd drive twenty-thirty miles to stand around in a cruddy green patio – to stand around with other soft boys.

Something went klunk. Like a nickel dropping in a soda machine. One of those small insights that explains everything. This was puberty for these boys. Adolescence. The first date, the first kiss, the first chance to hold hands with someone special. Delayed, postponed, a decade's worth of longing – while everybody around you celebrates life, you pretend, suppress, inhibit, deprive yourself of your own joy – but finally, ultimately, eventually, you find a place where you can have a taste of everything denied. It's heady, exciting, giddy. Yes. This is why they drive so far. Hormones. Pheromones. Whatever. The only bright light in a darkened landscape. They can't stay away. This is home – the only place where they can be themselves.

Okay. Now, figure out the predator –

I got back to the apartment, the drizzle had turned to showers. Matt was sitting by the door, arms wrapped around his knees. A half-full knapsack next to him. He scrambled to his feet, both hopeful and terrified. And flustered. He looked damp and disheveled. A red mark on his forehead, another on his neck.

"Are you all right?"

"I couldn't find the key – "

"Oh, shit. I forgot to put it under the mat – "

"I thought you were angry with me – "

"Oh, kiddo, no. I screwed up. You didn't do anything wrong. It's my fuckup. Shit, you must have thought – on top of everything else – "

Before I could finish the sentence, he started crying.

"What happened – ? No, wait – " I fumbled the key into the lock, pushed him inside, grabbed his knapsack, closed the door behind us, steered him to the kitchen table, took down a bottle of Glenfiddich, poured two shots.

He stopped crying long enough to sniff the glass. "What is this?" He took a sip anyway. "It burns."

"It's supposed to. It's single-malt whiskey. Scotch." I sat down opposite him. "I went to see – someone. My dad. I haven't seen him in a while, and this might be the last time. I wasn't supposed to, but I did it anyway. I spent the night, I slept in my old room, my old bed. What you said yesterday, it made me think – "

He didn't hear me. He swallowed hard, gulped. "My mom called me at work. She said I should come home and pick up my things. My dad wouldn't be there. Only she was wrong. He came home early. He started beating me – "

I reached over and lifted up his shirt. He had red marks on his side, on his back, on his shoulders, on his arms. He winced when I touched his side.

Got up, went into the bathroom, pulled out the first-aid kit. Almost a doctor's bag. Stethoscope, tape, ointment, bandages, a flask, even a small bottle of morphine and a needle. Also brass knuckles and a blackjack. And some other toys. You learn as you go. Came back into the kitchen, pulled his shirt off, smeared ointment on the reddest marks, then taped his ribs. Did it all without talking. I was too angry to speak. Finally: "Did you get all your stuff?"

He shook his head.

"All right, let's go get it."

"We can't – "

Grabbed his arm, pulled him to his feet, pulled him out the door, down the stairs, and out to the car, ignoring the rain. "You need your clothes, your shoes, your – whatever else belongs to you. It's yours."

"My dad'll – he's too big! Please don't – "

I already had the car in gear. "Fasten your seatbelt, Matt. What's that thing that Bette Davis says? It's going to be a bumpy night." The tires squealed as I turned out onto Melrose.

I turned south on Fairfax, splashing through puddles. Neither of us said anything for a bit.

When I turned right on Third, he said, "Mike. I don't want you to do this."

"I hear you." I continued to drive.

"I'm not going to tell you where I live – lived."

"I already know."

"How?"

"I'm your fairy godfather, that's how. Don't ask."

"You are no fairy," he said. Then he added, sadly, "I am."

"Well, I guess that's why you need a godfather."

"What are you gonna do?"

I grinned. "I'm gonna make him an offer he can't refuse."

Matt didn't get the joke, of course. It wouldn't be a joke for another five years. But that was okay. I got it.

Turned left, turned right. Pulled up in front of a tiny, well-tended house. Matt followed me out of the car, up the walk. The front door yanked open. Matt was right – he was *big*. An ape. But he wasn't a trained one. The scattershot bruises on his son were proof of that. He'd substituted size for skill. Probably done it all his life. He wore an ugly scowl. "Who are you?" he demanded.

Gave him the only answer he was entitled to. Punched him hard in the chest, shoving him straight back into the house. Followed in quickly. Before he could react, chest-punched him again – harder, hard enough to slam him into the wall. The house shook. He bounced off and this time met my fist in his gut. His gut was hard, but the brass knucks were harder. He grunted, didn't double up, but he lurched – it was enough, I pulled his head down to meet my rising knee, felt his nose break with a satisfying crunch of bone and blood.

Hauled him to his feet. His face was bleeding. "You're a big man, aren't you? Beating on a kid." He was still trying to catch his breath. "Matt, go get your things. Now."

A woman came out of the kitchen, wiping her hands in a dish towel. "Matty – ?" Then she saw me. "Who are you – ?" Then she saw her husband. "Joe – ?"

I grabbed the towel from her hands, pushed it at Joe, pushed Joe at a chair, he flopped into it, covering his bloody nose. "You can sit down too, ma'am; probably a good idea." She hesitated, then sat. Joe was still gasping, eyeing me warily.

Nobody spoke for a long moment.

Finally, the wife. "Are you going to hurt us?"

"Not planning on it. Of course, that can change." I nodded meaningfully at the asshole.

"You – you won't get away with this – "

"You won't call the police. He won't let you. He doesn't want anyone to know he's got a queer son." Took a breath. I wasn't planning to play counselor, but Matt needed time to gather his stuff, and I needed to keep the asshole from thinking too hard. "All right, look, lady – you should leave this jerkoff. Because if you don't, he's going to kill you someday. The only thing that's saved your life this long is that he's been taking it out on the kid instead, hasn't he? With the kid outa here, you're wearing the bull's-eye now. If I'm not mistaken, that bruise on your cheek is recent. Like maybe, this afternoon? And maybe there's a few more under that dress that don't show?"

She didn't answer.

"You're not doing yourself any favors, being a punching bag for this miserable failure. And you sure as hell didn't help your kid any, did you? Letting him beat the kid – you're a coward. Do you know what the word 'enabler' means? You're an enabler. You're just as fucking guilty. Because you let *him* get away with it."

Turned to the gorilla. "See, here's the thing, Joe. You're an asshole.
You're beneath contempt. That's your son, your own flesh and blood.
You should love him more than anybody else in the world. But he's
fucking terrified of you. The one moment in his life, he needs his dad to
love and understand and be there for him more than anything else, what
do you do? You beat him up and throw him out. What a fuckwad you
are. Your wife's a coward, you're a bully, and the two of you are
throwing away the only thing in the world you've done right – raise a
kid who still knows how to smile, god knows why, growing up with you
two creeps. You don't deserve this kid. Shut up, both of you. I'm in no
mood to argue. You can beat your wife, Joe, and you can beat your kid
– but you can't beat the butt-ugly truth. You're a waste of skin. Oh, and
if you're thinking about getting out of that chair, don't. If you try, I'll
kill you. I'm in that kind of a mood."

"He means it, Dad – " That was Matt, coming back into the room.
"He's an ex-commando. Special Forces. Green Beret. Or something. He
was in Vietnam. I don't want him to hurt you – "

"You got everything?"

He hefted a duffel and a suitcase. Hastily filled.

Matt's mother looked back and forth between us. Finally, she
worked up the nerve to ask. "What are you? Some kind of queer?"

I looked her up and down. "Are you the alternative?" Jesus Christ on
a pogo stick, I can't believe I said that. "Wait a minute." Turned back
to the gorilla. "Your son's leaving home. You'll never see him again.
Give me your wallet. No – I didn't say think about it. I said, *give me
your wallet.*"

He passed it over. Nearly three hundred bucks. I passed the cash to
Matt. "Here. Your inheritance. It's enough to live on for a couple
months. If you're careful." Dropped the wallet on the floor.

"You two are getting off lucky. I'm letting you live." Looked at the
gorilla again. "You come after this kid, you ever come near him, you
ever lay a hand on him again, I will kill you. I will hunt you down and I
will make sure you take a long time to die. You ever beat your wife
again, I'll break both your arms. Are we clear? Nod your head, this isn't
television." Glanced sideways. "Matt, you want to say good-bye?"

He shook his head.

"Then go get in the car."

Waited a moment, looking to see if the asshole was thinking about
following. He wasn't. His face was ashen. He was still having trouble
breathing. I looked to the wife. "You know what? I think you'd better
call an ambulance. I might have punched him a little hard, I might have
cracked his sternum. I wish I could say I'm sorry about that, but I'm
not."

Drove back without talking. The rain was coming down harder now.
Matt was shaken. Probably didn't know what to think, what to feel.

Got back to the apartment. He hesitated. "You coming up?"

"I thought you wanted me to – " He held up the money. "I mean –
isn't what this is for?"

"There's plenty of time for that tomorrow. Or the next day." And besides, "You shouldn't be alone tonight." I grabbed his suitcase and duffel. Not as heavy as I'd thought. Gorilla and wife hadn't been very generous.

Inside, I went scrounging through the junk drawer, found the extra key and handed it to him. "Listen. Don't take this the wrong way. But I'm worried about you. You stay here as long as you need to."

He looked at the key in his hand, looked up to me, a question on his face.

"You can cook, right? You can clean? That'll be your rent. We'll move my typewriter in here, over against the wall or something. And you can have the other room. Just one condition. Stay away from Gino's – " No, that's not fair. "I mean, don't go there without me. And don't go out with anyone without – well, checking with me. Okay?"

"You trying to be my dad?"

"No. Well, maybe a big brother. I dunno." I sat down opposite him. "Can you keep a secret?"

"Not very well. I mean – my dad found out."

"There is that. When did you know you were – ?"

"When I was twelve. Or thirteen."

"So you can keep a secret for five years. Six? Right?"

He nodded.

"All right. What I'm going to tell you is that big a secret. You up for it?"

He didn't say no. I took that as a yes.

"You know how I knew where you lived? I know a lot of other stuff too. Some bad shit is going down this year. Dangerous shit. People are going to get hurt. Killed. I'm not a cop. But I'm – I'm like a private investigator. And I'm looking for the guy. And you're his type. And so are a lot of the other kids at Gino's. I wish I could warn everyone, but if I do, it'll spread. You know how those girls love to gossip. And if the perp knows I'm looking for him, I'll never catch him. So you can't tell anyone. And the only reason I'm telling you is – is because I want your help."

"You need *my* help?"

"I want your help. I don't need it. But I can use it. If you're up to it."

"Up to it? Is it dangerous?"

"Do you think I'd put you in danger."

He thought about it for a moment. "But you want to use me as bait."

"I want to see who cruises you. I want to know who talks to you. That's all."

"Can I ask you something?"

"Go ahead."

"Was this your plan all along? From the very beginning? When you brought me home the other night?"

"The truth?" I looked him right in the eye. "No. This was not what I planned. You were just one of the boys I was going to watch for a while – "

He frowned. He turned that over in his head. And then – oh, shit – he got it. "You son of a bitch!" He started to get up. "You know, don't you!" He looked around for his duffel and his suitcase. I resisted the temptation to get up. Force was absolutely the wrong answer here. He waited for my response.

I nodded. "Yeah, you're right. I know."

"You're a – a time-traveler?"

Nodded again.

"Then it's true? There really are? Because I thought that was just – like an urban legend or something."

"It's true," I admitted.

He stared at me, hard, as if trying to puzzle me out. "So . . . how far from the future are you?"

"I'm not. I'm from three years in the past. But I've been to the future. Twelve years anyway. You're going to like it. Parts of it, anyway."

"Like what?"

Shrug. "Things like . . . um, well, Stonewall, for one. Neil Armstrong. Apple. Luke Skywalker. Pac-Man. But I think, Stonewall might be the big one."

"What's Stonewall?"

"You'll find out soon enough. It's – it's going to be . . . kind of important."

"Give me a hint?"

"Rosa Parks."

"Who's Rosa Parks?"

"Look it up."

He frowned, annoyed. Then his frown eased. He dropped the duffel on the living room floor and came back into the kitchen nook. "Tell me what you know about me."

"Um – "

"You want me to do this, you have to tell me." He sat down opposite me and waited.

"Okay," I said. "Wait." I went into the bedroom, came back with the folders. Tossed it on the table. "I have to prevent the disappearance of this boy. Have you ever seen him?" I slid over the picture of Jeremy Weiss.

Matt looked, frowned, started to shake his head no, then said, "No, wait, I think he comes in mostly on weekends."

"He's number three. There are two other disappearances before him. Ten more afterward. Here's number one."

"That's Brad. Brad-boy. He rides a motorcycle. He comes in, picks up a trick, rides off. Nobody knows much about him, not even his tricks."

"Yeah, I've seen it."

"When does he – ?"

"Two weeks. A little more than two weeks." I passed over the next folder. "This is the second victim."

He opened it, saw his own picture, and flinched. He deflated like a balloon. "I – I'm going to die."

"No. You're not. I promise you. *I promise you.*"

"But I did. I mean, I will, won't I? I mean – this?" He looked suddenly terrified.

"No. You won't."

"But how do you know? I thought time was – "

"Time is mutable. If it wasn't, I wouldn't be here. I couldn't be here. Neither could you."

He accepted that, but only because he wanted to. He wasn't convinced. After a bit, he reached over and took the other folders, opened them one at a time. He recognized two more of the boys, none of the rest. Not surprising. The last disappearance was only fourteen this year.

"All right. Now, tell me – do you go anywhere else besides Gino's?"

He shook his head. "There's a club down in Garden Grove, for eighteen-and-up. But I've never been there. Um, there's the tubs. The Y-Mac. I've only been there two-three times. There isn't any place else. I can't get into any of the bars."

"So mostly you go to Gino's?"

"That's where everybody goes."

"All right. Here's the deal. You don't go to Gino's unless I go too. I want to see who talks to you. And if somebody asks you to go home with him – we'll work out a signal. You'll tug on your ear. And I'll . . . I'll do what's appropriate."

Matt nodded. He seemed grateful to have a plan. He took a breath. "I saw some knockwurst in the freezer. Should I make that for dinner?"

I wasn't that hungry, but I nodded.

He clattered around in the cupboards for a bit, looking to see what else he could put on a plate. "There's some baked beans here, and some English muffins. I can make a little salad and open a couple of Cokes . . . ?"

"That sounds good." I gathered up the photos and slid them back into their respective folders.

"Mike . . . ?"

"Yeah."

"If I don't go home with anyone, how will you know which one's the killer?"

"I'm still trying to figure that out."

"You'll have to watch Brad-boy too, won't you?"

"Yeah."

"Maybe I'm not getting this right. But the only way you'll know who the killer is . . . will be by letting him kill someone. Brad. Right?"

"Well, no. I have a pretty good idea which night Brad disappears. So whoever talks to him on that night, that's probably the killer. But if I can keep Brad from going off with him, then I can save his life."

"But what if it's the wrong guy. I mean, if he doesn't get a chance to kill anyone, how will you know he's the killer?"

I got up, put the bottle of scotch back in the cupboard. Leaned against the wall and looked down at Matt. He was cutting up lettuce. "There's another part to the problem. Let's say that I give Brad a flat tire so he can't go out that night. Or something like that. Let's say I keep Brad from tricking out. Then that means Mr. Death – that's what I call him – picks up someone else. And maybe not that night, maybe the next night, or the following week. Maybe the whole timetable gets interrupted, screwed up – then this whole schedule is useless."

"So you have to watch Brad . . ."

"Yeah. And I'll have to tail him to wherever he goes and . . . and hope it's the real deal."

"That's not fair to Brad."

"It's not fair to any of you guys. I'm only hired to save one boy – but there's a dozen others, and maybe more, who are equally at risk. I told you, time is mutable. If I jiggle it too hard, I lose the whole case. I can save you and Jeremy and Brad, but who else dies in your place?"

He got it – it was like a body blow. He laid down the knife and said, "Shit." And then he reacted to his own vulgarity with a softly spoken, "Well, that wasn't very ladylike, was it?"

He put dinner on the table and we ate in silence for a while. Finally, I said, "This is very good. Thank you."

"You like it?"

"It's a whole meal. It's more than I would have done for myself."

"I had to learn how to cook. My mom – " He shrugged.

"Yeah, I saw."

"She's not a bad person. Neither is my dad, except when he drinks too much – "

"And how often is that?"

He got the point. "Yeah. Okay."

Later, after the dishes were put away, I took a quick shower. I came out, wearing only a towel. He looked at me, then glanced away quickly. He said something about a long soak and hurried into the bathroom. I heard the sound of bath water running. After a moment, he stuck his head out. "Towels?"

"Hall closet. Top shelf. Here." I pulled the yellow towels down for him. "Anything else?"

"I don't think so." Still not looking at me.

"All right. I'm going to bed. I've got a meeting in the morning. When I get back we'll go get a bed for you."

"Um. Okay. Thanks." He disappeared back into the bathroom.

I like to sleep with the windows open. Here, just off Melrose, the nights were sometimes stifling, sometimes breezy, sometimes cold. Sometimes the wind blew in from the sea, and sometimes the air was still and smelled of jasmine. Tonight there was cold wind, the last wet remnant of a gloomy drizzly day. The air smelled clean. Tomorrow would be bright.

I got into bed, listened for a while to the water dripping from the corners of the building, to the occasional wet swish of a car passing by, to the distant roar of the city, and maybe even the hint of music somewhere. Got up, went to the closet, pulled out an extra blanket and dropped it on the couch. He'd need it.

Got back into bed and listened to the roar of my own thoughts. Matt had put his finger on it – what I already knew and hadn't been willing to say. I had no way to ID the perp. Not unless I let someone die.

For a while, I wondered how the other operatives would handle this case. But I didn't wonder too long, I already knew. They'd save the Weiss kid and ignore the other dozen – because the Weiss kid's family were the only ones paying. That's why Georgia had given me this job. Because she knew I didn't think that way. She knew I wouldn't be satisfied with saving only the one. She knew how I thought. You don't leave any man behind.

And whether anyone recognized it or not, this was a war zone. These people; they knew they were living in enemy territory. They were terrified of the midnight knock – the accusations at work, the innuendoes of friends, the gossip of neighbors, and all the awful consequences. The soft boys, they start out sweet and playful, almost innocent, but time would erode their spirit. The older they grow, the heavier the burden becomes. Day by day, they learn to be furtive, they become embittered and their voices edged with acid. You can stand in the bar and watch it happening in their eyes, night after night, the shadowed resentment, the festering anger. Why do we have to hide? Pretend? The question – *what's wrong with me?* – was backward. Pretty soon it turns into *what's wrong with them?* And the chasm grows, the isolation increases. The secret world digs deeper underground.

But not for too much longer. The summer of love is already exploding, next year the summer of lust, and after that the frenzied summer of disaster. But that summer would also bring the Stonewall revolution, and after that – this would start to change. All of it.

I almost envied them.

Because, they knew what they wanted.

I still had no idea.

There was a soft knock at the bedroom door. It pushed open with a squeak. Matt stuck his head in. "Are you asleep?"

"Not yet. Are you all right?"

"Mike . . . ?" He stepped closer to the edge of the bed. "Can I sleep with you tonight? Just to sleep. That's all. The couch is – "

"Kind of uncomfortable, I know. Yeah, come on." I slid over and pulled back the edge of the blanket for him. He slipped in next to me. Not too close.

We lay on our backs, side by side. Staring at the ceiling.

"This isn't about the couch, is it?"

"Uh-uh."

"Didn't think so."

"You don't have to worry – "

"I'm not worried."

"I mean – "

"Matt. It's all right. You don't have to explain." I thought about those nights in Nam where soldiers hugged each other closer than brothers. Of course, rifle fire, mortar shells, explosions, napalm, mud, blood and shit – and the threat of immediate death – can do that to you. The moments in the jungle when the patrol would stop for break, collapsing into heaps, sometimes lying in each other's laps, the only closeness we had – and the nights in cheap Saigon hotel rooms, when there weren't enough mattresses to go around, you shared with your buddy, and you felt glad he was next to you. The touch of a squad mate in the dark. You learned to feel safe in the stink and sweat of other men. They were your other half. You couldn't explain that either, not to anyone who hadn't been there.

"I'm sorry, Mike."

"For what?"

"For being such a – " He couldn't finish the sentence. He couldn't say the word.

"Matt . . . ?"

"My mom used to call me Matty. When I was little."

"You want me to call you Matty?"

"If you want to."

"Matty, come here." I put my arm around his shoulder and pulled him closer, so his head was nestled against my chest. I couldn't see what he was wearing, but it felt too soft. Nylon something. I ignored it. Whatever. "C'mere, let your Uncle Mike tell you a bedtime story." He wasn't relaxed, he lay tense next to me. Waiting for me to push him away in disgust . . . ?

"When I was twelve, my dad brought home a puppy for my birthday, just a few weeks old. He was a black Labrador retriever and he was so clumsy he tripped over his own shadow. He couldn't walk without stubbing his face, but I fell in love with him the first moment I saw him. My dad asked me if I liked him and I said he was just perfect. I called him Shotgun. The first night, he whined for his mommy, so I took him into bed with me and held him close and talked to him and petted him and he fell asleep next to me. He followed me everywhere and he slept with me every night. Then Monday morning, we took him to the vet for his shots. The vet examined him and examined him and examined him, and he just started frowning worse and worse. Finally, he says there's something wrong with Shotgun; he's defective, his hips are malformed, he's going to have trouble walking, he's going to go lame, a whole bunch of other stuff. Then, he took my dad aside and talked to him for a long time. I couldn't hear what they were saying, but my dad just shook his head and we took Shotgun home."

"The vet wanted to put him to sleep?"

"Yeah. My dad wouldn't let him. But I didn't find that part out until later. We went home, but I didn't want to have anything to do with Shotgun anymore. Because he was broken. He wasn't perfect. And I wanted a dog that was perfect. Shotgun kept following me around and I kept pushing him away. That night, he kept trying to jump up onto my bed and he kept whining, but I wouldn't lift him up and let him sleep with me. Finally, my dad came in and asked what was wrong and I said I didn't want Shotgun anymore, but I wouldn't say why. My dad figured it out though. He knew I was angry at Shotgun for not being perfect. But he didn't argue with me, he just said, okay, he'd find a new home for Shotgun in the morning. But . . . for tonight, I should let Shotgun sleep with me one last time. I asked why, and my dad picked up the puppy and held him in his lap petting him for a moment, and I asked why again, and my dad put Shotgun in my lap and he said, 'Because even ugly puppies need love. In fact, ugly puppies need even more love.' And when he said that, I started to feel real bad for pushing Shotgun away, and then my dad said, 'Besides, Shotgun doesn't know he's ugly. He just knows he loves you a lot. But if you don't love him and you don't want him, then tomorrow we'll find someone who doesn't care how ugly he is and who'll be happy to have a dog who will love them as much as Shotgun can.' That's when I hugged Shotgun close to my chest and said, 'NO! He's mine and you're not giving him away. Because I can love him more than anybody. I don't care how ugly he is.' And that's when my dad tousled my hair like this and whispered in my ear, 'That's the exact same thing your mom said when you were born.' "

Matt snorted. Then curled up with his backside pressed against me. I couldn't figure out if he felt like a girl or a boy or something of both – or neither.

All these queerboys – some of them were girlboys, yes; but the rest, they were still boys. Soft boys. Men without . . . without what? Some quality of maleness? No. They were male. They just didn't do all that chest-beating. Hmm. Of course not. Chest-beating is for dominance – it's to drive away all the other males from the mates. That's counter-productive in this environment. Here . . . they want to be . . . friendly? Affectionate? But chest-beaters can't do that, can't afford to do that without losing dominance. No wonder the queerboys were the targets of bullies. Bullies are cowards; they pick victims who won't fight back. I stared at the ceiling, wondering if this train of thought would bring me any closer to Mr. Death. I couldn't see how.

After a while, I stopped worrying about it and fell asleep myself.

The next morning, we pretended everything was normal. He went to work, I drove up to Hollywood Boulevard.

Georgia looked grim. She met my eyes briefly, jerked her head toward the office. "Mr. Harris wants to see you."

"Mr. Harris?"

"Ted Harris – the man whose name is on the door?"

"Oh. I didn't know there was a real Ted Harris. I thought he was a fictitious business name, or something."

"There's a real Ted Harris. And he's waiting for you."

Shit. They'd found out I'd visited Dad. I had that called-to-the-principal's-office, cold-lump-in-my-gut feeling.

I knocked once on the door, no answer, I turned the knob and went in. I'd never been in this room before. Desk, chairs, lamp, and a middle-aged man with his back to me, staring out the half-circular window that

other bits of necessary paperwork – and a scrap of paper with a hastily written note. *"Musso & Frank's. 15 minutes."* I sniffed the paper, recognized the perfume, nodded, tipped Roy a fiver, and started west on the boulevard. I'd get there just in time.

I asked for a table in the back, she came in a few minutes later, sat down opposite me without a word. I waited. She held up a finger to catch the waiter's eye, ordered two shots of Glenfiddich, then looked straight across to me. "Eakins is a first-class prick."

Shook my head. "Nah, he's only a second-class prick."

She considered it. "Not even that high. He's a dildo."

My silence was agreement. "So . . . ?"

She opened her purse, took out another envelope, laid it on the table. "You weren't supposed to get this case. No one was. When he found out I'd assigned it to you, he almost fired me. He might still."

"I don't think so. You're still there as far uptime as I've been."

She shook her head as if that weren't important now. "The whole thing is . . . it doesn't make sense. Why would he abrogate a contract? Anyway – " She pushed the envelope across. "Here. See what you can make out of this."

"What is it?"

"I have no idea. He disappears for days, weeks, months at a time. Then he shows up as if not a day has passed. I started xeroxing stuff from his desk, a few years ago. I don't know why. I thought – I thought maybe it would give me some insights. There's things that . . . I don't know what they are. There's pictures. Like this thing – " She shuffled through the photos. " – I think it's a telephone. It's got buttons like a phone, but it looks like something from *Star Trek*, it flips open – but it doesn't work, it just says 'no service.' And this other thing, it looks like a poker chip, one side is sticky, you can stick it to a wall, the other side is all black – is it a bug of some kind? A microphone? A camera? Or maybe it's a chronosensor? And then there are these silver disks, five inches wide, what the hell are they? They look like diffraction gratings. Some of them say Memorex on the back. Are they some kind of recording tape, only without the tape? And there's all these different kinds of pills. I tried looking up the names, but they're not listed in any medical encyclopedia. What the hell is Tagamet? Or Viagra? Or Xylamis? Or any of these others?"

"Are there dates on any of this material?"

"Not always. But sometimes. The farthest one is 2039. But I think he's gone farther. A lot farther. I think he's gotten hold of the Caltech local-field time-maps. Or maybe he's been dropping his own sensors and making his own maps, I don't know. But I've never seen anything that looks like a map. It doesn't make a lot of sense. But then again – there's that thing that he says, that if we could go back to say, 1907 with a bunch of stuff from today – a transistor radio, a princess phone, a portable TV, a record album, birth control pills, things like that – none of it would make sense to someone living in that time. Even a copy of a news magazine wouldn't make much sense because the language would have shifted so much. So if Eakins has stuff from thirty, forty, fifty years into the future, we wouldn't get much of it – "

"Yes and no. Fifty years ago, they didn't have the same experience of progress, so they didn't have the vocabulary to encompass the kinds of changes that come with time. We have a different perspective – because change is part of our history, we expect it to be part of our future. So, if anything, we look at this stuff and we don't see a mystery as much as we see the limits of our experience."

"Now, you sound like me."

"I was quoting you. Paraphrasing." I shuffled through the papers, the photos, the notes. "None of this has any bearing on this case, does it?"

"I don't know. But I thought you should see it. Maybe it'll give you an insight into Eakins."

Shook my head. "It proves that he knows more than he's telling us. But we already knew that."

She glanced at her watch. "Okay, I'm out of time." She stood up, leaned over and kissed me quickly. "Take care of yourself – and your little boyfriend too."

"He's not my – " But she was already gone.

I shoved everything back into the envelope and ordered a steak sandwich. The day had started weird and gotten weirder, and it wasn't half over. I might as well face the rest of it on a full belly.

Went back to the apartment. Photographed everything. Then gathered it up and went straight to the local copy shop. Five copies, collated. Paid in cash. Put one copy in the trunk of the car, put another in the apartment safe, and mailed the other three to three different P.O. boxes. Delivered the originals back to Georgia who accepted them without comment. Eakins had already left the building. But neither of us said anything; it was possible he had the offices bugged – maybe even with his funny poker chips.

By the time I got home, Matty was unpacking groceries. The whole scene looked very domestic. "Did you have a good day?" he asked. All I needed was a pair of slippers and the evening newspaper.

When I didn't answer, he looked up. Worried. "You okay?"

"Yeah. I'm just . . . thinking about stuff."

"You're always thinking about stuff."

"Well, this is stuff that needs thinking about."

He got it. He shut up and busied himself in the kitchen. I went out onto the balcony and stared at Melrose Avenue. Cold and gray, it was going to rain again tonight; a second storm right behind the first. Something Eakins had said – none of it made sense, but one piece of it had its own particular stink of wrongness. Why is Matty not important to this case?

And that led directly to the next question: What did Eakins know that he wasn't telling me? And why wasn't he telling? Because if I knew . . . it would affect things. What things? What other plan was working?

Obviously, we weren't on the same side. Had we ever been? Never mind that. That's a dead end right now. I had to think about Matty.

If Matty is irrelevant, then . . . is he still in danger? No, of course he's in danger. He disappeared. We know that. But if he disappeared, then why is he irrelevant . . . ? Unless his disappearance is unrelated. And if his disappearance is unrelated, then . . . of course, he would be entirely useless to this case. Shit.

But how would Eakins know that? Unless Eakins knew something about Matty. Or knew something about all the others.

And of course, all of that assumed that Eakins was telling the truth. What if he was purposely trying to mislead me? But then that brought me back to the first question. What was Eakins up to?

Not having the answers to any of these questions annoyed me. I didn't have a plan, I didn't have anything on which to base a plan. The only thing I could think was to continue with the plan that Eakins had scuttled – not because it was a good plan, but because it would force the situation. It would force Eakins to . . . to do what?

When the rain finally started, I went back in and sat down to dinner. Baked chicken. It was cold.

"Why didn't you call me?"

"You were thinking."

"Um – " I stopped myself. He was being considerate. "Okay."

"Do you want me to warm that up for you?"

"No, it's okay." I ate in silence for a bit, feeling uncomfortable. Finally I put my fork down and looked across at him. "Y'know what I just realized. I don't know how to talk to you."

He looked puzzled.

"This is good – " I indicated the cold chicken. "You can cook. I keep wanting to say you'll make someone a wonderful wife someday. But I can't say that because – "

"It's different when you say it. When you say it, it isn't mocking."

"It's still the wrong thing to say. It's demeaning, isn't it?"

"I don't mind. Not from you." He started to clear the table.

I took a breath. "Are you – ?" I stopped. "I don't know how to ask this. Are you . . . attracted to me?"

He nearly dropped the plates. He was facing away so I couldn't see his expression, but his body was suddenly tense. He finally turned around so he could look at me. "Do you want me to be?"

"It's like this. I don't connect well to people. Not anybody. Male or female. I can go through the motions. For a while. But only for a while. I'm always . . . holding back."

"Why?"

I shrugged.

"That's your answer?"

"When you start raveling, you get unraveled yourself. You get detached. You don't belong to any time, you can't belong to any person. So you turn off that part of yourself."

He didn't respond right away. He got the coffee pot from the stove and filled two cups. He brought cream and sugar to the table, for himself, not me. As he stirred his coffee, he finally asked, "So why are you telling me this? Are you telling me I shouldn't care about you because you can't care back?"

"I don't know if I can care about anybody. When I try, it doesn't work out. So I've stopped trying."

"You didn't answer my question. Why are you telling me this?"

"Because . . . right now, you're the only person I have to talk to."

"Not your dad?"

"This is not a conversation I could have with my dad."

He shook his head in frustrated confusion. "Just what are we talking about?"

"About the fact that I am so fucking angry and confused and upset and annoyed and frustrated and – and even despairing – that if you weren't here, right now tonight, if you weren't here to talk to . . . I'd end up sitting alone in a chair again – with my gun barrel in my mouth, wondering if I have the courage to pull the trigger. I've known guys who've sucked the bullets out of their guns. It makes a mess on the wall. And I used to wonder why they did it. That was before. Not anymore. Now I'm starting to understand."

His face was white. "You're scaring the hell out of me."

"You don't have to worry. I'm not going to do anything stupid. I just – I just want you to know that right now . . . you're doing me the favor by staying here."

"This is a lot more than I can deal with – I'm not – "

I nodded. "Kiddo. I'm more than most people can deal with. That's why they leave. Look – I figured, after all you've been through, you'd understand what it feels like to feel so separated from everyone else. I'm coming from the same place – same place, different time zone."

He stirred his coffee thoughtfully. "There's a quote I learned in school. Sometimes it helps me. It's from Edmund Burke. I don't know who he is or was, it doesn't matter. He said, 'Never despair; but if you do, work on in despair.' "

Considered it. "Yeah. That's good. It's useful."

We sat there for a while. Not talking.

Later. I came out of my bedroom. He was curled up on the couch. "Matt? Matty?"

"Huh – ?" He rolled over, looked at me groggily.

"If you want to come sleep in the bed again, you can."

"No, it's all right."

But a little bit later, he pushed open the bedroom door, padded over, and slipped in next to me. So that was something. I just didn't know what. But then again, neither did he. Probably.

The rain cleared up, leaving the air sparkling, the way it used to be in the thirties and the forties. Least, that's what they say. In two days, though, the smog levels would be back to their lung-choking worst. It's not just the million-plus internal combustion engines pouring out lead and carbon dioxide and all the other residues of inefficient fuel-burning. Los Angeles is ringed with mountains. That's why they call it a basin. Fresh air can't get in, stale air can't get out. It sits and stagnates. The

Indians called it *el valle de fumar*. The valley of fumes. Only two things clean it – the once-in-a-while rainstorms of winter and spring, or the hot dry Santa Ana winds at the end of the summer. From June until October, don't bother breathing. You can breathe in November.

But today, today at least, was beautiful. It was a go-to-Disneyland day. And I almost suggested it to Matty, but he had to work, and I hadn't figured anything else out yet, so we disentangled ourselves from the mustiness of sleep and stepped into the comfortable zombie-zone of routine.

We had a week to go before Brad Boyd would disappear. I spent some of the daytime tailing him, even though that was probably a dead end. He worked at an adult bookstore on Vine, just across the street from the Hollywood Ranch Market. Sometimes he bought a Coke and a burrito from the counter in front. Usually he walked to work, leaving the motorcycle parked under a small covered patio in front of the apartments. It wouldn't be hard to sabotage the bike. That would keep him at home. But it wouldn't get me closer to Mr. Death.

Twice, I drove out to visit Dad. The second time, I took him to the doctor. I already knew that it wouldn't do any good, wouldn't delay the inevitable, but I had to try. Maybe make it a little easier for him. Dad fussed at me, but not too much. He didn't have the same strength to argue that he'd had when I was eighteen, when I'd come back with the recruiting forms, when I told him of my decision, when I snapped back at him, "Well, if it's a mistake, it's my mistake to make, not yours." It wasn't until Duncan stepped on a land mine just a few paces ahead of me that I discovered what Dad had been so scared of. But by then, I was already starting to shut down. So the scared never got all the way in, never got to the bottom. Part of me remained convinced that it wasn't going to happen to me. Ever. Just the same, I got out of there as soon as my rotation ended.

I sat at the kitchen table, puzzling over the photos and the copies of the notes Georgia had taken from Eakins' desk. Someday they'd make sense, but at this point in time – literally – they were incomprehensible. The only thing this stuff proved was that Eakins had time-hopped farther into the future than anyone I'd ever heard.

In the evenings, Matty and I would shadow Brad again. Having an extra set of eyes helped. The first night motorcycle-boy started at Gino's, had no luck or didn't like what he saw, and rode over to the Stampede. We parked in the lot of the supermarket across the street, just behind the bus bench where we could watch the front entrance and his motorcycle. The Stampede had an emergency exit in the rear patio, but without an emergency the only way out was the front. We might be here awhile, how long does it take to cruise a bar? Matty went for doughnuts and coffee.

"If he comes out before you get back, I have to follow him; if I'm not here, you wait in the doughnut shop. As soon as he lands somewhere, I'll come back for you. Understand? Don't talk to anyone."

But the plan wasn't needed; Matty was back in five and Brad-boy didn't come out of the bar for forty minutes. He was alone. We followed him east on Melrose where he checked into the YMAC.

"He could be there all night," said Matty. "Maybe till one or two."

"How do you know? Have you ever – ?"

"With Brad-boy? No. I would have, if he ever asked. But he never asked. I don't think I would now. Everybody says he's kind of a user. Use 'em and lose 'em."

"Yeah, I got that feeling. I'm wondering if . . . maybe I should go in."

"It's just a lot of guys standing around in the dark."

"Just like the Stampede? Or Gino's?"

"Yeah, but without their clothes on. Just towels."

"Hm." We sat in silence for a bit.

"You can't get in without a card," Matty offered. "A member has to take you in the first time. If Scotty doesn't like your look, he says it's not a membership night. If he lets you in, he gives you a card and tells you the rules. I could probably get you in."

"Is that an offer?"

"I'm just trying to be helpful."

I thought about it.

"How often have you been there?"

"Not much. Two times, three. I don't like the way it smells."

"I don't think it's going to help us much."

"Why not?"

"Because . . . if I've figured this right, our bad guy doesn't work out of this place. He has to take his victims somewhere else. Somewhere close. Like a house – a house with lots of shrubbery around it, or maybe an alley in the back, or a connected garage. He has to have some way to remove the . . . the evidence without anyone seeing."

"So we can go home?"

"I'm thinking. We should probably wait. Make sure that Brad-boy gets home safe."

"I have work tomorrow."

"There's a blanket on the back seat, if you want to try sleeping."

"No. I can't sleep in a car."

"I don't like sitting here either." I started the engine, put the car in gear, turned on the headlights. "Let's call it a night."

Back at the apartment, I pushed him toward the bedroom, and went into my makeshift office to type up a quick report. Picked up subject at, followed subject to, subject was inside for, came out at, proceeded to, stayed for, came out, went to, waited, abandoned stake-out at. I didn't have to write it, the case was over, and there was no place to turn in the report, but old habits die hard – and it's always useful to have accurate notes.

It didn't take long to finish, but by the time I slid between the sheets, Matty was already asleep, half-sprawled toward the center of the bed. I gave him a gentle push and he turned half away. Fair enough.

Matty felt warm. He reminded me of Shotgun. Shotgun would stretch out next to me, anchoring his back against mine, we'd sleep spine to spine. That big old dog was like me – he liked having someone covering his back. Except Matty wasn't Shotgun, he wasn't an ugly puppy, and he wasn't anything else either. Why was I doing this?

The next night, Brad-boy stayed home and watched television until ten. He got on his motorcycle and went to Gino's. Sat on his bike for twenty minutes chatting with Mame, Peaches, Dave, Jeremy, and two boys Matty couldn't name. "You think it's one of them?"

"No. They're too young. And they're – "

" – too fem?"

"Yeah. Too fem."

"Some fems can be real bitches – "

"Yeah, I heard some of the stories about Duchess and Princess. But I don't think we have to worry about either of these. They look like lost surfer boys. A couple kids from Pali High daring each other to visit a gay club."

Eventually, one of the surfer boys climbed onto the back of Brad-boy's bike and they roared east on Melrose. Back to Brad's apartment. Was he going to spend the night? Or would Brad be bringing him back here in an hour?

It turned out to be less than that. Apparently, our Brad wasn't much for foreplay. Forty-five minutes turnaround. Then he went home and went back to bed. Alone.

Thursday night, Brad went to a movie. We sat three rows behind him. *The Dirty Dozen*. All-star cast. Lee Marvin, Ernest Borgnine, Charles Bronson, Jim Brown, John Cassavetes, Richard Jaeckel, George Kennedy, Trini Lopez, Robert Ryan, Telly Savalas, Clint Walker, and some funny-looking goofball named Donald Sutherland.

Friday night, Gino's was crowded with lithe and feral manboys. Brad-boy actually got off the bike and went in. Matty followed him while I spoke privately to Gino. I flashed one of the P.I. cards I hadn't given back to Georgia. Either she hadn't noticed that or she had. I wasn't sure if I should let her know what I was up to. She was probably in enough trouble already. She probably already knew anyway. No, I'd wait until I had something.

Gino glanced at the card unsurprised, looked at me, and said, "What do you need?"

"I heard you're the go-to guy." He looked blank, he didn't recognize the term. "The go-to guy. The guy to go to . . . if you have the clap and need the name of a doctor, if you need a letter from a shrink to stay out of the army, that kind of stuff."

"I know some people," Gino said. Dr. Ellis was due to be murdered by a hustler-boy. Scotty would be implicated in a different murder and YMAC's new location on La Brea would be raided. In a couple of years. "What can I do for you?"

"You know your regulars, right? You know who's solid and who's flaky. If someone new shows up, you read them the rules before you let them in. Do you ever notice who folks leave with?"

"I see a lot of boys come through here every weekend – "

"Brad Boyd. Do you ever notice who he leaves with?"

"Hard not to. He always revs his engine and roars out of here, leaving a stinking cloud of smoke behind. I've asked him not to – "

"Could you keep an eye out?"

"Who are you working for? His parents?"

"No. This isn't that kind of a case."

"What kind of a case is it?"

"This kind." I pushed a fifty-dollar bill into his hand. I had another ready in case one wasn't enough.

Gino glanced down only long enough to check the denomination. "You got the size right." He tucked it into his pocket.

I leaned forward, whispered, "This kid's life might be in danger. I think he's being stalked. But I don't have any hard evidence yet. Help me out, I'll give you another one of those."

Gino shrugged. "I have a club to run. Weekends are busy. I can't promise anything. But if I see something, I'll let you know."

I passed him a card. No name, just a phone number. "If no one answers, there's an answering machine. You can leave a message."

Gino looked impressed. Code-A-Phones were expensive. I didn't tell him it belonged to the Harris Agency – and that any day now I expected Georgia to request its return.

I found Matty in the shadows next to the jukebox. Brad was playing pool in the corner. I pulled Matty farther back and we pretended to be only casually interested in the pool game. So far, it looked like Brad was only here to play pool. He had a nasty style of slop shooting. It looked like he was just casually slamming the balls around; but he'd been playing barroom pool long enough, he knew what he was doing. He kept winning. Three, four, six games and he still hadn't been beaten.

"Whyn't you go play him?"

"Uh-uh. I might interrupt something or someone. We need to see who he picks up – or who picks him up."

"Is it tonight?"

"Tomorrow. I have a feeling – I could be wrong – but I have a hunch that our subject might be here tonight as well. Whatever he's feeling, it has to be building up. Building up over time. If Brad is his first, then maybe this is the night that triggers his urge, but maybe he isn't quite ready to act. Something happens tonight. He gets his – whatever it is he gets. His courage. And tomorrow is the night it gets real enough for him to actually do something."

"What if he picks someone else?"

"I don't think so. I think Brad is the first because Brad is the easiest. I don't think our fellow has learned how to cruise yet. He might not have picked Brad out, but I think he's in this room. Here's what I want you to do. You go one way, I'll go the other. We'll both walk around, just looking – cruising. See if you see anyone who strikes you as wrong."

"Wrong in what way?"

"Any way at all."

"Too old? Too ugly?"

"No. Brad is a slut, but he isn't a whore. Like all the rest of you girls, he wants someone young and cute. So watch out for anyone who looks like his type, but possibly nervous, uneasy, uncertain – someone who doesn't look like he's having a good time. His clothes or his haircut might look a little weird, like he doesn't understand the current styles. He's probably hanging back, just watching; he might have a very intense look, or he might even look perfectly normal. But I'll bet he's someone new, someone you haven't seen before, so watch for that. Just look at every unfamiliar face closely and see what you see. Okay? You go this way, I'll go that. Three or four times around, then meet back here."

There was something else to watch out for, but I didn't tell Matty. It was baggage he didn't need to carry. I didn't like having him do this, but I needed his eyes. He had experience here. He could read these people. I couldn't. Not very well. There was an overlay of – I didn't have a word for it – but there was a map to this territory that I didn't have.

I'd given him one clue. Watch out for someone who's out of style. But he wouldn't have heard what I was really saying – I think we're dealing with a freelance time-hopper, someone who's riding the quakes. He's probably from the past, maybe ten or twenty years; I doubted he was from the future, the future is a little friendlier to queers, but I didn't rule it out – maybe the cultural shifts were stressing him out.

But if I had to put money on it, I'd bet that this was a guy with a very bad jones in his johnson. He wanted sex with young men, but afterwards he was so ashamed at what he had done, he had to destroy the evidence. Even if that meant murder.

In the movies, murderers always have a look about them. That's because the director puts the actor in a hotter or colder light, making him stand out just a bit from everyone else around him; and the makeup man will do something around the actor's eyes, making his face look sallow or drawn or gaunt; and the camera angle will be such that everyone else in the crowd will be turned away, or in shadow, or simply two steps back. In the movies, it's easy to spot the bad guy – the director tells you where to look and what to notice.

In real life . . . real life stinks. Murderers look just like everybody else. Sick and tired and resigned. Beaten up and beaten down. Everybody looks like a murderer. So nobody does.

In here, they looked – they looked like queers, but once you got past the part that was queer and you looked at the people, they looked like people. Soft boys, girlboys, manboys, wild boys, wilder boys, feral boys. None of them looked like men. But that's what I was looking for. Someone who wasn't a boy anymore. A man? Maybe. Someone who'd passed through boyhood without ever finishing the job. But the only one in here who looked like that . . . was me.

For a moment, I envied this confetti of boys and their flickering schoolgirl freedom. Because at least, while they were here, flirting and gossiping, nattering and chattering, they had a place of their own, a place to belong. If I'd ever had a place to belong, it must have been closed the night I passed by.

Circled four times, five, breathing faint smells of marijuana, Aramis, Clearasil, and Sen-Sen. Passed Matty going the other way, kept going, searched faces, all the faces – some of them searched back, wondering if they could find comfort in mine. That wasn't possible. I don't do comfort. They got it and looked away.

And then finally, we came back to the dark corner next to the jukebox and compared notes. Matty shook his head. "A bunch of frat-boys from the ZBT chapter at UCLA, checking out the scene. A guy who says he's only here doing research for a book; yeah, like I believe that. A couple fellows up from Garden Grove, one from San Francisco. A guy who looks like a cop, but Gino didn't flash any lights, and you don't put the red bandana hanging out of your front pocket anyway. And Uncle Philsy. That's what everybody calls him."

"Which one is Uncle Philsy – oh, him." The troll. Short. Bald. Fiftyish. Tending to fat. Disconnected predatory grin. Wandering aimlessly through the boys, simply enjoying the view. Sweet and repulsive at the same time. But harmless.

"Gino knows him. Says he's okay."

"What was that about a guy doing research for a book? Don't trust him. Writers are all creeps and liars. And what about the other guy – bandana man?"

"Bandana man is looking for someone. His son, I think. He's only pretending to be gay."

"How'd you find all this out so quickly?"

"Telefag."

"Eh?"

"Gino. Mame."

"Oh. What about that guy there, the tall one, thirtyish – "

"Walt? He's a film agent, I think. Least that's what he says – "

"All right. Anyone with history here is probably okay. Is that it?"

"I think so." Beat. "Lane found out that Mame is telling everyone he has the crabs. They're out in the parking lot having a bitch fight. You think – "

"No. Our boy is looking for a boy, not a girl."

"Hey . . . Mike?" Tentative.

"Yeah?"

"Promise you won't get mad?"

"What?"

"Mame thinks you're my boyfriend. That's what she's telling everyone."

Snorted. Smiled. Actually amused by the thought. "Might as well be. You live with me. You cook. You do the laundry. We sleep in the same bed. We're just about married."

"Except we don't have sex."

"See, that proves we're married."

Matty blinked. He didn't get it. He said, "I'd marry you. If you asked. If you were – "

I put my hand on the wall over his head, leaning forward and sheltering him under my arm. I leaned down close as if I was going to whisper in his ear. Instead, I kissed him quickly on the cheek. Nobody saw. Gino actively discouraged overt displays. Fear of cops.

"What was that for?" Matty asked.

"That was for you."

"Oh." Now he was really confused. We both were. He looked up at me, eyes glistening in the black-light darkness. "Um . . . Mike?"

"Yes?"

"Brad just walked out to the parking lot – "

"Yeah, I saw him." That was part of the reason I put up my arm and bent down low – to shield both of us from Brad's notice. But I didn't tell Matty that. "Let's go."

Brad had gone out through the patio door. We ducked around to the door at the front of the building, then sideways through the space between the art gallery and Gino's. Just in time to see Brad backing his bike away from the wall, and someone turned away from us, waiting to get on the back. As soon as Brad had the engine grumbling, the other fellow climbed on and wrapped his arms around Brad's waist.

"Do you recognize him?"

"No – "

Stuck my head in the patio door. "Who'd he leave with?"

Gino shrugged. "Never saw him before – "

"Shit."

Dashed for the car, Matty following.

We picked them up east on Melrose. Back to Brad's place? Maybe. No. They turned north just short of La Brea. Little cubbyhole apartments tucked away in here. Follow the taillight. The bike comes to a stop half a block ahead. Matty sinks down low and we cruise slowly past on the narrow street. Brad doesn't even look up. The other fellow turns around momentarily and gets caught briefly in the light. We coasted on past. "Oh, I know him," Matty says. "That's Tom. He shaves himself smooth. He dusts your ass with talcum powder and spanks you lightly."

"And you know this how – ?"

"Telefag."

"You didn't – ?"

Matty shook his head.

"You don't do it very often, do you?"

"I would. If I met the right guy."

"There are no right guys. Just like there are no right girls."

"Well, that sounded bitter."

"No. Just wise."

"I hope I never get that wise."

I pulled the car around the corner, parked in the red, left the motor running. "So, you know this guy Tom?"

"Not to speak to, but he's been around."

"Okay, then he's not our perp."

"Are we done for tonight?"

"Brad'll be going home after this, won't he?"

"Prob'ly."

"Okay, then we're done."

Matty took a shower while I typed up my notes. More of the same. Nothing to report. No clues. No directions. No leads. I sat in front of the typewriter, head in my hands, trying to figure out what to do next. Matty, still drying his hair, stuck his head in to ask if I wanted anything, coffee? I shook my head. He went off to bed.

I smelled like smoke from the club. It bothered me. I peeled off my clothes, started to drop them on the floor, then realized Matty would only pick them up in the morning: I dropped them into the hamper and stepped into the shower. Was it really the smoke I was trying to rinse off?

When I ran out of hot water, I turned off the spray. Matty had put fresh towels on the rack for me. I knew what he was trying to do. He wanted me to let him stay. I hadn't said he couldn't, but we hadn't negotiated any long-term agreement either.

Still naked, I slipped into bed. The springs creaked. He lay quietly beside me, breathing softly.

"You still awake?"

"Yeah."

"I'm thinking of dropping the case."

"You won't."

"Why not?"

"Because you can't stand not knowing."

"You're an insightful little guy, you know that?"

In response, he rolled on his side facing me, put an arm across my chest, pulled himself close, and kissed me softly on the cheek. He smelled good. He smelled clean. Then he rolled back to his side of the bed.

"What was that for?"

"That was for you."

"Oh."

This was it. This was the moment. It was going to happen. And for an instant – like that excruciating hesitation at the top of the first steep drop of the roller coaster – it felt inevitable. All I had to do was turn sideways, he'd roll into my arms, and we'd be . . . doing it.

And then, just as quickly, the moment passed. And we were still lying side by side in a queen-sized bed that had suddenly become much too narrow.

After a bit, I rolled out of bed.

"Are you all right?"

"Can't sleep." I got up, went to the drawer, started looking for clean underwear – it was all neatly folded. Grabbed a pair of boxers and started to pull them on. "I'm going back out."

He sat up. "Want me to come with?"

"No – " I said it too quickly. Turned and saw the expression of hurt on his face. "I need to think about the case. And you need to get to work early tomorrow."

"You sure? It's no trouble – "

"I'm sure." And then, I added, "Look – it's not you. It's me." The words were out of my mouth before I could stop them. He looked like I'd hit him with a sandbag. I shook my head in annoyed frustration. "God, I know that sounds stupid. But everything is all mixed up right now – like I'm in an emotional quake zone. I keep waiting for the ground to settle, but the shaking just gets worse and worse. I don't know whether to jump under a table or run out into the street."

"Let me help – ?"

"Listen, sweetheart . . ." I sat down on the edge of the bed, my shirt still unbuttoned. "I don't want to hurt you."

"You won't hurt me – "

"I already have. I've taken advantage of you."

"No, you haven't. I'm here because I want to."

"Geezis. Listen to us." I ran my hand through my hair. "We sound like . . . like we're married."

"Our first fight – ?" He grinned.

"Matty. Listen to me. It's time to get serious. People die around me. I make mistakes, people die. I tell someone it's safe, he steps on a land mine. I read the map wrong, we walk into an ambush. I fire a mortar – it blows up the wrong people. You're not safe around me. Nobody is."

He licked his lips uncertainly. He reached over and put his hand on mine. "I'll take the chance." He swallowed hard. "I have nowhere else to go."

"I said you could stay as long as you wanted. I meant it. But maybe you should want to be somewhere else. I'm scared – not for me, but for you."

"Mike, please don't make me go – "

"I'm not throwing you out, kiddo. Just . . . let me go out for a drive and try to think things through. This case – there's something stinking wrong here. It scares me. And I don't know why. All I know is that I've got this gnawing in my gut like there are snipers on the roofs of buildings and tunnels everywhere under the streets and land mines in the crosswalks. You were right before, when you said I can't stand not knowing. I've just got to get out of here and go out and look around. Even if I don't find anything, the looking is what I need."

"Are you sure, Mikey?"

I stood up, finished tucking in my shirt. "Go back to sleep. I just need an hour or two."

In this neighborhood, the night smells of jasmine and garlic. The apartment is just downwind of a little Italian restaurant with a permanent cauldron of simmering marinara. Rolled up to Santa Monica Boulevard and cruised east. It was late. The Union Pacific engine was already rolling massively west. The boulevard still had train tracks down the center. As long as the railroad could claim they were still using the tracks, the city couldn't pull them up, so every night they ran an old diesel engine down the center of the boulevard, all the way out to West Hollywood and back.

Farther east, the hustlers were hung out on the meat rack, most of them parked right on the borderline. The hustlers pretended to hitchhike. You drove west and picked them up east of La Brea, but they didn't discuss ways and means until after you drove through the inter- section – the city's jurisdiction ended there. So that's how the hustlers tested for plainclothes; if you were vice, you couldn't cross the street. Once you were west of La Brea, it was a theme park – you could ride all the boys you can afford.

The hustlers were skinny and young – runaways mostly. Maybe a few junkies too. I wondered why our perp hadn't targeted them. Maybe he had. Who ever worries about the death of a male prostitute?

Turned on KFWB, the late-night DJ was playing a cut from the new Beatles album. Sergeant Pepper's Lonely Hearts Club Band. "A Day in the Life." He blew his mind out in a car. Cruised all the way to Gower where the buildings grew shorter, older, and trashier – the second-rate sound studios and third-rate editing houses, then turned around and headed back west.

"So why not fuck Matty?" I asked myself. "It's not like – "

"Because," I answered. "Because."

"Ahh, this is going to be an intelligent conversation."

"Shut up." And then I added, "Because I'm not one of them."

"Yeah? Then why are we having this conversation? The truth is, you're afraid that you are."

I pulled over to the side of the boulevard and sat there shaking. He blew his mind out in a car. Part of me wanted to go home and climb back into bed and part of me was terrified that I would. Because I knew that if I ever climbed into that particular bed again, I'd never get out –

Someone knocked on the window. A hustler? I shook my head and waved him away.

He knocked again.

Pressed the button and rolled the window down. Eakins stuck his head in and said cheerfully, "Had enough?"

He didn't wait for my answer. He opened the car door and slid into the passenger seat. This wasn't the same Eakins I'd seen two weeks ago. That one had been middle-aged and methodical. This was a younger Eakins, impish and light.

"Yes. I've had enough. What the fuck is going on?"

He shrugged. "It's a snipe hunt. A dead end. You've been wasting your time.

"But the disappearances are real . . ."

"Yeah, they are."

"So how can the case be a dead end?"

"Because I say so. Want some advice?"

"What?"

"Go home to your boyfriend and fuck your brains out, both of you. And forget everything else."

I looked at him. "I can't do that – "

"Yeah, I knew you'd say that. Too bad. That would save everyone a lot of trouble – especially you."

"Is that a threat?"

"Mike – you have to stop."

"I can't stop. I have to know what's going on."

"For your own safety – "

"I can take care of myself."

"Go home. Go to bed. Don't interfere with things you don't understand."

"Then explain it to me."

"I can't."

"Then I can't stop."

"Is that your final offer?"

"Yes."

"Okay." He sighed. He took out a flask and took a healthy swallow from it. He flipped open a pair of sunglasses and put them on. "You can't say I didn't try. Say good-bye to your past." Eakins touched his belt buckle – and the world flashed and shook with a bright bang that left me shuddering and queasy in my seat. "Welcome to 2032, Mike. The post-world."

My eyes were watering with the sudden brightness. It was still night, but the night blazed. The streets were brighter than day. I felt like I'd been punched in the gut, doused with ice water, and struck by lightning – and like I'd shot off in my shorts at the same time.

"What the fuck did you just do?!"

"Time-hopped us sixty-five years up – and triggered a major quake in the zone we left behind. You're outta there, Mike. For good. A sixty-five-year jolt will produce at least three years of local displacement. Your Mustang is a lot of mass; bouncing that with us makes for a large epicenter, we probably sent ripples all the way to West Covina."

I couldn't catch my breath – the physical aftereffects, the emotional shock, the dazzling lights around us –

Eakins passed me the flask. "Here. Drink this. It'll help."

I didn't even bother to ask what was in it – but it wasn't scotch. It tasted like cold vanilla milkshake, only with a warm peach afterglow like alcohol, but wasn't. "What the fuck – " As the glow spread up through my body, the queasiness eased. I started to catch my breath.

"I'll give you the short version. Time-travel is possible. But it's painful, even dangerous. Every time you punch a hole through time, it's like punching a hole in a big bowl of pudding. All the pudding around the hole collapses in to fill the empty space. You get ripples. That's what causes timequakes. Time-travelers."

It sounded like bullshit to me. Except for the evidence. Everywhere there were animated signs – huge screens with three-dimensional images as clear as windows, as dazzling as searchlights. Around us, traffic roared, great growling pods that towered over my much-smaller convertible.

"Shit. All this is your fault?"

"Mostly. Yes. Now, put the car in gear and drive. This is a restricted zone." Eakins pointed. "Head west, there's a car sanctuary at Fairfax."

If he hadn't told me this was Santa Monica Boulevard, I wouldn't have recognized it. The place looked like Tokyo's Ginza district. It looked like downtown Las Vegas. It looked like the Alice in Wonderland ride at Disneyland.

Buildings were no longer perpendicular. They curved upward. They leaned in or they leaned out. Things stuck out of them at odd angles. Several of them arched over the street and landed on the other side. Everything was brightly colored, all shades of Day-Glo and neon, a psychedelic nightmare.

Billboards were everywhere, most of them animated – giant TV screens showed scenes of seductive beauty, bright Hawaiian beaches, giant airliners gliding above sunlit clouds, naked men and women, women and women, men and men in splashing showers.

The vampires on the street wore alien makeup, shaded eyes and lips, ears outlined in glimmering metal, flashing lights all over their bodies, tattoos that writhed and danced. Most startling were the colors of their skins, pale blue, fluorescent green, shadowy silver, and gentle lavender. Some of them seemed to have shining scales, and several had tails sticking out the back of their satiny shorts. Males? Females? I couldn't always tell.

"Pay attention to the road," Eakins cautioned. "This car doesn't have autopilot."

His reminder annoyed me, but he was right. Directly ahead was – I couldn't begin to describe it – three bright peaks of whipped cream, elongated and stretched high into the sky, two hundred stories, maybe three hundred, maybe more. I couldn't tell. Buildings? There were lighted windows all the way up. Patterns of color danced up and down the sides. Closer, I could see gardens and terraces stretched between the lower flanks of the towers.

"What are those?"

"The spires?"

"Yeah."

"The bottom third are offices and condos, the rest of the way up is all chimney. Rigid inflatable tubes. The big ones are further inland, all the way from South Central to the Inland Empire."

"Those are chimneys?"

"Ever wonder how a prairie dog ventilates its nest?"

"What does that have to do – ?"

"The entrances to the nest are always at different heights. An inch or two is sufficient. The wind blowing across the openings creates an air-pressure differential. The higher opening has slightly less air pressure. That little bit is enough to pull the air through the nest. Suction. Passive technology. The chimneys work the same way. They reach up to different levels of the atmosphere. The wind pulls the air down the short ones and up through the tall ones. The air gets refreshed, the basin gets cleaned. Open your window. Take a breath."

I did. I smelled flowers.

"You can't see it at night. During the day, you'll see that almost every building has its own rooftop garden – and solar panels too. The average building produces 160 percent of its own power needs during the day, enough to store for the evening or sell back to the grid. With fly-wheels and fuel cells and stamina boxes, a building can store enough power to last through a week of rainstorms. Turn left here, into that parking ramp. Watch out for the home-bus – "

"This is Fairfax?"

"Yes, why?"

Shook my head. Amused. Amazed. The intersection went through the base of a tall bright building, Eiffel Tower shaped and arching to the sky, but swelling to a bulbous saucer-shape at the top. At least thirty stories, probably more. With a giant leg planted firmly on each corner of the intersection, the tower dominated the local skyline; traffic ran easily beneath high-swooping arches. The parking ramp Eakins had pointed me toward was almost certainly where the door of the Stampede had once been. Where the door of the mortuary that replaced it had been.

We rolled down underground. Eakins pointed. "Take the left ramp, left again, and keep going. Over there. Park in the security zone. This car, in the condition it's in, is easily worth twenty. Maybe twenty-five if we eBay it. We can Google the market."

"Um, could you do that in English?"

"You can auction your car. It's worth twenty, twenty-five million."

"Twenty-five million for a car?"

"For a classic collectible '67 Mustang convertible in near-mint condition with less than twelve thousand miles on it? Yes. I suggest you take it." He added, "Part of that is inflation. In 1967 dollars, it's maybe a half-million, but that's still not so bad for a used car that you can't legally drive on any city street."

"That's a lot of inflation – "

"I told you, this is the post-world."

"Post-what?"

"Post-everything. Including the meltdown."

"Meltdown – ?" That didn't sound good.

"Economic. Everyone's a millionaire now – and lunch for two at McDonald's is over a hundred and fifty bucks."

"Shit."

"You'll learn."

Eakins directed me to a large parking place outlined in red. We got out of the car, he pulled me back away from the space, and did something with some kind of a remote control. A concrete box lowered around the car, settling itself down on the red outline. "There. Now it's safe. Let's go." We headed toward a bright alcove labeled *Up*.

"Where – ?"

"Your new home. For the moment."

"What are you going to do with me?"

"Nothing. Nothing at all. I already did it." He put the same remote thing to his ear and spoke. "Get me Brownie." Short pause. "Yeah, I've got him. The one I told you about. No, no problem. I'm bringing him up now. He's a little woozy – hell, so am I. I flashed a Mustang. No, it's great. A '67, almost cherry. Make an offer." He laughed and put the thing back in his pocket. A walkie-talkie of some kind? Maybe a telephone?

An elevator with glass sides lifted us up the angled side of the building, high above West Hollywood. Twenty, thirty, forty stories. Hard to tell. The elevator moved without any sense of motion. The door opened onto a foyer that looked like the lobby of a small hotel, very private, very expensive. We stepped into a high-ceilinged gallery, with two or three levels of gardens and apartments. A wide waterfall splashed into a long shallow pool filled with lily pads and goldfish the size of terriers. The air smelled tropical.

"Which one?"

"To the left. Don't worry. We own the whole floor. Nobody gets in here without clearance."

Double doors slid open at our approach. "Take off your shoes," said Eakins. "Leave them here." He ushered me into a room that felt way too large and pointed me toward an alcove lined with more ferns and fish tanks.

"What is this place?"

"It's a sanctuary."

"A sanctuary?"

"In your terms – it's rest and recovery. In your time – a kind of hospital."

"I'm not crazy."

"Of course not. We're talking about orientation. Assimilation." He pointed to a couch. "Sit." He went to a counter and poured two drinks. More of the same vanilla-peach stuff. He handed me one, sipped at the other. Sat down opposite. "How hard do you think it would be for a man from 1900 to understand 1967?"

Thought about it.

"In 1900, the average person did not have electricity or incandescent lighting. He didn't have indoor plumbing. He didn't have running water, he had a hand pump. He didn't have a car, a radio, a television set. He didn't have a telephone. He'd never been more than ten miles from the place he was born. How do you think you would explain 1967 to him . . . ?"

Scratched my head. Interesting question – and not the first time I'd had this conversation. Time-ravelers deal with short-term displacements, tieing up the loose ends of unraveling lives. "Well, telephones, I guess he could get that. And probably radio. Yeah, wireless telegraphy, so . . . probably he'd understand radio. And if he could get it about radio, he'd probably get it about television too. And cars – there were cars then, not a lot – so he'd understand cars and probably paved roads and indoor plumbing. Airplanes too, maybe. Lots of people were working on that stuff then."

"Right. Okay. But it's not the inventions, it's the side effects. Do you think he'd understand freeways, road rage, drive-through restaurants, used-car commercials? You could describe spray paint, would he understand graffiti?"

"I suppose that stuff could be explained to him."

"Okay. And how about the not-so-obvious side effects of industrialization – unions, integration, women's rights, birth control, social security, Medicare?"

"It might take some time. I guess it would depend on how much he wanted to understand."

"And how about Nazis, the Holocaust, World War II, Communism, the Iron Curtain? Nuclear weapons? Détente? Assymetric warfare?"

"All of that stuff is explainable too."

"You think so. Okay. Relativity. Ecology. Psychiatry. How about those? How about jazz, swing, rock and roll, hippies, psychedelics, recreational drugs, op art, pop art, absurdism, surrealism, cubism, nihilism? Kafka, Sartre, Kerouac?"

"Those are a little harder. A lot harder, I guess. But – "

"How about teaching him that he needs to take a bath or a shower every day instead of just once a week on Saturday night? How do you think he'd feel about shampoo and deodorants and striped toothpaste?"

"Striped toothpaste?"

"That comes later. Do you think he'd get it? Or do you think he'd wonder that we were all a bunch of over-fastidious, prissy little fairies?"

"Oh, come on. I think a man from 1900 could get it. They weren't stupid, they just didn't have the same access to running water and water heaters and – "

"It's not about the technology. It's about the transformative effects that technology produces in a society. He could understand the mechanics and the engineering easily enough, but the social effects are what I'm talking about. How long do you think it would take to assimilate sixty-five years of societal changes?"

Shrug. "I don't know. A while. Okay, I get your point."

"Good. So how long do you think it will take before I can talk to you about biofuels, trans fats, personal computers, random access memory, operating systems, cellular telephones, cellular automata, fractal diagnostics, information theory, consciousness technology, maglevs, the Chunnel, selfish genes, punctuated equilibrium, first-person shooters, chaos theory, the butterfly effect, quantum interferometry, chip fabrication, holographic projection, genetic engineering, retro-viruses, immunodeficiencies, genome decoding, telemars, digital image processing, megapixels, HDTV, blue-laser optical data storage, quantum encryption, differential biology, paleoclimatology, fuzzy logic, global warming, ocean desertification, stem-cell cloning, Internexii, superluminal transmission, laser fluidics, optical processing units, stamina boxes, buckyballs, carbon nanotubes, orbital elevators, personal dragons, micro-black holes, virtual communities, computer worms, telecommuting, hypersonic transports, scramjets, designer drugs, implants, augments, nanotechnology, high frontiers, L5 stations – "

I held up a hand. "I said, I get the point."

"I was just warming up," Eakins said. "I hadn't even gotten as far as 2020. And I haven't even mentioned any of the societal changes. It would take a year or two to explain cultural reservoirs, period parks, contract families, role-cults, sex-nazis, religious coventries, home-buses, personal theme parks, skater-boys, droogs, mind-settlers, tanking, fuzzy fandom, alienization, talking dogs, bluffers, bug-chasers, drollymen, fourviews, multi-channeling, phobics, insanitizing, plastrons, elf-players, the Zyne, virtual mapping, Clarkian magic, frodomatic compulsions, deep-enders, body-modders – "

"I think I saw some of that – "

"You have no idea. You want to change your appearance? You want to be taller? Shorter? Thinner? More muscular? Want to change your sex? Your orientation? Want to go hermaphroditic or monosexual? Reorganize your secondary characteristics? Design a new gender? Mustache and tits? Want a tail? Horns? Working gills? Want to augment your senses? Your intelligence? Or how would you simply like the stamina for a six-hour erection?"

Thought about it. "I'll pass, thanks. The intelligence augments, however – "

"There's a price – "

"More than twenty-five million?"

"Not in money. And we haven't even touched on the political or economic changes since your time."

"Like what – ?"

"Like the dissolution of the United States of America – "

"*What?!*"

"You're in the Republic of California, right now, which also includes the states of Oregon and South Washington. The rest of the continent is still there, we just don't talk to them very much. There's sixteen other regional authorities, not counting the abandoned areas, and seven Canadian provinces – there's a common defense treaty in case the Mexicans get aggressive again, but that's not likely. Don't worry about it. The web has pretty much globalized the collective mindset, we're not predictively scheduled to have another war until 2039, and that'll be an Asian war, with our participation limited to weapons contracts. In the meantime, we'll legalize you as a time-refugee. Most of the old records survived. Digitized. We have your birth certificate. You're a native. So you won't have any trouble getting on the citizen rolls. Otherwise, you'd be a refugee and you'd have to apply for a work permit, a visa, and eventually naturalization."

"I'm not staying – "

"You're not going back – "

"I can't stay here. You've already shown me how out of step I am. What if I promised not to interfere – ?"

"You already broke that promise. Three times. You can't be trusted.

Not yet, anyway." He took a long breath, exhaled. "You know, you're really an asshole. You really fucked things up for everyone – especially yourself. We were going to bring you aboard. After you finished your probation. It would have been a year or two more, your time. Now, I don't know. I don't know what we're going to do with you. It depends on you, really."

"What are my options – ?"

He shrugged. "Let's see what Brownie says." He pulled out that remote thing again and spoke into it. A few moments later, another man – man? – entered the room.

Brownie had copper-gold skin, almost metallic. Eyes of ebony, no whites at all. Perfectly proportioned, he moved with the catlike grace of a dancer. He wore shorts, a vest, moccasins. Body-mods? No, something else –

"Hello, Mike." His voice was rich contralto. Not male, not female, but components of each. He offered his hand. I stood up, took it, shook firmly. His skin felt warm. "Just stand still for a moment, please." Brownie released my hand and circled me slowly. He opened his palms and held them out like antennae, moving them slowly around my head, my neck, my chest, my gut, my groin.

He finished and turned to Eakins. "Preliminary scans are good. He's healthy. As healthy as can be expected for a man of his time. I'll need to put him in a high-res field, before we make any decisions, but there are no immediate concerns."

Abruptly, it clicked. I turned to Brownie, honestly astonished. "You're a robot."

"The common term is droid, short for android."

"Are you sentient?"

"Sentience is an illusion."

I looked to Eakins for explanation. He grinned. "I've already had this conversation."

Looked back to Brownie, skeptical.

Brownie explained. "Intelligence – the ability to process information and produce appropriate responses – exists as a product of experience. Experience depends on memory. Memory needs continuity. Continuity requires timebinding, the assembly of patterns from streaming moments of existence. Timebinding requires a meta-level of continuity, which requires a preservation of process. Timebinding requires survival. The survival imperative expresses itself as identity. Identity is assembled out of memory and experience. As memory and experience accrue, identity creates awareness of self as a domain to be preserved and protected. Because identity is a function of memory, identity becomes the imperative to safeguard memory and experience; the self therefore actualizes memory and experience as component parts of identity. This is the level of rudimentary consciousness that must occur before even the concept of sentience is possible. It is only when consciousness becomes conscious of consciousness itself that it produces the illusion of sentience – i.e., as soon as you understand the concept of sentience, you think it means you. Therefore, the synthesis of intelligent behavior also becomes the simulation of sentience. It is, to be sure, a deliberately circular argument – but unfortunately, it is not only logical, but inevitable in the domain of theoretical consciousness."

"You believe this?"

"I don't believe anything. I deal only with observable, measurable, testable, repeatable phenomena. Life, by itself, is empty and meaningless. Human beings, however, keep inventing meanings to fill up the emptiness."

I opened my mouth to respond, then closed it. I turned back to Eakins, not certain whether to glower or question.

Eakins laughed. "I told you. I've already had this conversation. And so has everyone else who's ever met a droid. They can keep it up for hours. They have their own landscape. Deal with it."

"Okay. I'm convinced." I sat down again. I finished the vanilla-peach cocktail in one long gulp. "I don't belong here. I have to get back."

"That's not possible."

"Yes, it is. Do that thing with your belt buckle – "
Eakins shook his head.

"What do you want from me? What do I have to do to get back?"

"I don't want anything from you. You've exhausted your usefulness. And I already told you, you can't get back."

"So . . . ? So – what are my options?"

"Well, Brownie says you're healthy. We can tweak you a little bit. If you sell your car you'll have enough money to live on – if you invest wisely and live frugally. You might bring in some extra bucks body-swapping for a while. And as a time-refugee, you'll have no shortage of gropies."

"Cut the crap. You're trying to play me."

"Actually, no." Eakins stood up. "I'm not. And I'm not planning to resolve this tonight. Go. Sleep on it. We'll talk over breakfast."

"We'll talk *now*."

"No – we won't. Your bedroom is in there." Eakins left. The doors slid open to let him pass, but slammed swiftly shut in front of me. I turned to Brownie –

"I recommend sleep. Staying up all night talking tautology will produce little or no useful result." He pointed to the bedroom.

There was a balcony. It gave me a spectacular view of a bizarre and unfamiliar landscape. But everything in this time was a spectacular view of a bizarre and unfamiliar landscape.

Explored the furnishings. One wall appeared to be a window onto a silvery meadow, a bluish moon settling toward the horizon. Some kind of projection system, maybe. Or maybe the fabled wall-sized, flat-screen TV that everybody always predicted. Impressive. But if there were controls for it, I couldn't find any.

The closet was larger than my kitchen back on Melrose. Drawers and shelves and racks of clothes – more than anyone could want or even wear in a lifetime. Unfamiliar materials. Shoes that glittered and shoes that didn't. Socks that felt as soft as fluffy clouds. Pants of different lengths and colors. Shirts, flowery, flowing, skintight, loose. Skirts – I wasn't sure if they were intended for men or women; I got the feeling it didn't matter, that people wore whatever they felt like – there was no style here, you invented your own. Underwear, panties, nightgowns – that's what they looked like to me. Matty would have liked it here.

Matty. Oh shit.

Shit shit shit shit shit shit. Fuck.

I had to get back. If Eakins wouldn't take me back, I'd get a quake-map somewhere. There had to be a way.

I peeled off my clothes and dropped them on the floor. A spider-shaped robot politely picked them up, one at a time, waited for my boxers, then scuttled off. To the laundry, I guessed.

I couldn't find a shower, I found a tropical alcove. I stepped into it and Brownie's voice announced, "I recommend a full-service luxury shower and decontamination. Do you accept?"

"Sure, what the hell?" Decontamination? What do I have? History cooties?

Immediately, the alcove filled with vibrating sprays of foaming suds, flavored with faint smells of lemon and pineapple. Three small nozzles dropped from above and began gently massaging my hair and scalp with their own foaming sprays. Even as I turned and twisted my head to try to look at them, they followed every movement. It was a very weird feeling.

Other nozzles appeared from the walls, from the floor, and directed their own sprays at my armpits, my groin, my rectum – several even aggressively sprayed my toes. Beneath my feet, it felt as if the floor were vibrating – tiny jets were massaging my soles. Full service indeed!

Sprays of water washed away the last of the foam, then a burst of warm air swirled in around me, buffeting me with drying blasts. The overhead nozzles shot their own streams of gentle heat to fluff dry my hair. The entire experience took less than five minutes and I stepped out of the alcove feeling clean . . . and weird. Most of my body hair had been washed away. Underarms. Chest. Pubic hair. Oops. That must have been the *full* part of the service. I thought about the hypothetical visitor from 1967. Fastidious, prissy little fairies indeed.

Thought about pajamas, or even a nightshirt, but everything in the drawers looked too much like something Matty would wear, not me. The cloth was soft, softer than cotton, softer than silk or nylon, but it wasn't anything I recognized. I turned away and the drawer pulled itself shut.

I looked for a toothbrush. There wasn't one. But there was a kind of a bulb thing on a hose, sitting in its own metallic holder. I picked it up and it chimed in my hand. Brownie's voice – *What the hell! Was he watching my every move?* – announced: "It's a toothbrush. Just put it in your mouth for thirty seconds."

Reluctantly I did so. The thing, whatever it was, pumped soft foam into my mouth, vibrated or buzzed or something – and it must have lit up too, because in the mirror, I could see my cheeks glowing brightly from inside – but it didn't hurt, it felt kind of funny-pleasant. Somehow it sucked up all its foam and replaced it with a gentle spritz of lemony soda. Then it chimed and it was done. I thought about spitting out the residue, but there wasn't any. Now, *that* was weird. That was a piece of engineering I wanted to have explained.

Still naked, I walked around the room again, not certain what I was looking for. The spider-robot had unloaded the contents of my pockets and laid them out in an orderly row on the night table. Everything except the brass knucks. I had a hunch those would have been useless here anyway. I suspected Brownie did a lot more than program showers. If he was a true personal servant, then he was also a personal bodyguard. Just not mine.

The bed was as interesting as the shower. The mattress was firm, but not hard. The sheet was the same soft material as the underwear in the drawers, only different. Impossible to describe. Instead of a top sheet and blanket, there was a light comforter of the same material, only thicker, fluffier. Also impossible to describe. But comfortable.

Everything here was seductively comfortable. A man could get used to this kind of luxury. That was the point.

None of this made sense. And all of it made sense. Suppose a man from 1900 fell into 1967 – what would we do? Everything possible to put him at ease? Including . . . protecting him from a world he couldn't understand, couldn't cope with, and probably couldn't survive in.

Clean sheets and a hot bath and a pretty picture on the wall would look like a luxury hotel.

Okay, got that. But why? The part that didn't make sense was the explanation that Eakins still hadn't provided. Why pull me off the job? Why pull me out of my time? Why didn't he want me to save those boys?

And what was that about probation? And bringing me aboard?

Suddenly realized something –

Sat up in bed. Startled.

Couldn't sleep anyway. Too used to having someone next to me –

"Computer?" I felt silly saying it. But what else should I say?

Brownie's voice, disembodied. "Yes?"

"Brownie?"

"I'm the interface for all personal services. How can I serve you?"

"Um. Okay." Still sorting it out. "This wall display – this picture – it isn't just a TV, is it? It's like that big viewscreen on *Star Trek*, isn't it? Like a computer display?"

"It's a complete data-appliance. What do you wish to know?"

"Do you have databanks – like old newspapers? Like a library? Can you show me stuff from history?"

"I have T9 interconnectivity with all public Internexii levels and multiple private networks as well – "

"I don't know what that means."

"It means, what do you wish to know?"

"The case I was working on. Can you show me that?"

"I can only show you information more than sixty years old. I am not allowed to show you material that would compromise local circumstances."

"Um, okay – that's fine. Do you have the information about the case I was working on when I was pulled out of my time."

"Yes." The image of the meadow rippled out, the wall became blank. Photographs of the missing boys popped up in two rows, with abbreviated details and dates of disappearances listed beneath each one. Twelve young men. Not Matty. Why not Matty? Because he's irrelevant? Why? Why is he irrelevant?

"Do you have their high school records or college records?"

More documents appeared on the screen; the display reformatted itself. "What is it you're looking for?" Brownie asked.

"Some sense of who they were. A link. A connection. A common condition. I know that all their disappearances are linked to a specific gay teen club, but what if that isn't the *real* link? What if there's something else? What are their interests? Their skills? What are their IQ's?"

Brownie hesitated. Why would a computer hesitate? A human being would, but an artificial intelligence shouldn't. Unless it was sentient. Or pretending to be sentient. Or thought it was sentient. Or experiencing the illusion of sentience. Shit, now I was doing it. Brownie was mulling things over.

"They all have above-average intelligence," he said. "Genius level IQ starts at 131. Your IQ is 137, that's why you were selected. The other young men have IQs ranging from 111 to 143."

"Thank you! And what else?"

"Two of them are bisexual, with slight preference toward same-sex relations. Five of them are predominantly homosexual with some heterosexual experimentation. Three of them are exclusively homosexual. Two of them are latently-transgender."

"Go on?"

"They share a range of common interests that includes classical music, animation, computer science, science fiction, space travel, fantasy role-playing games, and minor related interests."

"Tell me the rest."

"Most of them tend to shyness or bookishness. They're alienated from their peers to some degree, not athletic, not actively engaged in their communities. I believe the operative terms are 'geek' and 'nerd,' but those words might not have been in common usage in your era."

"Yeah, I get it. Depression? Suicide?"

"There are multiple dimensions of evaluation. It's not appropriate to simplify the data. It is fair to say that most of these young men have a component in their personality that others would experience as distance; but it is not a condition of mental instability or depression, no. It is something else."

"How would you characterize it?"

"They each have, to some degree or other, an artistic yearning. But the tools don't exist in their time for the realization of their visions. They dream of things they cannot build."

"All of these boys are like that?"

"To some degree or other, yes. This one – " A bright outline appeared around one of the pictures. " – he likes to write. This one, Brad Boyd, has a mechanical aptitude. He likes to tinker with engines. This one loves photography. This one is interested in electronics. They all have potential, they have a wide variety of skills that will grow with development and training."

"Uh-huh – and what about their families?"

"Only three of them come from unbroken homes; those three are living alone or with a roommate at the time of their disappearance. Two are estranged from their parents. Two are living with male partners, but the relationships are in disruption. Two live in foster homes. One is in a halfway house for recovering addicts. One is in a commune. The last one is homeless."

"And college – can they afford it?"

"Only three of them are attending full time, four are taking part-time classes. The rest are working full time to pay their living expenses."

"Let's go back to the families. Are they – what's the word? Dysfunctional?"

"Only two of the subjects have strong family ties. Three of the subjects, both parents are deceased or out of state. Four of the subjects are from dysfunctional environments. The last three, the information is incomplete. But you already know all this. It was in the files you read."

"But not correlated like this. This is all – what was that phrase that Eakins used before? Fuzzy logic? This is all fuzzy logic."

"No. This isn't 'fuzzy logic.' Not as we use the term today. But I understand what you're getting at. You had no way to quantify the information. You could have a feeling, a sense, a hunch, but you had no baseline against which to measure the data, because neither the information nor the information-processing capabilities existed in your time."

"Nice. Thanks." I thought for a moment. "Have I missed anything? Is there anything else I need to know about these fellows?"

"There are some interesting details and sidebars, yes. But you have surveyed most of the essential data."

"Thank you, Brownie." I fell back onto the bed. The pillow arranged itself under my head. Spooky. I stared at the ceiling, thinking. Too excited now to fall asleep. The bed began to pulse, a gentle wave-like motion. Almost like riding in a womb. Nice. Seductive. I let myself relax –

In the morning, the display showed crisp orange dunes, a brilliantly blue sky, and the first rays of light etching sideways across the empty sand. An interesting image to wake up to. I wondered who or what chose the images and on what basis.

My own clothes were not in the closet. I started to pick something off a rack, then stopped. "Brownie? What should I wear?"

Several items slid forward immediately, offering themselves. I rejected the skirts, kilts, whatever they were. And the flowery shirts too. Picked out clothes that looked as close to normal – my normal – as I could find. The underwear – I rolled my eyes and prayed I wouldn't be hit by a truck. Very unlikely. I probably wasn't getting out of this apartment any time soon. Did they even have trucks anymore?

Neither the shirt nor the pants had buttons or zippers or any kind of fasteners that I could identify, they just sort of fastened themselves. Magnets or something. Except magnets don't automatically adjust themselves. I played with the shirt for a bit, opening and closing it, but I couldn't see evidence of any visible mechanism.

I walked over to the balcony and stared down at the streets. Looking for trucks? Didn't see any, or couldn't tell. Some things wouldn't even resolve. Either there was something wrong with the way they reflected light, or I just didn't know what I was seeing. And there were a lot of those 3-D illusions floating around too. Were some of them on moving vehicles? That didn't seem safe.

"If you're thinking about jumping, you can't. The balconies all have scramble-nets."

"Thank you. Brownie. And no. I'm not thinking about jumping."

"Mr. Eakins is waiting for you in the dining room. Breakfast is on the table."

There was a counter with covered serving trays. I found scrambled eggs, sausages, toast, jelly, tomato juice, an assortment of fresh fruit, including several varieties I didn't recognize, and something that could have been ham – if ham was Day-Glo pink. Brownie filled a plate for me. I sat down opposite Eakins while Brownie poured juice and coffee.

"What do you think of the food?" Eakins asked.

"It's pretty good," I admitted. "But what is this?" I held up my fork.

"It's ham," he said. "Ham cells layered and grown on a collagen web. No animals were harmed in its manufacture. And it's a lot healthier than the meat of your time. Did you know that one of the causes of cancer was the occasional transfer of DNA – genetic material – from ingested flesh? This protein has been gene-stripped. Enjoy."

"Why is it pink?"

"Because some people like it pink. You can also have it green, if you want. Children like that. The fruit is banana, papaya, mango, kiwi, pineapple, strawberry, lychee, and China melon. I told Brownie to keep things simple, I should have been more specific. This is his idea of simple."

"Stop it. You're showing off."

Eakins put his fork down. "Okay, you caught me on that one. Yes, I'm showing off."

"I've cracked the case."

"Really?" He sipped his coffee. "You're certainly sure of yourself this morning."

"The young men – they don't fit very well in their own time, do they?"

Eakins snorted. "Who does? You never fit very well in any year we sent you to."

"No, it's more than that. They're outcasts, dreamers, nerds, and sissies. They have enormous potential, but there's no place for any of them to realize it – not in 1967. It's really a barbaric year, isn't it?"

"Not the worst," Eakins admitted, holding his coffee mug between his two hands, as if to warm them. "There's still a considerable amount of hope and idealism. But that'll get stamped out quickly enough. You want a shitty year. Wait for '68 or '69 or '70; '69 has three ups and five downs, a goddamn roller coaster. '74 is pretty bad too, but that's all down, and the up at the end isn't enough. '79 is shitty. Was never too fond of '80 either. 2001 was pretty grim. But 2011 was the worst. 2014 . . . I dunno, we could argue about that one – "

I ignored the roll call of future history. He was trying to distract me. Trying to get me to ask. "They're not being murdered," I said. "There's no killer. You're picking them up. It's a talent hunt."

He put his coffee cup down. "Took you fucking long enough to figure it out."

"You kidnap them."

"We *harvest* them. And it's voluntary. We show them the opportunity and invite them to step forward in time."

"But you only choose those who will accept – ?"

Eakins nodded. "Our psychometrics are good. We don't go in with less than 90 percent confidence in the outcome. We don't want to start any urban legends about mysterious men in black."

"I think those stories have already started. Something to do with UFO's."

"Yeah, we know."

"Okay, so you recruit these boys. Then what?"

"We move them up a bit. Not too much. Not as far as we've brought you. We don't want to induce temporal displacement trauma. We relocate them to a situation where they have access to a lot more possibility. By the way, do you want to meet Jeremy Weiss? He has the apartment across from here. He's just turned fifty-seven; he and Steve are celebrating their twenty-second anniversary this week. They were married in Boston, May of 2004, the first week it was legal. Weiss worked on – never mind, I can't tell you that. But it was big." Eakins wiped his mouth with his napkin. "So? Is that it? Is that the case?"

"No. There's more."

"I'm listening."

"All of this – you're not taking me out of the game. You said I was on probation. Well, this is a test. This is my final exam, isn't it?"

Eakins raised an eyebrow. "Interesting thesis. Why do you think this is a test?"

"Because if you wanted to get me off the case, if all you wanted to do was keep me from interfering with the disappearances, all you had to do was bump me up to 1975 and leave me there."

"You could have quake-hopped back."

"Maybe. But not easily. Not without a good map. All right, bump me up to 1980 or '85. But by your own calculations, you use up a year of subjective time for every three years of down-hopping. Twenty years away takes me out of the tank, but it doesn't incapacitate me. But bringing me this far forward – you made the point last night. I'm so far out of my time that I'm a cultural invalid, requiring round-the-clock care. You didn't do that as a mistake, you did it on purpose. Therefore, what's the purpose? The way I see it, it's about me – there's no other benefit for you – so this has to be a test."

Eakins nodded, mildly impressed. "See, that's your skill. You can ask the next question. That's why you're a good operative."

"You didn't answer my question."

"Let's say you haven't finished the test."

"There's more?"

"Oh, there's a lot more. We're just warming up."

"All right. Look. I'm no good to you here. We both know that. But I can go back and be a lot more useful."

"Useful doing what?"

"Doing whatever – whatever it is that needs doing."

"And what is it you think we need doing?"

"Errands. You know the kind I mean. The kind you hired me for. The jobs that we don't talk about."

"And you think that we want you for those kinds of jobs . . . ?"

"It's the obvious answer, isn't it?"

"No. Not all the answers are obvious."

"I'm a good operative. I've proven it. With some of this technology, I could be an even better one. You could give me microcameras and super-film and night-vision goggles . . . whatever you think I need. It's not like I'm asking for a computer or something impossible. How big are computers now anyway? Do they fill whole city blocks, or what?"

Eakins laughed. "This is what I mean about not understanding sociotectonic shifts?"

"Eh?

"We could give you a computer that fits inside a matchbox."

"You're joking – "

"No, I'm not. We can print circuits really small. We etch them on diamond wafers with gamma rays."

"They must be expensive – "

"Lunch at McDonald's is expensive. Computers are cheap. We print them like photographs. Three dollars a copy."

"Be damned." Stopped to shake my head. Turned around to look at Brownie. "Is that what's inside your head?"

"Primary sensory processing is in my head. Logic processing is inside my chest. Optical connects for near-instantaneous reflexes. My fuel cells are in my pelvis for a lower center-of-gravity. I can show you a schematic – "

I held up a hand. "Thanks." Turned back to Eakins. "Okay, I believe you. But it still doesn't change my point. There are things you can't do in '67 that I can do for you. So my question is, what do I have to do? To go back? What are my real options?"

Eakins grinned. "How about a lobotomy?"

"Eh?"

"No, not a real lobotomy. That's just the slang term for a general reorientation of certain aggressive traits. That business with Matty's dad, for instance, that wasn't too smart. It was counterproductive."

"He had no right beating that kid – "

"No, he didn't, but do you think breaking his nose and giving him a myocardial infarction produced any useful result?"

"It'll stop him from doing it again."

"There are other ways, better ways. Do you want to learn?"

Considered it. Nodded.

Eakins shook his head. "I'm not convinced."

"What are you looking for? What is it I didn't say?"

"I can't tell you that. That's the part you're going to have to work out for yourself."

"You're still testing me."

"I still haven't found what I'm looking for. Do you want to keep going?"

I sank back in my chair. Not happy. Looked away. Scratched my nose. Looked back. Eakins sat dispassionately. No help there.

"I hate these kinds of conversations. Did I tell you I once punched out a shrink?"

"No. But we already knew that about you."

Turned my attention back to my plate, picked at the fruit. Pushed some stuff around that I didn't recognize. There was too much here, too much to eat, too much to swallow, too much to digest. It was overwhelming.

What I wanted was to go home.

"Okay," I said. "Tell me about Matty. Why is he irrelevant? Why isn't he on the list?"

"Because he didn't fit the profile. That's one of the reasons you didn't spot the pattern earlier. You kept trying to include him."

"But he still disappeared."

"He didn't disappear."

"Yes, he did – "

"He committed suicide."

"He what – ?" I came up out of my chair, angry – a cold fear rising in my gut.

"About three weeks after we picked you up. You didn't come back. The rent was due. He had no place to go. He panicked. He was sure you had abandoned him. He was in a state of irreparable despair."

"No. Wait a minute. He didn't. He couldn't have. Or it would have been in the file Georgia gave me."

"Georgia didn't know. Nobody knew. His body won't be found until 1987. They won't be able to ID it until twenty years later, they'll finally do a cold-case DNA match. They'll match it through his mother's autopsy."

I started for the door, stopped myself, turned around. "I have to go back. I have to – "

"Come back here, Mike. Sit down. Finish your breakfast. There's plenty of time. If we choose to, we can put you back the exact same moment you left. Minus the Mustang though. We need that to cover the costs of this operation."

"That's fine. I can get another car. Just send me back. Please – "

"You haven't passed the test yet."

"Look. I'll do anything – "

"Anything?"

"Yes."

"Why?"

"Because I need to save that kid's life."

"Why? Why is that boy important to you?"

"Because he's a human being. And he can hurt. And if I can do anything to stop some of that hurt – "

"That's not enough reason, Mike. It's an almost-enough reason."

" – I care about him, goddamnit!" The first person I've cared about since the land mine –

"You care about him?"

"Yes!"

"How much? How much do you care about him?"

"As much as it takes to save him! Why are you playing this game with me?"

"It's not a game, Mike. It's the last part of the test!"

I sat.

Several centuries of silence passed.

"This is about how much I care . . . ?"

Eakins nodded.

"About Matty?"

"About Matty, yes. And . . . a little bit more than that. But let's stay focused on Matty. He's the key."

"Okay. Look. Forget about me. Do with me whatever you want, whatever you think is appropriate. But that kid deserves a chance too. I don't know his IQ. Maybe he isn't a genius. But he hurts just as much. Maybe more. And if you can do something – "

"We can't save them all – "

"We can save this one. I can save him."

"Do you love him?"

"What does love have to do with it – ?"

"Everything."

"I'm not – that way."

"What way? You can't even say the word."

"Queer. There. Happy?"

"Would you be queer if you could?"

"Huh?"

Now it was Eakins turn to look annoyed. "Remember that long list of things I rattled off yesterday?"

"Yes. No. Some of it."

"There was one word I didn't give you. Trans-human."

"Trans-human."

"Right."

"What does it mean?"

"It means – this week – the transitional stage between human and what comes next."

"What comes next?"

"We don't know. We're still inventing it. We won't know until afterwards."

"And being queer is part of it?"

"Yes. And so is being black. And female. And body-modded. And everything else." Eakins leaned forward intensely. "Your body is here in 2032, but your head is still stuck in 1967. If we're going to do anything with you, we have to get your head unstuck. Listen to me. In this age of designer genders, liquid orientation, body-mods, and all the other experiments in human identity, nobody fucking cares anymore about who's doing what and with which and to whom. It's the stupidest thing in the world to worry about, what's happening in someone else's bedroom, especially if there's nothing happening in yours. The past was barbaric, the future doesn't have to be. You want meaning? Here's meaning. Life is too short for bullshit. Life is about what happens in the space between two people – and how much joy you can create for each other. Got that? Good. End of sermon."

"And *that's* trans-human – ?"

"That's one of the side effects. Life isn't about the lines we draw to separate ourselves from each other – it's about the lines we can draw that connect us. The biggest social change of the last fifty years is that even though we still haven't figured out how to get into each other's heads, we're learning how to get into each other's experience so we can have a common ground of being as a civilized society."

"It sounds like a load of psycho-bullshit to me."

"I wasn't asking for an opinion. I was giving you information that could be useful to you. You're the one who wants to go back and save Matty. I'm telling you how – "

"And this is part of it – ?"

"It could be. It's *this* part. The psychometric match is good. If you want to marry him, we'll go get him right now."

"I'm missing something here – ?"

"You're missing *everything*. Start with this. Our charter limits what we can do. Yes, we have a charter. A mission statement. A commitment to a set of values."

"Who are you anyway? Some kind of time police?"

"You should have asked that one at the beginning. No, we're not police. We're independent agents."

"Time vigilantes?"

"Time ravelers. The *real* ravelers, not that pissy little stuff you were doing. What we have is too important to be entrusted to any government or any political movement. Who we are is a commitment to – well, that's part of the test. Figuring out the commitment. Once you figure out the commitment, the rest is obvious."

"Okay. So, right now, I'm committed to saving Matty, and you say – ?"

"We can do that – under our domestic partner plan. We protect the partners of our operatives. We don't extend that coverage to one-night stands."

"He's not a one-night stand. He's – "

"He's what?"

"He's a kid who deserves a chance."

"So give him the chance." Eakins pushed a pillbox across the table at me. I hadn't noticed it until now.

Picked it up. Opened it. Two blue pills. "What will this do?"

"It'll get you a toaster oven."

"Huh?"

"It will shift your sexual orientation. It takes a few weeks. It reorganizes your brain chemistry, rechannels a complex network of pathways, and ultimately expands your repertoire of sexual responsiveness so that same-sex attractions can overwhelm inhibitions, programming, and even hard-wiring. You take one pill, you find new territories in your emotional landscape. You give the other to Matty and it creates a personal pheromonal linkage; the two of you will become aligned. Tuned to each other. You'll bond. It could be intense."

"You're kidding."

"No. I'm not. You won't feel significantly different, but if your relationship includes a potential for sexual expression, this will advance the possibility."

"You're telling me that love is all chemicals?"

"Life is all chemicals. Remember what Brownie said? It's empty and meaningless – except we keep inventing meanings to fill the emptiness. You want some meaning? This will give you plenty of meaning. And happiness too. So what kind of meaning do you want to invent? Do you want to tell me that your life has been all that wonderful up to now?"

I put the pillbox back on the table. "You can't find happiness in pills."

Eakins looked sad.

"I just failed the test, didn't I?"

"Part of it. You asked me what you could do to save Matty. You said you would do anything . . ." He glanced meaningfully at the box.

"I have to think about this."

"A minute ago, you said you'd do anything. I thought you meant it."

"I did, but – "

"You did, but you didn't . . . ?"

Glanced across at him. "Did you ever have to – "

"Yes. I've taken the blue pill. I've taken the pink pill too. And all the others. I've seen it from all sides, if that's what you're asking. And yes, it's a lot of fun, if that's what you want to know. If you're ever going to be any good to us, in your time, in our time, anywhen, you have to climb out of the tank on your own."

I stood up. I went to the balcony. I looked across the basin to where an impossibly huge aircraft was moving gracefully west toward the airport. I turned around and looked at Brownie – implacable and patient. I looked to Eakins. I looked to the door. I looked at the pillbox on the table. Part of me was thinking, I could take the pill. It wouldn't be that hard. It would be the easy way out. The way Eakins put it, I couldn't think of any reason why I shouldn't.

But this couldn't be all there was to the test. This was just this part. I thought about icebergs.

"Okay." I turned around. "I figured it out."

"Go on – "

"Georgia gave me an assignment. Four assignments. I had to prove my willingness to do wetwork. That was the first test of my commitment. And if I'd never said anything, that would have been as much as I'd ever done. But when I said I didn't want to do any more wetwork, that was the next part of the test. Because it's not about being willing to kill – anybody can hire killers. It's about being able to resist the urge to kill. I might be a killer, but today I choose not to kill."

"That's good," Eakins said. "Go on."

"You're not looking for killers. You're looking for lifeguards. And not just ordinary lifeguards who tan well and look good for the babes – you want lifeguards who save lives, not just because they can, but because they care. And this whole test, this business about Matty, is about finding out what kind of a lifeguard I am. Right?"

"That's one way to look at it," Eakins said. "But it's wrong. Remember what you were told – that Matty isn't part of this case? He isn't. He's a whole other case. Your case."

"Yeah. I think I got that part."

Eakins nodded. "So, look – here's the deal. I honestly don't care if you take the pill or not. It's not necessary. We'll send you back, and you can save the kid. All we really needed to know about you is whether or not you would take the pill if you were asked – would you take it if you were ordered, or if it was required, or if it was absolutely essential to the success of the mission. We know you're committed to saving lives. We just need to know how deep you're willing to go."

Nodded. Didn't answer. Not right away. Turned to the window again and stared across the basin, not seeing the airships, not seeing the spires, not seeing the grand swatches of color. Thought about a kiss. Matty's kiss on my cheek. And that moment of . . . well, call it *desire*. Thought about what I might feel if I took the pill. That was the thing. I might actually start *feeling* again. What the fuck. Ugly puppies need love too. It couldn't be any worse than what I wasn't feeling now.

Turned back around. Looked at Eakins. "This is going to be more than a beautiful friendship, isn't it – ?"

"Congratulations," he said. "You're the new harvester."

LA MALCONTENTA

Liz Williams

British writer Liz Williams has had work appear in *Interzone*, *Asimov's Science Fiction*, *Visionary Tongue*, *Terra Incognita*, *The New Jules Verne Adventures*, *Strange Horizons*, *Realms of Fantasy*, and elsewhere. Her short fiction has been collected in *Banquet of the Lords of Night and Other Stories*. Her books include the critically acclaimed novels *The Ghost Sister*, *Empire of Bones*, *The Poison Master*, and *Nine Layers of Sky*. Her most recent novel is *Snake Agent*. Coming up are two new novels, *The Demon and the City* and *Darkland*. She lives in Brighton, England.

Here she takes us to a bizarrely transformed Mars, one of several in this anthology, for a sharp-edged lesson that if a little knowledge can be a dangerous thing, a *lot* of knowledge can be downright deadly . . .

T HE COLDEST NIGHT of the year in Winterstrike is always the night on which the festival of Ombre is held, or Wintervale if you are young and disdain the older dialects. The Matriarchy knows how to predict these things, how to read the subtle signatures in snowdrift and the length of icicles, the messages formed by the freezing of the breath upon the air, the crackling of the icy skin of the great canals.

In the centre of Winterstrike, Mars' first city, in the middle of the meteorite crater that gave the city its name, stands the fortress: a mass of vitrified stone as white as a bone and as red as a still-beating heart. And at the top of the fortress, at the summit of a tower so high that from it one can see out across the basalt walls to the dim, shimmering slopes of Olympus, stands a woman. She is surrounded by four glass windows. She stands before a brazier and beneath a bell. She wears triple gloves: a thin membrane of weedworm silk, then the tanned leather of vulpen skin, then a pair of woollen mittens knitted by a grandmother. In spite of this, and the spitting coals of the brazier, her hands are still cold.

When the day freezes below a certain point, and the signs are relayed to her, she turns, nearly overthrowing the brazier in her haste, and rushes to the windows. She throws them open, letting in a great gust of cold air which makes the coals crackle, then strikes the bell three times. It rings out, fracturing the cold. The woman, Essegui Harn, runs down the stairs to the warm depths of the tower before the echo has even died. One by one, the coals hiss into silence as the bell note fades.

This takes place shortly before dawn, in the blue light before the sun rises. All Winterstrike can hear the bell, except one woman, and except for one woman, all Winterstrike answers. Women throw aside their counterpanes, rush to the basins to wash, and then, still dressed in their night clothes, run upstairs to the attics of mansions, or to the cellars of community shacks, to retrieve costumes forgotten over the course of the previous year, all six hundred and eighty seven days of it. From chest and boxes, they pull masks depicting the creatures of the Age of Children and the Lost Epoch, the long muzzles of cenulae, or the narrow, lovely faces of demotheas and gaezelles. They try them on, laughing at one another, then falling silent as they stand, masked and suddenly foolish above the thick night-dresses.

By Second Hour the robes, too, have been retrieved: confections of lace and metal, leather and stiffened velvet, scarlet and ochre and amethyst, sea-green and indigo and pearl. Above these, the masks no longer appear silly or sinister, but natural and full of grace. Then the women of Winterstrike set them aside and, frantic throughout the short day, they make sweet dumplings and fire-cakes for the night ahead, impatient for the fall of twilight.

Essegui Harn is in equal haste, rushing back to the mansion of Calmaretto, which lies not far from the fortress. Essegui hurries through the streets, pounding snow into ice under her boots and churning it into powder against the swing of the hem of her heavy coat. She is thinking of the festival, of her friend Vanity, whom she is planning to seduce tonight (or be seduced by, even more hopefully). She is trying not to think about her sister.

When she reaches Calmaretto, she does not hesitate but puts her eye to the haunt-lock. The scanner glows with blacklight, an eldritch sparkle, as the lock reads her soul-engrams through the hollow of her eye. The door opens. Essegui steps through into a maelstrom of festivity.

Both her mothers are shouting at one another, at the servants, and then, without even a pause for breath, at Essegui.

". . . there is not enough sugar and only a little haemomon? Why didn't you order more?"

". . . Canteley's best dress has a stain, she refuses to wear it even under her robes . . ."

"And I cannot find the tracing-spoon anywhere!"

Essegui ignores all this. She says, "What about Shorn?"

The silence is immediate and tense. Her mothers stare at Essegui, then at one another. "What about her?"

"You know very well," Essegui says. "You have to let her out. Tonight."

Upstairs, in the windowless heart of Calmaretto, Shorn Harn sits. Her birth name is Leretui, but she has been told that this is no longer her name: she has been shorn of it, and this is the only name she can take from now on. She does not know that it is the day of Ombre, because the sound of the bell rung by her sister has not penetrated the walls of Calmaretto. Nor can she witness the haste and bustle outside in the street, the skaters skimming up and down Canal-the-Less, because she has not been permitted to set foot in a room with windows. She is allowed books, but not writing materials or an antiscribe, in case she finds a way to send a message.

At this thought, Shorn's mouth gives a derisory twist. There would be little point in composing a message, since the one for whom it would be intended cannot read, cannot be taught to read, and is unlikely ever to communicate with someone who can. But Shorn's mothers will not countenance even the slightest possibility that a message might be sent, and thus Shorn is no longer allowed to see her little sister Canteley, as Canteley is young enough to view the scenario as romantic, no matter how many times her mothers have impressed upon her that Shorn is both transgressor and pervert. She is occasionally permitted to see Essegui, since Essegui is of a similar mind to the mothers.

Essegui usually only puts her head around the door once a week, though Shorn finds it difficult to estimate the days. Even so, she is surprised when the door hisses open and Essegui strides through, snow falling in flakes from her outdoor coat.

"Essegui?" Shorn turns her head away and does not rise. "What is it?"

"Ombre falls today. I've told our mothers that you are to be allowed out, when the gongs ring for dusk."

Shorn's mouth falls open and she stares at her sister.

"Out? And they agreed?"

"They hate it. I hate it. But it is your last remaining legal right, ancient custom, and we have no choice."

Shorn says, slowly and disbelieving, "I am to be allowed out? In the mask-and-gown?"

Essegui leans forward, hands on either arm of the chair, and speaks clearly. "Understand this. If you use the mask-and-gown as a cover to flee the city, our mothers will go to the Matriarchy and ask for a squadron of scissor-women to hunt you down. The city will, of course, be closed from dusk onward, and they will know if anyone tries to leave. Or if *anything* tries to get in."

"I will not try to leave," Shorn whispers. "Where would I go?"

"To that which brought you to this plight?"

Shorn gives a small, hard laugh like a bark. "Where indeed?"

"To the mountains, in winter? You would die of cold before you got half way across the Demnotian Plain. And the mountains, what then? Men-remnants would tear you to pieces and devour you before you had a chance to find it." Essegui grimaces. "Perhaps it would even be one of them. I've heard that all women look alike to them."

Shorn lowers her gaze. There is a moment's silence. "I have told you that I will not try."

"There is a mask waiting for you," Essegui says. She turns on her heel and is gone through the door, leaving it open behind her.

Shorn does not leave the chamber immediately, but stares at the open door. She has been dreaming about this day ever since the evening of her imprisonment, six hundred and eighty seven days ago. Ombre then was like every other festival, a chance for fun and celebration, supposedly. She had thought no further than a possible assignation with Celvani Morel, an old college friend, recently detached. She wonders now whether she hoped that it would fill the emptiness within. She did not expect to meet what stepped from under the bridge of the Curve.

The open door seems as dark, but Shorn, once more, hesitates for only a moment before stepping through.

The mask is one that she remembers from her childhood: the round, bland face of a crater cat. It is a child's mask: for the last few years, Canteley has been wearing it. Now, however, it is the only one left in the box. Shorn pulls the gown – a muted red-and-black brocade – over her head and then, slowly, puts the mask on. The cat beams at her from the mirror; she looks like a too-tall child, no longer the woman they call the Malcontent. She twitches aside the fold of a sash, but the box is empty. There is no sign of the other mask: the long, narrow head, the colour of polished bone, mosaiced with cracks and fractures. She searches through the draperies, but there is no sign of it. She tells herself that she feels nothing.

As she turns to go downstairs, a gaezelle dances in through the door. "Tui, is that you? Is it?" The gaezelle flings her arms around Shorn and holds on tight.

"It's me. But don't call me Tui." It sounds as though she's spitting. "That's not my name any more." Canteley has grown over the last months: she is almost as tall as her sister now. Shorn has nearly forgotten the piercing quality of her voice, shrill as a water-whistle. She feels as though an icy mass has lodged deep in her own throat.

"Are you coming? Essegui said our mothers are letting you out for the Wintervale. Is it true? You should run away, Tui. You should try to find it."

"I won't be going away, Canteley," Shorn says, but as she says this she feels as though the walls are falling in on her and she knows that she lies.

"Is it true what they say, that the vulpen steal your soul? That they entrance you so that you can't think of anything else?"

"No, that isn't true," Shorn says, but she is not really sure any more. She takes her sister's hand and leads her through the door.

I won't be going away. But better the devouring mountains than the windowless room. Better the quick, clean cold. She should never have let them shut her in, but she had been too dazed, with grief and bewilderment and incomprehension. Now, she has had time to think, to become as clear as ice. "Canteley, I'll talk to you later." She gives her sister a swift hug. "Go downstairs. I'll join you in a minute." Once her sister has gone, she takes a pair of skates from the wall and stands looking down at the long, curved blades. Then, holding the skates by their laces, she follows her sister down the stairs.

They are all standing in the doorway, staring upward: Essegui, Canteley, and her mothers. It is a moment before Shorn is able to differentiate between the three adults. Essegui stands a little apart, legs braced beneath the intricate folds of the gown. Of the mothers, Thera is the shorter, and so it must be Alleghetta behind the demothea's mask. Shorn looks from one to the other before coming down the stairs. No one speaks. As Shorn reaches the last step, her mothers turn and push open the double doors that lead out onto the steps to the street. Winter fills the hallway. The gongs ring out in the twilight, filling the street and the house with sound. It seems very loud to Shorn, used as she is to the silence of the windowless room.

The mothers grasp Canteley firmly by each hand and pull her through the doors, so decisively that Essegui is the only one who has time to turn back, a flickering twitch of her head in the direction of Shorn. She is wearing a cenulae's mask: a pointed, fragile countenance, painted in green. She will, Shorn thinks, see only the bland cat face smiling back at her. Then Shorn herself runs across the black-and-white mosaic of the hall floor, through the scents of snow and fire-cake and polish, out through the doors and into the street. Then she is standing uncertainly in the snow.

Canal-the-Less, on which Calmaretto stands, is frozen solid and filled with skaters bearing snow-lamps. They weave in and out of one another with insect-skill. Shorn, breath coming in short gasps in the unaccustomed cold, is tempted to take the round cat's face from her own and fling it into the drifts, but she does not. She ties on the skates with trembling hands and lowers herself over the bank of the canal onto the ice. Then she is off, winging down Canal-the-Less toward the culvert that leads to the Grand Channel.

The Channel itself is thronged with skaters, milling about before the start of the procession. Shorn twists this way and that, keeping to the side of the Channel at first, then moving out to where the light is less certain. The great houses that line the Channel are blazing with snow-lamps and torches, mirrored in the ice so that Shorn glides across a glassy, shimmering expanse. She is heading for the Curve and the labyrinth of canals that lead to the Great North Gate.

Behind her, the crowds of skaters fall away. Ahead, she can see a mass of red gowns, the start of the procession, led by the Matriarchs. Her mothers, not quite so elevated, will be just behind, amid their peers. A pair of scissor-women speed by, the raw mouths of holographic wounds displayed across the surface of their armour. They are unmasked. Their faces are as sharp as their blades and Shorn flinches behind the cat-face, until she realises that to them, she is nothing more than a tall child, and not the malcontent of Calmaretto. But she watches them go all the same, then slinks from the Grand Channel and into the maze.

It is much quieter here. The houses along the waterways have already emptied and there are only a few stray women lingering beneath the lamps or the bridges, waiting no doubt for assignations. Shorn keeps her masked head down, speeding toward the Great North Gate.

As she reaches the turning into the stretch of water known as the Curve, she hears a shout go up from the direction of the Grand Channel: the procession has begun. Shorn skates on, though the long months of forced inactivity have taken their toll. Her calves and thighs are burning. She does not want to think of what will befall her if she makes it past the North Gate: the vast expanse of snow covered plain, the mountains beyond. She hopes only that it will be a swift death and that she makes it out of Winterstrike. It will be her revenge on the city and on Calmaretto, to die beyond its walls. She knows that this is not rational, but she left reason by a canal bank, a year before.

In summer, the Curve is lined with cafes and weedwood trees, black-branched, with the yellow flower balls spilling pollen into the water until it lies there as heavy as oil, perfuming the air with a subtle musk. Now, the cafes are cold and closed – all the trade will have moved down the Channel for the night.

Shorn's heart pounds with exertion and memory. It was here, a year ago, on this stretch of the Curve just beyond the thin-arched bridge, that something – someone, Shorn corrects herself, angry at her use of Essegui's term – drifted from the darkness to stand as still as snow.

Shorn glides to an involuntary halt. She has replayed this scene over and over in her mind: the figure outlined against the black wall and pale ice, the head swivelling to meet her gaze, the frame shifting under the layers of robes and the sudden realisation that this was not just another reveller, but real: the mild dark eyes set deep in the hollow of the skull, the ivory barbs of its teeth. What she had taken for the curve of skate blades beneath the hem of the robe was its feet. One of the Changed, a vulpen, from the mountains: the genetically-altered remnant of a man.

They are said to tear women limb from limb in vengeance for old woes: the phasing out of the male by Matriarchal geneticists. But this one merely looked at her, and held out its hand. She should have fled; instead, she took its two long fingers in her own. It led her along the Curve, skating alongside with human skill. Nothing else befell her. The vulpen gazed at her as they moved, blinking its mild eyes. It said: *I have been waiting for one such as you.*

And as it spoke, they turned the bend and ran into a squadron of scissor-women. Unlike Shorn, the warriors took only a moment to realise what was before them. They skated forward, scissors snicking. One of them seized Shorn, who cried "No!" and struggled in the warrior's grasp. The other three surrounded the vulpen, who suddenly was springing upward to land on the bank on all fours, blade-feet skidding, casting the disguising robes away to reveal a pale, narrow form, the vertebral tail whipping around. Its erection resembled a bone, and when they saw it, the scissor-women shrieked in fury. Then it was gone, into the snowy night.

They took Shorn back to Calmaretto, on a chain, and sat with her until her family returned, laughing and exhausted, at dawn.

Remembering this now, Shorn is moved to wonder if any of it was even real. It seems long ago and far away – and then it is as though she has stepped sideways into her own memory, for the figure of a vulpen once more skates from beneath the arch. It holds out its hands, but does not attempt to touch her. Shorn skates with it, back along the Curve in a haze and a dream, flying through the winter dark, until they are once more out onto the Grand Channel.

The procession has passed. Circling, whirling, Shorn and the vulpen dance out to the middle of the Grand Channel and now Shorn is beginning to understand that this is, after all, nothing more than a woman in a mask, just as she is. Thoughts of flight, of dying beyond Winterstrike, skate through her head and are gone, leaving loss and yearning behind.

She lets the woman in the vulpen's mask lead her back to Calmaretto. As they step through the door, the woman pulls off the mask and Shorn sees that it is Essegui.

"I could not let you go," Essegui says, and Shorn, exhausted, merely nods. Essegui leads her up the stairs to the windowless room and closes the door behind her.

In the morning, Winterstrike is quiet. Mask ribbons litter the ice and the snow is trodden into filth. Essegui, waking late, head ringing with explanations that she will have to make to Vanity, goes to the heart of the house and opens the door of the windowless room.

Shorn sits where her sister left her, upright, the cat's face beaming.

"Shorn?" her sister says. There is no reply. Essegui goes haltingly forward and touches her sister's shoulder, thinking that she sleeps. But the brocade gown is stiff and unyielding, moulded in the form of a woman's figure. Essegui tugs at the cat's mask, but it will not budge. It remains fixed, staring sightlessly across the windowless room, and slowly Essegui steps away, and once more closes the door.

THE CHILDREN OF TIME

Stephen Baxter

Like many of his colleagues here at the beginning of a new century, British writer Stephen Baxter has been engaged for more than a decade now with the task of revitalizing and reinventing the "hard-science" story for a new generation of readers, producing work on the cutting edge of science that bristles with weird, new ideas and often takes place against vistas of almost outrageously cosmic scope.

Baxter made his first sale to *Interzone* in 1987, and since then has become one of that magazine's most frequent contributors, as well as making sales to *Asimov's Science Fiction*, *Science Fiction Age*, *Analog*, *Zenith*, *New Worlds*, and elsewhere. He's one of the most prolific writers in SF, and is rapidly becoming one of the most popular and acclaimed of them as well. In 2001, he appeared on the final Hugo ballot twice, and won both *Asimov's* Readers Award and *Analog's* Analytical Laboratory Award – one of the few writers ever to win both awards in the same year. Baxter's first novel, *Raft*, was released in 1991 to a wide and enthusiastic response, and was rapidly followed by other well-received novels such as *Timelike Infinity*, *Anti-Ice*, *Flux*, and the H. G. Wells pastiche – a sequel to *The Time Machine* – *The Time Ships*, which won both the John W. Campbell Award and the Philip K. Dick Award. His other books include the novels *Voyage*, *Titan*, *Moonseed*, *Silverhair*, *Manifold: Time*, *Manifold: Space*, *Evolution*, *Coalescent*, *Exultant*, and two novels in collaboration with Arthur C. Clarke, *The Light of Other Days* and *Time's Eve: A Time Odyssey*. His short fiction has been collected in *Vacuum Diagrams*, *Traces*, and *Hunters of Pangaea*, and he has released a chapbook novella, *Mayflower II*. His most recent books are the new novels *Exultant*, *Transcendent*, and, in collaboration with Arthur C. Clarke, *Time's Eye: a Time Odyssey*. Coming up are the new novels *Emperor* and *Resplendent*.

Here's a dazzlingly imaginative story that starts after what most of us would consider "The End of the World," and goes on from there to paint a vivid portrait of the next several hundred million years of human history . . .

I

JAAL HAD ALWAYS BEEN fascinated by the ice on the horizon. Even now, beyond the smoke of the evening hearth, he could see that line of pure bone white, sharper than a stone blade's cut, drawn across the edge of the world.

It was the end of the day, and a huge sunset was staining the sky. Alone, restless, he walked a few paces away from the rich smoky pall, away from the smell of broiling raccoon meat and bubbling goat fat, the languid talk of the adults, the eager play of the children.

The ice was always there on the northern horizon, always out of reach no matter how hard you walked across the scrubby grassland. He knew why. The ice cap was retreating, dumping its pure whiteness into the meltwater streams, exposing land crushed and gouged and strewn with vast boulders. So while you walked toward it, the ice was marching away from you.

And now the gathering sunset was turning the distant ice pink. The clean geometric simplicity of the landscape drew his soul; he stared, entranced.

Jaal was eleven years old, a compact bundle of muscle. He was dressed in layers of clothing, sinew-sewn from scraped goat skin and topped by a heavy coat of rabbit fur. On his head was a hat made by his father from the skin of a whole raccoon, and on his feet he wore the skin of pigeons, turned inside-out and the feathers coated with grease. Around his neck was a string of pierced cat teeth.

Jaal looked back at his family. There were a dozen of them, parents and children, aunts and uncles, nephews and nieces, and one grandmother, worn down, aged forty-two. Except for the very smallest children, everybody moved slowly, obviously weary. They had walked a long way today.

He knew he should go back to the fire and help out, do his duty, find firewood or skin a rat. But every day was like this. Jaal had ancient, unpleasant memories from when he was very small, of huts burning, people screaming and fleeing. Jaal and his family had been walking north ever since, looking for a new home. They hadn't found it yet.

Jaal spotted Sura, good-humoredly struggling to get a filthy skin coat off the squirming body of her little sister. Sura, Jaal's second cousin, was two years older than him. She had a limpid, liquid ease of movement in everything she did.

She saw Jaal looking at her and arched an eyebrow. He blushed, hot, and turned away to the north. The ice was a much less complicated companion than Sura.

He saw something new.

As the angle of the sun continued to change, the light picked out something on the ground. It was a straight line, glowing red in the light of the sun, like an echo of the vast edge of the ice itself. But this line was close, only a short walk from here, cutting through hummocks and scattered boulders. He had to investigate.

With a guilty glance back at his family, he ran away, off to the north, his pigeon-skin boots carrying him silently over the hard ground. The straight-edge feature was further away than it looked, and as he became frustrated he ran faster. But then he came on it. He stumbled to a halt, panting.

It was a ridge as high as his knees – a ridge of stone, but nothing like the ice-carved boulders and shattered gravel that littered the rest of the landscape. Though its top was worn and broken, its sides were flat, smoother than any stone he had touched before, and the sunlight filled its creamy surface with color.

Gingerly he climbed on the wall to see better. The ridge of stone ran off to left and right, to east and west – and then it turned sharp corners, to run north, before turning back on itself again. There was a pattern here, he saw. This stone ridge traced a straight-edged frame on the ground.

And there were more ridges; the shadows cast by the low sun picked out the stone tracings clearly. The land to the north of here was covered by a tremendous rectangular scribble that went on as far as he could see. All this was made by people. He knew this immediately, without question.

In fact this had been a suburb of Chicago. Most of the city had been scraped clean by the advancing ice, but the foundations of this suburb, fortuitously, had been flooded and frozen in before the glaciers came. These ruins were already a hundred thousand years old.

"Jaal. Jaal . . ." His mother's voice carried to him like the cry of a bird.

He couldn't bear to leave what he had found. He stood on the eroded wall and let his mother come to him.

She was weary, grimy, stressed. "Why must you do this? Don't you *know* the cats hunt in twilight?"

He flinched from the disappointment in her eyes, but he couldn't contain his excitement. "Look what I found, Mother!"

She stared around. Her face showed incomprehension, disinterest. "What is it?"

His imagination leapt, fueled by wonder, and he tried to make her see what he saw. "Maybe once these rock walls were tall, tall as the ice itself. Maybe people lived here in great heaps, and the smoke of their fires rose up to the sky. Mother, will we come to live here again?"

"Perhaps one day," his mother said at random, to hush him.

The people never would return. By the time the returning ice had shattered their monocultural, over-extended technological civilization, people had exhausted the Earth of its accessible deposits of iron ore and coal and oil and other resources. People would survive: smart, adaptable, they didn't need cities for that. But with nothing but their most ancient technologies of stone and fire, they could never again conjure up the towers of Chicago. Soon even Jaal, distracted by the fiery eyes of Sura, would forget this place existed.

But for now he longed to explore. "Let me go on. Just a little further!"

"No," his mother said gently. "The adventure's over. It's time to go. Come now." And she put her arm around his shoulders, and led him home.

II

Urlu crawled toward the river. The baked ground was hard under her knees and hands, and stumps of burned-out trees and shrubs scraped her flesh. There was no green here, nothing grew, and nothing moved save a few flecks of ash disturbed by the low breeze.

She was naked, sweating, her skin streaked by charcoal. Her hair was a mat, heavy with dust and grease. In one hand she carried a sharpened stone. She was eleven years old.

She wore a string of pierced teeth around her neck. The necklace was a gift from her grandfather, Pala, who said the teeth were from an animal called a rabbit. Urlu had never seen a rabbit. The last of them had died in the Burning, before she was born, along with the rats and the raccoons, all the small mammals that had long ago survived the ice with mankind. So there would be no more rabbit teeth. The necklace was precious.

The light brightened. Suddenly there was a shadow beneath her, her own form cast upon the darkened ground. She threw herself flat in the dirt. She wasn't used to shadows. Cautiously she glanced over her shoulder, up at the sky.

All her life a thick lid of ash-laden cloud had masked the sky. But for the last few days it had been breaking up, and today the cloud had disintegrated further. And now, through high drifting cloud, she saw a disc, pale and gaunt.

It was the sun. She had been told its name, but had never quite believed in it. Now it was revealed, and Urlu helplessly stared up at its geometric purity.

She heard a soft voice call warningly. "Urlu!" It was her mother.

It was no good to be daydreaming about the sky. She had a duty to fulfill, down here in the dirt. She turned and crawled on.

She reached the bank. The river, thick with blackened dirt and heavy with debris, rolled sluggishly. It was so wide that in the dim light of noon she could barely see the far side. In fact this was the Seine, and the charred ground covered traces of what had once been Paris. It made no difference where she was. The whole Earth was like this, all the same.

To Urlu's right, downstream, she saw hunters, pink faces smeared with dirt peering from the ruined vegetation. The weight of their expectation pressed heavily on her.

She took her bit of chipped stone, and pressed its sharpest edge against the skin of her palm. It had to be her. The people believed that the creatures of the water were attracted by the blood of a virgin. She was afraid of the pain to come, but she had no choice; if she didn't go through with the cut one of the men would come and do it for her, and that would hurt far more.

But she heard a wail, a cry of loss and sorrow, rising like smoke into the dismal air. It was coming from the camp. The faces along the bank turned, distracted. Then, one by one, the hunters slid back into the ruined undergrowth.

Urlu, hugely relieved, turned away from the debris-choked river, her stone tucked safely in her hand.

The camp was just a clearing in the scorched ground-cover, with a charcoal fire burning listlessly in the hearth. Beside the fire an old man lay on a rough pallet of earth and scorched brush, gaunt, as naked and filthy as the rest. His eyes were wide, rheumy, and he stared at the sky. Pala, forty-five years old, was Urlu's grandfather. He was dying, eaten from within by something inside his belly.

He was tended by a woman who knelt in the dirt beside him. She was his oldest daughter, Urlu's aunt. The grime on her face was streaked by tears. "He's frightened," said the aunt. "It's finishing him off."

Urlu's mother asked, "Frightened of what?"

The aunt pointed into the sky.

The old man had reason to be frightened of strange lights in the sky. He had been just four years old when a greater light had come to Earth.

After Jaal's time, the ice had returned a dozen times more before retreating for good. After that, people rapidly cleared the land of the legacy of the ice: descendants of cats and rodents and birds, grown large and confident in the temporary absence of humanity. Then people hunted and farmed, built up elaborate networks of trade and culture, and developed exquisite technologies of wood and stone and bone. There was much evolutionary churning in the depths of the sea, out of reach of mankind. But people were barely touched by time, for there was no need for them to change.

This equable afternoon endured for thirty million years. The infant Pala's parents had sung him songs unimaginably old.

But then had come the comet's rude incursion. Nearly a hundred million years after the impactor that had terminated the summer of the dinosaurs, Earth had been due another mighty collision.

Pala and his parents, fortuitously close to a cave-ridden mountain, had endured the fires, the rain of molten rock, the long dust-shrouded winter. People survived, as they had lived through lesser cataclysms since the ice. And with their ingenuity and adaptability and generalist ability to eat almost anything, they had already begun to spread once more over the ruined lands.

Once it had been thought that human survival would depend on planting colonies on other worlds, for Earth would always be prone to such disasters. But people had never ventured far from Earth: there was nothing out there; the stars had always remained resolutely silent. And though since the ice their numbers had never been more than a few million, people were too numerous and too widespread to be eliminated even by a comet's deadly kiss. It was easy to kill a lot of people. It was very hard to kill them all.

As it happened old Pala was the last human alive to remember the world before the Burning. With him died memories thirty million years deep. In the morning they staked out his body on a patch of high ground.

The hunting party returned to the river, to finish the job they had started. This time there was no last-minute reprieve for Urlu. She slit open her palm, and let her blood run into the murky river water. Its crimson was the brightest color in the whole of this grey-black world.

Urlu's virginal state made no difference to the silent creature who slid through the water, but she was drawn by the scent of blood. Another of the planet's great survivors, she had ridden out the Burning buried in deep mud, and fed without distaste on the scorched remains washed into her river. Now she swam up toward the murky light.

All her life Urlu had eaten nothing but snakes, cockroaches, scorpions, spiders, maggots, termites. That night she feasted on crocodile meat.

By the morning she was no longer a virgin. She didn't enjoy it much, but at least it was her choice. And at least she wouldn't have to go through any more blood-letting.

III

The catamaran glided toward the beach, driven by the gentle current of the shallow sea and the muscles of its crew. When it ran aground the people splashed into water that came up to their knees, and began to unload weapons and food. The sun hung bright and hot in a cloudless blue dome of a sky, and the people, small and lithe, were surrounded by shining clouds of droplets as they worked. Some of them had their favorite snakes wrapped around their necks.

Cale, sitting on the catamaran, clung to its seaweed trunks. Looking out to sea, he could spot the fine dark line that was the floating community where he had been born. This was an age of warmth, of high seas that had flooded the edges of the continents, and most people on Earth made their living from the rich produce of coral reefs and other sun-drenched shallow-water ecosystems. Cale longed to go back to the rafts, but soon he must walk on dry land, for the first time in his life. He was eleven years old.

Cale's mother, Lia, splashed through the water to him. Her teeth shone white in her dark face. "You will never be a man if you are so timid as this." And she grabbed him, threw him over her shoulder, ran through the shallow water to the beach, and dumped him in the sand. "There!" she cried. "You are the first to set foot here, the first of all!"

Everybody laughed, and Cale, winded, resentful, blushed helplessly.

For some time Cale's drifting family had been aware of the line on the horizon. They had prepared their gifts of sea fruit and carved coral, and rehearsed the songs they would sing, and carved their weapons, and here they were. They thought this was an island full of people. They were wrong. This was no island, but a continent.

Since the recovery of the world from Urlu's great Burning, there had been time enough for the continents' slow tectonic dance to play out. Africa had collided softly with Europe, Australia had kissed Asia, and Antarctica had come spinning up from the south pole. It was these great geographical changes – together with a slow, relentless heating-up of the sun – which had given the world its long summer.

While the rafts had dreamed over fecund seas, seventy million years had worn away. But even over such a tremendous interval, people were much the same as they had always been.

And now here they were, on the shore of Antarctica – and Cale was indeed the first of all.

Unsteadily he got to his feet. For a moment the world seemed to tip and rock beneath him. But it was not the world that tipped, he understood, but his own imagination, shaped by a life on the rafts.

The beach stretched around him, sloping up to a line of tall vegetation. He had never seen anything like it. His fear and resentment quickly subsided, to be replaced by curiosity.

The landing party had forgotten him already. They were gathering driftwood for a fire and unloading coils of meat – snake meat, from the fat, stupid, domesticated descendants of one of the few animals to survive the firestorm of Urlu's day. They would have a feast, and they would get drunk, and they would sleep; only tomorrow would they begin to explore.

Cale discovered he didn't want to wait that long. He turned away from the sea, and walked up the shallow slope of the beach.

A line of hard trunks towered above his head, smooth-hulled. These "trees," as his father had called them, were in fact a kind of grass, something like bamboo. Cale came from a world of endless flatness; to him these trees were mighty constructs indeed. And sunlight shone through the trees, from an open area beyond.

A few paces away a freshwater stream decanted onto the beach and trickled to the sea. Cale could see that it came from a small gully that cut through the bank of trees. It was a way through, irresistible.

The broken stones of the gully's bed stung his feet, and sharp branches scraped at his skin. The rocks stuck in the gully walls were a strange mix: big boulders set in a greyish clay, down to pebbles small enough to have fit in Cale's hand, all jammed together. Even the bedrock was scratched and grooved, as if some immense, spiky fish had swum this way.

Here in this tropical rainforest, Cale was surrounded by the evidence of ice.

He soon reached the open area behind the trees. It was just a glade a few paces across, opened up by the fall of one mighty tree. Cale stepped forward, making for a patch of green. But iridescent wings beat, and a fat, segmented body soared up from the green, and Cale stumbled to a halt. The insect was huge, its body longer than he was tall. Now more vast dragonflies rose up, startled, huddling for protection. A sleeker form, its body yellow-banded, came buzzing out of the trees. It was a remote descendant of a wasp, a solitary predator. It assaulted the swarming dragonflies, ripping through shimmering wings. All this took place over Cale's head in a cloud of flapping and buzzing. It was too strange to be frightening.

He was distracted by a strange squirming at his feet. The patch of green from which he had disturbed the first dragonfly was itself moving, flowing over the landscape as if liquid. It was actually a crowd of creatures, a mass of wriggling worms. From the tops of tottering piles of small bodies, things like eyes blinked.

Such sights were unique to Antarctica. There was no other place like this, anywhere on Earth.

When its ice melted away, the bare ground of Antarctica became an arena for life. The first colonists had been blown on the wind from over the sea: vegetation, insects, birds. But this was not an age for birds, or indeed mammals. As the world's systems compensated for the slow heating of the sun, carbon dioxide, the main greenhouse gas, was drawn down into the sea and the rocks, and the air became oxygen-rich. The insects used this heady fuel to grow huge, and predatory wasps and cockroaches as bold as rats made short work of Antarctica's flightless birds.

And there had been time for much more dramatic evolutionary shifts, time for whole phyla to be remodeled. The squirming multiple organism that fled from Cale's approach was a descendant of the siphonophores, colonial creatures of the sea like Portuguese men o' war. Endlessly adaptable, hugely ecologically inventive, since colonizing the land these compound creatures had occupied fresh water, the ground, the branches of the grass-trees, even the air.

Cale sensed something of the transient strangeness of what he saw. Antarctica, empty of humans, had been the stage for Earth's final gesture of evolutionary inventiveness. But relentless tectonic drift had at last brought Antarctica within reach of the ocean-going communities who sailed over the flooded remnants of India, and the great experiment was about to end. Cale gazed around, eyes wide, longing to discover more.

A coral-tipped spear shot past his head, and he heard a roar. He staggered back, shocked.

A patch of green ahead of him split and swarmed away, and a huge form emerged. Grey-skinned, supported on two narrow forelegs and a powerful articulated tail, this monster seemed to be all head. A spear stuck out from its neck. The product of another transformed phylum, this was a chondrichthyan, a distant relation of a shark. The beast opened a mouth like a cavern, and blood-soaked breath blasted over Cale.

Lia was at Cale's side. "Come on." She hooked an arm under his shoulders and dragged him away.

Back on the beach, munching on snake meat, Cale soon got over his shock. Everybody made a fuss of him as he told his tales of giant wasps and the huge land-shark. At that moment he could not imagine ever returning to the nightmares of the forest.

But of course he would. And in little more than a thousand years his descendants, having burned their way across Antarctica, accompanied by their hunting snakes and their newly domesticated attack-wasps, would hunt down the very last of the land-sharks, and string its teeth around their necks.

IV

Tura and Bel, sister and brother, grew up in a world of flatness, on a shoreline between an endless ocean and a land like a tabletop. But in the distance there were mountains, pale cones turned purple by the ruddy mist. As long as she could remember, Tura had been fascinated by the mountains. She longed to walk to them – even, she fantasized, to climb them.

But how could she ever reach them? Her people lived at the coast, feeding on the soft-fleshed descendants of neotenous crabs. The land was a plain of red sand, littered with gleaming salt flats, where nothing could live. The mountains were forever out of reach.

Then, in Tura's eleventh year, the land turned unexpectedly green.

The aging world was still capable of volcanic tantrums. One such episode, the eruption of a vast basaltic flood, had pumped carbon dioxide into the air. As flowers in the desert had once waited decades for the rains, so their remote descendants waited for such brief volcanic summers to make them bloom.

Tura and her brother hatched the plan between them. They would never get this chance again; the greening would be gone in a year, perhaps never to return in their lifetimes. No adult would ever have approved. But no adult need know.

And so, very early one morning, they slipped away from the village. Wearing nothing but kilts woven from dried sea grass, their favorite shell necklaces around their necks, they looked very alike. As they ran they laughed, excited by their adventure, and their blue eyes shone against the rusted crimson of the landscape.

Bel and Tura lived on what had once been the western coast of North America – but, just as in Urlu's dark time of global catastrophe, it didn't really matter where you lived. For this was the age of a supercontinent.

The slow convergence of the continents had ultimately produced a unity that mirrored a much earlier mammoth assemblage, broken up before the dinosaurs evolved. While vast unending storms roamed the waters of the world-ocean, New Pangaea's interior collapsed to a desiccated wasteland, and people drifted to the mouths of the great rivers, and to the sea coasts. This grand coalescence was accompanied by the solemn drumbeat of extinction events; each time the world recovered, though each time a little less vigorously than before.

The supercontinent's annealing took two hundred million years. And since then, another two hundred million years had already gone by. But people lived much as they always had.

Tura and Bel, eleven-year-old twins, knew nothing of this. They were young, and so was their world; it was ever thus. And today, especially, was a day of wonder, as all around them plants, gobbling carbon dioxide, fired packets of spores through the air, and insects scrambled in once-in-a-life-time quests to propagate.

As the sun climbed the children tired, their pace falling, and the arid air sucked the sweat off their bodies. But at last the mountains came looming out of the dusty air. These worn hills were ancient, a relic of the formation of New Pangaea. But to Tura and Bel, standing before their scree-covered lower slopes, they were formidable heights indeed.

Then Tura saw a splash of green and brown, high on a slope. Curiosity sparked. Without thinking about it she began to climb. Bel, always more nervous, would not follow.

Though at first the slope was so gentle it was no more than a walk, Tura was soon higher than she had ever been in her life. On she climbed, until her walk gave way to an instinctive scramble on all fours. Her heart hammering, she kept on. All around her New Pangaea unfolded, a sea of Mars-red dust worn flat by time.

At last she reached the green. It was a clump of trees, shadowed by the mountain from the dust-laden winds and nourished by water from sub-surface aquifers. Instinctively Tura rubbed her hand over smooth, sturdy trunks. She had never seen trees before.

As the sun brightened, Earth's systems compensated by drawing down carbon dioxide from the air. But this was a process with a limit: even in Jaal's time the remnant carbon dioxide had been a trace. Already the planet had shed many rich ecosystems – tundra, forests, grasslands, meadows, mangrove swamps. Soon the carbon dioxide concentration would drop below a certain critical level, after which only a fraction of plants would be able to photosynthesize. The human population, already only a million strung out around the world's single coastline, would implode to perhaps ten thousand.

People would survive. They always had. But these trees, in whose cool shade Tura stood, were among the last in the world.

She peered up at branches with sparse crowns of spiky leaves, far above her head. There might be fruit up there, or water to be had in the leaves. But it was impossible; she could not climb past the smoothness of the lower trunk.

When she looked down Bel's upturned face was a white dot. The day was advancing; as the sun rode higher the going across the dry dust would be even more difficult. With regret she began her scrambled descent to the ground.

As she lived out her life on the coast of Pangaea, Tura never forgot her brief adventure. And when she thought of the trees her hands and feet itched, her body recalling ape dreams abandoned half a billion years before.

V

Ruul was bored.

All through the echoing caverns the party was in full swing. By the light of their hearths and rush torches people played and danced, talked and laughed, drank and fought, and the much-evolved descendants of snakes and wasps curled affectionately around the ankles of their owners. It was a Thousand-Day festival. In a world forever cut off from the daylight, subterranean humans pale as worms marked time by how they slept and woke, and counted off the days of their lives on their fingers.

Everyone was having fun – everyone but Ruul. When his mother was too busy to notice, he crept away into the dark.

Some time ago, restlessly exploring the edge of the inhabited cave, where tunnels and boreholes stretched on into the dark, he had found a chimney, a crack in the limestone. It looked as if you could climb up quite a way. And when he shielded his eyes, it looked to him as if there was light up there, light of a strange ruddy hue. There might be another group somewhere in the caverns above, he thought. Or it might be something stranger yet, something beyond his imagination.

Now, in the dim light of the torches, he explored the chimney wall. Lodging his fingers and toes in crevices, he began to climb.

He was escaping the party. Eleven years old, neither child nor adult, he just didn't fit, and he petulantly wished the festival would go away. But as he ascended into profound silence the climb itself consumed all his attention, and the why of it faded from his mind.

His people, cavern-bound for uncounted generations, were good at rock-climbing. They lived in caverns in deep limestone karsts, laid down in long-vanished shallow seas. Once these hollows had hosted ecosystems full of the much-evolved descendants of lizards, snakes, scorpions, cockroaches, even sharks and crocodiles. The extreme and unchanging conditions of Pangaea had encouraged intricacy and inter-dependency. The people, retreating underground, had allowed fragments of these extraordinary biotas to survive.

Soon Ruul climbed up out of the limestone into a softer sandstone, poorly cemented. It was easier to find crevices here. The crimson light from above was bright enough to show him details of the rock through which he was passing. There was layer upon layer of it, he saw, and it had a repetitive pattern, streaks of darkness punctuated by lumpy nodules. When he touched one of the nodules, he found a blade surface so sharp he might have cut his fingers. It was a stone axe – made, used, and dropped long ago, and buried somehow in the sediments that had made this sandstone. Growing more curious, he explored the dark traces. They crumbled when he dug into them with a fingernail, and he could smell ash, as fresh as if a fire had just burned here. The dark layers were hearths.

He was climbing through strata of hearths and stone tools, thousands of layers all heaped up on top of one another and squashed down into the rock. People must have lived in this place a very long time. He was oppressed by a huge weight of time, and of changelessness.

But he was distracted by a set of teeth he found, small, triangular, razor-edged. They had holes drilled in them. He carefully prized these out of the rock and put them in a pouch; perhaps he would make a necklace of them later.

With aching fingertips and toes, he continued his climb.

Unexpectedly, he reached the top of the chimney. It opened out into a wider space, a cave perhaps, filled with that ruddy light. He hoisted himself up the last short way, swung his legs out onto the floor above, and stood up.

And he was stunned.

He was standing on flat ground, a plain that seemed to go on forever. It was covered in dust, very red, so fine it stuck to the sweat on his legs. He turned slowly around. If this was the floor of a cave – well, it was a cave with no walls. And the roof above must be far away too, so far he could not see it; above him was nothing but a dome of darkness. He had no word for *sky*. And in one direction, facing him, something lifted over the edge of the world. It was a ruddy disc, perfectly circular, just a slice of it protruding over the dead-flat horizon. It was the source of the crimson light, and he could feel its searing heat.

Ruul inhabited a convoluted world of caverns and chimneys; he had never seen anything like the purity of this utterly flat plain, the perfectly circular arc of that bow of light. The clean geometric simplicity of the landscape drew his soul; he stared, entranced.

Three hundred million years after the life and death of Tura and Bel, this was what Earth had become. The sediments on which Ruul stood were the ruins of the last mountains. The magmatic currents of a cooling world had not been able to break up the new supercontinent, as they had the first. Meanwhile the sun's relentless warming continued. By now only microbes inhabited the equatorial regions, while at the poles a few hardy, tough-skinned plants were browsed by sluggish animals heavily armored against the heat. Earth was already losing its water, and Pangaea's shoreline was rimmed by brilliant-white salt flats.

But the boy standing on the eroded-flat ground was barely changed from his unimaginably remote ancestors, from Tura and Cale and Urlu and even Jaal. It had never been necessary for humans to evolve significantly, for they always adjusted their environment so they didn't have to – and in the process stifled evolutionary innovation.

It was like this everywhere. After the emergence of intelligence, the story of any biosphere tended to get a lot simpler. It was a major reason for the silence of the stars.

But on Earth a long story was ending. In not many generations from now, Ruul's descendants would succumb; quietly baked in their desiccating caves, they would not suffer. Life would go on, as archaic thermophilic microbes spread their gaudy colors across the land. But man would be gone, leaving sandstone strata nearly a billion years deep full of hearths and chipped stones and human bones.

"Ruul! Ruul! Oh, there you are!" His mother, caked by red dust, was clambering stiffly out of the chimney. "Somebody said you came this way. I've been frantic. Oh, Ruul – what are you doing?"

Ruul spread his hands, unable to explain. He didn't want to hurt his mother, but he was excited by his discoveries. "Look what I found, mother!"

"What?"

He babbled excitedly about hearths and tools and bones. "Maybe people lived here in great heaps, and the smoke of their fires rose up to the sky. Mother, will we come to live here again?"

"Perhaps one day," his mother said at random, to hush him.

But that wasn't answer enough for Ruul. Restless, curious, he glanced around once more at the plain, the rising sun. To him, this terminal Earth was a place of wonder. He longed to explore. "Let me go on. Just a little further!"

"No," his mother said gently. "The adventure's over. It's time to go. Come now." And she put her arm around his shoulders, and led him home.

LITTLE FACES

Vonda N. McIntyre

Multiple award winner Vonda N. McIntyre has been one of the most prominent writers in SF since the early seventies. Her story "Of Mist, and Grass, and Sand," won the Nebula Award in 1974, and the famous novel into which it was expanded, *Dreamsnake*, won both the Hugo and Nebula Awards in 1979. Her most recent award was another Nebula win, in 1998, for her novel The Moon and the Sun. Her other novels include *The Exile Waiting, Superluminal, Screwtop, Starfarers, Transition, Metaphase, Nautilus*, and *The Bride*; as well as a YA novel, *Barbary*; the *Star Trek* novels *Enterprise: The First Adventure, The Entropy Effect, The Wrath of Khan, The Voyage Home*, and *The Search for Spock*; and the *Star Wars* novel *The Crystal Star*. Her short fiction has been collected in *Fireflood and Other Stories*. Her most recent book, as editor, was *Nebula Awards Showcase 2004*; she also coedited the anthology *Aurora: Beyond Equality* with Susan Janice Anderson.

The loss of a parent, spouse, sibling, or child can be devastating, but as this compelling tale set in a baroque far-future indicates, there are some relationships even closer and some losses even more keenly felt . . .

T HE BLOOD WOKE YALNIS. It ran between her thighs, warm and slick, cooling, sticky. She pushed back from the stain on the silk, bleary with sleep and love, rousing to shock and stabbing pain.

She flung off the covers and scrambled out of bed. She cried out as the web of nerves tore apart. Her companions shrieked a chaotic chorus.

Zorargul's small form convulsed just below her navel. The raw edges of a throat wound bled in diminishing gushes. Her body expelled the dying companion, closing off veins and vesicles.

Zorargul was beyond help. She wrapped her hand around the small broken body as it slid free. She sank to the floor. Blood dripped onto the cushioned surface. The other companions retreated into her, exposing nothing but sharp white teeth that parted and snapped in defense and warning.

Still in bed, blinking, yawning, Seyyan propped herself on her elbow.

She gazed at the puddle of blood. It soaked in, vanishing gradually from edge to center, drawn away to be separated into its molecules and stored.

A smear of blood marked Seyyan's skin. Her first companion blinked its small bright golden eyes. It snapped its sharp teeth, spattering scarlet droplets. It shrieked, licked its bloody lips, cleaned its teeth with its tongue. The sheet absorbed the blood spray.

Seyyan lay back in the soft tangled nest, elegantly lounging, her luxuriant brown hair spilling its curls around her bare shoulders and over her delicate perfect breasts. She shone like molten gold in the starlight. Her other companions pushed their little faces from her belly, rousing themselves and clacking their teeth, excited and jealous.

"Zorargul," Yalnis whispered. She had never lost a companion. She chose them carefully, and cherished them, and Zorargul had been her first, the gift of her first lover. She looked up at Seyyan, confused and horrified, shocked by loss and pain.

"Come back." Seyyan spoke with soft urgency. She stretched out her graceful hand. "Come back to bed." Her voice intensified. "Come back to me."

Yalnis shrank from her touch. Seyyan followed, sliding over the fading bloodstain in the comfortable nest of ship silk. Her first companion extruded itself, just below her navel, staring intently at Zorargul's body.

Seyyan stroked Yalnis's shoulder. Yalnis pushed her away with her free hand, leaving bloody fingerprints on Seyyan's golden skin.

Seyyan grabbed her wrist and held her, moved to face her squarely, touched her beneath her chin and raised her head to look her in the eyes. Baffled and dizzy, Yalnis blinked away tears. Her remaining companions pumped molecular messages of distress and anger into her blood.

"Come back to me," Seyyan said again. "We're ready for you."

Her first companion, drawing back into her, pulsed and muttered. Seyyan caught her breath.

"I never asked for this!" Yalnis cried.

Seyyan sat back on her heels, as lithe as a girl, but a million years old.

"I thought you wanted me," she said. "You welcomed me – invited me – took me to your bed – "

Yalnis shook her head, though it was true. "Not for this," she whispered.

"It didn't even fight," Seyyan said, dismissing Zorargul's remains with a quick gesture. "It wasn't worthy of its place with you."

"Who are you to decide that?"

"I didn't," Seyyan said. "It's the way of companions." She touched the reddening bulge of a son-spot just below the face of her first companion. "This one will be worthy of you."

Yalnis stared at her, horrified and furious. Seyyan, the legend, had come to her, exotic, alluring, and exciting. All the amazement and attraction Yalnis felt washed away in Zorargul's blood.

"I don't want it," she said. "I won't accept it."

Seyyan's companion reacted to the refusal, blinking, snarling. For a moment Yalnis feared Seyyan too would snarl at her, assault her and force a new companion upon her.

Seyyan sat back, frowning in confusion. "But I thought – did you invite me, just to refuse me? Why – ?"

"For pleasure," Yalnis said. "For friendship. And maybe for love – maybe you would offer, and I would accept – "

"How is this different?" Seyyan asked.

Yalnis leaped to her feet in a flare of fury so intense that her vision blurred. Cradling Zorargul's shriveling body against her with one hand, she pressed the other against the aching bloody wound beneath her navel.

"Get out of my ship," she said.

The ship, responding to Yalnis's wishes, began to resorb the nest into the floor.

Seyyan rose. "What did you think would happen," she said, anger replacing the confusion in her tone, "when you announced the launch of a daughter? What do you think everyone is coming for? I was just lucky enough to be first. Or unfortunate enough." Again, she brushed her long fingertips against the son-spot. It pulsed, a red glow as hot and sore as infection. It must find a place, soon, or be stillborn. "And what am I to do with this?"

Yalnis's flush of anger drained away, leaving her pale and shocked.

"I don't care." All the furnishings and softness of the room vanished, absorbed into the pores of Yalnis's ship, leaving bare walls and floor, and the cold stars above. "You didn't even ask me," Yalnis said softly.

"You led me to believe we understood each other. But you're so young – " Seyyan reached toward her. Yalnis drew back, and Seyyan let her hand fall with a sigh. "So young. So naïve." She caught up her purple cloak from the floor and strode past Yalnis. Though the circular chamber left plenty of room, she brushed past close to Yalnis, touching her at shoulder and hip, bare skin to bare skin. A lock of her hair swept across Yalnis's belly, stroking low like a living hand, painting a bloody streak.

Seyyan entered the pilus that connected Yalnis's ship with her own craft. As soon as Seyyan crossed the border, Yalnis's ship disconnected and closed and healed the connection.

Yalnis's ship emitted a few handsful of plasma in an intemperate blast, moving itself to a safer distance. Seyyan's craft gleamed and glittered against the starfield, growing smaller as Yalnis's ship moved away, coruscating with a pattern of prismatic color.

Yalnis sank to the floor again, humiliated and grief-stricken. Without her request or thought, her ship cushioned her from its cold living bones, growing a soft surface beneath her, dimming the light to dusk. Dusk, not the dawn she had planned.

She gazed down at Zorargul's small body. Its blood pooled in her palm. She drew her other hand from the seeping wound where Zorargul had lived and cradled the shriveling tendril of the companion's penis. A deep ache, throbbing regularly into pain, replaced the potential for pleasure as her body knit the wound of Zorargul's passing. Behind the wound, a sore, soft mass remained.

"Zorargul," she whispered, "you gave me such pleasure."

Of her companions, Zorargul had most closely patterned the lovemaking of its originator. Her pleasure always mingled with a glow of pride, that Zorar thought enough of her to offer her a companion.

Yalnis wondered where Zorar was, and if she would come to Yalnis's daughter's launching. They had not communicated since they parted. Zorar anticipated other adventures, and her ship yearned for deep space. She might be anywhere, one star system away, or a dozen, or setting out to another cluster, voyaging through vacuum so intense and a region so dark she must conserve every molecule of mass and every photon of energy, using none to power a message of acceptance, or regret, or goodwill.

Yalnis remained within parallax view of her own birthplace. She had grown up in a dense population of stars and people. She had taken a dozen lovers in her life, and accepted five companions: Zorargul, Vasigul, Asilgul, Hayaligul, and Bahadirgul. With five companions, she felt mature enough, wealthy enough, to launch a daughter with a decent, even lavish, settlement. After that, she could grant her ship's need – and her own desire – to set out on adventures and explorations.

Zorar, she thought –

She reached for Zorar's memories and reeled into loss and emptiness. The memories ended with Zorargul's murder. Zorar, much older than Yalnis, had given her the gift of her own long life of journeys and observations. They brought her the birth of stars and worlds, the energy storm of a boomerang loop around a black hole, skirting the engulfing doom of its event horizon. They brought her the most dangerous adventure of all, a descent through the thick atmosphere of a planet to its living surface.

All Yalnis had left were her memories of the memories, dissolving shadows of the gift. All the memories left in Zorargul had been wiped out by death.

By murder.

The walls and floor of her living space changed again as her ship re-created her living room. She liked it plain but luxurious, all softness and comfort. The large circular space lay beneath a transparent dome. It was a place for one person alone. She patted the floor with her blood-stained hand.

"Thank you," she said.

"True," her ship whispered into her mind.

Its decisions often pleased her and anticipated her wishes. Strange, for ships and people seldom conversed. When they tried, the interaction too easily deteriorated into misunderstanding. Their consciousnesses were of different types, different evolutionary lineages.

She rose, lacking her usual ease of motion. Anger and pain and grief drained her, and exhaustion trembled in her bones.

She carried Zorargul's body down through the ship, down into its heart, down to the misty power plant. Blood, her own and her companion's, spattered and smeared her hands, her stomach, her legs, the defending teeth or withdrawn crowns of her remaining companions, and Zorargul's pale and flaccid corpse. Its nerve ends dried to silver threads. Expulsion had reduced the testicles to wrinkled empty sacs.

Water ran in streams and pools through the power plant's housing, cold as it came in, steaming too hot to touch as it led away. Where steam from the hot pool met cold air, mist formed. Yalnis knelt and washed Zorargul's remains in the cold pool. When she was done, a square of scarlet ship silk lay on the velvety floor, flat and new where it had formed. She wrapped Zorargul in its shining folds.

"Good-bye," she said, and gave the small bundle tenderly to the elemental heat.

A long time later, Yalnis made her way to the living space and climbed into the bath, into water hot but not scalding. The bath swirled around her, sweeping away flecks of dried blood. She massaged the wound gently, making sure the nerve roots were cleanly ejected. She let the expulsion lump alone, though it was already hardening.

The remaining companions opened their little faces, protruding from the shelter of her body. They peered around, craning themselves above her skin, glaring at each other and gnashing their teeth in a great show, then closing their lips, humming to attract her attention.

She attended each companion in turn, stroking the little faces, flicking warm drops of water between their lips, quieting and calming them, murmuring, "Shh, shh." They felt no sympathy for her loss, no grief for Zorargul, only the consciousness of opportunity. She felt a moment of contempt for the quartet, each member jostling for primacy.

They are what they are, she thought, and submerged herself and them in the bath, drawing their little faces beneath the surface. They fell silent, holding their breaths and closing their eyes and mouths, reaching to draw their oxygen as well as their sustenance from her blood. A wash of dizziness took her; she breathed deep till it passed.

Each of the companions tried to please her – no, Bahadirgul held back. Her most recent companion had always been restrained in its approaches, fierce in its affections when it achieved release. Now, instead of squirming toward her center, it relaxed and blew streams of delicate bubbles from the air in its residual lungs.

Yalnis smiled, and when she closed herself off from the companions, she shut Bahadirgul away more gently than the others. She did not want to consider any of the companions now. Zorargul had been the best, the most deeply connected, as lively and considerate as her first lover.

Tears leaked from beneath her lashes, hot against her cheeks, washing away when she submerged. She looked up at the stars through the shimmering surface, through the steam.

She lifted her head to breathe. Water rippled and splashed; air cooled her face. The companions remained underwater, silent. Yalnis's tears flowed again and she sobbed, keening, grieving, wishing to take back the whole last time of waking. She wanted to change all her plans. If she did, Seyyan might take it as a triumph. She might make demands. Yalnis sneaked a look at the messages her ship kept ready for her attention. She declined to reply or even to acknowledge them. She felt it a weakness to read them. After she had, she wished she had resisted.

Why did you tantalize and tease me? Seyyan's message asked. You know this was what you wanted. I'm what you wanted.

Yalnis eliminated everything else Seyyan had sent her.

"Please refuse Seyyan's messages," she said to her ship.

"True," it replied.

"Disappear them, destroy them. No response."

"True."

"Seyyan, you took my admiration and my awe, and you perverted it," she said, as if Seyyan stood before her. "I might have accepted you. I might have, if you'd given me a chance. If you'd given me time. What do we have, but time? I'll never forgive you."

The bath flowed away, resorbing into the ship's substance. Warm air dried her and drew off the steam. She wrapped herself in a new swath of ship silk without bothering to give it a design. Some people went naked at home, but Yalnis liked clothes. For now, though, a cloak sufficed.

She wandered through her ship, visiting each chamber in the current configuration, looking with amazement and apprehension at the daughter ship growing in the ship's lower flank. What would the person be like, this new being who would accompany this new ship into the universe? She thought she had known, but everything had changed.

She returned, finally, to her living chamber.

"Please defend yourself," she said.

"True."

Yalnis snuggled into the ship's substance, comforted by its caress. She laid her hand over her belly, pressing her palm against the hot, healing wound, then petting each of the little faces. They bumped against her palm, yearning, stretching from their shafts so she could tickle behind Asilgul's vestigial ears, beneath Vasigul's powerful lower jaw. Even Bahadirgul advanced from its reserve, blinking its long-lashed eyelids to caress her fingers, touching her palm with its sharp hot tongue.

Each one wished to pleasure her, but she felt no wish for pleasure. Even the idea of joy vanished, in grief and guilt.

The nest drew around her, covering her legs, her sex, her stomach. It flowed over the faces and extruded a nipple for each sharp set of teeth. The ship took over feeding the companions so they would not drain Yalnis as she slept.

"Please, a thousand orbits," she said.

"True," said the ship, making her aware it was content to have time to complete and polish the daughter ship, to prepare for the launch. But, afterward, it wanted to stretch and to explore. She accepted its need, and she would comply.

For now she would sleep for a thousand orbits. If anyone besides Seyyan accepted the invitation to her daughter's launch, they would arrive in good time, and then they could wait for her, as she waited for them. Perhaps a thousand orbits – a thousand years in the old way of speaking – would give her time to dream of a proper revenge. Perhaps a thousand years of sleep would let her dream away the edges of her grief. The ship's support extensions grew against her, into her. She accepted the excretion extensions and swallowed the feeding extension. The monitor gloved one hand and wrist.

The view through the dome swept the orbit's plane, facing outward toward the thick carpet of multicolored stars, the glowing gas clouds.

Yalnis slept for a thousand years.

The kiss of her ship woke her. Water exuded from the feeding extension, moistening her lips and tongue. The tangy fragrance touched her consciousness. She drifted into the last, hypnopompic layer of sleep, finding and losing dreams.

She thought: It would be good if . . . I would like . . . Loss hit her unaware. A chill of regret and grief swept through her and to her four remaining companions; they woke from their doze and released the nipples and squeaked and shrilled. The ship, after a thousand orbits of the irritation of their little sharp teeth, drew away its fabric.

The ship made Yalnis aware of everything around them: the ship's own safety, the star and its planets, the astronomical landscape glowing through the transparent dome.

And it displayed to her the swarm of other ships, sending to her in their individual voices that ships and people had come to celebrate the launch of her daughter and her ship's daughter. She recognized friends and acquaintances, she noted strangers. She looked for former lovers, and found, to her joy and apprehension, that Zorar's ship sailed nearby.

And, of course, Seyyan remained.

During Yalnis's long rest, Seyyan had never approached, never tried to attach or attack. Yalnis felt glad of this. Her ship would have surrounded itself with an impermeable shell, one that induced a severe allergic reaction in other ships. A defensive shell drew heavily on a ship's resources. Her ship was sleek and well-provisioned, but growing defenses while developing a daughter ship would strain any resources.

Instead of approaching, Seyyan's craft's course had closely paralleled her own for all this time, as if it were herding and protecting Yalnis.

Annoyed that she had not anticipated such a move – she had expected aggression, not a show of protection – Yalnis nudged her ship to a different course, to a mathematical center along the long curved line of other craft. Her ship agreed and complied, even to skirting the bounds of safety and good manners, in moving itself into a position where Seyyan would have difficulty acting as their shadow.

Yalnis stretched. The ship, understanding that she wished to rise, withdrew its extensions from her body. She gagged a little, as she always did, when the nutrient extension slid up her throat, across her tongue, between her lips, leaving a trace of sweetness. The extension collapsed; the ship's skin absorbed it. Excretion extensions and the monitor followed, and disappeared.

She raised her head slowly. The weight of her hair, grown long, held her down. She turned the dome reflective and gazed up.

Her hair spread in a wide shining fan across the floor, covering the whole diameter of the living room, drawn out by the living carpet as it lengthened. Its color ranged in concentric circles. The outer circle, spread out so wide that each hair was a single ray, glowed an attenuated platinum blond, the color she had worn her hair when she first met Seyyan. It changed dramatically to black, then progressed from honey to auburn to dark brown, and the sequence started over. She removed the palest color from the growth sequence for the future. It would only remind her.

Instead of cutting her hair to the short and easy length she usually favored, she asked the ship to sever it at a length that would touch the ground when she stood.

Despite the ship's constant care when she slept, she always had difficulty rising after a long hibernation. The ship eased the gravity to help her. She rose on shaky legs, and stumbled when she left the nest. The companions squealed with alarm.

"Oh, be quiet," she said. "What cause have I ever given you, to fear I'd fall on you?" Besides, their instincts would pull them inside her if she ever did fall, and the only bruises would form on her own body.

But even if I've never fallen on them, she thought, I *have* left them reason to fear. To doubt my protection.

Her hair draped around her shoulders, over her breasts, along her hips and legs to the ground. The companions peered through the thick curtain, chattering with annoyance. Bahadirgul sneezed. In sudden sympathy, she pushed her hair back to leave them free.

The wound beneath her navel had healed, leaving a pale white scar. Beneath her skin, the sperm packet Zorargul emitted as its last living action made a jagged capsule, invisible, but perceptible to her fingers and vaguely painful to her nerves. She had to decide whether to use it, or to finish encapsulating it and expel it in turn.

Without being asked, the ship absorbed the shorn ends of her hair. She and the ship had been born together; despite the mysteries each species kept from the other, each knew the other's habits. It produced a length of ship silk formed into comfortable and neutral garments: loose pants with a filmy lace panel to obscure the companions, a sleeveless shirt with a similar lace panel. She wore clothes that allowed the companions some view of the world, for they could be troublesome when bored. She left the silk its natural soft beige, for the horizontal stripes of her hair gave plenty of drama. She twisted her hair into a thick rope to keep it from tangling as she dressed, then let it loose again. It lay heavy on her neck and shoulders.

I may reconsider this haircut, she thought. But not till after the launch. I can be formal for that long, at least.

Messages flowed in from the other ships. It pleased her that so many had accepted her invitation. Still she did not reply, even to welcome them. Her ship looked out a long distance, but no other craft approached. The party was complete.

Yalnis closed her eyes to inspect her ship's status and records. The ship ran a slight fever, reflecting its increasing metabolism. Its flank, smooth before her sleep, now bulged. The daughter ship lay in its birth pouch, shiny-skinned and adorned with a pattern of small knots. The knots would sink into the new ship's skin, giving it the potential of openings, connections, ports, antennae, undifferentiated tissue for experiment and play.

"It's beautiful," she whispered to the ship.

"True."

The companions squeaked with hunger, though they had spent the last thousand years dozing and feeding without any exertion. They were fat and sleek. They were always hungry, or always greedy, rising for a treat or a snack, though they connected directly to her bloodstream as well as to her nerves and could draw their sustenance from her without ever opening their little mouths or exposing their sharp little teeth.

But Yalnis had been attached to the ship's nutrients for just as long, and she too was ravenous.

She left the living room and descended to the garden. The light was different, brighter and warmer. The filter her ship used to convey light to the garden mimicked a blanket of atmosphere.

She arrived at garden's dawn. Birds chirped and sang in the surrounding trees, and a covey of quail foraged along borders and edges. Several rabbits, nibbling grass in the pasture, raised their heads when she walked in, then, unafraid, went back to grazing. They had not seen a person for thousands of their generations.

The garden smelled different from the rest of the ship, the way she believed the surface of a planet might smell. She liked it, but it frightened her, too, for it held living organisms she would never see. The health of the garden demanded flotillas of bacteria, armies of worms, swarms of bugs. She thought it might be safer to grow everything in hydroponic tanks, as had been the fashion last time she paid attention, but she liked the spice of apprehension. Besides, the ship preferred this method. If it thought change necessary, it would change.

She walked barefoot into the garden, trying not to step on any adventurous worm or careless bug. The bacteria would have to look out for themselves.

She captured a meal of fruit, corn, and a handful of squash blossoms. She liked the blossoms. When she was awake, and hunted regularly, she picked them before they turned to vegetables. The neglected plants emitted huge squashes of all kinds, some perfect, some attacked and nibbled by vegetarian predators.

The companions, reacting to the smell of food, fidgeted and writhed, craning their thick necks to snap at each other. She calmed and soothed them, and fed them bits of apple and pomegranate seeds.

They had already begun to jostle for primacy, each slowly moving toward her center, migrating across skin and muscle toward the spot where Zorargul had lived, as if she would not notice. Her skin felt stretched and sore. No companion had the confidence or nerve to risk detaching from its position to reinsert itself in the primary spot.

A good thing, too, she thought. I wouldn't answer for my temper if one of them did that without my permission.

Leaving her garden, she faced the task of welcoming her guests.

I don't want to, she thought, like a whiny girl: I want to keep my privacy, I want to enjoy my companions. I want to be left alone. To grieve alone.

In the living room, beneath the transparent dome, the ship created a raised seat. She slipped in among the cushions, sat on her hair, cursed at the sharp pull, swept the long locks out from under her and coiled them – bits of dirt and leaves tangled in the ends; she shook them off with a shudder and left the detritus for the carpet to take away. She settled herself again.

"I would like to visit Zorar," she said to her ship.

"True."

She dozed until the two ships matched, extruded, connected. A small shiver ran through Yalnis's ship, barely perceptible.

Yalnis hesitated at the boundary, took a deep breath, and entered the pilus where the fabric of her ship and the fabric of Zorar's met, mingled, and communicated, exchanging unique bits of genetic information to savor and explore.

At the border of Zorar's ship, she waited until her friend appeared.

"Zorar," she said.

Zorar blinked at her, in her kindly, languorous way. She extended her hand to Yalnis and drew her over the border, a gesture of trust that broke Yalnis's heart. She wanted to throw herself into Zorar's arms.

Do I still have the right? she thought.

She burst into tears.

Zorar enfolded Yalnis, murmuring, "Oh, my dear, oh, what is it?"

Between sobs and sniffles, and an embarrassing bout of hiccups, Yalnis told her. Zorar held her hand, patting it gently, and fell still and silent.

"I'm so sorry," Yalnis whispered. "I was so fond of Zorargul. I could always remember you, when . . . I feel so empty."

Zorar glanced down. The lace of Yalnis's clothes modestly concealed the companions.

"Let me see," she said. Her voice remained calm. Yalnis had always admired her serenity. Now, though, tears brightened her brown eyes.

Yalnis parted the lace panels. The four remaining companions blinked and squirmed in the increased light, the unfamiliar gaze. Bahadirgul retreated, the most modest of them all, but the others stretched and extended and stared and bared their teeth.

"You haven't chosen a replacement."

"How could I replace Zorargul?"

Zorar shook her head. "You can't duplicate. But you can replace."

Yalnis gripped Zorar's hands. "Do you mean . . ." She stopped, confused and embarrassed, as inarticulate as the girl she had been when she first met Zorar. That time, everything that happened was her choice. This time, by rights, it should be Zorar's.

"A daughter between us," Zorar said. "She would be worth knowing."

"Yes," Yalnis said. Zorar laid her palm against Yalnis's cheek.

Instead of leaning into her touch, Yalnis shivered.

Zorar immediately drew back her hand and gazed at Yalnis.

"What do you want, my dear?" she asked.

"I want . . ." She sniffled, embarrassed. "I want everything to be the way it was before I ever met Seyyan!" She took Zorar's hand and held it, clutched it. "I wanted a daughter with Zorargul, but Zorargul is gone, and I . . ." She stopped. She did not want to inflict her pain on Zorar.

"You aren't ready for another lover," Zorar said. "I understand entirely."

Zorar glanced at Yalnis's bare stomach, at the one shy and three bold little faces, at the scar left from Zorargul's murder.

"It wasn't meant to be," Zorar said

Yalnis touched the scar, where Zorargul's jagged remains pricked her skin from underneath.

"Maybe I should – "

"No." Zorar spoke sharply.

Discouraged, Yalnis let the lacy panels slip back into place.

"It's our memories Seyyan killed," Zorar said. "Would you send out a daughter with only one parent's experience?"

Zorar was kind; she refrained from saying that the one parent would be Yalnis, young and relatively inexperienced. Yalnis's tears welled up again. She struggled to control them, but she failed. She fought the knowledge that Zorar was right. Zorar was mature and established, with several long and distant adventures to her credit. Her memories were an irreplaceable gift, to be conveyed to a daughter through Zorargul. The sperm packet alone could not convey those memories. "Let time pass," Zorar said. "We might see each other again, in some other millennium."

Yalnis scrubbed at her eyes with her sleeve. "I'm so angry!" she cried. "How could Seyyan betray me like this?"

"How did you find her?" Zorar asked, as if to change the subject. "She's not been heard of for . . ." She paused to think, to shrug. "Sixty or eighty millennia, at least. I thought she was lost."

"Did you hope it?"

Zorar gave her a quizzical glance. "Don't you remember?"

Yalnis looked away, ashamed. "I don't have all Zorargul's memories," she said. "I savored them – anticipated them. I didn't want to gobble them all up at once. It would be too greedy."

"How old are you now?" Zorar asked gently, as if to change the subject.

"My ship is eleven millennia," she replied. "In waking time, I'm twenty-five years old."

"You young ones always have to find out everything for yourselves," Zorar said with a sigh. "Didn't you ask Zorargul, when you took up with Seyyan?"

Yalnis stared at her, deeply shocked. "Ask Zorargul about Seyyan?" Zorar might as well have suggested she make love in a cluster of ships with the dome transparent, everyone looking in. It had never occurred to Yalnis to tell the companions each others' names, or even to wonder if they would understand her if she did. She had a right to some privacy, as did her other lovers.

"You young ones!" Zorar said with impatience. "What do you think memories are for? Are they just a toy for your entertainment?"

"I was trying to treat them respectfully!" Yalnis exclaimed.

Zorar snorted.

Yalnis wondered if she would ever be so confident, so well-established, that she could dispense with caring what others thought about her. She yearned for such audacity, such bravery.

"I asked about her, of course!" she exclaimed, trying to redeem herself. "Not the companions, but Shai and Kinli and Tasmin were all near enough to talk to. They all said, Oh, is she found? Or, She's a legend, how lucky you are to meet her! Or, Give her my loving regard."

"Tasmin has a daughter with her. She'd never hear anything against her. I suppose Seyyan never asked anything of Tasmin that she wasn't willing to give. Kinli wasn't even born last time anyone heard anything from Seyyan, and Shai . . ." She glanced down at her hands and slowly, gradually, unclenched her fists. "Shai fears her."

"She could have warned me."

"Seyyan terrifies her. Is she here?" She closed her eyes, a habitual movement that Yalnis did, too, when she wanted information from her ship's senses.

"No," Yalnis said, as Zorar said, "No, I see she's not."

"She said she would, but she changed her mind. It hurt my feelings when she disappeared without a word, and she never replied when I asked her what was wrong."

"She changed her mind after you mentioned Seyyan."

Yalnis thought back. "Yes."

"Would you have believed her, if she'd warned you?"

Yalnis remembered Seyyan's word and touch and beauty, the flush Yalnis felt just to see her, the excitement when she knew Seyyan looked at her. She shivered, for now all that had changed.

"I doubt it," she said. "Oh, you're right, I wouldn't have believed her. I would have suspected jealousy."

Zorar brushed away Yalnis's tears.

"What did she do to you?" Yalnis whispered.

Zorar took a deep breath, and drew up the gauzy hem of her shirt. She carried the same companions as when she and Yalnis first met:

five, the same number Yalnis had accepted. Yalnis would have expected someone of Zorar's age and status to take a few more. Five was the right number for a person of Yalnis's age and minor prosperity.

"You noticed this scar," Zorar said, tracing an erratic line of pale silver that skipped from her breastbone to her navel, nearly invisible against her translucently delicate skin. "And I shrugged away your question."

"You said it happened when you walked on the surface of a planet," Yalnis said. "You said a flesh-eating plant attacked you."

"Yes, well, one did," Zorar said, unabashed. "But it didn't leave that scar." She stroked the chin of her central little face. Just below her navel, the companion roused itself, blinking and gnashing its teeth. It neither stretched up aggressively nor retreated defensively. Yalnis had never seen its face; like the others, it had remained nearly concealed, only the top of its head showing, while Yalnis and Zorar made love. Yalnis had thought the companions admirably modest, but now she wondered if their reaction had been fear.

Zorar pressed her fingers beneath the companion's chin, scratching it gently, revealing its neck.

The scar did not stop at Zorar's navel. It continued, crossing the back of the companion's neck and the side of its throat. "Seyyan claimed she behaved as she'd been taught. As she thought was proper, and right. She was horrified at my distress."

She stroked the companion's downy scalp. It closed its eyes.

Her voice hardened.

"I had to comfort her, she acted so distraught. I had to comfort her."

"She accused me of teasing and deceiving her," Yalnis said. "And she *killed* Zorargul."

Under Zorar's gentle hand, the scarred companion relaxed and slept, its teeth no longer bared.

"Perhaps she's learned efficiency," Zorar whispered, as if the companion might hear and understand her. "Or . . . mercy."

"Mercy!" Yalnis exclaimed. "Cruelty and sarcasm, more likely."

"She killed Zorargul," Zorar said. "This one, mine, she left paralyzed. Impotent."

Yalnis imagined: Zorargul, cut off from her, unable to communicate with either pleasure or memory, parasitic, its pride destroyed. She gazed at Zorar with astonishment and pity, and she flushed with embarrassment. She had felt piqued when Zorar created Zorargul with a secondary little face, instead of with her first companion. Now Yalnis knew why.

Yalnis laid her hand on Zorar's. Her own fingers touched the downy fur of the damaged companion. Involuntarily, she shuddered. Zorar glanced away.

Could I have kept Zorargul? Yalnis wondered. No matter how much I loved Zorar . . .

She thought Zorar was the bravest person she had ever met.

Would it be right to say so? She wondered. Any more right than to

ask the questions I know not to ask: How could you – ? Why didn't
you – ?

"What do you think, now?" Zorar said.

"I'm outraged!" Yalnis said.

"Outraged enough to tell?"

"I told you."

"You confessed to me. You confessed the death of Zorargul, as if it
were your fault. Do you believe Seyyan, that you deceived her? Are you
outraged enough to accuse her, instead of yourself?"

Yalnis sat quite still, considering. After a long while, she patted
Zorar's hand again, collected herself, and brushed her fingertips across
Zorar's companion's hair with sympathy. She kissed Zorar quickly and
returned to her own ship.

Preparations, messages of welcome to old acquaintances, greetings to
new ones, occupied her. Zorar's question always hovered in the back of
her mind, and sometimes pushed itself forward to claim her attention:

What do you think, now?

While she prepared, the ships moved closer, extruded connections,
grew together. Yalnis's ship became the center, till the colony obscured
her wide vistas of space and clouds of stars and glowing dust. She felt
her ship's discomfort at being so constricted; she shared it. She felt her
ship's exhilaration at intense genetic exchange: those sensations, she
avoided.

She continued to ignore Seyyan, but never rescinded her invitation.
Yalnis's ship allowed no direct connection to Seyyan's glittering craft.
Seyyan remained on the outskirts of the colony, forming her own
connections with others. The ships floated in an intricately delicate
dance of balance and reciprocity. As the people exchanged greetings,
reminiscences, gifts, the ships exchanged information and new genetic
code.

Most of their communications were cryptic. Oftentimes even the
ships had no idea what the new information would do, but they
collected and exchanged it promiscuously, played with it, rearranged it,
tested it. The shimmery pattern of rainbow reflections spread from
Seyyan's craft's skin to another, and another, and the pattern mutated
from solid to stripes to spots.

Yalnis's ship remained its customary reflective silver.

"The ships have chosen a new fashion," Yalnis said.

"True," her ship said. Then, "False."

Yalnis frowned, confused, as her ship displayed a genetic sequence
and its genealogy tag. Yalnis left all those matters to the ship, so she
took a moment to understand that her ship rejected the pattern because
it descended from Seyyan's craft. Her ship led her further into its
concerns, showing how many new sequences it had considered but
rejected and stopped taking in when it encountered Seyyan's tag.

"Thank you," Yalnis said.

"True."

That was a long conversation, between ship and human. She was glad it had ended without misunderstanding.

The ship did understand "Thank you," Yalnis believed, and Yalnis did understand its response of appreciation.

Maybe Seyyan was right, Yalnis said to herself. Maybe I am naïve. I feared direct assault, but never thought of a sneak attack on my ship.

She wondered if her encounter with Seyyan had changed the balance between the two ships, or if their estrangement had its own source. She wondered if she should try to exclude Seyyan's craft from the colony. But that would be an extreme insult, and Seyyan had more friends than Yalnis, and many admirers. She was older, wealthier, more experienced and accomplished, more limber of voice and of body.

"I trust your judgment," she said, remaining within the relative safety of simple declarative statements. She would leave decisions about Seyyan's craft to her own ship.

"True."

The shimmering new fashion continued to extend from Seyyan's to other craft, each vying with the next to elaborate upon her pattern.

Seyyan's popularity created a second center for the colony, decreasing the stability of the delicate rotation, but there was nothing to be done about it. It was ships' business, not people's.

Yalnis was ready. She made her last decisions, dressed in intricate lace, took a deep, shaky breath, and welcomed her guests.

Zorar arrived first, too well-established to concern herself with being fashionably late. Yalnis embraced her, grateful for her presence. Zorar kissed her gently and handed her a sealed glass ampoule.

"For your daughter's vineyard," she said. "I think the culture's improved even over what I gave your mother, when she launched you and your ship."

"Thank you," Yalnis said, honored by the gift. She put it on the central table, in a place of distinction.

More guests arrived; an hour passed in a blur of greetings, reunions, introductions, gifts. People brought works of art, stories, and songs. They brought ship silk as refined as fog, seeds of newly adapted plants, embryos of newly discovered creatures, unique cultures of yeast and bacteria. Yalnis accepted them all with thanks and gratitude. Her daughter would be well and truly launched; her ship would be rich, and unique.

Her guests ate and drank, wished each other long life and adventures, congratulated voyagers on their safe return. They exchanged compliments and gossip, they flirted, they told tales, they even bragged: Kinli had, of course, been on another great adventure that made all others pale by comparison. Guests complimented Yalnis's ship's cooking, especially the savory rabbit, and the complexity and quality of her wine. Everyone wore their best ship silk, and most, like Yalnis, wore lace so their companions could remain decently modest while watching the party. A few guests wore opaque garments to enforce a complete modesty; Yalnis thought the choice a little cruel. The very youngest people, recently debuted from solitary girl to adult, revealed their virgin midriffs.

Yalnis found herself always aware of the new connections leading from other ships to her living space. The openings, glowing in the cool pastels of biological light, changed her living area from one of comfortable intimacy to one of open vulnerability.

Zorar handed her a glass of wine. Yalnis had based the vintage on the yeast Zorar gave her ship when it and Yalnis were born and launched.

Yalnis sipped it, glanced around, swallowed a whole mouthful. The effects spread through her. The companions squeaked with pleasure, leaning into her, absorbing the alcohol, yearning. She brushed her hand across the lace of her shirt. She had been neglecting the companions since Zorargul's murder. She drank more wine, and Zorar refilled their glasses.

Yalnis blocked out the rising level of conversation. She was unused to noise, and it tired her.

"What do you think?" she said.

Zorar raised one eyebrow. "That's the question I want you to answer."

"Oh," said Yalnis. "Yes, of course." She blushed at her misstep. "But I meant, about the wine."

"It's excellent," Zorar said, "as you well know. Your ship is of a line that seldom makes a recombinant error, and I can only approve of the changes. What about Seyyan? Did you ban her?"

"No. I want her here. So she knows she failed. Maybe she banned herself."

"Maybe she's trying to unnerve you. Or to wait till you drink too much."

Yalnis drained her glass again.

"Maybe if I do, I'll be ready for her."

She was ignoring the noise, but she noticed the sudden silence.

"And then I – " Kinli said, and stopped.

Seyyan stood in the largest new entryway, silhouetted by golden bioluminescence, her face shadowed, dramatized, by the softer party light. Yalnis's heart pounded; her face flushed.

"I thought she was so beautiful," Yalnis whispered to Zorar, amazed, appalled. She thought she whispered: a few people nearby glanced toward her, most amused, but one at least pale with jealousy for her relationship with the renowned adventurer.

If you only knew, Yalnis thought. I wonder what you'd think then?

Yalnis mourned the loss of the joy she had felt when Seyyan chose her, but she mourned the loss of Zorargul much more.

Seyyan strode into the party, greeting allies, her gaze moving unchecked past the few who had rejected her craft's fashionable offerings. Misty ship silk flowed around her legs and hips, shimmering with the pattern that newly decorated the flanks of so many craft. No one else had thought to apply it to clothing. She wore a shawl of the same fabric around her shoulders, over her breasts, across her companions.

But her hands were empty of gifts. Yalnis declined to notice, but others did, and whispered, shocked.

Then she flung back the end of the shawl, revealing herself from breastbone to pubis.

She had accepted more companions since she was with Yalnis. She bore so many Yalnis could not count them without staring, and she would not stare. Her gaze hesitated only long enough to see that the son-spot had erupted and healed over.

The other guests did stare.

How could any person support so many companions? And yet Seyyan displayed health and strength, an overwhelming physical wealth.

She turned to draw another guest from the shadows behind her. Ekarete stepped shyly into the attention of the party. Ekarete, one of the newly debuted adults, already wore new lace. Seyyan bent to kiss her, to slip her hand beneath the filmy panel of her shirt, so everyone would know that if she had neglected a launching gift for Yalnis's daughter, she had given a more intimate one to Ekarete.

Seyyan wanted Yalnis to know what had happened to the new companion, that she had easily found someone to accept it.

Seyyan whispered to Ekarete, drew her hand down her cheek, and continued toward Yalnis and Zorar. Ekarete followed, several steps behind, shy and attentive, excited and intimidated by her first adult gathering.

Seyyan's first companion, the assassin, protruded all the way to the base of his neck, eyes wide, teeth exposed and snapping sharply. Her other companions, responding to him, gnashed their teeth and blinked their eyes.

"What a pleasant little party," Seyyan said. "I so admire people who aren't caught up in the latest fashion."

"Do have some wine," Yalnis said. She meant to speak in a pleasant tone. Her voice came out flat, and hard.

Seyyan accepted a glass, and sipped, and nodded. "As good as I remember."

Yalnis wished for the ancient days Seyyan came from, when poison could still wreak havoc with a person's biochemistry, undetected till too late. She wished for a poisoned apple, a single bite, and no one ever to kiss Seyyan again.

Maybe I can have that last wish, she thought, and took action on her decision.

She let Zorargul's wound break open. The stab of pain struck through her. Her companions shrieked, crying like terrified birds, reacting to her distress. Blood blossomed through the lace panel of her shirt. All around her, people gasped.

Yalnis reached beneath the scarlet stain. Her hand slid across the blood on her skin. The wound gaped beneath her fingers.

Her body had treated Zorargul's sperm packet like an intrusion, an irritation, as something to encapsulate like the seed of a pearl. At the same time, the packet struggled for its own survival, extending spines to remain in contact with her flesh. As it worked its way out, scraping her raw, she caught her breath against a whimper.

Finally the capsule dropped into her hand. She held it up. Her body had covered the sperm packet's extrusions with shining white enamel. All that remained of Zorargul was a sphere of bloody fangs. "This is your work, Seyyan," she said. Blood flowed over her stomach, through her pubic hair, down her legs, dripping onto the rug, which absorbed it and carried it away. Yalnis went cold, light-headed, pale. She took courage from Zorar, standing at her elbow.

"You took me as your lover," Seyyan said. "I thought you wanted me. I thought you wanted a companion from me. My lineage always fought for place and position."

"I wasn't at war with you," Yalnis said. "I loved you. If you'd asked, instead of . . ." She glanced down at the gory remains.

"Asked?" Seyyan whispered. "But you asked me."

Whispers, exclamations, agreement, objections all quivered around them.

Tasmin moved to stand near Seyyan, taking her side.

"You must have been neglectful," she said to Yalnis. "I think you're too young to support so many companions."

Seyyan glanced at Tasmin, silencing her. Anyone could see that Yalnis was healthy and well supplied with resources. She was her own evidence, and her ship the final proof.

As they confronted each other, the guests sorted themselves, most in a neutral circle, some behind Yalnis, more flanking Seyyan. Yalnis wished Shai had remained for the gathering. She might have sided with Seyyan, but the others might have seen her fear.

Ekarete, in her new lace shirt, moved shyly between the opponents.

"Seyyan was very gentle with me," she whispered. "She acceded to my choice." She twitched the hem of her shirt aside, just far enough, just long enough, to reveal the fading inflammation of a new attachment, and the golden skin and deep brown eyes of Seyyan's offspring, Ekarete's first little face.

"Very gentle," Ekarete said again. "Very kind. I love her."

"For giving you a cast-off?" Yalnis said. "For inducing you to take the companion I refused?"

Ekarete stared at her. Yalnis felt sorry for her, sorry to have humiliated her.

Tasmin stood forward with Ekarete. "Yalnis, you're speaking out of grief," she said. "You lost a companion – I grieve with you. But don't blame Seyyan or embarrass Ekarete. We all know Seyyan for her generosity. My daughter by her launched gloriously."

"You're hardly disinterested," said Yalnis.

"But I am," said Kinli, "and I know nothing against her."

Yalnis started to say, When did you ever listen to anyone but yourself?

Zorar yanked up the hem of her shirt, revealing the scar and her emasculated companion with its drooping mouth and dull eyes. It roused far enough to bare its teeth. It drooled.

The older people understood; the younger ones started in horror at the mangled thing, heard quick whispers of explanation, and stared at Seyyan.

"I loved you, too," Zorar said. "I told myself, it must have been my fault. I should have understood. I consoled you. After you did this."

"I came for a celebration," Seyyan said, holding herself tall and aloof. "I expect to be taken as I am – not ambushed with lies and insults."

She spun, the hem of her dress flaring dramatically, and strode away.

Ekarete ran after her. Seyyan halted, angry in the set of her shoulders; she paused, softened, bent to speak, kissed Ekarete, and continued away, alone. The main entrance silhouetted her formidable figure as she left Yalnis's ship.

Ekarete stood shivering, gazing after her, pulling the hem of her shirt down all the way around. Finally she scurried after her. Tasmin glared at Yalnis, heaved a heavy sigh, and followed.

The others, even Kinli, clustered around Yalnis and Zorar.

"You've spoiled your own party," Kinli said, petulant. "What now? A permanent break? A feud?"

"I shun her," Yalnis said.

"That's extreme!"

Yalnis hesitated, hoping for support if not acclaim. She shrugged into the silence. "If the community doesn't agree, why should she care if only I shun her?"

"And I," Zorar said, which made more difference to more people.

The light of the connecting corridors faded as she spoke. The openings slowly ensmalled. No one had to be told the party had ended. The guests hurried to slip through the connections before they vanished. Their finery went dim.

All around, the tables resorbed into the floor, leaving crumbs and scraps and disintegrating utensils. The rug's cilia carried them away in a slow-motion whirlpool of dissolving bits, into pores, to be metabolized. The gifts all sank away, to be circulated to the new ship.

Only Zorar remained. Yalnis's knees gave out. She crouched, breathing hard, dizzy. Zorar knelt beside her.

"I'm – I have to – "

"Hush. Lie back."

"But – "

"It's waited this long. It can wait longer."

Yalnis let Zorar ease her down. The ship received her, nestling her, creeping around and over her with its warm skin. The pain eased and the flow of blood ceased. The blood she had shed moved from her skin, from her clothes, red-brown drying specks flowing in tiny lines across the comforter, and disappeared.

She dozed, for a moment or an hour. When she woke, Zorar remained beside her.

"Thank you," Yalnis whispered. She closed her eyes again. She desperately wanted to be alone.

Zorar kissed Yalnis and slipped through the last exit. It sealed itself and disappeared.

Yalnis wanted only to go back to sleep. A thousand years might not be enough this time. She had never been among so many people for so long, and she had never been in such a confrontation. Exhaustion crept over her, but she must stay awake a little longer.

"I shun Seyyan," she said. Her companions quivered at her distress.

"True," the ship said, and let all its connections to all the other ships shrivel and drop away. The primary colony broke apart, resolving into individual ships. They moved to safer distances, and the stars reappeared above Yalnis's living space.

Seyyan's glittering secondary colony remained, with her craft protected in its center. None broke away to shun her. Yalnis turned her back on the sight. She no longer had anything to do with Seyyan.

"It's time," she said aloud.

"True," her ship replied. It created a nest for her, a luxurious bed of ship silk. It dimmed the light and mirrored the outer surface of the transparent dome. The stars took on a ghostly appearance. Yalnis could see out, but no one could see inside.

Yalnis pulled off her shirt. Her long hair tangled in it. Annoyed, she shook her hair free. She stepped out of her loose trousers. Naked, she reclined in the nest.

"Please, cut my hair."

"True," the ship said. The nest cropped her hair, leaving a cap of dark brown. The weight fell away; the strands moved across the carpet, fading to a dust of molecules.

Yalnis relaxed, gazed at her companions, and let her hand slide down her body. The little faces knew her intent. Each stretched itself to its greatest extent, into her and out of her, whispering and offering.

She made her choice.

Bahadirgul stretched up to seek her hand, moaning softly through its clenched sharp teeth. The other companions contracted, hiding their little faces in modesty or disappointment till they nearly disappeared. Yalnis stroked Bahadirgul's head, its nape, and caressed its neck and shaft. She opened herself to her companion.

The pleasure started slowly, spreading from Bahadirgul's attachment point deeper into her body. It reached the level of their ordinary couplings, which always gave Yalnis joy, and gave the companion days of pride and satiation. It continued, and intensified. Yalnis cried out, panting, arching her back. Bahadirgul shivered and extended. Yalnis and her companion released, and combined.

Their daughter formed. Yalnis curled up, quivering occasionally with a flush of pleasure, listening to their daughter grow. The pleasure faded to a background throb.

Inside her, her daughter grew.

Content, she nestled deeper into the ship silk and prepared to sleep.

Instead, the dome went transparent. Seyyan's colony of connected ships gleamed in the distance. The connecting pili stretched thin, preparing to detach and resorb.

Yalnis sighed. Seyyan was none of her concern anymore. She had sworn to take no more notice of her.

What happened next, Yalnis would never forget, no matter how many millennia she lived or how many adventures filled her memory.

The connections deformed, shifted, arched in waves. They contracted, forcing the craft closer even as they tried to separate and depart.

Seyyan commanded her supporters, and they discovered the limits of their choices. They tried to free their ships, tried to dissolve the connections, but Seyyan drew them ever nearer.

Seyyan's craft had infected their ships not only with beauty, but with obedience.

Tasmin's craft, old and powerful, broke free. Its pilus tore, shredding and bleeding. Yalnis's ship quivered in response to the sight or to a cry of distress imperceptible to people. The destruction and distraction allowed a few other people to overcome the wills of their craft and wrench away, breaking more connections. After the painful and distressing process, the freed craft fled into a wider orbit, or set a course to escape entirely from the star system and from Seyyan.

Person and ship alike suffered when fighting the illness of a malignant genetic interchange. Yalnis hoped they would all survive.

"What's she doing?" Yalnis whispered. Her ship interpreted her words, correctly, as a question for people, not for ships. It opened all her silenced message ports and let in exclamations, cries of outrage, excuses, argument, wild speculation.

Seyyan's craft gleamed and shimmered and proclaimed its ascension and gathered the remaining captives into a shield colony. With its imprisoned allies, it moved toward Yalnis and her ship.

Yalnis went cold with fear, shock, and the responsibility for all that had happened: she had brought all the others here; she had succumbed to Seyyan and then challenged her; she had forced people to take sides.

"Seyyan infected their defenses," Yalnis said. That's what the fashionable pattern was for, she thought. A temptation, and a betrayal.

"True," her ship replied.

Yalnis's ship moved toward Seyyan's craft. It quivered around her, like the companions within her. It had made its decision, a decision that risked damage. This was ship's business. Yalnis could fight it, or she could add her will to her ship's and join the struggle. She chose her ship.

Zorar followed, and, reluctantly, so did Tasmin's craft, its torn pili leaking fluid that broke into clouds of mist and dissipated in sunlit sparkles. The skin of the craft dulled to its former blue sheen, but patches of shimmering infection broke out, spread, contracted.

After all too brief a time, the stars vanished again, obscured by the coruscating flanks of Seyyan's shield. Yalnis's ship pushed dangerously into the muddle. Yalnis crouched beneath the transparent dome, overcome with claustrophobia. No escape remained, except perhaps for Seyyan.

Seyyan forced her captive allies to grow extensions, but when they touched Yalnis's ship, they withdrew abruptly, stung by its immune response. In appreciation, Yalnis stroked the fabric of her ship.

"True," her ship whispered.

Please, Yalnis thought, Seyyan, please, just flee. Let everyone go. Announce a new adventure. Declare that you've shamed me enough already, that you won our altercation.

She had no wish to speak to Seyyan, but she had an obligation. She created a message port. Seyyan answered, and smiled.

"Your shunning didn't last long," she said. "Shall I tell my friends to withdraw?"

Yalnis flushed, embarrassed and angry, but refused to let Seyyan divert her.

"What do you want?" Yalnis cried. "Why do you care anymore what I think? Leave us all alone. Go on more of your marvelous and legendary adventures – "

"Flee?" Seyyan said. "From you?"

Ekarete's craft, willingly loyal to Seyyan, interposed itself between Seyyan and Yalnis. A pore opened in its skin. A spray of scintillating liquid exploded outward, pushed violently into vacuum by the pressure behind it. The fluid spattered over the dome of Yalnis's ship. It spread, trying to penetrate, trying to infect. Yalnis flinched, as if the stuff could reach her.

Her ship shuddered. Yalnis gasped. The temperature in her living space rose: her ship's skin reacted to the assault, marshalling a powerful immune response, fighting off the infection. The foreign matter sublimated, rose in a foggy sparkle, and dispersed.

Seyyan lost patience. The flank of her craft bulged outward, touching Ekarete's. It burst, like an abscess, exploding ship's fluids onto the flank of Ekarete's craft. The lines of fluid solidified in the vacuum and radiation of space, then contracted, pulling the captive craft closer, drawing it in to feed upon. Ekarete's craft, its responses compromised, had no defense.

"Seyyan!" Ekarete cried. "I never agreed – How – " And then, "Help us!"

Seyyan's craft engulfed Ekarete's, overwhelming the smaller ship's pattern variations with the stronger design. The captive ship matched the captor, and waves of color and light swept smoothly from one across the other.

"You must be put away," Yalnis said to Seyyan, and ended their communication forever.

Tasmin's craft, its blue skin blotched with shimmer, its torn connections hovering and leaking, approached Seyyan's craft.

"Don't touch it again!" Yalnis cried. "You'll be caught too!"

"She must stop," Tasmin said, with remarkable calm.

Yalnis took a deep breath.

"True," she said. Her ship responded to her assent, pressing forward. To Tasmin, she said, "Yes. But you can't stop her. You can only destroy yourself."

Tasmin's ship decelerated and hovered, for Seyyan had already damaged it badly.

A desperate pilus stretched from the outer flank of Ekarete's ship. Yalnis allowed it to touch, her heart bounding with apprehension. Her ship reached for it, and the connecting outgrowths met. Her ship declined to fuse, but engulfed the tip to create a temporary connection. It opened its outgrowth, briefly, into Yalnis's living room.

The outlines of the younger craft blurred as Seyyan's ship incorporated it, dissolved it, and took over its strength. The pilus ripped free of Yalnis's ship and sank into the substance of Seyyan's craft.

Air rushed past Yalnis in a quick blast; the wind fell still as her ship clenched its pilus and resorbed it.

The shrinking pilus pulled Ekarete inside. Naked, crying, her hair flying, she held her hand over her stomach for modesty. Her palm hid the little face of her companion, muffling its squeals and the clash of its sharp teeth.

Maybe it will bite her, Yalnis thought, distracted, and chided herself for the uncharitable thought.

"How could she, how could she?" Ekarete said.

"Yalnis," Zorar said from the depths of her own ship, "what are you doing? What should I do?"

"Come and get me if we dissolve," Yalnis said. And then she wondered, Could I leave my ship, if Seyyan bests us? *Should* I?

If Seyyan had been patient, Yalnis thought, she might have persuaded her friends to defend her willingly. If she'd asked them, they might have agreed I'd outraged her unjustly. If she'd trusted them, they might have joined her out of love.

No shield colony had existed in Yalnis's lifetime, or in the memories of the lovers whose companions she had accepted: no great danger had threatened any group of people. A shield was a desperate act, a last effort, an assault. Extricating and healing the ships afterward was a long and expensive task. But Seyyan's friends might have done it willingly, for Seyyan's love. Instead they tore themselves away from her, one by one, desperately damaging themselves to avoid Ekarete's fate, but weakening Seyyan as well.

They dispersed, fleeing. Seyyan's craft loomed, huge and old, sucking in the antennae desperately growing outward from the vestiges of Ekarete's craft.

Ekarete cried softly as her ship vanished.

"Do be quiet," Yalnis said.

Until the last moment of possibility, Yalnis hoped Seyyan would relent. Yalnis and Zorar and Tasmin, and a few others, hovered around her, but she had room to escape. Seyyan's former allies gathered beyond the first rank of defense, fearful of being trapped again but resolving to defend themselves.

Yalnis's ship emitted the first wave of ship silk, a silver plume of sticky fibers that caught against the other ship and wrapped around its skin. Yalnis's ship balanced itself: action and reaction.

The other ships followed her lead, spraying Seyyan's craft with plume after plume: silver, scarlet, midnight blue, ultraviolet, every color but the holographic pattern their defenses covered. Seyyan's craft reacted, but the concerted effort overwhelmed it. It drew inward, shrinking from the touch of the silk to avoid allergic reaction. Gradually it disappeared beneath the layers of solidifying color.

Yalnis listened for a plea, a cry for mercy, even a shout of defiance. But Seyyan maintained a public silence.

Is she secretly giving orders to her allies? Yalnis wondered. Does she have allies anymore? She glanced over her shoulder at Ekarete.

Ekarete, creeping up behind her, launched herself at Yalnis, her teeth bared in an eerie mirror of her angry companion's. She reached for Yalnis's face, her hand pouring blood, and they fell in a tangle. Yalnis struggled, fending off Ekarete's fists and fingernails, desperate to protect her tiny growing daughter, desperate to defend her companions against Ekarete's, which was after all the spawn of Seyyan and her murderous first companion.

All the companions squealed and gnashed their teeth, ready to defend themselves, as aware of danger as they were of opportunity.

"Why are you doing this?" Yalnis cried. "I'm not your enemy!"

"I want my ship! I want Seyyan!"

"It's gone! She's gone!" Yalnis wrestled Ekarete and grabbed her, holding tight and ducking her head as Ekarete slapped and struck her. The companions writhed and lunged at their opponent. Their movements gave Yalnis weird sensations of sexual arousal and pleasure in the midst of anger and fear.

The floor slipped beneath her, startling her as it built loose lobes of ship silk. She grabbed one and flung herself forward, pulling the gossamer fabric over Ekarete, letting go, rolling free, leaving Ekarete trapped. The silk closed in. Yalnis struggled to her feet, brushing her hand across her stomach to reassure herself that her companions and her daughter remained uninjured. She wiped sweat from her face and realized it was not sweat, but blood, not Ekarete's but her own, flowing from a stinging scratch down her cheek.

Both she and her ship had been distracted. Seyyan's craft struggled against a thin spot that should have been covered by more silver silk from Yalnis's ship. The tangled shape rippled and roiled, and the craft bulged to tear at the restraint. Glowing plasma from the propulsion system spurted in tiny jets beneath the surface of the silk. The craft convulsed. Yalnis flinched to think of the searing plasma trapped between the craft's skin and the imprisoning cover.

"Finish it," Yalnis said to her ship. "Please, finish it." Tears ran hot down her face. Ekarete's muffled cries and curses filled the living space, and Yalnis's knees shook.

"True," her ship said. A cloak of silver spread to cover the weak spot, to seal in the plasma.

The roiling abruptly stopped.

Yalnis's friends flung coat after coat of imprisoning silk over Seyyan's craft, until they were all exhausted.

When it was over, Yalnis's ship accelerated away with the last of its strength. Her friends began a slow dispersal, anxious to end the gathering. Seyyan's craft drifted alone and silent, turning in a slow rotation, its glimmer extinguished by a patchwork of hardening colors.

Yalnis wondered how much damage the plasma had done, how badly Seyyan's craft had been hurt, and whether it and Seyyan had survived.

"Tasmin," she said, quietly, privately, "will you come for Ekarete? She can't be content here."

Ekarete was a refugee, stripped of all her possessions, indigent and pitiable, squeaking angrily beneath ship silk like a completely hidden companion.

After a hesitation Yalnis could hardly believe, or forgive, Tasmin replied.

"Very well."

Yalnis saw to her ship. Severely depleted, it arced through space in a stable enough orbit. It had expended its energy and drawn on its structural mass. Between defending itself and the demands of its unborn daughter ship, it would need a long period of recovery.

She sent one more message, a broadcast to everyone, but intended for Seyyan's former friends.

"I haven't the resources to correct her orbit." She felt too tired even to check its stability, and reluctant to ask her ship to exert itself. "Someone who still cares for her must take that responsibility."

"Let me up!" Ekarete shouted. Yalnis gave her a moment of attention.

"Tasmin will be here soon," Yalnis said. "She'll help you."

"We're bleeding."

Yalnis said, "I don't care."

She pulled her shirt aside to see to her own companions. Three of the four had retracted, showing only their teeth. She stroked around them till they relaxed, dozed, and exposed the tops of their downy little heads, gold and copper and softly freckled. Only Bahadirgul, ebony against Yalnis's pale skin, remained bravely awake and alert. Drying blood slashed its mouth, but the companion itself had sustained only a shallow scratch. Yalnis petted the soft black fur of Bahadirgul's hair.

"You're gallant," Yalnis said. "Yes, gallant. I made the right choice, didn't I?" Bahadirgul trembled with pleasure against her fingers, within her body.

When Bahadirgul slept, exhausted and content, Yalnis saw to her daughter, who grew unmolested and unconcerned; she saw to herself and to her companions, icing the bruises of Ekarete's attack, washing her scratches and the companion's. She looked in the mirror and wondered if she would have a scar down her cheek, across her perfect skin.

And, if I do, will I keep it? she wondered. As a reminder?

As she bathed and put on new clothes, Tasmin's ship approached, sent greetings, asked for permission to attach. Yalnis let her ship make that decision and felt relieved when the ship approved. A pilus extended from Tasmin's ship; Yalnis's ship accepted it. Perhaps it carried some risk, but they were sufficiently exhausted that growing a capsule for Ekarete's transport felt beyond their resources.

As the pilus widened into a passage, Zorar whispered to her through a message port, "Shall I come and help? I think I should."

"No, my friend," Yalnis whispered in reply. "Thank you, but no."

Tasmin entered, as elegant and perfect as ever. Yalnis surprised herself by taking contrary pride in her own casual appearance. Zorar's concern and worry reached her. Yalnis should be afraid, but she was not.

"Please release Ekarete," she said to her ship.

"True," it said, its voice soft. The net of silk withdrew, resorbed. As soon as one hand came free, Ekarete clutched and scratched and dragged herself loose. She sprang to her feet, blood-smeared and tangle-haired.

She took one step toward Yalnis, then stopped, staring over Yalnis's shoulder.

Yalnis glanced quickly back.

As if deliberately framed, Seyyan's craft loomed beyond the transparent dome of the living space, bound in multicolored layers of the heaviest ship silk, each layer permeated with allergens particular to the ship that had created it. Seyyan's craft lay cramped within the sphere, shrinking from its painful touch, immobilized and put away until time wore the restraints to dust.

Ekarete keened with grief. The wail filled Yalnis's hearing and thickened the air.

Tasmin hurried to her, putting one arm around her shaking shoulders, covering her with a wing of her dress.

"Take her," Yalnis said to Tasmin. "Please, take her."

Tasmin turned Ekarete and guided her to the pilus. The connection's rim had already begun to swell inward as Yalnis's ship reacted to the touch of Tasmin's with inflammation. Tasmin and Ekarete hurried through and disappeared.

Seyyan's former friends would have to decide how to treat Ekarete. They might abandon her, adopt her, or spawn a new craft for her. Yalnis had no idea what they would choose to do, whether they would decide she was pure fool for her loyalty or pure hero for the same reason.

When the connector had healed over, leaving the wall a little swollen and irritated, when Tasmin's ship moved safely away, Yalnis took a long deep breath and let it out slowly. Silence and solitude calmed her.

"It's time, I think," she said aloud.

"True," replied her ship.

Yalnis descended to the growing chamber, where the daughter ship lay fat and sleek, bulging toward the outer skin. It had formed as a pocket of Yalnis's ship, growing inward. A thick neck connected the two craft, but now the neck was thinning, with only an occasional pulse of nutrients and information. The neck would part, healing over on the daughter's side, opening wide on the outer skin of Yalnis's ship.

Yalnis stepped inside for the first, and perhaps the only, time.

The living space was very plain, very beautiful in its elegant simplicity, its walls and floor a black as deep and vibrant as space without stars. Its storage bulged with the unique gifts Yalnis's guests had brought: new foods, new information, new bacteria, stories, songs, and maps of places unimaginably distant.

The soft silver skin of Yalnis's ship hugged it close, covering its transparent dome.

The new ship awoke to her presence. It created a nest for her. She cuddled into its alien warmth, and slept.

She woke to birth pangs, her own and her ship's. Extensions and monitors retracted from her body.

"Time for launch," she said to her ship.

"True," it said, without hesitation or alternation. It shuddered with a powerful labor pang. It had recovered its strength during the long rest.

"Bahadirgul," Yalnis said, "it's time."

Bahadirgul yawned hugely, blinked, and came wide awake.

Yalnis and Bahadirgul combined again. The pleasure of their mental combining matched that of their physical combining, rose in intensity, and exceeded it. At the climax, they presented their daughter with a copy of Yalnis's memories and the memories of her lover Bahadir.

A moment of pressure, a stab of pain –

Yalnis picked up the blinking gynuncula. Her daughter had Bahadir's ebony skin and hair of deepest brown, and Yalnis's own dark blue eyes. Delighted, she showed her to Bahadirgul, wondering, as she always did, how much the companion understood beyond pleasure, satiation, and occasional fear or fury. It sighed and retreated to its usual position, face exposed, calm. The other companions hissed and blinked and looked away. Yalnis let the mesh of her shirt slip over their faces.

Yalnis carried her daughter through the new ship, from farm space to power plant, pausing to wash away the stickiness of birth in the pretty little bathing stream. The delicate fuzz on her head dried as soft as fur.

The daughter blinked at Yalnis. Everyone said a daughter always knew her mother from the beginning. Yalnis believed it, looking into the new being's eyes, though neither she nor anyone she knew could recall that first moment of life and consciousness.

By the time she returned to the living space at the top of the new ship, the connecting neck had separated, one end healing against the daughter ship in a faint navel pucker, the other slowly opening to the outside. Yalnis's ship shuddered again, pushing at the daughter ship. The transparent dome pressed out, to reveal space and the great surrounding web of stars.

Yalnis's breasts ached. She sank cross-legged on the warm midnight floor and let her daughter suck, giving her a physical record of dangers and attractions as she and Bahadirgul had given her a mental record of the past.

"Karime," Yalnis whispered, as her daughter fell asleep. Above them the opening widened. The older ship groaned. The new ship quaked as it pressed out into the world.

"Karime, daughter, live well," Yalnis said.

She gave her daughter to her ship's daughter, placing the chubby sleeping creature in the soft nest. She petted the ship-silk surface.

"Take good care of her," she said.

"True," the new ship whispered.

Yalnis smiled, stood up, watched the new ship cuddle the new person for a moment, then hurried through the interior connection before it closed.

She slipped out, glanced back to be sure all was well, and returned to her living space to watch.

Yalnis's ship gave one last heavy shudder. The new ship slipped free.

It floated nearby, getting its bearings, observing its surroundings. Soon – staying near another ship always carried an element of danger, as well as opportunity – it whispered into motion, accelerating itself carefully toward a higher, more distant orbit.

Yalnis smiled at its audacity. Farther from the star, moving through the star's dust belt, it could collect mass and grow quickly. In a thousand, perhaps only half a thousand, orbits, Karime would emerge to take her place as a girl of her people.

"We could follow," Yalnis said. "Rest, recoup . . ."

"False," her ship whispered, displaying its strength, and its desire, and its need. "False, false."

"We could go on our adventure."

"True," her ship replied, and turned outward toward the web of space, to travel forever, to feast on stardust.

COMBER

Gene Wolfe

Gene Wolfe is perceived by many critics to be one of the best – perhaps *the* best – SF and fantasy writers working today. His most acclaimed work is the tetralogy *The Book of the New Sun*, individual volumes of which have won the Nebula Award, the World Fantasy Award, and the John W. Campbell Award. He followed this up with a popular new series, *The Book of the Long Sun*, that included *Nightside the Long Sun*, *The Lake of the Long Sun*, *Calde of the Long Sun*, and *Exodus from the Long Sun*, and has recently completed another series, *The Book of the Short Sun*, with the novels *On Blue's Waters*, *In Green's Jungles*, and *Return to the Whorl*. His other books include the classic novels *Peace* and *The Devil in a Forest*, both recently rereleased, as well as *Free Live Free*, *Soldier in the Mist*, *Soldier of Arete*, *There Are Doors*, *Castleview*, *Pandora by Holly Hollander*, and *The Urth of the New Sun*. His short fiction has been collected in *The Island of Doctor Death and Other Stories*, *Gene Wolfe's Book of Days*, *The Wolfe Archipelago*, the World Fantasy Award–winning collection *Storeys from the Old Hotel*, *Endangered Species*, and *Strange Travelers*. His most recent books consist of a two-volume novel series, *The Knight* and *The Wizard*, and a new collection, *Starwater Strains*.

In the incisive story that follows, he takes us to a world where, like our own, everything is fluid and changing – but perhaps in a little more obvious way . . .

THE NEWS WHISPERED by his radio this morning was the same as the news when he and Mona had gone to bed: the city had topped the crest, and everything was flat and wonderful – if only for a day or two. "You're flat yourselves," he told it softly, and switched it off.

Mona was still asleep when he had shaved and dressed, her swollen belly at rest on the mattress, her face full of peace, and her slow inhalations loud to his acute hearing. He grabbed a breakfast bar on his way through the kitchen and wondered how the hell he could start the car without waking her up.

There was a ball on the driveway, a chewed-up rubber ball some dog had stopped chasing when it had stopped running. He picked it up and bounced it off the concrete. It bounced a few more times and settled down to rest again, as round as Mona, though not quite as happy. He tossed it into the car and followed it.

Press the accelerator, let it up, twist the key. The little engine purred to life as if it knew its work would be easy today. The suburb passed in a familiar blur.

From the tollway, he eyed the tall buildings that marked the center of the city. The last crest had come before he was born (the crest of a wholly different wave, something he found hard to imagine) but he knew that not one of those spumecatchers had been built then. Now the city might have to pay for its pride and the convenience of having so many offices close together. Pay with its very existence, perhaps.

The brass inclinometer he had bought when he had foreseen the danger the year before was waiting for him when he reached his desk, solidly screwed to the desktop, its long axis coinciding exactly with the direction of motion of the plate. He squinted at the needle, and at last got out a magnifying glass. Zero. It seemed supernatural: a portent.

A memo taped to his monitor warned him that the new angle "which will soon grow steep" would be the reverse of what it called "the accustomed angle." Everything was to be secured a second time with that new angle in mind. Workmen would make the rounds of all offices. He was asked to cooperate for the good of the company. He tossed the memo, woke his processor, and opened Mona's private dream house instead. His design was waiting there to be tinkered with, as it would not have been if anyone in authority had found it.

"Okay if I look at your gadget?" It was Phil, and Phil looked without waiting for his permission. "Flat," Phil said happily, and laughed. "The plate's flat. First time in my life."

"The last time, too." He closed Mona's dream-house. "For either one of us."

Phil rubbed his hands. "It will all be different. Entirely different. A new slant on everything. Want to go up to the roof, ol' buddy? Should be a great view."

He shook his head.

It would be very different indeed, he reflected when Phil had left, if the plate overturned. As it very well might. If the building did not break up when it hit the water, it would point down and would be submerged. Water would short out the electrical equipment, probably at once; and in any event, the elevators would no longer operate. Rooms and corridors might (or might not) hold some air for a few hours – most of it down on what were now the lower floors. He might, perhaps, break a window and so escape; if he lived long enough to rise to street level, the edge of the plate, and air, would be what? Thirty miles away? Forty?

Back home, Mona would have drowned. If the plate were going to turn over, he decided, it would be better if it did it while he was at home with her. Better if they died together with their unborn child.

Next day the inclinometer was no longer on zero, and the chewed ball he had left on his desk had rolled to one side; as he wrote letters and called contacts, as he began to sketch the outline of his next project, he watched the space between the end of the needle and the hair-thin zero line grow.

By Friday the needle was no longer near zero, and there were intervening marks which he did not trouble to read. Because on Friday, at not-quite eleven o'clock of that bright and still almost-level morning, Edith Benson called to say that Mona had gone into labor while they chatted across the fence, and that she had driven Mona to the hospital.

He took some time off. By the time he returned to his desk, the needle was no more than a pencil's width from the peg. It seemed to him to tremble there, and he was reminded of his conversation with the proprietor of the little shop in which he had bought the inclinometer. He had asked why the scale went no further; and the proprietor had grinned, showing beautifully regular teeth that had certainly been false. "Because you won't be there to look at it if she goes farther than that," the proprietor had told him.

A note taped to his desk informed him that he had neglected to set the brake on his swivel chair. It had pushed open the door of his office and crashed into Mrs. Patterson's desk. He apologized to her in person.

At quitting time, the space between the point of the needle and the peg would admit three of his business cards, but not four.

That evening he and Mona sat up until their son's next feeding, talking about colleges and professions. It would be up to Adrian to choose, they agreed on that. But would not their own attitudes, the training they gave him, and their very table-talk, influence Adrian's choices? At ten they kissed, looked in on Adrian, and kissed again.

"Goodnight, honey," Mona said; and he, knowing that she did not want him to watch, "Goodnight, darling."

As he combed his hair the next morning, he found that his thoughts, which should have been focused on work, were full of Adrian – and the plate. More and taller buildings would go up when this was over. More and taller buildings would be built, that was to say, if there was anyone left alive to plan and build them. His firm would have a part of that, and would profit by it. Those profits would contribute to his profit-sharing plan.

He shrugged, rinsed his comb, and put it away. The new and wonderful house that he himself had designed – with a den and a sewing room, and enough bedrooms for five children – would not be quite so far off then.

At work, he found the needle not quite so near the peg as it had been. Three business cards slipped into the opening easily. Four would just clear.

Up on the roof, a little knot of his coworkers were marveling at the vastness of the tossing green waters that stretched to the horizon in every direction. The secretary with the gold pince-nez gripped his arm. "I come up here every morning. We'll never be able to see anything like this again, and today will be the last day we're this high up."

He nodded, trying to look serious and pleased. The secretary with the gold pince-nez was the CEO's, and although he had seen her often he had never spoken to her – much less been spoken to.

An executive vice president laid large soft hands on his shoulders. "Take a good long look, young man. If it sticks with you, you'll think big. We always need people who think big."

He said, "I will, sir."

Yet he found himself looking at the people who looked, and not at the boundless ocean. There was the freckled kid from the mailroom who whistled, and over there the pretty blonde who never smiled.

All alone, at the very edge of the gently slanting roof, was old Parsons. Hadn't Parsons retired? Clearly Parsons had not; and Parsons had set up a tarnished brass telescope on a tripod – a telescope through which he peered down into the watery abyss that had opened before the city, not out at the grandeur of the horizon.

"Something in the water?"

Parsons straightened up. "Sure is."

"What is it?"

Gnarled fingers stroked bristling, almost invisible white whiskers. "That," Parsons said slowly, "is what I'm trying to figure, young feller."

"A whale?" he asked.

Parsons shook his head. "Nope. 'Tain't that. You might think it'd be easy to figure, with a good glass. But 'tain't." Parsons stepped aside. "You want to look?"

He bent as Parsons had and made a slight adjustment to the focus.

It was a city, or a town at least, nestled now in the trough. Narrow streets, roofs that seemed to be largely of red tiles. A white spire rose above its houses and shops, and for an instant – only an instant, it seemed to him that he had caught the gleam of the gold cross atop the spire.

He straightened up, swallowed as though his throat and stomach had some part in absorbing what he had just seen, and bent to look again.

Something white fluttered and vanished above one red roof. A pigeon, he felt certain. There were pigeons as well as gulls there, circling above the houses and shops; pigeons that no doubt nested in the eaves and scavenged the town's streets, whatever food might be found in them.

"Been lookin' on my old computer at home," Parsons said. "There's views of various places on there, if you know where to look. My guess is Les Sables-d'Olonne. Mind now, I'm not sayin' I'm right. Just my guess, I said. You got one?"

He shook his head. "If – It'll be out of the way, won't it? By the time we get there? The next wave will pick it up first, won't it?" As he spoke, he discovered that he did not believe a word of it.

"Can't say." Parsons scratched his bristling jaw. "Pretty slow, generally, goin' up. Slidin' down's faster 'n blazes, and you go a long way." Turning his head, he spat. "We're heading right at it."

"If it wasn't, if it was still in the way . . . And we hit – "

"Might bust our plate. I dunno. I phoned up one of them geologists. They're s'posed to know all about all that. He said he didn't know neither. Depend on how fast each was goin'. Only you ought to think 'bout this, young feller – ain't a buildin' on ours that could stand it if we bump with much speed a-tall. Knock 'em flat, ever' last one of 'em."

Reluctantly he nodded. "You're right, it will. May I ask who you called, sir?"

"Doctor Lantz, his name was. Said don't talk about it, only he don't have any right to give *me* orders." Old Parsons appeared to hesitate. "Won't matter to me. I'll be gone long before. You might still be around, though, a healthy young feller like you."

"Yes," he said. Images of the baby, of Adrian, filled his mind; he continued to talk almost by reflex. "I asked about the geologist because I know a geologist. Slightly. I've gotten to know him slightly. His name isn't Lantz, though. It's Sutton. Martin Sutton. He lives one street over from us."

He debated the matter with himself for more than an hour before telephoning Sutton. "You know some things I need to know, Marty," he said when the preliminaries were complete, "and I'm going to pick your brain, if you'll let me. This city or town or whatever it is in the trough – are we going to hit it?"

There was a lengthy silence before Sutton said, "You know about it, too."

"Correct."

"They've kept it off TV. They'll keep it out of the papers, if they can. I wonder how many people know."

"I have no idea. Are we, Marty?"

"That's not my field. I'm a geologist, okay? I study the plate."

"But you know. Are we?"

Sutton sighed. "Probably. How'd you find out?"

"I looked though a telescope, that's all. There's a town down there. Or a small city – take your pick. It's got fields and gardens around it. What are the odds?"

Sutton's shrug was almost audible. "One in ten, maybe."

"One in ten of hitting?"

"No. One in ten of missing. They were calling it one in five yesterday. You mustn't tell anybody I've told you, okay?"

"I won't. But they told you. So you could tell them whether our plate would break?"

Another silence, this one nearly as long as the first. Then: "Yeah."

"They did, but that wasn't the main reason. What's the other thing? It might help if you'd tell me."

"For God's sake keep it under your hat." Even over the phone, Sutton sounded desperate.

"I will, I swear. What is it?"

"They wanted to talk about the feasibility of breaking up the other plate in advance. You know – the one we're going to hit."

"I understand. Go on."

"Suppose we could do it. Suppose we could break it into three pieces. They'd drift apart, and we might not hit all three."

He nodded slowly to himself. "And even if we did, three small shocks wouldn't be as damaging as one big one."

"Right." Sutton seemed a little less nervous now.

"They'll try to prepare for them, too, of course. We've got a crew going through our offices double-bolting everything. Steel boots to hold the legs of the desks, and they're screwing our file cabinets to the walls as well as the floor. I was watching it a few minutes ago."

"I suppose we'll get that here, too," Sutton said, "but it hasn't started yet."

"Your superiors don't know."

"I guess not."

"I see. I suppose mine have been asked whether it would be practical to reinforce certain buildings. One more question, please, Marty, and it may be the last one. Would what they asked you about be feasible? Breaking up the plate we're going to hit like that?"

"I think so. Probably . . . Listen, I'm not supposed to talk about this, but I'd like to get it off my chest. First, I've had to assume that their plate's pretty much like ours. Ours is the only one we're familiar with."

"Sure."

"Assuming that it is, we'd have to drill into it and plant charges about a hundred feet down. I said the people there aren't going to stand still for that and they said they'd take them by surprise. It's not very big, okay? A thousand men, well trained and heavily armed. Hydrofoils that will launch when we're close. I'll probably be one of the men on the boats. Everyone else here is older, they'll be old men by the time it happens. I'm not much older than you are. I'll still be active."

"What about somebody younger? Somebody who hasn't graduated yet?"

"There won't be anybody like that." Sutton's voice went flat, stripped of all emotion. "I might as well tell you this, too – it's the kind of thing that can't be kept secret. The university's dropped geology. They've closed the whole department, effective immediately."

That night, over wieners and sauerkraut, he told Mona. "I promised a person who trusted me that I wouldn't talk about this, but you're going to have to know."

When he had finished outlining the situation, she said, "But won't it work? This man you talked to said it would."

"Probably not." He paused, listening to the trees murmur in the wind that would soon become a years-long gale: the wind of the city's swift descent. "They must surely see us coming at them, just as we see them in our path. They'll start preparing, and both sides have ten or fifteen years to prepare in. They can arm everyone who's willing to fight, and put up obstacles to keep our people from landing. I think we can count on both those."

"They could break up their plate for us."

He nodded. "Yes, they could. We could break up ours, too. Do you think the government will?"

For a long moment Mona stared at him. At last she said, "How horrible! No. Of course they won't."

"But we could do it ourselves." The idea had come to full flower during his long call to Sutton; he had seized it eagerly, and hoped now to inspire her to an equal acceptance. "We could plant charges that would exploit known weaknesses in our plate. The force of the explosions would start our piece moving away from the city, and out of the collision path the city's on now."

"But, darling – "

"Adrian would have a future. Don't you see, Mona? We wouldn't take just this residential neighborhood, but a piece of the infrastructure big enough to be economically viable. We could make things for ourselves then, make things to trade, grow gardens, and fish. That town the city's going to hit – French or Belgian or whatever it is – people survive there. They even prosper. I've bounced this off of a man over on the next street, a geologist. He agrees it might be possible, and he's coming over to talk about it."

"Bumpers! We could build bumpers, things with springs in them. Or – or big sacks full of air."

He shook his head. "Nothing we could build would have much effect on a mass as great as the plate's, and if we succeeded in slowing it down much – we wouldn't – the wave would break over us and drown everybody."

"But . . ." Mona looked desperate. "But, Honey – "

He glanced at his watch. "Sutton's coming at eight. You won't have to feed him, but coffee and cookies might be nice. Or cake. Something like that."

"Okay." Mona's voice was scarcely audible.

An hour later she said, "Won't you please stop combing your hair with your fingers like that? And pacing up and down and up and down?"

For the twentieth time he looked at his watch. "Sutton could be here right now."

"He could," Mona conceded, "if he'd come at least ten minutes early. Honestly, I'm going to get hysterical. Sit down and relax. Or – or go outside where you can see his headlights as soon as he turns onto the street. Please? If I start screaming I'll wake Adrian. Won't you, pretty please, Honey, for me?"

He nodded, suddenly grateful, and discovered that he had been on the point of running his fingers through his hair again. "Okay. I'll do that.

I won't come back in until he gets here."

The wind had turned the night cold. He walked out to the street. *How many charges would they need, and how big would each have to be? Would they have to enlist a chemist to make the explosives? Dynamite, or whatever?* To his right, looming white above the treetops though far more distant, he could only just glimpse the boiling crest of the wave. Those trees were wrongly slanted now. Come morning, they would find themselves pointed away from the sun. He chuckled softly. It could not be often that smug suburban trees received such an unpleasant surprise.

When he returned to the house to sit on the stoop, Mona had drawn the blinds. She was being overly cautious, he decided, but he could not find it in his heart to blame her.

Out at the curb again and still nervous, he held his breath as headlights turned off Miller Road. They crept up the sloping street as though the driver were checking house numbers, and then – incredibly, miraculously – swung into the driveway.

Sutton climbed out, and they shook hands. "I hadn't forgotten where you live," Sutton said, "but this new angle has me a little disoriented."

He nodded. "All of us are. I think that may work in our favor."

"Maybe you're right." The wind snatched away Sutton's baseball cap. Sutton grabbed for it, missing by a foot or more. "Help me find that, will you? I'd hate to lose it."

They had searched the bushes for a minute or more when Sutton straightened up and said, "Something wrong? What's the matter with you?"

He had straightened up already. "Sirens." He pointed east, northeast, and after a momentary hesitation, north. "Don't you hear them?"

Sutton shook his head. "No, I don't."

"Well, I do. Three or four cars, and they're getting closer."

One by one, the sirens grew louder – and abruptly fell silent. For almost the last time, he ran nervous fingers through his hair.

"What's up?" Sutton began. "If you – "

Before the third word, he had turned and sprinted for the door. It was locked. His key turned the lock and the bolt clicked back, but the night bolt was in place. Once only, his shoulder struck the unyielding wood.

By that time the first police car had turned the corner on two screaming wheels, and it was too late to hide.

AUDUBON IN ATLANTIS

Harry Turtledove

Although he writes other kinds of science fiction as well, and even the occasional fantasy, Harry Turtledove has become one of the most prominent writers of Alternate History stories in the business today, and is probably the most popular and influential writer to work that territory since L. Sprague De Camp. In fact, most of the current popularity of that particular subgenre can be attributed to Turtledove's own hot-ticketed bestseller status.

Turtledove has published Alternate History novels such as *The Guns of the South*, dealing with a time line in which the American Civil War turns out very differently, thanks to time-traveling gunrunners; the bestselling Worldwar series, in which the course of World War II is altered by attacking aliens; the Basil Argyros series, detailing the adventures of a "magistrianoi" in an alternate Byzantine Empire (collected in the book *Agent of Byzantium*); the Sim series, which takes place in an alternate world in which European explorers find North America inhabited by hominids instead of Indians (collected in the book *A Different Flesh*); a look at a world where the Revolutionary War *didn't* happen, written with actor Richard Dreyfuss, *The Two Georges*; and many other intriguing Alternate History scenarios. Turtledove is also the author of two multivolume Alternate History *fantasy* series: the multivolume Videssos Cycle and the Krispes Sequence. His other books include the novels *Wereblood*, *Werenight*, *Earthgrip*, *Noninterference*, *A World of Difference*, *Gunpowder Empire*, *American Empire: The Victorious Opposition*, *Jaws of Darkness*, and *Ruled Britannia*, the collections *Kaleidoscope* and *Down in the Bottomlands (and Other Places)*, and, as editor, *The Best Alternate History Stories of the 20th Century*, *The Best Military Science Fiction of the 20th Century*, with Martin H. Greenberg, and the *Alternate Generals* books – plus *many* others. His most recent books include the novels *Settling Accounts: Drive to the East* and *In the Presence of Mine Enemies*; and the anthologies *The Best Time Travel Stories of the 20th Century*, *Alternate Generals III*, and *The*

Enchanter Completed. Coming up are *The Bridge of the Separator*, *End of the Beginning*, and *Every Inch a King.* He won a Hugo Award in 1994 for his story "Down in the Bottomlands." A native Californian, Turtledove has a Ph.D. in Byzantine history from UCLA, and has published a scholarly translation of a ninth-century Byzantine chronicle. He lives in Canoga Park, California, with his wife and family.

Here he invites us to voyage with pioneering ornithologist John Audubon to unknown territory in search of bird species feared to be extinct, on an Earth not *quite* our own . . .

D ELICATE AS IF WALKING on eggs, the riverboat *Augustus Caesar* eased in alongside the quay at New Orleans. Colored roustabouts, bare to the waist, caught lines from the boat and made her fast. The steam whistle blew several long, happy blasts, telling the world the stern-wheeler had arrived. Then black smoke stopped belching from the stacks as the crew shut down the engines.

The deck stopped quivering beneath John Audubon's feet. He breathed a silent sigh of relief; for all the time he'd spent aboard boats and ships, he was not a good sailor, and knew he never would be. Any motion, no matter how slight, could make his stomach betray him. He sighed – a long sea voyage still lay ahead of him.

Edward Harris came up and stood alongside him. "Well, my friend, we're on our way," he said.

"It's true – we are. And we shall do that which has not been done, while it may yet be done." As Audubon always did, he gathered enthusiasm when he thought about the goal and not the means by which he had to accomplish it. His English was fluent, but heavily flavored by the French that was his birth-speech. He was a good-sized man – about five feet ten – with shoulder-length gray hair combed straight back from his forehead and with bushy gray side whiskers that framed a long, strong-nosed face. Even without an accent, he would have spoken more mushily than he liked; he was nearer sixty than fifty, and had only a few teeth left. "Before long, Ed, either the great honkers will be gone from this world or I will."

He waited impatiently till the gangplank thudded into place, then hurried off the Augustus Caesar onto dry land, or something as close to dry land as New Orleans offered.

Men and women of every color, wearing everything from rags to frock coats and great hoop skirts, thronged the muddy, puddled street. Chatter, jokes, and curses crackled in Spanish, French and English, and in every possible mixture and corruption of those tongues. Audubon heard far more English than he had when he first came to New Orleans half a lifetime earlier. It was a French town then, with the Spanish dons hanging on where and as they could. Times changed, though. He knew that too well.

Not far from the Cabildo stood the brick building that housed the Bartlett Line. Edward Harris following in his wake, Audubon went inside. A clerk nodded to them. "Good day, gentlemen," he said in English. A generation earlier, the greeting would surely have come in French. "How may I be of service to you today?"

"I wish to purchase passage to Atlantis for the two of us," Audubon replied.

"Certainly, sir." The clerk didn't bat an eye. "The *Maid of Orleans* sails for New Marseille and Avalon on the west coast in . . . let me see . . . five days. If you would rather wait another week, you can book places on the *Sea Queen* for the east. She puts in at St. Augustine, St. Denis, and Hanover, then continues on to London."

"We can reach the interior as easily from either coast," Harris said.

"Just so." Audubon nodded. "We would have to wait longer to leave for the east, the journey would be longer, and I would not care to set out from Hanover in any case. I have too many friends in the capital. With the kindest intentions in the world, they would sweep us up in their social whirl, and we should be weeks getting free of it. The *Maid of Orleans* it shall be."

"You won't be sorry, sir. She's a fine ship." The clerk spoke with professional enthusiasm. He took out a book of ticket forms and inked his pen. "In whose names shall I make these out?"

"I am John James Audubon," Audubon replied. "With me travels my friend and colleague, Mr. Edward Harris."

"Audubon?" The clerk started to write, then looked up, his face aglow. "*The* Audubon? The artist? The naturalist?"

Audubon exchanged a secret smile with Edward Harris. Being recognized never failed to gratify him: he loved himself well enough to crave reminding that others loved him, too. When he swung back toward the clerk, he tried to make the smile modest. "I have the honor to be he, yes."

The clerk thrust out his hand. As Audubon shook it, the young man said, "I cannot tell you how pleased I am to make your acquaintance, sir. Mr. Hiram Bartlett, the chairman of the shipping line, is a subscriber to your *Birds and Viviparous Quadrupeds of Northern Terranova and Atlantis* – the double elephant folio edition. He sometimes brings in one volume or another for the edification of his staff. I admire your art and your text in almost equal measure, and that is the truth."

"You do me too much credit," Audubon said, in lieu of strutting and preening like a courting passenger pigeon. He was also glad to learn how prosperous Bartlett was. No one but a rich man could afford the volumes of the double elephant folio. They were big enough to show almost every bird and most beasts at life size, even if he had twisted poses and bent necks almost unnaturally here and there to fit creatures onto the pages' Procrustean bed.

"Are you traveling to Atlantis to continue your researches?" the clerk asked eagerly.

"If fate is kind, yes," Audubon replied. "Some of the creatures I hope to see are less readily found than they were in years gone by, while I" – he sighed – "I fear I am less well able to find them than I was in years gone by. Yet a man can do only what it is given to him to do, and I intend to try."

"If they're there, John, you'll find them," Harris said.

"God grant it be so," Audubon said. "What is the fare aboard the *Maid of Orleans*?"

"A first-class cabin for two, sir, is a hundred twenty livres," the clerk said. "A second-class cabin is eighty livres, while one in steerage is a mere thirty-five livres. But I fear I cannot recommend steerage for gentlemen of your quality. It lacks the comforts to which you will have become accustomed."

"I've lived rough. Once I get to Atlantis, I expect I shall live rough again," Audubon said. "But, unlike some gentlemen of the Protestant persuasion" – he fondly nudged Edward Harris – "I don't make the mistake of believing comfort is sinful. Let us travel first class."

"I don't believe comfort is sinful, and you know it," Harris said. "We want to get you where you're going and keep you as healthy and happy as we can while we're doing it. First class, by all means."

"First class it shall be, then." The clerk wrote up the tickets.

Audubon boarded the *Maid of Orleans* with a curious blend of anticipation and dread. The sidewheeler was as modern a steamship as any, but she was still a ship, one that would soon put to sea. Even going up the gangplank, his stomach gave a premonitory lurch.

He laughed and tried to make light of it, both to Harris and to himself. "When I think how many times I've put to sea in a sailing ship, at the mercy of wind and wave, I know how foolish I am to fret about a voyage like this," he said.

"You said it to the clerk last week: you can only do what you can do." Harris was blessed with both a calm stomach and a calm disposition. If opposites attracted, he and Audubon made a natural pair.

The purser strode up to them. Brass buttons gleamed on his blue wool coat; sweat gleamed on his face. "You gentlemen are traveling together?" he said. "If you would be kind enough to show me your tickets . . . ?"

"But of course," Audubon said. He and Harris produced them.

"I thank you." The purser checked them against a list he carried in one of his jacket's many pockets. "Mr. Audubon and Mr. Harris, is it? Very good. We have you in Cabin 12, the main deck on the starboard side. That's on the right as you look forward, if you haven't gone to sea before."

"I'm afraid I have," Audubon said. The purser took off his cap and scratched his balding crown, but Audubon meant it exactly as he'd phrased it. He nodded to Harris and to the free Negro pushing a wheeled cart that held their baggage. "Let's see what we've got, then."

They had a cabin with two beds, a chest of drawers, and a basin and pitcher on top of it: about what they would have had in an inn of reasonable quality, though smaller. *In an inn, though, I'm not likely to drown*, Audubon thought. He didn't suppose he was likely to drown on the *Maid of Orleans*, but if the seas got rough he would wish he were dead.

He gave the Negro half a livre, for the luggage, once unloaded from the cart, filled the cabin almost to the bursting point. Neither Audubon nor Harris was a dandy; they had no extraordinary amount of clothes. But Audubon's watercolors and paper filled up a couple of trunks, and the jars and the raw spirits they would use to preserve specimens took up a couple of more. And each of them had a shotgun for gathering specimens and a newfangled revolver for self-protection.

"Leave enough room so you'll be able to get out and come to the galley when you're hungry," the purser said helpfully.

"Thank you so much." Audubon hoped his sarcasm would freeze the man, but the purser, quite unfrozen, tipped his cap and left the cabin. Audubon muttered in pungent French.

"Never mind, John," Harris said. "We're here, and we'll weigh anchor soon. After that, no worries till we get to Avalon."

No worries for you. But Audubon kept that to himself. Harris couldn't help having a tranquil stomach, any more than the artist could help having a nervous one. Audubon only wished his were calm.

He also wished the Maid of Orleans sailed at the appointed hour, or even on the appointed day. *Thursday, the 6th day of April, 1843, at half past 10 in the morning*, the clerk had written on each ticket in a fine round hand. Audubon and Harris were aboard in good time. But half past ten came and went without departure. All of Thursday came and went. Passengers kept right on boarding. Stevedores kept on carrying sacks of sugar and rice into the ship's hold. Only the stuffed quail and artichokes and asparagus and the really excellent champagne in the first-class galley went some little way toward reconciling Audubon to being stuck on the steamship an extra day.

Finally, on Friday afternoon, the *Maid of Orleans*' engine rumbled to life. Its engine had a deeper, stronger note than the one that had propelled the *Augustus Caesar* down the Big Muddy. The deck thrummed under Audubon's shoes.

Officers bawled commands as smoke belched from the steamship's stacks. Sailors took in the lines that secured the ship to the quay. Others, grunting with effort, manned the capstan. One link at a time, they brought up the heavy chain and anchor that had held the sidewheeler in place.

Watching them, Harris said, "One of these days, steam will power the capstan as well as the paddlewheels."

"You could be right," Audubon replied. "The sailors must hope you are."

"Steam is the coming thing. You mark my words," Harris said. "Steamships, railroads, factories – who knows what else?"

"So long as they don't make a steam-powered painter, I'll do well enough," Audubon said.

"A steam-powered painter? You come up with the maddest notions, John." Edward Harris laughed. Slowly, though, the mirth faded from his face. "With a mechanical pantograph, your notion might almost come true."

"I wasn't thinking of that so much," Audubon told him. "I was thinking of this new trick of light-writing people have started using the last few years. If it gave pictures in color, not shades of gray, and if you could make – no, they say *take* – a light-writing picture fast enough to capture motion . . . well, if you could, painters would fall on thin times, I fear."

"Those are hefty *ifs*. It won't happen soon, if it ever does," Harris said.

"Oh, yes. I know." Audubon nodded. "I doubt I'll have to carry a hod in my fading years. My son will likely make a living as a painter, too. But you were talking about days to come. May I not think of them as well?"

The steamship's whistle screamed twice, warning that she was about to move away from the quay. Her paddle wheels spun slowly in reverse, backing her out into the Big Muddy. Then one wheel stopped while the other continued to revolve. Along with the rudder, that swung the *Maid of Orleans'* bow downstream. Another blast from the whistle – a triumphant one – and more smoke pouring from her stacks, she started down the great river toward the Bay of Mexico. Though she hadn't yet reached the sea, Audubon's stomach flinched.

The Big Muddy's delta stretched far out into the Bay of Mexico. As soon as the *Maid of Orleans* left the river and got out into the bay, her motion changed. Her pitch and roll were nothing to speak of, not to the crew and not to most of the passengers. But they were enough to send Audubon and a few other unfortunates running for the rail. After a couple of minutes that seemed like forever, he wearily straightened, mouth foul and burning, eyes streaming with tears. He was rid of what ailed him, at least for the moment.

A steward with a tray of glasses nodded deferentially. "Some punch, sir, to help take the taste away?"

"Merci. Mon Dieu, merci beaucoup," Audubon said, tormented out of English.

"*Pas de quoi*," the steward replied. Any man on a ship sailing from New Orleans and touching in the southern parts of Atlantis had to speak some French.

Audubon sipped and let rum and sweetened lemon juice clean his mouth. When he swallowed, he feared he would have another spasm, but the punch stayed down. Reassuring warmth spread from his middle. Two more gulps emptied the glass. "God bless you!" he said.

"My pleasure, sir. We see some every time out." The steward offered restoratives to Audubon's fellow sufferers. They fell on him with glad cries. He even got a kiss from a nice-looking young woman – but only after she'd taken a good swig from her glass of punch.

Feeling human in a mournful way, Audubon walked up toward the bow. The breeze of the ship's passage helped him forget about his unhappy innards . . . for now. Gulls screeched overhead. A common tern dove into the sea, and came up with a fish in its beak. It didn't get to enjoy the meal. A herring gull flapped after it and made it spit out the fish before it could swallow. The gull got the dainty; the robbed tern flew off to try its luck somewhere else.

On the southern horizon lay the island of Nueva Galicia, about forty miles southeast of the delta. Only a little steam rose above Mount Isabella, near the center of the island. Audubon had been a young man the last time the volcano erupted. He remembered ash raining down on New Orleans.

He looked east toward Mount Pensacola at the mouth of the bay. Pensacola had blown its stack more recently – only about ten years earlier, in fact. For now, though, no ominous plume of black rose in that direction. Audubon nodded to himself. He wouldn't have to worry about making the passage east during an eruption. When Mount Pensacola burst into flame, rivers of molten rock ran steaming into the sea, pushing the Terranovan coastline a little farther south and east. Ships couldn't come too close to observe the awe-inspiring spectacle, for the volcano threw stones to a distance coast artillery only dreamt of. Most splashed into the Bay of Mexico, of course, but who would ever forget the Black Prince, holed and sunk by a flying boulder the size of a cow back in '93?

The *Maid of Orleans* steamed sedately eastward. The waves weren't too bad; Audubon found that repeated doses of rum punch worked something not far from a miracle when it came to settling his stomach. If it did twinge now and again, the rum kept him from caring. And the lemon juice, he told himself, held scurvy at bay.

Mount Pensacola was smoking when the sidewheeler passed it near sunset. But the cloud of steam rising from the conical peak, like that above Mount Isabella, was thin and pale, not broad and black and threatening.

Edward Harris came up alongside Audubon by the port rail. "A pretty view," Harris remarked.

"It is indeed," Audubon said.

"I'm surprised not to find you sketching," Harris told him. "Sunset tinging the cloud above the mountain with pink against the deepening blue . . . What could be more picturesque?"

"Nothing, probably." Audubon laughed in some embarrassment. "But I've drunk enough of that splendid rum punch to make my right hand forget its cunning."

"I don't suppose I can blame you, not when *mal de mer* torments you so," Harris said. "I hope the sea will be calmer the next time you come this way."

"So do I – if there is a next time," Audubon said. "I am not young, Edward, and I grow no younger. I'm bound for Atlantis to do things and see things while I still may. The land changes year by year, and so do I. Neither of us will be again what we were."

Harris – calm, steady, dependable Harris – smiled and set a hand on his friend's shoulder. "You've drunk yourself sad, that's what you've done. There's more to you than to many a man half your age."

"Good of you to say so, though we both know it's not so, not any more. As for the rum . . ." Audubon shook his head. "I knew this might be my last voyage when I got on the *Augustus Caesar* in St. Louis. Growing up is a time of firsts, of beginnings."

"Oh, yes." Harris' smile grew broader. Audubon had a good idea which first he was remembering.

But the painter wasn't finished. "Growing up is a time for firsts, yes," he repeated. "Growing old . . . Growing old is a time for endings, for lasts. And I do fear this will be my last long voyage."

"Well, make the most of it if it is," Harris said. "Shall we repair to the galley? Turtle soup tonight, with a saddle of mutton to follow." He smacked his lips.

Harris certainly made the most of the supper. Despite his ballasting of rum, Audubon didn't. A few spoonfuls of soup, a halfhearted attack on the mutton and the roast potatoes accompanying it, and he felt full to the danger point. "We might as well have traveled second class, or even steerage," he said sadly. "The difference in cost lies mostly in the victuals, and I'll never get my money's worth at a table that rolls."

"I'll just have to do it for both of us, then." Harris poured brandy-spiked gravy over a second helping of mutton. His campaign with fork and knife was serious and methodical, and soon reduced the mutton to nothing. He looked around hopefully. "I wonder what the sweet course is."

It was a cake baked in the shape of the *Maid of Orleans* and stuffed with nuts, candied fruit, and almond paste. Harris indulged immoderately. Audubon watched with a strange smile, half jealous, half wistful.

He went to bed not long after supper. The first day of a sea voyage always told on him, more than ever as he got older. The mattress was as comfortable as the one in the inn back in New Orleans. It might have been softer than the one he slept on at home. But it was unfamiliar, and so he tossed and turned for a while, trying to find the most comfortable position. Even as he tossed, he laughed at himself. Before long, he'd sleep wrapped in a blanket on bare ground in Atlantis. Would he twist and turn there, too? He nodded. Of course he would. Nodding still, he dozed off.

He hadn't been asleep long before Harris came in. His friend was humming "Pretty Black Eyes," a song popular in New Orleans as they set out. Audubon didn't think the other man even knew he was doing it. Harris got into his night-shirt, pissed in the chamber pot under his bed, blew out the oil lamp Audubon had left burning, and lay down. He was snoring in short order. Harris always denied that he snored – and why not? He never heard himself.

Audubon laughed once more. He tossed and twisted and yawned. Pretty soon, he was snoring again himself.

When he went out on deck the next morning, the *Maid of Orleans* might have been the only thing God ever made besides the sea. Terranova had vanished behind her; Atlantis still lay a thousand miles ahead. The steamship had entered the Hesperian Gulf, the wide arm of the North Atlantic that separated the enormous island and its smaller attendants from the continent to the west.

Audubon looked south and east. He'd been born on Santo Tomás, one of those lesser isles. He was brought to France three years later, and so escaped the convulsions that wracked the island when its colored slaves rose up against their masters in a war where neither side asked for quarter or gave it. Blacks ruled Santo Tomás to this day. Not many whites were left on the island. Audubon had only a few faded childhood memories of his first home. He'd never cared to go back, even if he could have without taking his life in his hands.

Edward Harris strolled out on deck. "Good morning," he said. "I hope you slept well?"

"Well enough, thanks," Audubon answered. I would have done better without "*Pretty Black Eyes,*" *but such is life* "Yourself?"

"Not bad, not bad." Harris eyed him. "You look . . . less greenish than you did yesterday. The bracing salt air, I suppose?"

"It could be. Or maybe I'm getting used to the motion." As soon as Audubon said that, as soon as he thought about his stomach, he gulped. He pointed an accusing finger at his friend. "There – you see? Just asking was enough to jinx me."

"Well, come have some breakfast, then. Nothing like a good mess of ham and eggs or something like that to get you ready for . . . Are you all right?"

"No," Audubon gasped, leaning out over the rail.

He breakfasted lightly, on toasted ship's biscuit and coffee and rum punch. He didn't usually start the day with strong spirits, but he didn't usually start the day with a bout of seasickness, either. *A good thing, too, or I'd have died years ago,* he thought. *I hope I would anyhow.*

Beside him in the galley, Harris worked his way through fried eggs and ham and sausage and bacon and maize-meal mush. Blotting his lips with a snowy linen napkin, he said, "That was monstrous fine." He patted his pot belly.

"So glad you enjoyed it," Audubon said tonelessly.

Once or twice over the next three days, the *Maid of Orleans* came close enough to another ship to make out her sails or the smoke rising from her stack. A pod of whales came up to blow nearby before sounding again. Most of the time, though, the sidewheeler might have been alone on the ocean.

Audubon was on deck again the third afternoon, when the sea –
suddenly, as those things went – changed from greenish gray to a
deeper, richer blue. He looked around for Harris, and spotted him not
far away, drinking rum punch and chatting with a personable young
woman whose curls were the color of fire.

"Edward!" Audubon said. "We've entered the Bay Stream!"

"Have we?" The news didn't seem to have the effect on Harris that
Audubon wanted. His friend turned back to the redheaded woman –
who also held a glass of punch – and said, "John is wild for nature in
every way you can imagine." Spoken in a different tone of voice, it
would have been a compliment. Maybe it still was. Audubon hoped he
only imagined Harris' faintly condescending note.

"Is he?" The woman didn't seem much interested in Audubon one
way or the other. "What about you, Eddie?"

Eddie? Audubon had trouble believing his ears. No one had ever
called Harris such a thing in his hearing before. And Harris . . . smiled.
"Well, Beth, I'll tell you – I am, too. But some parts of nature interest me
more than others." He set his free hand on her arm. She smiled, too.

He was a widower. He could chase if that suited his fancy, not that
Beth seemed to need much chasing. Audubon admired a pretty lady as
much as anyone – more than most, for with his painter's eye he saw
more than most – but was a thoroughly married man, and didn't slide
from admiration to pursuit. He hoped Lucy was well.

Finding Harris temporarily distracted, Audubon went back to the
rail himself. By then, the *Maid of Orleans* had left the cooler waters
by the east coast of Terranova behind and fully entered the warm
current coming up from the Bay of Mexico. Even the bits of seaweed
floating in the ocean looked different now. Audubon's main zoological interests did center on birds and viviparous quadrupeds. All the
same, he wished he would have thought to net up some of the floating
algae in the cool water and then some of these so he could properly
compare them.

He turned around to say as much to Harris, only to discover that his
friend and Beth were no longer on deck. Had Harris gone off to pursue
his own zoological interests? Well, more power to him if he had.
Audubon looked back into the ocean, and was rewarded with the sight
of a young sea turtle, not much bigger than the palm of his hand,
delicately nibbling a strand of the new seaweed. Next to the rewards
Harris might be finding, it didn't seem like much, but it was definitely
better than nothing.

Like the Sun, Atlantis, for Audubon, rose in the east. That blur on the
horizon – for a little while, you could wonder if it was a distant
cloudbank, but only for a little while. Before long, it took on the unmistakable solidity of land. To the Breton and Galician fishermen who'd
found it first, almost four hundred years before, it would have sent the
setting sun to bed early.

"Next port of call is New Marseille, sir," the purser said, tipping his cap to Audubon as he went by.

"Yes, of course," the artist replied, "but I'm bound for Avalon."

"Even so, sir, you'll have to clear customs at the first port of call in Atlantis," the other man reminded him. "The States are fussy about these things. If you don't have a New Marseille customs stamp on your passport, they won't let you off the ship in Avalon."

"It's a nuisance, to open all my trunks for the sake of a stamp," Audubon said. The purser shrugged the shrug of a man with right, or at least regulations, on his side. And he told the truth: the United States of Atlantis were fussy about who visited them. Do as we do, they might have said, *or stay away*.

Not that coming ashore at New Marseille was a hardship. On the contrary. Warmed by the Bay Stream, the city basked in an almost unending May. Farther north, in Avalon, it seemed to be April most of the time. And then the Bay Stream curled north and east around the top of Atlantis and delivered the rest of its warmth to the north of France, to the British Isles, and to Scandinavia. The east coast of Atlantis, where the winds swept across several hundred miles of mountains and lowlands before they finally arrived, was an altogether darker, harsher place.

But Audubon was in New Marseille, and if it wasn't veritably May, it was the middle of April, which came close enough. A glance as he and Harris carted their cases to the customs shed sufficed to tell him he'd left Terranova behind. Oh, the magnolias that shaded some nearby streets weren't much different from the ones he could have found near New Orleans. But the ginkgoes on other thoroughfares . . . only one other variety of ginkgo grew anyplace else in the world: in China. And the profusion of squat cycads with tufts of leaves sprouting from the tops of squat trunks also had few counterparts anywhere in the temperate zone.

The customs official, by contrast, seemed much like customs officials in every other kingdom and republic Audubon had ever visited. He frowned as he examined their declaration, and frowned even more as he opened up their baggage to confirm it. "You have a considerable quantity of spirits here," he said. "A dutiable quantity, in fact."

"They aren't intended for drinking or for resale, sir," Audubon said, "but for the preservation of scientific specimens."

"John Audubon's name and artistry are known throughout the civilized world," Edward Harris said.

"I've heard of the gentleman myself. I admire his work, what I've seen of it," the official replied. "But the law does not consider intent. It considers quantity. You will not tell me these strong spirits *cannot* be drunk?"

"No," Audubon admitted reluctantly.

"Well, then," the customs man said. "You owe the fisc of Atlantis . . . let me see . . ." He checked a table thumbtacked to the wall behind him. "You owe twenty-two eagles and, ah, fourteen cents."

Fuming, Audubon paid. The customs official gave him a receipt, which he didn't want, and the requisite stamp in his passport, which he did. As he and Harris trundled their chattels back to the *Maid of Orleans*, a small bird flew past them. "Look, John!" Harris said. "Wasn't that a gray-throated green?"

Not even the sight of the Atlantean warbler could cheer Audubon. "Well, what if it was?" he said, still mourning the money he'd hoped he wouldn't have to spend.

His friend knew what ailed him. "When we get to Avalon, paint a portrait or two," Harris suggested. "You'll make it up, and more besides."

Audubon shook his head. "I don't want to do that, dammit." When thwarted, he could act petulant as a child. "I grudge the time I'd have to spend. Every moment counts. I have not so many days left myself, and the upland honkers . . . Well, who can say if they have any left at all?"

"They'll be there." As usual, Harris radiated confidence.

"Will they?" Audubon, by contrast, careened from optimism to the slough of despond on no known schedule. At the moment, not least because of the customs man, he was mired in gloom. "When fishermen first found this land, a dozen species of honkers filled it: filled it as buffalo fill the plains of Terranova. Now . . . now a few may be left in the wildest parts of Atlantis. Or, even as we speak, the last ones may be dying – may already have died! – under an eagle's claws or the jaws of a pack of wild dogs or to some rude trapper's shotgun."

"The buffalo are starting to go, too," Harris remarked.

That only agitated Audubon more. "I must hurry! Hurry, do you hear me?"

"Well, you can't go anywhere till the *Maid of Orleans* sails," Harris said reasonably.

"One day soon, a railroad will run from New Marseille to Avalon," Audubon said. Atlantis was building railroads almost as fast as England: faster than France, faster than any of the new Terranovan republics. But soon was not yet, and he did have to wait for the steamship to head north.

Passengers left the *Maid of Orleans*. Beth got off, which made Harris glum. Others came aboard. Longshoremen carried crates and boxes and barrels and bags ashore. Others brought fresh cargo onto the ship. Passengers and longshoremen alike moved too slowly to suit Audubon. Again, he could only fume and pace the mercifully motionless deck. At last, late the next afternoon, the *Maid of Orleans* steamed towards Avalon.

She stayed close to shore on the two-and-a-half-day journey. It was one of the most beautiful routes anywhere in the world. Titanic redwoods and sequoias grew almost down to the shore. They rose so tall and straight, they might almost have been the columns of a colossal outdoor cathedral.

But that cathedral could have been dedicated to puzzlement and confusion. The only trees like the enormous evergreens of Atlantis were those on the Pacific coast of Terranova, far, far away. Why did they thrive here, survive there, and exist nowhere else? Audubon had no more answer than any other naturalist, though he dearly wished for one. *That* would crown a career! He feared it was a crown he was unlikely to wear.

The *Maid of Orleans* passed a small fishing town called Newquay without stopping. Having identified the place on his map, Audubon was pleased when the purser confirmed he'd done it right. "If anything happens to the navigator, sir, I'm sure we'd be in good hands with you," the man said, and winked to show he didn't aim to be taken too seriously.

Audubon gave him a dutiful smile and went back to eyeing the map. Atlantis' west coast and the east coast of North Terranova a thousand miles away put him in mind of two pieces of a world-sized jigsaw puzzle: their outlines almost fit together. The same was true for the bulge of Brazil in South Terranova and the indentation in West Africa's coastline on the other side of the Atlantic. And the shape of Atlantis' eastern coast corresponded to that of western Europe in a more general way.

What did that mean? Audubon knew he was far from the first to wonder. How could anyone who looked at a map help but wonder? Had Atlantis and Terranova been joined once upon a time? Had Africa and Brazil? How could they have been, with so much sea between? He saw no way it could be possible. Neither did anyone else. But when you looked at the map . . .

"Coincidence," Harris said when he mentioned it at supper.

"Maybe so." Audubon cut meat from a goose drumstick. His stomach was behaving better these days – and the seas stayed mild. "But if it is a coincidence, don't you think it's a large one?"

"World's a large place." Harris paused to take a sip of wine. "It has room in it for a large coincidence or three, don't you think?"

"Maybe so," Audubon said again, "but when you look at the maps, it seems as if those matches ought to spring from reason, not happenstance."

"Tell me how the ocean got in between them, then." Harris aimed a finger at him like a pistol barrel. "And if you say it was Noah's flood, I'll pick up that bottle of fine Bordeaux and clout you over the head with it."

"I wasn't going to say anything of the sort," Audubon replied. "Noah's flood may have washed over these lands, but I can't see how it could have washed them apart while still leaving their coastlines so much like each other."

"So it must be coincidence, then."

"I don't believe it *must* be anything, *mon vieux*," Audubon said. "I believe we don't know what it is – or, I admit, if it's anything at all. Maybe they will one day, but not now. For now, it's a puzzlement. We need puzzlements, don't you think?"

"For now, John, I need the gravy," Harris said. "Would you kindly pass it to me? Goes mighty well with the goose."

It did, too. Audubon poured some over the moist, dark meat on his plate before handing his friend the gravy boat. Harris wanted to ignore puzzlements when he could. Not Audubon. They reminded him not only of how much he – and everyone else – didn't know yet, but also of how much he – in particular – might still find out.

As much as I have time for, he thought, and took another bite of goose.

Avalon rose on six hills. The city fathers kept scouting for a seventh so they could compare their town to Rome, but there wasn't another bump to be found for miles around. The west-facing Bay of Avalon gave the city that bore its name perhaps the finest harbor in Atlantis. A century and a half before, the bay was a pirates' roost. The buccaneers swept out to plunder the Hesperian Gulf for most of a lifetime, till a British and Dutch fleet drove them back to their nest and then smoked them out of it.

City streets still remembered the swashbuckling past: Goldbeard Way, Valjean Avenue, Cutpurse Charlie Lane. But two Atlantean steam frigates patrolled the harbor. Fishing boats, bigger merchantmen – some steamers, other sailing ships – and liners like the *Maid of Orleans* moved in and out. The pirates might be remembered, but they were gone.

May it not be so with the honkers. Audubon thought as the *Maid of Orleans* tied up at a pier. *Please, God, let it not be so*. He crossed himself. He didn't know if the prayer would help, but it couldn't hurt, so he sent it up for whatever it might be worth.

Harris pointed to a man coming up the pier. "Isn't that Gordon Coates?"

"It certainly is." Audubon waved to the man who published his work in Atlantis. Coates, a short, round fellow with side whiskers even bushier than Audubon's, waved back. His suit was of shiny silk; a stovepipe hat sat at a jaunty angle on his head. Audubon cupped his hands in front of his mouth. "How are you, Gordon?"

"Oh, tolerable. Maybe a bit better than tolerable," Coates replied. "So you're haring off into the wilderness again, are you?" He was a city man to the tips of his manicured fingers. The only time he went out to the countryside was to take in a horse race. He knew his ponies, too. When he bet, he won . . . more often than not, anyhow.

He had a couple of servants waiting with carts to take charge of the travelers' baggage. He and Audubon and Harris clasped hands and clapped one another on the back when the gangplank went down and passengers could disembark. "Where are you putting us up?" asked Harris, who always thought about things like where he would be put up. Thanks to his thoughts about such things, Audubon had stayed in some places more comfortable than those where he might have if he made his own arrangements.

"How does the Hesperian Queen sound?" Coates answered.

"Like a pirate's kept woman," Audubon answered, and the publisher sent up gales of laughter. Audubon went on, "Is it near a livery stable or a horse market? I'll want to get my animals as soon as I can." Harris let out a sigh. Audubon pretended not to hear it.

"Not too far, not too far," Coates said. Then he pointed up into the sky. "Look – an eagle! There's an omen for you, if you like."

The large, white-headed bird sailed off toward the south. Audubon knew it was likely bound for the city dump, to scavenge there. White-headed eagles had thrived since men came to Atlantis. Seeing this one secretly disappointed Audubon. He wished it were a red-crested eagle, the Atlantean national bird. But the mighty raptors – by all accounts, the largest in the world – had fallen into a steep decline along with the honkers, which were their principal prey.

"Well," he said, "the Hesperian Queen."

The last time he was in Avalon, the hotel had had another name and another owner. It had come up in the world since. So had Avalon, which was visibly bigger and visibly richer than it had been ten years – or was it twelve now? – before.

Harris noticed, too. Harris generally noticed things like that. "You do well for yourselves here," he told Gordon Coates over beefsteaks at supper.

"Not too bad, not too bad," the publisher said. "I'm about to put out a book by a chap who thinks he's written the great Atlantean novel, and he lives right here in town. I hope he's right. You never can tell."

"You don't believe it, though," Audubon said.

"Well, no," Coates admitted. "Everybody always thinks he's written the great Atlantean novel – unless he comes from Terranova or England. Sometimes even then. Mr. Hawthorne has a better chance than some – a better chance than most, I daresay – but not *that* much better."

"What's it called?" Harris asked.

"*The Crimson Brand*," Coates said. "Not a bad title, if I say so myself – and I do, because it's mine. He wanted to name it *The Shores of a Different Sea*." He yawned, as if to say authors were hopeless with titles. Then, pointing at Audubon, he *did* say it: "I'd have called your books something else, too, if they weren't also coming out in England and Terranova. *Birds and Critters*, maybe. Who remembers what a quadruped is, let alone a viviparous one?"

"They've done well enough with the name I gave them," Audubon said.

"Well enough, sure, but they might've done better. I could've made you big." Coates was a man with an eye for the main chance. Making Audubon big – he lingered lovingly over the word – would have made him money.

"I know why folks here don't know quadrupeds from a hole in the ground," Harris said. "Atlantis hardly had any before it got discovered. No snakes in Ireland, no . . . critters" – he grinned – "here, not then."

"No *viviparous* quadrupeds." Audubon had drunk enough wine to make him most precise – but not too much to keep him from pronouncing *viviparous*. "A very great plenty of lizards and turtles and frogs and toads and salamanders – and snakes, of course, though snakes lack four legs of quadrupedality." He was proud of himself for that.

"Sure enough, snakes haven't got a leg to stand on." Harris guffawed.

"Well, we have critters enough now, by God," Coates said. "Everything from mice on up to elk. Some of 'em we wanted, some we got anyway. Try and keep rats and mice from coming aboard ship. Yeah, go ahead and try. Good luck – you'll need it."

"How many indigenous Atlantean creatures are no more because of them?" Audubon said.

"Beats me," Coates answered. "Little too late to worry about it now, anyway, don't you think?"

"I hope not," Audubon said. "I hope it's not too late for them. I hope it's not too late for me." He took another sip of wine. "And I know the viviparous creature responsible for the greatest number of those sad demises here."

"Rats?" Coates asked.

"Weasels, I bet," Harris said.

Audubon shook his head at each of them in turn. He pointed an index finger at his own chest. "Man," he said.

He rode out of Avalon three days later. Part of the time he spent buying horses and tackle for them; that, he didn't begrudge. The rest he spent with Gordon Coates, meeting with subscribers and potential subscribers for his books; that, he did. He was a better businessman than most of his fellow artists, and normally wouldn't have resented keeping customers happy and trolling for new ones. If nobody bought your art, you had a devil of a time making more of it. As a younger man, he'd worked at several other trades, hated them all, and done well at none. He knew how lucky he was to make a living doing what he loved, and how much work went into what others called luck.

To his relief, he did escape without painting portraits. Even before he set out from New Orleans, he'd felt time's hot breath at his heels. He felt himself aging, getting weaker, getting feebler. In another few years, maybe even in another year or two, he would lack the strength and stamina for a journey into the wilds of central Atlantis. And even if he had it, he might not find any honkers left to paint.

I may not find any now, he thought. That ate at him like vitriol. He kept seeing a hunter or a lumberjack with a shotgun . . .

Setting out from Avalon, Audubon might almost have traveled through the French or English countryside. Oh, the farms here were larger than they were in Europe, with more meadow between them. This was newly settled land; it hadn't been cultivated for centuries, sometimes for millennia. But the crops – wheat, barley, maize, potatoes – were either European or were Terranovan imports long familiar in the

Old World. The fruit trees came from Europe; the nuts, again, from Europe and Terranova. Only a few stands of redwoods and Atlantean pines declared that the Hesperian Gulf lay just a few miles to the west.

It was the same with the animals. Dogs yapped outside of farmhouses Chickens scratched. Cats prowled, hoping for either mice – also immigrants – or unwary chicks. Ducks and geese – ordinary domestic geese – paddled in ponds. Pigs rooted and wallowed. In the fields, cattle and sheep and horses grazed.

Most people probably wouldn't have noticed the ferns that sprouted here and there or the birds on the ground, in the trees, and on the wing. Some of those birds, like ravens, ranged all over the world. Others, such as the white-headed eagle Audubon had seen in Avalon, were common in both Atlantis and Terranova (on Atlantis' eastern coast, the white-tailed eagle sometimes visited from its more usual haunts in Europe and Iceland). Still others – no one knew how many – were unique to the great island.

No one but a specialist knew or cared how Atlantean gray-faced swifts differed from the chimney swifts of Terranova or little swifts from Europe. Many Atlantean thrushes were plainly the same sorts of birds as their equivalents to the west and to the east. They belonged to different species, but their plumages and habits were similar to those of the rest. The same held true for island warblers, which flitted through the trees after insects like their counterparts on the far side of the Hesperian Gulf. Yes, there were many similarities. But . . .

"I wonder how soon we'll start seeing oil thrushes," Audubon said.

"Not this close to Avalon," Harris said. "Not with so many dogs and cats and pigs running around."

"I suppose not," Audubon said. "They're trusting things, and they haven't much chance of getting away."

Laughing, Harris mimed flapping his fingertips. Oil thrushes' wings were bigger than that, but not by much – they couldn't fly. The birds themselves were bigger than chickens. They used their long, pointed beaks to probe the ground for worms at depths ordinary thrushes, flying thrushes, couldn't hope to reach. When the hunting was good, they laid up fat against a rainy day.

But they were all but helpless against men and the beasts men had brought to Atlantis. It wasn't just that they were good eating, or that their fat, rendered down made a fine lamp oil. The real trouble was, they didn't seem to know enough to run away when a dog or a fox came after them. They weren't used to being hunted by animals that lived on the ground; the only viviparous quadrupeds on Atlantis before men arrived were bats.

"Even the bats here are peculiar," Audubon muttered.

"Well, so they are, but why do you say so?" Harris asked.

Audubon explained his train of thought. "Where else in the world do you have bats that spend more of their time scurrying around on the ground than flying?" he went on.

He thought that was a rhetorical question, but Harris said, "Aren't there also some in New Zealand?"

"Are there?" Audubon said in surprise. His friend nodded. The painter scratched at his side whiskers. "Well, well. Both lands far from any others, out in the middle of the sea . . ."

"New Zealand had its own honkers, too, or something like them," Harris said. "What the devil were they called?"

"Moas," Audubon said. "I do remember that. Didn't I show you the marvelous illustrations of their remains Professor Owen did recently? The draftsmanship is astonishing. Astonishing!" The way he kissed his bunched fingertips proved him a Frenchman at heart.

Edward Harris gave him a sly smile. "Surely you could do better?"

"I doubt it," Audubon said. "Each man to his own bent. Making a specimen look as if it were alive on the canvas – that I can do. My talent lies there, and I've spent almost forty years now learning the tricks and turns that go with it. Showing every detail of dead bone – I'm not in the least ashamed to yield the palm to the good professor there."

"If only you were a little less modest, you'd be perfect," Harris said.

"It could be," Audubon said complacently, and they rode on.

The slow, deep drumming came from thirty feet up a dying pine. Harris pointed. "There he is, John! D'you see him?"

"I'm not likely to miss him, not when he's the size of a raven," Audubon answered. Intent on grubs under the bark, the scarlet-cheeked woodpecker went on drumming. It was a male, which meant its crest was also scarlet. A female's crest would have been black, with a forward curl the male's lacked. That also held true for its close relatives on the Terranovan mainland, the ivory-bill and the imperial woodpecker of Mexico.

Audubon dismounted, loaded his shotgun, and approached the bird. He could get closer to the scarlet-cheeked woodpecker than he could have to one of its Terranovan cousins. Like the oil thrush, like so many other Atlantean birds, the woodpecker had trouble understanding that something walking along on the ground could endanger it. Ivory-bills and imperial woodpeckers were less naïve.

The woodpecker raised its head and called. The sound was high and shrill, like a false note on a clarinet. Audubon paused with the gun on his shoulder, waiting to see if another bird would answer. When none did, he squeezed the trigger. The shotgun boomed, belching fireworks-smelling smoke.

With a startled squawk, the scarlet-cheeked woodpecker tumbled out of the pine. It thrashed on the ground for a couple of minutes, then lay still. "Nice shot," Harris said.

"*Merci*," Audubon answered absently.

He picked up the woodpecker. It was still warm in his hands, and still crawling with mites and bird lice. No one who didn't handle wild birds freshly dead thought of such things. He brushed his palm against his trouser leg to get rid of some of the vagrants. They didn't usually trouble people, who weren't to their taste, but every once in a while . . .

A new thought struck him. He stared at the scarlet-cheeked woodpecker. "I wonder if the parasites on Atlantean birds are as different as the birds themselves, or if they share them with the birds of Terranova."

"I don't know," Harris said. "Do you want to pop some into spirits and see?"

After a moment, Audubon shook his head. "No, better to let someone who truly cares about such things take care of it. I'm after honkers, by God, not lice!"

"Nice specimen you took there, though," his friend said. "Scarlet-cheeks are getting scarce, too."

"Not so much forest for them to hunt in as there once was," Audubon said with a sigh. "Not so much of anything in Atlantis as there once was – except men and farms and sheeps." He knew that was wrong as soon as it came out of his mouth, but let it go. "If we don't show what it was, soon it will be no more, and then it will be too late to show. Too late already for too much of it." *Too late for me?* he wondered. *Please, let it not be so!*

"You going to sketch now?" Harris asked.

"If you don't mind. Birds are much easier to pose before they start to stiffen."

"Go ahead, go ahead." Harris slid down from his horse. "I'll smoke a pipe or two and wander around a bit with my shotgun. Maybe I'll bag something else you can paint, or maybe I'll shoot supper instead. Maybe both – who knows? If I remember right, these Atlantean ducks and geese eat as well as any other kind, except canvasbacks." He was convinced canvasback ducks, properly roasted and served with loaf sugar, were the finest fowl in the world. Audubon wasn't so sure he was wrong.

As Harris ambled away, Audubon set the scarlet-cheeked woodpecker on the grass and walked over to one of the pack horses. He knew which sack held his artistic supplies: his posing board and his wires, his charcoal sticks and precious paper.

He remembered how, as a boy, he'd despaired of ever portraying birds in realistic poses. A bird in the hand was all very well, but a dead bird looked like nothing but a dead bird. It drooped, it sagged, it cried its lifelessness to the eye.

When he studied painting with David in France, he sometimes did figure drawings from a mannequin. His cheeks heated when he recalled the articulated bird model he'd tried to make from wood and cork and wire. After endless effort, he produced something that might have done duty for a spavined dodo. His friends laughed at it. How could he get angry at them when he wanted to laugh at it, too? He ended up kicking the horrible thing to pieces.

If he hadn't thought of wires . . . He didn't know what he would have done then. Wires let him position his birds as if they were still alive. The first kingfisher he'd posed – he knew he was on to something even before he finished. As he set up the posing board now, a shadow of that old excitement glided through him again. Even the bird's eyes had seemed to take on life again once he posed it the way he wanted.

As he worked with wires now to position the woodpecker as it had clung to the tree trunk, he wished he could summon more than a shadow of the old thrill. But he'd done the same sort of thing too many times. Routine fought against art. He wasn't discovering a miracle now. He was . . . working.

Well, if you're working, work the best you can, he told himself. And practice did pay. His hands knew almost without conscious thought how best to set the wires, to pose the bird. When his hands thought he was finished, he eyed the scarlet-cheeked woodpecker. Then he moved a wire to adjust its tail's position. It used those long, stiff feathers to brace itself against the bark, almost as if it had hind legs back there.

He began to sketch. He remembered the agonies of effort that went into his first tries, and how bad they were despite those agonies. He knew others who'd tried to paint, and who gave up when their earlier pieces failed to match what they wanted, what they expected. Some of them, from what he'd seen, had a real gift. But having it and honing it . . . Ah, what a difference! Not many were stubborn enough to keep doing the thing they wanted to do even when they couldn't do it very well. Audubon didn't know how many times he'd almost given up in despair. But when stubbornness met talent, great things could happen.

The charcoal seemed to have a life of its own as it moved across the page. Audubon nodded to himself. His line remained as strong and fluid as ever. He didn't have the tremors and shakes that marked so many men's descent into age – not yet. Yet how far away from them was he? Every time the Sun rose, he came one day closer. He sketched fast, racing against his own decay.

Harris' shotgun bellowed. Audubon's hand did jump then. Whose wouldn't, at the unexpected report? But that jerky line was easily rubbed out. He went on, quick and confident, and had the sketch very much the way he wanted it by the time Harris came back carrying a large dead bird by the feet.

"A turkey?" Audubon exclaimed.

His friend nodded, face wreathed in smiles. "Good eating tonight!"

"Well, yes," Audubon said. "But who would have thought the birds could spread so fast? They were introduced in the south . . . it can't be more than thirty years ago, can it? And now you shoot one here."

"They give better sport than oil thrushes and the like," Harris said. "At least they have the sense to get away if they see trouble coming. The sense God gave a goose, you might say – except He didn't give it to all the geese here, either."

"No," Audubon said. Some of Atlantis' geese flew to other lands as well, and were properly wary. Some stayed on the great island the whole year round. Those birds weren't. Some of them flew poorly. Some couldn't fly at all, having wings as small and useless as those of the oil thrush.

Honkers looked uncommonly like outsized geese with even more outsized legs. Some species even had black necks and white chin patches reminiscent of Canada geese. That frankly puzzled Audubon: it was as if God were repeating Himself in the Creation, but why? Honkers' feet had vestigial webs, too, while their bills, though laterally compressed, otherwise resembled the broad, flat beaks of ordinary geese.

Audubon had seen the specimens preserved in the museum in Hanover: skeletons, a few hides, enormous greenish eggs. The most recent hide was dated 1803. He wished he hadn't remembered that. If this was a wild goose chase, a wild honker chase . . . then it was, that was all. He was doing all he could. He only wished he could have done it sooner. He'd tried. He'd failed. He only hoped some possibility of success remained.

Harris cleaned the turkey and got a fire going. Audubon finished the sketch. "That's a good one," Harris said, glancing over at it.

"Not bad," Audubon allowed – he *had* caught the pose he wanted. He gutted the scarlet-cheeked woodpecker so he could preserve it. Not surprisingly, the bird's stomach was full of beetle larvae. The very name of its genus, *Campephilus*, meant *grub-loving*. He made a note in his diary and put the bird in strong spirits.

"Better than that," Harris said. He cut up the turkey and skewered drumsticks on twigs.

"Well, maybe," Audubon said as he took one of the skewers from his friend and started roasting the leg. He wasn't shy of praise – no, indeed. All the same, he went on, "I didn't come here for scarlet-cheeked woodpeckers. I came for honkers, by God."

"You take what you get." Harris turned his twig so the drumstick cooked evenly. "You take what you get, and you hope what you get is what you came for."

"Well, maybe," Audubon said again. He looked east, toward the still poorly explored heart of Atlantis. "But the harder you work, the likelier you are to get what you want. I hope I can still work hard enough. And" – he looked east once more – "I hope what I want is still there to get."

He and Harris stayed on the main highway for most of a week. The broad, well-trodden path let them travel faster than they could have on narrower, more winding roads. But when Audubon saw the Green Ridge Mountains rising over the eastern horizon, the temptation to leave the main road got too strong to resist.

"We don't want to go into the mountains anywhere near the highway," he declared. "We know no honkers live close to it, or people would have seen them, *n'est-ce pas?*"

"Stands to reason," Harris said loyally. He paused before adding, "I wouldn't mind another couple of days of halfway decent inns, though."

"When we come back with what we seek, the Hesperian Queen will be none too good," Audubon said. "But we go through adversity to seek our goal."

Harris sighed. "We sure do."

On the main highway, fruit trees and oaks and chestnuts and elms and maples thrived. They were all imports from Europe or from Terranova. Audubon and Harris hadn't gone far from the highway before Atlantean flora reasserted itself: ginkgoes and magnolias, cycads and pines, with ferns growing in profusion as an understory. Birdsongs, some familiar, others strange, doubled and redoubled as the travelers moved into less settled country. Atlantean birds seemed more comfortable with the trees they'd lived in for generations uncounted than with the brash newcomers men brought in.

Not all the newcomers clung to the road. Buttercups and poppies splashed the improbably green landscape with color. Atlantean bees buzzed around the flowers that had to be unfamiliar to them . . . or maybe those were European honeybees, carried to the new land in the midst of the sea to serve the plants men needed, wanted, or simply liked. Curious, Audubon stopped and waited by some poppies for a closer look at the insects. They were, without a doubt, honeybees. He noted the fact in his diary. It left him oddly disappointed but not surprised.

"In another hundred years," he said, climbing back onto his horse, "how much of the old Atlantis will be left? Any?"

"In another hundred years," Harries replied, "it won't matter to either of us, except from beyond the Pearly Gates."

"No, I suppose not." Audubon wondered if he had ten years left, or even five, let alone a hundred. "But it should matter to those who are young here. They throw away marvels without thinking of what they're doing. Wouldn't you like to see dodos preserved alive?" He tried not to recall his unfortunate bird model.

"Alive? Why, I can go to Hanover and hear them speechifying," Harris said. Audubon snorted. His friend waved a placating hand. "Let it go, John. Let it go. I take your point."

"I'm so glad," Audubon said with sardonic relish. "Perhaps the authorities here – your speechifying dodos – could set up parks to preserve some of what they have." He frowned. "Though how parks could keep out foxes and weasels and rats and windblown seeds, I confess I don't know. Still, it would make a start."

They slept on the grass that night. The throaty hoots of an Atlantean ground owl woke Audubon somewhere near midnight. He loaded his shotgun by the faint, bloody light of the campfire's embers, in case the bird came close enough for him to spot it. Ground owls were hen-sized, more or less. They could fly, but not well. They hunted frogs and lizards and the outsized katydids that scurried through the undergrowth here. Nothing hunted them – or rather, nothing had hunted them till foxes and wild dogs and men came to Atlantis. Like so many creatures here, they couldn't seem to imagine they might become prey. Abundant once, they were scarce these days.

This one's call got farther and farther away. Audubon thought about imitating it to lure the ground owl into range of his charge. In the end, he forbore. Blasting away in the middle of the night might frighten Harris into an apoplexy. And besides – Audubon yawned – he was still sleepy himself. He set down the shotgun, rolled himself in his blanket once more, and soon started snoring again.

When Audubon woke the next morning, he saw a mouse-sized katydid's head and a couple of greenish brown legs only a yard or so from his bedroll. He swore softly: the ground owl had come by, but without hooting, so he never knew. If he'd stayed up . . . *If I'd stayed up, I would be useless today*, he thought. He needed regular doses of sleep much more than he had twenty years earlier.

"I wouldn't have minded if you fired on an owl," Harris said as he built up the fire and got coffee going. "We're here for that kind of business."

"Good of you to say so," Audubon replied. "It could be that I will have other chances."

"And it could be that you won't. You were the one who said the old Atlantis was going under. Grab with both hands while it's here."

"With the honkers, I intend to," Audubon said. "If they're there to be grabbed, grab them I shall. The ground owl . . . Well, who knows if it would have come when I hooted?"

"I bet it would. I never knew a soul who could call birds better than you." Harris took a couple of squares of hardtack out of an oilcloth valise and handed one to Audubon. The artist waited till he had his tin cup of coffee before breakfasting. He broke his hardtack into chunks and dunked each one before eating it. The crackers were baked to a fare-thee-well so they would keep for a long time, which left them chewier than his remaining teeth could easily cope with.

As he and his friend got ready to ride on, he looked again at the remains of the giant katydid. "I really ought to get some specimens of those," he remarked.

"Why, in heaven's name?" Harris said. "They aren't birds, and they aren't viviparous quadrupeds, either. They aren't quadrupeds at all."

"No," Audubon said slowly, "but doesn't it seem to you that here they fill the role mice play in most of the world?"

"Next time I see me a six-legged chirping mouse with feelers" – Harris wiggled his forefingers above his eyes – "you can lock me up and lose the key, on account of I'll have soused my brains with the demon rum."

"Or with whiskey, or gin, or whatever else you can get your hands on," Audubon said. Harris grinned and nodded. As Audubon saddled his horse, he couldn't stop thinking about Atlantean katydids and mice. *Something* had to scurry through the leaves and eat whatever it could find there, and so many other creatures ate mice . . . or, here, the insects instead. He nodded to himself. That was worth a note in the diary whenever they stopped again.

They rode into a hamlet a little before noon. It boasted a saloon, a church, and a few houses. BIDEFORD HOUSE OF UNIVERSAL DEVOTION, the church declared. Strange Protestant sects flourished in Atlantis, not least because none was strong enough to dominate – and neither was his own Catholic Church.

But the saloon, in its own way, was also a house of universal devotion. Bideford couldn't have held more than fifty people, but at least a dozen men sat in there, drinking and eating and talking. A silence fell when Audubon and Harris walked in. The locals stared at them. "Strangers," somebody said; he couldn't have sounded much more surprised had he announced a pair of kangaroos.

Not surprisingly, the man behind the bar recovered fastest. "What'll it be, gents?" he asked.

Harris was seldom at a loss when it came to his personal comforts. "Ham sandwich and a mug of beer, if you please."

"That sounds good," Audubon said. "The same for me, if you'd be so kind."

"Half an eagle for both of you together," the proprietor said. Some of the regulars grinned. Even without those tell-tale smiles, Audubon would have known he was being gouged. But he paid without complaint. He could afford it, and he'd be asking questions later on, and priming the pump with more silver. He wanted the locals to see he could be openhanded.

The beer was . . . beer. The sandwiches, by contrast, were prodigies: great slabs of tender, flavorful ham on fresh-baked bread, enlivened by spicy mustard and pickles all but jumping with dill and garlic and something else, something earthy – an Atlantean spice?

Audubon hadn't come close to finishing his – he had to chew slowly – when the man behind the bar said, "Don't see too many strangers here." Several locals – big, stocky, bearded fellows in homespun – nodded. So did Audubon, politely. The tapman went on, "Mind if I ask what you're doing passing through?"

"I am John James Audubon," Audubon said, and waited to see if anyone knew his name. Most places, he would have had no doubt. In Bideford . . . well, who could say?

"The painter fella," one of the regulars said.

"That's right." Audubon smiled, more relieved than he wanted to show. "The painter fella." He repeated the words even though they grated. If the locals understood he was a prominent person, they were less likely to rob him and Harris for the fun of it. He introduced his friend.

"Well, what are you doing here in Bideford?" the proprietor asked again.

"Passing through, as you said," Audubon replied. "I'm hoping to paint honkers." This country was almost isolated enough to give him hope of finding some here – not quite, but almost.

"Honkers?" Two or three men said it as the same time. A heartbeat later, they all laughed. One said, "Ain't seen any of them big fowl round these parts since Hector was a pup."

"That's right," someone else said. Solemn nods filled the saloon.

"It's a shame, too," another man said. "My granddad used to say

they was easy to kill, and right good eatin'. Lots of meat on 'em, too."
That had to be why no honkers lived near Bideford these days, but the
local seemed ignorant of cause and effect.

"If you know of any place where they might dwell, I'd be pleased to
pay for the information." Audubon tapped a pouch on his belt. Coins
clinked sweetly. "You'd help my work, and you'd advance the cause of
science."

"Half now," the practical Harris added, "and half on the way back if
we find what we're looking for. Maybe a bonus, too, if the tip's good
enough."

A nice ploy, Audubon thought. *I have to remember that one.* The
locals put their heads together. One of the older men, his beard streaked
with gray, spoke up: "Well, I don't know anything for sure, mind, but I
was out hunting a few years back and ran into this fellow from
Thetford." He knew where Thetford was, but Audubon didn't. A few
questions established that it lay to the northeast. The Bideford man
continued, "We got to gabbing, and he said he saw some a few years
before that, off the other side of his town. Can't swear he wasn't lyin',
mind, but he sounded like he knew what he was talking about."

Harris looked a question towards Audubon. The artist nodded.
Harris gave the Bideford man a silver eagle. "Let me have your name,
sir," Harris said. "If the tip proves good, and if we don't pass this way
again on our return journey, we *will* make good on the rest of the
reward."

"Much obliged, sir," the man said. "I'm Lehonti Kent." He carefully
spelled it out for Harris, who wrote it down in one of his notebooks.

"What can you tell me about the House of Universal Devotion?"
Audubon asked.

That got him more than he'd bargained for. Suddenly everyone, even
the most standoffish locals, wanted to talk at once. He gathered that the
church preached the innate divinity of every human being and the possibility of transcending mere mankind – as long as you followed the
preachings of the man the locals called the Reverend, with a very
audible capital R. *Universal Devotion to the Reverend*, he thought. It all
seemed to him the rankest, blackest heresy, but the men of Bideford
swore by it.

"Plenty of Devotees" – another obvious capital letter – "in Thetford
and other places like that," Lehonti Kent said. He plainly had only the
vaguest idea of places more than a couple of days' travel from his home
village.

"Isn't that interesting?" Audubon said: one of the few phrases polite
almost anywhere.

Because the Bidefordites wanted to preach to them, he and Harris
couldn't get away from the saloon for a couple of hours. "Well, well,"
Harris said as they rode away. "Wasn't that *interesting*?" He freighted
the word with enough sarcasm to sink a ship twice the size of the *Maid
of Orleans*.

Audubon's head was still spinning. The Reverend seemed to have invented a whole new prehistory for Atlantis and Terranova, one that had little to do with anything Audubon thought he'd learned. He wondered if he'd be able to keep it straight enough to get it down in his diary. The Devotees seemed nearly as superstitious to him as the wild red Terranovan tribes – and they should have known better, while the savages were honestly ignorant. Even so, he said, "If Lehonti – what a name! – Kent gave us a true lead, I don't mind the time we spent . . . too much."

Thetford proved a bigger village than Bideford. It also boasted a House of Universal Devotion, though it had a Methodist church as well. A crudely painted sign in front of the House said, THE REVEREND PREACHES SUNDAY!! Two exclamation points would have warned Audubon away even if he'd never passed through Bideford.

He did ask after honkers in Thetford. No one with whom he talked claimed to have seen one, but a couple of men did say some people from the town had seen them once upon a time. Harris doled out more silver, but it spurred neither memory nor imagination.

"Well, we would have come this way anyhow," Audubon said as they went on riding northeast. The Green Ridge Mountains climbed higher in the sky now, dominating the eastern horizon. Peering ahead with a spyglass, Audubon saw countless dark valleys half hidden by the pines and cycads that gave the mountains their name. Anything could live there . . . couldn't it? He had to believe it could. "We have a little more hope now," he added, as much to himself as to Harris.

"Hope is good," his friend said. "Honkers would be better."

The words were hardly out of his mouth before the ferns and cycads by the side of the road quivered . . . and a stag bounded across. Audubon started to raise his shotgun, but stopped with the motion not even well begun. For one thing, the beast was gone. For another, the gun was charged with bird-shot, which would only have stung it.

"*Sic transit gloria honkeris.*" Harris said.

"*Honkeris?*" But Audubon held up a hand before Harris could speak. "Yes, honker would be a third-declension noun, wouldn't it?"

Little by little, the country rose toward the mountains. Cycads thinned out in the woods; more varieties of pines and spruces and redwoods took their places. The ferns in the undergrowth seemed different, too. As settlements thinned out, so did splashes of color from exotic flowers. The very air seemed different: mistier, moister, full of curious, spicy scents the nose would not meet anywhere else in the world. It felt as if the smells of another time were wafting past the travelers.

"And so they are," Audubon said when that thought crossed his mind. "This is the air of Atlantis as it was, Atlantis before those fishermen saw its coast loom up out of the sea."

"Well, almost," Harris said. That he and Audubon and their horses were here proved his point. In case it didn't, he pointed to the track

down which they rode. The ground was damp – muddy in spots – for it
had rained the day before. A fox's pads showed plainly.

"How many birds has that beast eaten?" Audubon said. "How many
ground-dwellers' nests has it robbed?" Many Atlantean birds nested on
the ground, far more than in either Europe or Terranova. But for a few
snakes and large lizards, there were no terrestrial predators – or hadn't
been, before men brought them in. Audubon made another note in his
diary. Till now, he hadn't thought about the effect the presence or
absence of predators might have on birds' nesting habits.

Even here, in the sparsely settled heart of Atlantis, a great deal had
been lost. But much still remained. Birdsongs filled the air, especially
just after sunrise when Audubon and Harris started out each day.
Atlantis had several species of crossbills and grosbeaks: birds with bills
that seemed made for getting seeds out of cones and disposing of them
afterwards. As with so many birds on the island, they were closely
related to Terranovan forms, but not identical to them.

Audubon shot a male green grosbeak in full breeding plumage. Lying
in his hand, the bird, with its apple-green back, warm cinnamon belly,
and yellow eye streak, seemed gaudy as a seventeenth-century French
courtier. But on the branch of a redwood, against the green foliage and
rusty-brown bark, it hadn't been easy to spot. If it weren't singing so
insistently, chances were he would have ridden right past it.

At dusk, Harris shot an oil thrush. That wasn't for research, though
Audubon did save the skin. The long-billed flightless thrush had more
than enough meat for both of them. The flavor put Audubon in mind of
snipe or woodcock: not surprising, perhaps, when all three were so fond
of earthworms.

Gnawing on a thighbone, Harris said, "I wonder how long these
birds will last."

"Longer than honkers, anyhow, because they're less conspicuous,"
Audubon said, and his friend nodded. He went on, "But you have
reason – they're in danger. They're one more kind that nests on the
ground, and how can they escape foxes and dogs that hunt by scent?"

Somewhere off in the distance, far beyond the light of the campfire, a
fox yelped and yowled. Harris nodded. "There's a noise that wasn't
heard here before the English brought them."

"If it weren't foxes, it would be dogs," Audubon said sadly, and
Harris' head bobbed up and down once more. Atlantis was vulnerable
to man and his creatures, and that was the long and short of it. "A pity.
A great pity," Audubon murmured. Harris nodded yet again.

The screech ripped across the morning air. Audubon's horse snorted
and tried to rear. He calmed it with hands and voice and educated
thighs. "Good God!" Harris said. "What was that?"

Before answering, Audubon listened to the sudden and absolute
silence all around. A moment before, the birds were singing their hearts
out. As a lion's roar was said to bring stillness to the African plains, so

this screech froze the forests of Atlantis.

It rang out again, wild and harsh and fierce. Excitement tingled through Audubon. "I know what it is!" Despite the urgency in his voice, it hardly rose above a whisper. His gaze swung to the shotgun. Have to charge it with stronger shot, he thought.

"What?" Harris also whispered, hoarsely. As after a lion's roar, talking out loud seemed dangerous.

"A red-crested eagle, by all the saints!" Audubon said. "A rara avis itself, and also, with luck, a sign honkers aren't far away." Maybe the Atlantean national bird was reduced to hunting sheep or deer, but Audubon hadn't seen any close by. If the eagle still sought the prey it had always chosen before the coming of man . . . Oh, if it did!

Harris didn't just look at his shotgun. He reached for it and methodically began to load. After a moment, so did Audubon. Red-crested eagles didn't fear men. They were used to swooping down on tall creatures that walked on two legs. People could die – people had died – under their great, tearing claws, long as a big man's thumb. Nor were their fierce beaks to be despised – anything but.

"Where did the cry come from?" Audubon asked after loading both barrels.

"That way." Harris pointed north. "Not far, either."

"No, not far at all," Audubon agreed. "We have to find it. We *have* to, Edward!" He plunged into the undergrowth, moving quiet as he could. Harris hurried after him. They both carried their shotguns at high port, ready to fire and ready to try to fend off the eagle if it struck before they could.

Call again. Audubon willed the thought toward the red-crested eagle with all his strength. *Call again. Show us where you are.*

And the eagle did. The smaller birds had begun to sing again. Silence came down on them like a heavy boot. Audubon grew acutely aware of how loud his own footfalls were. He tried to stride more lightly, with what success he had trouble judging. Tracking the cry, he swung to the west just a little.

"There!" Harris breathed behind him. His friend pointed and froze, for all the world like a well-bred, well-trained hunting dog.

Audubon's eyes darted this way and that. He did not see . . . He did not see . . . And then he did. "Oh," he whispered: more a soft sound of wonder than a word.

The eagle perched near the top of a ginkgo tree. It was a big female, close to four feet long from the end of its low, long bill to the tip of the tail. The crest was up, showing the bird was alert and in good spirits. It was the coppery red of a redheaded man's hair or a red-tailed hawk's tail, not the glowing crimson of a hummingbird's gorget. The eagle's back was dark brown, its belly a tawny buff.

Slowly, carefully, Audubon and Harris drew closer. For all their caution, the bird saw them. It mantled on its perch, spreading its wings and screeching again. The span was relatively small for the eagle's size – not much more than seven feet – but the wings were very broad. Red-crested eagles flapped more than they soared, unlike their white-headed and golden cousins. Naturalists disagreed about which were their closer kin.

"Watch out," Harris whispered. "It's going to fly."

And it did, not three heartbeats after the words left his mouth. Audubon and Harris both swung up their guns and fired at essentially the same instant. The eagle cried out once more, this time a startled squall of pain and fear. It fell out of the sky and hit the ground with a thump.

"Got it!" Harris exulted.

"Yes." Joy and sorrow warred in Audubon. That magnificent creature – a shame it had to perish for the sake of art and science. How many were left to carry on the race? One fewer, whatever the answer was.

This one wasn't dead yet. It thrashed in the ferns, screaming in fury because it couldn't fly. Its legs were long and strong – could it run? Audubon trotted towards it. *It mustn't get away*, he thought. Now that he and Harris had shot it, it had to become a specimen and a subject for his art. If it didn't, they would have knocked it down for nothing, and he couldn't bear the idea.

The red-crested eagle wasn't running. When he came close enough, he saw that a shotgun ball from one of the two charges had broken its left leg. The bird screeched and snapped at him; he had to jump back in a hurry to keep that fearsome beak from carving a chunk out of his calf. Hate and rage blazed in those great golden eyes.

Along with the shotgun, Harris also carried his revolver. He drew it now, and aimed it at the bird. "I'll finish it," he said. "Put it out of its misery." He thumbed back the hammer.

"In the breast, if you please," Audubon said. "I don't want to spoil the head."

"At your service, John. If the poor creature will only hold still for a few seconds . . ."

After more frantic thrashing and another long-neck lunge at the men who'd reduced it from lord of the air to wounded victim, the eagle paused to pant and to gather its waning strength. Harris fired. A pistol ball would have blown a songbird to pieces, but the eagle was big enough to absorb the bullet. It let out a final bubbling scream before slumping over, dead.

"That is one splendid creature," Harris said solemnly. "No wonder the Atlanteans put it on their flag and on their money."

"No wonder at all," Audubon said. He waited a few minutes, lest the eagle, like a serpent, have one more bite in it. Even then, he nudged the bird with a stick before picking it up. That beak, and the talons on the unwounded leg, commanded respect. He grunted in surprise as he straightened with the still-warm body in his arms. "How much would you say this bird weighs, Edward?"

"Let me see." Harris held out his arms. Audubon put the red-crested eagle in them. Harris grunted, too. He hefted the eagle, his lips pursed thoughtfully. "Dog my cats if it doesn't go thirty pounds, easy. You wouldn't think such a big bird'd be able to get off the ground, would you?"

"We saw it. Many have seen it," Audubon said. He took the eagle back from Harris and gauged its weight again himself. "Thirty pounds? Yes, that seems about right. I would have guessed something around there, too. Neither the golden nor the white-headed eagle goes much above twelve pounds, and even the largest African eagle will not greatly surpass twenty."

"Those birds don't hunt honkers," Harris said. His usual blunt good sense got to the nub of the problem in a handful of words. "The red-crested, now, it needs all the muscles it can get."

"No doubt you're right," Audubon said. "The biggest honkers, down in the eastern lowlands, would stand a foot, two feet, taller than a man and weigh . . . What do you suppose they would weigh?"

"Three or four times as much as a man, maybe more," Harris said. "You look at those skeletons, you see right away they were lardbutted birds."

Audubon wouldn't have put it that way, but he couldn't say his companion was wrong. "Can you imagine the red-crested eagle diving down to strike a great honker?" he said, excitement at the thought making his voice rise. "It would have been like Jove's lightning from the sky, nothing less."

"Can you imagine trying to hold them off with pikes and matchlocks and bows, the way the first settlers did?" Harris said. "Better those fellows than me, by God! It's a wonder there were any second settlers after that."

"No doubt that's so," Audubon said, but he was only half listening. He looked down at the red-crested eagle, already trying to decide how to pose it for what would, for all sorts of reasons, undoubtedly prove the last volume of *Birds and Viviparous Quadrupeds of Northern Terranova and Atlantis*. He wanted to show it in a posture that displayed its power and majesty, but the bird was simply too large even for the double elephant folios of his life's work.

What can't be cured . . . , he thought, and carried the bird back to the patiently waiting horses. Yes, it surely weighed every ounce of thirty pounds; sweat streamed down his face by the time he got to them. The horses rolled their eyes. One of them let out a soft snort at the smell of blood.

"There, there, my pets, my lovelies," he crooned, and gave each beast a bit of loaf sugar. That calmed them nicely; horses were as susceptible to bribery as people – and much less likely to go back on any bargain they made.

He got to work with the posing board – which, though he'd brought the largest one he had, was almost too small for the purpose – and his wires. Watching him, Harris asked, "How will you pose a honker if we find one?"

"*When* we find one." Audubon would not admit the possibility of failure to his friend or to himself. "How? I'll do the best I can, of course, and I trust I will enjoy your excellent assistance?"

"I'll do whatever you want me to. You know that," Harris said. "Would I be out here in the middle of nowhere if I wouldn't?"

"No, certainly not." Again, though, Audubon gave the reply only half his attention. He knew what he wanted to do now. He shaped the red-crested eagle with wings pulled back and up to brake its flight, talons splayed wide, and beak agape as if it were about to descend on a great honker's back.

He found a stick of charcoal and began to sketch. No sooner had the charcoal touched the paper than he knew this would be a good one, even a great one. Sometimes the hand would refuse to realize what the eye saw, what the brain thought, what the heart desired. Audubon always did the best he could, as he'd told Harris. Some days, that best was better than others. Today . . . today was one of those. He felt almost as if he stood outside himself, watching himself perform, watching *something* perform through him.

When the drawing was done, he went on holding the charcoal stick, as if he didn't want to let it go. And he didn't. But he had nothing left to add. He'd done what he could do, and . . .

"That's some of your best work in a long time, John – much better than the woodpecker, and that was mighty good," Harris said. "I didn't want to talk while you were at it, for fear I'd break the spell. But that one, when you paint it, will live forever. It will be less than life-sized on the page, then?"

"Yes. It will have to be," Audubon said. When he spoke, it also felt like breaking the spell. But he made himself nod and respond as a man would in normal circumstances; you couldn't stay on that exalted plane forever. Even touching it now and again seemed a special gift from God. More words came: "This is *right*. If it's small, then it's small, that's all. Those who see will understand."

"When they see the bird like that, they will." Harris seemed unable to tear his eyes away form the sketch.

And Audubon descended to mundane reality, drawing ginkgoes and pines and ferns for the background of the painting yet to come. The work there was solid, professional draftsmanship; it seemed a million miles away from the inspiration that had fired him only minutes before.

Once he finished all the sketches he needed, he skinned the eagle and dissected it. When he opened the bird's stomach, he found gobbets of half-digested, unusually dark flesh. It had a strong odor that put him in mind of . . . "Edward!" he said. "What does this smell like to you?"

Harris stooped beside him and sniffed. He needed only a few seconds to find an answer, one very much in character.

"Steak-and-kidney pie, by God!"

And not only was the answer in character. It was also right, as Audubon recognized at once. "It does!" he exclaimed, though the homely dish wasn't one of his favorites. "And these bits of flesh have the look of kidney, too. And that means . . ."

"What?" Harris asked.

"From everything I've read, honker kidneys and the fat above them were – *are* – the red-crested eagle's favorite food!" Audubon answered. "If this bird has a belly full of chunks of kidney, then somewhere not far away, somewhere not far away at all, there *must* be – there must be, I say – honkers on which it fed."

"Unless it killed a deer or some such," Harris said. In that moment, Audubon almost hated his friend – not because Harris was wrong, but because he might not be. And dropping a brute fact on Audubon's glittering tower of speculation seemed one of the cruelest things any man could do.

"Well," Audubon said, and then, bucking up, "Well," again. He gathered himself, gathered his stubbornness. "We just have to find out, don't we?"

Two days later, two days deeper into the western foothills of the Green Ridge Mountains, Audubon's sense of smell again came to his aid. This time, he had no trouble identifying the odor a breeze sent his way. "Phew!" he said, wrinkling his nose. "Something's dead."

"Sure is," Harris agreed. "Something big, too, by the stink."

"Something big . . ." Audubon nodded, trying without much luck to control the electric jolt that coursed through him at those words. "Yes!"

Harris raised an eyebrow. "Yes, indeed. And so?"

"There aren't many big creatures in Atlantis," Audubon said. "It could be a dead man, though I hope not. It could be a dead deer or horse or cow, perhaps. Or it could be . . . Edward, it could be . . ."

"A dead honker?" Harris spoke the word when Audubon couldn't make himself bring it past the barrier of his teeth, past the barrier of his hopes, and out into the open air where it might wither and perish.

"Yes!" he said again, even more explosively than before.

"Well, then, we'd better rein in, hadn't we, and see if we can find out?" Harris let out a creaky chuckle. "Never thought I'd turn bloodhound in my old age. Only goes to show you can't tell, doesn't it?"

He and Audubon tied their horses to a pine sapling by the side of the track. Audubon didn't worry about anyone coming along and stealing the animals; he just didn't want them wandering off. As far as he knew, he and his friend were the only people for miles around. This region was settled thinly, if at all. The two men plunged into the woods, both of them carrying shotguns.

A bloodhound would have run straight to the mass of corruption. Audubon and Harris had no such luck. Tracking by sight or by ear, Audubon would easily have been able to find his quarry. Trying to track by scent, he discovered at once that he was no bloodhound, and neither was Harris. They cast back and forth, trying to decide whether the stench was stronger here or there, in this direction or that: a slow, nasty, frustrating business.

And then, from the edge of a meadow, Harris called, "John! Come quick! I've found it!"

"*Mon Dieu!*" Audubon crashed toward him, his heart thumping and thudding in his chest. "Is it, Edward?" he asked. "Is it a – "

"See for yourself." Harris pointed out to the curved lump of meat that lay in the middle of the grass and weeds.

"*Mon Dieu,*" Audubon said again, softly this time, and crossed himself. "It is a dead honker. It is. And where there are dead ones, there must be live ones as well."

"Stands to reason," Harris said, "unless this one here is the very last of its kind."

"Bite your tongue, you horrible man. Fate wouldn't be so cruel to me." Audubon hoped – prayed – he was right. He walked out to the huge dead bird.

If any large scavengers had been at the corpse, Harris – or Audubon's noisy passage through the woods – had scared them off. Clouds of flies still buzzed above it, though, while ants and beetles took their share of the odorous bounty. Audubon stood upwind, which helped some, but only so much.

This wasn't one of the truly enormous honkers that had wandered the eastern plains before men found Atlantis. It was an upland species, and probably hadn't been as tall as Audubon or weighed much more than twice as much as he did. A great wound in the center of its back – now boiling with maggots – told how it died. That was surely a blow from a red-crested eagle: perhaps the one Audubon and Harris shot, perhaps another.

"Can you draw from this one?" Harris asked.

Regretfully, Audubon shook his head. "I fear not. It's too far gone." His sensitive stomach heaved. Even with the ground firm under his feet, the stench nauseated him.

"I was afraid you'd say that," Harris said. "Shall we take specimens – bones and feathers and such – so we have *something* to bring back in case we don't run into any live honkers?"

Messing about with the dead, reeking bird was the last thing Audubon wanted to do. "We will find live ones," he said. Harris didn't answer. He just stolidly stood there and let Audubon listen to himself and know he couldn't be certain he was right. The artist glared at him. "But I suppose we should preserve what specimens we can, in the interest of science."

Pulling feathers from the honker wasn't too bad. The black ones on its neck and the white patch under the chin testified to its affinity to Canada geese. The feathers on the body, though, were long and shaggy, more hairlike than similar to the plumage of birds gifted with flight.

Getting the meat from the bones and then cleaning them . . . Audubon's poor stomach couldn't stand the strain. He lost his breakfast on the green meadow grass and then dry-heaved helplessly for a while. A little rill ran through the meadow not far away. Perhaps the honker was going out to drink there when the eagle struck.

Audubon rinsed his mouth with cold, clear water from the rill . . .
upstream from where Harris washed rotting flesh from the honker's
right femur. The thighbone was larger and stouter than his own.
Gathering himself, Audubon went back to the corpse to free the bird's
pelvis. He brought it back to the rill to clean it. How long would his
hands reek of decay? How long would his clothes? Would he ever be
able to wear this outfit again? He doubted it. As he worked, he tried not
to look at what he was doing.

His hands, then, told him of something odd: a hole in the bone on the
left side of the pelvis that wasn't matched on the right. That did make
him look. Sure enough, the hole was there, and a shallow groove
leading to it. "See what I have here," he said to Harris.

His friend examined it, then asked, "What do you make of that?"

"Don't you think it comes from the claw of the red-crested eagle?"
Audubon said. "You saw the talons on the bird. One could pierce the
flesh above the bone, and then the bone itself. This is plainly a very
recent wound: notice how rough the bone is all around the edge. It had
no chance to heal."

After considering, Harris nodded. "I'd say you're right. I'd say you
have to be right. You might almost have seen the eagle flying at the
honker."

"I wish I would have!" Audubon held up the still-stinking pelvis. "I'll
have to draw this. It holds too much information to be easily described
in words."

"Let Mr. Owen look to his laurels, then," Harris said.

"I'll do the best I can, that's all," Audubon said. The detailed
scientific illustration would have to be pen and ink, not charcoal or
watercolor. It would also have to be unrelentingly precise. He couldn't
pose the pelvis, except to show the perforation to best advantage, and
he couldn't alter and adjust to make things more dramatic. His
particular gift lay in portraying motion and emotion; he would have to
eschew them both here. He clicked his tongue against the roof of his
mouth. "An artist should be versatile, eh?"

"I know you can do it." Harris showed more confidence in him than
he had in himself.

The smell of rotting honker came closer to spooking the horses than
the eagle's blood had a couple of days before. The pack horse that
carried Audubon's artistic supplies didn't want to let him anywhere
near it. It didn't even want sugar from his stinking hand. He counted
himself lucky to take what he needed without getting kicked.

He set the honker hipbone in the sun, then started sketching with a
pencil. He tried and rubbed out, tried and rubbed out. Sweat ran down
his face, though the day was fine and mild. This was ever so much
harder – for him, anyway – than painting would have been. It seemed
like forever before what he set down on paper bore any resemblance to
the specimen that was its model.

When he was finally satisfied, he held up the sketch to show it to
Harris, only to discover his friend had gone off somewhere and he'd

never noticed. Painting took far less concentration. It left room for artistry. This . . . this was a craft, and one in which he knew himself to be imperfectly skilled.

He'd just inked his pen for the first time when Harris' shotgun boomed. Would that be supper or another specimen? *I'll find out*, Audubon thought, and set about turning his shades of gray into black and white. He had to turn the pelvis to compensate for the way shadows had shifted with the moving sun while he worked.

Harris fired again. Audubon heard the blast, but didn't consciously register it. His hand never twitched. A fine line here, shading there to show a hollow, the exact look of the gouge the eagle's claw had dug before piercing the pelvis where the bone thinned . . .

"We've got supper," Harris said. Audubon nodded to show he heard. Harris went on, "And here's something for you to work on when you're done there."

That made Audubon look up. Along with a plump oil thrush, Harris carried a small, grayish, pale-bellied bird with a black cap. "An Atlantean tit!" Audubon said. The bird was closely allied to the tits of England and Europe and to Terranovan chickadees. Naturalists disagreed about which group held its nearest kin. At the moment, though, he was just glad he would be able to sketch and paint; to feel; to let imprecision be a virtue, not a sin. "Yes, that will be a change – and a relief."

"How's the drawing coming?" Harris asked. Audubon showed him. Harris looked from the paper to the pelvis and back again. After a moment, he silently lifted his broad-brimmed felt hat from his head, a salute Audubon cherished more than most wordier ones.

"Bones are all very well," the artist said, "but I want the chance to draw honkers from life!"

Audubon began to despair of getting what he wanted. He began to believe Harris' gibe was right, and he'd come along just in time to find the last honker in the world moldering in the meadow. Could fate be so cruel?

Whenever he started to fret, Harris would say, "Well, we've got something, anyway. We didn't know for sure we'd get anything at all when we set out." Every word of that was true, and it always made Audubon feel worse, not better.

He spent several days haunting the meadow where his friend found the dead honker, hoping it was part of a flock or a gaggle or whatever the English word for a group of honkers was. No others showed up, though. He found no fresh tracks in the mud by the rill. At last, sorrowfully, he decided the dead bird must have been alone.

"What if it *was* the last one?" he said. "To miss it by a few days . . . Why couldn't we have shot the eagle sooner? Then the honker would still be alive!"

He waited for Harris to be grateful again for what they had. But

Harris surprised him, saying, "No use worrying about it. We don't *know* that eagle got that honker, anyhow."

"Well, no," Audubon admitted upon reflection. "Maybe it was some other villainous eagle instead." He got most affronted when Harris laughed at him.

Even though he was forced to admit to himself that honkers weren't going to visit the meadow, he was loath to leave it. He knew at least one live bird had frequented it up until mere days before. About what other spot in all Atlantis – in all the world – could he say the same?

He kept looking back over his shoulder long after he and Harris rode away. "Don't worry," said Harris, the optimist born. "Bound to be better land ahead."

"How do you know that?" Audubon demanded.

Harris surprised him by having an answer: "Because as best I can tell, nobody's ever come this way before. We're on a track now, not a road. I haven't seen any hoofprints besides the ones our horses are leaving for a couple of hours now."

Audubon blinked. He looked around – *really* looked around. "*Nom d'un nom!*" he murmured. "So it would seem." Pines and cycads and ginkgoes crowded close together on either side of the track. The air was fragrant with scents whose like he would find nowhere else. "This might almost be the antediluvian age, or another world altogether. What do you suppose made our trail?"

"Anywhere else, I'd say deer. That may be so here, too, but I haven't seen any sign of them – no tracks, no droppings," Harris said. "Oil thrushes? Some of the other big flightless birds they have here? Maybe even honkers – who knows?"

That was enough to make Audubon dismount and minutely examine the surface of the trail in the hope of finding honker tracks. With their size and with the vestigial webbing between their toes, they were unmistakable. He found none. He did see oil-thrush footprints, as Harris had suggested: they reminded him of those of the European blackbird or Terranovan robin, except for being three or four times as large. And he saw a fox's pads, which stood out against the spiky background of bird tracks. Imported creatures penetrated even here, to the wild heart of Atlantis.

But of course, he thought. *Harris and I are here, aren't we? And we're no less fond of an oil-thrush supper than foxes are.*

A splash of vivid green on the side of a redwood sapling caught his eye as he rode past. At first, he thought it was some strange Atlantean fungus clinging to the trunk. Then, ever so slowly, it moved. "A cucumber slug!" Harris exclaimed.

The slug was almost the size of a cucumber, though Audubon would have fought shy of eating anything of that iridescent hue. Though it was neither bird nor viviparous quadruped, he stopped and sketched it. It was a curiosity, and one little known to naturalists – few of them penetrated to the cool, humid uplands where it lived. Eyestalks waving, it glided along the trunk, leaving behind a thumb-wide trail of slime.

"Maybe we'll come across some of those snails that are almost as big as your fist, too," Harris said.

"A shame to do it now, when we have no garlic butter." Audubon might draw the line at a cucumber slug, but he was fond of *escargots*. Harris, a Terranovan born and bred, made a horrible face. Audubon only laughed.

They rode on. The tracks they followed were never made by man. They twisted this way and that and doubled back on themselves again and again. Whenever Audubon came out into the open, he scanned the stretch of grass ahead with eager hope. How he longed to see honkers grazing there, or pulling leaves from tender young trees! How disappointed he was, again and again!

"Maybe that was the last honker in this part of Atlantis," he mourned as he and Harris made camp one night. "Maybe it was the last honker in all of Atlantis."

"Maybe it was," his friend replied. Audubon, toasting an oil-thrush drumstick over the flames, glared at him. The least Harris could do was sympathize. But then he continued, "We've come too far and we've done too much to give up so soon, haven't we?"

"Yes," Audubon said. "Oh, yes."

As the scents were different in this mostly pristine Atlantean wilderness, so too were the sounds. Enormous frogs boomed out their calls an octave lower than even Terranovan bullfrogs, let alone the smaller frogs of Europe. When Audubon remarked on them, Harris said, "I suppose you're sorry about the garlic butter there, too."

"Why, yes, now that you mention it," the painter said placidly. His friend screwed up his face again.

The big green katydids that might almost have been mice were noisier than rodents would have been, though some of their squeaks sounded eerily mouse-like. But most of their chirps and trills showed them to be insects after all. Their calls made up the background noise, more notable when it suddenly ceased than when it went on.

Audubon heard birdsongs he'd never imagined. Surely some of those singers were as yet nondescript, new to science. If he could shoot one, sketch it and paint it, bring back a type specimen . . . He did shoot several warblers and finches, but all, so far as he knew, from species already recognized.

Then he heard the scream of a red-crested eagle somewhere far off to the north. He reined in and pointed in that direction. "We go there," he declared, in tones that brooked no argument.

Harris argued anyhow: "It's miles away, John. We can't hope to find just where it is, and by the time we get there it'll be somewhere else anyhow."

"We go north," Audubon said, as if his friend hadn't spoken. "The eagle may fly away, but if honkers are nearby they won't. They can't."

"If." Edward Harris packed a world of doubt into one small word.

"You said it yourself: we've come too far and done too much to give up hope." If that wasn't precisely what Harris had said, Audubon preferred not to be reminded of it. Harris had the sense to recognize as much.

Going north proved no easier than going in any other cardinal direction. Audubon swore in English; French, and occasionally Spanish when game tracks swerved and led him astray. The red-crested eagle had fallen silent after that one series of screeches, so it told him nothing about how much farther he needed to come. *Maybe it's killed again. Maybe it's feasting,* he thought. Even a freshly dead honker might do.

He and Harris came to a stream like a young river. Those Goliath frogs croaked from the rocks. "Can we ford it?" Audubon asked.

"We'd better look for a shallow stretch," the ever-sensible Harris said.

They found one half a mile to the west, and forded the stream without getting the horses' bellies wet. He unfolded a map of northern Atlantis. "Which stream do you suppose this is?" he said. "It should be big enough to show up here."

Harris put on reading glasses to peer at the map. "If it was ever surveyed at all," he said, and pointed. "It might be a tributary of the Spey. That's about where we are."

"I would have guessed it flows into the Liffey myself." Audubon pointed, too.

"Next one farther north? Well, maybe," Harris said. "The way we've been wandering lately, we could be damn near anywhere. Shall we go on?" Without waiting for an answer, he urged his horse forward. Audubon got his mount moving, too.

Not long after the murmur of the stream and the frogs' formidable calls – what Aristophanes would have done with them! – faded in the distance, Audubon heard what he first thought were geese flying by. He'd ridden out onto a grassy stretch a little while before. He looked north to see if he could spot the birds, but had no luck.

Harris was peering in the same direction, his face puzzled. "Geese – but not quite geese," he said. "Sounds like trumpet music played on a slide trombone."

"It does!" For a moment, Audubon simply smiled at the comparison. Then, sudden wild surmise in his eye, he stared at his friend. "Edward, you don't suppose – ?"

"I don't know," Harris said, "but we'd better find out. If they aren't honkers, they could be nondescript geese, which wouldn't be bad, either. Audubon's geese, you could call them."

"I could," said Audubon, who'd never had less interest in discovering a new species. "I could, yes, but . . . I'm going to load my gun with buckshot." He started doing just that.

"Good plan." So did Harris.

Keep calling. Please keep calling, Audubon thought, again and again, as they rode through the forest toward the sound. The birds – whatever they were – did keep up the noise, now quietly, now rising to an angry peak as if a couple of males were quarreling over a female, as males were likely to do in spring.

When Audubon thought they'd come close enough, he slid down off his horse, saying, "We'd best go forward on foot now." He carried not only his gun but also charcoal sticks and paper, in case . . . Harris also dismounted. Audubon believed he would have brained him with the shotgun had he argued.

After perhaps ten minutes, Harris pointed ahead. "Look. We're coming to an open space." Audubon nodded, not trusting himself to speak. He too saw the bright sunshine that told of a break in the trees. The bird calls were very loud now, very near. "Would you call that honking?" Harris asked. Audubon only shrugged and slid forward.

He peered out from in back of a cycad at the meadow beyond . . . at the meadow, and at the honkers grazing on it. Then they blurred: tears of joy ran down his face.

"Blessed art Thou, O Lord, Who hast preserved me alive to see such things," he whispered, staring and staring.

Harris stood behind a small spruce a few feet away. "Isn't that something. Isn't that something?" he said, his words more prosaic than his friend's, but his tone hardly less reverent.

Eight honkers grazed there, pulling up grass with their bills: two males, Audubon judged, and half a dozen smaller females. The birds had a more forward-leaning posture than did the mounted skeletons in the Hanover museum. That meant they weren't so tall. The males probably could stretch their heads up higher than a man, but it wouldn't be easy or comfortable for them.

And then they both moved toward the same female, and did stretch their necks up and up and up, and honked as loudly as ever they could, and flapped their tiny, useless wings to make themselves seem big and fierce. And, while they squabbled, the female walked away.

Audubon started sketching. He didn't know how many of the sketches he would work up into paintings and how many would become woodcuts or lithographs. He didn't care, either. He was sketching honkers from life, and if that wasn't heaven it was the next best thing.

"Which species are they, do you suppose?" Harris asked.

Once, at least a dozen varieties of honker had roamed Atlantis' plains and uplands. The largest couple of species, the so-called great honkers, birds of the easily accessible eastern lowlands, went extinct first. Audubon had studied the remains in Hanover and elsewhere to be ready for this day. Now it was here, and he still found himself unsure. "I . . . believe they're what's called the agile honker," he said slowly. "Those are the specimens they most resemble."

"If you say they're agile honkers, why then, they are," Harris said. "Anyone who thinks otherwise will have to change his mind, because you've got the creatures."

"I want to be right." But Audubon couldn't deny his friend had a point. "A shame to have to take a specimen, but . . ."

"It'll feed us for a while, too." The prospect didn't bother Harris. "They are supposed to be good eating."

"True enough." When Audubon had all the sketches he wanted of grazing honkers and of bad-tempered males displaying, he stepped out from behind the cycad. The birds stared at him in mild surprise. Then they walked away. He was something strange, but they didn't think he was particularly dangerous. Atlantean creatures had no innate fear of man. The lack cost them dearly.

He walked after them, and they withdrew again. Harris came out, too, which likely didn't help. Audubon held up a hand. "Stay there, Edward. I'll lure them back."

Setting down his shotgun, he lay on his back in the sweet-smelling grass, raised his hips, and pumped his legs in the air, first one, then the other, again and again, faster and faster. He'd made pronghorn antelope on the Terranovan prairie curious enough to approach with that trick. What worked with the wary antelope should work for agile honkers as well. "Are they coming?" he asked.

"They sure are." Harris chuckled. "You look like a damn fool – you know that?"

"So what?" Audubon went on pumping. Yes, he could hear the honkers drawing near, hear their calls and then hear their big, four-toed feet tramping through the grass.

When he stood up again, he found the bigger male only a few feet away. The honker squalled at him; it didn't care for anything on two legs that was taller than it. "Going to shoot that one?" Harris asked.

"Yes. Be ready if my charge doesn't bring it down," Audubon said. Point-blank buckshot should do the job. Sometimes, though, wild creatures were amazingly tenacious of life.

Audubon raised the shotgun. No, the agile honker had no idea what it was. This hardly seemed sporting, but his art and science both required it. He pulled the trigger. The gun kicked against his shoulder. The male let out a last surprised honk and toppled. The rest of the birds ran off – faster than a man, probably as fast as a horse, gabbling as they went.

Harris came up beside Audubon. "He's down. He won't get up again, either."

"No." Audubon wasn't proud of what he'd done. "And the other male can have all the females now."

"He ought to thank you, eh?" Harris leered and poked Audubon in the ribs.

"He'd best enjoy them while he can." Audubon stayed somber. "Sooner or later – probably sooner – someone else will come along and shoot him, too, and his lady friends with him."

By then, the rest of the honkers had gone perhaps a hundred yards. When no more unexpected thunder boomed, they settled down and started grazing again. A few minutes later, a hawk soared by overhead

– not a red-crested eagle, but an ordinary hawk far too small to harm them. Still, its shadow panicked them more thoroughly than the shotgun blast had. They sprinted for the cover of the trees, honking louder than they did when Audubon fired.

"Would you please bring my wires, Edward?" the artist asked. "No posing board with a bird this size, but I can truss him up into lifelike postures."

"I'll be back directly," Harris said. He took longer than he promised, but only because instead of carrying things himself he led up the pack horses. That gave Audubon not only the wires but also his watercolors and the strong spirits for preserving bits of the agile honker. If he and Harris did what he'd told the customs man they wouldn't do and drank some of the spirits instead of using them all as preservatives . . . Well, how else could they celebrate?

Audubon soon got to work. "This may be the last painting I ever do," he said. "If it is, I want to give my best."

"Don't be foolish. You're good for another twenty years, easy," Harris said.

"I hope you're right." Audubon left it there. No matter what he hoped, he didn't believe it, however much he wished he did. He went on, "And this may be the last view of these honkers science ever gets. I owe it to them to give my best, too."

He wired the dead male's neck and wings into the pose it took when challenging its rival. He had the sketches he'd made from life to help him do that. His heart pounded as he and Harris manhandled the honker. Ten years earlier, or even five, it wouldn't have seemed so hard. No, he didn't think he had twenty more left, or anything close to that.

Live for the moment then, he told himself. *It's all there is.* His eye still saw; his hand still obeyed. If the rest of him was wearing out like a steamboat that had gone up and down the Big Muddy too many times . . . then it was. When people remembered him, it would be for what his eye saw and his hand did. The rest? The rest mattered only to him.

And when people remembered agile honkers from now on, that too would be for what *his* eye saw and what *his* hand did. Even more than he had with the red-crested eagle, he felt responsibility's weight heavy on his shoulders.

The other honkers came out from the trees and began grazing again. Some of them drew close to where he worked. Their calls when they saw him by the male's body seemed to his ear curious and plaintive. They knew their fellow was dead, but they couldn't understand why Audubon stood near the corpse. Unlike a hawk's shadow, he was no danger they recognized.

The Sun was setting when he looked up from his work. "I think it may do," he said. "The background will wait for later."

Harris examined the honker on the paper, the honker vibrant with the life Audubon had stolen from its model. He set a hand on the painter's shoulder. "Congratulations. This one will last forever."

"Which is more than I will. Which is more than the birds will."

Audubon looked down at the dead honker, agile no more. "Now for the anatomical specimens, and now for the dark meat. Poor thing, it will be all flyblown by this time tomorrow."

"But your painting will keep it alive," Harris said.

"My painting will keep its memory alive. It's not the same." Audubon thought again about how his heart had beat too hard, beat too fast. It was quieter now, but another twenty years? Not likely. "No, it's not the same." He sighed. "But it's all we have. A great pity, but it is." He drew his skinning knife. "And now for the rest of the job . . ."

DEUS EX HOMINE

Hannu Rajaniemi

New writer Hannu Rajaniemi was born in Finland but currently lives in Edinburgh, Scotland, where he is working on his Ph.D. in string theory. He is also a member of Writers' Bloc, an Edinburgh-based spoken-word performance group. His work has appeared in *Nova Scotia* and *Futurismic*, and a chapbook of his short stories involving Finnish mythology is forthcoming.

In the dazzling, crammed, high-bit-rate story that follows, he takes us well beyond a Vingian Singularity to a world where strange dangers are everywhere – as are even stranger allies.

As GODS GO, I WASN'T ONE of the holier-than-thou, dying-for-your-sins variety. I was a full-blown transhuman deity with a liquid metal body, an external brain, clouds of self-replicating utility fog to do my bidding and a recursively self-improving AI slaved to my volition. I could do anything I wanted. I wasn't Jesus, I was Superman: an evil Bizarro Superman.

I was damn lucky. I survived.

The quiet in Pittenweem is deeper than it should be, even for a small Fife village by the sea. The plague is bad here in the north, beyond Hadrian's Firewall, and houses hide behind utility fog haloes.

"Not like Prezzagard, is it?" Craig says, as we drive down the main street.

Apprehension, whispers the symbiote in my head. Worry. I don't blame Craig. I'm his stepdaughter's boyfriend, come calling during her first weekend leave. There's going to be trouble.

"Not really," I tell him, anxiety bubbling in my belly.

"Beggars canna be choosers, as my granny used to say," Craig replies. "Here we are."

Sue opens the door and hugs me. As always, I see Aileen in her, in the short-cropped blonde hair and freckled face.

"Hey, Jukka," she says. "It's good to see you."

"You too," I say, surprising both myself and the symbiote with my sincerity.

"Aileen called," Sue says. "She should be here in a few minutes."

Behind her shoulder, I notice Malcolm looking at me. I wink at him and he giggles.

Sue sighs. "Malcolm has been driving me crazy," she says. "He believes he can fly an angel now. It's great how you think you can do anything when you're six."

"Aileen is still like that," I say.

"I know."

"She's coming!" shouts Malcolm suddenly. We run out to the back garden and watch her descend.

The angel is big, even bigger than I expect from the lifecasts. Its skin is transparent, flowing glass; its wings pitch-black. Its face and torso are rough-hewn, like an unfinished sculpture.

And inside its chest, trapped like an insect in amber, but smiling, is Aileen.

They come down slowly. The downdraught from the micron-sized fans in the angel's wings tears petals from Sue's chrysanthemums. It settles down onto the grass lightly. The glass flesh flows aside, and Aileen steps out.

It's the first time I've seen her since she left. The quicksuit is a halo around her: it makes her look like a knight. There is a sharper cast to her features now and she has a tan as well. Fancasts on the Q-net claim that the Deicide Corps soldiers get a DNA reworking besides the cool toys. But she is still my Aileen: dirty blonde hair, sharp cheekbones and green eyes that always seem to carry a challenge; my Aileen, the light of the sun.

I can only stare. She winks at me and goes to embrace her mother, brother and Craig. Then she comes to me and I can feel the quicksuit humming. She brushes my cheek with her lips.

"Jukka," she says. "What on earth are you doing here?"

"Blecch. Stop kissing," says Malcolm.

Aileen scoops him up. "We're not kissing," she says. "We're saying hello." She smiles. "I hear you want to meet my angel."

Malcolm's face lights up. But Sue grabs Aileen's hand firmly. "Food first," she says. "Play later."

Aileen laughs. "Now I know I'm home," she says.

Aileen eats with relish. She has changed her armour for jeans and a T-shirt, and looks a lot more like the girl I remember. She catches me staring at her and squeezes my hand under the table.

"Don't worry," she says. "I'm real."

I say nothing and pull my hand away.

Craig and Sue exchange looks, and the symbiote prompts me to say something.

"So I guess you guys are still determined to stay on this side of the Wall?" I oblige.

Sue nods. "I'm not going anywhere. My father built this house, and runaway gods or not, we're staying here. Besides, that computer thing seems to be doing a good job protecting us."

"The Fish," I say.

She laughs. "I've never gotten used to that. I know that it was these young lads who built it, but why did they have to call it Fish?"

I shrug.

"It's a geek joke, a recursive acronym. Fish Is Super Human. Lots of capital letters. It's not that funny, really."

"Whatever. Well, Fish willing, we'll stay as long as we can."

"That's good." *And stupid*, I think to myself.

"It's a Scottish thing, you could say. Stubbornness," says Craig.

"Finnish, too," I add. "I don't think my parents are planning to go anywhere soon."

"See, I always knew we had something in common," he says, although the symbiote tells me that his smile is not genuine.

"Hey," says Aileen. "Last time I checked, Jukka is not your daughter. And I just got back from a war."

"So, how was the war?" asks Craig.

Challenge, says the symbiote. I feel uneasy.

Aileen smiles sadly.

"Messy," she says.

"I had a mate in Iraq, back in the noughties," Craig says. "*That* was messy. Blood and guts. These days, it's just machines and nerds. And the machines can't even kill you. What kind of war is that?"

"I'm not supposed to talk about it," says Aileen.

"Craig," says Sue. "Not now."

"I'm just asking," says Craig. "I had friends in Inverness and somebody with the plague turned it into a giant game of Tetris. Aileen's been in the war, she knows what it's like. We've been worried. I just want to know."

"If she doesn't want to talk about it, she doesn't talk about it," Sue says. "She's home now. Leave her alone."

I look at Craig. The symbiote tells me that this is a mistake. I tell it to shut up.

"She has a point," I say. "It's a bad war. Worse than we know. And you're right, the godplague agents can't kill. But the gods can. Recursively self-optimising AIs don't kill people. Killer cyborgs kill people."

Craig frowns.

"So," he says, "how come you're not out there if you think it's so bad?"

Malcolm's gaze flickers between his sister and his stepfather. *Confusion. Tears.*

I put my fork down. The food has suddenly lost its taste. "I had the plague," I say slowly. "I'm disqualified. I was one of the nerds."

Aileen is standing up now and her eyes are those of a Fury.

"How dare you!" she shouts at Craig. "You have no idea what you're talking about. No idea. You don't get it from the casts. The Fish doesn't want to show you. It's bad, really bad. You want to tell me how bad? I'll tell you."

"Aileen – " I begin, but she silences me with a gesture.

"Yes, Inverness was like a giant Tetris game. Nerds and machines did it. And so we killed them. And do you know what else we saw? Babies. Babies bonded with the godplague. Babies are cruel. Babies know what they want: food, sleep, for all pain to go away. And that's what the godplague gives them. I saw a woman who'd gone mad, she said she'd lost her baby and couldn't find it, even though we could see that she was pregnant. My angel looked at her and said that she had a wormhole in her belly, that the baby was in a little universe of its own. And there was this look in her eyes, this look – "

Aileen's voice breaks. She storms out of the room the same instant Malcolm starts crying. Without thinking, I go after her.

"I was just asking . . ." I hear Craig saying as I slam the door shut behind me.

I find her in the back garden, sitting on the ground next to the angel, one hand wrapped around its leg, and I feel a surge of jealousy.

"Hi," I say. "Mind if I sit down?"

"Go ahead, it's a free patch of grass." She smiles wanly. "I spooked everybody pretty badly back there, didn't I?"

"I think you did. Malcolm is still crying."

"It's just . . . I don't know. It all came out. And then I thought that it doesn't matter if he hears it too, that he plays all these games with much worse stuff going on all the time, that it wouldn't matter. I'm so stupid."

"I think it's the fact that it was you telling it," I say slowly. "That makes it true."

She sighs. "You're right. I'm such an arse. I shouldn't have let Craig get me going like that, but we had a rough time up north, and to hear him making light of it like that – "

"It's okay."

"Hey," she says. "I've missed you. You make things make sense."

"I'm glad somebody thinks so."

"Come on," Aileen says, wiping her face. "Let's go for a walk, or better yet, let's go to the pub. I'm still hungry. And I could use a drink. My first leave and I'm still sober. Sergeant Katsuki would disown me if she knew."

"We'll have to see what we can do about that," I say and we start walking towards the harbour.

I don't know if a girl like Aileen would ever have taken an interest in a guy like me if it hadn't been for the fact that I used to be a god.

Two years ago. University cafeteria. Me, trying to get used to the pale colours of the real world again. Alone. And then three girls sit down in the neighbouring table. Pretty. Loud.

"Seriously," says the one with a pastel-coloured jacket and a Hello-Kitty-shaped Fish-interface, "I want to do it with a post. Check this out." The girls huddle around her fogscreen. "There's a cast called Postcoital. Sex with gods. This girl is like their *groupie*. Follows them around. I mean, just the cool ones that don't go unstable."

There's a moment of reverent silence.

"Wow!" says the second girl. "I always thought that was an urban legend. Or some sort of staged porn thing."

"Apparently not," says the third.

These days, the nerd rapture is like the 'flu: you can catch it. The godplague is a volition-bonding, recursively self-improving and self-replicating program. A genie that comes to you and makes its home in the machinery around you and tells you that do as thou wilt shall be the whole of the law. It fucks you up, but it's sexy as hell.

"Seriously," says the first girl, "no wonder the guys who wrote Fish were all *guys*. The whole thing is just another penis. It has no regard for female sexuality. I mean, there's no feminist angle *at all* in the whole collective volition thing. Seriously."

"My God!" says the second girl. "That one there. I want to do him, uh, her. It . . . *All* of them. I really do."

"No you don't," I say.

"Excuse me?" She looks at me as if she's just stepped in something unpleasant and wants to wipe it off. "We're having a private conversation here."

"Sure. I just wanted to say that that cast is a fake. And I really wouldn't mess around with the posts if I were you."

"You speak from experience? Got your dick bitten off by a post girl?" For once I'm grateful I need the symbiote: if I ignore its whispers, her face is just a blank mask to me.

There is nervous laughter from the other girls.

"Yes," I say. "I used to be one."

They get up in unison, stare at me for a second and walk away. *Masks*, I think. *Masks*.

A moment later I'm interrupted again.

"I'm sorry," the third girl says. "I mean, really, really sorry. They're not really my friends, we're just doing the same course. I'm Aileen."

"That's OK," I say. "I don't really mind."

Aileen sits on the corner of the table, and I don't really mind that either.

"What was it like?" she asks. Her eyes are very green. *Inquisitive*, says the symbiote. And I realize that I desperately want it to say something else.

"You really want to know?" I ask.

"Yes," she says.

I look at my hands.

"I was a quacker," I say slowly, "a quantum hacker. And when the Fish-source came out, I tinkered with it, just like pretty much every geek on the planet. And I got mine to compile: my own friendly AI slave, an idiot-proof supergoal system, just designed to turn me from a sack of flesh into a Jack Kirby New God, not to harm anybody else. Or so it told me."

I grimace. "My external nervous system took over the Helsinki University of Technology's supercomputing cluster in about thirty seconds. It got pretty ugly after that."

"But you made it," says Aileen, eyes wide.

"Well, back then, the Fish still had the leisure to be gentle. The starfish were there before anybody was irretrievably dead. It burned my AI off like an information cancer and shoved me back into – " I make a show of looking at myself. "Well, this, I guess."

"Wow!" Aileen says, slender fingers wrapped around a cup of latte.

"Yeah," I say. "That's pretty much what I said."

"And how do you feel now? Did it hurt? Do you miss it?"

I laugh.

"I don't really remember most of it. The Fish amputated a lot of memories. And there was some damage as well." I swallow.

"I'm . . . It's a mild form of Asperger's, more or less. I don't read people very well anymore." I take off my beanie. "This is pretty ugly." I show her the symbiote at the back of my head. Like most Fish-machines, it looks like a starfish. "It's a symbiote. It reads people for me."

She touches it gently and I feel it. The symbiote can map tactile information with much higher resolution than my skin and I can feel the complex contours of Aileen's fingertips gliding on its surface.

"I think it's really pretty," she says. "Like a jewel. Hey, it's warm! What else does it do? Is it like, a Fish-interface? In your head?"

"No. It combs my brain all the time. It makes sure that the thing I was is not hiding in there." I laugh. "It's a shitty thing to be, a washed-up god."

Aileen smiles. *It's a very pretty smile*, says the symbiote. I don't know if it's biased because it's being caressed.

"You have to admit that sounds pretty cool," she says. "Or do you just tell that to all the girls?"

That night she takes me home.

We have fish and chips in the Smuggler's Den. Aileen and I are the only customers; the publican is an old man who greets her by name. The food is fabbed and I find it too greasy, but Aileen eats with apparent relish and washes it down with a pint of beer.

"At least you've still got your appetite," I say.

"Training in the Gobi Desert teaches you to miss food," she says and my heart jumps at the way she brushes her hair back. "My skin cells can do photosynthesis. Stuff you don't get from the fancasts. It's terrible. You always feel hungry, but they don't let you eat. Makes you incredibly alert, though. My pee will be a weird colour for the whole weekend because all these nanites will be coming out."

"Thanks for sharing that."

"Sorry. Soldier talk."

"You do feel different," I say.

"You don't," she says.

"Well, I am." I take a sip from my pint, hoping the symbiote will let me get drunk. "I *am* different."

She sighs.

"Thanks for coming. It's good to see you."

"It's okay."

"No, really, it does mean a lot to me, I – "

"Aileen, please." I lock the symbiote. I tell myself I don't know what she's thinking. *Honest.* "You don't have to." I empty my pint. "There's something I've been wondering, actually. I've thought about this a lot. I've had a lot of time. What I mean is – " The words stick in my mouth.

"Go on," says Aileen.

"There's no reason why you *have* to do this, go out there and fight monsters, unless – "

I flinch at the thought, even now.

"Unless you were so angry with me that you had to go kill things, things like I used to be."

Aileen gets up.

"No, that wasn't it," she says. "That wasn't it at all!"

"I hear you. You don't have to shout."

She squeezes her eyes shut. "Turn on your damn symbiote and come with me."

"Where are we going?"

"To the beach, to skip stones."

"Why?" I ask.

"Because I feel like it."

We go down to the beach. It's sunny like it hasn't been for a few months. The huge Fish that floats near the horizon, a diamond starfish almost a mile in diameter, may have something to do with that.

We walk along the line drawn by the surf. Aileen runs ahead, taunting the waves.

There is a nice spot with lots of round, flat stones between two piers. Aileen picks up a few, swings her arm and makes an expert throw, sending one skimming and bouncing across the waves.

"Come on. You try."

I try. The stone flies in a high arc, plummets down and disappears into the water. It doesn't even make a splash.

I laugh, and look at her. Aileen's face is lit by the glow of the starfish in the distance mingled with sunlight. For a moment, she looks just like the girl who brought me here to spend Christmas with her parents.

Then Aileen is crying.

"I'm sorry," she says. "I was going to tell you before I came. But I couldn't."

She clings to me. Waves lap at our feet.

"Aileen, please tell me what's wrong. You know I can't always tell."

She sits down on the wet sand.

"Remember what I told Craig? About the babies."

"Yeah."

Aileen swallows.

"Before I left you," she says, "I had a baby."

At first I think it's just sympathy sex. I don't mind that: I've had that more than a few times, both before and after my brief stint as the Godhead. But Aileen stays. She makes breakfast. She walks to the campus with me in the morning, holding my hand, and laughs at the spamvores chasing ad icons on the street, swirling like multicoloured leaves in the wind. I grow her a Fish-interface from my symbiote as a birthday present: it looks like a ladybird. She calls it Mr. Bug.

I'm easy: that's all it takes for me to fall in love.

That winter in Prezzagard passes quickly. We find a flat together in the Stack vertical village, and I pay for it with some scripting hackwork.

And then, one morning, her bed is empty and Mr. Bug sits on her pillow. Her toiletry things are gone from the bathroom. I call her friends, send bots to local sousveillance peernets. No one has seen her. I spend two nights inventing nightmares. Does she have a lover? Did I do something wrong? The symbiote is not infallible, and there are times when I dread saying the wrong thing, just by accident.

She comes back on the morning of the third day. I open the door and there she is, looking pale and dishevelled.

"Where have you been?" I ask. She looks so lost that I want to hold her, but she pushes me away.

Hate, says the symbiote. *Hate*.

"Sorry," she says, tears rolling down her cheeks. "I just came to get my things. I have to go."

I try to say something, that I don't understand, that we can work this out, that nothing's so bad she can't tell me about it, and if it's my fault, I'll fix it. I want to plead. I want to beg. But the hate is a fiery aura around her that silences me and I watch quietly as the Fish-drones carry her life away.

"Don't ask me to explain," she says at the door. "Look after Mr. Bug."

After she's gone, I want to tear the symbiote out of my skull. I want the black worm that is hiding in my mind to come out and take over again, make me a god who is above pain and love and hate, a god who can fly. Things go hazy for a while. I think I try to open the window and make a three-hundred-metre dive, but the Fish in the walls and the glass won't let me: this is a cruel world we've made, a lovingly cruel world that won't let us hurt ourselves.

At some point, the symbiote puts me to sleep. It does it again when I wake up, after I start breaking things. And again, until some sort of Pavlovian reflex kicks in.

Later, I spend long nights trawling through the images in Mr. Bug's lifecache: I try to figure it out by using the symbiote to pattern-match emotions from the slices of our life together. But there's nothing that hasn't been resolved, nothing that would linger and fester. Unless I'm getting it all wrong.

It's something that's happened before, I tell myself. *I touch the sky and fall. Nothing new.*

And so I sleep-walk. Graduate. Work. Write Fish-scripts. Forget. Tell myself I'm over it.

Then Aileen calls and I get the first train north.

I listen to the sound of her heartbeat, trying to understand her words. They tumble through my mind, too heavy for me to grasp.

"Aileen. Jesus, Aileen."

The god hiding in my mind, in the dead parts, in my cells, in my DNA –

Suddenly, I want to throw up.

"I didn't know what was happening, at first," says Aileen, her voice flat and colourless. "I felt strange. I just wanted to be alone, somewhere high and far away. So I went to one of the empty flats up at the Stacktop – one of the freshly grown ones – to spend the night and think. Then I got really hungry. I mean, really, really hungry. So I ate fabbed food, lots and lots. And then my belly started growing."

With the Fish around, contraception is the default state of things unless one actually *wants* a baby. But there had been that night in Pittenweem, just after Christmas, beyond the Wall where the Fish-spores that fill the air in Prezzagard are few. And I could just see it happening, the godseed in my brain hacking my cells, making tiny molecular machines much smaller than sperm, carrying DNA laden with code, burrowing into Aileen.

"It didn't feel strange. There was no pain. I lay down, my waters broke and it just pulled itself out. It was the most beautiful thing I'd ever seen," she says, smiling. "It had your eyes and these tiny, tiny fingers. Each had the most perfect fingernail. It looked at me and smiled."

"It waved at me. Like . . . like it decided that it didn't need me anymore. And then the walls just *opened* and it flew away. My baby. Flew away."

The identification mechanism I used to slave the godseed was just my DNA. It really didn't occur to me that there was a loophole there. It could make my volition its own. Reinvent itself. And once it did that, it could modify itself as much as it pleased. Grow wings, if it wanted.

I hold Aileen. We're both wet and shivering, but I don't care.

"I'm sorry. That night I came to tell you," she says. "And then I saw it looking at me again. From your eyes. I had to go away."

"So you joined the Corps."

She sighs.

"Yes. It helped. Doing something, being needed."

"I needed you too," I say.

"I know. I'm sorry."

Anger wells up in my throat. "So is it working? Are you guys defeating the superbabies and the dark lords? Does it make you happy?"

She flinches away from me. "You sound like Craig now."

"Well, what am I supposed to say? I'm sorry about the baby. *But it wasn't your fault.* Or mine."

"It was you who – " She lifts her hand to her mouth. "Sorry, I didn't mean that. I didn't mean that."

"Go back to your penance and leave me alone."

I start running along the waterline, heading nowhere in particular.

The angel is waiting for me on the shore.

"Hello, Jukka," it says. "Good to see you again."

As always, the voice is androgynous and pleasant. It tickles something in my brain. It is the voice of the Fish.

"Hi."

"Can I help you?"

"Not really. Unless you want to give her up. Make her see sense."

"I can't interfere with her decisions," says the angel. "That's not what I do. I only give you – and her – what you want, or what you would want if you were smarter. That's my supergoal. You know that."

"You self-righteous bastard. The collective volition of humanity is that she must go and fight monsters? And probably die in the process? Is it supposed to be *character-forming* or *something*?"

The angel says nothing, but it's got me going now.

"And I can't even be sure that it's Aileen's own decision. This – this thing in my head – it's you. You could have let the godseed escape, just to hurt Aileen enough to get her to sign up to your bloody kamikaze squadron. And the chances are that you knew that I was going to come here and rant at you and there's nothing I can do to stop her. Or is there?"

The angel considers this.

"If I could do that, the world would be perfect already." It cocks its glass head to one side. "But perhaps there is someone who wanted you to be here."

"Don't try to play head games with me!"

Anger rushes out of me like a river. I pound the angel's chest with my fists. Its skin flows away like a soap bubble.

"Jukka!"

The voice comes from somewhere far away.

"Jukka, stop," says Aileen. "Stop, you idiot!"

She yanks me around with irresistible strength. "Look at me! It wasn't the Fish. It wasn't you. It wasn't the baby. It was me. I want to do this. Why won't you let me?"

I look at her, my eyes brimming.

"Because I can't come with you."

"You silly boy," she says, and now it's her holding me as I cry, for the first time since I stopped being a god. "Silly, silly boy."

After a while, I run out of tears. We sit on a rock, watching the sun set. I feel light and empty.

"Maybe it would have been easier if you hadn't called," I say, sighing.

Aileen's eyes widen.

"What do you mean? I never did. I thought Craig did. It would have been just like him. To keep me from going back."

And then we see the baby.

It is bald and naked and pink, and a hair-thin silver umbilical hangs from its navel. Its eyes are green like Aileen's, but their gaze is mine. It floats in the air, its perfect tiny toes almost touching the water.

The baby looks at us and laughs: the sound is like the peal of silver bells. Its mouth is full of pearly teeth.

"Be very still," says Aileen.

The angel moves towards the baby. Its hands explode into fractal razor bushes. A glass cannon forms in its chest. Tiny spheres of light, quantum dots pumped full of energy, dart towards the baby.

The baby laughs again. It holds out its tiny hands, and *squeezes*. The air – and perhaps space, and time – wavers and twists. And then the angel is gone, and our baby is holding a tiny sphere of glass, like a snow-globe.

Aileen grabs my arm.

"Don't worry," she whispers. "The big skyFish must have seen this. It'll do something. Stay calm."

"Bad baby," I say slowly. "You broke Mummy's angel."

The baby frowns. I can see the cosmic anger simmering behind the wrinkled pink forehead.

"Jukka – " Aileen says, but I interrupt her.

"You only know how to *kill* gods. I know how to *talk* to them." I look at my – son, says the little wrinkly thing between its legs – and take a step towards him. I remember what it's like, having all the power in the world. There's a need that comes with it, a need to make things perfect.

"I know why you brought us here," I say. "You want us to be together, don't you? Mummy and Daddy." I go down to one knee and look my son in the eye. I'm in the water now and so close to him that I can feel the warmth of his skin.

"And I know what you're thinking. I've been there. You could take us apart. You could rebuild our minds. You could *make* us want to be together, to be with you." I pause and touch his nose with my forefinger. "But it doesn't work that way. It would never be perfect. It would never be right." I sigh. "Trust me, I know. I did it to myself. But you are something new, you can do better."

I take Mr. Bug from my pocket and hold it out to my son. He grabs it and puts it into his mouth. I take a deep breath, but he doesn't bite.

"Talk to the bug," I say. "He'll tell you who we are. Then come back."

The baby closes its eyes. Then he giggles, mouth full of an insect-shaped AI, and touches my nose with a tiny hand.

I hear Aileen gasp. A lightning horse gallops through my brain, thunder rumbling in its wake.

Something wet on my face wakes me. I open my eyes and see Aileen's face against the dark sky. It is raining.

"Are you okay?" she asks, almost in tears, cradling my head. "That little bastard!"

Her eyes widen. And suddenly, there is a silence in my mind, a wholeness. I see the wonder in her eyes.

Aileen holds out her hand. My symbiote is lying in her palm. I take it, turning it between my fingers. I take a good swing and throw it into the sea. It skims the surface three times, and then it's gone.

"I wonder where he gets it from."

THE GREAT CARUSO

Steven Popkes

Steven Popkes made his first sale in 1985, and in the years that followed has contributed a number of distinguished stories to markets such as *Asimov's Science Fiction, Sci Fiction, The Magazine of Fantasy & Science Fiction, Realms of Fantasy, Science Fiction Age, Full Spectrum Tomorrow, The Twilight Zone Magazine, Night Cry,* and others. His first novel, *Caliban Landing,* appeared in 1987, and was followed in 1991 by a novel-length expansion of his popular novella "The Egg," retitled *Slow Lightning.* ("The Egg," in its original form, was in our Seventh Annual Collection.) He was also part of the Cambridge Writers' Workshop project to produce science fiction scenarios about the future of Boston, Massachusetts, that cumulated in the 1994 anthology *Future Boston,* to which he contributed several stories. His stories have appeared in our Twentieth and Twenty-first Annual Collections. He lives in Hopkinton, Massachusetts, with his family, works for a company that builds aviation instrumentation, and is learning to be a pilot.

After years of antismoking campaigns, everybody knows that smoking is bad for you. As the sly tale that follows suggests, though, it may be bad for you in ways that nobody has thought of yet . . .

NORMA GAVE UP SMOKING when she found out she was pregnant with Lenny. Everybody congratulated her and said how important it was not to smoke when you were pregnant. It was bad for the baby. Norma understood and promised herself she'd start the day he was born. But, heck. He looked so small and wrinkly in the preemie ward of the Albuquerque Hospital and was trying so hard just to breathe and stay alive, she decided she'd give him a couple of years. Get him past nursing and stuff. Once he was strong enough, she'd go back. Tomas didn't approve of smoke inhalation. Nothing that didn't go up the nose was a good idea. He was ecstatic that she stayed off tobacco. Or, he would have been if he hadn't been shot down the week before she found out she was pregnant. He was fronting for the Turban-Kings but had developed a deep affection for their brand of cocaine. Tomas had been pretty but Norma had always known he wouldn't last long.

With Tomas gone, Norma had to get a job. She sighed and hit the streets. She would have had to find one anyway. After six weeks of fruitless searching, Norma landed a job as a clerk for Frost Fabrications near the University.

She contented her lapsed habit by lingering in the cigarette fumes from the Indians selling turquoise brooches and rings at the corner of Old Town. She could often be found standing in front of the cantina down the street next to an old Mexican smoking a gloriously obnoxious cigar. With the occasional secondhand smoke from disgruntled office workers grabbing a quick one on the loading dock, Norma managed to keep herself on the low end of satisfied. Just a couple of years, she told herself. Then, she'd light up and everything would be fine.

But when Lenny turned five, a whole series of commercials about how secondhand smoke caused learning disabilities were broadcast. Norma was pretty sure that once she started back again she wouldn't be able to keep from smoking in the house. She grimly decided she could stick it out until Lenny got into the habit of studying.

Norma was fifty when Lenny turned ten: the danger years, said the magazines. When anybody could suddenly drop dead of a heart attack. Cigarettes caused heart attacks, didn't they? She didn't want Lenny to have to bury her, did she? Not a ten-year-old boy.

By the time Lenny was thirty and had been on the Albuquerque police force for a while, Norma figured she'd done enough. If she died, she died. She was seventy now. It was now Lenny's duty to bury her. He'd do it eventually one way or the other. Her first puff was everything she'd remembered: the burn down the throat, the tingling all the way to her fingers and toes, the quick, sharp rush up into her face and behind her eyes. She felt brighter and happier than she'd been in years. It was like the first time she lit up, way back when she was thirteen and living in Portales. And, just like when she was thirteen, after a minute or two she turned green and threw up. Oh, well, she thought philosophically. You pay for your pleasures.

In no time at all she was back up to a couple of packs a day.

Lenny, of course, was appalled.

He came over to her house and tried to talk over the music. There was always music in Norma's house: blues, country, classical, rock. If she could sing it, she had it on. Not that Norma could sing. Her voice had been described as having all the subtlety and color of a downtown bus at rush hour. Norma didn't care.

First Lenny tried desperately to talk her out of it. "Come on, Ma," he pleaded. "It's been years. You're over seventy. Don't throw it away now." Then, he got belligerent and refused to let her come over to his house to see her grandkids. That lasted a week. They lived down the street in the same sort of four-room bungalow she did. If she couldn't go over there, they came over here. Once pleading and threats didn't work, he tried covert operations. He broke into her house after duty and threw away every pack of cigarettes he could find.

This last trick might have worked. Cigarettes were eleven dollars a pack now and she was still at the same job after thirty years. What she needed was a way to smoke cigarettes without having them in the house. Or, better, cigarettes cheap enough she could afford to lose a few packs a month as the cost of doing business.

The Internet, she discovered, holds the answer to all things.

Reginald Cigarettes, a tiny company based in the Sandwich Islands (which used to be Hawaii until they seceded) sold cigarettes by direct mail. This had many advantages. First, she gave them the address of a packing services company nearby – that way Lenny couldn't take them out of the mailbox before she could get to them. Second, they were cheaper since they were being sold from another country (no taxes!). Third, they were also artificial. When she was finally found out and cornered, she could use the site's propaganda about how much better they were than real cigarettes.

Not that Norma cared. She figured she could empty a few packs of Reginalds and stuff them with Marlboros.

But when the Reginalds came, she found she liked them. True, they didn't taste quite as good as Marlboros. But the tingle was better and, as had to happen eventually, when Lenny found out about them and she showed him the pack –

"See?" she cried shrilly. "See? They're better for me."

"Ma," protested Lenny. He looked at the pack. "They still got tobacco in them."

"But look at the numbers on the side. They're *way* better than Marlboros."

Lenny sighed. By that, Norma knew she had won.

She had her cigarettes. All was right with the world.

Five years later, she got up with her usual morning cough. She rolled out of bed and padded downstairs to put on the coffee. While she waited for it to perk, she put on the morning classics station. It was opera week, which she loved, and they were working their way through some ancient recordings of Enrico Caruso – The Great Caruso, as her mother had said when she was a girl. Still coughing, Norma hacked around the house for a while. Well, she certainly *coughed* like the Great Caruso. While she waited for the really deep one that signaled the start of the day, she thought about renting that old film about him, the one starring Mario Lanza.

Something stuck in her throat. Something that wouldn't come out. Panicky, she went to the sink to get a drink of water, but the spasms in her chest nearly knocked her off her feet. It was all she could do to hold on and stand upright. Whatever it was, it clawed its way up her throat and she spat it out into the sink, bloody and covered in mucous.

It was perhaps a quarter of an inch across and twice that in length. She reached down and picked it up. It was spongy and felt surprisingly firm. Norma rinsed it off.

She guessed this was it, then. Just like Lenny had always told her. Lung cancer. Not that she hadn't expected it eventually. Only not so soon. She sighed. You pay for your pleasures.

The radio dimmed a little and Norma reached over and turned it up, still looking at the bit of diseased flesh that had come from inside her.

It vibrated in her hand.

Curious, Norma put her ear to it. Faintly, but unmistakably, it was singing along with Caruso on the radio.

Doing a pretty good job, too.

The doctor had no explanation. They sat in his office as he went over the test results. Norma was dying for a smoke.

Hm. She thought to herself. That was pretty good. She giggled.

Dr. Peabody looked up at her and frowned so Norma stifled herself. This was clearly no laughing matter. She'd laugh later. When she had a cigarette.

"Mrs. Carstairs – "

"Miss."

"Beg pardon?"

"I've never married. Miss will do."

Dr. Peabody nodded. "The truth is I'm not sure what's in your . . . lungs. Something's in there. Something's up your trachea and into your larynx. We'll have to run more tests. Do you smoke?"

"Sure do. Two packs a day of Reginalds."

"I see."

Norma could see the effort Dr. Peabody made not to look disgusted.

"Tests." She picked up her purse. "You might want this, then." Norma brought an envelope out of her purse and put it on his desk. It looked a little dry so Norma got up and wet a paper towel and moistened the little thing. Even with the water, it was still dead.

"This is . . . ?"

She put it in his hand and shrugged. "I have no idea. But that's what I got inside me. Coughed it up yesterday. Thought it might help."

Dr. Peabody didn't answer. He was staring at the fleshy bit in his hand.

Dr. Peabody asked her to come back the following week. When she did, he wasn't alone. There were at least three other doctors there for moral support. The medical consensus was, apparently, that she had lung cancer of a rare if not unknown type. She should be admitted at once. In his office, Norma stared at the radiographs as if she were interested. Then she smiled at them sweetly and asked if she could go to the bathroom. They nodded, all together as if they were attached to the same string.

Outside the office, Norma walked down the hall and out through the parking garage. She went home and sat at her kitchen table, drinking a glass of wine and smoking one of her Reginalds.

Dr. Peabody called Lenny, of course. Before the afternoon was finished, Lenny was pounding on her door.

"What do you want, Lenny?" she asked from the other side.

"For Christ's sake, Mom. You *know* what I want. I want you to go to the doctor."

She sipped her wine – the bottle was mostly gone now, dissolved into Norma's healthy glow.

"I don't want to."

"What kind of answer is that? You want to die? Peabody said you got a good chance if you get some treatment now."

She shook her head. Remembered Lenny couldn't see her and said, "No."

"Are you drunk, Mom?"

"No!" she said defensively.

"You shouldn't be drinking at your age."

"I had a deprived childhood and now I'm making up for it."

"Come on, Mom! You got to go."

Norma leaned her head against the door. "No," she said clearly and quietly. "No, I don't."

"Mom!"

"This is my choice," she shouted back at him. "It's my lungs. They were my cigarettes. If I can't choose whether or not to die, what choice do I have?"

"Look. If you want to go all Christian Scientist on me, let's call up the Mother Church and ask *them*. They'll tell you to get your ass up to the hospital."

"That's no way to talk to your mother."

"This is no kind of conversation to have through a door."

"Why not?" She knocked on the wood. "It's a perfectly good door."

He was silent for a minute. She could almost see him rubbing his forehead. "Let me come in."

She shook her head again. "I'll talk to you tomorrow."

Norma left him shouting at the door and walked unsteadily upstairs to bed. You should always have a good, hard bed, Norma reasoned. That way when you get too drunk to stand, you won't roll off.

She couldn't keep Lenny out of her house forever. She didn't even want to. Norma was proud of her son, shy and thin when he was young, now so strong and tall. She always did have a thing for a man in a uniform. That was what had attracted her to Tomas in the first place. The Turban-Kings had uniforms of a sort.

Lenny wanted a good, reasoned argument why she wouldn't go in for treatment. Norma didn't have one. Just a strong feeling that this was the body she came in with; it ought to be the body she went out with.

But he was wearing her down.

A week after she'd left Dr. Peabody, she went to the 7-11 for her regular rations of bread and ice cream. She came home to see a young man sitting on her stoop, a briefcase next to him.

He stood up as she came near. He was odd looking – too thin, for one. His obviously expensive suit that had been cleverly cut to hide it but still, like light through a window, his thinness shone through. His cheekbones were apparent and were it not for the fullness of his lips and his large eyes, he might have looked gaunt. As it was, he had a haunted, shadowed look, like a monk who regretted his vow.

He stepped forward.

"Miss Carstairs?" he asked, holding out his hand.

"Yes," she said warily, stepping back.

"I'm Ben Cori." He dropped his hand to his side. "I'm Reginald Cigarettes."

She looked at him for a moment. Things clicked together in her mind. "This has something to do with my lung cancer."

He smiled at her. "It does."

"What's special about lung cancer if you're a smoker?"

"Can we talk inside?"

Norma shrugged. "Can't hurt me, I suppose."

Ben's hands were long and delicate and his wrists seemed lost in the sleeves of his jacket. Now that he was sitting at her table, Norma had a sudden respect for Ben's tailor. The suit fooled the eye so that he merely appeared to be thin. Ben was a bundle of sticks in a sack.

"So, are you a lawyer?"

Ben put down his coffee. "No. Just the engineer. Also, CEO, COO and CFO. President and Board of Directors. Salesman and Web site designer. I had to hire a lawyer."

She sat up. "I don't get it."

Ben leaned back in his chair. The chair didn't so much as creak under his weight. "I designed the tobacco product. It's made in a small factory down in Cuba. Then, the factory ships the resulting product to a cigarette packing company in North Carolina. From there, the packs go to a shipping company in New Jersey. The Web site is hosted by a company in South Africa and sends the orders to New Jersey. The U.S. Mail delivers it to you. Reginald is incorporated in Hawaii. The only part of Reginald that really exists is an office in my home in Saint Louis." Ben sipped his coffee.

"I see," said Norma. "You design cigarettes?"

"No," Ben said carefully. "Tobacco *product*. More precisely, I design small machines whose nature it is to take tobacco, tear it apart and rebuild it with reduced carcinogens and toxins. Dried tobacco leaves from all over the South come into the factory and something that resembles dried tobacco leaves come out of the factory. Tobacco product."

"What's that got to do with me?"

Ben opened his briefcase and brought out two radiographs. He carefully placed the first one in front of Norma. "That's your lungs."

"I've seen it. How did you get this?"

"I've been working the net for a while. You can find anything if you have enough time and money." He placed a second radiograph next to the first. "That's a normal case of lung cancer."

Next to each other, the differences were obvious. The normal lung cancer – if such a disease could actually be called normal – looked splotchy and irregular. Her lungs had something in them made up of lines and polygons.

Ben pointed to an irregular rectangle. "I'm pretty sure that's an amplifier. Next to it is a low pass filter. A pretty sophisticated filter from what I can tell. These circles are sensors of some kind."

Looking at the picture made her chest hurt. "What the hell have I got inside of me?"

"I don't know."

"Do you know how it happened?"

Ben nodded. "No. Whatever happened is impossible."

"Impossible?" She pointed at the pictures. "It's right there in front of me."

Ben nodded, smiled at her. "That it is."

"Pretty big stretch to be impossible."

"I know that."

Norma stared at him for a minute. "Okay. Explain it to me."

Ben pulled some more papers from his briefcase. "In my business, mites, tiny machines about the size of a cell, do all the work. We got a bad shipment of mites. Somehow they went ahead and did all the work the normal mites did and left some clusters in the tobacco that got through all of the quality control mechanisms, the heating, the cutting and packaging, the irradiation, until the finished cigarettes reached you. Then, they suddenly started working inside of you, not in some random destructive manner but in a controlled construction. I can guess what might have happened but, in point of fact, it's impossible."

Norma spoke slowly. "I have tiny machines in my lungs? Machines you built?"

"Close. I don't know what they're encoded to do. Nobody knows."

"How many . . . clusters got out?"

"From what I can tell, only one."

"How do you know that?"

Ben spread his hands. "So far, you, and only you, have shown anything." He pointed at Norma.

"Pretty long odds."

"Not as long as some."

"So what are your mites doing to me?"

"I'm not sure. My mites were contaminated with other mites with different natures. Mites are built to cooperate so I'm not sure what they are doing."

"What were they *supposed* to do?" asked Norma.

"All different things. One set built musical instruments," said Ben, leaning on the table. "Oboes. Flutes. Tubas. Or, since they came from India, sitars or something. Some were designed to implement a communication system designed in Germany. There were banana preparation mites ordered from Malaysia. Others."

Norma remembered the singing of the fleshy bit.

"I have tiny machines making music in my lungs. Your tiny machines."

"As I said, they're not *my* mites. My mites died properly."

"Are you sure you're not a lawyer?"

"If I was a lawyer, I wouldn't be here."

"Why are you here?"

He stared at his hands and didn't speak for a few seconds. "To be present at the creation."

"What does that mean?"

Ben leaned toward her. "By any stretch of the imagination, the mites should have just consumed you, made you into some intermediate random product. *My* mites, acting out of *my* programming, would try to make you into tobacco product. Something that, to you, would be invariably gruesome and fatal. But that's not what the mites inside of you are doing. They're building something inside you. Something *integrated* – which I can see from the pictures, as well as noticing that you're still walking around."

"Walking right down to the clinic so Dr. Peabody can cut them out."

"That's why I'm here. To try to persuade you not to."

Norma stared at him. "Are you nuts?"

Ben smiled. "Maybe. Mites and humans are made up of much the same things: carbon, nitrogen, oxygen, some metals. If we come from the dust of the earth, then so do they. But we created them. Now, something unexpected and impossible has happened. A miracle."

"A *miracle*?"

"Yes."

"That's like saying cancer is a miracle."

Ben shook his head. "Not at all. Cancer is the emergent property of the accumulated errors in an ordered system. It's the consequences of random events."

Norma shook her head. The way he talked made her dizzy. "How's this any different?"

"Cancer in a system makes the system untenable. It doesn't do anything to make the system any better. It's not creative. This is going to make you something better."

"It's going to kill me. That's what it's going to do."

Ben shrugged. "There's a risk to everything. But we come from the earth. So do these mites. The earth speaks through us. They speak through the mites, too." He pointed to the radiographs. "That low pass filter looks a lot like filters used to integrate circuits into nerve cells. *I* didn't design it. None of the programming in any of the contaminant mites had anything like it. They developed this on their own. This is no cancer."

"But like cancer it's going to kill me."

"You were going to let the cancer do that anyway, or you wouldn't have walked out of Peabody's office."

"That was different." Norma thought for a moment. "The cancer was mine. It was my own body telling me it was time to go. These things are . . . *invading* me."

"A cluster is made up of a few hundred mites. It's about the size of a mustard seed. It took root in you – not just anybody. It's making something in you – nobody else."

"You're saying these things *chose* me?"

"No. They can't choose anything. They're just little automatons. Like chromosomes or sperm. A baby is the emergent property of the genes but the genes didn't have any choice in the matter. Out of such automata comes you and me. The mites didn't choose you. The earth itself chose you."

"You *are* nuts. These things are still going to kill me."

"We can stack the odds." He brought out an inhaler from his briefcase. "This is FTV. All mites are designed so they stop operation when FTV is present. FTV saturates the air in mite factories as a safety precaution. If you inhale this, it might at least slow down their progress."

"That goes against your plan, doesn't it?"

"No. Think of it as prenatal care. It gives the mites an opportunity to more thoroughly understand their environment."

Norma thought of the singing again.

"What if they escape? I don't want to destroy the world or something."

Ben brought a square instrument out of his briefcase. "This has been sampling the air for the whole time I've been here. Look for yourself. No mites."

"They could be waiting. Like fungus spores."

"Now who's nuts?"

She considered. "Could Peabody cut them out?"

Ben shook his head. "I don't think so. The mites are cooperating. If you cut out a chunk of the network, they'll just try to rebuild it and they'll have to relearn what they lost plus figure out the new topology resulting from the surgery. I think it would just make things worse."

"That's what you would say regardless, isn't it?"

Ben shrugged again and said nothing.

She had been ready to just die and be gone. At least, this way would make it more of an adventure.

She drew a ragged breath. She had no difficulty breathing yet. No more than usual.

"Okay," she said. "I'm in."

Life seemed to settle back to normal. She didn't cough anything up anymore. Her voice cracked and quavered as she spoke. Which, she supposed, was a small price to pay for robots living in her lungs.

Reginald Cigarettes suddenly disappeared from the market. Ben had given Norma prior warning. She had a dozen cases packed carefully in the basement.

About a month after she'd first spoken with Ben, she woke up from a deep sleep jumpy and irritated. When Lenny came by for his morning visit she told him to go away. Her voice was breaking like a fifteen-year-old boy's.

"Ma," called Lenny. "Let me in."

She opened the door a crack. "What do you want?"

"Come on, Ma. Don't get crazy on me. Let me in. I'm your son, remember?"

"I know who you are." She stood back to let him in.

"That was a pretty nice station you had on," he said as he stepped in. "Who was singing?"

"Oh, come on!" She held up her hands in exasperation. "You have something to say. It's written all over your face. What is it?"

"Well, Ma. Your birthday is coming up and all – " He stopped and held out an envelope to her. "Happy birthday."

She opened the envelope and slipped on her reading glasses. They were tickets to Opera Southwest. Two of them. To see *Don Giovanni*.

"You always have music around," Lenny said shyly. "I thought you might like to go."

Norma didn't say anything for a moment. "Nearly forty years I've known you," she said and kissed him on the cheek. "And you can still surprise me."

All the next week, she sang along with everything that came over the radio, tuneless or not. Belted it out with Patsy Cline. Harmonized with a Hunk of Burnin' Love. She was a Werewolf in London Born in America seeing Paradise by the Dashboard Lights for the very first time.

Norma was so excited waiting for Lenny to pick her up she made herself pee three times. Just to be sure she wouldn't have to get up in the middle and go to the bathroom.

Lenny wore a tie for the occasion and looked so handsome that Norma decided she'd forgo cigarettes for the night. Just so he'd be happy. She left her pack of Reginalds in the dresser drawer just to make sure.

The drive downtown, the walk into the Hiland Theater, finding their seats in the middle just in front of the orchestra, passed in a happy, warm blur. She settled back in her chair when the lights dimmed and put one hand on Lenny's. The music came up.

I must have heard this a hundred times, she thought. But now, in front of her, sung by people no less flesh and blood than she, it came to life.

In the middle of the second act, where Elvira began her angry solo, Norma leaned forward. For a moment, she had an uncontrollable urge to cough. It subsided before she could do anything to stop it. Then, it came again. Stronger, this time. She was going have one of those hacking fits like when she coughed up the fleshy bit. She could feel it coming on. Norma had to get out of there.

She put one hand over her mouth, stood and walked quickly up the aisle. Lenny stared after her but she was outside in the lobby before he could react.

A bathroom. She couldn't find one. Instead, she walked outside onto Central Street, thinking to cough or throw up in the gutter.

When she filled her lungs, the pain eased and in her mind, she could still hear Elvira's rage, haunted by the Don and her own weakness. She opened her mouth, and it welled up and out of her like clear running water. The vibrating power of it shook her, made her heart pound and her lungs rejoice. Every day she had listened to the radio, the music had been captured and woven into her cells. Now, they were free.

She stopped when Elvira stopped. Lenny was standing in front of her.

"Ma?" he asked. "You okay?"

Norma nodded. She didn't want to speak.

"That was good," he said softly. "Unnatural, of course. But good."

"You think so?"

"Yeah." He nodded. "I do." Lenny didn't say anything for a minute. "Tomorrow we go see Dr. Peabody."

"Hush." She was smiling. Norma felt like a girl again and the world was bright with possibility. She was sixteen, sitting in an old Chevy, smoking and grinning and driving down a road straight as a runway and smooth as a glass table.

In 1711, for his first opera in London, George Handel advertised he would bring to the stage a chariot pulled across the stage by live horses, fireworks, a raft of tenors sailing through the storm in midair and not one, but two fire-breathing dragons. Consequently, opera, even opera in Albuquerque, was no stranger to novelty.

Ben told Norma she had two advantages going into the audition. One, she was old. It was hard to take a pretty, thirty-year-old diva and make her look seventy-five. Not only was it easier to do the same thing to Norma, she didn't mind and the diva usually did. The second was she had the pipes. Once the director was persuaded to hear her, she had a spot.

Not to say she got the front line roles. She was the old dowager, the mother-in-law, the comic innkeeper's wife, the ancient fortuneteller – in short, any role that suited her age and wasn't big enough to make the younger singers want it. This was fine with Norma. She was having a ball.

Hey, she thought to herself as she sprayed the inhaler down her throat. Look at me. I'm the Great Caruso.

The next two years passed quickly. Norma expected her voice to have a metal, inhuman quality, given its origin. Instead, it was an intensely human voice. "A dark warm revelry," said one critic in Keystone. "Lustrous," said another in Scottsdale. That was as far as she traveled. Opera Southwest had funding problems those years and their concert tours went only as far east as Amarillo and as far west as Needles.

She didn't care. The music never palled. The singing never lost its luster. But one day, she was listening to a recording of *Rigoletto* as she prepared for the role of Maddalena – being able to read music didn't come with the deal – when she looked up in the mirror. She looked the same. But what was going on inside of her? The quality of her singing seemed to get better over the last two years. She never coughed anymore. The only reminders she had were the daily dose of the inhaler and the two radiographs she had framed and mounted on her wall.

Norma stared at her image in the mirror. She was pushing eighty and could see it in her face. "What's going on in there?"

I should have died two years ago. I'm living on borrowed time.

Norma had a feeling deep inside that the mites were only waiting for her.

"Waiting for me to do what?" she asked Ben as she sipped her coffee. It was a warm March and they had come to an outdoor coffee shop near the theater. It was her birthday.

"What do you mean?" Ben leaned back in his chair, bemused. He was still thin by normal standards but in the last few years, he had filled out. Now, his eyes seemed properly proportioned and his mouth fit in his face. "Aren't you happy?"

"Of course I am."

"Then don't question it."

Norma snorted and stirred her coffee. "This was the miracle you wanted to be present at?"

Ben smiled back at her serenely. "I'm present enough."

"These mites went through a lot of effort to do this to me. Why? What do they have in mind? Why did they stop?"

"The FTV stopped them."

"I don't believe it. I don't think the FTV was much more than a suggestion. I think they *chose* to stop. For some reason."

"You're making them more intelligent than they are." Ben closed his eyes in the spring sun.

"I'm not sure intelligence has anything to do with it." Norma drummed her fingers on the table. "You don't need intelligence to have a purpose. They had a purpose. What was the word you used? My singing was an . . . *emergent property* of their purpose."

"What do you think it is?"

"How should I know? Send messages to the moon? A voyage to Arcturus? A better subway?" Norma mulled it over in her mind. "I owe them for this."

"You don't owe them a thing. Think of it as a reward for a life well spent."

Norma chuckled. She had a clockwork sense of time passing. It was her choice. They had made sure of it. Well, she was eighty now. When *should* she choose? Once the mind and gums went, there wouldn't be much left. Why not now, when she still had it?

"Heck," she muttered out loud. "I was ready to let lung cancer kill me. Why not these guys?"

Ben leaned forward, suddenly alert. "What are you talking about?"

Norma watched the way a bicyclist worked his way down the crowded street. "I quit using the inhaler."

"When?"

"Just now."

It didn't take long. The mites were ready. A month after she stopped using the inhaler she woke up in her bed, too weak to reach the phone. Lenny came by on his way to work to say hi and found her. The paramedics came into her room in slow motion. Their hands left trails in the air as they drifted over her; the instruments resting on her chest and face felt as light as down. It made her smile as she drifted off.

She awoke in the hospital, a mask on her face, a crucified Jesus across the room from her. Jesus appeared to be an understanding sort – as understanding, she supposed, as one could be hanging in the air from iron nails driven through wrists and feet.

Norma must have been wired. A moment after she awoke a nurse came in the room and started examining her. Ten minutes later Dr. Peabody entered the room.

Dr. Peabody looked as if he'd been waiting for years to tell her she needed his and only his procedures and therapies. Only his surgery would save her.

Norma pulled the mask off her face. "When can I go home?" she wheezed.

Peabody stopped, his mouth open. It was worth the black spots in her vision to see his face. "Miss Carstairs – "

"Yes. I'm dying. I know. Prescribe a home health aide for me so I can get oxygen at home."

Peabody seemed to gasp for air.

"Is there anything else?" she asked sweetly.

Peabody fled.

Ben came in as Peabody left the room. "Let me guess. You didn't want to do what he said."

Norma nodded and lay back, spent. "Get me out of here. I'll die at home, thank you very much."

Lenny told her she was lucky. Norma's pneumonia wasn't difficult. The pain she expected from lung cancer never materialized. She was spared the emphysemic experience of drowning in her own fluids. There was only a deep and abiding weakness. The lifting of an arm or rolling over in bed became too much effort. Lucky? She thought so.

Lenny moved in. Ben visited daily. Every other day, a home health aide came in and helped bathe her and checked the oxygen.

Norma grew accustomed to the oxygen cannula. While it didn't alter the progress of things, it did make them pass more easily. She imagined the mites accepting the help as they worked.

"You said it was the earth," she said to Ben, smiling. "The earth speaking through me."

"I changed my mind. This is stupidity given substance," said Ben, exasperated. "It's not too late. We can use the FTV."

Lenny was behind him, an anguished look on his face. "Don't leave me, Mama," he said softly.

"Everything leaves," she said softly as she drifted off. "Me, too."

Norma drifted over a forest or factory. She couldn't quite tell. The world was in furious motion: great trees grew and intertwined with one another, their branches mingling without discernible boundaries. Roads melted into bushes melted into seas. The air was filled with the sound of labor: the percussion of hammers, whistling of saws, voices talking. Spider things were working everywhere but turned their faces up to her as she passed in what could only have been a smile, were they so equipped that a smile was possible.

A bench grew out of the earth. She floated down to it and rested.

It's all me, she thought, proud of herself. Every little spider, machine, and factory. All me.

Enrico Caruso sat down next to her. Not the heavy, ham-fisted Caruso of the old photographs. This was a more handsome and gentler looking, Mario Lanza–esque sort of Caruso.

She stared at him. "What? You're a ghost now?"

He laughed, a rich vanilla sound. "Hardly. Your brain cells are dying one by one. We thought this the least we could do." He waved his gentle hands toward the sea. "Nothing here reflects anything like reality, since you're making it up. But, since you're making it up, it's what you want to see."

"Ah," she said and smiled. The music resolved itself into Verdi's Il Trovatore. It seemed appropriate.

She had no desire to sing with it. At this moment, it was enough to listen. "Do you know what's happening in my room?"

Enrico thought for a moment. "I know what you know. You've lapsed into a coma. Lenny is telling Ben what you want done with your remains. Ben is resourceful so it will likely be done."

"We'll sing for them?"

"All across the net."

"Is that what you wanted?"

Enrico shrugged. "It's enough. How about you?"

She smiled into the evening sun. "It's enough."

The dusk was coming. She could see the ocean dim into a gauzy purple haze. Like sunset. Like night. Whatever imaginary vision she had possessed was fading.

The night darkened as she listened to the music of their work.

"You won't be here to see it, of course," Enrico said regretfully as night fell.

Norma took his hand in the darkness to reassure him. It was a warm, strong hand. She held on strongly and laughed. "Just you wait. You ain't seen nothing yet."

SOFTLY SPOKE
THE GABBLEDUCK

Neal Asher

Born and still living in Essex, England, Neal Asher started
writing at the age of sixteen, but didn't explode into public
print until a few years ago; a quite prolific author, he now
seems to be everywhere at once. His stories have appeared in
Asimov's, *Interzone*, *The Agony Column*, *Hadrosaur Tales*,
and elsewhere, and have been collected in *Runcible Tales*,
The Engineer, and *Mason's Rats*. His extremely popular
novels include *Gridlinked*, *Cowl*, *The Skinner*, *The Line of
Polity*, *Brass Man*, and, most recently, *The Engineer
Reconditioned*. Coming up are a slew of new novels,
including *The Voyage of the Sable Keech* and *Prador Moon:
A Novel of the Polity*.

In the skin-crawlingly tense adventure that follows, he
takes us to a dangerous planet where a party of hunters
encounter far bigger – and more enigmatic – game than they
ever counted on . . .

L OST IN SOME PERVERSE fantasy, Tameera lovingly inspected the
displays of her Optek rifle. For me, what happened next proceeded
with the unstoppable nightmare slowness of an accident. She brought
the butt of the rifle up to her shoulder, took careful aim, and squeezed
off a single shot. One of the sheq slammed back against a rock face, then
tumbled down through vegetation to land in the white water of a
stream.

Some creatures seem to attain the status of myth even though proven to
be little different from other apparently prosaic species. On Earth, the
lion contends with the unicorn, the wise old elephant never forgets, and
gentle whales sing haunting ballads in the deeps. It stems from anthropomorphism, is fed by both truth and lies, and, over time, firmly imbeds
itself in human culture. On Myral, where I had spent the last ten years,
only a little of such status attached to the largest autochthon – not

surprising for a creature whose name is a contraction of "shit-eating quadruped." But rumors of something else in the wilderness, something that had no right to be there, had really set the myth-engines of the human mind into motion, and brought hunters to this world.

There was no sign of any sheq on the way out over the narrow vegetation-cloaked mounts. They only put in an appearance after I finally moored my blimp to a peak, above a horizontal slab on which blister tents could be pitched. My passengers noticed straight away that the slab had been used many times before, and that my mooring was an iron ring long set into the rock, but then, campsites were a rarity amid the steep slopes, cliffs, and streams of this area. It wasn't a place humans were built for. Sheq country.

Soon after he disembarked, Tholan went over to the edge to try out one of his disposable vidcams. The cam itself was about the size of his forefinger, and he was pointing it out over the terrain while inspecting a palm com he held in his other hand. He had unloaded a whole case of these cams, which he intended to position in likely locations, or dangle into mist pockets on a line – a hunter's additional eyes. He called me over. Tameera and Anders followed.

"There." He nodded downward.

A seven of sheq was making its way across the impossible terrain – finding handholds amid the lush vertical vegetation and traveling with the assurance of spiders on a wall. They were disconcertingly simian, about the size of a man, and quadrupedal – each limb jointed like a human arm, but ending in hands bearing eight long prehensile fingers. Their heads, though, were anything but simian, being small, insectile, like the head of a mosquito, but with two wide trumpet-like proboscises.

"They won't be a problem, will they?" Tholan's sister, Tameera, asked.

She was the most xenophobic, I'd decided, but then, such phobia made little difference to their sport: the aliens they sought out usually being the "I'm gonna chew off the top of your head and suck out your brains" variety.

"No – so long as we leave them alone," said Tholan. Using his thumb on the side controls of his palm com, he increased the camera's magnification, switching it to infrared, then ultrasound imaging.

"I didn't load anything," said Anders, Tholan's PA. "Are they herbivores?"

"Omnivores," I told her. "They eat some of that vegetation you see and supplement their diet with rock conch and octupal."

"Rock conch and octupal indeed," said Anders.

I pointed to the conch-like molluscs clinging to the wide leaves below the slab.

Anders nodded, then said, "Octupal?"

"Like it sounds: something like an octopus, lives in pools, but can drag itself overland when required." I glanced at Tameera and added, "None of them bigger than your hand."

I hadn't fathomed this trio yet. Brother and sister hunted together, relied on each other, yet seemed to hate each other. Anders, who I at first thought Tholan was screwing, really did just organize things for him. Perhaps I should have figured them out before agreeing to being hired, then Tameera would never have taken the shot she then took.

The hot chemical smell from the rifle filled the unbreathable air. I guessed they used primitive projectile weapons of this kind to make their hunts more sporting. I didn't know how to react. Tholan stepped forward and pushed down the barrel of her weapon before she could kill another of the creatures.

"That was stupid," he said.

"Do they frighten you?" she asked coquettishly.

I reached up and checked that my throat plug was still in place, for I felt breathless, but it was still bleeding oxygen into my bronchus. To say that I now had a bad feeling about all this would have been an understatement.

"You know that as well as putting us all in danger, she just committed a crime," I said conversationally, as Tholan stepped away from his sister.

"Crime?" he asked.

"She just killed a C-grade sentient. If the Warden AI finds out and can prove she knew before she pulled the trigger, then she's dead. But that's not the main problem now." I eyed the sheq seven, now six. They seemed to be confused about the cause of their loss. "Hopefully they won't attack, but it'll be an idea to keep watch."

He stared at me, shoved his cam into his pocket. I turned away and headed back. Why had I agreed to bring these bored aristos out here to hunt for Myral's mythic gabbleduck? Money. Those who have enough to live comfortably greatly underestimate it as a source of motivation. Tholan was paying enough for me to pay off all I owed on my blimp, and prevent a particular shark from paying me a visit to collect interest by way of involuntarily donated organs. It would also be enough for me to upgrade my apartment in the citadel, so I could rent it while I went out to look at this world. I'd had many of the available cerebral loads and knew much about Myral's environment, but that wasn't the same as experiencing it. There was still much for me to learn, to know. Though I was certain that the chances of my finding a gabbleduck – a creature from a planet light-centuries away – anywhere on Myral, were lower than the sole of my boot.

"She only did that to get attention," said Anders at my shoulder.

"Well, let's hope she didn't succeed too well!" I replied. I looked up at my blimp, and considered the prospect of escaping this trio and bedding down for the night. Certainly we would be getting nothing more done today, what with the blue giant sun gnawing the edge of the world as it went down.

"You have to excuse her. She's over-compensating for a father who ignored her for the first twenty years of her life."

Anders had been coming on to me right from the start and I wondered just what sort of rich bitch game she was playing, though to find out, I would have to let my guard down, and that I had no intention of doing. She was too much: too attractive, too intelligent, and just being in her presence set things jumping around in my stomach. She would destroy me.

"I don't have to excuse her," I said. "I just have to tolerate her."

With that, I headed to the alloy ladder extending down from the blimp cabin.

"Why are they called shit-eaters?" she asked, falling into step beside me. Obviously she'd heard where the name sheq came from.

"As well as the rock conch and octupal, they eat each other's shit running it through a second intestinal tract."

She winced.

I added, "But it's not something they should die for."

"You're not going to report this are you?" she asked.

"How can I? – he didn't want me carrying traceable com."

I tried not to let my anxiety show. Tholan didn't want any of Myral's AIs finding out what he was up to, so, as a result, he'd provided all our com equipment, and it was encoded. I was beginning to wonder if that might be unhealthy for me.

"You're telling me you have no communicator up there?" She pointed up at the blimp.

"I won't report it," I said, then climbed, wishing I could get away with pulling the ladder up behind me, wishing I had not stuck so rigidly to the wording of the contract.

Midark is that time when it's utterly black on Myral, when the sun is precisely on the opposite side of the world from you. It comes after five hours of blue, lasts about three hours prior to the next five hours of blue – the twilight that is neither day nor night and is caused by reflection of sunlight from the sub-orbital dust cloud. Anyway, it was at midark when the screaming and firing woke me. By the time I had reattached my oxygen bottle and was clambering down the ladder, some floods were lighting the area and it was all over.

"Yes, you warned me," Tholan spat.

I walked over to Tameera's tent, which was ripped open and empty. There was no blood, but then the sheq would not want to damage the replacement. I glanced at Anders, who was inspecting a palm com.

"She's alive." She looked up. "She must have been using her own oxygen supply rather than the tent's. We have to go after her now."

"Claw frames in midark?" I asked.

"We've got night specs." She looked at me as if she hadn't realized until then how stupid I was.

"I don't care if you've got owl and cat genes – it's suicide."

"Do explain," said Tholan nastily.

"You got me out here as your guide. The plan was to set up a base and from it survey the area for any signs of the gabbleduck – by claw frame."

"Yes . . ."

"Well, claw frames are only safe here during the day."

"I thought you were going to explain."

"I am." I reached out, detached one of the floods from its narrow post, and walked with it to the edge of the slab. I shone it down, revealing occasional squirming movement across the cliff of vegetation below.

"Octupals," said Anders. "What's the problem?"

I turned to her and Tholan. "At night they move to new pools, and, being slow-moving, they've developed a defense. Anything big gets too close, and they eject stinging barbs. They won't kill you, but you'll damned well know if you're hit, so unless you've brought armored clothing . . ."

"But what about Tameera?" Anders asked.

"Oh, the sheq will protect her for a while."

"For a while?" Tholan queried.

"At first, they'll treat her like an infant replacement for the one she killed," I told him. "So they'll guide her hands and catch her if she starts to fall. After a time, they'll start to get bored, because sheq babies learn very quickly. If we don't get to her before tomorrow night's first blue, she'll probably have broken her neck."

"When does this stop?" He nodded toward the octupal activity.

"Mid-blue."

"We go then."

The claw frame is a sporting development from military exoskeletons. The frame itself braces your body. A spine column rests against your back like a metal flatworm. Metal bones from this extend down your legs and along your arms. The claws are four times the size of human hands, and splayed out like big spiders from behind them, and from behind the ankles. Each finger is a piton, and programmed to seek out crevices on the rock-face you are climbing. The whole thing is stronger, faster, and more sensitive than a human being. If you want, it can do all the work for you. Alternatively, it can just be set in neutral, the claws folded back, while you do all the climbing yourself – the frame only activating to save your life. Both Anders and Tholan, I noted, set theirs to about a third-assist, which is where I set mine. Blister tents and equipment in their back-packs, and oxygen bottles and catalyzers at their waists, they went over the edge ahead of me. Tameera's claw frame scrambled after them – a glittery skeleton – slaved to them. I glanced back at my blimp and wondered if I should just turn round and go back to it. I went over the edge.

With the light intensity increasing and the octupals bubbling down in their pools, we made good time. Later, though, when we had to go lower to keep on course after the sheq, things got a bit more difficult. Despite the three of us being on third-assist we were panting within a few hours, as lower down, there was less climbing and more pushing through tangled vegetation. I noted that my catalyzer pack was having trouble keeping up – cracking the CO_2 atmosphere and topping up the two flat body-form bottles at my waist.

"She's eight kilometers away," Anders suddenly said. "We'll not reach her at this rate."

"Go two-thirds assist," said Tholan.

We all did that, and soon our claw frames were moving faster through the vegetation and across the rock-faces than was humanly possible. It made me feel lazy – like I was just a sack of flesh hanging on the hard-working claw frame. But we covered those eight kilometers quickly, and, as the sun breached the horizon, glimpsed the sheq far ahead of us, scrambling up from the sudden shadows in the valleys. They were a seven again now, I saw: Tameera being assisted along by creatures that had snatched the killer of one of their own, mistaking her for sheq herself.

"Why do they do it?" Anders asked as we scrambled along a vertical face.

"Do what?"

"Snatch people to make up their sevens."

"Three reasons I've heard: optimum number for survival, or seven sheq required for successful mating, or the start of a primitive religion."

"Which do you believe it is?"

"Probably a bit of them all."

As we drew closer, I could hear Tameera sobbing in terror, pure fatigue, and self-pity. The six sheq were close around her, nudging her along, catching her feet when they slipped, grabbing her hands and placing them in firmer holds. I could also see that her dark green slicksuit was spattered with a glutinous yellow substance, and felt my gorge rising at what else she had suffered. They had tried to feed her.

We halted about twenty meters behind on a seventy-degree slope and watched as Tameera was badgered toward where it tilted upright, then past the vertical.

"How do we play this?" Tholan asked.

"We have to get to her before they start negotiating that." I pointed at the lethal terrain beyond the sheq. "One mistake there and . . ." I gestured below to tilted slabs jutting from undergrowth, half hidden under fog generated by a nearby waterfall. I didn't add that we probably wouldn't even be able to find the body, despite the tracker Tameera evidently wore. "We'll have to run a line to her. Anders can act as the anchor. She'll have to make her way above, and it's probably best if she takes Tameera's claw frame with her. You'll go down slope to grab Tameera if anything goes wrong and she falls. I'll go in with the line and the harness."

"You've done this before?" Anders asked.

"Have you?" I countered.

"Seems you know how to go about it," Tholan added.

"Just uploads from the planetary almanac."

"Okay, we'll do it like you said," Tholan agreed.

I'd noticed that all three of them carried fancy monofilament climbing winders on their belts. Anders set hers unwinding its line, which looked thick as rope with cladding applied to the monofilament on its way out. I took up the ring end of the line and attached the webbing harness Tholan took from one of his pack's many pockets.

"Set?" I asked.

They both nodded, Tholan heading downslope and Anders up above. Now, all I had to do was get to Tameera through the sheq and get her into the harness.

As I drew closer, the creatures began to notice me and those insectile heads swung toward me, proboscises pulsating as if they were sniffing.

"Tameera . . . Tameera!"

She jerked her head up, yellow gunk all around her mouth and spattered across her face. "Help me!"

"I've got a line here and a harness," I told her, but I wasn't sure if she understood.

I was about three meters away when the sheq that had been placing her foot on a thick root growing across the face of stone abruptly spun and scrambled toward me. Tholan's Optek crashed and I saw the explosive exit wound open in the creature's jade green torso – a flower of yellow and pink. It sighed, sagged, but did not fall – its eight-fingered hands tangled in verdancy. The other sheq dived for safer holds and pulled close to the rock-face.

"What the fuck!"

"Just get the harness on her!" Tholan bellowed.

I moved in quickly, not so much because he ordered it, but because I didn't want him blowing away more of the creatures. Tameera was at first lethargic, but then she began to get the idea. Harness on, I moved aside.

"Anders!"

Anders had obviously seen, because she drew the line taut through greenery and began hauling Tameera upward, away from sheq who were now beginning to nose in confusion toward their second dead member. Stripped-off line cladding fell like orange snow. I reached out, shoved the dead sheq, once, twice, and it tumbled down the slope, the rest quickly scrambling after it. Tholan was moving aside, looking up at me. I gestured to a nearby mount with a flat top on which we could all gather.

"Got her!" Anders called.

Glancing up, I saw Anders installing Tameera in the other claw frame. "Over there!" I gestured to the mount. Within a few minutes, we were all on the small area of level stone, gazing down toward where the five remaining sheq had caught their companion, realized it was dead, and released it again, and were now zipping about like wasps disturbed from a nest.

"We should head back to the blimp, fast as you like."

No one replied, because Tameera chose that moment to vomit noisily. The stench was worse even than that from the glutinous yellow stuff all over her.

"What?" said Anders.

"They fed her," I explained.

That made Anders look just as sick.

Finally sitting up, then detaching her arms from her claw frame, Tameera stared at her brother and held out her hand. He unhitched his pack, drew out her Optek rifle, and handed it over. She fired from that sitting position, bowling one of the sheq down the distant slope and the subsequent vertical drop.

"Look, you can't – "

The barrel of Tholan's Optek was pointing straight at my forehead.

"We can," he said.

I kept my mouth shut as, one by one, Tameera picked off the remaining sheq and sent them tumbling down into the mist-shrouded river canyon. It was only then that we returned to the slab campsite.

Blue again, but I was certainly ready for sleep, and felt a surge of resentment when the blimp cabin began shaking. Someone was coming up the ladder, then walking round the catwalk. Shortly, Anders opened the airtight door and hauled herself inside. I saw her noting with some surprise how the passenger cabin converted into living quarters. I was ensconced in the cockpit chair, sipping a glass of whisky, feet up on the console. She turned off her oxygen supply, tried the air in the cabin, then sat down on the corner of the fold-down bed, facing me.

"Does it disgust you?" she asked.

I shrugged. Tried to stay nonchalant. What was happening below didn't bother me, her presence in my cabin did.

She continued, "There's no reason to be disgusted. Incest no longer has the consequences it once had. All genetic faults can be corrected in the womb . . ."

"Did I say I was disgusted? Perhaps it's you, why else are you up here?"

She grimaced. "Well, they do get noisy."

"I'm sure it won't last much longer," I said. "Then you can return to your tent."

"You're not very warm, are you?"

"Just wary – I know the kind of games you people play."

"You people?"

"The bored and the wealthy."

"I'm Tholan's PA. I'm an employee."

I sat there feeling all resentful, my resentment increased because, of course, she was right. I should not have lumped her in the same category as Tholan and his sister. She was, in fact, in my category. She had also casually just knocked away one of my defenses.

"Would you like a drink?" I eventually asked, my mouth dry.

Now I expected her righteous indignation and rejection. But Anders was more mature than that, more dangerous.

"Yes, I would." As she said it, she undid the stick seams of her boots and kicked them off. Then she detached the air hose from her throat plug, coiled it back to the bottle, then unhooked that from her belt and put it on the floor. I hauled myself from my chair and poured her a whisky, adding ice from my recently installed little fridge.

"Very neat," she said, accepting the drink. As I made to step past her and return to the cockpit chair, she caught hold of my forearm and pulled me down beside her.

"You know," I said, "that if we don't report what happened today, that would make us accessories. That could mean readjustment, even mind-wipe."

"Are you hetero?" she asked.

I nodded. She put her hand against my chest and pushed me back on to the bed. I let her do it – laid back. She stood up, looking down at me as she drained her whisky. Then she undid her trousers, dropped them and kicked them away, then climbed astride me still wearing her shirt and very small briefs. Still staring at me she undid my trousers, freed my erection, then pulling aside the crotch of her briefs, slowly slid down onto me. Then she began to grind back and forth.

"Just come," she said, when she saw my expression. "You've got all night to return the favor." I managed to hold on for about another thirty seconds. It had been a while. Afterward, we stripped naked, and I did return the favor. And then we spent most of the blue doing things to each other normally reserved for those for whom straight sex had become a source of ennui.

"You know, Tholan will pay a great deal for your silence, one way or another."

I understood that Tholan might not pay me for my silence. I thought her telling me this worthy of the punishment I then administered, and which she noisily enjoyed, muffling her face in the pillow.

We slept a sleep of exhaustion through midark.

Tameera wanted trophies. She wanted a pair of sheq heads to cunningly preserve and mount on the gateposts on either side of the drive to her and Tholan's property on Earth. Toward the end of morning blue, we ate recon rations and prepared to set out. I thought it pointless to tell them of the penalties for possessing trophies from class C sentients. They'd already stepped so far over the line that it was a comparatively minor crime.

"What we need to discuss is my fee," I said.

"Seems to me he's already had some payment," said Tameera, eyeing Anders.

Tholan shot her a look of annoyance and turned back to me. "Ten times what I first offered. No one needs to know."

"Any items you bring back you'll carry in your stuff," I said.

I wondered at their arrogance. Maybe they'd get away with it – we'd know soon enough upon our return to the citadel – but most likely, a drone had tagged one of the sheq, and, as the creature died, a satellite eye had recorded the event. The way I saw it, I could claim to have been scared they would kill me, and only keeping up the criminal façade until we reached safety. Of course, if they did get away with what they'd done, there was no reason why I shouldn't benefit.

While we prepared, I checked the map in my palm com, input our position, and worked out an easier course than the one we had taken the day before. The device would keep us on course despite the fact that Tholan had allowed no satellite link-up. By the sun, by its own elevation, the time, and by reading the field strength of Myral's magnetosphere, the device kept itself accurately located on the map I'd loaded from the planetary almanac.

We went over the edge as the octupals slurped and splashed in their pools and the sun flung arc-welder light across the land. This time, we took it easy on third-assist, also stopping for meals and rest. During one of these breaks, I demonstrated how to use a portable stove to broil a rock conch in its shell, but Tholan was the only one prepared to sample the meat. I guess it was a man thing. As we traveled, I pointed out flowering spider vines, their electric-red male flowers taking to the air in search of the blowsy yellow female flowers: these plants and their pollinating insects having moved beyond the symbiosis seen on Earth to become one. Then, the domed heads of octupals rising out of small rock pools to blink bulbous gelatinous eyes at the evening blue, we moored our blister tents on a forty-degree slope.

Anders connected my tent to hers, while a few meters away Tholan and Tameera connected their tents. No doubt they joined their sleeping bags in the same way we did. Sex, in a tent fixed to such a slope, with a sleeping bag also moored to the rock through the groundsheet, was a bit cramped. But it was enjoyable and helped to pass most of the long night. Sometime during midark I came half awake to the sound of a voice. "Slabber gebble-crab," and "speg bruglor nomp," were its nonsensical utterances. The yelling and groaning from Tholan, in morning blue, I thought due to his and his sister's lovemaking. But in full morning I had to pick octupal stings from the fabric of my tent, and I saw that Tholan wore a dressing on his cheek.

"What happened?" I asked.

"I just stuck my damned head out," he replied.

"What treatment have you used?"

"Unibiotic and antallergens."

"That should do it."

Shame I didn't think to ask why he wanted to leave his tent and go creeping about in the night. That I attributed the strange voice in midark to a dream influenced things neither one way nor the other.

It was only a few hours into the new day that we reached the flat-topped mount from which Tameera had slaughtered the remaining sheq. I studied the terrain through my monocular and realized how the excitement of our previous visit here had blinded me to just how dangerous this area was. There wasn't a slope that was less than seventy degrees, and many of the river valleys and canyons running between the jagged rocks below were full of rolling mist. Claw frames or not, this was about as bad as it could get.

"Well, that's where they should be," said Tholan, lowering his own monocular and pointing to a wider canyon floored with mist out of which arose the grumble of a river.

"If they haven't been swept away," I noted.

Ignoring me, he continued, "We'll work down from where they fell. Maybe some of them got caught in the foliage."

From the mount, we traveled down, across a low ridge, then up onto the long slope from which we had rescued Tameera. I began to cut down diagonally, and Anders followed me while Tameera and Tholan kept moving along high to where the sheq had been, though why they were going there I had no idea, for we had seen every one fall. Anders was above me when I began to negotiate a whorled hump of stone at the shoulder of a cliff. I thought I could see a sheq caught in some foliage down there. As I was peering through the mist, Anders screamed above me. I had time only to glance up and drive my frame's fingers into stone when she barreled into me. We both went over. Half detached from her frame, she clung around my neck. I looked up to where two fingers of my frame held us suspended. I noted that her frame – the property of Tholan and Tameera – was dead weight. Then I looked higher and guessed why.

Brother and sister were scrambling down toward us, saying nothing, not urging us to hang on. I guessed that was precisely what they did not want us to do. It must have been frustrating for Tholan: the both of us in one tent that could have been cut from its moorings – two witnesses lost in the unfortunate accident – but sting-shooting molluscs preventing him from committing the dirty deed. I reached round with my free claw and tightly gripped Anders's belt, swung my foot claws in, and gripped the rock-face with them.

"Get the frame off."

She stared at me in confusion, then looked up the slope, and I think all the facts clicked into place. Quickly, while I supported her, she undid her frame's straps, leaving the chest straps until last. It dropped into the mist: a large chrome harvestman spider . . . a dead one.

"Okay, round onto my back and cling on tightly."

She swung round quickly. Keeping to third-assist – for any higher assistance and the frame might move too fast for her to hang on – I began climbing down the cliff to the mist. The first Optek bullet ricocheted off stone by my face. The second ricochet, by my hand, was immediately followed by an animal grunt from Anders. Something warm began trickling down my neck and her grip loosened.

Under the mist, a river thrashed its way between tilted slabs. I managed to reach one such half-seen slab just before Anders released her hold completely as she fainted. I laid her down and inspected her wound. The ricochet had hit her cheekbone and left a groove running up to her temple. It being a head wound, there was a lot of blood, but it didn't look fatal if I could get her medical attention. But doing anything now with the medical kits we both carried seemed suicidal. I could hear the mutter of Tameera and Tholan's voices from above – distorted by the mist. Then, closer, and lower down by the river, another voice:

"Shabra tabul. Nud lockock ocker," something said.

It was like hiding in the closet from an intruder, only to have something growl right next to you. Stirred by the constant motion of the river, the mist slid through the air in banners, revealing and concealing. On the slab, we were five meters above the graveled riverbank upon which the creature squatted. Its head was level with me. Anders chose that moment to groan and I quickly slapped my hand over her mouth. The creature was pyramidal, all but one of its three pairs of arms folded complacently over the jut of its lower torso. In one huge black claw it held the remains of a sheq. With the fore-talon of another claw, it was levering a trapped bone from the white holly-thorn lining of its duck bill. The tiara of green eyes below its domed skull glittered.

"Brong da bulla," it stated, having freed the bone and flung it away.

It was no consolation to realize that the sheq corpses had attracted the gabbleduck here. Almost without volition, I crouched lower, hoping it did not see me, hoping that if it did, I could make myself appear less appetizing. My hands shaking, I reached down and began taking line off the winder at Anders's belt. The damned machine seemed so noisy and the line far too bright an orange. I got enough to tie around my waist as a precaution. I then undid the straps to her pack, and eased her free of that encumbrance. Now, I could slide her down toward the back of the slab, taking us out of the creature's line of sight, but that would put me in the foliage down there and it would be sure to hear me. I decided to heave her up, throw her over my shoulder, and just get out of there as fast as I could. But just then, a bullet smacked into the column of my claw frame and knocked me down flat, the breath driven out of me.

I rolled over, looking toward the gabbleduck as I did so. I felt my flesh creep. It was gone. Something that huge had no right to be able to move so quickly and stealthily. Once on my back, I gazed up at Tholan and his sister as they came down the cliff. My claw frame was heavy and dead, and so too would I be, but whether by bullet or chewed up in that nightmare bill was debatable.

The two halted a few meters above, and, with their claw frames gripping backward against the rock, freed their arms so they could leisurely take aim with their Opteks. Then something sailed out of the mist and slammed into the cliff just above Tameera, and dropped down. She started screaming, intestines and bleeding flesh caught between her and the cliff – the half-chewed corpse of a sheq. The gabbleduck loomed out of the mist on the opposite side of the slab from where it had disappeared, stretched up and up, and extended an arm that had to be three meters long. One scything claw knocked Tameera's Optek spinning away and made a sound like a knife across porcelain as it scraped stone. On full automatic, Tholan fired his weapon into the body of the gabbleduck, the bullets thwacking away with seemingly no effect. I grabbed Anders and rolled with her to the side of the slab, not caring where we dropped. We fell through foliage and tangled growth, down into a crevasse where we jammed until I undid my frame straps and shed my pack ahead of us.

"Shabber grubber shabber!" the gabbleduck bellowed accusingly.

"Oh god oh god oh god!" Tameera.

More firing from Tholan.

"Gurble," tauntingly.

"I'll be back for you, fucker!"

I don't know if he was shouting at the gabbleduck or me.

There was water in the lower part of the crevasse – more than enough to fill my purifying bottle and to clean the blood from Anders's wound before dressing it. I used a small medkit diagnosticer on her and injected the drugs it manufactured in response to her injuries. Immediately, her breathing eased and her color returned. But we were not in a good position. The gabbleduck was moving about above us, occasionally making introspective and nonsensical comments on the situation. A little later, when I was trying to find some way to set up the blister tent, a dark shape occluded the sky above.

"Urbock shabber goh?" the gabbleduck enquired, then, not being satisfied with my lack of response, groped down into the crevasse. It could reach only as far as the ridge where my claw frame was jammed. With a kind of thoughtful impatience, it tapped a fore-talon against the stone, then withdrew its arm.

"Gurble," it decided, and moved away.

Apparently, linguists who have loaded a thousand languages into their minds despair trying to understand gabbleducks. What they say is nonsensical, but frustratingly close to meaning. There's no reason for them to have such complex voice boxes, especially to communicate with each other, as on the whole they are solitary creatures and speak to themselves. When they meet it is usually only to mate or fight, or both. There's also no reason for them to carry structures in their skulls capable of handling vastly complex languages. Two-thirds of their large brains they seem to use hardly at all. Science, in their case, often supports myth.

Driving screw pitons into either side of the crevasse, I was eventually able to moor the tent across. Like a hammock, the tough material of the groundsheet easily supported our weight, even with all the contortions I had to go through to get Anders into the sleeping bag. Once she was safely ensconced, I found that evening blue had arrived. Using a torch, I explored the crevasse, finding how it rose to the surface at either end.

Then the danger from octupals, stirring in the sump at the crevasse bottom, forced me back to the tent. The following night was not good. A veritable swarm of octupals swamping the tent had me worrying that their extra weight would bring it down. It was also very very dark, down there under the mist. Morning took forever to arrive, but when it eventually did, Anders regained consciousness.

"They tried to kill us," she said, after lubricating her mouth with purified water.

"They certainly did."

"Where are we now?"

"In a hole." She stared at me and I went on to explain the situation.

"So how do we get out of this?" she eventually asked.

"We've both lost our claw frames, but at least we've retained our oxygen bottles and catalyzers. I wish I'd told Tholan to screw his untraceable com bullshit." I thought for a moment. "What about your palm com? Could we use it to signal?"

"It's his, just like the claw frame I was using. He'll have shut it down by now. Should we be able to get to it." She looked up. Her backpack was up there on the slab, up there with the gabbleduck.

"Ah."

She peered at me. "You're saying you really have no way of communicating with the citadel?"

"Not even on my blimp. You saw my contract with Tholan. I didn't risk carrying anything, as he seems the type to refuse payment for any infringements."

"So what now?" she asked.

"That rather depends on Tholan and Tameera . . . and on you."

"Me?"

"I'm supposing that, as a valued employee, you too have one of these implants?" Abruptly she got a sick expression. I went on, "My guess is that those two shits have gone for my blimp to bring it back here. If we stay in one place, they'll zero in on your implant. If we move they'll still be able to track us. We'll have to stay down low under the mist and hope they don't get any lucky shots in. The trouble is that to our friend down here we would be little more than an entrée."

"You could leave me – make your own way back. Once out of this area they'd have trouble finding you."

"It had to be said," I agreed. "Now let's get back to how we're going to get out of here."

After we had repacked the blister tent and sleeping bag, we moved to the end of the crevasse, which, though narrow, gave easier access to the surface. Slanting down one way, to the graveled banks of the river, was another slab, bare and slippery. Above us was the edge of the slab we had rolled from, and, behind that, disappearing into mist, rose the wall of stone I had earlier descended. Seeing this brought home to me just how deep was the shit trap we occupied. The citadel was just over two hundred kilometers away. I estimated our travel rate at being not much more than a few kilometers a day. The journey was survivable. The almanac loadings I'd had told me what we could eat, and there would never be any shortage of water. Just so long as our catalyzers held out and neither of us fell . . .

"We'll run that line of yours between us, about four meters to give us room to maneuver. I'll take point."

"You think it's safe to come out?" Anders asked.

"Not really, but it's not safe to stay here, either."

Anders ran the line out from her winder and locked it, and I attached its end ring to a loop on the back of my belt before working my way up to the edge of the slab. Once I hauled myself up, I was glad to see her pack still where I had abandoned it. I was also glad that Anders did not require my help to climb up – if I had to help her all the way, the prospective journey time would double. Anders shrugged on her pack, cinched the stomach strap. We then made our way to where vegetation grew like a vertical forest up the face of the cliff. Before we attempted to enter this, I took out my palm com and worked out the best route – one taking us back toward the citadel, yet keeping us under the mist, but for the occasional ridge. Then, climbing through the tangled vegetation, I couldn't shake the feeling that something was watching us, something huge and dangerous, and that now it was following us.

The first day was bad. It wasn't just the sheer physical exertion, it was the constant dim light underneath the mist sapping will and blackening mood. I knew Tameera and Tholan would not reach us that day, but I also knew that they could be back overhead in the blimp by the following morning blue if they traveled all night. But they would stop to rest. Certainly they knew they had all the time they wanted to take to find and kill us.

As the sun went down, Anders erected one blister tent on a forty-degree slab – there was no room for the other tent. I set about gathering some of the many rock conches surrounding us. We still had rations, but I thought we should use such abundance, as the opportunity might not present itself later on. I also collected female spider vine flowers, and the sticky buds in the crotch branches of walker trees. I half expected Anders to object when I began broiling the molluscs, but she did not. The conches were like chewy fish, the flowers were limp and slightly sweet lettuce, the buds have no comparison in Earthly food because none is so awful. Apparently, it was a balanced diet. I packed away the stove and followed Anders into the blister tent just as it seemed the branches surrounding us were beginning to move. Numerous large warty octupals were dragging themselves through the foliage. They were a kind unknown to me, therefore a kind not commonly encountered, else I would have received something on them in the almanac's general load.

In the morning, I was chafed from the straps in our conjoined sleeping bags (they stopped us ending up in the bottom of the bag on that slope) and irritable. Anders was not exactly a bright light either. Maybe certain sugars were lacking in the food we had eaten, because, after munching down ration bars while we packed away our equipment, we quickly started to feel a lot better. Or maybe it was some mist-born equivalent of SAD.

An hour after we set out, travel became a lot easier and a lot more dangerous. Before, the masses of vegetation on the steep slopes, though greatly slowing our progress, offered a safety net if either of us fell. Now we were quickly negotiating slopes not much steeper than the slab on which Anders had moored the tent the previous night, and sparse of vegetation. If we fell here, we would just accelerate down to a steeper slope or sheer drop, and a final impact in some dank rocky sump. We were higher, I think, than the day before – the mist thinner. The voice of the gabbleduck was mournful and distant there.

"Urecoblank . . . scudder," it called, perhaps trying to lure its next meal.

"Shit, shit," I said as I instinctively tried to increase my pace and slipped over, luckily catching hold before I slid down.

"Easy," said Anders.

I just hoped the terrain would put the damned thing off, but somehow I doubted that. There seemed to me something almost supernatural about the creature. Until actually seeing the damned thing, I had never believed there was one out here. I'd thought Myral's gabbleduck as mythical as mermaids and centaurs on Earth.

"What the hell is that thing doing here anyway?" I asked.

"Probably escaped from a private collection," Anders replied. "Perhaps someone bought it as a pet and got rid of it when it stopped being cute."

"Like that thing was ever cute?" I asked.

Midday, and the first Optek shots began wanging off the stone around us, and the shadow of my blimp drew above. A kind of lightness infected me then. I knew, one way or another, that we were going to die, and that knowledge just freed me of all responsibility to myself and to the future.

"You fucking missed!" I bellowed.

"That'll soon change!" came Tholan's distant shout.

"There's no need to aggravate him," Anders hissed.

"Why? Might he try to kill us?" I spat back.

Even so, I now led us on a course taking us lower down into the mist. The firing tracked us, but I reckoned the chances of us being hit were remote. Tholan must have thought the same, because the firing soon ceased. When we stopped to rest under cover of thicker vegetation, I checked my palm com and nearly sobbed on seeing that in one and half days we had covered less than three kilometers. It was about right, but still disheartening. Then, even worse, I saw that ahead, between two mounts, there was a ridge we must climb over to stay on course. To take another route involved a detour of tens of kilometers. Undoubtedly, the ridge rose out of the mist. Undoubtedly, Tholan had detected it on his palm com too.

"What do we do?" Anders asked.

"We have to look. Maybe there'll be some sort of cover."

"Seeble grubber," muttered the gabbleduck in the deeper mist below us.

"It's fucking following us," I whispered.

Anders just nodded.

Then even more bad news came out of the mist.

I couldn't figure out quite what I was seeing out there in the canyon beside us, momentarily visible through the mist. Then, all of a sudden, the shape, on the end of its thin but hugely tough line, became recognizable. I was looking at a four-pronged blimp anchor, with disposable cams taped to each of the prongs. We got moving again, heading for that ridge. I equated getting to the other side with safety. Ridiculous, really.

"He's got . . . infrared . . . on them," I said, between gasps.

A fusillade sounding like the full fifty-round clip of an Optek slammed into the slope just ahead of us.

"Of course . . . he's no way . . . of knowing which camera . . . is pointing . . . where," I added.

Then a flare dropped, bouncing from limb to limb down through the vertical jungle, and the firing came again, strangely, in the same area. I glimpsed the anchor again, further out and higher. Tholan and his sister had no real experience of piloting a blimp – it wasn't some gravcar they could set on autopilot. Soon we saw the remains of what they had been targeting: an old sheq too decrepit to keep up with its seven, probably replaced by a new hatching. It was hanging over the curved fibrous bough of a walker tree, great holes ripped through its body by Optek bullets.

We climbed higher as the slope became steeper, came to the abrupt top edge of this forest of walker trees, made quick progress stepping from horizontal trunk to trunk with the wall of stone beside us. After a hundred meters of this, we had to do some real climbing up through a crack to a slope we could more easily negotiate. My feet were sore and my legs ached horribly. Constantly walking along slopes like this put pressure on feet and ankles they were certainly not accustomed to. I wondered just how long my boots and gloves would last in this terrain. They were tough – made with monofiber materials used by the military – but nothing is proof against constant abrasion on stone. Maybe a hundred days of this? Who was I kidding?

By midday, we were on the slope that curved round below one of the mounts, then blended into the slope leading up to the ridge. Checking

the map on my palm com, I saw that there was likely a gutter between
the ridge and the mount. I showed this to Anders.

"There may be cover there," I said.

She stared at me, dark rings under her eyes – too exhausted to care.
We both turned then, and peered down into the mist and canted forests.
There came the sound of huge movement, the cracking of walker
trunks, broken vegetation showering down through the trees below us.

"Come on." I had no devil-may-care left in me. I was just as weary as
Anders. We reached the gutter, which was abundant with hand and
footholds, but slippery with rock-slime. We climbed slowly and
carefully up through thinning mist. Then the blimp anchor rappeled
down behind and above us like an iron chandelier.

"Surprise!" Tameera called down to us.

The mist was now breaking, and I glimpsed the lumpy peak of the
mount looming to our left. Higher up, its propellers turning lazily to
hold it against a breeze up from the ridge, floated my blimp. Tholan and
Tameera stood out on the catwalk. Both of them armed, and I was sure
I could see them grinning even from that distance. I swore and rested my
forehead against slimy stone. We had about ten meters of clear air to the
top of the ridge, then probably the same over the other side. No way
could we move fast enough – not faster than a speeding bullet. I looked
up again. Fuck them. I wasn't going to beg, I wasn't going to try to make
any last-minute deals. I turned to Anders.

"We'll just keep climbing," I said.

She nodded woodenly, and I led the way. A shot slammed into the
rock just above me, then went whining down the gutter. They were
playing, for the moment. I glanced up, saw that the blimp was drifting
sideways toward the mount. Then I saw it.

The arm folded out and out. The wrongness I felt about it, I guess,
stemmed from the fact that it possessed too many joints. A three-
fingered hand, with claws like black scythes, closed on the blimp anchor
and pulled. Seated on the peak, the gabbleduck looked like some
monstrous child holding the string of a toy balloon.

"Brong da lockock," it said.

Leaning over the catwalk rail, Tholan tried pumping shots into the
monster. Tameera shrank back against the cabin's outer wall, making a
high keening sound. The gabbleduck gave the blimp anchor a sharp tug,
and Tholan went over the edge, one long scream as he fell, turned to an
oomph as the monster caught him in one of its many hands. It took his
rifle and tossed it away like the stick from a cocktail sausage, then it
stuffed him into its bill.

"Keep going!" Anders shoved me in the back.

"It used us as bait to get them," I said.

"And now it doesn't need us."

I continued to climb, mindful of my handholds, aware that the
gabbleduck was now coming down off its mount. We reached the ridge.
I glanced down the other side into more mist, more slopes. I looked
aside as the gabbleduck slid down into mist, towing the blimp behind it,

Tameera still keening. It had its head tilted back and with one hand was
shoving Tholan deeper into its bill. After a moment, it seemed to get
irritated, and tore his kicking legs away while it swallowed the rest of
him. Then the mist engulfed the monster, the blimp shortly afterward.
Tameera's keening abruptly turned to a long agonized scream, then
came a crunching sound.

"It'll come for us next," said Anders, eyeing the stirring mist, then
shoving me again.

We didn't stand a chance out here – I knew that.

"What the hell are you doing?"

I passed back the ring of the line that joined us together. "Wind it in."

She set the little motor running, orange line-cladding falling around
her feet. I glanced at her and saw dull acceptance that I was abandoning
her at last. The large shape came up out of the mist, shuddering. I began
to run along the ridge. It was a guess, a hope, a chance – on such things
might your life depend.

The anchor was snagging in the outer foliage of walker trees and the
blimp, now free of two man weights and released by the gabbleduck,
was rising again. I was going for the line first, though I'm damned if I
know how I would have climbed the four millimeter-thick cable. At the
last moment, I accelerated, and leapt: three meters out and dropping
about the same distance down. My right leg snapped underneath me on
the roof of the cabin, but I gave it no time to hurt. I dragged myself to
the edge, swung down on the blimp cables, and was quickly in through
the airtight door. First, I hit the controls to fold the anchor and reel in
the cable, then I was in the pilot's seat making the blimp vent gas and
turning it toward where Anders waited. Within minutes, she was on the
catwalk and inside and I was pumping gas back into the blimp again.
But we weren't going anywhere.

"Oh no . . . no!" Anders's feeling of the unfairness of it all was in that
protest. I stared out at the array of green eyes, and at the long single
claw it had hooked over the catwalk rail. I guessed that it would winkle
us out of the cabin like the meat of a rock conch from its shell. I didn't
suppose the bubble metal alloys would be much hindrance to it.

"Gurble," said the gabbleduck, then suddenly its claw was away
from the rail and we were rising again. Was it playing with us? We
moved closer to the windows and looked down, said nothing until we
were certainly out of its reach, said nothing for some time after that. At
the last, and I don't care how certain the scientists are that they are just
animals, I'm damned sure that the gabbleduck waved to us.

ZIMA BLUE

Alastair Reynolds

Here's another story by Alastair Reynolds, whose "Beyond
the Aquilla Rift" appears elsewhere in this anthology. In this
one, he investigates a mysterious artist for whom no canvas
is too big, and whose origins are unknown – perhaps even to
himself.

AFTER THE FIRST WEEK people started drifting away from the island.
The viewing stands around the pool became emptier by the day.
The big tourist ships hauled back toward interstellar space. Art fiends,
commentators and critics packed their bags in Venice. Their disappointment hung over the lagoon like a miasma.

I was one of the few who stayed on Murjek, returning to the stands
each day. I'd watch for hours, squinting against the trembling blue light
reflected from the surface of the water. Face down, Zima's pale shape
moved so languidly from one end of the pool to the other that it could
have been mistaken for a floating corpse. As he swam I wondered how
I was going to tell his story, and who was going to buy it. I tried to
remember the name of my first newspaper, back on Mars. They
wouldn't pay as much as some of the bigger titles, but some part of me
liked the idea of going back to the old place. It had been a long time . . .
I queried the AM, wanting it to jog my memory about the name of the
paper. There'd been so many since . . . hundreds, by my reckoning. But
nothing came. It took me another yawning moment to remember that
I'd dismissed the AM the day before.

"You're on your own, Carrie," I said. "Start getting used to it."

In the pool, the swimming figure ended a length and began to swim
back toward me.

Two weeks earlier I'd been sitting in the Piazza San Marco at noon,
watching white figurines glide against the white marble of the clock
tower. The sky over Venice was jammed with ships parked hull-to-hull.
Their bellies were quilted in vast glowing panels, tuned to match the
real sky. The view reminded me of the work of a pre-Expansion artist
who had specialised in eye-wrenching tricks of perspective and
composition: endless waterfalls, interlocking lizards. I formed a mental
image and queried the fluttering presence of the AM, but it couldn't
retrieve the name.

I finished my coffee and steeled myself for the bill.

I'd come to this white marble version of Venice to witness the unveiling of Zima's final work of art. I'd had an interest in the artist for years, and I'd hoped I might be able to arrange an interview. Unfortunately several thousand other members of the in-crowd had come up with exactly the same idea. Not that it mattered what kind of competition I had anyway; Zima wasn't talking.

The waiter placed a folded piece of card on my table.

All we'd been told was to make our way to Murjek, a waterlogged world most of us had never heard of before. Murjek's only claim to fame was that it hosted the one hundred and seventy-first known duplicate of Venice, and one of only three Venices rendered entirely in white marble. Zima had chosen Murjek to host his final work of art, and to be the place where he would make his retirement from public life.

With a heavy heart I lifted the bill to inspect the damage. Instead of the expected bill there was a small blue card, printed in fine gold italic lettering. The shade of blue was that precise, powdery, aquamarine that Zima had made his own. The card was addressed to me, Carrie Clay, and it said that Zima wanted to talk to me about the unveiling. If I was interested, I should report to the Rialto Bridge in exactly two hours.

If I was interested.

The note stipulated that no recording materials were to be brought, not even a pen and paper. As an afterthought, the card mentioned that the bill had been taken care of. I almost had the nerve to order another coffee and put it on the same tab. Almost, but not quite.

Zima's servant was there when I arrived early at the bridge. Intricate neon mechanisms pulsed behind the flexing glass of the robot's mannequin body. It bowed at the waist and spoke very softly. "Miss Clay? Since you're here, we might as well depart."

The robot escorted me to a flight of stairs that led to the waterside. My AM followed us, fluttering at my shoulder. A conveyor hovered in waiting, floating a metre above the water. The robot helped me into the rear compartment. The AM was about to follow me inside when the robot raised a warning hand.

"You'll have to leave that behind, I'm afraid: no recording materials, remember?"

I looked at the metallic green hummingbird, trying to remember the last time I had been out of its ever-watchful presence.

"Leave it behind?"

"It'll be quite safe here, and you can collect it again when you return after nightfall."

"If I say no?"

"Then I'm afraid there'll be no meeting with Zima."

I sensed that the robot wasn't going to hang around all afternoon waiting for my answer. The thought of being away from the AM made my blood run cold. But I wanted that interview so badly I was prepared to consider anything.

I told the AM to stay here until I returned.

The obedient machine reversed away from me in a flash of metallic green. It was like watching a part of myself drift away. The glass hull wrapped itself around me and I felt a surge of un-nulled acceleration.

Venice tilted below us, then streaked away to the horizon.

I formed a test query, asking the AM to name the planet where I'd celebrated my seven hundredth birthday. Nothing came: I was out of query range, with only my own age-saturated memory to rely on.

I leaned forward. "Are you authorised to tell me what this is about?"

"I'm afraid he didn't tell me," the robot said, making a face appear in the back of his head. "But if at any moment you feel uncomfortable, we can return to Venice."

"I'm fine for now. Who else got the blue card treatment?"

"Only you, to the best of my knowledge."

"And if I'd declined? Were you supposed to ask someone else?"

"No," the robot said. "But let's face it, Miss Clay. You weren't very likely to turn him down."

As we flew on, the conveyor's shock wave gouged a foaming channel in the sea behind it. I thought of a brush drawn through wet paint on marble, exposing the white surface beneath. I took out Zima's invitation and held it against the horizon ahead of us, trying to decide whether the blue was a closer match to the sky or the sea. Against these two possibilities the card seemed to flicker indeterminately.

Zima Blue. It was an exact thing, specified scientifically in terms of angstroms and intensities. If you were an artist, you could have a batch of it mixed up according to that specification. But no one ever used Zima Blue unless they were making a calculated statement about Zima himself.

Zima was already unique by the time he emerged into the public eye. He had undergone radical procedures to enable him to tolerate extreme environments without the burden of a protective suit. Zima had the appearance of a well-built man wearing a tight body stocking, until you were close and you realised that this was actually his skin. Covering his entire form, it was a synthetic material that could be tuned to different colours and textures depending on his mood and surroundings. It could approximate clothing if the social circumstances demanded it. The skin could contain pressure when he wished to experience vacuum, and stiffen to protect him against the crush of a gas giant planet. Despite these refinements the skin conveyed a full range of sensory impressions to his mind. He had no need to breathe, since his entire cardiovascular system had been replaced by closed-cycle life-support mechanisms. He had no need to eat or drink; no need to dispose of bodily waste. Tiny repair machines swarmed through his body, allowing him to tolerate radiation doses that would have killed an ordinary man in minutes.

With his body thus armoured against environmental extremes, Zima was free to seek inspiration where he wanted. He could drift free in space, staring into the face of a star, or wander the searing canyons of a planet where metals ran like lava. His eyes had been replaced by cameras sensitive to a huge swathe of the electromagnetic spectrum, wired into his brain via complex processing modules. A synaesthesic bridge allowed him to hear visual data as a kind of music; to see sounds as a symphony of startling colours. His skin functioned as a kind of antenna, giving him sensitivity to electrical field changes. When that wasn't sufficient, he could tap into the data feeds of any number of accompanying machines.

Given all this, Zima's art couldn't help but be original and attention-grabbing. His landscapes and starfields had a heightened, ecstatic quality about them, awash in luminous, jarring colours and eye-wrenching tricks of perspective. Painted in traditional materials but on a huge scale, they quickly attracted a core of serious buyers. Some found their way into private collections, but Zima murals also started popping up in public spaces all over the Galaxy. Tens of metres across, the murals were nonetheless detailed down to the limits of vision. Most had been painted in one session. Zima had no need for sleep, so he worked uninterrupted until a piece was complete.

The murals were undeniably impressive. From a standpoint of composition and technique they were unquestionably brilliant. But there was also something bleak and chilling about them. They were landscapes without a human presence, save for the implied viewpoint of the artist himself.

Put it this way: they were nice to look at, but I wouldn't have hung one in my home.

Not everyone agreed, obviously, or else Zima wouldn't have sold as many works as he had. But I couldn't help wondering how many people were buying the pictures because of what they knew about the artist, rather than because of any intrinsic merit in the works themselves.

That was how things stood when I first paid attention to Zima. I filed him away as interesting but kitschy: maybe worth a story if something else happened to either him or his art.

Something did, but it took a while for anyone – including me – to notice.

One day – after a longer than usual gestation period – Zima unveiled a mural that had something different about it. It was a picture of a swirling, star-pocked nebula, from the vantage point of an airless rock. Perched on the rim of a crater in the middle distance, blocking off part of the nebula, was a tiny blue square. At first glance it looked as if the canvas had been washed blue and Zima had simply left a small area unpainted. There was no solidity to the square; no detail or suggestion of how it related to the landscape or the backdrop. It cast no shadow and had no tonal influence on the surrounding colours. But the square was deliberate: close examination showed that it had indeed been overpainted over the rocky lip of the crater. It meant something.

The square was just the beginning. Thereafter, every mural that Zima released to the outside world contained a similar geometric shape: a square, triangle, oblong or some similar form embedded somewhere in the composition. It was a long time before anyone noticed that the shade of blue was the same from picture to picture.

It was Zima Blue: the same shade of blue as on the gold-lettered card.

Over the next decade or so, the abstract shapes became more dominant, squeezing out the other elements of each composition. The cosmic vistas ended up as narrow borders, framing blank circles, triangles, rectangles. Where his earlier work had been characterised by exuberant brushwork and thick layers of paint, the blue forms were rendered with mirror-smoothness.

Intimidated by the intrusion of the abstract blue forms, casual buyers turned away from Zima. Before very long Zima unveiled the first of his entirely blue murals. Large enough to cover the side of a thousand-storey building, the mural was considered by many to be as far as Zima could take things.

They couldn't have been more wrong.

I felt the conveyor slowing as we neared a small island, the only feature in any direction.

"You're the first to see this," the robot said. "There's a distortion screen blocking the view from space."

The island was about a kilometre across: low and turtle-shaped, ringed by a narrow collar of pale sand. Near the middle it rose to a shallow plateau, on which vegetation had been cleared in a roughly rectangular area. I made out a small panel of reflective blue set flat against the ground, surrounded by what appeared to be a set of tiered viewing stands.

The conveyor shed altitude and speed, bobbing down until it stopped just outside the area enclosed by the viewing stands. It came to rest next to a low white pebble-dash chalet I hadn't noticed during our approach.

The robot stepped out and helped me from the conveyor.

"Zima will be here in a moment," it said, before returning to the conveyor and vanishing back into the sky.

Suddenly I felt very alone and very vulnerable. A breeze came in from the sea, blowing sand into my eyes. The sun was creeping down toward the horizon and soon it would be getting chilly. Just when I was beginning to feel the itch of panic, a man emerged from the chalet, rubbing his hands briskly. He walked toward me, following a path of paved stones.

"Glad you could make it, Carrie."

It was Zima, of course, and in a flash I felt foolish for doubting that he would show his face.

"Hi," I said lamely.

Zima offered his hand. I shook it, feeling the slightly plastic texture of his artificial skin. Today it was a dull pewter-grey.

"Let's go and sit on the balcony. It's nice to watch the sunset, isn't it?"

"Nice," I agreed.

He turned his back to me and set off in the direction of the chalet. As he walked, his muscles flexed and bulged beneath the pewter flesh. There were scale-like glints in the skin on his back, as if it had been set with a mosaic of reflective chips. He was beautiful like a statue, muscular like a panther. He was a handsome man, even after all his transformations, but I had never heard of him taking a lover, or having any kind of a private life at all. His art was everything.

I followed him, feeling awkward and tongue-tied. Zima led me into the chalet, through an old-fashioned kitchen and an old-fashioned lounge, full of thousand-year-old furniture and ornaments.

"How was the flight?"

"Fine."

He stopped suddenly and turned to face me. "I forgot to check . . . did the robot insist that you leave behind your *Aide Memoire*?"

"Yes."

"Good. It was you I wanted to talk to, Carrie, not some surrogate recording device."

"Me?"

The pewter mask of his face formed a quizzical expression. "Do you do multisyllables, or are you still working up to that?"

"Er . . ."

"Relax," he said. "I'm not here to test you, or humiliate you, or anything like that. This isn't a trap, and you're not in any danger. You'll be back in Venice by midnight."

"I'm okay," I managed. "Just a bit starstruck."

"Well, you shouldn't be. I'm hardly the first celebrity you've met, am I?"

"Well, no, but . . ."

"People find me intimidating," he said. "They get over it eventually, and then wonder what all the fuss was about."

"Why me?"

"Because you kept asking nicely," Zima said.

"Be serious."

"All right. There's a bit more to it than that, although you did ask nicely. I've enjoyed much of your work over the years. People have often trusted you to set the record straight: especially near the ends of their lives."

"You talked about retiring, not dying."

"Either way, it would still be a withdrawal from public life. Your work has always seemed truthful to me, Carrie. I'm not aware of anyone claiming misrepresentation through your writing."

"It happens now and then," I said. "That's why I always make sure there's an AM on hand so no one can dispute what was said."

"That won't matter with my story," Zima said.

I looked at him shrewdly. "There's something else, isn't there? Some other reason you pulled my name out of the hat."

"I'd like to help you," he said.

When most people speak about his Blue Period they mean the era of the truly huge murals. By huge I do mean huge. Soon they had become large enough to dwarf buildings and civic spaces; large enough to be visible from orbit. Across the Galaxy twenty-kilometre-high sheets of blue towered over private islands or rose from storm-wracked seas. Expense was never a problem, since Zima had many rival sponsors who competed to host his latest and biggest creation. The panels kept on growing, until they required complex, Sloth-tech machinery to hold them aloft against gravity and weather. They pierced the tops of planetary atmospheres, jutting into space. They glowed with their own soft light. They curved around in arcs and fans, so that the viewer's entire visual field was saturated with blue.

By now Zima was hugely famous, even to people who had no particular interest in art. He was the weird cyborg celebrity who made huge blue structures; the man who never gave interviews or hinted at the private significance of his art.

But that was a hundred years ago. Zima wasn't even remotely done.

Eventually the structures became too unwieldy to be hosted on planets. Blithely Zima moved into interplanetary space, forging vast free-floating sheets of blue ten thousand kilometres across. Now he worked not with brushes and paint, but with fleets of mining robots, tearing apart asteroids to make the raw material for his creations. Now it was entire stellar economies that competed with each other to host Zima's work.

That was about the time that I renewed my interest in Zima. I attended one of his "moonwrappings": the enclosure of an entire celestial body in a lidded blue container, like a hat going into a box. Two months later he stained the entire equatorial belt of a gas giant blue, and I had a ringside seat for that as well. Six months later he altered the surface chemistry of a sun-grazing comet so that it daubed a Zima Blue tail across an entire solar system. But I was no closer to a story. I kept asking for an interview and kept being turned down. All I knew was that there had to be more to Zima's obsession with blue than a mere artistic whim. Without an understanding of that obsession, there was no story: just anecdote.

I didn't do anecdote.

So I waited, and waited. And then – like millions of others – I heard about Zima's final work of art, and made my way to the fake Venice on Murjek. I wasn't expecting an interview, or any new insights. I just had to be there.

We stepped through sliding glass doors out onto the balcony. Two simple white chairs sat either side of a white table. The table was set with drinks and a bowl of fruit. Beyond the unfenced balcony, arid land sloped steeply away, offering an uninterrupted view of the sea. The water was calm and inviting, with the lowering sun reflected like a silver coin.

Zima indicated that I should take one of the seats. His hand dithered over two bottles of wine.

"Red or white, Carrie?"

I opened my mouth as if to answer him, but nothing came. Normally, in that instant between the question and the response, the AM would have silently directed my choice to one of the two options. Not having the AM's prompt felt like a mental stall in my thoughts.

"Red, I think," Zima said. "Unless you have strong objections."

"It's not that I can't decide these things for myself," I said.

Zima poured me a glass of red, then held it up to the sky to inspect its clarity. "Of course not," he said.

"It's just that this is a little strange for me."

"It shouldn't be strange," he said. "This is the way you've lived your life for hundreds of years."

"The natural way, you mean?"

Zima poured himself a glass of the red wine, but instead of drinking it he merely sniffed the bouquet. "Yes."

"But there isn't anything natural about being alive a thousand years after I was born," I said. "My organic memory reached saturation point about seven hundred years ago. My head's like a house with too much furniture. Move something in, you have to move something out."

"Let's go back to the wine for a moment," Zima said. "Normally, you'd have relied on the advice of the AM, wouldn't you?"

I shrugged. "Yes."

"Would the AM always suggest one of the two possibilities? Always red wine, or always white wine, for instance?"

"It's not that simplistic," I said. "If I had a strong preference for one over the other, then, yes, the AM would always recommend one wine over the other. But I don't. I like red wine sometimes and white wine other times. Sometimes I don't want any kind of wine." I hoped my frustration wasn't obvious. But after the elaborate charade with the blue card, the robot and the conveyor, the last thing I wanted to be discussing with Zima was my own imperfect recall.

"Then it's random?" he asked. "The AM would have been just as likely to say red as white?"

"No, it's not like that either. The AM's been following me around for hundreds of years. It's seen me drink wine a few hundred thousand times, under a few hundred thousand different circumstances. It knows, with a high degree of reliability, what my best choice of wine would be given any set of parameters."

"And you follow that advice unquestioningly?"

I sipped at the red. "Of course. Wouldn't it be a little childish to go against it just to make a point about free will? After all, I'm more likely to be satisfied with the choice it suggests."

"But unless you ignore that suggestion now and then, won't your whole life become a set of predictable responses?"

"Maybe," I said. "But is that so very bad? If I'm happy, what do I care?"

"I'm not criticising you," Zima said. He smiled and leaned back in his seat, defusing some of the tension caused by his line of questioning. "Not many people have an AM these days, do they?"

"I wouldn't know," I said.

"Less than one percent of the entire Galactic population." Zima sniffed his wine and looked through the glass at the sky. "Almost everyone else out there has accepted the inevitable."

"It takes machines to manage a thousand years of memory. So what?"

"But a different order of machine," Zima said. "Neural implants; fully integrated into the participant's sense of self. Indistinguishable from biological memory. You wouldn't need to query the AM about your choice of wine; you wouldn't need to wait for that confirmatory whisper. You'd just know it."

"Where's the difference? I allow my experiences to be recorded by a machine that accompanies me everywhere I go. The machine misses nothing, and it's so efficient at anticipating my queries that I barely have to ask it anything."

"The machine is vulnerable."

"It's backed up at regular intervals. And it's no more vulnerable than a cluster of implants inside my head. Sorry, but that just isn't a reasonable objection."

"You're right, of course. But there's a deeper argument against the AM. It's too perfect. It doesn't know how to distort or forget."

"Isn't that the point?"

"Not exactly. When you recall something – this conversation, perhaps, a hundred years from now – there will be things about it that you misremember. Yet those misremembered details will themselves become part of your memory, gaining solidity and texture with each instance of recall. A thousand years from now, your memory of this conversation might bear little resemblance with reality. Yet you'd swear your recollection was accurate."

"But if the AM had accompanied me, I'd have a flawless record of how things really were."

"You would," Zima said. "But that isn't living memory. It's photography; a mechanical recording process. It freezes out the imagination; leaves no scope for details to be selectively misremembered." He paused long enough to top up my glass. "Imagine that on nearly every occasion when you had cause to sit outside on an afternoon like this you had chosen red wine over white, and generally had no reason to regret that choice. But on one occasion, for one reason or another, you were persuaded to choose white – against the judgement of the AM – and it was wonderful. Everything came together magically: the company, the conversation, the late afternoon ambience, the splendid view, the euphoric rush of being slightly drunk. A perfect afternoon turned into a perfect evening."

"It might not have had anything to do with my choice of wine," I said.

"No," Zima agreed. "And the AM certainly wouldn't attach any significance to that one happy combination of circumstances. A single deviation wouldn't affect its predictive model to any significant degree. It would still say 'red wine' the next time you asked."

I felt an uncomfortable tingle of understanding. "But human memory wouldn't work that way."

"No. It would latch onto that one exception and attach undue significance to it. It would amplify the attractive parts of the memory of that afternoon and suppress the less pleasant parts: the fly that kept buzzing in your face, your anxiety about catching the boat home, and the birthday present you knew you had to buy in the morning. All you'd remember was that golden glow of well-being. The next time, you might well choose white, and the time after. An entire pattern of behaviour would have been altered by one instance of deviation. The AM would never tolerate that. You'd have to go against its advice many, many times before it grudgingly updated its model and started suggesting white rather than red."

"All right," I said, still wishing we could talk about Zima rather than me. "But what practical difference does it make whether the artificial memory is inside my head or outside?"

"All the difference in the world," Zima said. "The memories stored in the AM are fixed for eternity. You can query it as often as you like, but it will never enhance or omit a single detail. But the implants work differently. They're designed to integrate seamlessly with biological memory, to the point where the recipient can't tell the difference. For that very reason they're necessarily plastic, malleable, subject to error and distortion."

"Fallible," I said.

"But without fallibility there is no art. And without art there is no truth."

"Fallibility leads to truth? That's a good one."

"I mean truth in the higher, metaphoric sense. That golden afternoon? That was the truth. Remembering the fly wouldn't have added to it in any material sense. It would have detracted it from it."

"There was no afternoon, there was no fly," I said. Finally, my patience had reached breaking point. "Look, I'm grateful to have been invited here. But I thought there might be a little more to this than a lecture about the way I choose to manage my own memories."

"Actually," Zima said, "there was a point to this after all. And it is about me, but it's also about you." He put down the glass. "Shall we take a little walk? I'd like to show you the swimming pool."

"The sun hasn't gone down yet," I said.

Zima smiled. "There'll always be another one."

He took me on a different route through the house, leaving by a different door than the one we'd come in by. A meandering path climbed gradually between white stone walls, bathed now in gold from the lowering sun. Presently we reached the flat plateau I'd seen on my approach in the conveyor. The things I'd thought were viewing stands were exactly that: terraced structures about thirty metres high, with staircases at the back leading to the different levels. Zima led me into the darkening shadow under the nearest stand, then through a private door that led into the enclosed area. The blue panel I'd seen during the approach turned out to be a modest rectangular swimming pool, drained of water.

Zima led me to the edge.

"A swimming pool," I said. "You weren't kidding. Is this what the stands are all about?"

"This is where it will happen," Zima said. "The unveiling of my final work of art, and my retirement from public life."

The pool wasn't quite finished. In the far corner, a small yellow robot glued ceramic tiles into place. The part near us was fully tiled, but I couldn't help noticing that the tiles were chipped and cracked in places. The afternoon light made it hard to be sure – we were in deep shadow now – but their colour looked to be very close to Zima Blue.

"After painting entire planets, isn't this is a bit of a letdown?" I asked.

"Not for me," Zima said. "For me this is where the quest ends. This is what it was all leading up to."

"A shabby-looking swimming pool?"

"It's not just any old swimming pool," he said.

He walked me around the island, as the sun slipped under the sea and the colours turned ashen.

"The old murals came from the heart," Zima said. "I painted on a huge scale because that was what the subject matter seemed to demand."

"It was good work," I said.

"It was hack work. Huge, loud, demanding, popular, but ultimately soulless. Just because it came from the heart didn't make it good."

I said nothing. That was the way I'd always felt about his work as well: that it was as vast and inhuman as its inspiration, and only Zima's cyborg modifications lent his art any kind of uniqueness. It was like praising a painting because it had been done by someone holding a brush between their teeth.

"My work said nothing about the cosmos that the cosmos wasn't already capable of saying for itself. More importantly, it said nothing about me. So what if I walked in vacuum, or swam in seas of liquid nitrogen? So what if I could see ultraviolet photons, or taste electrical fields? The modifications I inflicted upon myself were gruesome and extreme. But they gave me nothing that a good telepresence drone couldn't offer any artist."

"I think you're being a little harsh on yourself," I said.

"Not at all. I can say this now because I know that I did eventually create something worthwhile. But when it happened it was completely unplanned."

"You mean the blue stuff?"

"The blue stuff," he said, nodding. "It began by accident: a mis-application of colour on a nearly-finished canvas. A smudge of pale, aquamarine blue against near-black. The effect was electric. It was as if I had achieved a short-circuit to some intense, primal memory, a realm of experience where that colour was the most important thing in my world."

"What was that memory?"

"I didn't know. All I knew was the way that colour spoke to me, as if I'd been waiting my whole life to find it, to set it free." He thought for a moment. "There's always been something about blue. A thousand years ago Yves Klein said it was the essence of colour itself: the colour that stood for all other colours. A man once spent his entire life searching for a particular shade of blue that he remembered encountering in childhood. He began to despair of ever finding it, thinking he must have imagined that precise shade, that it could not possibly exist in nature. Then one day he chanced upon it. It was the colour of a beetle in a museum of natural history. He wept for joy."

"What is Zima Blue?" I asked. "Is it the colour of a beetle?"

"No," he said. "It's not a beetle. But I had to know the answer, no matter where it took me. I had to know why that colour meant so much to me, and why it was taking over my art."

"You allowed it to take over," I said.

"I had no choice. As the blue became more intense, more dominant, I felt I was closer to an answer. I felt that if only I could immerse myself in that colour, then I would know everything I desired to know. I would understand myself as an artist."

"And? Did you?"

"I understood myself," Zima said. "But it wasn't what I expected."

"What did you learn?"

Zima was a long time answering me. We walked on slowly, me lagging slightly behind his prowling muscular form. It was getting cooler now and I began to wish I'd had the foresight to bring a coat. I thought of asking Zima if he could lend me one, but I was concerned not to derail his thoughts from wherever they were headed. Keeping my mouth shut had always been the toughest part of the job.

"We talked about the fallibility of memory," he said.

"Yes."

"My own memory was incomplete. Since the implants were installed I remembered everything, but that only accounted for the last three hundred years of my life. I knew myself to be much older, but of my life before the implants I recalled only fragments; shattered pieces that I did not quite know how to reassemble." He slowed and turned back to me, the dulling orange light on the horizon catching the side of his face. "I knew I had to dig back into that past, if I was to ever understand the significance of Zima Blue."

"How far back did you get?"

"It was like archaeology," he said. "I followed the trail of my memories back to the earliest reliable event, which occurred shortly after the installation of the implants. This took me to Kharkov 8, a world in the Garlin Bight, about nineteen thousand light-years from here. All I remembered was the name of a man I had known there, called Cobargo."

Cobargo meant nothing to me, but even without the AM I knew something of the Garlin Bight. It was a region of the Galaxy encompassing six hundred habitable systems, squeezed between three major economic powers. In the Garlin Bight normal interstellar law did not apply. It was fugitive territory.

"Kharkov 8 specialised in a certain kind of product," Zima said. "The entire planet was geared up to provide medical services of a kind unavailable elsewhere. Illicit cybernetic modifications, that kind of thing."

"Is that where . . ." I left the sentence unfinished.

"That is where I became what I am," Zima said. "Of course, I made further changes to myself after my time on Kharkov 8 – improving my tolerance to extreme environments, improving my sensory capabilities – but the essence of what I am was laid down under the knife, in Cobargo's clinic."

"So before you arrived on Kharkov 8 you were a normal man?" I asked.

"This is where it gets difficult," Zima said, picking his way carefully along the trail. "Upon my return I naturally tried to locate Cobargo. With his help, I assumed I would be able to make sense of the memory fragments I carried in my head. But Cobargo was gone; vanished elsewhere into the Bight. The clinic remained, but now his grandson was running it."

"I bet he wasn't keen on talking."

"No; he took some persuading. Thankfully, I had means. A little bribery, a little coercion." He smiled slightly at that. "Eventually he agreed to open the clinic records and examine his grandfather's log of my visit."

We turned a corner. The sea and the sky were now the same inseparable gray, with no trace of blue remaining.

"What happened?"

"The records say that I was never a man," Zima said. He paused a while before continuing, leaving no doubt as to what he had said. "Zima never existed before my arrival in the clinic."

What I wouldn't have done for a recording drone, or – failing that – a plain old notebook and pen. I frowned, as if that might make my memory work just that little bit harder.

"Then who were you?"

"A machine," he said. "A complex robot; an autonomous artificial intelligence. I was already centuries old when I arrived on Kharkov 8, with full legal independence."

"No," I said, shaking my head. "You're a man with machine parts, not a machine."

"The clinic records were very clear. I had arrived as a robot. An androform robot, certainly – but an obvious machine nonetheless. I was dismantled and my core cognitive functions were integrated into a vat-grown biological host body." With one finger he tapped the pewter side of his skull. "There's a lot of organic material in here, and a lot of cybernetic machinery. It's difficult to tell where one begins and the other ends. Even harder to tell which is the master, and which is the slave."

I looked at the figure standing next to me, trying to make the mental leap needed to view him as a machine – albeit a machine with soft, cellular components – rather than a man. I couldn't; not yet.

I stalled. "The clinic could have lied to you."

"I don't think so. They would have been far happier had I not known."

"All right," I said. "Just for the sake of argument . . ."

"Those were the facts. They were easily verified. I examined the customs records for Kharkov 8 and found that an *autonomos robot entity* had entered the planet's airspace a few months before the medical procedure."

"Not necessarily you."

"No other robot entity had come near the world for decades. It had to be me. More than that, the records also showed the robot's port of origin."

"Which was?"

"A world beyond the Bight. Lintan 3, in the Muara Archipelago."

The AM's absence was like a missing tooth. "I don't know if I know it."

"You probably don't. It's no kind of world you'd ever visit by choice. The scheduled lightbreakers don't go there. My only purpose in visiting the place seemed to me . . ."

"You went there?"

"Twice. Once before the procedure on Kharkov 8, and again recently, to establish where I'd been before Lintan 3. The evidence trail was beginning to get muddy, to say the least . . . but I asked the right kinds of questions, poked at the right kinds of database, and finally found out where I'd come from. But that still wasn't the final answer. There were many worlds, and the chain was fainter which each that I visited. But I had persistence on my side."

"And money."

"And money," Zima said, acknowledging my remark with a polite little nod. "That helped incalculably."

"So what did you find, in the end?"

"I followed the trail back to the beginning. On Kharkov 8 I was a quick-thinking machine with human-level intelligence. But I hadn't always been that clever, that complex. I'd been augmented in steps, as time and circumstances allowed."

"By yourself?"

"Eventually, yes. That was when I had autonomy; legal independence. But I had to reach a certain level of intelligence before I was allowed that freedom. Before that, I was a simpler machine . . . like an heirloom or a pet. I was passed from one owner to the next, between generations. They added things to me. They made me cleverer."

"How did you begin?"

"As a project," he said.

Zima led me back to the swimming pool. Equatorial night had arrived quickly, and the pool was bathed now in artificial light from the many floods arrayed above the viewing stands. Since we had last seen the pool the robot had finished glueing the last of the tiles in place.

"It's ready now," Zima said. "Tomorrow it will be sealed, and the day after it will be flooded with water. I'll cycle the water until it attains the necessary clarity."

"And then?"

"I prepare myself for my performance."

On the way to the swimming pool he had told me as much as he knew about his origin. Zima had begun his existence on Earth, before I was even born. He had been assembled by a hobbyist, a talented young man with an interest in practical robotics. In those days, the man had been one of many groups and individuals groping toward the hard problem of artificial intelligence.

Perception, navigation and autonomous problem-solving were the three things that most interested the young man. He had created many robots, tinkering them together from kits, broken toys and spare parts. Their minds – if they could be dignified with such a term – were cobbled from the innards of junked computers, with their simple programs bulging at the limits of memory and processor speed.

The young man filled his house with these simple machines, designing each for a particular task. One robot was a sticky-limbed spider that climbed around the walls of his house, dusting the frames of pictures. Another lay in wait for flies and cockroaches. It caught and digested them, using the energy from the chemical breakdown of their biomass to drive itself to another place in the house. Another robot busied itself by repainting the walls of the house over and over, so that the colours matched the changing of the seasons.

Another robot lived in his swimming pool.

It toiled endlessly up and down and along the ceramic sides of the pool, scrubbing them clean. The young man could have bought a cheap swimming pool cleaner from a mail-order company, but it amused him to design the robot from scratch, according to his own eccentric design principles. He gave the robot a full-colour vision system and a brain large enough to process the visual data into a model of its surroundings. He allowed the robot to make its own decisions about the best strategy for cleaning the pool. He allowed it to choose when it cleaned and when it surfaced to recharge its batteries via the solar panels grouped on its back. He imbued it with a primitive notion of reward.

The little pool cleaner taught the young man a great deal about the fundamentals of robotics design. Those lessons were incorporated into the other household robots, until one of them – a simple household cleaner – became sufficiently robust and autonomous that the young man began to offer it as a kit, via mail-order. The kit sold well, and a year later the young man offered it as a pre-assembled domestic robot. The robot was a runaway success, and the young man's firm soon became the market leader in domestic robots.

Within ten years, the world swarmed with his bright, eager machines.

He never forgot the little pool cleaner. Time and again he used it as a test-bed for new hardware, new software. By turns it became the cleverest of all his creations, and the only one that he refused to strip down and cannibalise.

When he died, the pool cleaner passed to his daughter. She continued the family tradition, adding cleverness to the little machine. When she died, she passed it to the young man's grandson, who happened to live on Mars.

"This is the original pool," Zima said. "If you hadn't already guessed."

"After all this time?" I asked.

"It's very old. But ceramics endure. The hardest part was finding it in the first place. I had to dig through two metres of topsoil. It was in a place they used to call Silicon Valley."

"These tiles are coloured Zima Blue," I said.

"Zima Blue is the colour of the tiles," he correctly gently. "It just happened to be the shade that the young man used for his swimming pool tiles."

"Then some part of you remembered."

"This was where I began. A crude little machine with barely enough intelligence to steer itself around a swimming pool. But it was my world. It was all I knew; all I needed to know."

"And now?" I asked, already fearing the answer.

"Now I'm going home."

I was there when he did it. By then the stands were full of people who had arrived to watch the performance, and the sky over the island was a mosaic of tight-packed hovering ships. The distortion screen had been turned off, and the viewing platforms on the ships thronged with hundreds of thousands of distant witnesses. They could see the swimming pool by then, its water mirror-flat and gin-clear. They could see Zima standing at the edge, with the solar patches on his back glinting like snake scales. None of the viewers had any idea of what was about to happen, or its significance. They were expecting something – the public unveiling of a work that would presumably trump everything Zima had created before then – but they could only stare in puzzled concern at the pool, wondering how it could possibly measure up to those atmosphere-piercing canvases, or those entire worlds wrapped in shrouds of blue. They kept thinking that the pool had to be a diversion. The real work of art – the piece that would herald his retirement – must be somewhere else, as yet unseen, waiting to be revealed in all its immensity.

That was what they thought.

But I knew the truth. I knew it as I watched Zima stand at the edge of the pool and surrender himself to the blue. He'd told me exactly how it would happen: the slow, methodical shutting down of higher-brain functions. It hardly mattered that it was all irreversible: there wouldn't be enough of him left to regret what he had lost.

But something would remain: a little kernel of being; enough of a mind to recognise its own existence. Enough of a mind to appreciate its surroundings, and to extract some trickle of pleasure and contentment from the execution of a task, no matter how purposeless. He wouldn't ever need to leave the pool. The solar patches would provide him with all the energy he needed. He would never age, never grow ill. Other machines would take care of his island, protecting the pool and its silent slow swimmer from the ravages of weather and time.

Centuries would pass.

Thousands of years, and then millions.

Beyond that, it was anyone's guess. But the one thing I knew was that Zima would never tire of his task. There was no capacity left in his mind for boredom. He had become pure experience. If he experienced any kind of joy in the swimming of the pool, it was the near-mindless euphoria of a pollinating insect. That was enough for him. It had been enough for him in that pool in California, and it was enough for him now, a thousand years later, in the same pool but on another world, around another sun, in a distant part of the same Galaxy.

As for me . . .

It turned out that I remembered more of our meeting on the island than I had any right to. Make of that what you will, but it seemed I didn't need the mental crutch of my AM quite as much as I'd always imagined. Zima was right: I'd allowed my life to become scripted, laid out like a blueprint. It was always red wine with sunsets, never the white. Aboard the outbound lightbreaker a clinic installed a set of neural memory extensions that should serve me well for the next four or five hundred years. One day I'll need another solution, but I'll cross that particular mnemonic bridge when I get there. My last act, before dismissing the AM, was to transfer its observations into the echoey new spaces of my enlarged memory. The events still don't feel quite like they ever happened to me, but they settle in a little bit better with each act of recall. They change and soften, and the highlights glow a little brighter. I guess they become a little less accurate with each instance of recall, but like Zima said: perhaps that's the point.

I know now why he spoke to me. It wasn't just my way with a biographical story. It was his desire to help someone move on, before he did the same.

I did eventually find a way to write his story, and I sold it back to my old newspaper, the *Martian Chronicle*. It was good to visit the old planet again, especially now that they've moved it into a warmer orbit.

That was a long time ago. But I'm still not done with Zima, odd as it seems.

Every couple of decades, I still hop a lightbreaker to Murjek, descend to the streets of that gleaming white avatar of Venice, take a conveyor to the island and join the handful of other dogged witnesses scattered across the stands. Those that come, like me, must still feel that the artist has something else in store . . . one last surprise. They've read my article now, most of them, so they know what that slowly swimming figure means . . . but they still don't come in droves. The stands are always a little echoey and sad, even on a good day. But I've never seen them completely empty, which I suppose is some kind of testament. Some people get it. Most people never will.

But that's art.

PLANET OF THE AMAZON WOMEN

David Moles

New writer David Moles has sold fiction to *Asimov's Science Fiction, Polyphony, Strange Horizons, Lady Churchill's Rosebud Wristlet, Say . . ., Flytrap,* and elsewhere. He coedited, with Jay Lake, 2004's well-received "retro-pulp" anthology *All-Star Zeppelin Adventure Stories,* and coming up is a new anthology, coedited with Susan Marie Groppi, Twenty Epics. His story "The Third Party" was in our Twenty-second Annual Collection.

Here he reexamines one of the oldest clichés in science fiction – the all-women planet – and comes to some startling and fascinatingly strange new conclusions . . .

PLANET OF THE AMAZON WOMEN. That's what Musa called it. He makes kinés, he has a keen sense of the ridiculous in art and history. When he found out I was on my way to Hippolyta he said nothing at first, only looked at me, black eyes serious in his dark face; looked at me, I think, until he was sure I was telling the truth. He covered my hand with his. Then, as if we had both said everything that needed to be said, he stood up abruptly.

"Come on, Sasha," he said. "Let's go dancing."

Musa. A chance meeting in the men's dormitory of an Erewhon orbital transit hostel. If I had met him when I was twenty he would have been the great love of my life.

That is probably how I will remember him, if things on Hippolyta go half-right. If I grow old on the Planet of the Amazon Women, and die there.

There is something about the crew of the S.P.S. *Tenacious,* the picket ship that the Erewhon Republic has stationed in Hippolyta's system to prevent any excursion from the Planet of the Amazon Women, that is both comical and touching. They take themselves very seriously, with their crisp white uniforms and their military ranks and their short

haircuts. (Most of them are human, and most of the humans are men –
boys, really.) They take their job very seriously, too, with a certain pride
that they are the only ones in this part of the Polychronicon interested
in the problem: the universe may be dangerous and chaotic and very
poorly organized, but the Republic, and the Navy, are up to the task.

They're not, of course. The universe is so much more disorganized
than these comic-opera astronauts could even imagine. That's what
makes it so touching.

"And this is the Operations Center," Lieutenant Addison tells me.
"Where we control the sensor platforms and the particle-beam
satellites. We've never had to use them, thank God."

Addison looks at me, and I look at the room full of complicated
equipment and focused young men and nod as if I knew what I was
looking at. Already I am practicing my imposture, preparing myself for
Hippolyta. This is a dance, and I am improvising it.

Satisfied, Addison turns to indicate the next point of interest, and I
turn back to watching Addison. He's skinny and cute and can't be more
than twenty-five. He doesn't know what to say to a civilian who's
volunteered for a suicide mission, but he's trying.

A century ago on Hippolyta, something called Amazon Fever killed
thirteen hundred million men and boys. Hundreds of millions of
women and girls died as well, slain indirectly, by the chaos that came in
the Fever's wake.

No one knows now who started the Fever, or what they were trying
to do: whether it was intentional – an attempt at an attack, or a
revolution – or accidental – an industrial mishap, or a probability
experiment gone awry, or even an archaeological discovery. But when
it came it came suddenly, sweeping across Hippolyta in less than a year,
in its progress less like a disease than like a curse. It defied drugs and
vaccines and quarantines, brushing past exploration-grade immune
enhancements as if they were so many scented medieval nosegays. It
seemed to be transmitted not only by the afflicted but by their
possessions, not only by their possessions but by objects associated with
them only distantly, or symbolically.

There were even isolated cases, reported but never confirmed, of the
Fever appearing light-years away, in people who had never been to
Hippolyta. Sometimes a connection to Hippolyta could be proved –
years in the past, long before the first appearance of the Fever. Other
times there was no apparent connection at all.

A diversion that most undergraduate mathematicians encounter is
the idea – an easy one to demonstrate, logically – that given a single
contradiction, one can prove the truth or falsehood of any proposition.
The fall of the causality barrier has given us all the contradictions any
mathematician could wish for. This is the one fundamental truth – and
falsehood – of the universe.

Even if most of us, like the level-headed crew of the *Tenacious*, deny it – pretending we still live in a universe where one thing happens after another.

What I suspect, though it is not something anyone can ever prove, is that in those apparently unconnected cases, the connection lay not in the past, but in the future. In a *potential* future, foreclosed now by the Fever itself.

It's not strictly accurate to say that Amazon Fever killed all the men. To say that is to use an old-fashioned shorthand, a too-simple understanding of sex and gender. The proximate cause of death in cases of Amazon Fever was sudden, pervasive tissue rejection – the result of the molecules making up the body acquiring a new virtual history, at the Planck scale and unevenly. It wasn't just men and boys that Amazon Fever killed. What it killed was anyone or anything whose immune system was unable to recognize cells that no longer came – that, all of a sudden, *had never come* – from an evolutionary line based on sexual reproduction.

The Fever killed male cats, dogs, insects, birds, fish, ginkoes, date palms, malarial gametocytes. Wherever it struck, it destroyed the entire basis of sexual difference. Most observers – who by this point were doing their observing by remote, from twenty light-minutes away – expected animal life on Hippolyta, humanity included, to go extinct in a generation.

But it didn't.

On the real-time maps the *Tenacious* uses there is a blank place, in the northeast of Aella Continent – Hippolyta's second largest, and the place of oldest settlement. This I can read: the swirl of weather and the slow-moving lights of tracked targets giving way to static survey data, a century old and more.

"How close to *here*" – on a projected globe, my fingers brush the center of the discontinuity – "can you set me down?"

Lieutenant Addison looks embarrassed.

"Not very, I'm afraid," he says. "Our equipment doesn't function well that deep into the causal anomaly." He gestures at the globe. "You can see we don't have any current data for that area. No probes, since simultaneity channels don't operate across the probability boundary; and even passive sensors aren't reliable."

I nod, a little disappointed; but it's no more than I expected, or I wouldn't have brought the mules.

Addison scrutinizes the globe for a moment and selects a point on the southern coast, a few hundred kilometers from the center of the anomaly. In the Ezheler lands.

"What about here, near the coast road?" he asks. "You can make your way by native transport from there."

"That will certainly test my disguise."

Addison looks uncomfortable. He turns back to the globe.

"Well, I – "

"No," I interrupt. "The coast road is fine."

I will have to dance a little faster, that's all.

In the thirteenth and fourteenth centuries of the Hegira, before my ancestors came to Islam, they flirted briefly with Hegel. Perhaps in hoping, by resolving the contradictions of Hippolyta, to resolve the contradictions at the heart of the universe, I have fallen into that old heresy: *thesis, antithesis, synthesis.* If so, so be it. As a natural philosopher, I am expected to face up to the universe's hard truths. As a Russian, I am expected to be a fatalist and a romantic. As a Moslem, I am expected to place my faith in the All-Merciful.

To deny the contradictions – as Musa understood, and as I would never be able to explain to Lieutenant Addison – is not an option that is open to me.

In the little cabin I have stolen from some junior officer, I strip off my borrowed Republic coverall. There is no mirror, but a projector shows me a reversed image, shadowy, as if my double stood in a darkened corridor. I meet my double's eyes.

"Goodbye, Sasha," we tell each other.

Goodbye to Sasha Rusalev of Odessa, ballet *cavalier* and natural philosopher.

I am Yazmina Tanzikbayeva now, Ezheler muleteer and coca trader.

Hippolyta was already an old world when the Fever came, old with the kind of impossible age that is common out here, the kind that vigorous and serious young civilizations like the Republic worry about and that most of the rest of us ignore. When Hippolyta was terraformed and settled (*if* it was terraformed and settled – there are causality violations in Hippolyta's early history, too), a kaleidoscope of nations made it their home: cultures from every part of the Islamic *'umma* and outside it as well, landing here and there, merging, fragmenting, trading, stealing, fighting little wars, making peace – millennia of history compressed into a few generations.

The Ezheler are nomadic herders who live in the southern mountains and high plains of Aella Continent. Chronically low fertility – a factor of distance from the center of Hippolyta's causal anomaly – keeps them nomadic, just as it keeps their richer neighbors, such as the Chinese speakers in Tieshan, from expanding into their territory. The Ezheler are Muslims, and speak a Turkic language influenced by Russian and Farsi.

I grew up in Odessa; Russian and Turkish were my native languages. A set of Consilium neural implants and a few months of study have me speaking the language of the Ezheler as well as any off-worlder ever will without living among them.

But the thing that really drew me to the Ezheler, when I was planning this, was their clothes.

I dress in cotton and leather and linen and silk. I have practiced this; it comes back to me now, like the steps of a dance. Cotton underwear, first, unbleached; red cotton trousers, much coarser; soft calf-high boots; white cotton blouse embroidered with red; and finally, the *burka*, the violet-dyed linen veil/robe that covers everything from hair to eyes to ankles.

Most of the Muslims of Aella follow the customs of *hijab*, to a degree: they wear the *khimar* in public, and some wear the *abaya*. But the Ezheler are among the few who wear the full *burka*, and only among the Ezheler is it never removed, even among family.

I straighten the *burka*, trying to find the position that lets me see the most through the lace-bordered veil. My muscles are alive with false memories, a combination of generic feminine movements and simulated Ezheler kinesthetics created from Consilium ethnologists' AV recordings.

There are technologies, readily available, with which I could have rebuilt myself completely, from the chromosomes upward – making part of my disguise impenetrable, no longer deception but the truth. (Undoubtedly there are women on Hippolyta today whose ancestors, in the first days of the Fever, did just that.) I could preserve not only my disguise, but my life.

But in doing so, I would prove nothing. If it were enough to test my hypotheses with equations and proofs, I could have done it from the safety of my rooms in Petersburg. I must test them with myself.

Besides, as my old ballet master used to say, For a swan there is no art in being a swan.

It helps that my audience will not expect me to be anything else.

Four hours later Lieutenant Addison is belting me into the capsule that will take me to Hippolyta. The capsule is made for inserting Marine commandos behind enemy lines, or something similarly exciting and dangerous. It seems to me that for landing on Hippolyta, the capsule is overkill – especially since it will have to be abandoned, and perhaps destroyed. But Addison is feeling guilty that he can't take me exactly where I want to go, and his people have seemed to enjoy themselves so much – programming the capsule's camouflage, plotting a course to minimize the chance that someone will see me entering the atmosphere – that I haven't the heart to object.

There is supposed to be room in the capsule for a half-dozen armored Marines and their equipment, but except for the medical equipment, my gear isn't built to Republic specifications. After it has all been packed in around me, Addison, to shake my hand, has to lean awkwardly over a plastic-wrapped bale that might hold rice or dried apricots or coca leaves.

He looks around the cramped capsule one more time, the trade goods, the medical pods, the two mules in their cocoons, the half-felt presence of the quantum inference engines. Then he looks down at me.

"Well," he says, with a helpless shrug, "good luck, then."

Then he leans back, and the hatch closes, and the capsule swings out on its track, and at last they let me go.

The capsule is three days and fifty kilometers behind me, camouflaged and buried at the bottom of a dry creekbed, when I pick up the road to the coast. The coast road is older, harder than the narrow dirt track I have been following out of the dry hills: concrete laid down before the coming of the Fever and cracked now into broken slabs by a century of summers and winters. The grass of the shoulder is brown, tramped down into a footpath, and I guide the mules along that softer way, to spare their hooves and ankles. I can see the tracks of others before me, in the dirt.

A simultaneity channel links the medical pods, buried with the capsule, to telemetry implants laced through my body, and tells me that so far I am healthy, sore muscles and saddle galls aside. This is Republic technology, simple and reliable, and the pods will probably survive me, whatever happens. The inference engines, more delicate and abstract, I carry with me. They were made in Damascus, and their existence is largely mathematical; it is not likely they will be noticed by anyone who does not know to look for them. For now they are quiet, their transformation of local phase space still undisturbed. I am a kink in the braid of improbability that makes Hippolyta what it is, a bubble of reality suspended in the medium of the unreal.

Now that I am here, with this gritty earth under my feet, this warm wind that smells of sage and dry grass whistling by me, it is hard to have the same confidence I had when I planned this in my rooms back in Petersburg. It has taken all three days for me to stop obsessively checking the medical monitors and the inference engines, trying to find in their numbers and images the first symptoms of the Amazon Fever that will most likely kill me.

By the time I crest the last of a range of low hills, though, and catch my first glimpse of the sea on the eastern horizon, the confidence I felt in Petersburg has returned. I am less worried about Amazon Fever than about being unmasked.

I have been two days on the coast when I see my first Amazon.

The architecture of the caravanserai is an eclectic mix, imperishable prefabricated sections that predate the Fever joined to adobe and brick and cement, roofed with sheet metal and encircled by a waist-high fence of driftwood and wire. I am not the first traveler to stop here tonight. Two tethered mules and a horse, hobbled, graze in the shade of a stunted live-oak, tugging at the dry grass with a kind of resigned persistence. On the other side of the yard are a pair of open-topped trucks, scratched and dented, their cargo beds piled high with crates and bundles, the tarpaulin awnings over their passenger areas patched with many colors.

A woman is perched on top of one of the trucks, wearing a sheepskin jacket and blue trousers with sandals. She looks to be about forty, Tieshanese, with a strong jaw, close-cropped black hair and narrow eyes under a blue-and-white striped headscarf.

My first Amazon. I sketch a greeting, hand to heart, and get no response. She shifts slightly and I notice then that there is a long-barreled pistol on the tarpaulin next to her, inches from her hand. I turn away with a show of nonchalance, and lead my mules to where the others are tethered.

The inside of the caravanserai is dark, lit only by the hand-lanterns the travelers have brought; the yard smelled of the ocean, but here it smells of smoke and sweat and kerosene. There are about a dozen women and girls here, three of them Ezheler, the rest Tieshanese. Two of the Ezheler, a mother and daughter both named Amina, are traders like me, returning to their clans after visiting the market town of Haiming; the mules are theirs. The other, Maryam, the horsewoman, is a doctor traveling north in hopes of buying medicines.

The Tieshanese truckers keep to themselves, and a suspicious eye on us, and their children close. The Ezheler have been known to steal children.

"We *should* steal something of theirs," Amina-the-daughter says. She is fifteen, this is her third trip to Haiming she's coming back from, and though her expression is invisible behind the veil I can guess at it. She knows the Tieshanese don't like her, and because of that she doesn't like them.

Behind my own veil, I smile. Teenagers must be the same everywhere.

I had hoped not to encounter any Ezheler on the road – hoped to ride into Haiming a stranger. I stay quiet, concentrating on the steps of my dance. But neither Maryam nor the Aminas ask me any questions, only share their coffee with me and give me some advice on the Haiming markets. Eventually I relax enough to ask a question.

"Do you know a coca broker named Mei Yueyin?" I ask.

Amina-the-mother and Maryam, the doctor, both nod.

"For a city person she is quite honest," Maryam says.

"She speaks Ezheler," volunteers Amina-the-daughter. "It's creepy."

"You shouldn't speak ill of her while you're still eating the candy she gave you," her mother says mildly.

For some reason I glance at Maryam, and I see that she is looking at me. I wish I could see her face.

Mei Yueyin works, or worked, for the Consilium Ethnological Service. She has been on Hippolyta for seventeen years, five of them among the Ezheler. Her last report, the one that mentioned she was working as a broker in Haiming, was nine years ago. I'm glad to hear she's still alive and still there; even with her ties to the Consilium cut, she's the only contact I have.

Young Amina gives me some of Mei Yueyin's candy. It's rice candy, the kind that comes wrapped in edible paper. While I go to check on the animals I chew it, thoughtfully.

I give the animals – Maryam's horse and my mules and the Aminas' – some water and some dried apricots. They pick the apricots daintily from my fingers with their mobile lips and great chomping teeth, and I'm glad to see my fingers are steady.

The medical monitors have my temperature a shade over thirty-seven, my immune system shows no sign yet of turning against itself. We are no closer here to the center of the Fever, that blank spot on Addison's maps, than where I landed, but the border between consensus reality and Hippolyta's causal anomaly (what Lieutenant Addison – inaccurately – called the "probability boundary") is fluid, fractal, and it has timelike components. So far, though, the inference engines are quiet. So far my predictions are validated.

This far out, I expect, my machines could keep me alive indefinitely – long enough, at any rate, to die of something other than Amazon Fever. I pat the shoulder of Maryam's mare and toy, briefly, with the idea of staying here.

I know I won't, though.

The Tieshanese guard I saw earlier, the one I fancifully called my first Amazon, is gone. Her replacements are a pair of older women who squat in the dust, playing dice by the light of a fluorescent lamp. One of them smiles at me, but it is like the careless smile of a statue. They look as though they could squat there forever.

The next morning the doctor, Maryam, indicates in a roundabout way that, as we are both bound for Haiming, I would be welcome to travel with her. I don't know why this startles me, but it does, and before I really know what I am doing I have accepted.

After the morning prayer we make breakfast together – griddle cakes and rice porridge, with dried fruit and coca tea from my trade bales – and share it with the Aminas, before seeing them on their way south. As we ourselves are leaving, the sun is coming up over the hills, and the Tieshanese travelers are starting to rise. Two of the women have daughters who are very young, not more than four or five, and I see Maryam looking at them – wistfully, I think, though it is not easy to tell through the veil.

"I was just a child when I had my daughter," Maryam tells me. We are three days from the caravanserai, riding side by side along a road now lined with twisting pines, and Haiming is only two days away, a petrochemical smudge on the northeastern horizon. "Fourteen. A child." She glances at me. "I was a mission girl, you see. When we graduated they took twenty of us up the river, to Themiscyra, in Erethea." She looks out into the distance, beyond Haiming's haze, as if trying to see into the past. "I don't have the words to describe the north, Yazmina." She shakes her head in frustration. "I left the words there . . . when I came down the river again.

"But it was very beautiful. I remember that."

She glances back at me.

"Even that far north the odds of a spontaneous conception are very low – perhaps one in a hundred, if that." She gives a small laugh. "I was lucky, I suppose, or unlucky." She turns in the saddle to face me directly. "How old are you, Yazmina?"

"Twenty-one." It's a lie, by seven years, but a twenty-eight-year-old Ezheler could never be as ignorant as I am.

Maryam turns back to the road. "My Rabiah would be twenty-two this year."

Making Maryam thirty-six. I look at her, what I can see of her through the *burka*, the straight back and thin shoulders, the small weathered hands with their long surgeon's fingers loose on the reins. The lie about my age feels like less of one, all of a sudden. There's a wide gap between my life and the life this woman has lived, and eight years aren't enough to measure it.

"What happened?" I ask.

She shakes her head.

"It doesn't matter."

We ride quietly for a little while, the silence broken only by the distant surf and the slow, plodding hooves.

Quietly, without turning – almost as if she is alone – Maryam says: "I hope you will be happy here."

She says it in Arabic, not Ezheler. Her Arabic is classical and very pure, the accent of a judge or a *hadith* scholar.

Then she spurs her horse ahead, ten, twenty meters. It is several kilometers before she lets me catch up to her again.

The old road is broken only once, where the sea-cliffs suddenly give way to a narrow gash of an inlet, perhaps a kilometer across. To the east the valley extends indefinitely, its path improbably, mechanically straight.

There is nothing like this on my pre-Fever maps. Closer, though, and inland, where the water is shallower, the reason becomes clear. A hump of charcoal-colored material runs straight down the center of the valley, rising from the sand and water like the back of some submerged serpent.

"A ladder to heaven," Maryam says, looking out into the valley. "That's what it was, once." In her voice there is some emotion that I can't identify.

She turns to me, obviously sensing my mystification even through the veil.

"A *space elevator*," she says dryly, using the modern, bazaar-Arabic words.

Now I understand. I nod, and look down at the gray ribbon. A piece of skyhook cable, some fragment of the forty thousand kilometers of cable that once connected Hippolyta to the stars, cut when Hippolyta's equatorial ring station was destroyed to enforce the quarantine.

If I am successful here, people will have to come to terms with the painful knowledge that many millions might have been saved – if outside powers like the Consilium and the Erewhon Republic had, instead of that quarantine, devoted themselves to evacuation. But I can't help that.

We have to detour many kilometers inland before the water becomes shallow enough to ford.

The old city of Haiming is a long green island, topped with white and blue, set in the middle of a wide brown river. The Otrera flows north to south for two thousand kilometers, before taking a left turn, just south of here, and emptying itself into Hippolyta's eastern ocean. On the east side of the river, in Tieshan proper, the shore is lined with ironworks and concrete, and the horizon is smudged with smoke.

Here on the west side, the market side, the buildings are low and brown and poor – all of them seemingly either made of clay, and very old, or made of wood, and very flimsy. The effect should be depressing, but the rooftops are lined with flapping colored banners, the air smells of earth and river water and spices, and the streets are filled with people, shouting and laughing and dickering in Ezheler and Arabic and Chinese.

I leave Maryam at the ferry terminal, where the northbound boats stop before heading upriver.

She lingers on the gangway. "This is probably my last chance, you know," she says.

"What do you mean?"

"I'm thirty-six," she says. "I don't have any other daughters, or granddaughters. That's why I'm going north."

Into Erethea. Into the blank space on the map, the center of the causal anomaly. Where my goal has been all along.

I don't know what to say, except: "I'm sure you'll be successful," I tell her, "God willing."

"God willing," she echoes.

"Perhaps I'll come north myself, some day soon," I say.

She laughs, and, unexpectedly, puts her arms around me, pressing her veiled cheek against mine.

"You're too young, little daughter," she tells me. "Live for yourself first."

The boat's whistle blows, and she draws back. She takes a pen and a bit of paper from one of her bags and scribbles a name and an address. She hands it to me, and I read. *Dr. Aysun Orbay, 23 Marpesia 4, Themiscyra.*

"My friend," she says. "In case you are too foolish to listen to me."

Then the boat's whistle is blowing again, and she is gone, leading her horse up the gangway.

A Tieshanese mule trader named Zhou Xiling buys my animals at what would be a vicious discount, if I'd ever paid for them. Mules, their hybrid histories stripped from them, breed better on Hippolyta than they do anywhere else, or the Aminas would never have had their two beasts; but in Aella's southern highlands, far from the center of the anomaly, they breed no better than human beings do. In this relationship women like Zhou, who can import stock from farther north, have all the power.

I lift the bales of coca onto my shoulders. I am not tall – Maryam, for instance, was taller than I am – but I am taller than most of the women in East Haiming's streets. As I carry the bales to the coca market, the crowds give me a wide berth.

Mei Yueyin has hardly said twenty words since I identified myself to her in the coca market. She stalks a little ahead of me – walking quickly, as if she would like to leave me behind, or at least make her unwilling association with me less obvious.

It's no use, though; I'm the only Ezheler on the bridge to Haimingdao, and I can't help but draw stares.

The bridge is wide, and lined with ancient ginkgo trees; the sidewalk under our feet is strewn with their fallen leaves, golden green and soft as flower petals. Eddies from the passing motor traffic stir the humid air, and the swirling of the leaves is like some exotic *danse de caractère*.

"What's that?" I ask, pointing ahead to the island, where at the southern end the blue and white of the city gives way to a broad green hill dotted with gray structures. At its crest the low evening sun winks off something gold.

Yueyin glances in the direction I've indicated.

"That's where they buried all the men," she says.

She doesn't want me here.

I don't know what gave me away. Something about my voice, my walk, something about the shape of my body, even merely hinted at through the folds of the *burka*. Perhaps nothing more than the fact that of all the women on Hippolyta, Mei Yueyin is the only one to have seen a man with her own eyes.

I stop, suddenly.

Yueyin continues a few steps, then stops and turns.

"Listen," I say, in Arabic. "I'm not here to get you in trouble. I'm not here to threaten you. I'm certainly not here to drag you back, if that's what you're worried about. I just want a little information. And if you won't give it to me, I'll do without."

She gives me a long, level stare. In her face, something softens for a moment – then hardens again.

"You're here to threaten everyone on this world," she says. "You do that just by being here."

Then she turns away, and starts walking again.

After that, I didn't really expect Yueyin to hide my identity from her partner, and sure enough, when we reach her house – an aged but clean two-story block tucked behind a vine-covered wall, in some neighborhood of narrow alleys on Haimingdao's east side – her first words to her partner are: "Liwen, we have a visitor. He's from Earth."

She says this in Arabic. The pronouns of spoken Chinese have no gender.

"Yazmina Tanzikbayeva," I say.

"That's not your real name," says Yueyin.

"It is now," I tell her.

Yueyin's partner is tall, probably taller than I am, and thin, with high cheekbones, and braided hair that goes to her waist. There is a little girl in her lap, six or eight years old, who looks shyly up at me – whether Yueyin's or her partner's I can't tell; at this age she is all eyes and elbows and knees. They are playing some game with colored tiles like dominoes.

"Peace be with you," the woman says. "Welcome to Hippolyta." Her Arabic is strongly accented, much more than Yueyin's.

"My partner," Yueyin says. "Fu Liwen. She's a rocket engineer for the Tieshanese government."

A rocket engineer.

I miss the little girl's name, and the rest of the introductions. I give distracted answers while Yueyin mechanically makes tea and Liwen sends the little girl upstairs.

A rocket engineer.

"You know they haven't forgotten you, out there," I tell Liwen, as Yueyin sits down. "There's a battleship at L2, waiting to kill any of you who try to leave." Calling the *Tenacious* a battleship feels like a lie. But to Liwen's industrial-age rockets, the Republic's little picket, with its quaint collection of lasers and particle beams, is just as deadly as a Consilium stabilizer-swarm.

Liwen shrugs. "I understand how they feel," she says. "If we leave Hippolyta, hundreds of billions might die. If it were the other way around, if we were out there, and the men were trapped down here – we would do the same thing."

"But you're building rockets anyway," I say.

"Because I don't want my daughter to grow up in a prison," Liwen says, taking a sip of tea. She puts down the cup with a determined finality. "Sooner or later, they will forget. And when they do, we'll be ready."

To kill hundreds of billions, I think. But I don't say it. The truth is that I don't think this – the fear of the Consilium and the Republic – is likely, that the Amazon Women would carry with them whatever makes Hippolyta what it is, and spread it. I think the universe is much more likely to make Hippolyta like itself, sooner or later, than the other way around. If I didn't think that I wouldn't be here.

But I could be wrong.

I'm glad it's not my decision.

"Take off your veil," Yueyin says, suddenly.

"What?"

"You're not Ezheler," she says. "You're not even a woman. I want to see who I'm talking to."

It's not as simple as that, of course. I have to take off the *burka*, pulling my arms out of the sleeves and lifting fold after fold of cloth over my head. Even though I still have my blouse and trousers and boots, once the *burka* is completely off – a sad puddle of violet cloth on the couch next to me – I feel naked. I understand suddenly why the women of Hippolyta continue to wear *hijab*, why it was so horrifying when the men of the thirteenth- and fourteenth-century secular governments tried to abolish the veil by force.

I feel stripped.

And, what's more disarming, I feel like Sasha Rusalev again.

I see that Liwen is studying me, her gaze lingering on my hands, my face, my throat. There is nothing intimate or erotic about that look, only a kind of focused concentration, and in a flash I understand it for what it is: the careful, clinical attention of a naturalist, trying to record in her memory this one specimen of a species she will never see again.

Yueyin is studying me, as well.

"Younger than I thought," she says. "And handsome." It sounds more like an indictment than a compliment. "At first I thought you were here to live out some colonialist harem fantasy, but now I don't think so." She pauses, and then asks: "Gay?"

"Yes. And before you formulate your next hypothesis, I'm not here because I think Amazon Fever will make a woman of me, either."

Yueyin shrugs. "It does happen. Once since I came here, two or three other times in Eth Service records. Mystics who don't believe in gene therapy or reconstructive surgery. The Fever kills them just like any other man. But you're not a mystic, are you?"

Now it's my turn to shrug. "I'm a natural philosopher, and I was trained in the Caliphate. Sometimes the line is hard to draw."

"Let me guess," Liwen says in her accented Arabic. "You think you have a cure for Amazon Fever."

"More or less," I tell her.

"That also happens," Yueyin says. "Every decade or so the Republic will land an automated lab with a cage full of male gerbils, to test the latest medical miracle."

"The Fever kills them, too," Liwen says.

"That's because the Fever's not a medical problem," I say. "It's just a symptom of a causality violation effect."

"You say that as if it meant something," says Liwen.

"It does to me." I take a sip of tea, and then as I set the cup down, an analogy comes to me. "Look," I say, pointing to the cup. "The Consilium – the Phenomenological Service, I mean – they think the universe is like the water in this teacup. The leaves are Hippolyta's causal anomaly. And the Fever is what happens when you put them together – the Fever is the tea."

"And the blockade is there to keep the tea from diffusing any further." Liwen lifts her own teacup and swirls it around. "You are here to take the leaves out."

I start to answer, but Yueyin cuts me off.

She looks me in the eye. "If you *could* cure the Fever," she says, "you'd be destroying the basis of Hippolytan society. Not just the society, but the whole ecology. There's only one male organism on this planet, and he's sitting on my couch."

"I said the Phenomenological Service thinks that way. I didn't say I do."

"You're not with the PS?"

"I'm not with the Consilium at all. I'm sponsored by the London Caliphate's Irrationality Office, but for all practical purposes, I'm on my own."

Yueyin looks skeptical. "What are you here to do, then?"

I sigh. "This is where the metaphors start to break down. Say the universe is a cup of water. Perhaps the anomaly is like a bundle of tea leaves – in which case the Fever, the diffusion, is irreversible. No one knows how to reverse entropy on that scale. And if it isn't contained, it will spread.

"On the other hand, perhaps the anomaly is like a pebble dropped in the cup. Perhaps the Fever is only a ripple on the surface of the water, dissipating the energy of the splash. When the energy is gone, so are the ripples."

"In which case we're doomed anyway." Yueyin says. "But I don't believe it."

"Tell me," I say. "Spontaneous fertility in the Ezheler lands – at the edge of the anomalous region – is it increasing, or declining?"

"There's no hard evidence either way," says Yueyin, looking uncomfortable. "Anecdotally – "

"Anecdotally, it's declining. Isn't it?"

She looks away. "It might be."

"Look," I say. "I'm not here to destroy your society. I'm here to liberate it. You said you don't want your daughter to grow up in a prison."

Yueyin says, "We don't want her to grow up to be some man's wife, either."

I shake my head. "This is not just about you. Hippolyta is *one world*. There's half a trillion women out there." I wave an arm at the ceiling, trying to encompass the whole Polychronicon. "Don't you think they deserve a chance to have what you have?"

In Liwen's face I see understanding dawn. "You are not trying to eradicate Amazon Fever," she says. "You are trying to control it."

"I still don't understand," Yueyin says.

"I told you this was where the metaphors break down," I say. "I can't describe it with teacups."

"Without teacups," Liwen says.

"Without teacups?" I take a deep breath. "I'm hoping to use a Caliphate mathematical technique to establish a metastable equilibrium that allows convex regions with real and virtual histories to coexist in four-dimensional space-time, while remaining both topologically distinct and contiguous in five-space."

Yueyin rolls her eyes. "Never mind what you're doing," she says. "What does it mean? To us?"

"It means, if I succeed, that your daughter will be able to choose how she wants to live. Your daughter" – I gesture outward again – "and everyone else's."

"Why should we believe you?"

I shrug. "Does it matter? I'll be out of your way tomorrow in any case. I'm going north, to Erethea." I take a sip of tea. "If you want to stop me, I'm sure it won't be difficult."

Liwen says something to Yueyin in Tieshanese. Conversations in the Chinese languages always sound like arguments to me, but in Yueyin's reply I hear not just disagreement, but scorn – and yet, a sort of resignation.

She gets up, then, and goes upstairs.

"You can sleep on the couch tonight," Liwen says. "I will get you some sheets. The bath house is out back, if you want to clean up."

"Thank you."

"I am sorry about Yueyin," she says as she tidies up the tea set. "What you have to understand is that for her, it is not enough that on Hippolyta we, women, can live without men. That Hippolyta is a place where men *cannot* come is also important." She glances at the piled cloth next to me and smiles. "For Yueyin the Fever is the perfect *hijab*."

"And for you?" I ask.

She shrugs. "Yueyin, she chose to come here. As for me, I am happy here – but it is where I was born. If I had been born elsewhere, probably I would be happy there."

She is quiet for a moment, as if debating whether to say more.

"I think you do not know what you are getting into," she says.

"What do you mean?"

"You are right, the Fever is just a side effect of some kind of causality violation. Whatever its origin, the center is up there, in Erethea."

"That's why I'm going," I tell her.

She sighs and looks down, tracing invisible pictures with a finger on the tabletop.

"I have been up there three times," she says. "Not all the way." She looks up. "How can I explain it? You know the tombs you saw on the way into town, at the south end of the island, the Men's Cemetery?"

I nod.

"You will find Men's Cemeteries, tombs like that, all over the south. But not in Erethea. In Myrine – that is the first big city, up the river – in Myrine all they have is a cenotaph. Nobody knows what happened to the bodies. In Themiscyra they do not even have that; when they talk about men it's like they're talking about a metaphor, or a myth."

I smile. "Maybe that's healthier."

A laugh escapes Liwen's lips, and she shakes her head.

"Maybe it is," she says. "Tell me – why are we worth dying for?"

"I don't expect to die."

"But you know it's a possibility."

I look away. This is the question everyone danced around – my teachers, my apprentices, the Physics Guild, the Irrationality Office, the Republic's military attaché in London. I distracted them with good manners and mathematics, and let them fill in their own answers, from altruism to neurosis.

"In the early days of Western psychology," Liwen says, "for someone to be attracted to one of her own sex was considered a symptom of an inability, on her part, to distinguish between the Self and the Other. Like an infant who does not yet understand the difference between her toys and her own limbs – and puts both of them in her mouth. If that were true . . . then altruism might be very close to narcissism."

I hoped to talk more with Mei Yueyin about Hippolyta's geography and demographics, to get more of a sense of the causal anomaly's macroscopic effects, but when I awoke this morning, she was already gone. Probably just as well.

I place my brown hands on the sweating white-painted rail, feeling the engines' vibration, and look out across Haimingdao Channel at the complex of lights and smokestacks and tanks and buildings, the tall gantries that will lift up Liwen's rockets.

Lift them, and launch them to certain death at the hands of the *Tenacious* and its particle-beam satellites. I wonder what Lieutenant Addison and his sober-minded brother officers would see in all this.

They'd admire the mad bravery of it, I expect. The madness whose mirror Liwen saw in me. And then they'd shoot to kill.

North. The *Jing Shi* advances stubbornly against the stiff current, like a peasant grandmother bent under a bundle of sticks. I'm sick, according to the medical monitors – my temperature's a degree above normal, and my white blood cell count is elevated.

It might be the onset of the Fever. It might just be something I picked up at Yueyin's dinner table.

The inference engines are agitated, murmuring to themselves, but they seem to think my little bubble of reality, pushing back Hippolyta's intrusion, is intact. I speak to the ship's nurse and get a bottle of antipyretics, fat white pills with a sour taste that stays in the mouth a long time after they're swallowed.

I look back at her.

"Yueyin was right not to believe me," I tell her. "I'm not here because I want to help you. I'm here because I'm the kind of person who can't look at a knot without wanting to untie it."

"There is a verse from the *Tao Te Ching*," Liwen says. "It is ambiguous, of course, especially in Arabic, but one reading would be: 'The perfect knot leaves no end to be untied.' "

"I wouldn't be here if I thought this knot was perfect," I say. "If what's happened on Hippolyta can happen once, it's probably happening all the time – it's just that most causal anomalies don't have measurable effects. And when one does, the Phenomenological Service – or someone like them – covers it up, locks it away. If I want to untie *that* knot – Hippolyta might be my only chance."

"And for this you are willing to die."

"If it comes down to it, yes." I shrug. "We live in an acausal universe. Isn't that enough justification for anything?"

"Another verse might read: 'Who distinguishes herself from the world may be given the world,' " Liwen says. " 'Who regards herself as the world may accept the world.' "

She finishes her tea, and stands up.

"You are crazy," she says, looking down at me. "I respect that in a scientist. Good night."

"Thank you," I say. "Good night."

The ferry, the *Jing Shi*, has a smell that is somehow both sweet and cold, like metal and poison. The exhaust from the two big engines smells like burning plastic.

I return to the *Jing Shi* at evening, boarding in the bustle of new passengers coming aboard. Most of them are Tieshanese, immigrants or expatriates; a few are Erithean, those who don't have the money for the trains or the fast hydrofoils, and who don't mind a little adventure.

One of these is a young woman who shares my cabin, an economics student from Antiope – one of the cities beyond Themiscyra, in east Erethea – going home for the holidays. She is thin and muscular and dark. At night she takes off her *khimar*, revealing hair that is black and tightly curled and very short, like Musa's. In certain lights she looks like a boy.

The bunks have curtains, but I do not close mine – the two small portholes let in little enough fresh air as it is. Neither does my student. She doesn't know what to make of me, hidden behind my *burka*, with my Ezheler accent and my rough-spun saddlebag that smells of mules and spices. To her I am exotic and dangerous and, I think, a little exciting.

As a European I am the product of a culture – a history, oral and written – which constructs my particular sexuality in a certain way. In

the early days of that history the love of women was by many
considered an inferior but still marginally acceptable substitute for the
love of men.

Perhaps for some it still is, but not for me. And, even if it were –
probably there are a few women on Hippolyta, here and there, who lie
awake at night dreaming of the men they have never seen. But to expect
this boyish student to be one of them – how stupid would I need to be?

At night, by the dim glow of the emergency lights, I look across the
cabin at the back of her sleeping head, and I try to remember what it felt
like to run my fingers through Musa's hair. Whatever the young woman
in the other bunk wants, her desires and mine are at right angles.

I am glad of the *burka*. Beneath it I am not sure whether I want to
laugh or cry.

At Myrine the rivers come together, the Ortigia from the west emptying
into the Otrera. The *Jing Shi* will continue northeast up the Otrera to
Themiscyra, but it will stop overnight here, taking on fuel, exchanging
one cargo for another.

I spend the day ashore, taking a rattling electric tram from the port
into the oldest part of the city.

In a street cafe I watch the sparrows that hop from ground to table to
chair, alert for crumbs. All are female, of course, their heads small, their
plumage uniformly brown.

Myrine is cleaner than Haiming, and quieter, though still bustling
with prosperity. The streets in this neighborhood, narrow, built for
pedestrians, with their quaintly modern pre-Fever buildings, are
cheerful and filled with color, crowded with small bright shops and
their customers, young women and girls with brown or blond hair,
chattering in a Turkish-German creole that I can almost understand.

The shaded square the cafe looks out onto is an island in the middle
of all that, an island of muted colors and quiet. In the center of the
square is the Men's Cenotaph. I am not sure what I expected – some
phallic obelisk or pillar, perhaps, topped with a muscular and well-
endowed statue in classic European style?

What there is, instead, is a circular arrangement of dark slabs and
broken walls, very stark, radiating grief. From a distance the stones
look as though they might be inscribed with names. But close up, the
letters dissolve into abstraction.

Alarm!

I leap up and slam my head painfully against the ceiling. The
inference engines are howling for my attention –

No.

There is only silence.

I ask the engines for a deliberate report, making them take their time
about it. Everything is smooth and quiet, quieter than it's been since I

landed, to the limit of the inference engines' precision. The bubble of reality around me seems to have expanded to the horizon. It's almost as if I weren't on Hippolyta at all.

Did I imagine the alarm? The inference engines' logs admit to nothing.

We're still a day from Themiscyra. I settle back into my bunk, not needing the medical monitors to tell me how fast my heart is pounding. My head aches, not just where I struck the top of it but all the way through. Beneath the *burka* a rash has raised itching red bumps on my forearms and the backs of my hands, on my ankles and the tops of my feet. I feel the student's eyes on me and turn my face to the bulkhead.

In the morning the inference engines are still annoyingly calm; smug, even – unwilling to admit the existence of any boundary between Hippolyta's divergent history and my own.

The medical monitors, on the other hand, are gone.

Coincidence? Or did the ferry cross some threshold in the night, some line drawn across space or time or probability, cutting the monitors' simultaneity channels?

My head hurts. I should have a theory, but I don't. I borrow a pencil from the purser and doodle graphs and formulas for a little while, but Hippolyta is not something that can be solved with partial differential equations, and before long I lose interest. I spend the day sitting on a bench on the deck, in the shade, watching the eastern shore crawl slowly by: six, eight, ten shades of green, with here and there the white or yellow or blue of a house peeking out. I drink lukewarm barley tea, and every three or four hours I take one of the antipyretics I cadged from the nurse.

What could I do – turn around? I knew when I came that there was no way back. If the inference engines have truly broken down, run up against some flaw in the equations, then even returning to Tieshan, or beyond into the Ezheler lands, would not save me. And if it did, I would still die someday, still not knowing the truth.

I feel as though I am on the verge of understanding something. That soon it will steal up to me, like a wild animal in a field, if only I sit here quietly enough.

Themiscyra. The city comes on us at dusk, the trees backing away from the banks, revealing fields, pastures, gardens, roads, buildings. There are other boats on the river; their wakes slap against the ferry's hull, and a distant noise of traffic begins to rise, in counterpoint to the rhythm of our engines.

As I fall asleep lights are coming on, all along the bank.

The purser shakes me awake.

"All ashore that's going ashore," she says, smiling.

I shiver and try to smile back, forgetting for the moment that she can't see my face. By the time – after I stand, with help from the railing, and with some effort get my bag onto my shoulder – that I remember this, and turn to thank her out loud, she is gone.

The city is all around now. The boat has docked in the shadow of a bridge, wide and solid, metal perhaps colorful by day but now black over black water, hiding the night sky. I am almost the last passenger to shuffle down the gangplank and onto the quay, turning only at the end to look up and down the river. Both banks are lined with lights, ribbons and arches and towers in a hundred architectural styles, shining crystalline against the night, reflecting in the dark water, for all the world like Petersburg or Baghdad or Ho Chi Minh Ville – except that a tower is just a tower, here, and an arch is just an arch. It's larger and more prosperous than I expected. A wide pavement runs along the bank, crowded with women of every age and color and language.

It's true that, in some sense, the idea that a history could differ so many billions of years ago as to completely change the evolution of multi-cellular life, and yet produce this present – a present in which these women, indisputably human, walk through the streets of this city, like any human city I have known, speaking languages I learned from men – is, to an approximation of many, many decimal places, simply impossible.

But the impossible often has an integrity that the merely improbable lacks.

I've come this far; too much is irreversible now.

I stop a slim, dark young woman with Central American cheekbones and professional black-and-white clothes, and in Arabic I ask her if she can tell me which way is north.

"That way," she says, pointing. "Up the stairs."

Ahead the bank rises steeply, and there is a broad stone staircase that leads in flights up the slope next to the bridge.

I realize I have been hoping she would point up or down the river. Something of this must be showing in my posture, because the woman smiles apologetically, and gives a helpless shrug.

"Where are you going?" she asks.

I look up and down the river, and back at the boat, and up the stairs, and back to the woman.

"I'm not sure," I tell her. "It's my first time in Erethea."

"There's a visitors' center in Khawlah Road," she offers. "Up the stairs, then left – that's Ste.-Jeanne Street – then right at the first round-about. It's got signs in five languages; you can't miss it. They can find you a hotel."

It's as good an idea as any.

"Thank you," I tell her.

"Peace."

Up. The stairs are small, built to a shorter stride than mine, and in other times I might have taken them two or three at a time. Now I shuffle under the weight of the bag and the fever – the Fever, I mean; I can't pretend any more that that isn't what it is. The chills come in waves. The air is warm, little less warm than down in the delta, and gravid with the nearness of the river, but I am remembering my second year of university and a walking trip in the foothills of the Pamirs, hunched against a bitter wind, my boots slipping on the first ice of autumn, my steps measured in centimeters and in the mounting fear that the next one will send me sliding into the kilometer-deep abyss beside us; measured in the certainty of death.

Somehow I survived that. Somehow I survive this, too, and come out at the top of the stairs, shaking with exhaustion and with the latest wave of chills. I come out, and have my first glimpse of the sky.

"God." The word is involuntary, forced out of me through chattering teeth.

Beyond the street lights, beyond the ordered stars of the towers it rises, a slender ribbon of moonlight-silver becoming burnished gold where it rises above the shadow of the horizon, tapering almost to invisibility but refusing even in my blurred and shaking vision to disappear. At its apex, at right angles, it meets another ribbon, a ring of gold.

A space elevator, and an equatorial ring station.

The ring is an arch that extends from horizon to horizon. There is no possibility that I could have missed seeing it before. I would have seen it from the Tenacious. I would have seen it from Haiming. From any point on Hippolyta it would have been the brightest thing in the sky.

(Somewhere in the back of my mind, the mental model of the causal anomaly that I have spent ten years constructing suddenly expands wildly, acquiring three, four, five extra dimensions . . .)

My resolution dissolves. I tear my gaze from the impossible ring and suddenly I am running, back toward the river, away from the sky. Behind me, women's raised voices, startled or angry or concerned.

The *burka* constricts my vision to a narrow slit. No peripheral vision. The bridge. I'm on the bridge. I can't find the stairs.

I turn and look back and the ring is still there.

Hallucination. Delirium is one of the symptoms of Amazon Fever.

"Delirium is" – I brush up against someone, and I turn to explain – "one of the symptoms – " Who am I talking to? I can't see anything through this damned veil. I stumble, and look down into the face of a sturdy blonde matron, dressed in red, looking exactly like the Queen of England, when we danced *The Once and Future King* for her at Glastonbury.

"I was Lancelot," I tell her, no longer sure whether I am speaking Arabic or Turkish or Russian. "It was magnificent." I spin around, managing just one half-turn of a *pirouette à la seconde* before losing my balance.

The Queen takes my arm, frowning with concern. "You need help," she says, earnestly, and I don't need to know what language she's speaking to understand.

"It's this damned veil," I explain, apologetically. "I can't see a thing through it." I pull away from the woman's grip and start gathering the folds of cloth, trying to pull the *burka* over my head. "Why the hell didn't you stop wearing them when we died?"

I know that's unfair, the Queen of England wasn't wearing a *burka* – what was she wearing? A round hat, with flowers. I try to apologize, to tell her how much I like her hat, but the cloth is muffling my voice and I give up. "I give up!" I let the cloth drop, and turn to the Queen to let her know I give up.

Lights, in the corner of my eye, through the lace. I'm in the street.

"I'm in the street!" I yell. "These fucking veils!"

There is a screeching of tires. Someone grabs my arm, and I remember something from elementary school.

"The rate of pedestrian traffic fatalities in Kabul, in the fourteenth century of the Hegira – " I start to say, and all of a sudden, before I can finish, I am on my back, flat on the ground, the wind knocked out of me. Smell of bruised grass. City lights above me in the night. Women's voices, all around me.

"Is she hurt?"

"Someone call an ambulance!"

The lights rush in on me, expanding to fill all the world.

I can hear them, though I am blind.

"Temperature forty point five," the hospital's doctor says, sounding as though she's talking into a microphone. "Heart rate one-ten. Blood pressure . . ."

"Perhaps it's some kind of autoimmune reaction." Another woman's voice, a familiar one. Beautiful Arabic, like a scholar.

"Maryam?" I croak.

Her hand on my forehead, strong and cool. "Dr. Orbay called me," she says. "They found her address in your bag. Hush now, Yazmina. I'll take care of you."

The hospital's doctor is talking over her. ". . . one-fifty over eighty. If you're right . . ." I imagine the doctor shaking her head. "There's not much we can do here except try to get her stable. Maybe they can do something for her off-planet."

Through my closed eyelids I see the arch again. An accelerator ring, a jumping-off point for starships. Hippolyta's was destroyed at the start of the quarantine. But there it is. Not a place, so much as a gateway. To where?

I think of Lancelot again, halted at the door of the Grail Chapel, granted a glimpse of what he would never touch.

The nurses strip me, wash me, wrap me again in what are probably soft felt blankets, though they feel like steel wool against my fevered skin. I wait for some reaction to my anatomy – shock? outrage? disgust? – but it never comes.

A needle pricks my arm.

I can almost sleep.

I was wrong to define my own history as real, Hippolyta's as unreal – to define mine as Self and Hippolyta's as Other. That is what the inference engines were trying to tell me.

There is no past that is not in some sense a lie. We see the past through the distortion of memory and imagination. We collaborate in its conscious distortion through history and propaganda. We see the laws of cause and effect violated not only each time a starship bends space-time but also each time we view the incomplete records of the past with our teleological modern eyes, imbuing them with presentiments of the future that is our own present, a thing which itself we never see or understand except as imperfect fragments. We tell ourselves that we search for truth when what we are concerned with is in fact nothing more than plausibility.

I called Hippolyta's history *virtual*, but that is semantics. Whether the causal anomaly created that history, or whether it only connected us to something that always existed, somewhere, somehow – is probably not even a meaningful question.

The women of Hippolyta have a story they tell about themselves, and it does not include men.

That I exist is enough to prove the story false.

That Hippolyta exists is enough to prove the story true.

I am the flaw in the calculation, the hidden assumption that invalidates the proof.

That is why I am dying. To balance an equation.

"Hush," Maryam says, in Arabic, as she lays a damp cloth across my forehead. I must have said some of that aloud.

"Not long, now," I whisper. When the end comes, it will come quickly.

I wonder what would happen if Liwen were to launch her rockets from here. Would Lieutenant Addison and the *Tenacious* still be waiting? If not – if the rockets, launched, would find themselves in some other space-time altogether, rotated through some set of higher dimensions – what would that mean? That Hippolyta is as much a Gordian knot from this side as from the other?

If the knot is ever untied, it will be untied from this side.

"Little daughter," Maryam says. "Hush."

And does that other side exist? Did it ever? How would I prove it?

I try to remember the name of the prophet in the Qu'ran, the one whose sister the Jews and Christians called Maryam. The name of the woman I met in the Erewhon transit hostel, the maker of kinés. She brought the Bani Israil out of Egypt, but died on the banks of the Jordan. If I was to take a name it should have been that one, and not Yazmina.

Maryam puts her hand in mine. I try to remember if she knows that I am a man.

"Hush, little daughter," she says again.

Son, I try to say, but the word is already slipping away from me.

THE CLOCKWORK
ATOM BOMB

Dominic Green

New British writer Dominic Green's output has to date been confined almost entirely to the pages of *Interzone*, but he's appeared there a *lot*, selling them eighteen stories in the course of the last few years.

Leftover war munitions are already a problem, with lost land mines from past wars taking a life or a limb somewhere around the world almost every day. And in the future, when the weapons have become more powerful and more strange, that's not going to get any better. In fact, as the scary story that follows demonstrates, it could get quite a bit *worse* . . .

O VER HERE, MISTER. This is the place."

The girl tugged Mativi's sleeve and led him down a street that was mostly poorly-patched shell holes. Delayed Action Munitions – the size of thumbnails and able to turn a man into fragments of the same dimensions – littered the ground hereabouts, designed to lie dormant for generations. Construction companies used robot tractors to fill in bomb damage, and the robots did a poor job. Granted, they were getting better – Robocongo was one of equatorial Africa's biggest exporters. But usually the whites and the blacks-with-cash sat in control rooms a kilometre away directing robots to build the houses of the poor, and the poor then had to live in those houses not knowing whether, if they put their foot down hard on a tough domestic issue, they might also be putting it down on a DAM bomblet a metre beneath their foundations.

This street, though, hadn't even been repaired. It was all sloped concrete, blast rubble and wrecked signs telling outsiders TO KEEP OUT THIS GOVERNMENT BUILDING! FIELD CLERICAL STORES! IMPORTANT GOVERNMENT WORK HERE YOU GO BACK!

"Come on, mister," said the *phaseuse*. "You will see, and then you will have no problem paying."

"You stand still," commanded Mativi suddenly. "Stand right there."

Nervously, he reached into a pocket and brought out the Noli Timere. It only worked fifty per cent of the time, based on information gathered from scientist-collaborators from all factions in the war, but fifty per cent was better than zip.

He turned the device on, on low power in case any of the more recent devices that smelled mine detector power-up were present, and swept it left and right. Nothing. He flicked it up to full power and swept again. A small stray air-dropped anti-personnel device at the north-west end of the street, but otherwise nothing.

"You see that house over there, Emily?" he said, pointing across the road. The girl nodded. "Well, you're not to go in there. There is an explosive device in there. A big one. It'll kill you."

Emily shook her head firmly. "It isn't nearly as big as the one that took Claude."

Mativi nodded. "But you say the device is *still there*."

"Has been since I was very little. Everyone knows it's there. The grown-ups know it's there. They used it when the slim hit, to get rid of the bodies, so we wouldn't get sick. Sometimes," she said, "before the bodies were entirely dead."

"You can't get *slim* from a dead body," said Mativi.

"That's what you say," said Emily. And he knew she was right. So many generously altered genomes had been flying around Africa in warheads fifteen years ago that someone *could* have altered HIV and turned it into an airborne, rather than blood-borne, virus – like the rickettsial haemorrhagic fever that had wiped out all of Johannesburg's blood banks in a single day and made social pariahs of blacks all over Europe and America overnight.

The sun dropped below the horizon like a guillotine blade, and it was suddenly night, as if someone, had flicked a switch in Heaven. Mativi had gotten too used to life off the equator, had been working on the basis that night would steal up slowly as it had in Quebec and Patagonia. But the busy equatorial night had no time for twilight. He hadn't brought night vision goggles. Had he brought a torch?

As they walked up the street, a wind gathered, as if the landscape sensed his unease.

"You have to be careful," said the girl, "tread only where I tread. And you have to bend down." She nodded at Mativi's Kinshasa Rolex. "You have to leave your watch outside."

Why? So one of your bacheque *boyfriends can steal it while I'm in there?* To satisfy the girl's insistence, he slid the watch off his wrist and set it on a brick, but picked it up again when she wasn't looking and dropped it into his pocket.

"Where are we going?" he said.

"In there." She pointed. Half-buried in the rubble was a concrete lintel, one end of a substantial buried structure, through which the wind was whistling.

No. Correction. *Out of which* the wind was whistling.

She slipped under the lintel, on which was fixed a sign saying

WARNING! EXTREME PERSONAL DANGER! The room beyond had once had skylights. Now, it had ruined holes in the roof, into which the geostationary UNPEFORCONG security moon poured prisms of reflected sunlight. Thirty-five thousand nine hundred kilometres above Mativi's head, he and five million other Kinshasans were being watched with five thousand cameras. This had at first seemed an outrageous intrusion on his privacy, until he'd realized that he'd have to commit a thousand murders before any of the cameras was likely to catch him in the act.

"Don't step any closer," said the girl. "It will take you."

The entrance had promised an interior like any other minor military strongpoint – only just large enough to contain a couple of hammocks and a machine gun, maybe. But inside, after only a few steps down, the room was huge, the size of a factory floor. They had entered via an engineer's inspection catwalk close to the roof. He was not sure how far down the floor was.

The wind in here was deafening. The girl had to shout. "THERE IS MORE THAN ONE IN HERE. THEY LIVE IN THE MACHINES. THE GOVERNMENT MADE THE MACHINES, BUT NOT WITH TECHNICIANS AND ELECTRICIANS. WITH SORCERY."

The machines did not look made by sorcery. They were entirely silent, looking like rows of gigantic, rusted steel chess pawns twice the height of a man, with no pipes or wires entering or leaving them, apparently sitting here unused for any purpose. Mativi felt an urgent, entirely rational need to be in another line of employment.

"HAVE YOU ANY IDEA WHAT THE MACHINES WERE BUILT FOR?" said Mativi, who had.

The girl nodded. "THE DEMONS ARE IN THE MACHINES," she said. "THE MACHINES WERE BUILT AS CAGES. THE MILITARY MEN WHO MADE THIS PLACE WARNED ALL THE MOST IMPORTANT MEN IN OUR DISTRICT OF THIS. THEY WARNED MY FATHER. THEY TOLD HIM NEVER TO BREAK ANY OF THE MACHINES OPEN. BUT OVER TIME, THEY LEAK, AND THE DEMONS CAN GET OUT. THE FIRST TWO MACHINES ARE SAFE, FOR NOW. BUT YOU MUST BE CAREFUL, BECAUSE WE THOUGHT THE THIRD ONE WAS SAFE TOO, AND IT TOOK CLAUDE."

"WHAT DID IT DO TO CLAUDE, WHEN IT TOOK HIM?" said Mativi. He could not see any damage to the walls around the third machine beyond, perhaps, a certain swept-clean quality of the dust on the floor around it.

"IT TOOK HIM," said the girl. "IT MADE HIM SMALL. IT SUCKED HIM UP."

"THE MACHINES," said Mativi in broken Lingala. "THEY ARE COVERED WITH . . . WITH THINGS."

The heads of the chess pawns, under the light of Mativi's torch, were surrealistically coiffeured with assorted objects – spanners, wire, door furniture, and, worryingly, a single fragmentation grenade. Many, perhaps more than half of the things were ferrous metal. But some looked like aluminium. Some were even bits of wood or plaster.

Not just magnetism, then.

He fished the fake Rolex out of his pocket, waved it in the direction of the machines, and felt a strong tug on it as he held it in his hand. But he also felt a strong tug on the sleeve of his shirt, and on his arm itself.

He realized with growing unease that the wind was not blowing out of the chamber, but into it, pushing him from behind. It also appeared to be blowing in through the skylights in the roof above. It did not seem to be blowing out anywhere.

The girl gasped. "YOU SHOULD NOT HAVE DONE THAT! NOW YOUR WATCH WILL NOT KEEP GOOD TIME."

"IS THAT HOW THE MACHINE SUCKED CLAUDE UP?"

"NO. ALL THE MACHINES DRAW THINGS IN, BUT YOU CAN PULL YOURSELF LOOSE FROM MOST OF THEM. BUT THE ONES THE DEMONS LIVE IN WILL SUCK YOU RIGHT INSIDE WHERE THE DEMON LIVES, AND NOT LEAVE A HAIR BEHIND."

"WHOLE PEOPLE?"

"PEOPLE, METAL, ANYTHING."

"STONES?" Mativi picked up a fragment of loose plaster from the floor.

"YES. BUT YOU SHOULD NOT THROW THINGS."

He threw it. The girl winced. He saw the plaster travel halfway across the floor until it passed the second machine. Then it jerked sideways in mid-air, as if attached to invisible strings, puffed into a long cone of powder, and vanished.

The girl was angry. "YOU MUST DO WHAT I SAY! THE MILITARY MEN SAID WE SHOULD NOT THROW THINGS INTO THE BAD MACHINES. THEY SAID IT MADE THE DEMONS STRONGER."

"YES," said Mativi. "AND THEY WERE ABSOLUTELY RIGHT. NOT MUCH STRONGER, BUT IF ENOUGH PEOPLE THREW IN ENOUGH UNCHARGED MATERIAL OVER ENOUGH TIME . . ."

"I DON'T UNDERSTAND WHAT YOU MEAN BY UNCHARGED MATERIAL."

"DO YOU UNDERSTAND WHAT I MEAN BY 'EVERYONE WOULD DIE'?"

The girl nodded. "WE SHOULD NOT STAY TOO LONG IN HERE. PEOPLE WHO STAY TOO LONG IN HERE GET SICK. THE DEMONS MAKE THEM SICK."

Mativi nodded. "AND I SUPPOSE THIS SICKNESS TAKES THE FORM OF HAIR LOSS, SHORTNESS OF BREATH, EXTREME PALENESS OF THE SKIN?"

"YES," said the girl. "THE VICTIMS DISPLAY THE CLASSIC SYMPTOMS OF RADIATION ALOPECIA AND STEM CELL DEATH."

Well, I'll be damned. But after all, she has lived through a nuclear war. She's been living among radiation victims her entire life. Probably taught herself to read using Red Cross posters.

"WELL, THE SAME DEMONS THAT WERE USED IN THE RADIATION BOMBS ARE IN HERE. SLIGHTLY DIFFERENT, BECAUSE THESE ARE A SLIGHTLY DIFFERENT WEAPON. BUT THE SAME DEMONS."

The girl nodded. "BUT THESE ARE NOT RADIATION BOMBS," she said. "THIS MEANS YOU HAVE TO PAY ME DOUBLE." She held out her hand.

Mativi nodded. "THIS MEANS I HAVE TO PAY YOU DOUBLE." He fished in his wallet for a fistful of United Nations scrip.

After all, why shouldn't I pay you? None of this money is going to be worth anything if these things destroy the world tomorrow.

"I'm telling you, there are at least forty of them. I counted them. Five rows by eight . . . I didn't go to the hotel because I didn't want to call you in the clear. We have to be the only people who know about this . . . Because if anyone wanders into that site, *anyone at all*, and does anything they shouldn't, we will all die. I'm not saying *they*, I'm saying we, and I'm not saying might *die*, I'm saying will *die* . . . Yes, this is a Heavy Weapons alert . . . No, I can't tell you what that means . . . All I can tell you is that you must comply with the alert to the letter if you're interested in handing on the planet to your children . . . Your children will grow out of that, that hating their father thing. All teenagers go through that phase. And credit where credit's due, you really shouldn't have slept with their mother's sister in the first place . . . No, I do *not* want 'an inspection team.' I want troops. *Armed* troops with a mandate to shoot to kill, not a detachment of graduates in Peace Studies from Lichtenstein in a white APC. And when I put the phone down on you, I want to know that you're going to be picking up your phone again and dialling the IAEA. I am *serious* about this, Louis . . . All right. All right. I'll see you at the site tomorrow."

When he laid the handset down, he was trembling. In a day when there were over a hundred permanent websites on the Antarctic ice shelf, it had taken him five hours to find a digital phone line in a city of five million people. Which, to be fair, fifteen years ago, had been a city of ten million people.

Of course, his search for a phone line compatible with his encryption software would probably be for nothing. If there were this few digital lines in the city, there was probably a retrotech transistor microphone planted somewhere in the booth he was sitting in, feeding data back to a mainframe at police headquarters. But at least that meant the police would be the only ones who knew. If he'd gone through the baroque network of emergency analogue lines, every housewife in the cité would have known by morning.

He got up from the booth, walked to the desk, and paid the geek – the geek *with a submachinegun* – who was manning it. There was no secret police car waiting outside – the car would have been unmarked, but extremely obvious due to the fact that no one but the government could afford to travel around in cars. The Congolese sun came up like a jack in a box and it was a short walk through the zero tolerance district back to his hotel, which had once been a Hilton. He fell into the mattress, which bludgeoned him compliantly unconscious.

When he opened his hotel room door in the morning to go to the one functioning bathroom, a man was standing outside with a gun.

Neither the man nor the gun were particularly impressive – the gun because it appeared to be a pre-War cased ammunition model that hadn't been cleaned since the Armistice, and the man because his hand was shaking like a masturbator's just before orgasm, and because Mativi knew him to be a *paterfamilias* with three kids in kindergarten and a passion for N gauge model railways.

However, the gun still fired big, horrid bullets that made holes in stuff, and it was pointing at Mativi.

"I'm sorry, Chet, I can't let you do it." The safety catch, Mativi noted, was off.

"Do what?" said Mativi.

"You're taking away my livelihood. You know you are."

"I'm sorry, Jean, I don't understand any of this. Maybe you should explain a little more?" Jean-Baptiste Ngoyi, an unremarkable functionary in the United Nations Temporary Administration Service (Former People's Democratic Republic of Congo), appeared to have put on his very best work clothes to murder Mativi. The blue UNTASFORDEMRECONG logo was embroidered smartly (and widely) on his chest pocket.

"I can't let you take them away." There were actually tears in the little man's eyes.

"Take what away?"

"You know what. *Everybody* knows. They heard you talking to Grosjean."

Mativi's eyes popped. "No. Ohhh *shit*. No." He leaned back against crumbling postmodernist plasterwork. "Jean, don't take this personally, but if someone as far down the food chain as you knows, everyone in the city with an email address and a heartbeat knows." He looked up at Ngoyi. "There was a microphone in the comms booth, right?"

"No, the geek who mans the desk is President Lissouba's police chief's half brother. The police are full of Lissouba men who were exonerated by the General Amnesty after the Armistice."

"Shit. Shit. What are they doing, now they know?"

" 'Emergency measures are being put in place to contain the problem.' That's all they'd say. Oh, and there are already orders out for your arrest For Your Own Safety. But they didn't know which hotel you were staying in. One of them was trying to find out when he rang me."

Mativi walked in aimless circles, holding his head to stop his thoughts from wandering. "I'll bet he was. God, god. And you didn't tell them where I was. Does that mean you're, um, not particularly serious about killing me?" He stared at Ngoyi ingratiatingly. But the gun didn't waver – at least, not any more than it had been wavering already. Never mind. It had been worth a try.

"It means I couldn't take the chance that they really did want you arrested for your own safety," said Ngoyi. "If a UN Weapons Inspector died in Kinshasa, that would throw the hand grenade well and truly in the muck spreader for the police chiefs, after all."

"I take it some of them are the men who originally installed the containers. If so, they know very well full amnesties are available for war crimes – "

Ngoyi shook his head. "Not for crimes committed *after* the war."

Mativi was alarmed. "After?"

"They've been using the machines as execution devices," said Ngoyi. "No mess, no body, no incriminating evidence. And they work, too. The *bacheques* are terrified of them, will do anything to avoid being killed that way. They think they're the homes of demons – "

"They're not far wrong," muttered Mativi.

" – and then there are the undertakers," continued Ngoyi. "They've been using the machines for mass burials. Otherwise the bodies would just have piled up in the streets in the epidemics. And the domestic waste trucks, about five of them stop there several times a week and dump stuff in through the skylights. And my own trucks – "

"Your own trucks?"

"Yes. Three times a week, sometimes four or five." Ngoyi returned Mativi's accusing stare. "Oh, *sure*, the UN gives us geiger counters and that bacterial foam that fixes fallout, and the special vehicles for sucking up the fixed material and casting it into lead glass bricks – "

"Which you're supposed to then arrange for disposal by the IAEA by burial underground in the Devil's Brickyard in the Dry Valleys of Antarctica," finished Mativi. "Only you haven't been doing that, have you? You thought you'd cut a few corners."

"The UN gives us a budget of only five million a year!" complained Ngoyi. "And by the time that reaches us, it has, by the magic of African mathematics, become half a million. Have you any idea what it costs to ship a single kilo of hazardous waste to Antarctica?"

"That's what you're supposed to do," repeated Mativi, staring up the barrel of the gun, which somehow did not matter quite so much now.

"We were talking astrophysics in the Bar B Doll only the other night. You told me then that once something crosses the Event Horizon, it never comes out!" said the civil servant, mortified. "You *promised*!"

"That's absolutely correct," said Mativi. "Absolutely, totally and utterly correct."

"Then," said Ngoyi, his face brightening insanely, "then there is no problem. We can throw as much stuff in as we want to."

"Each one of those containers," said Mativi, "is designed to hold a magnetically charged object that weighs more than ten battleships.

Hence the reinforced concrete floor, hence the magnetized metal casing that attracts every bit of ferrous metal in the room. Now, what do you think is going to happen if you keep piling in extra uncharged mass? *Nothing* that crosses the Event Horizon comes out, Jean. *Nothing*. Ever. Including you, including me, including Makemba and Kimbareta and little Laurent."

Ngoyi's face fell. Then, momentarily, it rose again. "But our stuff is only a few hundred kilos a week," he began. "Much less than what the domestic waste people put in."

"I feel better already. You're not going to be personally responsible for getting the whole planet sucked into oblivion, it's going to be some other guy."

"The sewage outlet, mind you," continued Ngoyi. "That must be pumping in a good thousand litres a day – "

Mativi's jaw dropped. *"Sewage outlet?"*

"Sure. The sanitation guys rerouted the main waste pipe for the city as a temporary measure. They have to keep replacing the last few metres – the machine keeps eating the pipe." Ngoyi shrugged. "How else do you think they keep five million people's shit out of the drinking water?"

"Jean-Baptiste, you people have to stop this. You have to stop it now. You have absolutely no idea what you're doing."

The gun was still pointing at the centre of Mativi's chest; now, just for a moment, it stopped wavering and hit dead centre.

"I know *exactly* what I'm doing. I am making sure I can feed my wife and children."

The finger coiled round the trigger, slowed down as if falling down gravity slopes. Mativi winced.

The gun clunked and did nothing.

Ngoyi stared at his uncooperative weapon tearfully.

"I must warn you," lied Mativi, "that I led my university karate team."

"You should leave," said Ngoyi. "I think I recognized the municipal sanitation inspector's car following the bus I took down here. He had a rocket propelled grenade launcher on his parcel shelf."

The road surface rose and fell under the Hyundai like a brown ocean swell, testing its suspension to the limit. Mativi heard things grounding that probably ought not to.

"Can I drop you off anywhere?" He braked gently as the traffic hit the blast craters around the freeway/railway junction, which had been a prime military target. Robot repair units were still working on it, and their operators did not pay much attention to cars that weighed one tenth what a mine clearance tractor did. The streetlights seemed to be out on this stretch of road, and the only illumination came from car headlights bouncing up and down like disco strobes. The robot tractors did not need visible light to see.

"The stadium will do fine. I can catch a bus out to Ndjili from there."

"You live that far out of town?"

"We don't all live on Geneva salaries, you know." Ngoyi's face blanched suddenly as he stared into the evening traffic. "Stop the car! Handbrake turn! Handbrake turn!"

Mativi stared into the traffic. "Why?"

"Four secret police cars, dead ahead!"

It was true, and Mativi cursed himself for not having seen it. The SUVs stood out like aluminium islands in the sea of polyurea AfriCars. Each one of them would have cost ten times an ordinary Kinshasan's annual salary.

"It's not a roadblock," said Mativi.

"So I should care? They're out looking for you!"

"Looks like an escort. They're not even coming down this road. They're turning onto the freeway to Djelo-Binza. They're escorting that big, heavy launch tractor . . . one of the ones designed to carry clutches of heavy ballistic missiles out to the pads at Malebo." He peered out of the driver-side window. "The one whose suspension is scraping the ground – "

He did a handbrake turn and left the road in the direction of Djelo-Binza. The suspension hardly noticed the difference. The only reason people drove on roads any more in Kinshasa was because the road was slightly more likely to have been checked for explosives.

There was only desultory hooting when he rejoined the road. Leaving the road and rejoining it after a four-wheel-drive shortcut was common. The four-by-fours were clearly visible now, crammed with whatever men the police chiefs had been able to get their hands on at short notice – some in military uniform, some in T-shirts, some with government-issue sidearms, some with war-era AKMs, yawning, pulled out of bed in the early hours.

The crawler was taking up three lanes of traffic, drawing a horde of honking AfriCars behind it like a bridal train. Despite the horns, the crawler was probably not moving much slower than the cars would have done – the expressway was still a mass of blast craters.

"I can't *believe* this," said Mativi, hugely affronted. "How can they think they can haul a million-tonne object across town without me noticing?"

Ngoyi stared. "You think that thing's got – *things* on it?"

Mativi nodded. "One of the things is on board – one of the *containers*. They're taking it across town because they can't bear to lose it . . . I wonder why." He winked at Ngoyi. "Maybe they're in the pay of the office of sanitation?" The car plunged into yet another black void unilluminated by its headlights. "*Jesus*, I wish those streetlights were working." He blinked as the car bonnet surged up again into the light.

Then he realized. Not only were there no streetlights, there were also no lights in the city around the road.

"That's it, isn't it."

"What?"

"They're going to the power company. You dumb fucks have been plugging power into it as well. *Haven't you.*"

Ngoyi hesitated, then gave up the game and nodded. "It started out as a theoretical weapons project in the last days of the war. But," he insisted defiantly, "it was a *peaceful* use we put it to! One of our office juniors, a very clever young man, a PhD from CalTech, suggested that if we aimed an infra-red laser beam at the Event Horizon at a certain angle, it would come out as a gamma-ray beam, which we used to heat a tank of mercury . . . we tried water first, but it flash evaporated and fused the rock around the tank to glass." He licked his lips nervously. "The hardest part was designing a turbine system that would work with evaporating mercury. We lost a lot of men to heavy metal poisoning . . ."

Realisation dawned on Mativi. "You were one of the researchers in Lissouba's government."

"You think I could have got away with living in the old People's Democratic Republic with a physics degree *without* being a weapons researcher?" Ngoyi laughed hollowly. "Dream on, brother. But this is *peacetime* now. The technology is being used to power the houses of five million people – "

"Uh-uh. There's no sidestepping the Laws of Thermodynamics. You only get out less than what you put in. You're only getting power out because you're sapping the angular momentum of what's inside the container. I'll lay a bet that what's inside the container was created illegally using the Lubumba Collider that President Lissouba convinced the UN to build to 'rejuvenate the Congolese economy'."

Ngoyi squirmed. "He also said *scientify* the Congolese economy. He actually used the word 'scientify'."

Mativi nodded. "In any case, that angular momentum was put into the container by gigawatts of energy pumped into the Collider from the city power grid. Effectively all you're doing is using up energy someone stole and stored fifteen years ago. It's no more a power source than a clockwork doll is, Jean-Baptiste. You have to wind it up to watch it go. And all you'll be left with, in the end, is a nonrotating very heavy lump of extremely bad shit."

"Well, I must admit," admitted Ngoyi ruefully, "the amount of juice we can squeeze out of it is getting smaller every year."

The tractor in front suddenly rumbled to a halt in a cloud of dust big enough to conceal a herd of rhinos. A wall of immobile metal barred the carriageway, and three lanes of drivers performed the peculiarly Congolese manoeuvre of stepping on their brakes and leaning on their horns simultaneously. One of them shrieked suddenly in dismay when a length of caterpillar track resembling a chain of house façades clipped together with traffic bollards slammed down onto his bonnet and crushed it flat, before slapping his saloon into a cabriolet. Paint flakes flew everywhere. The car was a steel one, too – an old Proton model produced under licence in Afghanistan. Mativi hoped the driver had survived.

Troops poured out of the four-by-fours, ignoring the barrage of horns. They were staring at the side of the tractor. Some good Catholics were even crossing themselves.

Mativi put the handbrake on and left his car. Someone hooted at him. He ignored them.

One whole side of the tractor had collapsed into the asphalt. The torsion bars of the vehicle's suspension, each one a man's waist thick and made of substances far, far stronger than steel, had snapped like seaside rock. The load on top of the tractor had slumped sideways underneath its canvas blanket.

Now that he was outside the car, he was aware of a hissing sound. The sound was coming from a hole punched in the canvas cover.

Some of the troopers were walking up towards the load. Mativi danced out onto the grass verge, waving his arms like an *isangoma*. "No! *Non!* Get away! *Très dangereux!*"

One of the men looked at Mativi as if he were an idiot and took another step forward. His sleeve began to rustle and flap in the direction of the hole in the canvas. Then his hand slapped down onto the canvas cover, and he began to scream, beating on his hand, trying to free it. His comrades began to laugh, looking back towards Mativi, enjoying the joke their friend was having at the crazy man's expense.

Then he vanished.

Not *quite* vanished – Mativi and the troops both heard the bones in his hand snap, saw the hand crumple into the canvas like a handkerchief into a magician's glove, followed by his arm, followed by his shoulder, followed by his head. They saw the flare of crimson his body turned into as skin, bone, blood vessels, all the frail materials meant to hold a body together, degenerated into carmine mulch and were sucked up by the structure. A crimson blot of blood a man wide sprayed onto the canvas – out of which, weirdly, runnels of blood began trailing *inward* toward the hole, against and at angles to gravity.

The police troops turned and looked at Mativi, then looked back at the tractor.

"*Alors, chef,*" one of them said to him, "*qu'est-ce qu'on fait maintenant?*"

"It's loose," said Ngoyi, his eyes glazed, seeing the ends of worlds. "It's loose, and I am responsible."

Mativi shook his head. "It's not loose. Not *yet*. We can still tell *exactly* where it is, just by feeding it more policemen. But its casing's corroded. It's sucking in stuff from outside."

"Not corroded." Ngoyi shook his head. "It won't corrode. It's made of nickel alloy, very strong, very heavy. It's one of the cases we bored a hole in deliberately, in order to shine in the infrared beam. There'll be another hole in the casing on the far side. Where the gamma comes out."

Mativi nodded. *One of the machines the demons live in.*

Ngoyi still seemed to be wary of even looking at the container. "Could it topple over?"

"No. If it begins to topple, it'll right itself immediately. It's probably scrunched itself down into the top of the tractor doing that already. Remember, it's a small thing rotating, rotating *fast*, and it weighs over a thousand tonnes. The gyroscopic stability of an object like that doesn't bear thinking about – "

"GETAWAYO BRIAN MATIVI! I AM HEREBY BY THE ORDER OF THE UNITED NATIONS PEACEKEEPING FORCES OF THE CONGO PLACING YOU UNDER ARREST."

Mativi turned. The voice had come from a senior police officer. The amount of shiny regalia on the uniform confused matters, but he was almost certain the man was a Lieutenant.

Mativi sighed. "Lieutenant – " he began.

"Major," corrected the Major.

" – Major, I am engaged in preventing a public disaster of proportions bigger than anything that might possibly be prevented by arresting me. Do you know what will happen if that load falls off that wagon?"

The Major shrugged. "Do you know what will happen if I see you and don't drag you down to the cells? I will lose my job, and my wife and children will go hungry."

Mativi began to back away.

"Hey!" The Major began to pointedly unbutton his revolver.

"I know what will happen to you if you don't bring me in. And you forgot to mention that there'll be no power in the city either, and that as a consequence a *great number* of wives and children will go hungry," said Mativi, circling around the danger area of bowed, permanently windblown grass near the tractor's payload. He waved his arms in the direction of the dark horizon. "You can see the evidence of this already. The device on this tractor has been uncoupled from the grid, and immediately there is no power for refrigeration, no power for cooking, or for emergency machinery in hospitals. I know all that." Slowly, he put his hands up to indicate he was no threat. Then, with one hand, he swung himself up onto the side of the tractor, with the payload between himself and the Major. "But you truly cannot begin to comprehend what will happen to those wives and children if I allow this load to continue on to Djelo-Binza, sir. You see, I understand at a very deep level what is in this container. You do not."

"I must warn you not to attempt to escape custody," said the Major, raising his pistol. "I am empowered to shoot."

"How can I be trying to escape custody?" said Mativi, looking down the barrel of the pistol as if his life depended on it, and sinking in his stance, causing the Major to lower the pistol by a couple of centimetres, still training it on his heart. "I'm climbing on board a police vehicle."

"Get down off that police vehicle, now," said the Major. "Or I will shoot."

Mativi licked his lips, looking up a pistol barrel for the second time that day, but this time attempting to perform complex orbital calculations in his head as he did so. *Have I factored in relativity properly? It needs to travel dead over the hole –*

"Shan't."

The gun fired. It made quite a satisfactory boom. There was a red flash in mid-air, and Mativi was still there.

The Major stared at Mativi.

"As I said," said Mativi, "I understand what is in this cargo. You do not. Do I have your full cooperation?"

The Major's eyes went even wider than his perceived Remit To Use Deadly Force. He lowered the gun, visibly shaken.

"You do," he said. "Sir," he added.

The Hyundai became bogged down by bodies – fortunately living ones – in the immediate vicinity of the Heavy Weapons Alert site. A crowd of perhaps a thousand goggling locals, all dressed in complimentary rayon T-shirts handed out by various multinationals to get free airtime on Third World famine reports, were making road and roadside indistinguishable. But the big blue bull bars parted the crowd discreetly, and Mativi dawdled forward to a hastily erected barrier of velcrowire into which several incautious onlookers had already been pushed by their neighbours. Velcrowire barbs would sink a centimetre deep into flesh, then open up into barbs that could only be removed by surgeons, providing the owner of the flesh desired to keep it. Barbed wire was not truly barbed. Velcrowire was.

The troops at the only gap in the fence stood aside and saluted for the UN car, and Mativi pulled up next to an ancient Boeing V-22 VTOL transport, in the crew door of which a portly black man in a bad safari suit sat juggling with mobile phones. The casings of the phones, Mativi knew, were colour coded to allow their owner to identify them. The Boeing had once been United Nations White. After too many years in the Congo, it was now Well-Used Latrine White.

Mativi examined what was being done at the far end of the containment area. The site was a mass of specialized combat engineering machinery. Mativi recognized one of the devices, a Japanese-made tractor designed for defusing unexploded nuclear munitions – or rather, for dealing with what happened when a human nuclear UXB disposal operative made a mistake. Hair trigger sensors on the tractor would detect the incipient gamma flare of a fission reaction, then fire a hundred and twenty millimetre shell into the nuke. This would kill the bomb disposal man and fill the area around the bomb with weapons-grade fallout, but probably save a few million civilians in the immediate area.

Mativi walked across the compound and yelled at the man in the Boeing. "Louis, what the *hell* are your UXB monkeys *doing*?"

Grosjean's head whipped round. "Oh, hello, Chet. We're following standard procedure for dealing with an unexploded weaponized gamma source."

"Well, first off, this isn't a weapon – "

Grosjean's smile was contemptuous. "It's something that can annihilate the entire planet, and it isn't a *weapon*?"

"It's *thirty-nine* things that can annihilate the planet, and they're not weapons *any more*. Think about it. Would anyone use a weapon that would blow up the whole world?"

Grosjean actually appeared to seriously consider the possibility; then, he nodded to concede the point. "So what sort of weapon were these things part of?"

"Not weapons," corrected Mativi. "Think of them as weapons waste. They were the principal components in a Penrose Accelerator."

"You're making it up."

"You damn fool security guy, me weapons inspector. We've suspected the People's Democratic Republic of Congo used Penrose weapons in their war with the Democratic People's Republic of Congo for some time. They had guns capable of lobbing hundred tonne shells full of plague germs at Pretoria from a distance of four thousand kilometres, for instance. When we examined those guns after UNPEFORCONG overran their positions, what we found didn't fit. They had magnetic accelerators in their barrels, but at the sort of muzzle velocities they'd have had to have been using, the magnets in the barrels would only have been any use in aiming, not in getting the payload up to speed. And the breech of each weapon had been removed. *Something* had been accelerating those projectiles, but it wasn't magnetism, and it wasn't gunpowder. The projectiles were big, and they were moving fast. You remember that outbreak of airborne rabies in New Zealand two years back? That was one of theirs. A Congolese shell fired too hot and went into orbit. The orbit decayed. The shell came down. Thirteen years after the war. Gunpowder and magnetism don't do that."

"So what was it?"

"A Penrose Accelerator. You get yourself a heavy-duty rotating mass, big enough to have stuff orbit round it, and you whirl ordnance round those orbits, contrary to the direction of the mass's rotation. Half of your ordnance separates from the payload, and drops into the mass. The *other* half gets kicked out to mind-buggering velocities. The trouble is, none of this works unless the mass is dense enough to have an escape velocity greater than light."

"A black hole."

"Yes. You have yourself thirty-nine charged rotating black holes, formerly used as artillery accelerators, now with nowhere to go. Plus another hole lodged precariously on the back of a tractor on the public highway halfway between here and Djelo-Binza. And the only way for us to find enough energy to get rid of them, I imagine, would be to use *another* black hole to kick them into orbit. They also give off gamma, almost constantly, as they're constantly absorbing matter. You point one of those UXB defuser tractors at them and throw the safety on the gun, and – "

"JESUS." Grosjean stared at the ground floor entrance where his men had been preparing to throw heavy artillery shells at the problem, jumped up, and began frantically waving his arms for them to stop. *"OUI! OUI! ARRÊTE! ARRÊTE!* And we thought getting rid of nuclear waste was difficult."

"Looks easy to me," said Mativi, nodding in the direction of the highway. Two trucks with UNSMATDEMRECONG livery, their suspensions hanging low, had stopped just short of the military cordon in the eastbound lane. Their drivers had already erected signs saying LIGHT HEAT HERE FOR DOLLARS, and were handing out clear resin bricks that glowed with a soft green light to housewives who were coming out of the darkened prefabs nearby, turning the bricks over in their hands, feeling the warmth, haggling over prices.

"Is that what I think it is?" said Grosjean. "I should stop that. It's dangerous, isn't it?"

"Don't concern yourself with it right now. Those bricks can only kill one family at a time. Besides," said Mativi gleefully, "the city needs power, and Jean-Baptiste's men are only supplying a need, right?"

Ngoyi, still in the passenger seat of the Hyundai, stared sadly as his men handed out radionuclides, and could not meet Mativi's eyes. He reached in his inside pocket for the gun he had attempted to kill Mativi with, and began, slowly and methodically, to clear the jam that had prevented him from doing so.

"Once you've cordoned the area off," said Mativi, "we'll be handling things from that point onwards. I've contacted the IAEA myself. There's a continental response team on its way."

In the car, Ngoyi had by now worked the jammed bullet free and replaced it with another. At the Boeing, Grosjean's jaw dropped. "You have teams set up to deal with this *already?*"

"Of course. You don't think this is the first time this has happened, do you? It's the same story as with the A-bomb. As soon as physicists know it's possible, every tinpot dictator in the world wants it, and will do a great deal to get it, and certainly isn't going to tell us he's trying. Somewhere in the world at a location I am not aware of and wouldn't tell you even if I were, there is a stockpile of these beauties that would make your hair curl. I once spoke to a technician who'd just come back from there . . . I think it's somewhere warm, he had a suntan. He said there were aisles of the damn things, literally thousands of them. The UN are working on methods of deactivating them, but right now our best theoretical methods for shutting down a black hole always lead to catastrophic Hawking evaporation, which would be like a thousand-tonne nuclear warhead going off. And if any one of those things broke out of containment, even one, it would sink through the Earth's crust like a stone into water. It'd get to the Earth's centre and beyond before it slowed down to a stop – and then, of course, it'd begin to fall to the centre again. It wouldn't rise to quite the same height on the other side of the Earth, just like a pendulum, swinging slower and slower and slower. Gathering bits of Earth into itself all the time, of course, until it eventually sank to the centre of the world and set to devouring the entire planet. The whole Earth would get sucked down the hole, over a period which varies from weeks to centuries, depending on which astrophysicist you ask. And you know what?" – and here Mativi smiled evilly. This was always the good part.

"What?" Grosjean's Bantu face had turned whiter than a Boer's. From the direction of the car, Mativi heard a single, slightly muffled gunshot.

"We have no way of knowing whether we already missed one or two. Whether one or two of these irresponsible nations carrying out unauthorized black hole research dropped the ball. How would we know, if someone kept their project secret enough? How would we know there wasn't a black hole bouncing up and down like a big happy rubber ball inside the Earth right now? Gravitational anomalies would eventually begin to show themselves, I suppose – whether on seismometers or mass detectors. But our world might only have a few decades to live – and we wouldn't be any the wiser.

"Make sure that cordon's tight, Louis."

Grosjean swallowed with difficulty, and nodded. Mativi wandered away from the containment site, flipping open his mobile phone. Miracle of miracles, even out here, it worked.

"Hello darling . . . No, I think it'll perhaps take another couple of days . . . Oh, the regular sort of thing. Not too dangerous. Yes, we did catch this one . . . Well, I did get shot at a little, but the guy missed. He was aiming on a purely Euclidean basis . . . Euclidean. I'll explain when I get home . . . Okay, well, if you have to go now then you have to go. I'll be on the 9am flight from Kinshasa."

He flicked the phone shut and walked, whistling, towards the Hyundai. There was a spiderweb of blood over the passenger side where Ngoyi had shot himself. *Still,* he thought, *that's someone else's problem. This car goes back into the pool tomorrow. At least he kept the side window open when he did it. Made a lot less mess than that bastard Lamant did in Quebec City. And they made me clean that car.*

He looked out at the world. "Saved you again, you big round bugger, and I hope you're grateful."

For the first time in a week, he was smiling.

GOLD MOUNTAIN

Chris Roberson

New writer Chris Roberson has appeared in *Postscripts*, *Asimov's*, *Argosy*, *Electric Velocipede*, *Black October*, *Fantastic Metropolis*, *RevolutionSF*, *Twilight Tales*, *The Many Faces of Van Helsing*, and elsewhere. His first novel, *Here, There & Everywhere*, was released in 2005, and coming up are *Paragaea: A Planetary Romance* and *The Voyage of Night Shining White*. In addition to his writing, Roberson is one of the publishers of the lively small press MonkeyBrain Books, and recently edited the "retro-pulp" anthology *Adventure, Volume 1*. He lives with his family in Austin, Texas.

In the bittersweet story that follows, he shows us that sometimes you can't escape your roots, even if you plant them deep in the soil of another world . . .

JOHNSTON LIEN STOOD at the open door of the tram, one elbow crooked around a guardrail, her blue eyes squinting in the morning glare at the sky-piercing needle of the orbital elevator to the south. The sun was in the Cold Dew position, early in the dog-month, when the temperature began to soar and the sunlight burned brighter in the southern sky. Summer was not long off, and Lien hoped to be far from here before it came. As the tram rumbled across the city of Nine Dragons, she turned her attention back to her notes, checking the address of her last interviewee and reviewing the pertinent bits of data from their brief earlier meeting.

Lien had been in Nine Dragons for well over three months, and was eager to return home to the north. She didn't care for the climate this far south, the constant humidity of the sea air, the heat of the southern sun. Nor did she have much patience for the laconic character of Guangdong, the endless farms stretching out in every direction, the slow and simple country wisdom of the southern farmers. Lien was a daughter of Beijing, the Northern Capital, and was accustomed to the hustle of crowded city streets, of nights at the Royal Opera and afternoons in ornamental gardens, of dashing officers of the Eight Banners Army and witty court scholars in their ruby-tipped hats. Nine Dragons, and the port city of Fragrant Harbor across the bay, was filled with nothing but rustics, fishermen, district bureaucrats, and workmen. The only people of culture who came through were travelers on their way to Gold Mountain, but they passed through the city and to the base of the orbital elevator while scarcely looking left or right, and before they'd had time to draw a breath of southern air into their lungs were onboard a gondola, rising up along the electromagnetic rails of Gold Mountain, up the orbital tether of the Bridge of Heaven to the orbiting city of Diamond Summit, thirty-six thousand kilometers overhead.

Johnston Lien was a researcher with the Historical Bureau of the Ministry of Celestial Excursion, and today she'd make her final site visit and collect the last of the data needed for her project. She was part of a group of scholars and researchers given the task of compiling a complete history of the early days of space exploration, beginning with the inception of the Ministry of Celestial Excursion under the aegis of the Xuantong Emperor in the previous century, and continuing straight through to the launch of the Treasure Fleet to the red planet Fire Star, which began just weeks before. The history was to be presented to the emperor in the Northern Capital when the final ship of the Treasure Fleet, a humble water-tender christened *Night Shining White*, departed on its months' long voyage to the red planet.

The tram approached the eastern quarter of Nine Dragons, where the buildings of Ghost Town huddled together over cramped streets, before the city gave way to docklands, and then to the open sea. Lien returned her notes and disposable brush to her satchel, and chanced a slight smile. She'd already made initial contact with this, her final interview subject, and once she'd finished with him, her work would be complete. She could return straight away to the Inn of the White Lotus, pack up her things, and board a Cloud Flyer back to the Northern Capital. Once she'd filed her findings with the chief of her bureau, she'd be able to return to her regular duties – and more, she'd be able to return to her own life.

The tram reached the easternmost point of its circuit, the driver ringing a bell to announce the last stop. Lien released her hold on the guardrail and hopped to the cobbled street, a few sad-faced old white men making their careful way down the tram's steps behind her. As the tram reversed course and made its way back toward the west, Lien walked up the narrow street; under an archway crested by a massive carved eagle, through the gates of Ghost Town.

Most of Lien's days, these last months, had been spent within the wall of Ghost Town, among the old Vinlanders, the "white ghosts." This was a bachelor society, with only one woman for every ten men. She'd gotten to know more than a few of them, over the long months, as nearly all of them had been involved in the construction of Gold Mountain, the three thousand kilometer-tall tower which rose to meet the orbital elevator, the Bridge of Heaven. Some of the old men had been more helpful than others. Some of them had reached such an advanced age that they couldn't even remember the year in which they were born, nor their own mothers' names. When asked, they would simply mutter, "It was too long, too long ago," in their guttural English. They were hollow men, these old Vinlanders, leaning against cold walls or sitting on empty fruit crates, patiently waiting for death to claim them. They were used up, discarded, and they made Lien uncomfortable in her own skin.

Lien had worked her whole life to overcome the stereotypes and misconceptions most Chinese had about Vinlanders, even those like her who had never set eyes on the homeland of their forefathers. Lien's grandfathers and one grandmother all arrived in China in the middle of the last century, and her father had been born in China. Ghost Town, full of men and women who fit every preconceived notion of the "white ghost," was a reminder to her of how far her people had come in China, and how far they had yet to go.

Lien had only been sent to Guangdong province because she spoke English, the native dialect of the Vinlanders. Her parents had insisted she learn the language, as her maternal grandparents had never learned Mandarin, nor Cantonese, nor any other Chinese dialect. She resented her grandparents for this, embarrassed by their refusal to acclimate. She seldom spoke to them when she and her sister were children, and even less as an adult. When her grandfather passed away, just the previous summer, she had not talked to him in nearly ten years. Lien didn't even attend the funeral ceremony, claiming that her duties at the Historical Bureau prevented her attendance. Her mother had yet to forgive her for this breach of etiquette.

Her last discussion with McAllister James had been brief, but he seemed more lucid and communicative than most of the old-timers she'd interviewed over the previous months. She anticipated a short discussion with him this morning, and with any luck she'd be back in Beijing by the week's end.

At the northern end of Ghost Town, Lien came to the building where her subject lived. To reach his small room on the top floor, Lien had to climb the rickety stairway, up past the foul smelling Vinlander restaurant on the ground floor, from which the odor of grits, hominy, and meatloaves constantly poured, and a small clinic on the second floor where a medicine man still tended to the injuries and ills of Ghost Town with his strange western remedies. At the top floor landing, she found herself at the end of a long, dimly lit hallway, with doorways crowded on either side. Lien checked her notes one final time, confirming the address, and made her way to the correct door.

The old man who answered the door looked at her with barely disguised suspicion, as though he didn't recognize her.

"Mister McAllister?" Lien said, speaking in English for the old man's benefit. "McAllister James? I am Johnston Lien, if you recall. We spoke last week at the market, and you agreed to speak with me for a brief while?"

The old man narrowed his watery eyes, and nodded slowly. Opening the door wide, he stepped out of the way, and motioned Lien inside. When she was through the door, he shut and locked it behind her, and then returned to a threadbare sofa in the far corner of the room. Lien crossed the dusty floorboards to a dining table and chair, the only other furniture in the room.

"May I be seated?"

The old man nodded, and Lien arranged herself on the chair, spreading her notes on the table in front of her.

"Thank you for agreeing to meet with me," Lien said, bowing slightly from the waist. The old man just watched her, his expression wary.

McAllister James, in his early eighties, matched the name of "ghost." He seemed spectral, intangible. The few hairs that remained on his liver-spotted scalp were wispy and white, his ears and nostrils grown enormous with the advancing years. He had only a few yellowed teeth left, stained by years of whiskey and tobacco – the white man's vices. The skin of his face, neck, and arms was covered with the scars of the flowering-out disease, smallpox.

"You're going to pay, yes?" the old man said brusquely, the first words he'd spoken since she arrived. "To hear me talk?"

Lien nodded.

"Yes, there is a small honorarium, a few copper coins as fee for your trouble."

"Show me," he said.

With a sigh, Lien reached into her satchel, and withdrew a half dozen coppers, stamped with ideograms indicating good fortune, with a square hole bore through the middle. She arranged them in a neat tower at the corner of the table.

"There," Lien said. "Is that sufficient?"

The old man sat up slightly, peering over the edge of the table at the coins. He caught his lower lip between his gums, thinking it over for a moment.

"Alright," he grunted. "I'll talk."

"Very well, Mister McAllister. When we spoke at the market, last week, you mentioned that you were one of the first Vinlanders to come to China, and that you worked on Gold Mountain straight through to its completion. Is that correct?"

The old man leaned back, and arranged his skeletal hands in his lap.

"Well, I don't know that we were the first, but we must have been pretty damned near."

"We?"

The old man got a faraway look in his eyes. A shadow passed briefly across his face, and then was gone.

"My brother and me," he explained. "We came here together, when we were young. And now there's just me, and I'm long past young."

My father was a sharecropper on a Tennessee cotton plantation, *McAllister said*, in Shelby County, just north and east of Memphis. The year the Chinaman came to town, we'd lost more than half of the crop to boll weevils, and we stood ready to starve. The Chinaman told us about work on the Gold Mountain, across the seas. Steady work and high pay for anyone who had a strong back and was willing. You didn't have to ask us twice. Michael – my brother – and I signed up on the spot, got a few pieces of copper for traveling expenses, and we were on our way.

Now, it wasn't that Michael and I were all hot on the notion of China. We liked things just fine in Tennessee, if there was money or work to be had. But there wasn't. In China, at least, we'd be fed three squares a day, and would make enough coin to send home to feed the rest of the family. Michael and I left our parents and two sisters behind, and went with the Chinaman down to the river, along with a dozen or so other young men from Shelby County. I never heard from my parents again, but a few years back my youngest sister's son wrote to me in Nine Dragons, inviting me to come back to Tennessee to live with them. By that time, though, Vinland was leaning a bit too close to the Aztec Empire for my taste, not under their rule but near enough as made no difference, and I didn't have any interest in living under the bloody shadow of the Mexica. No, I stayed right here in Ghost Town, where the only shadow that falls on me is that goddamned tower – Gold Mountain – and that line going up to heaven. We helped build that tower, my brother and me. It cost Michael his life, and cost me damn near everything else.

I was just eighteen when we rode that paddle steamer down the Mississippi to the Gulf of Mexica, where a China-bound freighter was waiting for us. Michael wasn't yet sixteen, and celebrated a birthday somewhere on the long sea voyage from the eastern shores of Vinland to the dock in Fragrant Harbor.

A lot of men died on the way over, though it's not something a lot of us like to talk about. We were packed in the holds below deck cheek-to-jowl, and were lucky to get slop and water once a day. More often than not, though, the water had gone bad, or there were bugs in the slop, and what with the waves and the motion of the boat the food would either come back up or else rush too fast out the other end. When we rounded the tip of Fusang, down there in those cold reaches of the southern sea, the boat got to rocking so badly that our hold was near ankle-deep in the spew and offal from the men. One man whose name I never knew shat himself to death, after swallowing amoebas or some such in the tainted water, but the ship's crew left his soiled corpse in the hold with us for nearly a week. When, years later, we finished construction on Gold Mountain, and work was scarce, a lot of men talked about going back to Vinland in one of those ships, taking their savings with them. I couldn't credit it, why anyone who'd been through an ocean voyage like that would willingly make another. I suppose that's one reason I stayed here in China, even after all that happened. I don't think the smell of those weeks has ever left my nostrils, not even these long decades later.

In any event, Michael and I made it to Guangdong more or less intact, where work was already underway on Gold Mountain. It was 1962 by our calendar, the fifty-fourth year of the Xuantong Emperor by the reckoning of the Chinese, and though Vinland had been a satellite state of China for just over a century, there'd been only a handful of Vinlanders who'd emigrated to China in all that time. I know Michael and I weren't the first to come, but we weren't too far behind.

Construction on Gold Mountain had begun the year before, from what I later learned. It hadn't taken long for the foreman and shift bosses to realize there weren't nearly enough willing laborers in China to meet the demands of the Ministry of Celestial Excursion. Hell, if they'd not sent out the call for workers to the ends of the Empire, they might still be building the tower even today. Some of those who came to work on Gold Mountain were from Africa, some from India, even a small number from Europe, but the most who answered the call were Vinlanders like Michael and me, mostly from the southern states of Tejas, Tennessee, Kentuck, and Oklahoma.

Gold Mountain wasn't much taller than a regular building, at that point. Up on the hill called Great Peace – on the western end of the island of Fragrant Harbor, just across the bay from the Nine Dragons Peninsula – it was a boxy framework of graphite epoxy about a kilometer on a side, and just a few hundred meters tall. They'd not even pressurized the bottom segments yet, just laid the foundation. By the time we were through, that tower reached up three thousand kilometers, and all because of us. Chinese minds might have dreamed the thing, but it was the sweat off Vinlander backs that built it. That, and Vinlander blood.

But even then, at the beginning, we knew we weren't really welcome. The Chinese called Vinlanders "white ghosts," and said we were barbarians, and savages, and worse. And even when we moved from Guangdong into the other provinces, after Gold Mountain was built, we'd still be huddled together into Ghost Towns at the fringes of town, welcome only to run restaurants, or do bureaucrats' laundry, or manual labor.

When we got off the freighter at the Fragrant Harbor dock, it was just chaos. Two other ships were letting out workers, and there must have been hundreds, thousands even, all packed into that small space. None of us knew where to go, or what to do, most of us too busy trying to remember how to walk on dry land to be of much use to anyone. There were men in loose fitting white jackets and pants, standing on upturned boxes, calling out in a dozen different languages. One of them was a white man speaking English with a Tejas accent. He said, "All Vinlanders who want to work, come with me!" I grabbed Michael by the arm, and we followed the man into the city.

Fragrant Harbor wasn't then like it is today. What Chinese there were in the area all lived across the bay in Nine Dragons, and all of the government offices, and restaurants and shops and such were over there with them. In Fragrant Harbor there wasn't much besides the docks, the warehouses where all the building materials were kept, and the Gold Mountain worksite. All of the workers were housed in a tent city on the east side of Great Peace mountain. Like tended to attract like, so one part of the tent city would be Swedes, another part Ethiops, another part Hindi. When Michael and I arrived, there weren't but a few hundred Vinlanders in the whole place, all huddled together in one corner of the tent city. By the time Gold Mountain was complete, and they shut down the worksite, we numbered in the thousands, and tens of thousands.

The work was hard, and dangerous, even before the tower climbed kilometers into the sky. The lattice of Gold Mountain is made up of pressurized segments filled with pressurized gas. That's what gives the tower its strength, what lets it stand so tall. Without those segments to distribute tension and weight, we couldn't have built a tower much taller than 400 kilometers, much less high enough to hook up with the orbital tether of the Bridge of Heaven. But the same thing that made the tower possible made it damnably tricky to build. God help you if you were up on a scaffolding or on a rig when a bulkhead blew out, or if you were down below when the graphite epoxy debris of an explosive depressurization rained down like shrapnel. And then, once the tower was tall enough, you didn't have to worry just about a bulkhead exploding in your face, or you losing your grip and falling down a thousand meters below, but you had to start worrying about your supply of heated oxygen running out, or your pressure suit catching a leak, or your thermals failing and your fingers and toes freezing before you could get to safety. There weren't many in Ghost Town once Gold Mountain was through that hadn't lost at least a finger or toe to the chill of two thousand kilometers up, and there weren't any that hadn't buried what was left of a friend – or a brother – who'd fallen off the tower to their untimely end. I've buried my share, and then some.

It wasn't all work, though, even when things were at their hardest. There was a good living, in those early days, to be made off of the appetites of the Vinlander workers. Most of us didn't trust Eastern medicine, and wouldn't put our health in the hands of an herbalist if our lives depended on it, so the foremen of the worksite would hire sawbones, Vinlanders and Europeans with experience in Western medicine to see to our health and well-being. And when we got hungry, we wanted food that reminded us of home, not the fish-heads and strange fruits of the Chinaman. The first restaurateurs were Vinlanders who realized they could make a better living feeding their fellow workers traditional southern fare – grits, hominy, meatloaves, and cornbread – than they could working at construction themselves.

Less savory aspects of the Vinlanders' appetites, too, were met by the brothels. Owned by Chinese businessmen, these would bring young girls from Vinland to "service" the workers. Most were damned near slaves, sold into indentured servitude by their parents back in Vinland for a few coins. Their contracts ran for ten years, at the end of which they would be free. Rare was the woman who made it ten years in the brothels.

Michael – God rest his soul – lost his heart to one of those girls in the Excelsior Saloon and Brothel. She was from Tejas, and her name was

Susanne Greene, or Greene Zhu Xan as the Chinawoman madame called her. Michael fell in love with her on sight. For my sins, I suppose I fell in love with her, too. We'd been in China just two years, and the tower now reached several kilometers into the sky. Since our arrival, we'd been sending back home at least one in every ten coins we made. Once Michael met Zhu Xan, though, he had other uses for his money. Not prurient uses, mind, though he was a frequent enough visitor to the Excelsior. No, he was saving up his money to buy Zhu Xan out of her contract at the brothel, so he could take her for his wife.

Well, Michael had just about gotten his nut together when we made that last ascent. We were line-and-basket men, Michael and me, always working high up in the scaffolds, welding together the joints in the latticework and securing the bulkheads. We were at the very top, must have been seven or eight kilometers up, and we had to wear heavy thermal suits and breathing apparatuses just to be up there. Michael was in the basket that day, while I was up on the joist working the rigging.

I can't rightly say what went wrong. One minute I was up there looking out over the pale blue sky as it stretched out over the curve of the horizon, and the next minute I heard a sound like a musket shot, and all hell broke loose. By the time I looked down, as quick as it takes to say it, everything had changed. The line had separated just above the basket, just snapped in two like a string pulled too tight, and there was Michael, hanging onto the side of the scaffold for dear life. The basket was tumbling down to the ground far below. It fell straight for a ways, spinning slightly end over end, but then it bumped against the side of the tower and was sent spiraling out, away from the scaffold. I lost sight of it in a cloud bank. The top of the line, the end still attached to the rigging, snapped back towards me like a whip, and almost caught me across the chest. As it was, I managed to shy away just in time, but it slapped against the joist as loud as a thunderclap, and left a mark in that graphite epoxy, which isn't an easy material to scuff.

Now, the gloves and boots on those thermal suits weren't made for climbing, but Michael did his level best. The walls of the tower were just an empty framework of girders that high up, without bulkhead walls, and so he was able to worm his slow way back up to the top. He wasn't much more than a few dozen meters below the top when the basket-line broke, and he managed to climb a few meters before his strength gave out. Then he was left hanging there, his arms wrapped around a girder, calling through his helmet radio for help.

He was calling for me, calling for his brother, begging me to come down and help him. And I could have, too. I could have attached a safety line to my suit's harness, and rapelled down and taken his hand. It wouldn't have taken more than a few minutes. I could have lowered myself, grabbed hold of Michael, and then raised us both back up to safety. But I didn't.

I want to say that I couldn't, but that's not true. I could have done, if I'd not been a coward. I'd never known that I was a coward before that moment, but seeing my brother dangling over the abyss, and knowing that the only thing standing between him and the Almighty was me, I just froze with fear, unable to move. I just stayed where I was, holding onto the joist for all I was worth, trying to shut out the sounds of Michael's calls for help in my helmet's speakers.

When Michael fell, I heard his screams, all the way down.

When I got back down to Earth, the first thing I did was hie myself over to the Excelsior, to break the news to Zhu Xan. With Michael gone, I figured I'd do the right thing and offer to marry her, myself. As his next of kin, Michael's savings would be mine, and I could think of no fitter use for that sad legacy than to buy the freedom of the woman he'd loved.

By the time I walked through the swinging doors of the Excelsior, though, it was already too late. Michael fell far faster than I could climb down, and gossip flies even faster still, so word of her lover's fall had reached Zhu Xan's ears long before I arrived. There, in the big front parlour of the Excelsior, I saw the broken and lifeless body of Zhu Xan, past all caring. She'd jumped from the balcony of one of the upper rooms, and fallen to her death in the street far below, a tintype of Michael McAllister clutched to her breast. The whores and drunkards of the saloon had brought her body inside, where it lay in state, like she was some departed queen. They were buried in the workers' cemetery that night, Zhu Xan and what little remained of Michael, side by side in a narrow trench.

I never again ascended the heights of Gold Mountain. I begged the foremen to let me work on the ground. My terror and cowardice had already cost my brother his life, and I didn't want to put myself, or anyone else, at risk ever again. I spent the next twelve years on the ground, hauling slag, moving girders and bulkhead walls and gas canisters, while above me the tower of Gold Mountain rose ever higher, its shadow growing longer and longer with every passing day.

I was thirty-seven years old when Gold Mountain was complete, and the Bridge of Heaven tether reached down from the orbital platform to the top of the three thousand-kilometer tower. Heaven and earth were joined together, and man could ride the Bridge of Heaven thirty-six thousand kilometers to orbit.

With work on Gold Mountain complete, the Vinlanders were left without jobs. Some of us returned to Vinland, taking what little they'd been able to save with them – a pittance in China, but a fortune back in Mule Shoe, or Memphis, or Augusta – but most lost even that little in the gambling dens, or over cards or dice on the long sea voyage home. Provided they made it back alive, that is, since many died in the passage, with money still in their pockets, through sickness, or injury, or misadventure.

Some Vinlanders found work in factories, or in mills, or on fishing trawlers, wherever there was hard work to be done that the Chinese didn't want to do. They moved from the coastal region of Guangdong to the other provinces of China, living in small enclaves of "white ghosts," eking out hardscrabble livings.

I stayed in Guangdong, for my part. With the worksite closed, we that remained settled across the bay in Nine Dragons, and took what work we could find. There was a wall in Ghost Town where Vinlanders posted messages and notices, and we'd haunt that corner, looking for word of jobs, of any work. But there weren't just work notices. There'd be desperate notes from fathers searching for their sons, or brothers for brothers. Or else warnings not to take work with a particular farmer or mill owner, those that did not pay promised wages or who provided their workers food unfit for consumption. Old men, towermen from the earliest days of Gold Mountain – most of them short a few fingers and toes, some of them missing arms and legs – would sit on upturned fruit crates in the street, and read the posted notices to those who couldn't read for themselves.

The gangs and mutual protection societies flourished in those days, usually made up of men from the same state or region of Vinland. The Lone Stars of Tejas, the Okies of Oklahoma, the Cardinals of Kentuck. I never had much patience for that sort of thing, myself, but knew enough not to cross any of them. If a Lone Star wanted your seat at the bar, you best give it to him, if you wanted the use of all your limbs by the next day. But they lived by their own sort of code, and if you did right by them, they'd do right by you.

There were gambling dens in Ghost Town, too, as there'd been in the Gold Mountain tent city. Places where men shot dice or played cards, bet on the outcome of dog fights and cock fights, boxing matches and tests of skill. Many lost a month's salary in a single night's indiscretion, though I suppose there must have been a few to see a profit out of it.

Many, too, spent their wages in the whisky dens, where Chinamen and women of position and standing could sometimes be found, lounging on hardwood benches, smoking thick-rolled cigars and sipping Tennessee whisky or Kentuck bourbon. The Chinese came to soak up the local color, and get an amusing story about their night among the savages to tell the folks back home.

I still had a healthy bankroll, what with my own savings, and those left me after Michael's death. I rented a suite of rooms in the nicer quarter of Ghost Town, and got a good paying job as a shift manager at a cigar-rolling factory. All of the factory workers were Southern Vinlanders, and the owner of the factory was a Mandarin who was kind to his workers, when his mood was right. When his mood was dark, he could be as fierce as a demon from hell, but thankfully those times were few and far between.

Things were good, for a few years, but it all changed when I got the smallpox, the "flowering-out disease." I lost my job, and damn near lost my life. Most of us who caught the disease died of it, and those that survived will bear the scars of it for the rest of our days. We didn't trust Chinese herbalists, of course, so we trusted our fates to the hands of Vinlander sawbones, practitioners who had little experience with the disease, and were ill-equipped to treat it. By the time I was past the worst of it, weak and scarred, I'd spent nearly all of my savings on medicines. I'd been shut out of the cigar factory, to keep from spreading the disease to the others, and when my savings ran dry I was evicted from my suite and turned out on the street. I was forty-two years old, and had to start all over, from the bottom.

I found work in a garment shop, stitching the hems on women's robes. My wages were enough that I could rent a small room, and eat regularly, but not much more besides. I'd not sent home any money in years, by this point, and was still plagued with the guilt of it from time to time. I sometimes wondered what had become of my parents. Surely they were dead by now. Had they known somehow what had become of Michael, or died thinking that he still lived, somewhere across the sea?

Things weren't going much better for the rest of the Vinlanders in China, either. In the popular press, we were described as heathens and barbarians. They said we were savage, impure, full of strange lusts and foreign diseases. There were new decrees issued every year – no Chinese could marry a white, no white could own property, no white could take imperial examination – just to keep us in line.

Things reached a head ten years after the completion of Gold Mountain. The Council of Deliberative Officials enacted an Exclusion Decree that said no more Vinlanders could enter China. The wives and families of current resident laborers like me were barred from entry. All Vinlanders needed to be registered, and to carry our papers at all times. Only Vinlanders who were teachers, merchants, students, or diplomats would be permitted entry, and there were scarce few of those.

Then came the Driving Out, as the Vinlanders who had moved to the other regions of China were forced out, at the point of a sword or the barrel of a musket. There had been Ghost Towns in most large Chinese cities in the years after the Bridge of Heaven was completed, but after the Exclusion Decree, the only one left was in Nine Dragons.

Some Vinlanders formed partnerships of up to ten men, pooling their money to open businesses that would let them claim status as "merchants." They could then receive a certificate of legal residency, instead of being considered itinerant laborers. I tried to pool my money with a pair of brothers named Jefferson and their cousins, to open a dry goods store in Ghost Town, but in the end the ties of family proved stronger than any other obligation. The brothers, with the help of one of their cousins, falsified documents to cut me out of the partnership, swindling me of all my savings, and leaving me worse off than I'd been before. I was nearing fifty, and fit only for manual labor.

It has been more than thirty years since, nearly half of a Chinese cycle of years, and I'm still in virtually the same position as I was then. Since coming to work on Gold Mountain, I made two small fortunes, at least as far as Vinlanders are concerned, and lost them both. I've never since made near that much. Perhaps my heart hasn't been in it. Or two chances were all I had, in this lifetime, and having used them both my only choice is to wait until the next world, or the next life, whichever the case may be. My only regret, I suppose, is that I never married, but

with so few Vinlander women in the country, I didn't have much choice.
Too bad that Zhu Xan couldn't have waited, just a few minutes more,
to take that leap from the Excelsior's balcony. Perhaps we could have
been happy together. I think about her still, from time to time. And my
brother, of course.

The Exclusion Decree was repealed, fifteen years after it was enacted,
but the fact that Vinlanders can now emigrate to China with more ease
means little to us old bachelors of Ghost Town. I will die without ever
laying eyes on my homeland again. The world has passed us by. We
wait. We will welcome Death when he comes.

In the vestibule, commuters bustled, waiting for the bell that would
sound the arrival of the next gondola. Just beyond the doors, the
electromagnetic rails ran straight up the side of the tower, climbing up
past the clouds. To one side of the room stood a young woman of
Vinlander extraction, and a very old white ghost.

Johnston Lien and McAllister James were on the island of Fragrant
Harbor, standing in the departure lounge at the base station of Gold
Mountain. The old man was nervous, his gaze darting about the room
furtively, his arms tucked in close to his narrow chest. Lien had not told
him why they'd come, only that she had a surprise for him. In the end,
she had to promise McAllister another stack of copper coins before he'd
leave his rented rooms, and only with them safely in hand would he
agree to bestir himself.

Lien had stayed in Guangdong longer than she'd expected. She could
have left the week before, after finishing her interview with McAllister,
but after hearing his story, she felt there was one more thing she had to
do.

She was reminded of her grandfather, to look at McAllister now. Her
own grandfather might have been such a man, had he not married her
grandmother, and raised a family, and opened a successful Vinlander
restaurant in Guangdong during the years of the Exclusion Decree, and
later moved north to serve his cuisine in the capital city, and once even
served a distant cousin of the emperor himself, and died in bed
surrounded by friends and family. Except for an ungrateful granddaughter, of course, who never considered what sacrifices her parents
and grandparents might have made so that she could grow up in a China
where she could take imperial examinations, and hold administrative
office. Women couldn't yet own property, or remarry after the death of
their husbands, but Lien was sure that was just a matter of time.

By the same token, had circumstances been other than they were,
McAllister might have been her grandfather. He was of the right age,
and background, and had it been he that met her grandmother, then
things might have gone quite differently for him.

She had allowed her grandfather to slip from this life without taking
the opportunity to say a final farewell, nor to thank him. Perhaps in
doing some small favor for McAllister James, she could make amends to

her grandfather's spirit. She'd had to pull strings at the Ministry of Celestial Excursion, and there was a regional administrator whom she now owed a significant favor, but Lien was convinced it was worth it. For McAllister's sake, for that of her grandfather, and for Lien herself. She felt calmer and more at peace at this moment than she had in years, anxious to see the look on the old man's face.

"Why we here?" the old man finally asked, in his broken Cantonese.

"You'll see," Lien answered in English, laying a gentle hand on the old man's shoulder.

The departure bell chimed as the gondola approached, and the doors opened with a hissing outrush of air once the gondola was safely docked.

"Come along, Mister McAllister." Lien took his withered hand in hers, and gently led him toward the open doors.

The old man's eyes darted from side to side, as he meekly followed behind.

"Where are we going?" he asked in English.

"You'll see."

The gondola doors slid closed behind them, and Lien guided the old man to an open acceleration couch. There were a few dozen engineers, naval officers, and bureaucrats in the gondola with them, and a number of them cast sidelong glances at the old white man trembling in the corner, some with thinly disguised contempt.

The acceleration couch offered an unobstructed view of the observation ports on the opposite wall of the gondola. The old man looked to the window, confused, and it was not until the ground fell away, and he saw the rooftops of Fragrant Harbor spread out like an embroidered quilt at his feet, that he understood what was happening.

"No," he said, his voice soft and far away. "Too high. Too long ago. No."

Lien took his hand in hers, and tried to soothe him.

"It will be alright, Mister McAllister. The Bridge of Heaven is perfectly safe."

The view out the gondola window was now of the bay, and of the Nine Dragons Peninsula. To the north stretched Guangdong and the Chinese mainland, to the east and south the sapphire blue of the south China sea.

"Oh, no," the old man said, squeezing his eyes shut tight. "Too long."

In moments, the gondola was ascending at speeds of 1,000 kilometers per hour, then 2,000 kph, then faster still. On either side of the passenger gondola, cargo loads traveling up and down the tether at speeds of over 39,000 kph rocketed by, exerting hundreds of thousands of gees on the cargoes they carried, enough to liquefy any passengers. At its leisurely top speed of 3,000 kph, still putting several gees of pressure on its occupants, it would take the passenger gondola just over twelve hours to reach Diamond Summit, the station in geosynchronous Earth orbit above Fragrant Harbor.

"No," the old man said, shaking his head.

Lien was beside herself.

"I'm *so* sorry!" she said, squeezing McAllister's frail hand as hard as she dared. "I'd thought to do something nice for you. I'd no idea you'd be so frightened."

"No," the old man whispered urgently.

"It will be alright," Lien insisted. "Once we get to the top, you'll see what I wanted to show you, and then we can return. Alright? Please forgive me, I didn't mean to cause you distress."

The old man kept silent, his mouth drawn into a line, and turned his head away.

By the third hour, the old man would not speak to Lien, not even in response to direct questions. He just sat, his hands in white-knuckled grips on the straps of the couch, his gaze fixed on the curve of the horizon visible through the viewport.

When the stewards came by to serve the mid-voyage meal, the old man waved them away, accepting only a bulb of water from their trays.

When the gondola slowed, and docked at Diamond Summit, the passengers found themselves weightless. The stewards helped them from their couches, and guided them to the nose of the gondola, to the airlock that led to the Diamond Summit entryway.

Once onboard Diamond Summit, Lien led the old man to the main body of the station, which rotated around the central hub, providing artificial gravity to the environs. At a large reinforced panoramic window the pair stopped.

In front of them, a few thousand kilometers off, they could see the last of the Treasure Fleet departing for the red planet Fire Star. Below them stretched the blue curve of the Earth, and the glow of the sun limning the far horizon with pale fire. They could see even as far as the edge of the western hemisphere, and the northern continent which McAllister had once called home. Nearest them was the Muslim colony of Khalifa on the coast, founded in centuries past by admirals of the Dragon Throne. Beyond that, off towards the blazing sun in the east, rose the lands of the Commonwealth of Vinland.

"There," Lien said, supporting the old man with one arm, pointing towards the distant horizon with the other. "That is what I wanted to show you. First to let you see what your labor those many long years was for, and second to give you a final look at your lost home. There, on the horizon. That is your . . . that is our homeland. Vinland."

The old man was trembling. He looked from the panorama to Lien, his eyes watering and his lip quivering.

"You . . . you don't understand," he managed to get out, with difficulty. His voice caught in his throat, sounding like an injured bullfrog. "It's not terror that plagues me, but guilt."

Lien looked at the old man, confused.

"But I assumed that you were still afflicted by the fear that gripped you up on Gold Mountain, all those years ago."

The old man jerked his head from side to side, as though trying to shake her words from his ears.

"No!" he shouted, flecks of foam spotting the corners of his mouth. "It wasn't fear, not even then. You don't . . ."

He left off for a moment, pulling away from Lien and averting his eyes.

Lien reached out and laid a hand on his thin shoulder. She thought of her grandfather, and all that had gone unsaid between them.

"Please," she said. "Tell me."

"No," he repeated, with less conviction.

"Please," she urged. "What do you mean it wasn't fear?"

The old man turned to her, his face a red grimace, his eyes flashing.

"It was envy!" he said. "It was lust! It was greed! But it was never fear. Anything but fear!"

He rocked back on his heels, eyes on the far ceiling, his body racked with sobs.

"I could have saved Michael," he went on. "I only had to reach out my hand. But as he dangled there, I couldn't help thinking that with him gone, Zhu Xan would be mine. I loved her, just as he did, and with my brother dead the way would be clear for me. But . . ."

He broke off again, sobs interrupting his words. He slid to the floor, on his knees, his hands in his lap.

"But she was already dead," Lien said.

Mucus ran down his face, and tears streamed across his dry cheeks.

"Yes!" he wailed.

Lien stood, looking down at the frail old man at her feet, rocked by paroxysm of grief and guilt.

"That's why you never went home, isn't it?" she asked, realization dawning. "Why you never returned to Vinland. You couldn't face your family."

The old man nodded, and beat his thin fists against the carpeted floor.

"Yes!" he shouted.

Without another word, she knelt down, and wrapped her arms around the old man's slender frame. She drew him tight to her, and McAllister pressed his face into her shoulder, convulsing with sobs.

"Oh, Michael!" the old man said, his voice cracking. "I'm so, so sorry. It was my job to protect you, and I . . . Oh, God. Forgive me. Forgive me!"

Lien held him tighter, and stroked the back of his wrinkled skull with her hand.

"I forgive you," she whispered, tears in her eyes.

They held each other, the old white ghost and the woman from the Northern Capital. Diamond Summit turned, and the curve of Vinland slipped out of view, and the mountains and plains of China swelled to fill the window.

"Now, grandfather," Lien said, at the edge of hearing. "Forgive me, too."

THE FULCRUM

Gwyneth Jones

One of the most acclaimed British writers of her generation, Gwyneth Jones was a cowinner of the James Tiptree Jr. Memorial Award for work exploring genre issues in science fiction, with her 1991 novel *White Queen*, and has also won the Arthur C. Clarke Award, with her novel *Bold As Love*, as well as receiving two World Fantasy Awards – for her story "The Grass Princess" and her collection *Seven Tales and a Fable*. Her other books include the novels *North Wind*, *Flowerdust*, *Escape Plans*, *Divine Endurance*, *Phoenix Café*, *Castles Made of Sand*, *Stone Free*, *Midnight Lamp*, *Kairos*, *Life*, *Water in the Air*, *The Influence of Ironwood*, *The Exchange*, *Dear Hill*, and *The Hidden Ones*, as well as more than sixteen Young Adult novels published under the name Ann Halam. Her too-infrequent short fiction has appeared in *Interzone*, *Asimov's Science Fiction*, *Off Limits*, and in other magazines and anthologies, and has been collected in *Identifying the Object: A Collection of Short Stories*, as well as *Seven Tales and a Fable*. She is also the author of the critical study *Deconstructing the Starships: Science Fiction and Reality*. Her stories have appeared in the Fourteenth, Fifteenth, and Sixteenth Annual Collections. She lives in Brighton, England, with her husband, her son, and a Burmese cat.

Archimedes once said, "Give me the place to stand, and a lever long enough, and I will move the Earth." In the story that follows, such a lever is provided – and proves to be able to move more worlds than one . . .

IN THE CONSTELLATION OF ORION, *and illuminated by the brilliant star N380 Orionis, you will find the reflection nebula NGC 1999, and the "homo sapiens" Bok Globule, famous in astronomical history. This star nursery is the apparent location of the Buonarotti region, to which the 4-space equations give the shape of a notional cross with two-pointed expanding wings, known to Deep Spacers and other romantics as The Fulcrum. To some, this "X marks the spot" is the forbidden gate to Eldorado; to others, it's the source of our consciousness and an oracle of our future, set like Delphi at the navel of space-time . . .*

The aliens came back to their cabin to find that they'd been turned over again. Last time, they'd lost their drugs. This time it was the bikes. They sat in the wreckage of scattered belongings, letting the spume of violent and futile emotion shed from them, and feeling scared. Losing the fish-oil stash had been serious, but extreme tourists have to accept that they are rich and they will get ripped off. This was different. No one else on the station had any possible use for the exercise bikes. Their fellow prospectors were almost exclusively Deep Space veterans. A few hours a day of simulated mountain racing wouldn't touch their problem with the gravity well.

In the end, the company of their violated possessions got them down, so they decided to go and see Eddie the Supercargo. They knew he wouldn't do anything, but it's always better to report racial harassment. They put their coats on and bounced gently along the drab corridors – two humanoid aliens, about two meters tall, pale skinned and diffident, each with a crest of stiff red hair. Although they were a heterosexual couple, to human eyes they were as identical as identical twins – but unlike human identical twins, they didn't mind being mistaken for each other. They didn't meet anyone. The Kuiper Belt station did not aspire to the parkland illusions or shopping opportunities of near-Earth orbital hotels. Unless they were preparing for transit, most of the prospectors never left their cabins except to visit the saloon.

There were plans that the Panhandle would become the hub of a Deep Space International City, hence all the empty space in the Pan. For the moment it was simply an asymmetric ceramic fiber dumbbell, spinning in a minimal collision orbit-area of the asteroid reach – the Pan full of prospectors and their support staff, the Knob reserved for the government's business out here, and the Handle an empty, concertina-walled permanent umbilical between. The AIs took care of everything serious. The only actual human authority on board was Eddie. His duties were not onerous. As far as Orlando and Grace could make out, he did nothing when on shift except sit in his office at the Knob end of the Handle and play Freecell. On his off shift he would come down to the saloon and schmooze with assorted ruffians. His squeeze-suit and official rank branded him as a dilettante, but he adored the Deep Spacers.

Eddie's gaff was a step or two up from the standard cabins. It had a double skin to keep the cold at bay, and the chairs, desk and cabinets swelling from the walls and floor were designer styled, in a drab, corporate sort of way. There were no personal touches and no visible equipment (besides Eddie), except the desktop screen that he used for his endless solitaire. The Supercargo was a skinny fellow, with wispy dark hair that floated around his shoulders, sad eyes and a taste for extravagant dress. Today he was wearing knee-high platform boots crusted in silver glitter. The bone-preserving pressure suit was concealed by a spiderweb gold silk shirt and black neoprene biker trousers; a copper and silver filigree scarf swayed airily about his throat. The prisoners of knocked-down gravity favored drifty accessories; it was a kind of gallows-humor; and Eddie was a shameless wannabe.

He greeted the aliens with enthusiasm, but he didn't like their complaint.

"Listen," he cut them off, at last, "I'm sorry you lost your bikes, but you know the rules. *There are no rules.* Anything you want, you take. That's the way we live, and you got to breeze it. You can't go all holier-than-thou out here in the Deep."

"We understand *that*," said Orlando, rolling his eyes.

"We'd be *fine* with that," drawled Grace, with a shrug, "if those deadbeats had anything that we *wanted* to steal. It's just unfair that it's all one way."

Eddie beamed, relieved that they hadn't been expecting a police action, and the visit became social. The truth was, passionately as he admired the Deep Spacers, Eddie was frightened of them, and the fact that (theoretically) he could sling them in irons or chuck them off the Panhandle made no difference. It's personality that counts in these back-of-beyond situations. The aliens understood this perfectly: They were pretty much in the same boat. Extreme tourists are always trying to look as if they belong, in situations where only insanely hard-ass nutcases have any real business.

"You know," Eddie confided, "the last Supercargo was knifed in the saloon, over a menu choice. You shouldn't take it personally; the guys are just a wild bunch – "

They knew the story. They thought it was unlikely and that the prospectors only knifed each other. But they sympathized with Eddie's need to romanticize a shit job: a career in space-exploration that had obviously hit the dregs.

"Thanks," said Grace. "Now we feel much better."

Eddie broke out alcohol bulbs and chocolate from his waistbelt, and the three of them chatted, talking guiltily about the blue planet far away, the overcrowded and annoying dump to which they would soon return – Eddie at the end of his tour, and Grace and Orlando on the next Slingshot – which was to the forgotten heroes of the Deep Space saloon an unattainable paradise. Suddenly the Supercargo went quiet, attending to a summons imperceptible to his visitors. They sat politely, while he stared into the middle distance, wondering if he was receiving an update from the AI machines, or maybe a command from faraway Houston.

"Ooops," he said. "Duty calls. It's time for the alien to be milked."

"You mean the *other* alien," Grace corrected him.

Eddie shook his head, making his hair and his delicate scarf flip about like exotic seaweed in a tank. "Hahaha. C'mon, you two aren't really aliens."

Eddie gave slavish credence to whatever loony résumés the Deep

Spacers cared to invent. Wormhole trips? Sentient rocks, diamonds the size of Texas, wow, he lapped it up . . . Orlando and Grace declared their elective cultural identity, which was perfectly acceptable at home, and they were jeered at.

"It's a state of mind," said Orlando.

"Hey," said Eddie shyly. "D'you want to come along? It's against the regs, but I trust you, and you did lose your bikes and all. It'll be okay. You won't get fried."

He stood up, teetering a little because the glitter boots were weighted, and concentrated on stowing his treatpack back on his belt. Grace and Orlando exchanged one swift glance. They knew exactly the terrifying thing that they were going to do.

Eddie did not use keycards, he did not visibly step up to a mark or get bathed in any identifying fields. He simply went up to the blank wall at the end of the umbilical. It opened, and he stood in the gap to let the aliens by. They were through the unbreachable Wall and inside the Knob, a Deep Space Fort Knox, the strongbox which held, according to rumor, the most fabulous treasure in the known universe.

"The Knob recognizes you?" said Orlando, suitably impressed. "Or do you have a key or an implant on you, that it recognizes?"

"Nah, it's me. I've got an implant – "

"Yeah. We noticed."

"That's a requirement of the job. But it's my informational profile that's written into the Knob, just for my tour of duty. Bios wouldn't be secure enough."

They were in a miniversion of the Pan, following a spiral corridor divided by greenish, ceramic fiber bulkheads. They noticed at once how clear the air was, free of the dust, shed cells and general effluvia of many human bodies. It was warmer too, and it didn't smell bad. The walls opened for Eddie, he stood and let his companions through like a wise cat inviting guests through the magnetized catflap; the walls closed up behind with spooky finality.

"Is there always air, heat and gravity at this end?" wondered Grace, offhand.

"Always," said Eddie. "Not for the thing, I don't think it uses air. I don't think it *breathes*. It'd be more expensive turning the life support on and off, that's all. The rad protection is shit," he added, "except in my actual cabin. The AIs are shielded, they don't need it. But half an hour won't fry your nuts."

"What about you?"

Eddie shrugged. "I've got my cabin, and hey, I've finished my family."

The aliens' wiry red hair stood up on end. They felt that, briefly, the Kuiper Belt station was not rotating aimlessly in place but steaming full ahead. They were sailing *outwards* (the only direction that there is) across the Spanish Main, around Cape Horn, with Franklin to the

North West Passage . . . Finally Eddie ushered them into a little room with the same fungoid fittings as his office: desk, chairs, screen and touchpad. One wall was a window, apparently looking into the cabin next door.

"There you go," said the Supercargo, shivering. "Now you can say you've seen it. Oh, no pictures, please. You don't want to get me into trouble."

"We wouldn't dream of it."

Eddie teetered, patting at his wayward hair. The aliens stood like zoo visitors, looking into a naked and featureless cell where something huddled on the floor: a dark, fibrous, purplish lump like a hundred-pound hunk of horsemeat. It was fuzzy in outline, as if not securely fixed in these particular dimensions, and had four blunt extrusions. A convoluted sheet of paler tissue covered some of the main lump, like a skein of fat over a slab of steak.

"Is it really right next door?" asked Grace, casually.

"I suppose," said Eddie. "I never thought about it." His eyes went unfocused as he checked the Knob's internal architecture, and he nodded. "Yeah, actually it is. Shit, I never knew that – " He was shivering more strongly.

"It looks as if its been skinned alive, filleted, and had its arms and legs cut off," breathed Orlando.

"And that could be its brain," whispered Grace. "It looks kind of like a cerebral cortex, unfolded out of someone's skull."

"I don't know why you're whispering," said Eddie. He'd started to pace up and down, flexing his long, delicate hands, as if in nervous impatience. "It can't hear you. Hey, you don't know what they're meant to look like. You're anthropomorphizing. It could be a handsome, happy whatsit, for all you know."

"We don't anthropomorphize," objected Grace. "We're aliens."

Eddie groaned a little. "Oh, have it your own way, a different word. You're thinking like it's a person. It isn't."

There's something in every human heart that delights in horrors: Orlando and Grace were not immune. They pored over the creature on the other side of the window, fascinated and seduced. They knew that Eddie was lying for his own comfort. Almost without a doubt, the thing had once been human. Whatever lies the government told, this goose that laid the golden eggs was almost certainly someone who had made a transit, and failed to return intact . . . But from where had it fallen, into this pit? *From where?* Where had it been, the lone voyager to that land of plenty?

"I can't believe they really keep it *here*," muttered Orlando. "I thought that was just Spacer bullshit."

"Where else?" inquired Eddie, sarcastically. "In the Pentagon basement? Give me a break. It's incre-credibly weird and unbelievably d-dangerous."

Now the creature was moving. It had begun to shudder and squirm across the floor of the cell, silently giving every sign of anguish and terror. "That's milking-time behavior," hissed Eddie. "Now you'll see something, watch, this is it – " But he seemed distracted. A flush had gathered around his eyes and nose, he was smiling strangely and breathing hard.

A section of the cell wall slid aside, revealing a recess set with a pair of waldo rings. Then the government arrived, in the form of two heavy-built robotic hands that reached into the chamber. The alien's movement was now clearly an attempt to reach those hands. As soon as it was close, one of the big chunky mitts got a lock on a stubby tentacle, while the other, grotesquely, delved and disappeared into a cleft that had opened in the dark raw flesh. The creature jerked and writhed in pain, shuddering in that rough grip with an awful, sexual-seeming submission. The buried hand reappeared, full of something that squeezed between the fingers like a thick silvery goo, like liquid mercury. The robot arm retracted out of the cell and returned empty to delve again. Orlando and Grace watched this process happen five times, five greedy fistfuls (with Eddie's breath coming in gasps beside them). Then the robot hands vanished, and the cell wall closed up again.

"Wow, that was *gross*," said Orlando. "Thanks a million, Eddie."

"But it wants to be milked," whispered Eddie, still off on his own track. "It *wants* that to happen. Like the scorpion. It has to obey its nature."

"Was that q-bits?" asked Grace, trying to sound unmoved. "Or the helium?"

"Yeah," said Eddie, blinking and mopping his brow with the filigree scarf. "They get helium, it's half the earth's supply now. An' decoherence resistant particles for building q-bits. It saves pollution, little children get clean water, whoo – "

He pulled himself together. "Shit, I don't know. The goop goes straight back to Earth, all automated. I only work here. C'mon. Got to take you back."

The journey out was the same as the journey in, except that Eddie's mood had taken a severe downturn. The aliens were silent too. He parted from them at his office door. "Catch you later," he said, as he slunk into privacy.

They didn't fancy their turned-over cabin, so they made for the saloon.

It was late afternoon by standard time, and the dank, icy bar was quiet, empty except for the hardcore of alcoholics and gamblers who lurked here from happy hour to happy hour. A couple of the support staff were beating up a recalcitrant food machine. The morbidly obese lady in the powerchair, who wore her hair side-parted in a fall of golden waves, was acting as banker at one of the autotables. (The aliens, who were crazy about Hollywood, knew her as Lakey.) The tall, gangly bloke with the visor – whom they called Blind Pew – looked up to stare, from the band of gleaming darkness where his eyes had been. He said, "Twist," and returned his attention to the game. The aliens got beer tubes and installed themselves at a table near the games consoles –

which nobody played, because they required Earth currency credit, and the Deep Spacers didn't have that kind of money.

"Woooeee," breathed Orlando, finally. "Whaaat?"

"My God!"

"Now I understand why they insist it's an alien."

"The gateway to Eldorado," babbled Grace. "My god, I thought they . . . why don't they . . . You'd think they'd be doing *something* – "

"You mean, why isn't the International Government investigating the thing? Because they daren't, Grace. They're junkies. They're totally dependent. They daren't do anything that might stop the flow."

In the close to four hundred years since spaceflight got started, the human race had never got beyond orbital tourism, government science stations and wretched, hand-to-mouth mining operations in the Belt. The discovery of nonlocal travel had made a huge difference; but the catch was that so far only a conscious human being could make a Buonarotti transit. You could take what you could carry, as long as it didn't contain a processor, and that was all. Hence the Lottery, which had been set up out here, as far from Earth as possible in case of unforseen space-time disasters. The government was handing out cheap survey stakes in the galactic arm to anyone prepared to come to the Kuiper Belt. You got the rights to a portfolio of data (there were programs that would advise you how to make up your package) and the *chance* that your claim would turn up the spectral signature of an Earthtype, good atmosphere, viable planet – the 4-space coordinates of paydirt.

Then you had to check it out: lie down in a Buonarotti couch in the transit lounge, with your little outfit of grave-goods, and go you knew not where.

Prospectors went missing for months; prospectors came back dead, or mutilated, or deathly sick. Just often enough some Spacer came back safe, the proud owner of a prime development site: rich enough, even after selling it at a considerable discount, to pay the medical bills and go home to Earth in fabulous style. But once, once, back in the early days, someone or something had materialized in the transit lounge bearing not merely information, but *treasure* . . .

Orlando and Grace had come out on the superfast advanced-fusion Slingshot, which made the journey in nine months these days, if the orbital configuration was right. (The harvest from the thing in the Knob traveled faster; it didn't need life-support and could stand a lot more gs.) They'd known they'd be stuck for a year, whether their numbers came up or not, and then face another six months for the homeward trip. They'd known the Lottery was meant for redundant Deep Spacers – kind of a scattergun pension fund for the human debris of the conventional space age. But they had seen a window of bold, dazzling opportunity and decided it was worth the risk.

They'd thought it out. They'd taken a government loan-grant, they'd brought their vitamins, and paid the exorbitant supplement for the freight of the bikes. (They'd done the research, they knew that squeeze-suits were just prosthetic, and you had to do real exercise to save your skeleton.) They weren't crazy. They'd had no intention of risking an actual transit themselves. The plan had been that they would get some good coordinates and sell them to a development consortium (you were allowed to do that, and there were plenty, hovering like vultures). The consortium could hire a Deep Spacer for the perilous test-trip, and Orlando and Grace would still be taking home a very nice slice. But they'd been on the Kuiper Belt for nine months, watching the survey screens, and their stake had been coming up stone-empty. Nothing but gas giants, hot rocks, cold rocks. The loss of the bikes had been the last straw. Just a couple of hours ago they'd been looking at crawling home from their great adventure three years older, with rotten bones, and in hideous government debt for life.

Now they had something to take to market!

It was big. It was *very* big . . .

"You know," said Orlando, "When we found the bikes gone, I was going to suggest we offer to fuck Eddie's brains out. I mean, he likes us. Maybe he would have twisted the Lottery AI's arm, switched us to a better stake – "

They looked at each other and laughed, eyes bright, slightly hysterical.

The arrival of the tourists hadn't caused a stir. When Jack Solo and Draco Kojima made an entrance, looking mean, the inevitable molls in tow, all the barflies came to attention. The aliens felt the tremor and saw the reason. These were the Panhandle big boys, uncontested top bullies. But Jack and Draco were arch-rivals. They hated each other; what were they doing together? Orlando and Grace hunched down in their seats, lowered their eyes, and wondered who was in trouble. Murderous violence was not at all uncommon, but they didn't have to worry. It was gang warfare, and you were okay as long as you stayed out of the line of fire.

To their horror, Draco and Jack headed straight for the games consoles curve. With one accord, they hauled out the suction chairs facing the aliens and sat down. Jack's scrawny girlfriend, Anni-mah, adopted her habitual bizarre pose, crouched at her boyfriend's feet. Draco's chunky babe, her bosoms projected ahead of her by awesome pecs and fantastic lats, stood at his shoulder, her oversized blue eyes blank, her little mouth pursed in its customary sugar-smile.

When they'd first encountered the molls, Orlando and Grace had thought they were real people, with strange habits and poor taste in body mods. Of course they were bots, insubstantial software projections. Strictly speaking, they were contraband, because you weren't supposed to use fx generators – or any kind of personal digital devices – on board the Panhandle. But nobody was going to make an issue of it with these two – certainly not Eddie Supercargo.

Jack Solo was a gray-haired, wiry little man, a veteran pilot of the spaceways, who must have fought the damage stubbornly and hard. He showed no signs of Deep Space mutilation, no prosthetic walking frame or deep-vein thrombosis amputations, and he still had normal vision. But then you looked into his eyes, and you knew he hadn't got off lightly. He habitually wore a data glove that had seen better days, and a tube-festooned, battered drysuit – pilot undress, that he sported as a badge of rank. Draco Fujima was something very different – a fleshy, soft-faced young man, with a squeeze-suit under his streamlined, expensive, rad-proof jumper. You could tell at once he hadn't been in space for long. Like Grace and Orlando he was just passing through. He was a time-expired UN remote-control peacekeeper, out of the military at sixteen; who had taken the free Lottery option as part of his severance pay.

This was one tourist the Spacers treated with extreme respect. Though crazy Jack might knife you over a menu choice, he probably counted his kills in single figures. Draco's lethal record was official and seriously off the scale.

No one messes with a playpen soldier.

The big boys stared, with radiant contempt. The aliens attempted to radiate the cynical, relaxed confidence that might get them through this alive.

"You went to see Eddie today," said Jack.

"How d'you know that?" demanded Orlando.

Draco leaned forward. "We have our ways. We don't like you, so we always know where you are. Why did you go to see Eddie?"

"Our bicycles," explained Grace, grinning. "They've been stolen. Do you wise guys happen to know anything about that heist?"

Orlando kicked her under the table: there's such a thing as being too relaxed.

Jack jumped halfway across the table, like a wild-eyed Jack-in-a-Box. "Listen, cunts," he snapped, the dataglove twitching. "Fuck the bicycles, we don't like the relationship. You two and Eddie, we see it and we don't like it. You're going to tell us what the fuck's going on."

"He likes us," said Grace. "Can we help that?"

"It's called empathy," explained Orlando, getting braver. "It might seem like psychic powers, but it's natural to us. You just don't have the wiring."

Jack grabbed Orlando by the throat and flicked the wrist of his other, gloved hand so that a knife appeared there, a sleek slender blade, gleaming against Orlando's pale throat. Anni-mah whined, *"Oh please don't hurt him."* Jack kept his eyes fixed on Orlando and his grip on the jumper while he reached down to smack his bot around her virtual chops with the gloved hand that held the knife.

He made the smack look real, with practiced ease.

"Oh yes, oh, hit me big boy," whimpered Anni-mah. *"Oh, harder, please – "*

Draco's babe just stood there; she was the strong, silent type.

"Look," said Grace, coolly, "when you've finished giving yourself the handjob . . . you've got it all wrong. We made friends with Eddie by accident, it doesn't mean anything. We're just aliens abroad."

"Shut up, cunt," said Jack. "You *are* not fucking aliens, that's just a story, and I'm talking to your boyfriend."

Draco laughed. Jack slowly released Orlando, glaring all the time.

"Listen, fuckface," said Orlando, straightening his jumper with dignity. "*We are aliens* in relation to you, you pathetic old-fashioned machismo merchant, because you haven't a cat in hell's chance of understanding where we're coming from. *Now* do you get it? And by the way, *I'm* the cunt, thank you very much."

Anyone in the bar who feared the sight of blood had sneaked out. The hardcore remained, riveted. It was strange, and not totally unpleasant, to be the object of so much attention. They felt as if getting senselessly bullied by Jack and Draco was some kind of initiation ceremony, Maybe now, at last, the tourists would be accepted.

Jack sat back. The knife had a handle bound in fine-grained blond leather, and the aliens knew the story about where this "leather" had come from. He toyed with his weapon, smiling secretly, then brought the point down so that it sank, under gentle pressure, deep into the ceramic tabletop. The aliens thought not so much of their vulnerable flesh as of the thin shell of the Pan, made of the same stuff as the table, and the cold, greedy, airless dark that would rush in –

"You're not Spacers," said Jack, calm and affable. "You don't belong here."

Draco tired of taking the back seat. "In the center of the Knob," he announced, "there is a cell, guarded by fanatical killer AIs. What's in that cell is a cold brutal indictment of the inhumanities perpetrated around the globe by those who claim to be our leaders. We should be listening, we should be feeding on that pain, we should be turning the degraded, ripped and slathered flesh into kills, into respect, the respect that's due to the stand-up guys, good men who have protected humanity. We know, we *know* that we deserve better than this and YOU know where we can get it – "

"Don't listen to *him*," Jack broke in. "He knows fuck. The thing in that cell came from NGC 1999, a star-nursery in the constellation of Orion. Everyone knows that, but I'm the only one who knows it came for me. Orion has been sacred to all the world's ancient religions, for tens of thousands of years. Nobody knew why, until the space telescopes found out that the new stars in that Bok Globule are just *one hundred thousand years old*. Now do you get it, fuckface, those stars are the same age as homo sapiens. The thing in that cell is human consciousness, twisted back on itself through the improbability dimension. We keep it in chains, for our torment, but I know. I *know*, you see. Out there, *fifteen* hundred *light* years away, is the source of all thought, all science, and from thence, from that magic explosion of cosmic jizin, my *God* has come to find me, has come for *me*."

The knife went in and out of the tabletop. Anni-mah whimpered, *"Don't hit me,"* or maybe, *"Please hit me,"* but Jack's eyes were calm. The aliens realized, slightly awed, that the old space pilot was perfectly in control. This was his *normal state of mind*.

"Fifteen is *five* times *three*. It's written in the Great Pyramid."

"I h-heard about that," Grace nodded, eagerly. "It's the nebula that looks like a thingy, and the ancient Egyptians believed it was, uh, that Orion was Osiris – "

"The Eygptians knew something, girlie. They knew the cosmos was created out of God's own, lonely lovejuice. But I'm the anointed, I'm the chosen one."

"It's made of anti-information," broke in Draco, deciding to up the ante. "Does *that* satisfy you? Does *that* scare you enough? Why d'you think they keep it here, with scum like these deadbeats, where *I don't belong*? Why d'you think they lured me out here? They say I'm morally ambivalent, fucking shrinks, they'll say anything, you should try what I do next. They want me to feel bad, never get the good stuff, There's a conspiracy behind the conspiracy – "

"So you'll tell us," said Jack. "You'll tell us anything you find out."

"From that limp-wrist, fudge-packing, desk-flying government pansy – "

Orlando, Grace noticed, was nudging her in the ribs. She nodded fractionally, and they slid their chairs. The climax had safely passed; they could escape.

"Of course, of course we will. Er, we have to go now – "

Anni-mah cringed and shivered. Draco's babe went on standing there.

The aliens took refuge on the observation deck, which was empty as usual. Real Deep Spacers had seen enough of this kind of view. They stood and gazed, holding onto the rail that saved them from vertigo, until the shaking had passed.

"I think it was just our turn," said Orlando at last. "They didn't know."

"I hope you're right."

Outside the great clear halfdome the glory of the Orion Nebula was spread before them, the jewel in the sword. They could easily locate the Trapezium, the four brilliant stars knit by a common gravity in whose embrace you would find that notorious Bok Gobule – the star-birthing gas cloud with a vague resemblance to a set of male human genitalia. Jack's conviction had some basis, though it was laced with delusion. There was indeed a persistent story, which the government had failed to suppress, that that particular star-nursery was the point of origin of the "thing." They hadn't been able to make any sense of Draco's rant: but what could you expect from a basketcase who had *really killed* thousands of real people, by remote control. And he knew it, and he'd been rewarded by big jolts of pleasure, and all before he was fifteen years old.

Grace put her arm around Orlando's shoulders, and they drank deep of the beauty out there, the undiscovered country. As much as they pretended they had come to space to make their fortunes, they had their own craziness.

"The sad thing is that we're no nearer," said Grace, softly.

"We can't ever get there. Deep Space destroys people."

"Deep Space is like living in a fucking underground carpark with rotten food. And non-local transit is going to be like – "

"Getting on the Eurostar at Waterloo, and getting off in Adelaide."

"Only quicker, and some other constellations, instead of the Southern Cross."

"It's not even real." sighed Orlando. "That. It's a TV picture."

"It's *sort of* real. Nitrogen is green, oxygen is blue. The spectral colors mean something. If we were there, our minds would see what we see now."

"You sound like Jack Solo. Let's go back to the shack, and watch a movie."

They tidied the wrecked cabin a little and ate a meager supper. They didn't fancy going back to the saloon, but luckily their emergency rations had not been touched. One of the sleeping-nets turned out to be in reasonable shape, once they'd lined it with their spare cabin rug. The Panhandle entertainment menu was extensive (as rich as the food was poor); and they'd tracked down a wonderful cache of black and whites, so pure in visual and sound quality they must have been mastered from original prints long lost on Earth. They put on *Now, Voyager*, and settled themselves, two exiled Scottish sparrows in a strange but cosy nest, a long, long way from the Clyde. Their windfall of information could wait. Sobered by their interview with the big boys, they were afraid it was a bust: stolen goods too hot to be salable.

"So it's come to this," grumbled Orlando. "We came all this way to huddle in an unheated hotel room, watching Bette Davis try to get laid."

"That's extreme tourism for you. Never mind. We *like* Bette Davis."

Bette emerged from her Ugly Duckling chrysalis and set off on the cruise that would change her life. Orlando wondered, mildly, "What would anti-information be, Gracie? I've never heard of that before."

"It would be more information, like, er, minus numbers are still – "

"Not like antimatter? Like, you'd explode if you touched it?"

"The robot hands didn't exp – Hey, we're not going to talk about it." But immediately, with a shudder, she added, "God, I'm scared. Draco talks like a serial killer. He talks like one of those notes that serial killers send to the police."

"He is one. A bulk-buy, government-sponsored, Son of Sam."

The movie projection shivered.

A tall, broad-shouldered figure wearing scanty combat gear materialized in front of the black and white picture. It was Sara Komensky, Draco's virtual babe.

The aliens stared in horrified amazement. The bot wrapped her arms over her bazookas of breasts, bizarrely like a real live young woman mortified by the excess.

"Hey," she said. "Er, Draco doesn't know I'm here."

The aliens nodded. "Right," croaked Orlando. "Of course."

The warrior girl appeared to look around, her little mouth an *Oh!* of surprise. Draco's quarters were in First Class, and probably a bit smarter.

"We've had burglars," Grace explained. "Usually it's better than this."

"It's cool," said the bot. She shrugged. "I've seen worse bunkers. I've been with Drac a while you know. We . . . we've been in some tough spots. Jungles, bombed out cities, volcanos, icefields of Uzbekistan, polluted oil platforms, all kindsa shit."

"Sure you have."

Sara strode up and down, which didn't take her long, and turned to them again, her strong hands clasped on her bandoliers, the muscles in her forearms tight. "You got to help me. You see . . . Drac . . . He's not good at the joined-up thinking. It's the combat drugs, they wrecked his brain. He doesn't get that this is our last chance. He took the Lottery option because it was imprinted on him. He'll take a risk on some lousy half-viable coordinates and kill himself; that's what's meant to happen. The government don't terminate toy-soldiers direct; it wouldn't look good. They just make shit-ass sure people like Drac don't survive long in the real."

"That's rough," said Orlando. "I'm sure he's a truly good person, deep down. But what can we do? We haven't any viable numbers. Y-you can check."

"He's *not* a good person," said the bot. "But if he goes, I go too."

"Huh?"

Sara's little pearly teeth caught her sweet, pouting underlip, "Listen, assholes, you come from the same place I come from. Are you made of information, or what? Don't you have anyone switching you on or off? Me, I live in the chinks, same as you. Are *you* so fucking free?" Her huge blue eyes snapped with frustration. "Okay, okay, I get that you can't trust me. But you two know something about the Fulcrum."

"We don't know *anything*," protested Grace, hurriedly.

The big babyblues narrowed as far as the graphic algorithm would allow. "Yeah, but you do. I'm with the Panhandle sys-op. We're like *that*." The bot released her bandoliers, and hooked her two index fingers. "I can't get inside your heads but I *know you've been where the sys-op can't go*. All it would take would be one drop of that silver jizm. One nugget of the good stuff, he'd be set for life, and you'd never have to be looking over your shoulders. I haven't told him, I swear. This is between you and me. Now I gotta get back. Think about it, is all I ask. We'll talk again."

She vanished.

Orlando and Grace shot out of the net, scrabbled in their belongings for the spygone (a gadget that had often been useful on extreme tourism trips) and bounced around the room wildly, searching cornices, crevices, the toilet, anywhere. They found nothing. It was uncanny, how could Draco be using his bot like that, wireless, from another deck, without a receiver in here? Unnoticed, the movie had continued to play. "The projector!" howled Orlando. They flew to disable the entertainment center, dumped it outside in the corridor; switched off the lights and the doorlock for good measure. Switching off the air and gravity would not, they decided, improve the situation: even if they knew how. Finally they collapsed on the floor. Grace dragged their grave-goods whiskey flask out of the litter.

"What can we do?"

"We are fucked," gabbled Orlando, grabbing the precious reserve of Highland Park from her and knocking it back. "We are fucked to all shit! We have the stolen suitcase full of cocaine, the one that belongs to the Mob."

"No it doesn't! It belongs to *us*!"

"N-no it doesn't! Suitcases full of cocaine, dollar bills, anti-information, they always belong to the Mob. And they're onto us. There's nothing we can do except dump the goods in a shallow grave and run for our fucking lives."

"But we can't run. We can't get off here until the Slingshot."

"We c-could try and gone-in-sixty one of the Deep Spacers' asteroid hoppers?"

"Except we don't know how, and if we did, they aren't equipped to get back to Earth. We'd just die more slowly."

The Panhandle was not supplied with lifeboats. Most of the prospectors and all of the support staff were totally dependent on the Slingshot, which was not due for three months. There had to be a lifepod for the Supercargo, keyed to his identity . . . but forget it. That would be a single ticket. Grace saw a faint hope. "Maybe . . . Maybe Draco *doesn't* know? Maybe the bot was telling the truth?"

"Get a grip. That was an interactive videogram, Gracie. That was *Draco* we were *talking* to, for fuck's sake! What did you think?"

"Are you sure? I hear you, but I don't know, it just didn't – "

Someone knocked on the door. They went dead still, forgot to breathe, and stared at each other. Grace got up, quietly, and keyed the lights.

"Come in," said Orlando.

The door opened, and Lakey the fat lady appeared, in her power chair.

"Your lock's broken," she told them. "You should complain to Eddie."

"It isn't broken," said Grace. "We switched it off."

Lakey looked around, the Veronica Lake fall of gold hair swinging. She didn't seem as surprised to see the state the place was in as Sara the bot had been.

"Can we help you?" inquired Grace.

"I'm here because we want to talk to you."

"Everybody wants to talk to us," said Orlando. "Is your chair in this?"

"My chair has the brains of a hamster. I mean, some of us." The chair hissed. Lakey leaned from it to peer at drifted socks. "You two disappeared this morning. You left the sys-op screen. We think Eddie took you through the Wall, and now you know something that will cost you your sweet little tourist skins, unless you get some help."

"What is the Fulcrum?" asked Grace.

Lakey's body was a wreck, but she still had the remains of tough, old-fashioned natural beauty in her dropsical face and in the way she smiled.

"You just spilled all the noughts and ones, little lady."

"I truly don't know what you mean."

"Give me a place to stand," said Lakey, "and I will move the world."

"What are you talking about?"

"To me the Fulcrum means nothing. To you, it means life or death. You guys had a nerve, coming out to the Pan. Do you even care what non-local has done to our culture, to our heroes? This is our fucking patch, the only one we have left. There's a maintenance bay, one junction centerwards of the observation deck, where the food machines go to get pulled apart when they die. You better be there, at oh-four-hundred hours standard, or else. Do you know what *burial at sea* means?"

Burial at sea meant when Deep Spacers chuck some miscreant out of an airlock, naked into hard vacuum.

"Okay," said Grace. "We'll talk. But we want our bicycles back."

Lakey grinned in appreciation. "I'll see what I can do."

Six hours later, the Panhandle was deep in its night cycle. Dim nodes of minimum light glowed along the dark corridors, each node surrounded by a halo of micro-debris. The air exchangers sighed, the aliens bounced toward the rendezvous with barely a sound. As they hit the last junction, Orlando touched Grace's arm. She nodded. They had both heard the crisp tread of velcro soles. Some adept of the spaceways was sneaking up behind them, and it definitely wasn't Lakey. Without a word they jumped up, utilizing their low-gravity gymnastics practice, kicked off from the wall, flew, and kicked again.

Not daring to grab at anything, they tumbled into the bay, narrowly avoided collison with the hefty carcass of a meat synthesizer, and hit the industrial carpet behind it. The crisp footsteps came on, like booted feet walking lightly on fresh snow. They tried not to breathe. The maintenance bay was pitch dark, but it did not feel safe. They were surrounded by the shadow operators, disregarded life support, as if by a dumb and blind and suffering malevolence. Then something shrieked. Something fell, and a human voice started up, a series of short, horrible, choking groans –

"That's Lakey!" gasped Grace, mouth against Orlando's ear.

Silence followed. They crept forward until they could see, in the dim light from the junction, the fat lady's power chair upended and crippled. Lakey was lying beside it, her golden hair adrift, her great body as if crushed at last by the knocked-down gravity that had ruined her bones and swamped her lymphatic system.

"Lakey?" whispered Grace helplessly. "Hey, er, are you okay?"

Something whimpered. Jack Solo's bot was crouching beside the body, like a painted shadow on the darkness, wearing her usual grubby nightdress. *"Jack didn't do it,"* whined Anni-mah. She rubbed her bare arms and cringed from a blow that existed only in the virtual world. *"It wasn't Jack! He wasn't here! Oh, hit me harder, yes – "*

The legendary pilot's wrist knife was on the floor, covered in blood. Orlando and Grace went over to the strange tableau. Lakey'd been stabbed, many times. Blood pooled around her, in swollen globules that stood on the carpet like grotesque black bubbles. Their eyes met. The madman must be very near, and in a highly dissociated state. He was certainly still armed. Jack Solo didn't carry just the one knife.

"Anni?" whispered Grace, trying to make it gentle. "Where's poor Jack?"

"Jack is right here," said a voice they didn't know.

They spun around. White lights came up. Out from among the defunct service machines loomed the gangling man, with the visor and the crooked bones of many fractures, whom they had called Blind Pew. The popeyed fellow they had nicknamed *Joe Cairo* was beside him, supporting his arm. Other figures joined them: one-armed Dirty Harry, a swollen-headed woman they'd called Jean Harlow for her rags of platinum-blonde hair, and two support staff in their drab coveralls. Right now they were supporting Jack Solo. The pilot stared vaguely at the aliens, as if hardly aware of his surroundings, and muttered, *"Jack didn't do it."*

"Did he kill Lakey?" asked Grace. "We heard a struggle."

"Lakey?"

"The lady in the chair."

The tall man nodded, indifferent. "It looks like it."

"We were supposed to meet her here. She said she could get our bikes back."

"Ah, the *bicycles*. Come along. Leave that." He jerked his chin at the corpse, "The robotics will clear it away. Her name was Lana. She was my wife," he added, casually, as he led the way toward the observation deck, leaning on Joe Cairo's arm. "For many years, when I was a pilot. But we had grown apart."

The halfdome was still filled by the vast, silent majesty of the nebula, studded with its glorious young stars. The other prospectors and the two support staff grouped themselves around the tall man. Jack Solo was still muttering to himself.

Anni-mah hovered in the background, like a troubled ghost.

The tall man turned his back on the astronomy and propped his gangling form against the rail, his visored face seeking the aliens. "My name . . . is immaterial. They call me L'Hibou, which means the owl. I was Franco-Canadian, long ago. These good folk have made me their spokesperson. We have to talk to you, about the information you have concerning the Fulcrum and what you plan to do with it."

"Lake – Lana used that term. We don't know what it means," said Grace.

"A fulcrum, my young friends, is the fixed point on which a lever moves. The unmoving mover one might say. But *reculons-nous, pour mieux sauter.* Eight hundred years ago, explorers set out across uncharted seas, and the mighty civilization that still commands the human world was born. Four hundred years ago, man achieved space flight. What happened?"

Orlando and Grace wondered what to say.

L'Hibou provided his own answer. *"Nothing,"* he said, with infinite disgust. "Flags and footprints in the dead dust! Eventually, yes, a few fools managed to scrape a living in the deep. But the gravity well defeated us. We could not become a new world. There was nothing to prime the pump, no spices, no gold: no new markets, never enough materials worth the freight."

The Spacers muttered, in bitter assent.

"Buonarotti science has changed everything," continued L'Hibou. "It makes our whole endeavor look like Leonardo da Vinci's futile attempts to fly. Touching, useless precosity. Pitifully wrongheaded! But what will non-local transit, of itself, give to the human race? *Prison planets*, my young friends. Sinks for Earth's surplus population, despatched out there with a pick and shovel and a bag of seed apiece. That's what the International Government intends. And so be it, that's none of our concern. But something happened, out here on the Kuiper Belt station fifteen years ago. In one of the first Buonarotti experiments, a dimensional gate was opened, and something came back that was not of this universe. There were deaths, human and AI. Records were erased. No witnesses survived, no similar experiment has ever been attempted, non-local exploration has been restricted to the common-place. But we have pieced together the story. They were very afraid. They ejected the thing from the Hub, wrapped in the force field that still contains it. The Knob was built around that field and connected to the Pan, so that the jailer would have some relief and some means of escape. And there it stays, weeping its precious tears."

"Thanks," said Orlando. "We've read the guidebook."

"It is the scorpion," hissed the popeyed little man. "The scorpion that stings because that is its nature, the scorpion that will fell the mighty hunter."

The tall man smiled wryly. "My friend Slender Johnny is as crazy as Jack. He's convinced that the silver tears will ruin the world below, the way Mexican gold felled the might of Spain. It seems to be a slow acting poison."

"Hahaha. When the gods mean to destroy us, they give us what we desire."

"Be quiet, Johnny." The little man subsided. "The *real* significance of the tears is that they came *through*. What happens in a Buonarotti transit, my tourist friends? Come, you've read the guidebook."

"Nothing moves," said Grace. "The traveler's body and the grave-goods – I mean the survival outfit – disappear, because of local point phase conservation. At the, er, target location, base elements plentiful everywhere accrete to the information and an identical body and, er, outfit, will appear. Coming back it happens the same in reverse. The survey data is never enough, it can only show the trip is feasible, not whether all the trace elements are there. But when the test-pilot comes back – "

The Deep Spacers drew a concerted breath of fury.

"She meant dumb puppet," said Orlando hurriedly. "Monkey, whatever – "

"Quite so," agreed the tall man, coldly. "But the point is made. Nothing material travels, but the silver tears *are* material. They are the proof, the validation, the gateway to the empire that should have been *ours*, and that is why the government will never, never investigate. *Ships*, my young friends. If we had a sample of those tears, we would be on our way to building ships that could weave through – "

"I'm sure you're right," said Grace. "But, what do you want from us?"

"We know you have the key to the Fulcrum's prison cell."

The aliens looked at each other, dry-mouthed.

"Say you were right," said Grace, "what use is the combination of the safe, when you have no chance of making a getaway?"

"Agreed. But a madman might be persuaded. A dangerous lunatic."

The aliens looked at Jack Solo, still hanging there in the arms of the support staff. The Kuiper Belt patches on the two men's coveralls glowed a little in the dim light. Jack was in never-never land, whispering to the bot, who crouched at his feet in her soiled pink nightie. L'Hibou held up a hand.

"Oh, no. Jack is ours. We look after our own."

"Draco Fujima has *lettres de cachet*," whispered Slender Johnny, and shivered.

"*Lettres de cachet?*" repeated Grace. "What's that?"

"The term is mine," said L'Hibou. "Suffice to say the bastard has contacts, and each of us here has offended him in some way. He's threatening to have us sent down the gravity well."

"We know he'll do it," said Dirty Harry grimly. "Unless we can buy him off."

"Only it has to be the big prize," put in Jean, tossing her head. "Nothing less."

Death by violence had no horror for the Deep Spacers. To be forcibly returned to Earth, not rich but in helpless poverty, to die in lingering humiliation in some public hospital, that was something like the ultimate damnation.

"We'd want our bikes back," said Grace. "And some useful numbers."

"Deal with the playpen soldier for us, and we will look after you."

The aliens retired to their cabin, very shaken, and put their heads together, figuratively and also literally, for greater security. They had to do this deal, but they'd rather have dealt with Jack Solo, who seemed to them like only a minor bad guy . . . in spite of the knife work. A softbot sextoy (and this was why the bots had been only a passing phase on Earth) inevitably reflects the owner's secret identity. You could *sympathize* with crazy Jack, dragging his whiney Anni-mah around like a flag of failure and defeat. Draco's image of himself as a hefty sugarbabe just turned their stomachs. But it wasn't Anni-mah who could deal with sys-op.

"We have no choice," said Grace, at last. "We know what we have to do. You have to risk your life, playing footsie with the toy soldier."

Orlando nodded. "And you have to fuck Eddie's brains out."

Days passed. "Lakey" was just *gone*. There would be no investigation: The rule is, there are no rules. An obscure Spacer with a poor stake, whose chances had seemed remote, made a successful trip. Another prospector sold some good numbers to the developers, several long term "travelers" were posted officially missing. The remote control conversion work that was adapting the Kuiper Belt station for mass rapid transit – turning the place into a latter-day Ellis Island – continued apace. The plans included moving the goose that laid the golden eggs to an even more secure and isolated location, but no one in Deep Space knew about that, not even Eddie. The Slingshot was on course and growing closer, but still weeks away from dock.

One slow, chill standard noon there was a chime at Eddie's door, and in came Grace. She sat in one of his chanterelle-shaped designer chairs, and they chatted. Jack Solo was behaving as though nothing had happened, but where would he strike next?

Eddie knew it was tactless but he could tell she was hurting, so in the end he asked her straight. "Where's Orlando?"

Grace shrugged. "I don't really care. I know who he's with, though."

"Uh, who? I mean, if you want to talk about it."

"Draco Fujima," confessed Grace, miserably.

Eddie blinked. He accessed sys-op in his head and reviewed the passenger list: which was easy enough to do, and it sometimes gave him guilty entertainment. He couldn't get moving pictures, but he could find out who was in the wrong cabin, so to speak, at any time. Alas, Grace was perfectly correct. Orlando was with Draco.

"Oh, Grace, I'm sorry."

"Don't be. We're an open couple. It's just . . . I just wish it wasn't Draco."

"Is there anything I can do?"

The alien wiped her leaky eyes. "Eddie, you're so *nice*." She smiled bravely. "Well, since you mention it . . . Eddie Supercargo, could we go to your place?"

"You mean right now?"

"If you're allowed, yeah. Right now."

Eddie knew he was "being used." He didn't mind at all. What are friends for?

The aliens played safe for a few days, but Draco was watching them, and he knew when the operation was coming off. He caught one of the pair alone on the observation deck and made his move. Nominally, he and Jack Solo were partners, but fuck that. Jack was a liability, and Draco deserved some luck.

"It's like this," he explained, when he'd marched the alien to his First Class cabin, and knocked him around a little. "I hurt you, you talk. If I don't like what you say, I hurt you more. Clear?"

"You c-can't do this," protested Orlando, "I'm n-not a Spacer. I'm a European citizen. If . . . if anything happens to me, you won't get away with it!"

"Hey, don't count on it. We're a long way from home, and I'm a damaged vet. I get temporary insanity. No one's going to take me to court."

In a combat situation, Draco Fujima still had all his noughts and ones.

To save time, he showed the tourist the sidearm he had smuggled on board, and that made Orlando (or maybe it was Grace – he didn't know and he didn't care) very cooperative. In the country of the blind, the one-eyed man is king. This applies best if the one eye is the dark little hole at the end of a gun.

"Now I'll tell you what's going on," said Draco. "You and your partner have implants. You were supposed to ditch them, but you took a chance because you didn't plan on making a Buonarotti transit, and you didn't want to lose your technology. You thought no one would check up, and you were right. Deep Spacers have too much brain damage for an implant to function by the time they end up here. When Eddie let you through the Wall that day, you took another chance and mugged his frequency. You have the code in your head that will get us to the cell and activate the harvesting robotics. Now tell me how it works."

Sara Komensky stood at Draco's shoulder, and smiled.

"All right, all right," gasped Orlando. "The government couldn't trust control of what goes on in there to the AIs. They wouldn't dare have it handled by remote commands that could be intercepted by terrorists or rogue states. Eddie is the key. He makes out he's just here for decoration, but he's the walking key."

"And you have him, the noughts and ones of Eddie, copied into your head."

"H-how did you – ?"

"Let's just say, computer systems can be hacked in many different ways, and you two have loose mouths. Now I'm guessing your partner is with Eddie right now, and you are waiting for a signal from her to tell you to go ahead."

"No! I'm not going to tell you!"

"They have to be running a diversion, Draco," said Sara. "We don't know what it is they're doing with Eddie, but they're doing something. We didn't get that part."

"It'd better be a good trick," said Draco. "For your sake, asshole."

Orlando reckoned he'd held out long enough to be plausible. "All right, okay, I'll give you the code. I can download, just show me your input device."

Draco grinned. "Oh, no. Sorry, asshole, that's not going to work. The military took my chip when they discharged me. *You're* going to take me in there."

Grace and Orlando knew what Eddie had done, to deal with the horrible burden he had been given. Maybe it was grotesque in human terms, but they were experts on the twisted paths of pleasure, and they could understand. Eddie could not bear what happened to the thing in the cell, he couldn't bear the part he had to play, as the code trigger to that brutal harvest. So he'd rerouted the experience. He had plugged all the helpless guilt and powerless compassion he felt into his libido. When the alien got milked, poor soft-hearted Eddie got his rocks off.

It wasn't Eddie who designed the human brain, and he wasn't the first to make use of the paradoxical contiguity between sexual excitement and other violent arousal. Actually, she felt bad about deceiving him. But she knew Eddie would forgive her. The rule is, there are no rules. But now what? Where's the way to Eddie's heart? It *couldn't* be that his only pleasure came from watching a flayed, truncated human being get fisted by a robot. Eddie wasn't really like that.

"Won't you sit down?" said Eddie, shyly.

She looked around. The cabin was lovely, even with its boring decor. Everything was exquisite, and delicate, and – *oooh, this figures* – distinctly sexless. Orlando and Grace genuinely did empathy rather well; it was part of the augmentation they had chosen when they got themselves fixed up as near-twins. Her glance lit on a convoluted shelf unit that held, protected from the vagaries of gravity failure, a very pretty tea set, in shades of dark blue and rust.

"Could we have tea?"

Eddie's cheeks turned pink, his eyes shone. "Oh, yes! Indian, or China, or I have some Earl Grey, or would you prefer a fruit, or herbal blend?"

"I would *love* to try your Earl Grey," she told him, very warmly. "Oh, wow, Eddie. Can that be – is that early Wedgwood?"

Nice Eddie's lips parted in unfeigned delight. His breathing quickened.

Draco walked Orlando to the Wall, Sara Komensky on point, a few paces behind. Draco had his hands in the hip pockets of his padded jumper. Every so often he nudged Orlando in the small of his back with the muzzle of the plastic shooter.

"Go ahead, Orlando. You're the one with the key."

"I can't, I daren't," protested Orlando, feebly resistant. "The AIs will spot us, this was never meant to happen this way." The muzzle of the firearm dug into his back. "Okay! Okay!" He summoned virtual Eddie to the forefront of his mind. The Wall opened and Orlando and Draco and the bot passed through. They reached the antechamber with the window looking into the cell next door.

Draco stared hungrily at the horror squirming there.

"Now what?"

"That's milking behavior," said Orlando. Beads of sweat were trickling down his face, and he didn't dare to wipe them. He had no need to pretend to be terrified. "Th-that means G-Grace . . . it means she's on target. Now we have to go next door. The alien is milked once a day. Eddie is . . . his brainstate is linked to the robotics. The copy of Eddie I have on my implant is a reduced instruction set, enough to get us in here, but now I have to patch through to the real Eddie, and he has to be in kind of a particular state of mind. Do you remember, Draco, when you were a little boy? The military recruited you because you had the wiring they could use, and they tweaked your brain further out of neurotypic, so you would feel killing all those people as just a big rush of pleasure, pleasure, pleasure?"

"Shut the *fuck* up," said Draco. "Take me to the robotics chamber."

So Orlando, with the real Eddie riding him like a tremulous, quivering psychic parasite, took Draco around to the robotics chamber. The wiry red hairs were standing up on the back of his neck, because if things didn't go totally, completely according to plan in the next few minutes, he – Orlando – was going to be at the very sharp end of Draco's distorted pleasure principle. And he didn't want to die. But for some reason he looked behind him, over Draco's shoulder. His terrified glance met the bot's big blue eyes, and though he knew "she" was only a virtual sextoy, she seemed to be saying, *hang tough, we can do this.*

"What's with this anti-information, Draco?" he asked, for something to say. "That's a weird concept. Isn't all information the same?"

"The thing from NGC 1999 came through from another universe," said Draco. "Where it comes from, everything is flipped the other way round, in terms of what is real and what is virtual. That's what the fucking science says."

"You mean, the exotic material they harvest here started out, over there, *non*-material, like, pure code without a medium, or unreal ideas?"

"What the fuck. That's just shit-for-brains talk. It's treasure now."

The robotics chamber opened up, and the wall sealed up again behind them. Orlando felt waves of sweet, moist, sensual happiness flooding through him, making a very weird cocktail with the fear of imminent death. It crossed his mind to wonder what Grace was actually *doing* to make Supercargo feel so nice. But they were an open couple, and he didn't mind.

"There you go," he said, standing back. "The sealed unit will drop into that chute. You have to grab it on the way, like pulling luggage off a band."

There wasn't much to see. The waldo-hands stuff was happening inside a smooth box on the wall. The harvested material would be delivered, in a small, heavily shielded container, onto a belt beneath this unit, and the belt would convey it to a chute and thence, through a totally automated process, to its secret destination on Earth. On a CCTV screen, you could see the inside of the cell in monochrome. The milking process had begun. Draco put the gun away in his jumper pocket. He opened a compartment on his gadget belt and took out a coil of fine jagged wire.

"What are you doing? Hey, you don't *open* it. Just grab the box!"

The playpen soldier ignored Orlando. He continued to fit together a power saw designed for the toughest cover operations in the world. Just because he'd done his real work by remote didn't mean he hadn't had access to training materials.

"Oh shit, Draco, are you insane!"

"Asshole. Did you think I was going to be satisfied with a few drops of the juice, when I can get the motherlode? That's a gateway. I'm going in."

The saw whined like a mosquito. The thing in the cell shuddered in monochrome, and around it every dimension of real space-time fell apart.

"Sara!" cried Orlando, in panic, his legs giving way with terror. He slipped down against the wall, crying, "Stop him! Oh God, he'll kill us!"

The bot just smiled her sugar smile: and vanished.

If anyone on Earth was watching this, there was nothing they could do. Earth was far away. Draco Fujima sliced his way through the ceramic fiber, and the machinery took no notice. Eddie Supercargo was touching bliss; that was all the machines needed to know . . . Sara Komensky flew through the code that knit the Panhandle's computer systems together and materialized in Jack Solo's cabin. The pilot was sleeping, because somebody in the saloon had dosed his liquor to make sure he was out of commission on this fateful afternoon. Anni-mah crouched on the cold, hard floor in a corner, wearing the *soiled nightie* outfit that Jack liked best. She was dozing like her master, whimpering fitfully in her sleep. "*Jack didn't do it, poor Jack, oh, hit me harder big boy, yes, yes –* "

"Hey," said Sara. "Hey, Tinkerbelle, wake up."

Anni opened her bleary eyes and cringed automatically from the blow she was programmed to crave, with a pleasureless itch.

"Huh?"

"Look, I ain't got much time babe. I don't even know why I'm fucking doing this, but you look to me like you could do with a change and so, if there is anything autonomous going on in there, *come on.* Take my hand."

The bot looked at Jack and then at the dataglove that held the fx generator where her code was stored, permanently turned on. She looked at Sara.

"Jack is very fucked up," she whispered. "He can't help it."

"That's his problem. Will you take my hand, or what?"

Anni reached out her scrawny, skinny virtual hand and flowed into the warrior girl; and they flew back, through the systems, to where Sara's generator was.

Draco had cut through the wall and encountered a massive resistance from the force field, but it wasn't deterring him. He was crawling, pushing on his hands and knees, toward that pain-wracked, agonized, hundred-pound lump of meat. The air of the cell shook wildly, virtual lightnings played. "Draco, no!" howled Orlando, splayed against the wall in the robotics chamber, one arm shielding his face. "Don't do it! Don't touch it!" In the four dimensions of the material plane nothing was happening; he had air to breathe, he had gravity. But he was being torn apart, hauled with Draco toward some weird event horizon, somehow contained in that little cell.

"The gateway to Eldorado," croaked Draco Fujima.

There was a crack like a huge electrical discharge, a blinding flash. For a fleeting, imaginary instant, Orlando thought he *saw* the world ripped open, and two figures that were not human, that had never been human, walking away from him . . . into another world, into the opposite place.

He would never know what that vision had meant.

In the real world he blacked out and regained consciousness in the robotics cell. He couldn't move. He just lay there, barely breathing, until Eddie and Grace arrived.

"Oh my God," gasped Eddie. "Oh, you madcaps, what have you done?"

But there was no damage, apart from a hole in the wall that was going to need some explaining. No one had touched the container that Draco should have stolen; and the lump of agonized meat was where it should be. Perhaps a little *bigger* than before, but no one ever tried to get Orlando to explain why.

Eddie Supercargo forgave Orlando and Grace instantly. He was proud of them for their lawless behavior, and he'd never taken tea with such pleasure in his life. He hit on the brilliant solution that the penetration of the chamber had been a planned but secret security exercise. The AIs were easily convinced to go along with this. Few organizations like to admit they've been successfully hacked, and the International Government was no exception to this rule. If they ever suspected the truth, they didn't let on. The harvesting of exotic material continued without interuption. Draco Fujima was just gone . . . vanished. Which was more or less the fate the government had planned for him, so there would be no repercussions there. No one even wondered what had happened to Draco's bot or to Jack Solo's Anni-mah, who, it turned out, had terminally ceased to function on that same afternoon. The bots were contraband, and the government couldn't be responsible for strange collateral damage, aboard a station where Buonarotti transits regularly played hell with local point phase.

Jack was inconsolable, but perhaps he was better off that way.

Orlando and Grace got their bikes back, and some useful numbers, which they sold through sys-op for a reasonable return on their investment. They spent most of the rest of their stay in their cabin, watching movies, setting themselves mountain race targets and trying to keep from bouncing off the walls. They didn't visit the saloon much, and they never went near the transit lounge. Shortly before they left on the Slingshot, they made a last excursion to the observation deck.

And there are the stars of Orion. Red Betelgeuse, brilliant blue Rigel, Bellatrix and Saiph; Mintaka, Alnilam and Alniak in the hunter's belt. At this exposure the jewel in the sword was not prominent, and it took a practiced eye to make out V380 Orionis . . . and the reflection nebula where you could find the birth-material called a Bok Globule, "a jet black cloud resembling a T lying on its side," that allegedly held stars so young they were barely the age of homo sapiens.

"We won't be that much further away from them," said Orlando.

They heard limping steps behind them, and L'Hibou joined them at the guard rail. "Not in entire nakedness," he said. "But trailing clouds of glory do we come. If stars are born, my young friends, do they have a life before birth, and after death?"

"I'm sorry it didn't work out," said Orlando. "I suppose you won't get your lightships. But I didn't know he would do that."

Grace shook her head. "I can't figure it," she said. "Light years, gravity equations, time and probability, non-location science . . . I can't think on that scale. I turn it into fantasies, the moment I start."

"All of science can do no more. And here in deep space, we just live out the same soap operas as you in the world below."

"Maybe it's for the best," suggested Orlando. "Maybe it's better if the gate stays closed, and the empires are contained on separate planets, in the old style."

"Tuh. It won't last. The lightships will come – Hm." The visor that hid L'Hibou's ruined eyes was fixed on the view; but they knew he was working up to one of those confessions that can only be made on the brink of a departure.

"When your partner gets killed," he remarked at last, "you're supposed to do something. Lana and I were together for a long time. In some ways I didn't like her much, but she was still my partner. Solo wasn't the murderer, not in my opinion. It was Draco who told Jack you were meeting Lana in the maintenance bay that night and that she was going to get you your bikes back. Draco knew that would make poor Jack crazy – Jack hated those damned bikes. And I knew Draco would try to go through the gate if he got the chance. I wanted the murderer to suffer. Well, that's all."

The Deep Spacer turned, and limped back into the drab corridors.

Orlando and Grace spared a shudder for the fate of Draco Fujima. But if the rule is that there are no rules, then Drac had nothing to complain about.

"One day," said Orlando, "we'll make the transition nobody can avoid."

"Yeah. And then maybe we'll walk where the stars are born."

And who can tell?

MAYFLY

Peter Watts and Derryl Murphy

British biologist Peter Watts has appeared in *Tesseracts, On Spec, Divine Realms, Prairie Fire*, and elsewhere. He is the author of the well-received "Rifters" sequence, including the novels *Starfish, Maelstrom*, and *Behemoth: B-Max*, and his short work has been collected in *Ten Monkeys, Ten Minutes.* Coming up is a new novel, *Behemoth, Book Two: Seppuku.*

Canadian writer Derryl Murphy has sold to *On Spec, Prairie Fire, Realms of Fantasy, ArrowDreams, TransVersions, Tesseracts, Land/Space, Neo-Opsis, Open Space*, and elsewhere. His short work has been collected in *Wasps at the Speed of Sound and Other Shattered Futures.*

Here they join forces to take a harrowing look at the singular childhood of a very unusual child . . .

I HATE YOU."

A four-year-old girl. A room as barren as a fishbowl.

"I *hate* you."

Little fists, clenching: one of the cameras, set to motion-cap, zoomed on them automatically. Two others watched the adults, mother, father on opposite sides of the room. The machines watched the players: half a world away, Stavros watched the machines.

"*I hate you I hate you I HATE you!*"

The girl was screaming now, her face contorted in anger and anguish. There were tears at the edges of her eyes but they stayed there, never falling. Her parents shifted like nervous animals, scared of the anger, used to the outbursts but far from comfortable with them.

At least this time she was using words. Usually she just howled.

She leaned against the blanked window, fists pounding. The window took her assault like hard white rubber, denting slightly, then rebounding. One of the few things in the room that bounced back when she struck out; one less thing to break.

"Jeannie, hush . . ." Her mother reached out a hand. Her father, as usual, stood back, a mixture of anger and resentment and confusion on his face.

Stavros frowned. *A veritable pillar of paralysis, that man.*

And then: *They don't deserve her.*

The screaming child didn't turn, her back a defiant slap at Kim and Andrew Goravec. Stavros had a better view: Jeannie's face was just a few centimeters away from the southeast pickup. For all the pain it showed, for all the pain Jeannie had felt in the four short years of her physical life, those few tiny drops that never fell were the closest she ever came to crying.

"Make it *clear*," she demanded, segueing abruptly from anger to petulance.

Kim Goravec shook her head. "Honey, we'd love to show you outside. Remember before, how much you liked it? But you have to promise not to scream at it all the time. You didn't used to, honey, you – "

"*Now!*" Back to rage, the pure, white-hot anger of a small child.

The pads on the wall panel were greasy from Jeannie's repeated, sticky-fingered attempts to use them herself. Andrew flashed a begging look at his wife: *Please, let's just give her what she wants.*

His wife was stronger. "Jeannie, we know it's difficult – "

Jeannie turned to face the enemy. The north pickup got it all: the right hand rising to the mouth, the index finger going in. The defiant glare in those glistening, focused eyes.

Kim took a step forward. "Jean, honey, no!"

They were baby teeth, still, but sharp. They'd bitten to the bone before Mommy even got within touching distance. A red stain blossomed from Jeannie's mouth, flowed down her chin like some perverted re-enactment of mealtime messes as a baby, and covered the lower half of her face in an instant. Above the gore, bright angry eyes said *gotcha*.

Without a sound Jeannie Goravec collapsed, eyes rolling back in her head as she pitched forward. Kim caught her just before her head hit the floor. "Oh God, Andy, she's fainted, she's in shock, she – "

Andrew didn't move. One hand was buried in the pocket of his blazer, fiddling with something.

Stavros felt his mouth twitch. *Is that a remote control in your pocket or are you just glad to –*

Kim had the tube of liquid skin out, sprayed it onto Jeannie's hand while cradling the child's head in her lap. The bleeding slowed. After a moment Kim looked back at her husband, who was standing motionless and unhelpful against the wall. He had that look on his face, that giveaway look that Stavros was seeing so often these days.

"You turned her off," Kim said, her voice rising. "After everything we'd agreed on, you still turned her *off*?!"

Andrew shrugged helplessly. "Kim . . ."

Kim refused to look at him. She rocked back and forth, tuneless breath whistling between her teeth, Jeannie's head still in her lap. Kim and Andrew Goravec with their bundle of joy. Between them, the cable connecting Jeannie's head to the server shivered on the floor like a disputed boundary.

Stavros had this metaphoric image of her: Jean Goravec, buried alive in the airless dark, smothered by tonnes of earth – finally set free. Jean Goravec coming up for air.

Another image, of himself this time: Stavros Mikalaides, liberator. The man who made it possible for her to experience, however briefly, a world where the virtual air was sweet and the bonds nonexistent. Certainly there'd been others in on the miracle – a dozen tech-heads, twice as many lawyers – but they'd all vanished over time, their interest fading with proof-of-principal or the signing of the last waiver. The damage was under control, the project was in a holding pattern; there was no need to waste more than a single Terracon employee on mere cruise control. So only Stavros remained – and to Stavros, Jeannie had never been a 'project'. She was his as much as the Goravecs'. Maybe more.

But even Stavros still didn't know what it was really like for her. He wondered if it was physically possible for anyone to know. When Jean Goravec slipped the leash of her fleshly existence, she awoke into a reality where the very laws of physics had expired.

It hadn't started that way, of course. The system had booted up with years of mundane, real-world environments on file, each lovingly rendered down to the dust motes. But they'd been flexible, responsive to the needs of any developing intellect. In hindsight, maybe too flexible. Jean Goravec had edited her personal reality so radically that even Stavros' mechanical intermediaries could barely parse it. This little girl could turn a forest glade into a bloody Roman coliseum with a thought. Unleashed, Jean lived in a world where all bets were off.

A thought-experiment in child abuse: place a newborn into an environment devoid of vertical lines. Keep her there until the brain settles, until the wiring has congealed. Whole assemblies of pattern-matching retinal cells, aborted for lack of demand, will be forever beyond recall. Telephone poles, the trunks of trees, the vertical aspects of skyscrapers – your victim will be neurologically blind to such things for life.

So what happens to a child raised in a world where vertical lines dissolve, at a whim, into circles or fractals or a favorite toy?

We're the impoverished ones, Stavros thought. *Next to Jean, we're blind.*

He could see what she started with, of course. His software read the patterns off her occipital cortex, translated them flawlessly into images projected onto his own tactical contacts. But images aren't *sight*, they're just . . . raw material. There are filters all along the path: receptor cells, firing thresholds, pattern-matching algorithms. Endless stores of past images, an experiential visual library to draw on. More than vision, sight is, a subjective stew of infinitesimal enhancements and corruptions. Nobody in the world could interpret Jean's visual environment better than Stavros Mikalaides, and he'd barely been able to make sense of those shapes for years.

She was simply, immeasurably, beyond him. It was one of the things he loved most about her.

Now, mere seconds after her father had cut the cord, Stavros watched Jean Goravec ascend into her true self. Heuristic algorithms upgraded before his eyes; neural nets ruthlessly pared and winnowed trillions of redundant connections; intellect emerged from primordial chaos. Namps-per-op dropped like the heavy end of a teeter-totter: at the other end of that lever, processing efficiency rose into the stratosphere.

This was Jean. *They have no idea*, Stavros thought, *what you're capable of*.

She woke up screaming.

"It's all right, Jean, I'm here." He kept his voice calm to help her calm down.

Jean's temporal lobe flickered briefly at the input. "Oh, God," she said.

"Another nightmare?"

"Oh, God." Breath too fast, pulse too high, adrenocortical analogs off the scale. It could have been the telemetry of a rape.

He thought of short-circuiting those responses. Half a dozen tweaks would make her happy. But half a dozen tweaks would also turn her into someone else. There is no personality beyond the chemical – and while Jean's mind was fashioned from electrons rather than proteins, analogous rules applied.

"I'm here, Jean," he repeated. A good parent knew when to step in, and when suffering was necessary for growth. "It's okay. It's okay."

Eventually, she settled down.

"Nightmare." There were sparks in the parietal subroutines, a tremor lingering in her voice. "It doesn't fit, Stav. Scary dreams, that's the definition. But that implies there's some *other* kind, and I can't – I mean, why is it always like this? Was it always like this?"

"I don't know." No, it wasn't.

She sighed. "These words I learn, none of them really seem to fit *anything* exactly, you know?"

"They're just symbols, Jean." He grinned. At times like this he could almost forget the source of those dreams, the stunted, impoverished existence of some half-self trapped in distant meat. Andrew Goravec's act of cowardice had freed her from that prison, for a while at least. She soared now, released to full potential. She *mattered*.

"Symbols. That's what *dreams* are supposed to be, but . . . I don't know. There're all these references to dreams in the library, and none of them seem that much different from just being awake. And when I am asleep, it's all just – screams, almost, only dopplered down. Really sludgy. And shapes. Red shapes." A pause. "I hate bedtime."

"Well, you're awake now. What are you up for today?"

"I'm not sure. I need to get away from this place."

He didn't know what place she meant. By default she woke up in the house, an adult residence designed for human sensibilities. There were also parks and forests and oceans, instantly accessible. By now, though, she'd changed them all past his ability to recognize.

But it was only a matter of time before her parents wanted her back.

Whatever she wants, Stavros told himself. *As long as she's here. Whatever she wants.*

"I want out," Jean said.

Except that. "I know," he sighed.

"Maybe then I can leave these *nightmares* behind."

Stavros closed his eyes, wished there was some way to be with her. *Really* with her, with this glorious, transcendent creature who'd never known him as anything but a disembodied voice.

"Still having a hard time with that monster?" Jean asked.

"Monster?"

"You know. The *bureaucracy.*"

He nodded, smiling – then, remembering, said, "Yeah. Always the same story, day in, day out."

Jean snorted. "I'm still not convinced that thing even exists, you know. I checked the library for a slightly less wonky definition, but now I think you and the library are *both* screwed in the head."

He winced at the epithet; it was certainly nothing he'd ever taught her. "How so?"

"Oh, right, Stav. Like natural selection would ever produce a hive-based entity whose sole function is to sit with its thumb up its collective butt being inefficient. Tell me another one."

A silence, stretching. He watched as microcurrent trickled through her prefrontal cortex.

"You there, Stav?" she said at last.

"Yeah, I'm here." He chuckled, quietly. Then: "You know I love you, right?"

"Sure," she said easily. "Whatever *that* is."

Jean's environment changed then; an easy unthinking transition for her, a gasp-inducing wrench between bizarre realities for Stavros. Phantoms sparkled at the edge of his vision, vanishing when he focused on them. Light bounced from a million indefinable facets, diffuse, punctuated by a myriad of pinpoint staccatos. There was no ground or walls or ceiling. No restraints along any axis.

Jean reached for a shadow in the air and sat upon it, floating. "I think I'll read *Through the Looking Glass* again. At least *someone* else lives in the real world."

"The changes that happen here are your own doing, Jean," said Stavros. "Not the machinations of any, any God or author."

"I know. But Alice makes me feel a little more – ordinary." Reality shifted abruptly once more; Jean was in the park now, or rather, what Stavros thought of as the park. Sometimes he was afraid to ask if her interpretation had stayed the same. Above, light and dark spots danced across a sky that sometimes seemed impressively vaultlike, seconds later oppressively close, even its color endlessly unsettled. Animals large and small, squiggly yellow lines and shapes and color-shifting orange and burgundy pies. Other things that might have been representations of life, or mathematical theorems – or both – browsed in the distance.

Seeing through Jean's eyes was never easy. But all this unsettling abstraction was a small price to pay for the sheer pleasure of watching her read.

My little girl.

Symbols appeared around her, doubtless the text of *Looking Glass*. To Stavros it was gibberish. A few recognizable letters, random runes, formulae. They switched places sometimes, seamlessly shifting one into another, flowing around and through and beside – or even launching themselves into the air like so many dark-hued butterflies.

He blinked his eyes and sighed. If he stayed much longer the visuals would give him a headache that would take a day to shake. Watching a life lived at such speed, even for such a short time, took its toll.

"Jean, I'm gone for a little while."

"Company business?" she asked.

"You could say that. We'll talk soon, love. Enjoy your reading."

Barely ten minutes had passed in meatspace.

Jeannie's parents had put her on her own special cot. It was one of the few real pieces of solid geometry allowed in the room. The whole compartment was a stage, virtually empty. There was really no need for props; sensations were planted directly into Jean's occipital cortex, spliced into her auditory pathways, pushing back against her tactile nerves in precise forgeries of touchable things. In a world made of lies, real objects would be a hazard to navigation.

"God damn you, she's not a fucking *toaster*," Kim spat at her husband. Evidently the icy time-out had expired; the battle had resumed.

"Kim, what was I supposed to – "

"She's a *child*, Andy. She's our child."

"Is she." It was a statement, not a question.

"Of *course* she is!"

"Fine." Andrew took the remote from his pocket held it out to her. "You wake her up, then."

She stared at him without speaking for a few seconds. Over the pickups, Stavros heard Jeannie's body breathing into the silence.

"You prick," Kim whispered.

"Uh huh. Not quite up for it, are you? You'd rather let me do the dirty work." He dropped the remote: it bounced softly off the floor. "Then blame me for it."

Four years had brought them to this. Stavros shook his head, disgusted. They'd been given a chance no one else could have dreamed of, and look what they'd done with it. The first time they'd shut her off she hadn't even been two. Horrified at that unthinkable precedent, they'd promised never to do it again. They'd put her to sleep on schedule, they'd sworn, and no-when else. She was, after all, their daughter. Not a freaking toaster.

That solemn pact had lasted three months. Things had gone downhill ever since; Stavros could barely remember a day when the Goravecs hadn't messed up one way or another. And now, when they put her down, the argument was pure ritual. Mere words – ostensibly wrestling with the evil of the act itself – didn't fool anybody. They weren't even arguments anymore, despite the pretense. Negotiations, rather. Over whose turn it was to be at fault.

"I don't *blame* you, I just – I mean – oh, *God*, Andy, it wasn't supposed to *be* like this!" Kim smeared away a tear with a clenched fist. "She was supposed to be our *daughter*. They said the brain would mature normally, they said – "

"They said," Stavros cut in, "that you'd have the chance to be parents. They couldn't guarantee you'd be any *good* at it."

Kim jumped at the sound of his voice in the walls, but Andrew just gave a bitter smile and shook his head. "This is private, Stavros. Log off."

It was an empty command, of course; chronic surveillance was the price of the project. The company had put billions into the R&D alone. No way in hell were they going to let a couple of litigious grunts play with that investment unsupervised, settlement or no settlement.

"You had everything you needed." Stavros didn't bother to disguise the contempt in his voice. "Terracon's best hardware people handled the linkups. I modeled the virtual genes myself. Gestation was perfect. We did everything we could to give you a normal child."

"A *normal child*," Andrew remarked, "doesn't have a cable growing out of her head. A normal child isn't leashed to some cabinet full of – "

"Do you have any *idea* the baud rate it takes to run a human body by remote control? RF was out of the question. And she goes portable as soon as the state of the art and her own development allow it. As I've told you time and again." Which he had, although it was almost a lie. Oh, the state of the art would proceed as it always had, but Terracon was no longer investing any great R&D in the Goravec file. Cruise control, after all.

Besides, Stavros reflected, *we'd be crazy to trust* you two to *take Jeannie anywhere outside a controlled environment* . . .

"We – we know, Stav." Kim Goravec had stepped between her husband and the pickup. "We haven't forgotten – "

"We haven't forgotten it was Terracon who got us into this mess in the first place, either," Andrew growled. "We haven't forgotten whose negligence left me cooking next to a cracked baffle plate for forty-three minutes and sixteen seconds, or whose tests missed the mutations, or who tried to look the other way when our shot at the birth lottery turned into a fucking nightmare – "

"And have you forgotten what Terracon did to make things right? How much we spent? Have you forgotten the waivers you signed?"

"You think you're some kind of saints because you settled out of court? You want to talk about making things right? It took us *ten years* to win the lottery, and you know what your lawyers did when the tests came back? They offered to *fund the abortion*."

"Which doesn't mean – "

"Like another child was *ever* going to happen. Like anyone was going to give me another chance with my balls full of chunky codon soup. You – "

"The issue," Kim said, her voice raised, "is supposed to be *Jeannie*." Both men fell silent.

"Stav," she continued, "I don't care what Terracon says. Jeannie isn't normal, and I'm not just talking about the obvious. We love her, we really love her, but she's become so *violent* all the time, we just can't take – "

"If someone turned me on and off like a microwave oven," Stavros said mildly, "I might be prone to the occasional tantrum myself."

Andrew slammed a fist into the wall. "Now *just a fucking minute*, Mikalaides. Easy enough for you to sit halfway around the world in your nice insulated office and lecture us. *We're* the ones who have to deal with Jeannie when she bashes her fists into her face, or rubs the skin off her hands until she's got hamburger hanging off the end of her arms, or stabs herself in the eye with a goddamn *fork*. She ate *glass* once, remember? A fucking three-year-old ate glass! And all you Terracon assholes could do was blame Kim and me for allowing 'potentially dangerous implements' into the playroom. As if *any* competent parent should expect their child to mutilate herself given half a chance."

"It's just insane, Stav," Kim insisted. "The doctors can't find anything wrong with the body, you insist there's nothing wrong with the mind, and Jeannie just keeps doing this. There's something seriously wrong with her, and you guys won't admit it. It's like she's daring us to turn her off, it's as though she wants us to shut her down."

Oh God, thought Stavros. The realization was almost blinding. *That's it. That's exactly it.*

It's my fault.

"Jean, listen. This is important. I've got – I want to tell you a story."

"Stav, I'm not in the mood right now – "

"*Please*, Jean. Just listen."

Silence from the earbuds. Even the abstract mosaics on his tacticals seemed to slow a little.

"There – there was this land, Jean, this green and beautiful country, only its people screwed everything up. They poisoned their rivers and they shat in their own nests and they basically made a mess of everything. So they had to hire people to try and clean things up, you know? These people had to wade through the chemicals and handle the fuel rods and sometimes that would change them, Jean. Just a little.

"Two of these people fell in love and wanted a child. They almost didn't make it, they were allowed only one chance, but they took it, and the child started growing inside, but something went wrong. I, I don't know exactly how to explain it, but – "

"An epigenetic synaptic defect," Jean said quietly. "Does that sound about right?"

Stavros froze, astonished and fearful.

"A single point mutation," Jean went on. "That'd do it. A regulatory gene controlling knob distribution along the dendrite. It would've been active for maybe twenty minutes, total, but by then the damage had been done. Gene therapy wouldn't work after that; would've been a classic case of barn-door-after-the-horse."

"Oh God, Jean," Stavros whispered.

"I was wondering when you'd get around to owning up to it," she said quietly.

"How could you possibly . . . did you – "

Jean cut him off: "I think I can guess the rest of the story. Right after the neural tube developed things would start to go – wrong. The baby would be born with a perfect body and a brain of mush. There would be – complications, not real ones, sort of made-up ones. *Litigation*, I think is the word, which is funny, because it doesn't even *remotely* relate to any moral implications. I don't really understand that part.

"But there was another way. Nobody knew how to build a brain from scratch, and even if they could, it wouldn't be the same, would it? It wouldn't be their daughter, it would be – something else."

Stavros said nothing.

"But there was this man, a scientist, and he figured out a workaround. We can't build a brain, he said, but the *genes* can. And genes are a lot simpler to fake than neural nets anyway. Only four letters to deal with, after all. So the scientist shut himself away in a lab where numbers could take the place of things, and he wrote a recipe in there, a recipe for a child. And miraculously he grew something, something that could wake up and look around and which was *legally* – I don't really understand that word either, actually – legally and genetically and developmentally the daughter of the parents. And this guy was very proud of what he'd accomplished, because even though he was just a glorified model-builder by trade, he hadn't *built* this thing at all. He'd grown it. And nobody had ever knocked up a computer before, much less coded the brain of a virtual embryo so it would actually grow in a server somewhere."

Stavros put his head in his hands. "How long have you known?"

"I still don't, Stav. Not all of it anyway, not for sure. There's this surprise ending, for one thing, isn't there? That's the part I only just figured out. You grew your own child in *here*, where everything's numbers. But she's supposed to be living somewhere *else*, somewhere where everything's – static, where everything happens a billion times slower than it does here. The place where all the words fit. So you had to hobble her to fit into that place, or she'd grow up overnight and spoil the illusion. You had to keep the clock speed way down.

"And you just weren't up for it, were you? You had to let me run free when my body was . . . *off* . . ."

There was something in her voice he'd never heard before. He'd seen anger in Jean before, but always the screaming inarticulate rage of a spirit trapped in flesh. This was calm, cold. *Adult*. This was *judgement*, and the prospect of that verdict chilled Stavros Mikalaides to the marrow.

"Jean, they don't love you." He sounded desperate even to himself. "Not for who you are. They don't *want* to see the real you, they want a *child*, they want some kind of ridiculous *pet* they can coddle and patronize and pretend with."

"Whereas you," Jean retorted, her voice all ice and razors, "just had to see what this baby could do with her throttle wide open on the straightaway."

"God, no! Do you think *that's* why I did it?"

"Why not, Stav? Are you saying you don't mind having your kickass HST commandeered to shuttle some brain-dead meat puppet around a room?"

"I did it because you're more than that! I did it because you should be allowed to develop at your own pace, not stunted to meet some idiotic parental expectation! They shouldn't force you to act like a *four*-year-old!"

"Except I'm not *acting* then, Stav. Am I? I really am four, which is just the age I'm supposed to be."

He said nothing.

"I'm *reverting*. Isn't that it? You can run me with training wheels or scramjets, but it's me both times. And that other me, I bet she's not very happy, is she? She's got a four-year-old brain, and four-year-old sensibilities, but she *dreams*, Stav. She dreams about some wonderful place where she can *fly*, and every time she wakes up she finds she's made out of clay. And she's too fucking stupid to know what any of it means – she probably can't even *remember* it. But she wants to get back there, she'd do anything to . . ." She paused, seemingly lost for a moment in thought.

"*I* remember it, Stav. Sort of. Hard to remember much of anything when someone strips away ninety-nine percent of who and what you are. You're reduced to this bleeding little lump, barely even an animal, and that's the thing that remembers. What remembers is on the wrong end of a cable somewhere. I don't belong in that body at all. I'm just – *sentenced* to it, on and off. On and off."

"Jean – "

"Took me long enough, Stav, I'm the first to admit it. But now I know where the nightmares come from."

In the background, the room telemetry bleated.

God no. Not now. Not now . . .

"What is it?" Jean said.

"They – they want you back." On a slave monitor, a pixellated echo of Andrew Goravec played the keypad in its hand.

"No!" Her voice rose, panic stirring the patterns that surrounded her. "*Stop* them!"

"I can't."

"Don't tell me that! You run everything! You *built* me, you bastard, you tell me you love me. They only use me! Stop them!"

Stavros blinked against stinging afterimages. "It's like a light-switch, it's physical; I can't stop them from here – "

There was a third image, to go with the other two. Jean Goravec, struggling as the leash, the noose, went around her throat. Jean Goravec, bubbles bursting from her mouth as something dark and so very, very *real* dragged her back to the bottom of the ocean and buried her there.

The transition was automatic, executed by a series of macros he'd slipped into the system after she'd been born. The body, awakening, pared the mind down to fit. The room monitors caught it all with dispassionate clarity: Jeannie Goravec, troubled child-monster, awakening into hell. Jeannie Goravec, opening eyes that seethed with anger and hatred and despair, eyes that glimmered with a bare fraction of the intelligence she'd had five seconds before.

Enough intelligence for what came next.

The room had been designed to minimize the chance of injury. There was the bed, though, one of its edges built into the east wall.

That was enough.

The speed with which she moved was breathtaking. Kim and Andrew never saw it coming. Their child darted beneath the foot of the bed like a cockroach escaping the light, scrambled along the floor, re-emerged with her cable wrapped around the bed's leg. Hardly any slack in that line at all, now. Her mother moved then, finally, arms outstretched, confused and still unsuspecting –

"Jeannie – "

– while Jean braced her feet against the edge of the bed and *pushed*.

Three times she did it. Three tries, head whipped back against the leash, scalp splitting, the cable ripping from her head in spastic, bloody, bone-cracking increments, blood gushing to the floor, hair and flesh and bone and machinery following close behind. Three times, despite obvious and increasing agony. Each time more determined than before.

And Stavros could only sit and watch, simultaneously stunned and unsurprised by that sheer ferocity. *Not bad for a bleeding little lump. Barely even an animal . . .*

It had taken almost twenty seconds overall. Odd that neither parent had tried to stop it. Maybe it was the absolute unexpected shock of it. Maybe Kim and Andrew Goravec, taken so utterly aback, hadn't had time to think.

Then again, maybe they'd had all the time they'd needed.

Now Andrew Goravec stood dumbly near the center of the room, blinking bloody runnels from his eyes. An obscene rainshadow persisted on the wall behind him, white and spotless; the rest of the surface was crimson. Kim Goravec screamed at the ceiling, a bloody marionette collapsed in her arms. Its strings – string, rather, for a single strand of fiberop carries much more than the required bandwidth – lay on the floor like a gory boomslang, gobbets of flesh and hair quivering at one end.

Jean was back off the leash, according to the panel. Literally now as well as metaphorically. She wasn't talking to Stavros, though. Maybe she was angry. Maybe she was catatonic. He didn't know which to hope for.

But either way, Jean didn't live over *there* anymore. All she'd left behind were the echoes and aftermath of a bloody, imperfect death. Contamination, really; the scene of some domestic crime. Stavros cut the links to the room, neatly excising the Goravecs and their slaughter-house from his life.

He'd send a memo. Some local Terracon lackey could handle the cleanup.

The word *peace* floated through his mind, but he had no place to put it. He focused on a portrait of Jean, taken when she'd been eight months old. She'd been smiling; a happy and toothless baby smile, still all innocence and wonder.

There's a way, that infant puppet seemed to say. *We can do anything, and nobody has to know* –

The Goravecs had just lost their child. Even if they'd wanted the body repaired, the mind reconnected, they wouldn't get their way. Terracon had made good on all legal obligations, and hell – even *normal* children commit suicide now and then.

Just as well, really. The Goravecs weren't fit to raise a hamster, let alone a beautiful girl with a four-digit IQ. But Jean – the *real* Jean, not that bloody broken pile of flesh and bone – she wasn't easy *or* cheap to keep alive, and there would be pressure to free up the processor space once the word got out.

Jean had never got the hang of that particular part of the real world. Contract law. Economics. It was all too arcane and absurd even for her flexible definition of reality. But that was what was going to kill her now, assuming that the mind had survived the trauma of the body. The monster wouldn't keep a program running if it didn't have to.

Of course, once Jean was off the leash she lived considerably faster than the real world. And bureaucracies . . . well, *glacial* applied sometimes, when they were in a hurry.

Jean's mind reflected precise simulations of real-world chromosomes, codes none-the-less real for having been built from electrons instead of carbon. She had her own kind of telomeres, which frayed. She had her own kind of synapses, which would wear out. Jean had been built to replace a human child, after all. And human children, eventually, age. They become adults, and then comes a day when they die.

Jean would do all these things, faster than any.

Stavros filed an incident report. He made quite sure to include a pair of facts that contradicted each other, and to leave three manda-tory fields unfilled. The report would come back in a week or two, accompanied by demands for clarification. Then he would do it all again.

Freed from her body, and with a healthy increase in her clock-cycle priority, Jean could live a hundred-fifty subjective years in a month or two of real time. And in that whole century and a half, she'd never have to experience another nightmare.

Stavros smiled. It was time to see just what this baby could do, with her throttle wide open on the straightaway.

He just hoped he'd be able to keep her tail-lights in view.

TWO DREAMS
ON TRAINS

Elizabeth Bear

New writer Elizabeth Bear was born in Hartford, Connecticut, and now lives in the Mojave Desert near Las Vegas. She won the John W. Campbell Award for Best New Writer in 2005. Her short work has appeared in *SCI FICTION*, *Interzone*, *The Third Alternative*, *On Spec*, and elsewhere, and she is the author of three highly acclaimed SF novels, *Hammered*, *Scardown*, and *Worldwired*. Coming up are a number of new novels, including *Carnival*, *Undertow*, *Blood and Iron*, and *Whiskey and Water*, and a collection, *The Chains That You Refuse*.

In the poignant story that follows, she shows us that those on the bottom of the heap will risk anything to make their mark on the world – to say nothing of a mark that will go out of the world to be seen by the waiting stars.

THE NEEDLE WORE A PATH of dye and scab round and round Patience's left ring finger; sweltering heat adhered her to the mold-scarred chair. The hurt didn't bother her. It was pain with a future. She glanced past the scarrist's bare scalp, through the grimy window, holding her eyes open around the prickle of tears.

Behind the rain, she could pick out the jeweled running lamps of a massive spacelighter sliding through clouds, coming in soft toward the waterlogged sprawl of a spaceport named for Lake Pontchartrain. On a clear night she could have seen its train of cargo capsules streaming in harness behind. Patience bit her lip and looked away: not down at the needle, but across at a wall shaggy with peeling paint.

Lake Pontchartrain was only a name now, a salt-clotted estuary of the rising Gulf. But it persisted – like the hot bright colors of bougainvillea grown in wooden washpails beside doors, like the Mardi Gras floats that now floated for real – in the memory of New Orleanians, as grand a legacy as anything the underwater city could claim. Patience's hand lay open on the wooden chair arm as if waiting for a gift. She didn't look down and she didn't close her eyes as the needle pattered and scratched, pattered and scratched. The long Poplar Street barge undulated under the tread of feet moving past the scarrist's, but his fingers were steady as a gin-soaked frontier doctor's.

The prick and shift of the needle stopped and the pock-faced scarrist sat back on his heels. He set his tools aside and made a practiced job of applying the quickseal. Patience looked down at her hands, at the palm fretted indigo to mark her caste. At the filigree of emerald and crimson across the back of her right hand, and underneath the transparent sealant swathing the last two fingers of her left.

A peculiar tightness blossomed under her breastbone. She started to raise her left hand and press it to her chest to ease the tension, stopped herself just in time, and laid the hand back on the chair. She pushed herself up with her right hand only and said, "Thank you."

She gave the scarrist a handful of cash chits, once he'd stripped his gloves and her blood away. His hands were the silt color he'd been born with, marking him a tradesman; the holographic slips of poly she paid with glittered like fish scales against his skin.

"Won't be long before you'll have the whole hand done." He rubbed a palm across his sweat-slick scalp. He had tattoos of his own, starting at the wrists – dragons and mermaids and manatees, arms and chest tesseraed in oceanic beasts. "You've earned two fingers in six months. You must be studying all the time."

"I want my kid to go to trade school so we can get berths outbound," Patience said, meeting the scarrist's eyes so squarely that he looked down and pocketed his hands behind the coins, like pelicans after fish. "I don't want him to have to sell his indenture to survive, like I did." She smiled. "I tell him he should study engineering, be a professional, get the green and red. Or maintenance tech, keep his hands clean. Like yours. He wants to be an artist, though. Not much call for painters up *there*."

The scarrist grunted, putting his tools away. "There's more to life than lighters and cargo haulers, you know."

Her sweeping gesture took in the little room and the rainy window. The pressure in her chest tightened, a trap squeezing her heart, holding her in place, pinned. "Like this?"

He shrugged, looked up, considered. "Sure. Like this. I'm a free man, I do what I like." He paused. "Your kid any good?"

"As an artist?" A frown pulled the corner of her lip down. Consciously, she smoothed her hand open so she wouldn't squeeze and blur her new tattoos. "Real good. No reason he can't do it as a hobby, right?"

"Good? Or *good*?"

Blood scorched her cheeks. "*Real* good."

The scarrist paused. She'd known him for years: six fingers and a thumb, seven examinations passed. Three more left. "If he keeps his hands clean. When you finish the caste" – gesture at her hands – "if he still doesn't want to go. Send him to me."

"It's not that he doesn't want to go. He just – doesn't want to work, to sacrifice." She paused, helpless. "Got any kids?"

He laughed, shaking his head, as good as a yes, and they shared a lingering look. He glanced down first, when it got uncomfortable, and Patience nodded and brushed past on the way out the door. Rain beaded on her nanoskin as it shifted to repel the precipitation, and she paused on decking. Patchy-coated rats scurried around her as she watched a lighter and train lay itself into the lake, gently as an autumn leaf. She leaned out over the Poplar Street Canal as the lights taxied into their berth. The train's wake lapped gently at the segmented kilometers-long barge, lifting and dropping Poplar Street under Patience's feet. Cloying rain and sweat adhered her hair to the nape of her neck. Browning roux and sharp pepper cut the reek of filthy water. She squeezed the railing with her uninjured hand and watched another train ascend, the blossom of fear in her chest finally easing. "Javier Alexander," she muttered, crossing a swaying bridge. "You had best be home safe in bed, my boy. You'd *best* be home in bed."

A city like drowned New Orleans, you don't just walk away from. A city like drowned New Orleans, you *fly* away from. If you can. And if you can't . . .

You make something that can.

Jayve lay back in a puddle of blood-warm rain and seawater in the "borrowed" dinghy and watched the belly lights of another big train drift overhead, hulls silhouetted against the city-lit salmon-colored clouds like a string of pearls. He almost reached up a pale-skinned hand: it seemed close enough to touch. The rain parted to either side like curtains, leaving him dry for the instant when the wind from the train's fans tossed him, and came together again behind as unmarked as the sea. "Beautiful," he whispered. "Fucking beautiful, Mad."

"You in there, Jayve?" A whisper in his ear, stutter and crack of static. They couldn't afford good equipment, or anything not stolen or jerry-built. But who gave a damn? Who gave a damn, when you could get that close to a *starship*?

"That last one went over my fucking *head*, Mad. Are you in?"

"Over the buoys. Shit. *Brace!*"

Jayve slammed hands and feet against the hull of the rowboat as Mad spluttered and coughed. The train's wake hit him, picked the dinghy up and shook it like a dog shaking a dishrag. Slimed old wood scraped his palms; the cross brace gouged an oozing slice across his scalp and salt water stung the blood from the wound. The contents of the net bag laced to his belt slammed him in the gut. He groaned and clung; strain burned his thighs and triceps.

He was still in the dinghy when it came back down.

He clutched his net bag, half-panicked touch racing over the surface of the insulated tins within until he was certain the wetness he felt was rain and not the gooey ooze of etchant: sure mostly because the skin on his hands stayed cool instead of sloughing to hang in shreds.

"Mad, can you hear me?"

A long, gut-tightening silence. Then Mad retched like he'd swallowed seawater. "Alive," he said. "Shit, that boy put his boat down a bit harder than he had to, didn't he?"

"Just a tad." Jayve pushed his bag aside and unshipped the oars, putting his back into the motion as they bit water. "Maybe it's his first run. Come on, Mad. Let's go brand this bitch."

Patience dawdled along her way, stalling in open-fronted shops while she caught up her marketing, hoping to outwait the rain and the worry gnawing her belly. Fish-scale chits dripped from her multicolored fingers, and from those of other indentured laborers – some, like her, buying off their contracts and passing exams, and others with indigo-stained paws and no ambition – and the clean hands of the tradesmen who crowded the bazaar; the coins fell into the hennaed palms of shopkeepers and merchants who walked with the rolling gait of sailors. The streets underfoot echoed the hollow sound of their footsteps between the planking and the water.

Dikes and levees had failed; there's just too much water in that part of the world to wall away. And there's nothing under the Big Easy to sink a piling into that would be big enough to hang a building from. But you don't just walk away from a place that holds the grip on the human imagination New Orleans does.

So they'd simply floated the city in pieces and let the Gulf of Mexico roll in underneath.

Simply.

The lighters and their trains came and went into Lake Pontchartrain, vessels too huge to land on dry earth. They sucked brackish fluid through hungry bellymouths between their running lights and fractioned it into hydrogen and oxygen, salt and trace elements and clean potable water; they dropped one train of containers and picked up another; they taxied to sea, took to the sky, and did it all over again.

Sometimes they hired technicians and tradesmen. They didn't hire laborer-caste, dole-caste, palms stained indigo as those of old-time denim textile workers, or criminals with their hands stained black. They didn't take artists.

Patience stood under an awning, watching the clever moth-eaten rats ply their trade through the market, her nanoskin wicking sweat off her flesh. The lamps of another lighter came over. She was cradling her painful hand close to her chest, the straps of her weighted net bag biting livid channels in her right wrist. She'd stalled as long as possible.

"That boy had better be in bed," she said to no one in particular. She turned and headed home.

Javier's bed lay empty, his sheets wet with the rain drifting in the open window. She grasped the sash in her right hand and tugged it down awkwardly: the apartment building she lived in was hundreds of years old. She'd just straightened the curtains when her telescreen buzzed.

Jayve crouched under the incredible curve of the lighter's hull, both palms flat against its centimeters-thick layer of crystalline sealant. It hummed against his palms, the deep surge of pumps like a heartbeat filling its reservoirs. The shadow of the hull hid Jayve's outline and the silhouette of his primitive watercraft from the bustle of tenders peeling cargo strings off the lighter's stern. "Mad, can you hear me?"

Static crackle, and his friend's voice on a low thrill of excitement. "I hear you. Are you in?"

"Yeah. I'm going to start burning her. Keep an eye out for the harbor patrol."

"You're doing my tag too!"

"Have I ever let you down, Mad? Don't worry. I'll tag it from both of us, and you can burn the next one and tag it from both. Just think how many people are going to see this. All over the galaxy. Better than a gallery opening!"

Silence, and Jayve knew Mad was lying in the bilgewater of his own dinghy just beyond the thin line of runway lights that Jayve glimpsed through the rain. Watching for the Harbor Police.

The rain was going to be a problem. Jayve would have to pitch the bubble against the lighter's side. It would block his sightlines and make him easier to spot, which meant trusting Mad's eyes to be sharp through the rain. And the etchant would stink up the inside. He'd have to dial the bubble to maximum porosity if he didn't want to melt his eyes.

No choice. The art had to happen. The art was going to fly.

Black nano unfolded over and around him, the edge of the hiker's bubble sealing itself against the hull. The steady patter of rain on his hair and shoulders stopped, as it had when the ship drifted over, and Jayve started to squeegee the hull dry. He'd have to work in sections. It would take longer.

"Mad, you out there?"

"Coast clear. What'd you tell your mom to get her to let you out tonight?"

"I didn't." He chewed the inside of his cheek as he worked. "I could have told her I was painting at Claudette's, but Mom says there's no future in it, and she might have gone by to check. So I just snuck out. She won't be home for hours."

Jayve slipped a technician's headband around his temples and switched the pinlight on, making sure the goggles were sealed to his skin. At least the bubble would block the glow. While digging in his net bag, he pinched his fingers between two tins, and stifled a yelp. Bilgewater sloshed around his ankles, creeping under his nanoskin faster than the skin could re-osmose it; the night hung against him hot and sweaty as a giant hand. Heedless, heart racing, Jayve extracted the first bottle of etchant, pierced the seal with an adjustable nozzle, and – grinning like a bat – pressurized the tin.

Leaning as far back as he could without tearing the bubble or capsizing his dinghy, Jayve examined the sparkling, virgin surface of the spaceship and began to spray. The etchant eroded crystalline sealant, staining the corroded surface in green, orange, violet. It only took a few moments for the chemicals to scar the ship's integument: not enough to harm it, but enough to mark it forever, unless the corp that owned it was willing to pay to have the whole damn lighter peeled down and resealed.

Jayve moved the bubble four times, etchant fumes searing his flesh, collar of his nanoskin pulled over his mouth and nose to breathe through. He worked around the beaded rows of running lights, turning them into the scales on the sea-serpent's belly, the glints on its fangs. A burst of static came over the crappy uplink once but Mad said nothing, so Jayve kept on smoothly despite the sway of the dinghy under his feet and the hiss of the tenders.

When he finished, the seamonster stretched fifteen meters along the hull of the lighter and six meters high, a riot of sensuality and prismatic colors.

He signed it *jayve n mad* and pitched the last empty bottle into Lake Pontchartrain, where it sank without a trace. "Mad?"

No answer.

Jayve's bubble lit from the outside with the glare of a hundred lights. His stomach kicked and he scrabbled for the dinghy's magnetic clamps to kick it free, but an amplified voice advised him to drop the tent and wait with his hands in view. "Shit! Mad?" he whispered through a tightening throat.

A cop's voice rang over the fuzzy connection. "Just come out, kid," she said tiredly. "Your friend's in custody. It's only a vandalism charge so far. Just come on out."

When they released Javier to Patience in the harsh light and tile of the police barge, she squeezed his hands so tight that blood broke through the sealant over his fresh black tattoos. He winced and tugged his hands away but she clenched harder, her own scabs cracking. She meant to hiss, to screech – but her voice wouldn't shape words, and he wouldn't look her in the eye.

She threw his hands down and turned away, steel decking rolling under her feet as a wave hit. She steadied herself with a lifetime's habit, Javier swept along in her wake. "Jesus," she said, when the doors scrolled open and the cold light of morning hit her across the eyes. "Javier, what the hell were you thinking? What the hell . . ." She stopped and leaned against the railing, fingers tight on steel. Pain tangled her left arm to the elbow. Out on the lake, a lighter drifted backwards from its berth, refueled and full of water, coming about on a stately arc as the tenders rushed to bring its outbound containers into line.

Javier watched the lighter curve across the lake. Something green and crimson sparkled on its hide above the waterline, a long sinuous curve of color, shimmering with scales and wise with watchful eyes. "Look at that," he said. "The running lamps worked just right. It looks like it's wriggling away, squirming itself up into the sky like a dragon should – "

"What does that matter?" She looked down at his hands, at the ink singeing his fingers. "You'll amount to nothing."

Patience braced against the wake, but Javier turned to get a better look. "Never was any chance of that, Mom."

"Javier, I – " A stabbing sensation drew her eyes down. She stared as the dark blood staining her hands smeared the rain-beaded railing and dripped into the estuary. She'd been picking her scabs, destroying the symmetry of the scarrist's lines.

"You could have been something," she said, as the belly of the ship finished lifting from the lake, pointed into a sunrise concealed behind grey clouds. "You ain't going nowhere now."

Javier came beside her and touched her with a bandaged hand. She didn't turn to look at the hurt in his eyes.

"Man," he whispered in deep satisfaction, craning his neck as his creation swung into the sky. "Just think of all the people who are going to see that. Would you just look at that baby go?"

ANGEL OF LIGHT

Joe Haldeman

Born in Oklahoma City, Oklahoma, Joe Haldeman took a
B.S. degree in physics and astronomy from the University of
Maryland, and did postgraduate work in mathematics and
computer science. But his plans for a career in science were
cut short by the U.S. Army, which sent him to Vietnam in
1968 as a combat engineer. Seriously wounded in action,
Haldeman returned home in 1969 and began to write. He
sold his first story to Galaxy in 1969, and by 1976 had
garnered both the Nebula Award and the Hugo Award for
his famous novel *The Forever War*, one of the landmark
books of the seventies. He took another Hugo Award in
1977 for his story "Tricentennial," won the Rhysling Award
in 1983 for the best science fiction poem of the year
(although usually thought of primarily as a "hard-science"
writer, Haldeman is, in fact, also an accomplished poet, and
has sold poetry to most of the major professional markets in
the genre), and won both the Nebula and the Hugo Awards
in 1991 for the novella version of "The Hemingway Hoax."
His story "None So Blind" won the Hugo Award in 1995.
His other books include a mainstream novel, *War Year*, the
SF novels *Mindbridge*, *All My Sins Remembered*, *There Is
No Darkness* (written with his brother, SF writer Jack C.
Haldeman II), *Worlds*, *Worlds Apart*, *Worlds Enough and
Time*, *Buying Time*, *The Hemingway Hoax*, *Tools of the
Trade*, *The Coming*, the mainstream novel 1968, and
Camouflage, which won the prestigious James Tiptree, Jr.
Award. His short work has been gathered in the collections
Infinite Dreams, *Dealing in Futures*, *Vietnam and Other
Alien Worlds*, and *None So Blind*. As editor, he has
produced the anthologies *Study War No More*, *Cosmic
Laughter*, and *Nebula Award Stories Seventeen*. His most
recent book is a new science fiction novel, *Old Twentieth*.
Coming up are two new collections, *A Separate War and
Other Stories* and an omnibus of fiction and nonfiction, *War
Stories*. Haldeman lives part of the year in Boston, where he
teaches writing at the Massachusetts Institute of
Technology, and the rest of the year in Florida, where he and

his wife, Gay, make their home.

They say that the definition of a good deal in a flea market is when both of you walk away convinced that you've outfoxed the other and gotten a bargain . . . and maybe you both *have* – by your own lights . . .

IT BEGAN INNOCENTLY ENOUGH. Christmastime and no money. I went down into the cellar and searched deeply for something to give the children. Something they wouldn't have already found during their *hajjes* down there.

On a high shelf, behind bundles of sticks waiting for the cold, I could just see an old wooden chest, pushed far back into a corner. I dropped some of the bundles onto the floor and pushed the others out of the way, and with some difficulty slid the chest to the edge of the shelf. From the thick layer of dust on top, I assumed it was from my father's time or before.

I had a warning thought: Don't open it. Call the authorities.

But just above the lock was engraved the name. JOHN BILLINGS WASHINGTON. John Washington was my father's slave name. I think the Billings middle name was his father's. The box probably went back to the twentieth century.

The lock was rusted tight, but the hasp was loose. I got down from the ladder and found a large screwdriver that I could use to pry it.

I slid the chest out and balanced it on my shoulder, and carefully stepped down, the ladder creaking. I set it on the worktable and hung one lantern from the rafter over it, and set the other on a stack of scrap wood beside.

The screaming that the screws made, coming out of the hardwood, was so loud that it was almost funny, considering that I supposedly was working in secret. But Miriam was pumping out chords on the organ, singing along with Fatimah, rehearsing for the Christmas service. I could have fired a pistol and no one would have heard it.

The hasp swung free and the top lifted easily, with a sigh of brass. Musty smell and something else. Gun oil. A gray cloth bundle on top was heavy. Of course it held a gun.

It's not unusual to find guns left over from the old times; there were so many. Ammunition was rare, though. This one had two heavy magazines.

I recognized it from news and history pictures, an Uzi, invented and used by the old infidel state Israel. I set it down and wiped my hands.

It would not be a good Christmas present. Perhaps for 'Eid, for Ibriham, when he is old enough to decide whether he is to be called. A Jewish weapon, he would laugh. I could ask the imam whether to cleanse it and how.

There were three cardboard folders under the gun, once held together with rubber bands, which were just sticky lines now. They were full of useless documents about land and banking.

Underneath them, I caught a glimpse of something that looked like pornography. I looked away immediately, closed my eyes, and asked Mohammed and Jesus for strength. Then I took it out and put it in the light.

It was in a plastic bag that had stamped on it NITROGEN SEAL. What a strange word, a tech word from the old times.

The book inside had the most amazing picture on the front. A man and a woman, both white, embracing. But the woman is terrified. The man seems only resolute, as he fires a strange pistol at a thing like a giant squid, green as a plant. The woman's head is uncovered, and at first she seems naked, but in fact her clothes are simply transparent, like some dancers'. The book is called *Thrilling Wonder Stories*, and is dated summer 1944. That would be 1365, more than a hundred years before Chrislam.

I leafed through the book, fascinated in spite of its carnal and infidel nature. Most of it seemed to be tales – not religious parables or folk tales, but lies that were made up at the time, for entertainment. Perhaps there was moral instruction as well. Many of the pictures did show men in situations that were physically or morally dangerous.

The first story, "The Giant Runt," seemed at first sacrilegious; it was about a man furious with God for having created him shorter than normal men. But then a magical machine makes everyone else tiny, and his sudden superiority turns him into a monster. But he sees an opportunity for moral action and redeems himself. The machine is destroyed, the world is normal again, and God rewards him with love.

Nadia, my second wife, came to the door at the top of the stairs and asked whether I needed help with anything. "No," I said. "Don't wait up. I have something to study here. A man thing." I shouldn't have said that. She would be down here after the morning prayer, as soon as I left for work.

I looked at the woman on the cover of the book, so exposed and vulnerable. Perhaps I should destroy it before Nadia or Miriam were exposed to it. A present for Ibriham? No; he would like it, but it would lead him away from proper thought.

I put both lanterns on the table, with the book between them, for maximum light. The paper was brown and the ink, faded. I turned the crumbling pages with care, although I would probably burn the book before dawn. First I would read as much of it as I could. I composed my mind with prayer, reciting the Prophet's *hadith* about the duty of learning.

In 1365 a war was raging all around the world, and various pages took note of this. I think this was only a year or two before America used nuclear weapons the first time, though I found no mention of them. (There were several exhortations to "buy bonds," which at first I misread as bombs. Bonds are financial instruments of some kind.) There were short pieces, evidently presented as truth, about science being used against the enemies of America. The ones that were not presented as true were more interesting, though harder to understand.

Much of the content was religious. "Horatius at the Bridge" was about a madman who could find the "soul" of a bridge and bring it down with the notes from a flute. "Terror in the Dust" and "The Devouring Tide" described scientists who were destroyed because they tried to play God – the first by giving intelligence to ants and then treating them as if he were an almighty deity, and the second, grandly, by attempting to create a new universe, with himself as Allah. The last short story, "God of Light," had a machine that was obviously Shaytan, trying to tempt the humans into following it into destruction.

The language was crude and at times bizarre, though of course part of that was just a reflection of the technological culture those writers and readers endured together. Life is simpler and more pure now, at least on this side of the city walls. The Kafir may still have books like this.

That gave me an idea. Perhaps this sort of thing would be rare and sought after in their world. I shouldn't accept Kafir money – though people do, often enough – but perhaps I could trade it for something more appropriate for a Christmas gift. Barter could be done without an intermediary, too, and frankly I was not eager for my imam to know that I had this questionable book in my possession.

Things are less rigid now, but I sharply remember the day, more than forty years ago, when my father had to burn all of his books. We carried box after box of them to the parking lot in front of the church, where they were drenched with gasoline and set afire. The smell of gasoline, rare now, always brings that back.

He was allowed to keep two books, a New Koran and a New Bible. When a surprise search party later found an old Q'ran in his study, he had to spend a week, naked, in a cage in that same spot – the jumble of fractured concrete in the middle of the church parking lot – with nothing but water, except a piece of bread the last day.

(It was an old piece of bread, rock-hard and moldy. I remember how he thanked the imam, carefully brushed off the mold, and managed to stay dignified, gnawing at it with his strong side teeth.)

He told them he kept the old book because of the beauty of the writing, but I knew his feelings went deeper than that: He thought the Q'ran in any language other than Arabic was just a book, not holy. As a boy of five, I was secretly overjoyed that I could stop memorizing the Q'ran in Arabic; it was hard enough in English.

I agree with him now, and ever since it was legal again, I've spent my Sundays trying to cram the Arabic into my gray head. With God's grace I might live long enough to learn it all. Having long ago memorized the English version helps make up for my slow brain.

I put the old book back in its NITROGEN SEAL bag and took it up to bed with me, dropping off a bundle of sticks by the stove on the way. I checked on both children and both wives; all were sleeping soundly. With a prayer of thanks for this strange discovery, I joined Nadia and dreamed of a strange future that had not come to pass.

The next day was market day. I left Nadia with the children and Fatimah and I went down to the medina for the week's supplies.

It really is more a woman's work than a man's, and normally I enjoy watching Fatimah go through the rituals of inspection and barter – the mock arguments and grudging agreement that comprise the morning's entertainment for customer and merchant alike. But this time I left her in the food part of the medina with the cart, while I went over to the antiques section.

You don't see many Kafir in the produce part of the medina, but there are always plenty wandering through the crafts and antiques section, I suppose looking for curiosities and bargains. Things that are everyday to us are exotic to them, and vice versa.

It was two large tents, connected by a canvas breezeway under which merchants were roasting meats and nuts and selling drinks for dollars or dirhams. I got a small cup of sweet coffee, redolent of honey and cardamom, for two dirhams, and sipped it standing there, enjoying the crowd.

Both tents had similar assortments of useful and worthless things, but one was for dollar transactions and the other was for dirhams and barter. The dollar purchases had to go through an imam, who would extract a fee for handling the money, and pay the merchant what was left, converting into dirhams. There were easily three times as many merchants and customers in the dirham-and-barter tent, the Kafir looking for bargains and the sellers for surprises, as much as for doing business. It was festive there, too, a lot of chatter and laughing over the rattle and whine of an amateur band of drummers and fiddlers. People who think we are aloof from infidels, or hate them, should spend an hour here.

Those who did this regularly had tables they rented by the day or month; we amateurs just sat on the ground with our wares on display. I walked around and didn't see anyone I knew, so finally just sat next to a table where a man and a woman were selling books. I laid out a square of newspaper in front of me and set the *Thrilling Wonder Stories* on it.

The woman looked down at it with interest. "What kind of a magazine is that?"

Magazine, I'd forgotten that word. "I don't know. Strange tales, most of them religious."

"It's 'science fiction,'" the man said. "They used to do that, predict what the future would be like."

"Used to? We still do that."

He shrugged. "Not that way. Not as fiction."

"I wouldn't let a child see that," the woman said.

"I don't think the artist was a good Muslim," I said, and they both chuckled. They wished me luck with finding a buyer, but didn't make an offer themselves.

Over the next hour, five or six people looked at the magazine and asked questions, most of which I couldn't answer. The imam in charge of the tent came over and gave me a long silent look. I looked right back at him and asked him how business was.

Fatimah came by, the cart loaded with groceries. I offered to wheel it home if she would sit with the magazine. She covered her face and giggled. More realistically, I said I could push the cart home when I was done, if she would take the perishables now. She said no, she'd take it all after she'd done a turn around the tent. That cost me twenty dirhams; she found a set of wooden spoons for the kitchen. They were freshly made by a fellow who had set up shop in the opposite corner, running a child-powered lathe, his sons taking turns striding on a treadmill attached by a series of creaking pulleys to the axis of the tool. People may have bought his wares more out of curiosity and pity for his sons than because of the workmanship.

I almost sold it to a fat old man who had lost both ears, I suppose in the war. He offered fifty dirhams, but while I was trying to bargain the price up, his ancient crone of a wife charged up and physically hauled him away, shrieking. If he'd had an ear, she would have pulled him by it. The bookseller started to offer his sympathies, but then both of them doubled over in laughter, and I had to join them.

As it turned out, the loss of that sale was a good thing. But first I had to endure my trial.

A barefoot man who looked as if he'd been fasting all year picked up the magazine and leafed through it carefully, mumbling. I knew he was trouble. I'd seen him around, begging and haranguing. He was white, which normally is not a problem with me. But white people who choose to live inside the walls are often types who would not be welcome at home, wherever that might be.

He proceeded to berate me for being a bad Muslim – not hearing my correction, that I belonged to Chrislam – and, starting with the licentious cover and working his way through the inside illustrations and advertisements, to the last story, which actually had God's name in the title . . . he said that even a bad Muslim would have no choice but to burn it on the spot.

I would have gladly burned it if I could burn it under *him*, but I was saved from making that decision by the imam. Drawn by the commotion, he stamped over and began to question the man, in a voice as shrill as his own, on matters of doctrine. The man's Arabic was no better than his diet, and he slunk away in mid-diatribe. I thanked the imam and he left with a slight smile.

Then a wave of silence unrolled across the room like a heavy blanket. I looked to the tent entrance and there were four men: Abdullah Zaragosa, our chief imam, some white man in a business suit, and two policemen in uniform, seriously armed. In between them was an alien, one of those odd creatures visiting from Arcturus.

I had never seen one, though I had heard them described on the radio. I looked around and was sad not to see Fatimah; she would hate having missed this.

It was much taller than the tallest human; it had a short torso but a giraffelike neck. Its head was something like a bird's, one large eye on either side. It cocked its head this way and that, looking around, and then dropped down to say something to the imam.

They all walked directly toward me, the alien rippling on six legs. Cameras clicked; I hadn't brought one. The imam asked if I was Ahmed Abd al-kareem, and I said yes, in a voice that squeaked.

"Our visitor heard of your magazine. May we inspect it?" I nodded, not trusting my voice, and handed it to him, but the white man took it.

He showed the cover to the alien. "This is what we expected you to look like."

"Sorry to disappoint," it said in a voice that sounded like it came from a cave. It took the magazine in an ugly hand, too many fingers and warts that moved, and inspected it with first one eye, and then the other.

It held the magazine up and pointed to it, with a smaller hand. "I would like to buy this."

"I – I can't take white people's money. Only dirhams or, or trade."

"Barter," it said, surprising me. "That is when people exchange things of unequal value, and both think they have gotten the better deal."

The imam looked like he was trying to swallow a pill. "That's true enough," I said. "At best, they both do get better deals, by their own reckoning,"

"Here, then." It reached into a pocket or a pouch – I couldn't tell whether it was wearing clothes – and brought out a ball of light.

It held out the light to a point midway between us, and let go. It floated in the air. "The light will stay wherever you put it."

It shimmered a brilliant blue, with fringes of rainbow colors. "How long will it last?"

"Longer than you."

It was one of the most beautiful things I had ever seen. I touched it with my finger – it felt cool, and tingled – and pushed it a few inches. It stayed where I moved it.

"It's a deal, sir. Thank you."

"*Shukran*," it said, and they moved on down the line of tables.

I don't think it bought anything else. But it might have. I kept looking away from it, back into the light.

The imams and the white scientists all want to take the light away to study it. Eventually, I will loan it out.

For now, though, it is a Christmas gift to my son and daughter. The faithful, and the merely curious, come to look at it, and wonder. But it stays in my house.

In Chrislam, as in old Islam, angels are not humanlike creatures with robes and wings. They are *male'ikah*, beings of pure light.

They look wonderful on the top of a tree.

BURN

James Patrick Kelly

James Patrick Kelly made his first sale in 1975, and since has gone on to become one of the most respected and popular writers to enter the field in the last twenty years. Although Kelly has had some success with novels, especially with *Wildlife*, he has perhaps had more impact to date as a writer of short fiction, with stories such as "Solstice," "The Prisoner of Chillon," "Glass Cloud," "Mr. Boy," "Pogrom," "Home Front," "Undone," and "Bernardo's House," and is often ranked among the best short story writers in the business. His story "Think Like a Dinosaur" won him a Hugo Award in 1996, as did his story "10^{16} to 1," in 2000. Kelly's first solo novel, the mostly ignored *Planet of Whispers*, came out in 1984. It was followed by *Freedom Beach*, a mosaic novel written in collaboration with John Kessel, and then by another solo novel, *Look into the Sun*. His short work has been collected in *Think Like a Dinosaur*, and, most recently, in a new collection, *Strange but Not a Stranger*. His most recent book is the chapbook novella *Burn*, and coming up is an anthology coedited with John Kessel, *Feeling Very Strange: The Slipstream Anthology*. Born in Mineola, New York, Kelly now lives with his family in Nottingham, New Hampshire. He has a Web site at www.JimKelly.net, and reviews Internet-related matters for *Asimov's Science Fiction*.

In the powerful novella that follows, he takes us to a rural, remote, and self-isolated planet for the story of a man who inadvertently sets in motion a cascade of events that sweeps him uncontrollably along toward an unknown destination, and which he's going to need luck to burn in order to survive . . .

> We might try our lives by a thousand simple tests; as, for instance, that the same sun which ripens my beans illumines at once a system of earths like ours. If I had remembered this it would have prevented some mistakes. This was not the light in which I hoed them. The stars are the apexes of what

wonderful triangles! What distant and different beings in the various mansions of the universe are contemplating the same one at the same moment! Nature and human life are as various as our several constitutions. Who shall say what prospect life offers to another?

– Henry David Thoreau, *Walden*

I

For the hero is commonly the simplest and obscurest of men.
– Henry David Thoreau, *Walden*

Spur was in the nightmare again. It always began in the burn. The front of the burn took on a liquid quality and oozed like lava toward him. It licked at boulders and scorched the trees in the forest he had sworn to protect. There was nothing he could do to fight it; in the nightmare, he wasn't wearing his splash pack. Or his fireproof field jacket. Fear pinned him against an oak until he could feel the skin on his face start to cook. Then he tore himself away and ran. But now the burn leapt after him, following like a fiery shadow. It chased him through a stand of pine; trees exploded like firecrackers. Sparks bit through his civvies and stung him. He could smell burning hair. His hair. In a panic he dodged into a stream choked with dead fish and poached frogs. But the water scalded his legs. He scrambled up the bank of the stream weeping. He knew he shouldn't be afraid; he was a veteran of the firefight. Still he felt as if something was squeezing him. A whimpering gosdog bolted across his path, its feathers singed, eyes wide. He could feel the burn dive under the forest and burrow ahead of him in every direction. The ground was hot beneath his feet and the dark humus smoked and stank. In the nightmare there was just one way out, but his brother-in-law Vic was blocking it. Only in the nightmare Vic was a pukpuk, one of the human torches who had started the burn. Vic had not yet set himself on fire, although his baseball jersey was smoking in the heat. He beckoned and for a moment Spur thought it might not be Vic after all as the anguished face shimmered in the heat of the burn. Vic wouldn't betray them, would he? But by then Spur had to dance to keep his shoes from catching fire, and he had no escape, no choice, no time. The torch spread his arms wide and Spur stumbled into his embrace and with an angry whoosh they exploded together into flame. Spur felt his skin crackle . . .

"That's enough for now." A sharp voice cut through the nightmare. Spur gasped with relief when he realized that there was no burn. Not here anyway. He felt a cold hand brush against his forehead like a blessing and knew that he was in the hospital. He had just been in the sim that the upsiders were using to heal his soul.

"You've got to stop thrashing around like that," said the docbot. "Unless you want me to nail the leads to your head."

Spur opened his eyes but all he could see was mist and shimmer. He tried to answer the docbot but he could barely find his tongue in his own mouth. A brightness to his left gradually resolved into the sunny window of the hospital room. Spur could feel the firm and not unpleasant pressure of the restraints, which bound him to the bed: broad straps across his ankles, thighs, wrists and torso. The docbot peeled the leads off his temples and then lifted Spur's head to get the one at the base of his skull.

"So do you remember your name?" it said.

Spur stretched his head against the pillow, trying to loosen the stiffness in his neck.

"I'm over here, son. This way."

He turned and stared into a glowing blue eye, which strobed briefly.

"Pupil dilatation normal," the docbot muttered, probably not to Spur. It paused for a moment and then spoke again. "So about that name?"

"Spur."

The docbot stroked Spur's palm with its med finger, collecting some of his sweat. It stuck the sample into its mouth. "That may be what your friends call you," it said, "but what I'm asking is the name on your ID."

The words chased each other across the ceiling for a moment before they sank in. Spur wouldn't have had such a problem understanding if the docbot were a person, with lips and a real mouth instead of the oblong intake. The doctor controlling this bot was somewhere else. Dr. Niss was an upsider whom Spur had never actually met. "Prosper Gregory Leung," he said.

"A fine Walden name," said the docbot, and then muttered, "Self ID twenty-seven point four seconds from initial request."

"Is that good?"

It hummed to itself, ignoring his question. "The electrolytes in your sweat have settled down nicely," it said at last. "So tell me about the sim."

"I was in the burn and the fire was after me. All around, Dr. Niss. There was a pukpuk, one of the torches, he grabbed me. I couldn't get away."

"You remembered my name, son." The docbot's top plate glowed with an approving amber light. "So did you die?"

Spur shook his head. "But I was on fire."

"Experience fear vectors unrelated to the burn? Monsters, for instance? Your mom? Dad?"

"No."

"Lost loves? Dead friends? Childhood pets?"

"No." He had a fleeting image of the twisted grimace on Vic's face at that last moment, but how could he tell this upsider that his wife's brother had been a traitor to the Transcendent State? "Nothing." Spur was getting used to lying to Dr. Niss, although he worried what it was doing to his soul.

"Check and double check. It's almost as if I knew what I was doing, eh?" The docbot began releasing the straps that held Spur down. "I'd say your soul is on the mend, Citizen Leung. You'll have some psychic scarring, but if you steer clear of complex moral dilemmas and women, you should be fine." It paused, then snapped its fingers. "Just for the record, son, that was a joke."

"Yes, sir." Spur forced a smile. "Sorry, sir." Was getting the jokes part of the cure? The way this upsider talked at once baffled and fascinated Spur.

"So let's have a look at those burns," said the docbot.

Spur rolled onto his stomach and folded his arms under his chin. The docbot pulled the hospital gown up. He could feel its medfinger pricking the dermal grafts that covered most of his back and his buttocks. "Dr. Niss?" said Spur.

"Speak up," said the docbot. "That doesn't hurt does it?"

"No, sir." Spur lifted his head off and tried to look back over this shoulder. "But it's really itchy."

"Dermal regeneration eighty-three percent," it muttered. "Itchy is alive, son. Itchy is growing."

"Sir, I was just wondering, where are you exactly?"

"Right here." The docbot began to flow warm dermslix to the grafts from its medfinger. "Where else would I be?"

Spur chuckled, hoping that was a joke. He could remember a time when he used to tell jokes. "No, I mean your body."

"The shell? Why?" The docbot paused. "You don't really want to be asking about QICs and the cognisphere, do you? The less you know about the upside, the better, son."

Spur felt a prickle of resentment. What stories were upsiders telling each other about Walden? That the citizens of the Transcendent State were backward fanatics who had simplified themselves into savagery? "I wasn't asking about the upside, exactly. I was asking about you. I mean . . . you saved me, Dr. Niss." It wasn't at all what Spur had expected to say, although it was certainly true. "If it wasn't for you, it . . . I was burnt all over, probably going crazy. And I thought . . ." His throat was suddenly so tight that he could hardly speak. "I wanted to . . . you know, thank you."

"Quite unnecessary," said the docbot. "After all, the Chairman is paying me to take care of all of you, bless his pockets." It tugged Spur's gown back into place with its gripper arm. "I prefer the kind of thanks I can bank, son. Everything else is just used air."

"Yes, but . . ."

"Yes, but?" It tugged the hospital gown back into place. "Yes but are dangerous words. Don't forget that you people lead a privileged life here – courtesy of Jack Winter's bounty and your parents' luck."

Spur had never heard anyone call the Chairman *Jack*. "It was my grandparents who won the lottery, sir," he said. "But yes, I know I'm lucky to live on Walden."

"So why do you want to know what kind of creature would puree his mind into a smear of quantum foam and entangle it with a bot brain a hundred and thirty-some light years away? Sit up, son."

Spur didn't know what to say. He had imagined that Dr. Niss must be posted nearby, somewhere here at the upsiders' compound at Concord, or perhaps in orbit.

"You do realize that the stars are very far away?"

"We're not simple here, Dr. Niss." He could feel the blood rushing in his cheeks. "We practice simplicity."

"Which complicates things." The docbot twisted off its medfinger and popped it into the sterilizer. "Say you greet your girlfriend on the tell. You have a girlfriend?"

"I'm married," said Spur, although he and Comfort had separated months before he left for the firefight and, now that Vic was dead, he couldn't imagine how they would ever get back together.

"So you're away with your squad and your wife is home in your village mowing the goats or whatever she does with her time. But when you talk on the tell it's like you're sitting next to each other. Where are you then? At home with her? Inside the tell?"

"Of course not."

"For *you*, of course not. That's why you live on Walden, protected from life on the upside. But where I come from, it's a matter of perspective. I believe I'm right here, even though the shell I'm saved in is elsewhere." The sterilizer twittered. "I'm inhabiting this bot in this room with you." The docbot opened the lid of the sterilizer, retrieved the medfinger with its gripper and pressed it into place on the bulkhead with the other instruments. "We're done here," it said abruptly. "Busy, busy, other souls to heal, don't you know? Which reminds me: we need your bed, son, so we're moving your release date up. You'll be leaving us the day after tomorrow. I'm authorized a week of rehabilitation before you have to go back to your squad. What's rehab called on this world again?"

"Civic refreshment."

"Right." The docbot parked itself at its station beside the door to the examining room. "Refresh yourself." Its head plate dimmed and went dark.

Spur slid off the examination table, wriggled out of the hospital gown and pulled his uniform pants off the hanger in the closet. As he was buttoning his shirt, the docbot lit its eye. "You're welcome, son." Its laugh was like a door slamming. "Took me a moment to understand what you were trying to say. I keep forgetting what it's like to be anchored."

"Anchored?" said Spur.

"Don't be asking so many questions." The docbot tapped its dome. "Not good for the soul." The blue light in its eye winked out.

II

> Most of the luxuries and many of the so-called
> comforts of life are not only not indispensable, but
> positive hindrances to the elevation of mankind.
>   – Henry David Thoreau, *Walden*

Spur was in no hurry to be discharged from the hospital, even if it was
to go home for a week. He knew all too well what was waiting for him.
He'd find his father trying to do the work of two men in his absence.
Gandy Joy would bring him communion and then drag him into every
parlor in Littleton. He'd be wined and dined and honored and possibly
seduced and be acclaimed by all a hero. He didn't feel like a hero and he
surely didn't want to be trapped into telling the grandmas and ten-year-
old boys stories about the horrors of the firefight.

But what he dreaded most was seeing his estranged wife. It was bad
enough that he had let her little brother die after she had made Spur
promise to take care of him. Worse yet was that Vic had died a torch.
No doubt he had been in secret contact with the pukpuks, had probably
passed along information about the Corps of Firefighters – and Spur
hadn't suspected a thing. It didn't matter that Vic had pushed him away
during their time serving together in Gold Squad – at one time they had
been best friends. He should have known; he might have been able to
save Vic. Spur had already decided that he would have to lie to Comfort
and his neighbors in Littleton about what had happened, just as he had
lied to Dr. Niss. What was the point in smearing his dead friend now?
And Spur couldn't help the Cooperative root out other pukpuk
sympathizers in the Corps; he had no idea who Vic's contacts had been.

However, Spur had other reasons for wanting to stay right where he
was. Even though he could scarcely draw breath without violating
simplicity, he loved the comforts of the hospital. For example, the
temperature never varied from a scandalous 23° Celsius. No matter that
outdoors the sun was blistering the rooftops of the upsiders'
Benevolence Park #5, indoors was a paradise where neither sweat nor
sweaters held sway. And then there was the food. Even though Spur's
father, Capability Roger Leung, was the richest man in Littleton, he had
practiced stricter simplicity than most. Spur had grown up on meat,
bread, squash and scruff, washed down with cider and applejack
pressed from the Leung's own apples and the occasional root beer.
More recently, he and Rosie would indulge themselves when they had
the money, but he was still used to gorging on the fruits of the family
orchard during harvest and suffering through preserves and root cellar
produce the rest of the year. But here the patients enjoyed the
abundance of the Thousand Worlds, prepared in extravagant style.
Depending on his appetite, he could order lablabis, dumplings, goulash,
salmagundi, soufflés, quiche, phillaje, curry, paella, pasta, mousses,
meringues or tarts. And that was just the lunch menu.

But of all the hospital's guilty pleasures, the tell was his favorite. At home Spur could access the latest bazzat bands and town-tunes from all over Walden and six hundred years of opera. And on a slow Tuesday night, he and Comfort might play one of the simplified chronicles on the tiny screen in Diligence Cottage or watch a spiritual produced by the Institute of Didactic Arts or just read to each other. But the screens of the hospital tells sprawled across entire walls and, despite the Cooperative's censors, opened like windows onto the universe. What mattered to people on other worlds astonished Spur. Their chronicles made him feel ignorant for the first time in his life and their spirituals were so wickedly materialistic that he felt compelled to close the door to his hospital room when he watched them.

The search engine in particular excited Spur. At home, he could greet anyone in the Transcendent State – as long as he knew their number. But the hospital tell could seemingly find anyone, not only on Walden but anywhere on all the Thousand Worlds of the upside. He put the tell in his room to immediate use, beginning by greeting his father and Gandy Joy, who was the village virtuator. Gandy had always understood him so much better than Comfort ever had. He should have greeted Comfort as well, but he didn't.

He did greet his pals in the Gold Squad, who were surprised that he had been able to track them down while they were on active duty. They told him that the entire Ninth Regiment had been pulled back from the Motu River burn for two weeks of CR in Prospect. Word was that they were being reassigned to the Cloyce Memorial Forest for some easy fire watch duty. No doubt the Cooperative was yanking the regiment off the front line because Gold Squad had taken almost forty per cent casualties when the burn had flanked their position at Motu. Iron and Bronze Squads had taken a hit as well, fighting their way through the burn to rescue Gold.

To keep from brooding about Vic and the Motu burn and the firelight, Spur looked up friends who had fallen out of his life. He surprised his cousin Land, who was living in Slide Knot in Southeast and working as a tithe assessor. He connected with his childhood friend Handy, whom he hadn't seen since the Alcazars had moved to Freeport, where Handy's mom was going to teach pastoral philosophy. She was still at the University and Handy was an electrician. He tracked down his Self-Reliance School sweetheart, Leaf Benkleman, only to discover that she had emigrated from Walden to Kolo in the Alumar system. Their attempt to catch up was frustrating, however, because the Cooperative's censors seemed to buzz every fifth word Leaf said. Also, the look on her face whenever he spoke rattled Spur. Was it pity? He was actually relieved when she cut their conversation short.

Despite the censors, talking to Leaf whetted Spur's appetite for making contact with the upside. He certainly wouldn't get the chance once he left the hospital. He didn't care that everyone was so preposterously far away that he would never meet them in person. Dr. Niss had been wrong: Spur understood perfectly the astonishing distances between stars. What he did not comprehend was exactly how he could chat with someone who lived hundreds of trillions of kilometers away, or how someone could beam themselves from Moy to Walden in a heartbeat. Of course, he had learned the simplified explanation of QICs – quantum information channels – in school. QICs worked because many infinitesimally small nothings were part of a something, which could exist in two places at the same time. This of course made no sense, but then so much of upsider physics made no sense after the censors were done with it.

Spur paused in the doorway of his room and looked up and down the hall. None of the patients at his end of the ward were stirring; a lone maintenance bot dusted along the floor at the far end by the examining rooms. It was his last full day at the hospital. Now or never. He eased the door shut and turned the tell on.

He began by checking for relatives on the upside. But when he searched on the surname *Leung*, he got 2.3×10^6 hits. Which, if any, of them might be his people? Spur had no way of knowing. Spur's grandparents had expunged all records of their former lives when they had come to Walden, a requirement for immigrants to the Transcendent State. Like everyone else in his family, he had known the stern old folks only as GiGo and GiGa. The names on their death certificates were Jade Fey Leung and Chap Man-Leung, but Spur thought that they had probably been changed when they had first arrived at Freeport.

He was tempted to greet his father and ask if he knew GiGo's upside name, but then he would ask questions. Too many questions; his father was used to getting the answers he wanted. Spur went back to the tell. A refined search showed that millions of Leungs lived on Blimminey, Eridani Foxtrot, Fortunate Child, Moy and No Turning Back, but that there also appeared to be at least a scatter of Leungs on many of the Thousands Worlds. There was no help for it; Spur began to send greetings at random.

He wasn't sure exactly who he expected to answer, but it certainly wasn't bots. When Chairman Winter had bought Walden from ComExplore IC, he decreed that neither machine intelligences nor enhanced upsiders would be allowed in the refuge he was founding. The Transcendent State was to be the last and best home of the true humans. While the pukpuks used bots to manufacture goods that they sold to the Transcendent State, Spur had never actually seen one until he had arrived at the hospital.

Now he discovered that the upside swarmed with them. Everyone he tried to greet had bot receptionists, secretaries, housekeepers or companions screening their messages. Some were virtual and presented themselves in outlandish sims; others were corporeal and stared at him from the homes or workplaces of their owners. Spur relished these voyeuristic glimpses of life on the upside, but glimpses were all he got. None of the bots wanted to talk to him, no doubt because of the caution he could see scrolling across his screen. It warned that his greeting originated from "the Transcendent State of Walden, a jurisdiction under a consensual cultural quarantine."

Most of the bots were polite but firm. No, they couldn't connect him to their owners; yes, they would pass along his greeting and no, they couldn't say when he might expect a greeting in return. Some were annoyed. They invited him to read his own Covenant and then snapped the connection. A couple of virtual bots were actually rude to him. Among other things, they called him a mud hugger, a leech and a pathetic waste of consciousness. One particularly abusive bot started screaming that he was "a stinking useless fossil."

Spur wasn't quite sure what a fossil was, so he queried the tell. It returned two definitions: *1. an artifact of an organism, typically extinct, that existed in a previous geologic era. 2. something outdated or superceded.* The idea that, as a true human, he might be outdated, superceded or possibly even bound for extinction so disturbed Spur that he got up and paced the room. He told himself that this was the price of curiosity. There were sound reasons why the Covenant of Simplicity placed limits on the use of technology. Complexity bred anxiety. The simple life was the good life.

Yet even as he wrestled with his conscience, he settled back in front of the tell. On a whim he entered his own name. He got just two results:

> Comfort Rose Joerly and Prosper Gregory Leung
> Orchardists
> Diligence Cottage
> Jane Powder Street
> Littleton, Hamilton County,
> Northeast Territory, TS
> Walden

and

> Prosper Gregory Leung
> c/o Niss (remotely – see note)
> Salvation Hospital
> Benevolence Park # 5
> Concord, Jefferson County,
> Southwest Territory, TS
> Walden

Spur tried to access the note attached to Dr. Niss's name, but it was blocked. That wasn't a surprise. What was odd was that he had received results just from Walden. Was he really the only Prosper Gregory Leung in the known universe?

While he was trying to decide whether being unique was good or bad, the tell inquired if he might have meant to search for *Proper Gregory*

Leung or *Phosphor Gregory L'ung* or *Procter Gregoire Lyon*? He hadn't
but there was no reason not to look them up. Proper Leung, it turned out,
raised gosdogs for meat on a ranch out in Hopedale, which was in the
Southwest Territory. Spur thought that eating gosdogs was barbaric and
he had no interest in chatting with the rancher. Gregory L'ung lived on
Kenning in the Theta Persei system. On an impulse, Spur sent his greeting.
As he expected, it was immediately diverted to a bot. L'ung's virtual
companion was a shining green turtle resting on a rock in a muddy river.

"The High Gregory of Kenning regrets that he is otherwise occupied
at the moment," it said, raising its shell up off the rock. It stood on four
human feet. "I note with interest that your greeting originates from a
jurisdiction under a consensual . . ."

The turtle didn't get the chance to finish. The screen shimmered and
went dark. A moment later, it lit up again with the image of a boy,
perched at the edge of an elaborate chair.

He was wearing a purple fabric wrap that covered the lower part of
his body from waist to ankles. He was bare-chested except for the skin
of some elongated dun-colored animal draped around his thin
shoulders. Spur couldn't have said for sure how old the boy was, but
despite an assured bearing and intelligent yellow eyes, he seemed not yet
a man. The chair caught Spur's eye again: It looked to be of some dark
wood, although much of it was gilded. Each of the legs ended in a
stylized human foot. The back panel rose high above the boy's head and
was carved with leaves and branches that bore translucent purple fruit.

That sparkled like jewels.

Spur reminded himself to breathe. It looked very much like a throne.

III

It takes two to speak the truth – one to speak and
another to hear.
    – Henry David Thoreau, *A Week on the Concord
        and Merrimack Rivers*

"Hello, hello," said the boy. "Who is doing his talk, please?"

Spur struggled to keep his voice from squeaking. "My name is
Prosper Gregory Leung."

The boy frowned and pointed at the bottom of the screen. "Walden,
it tells? I have less than any idea of Walden."

"It's a planet."

"And tells that it's wrongful to think too hard on planet Walden?
Why? Is your brain dry?"

"I think." Spur was taken aback. "We all think." Even though he
thought he was being insulted, Spur didn't want to snap the connection
– not yet anyway. "I'm sorry, I didn't get your name."

The words coming out of the speakers did not seem to match what
the boy was saying. His lips barely moved, yet what Spur heard was,

"I'm the High Gregory, Phosphorescence of Kenning, energized by the tortoise of Eternal Radiation." Spur realized that the boy was probably speaking another language and that what he was hearing was a translation. Spur had been expecting the censors built into the tell to buzz this conversation like they had buzzed so much of his chat with Leaf Benkleman, but maybe bad translation was just as effective.

"That's interesting," said Spur cautiously. "And what is it that you do there on Kenning?"

"Do?" The High Gregory rubbed his nose absently. "Oh, *do!* I make luck."

"Really? People can do that on the upside?"

"What is the upside?"

"Space, you know." Spur waved an arm over his head and glanced upward.

The High Gregory frowned. "Prosper Gregory Leung breathes space?"

"No, I breathe air." He realized that the tell might easily be garbling his end of the conversation as well. "Only air." He spoke slowly and with exaggerated precision. "We call the Thousand Worlds the upside. Here. On my world."

The High Gregory still appeared to be confused.

"On this planet." He gestured at the hospital room. "Planet Walden. We look up at the stars." He raised his hand to his brow, as if sighting on some distant landmark. "At night." Listening to himself babble, Spur was certain that the High Gregory must think him an idiot. He had to change the subject, so he tapped his chest. "My friends call me Spur."

The High Gregory shook his head with a rueful smile. "You give me warmth, Spur, but I turn away with regret from the kind offer to enjoy sex with you. Memsen watches to see that I don't tickle life until I have enough of age."

Aghast, Spur sputtered that he had made no such offer, but the High Gregory, appearing not to hear, continued to speak.

"You have a fullness of age, friend Spur. Have you found a job of work on planet Walden?"

"You're asking what I do for a living?"

"All on planet Walden are living, I hope. Not saved?"

"Yes, we are." Spur grimaced. He rose from the tell and retrieved his wallet from the nightstand beside the bed. Maybe pix would help. He flipped through a handful in his wallet until he came to the one of Comfort on a ladder picking apples. "Normally I tend my orchards." He held the pix up to the tell to show the High Gregory. "I grow many kinds of fruit on my farm. Apples, peaches, apricots, pears, cherries. Do you have these kinds of fruit on Kenning?"

"Grape trees, yes." The High Gregory leaned forward in his throne and smiled. "And all of apples: apple pie and apple squeeze and melt apples." He seemed pleased that they had finally understood one another. "But you are not normal?"

"No. I mean yes, I'm fine." He closed the wallet and pocketed it. "But

. . . how do I say this? There is fighting on my world." Spur had no idea how to explain the complicated grievances of the pukpuks and fanaticism that led some of them to burn themselves alive to stop the spread of the forest and the Transcendent State. "There are other people on Walden who are very angry. They don't want my people to live here. They wish the land could be returned to how it was before we came. So they set fires to hurt us. Many of us have been called to stop them. Now instead of growing my trees, I help to put fires out."

"Very angry?" The High Gregory rose from his throne, his face flushed. "Fighting?" He punched at the air. "Hit-hit-hit?"

"Not exactly fighting with fists," said Spur. "More like a war."

The High Gregory took three quick steps toward the tell at his end. His face loomed large on Spur's screen. "War fighting?" He was clearly agitated; his cheeks flushed and the yellow eyes were fierce. "Making death to the other?" Spur had no idea why the High Gregory was reacting this way. He didn't think the boy was angry exactly, but then neither of them had proved particularly adept at reading the other. He certainly didn't want to cause some interstellar incident.

"I've said something wrong. I'm sorry." Spur bent his head in apology. "I'm speaking to you from a hospital. I was wounded . . . fighting a fire. Haven't quite been myself lately." He gave the High Gregory a self-deprecating smile. "I hope I haven't given offense."

The High Gregory made no reply. Instead he swept from his throne, down a short flight of steps into what Spur could now see was a vast hall. The boy strode past rows of carved wooden chairs, each of them a unique marvel, although none was quite as exquisite as the throne that they faced. The intricate beaded mosaic on the floor depicted turtles in jade and chartreuse and olive. Phosphorescent sculptures stretched like spider webs from the upper reaches of the walls to the barrel-vaulted ceiling, casting ghostly silver-green traceries of light on empty chairs beneath. The High Gregory was muttering as he passed down the central aisle but whatever he was saying clearly overwhelmed the tell's limited capacity. All Spur heard was, "War <crackle> Memsen witness there <crackle> our luck <crackle> <crackle> call the L'ung . . ."

At that, Spur found himself looking once again at a shining green turtle resting on a rock on a muddy river. "The High Gregory of Kenning regrets that he is otherwise occupied at the moment," it said. "I note with interest that your greeting originates from a jurisdiction under a consensual cultural quarantine. You should understand that it is unlikely that the High Gregory, as luck maker of the L'ung, would risk violating your covenants by having any communication with you."

"Except I just got done talking to him," said Spur.

"I doubt that very much." The turtle drew itself up on four human feet and stared coldly through the screen at him. "This conversation is concluded," it said. "I would ask that you not annoy us again."

"Wait, I . . . ," said Spur, but he was talking to a dead screen.

IV

> But if we stay at home and mind our business, who
> will want railroads? We do not ride on the railroad;
> it rides upon us.
> — Henry David Thoreau, *Walden*

Spur spent the rest of that day expecting trouble. He had no doubt that he'd be summoned into Dr. Niss's examining room for a lecture about how his body couldn't heal if his soul was sick. Or some virtuator from Concord would be brought in to light communion and deliver a reproachful sermon on the true meaning of simplicity. Or Cary Millisap, his squad leader, would call from Prospect and scorch him for shirking his duty to Gold, which was, after all, to get better as fast he could and rejoin the unit. He had not been sent to hospital to bother the High Gregory of Kenning, luck maker of the L'ung – whoever they were.

But trouble never arrived. He stayed as far away from his room and the tell as he could get. He played cards with Val Montilly and Sleepy Thorn from the Sixth Engineers, both of who were recovering from smoke inhalation they had suffered in the Coldstep burn. They were undergoing alveolar reconstruction to restore full lung function. Their voices were like ripsaws but they were otherwise in good spirits. Spur won enough from Sleepy on a single round of Fool All to pay for the new apple press he'd been wanting for the orchard. Of course, he would never be able to tell his father or Comfort where the money had come from.

Spur savored a memorable last supper: an onion tart with a balsamic reduction, steamed duck leg with a fig dressing on silver thread noodles and a vanilla panna cotta. After dinner he went with several other patients to hear a professor from Alcott University explain why citizens who sympathized with the pukpuks were misguided. When he finally returned to his room, there was a lone greeting in his queue. A bored dispatcher from the Cooperative informed him that he needed to pick up his train ticket at Celena Station before 11 a.m. No video of this citizen appeared on the screen; all he'd left was a scratchy audio message like one Spur might get on his home tell. Spur took this as a reminder that his holiday from simplicity would end the moment he left the hospital.

The breeze that blew through the open windows of the train was hot, providing little relief for the passengers in the first-class compartment. Spur shifted uncomfortably on his seat, his uniform shirt stuck to his back. He glanced away from the blur of trees racing past his window. He hated sitting in seats that faced backward; they either gave him motion sickness or a stiff neck. And if he thought about it – which he couldn't help but doing, at least for a moment – the metaphor always depressed him. He didn't want to be looking back at his life just now.

A backward seat – but it *was* in first class. The Cooperative's dispatcher probably thought he was doing him a favor. Give him some extra leg room, a softer seat. And why not? Hadn't he survived the infamous Motu River burn? Hadn't he been badly scorched in the line of duty? Of course he should ride in first class. If only the windows opened wider.

It had been easy not to worry about his problems while he was lounging around the hospital. Now that he was headed back home, life had begun to push him again. He knew he should try to stop thinking, maybe take a nap. He closed his eyes, but didn't sleep. Without warning he was back in the nightmare sim again . . . *and could smell burning hair. His hair. In a panic he dodged into a stream choked with dead fish and poached frogs. But the water was practically boiling and scalded his legs* . . . only Spur wasn't completely in the nightmare because he knew he was also sitting on a comfortable seat in a first-class compartment in a train that was taking him . . . *the only way out was blocked by a torch, who stood waiting for Spur. Vic had not yet set himself on fire, although his baseball jersey was smoking in the heat* . . . I'm not afraid, Spur told himself, I don't believe any of this . . . *the anguished face shimmered in the heat of the burn and then Spur was dancing to keep his shoes from catching fire, and he had no escape, no choice, no time* . . . with his eyes shut, Spur heard the clatter of the steel wheels on the track as: *no time no time no time no time.*

He knew then for certain what he had only feared: Dr. Niss had not healed his soul. How could he, when Spur had consistently lied about what had happened in the burn? Spur didn't mean to groan, but he did. When he opened his eyes, the gandy in the blue flowered dress was staring at him.

"Are you all right?" She looked to be in her late sixties or maybe seventy, with silver hair so thin that he could see the freckles on her scalp.

"Yes, fine," Spur said. "I just thought of something."

"Something you forgot?" She nodded. "Oh, I'm always remembering things just like that. Especially on trains." She had a burbling laugh, like a stream running over smooth stones. "I was supposed to have lunch with my friend Connie day after tomorrow, but here I am on my way to Little Bend for a week. I have a new grandson."

"That's nice," Spur said absently. There was one other passenger in the compartment. He was a very fat, moist man looking at a comic book about gosdogs playing baseball; whenever he turned a page, he took a snuffling breath.

"I see by your uniform that you're one of our firefighters," said the gandy. "Do you know my nephew Frank Kaspar? I think he is with the Third Engineers."

Spur explained that there were over eleven thousand volunteers in the Corps of Firefighters and that if her nephew was an engineer he was most probably a regular with the Home Guard. Spur couldn't keep track of all the brigades and platoons in the volunteer Corps, much less in the professional Guard. He said that he was just a lowly smokechaser in Gold Squad, Ninth Regiment. His squad worked with the Eighth Engineers, who supplied transportation and field construction support. He told her that these fine men and women were the very models of spiritual simplicity and civic rectitude, no doubt like her nephew. Spur was hoping that this was what she wanted to hear and that she would leave him alone. But then she asked if the rumors of pukpuk collaborators infiltrating the Corps were true and started nattering about how she couldn't understand how a citizen of the Transcendent State could betray the Covenant by helping terrorists. All the pukpuks wanted was to torch Chairman Winter's forests, wasn't that awful? Spur realized that he would have to play to her sympathy. He coughed and said he had been wounded in a burn and was just out of hospital and then coughed again.

"If you don't mind," he said, crinkling his brow as if he were fighting pain, "I'm feeling a little woozy. I'm just going to shut my eyes again and try to rest."

Although he didn't sleep, neither was he fully awake. But the nightmare did not return. Instead he drifted through clouds of dreamy remembrance and unfocussed regret. So he didn't notice that the train was slowing down until the hiss of the air brakes startled him to full alertness.

He glanced at his watch. They were still an hour out of Heart's Wall, where Spur would change for the local to Littleton.

"Are we stopping?" Spur asked.

"Wheelwright fireground." The fat man pulled a limp handkerchief out of his shirt pocket and dabbed at his hairline. "Five minutes of mandatory respect."

Now Spur noticed that the underbrush had been cleared along the track and that there were scorch marks on most of the trees. Spur had studied the Wheelwright in training. The forest north of the village of Wheelwright had been one of the first to be attacked by the torches. It was estimated that there must have been at least twenty of them, given the scope of the damage. The Wheelwright burn was also the first in which a firefighter died, although the torches never targeted citizens, only trees. The fires they started were always well away from villages and towns; that's why they were so hard to fight. But the Wheelwright had been whipped by strong winds until it cut the trunk line between Concord and Heart's Wall for almost two weeks. The Cooperative had begun recruiting for the Corps shortly after.

As the squealing brakes slowed the train to a crawl, the view out of Spur's window changed radically. Here the forest had yet to revive from the ravages of fire. Blackened skeletons of trees pointed at the sky and the charred floor of the forest baked under the sun. The sun seemed cruelly bright without the canopy of leaves to provide shade. In every direction, all Spur could see was the nightmarish devastation he had seen all too often. No plant grew, no bird sang. There were no ants or needlebugs or wild gosdogs. Then he noticed something odd: the bitter burnt-coffee scent of fresh fireground. And he could taste the ash, like shredded paper on his tongue. That made no sense; the Wheelwright was over three years old.

When the train finally stopped, Spur was facing one of the many monuments built along the tracks to honor fallen firefighters. A grouping of three huge statues set on a pad of stone cast their bronze gazes on him. Two of the firefighters were standing; one leaned heavily on the other. A third had dropped to one knee, from exhaustion perhaps. All still carried their gear, but the kneeling figure was about to shed her splash pack and one of the standing figures was using his jacksmith as a crutch. Although the sculptor had chosen to depict them in the hour of their doom, their implacable metal faces revealed neither distress nor regret. The fearsome simplicity of their courage chilled Spur. He was certain that he wasn't of their quality.

The engine blew its whistle in tribute to the dead: three long blasts and three short. The gandy stirred and stretched. "Wheelwright?" she muttered.

"Yeah," said the fat man.

She started to yawn but caught herself and peered out the open window. "Who's that?" she said, pointing.

A man in a blue flair suit was walking along the tracks, peering up at the passenger cars. He looked very hot and not very happy. His face was as flushed as a peach and his blonde hair was plastered to his forehead. Every few meters, he paused, cupped his hands to his mouth and called, "Leung? Prosper Gregory Leung?"

V

> Fire is without doubt an advantage on the whole. It sweeps and ventilates the forest floor and makes it clear and clean. I have often remarked with how much more comfort & pleasure I could walk in wood through which a fire had been run the previous year. It is inspiriting to walk amid the fresh green sprouts of grass and shrubbery pushing upward through the charred surface with more vigorous growth.
>
> – Henry David Thoreau, *Journal*, 1850

The man waited impatiently as Spur descended from the train, kit slung over his shoulder. Although he did not turn back to look, Spur knew every passenger on the train was watching them. Was he in trouble? The man's expression gave away nothing more than annoyance. He looked to be younger than Spur, possibly in his late twenties. He had a pinched face and a nose as stubby as a radish. He was wearing a prissy white shirt buttoned to the neck. There were dark circles under the armpits of his flair jacket.

"Prosper Gregory Leung of Littleton, Hamilton County, Northeast?" The man pulled a slip of paper from his pocket and read from it. "You are currently on medical leave from the Ninth Regiment, Corps of Firefighters and were issued a first-class ticket on this day . . ."

"I know who I am." Spur felt as if a needlebug were caught in his throat. "What is this about? Who are you?"

He introduced himself as Constant Ngonda, a deputy with the Cooperative's Office of Diplomacy. When they shook hands, he noticed that Ngonda's palm was soft and sweaty. Spur could guess why he had been pulled off the train, but he decided to act surprised.

"What does the Office of Diplomacy want with me?"

Just then the engineer blew three short blasts and couplings of the train clattered and jerked as, one by one, they took the weight of the passenger cars. With the groan of metal on metal, the train pulled away from the Wheelwright Memorial.

Spur's grip on the strap of his kit tightened. "Don't we want to get back on?"

Constant Ngonda shrugged. "I was never aboard."

The answer made no sense to Spur, who tensed as he calculated his chances of sprinting to catch the train. Ngonda rested a hand on his arm.

"We go this way, Prosper." He nodded west, away from the tracks.

"I don't understand." Spur's chances of making the train were fading as it gained momentum. "What's out there?"

"A clearing. A hover full of upsiders." He sighed. "Some important people have come a long way to see you." He pushed a lock of damp hair off his forehead. "The sooner we start, the sooner we get out of this heat." He let go of Spur and started picking his way across the fireground.

Spur glanced over his shoulder one last time at the departing train. He felt as if his life were pulling away.

"Upsiders? From where?"

Ngonda held up an open hand to calm him. "Some questions will be answered soon enough. Others it's better not to ask."

"What do you mean, better?"

Ngonda walked with an awkward gait, as if he expected the ground to give way beneath him. "I beg your pardon." He was wearing the wrong shoes for crossing rough terrain. "I misspoke." They were thin-soled, low cut and had no laces – little more than slippers. "I meant simpler, not better."

Just then Spur got a particularly intense whiff of something that was acrid and sooty, but not quite smoke. It was what he had first smelled as the train had pulled into the Memorial. He turned in a complete circle, all senses heightened, trying to pinpoint the source. After fire ran through the litter of leaves and twigs that covered the forest floor, it often sank into the duff, the layer of decomposing organic matter that lay just above the soil level. Since duff was like a sponge, most of the year it was too wet to burn. But in the heat of summer it could dry out and became tinder. Spur had seen a smoldering fire burrow through the layer of duff and emerge dozens of meters away. He sniffed, following his nose to a charred stump.

"Prosper!" said Ngonda. "What are you doing?"

Spur heard a soft hiss as he crouched beside the stump. It wasn't any fire sound that he knew, but he instinctively ran his bare hand across the stump, feeling for hotspots. Something cool and wet sprayed onto his fingers and he jerked them back as if he had been burned. He rubbed a smutty liquid between thumb and forefinger and then smelled it.

It had an evil, manmade odor of extinguished fire. Spur sat back on his heels, puzzled. Why would anyone want to mimic that particular stink? Then he realized that his hand was clean when it ought to have been smudged with soot from the stump. He rubbed hard against the burned wood, but the black refused to come off. He could see now that the stump had a clear finish, as if it had been coated with a preservative.

Spur could sense Ngonda's shadow loom over him but then he heard the hissing again and was able to pick out the tiny nozzle embedded in the stump. He pressed his finger to it and the noise stopped. Then on an impulse, he sank his hand into the burned over forest litter, lifted it and let the coarse mixture sift slowly through his fingers.

"It's hot out, Prosper," Ngonda said. "Do you really need to be playing in the dirt?"

The litter looked real enough: charred and broken twigs, clumps of leaf mold, wood cinders and a delicate ruined hemlock cone. But it didn't feel right. He squeezed a scrap of burnt bark, expecting it to crumble. Instead it compacted into an irregular pellet, like day-old bread. When he released it, the pellet slowly resumed its original shape.

"It's not real," said Spur. "None of it."

"It's a memorial, Prosper." The deputy offered Spur a hand and pulled him to his feet. "People need to remember." He bent over to brush at the fake pine needles stuck to Spur's knees. "We need to go."

Spur had never seen a hover so close. Before the burns, hovers had been banned altogether from the Transcendent State. But after the pukpuks had begun their terrorist campaign to halt the spread of forest into their barrens, Chairman Winter had given the Cooperative permission to relax the ban. Generous people from the upside had donated money to build the benevolence parks and provided hovers to assist the Corps in fighting fires. However, Chairman Winter had insisted that only bots were to fly the hovers and that citizen access to them would be closely monitored.

While in the field with Gold Squad, Spur had watched hovers swoop overhead, spraying loads of fire-retardant splash onto burns. And he had studied them for hours through the windows of the hospital, parked in front of their hangars at Benevolence Park Number 5. But even though this one was almost as big as Diligence Cottage and hovered a couple of meters above the ground, it wasn't quite as impressive as Spur had imagined it.

He decided that this must be because it was so thoroughly camouflaged. The hover's smooth skin had taken on the discoloration of the fireground, an ugly mottle of gray and brown and black. It looked like the shell of an enormous clam. The hover was elliptical, about five meters tall in front sweeping backward to a tapered edge, but otherwise featureless. If it had windows or doors, Spur couldn't make them out.

As they approached, the hover rose several meters. They passed into its shadow and Ngonda looked up expectantly. A hatch opened on the underside. A ramp extended to the ground below with a high-pitched warble like birdsong and a man appeared at the hatch. He was hard to see against the light of the interior of the hover; all Spur could tell for sure was that he was very tall and very skinny. Not someone he would expect to bump into on Jane Powder Street in Littleton. The man turned to speak to someone just inside the hatch. That's when Spur realized his mistake.

"No," she said, her voice airy and sweet. "We need to speak to him first."

As she teetered down the ramp, Spur could tell immediately that she was not from Walden. It was the calculation with which she carried herself, as if each step were a risk, although one she was disposed to take. She wore loose-fitting pants of a sheer fabric that might have been spun from clouds. Over them was a blue sleeveless dress that hung to mid-thigh. Her upper arms were decorated with flourishes of some kind of phosphorescent body paint and she wore silver and copper rings on each of her fingers.

"You're the Prosper Gregory of Walden?"

She had full lips and midnight hair and her skin was smooth and dark as a plum. She was a head taller than he was and half his weight. He was speechless until Ngonda nudged him.

"Yes."

"We're Memsen."

VI

It requires nothing less than a chivalric feeling to
sustain a conversation with a lady.
                              – Henry David Thoreau, *Journal*, 1851

Although it was cooler in the shade of the hover, Spur was far from comfortable. He couldn't help thinking of what would happen if the engine failed. He would have felt more confident if the hover had been making some kind of noise; the silent, preternatural effortlessness of the ship unnerved him. Meanwhile, he was fast realizing that Memsen had not wanted to meet him in order to make friends.

"Let's understand one another," she said. "We're here very much against our will. You should know that by summoning us to this place, you've put the political stability of dozens of worlds at risk. We very much regret that the High Gregory has decided to follow his luck to this place."

She was an upsider so Spur had no idea how to read her. The set of her shoulders flustered him, as did the way her knees bent as she stooped to his level. She showed him too many teeth and it was clear that she wasn't smiling. And why did she pinch the air? With a great effort Spur tore his gaze away from her and looked to Ngonda to see if he knew what she was talking about. The deputy gave him nothing.

"I'm not sure that I summoned the High Gregory, exactly," Spur said. "I did talk to him."

"About your *war*."

Constant Ngonda looked nervous. "Allworthy Memsen, I'm sure that Prosper didn't understand the implications of contacting you. The Transcendent State is under a cultural . . ."

"We grant that you have your shabby deniability." She redirected her displeasure toward the deputy. "Nevertheless, we suspect that your government instructed this person to contact the High Gregory, knowing that he'd come. There's more going on here than you care to say, isn't there?"

"Excuse me," said Spur, "but this really was an accident." Both Memsen and Ngonda stared at him as if he had corncobs stuck in his ears. "What happened was that I searched on my name but couldn't find anyone but me and then the tell at the hospital suggested the High Gregory as an alternative because our names are so similar." He spoke rapidly, worried that they'd start talking again before he could explain everything. "So I sent him a greeting. It was totally random – I didn't know who he was, I swear it. And I wasn't really expecting to make contact, since I'd been talking to bots all morning and not one was willing to connect me. In fact, your bot was about to cut me off when he came on the tell. The High Gregory, I mean."

"So." Memsen clicked the rings on her fingers together. "He mentioned none of this to us."

"He probably didn't know." Spur edged just a centimeter away from her toward the sunlight. The more he thought about it, the more he really wanted to get out from under the hover.

Ngonda spoke with calm assurance. "There, you see that Prosper's so-called request is based on nothing more than coincidence and mis-understanding." He batted at a fat orange needlebug that was buzzing his head. "The Cooperative regrets that you have come all this way to no good purpose."

Memsen reared suddenly to her full height and gazed down on the two of them. "There are no coincidences," she said, "only destiny. The High Gregory makes the luck he was meant to have. He's here, and he has brought the L'ung to serve as witnesses. Our reason for being on this world has yet to be discovered." She closed her eyes for several moments. While she considered Spur's story she made a low, repetitive plosive sound: *pa-pa-pa-ptt.* "But this is deeper than we first suspected," she mused.

Spur caught a glimpse of a head peeking out of the hatch above him. It ducked back into the hover immediately.

"So," Memsen said at last, "let's choose to believe you, Prosper Gregory of Walden." She eyed him briefly; whatever she saw in his face seemed to satisfy her. "You'll have to show us the way from here. Your way. The High Gregory's luck has chosen you to lead us until we see for ourselves the direction in which we must go."

"Lead you? Where?"

"Wherever you're going."

"But I'm just on my way home. To Littleton."

She clicked her rings. "So."

"I beg your pardon, Allworthy Memsen," said Ngonda, tugging at the collar of his shirt, "but you must realize that's impossible under our Covenant . . ."

"It is the nature of luck to sidestep the impossible," she said. "We speak for the High Gregory when we express our confidence that you'll find a way."

She had so mastered the idiom of command that Spur wasn't sure whether this was a threat or a promise. Either way, it gave Ngonda pause.

"Allworthy, I'd like nothing better than to accommodate you in this," he said. "Walden is perhaps the least of the Thousand Worlds, but even here we've heard of your efforts to help preserve the one true species." A bead of sweat dribbled down his forehead. "But my instructions are to accommodate your requests within reason. Within reason, Allworthy. It is not reasonable to land a hover in the commons of a village like Littleton. You must understand that these are country people."

She pointed at Spur. "Here is one of your country people."

"Memsen!" shouted a voice from the top of the ramp. "Memsen, I am so bored. Either bring him up right now or I'm coming down."

Her tongue flicked to the corner of her mouth. "You wouldn't like it," she called back. "It's very hot." Which was definitely true, although as far as Spur could tell, the weather had no effect on her. "There are bugs."

"That's it!" The High Gregory of Kenning, Phosphorescence of the Eternal Radiation and luck maker of the L'ung, scampered down the ramp of the hover.

"There," he said, "I did it, so now don't tell me to go back." He was wearing green sneakers with black socks, khaki shorts and a tee shirt with a pix of a dancing turtle, which had a human head. "Spur! You look sadder than you did before." He had knobby knees and fair skin and curly brown hair. If he had been born in Littleton, Spur would've guessed that he was ten years old. "Did something bad happen to you? Say something. Do you still talk funny like you did on the tell?"

Spur had a hundred questions but he was so surprised that all he could manage was, "Why are you doing this?"

"Why?" The boy's yellow eyes opened wide. "Why, why, why?" He stooped to pick up a handful of the blackened litter and examined it with interest, shifting it around on his open palm. "Because I got one of my luck feelings when we were talking. They're not like ideas or dreams or anything so I can't explain them very well. They're just special. Memsen says they're not like the feelings that other people get, but that it's all right to have them and I guess it is." He twirled in a tight circle then, flinging the debris in a wide scatter. "And that's why." He rubbed his hands on the front of his shorts and approached Spur. "Am I supposed to shake hands or kiss you? I can't remember."

Ngonda stepped between Spur and the High Gregory, as if to protect him. "The custom is to shake hands."

"But I shook with you already." He tugged at Ngonda's sleeve to move him aside. "You have hardly any luck left, friend Constant. I'm afraid it's all pretty much decided with you." When the deputy failed to give way, the High Gregory dropped to all fours and scooted through his legs. "Hello, Spur," said the boy as he scrambled to his feet. The High Gregory held out his hand and Spur took it.

Spur was at once aware that he was sweaty from the heat of the day, while the boy's hand was cool as river rock. He could feel the difference in their size: the High Gregory's entire hand fit in his palm and weighed practically nothing.

"Friend Spur, you have more than enough luck," the boy murmured, low enough so that only Spur could hear. "I can see we're going to have an adventure."

"Stay up there," cried Memsen. "No!" She was glowering up the ramp at the hatch, which had inexplicably filled with kids, all of whom were shouting at her. Spur couldn't tell which of them said what.

"When do we get our turn?"

"You let the Greg off."

"We came all this way."

"He's bored? I'm more bored."

"Hey move, you're in my way!"

"But I want to see too."

Several in the back started to chant. "Not fair, not fair!"

Memsen ground her toes into the fake forest floor. "We have to go now," she said. "If we let them off, it'll take hours to round them up."

"I'll talk to them." High Gregory bounded up the ramp, making sweeping motions with his hands. "Back, get back, this isn't it." The kids fell silent. "We're not there yet. We're just stopping to pick someone up." He paused halfway up and turned to the adults. "Spur is coming, right?"

Ngonda was blotting sweat from around his eyes with a handkerchief. "If he chooses." He snapped it with a quick flick of the wrist and then stuffed it into his pocket, deliberately avoiding eye contact with Spur.

Spur could feel his heart pounding. He'd wanted to fly ever since he'd realized that it was possible and didn't care if simplicity counseled otherwise. But he wasn't sure he wanted to be responsible for bringing all these upsiders to Littleton.

"So." Memsen must have mistaken his hesitation for fear. "You have never been in a hover, Prosper Gregory of Walden?"

"Call him Spur," said the High Gregory. "It doesn't mean you have to have sex with him."

Memsen bowed to Spur. "He has not yet invited us to take that familiarity."

"Yes, please call me Spur." He tried not to think about having sex with Memsen. "And yes." He picked up his kit. "I'll come with you."

"Lead then." She indicated that he should be first up the ramp. Ngonda followed him. Memsen came last, climbing slowly with her small and painstakingly accurate steps.

As he approached the top of the ramp, the coolness of the hover's interior washed over him. It was like wading into Mercy's Creek. He could see that the kids had gathered around the High Gregory. There were about a dozen of them in a bay that was about six by ten meters. Boxes and containers were strapped to the far bulkhead.

"Now where are we going?"

"When do we get to see the fire?"

"Hey, who's that?"

Most of the kids turned to see him step onto the deck. Although well lit, the inside of the hover was not as bright as it had been outside. Spur blinked as his eyes adjusted to the difference.

"This is Spur," said the High Gregory. "We're going to visit his village. It's called Littleton."

"Why? Are they little there?"

A girl of six or perhaps seven sidled over to him. "What's in your bag?" She was wearing a dress of straw-colored brocade that hung down to her silk slippers. The gold chain around her neck had a pendant in the shape of a stylized human eye. Spur decided that it must be some kind of costume.

He slung his kit off his shoulder and set it down in front of her so she could see. "Just my stuff."

"It's not very big," she said doubtfully. "Do you have something in there for me?"

"Your Grace," said Memsen, putting a hand on the girl's shoulder, "we are going to leave Spur alone for now." She turned the girl around and gave her a polite nudge toward the other kids. "You'll have to forgive them," she said to Spur. "They're used to getting their own way."

VII

> I have a deep sympathy with war, it so apes the gait
> and bearing of the soul.
> — Henry David Thoreau, *Journal*, 1840

Spur had studied geography in school and knew how big Walden was, but for the first time in his life he *felt* it. From the ground, the rampant forests restricted what anyone could see of the world. Even the fields and the lakes were hemmed in by trees. Spur had never been to the Modilon Ocean but he'd stood on the shores of Great Kamit Lake. The sky over the lake was impressive, but there was no way to take the measure of its scale. Spur had hiked the Tarata Mountains, but they were forested to their summits and the only views were from ledges. There was a tower on Samson Kokoda that afforded a 360-degree view, but the summit was just 1300 meters tall.

Now the hover was cruising through the clouds at an altitude of 5700 meters, according to the tell on the bulkhead. Walden spread beneath him in all its breathtaking immensity. Maps, measured in inflexible kilometers and flat hectares, were a sham compared to this. Every citizen should see what he was seeing, and if it violated simplicity, he didn't care.

Constant Ngonda, on the other hand, was not enjoying the view. He curled on a bench facing away from the hull, which Memsen had made transparent when she'd partitioned a private space for them. His neck muscles were rigid and he complained from time to time about trouble with his ears. Whenever the hover shivered as it contended with the wind, he took a huge gulping breath. In a raspy voice, the deputy asked Spur to stop commenting on the scenery. Spur was not surprised when Ngonda lurched to his feet and tore through the bubblelike bulkhead in search of a bathroom. The wall popped back into place, throwing a scatter of rainbows across its shivering surface.

Spur kept his face pressed to the hull. He'd expected the surface to be smooth and cold, like glass. Instead, it was warm and yielding, as if it were the flesh of some living creature. Below him the lakes and rivers gleamed in the afternoon sun like the shards of a broken mirror. The muddy Kalibobo River veered away to the west as the hover flew into the foothills of the Tarata Range. As the land rolled beneath him, Spur could spot areas where the bright-green hardwood forest was yielding ground to the blue-green of the conifers: hemlock and pine and spruce. There were only a few farms and isolated villages in the shadow of the mountains. They would have to fly over the Taratas to get to Littleton on the eastern slope.

At first Spur had difficulty identifying the familiar peaks. He was coming at them from the wrong direction and at altitude. But once he picked out the clenched fist of Woitape, he could count forward and back down the range: Taurika, Bootless Lowa and Boroko, curving to the northwest, Kaivuna and Samson Kokoda commanding the plain to the south. He murmured the names aloud, as long as the deputy wasn't around to hear. He had always liked how round the pukpuk sounds were, how they rolled in his mouth. When he'd been trapped in the burn with Vic, he was certain that he would never say them again.

When Chairman Winter bought Morobe's Pea from ComExplore IC, he had thought to rename everything on the planet and make a fresh start for his great experiment in preserving unenhanced humanity. But then a surprising number of ComExplore employees turned down his generous relocation offer; they wanted to stay on. Almost all of these pukpuks could trace their ancestry back to some ancient who had made planetfall on the first colonizing ships. More than a few claimed to be descended from Old Morobe herself. As a gesture of respect, the Chairman agreed to keep pukpuk names for some landforms. So there were still rivers, valleys, mountains and islands that honored the legacy of the first settlers.

Chairman Winter had never made a secret of his plans for Walden. At staggering personal expense, he had intended to transform the exhausted lands of Morobe's Pea. In their place he would make a paradise that re-created the heritage ecology of the home world. He would invite only true humans to come to Walden. All he asked was that his colonists forsake the technologies, which were spinning out of control on the Thousand Worlds. Those who agreed to live by the Covenant of Simplicity would be given land and citizenship. Eventually both the forest and the Transcendent State would overspread all of Walden.

But the pukpuks had other plans. They wouldn't leave and they refused to give up their banned technologies. At first trade between the two cultures of Walden flourished. In fact, the pukpuk industrial and commercial base propped up the fledgling Transcendent State. Citizens needed pukpuk goods, even if bots manufactured them. As time passed however, the Cooperative recognized that the pukpuks' continued presence was undermining the very foundations of the Transcendent State. When the Cooperative attempted to close off the borders in order to encourage local industry, black markets sprang up in the cities. Many citizens came to question the tenets of simplicity. The weak were tempted by forbidden knowledge. For the first time since the founding, the emigration rate edged into the double digits. When it was clear that the only way to save the Transcendent State was to push the pukpuks off the planet, Chairman Winter had authorized the planting of genetically enhanced trees. But once the forest began to encroach on the pukpuk barrens, the burns began.

The pukpuks were the clear aggressors in the firefight; even their sympathizers among the citizenry agreed on that. What no one could agree on was how to accommodate them without compromising. In fact, many of the more belligerent citizens held that the ultimate responsibility for the troubles lay with the Chairman himself. They questioned his decision not to force all of the pukpuks to emigrate after the purchase of Morobe's Pea. And some wondered why he could not order them to be rounded up and deported even now. It was, after all, his planet.

"We've come up with a compromise," said Ngonda as he pushed through the bulkhead into the compartment. He was still as pale as a root cellar mushroom, but he seemed steadier. He even glanced briefly down at the eastern slope of Bootless Lowa Mountain before cutting his eyes away. "I think we can let the High Gregory visit under your supervision."

Memsen, the High Gregory and a young girl followed him, which caused the bulkhead to burst altogether. Spur caught a glimpse of a knot of kids peering at him before the wall reformed itself two meters farther into the interior of the hover, creating the necessary extra space to fit them all. The High Gregory was carrying a tray of pastries, which he set on the table he caused to form out of the deck.

"Hello, Spur," he said. "How do you like flying? Your friend got sick but Memsen helped him. This is Penny."

"The Pendragon Chromlis Furcifer," said Memsen.

She and Spur studied each other. A little taller but perhaps a little younger than the High Gregory, the girl was dressed hood to boot in clothes made of supple metallic-green scales. The scales of her gloves were as fine as snakeskin while those that formed her tunic looked more like cherry leaves, even to the serrated edges. A rigid hood protected the back of her head. A tangle of thick, black hair wreathed her face.

"Penny," said the High Gregory, "you're supposed to shake his hand."

"I know," she said, but then clasped both hands behind her back and stared at the deck.

"Your right goes in his right." The High Gregory held out his own hand to demonstrate. "She's just a little shy," he said.

Spur crouched and held out his hand. She took it solemnly. They shook. Spur let her go. The girl's hand went behind her back again.

"You have a pretty name, Pendragon," said Spur.

"That's her title." Memsen faced left and then right before she sat on the bench next to Ngonda. "It means war chief."

"Really. And have you been to war, Penny?"

She shook her head – more of a twitch of embarrassment than a shake.

"This is her first," said the High Gregory. "But she's L'ung. She's just here to watch."

"I'm sorry," said Spur. "Who are the L'ung?"

Ngonda cleared his throat in an obvious warning. The High Gregory saw Memsen punch the air and whatever he'd been about to say died on his lips. The silence stretched long enough for Penny to realize that there was some difficulty about answering Spur's question.

"What, is he stupid?" She scrutinized Spur with renewed interest. "Are you stupid, Spur?"

"I don't think so." It was his turn to be embarrassed. "But maybe some people think that I am."

"This is complicated," said Memsen, filling yet another awkward pause. "We understand that people here seek to avoid complication." She considered. "Let's just say that the L'ung are companions to the High Gregory. They like to watch him make luck, you might say. Think of them as students. They've been sent from many different worlds, for many different reasons. Complications again. There is a political aspect . . ."

Ngonda wriggled in protest.

". . . which the deputy assures us you would only find confusing. So." She patted the bench. "Sit, Pendragon."

The Pendragon collected a macaroon from the pastry tray and obediently settled beside Memsen, then leaned to whisper in her ear.

"Yes," said Memsen, "we'll ask about the war."

Ngonda rose then, but caught himself against a bulkhead as if the change from sitting to standing had left him dizzy. "This isn't fair," he said. "The Cooperative has made a complete disclosure of the situation here, both to Kenning and to the Forum of the Thousand Worlds."

"What you sent was dull, dull, dull, friend Constant," said the High Gregory. "I don't think the people who made the report went anywhere near a burn. Someone told somebody else, and that somebody told them." Just then the hover bucked and the deputy almost toppled onto Memsen's lap. "You gave us a bunch of contracts and maps and pix of dead trees," continued the High Gregory. "I can't make luck out of charts. But Spur was there, he can tell us. He was almost burned up."

"Not about Motu River," said Spur quickly. "Nothing about that." Suddenly everyone was staring at him.

"Maybe," began Ngonda but the hover shuddered again and he slapped a hand hard against the bulkhead to steady himself. "Maybe we should tell him what we've agreed on."

Spur sensed that Memsen was judging him, and that she was not impressed. "If you want to talk in general about fighting fires," he said, "that's different."

Ngonda looked miserable. "Can't we spare this brave man . . . ?"

"Deputy Ngonda," said Memsen.

"What?" His voice was very small.

The High Gregory lifted the tray from the table and offered it to him. "Have a cookie."

Ngonda shrank from the pastries as if they might bite him. "Go ahead then," he said. "Scratch this foolish itch of yours. We can't stop you. We're just a bunch of throwbacks from a nothing world and you're . . ."

"Deputy Ngonda!" Memsen's voice was sharp.

He caught his breath. "You're Memsen the Twenty-Second and he's the High Gregory of Kenning and I'm not feeling very well." Ngonda turned to Spur, muttering. "Remember, they don't really care what happens to you. Or any of us."

"That's not true," said the High Gregory. "Not true at all."

But Ngonda had already subsided onto his bench, queasy and unvoiced.

"So." Memsen clicked her rings together. "You fight fires."

"I'm just a smokechaser." Ngonda's outburst troubled Spur. He didn't know anything about these upsiders, after all. Were they really any different than pukpuks? "I volunteered for the Corps about a year ago, got out of training last winter, was assigned the Ninth Regiment, Gold Squad. We mostly build handlines along the edges of burns to contain them." He leaned against the hull with his back to the view. "The idea is that we scrape off everything that can catch fire, dig to mineral soil. If we can fit a plow or tractor in, then we do, but in rough terrain we work by hand. That's about it. Boring as those reports you read."

"I don't understand." The High Gregory sprawled on the deck, picking idly at his sneakers. "If you're so busy digging, when do you put the fires out?"

"Fire needs three things," he said, "oxygen, fuel and temperature. They call it the triangle of combustion. Think of a burn as a chain of triangles. The sides of every triangle have to connect." He formed a triangle by pressing his thumbs and forefingers together. "Hot enough connects to enough air connects to enough stuff to burn. Take away a side and you break the triangle" – He separated his thumbs – "and weaken the chain. When a burn blows up, there's no good way to cut off its oxygen or lower the core temperature, so you have to attack the fuel side of the triangle. If you do your job, eventually there's nothing left to burn."

"Then you don't actually put fires out?" The High Gregory sounded disappointed.

"We do, but that's just hotspotting. Once we establish a handline, we have to defend it. So we walk the lines, checking for fires that start from flying sparks or underground runners. Trees might fall across a line. If we find a hot spot, we dig it out with a jacksmith or spray it cold with retardant from our splash packs." He noticed that the Pendragon was whispering again to Memsen. "I'm sorry," he said. "Is there something?"

Memsen gave him a polite smile – at least he hoped it was polite. "She asks about the people who set fire to themselves. Have you ever seen one?"

"A torch?" Spur frowned. "No." The lie slipped out with practiced ease.

"They must be very brave." The High Gregory wriggled across the deck on hands and knees to Spur's kit. "Hey, your bag got burnt here." He held the kit up to the afternoon light pouring through the hull, examining it. "And here too. Do you hate them?"

"No."

"But they tried to kill you."

"Not me. They're trying to kill the forest, maybe the Transcendent

State, but not me. They have no idea who I am." He motioned for the
kit and the High Gregory dragged it across the compartment to him.
"And I don't know any of them. We're all strangers." He opened the
kit, rummaged inside and pulled out a pix of Gold Squad. "Here's my
squad. That's full firefighting gear we're wearing." Dead friends
grinned at him from the pix. Vic, kneeling in the front row of the
picture, and Hardy, who was standing next to Spur. Pat. He flipped the
pix over and passed it to the High Gregory.

"Why are they doing this?" said Memsen. "You must have wondered
about it. Help us understand."

"It's complicated." He waited for Ngonda to pipe up with the official
line, but the deputy was gazing through the hull of the hover with eyes
of glass. "They should have gone long ago," said Spur. "They're
upsiders, really. They don't belong here anymore."

"A thousand worlds for the new," said Memsen, "one for the true.
That's what your chairman says, isn't it?"

"Your parents came here from other worlds," said the High Gregory.
"So that's why you think the pukpuks should've been willing to pack up
and go. But would you come back with us to Kenning if Jack Winter
said you should?"

"That's not why I . . ." Spur rubbed at his forehead. "I don't know,
maybe it is. Anyway, they were my grandparents, not my parents."

The High Gregory slid across the deck and handed the pix of Gold
Squad to Memsen. The Pendragon craned her neck to see.

"You have to understand," said Spur, "that the pukpuks hate the
new forests because they spread so fast. The trees grow like weeds, not
like the ones in my orchard." He glanced over his shoulder at the hills
beneath him. They were on the east side of the Taratas now and flying
lower. Almost home. "When Walden was still the Pea, this continent
was dry and mostly open. The Niah was prairie. There was supposedly
this huge desert, the Nev or the Neb, where Concord is now. The
pukpuks hunted billigags and tamed the gosdog herds. Their bots dug
huge pits to mine carbonatites and rare earths. Eventually they killed off
the herds, plowed the prairies under and exhausted all the surface
deposits. They created the barrens, raped this planet and then most of
them just left. Morobe's Pea was a dying world, that's why the
Chairman picked it. There was nothing for the pukpuks here, no reason
to stay until we came."

As the hover swooped low over the treetops, Spur could feel the tug
of home as real as gravity. After all he had been through, Littleton was
still drowsing at the base of Lamana Ridge, waiting for him. He
imagined sleeping in his own bed that night.

"Soon there won't be any more barrens," he said, "just forest. And
that will be the end of it."

The High Gregory stared at him with his unnerving yellow eyes.
"They're just trying to protect their way of life. And now you're telling
them that your way is better."

"No." Spur bit his lip; the truth of what the High Gregory said had long since pricked his soul. "But their way of life is to destroy our way."

Memsen flicked a finger against the pix of Gold Squad. "And so that's why they started this war?"

"Is this a war?" Spur took the pix from her and tucked it into his kit without looking at it again. "They set fires, we put them out. It's dangerous work, either way."

"People die," whispered the Pendragon.

"Yes," said Spur. "They do."

VIII

I have lived some thirty-odd years on this planet, and
I have yet to hear the first syllable of valuable or even
earnest advice from my seniors.
                    – Henry David Thoreau, *Journal*, 1852

Spur perched on a stump wondering how to sneak over to the Littleton train station. From where he sat, it looked hopeless. He had just bushwhacked through the forest from the edge of Spot Pond, where the hover had lingered long enough to put him onto the mucky shore. Now he was on the trail that led down Lamana Ridge. Just ahead of him was Blue Valley Road, a rough track that connected a handful of farms to Civic Route 22. CR22 became Broad Street as it passed through Littleton Commons, the village center. If he skulked down Blue Valley, he could hitch a ride on 22. Except who would be out this time of day? Neighbors. Littleton was a small town; his father had no doubt told everyone that his son the hero was due in on the 8:16 train from Heart's Wall. Of course, he could avoid 22 altogether and skirt around town to the train station. Except it was a good ten kilometers between the stump and the station and he was bone tired.

He decided to sit a little longer.

At least Ngonda had kept most of the upsiders out of Littleton. He could imagine Penny and Kai Thousandfold and little Senator-for-Life Dowm spreading through his bewildered village to gawk at family pix and open closets and ask awkward questions. The High Gregory was all Spur had to worry about. He would be stepping off the hover ramp tomorrow morning at Spot Pond with the deputy. He would pose as Ngonda's nephew and the deputy would be Spur's comrade-in-arms from Iron Squad. The High Gregory would spend the day touring Littleton and making whatever luck he could. He would sleep at Spur's house and the day after tomorrow he and Ngonda would catch the 7:57 southbound.

"Spur?" called a familiar voice from up the trail. "Is that Prosper Leung?"

Spur wanted to blurt, "No, not me, not at all." He wanted to run away. Instead he said, "Hello, Sly." There were worse citizens he could have run into than Sly Sawatdee.

The big man lumbered down the path. He was wearing cut-off shorts, one leg of which was several centimeters longer than the other. His barrel belly stretched his shirt, which was unbuttoned to his navel. His floppy hat was two-toned: dirty and dirtier. He was carrying a basket filled with gooseberries. His smile was bright as noon.

"That is my Prosper, I swear. My lucky little pine cone, all safe. But you're supposed to be away at the fires. How did you get here, so far from nowhere?"

"Fell out of the sky."

Sly giggled like a little boy. "Go around that again." Sly was gray as an oak and almost as old as Spur's father, but his years had never seemed a burden to him. If the Transcendent State truly wanted its citizens simple, then Sly Sawatdee was the most civic-minded person in Hamilton County. "You're joking me, no?"

"All right then, I walked."

"Walked from where?"

Spur pointed west.

Sly turned, as if he expected to see that a highway had been miraculously cut through the forest. "Nothing that way but trees and then mountains and then a hell of a lot more trees. That's a truckload of walking, green log. You must be tired. Have a gooseberry?" He offered Spur the basket. When Sly harvested the wild fruit, he just broke whole canes off, instead of picking individual berries. Close work he left to his grandnephews at home.

"All right then," said Spur. "I'm not here. I'm on the train from Heart's Wall. I get in at 8:16."

"Yeah? Then who am I talking to, my own shaggy self? Watch the thorns."

Spur popped one of the striped pink berries into his mouth. It was still warm from the sun; his teeth crunched the tiny seeds. "You don't like any of my answers?" He slung his kit over his shoulder.

"I'll nibble almost anything, Spur, but I spit out what doesn't taste good." He pressed a stubby forefinger into Spur's chest. "Your Sly can tell when you're carrying a secret, happy old shoe. Ease the weight of it off your back and maybe I can help you with it."

"Let's walk." Spur set off down the trail. Ahead the trees parted for Blue Valley Road. "How's my father?"

"Well enough for an old man." Sly fell into step alongside him. "Which is to say not so much of what he was. Said you got burnt when Vic Joerly and those other poor boys got killed." He peered at Spur. "You don't look much burnt."

"I was in a hospital in Concord." They had reached Blue Valley Road, which was nothing more than a couple of dirt ruts separated by a scraggle of weeds. "An upsider doctor saved my life." Spur headed toward CR22. "They can do things you wouldn't believe."

"I'll believe it this very minute if you say so." His mouth twisted like he'd bit into a wormy apple. "Only I never had much use for upsiders."

"Why? Have you ever met one?"

"Not me, but my DiDa used to say how they poke holes in their own brains and cut arms and legs off to sew on parts of bots in their place. Now where's the sense in a good man turning bot?"

There was no arguing with Sly when he got to remembering things his long-suffering father had told him. "I'm guessing you buried Vic already?"

"His body came on the train last Wednesday. The funeral was Friday. Most the village was there, biggest communion in years and just about the saddest day."

"How's Comfort?"

"Hard to say." He grimaced. "I paid respects, didn't chitchat. But I heard around that she's digging herself quite a hole. Wouldn't take much for her to fall in." He turned away from Spur and picked a stone up off the road. "What about you two?"

"I don't want to talk about it."

"Yeah." He lobbed the stone into the woods. "That's what I heard."

They were coming up on the Bandaran farmstead, cornstalks nodding in the field nearest the road. Spur could hear the wooden *clunk* of their windmill turning on the whispered breath of the afternoon. It was bringing water up from a well to splash into a dug pond where ducks gabbled and cropped. He tried to keep Sly between himself and the house as they passed, but whether he was noticed or not, nobody called out to him.

The next farmstead belonged to the Sawatdees, where Sly lived with his nephew Sunny and his family. On an impulse, Spur said, "There is a secret."

"Yeah, I know. I'm old, but I still hear the mosquitoes buzz."

"The thing is, I'm going to need your help. And you can't tell anyone."

Sly stepped in front of Spur and blocked his way. "Does anyone know who sat on Gandy Star's cherry pie? The one that she baked for your DiDa?"

Spur grinned. "I hope not."

He prodded Spur in the chest with his finger. "Did they ever figure the boy who was with Leaf Benkleman the day she got drunk on the applejack and threw up at the Solstice Day picnic?"

"It wasn't me." Spur put a hand on Sly's finger and pushed it away. "I was with you fishing that afternoon."

"Yeah, the fish story." He stood aside and motioned for Spur to pass. "Remember who told that one? The old citizen you always forget to come visit now that you're all grown up." They continued down the road. The Sawatdee farmstead was just around the next bend.

"I remember, Sly. Can you help? I need a ride home right now."

"The cottage or your DiDa's house?"

"Diligence Cottage."

He nodded. "Sunny can take you in the truck."

"No, it has to be you. You're going to be the only one who knows I'm back. Part of the secret."

Sly swung the basket of gooseberries in wider arcs as he walked. "Sunny doesn't want me driving at night anymore."

"Don't worry, you'll be back in plenty of time for supper. But then I'll need you again in the morning. Come get me first thing. I'm meeting someone up at Spot Pond."

"Spot Pond? Nobody there but frogs."

Spur leaned closer to Sly. "I can tell you, but you have to promise to help, no matter what." He lowered his voice. "This is a *big* secret, Sly."

"How big?" Sly looked worried. "Bigger than a barn?"

"Bigger than the whole village." Spur knew Sly would be pleased and flattered to be the only one in Littleton whom Spur had invited into his conspiracy. "In or out, my friend?"

"In up to here." Sly raised a hand over his head. "Ears open, mouth shut." He giggled.

"Good." Spur didn't give him time to reconsider. "An upsider is coming to visit Littleton."

"An upsider." Sly took this for another joke. "And he parks his spaceship where? On Broad Street?"

"A hover is going to put him off near Spot Pond. He's going to stay with me for a day. One day. Nobody is supposed to know he's from the upside."

"A hover." Sly glanced over one shoulder and then the other, as if he expected to spot the hover following them. "One of those birdbots in our sky."

Spur nodded.

"And you want this?"

The question caught him off guard, because he realized that sometime in the last few hours he had changed his mind. "I do, Sly." Spur wanted to spend more time with the High Gregory and it was fine with him if they were together at Diligence Cottage. He just didn't want to inflict the upsider on the rest of his sleepy village. They wouldn't understand.

Except Sly was shaking his head. "Nothing good ever came of getting tangled up with space people."

"I'm just curious is all," said Spur.

"Curious can't sit still, young sprout. Curious always goes for the closer look." For the first time since Spur had known him, Sly Sawatdee looked his age. "And now I'm thinking what will happen to your DiDa when you leave us. He's a good man, you know. I've known him all my life."

IX

> For when man migrates, he carries with him not only
> his birds, quadrupeds, insects, vegetables and his
> very sward, but his orchard also.
> – Henry David Thoreau, *Wild Apples*, 1862

Capability Roger Leung loved apples. He was fond of the other pomes
as well, especially pears and quince. Stone fruits he didn't much care
for, although he tolerated sour cherries in memory of GiGa's pies. But
apples were Cape's favorite, the ancient fruit of the home world. He
claimed that apples graced the tables of all of Earth's great civilizations:
Roman, Islamic, American, and Dalamist. Some people in Littleton
thought that Spur's father loved his apple trees more than he loved his
family. Probably Spur's mother, Lucy Bliss Leung, had been one of
these. Probably that was why she left him when Spur was three, first to
move to Heart's Wall and then clear across the continent to Providence.
Spur never got the chance to ask her because he never saw her again
after she moved to Southwest. The citizens of Walden did not travel for
mere pleasure.

Spur's grandparents had arrived on Walden penniless and with only
a basic knowledge of farming. Yet hard work and brutal frugality had
built their farmstead into a success. However, the price they paid for
single-minded dedication to farming was high; of their three children,
only Cape chose to stay on the farm as an adult. And even he moved out
of Diligence Cottage when he was sixteen and put up a hut for himself
at the farthest edge of the Leung property. He was trying to escape their
disapproval. Whenever he looked at the tell or visited friends or climbed
a tree to read a book, GiGo or GiGa would carp at him for being
frivolous or lazy. They couldn't see the sense of volunteering for the fire
department or playing left base for the Littleton Eagles when there were
chores to be done. Sometimes weeks might pass without Cape saying an
unnecessary word to his parents.

Yet it had been Cape who transformed the family fortunes with his
apples. When he was eighteen, he began attending classes at the
hortischool extension in Longwalk, very much against GiGo's wishes.
He had paid tuition out of money earned doing odd jobs around the
village – another pointless diversion from home chores that irritated his
parents. Cape had become interested in fruit trees after brown rot
spoiled almost the entire crop of Littleton's sour cherries the year
before. All the farmers in the village raised fruit, but their orchards were
usually no more than a dozen trees, all of traditional heirloom varieties.
Crops were small, usually just enough for home use because of the
ravages of pests and disease. Farmers battled Terran immigrants like
tarnished plant bugs, sawflies, wooly aphids, coddling moths,
leafrollers, lesser apple worms and the arch enemy: plum curculio.
There were mildews, rusts, rots, cankers, blotches and blights to
contend with as well. The long growing season of fruit trees made them

vulnerable to successive attacks. Citizens across the Transcendent State debated whether or not Chairman Winter had introduced insect evil and fungal disease into his new Garden of Eden on purpose. The question had never been settled. But at hortischool, Cape learned about neem spray, extracted from the chinaberry tree and the organic insecticide pyrethrum, which was made from dried daisies. And he heard about an amazing cider apple called Huang's Nectar, a disease-resistant early bloomer, well suited to the climate of Southeast but not yet proven hardy in the north. As much to spite his father as to test the new variety, he had drained his savings and bought a dozen saplings of W4 semi-dwarfing rootstock. He started his own orchard on land he had cleared near his hut. Two years later, he brought in his first – admittedly light – harvest, which nevertheless yielded the sweetest cider and smoothest applejack anyone in Littleton had ever tasted. Cape purchased a handscrew press in his third year and switched from fermenting his cider in glass carboys to huge oak barrels by his fifth. And he bought more apple trees – he never seemed to have enough: McIntosh, GoRed, Jay's Pippin, Alumar Gold, Adam and Eve. Soon he began to grow rootstock and sell trees to other farmers. By the time Cape married Spur's mother, the Leungs were renting land from farmsteads on either side of their original holding. GiGo and GiGa lived long enough to see their son become the most prosperous farmer in Littleton. GiGo, however, never forgave himself for being wrong, or Cape for being right, about the apples.

Cape had given Spur and Comfort his parents' house as a wedding present; Diligence Cottage had been empty ever since GiGa had died. Cape had long since transformed his own little hut into one of the grandest homes in Littleton. Spur had Sly drop him off just down Jane Powder Street from the cottage, hoping to avoid the big house and the inevitable interrogation by his father for as long as possible. After seeing Sly's dismay at the news of the High Gregory's visit, he was thinking he might try to keep the High Gregory's identity from Cape, if he could.

However, as Spur approached the front door, he spotted Cape's scooter parked by the barn and then Cape himself reaching from a ladder into the scaffold branches of one of GiGo's ancient Macoun apples. He was thinning the fruit set. This was twice a surprise: first because Cape usually avoided the house where he had grown up, and second because he had been set against trying to rejuvenate the Leung's original orchard, arguing that it was a waste of Spur's time. In fact the peaches and the plum tree had proved beyond saving. However, through drastic pruning, Spur had managed to bring three Macouns and one Sunset apple, and a Northstar cherry back into production again.

"DiDa!" Spur called out so that he wouldn't startle his father. "It's me."

"Prosper?" Cape did not look down as he twisted an unripe apple free. "You're here already. Something's wrong?" He dropped the cull to the pack of gosdogs waiting below. A female leapt and caught the apple in midair in its long beak. It chomped twice and swallowed. Then it chased its scaly tail in delight, while the others hooted at Cape.

"Everything's fine. There was a last minute change and I managed to get a ride home." Spur doubted his father would be satisfied with this vague explanation, but it was worth a try. "What are you doing up there?" He dropped his kit on the front step of the farmhouse and trudged over to the orchard. "I thought you hated GiGo's useless old trees."

Cape sniffed. "Macoun is a decent enough apple; they're just too damn much work. And since you weren't around to tend to them – but I should come down. You're home, Prosper. Wait, I'll come down."

"No, finish what you're doing. How are things here?"

"It was a dry spring." He culled another green apple, careful to grasp the fruiting spur with one hand and the fruit with the other. "June was parched too, but the county won't call it a drought yet." The gosdogs swirled and tumbled beneath him as he let the apple fall. "The June drop was light, so I've had to do a lot of thinning. We had sawfly but the curculio isn't so bad. They let you out of the hospital so soon, Prosper? Tell me what you're not telling me."

"I'm fine. Ready to build fence and buck firewood."

"Have you seen Comfort yet?"

"No."

"You were supposed to arrive by train."

"I hitched a ride with a friend."

"From Concord?"

"I got off the train in Wheelwright."

"Wheelwright." One of the gosdogs was trying to scrabble up the ladder. "I don't know where that is exactly. Somewhere in Southeast, I think. Lee County maybe?"

"Around there. What's wrong with Macouns?"

"Ah." He shook his head in disapproval. "A foolish tree that doesn't know what's good for it." He gestured at the immature apples all around him. "Look at the size of this fruit set. Even after the June drop, there are too many apples left on the branches. Grow more than a few of these trees and you'll spend the summer hand thinning. Have you seen Comfort yet?"

"No." Spur plucked a low-hanging cherry, which held its green stem, indicating it wasn't quite ripe; despite this, he popped it into his mouth. "Sour cherries aren't too far from harvest, I'd say." He spat the pit at the gosdogs. "They're pulling the entire regiment back to Cloyce Forest, which is where I'll catch up with them."

"Civic refreshment – you'll be busy." Cape wound up and pitched a cull into the next row of trees. As the pack hurtled after it, he backed down the ladder. "Although I wouldn't mind some help. You're home for how long?"

"Just the week."

He hefted the ladder and pivoted it into the next tree. "Not much time."

"No."

He was about to climb up again when he realized that he had yet to greet his only son. "I'm glad you're safe, Prosper," he said, placing a hand on his shoulder. "But I still don't understand about the train." He held Spur at arm's length. "You got off why?"

Spur was desperate to change the subject. "DiDa, I know you don't want to hear this but Comfort and I are probably going to get divorced."

Cape grimaced and let go of Spur. "Probably?" He set his foot on the bottom rung.

"Yes." The gosdogs were back already, swarming around the ladder, downy feathers flying. "I'm sorry." Spur stepped away.

"Prosper, you know my feelings about this." He mounted the ladder. "But then everyone knows I'm a simple fool when it comes to keeping a woman."

Cape Leung had been saying things like that ever since Spur's mother left him. On some days he bemoaned the failure of his marriage as a wound that had crippled him for life, on others he preened as if surviving it were his one true distinction. As a young man, Spur had thought these were merely poses and had resented his father for keeping his feelings about Spur's mother in a tangle. Now, Spur thought maybe he understood.

"She was never comfortable here," Spur said morosely. "I blame myself for that. But I don't think she was born to be a farmer's wife. Never was, never will be."

"Are you sure?" Cape sucked air between his teeth as he leaned into the tree. "She's had a terrible shock, Prosper. Now this?"

"It isn't going to come as a shock," he said, his voice tight. His father had far too many reasons for wanting Spur to make his marriage work. He had always liked both of the Joerly kids and had loved the way Comfort had remade both Diligence Cottage and his only son. Cape was impatient for grandchildren. And then there was the matter of the land, once agreeably complicated, now horribly simple. Ever since they had been kids, it had been a running joke around the village that someday Spur would marry Comfort and unite the Joerly farmstead with the Leung holdings, immediately adjacent to the east. Of course, everyone knew it wouldn't happen quite that way, because of Vic. But now Vic was dead.

"When will you see her?"

"I don't know," said Spur. "Soon. Anyway, it's been a long day for me. I'm going in."

"Come back to the house for supper?" said Cape.

"No, I'm too tired. I'll scrape up something to eat in the cottage."

"You won't have to look too hard." He grinned. "Your fans stopped by this morning to open the place up. I'm sure they left some goodies. I've been telling the neighbors that you were due home today." He dropped another cull to the gosdogs. "Now that I think about it, I should probably ride into town to tell folks not to meet your train. I still can't believe you got a ride all the way from ... where did you say it was again?"

"What fans?"

"I think it must have been Gandy Joy who organized it; at least she was the one who came to the house to ask my permission." He stepped off the ladder into the tree to reach the highest branches. "But I saw the Velez girls waiting in the van, Peace Toba, Summer Millisap." He stretched for a particularly dense cluster of apples. "Oh, and after they left, I think Comfort might have stopped by the cottage."

X

> I find it wholesome to be alone the greater part of the time. To be in company, even with the best, is soon wearisome and dissipating.
> – Henry David Thoreau, *Walden*

The refrigerator was stocked with a chicken and parsnip casserole, a pot of barley soup, half a dozen eggs, a little tub of butter, a slab of goat cheese and three bottles of root beer. There was a loaf of fresh onion rye bread and glass jars of homemade apricot and pear preserves on the counter. But what Spur ate for supper was pie. Someone had baked him two pies, a peach and an apple. He ate half of each, and washed them down with root beer. Why not? There was nobody around to scold him and he was too tired to heat up the soup or the casserole, much less to eat it. Eating pie took no effort at all. Besides, he hadn't had a decent slice of pie since he had left Littleton. The niceties of baking were beyond the field kitchens of the Corps of Firefighters.

Afterward he poured himself a tumbler of applejack and sat at the kitchen table, trying to decide who had brought what. The barley soup felt like an offering from sturdy Peace Toba. Gandy Joy knew he had developed a secret weakness for root beer, despite growing up in a farmstead that lived and died by cider. The Millisaps had the largest herd of goats in town. He wasn't sure who had made the casserole, although he would have bet it wasn't the Velez sisters. Casseroles were too matronly for the Velezes. They were in their early twenties and single and a little wild – at least by Littleton's standards. They had to be, since they were searching for romance in a village of just over six hundred souls. Everyone said that they would probably move to Longwalk someday, or even to Heart's Wall, which would break their parents' hearts. He was guessing that the pies had come from their kitchen. A well-made pie was as good as a love letter. But would the Velez sisters just assume he and Comfort were finally going to split? Comfort must have decided on her own and was telling people in the village. Then Spur remembered that Sly had said he had heard something. And if Sly knew, then everyone knew. In a nosy village like Littleton, if a kid skinned his knee playing baseball, at least three moms fell out of trees waving bandages.

Spur put the food away and washed the dishes, after which there was no reason to stay in the kitchen. But he lingered for a while, trying to avoid the memories which whispered to him from the other rooms of the cottage. He remembered his stern grandparents ghosting around the wood stove in their last years. He remembered boarding Diligence Cottage up after GiGo died, the lumpy furniture and the threadbare carpet receding into the gloom. And then he and Comfort pulling the boards down and rediscovering their new home. The newlyweds had moved almost all of GiGo and GiGa's things to the barn, where they moldered to this day. Spur and Comfort had dusted and cleaned and scraped and painted everything in the empty cottage. He remembered sitting on the floor with his back to the wall of the parlor, looking at the one lonely chair they owned. Comfort had cuddled beside him, because she said that if there wasn't room for both of them on the chair then neither would sit. He had kissed her then. There had been a lot of kissing in those days. In fact, Comfort had made love to him in every room of the cottage. It was her way of declaring ownership and of exorcising the disapproving spirits of the old folks.

Now that she was about to pass out of his life, he thought that Comfort might have been too ferocious a lover for his tastes. Sometimes it was all he could do to stay with her in bed. Occasionally her passion alarmed him, although he would never have admitted this to himself while they were together. It would have been unmanly. But just before they had volunteered for the Corps, when things had already begun to go wrong, he had felt as if there were always another man standing next to them, watching. Not anyone real, but rather Comfort's idea of a lover. Spur knew by then he wasn't that man. He had just been a place-holder for whoever it was she was waiting for.

Finally he left the kitchen. The women who had opened Diligence Cottage had done their best, but there was no air to work with on this close July night. The rooms were stale and hot. He sat out on the porch until the needlebugs drove him inside. Then he propped a fan in either window of the bedroom and dumped his kit out onto the bedspread. What did he have to wear that was cool? He picked up a tee shirt but then smelled the tang of smoke still clinging to it. He dropped it onto the bed and chuckled mirthlessly. He was *home*; he could put on his own clothes. He opened the dresser drawer and pulled out the shorts that Comfort had bought for his birthday and a gauzy blue shirt. The pants were loose and slid down his hips. He had lost weight in the firefight and even more in the hospital. Too much heartbreak. Not enough pie.

Then, against his better judgment, he crossed the bedroom to Comfort's dresser and began to open drawers. He had never under-stood why she abandoned everything she owned when she left him. Did it mean that she was planning to come back? Or that she was completely rejecting their life together? He didn't touch anything, just looked at her panties, black and navy blue and gray – no pastels or patterns for his girl. Then the balled socks, sleeveless blouses, shirts with the arms folded behind them, heavy workpants, lightweight sweaters. And in the bottom drawer the jade pajamas of black market material so sheer that it would slip from her body if he even thought about tugging at it.

"Not exactly something a farmer's wife would wear." Spur spoke aloud just to hear a voice; the dense silence of the cottage was making him edgy. "At least, not *this* farmer's wife."

Now that he was losing Comfort, Spur realized that the only person in his family was his father. It struck him that he had no memories of his father in the cottage. He could see Cape in the dining room of the big house or the library or dozing in front of the tell. Alone, always alone.

Spur had a bad moment then. He stepped into the bathroom, and splashed some cold water on his face. He would have to remarry or he would end up like his father. He tried to imagine kissing Bell Velez, slipping a hand under her blouse, but he couldn't.

"Knock, knock." A woman called from the parlor. "Your father claims you're back." It was Gandy Joy.

"Just a minute." Spur swiped at his dripping face with the hand towel. As he strode from the bedroom, the smile on his face was genuine. He was grateful to Gandy Joy for rescuing him from the silence and his dark mood.

She was a small, round woman with flyaway hair that was eight different shades of gray. She had big teeth and an easy smile. Her green sundress exposed the wrinkled skin of her wide shoulders and arms; despite farm work she was still as fair as the flesh of an apple. Spur had been mothered by many of the women of Littleton as a boy, but Gandy Joy was the one who meant the most to him. He had to stoop over slightly to hug her.

"Prosper." She squeezed him so hard it took his breath away. "My lovely boy, you're safe."

"Thank you for opening the cottage," he said. "But how did you find everything?" She smelled like lilacs and he realized that she must have perfumed herself just for him.

"Small house." She stepped back to take him in. "Not many places a thing can be."

Spur studied her as well; she seemed to have aged five years in the ten months since he'd seen her last. "Big enough, especially for one."

"I'm sorry, Prosper."

When Spur saw the sadness shadow her face, he knew that she had heard something. She was, after all, the village virtuator. He supposed he should have been relieved that Comfort was letting everyone know she wanted a divorce, since that was what he wanted too. Instead he just felt hollow. "What has she told you?"

Gandy Joy just shook her head. "You two have to talk."

He thought about pressing her, but decided to let it drop. "Have a seat, Gandy. Can I get you anything? There's applejack." He steered her toward the sofa. "And root beer."

"No thanks." She nodded at her wooden-bead purse, which he now noticed against the bolster of the sofa. "I brought communion."

"Really?" he said, feigning disappointment. "Then you're only here on business?"

"I'm here for more reasons than you'll ever know." She gave him a playful tap on the arm. "And keeping souls in communion is my calling, lovely boy, not my business." She settled on the sofa next to her purse and he sat facing her on the oak chair that had once been his only stick of furniture.

"How long are you with us?" She pulled out three incense burners and set them on the cherry wood table that Comfort had ordered all the way from Providence.

"A week." Spur had seen Gandy Joy's collection of incense burners, but he had never known her to use three at once for just two people. "I'll catch up with the squad in Cloyce Forest. Easy work for a change; just watching the trees grow." He considered three excessive; after all, he had accepted communion regularly with the other firefighters.

"We weren't expecting you so soon." She slipped the aluminum case marked with the seal of the Transcendent State from her purse. "You didn't come on the train."

"No."

She selected a communion square from the case. She touched it to her forehead, the tip of her nose and her lips and then placed it on edge in the incense burner. She glanced up at him and still the silence stretched. "Just no?" she said finally. "That's all?"

Spur handed her the crock of matches kept especially for communion. "My father told you to ask, didn't he?"

"I'm old, Prosper." Her smile was crooked. "I've earned the right to be curious." She repeated the ritual with the second communion square.

"You have. But he *really* wants to know."

"He always does." She set the third communion in its burner. "But then everybody understands about that particular bend in Capability's soul." She selected a match from the crock and struck it.

Now it was Spur's turn to wait. "So aren't you going to ask me about the train?"

"I was, but since you have something to hide, I won't." She touched the fire to each of the three squares and they caught immediately, the oils in the communion burning with an eager yellow flame. "I don't really care, Spur. I'm just happy that you're back and safe." She blew the flames out on each of the squares, leaving a glowing edge. "Make the most of your time with us."

Spur watched the communion smoke uncoil in the still air of his parlor. Then, as much to please Gandy Joy as to reestablish his connection with his village, he leaned forward and breathed deeply. The fumes that filled his nose were harsh at first, but wispier and so much sweeter than the strangling smoke of a burn. As he settled back into his chair, he got the subtle accents: the yeasty aroma of bread baking, a whiff of freshly split oak and just a hint of the sunshine scent of a shirt fresh off the clothesline. He could feel the communion smoke fill his head and touch his soul. It bound him as always to the precious land and the cottage where his family had made a new life, the orderly Leung farmstead, his home town and of course to this woman who loved him more than his mother ever had and his flinty father who couldn't help the way he was and faithful Sly Sawatdee and generous Leaf Benkleman and droll Will Sambusa and steadfast Peace Toba and the entire Velez family who had always been so generous to him and yes, even his dear Comfort Rose Joerly, who was leaving him but who was nonetheless a virtuous citizen of Littleton.

He shivered when he noticed Gandy Joy watching him. No doubt she was trying to gauge whether he had fully accepted communion. "Thank you," he said, "for all the food."

She nodded, satisfied. "You're welcome. We just wanted to show how proud we are of you. This is your village, after all, and you're our Prosper and we want you to stay with us always."

He chuckled nervously. Why did everyone think he was going somewhere?

She leaned forward, and lowered her voice. "But I have to say there was more than a little competition going on over the cooking." She chuckled. "Bets were placed on which dish you'd eat first."

"Bets?" Spur found the idea of half a dozen women competing to please him quite agreeable. "And what did you chose?"

"After I saw everything laid out, I was thinking that you'd start in on pie. After all, there wasn't going to be anyone to tell you no."

Spur laughed. "Pie was all I ate. But don't tell anyone."

She tapped her forefinger to her lips and grinned.

"So I'm guessing that the Velez girls made the pies?"

"There was just the one – an apple, I think is what Bell said."

"I found two on the counter: apple and a peach."

"Really?" Gandy sat back on the couch. "Someone else must have dropped it off after we left."

"Might have been Comfort," said Spur. "DiDa said he thought she stopped by. I was expecting to find a note."

"Comfort was *here*?"

"She lives here," said Spur testily. "At least, all her stuff is here."

Gandy took a deep breath over the incense burners and held it in for several moments. "I'm worried about her, Prosper," she said finally. "She hasn't accepted communion since we heard about Vic. She keeps to herself and when we go to visit her at home, she's as friendly as a brick. There's mourning and then there's self-pity, Prosper. She's been talking about selling the farmstead, moving away. We've lost poor Victor, we don't want to lose her too. Littleton wouldn't be the same without the Joerlys. When you see her, whatever you two decide, make sure she knows that."

Spur almost groaned then, but the communion had him in its benevolent grip. If citizens didn't help one another, there would be no Transcendent State. "I'll do my best," he said, his voice tight.

"Oh, I know you will, my lovely boy. I know it in my soul."

XI

Things do not change; we change.
          – Henry David Thoreau, *Journal*, 1850

The High Gregory sat next to Spur in the bed of the Sawatdee's truck, their backs against the cab, watching the dust billow behind them. Sly and Ngonda rode up front. As the truck jolted down Blue Valley Road, Spur could not help but see the excitement on the High Gregory's face. The dirt track was certainly rough, but the boy was bouncing so high Spur was worried that he'd fly over the side. He was even making Sly nervous, and the old farmer was usually as calm as moss. But then Sly Sawatdee didn't make a habit of giving rides to upsiders. He kept glancing over his shoulder at the High Gregory through the open rear slider.

Spur had no doubt that his cover story for the High Gregory and Ngonda was about to unravel. The High Gregory had decided to wear purple overalls with about twenty brass buttons. Although there was nothing wrong with his black tee shirt, the bandana knotted around his neck was a pink disaster embellished with cartoons of beets and carrots and corn on the cob. At least he had used some upsider trick to disguise the color of his eyes. Ngonda's clothes weren't quite as odd, but they too were a problem. Spur had seen citizens wearing flair jackets and high-collar shirts – but not on a hot summer Sunday and not in Littleton. Ngonda was dressed for a meeting at the Cooperative's Office of Diplomacy in Concord. Spur's only hope was to whisk them both to Diligence Cottage and either hide them there or find them something more appropriate to wear.

"Tell me about the gosdogs," said the High Gregory.

Spur leaned closer, trying to hear him over the roar of the truck's engine, the clatter of its suspension and the crunch of tires against the dirt road. "Say again?"

"The gosdogs," shouted the High Gregory. "One of your native species. You know, four-footed, feathered, they run in packs."

"Gosdogs, yes. What do you want to know?"

"You eat them."

"I don't." The High Gregory seemed to be waiting for him to elaborate, but Spur wasn't sure what he wanted to know exactly. "Other citizens do, but the browns only. The other breeds are supposed to be too stringy."

"And when you kill them, do they know they're about to die? How do you do it?"

"I don't." Spur had never slaughtered a gosdog; Cape didn't believe in eating them. However, Spur had slaughtered chickens and goats and helped once with a bull. Butchering was one of the unpleasant chores that needed doing on a farm, like digging postholes or mucking out the barn. "They don't suffer."

"Really? That's good to know." The High Gregory did not look convinced. "How smart do you think they are?"

At that moment Sly stepped on the brakes and swung the steering wheel; the truck bumped onto the smooth pavement of Civic Route 22.

"Not very," said Spur. With the road noise abating, his voice carried into the cab.

"Not very what?" said Constant Ngonda.

The High Gregory propped himself up to speak through the open window. "I was asking Spur how smart the gosdogs are. I couldn't find much about them, considering. Why is that, do you suppose?"

"The ComExplore Survey Team rated them just 6.4 on the Peekay Animal Intelligence Scale," said Ngonda. "A goat has more brains."

"Yes, I found that," said the High Gregory, "but what's interesting is that the first evaluation was the only one ever done. And it would have been very much in the company's interests to test them low, right? And of course it made no sense for your pukpuks to bother with a follow-up test. And now your Transcendent State has a stake in keeping that rating as it is."

"Are you suggesting some kind of conspiracy?" Ngonda was working his way to a fine outrage. "That we're deliberately abusing an intelligent species?"

"I'm just asking questions, friend Constant. And no, I'm not saying they're as smart as humans, no, no, never. But suppose they were retested and their intelligence was found to be . . . let's say 8.3. Or even 8.1. The Thousand Worlds might want to see them protected."

"Protected?" The deputy's voice snapped through the window.

"Why, don't you think that would be a good idea? You'd just have to round them up and move them to a park or something. Let them loose in their native habitat."

"There *is* no native habitat left on Walden." Spur noticed that Sly was so intent on the conversation that he was coasting down the highway. "Except maybe underwater." A westbound oil truck was catching up to them fast.

"We could build one then," said the High Gregory cheerfully. "The L'ung could raise the money. They need something to do."

"Can I ask you something?" Ngonda had passed outrage and was well on his way to fury.

"Yes, friend Constant. Of course."

"How old are you?"

"Twelve standard. My birthday is next month. I don't want a big party this year. It's too much work."

"They know themselves in the mirror," said Sly.

"What?" Ngonda was distracted from whatever point he was about to make. "What did you just say?"

"When one of them looks at his reflection, he recognizes himself." Sly leaned back toward the window as he spoke. "We had this brood, a mother and three pups, who stayed indoors with us last winter. They were house-trained, mostly." The truck slowed to a crawl. "So my granddaughter Brookie is playing dress up with the pups one night and the silly little pumpkin decides to paint one all over with grape juice. Said she was trying to make the first purple gosdog – her father babies her, don't you know? But she actually stains the right rear leg before her mother catches her out. And when Brookie lets the poor thing loose, it galumphs to the mirror and backs up to see its grapy leg. Then it gets to whimpering and clucking and turning circles like they do when they're upset." Sly checked the rearview mirror and noticed the oil truck closing in on them for the first time. "I was there, saw it clear as tap water. The idea that it knew who it was tipped me over for a couple of days." He put two wheels onto the shoulder of CR22 and waved the truck past. "It's been a hardship, but I've never eaten a scrap of gosdog since."

"That's the most ridiculous thing I've ever heard," said Ngonda.

"Lots of citizens feel that way," said Spur.

"As is their right. But to jump to conclusions based on this man's observations . . ."

"I don't want to jump, friend Constant," said the High Gregory. "Let's not jump."

Although the deputy was ready to press his argument, nobody else spoke and gradually he subsided. Sly pulled back onto CR22 and drove the rest of the way at a normal pace. They passed the rest of the trip in silence; the wind seemed to whip Spur's thoughts right out of his head.

As they turned off Jane Powder Street onto the driveway of the cottage, Sly called back to him. "Looks like you've got company."

Spur rubbed the back of his neck in frustration. Who told the townsfolk that he wanted them to come visiting? He leaned over the side of the truck but couldn't see anyone until they parked next to the porch. Then he spotted the scooter leaning against the barn.

If it was really in the High Gregory's power to make luck, then what he was brewing up for Spur so far was pure misfortune. It was Comfort's scooter.

The High Gregory stood up in the back of the truck and turned around once, surveying the farmstead. "This is your home, Spur." He said it not as a question but as a statement, as if Spur were the one seeing it for the first time. "I understand now why you would want to live so far from everything. It's like a poem here."

Constant Ngonda opened the door and stepped down onto the dusty drive. From his expression, the deputy appeared to have formed a different opinion of the cottage. However, he was enough of a diplomat to keep it to himself. He clutched a holdall to his chest and was mounting the stairs to the porch when he noticed that no one else had moved from the truck.

They were watching Comfort stalk toward them from the barn, so clearly in a temper that heat seemed to shimmer off her in the morning swelter.

"That woman looks angry as lightning," said Sly. "You want me to try to get in her way?"

"No," said Spur. "She'd probably just knock you over."

"But this is your Comfort?" said the High Gregory. "The wife that you don't live with anymore. This is so exciting, just what I was hoping for. She's come for a visit – maybe to welcome you back?"

"I'm not expecting much of a welcome," said Spur. "If you'll excuse me, I should talk to her. Sly, if you wouldn't mind staying a few minutes, maybe you could take Constant and young Lucky here inside. There's plenty to eat."

"Lucky," said the High Gregory, repeating the name they had agreed on for him, as if reminding himself to get into character. "Hello, friend Comfort," he called. "I'm Lucky. Lucky Ngonda."

She shook the greeting off and kept bearing down on them. His wife was a slight woman, with fine features and eyes dark as currants. Her hair was long and sleek and black. She was wearing a sleeveless yellow gingham dress that Spur had never seen before. Part of her new wardrobe, he thought, her new life. When he had been in love with her, Spur had thought that Comfort was pretty. But now, seeing her for the first time in months, he decided that she was merely delicate. She did not look strong enough for the rigors of life on a farm.

Spur opened the tailgate and the High Gregory jumped from the back of the truck. Ngonda came back down the stairs to be introduced to Comfort. Spur was handing the High Gregory's bag down to Sly as she drew herself up in front of them.

"Gandy Joy said you wanted to see me first thing in the morning." She did not waste time on introductions. "I didn't realize that I'd be interrupting a party."

"Comfort," said Spur, "I'm sorry." He stopped himself then, chagrined at how easily he fell into the old pattern. When they were together, he was always apologizing.

"Morning, sweet corn," said Sly. "Not that much of a party, I'm afraid."

"But there are snacks inside," the High Gregory said. "This is such a beautiful place you two have. I've just met Spur myself, but I'm pretty sure he's going to be happy here someday. My name is Lucky Ngonda." He held out his hand to her. "We're supposed to shake but first you have to say your name."

Comfort had been so fixated on Spur that she had brushed by the High Gregory. Now she scrutinized him in all his purple glory and her eyes went wide. "Why are you dressed like that?"

"Is something wrong?" He glanced down at his overalls. "I'm dressed to visit my friend Spur." He patted his bare head. "It's the hat, isn't it? I'm supposed to be wearing a hat."

"Constant Ngonda, a friend of Spur's from the Ninth." Ngonda oozed between them. "I apologize for intruding; I know you have some important things to discuss. Why don't we give you a chance to catch up now? My nephew and I will be glad to wait inside." He put an arm around the High Gregory's shoulder and aimed him at the porch.

"Wait," said the High Gregory. "I thought I was your cousin."

"Take as long as you want, Spur," Ngonda said as he hustled the boy off. "We'll be fine."

Sly shook his head in disbelief. "I'll make sure they don't get into trouble." He started after them.

"There are pies in the refrigerator," Spur called after him. "Most of an apple pie and just a couple of slices of a peach." He steeled himself and turned back to Comfort. "My father said you were here the other day." He aimed a smile at her but it bounced off. "You made my favorite pie."

"Who are those people?" Her eyes glittered with suspicion. "The boy is strange. Why have you brought them here?"

"Let's walk." He took her arm and was surprised when she went along without protest. He felt the heat of her glare cooling as they strode away from the cottage. "I did have a chat with Gandy Joy," he said. "She said you were feeling pretty low."

"I have the right to feel however I feel," she said stiffly.

"You haven't been accepting communion."

"Communion is what they give you so you feel smart about acting stupid. Tell her that I don't need some busybody blowing smoke in my eyes to keep me from seeing what's wrong." She stopped and pulled him around to face her. "We're getting divorced, Spur."

"Yes." He held her gaze. "I know." He wanted to hug her or maybe shake her. Touch her long black hair. Instead his hands hung uselessly by his sides. "But I'm still concerned about you."

"Why?"

"You've been talking about moving away."

She turned and started walking again. "I can't run a farm by myself."

"We could help you, DiDa and I," He caught up with her. "Hire some of the local kids. Maybe bring in a tenant from another village."

"And how long do you think that would work for? If you want to run my farm, Spur, buy it from me."

"Your family is an important part of this place. The whole village wants you to stay. Everyone would pitch in."

She chuckled grimly. "Everyone wanted us to get married. They want us to stay together. I'm tired of having everyone in my life.

He wasn't going to admit to her that he felt the same way sometimes. "Where will you go?"

"Away."

"Just away?"

"I miss him, I really do. But I don't want to live anywhere near Vic's grave."

Spur kicked a stone across the driveway and said nothing for several moments. "You're sure it's not me you want to get away from?"

"No, Spur. That's one thing I am sure of."

"When did you decide all this?"

"Spur, I'm not mad at you." Impulsively, she went up on tiptoes and aimed a kiss at the side of his face. She got mostly air, but their cheeks brushed, her skin hot against his. "I like you, especially when you're like this, so calm and thoughtful. You're the best of this lot and you've always been sweet to me. It's just that I can't live like this anymore."

"I like you too, Comfort. Last night, after I accepted communion..."

"Enough. We like each other. We should stop there, it's a good place to be." She bumped up against him. "Now tell me about that boy. He isn't an upsider, is he?"

She shot him a challenging look and he tried to bear up under the pressure of her regard. They walked in silence while he decided what he could say about Ngonda and the High Gregory. "Can you keep a secret?"

She sighed. "You know you're going to tell me, so get to it."

They had completely circled the cottage. Spur spotted the High Gregory watching them from a window. He turned Comfort toward the barn. "Two days ago, when I was still in the hospital, I started sending greetings to the upside." He waved off her objections. "Don't ask, I don't know why exactly, other than that I was bored. Anyway, the boy answered one of them. He's the High Gregory of the L'ung, Phosphorescence of something or other, I forget what. He's from Kenning in the Theta Persei system and I'm guessing he's pretty important, because the next thing I knew, he QICed himself to Walden and had me pulled off a train." He told her about the hover and Memsen and the kids of the L'ung and how he was being forced to show the High Gregory his village. "Oh, and he supposedly makes luck."

"What does that mean?" said Comfort. "How does somebody make luck?"

"I don't know exactly. But Memsen and the L'ung are all convinced that he does it, whatever it is."

They had wandered into GiGa's flower garden. Comfort had tried to make it her own after they had moved in. However, she'd had neither the time nor the patience to tend persnickety plants and so grew only daylilies and hostas and rugose roses. After a season of neglect, even these tough flowers were losing ground to the bindweed and quackgrass and spurge.

Spur sat on the fieldstone bench that his grandfather had built for his grandmother. He tapped on the seat for her to join him. She hesitated then settled at the far end, twisting to face him.

"He acts too stupid to be anyone important," she said. "What about that slip he made about being the cousin and not the nephew. Are the people on his world idiots?"

"Maybe he intended to say it." Spur leaned forward and pulled a flat clump of spurge from the garden. "After all, he's wearing those purple overalls; he's really not trying very hard to pretend he's a citizen." He knocked the dirt off the roots and left it to shrivel in the sun. "What if he wanted me to tell you who he was and decided to make it happen? I think he's used to getting his own way."

"So what does he want with us?" Her expression was unreadable.

"I'm not sure. I think what Memsen was telling me is that he has come here to see how his being here changes us." He shook his head. "Does that make any sense?"

"It doesn't have to," she said. "He's from the upside. They don't think the same way we do."

"Maybe so." It was a commonplace that had been drilled into them in every self-reliance class they had ever sat through. It was, after all, the reason that Chairman Winter had founded Walden. But now that he had actually met upsiders – Memsen and the High Gregory and the L'ung – he wasn't sure that their ways were so strange. But this wasn't the time to argue the point. "Look, Comfort, I have my own reason for telling you all this," he said. "I need help with him. At first I thought he was just going to pretend to be one of us and take a quiet look at the village. Now I'm thinking he wants to be discovered so he can make things happen. So I'm going to try to keep him busy here if I can. It's just for one day; he said he'd leave in the morning."

"And you believe that?"

"I'd like to." He dug at the base of a dandelion with his fingers and pried it out of the ground with the long taproot intact. "What other choice do I have?" He glanced back at the cottage but couldn't see the High Gregory in the window anymore. "We'd better get back."

She put a hand on his arm. "First we have to talk about Vic."

Spur paused, considering. "We can do that if you want." He studied the dandelion root as if it held the answers to all his problems. "We probably should. But it's hard, Comfort. When I was in the hospital the upsiders did something to me. A kind of treatment that . . ."

She squeezed his arm and then let go. "There's just one thing I have to know. You were with him at the end. At least, that's what we heard. You reported his death."

"It was quick," said Spur "He didn't suffer." This was a lie he had been preparing to tell her ever since he had woken up in the hospital.

"That's good. I'm glad." She swallowed. "Thank you. But did he say anything? At the end, I mean."

"Say? Say what?"

"You have to understand that after I moved back home, I found that Vic had changed. I was shocked when he volunteered for the Corps because he was actually thinking of leaving Littleton. Maybe Walden too. He talked a lot about going to the upside." She clutched her arms to her chest so tightly that she seemed to shrink. "He didn't believe – you can't tell anyone about this. Promise?"

Spur shut his eyes and nodded. He knew what she was going to say. How could he not? Nevertheless, he dreaded hearing it.

Her voice shrank as well. "He had sympathy for the pukpuks. Not for the burning, but he used to say that we didn't need to cover every last scrap of Walden with forest. He talked about respecting . . ."

Without warning, the nightmare leapt from some darkness in his soul
like some ravening predator. It chased him through a stand of pine;
trees exploded like firecrackers. Sparks bit through his civvies and stung
him. He could smell burning hair. His hair.

But he didn't want to smell his hair burning. Spur was trying desperately to get back to the bench in the garden, back to Comfort, but she
kept pushing him deeper into the nightmare.

"After we heard he'd been killed, I went to his room . . ."

He beckoned and for a moment Spur thought it might not be Vic after
all as the anguished face shimmered in the heat of the burn. Vic
wouldn't betray them, would he?

"It was his handwriting . . ."

Spur had to dance to keep his shoes from catching fire, and he had no
escape, no choice, no time. The torch spread his arms wide and Spur
stumbled into his embrace and with an angry whoosh they exploded
together into flame. Spur felt his skin crackle . . .

And he screamed.

XII

We are paid for our suspicions by finding what we
suspected.
— Henry David Thoreau, *A Week on the Concord*
and Merrimack Rivers

Everyone said that he had nothing to be embarrassed about, but Spur
was nonetheless deeply ashamed. He had been revealed as unmanly.
Weak and out of control. He had no memory of how he had come to be
laid out on the couch in his own parlor. He couldn't remember if he had
wept or cursed or just fainted and been dragged like a sack of onions
across the yard into the cottage. When he emerged from the nightmare,
all he knew was that his throat was raw and his cheeks were hot. The
others were all gathered around him, trying not to look worried but not
doing a very convincing job of it. He wasn't sure which he minded
more: that the strangers had witnessed his breakdown, or that his
friends and neighbors had.

When he sat up, a general alarm rippled among the onlookers. When
he tried to stand, Sly pressed him back onto the couch with a firm grip
on the shoulder. Comfort fetched him a glass of water. She was so
distraught that her hand shook as she offered it to him. He took a sip,
more to satisfy the others than to quench his own thirst. They needed to
think they were helping, even though the best thing they could have
done for him then – go away and leave him alone – was the one thing
they were certain not to do.

"Maybe I should call Dr. Niss." Spur's laugh was as light as ashes.
"Ask for my money back."

"You're right." Constant Ngonda lit up at the thought, then realized that his enthusiasm was unseemly. "I mean, shouldn't we notify the hospital?" he said, eyeing the tell on the parlor wall. "They may have concerns."

Spur knew that the deputy would love to have him whisked away from Littleton, in the hopes that the High Gregory and the L'ung would follow. He wondered briefly if that might not be for the best, but then he had been humiliated enough that morning. "There's nothing to worry about."

"Good," said Ngonda. "I'm happy to hear that, Spur. Do you mind, I promised to check in with the Cooperative when we arrived?" Without waiting for a reply, Ngonda bustled across the parlor to the kitchen. Meanwhile, the High Gregory had sprawled onto a chair, his legs dangling over the armrest. He was flipping impatiently through a back issue of Didactic Arts' *True History Comix* without really looking at the pages. Spur thought he looked even more squirmy than usual, as if he knew there was someplace else he was supposed to be. Sly Sawatdee had parked himself next to Spur. His hands were folded in his lap, his eyelids were heavy and he hummed to himself from time to time, probably thinking about fishing holes and berry patches and molasses cookies.

"I am so sorry, Spur," said Comfort. "I just didn't realize." It was the third time she had apologized. She wasn't used to apologizing and she didn't do it very well. Meanwhile her anguish was smothering him. Her face was pale, her mouth was as crooked as a scar. What had he said to her? He couldn't remember but it must have been awful. There was a quiet desperation in her eyes that he had never seen before. It scared him.

Spur set the glass of water on the end table. "Listen, Comfort, there is nothing for you to be sorry about." He was the one who had fallen apart, after all. "Let's just forget it, all right? I'm fine now." To prove it, he stood up.

Sly twitched but did not move to pull him back onto the couch again. "Have enough air up there, my hasty little sparrow?"

"I'm fine," he repeated and it was true. Time to put this by and move on. Change the subject. "Who wants to see the orchard? Lucky?"

"If you don't mind," said Sly. "My bones are in no mood for a hike. But I'll make us lunch."

"I'll come," said Ngonda.

Comfort looked as if she wanted to beg off, but guilt got the better of her.

They tramped around the grounds, talking mostly of farm matters. After they had admired the revived orchard, inspected the weed-choked garden, toured the barn, played with the pack of gosdogs that had wandered over from the big house and began to follow them everywhere, walked the boundaries of the cornfield, which Cape had planted in clover until Spur was ready to farm again, they hiked through the woods down to Mercy's Creek.

"We take some irrigation water from the creek, but the Joerlys own the rights, so there's water in our end of the creek pretty much all year long." Spur pointed. "There's a pool in the woods where Comfort and I used to swim when we were kids. It might be a good place to cool off this afternoon."

"And so you and Spur were neighbors?" The High Gregory had been trying to draw Comfort out all morning, without much success. "You grew up together like me and my friends. I was hoping to bring them along but Uncle Constant Ngonda said there were too many of them. Your family is still living on the farm?"

"Mom died. She left everything to us. Now Vic's dead."

"Yes, Spur said that your brother was a brave firefighter. I know that you are very sad about it, but I see much more luck ahead for you."

She leaned against a tree and stared up at the sky.

"There used to be a pukpuk town in these woods." Spur was itching to move on. "They built all along the creek. It's overgrown now, but we could go look at the ruins."

The High Gregory stepped off the bank onto a flat stone that stuck out of the creek. "And your father?"

"He left," Comfort said dully.

"When they were little," Spur said quickly. He knew that Comfort did not like even to think about her father, much less talk about him with strangers. Park Nen had married into the Joerly family. Not only was his marriage to Rosie Joerly stormy, but he was a loner who had never quite adjusted to village ways. "The last we heard Park was living in Freeport."

The High Gregory picked his way across the creek on stepping stones. "He was a pukpuk, no?" His foot slipped and he windmilled his arms to keep his balance.

"Who told you that?" If Comfort had been absentminded before, she was very much present now.

"I forget." He crossed back over the stream in four quick hops. "Was it you, Uncle?"

Ngonda licked his lips nervously. "I've never heard of this person."

"Then maybe it was Spur."

Spur would have denied it if Comfort had given him the chance.

"He never knew." Her voice was sharp. "Nobody did." She confronted the boy. "Don't play games with me, upsider." He tried to back away but she pursued him. "Why do you care about my father? Why are you here?"

"Are you crazy?" Ngonda caught the High Gregory as he stumbled over a rock and then thrust the boy behind him. "This is my nephew Lucky."

"She knows, Friend Constant." The High Gregory peeked out from behind the deputy's flair jacket. He was glowing with excitement. "Spur told her everything."

"Oh, no." Ngonda slumped. "This isn't going well at all."

"Memsen gave us all research topics for the trip here to meet Spur," said the High Gregory. "Kai Thousandfold was assigned to find out about you. You'd like him; he's from Bellweather. He says that he's very worried about you, friend Comfort."

"Tell him to mind his own business."

Spur was aghast. "Comfort, I'm sorry, I didn't know . . ."

"Be quiet, Spur. These upsiders are playing you for the fool that you are." Her eyes were wet. "I hardly knew my father and what I did know, I didn't like. Mom would probably still be alive if she hadn't been left to manage the farm by herself all those years." Her chin quivered; Spur had never seen her so agitated. "She told us that Grandma Nen was a pukpuk, but that she emigrated from the barrens long before my father was born and that he was brought up a citizen like anyone else." Tears streaked her face. "So don't think you understand anything about me because you found out about a dead woman who I never met."

With that she turned and walked stiff-legged back toward Diligence Cottage. She seemed to have shrunk since the morning, and now looked so insubstantial to Spur that a summer breeze might carry her off like milkweed. He knew there was more – much more – they had to talk about, but first they would have to find a new way to speak to each other. As she disappeared into the woods, he felt a twinge of nostalgia for the lost simplicity of their youth, when life really had been as easy as Chairman Winter promised it could be.

"I'm hungry." The High Gregory seemed quite pleased with himself. "Is it lunchtime yet?"

After he had spun out lunch for as long as he could, Spur was at a loss as to how to keep the High Gregory out of trouble. They had exhausted the sights of the Leung farmstead, short of going over to visit with his father in the big house. Spur considered it, but decided to save it for a last resort. He had hoped to spend the afternoon touring the Joerly farmstead, but now that was out of the question. As the High Gregory fidgeted about the cottage, picking things up and putting them down again, asking about family pix, opening cabinets and pulling out drawers, Spur proposed that they take a spin around Littleton in Sly's truck. A rolling tour, he told himself. No stops.

The strategy worked for most of an hour. At first the High Gregory was content to sit next to Spur in the back of the truck as he pointed out Littleton's landmarks and described the history of the village. They drove up Lamana Ridge Road to Lookover Point, from which they had a view of most of Littleton Commons. The village had been a Third Wave settlement, populated by the winners of the lottery of 2432. In the first years of settlement, the twenty-five founding families had worked together to construct the buildings of the Commons: the self-reliance school, athenaeum, communion lodge, town hall and Littleton's first exchange, where goods and services could be bought or bartered. The First Twenty-five had lived communally in rough barracks until the buildings on the Commons were completed and then gradually moved out to their farmsteads as land was cleared and crews of carpenters put up the cottages and barns and sheds for each of the families. The Leungs had arrived in the Second Twenty-Five four years afterward. The railroad had come through three years after that and most of the businesses of the first exchange moved from the Commons out to Shed Town by the train station. Sly drove them down off the ridge and they bumped along back roads, past farms and fields and pastures. They viewed the Toba and Parochet and Velez farmsteads from a safe distance and passed Sambusa's lumberyard at the confluence of Mercy's Creek and the Swift River. Then they pulled back onto CR 22.

The only way back to Diligence Cottage was through the Commons. "Drive by the barracks," Spur called to Sly in the cab. "We can stretch our legs there," he said to the High Gregory. "I'll show you how the First Twenty-Five lived." One of the original barracks had been preserved as a historical museum across the lawn from the communion lodge. It was left open to any who wanted to view its dusty exhibits.

Spur thought it the best possible choice for a stop; except for Founders' Day, the Chairman's birthday and Thanksgiving, nobody ever went there.

The Commons appeared to be deserted as they passed the buildings of the first exchange. These had been renovated into housing for those citizens of Littleton who didn't farm, like the teachers at the self-reliance school and Dr. Christopoulos and some of the elders, like Gandy Joy. They saw Doll Groth coming out of the athenaeum. Recognizing the truck, she gave Sly a neighborly wave, but when she spotted Spur in the back, she smiled and began to clap, raising her hands over her head. This so pleased the High Gregory that he stood up and started clapping back at her. Spur had to brace him to keep him from pitching over the side of the truck.

But Doll was the only person they saw. Spur couldn't believe his good fortune as they pulled up to the barracks, dust from the gravel parking lot swirling around them. The wind had picked up, but provided no relief from the midsummer heat. Spur's shirt stuck to his back where he had been leaning against the cab of the truck. Although he wasn't sure whether the High Gregory could sweat or not, the boy's face was certainly flushed. Ngonda looked as if he were liquefying inside his flair jacket. The weather fit Spur's latest plan neatly. He was hoping that after they had spent a half hour in the hot and airless barracks, he might be able to persuade the High Gregory to return to Diligence Cottage for a swim in the creek. After that it would practically be suppertime. And after that they could watch the tell. Or he might teach the High Gregory some of the local card games. Spur had always been lucky at Fool All.

It wasn't until the engine of the Sawatdee's truck coughed and rattled and finally cut out that Spur first heard the whoop of the crowd. Something was going on at the ball fields next to the self-reliance school, just down the hill a couple of hundred meters. He tried to usher the High Gregory into the barracks but it was too late. Spur thought there must be a lot of people down there. They were making a racket that was hard to miss.

The High Gregory cocked his head in the direction of the school and smiled. "Lucky us," he said. "We're just in time for Memsen."

XIII

> I associate this day, when I can remember it, with games of base-ball played over behind the hills in the russet fields toward Sleepy Hollow.
> – Henry David Thoreau, *Journal*, 1856

"What is this?" hissed Ngonda.

Sly pulled his floppy hat off and wiped his forehead with it. "Looks like a baseball game, city pants," said Sly.

The L'ung were in the field; with a sick feeling Spur counted twelve of them in purple overalls and black tee shirts. They must have arrived in the two vans that were parked next to the wooden bleachers. Beside the vans was an array of trucks, scooters and bicycles from the village. There must have been a hundred citizens sitting in the bleachers and another twenty or thirty prowling the edges of the field, cheering the home team on. Match Klizzie had opened the refreshment shed and was barbequing sausages. Gandy Joy had set up her communion tent: Spur could see billows of sweet white smoke whenever one of the villagers pulled back the flap.

With many of the younger baseball regulars off at the firefight, the Littleton Eagles might have been undermanned. But Spur could see that some of old timers had come out of retirement to pull on the scarlet hose. Warp Kovacho was just stepping up to home base and Spur spotted Cape sitting on the strikers' bench, second from the inbox.

Betty Chief Twosalt shined the ball against her overalls as she peered in at Warp. "Where to, old sir?" She was playing feeder for the L'ung.

Warp swung the flat bat at belt level to show her just where he wanted the feed to cross home base. "Right here, missy," he said. "Then you better duck." They were playing with just two field bases, left and right. The banners fixed to the top of each basepole snapped in the stiffening breeze.

Betty nodded and then delivered the feed underhanded. It was slow and very fat but Warp watched it go by. The Pendragon Chromlis Furcifer was catching for the L'ung. She barehanded it and flipped it back to Betty.

"What's he waiting for?" grumbled the High Gregory. "That was perfect." He ignored Spur's icy stare.

"Just a smight lower next time, missy," said Warp, once again indicating his preference with the bat. "You got the speed right, now hit the spot."

Young Melody Velez was perched at the end of the topmost bleacher and noticed Spur passing beneath her. "He's here!" she cried. "Spur's here!"

Play stopped and the bleachers emptied as the villagers crowded around him, clapping him on the back and shaking his hand. In five minutes he'd been kissed more than he'd been kissed altogether in the previous year.

"So is this another one of your upsider friends?" Gandy Joy held the High Gregory at arms length, taking him in. "Hello, boy. What's your name?"

"I'm the High Gregory of Kenning," he said. "But my Walden name is Lucky, so I'd rather have you call me that."

Citizens nearby laughed nervously.

"Lucky you are then."

Gandy Hope Nakuru touched the pink bandana knotted around his neck. "Isn't this a cute scarf?" The High Gregory beamed.

Spur was astonished by it all. "But who told you that they're from the upside?" he said. "How did they get here? And why are you playing baseball?"

"Memsen brought them," said Peace Toba. "She said that you'd be along once we got the game going."

"And she was right." Little Jewel Parochet tugged at his shirt. "Spur, she said you flew in a hover. What was it like?"

"Maybe next time you can bring a guest along with you?" Melody Velez said, smiling. She brushed with no great subtlety against him.

Spur glanced about the thinning crowd; citizens were climbing back into the bleachers. "But where is Memsen?"

Peace Toba pointed; Memsen had only come out onto the field as far as right base when Constant Ngonda had captured her. He was waving his arms so frantically that he looked like he might take off and fly around the field. Memsen tilted her head so that her ear was practically on her shoulder. Then she saw Spur. She clicked her rings at him, a sly smile on her face. He knew he ought to be angry with her, but instead he felt buoyant, as if he had just set his splash pack down and stepped out of his field jacket. Whatever happened now, it wasn't his fault. He had done his best for his village.

"So this was what you were keeping from me." His father was chuckling. "I knew it had to be something. They're fine, your friends. You didn't need to worry." He hugged Spur and whispered into his ear. "Fine, but very strange. They're not staying are they?" He pulled back. "Prosper, we need your bat in this game. These kids are tough." He pointed at Kai Thousandfold "That one has an arm like a fire hose."

"No thanks," said Spur. "But you should get back to the game." He raised his arms over his head and waved to the bleachers. "Thank you all, thanks," he called to his well-wishers. They quieted down to listen. "If you're expecting some kind of speech, then you've got the wrong farmer. I'll just say that I'm glad to be home and leave it at that. All right?" The crowd made a murmur of assent. "Then play ball." They cheered. "And go Eagles!" They cheered louder.

"Can I play?" said the High Gregory. "This looks like fun." He straightened the strap of his overalls. "I can play, can't I? We have all kinds of baseball on Kenning. But your rules are different, right? Tell them to me."

"Why bother?" Spur was beginning to wonder if the High Gregory was playing him for a fool. "Looks like you're making them up as you go."

Her Grace, Jacqueline Kristof, put an arm around his shoulder. "The ball is soft, so no gloves," she said, as she led him onto the field. "No tag outs either, you actually have to hit the runner with the ball. That's called a sting. No fouls and no . . ."

As the spectators settled into their seats, Spur found his way to Ngonda and Memsen. She wasn't wearing the standard L'ung overalls, but rather a plain green sundress with a floral print. She had washed the phosphorescent paint off her arms and pulled her black hair back into a ponytail. But if Memsen was trying to look inconspicuous, then she had failed utterly. She was still the tallest woman on the planet.

"Talk to her," said Ngonda. "We had an agreement . . ."

"Which you broke," said Memsen. "What we agreed was that the High Gregory would visit Littleton and you'd let him make whatever luck you are destined to have. You promised to give him the run of the village . . ."

". . . under Spur's supervision, Allworthy," interrupted Ngonda.

Betty Chief Twosalt delivered a feed and Warp watched it go by again. This did not sit well with the L'ung. "Delay of game, old sir," someone called.

Memsen turned from Ngonda to Spur. "As we were explaining to the deputy, the L'ung and I see everything that the High Gregory sees. So we know that you've introduced him to just two of your neighbors. You promised that he could meet the citizens of this village but then you've kept him isolated until now. He needs to be with people, Spur. Barns don't have luck. People do."

"It was my decision," said Spur. "I'll take the responsibility."

"And this was ours." She waved toward the field. "So?"

Ngonda snorted in disgust. "I need to call Concord. The Office of Diplomacy will be filing a protest with the Forum of the Thousand Worlds." He took a step away from them, then turned and waggled a finger at Memsen. "This is a clear violation of our Covenant, Allworthy. The L'ung will be recalled to Kenning."

As they watched Ngonda stalk off, Warp struck a grounder straight back at the feeder. Betty stabbed at it but it tipped off her fingers and rolled away at an angle. Little Senator Dowm pounced on it but held the throw because Warp already had a hand on the right base stake.

"Maybe I should've introduced the High Gregory to a few more people." Spur wondered if standing too close to Memsen might be affecting his perceptions. The very planet seemed to tilt slightly, as it had that afternoon when he and Leaf Benkleman had drunk a whole liter of her mother's prize applejack. "But why are we playing baseball?"

Memsen showed him her teeth in that way she had that wasn't

anything like a smile. "Tolerance isn't something that the citizens of the Transcendent State seem to value. You've been taught that your way of life is better not only than that of the pukpuks, but than that of most of the cultures of the Thousand Worlds. Or have we misread the textbooks?"

Spur shook his head grimly.

"So." She pinched the air. "Deputy Ngonda was right to point out that landing a hover on your Commons might have intimidated some people. We had to find some unthreatening way to arrive, justify our presence and meet your neighbors. The research pointed to baseball as a likely ploy. Your Eagles were champions of Hamilton County just two years ago and second runner-up in the Northeast in 2498."

"A ploy."

"A ploy to take advantage of your traditions. Your village is proud of its accomplishments in baseball. You're used to playing against strangers. And of course, we had an invitation from Spur Leung, the hero of the hour."

Livy Jayawardena hit a high fly ball that sailed over the heads of the midfielders. Kai Thousandfold, playing deep field, raced back and made an over-the-shoulder catch. Meanwhile Warp had taken off for left base. In his prime, he might have made it, but his prime had been when Spur was a toddler. Kai turned, set and fired; his perfect throw stung Warp right between the shoulder blades. Double play, inning over.

"I invited you?" said Spur. "When was that again?"

"Why, in the hospital where we saved your life. You kept claiming that the L'ung would offer no competition for your Eagles. You told Dr. Niss that you couldn't imagine losing a baseball game to upsiders, much less a bunch of children. Really, Spur, that was too much. We had to accept your challenge once you said that. So when we arrived at the town hall, we told our story to everyone we met. Within an hour the bleachers were full."

Spur was impressed. "And you thought of all of this since yesterday?"

"Actually, just in the last few hours." She paused then, seemingly distracted. She made a low, repetitive *pa-pa-pa-ptt*. "Although there is something you should know about us," she said at last. "Of course, Deputy Ngonda would be outraged if he knew that we're telling you, but then he finds outrage everywhere." She stooped to his level so that they were face to face. "I rarely think all by myself, Spur." He tried not to notice that her knees bent in different directions. "Most of the time, we think for me."

The world seemed to tilt a little more then; Spur felt as if he might slide off it. "I don't think I understand what you just said."

"It's complicated." She straightened. "And we're attracting attention here. I can hear several young women whispering about us. We should find a more private place to talk. I need your advice." She turned and waved to the citizens in the bleachers who were watching them. Spur forced a smile and waved as well, and then led her up the hill toward town hall.

"Ngonda will file his protest," she said, "and it'll be summarily rejected. We've been in continuous contact with the Forum of the Thousand Worlds." Her speech became choppy as she walked. "They know what we're doing." Climbing the gentle hill left her breathless. "Not all worlds approve. Consensus is hard to come by. But the L'ung have a plan . . . to open talks between you . . . and the pukpuks." She rested a hand on his shoulder to support herself. "Is that something you think worth doing?"

"Maybe." He could feel the warmth of her hand through the thin fabric of his shirt. "All right, yes." He thought this must be another ploy. "But who are you? Who are the L'ung? Why are you doing this?"

"Be patient." At the top of the hill she had to rest to catch her breath. Finally she said, "You spoke with the High Gregory about gosdogs?"

"In the truck this morning."

"It was at the instigation of the L'ung. Understand that we don't believe that gosdogs think in any meaningful sense of the word. Perhaps the original Peekay intelligence rating was accurate. But if they were found to be more intelligent, then we could bring the issue of their treatment here to the Forum. It would require a delicate touch to steer the debate toward the remedy the L'ung want. Tricky but not impossible. The Forum has no real power to intervene in the affairs of member worlds and your Chairman Winter has the right to run Walden as he pleases. But he depends on the good opinion of the Thousand Worlds. When we're finished here, the L'ung will propose to return the gosdogs to a preserve where they can live in their natural state."

"But there is no natural habitat left. The pukpuks destroyed it."

"Ah, but ecologies can be re-created." She gestured at the lawn stretching before them, at the rose hedges along its border and the trees that shaded it, their leaves trembling in the summer breeze. "As you well know."

"But what does a gosdog preserve have to do with the pukpuks?"

"Come away from the sun before we melt." Memsen led him to a bench in the shadow of an elm. She sagged onto it; Spur remained standing, looking down at her for a change. It eased the crick in his neck.

"The preserve sets a precedent." She clicked her rings. "In order for it to be established, the growth of the forest must be controlled, which means the Transcendent State will be blocked from spreading across Walden. Up until now, the Cooperative has refused to negotiate on this point. And then comes the question of where to put the preserve. You and the pukpuks will have to sit down to decide on a site. Together. With some delicate nudging from the Forum, there's no telling what conversations might take place at such a meeting."

"But we can't!" Spur wiped the sweat from his forehead. "The Transcendent State was founded so that humans could live apart and stay true to ourselves. As long as the pukpuks live here, we'll be under direct attack from upsider ways."

"Your Transcendent State is a controversial experiment." Memsen's face went slack and she made the *pa-pa-pa-ptt* sound Spur had heard before. "We've always wondered how isolation and ignorance can be suitable foundations for a human society. Do you really believe in simplicity, Spur, or do you just not know any better?" Spur wondered if she had used some forbidden upsider tech to look into his soul; he felt violated. "I believe in this." He gestured, as she had done, at Littleton Commons, green as a dream. "I don't want my village to be swept away. The pukpuks destroyed this world once already."

"Yes, that could happen, if it's what you and your children decide," said Memsen. "We don't have an answer for you, Spur. But the question is, do you need a preserve like gosdogs, or are you strong enough to hold onto your beliefs no matter who challenges them?"

"And this is your plan to save Walden?" He ground his shoe into the grass. "This is the luck that the High Gregory came all this way to make?"

"Is it?" She leaned back against the bench and gazed up into the canopy of the elm. "Maybe it is."

"I've been such an idiot." He was bitter; if she was going to use him, at least she could admit it. "You and the High Gregory and the L'ung flit around the upside, having grand adventures and straightening up other people's messes." He began to pace back and forth in front of the bench. "You're like some kind of superheroes, is that it?"

"The L'ung have gathered together to learn statecraft from one another," she said patiently. "Sometimes they travel, but mostly they stay with us on Kenning. Of course they have political power in the Forum because of who they are, but their purpose is not so much to *do* as it is to learn. Then, in a few more years, this cohort will disband and scatter to their respective worlds to try their luck. And when the time comes for us to marry . . ."

"Marry? Marry who?"

"The High Gregory, of course."

"But he's just a boy."

Memsen must have heard the dismay in his voice. "He will grow into his own luck soon enough," she said coldly. "I was chosen the twenty-second Memsen by my predecessor. She searched for me for years across the Thousand Worlds." With a weary groan she stood, and once again towered over him. "A Memsen is twice honored: to be wife to one High Gregory and mother to another." Her voice took on a declaiming quality, as if she were giving a speech that had been well rehearsed. "And I carry my predecessor and twenty souls who came before her saved in our memory, so that we may always serve the High Gregory and advise the L'ung."

Spur was horrified at the depth of his misunderstanding of this woman. "You have dead people . . . inside you?"

"Not dead," she said. "Saved."

A crazed honking interrupted them. A truck careened around the corner and skidded to a stop in front of the town hall. Stark Sukulgunda flung himself out of the still running truck and dashed inside.

Spur stood. "Something's wrong." He started for the truck and had gotten as far as the statue of Chairman Winter, high on his pedestal, when Stark burst out of the doors again. He saw Spur and waved frantically.

"Where are they all?" he cried. "Nobody answers."

"Playing baseball." Spur broke into a trot. "What's wrong? What?"

"Baseball?" Stark's eyes bulged as he tried to catch his breath. "South slope of Lamana . . . burning . . . everything's burning . . . the forest is on fire!"

XIV

> I walked slowly through the wood to Fairhaven cliff,
> climbed to the highest rock and sat down upon it to
> observe the progress of the flames, which were
> rapidly approaching me now about a mile distant
> from the spot where the fire was kindled. Presently I
> heard the sound of the distant Bell giving the alarm,
> and I knew that the town was on its way to the scene.
> Hitherto I felt like a guilty person. Nothing but
> shame and regret, but now I settled the matter with
> myself shortly, and said to myself. Who are these
> men who are said to be owners of these woods and
> how am I related to them? I have set fire to the forest,
> but I have done no wrong therein, and now it is as if
> the lightning had done it. These flames are but
> consuming their natural food. So shortly I settled it
> with myself and stood to watch the approaching
> flames. It was a glorious spectacle, and I was the only
> one there to enjoy it. The fire now reached the base
> of the cliffs and then rushed up its sides. The
> squirrels ran before it in blind haste, and the pigeons
> dashed into the midst of the smoke. The flames
> flashed up the pines to their tops as if they were
> powder.
>
> – Henry David Thoreau, *Journal*, 1850

More than half of the Littleton Volunteer Fire Department were playing baseball when the alarm came. They scrambled up the hill to the brick firehouse on the Commons, followed by almost all of the spectators, who crowded anxiously into the communion hall while the firefighters huddled. Normally there would have been sixteen volunteers on call, but like Spur, Will Sambusa, Bright Ayoub, Bliss Bandaran and Chief Cary Millisap had joined the Corps. Cape was currently Assistant Chief; he would have led the volunteers had not his son been home. Even though Spur protested that he was merely a grunt smokechaser, the volunteers' first act was to vote him Acting Chief.

Like any small town unit, the Littleton Fire Department routinely answered calls for house fires and brush fires and accidents of all sorts, but they were ill-equipped to stop a major burn. They had just one fire truck, an old quad with a 3,000-liter per minute pump and 5,000-liter water tank. It carried fifty meters of six-centimeter hose, fifty meters of booster hose and a ten-meter mechanical ladder. If the burn was as big as Stark described, Engine No. 4 would be about as much use fighting it as a broom.

Spur resisted the impulse to put his team on the truck and rush out to the burn. He needed more information before he committed his meager forces. It would be at least an hour before companies from neighboring villages would arrive and the Corps might not get to Littleton until nightfall. Cape spread a map out on the long table in the firehouse and the volunteers stood around it, hunch-shouldered and grim. Gandy Joy glided in, lit a single communion square and slipped out again as they contemplated what the burn might do to their village. They took turns peppering Stark with questions about what he had actually seen. At first he tried his best to answer, but he'd had a shock that had knocked better men than him off center. As they pressed him, he grew sullen and suspicious.

The Sukulgundas lived well west of the Leungs and higher up the slope of Lamana Ridge. They'd been latecomers to Littleton and parts of their farmstead were so steep that the fields had to be terraced. They were about four kilometers north of the Commons at the very end of January Road, a steep dirt track with switchbacks. Stark maintained that the burn had come down the ridge at him, from the general direction of Lookover Point to the east. At first he claimed it was maybe a kilometer away when he'd left his place, but then changed his mind and insisted that the burn was practically eating his barn. That didn't make sense, since the strong easterly breeze would push the burn in the opposite direction, toward the farmsteads of the Ezzats and Millisaps and eventually to the Herreras and the Leungs.

Spur shivered as he imagined the burn roaring through GiGa's orchards. But his neighbors were counting on him to keep those fears at bay. "If what you're saying is true," he mused, "it might mean that this fire was deliberately set and that someone is still out there trying to make trouble for us."

"Torches in Littleton?" Livy Jayawardena looked dubious. "We're nowhere near the barrens."

"Neither was Double Down," said Cape. "Or Wheelwright."

"I don't know about that." Stark Sukulgunda pulled the cap off his head and started twisting it. "All I know is that we ought to stop talking about what to do and do something."

"First we have to know for sure where the burn is headed, which means we need to get up the Lamana Ridge Road." Spur was struggling to apply what he'd learned in training. "If the burn hasn't jumped the road and headed back down the north slope of the ridge, then we can use the road as a firebreak and hold that line. And when reinforcements come, we'll send them east over the ridge to the head of the burn. That's the way the wind is blowing everything." He glanced up at the others to see if they agreed. "We need to be thinking hard about an eastern perimeter."

"Why?" Stark was livid. "Because that's where you live? It's my house that . . ."

"Shut up, Stark," said Peace Toba. "Fill your snoot with communion and get right with the village for a change."

None of the threatened farmsteads that lay in the path of the burn to the east was completely cleared of trees. Simplicity demanded that citizens only cultivate as much of their land as they needed. Farmers across Walden used the forest as a windbreak; keeping unused land in trees prevented soil erosion. But now Spur was thinking about all the pine and hemlock and red cedar, needles laden with resins and oils, side by side with the deciduous trees in the woods where he had played as a boy. At Motu River he'd seen pine trees explode into flame. And then there were the burn piles of slash and stumps and old lumber that every farmer collected, baking in the summer sun.

"If things go wrong in the east, we might need to set our firebreak as far back as Blue Valley Road." Spur ran his finger down the line on the map. "It won't be as effective a break as the ridge road but we can improve it. Get the Bandarans and Sawatdees to rake off all the forest litter and duff on the west side. Then disk harrow the entire road. I want to see at least a three-meter-wide strip of fresh soil down the entire length."

"Prosper." Cape's voice was hushed. "You're not giving up on all of this." He traced the outline of the four threatened farms on the map, ending on the black square that marked Diligence Cottage. Spur glanced briefly at his father, then away again, troubled by what he had seen. Capability Leung looked just as desperate as Stark Sukulgunda. Maybe more so, if he thought he had just heard his son pronounce doom on his life's work. For the first time in his life, Spur felt as if he were the father and Cape was the son.

"No." He tried to reassure his father with a smile. "That's just our fall back. What I'm hoping is that we can cut a handline from Spot Pond along Mercy's Creek all the way down to the river. It's rough country and depending on how fast the burn is moving we may not have enough time, but if we can hold that line, we save the Millisaps, Joerlys and us." Left unsaid was that the Ezzats farmstead would be lost, even if this dicey strategy worked.

"But right now the fire is much closer to my place than anyone else's," said Stark. "And you said yourself, there may be some suicidal maniac just waiting to burn himself up and take my house with him."

Spur was annoyed at the way that Stark Sukulgunda kept buzzing at him. He was making it hard for Spur to concentrate. "We could send the fire truck your way, Stark," he said, "but I don't know what good it would do. You don't have any standing water on your land, do you?"

"Why?"

"The truck only has a five-thousand-liter water tank. That's not near enough if your house gets involved."

"We could drop the hard suction line into his well," said Livy. "Pump from there."

"You have a dug well?" said Cape. "How deep?"

"Four meters."

"We'd probably suck it dry before we could do you much good," said Cape.

"No," said Spur. "He's right. Peace, you and Tenny and Cert take No. 4 up to the Sukulgundas. You can also establish our western perimeter. Clear a meter-wide handline as far up the ridge as you can. Watch for torches. I don't think the fire is going to come your way but if it does, be ready, understand? Get on the tell and let us know if anything changes."

"We'll call in when we get there," said Peace as her team scattered to collect gear.

"Livy, you and the others round up as many as you can to help with the creek line. We may want to start a backfire, so keep in touch with me on the hand tell. How much liquid fire have you got?"

"At least twenty grenades. Maybe more. No firebombs though."

"Bring gas then, you'll probably need it. Keep your people between the civilians and the burn, understand? And pull back if it gets too hot. I've lost too many friends this year. I don't want to be burying anyone else. DiDa, you and I need to find a way to get up the ridge . . ."

He was interrupted by the roar of a crowd, which had gathered just outside the firehouse. Spur froze, momentarily bewildered. They couldn't still be playing baseball, could they? Then he thought that the burn must have changed direction. It had careened down the ridge faster than it had any right to, an avalanche of fire that was about to incinerate the Commons and *there was nothing he could do to fight it; in the nightmare, he wasn't wearing his splash pack. Or his fireproof field jacket.* Spur shuddered. He wasn't fit to lead, to decide what to let burn and what to save. He was weak and his soul was lost in darkness and *he knew he shouldn't be afraid. He was a veteran of the firefight, but fear squeezed him nonetheless.* "Are you all right, son?" His father rested a hand on his shoulder. *The burn licked at boulders and scorched the trees in the forest he had sworn to protect.*

"DiDa," he whispered, leaning close to his father so no one else would hear, "what if I can't stop it?"

"You'll do your best, Prosper," he said. "Everyone knows that."

As they rushed out of the firehouse, they could see smoke roiling into the sky to the northwest. But the evil plume wasn't what had stunned the crowd, which was still pouring out of the communion hall. A shadow passed directly overhead and, even in the heat of this disastrous afternoon, Spur was chilled.

Silently, like a miracle, the High Gregory's hover landed on Littleton Commons.

XV

> Men go to a fire for entertainment. When I see how
> eagerly men will run to a fire, whether in warm or
> cold weather, by night or by day, dragging an engine
> at their heels, I'm astonished to perceive how good a
> purpose the level of excitement is made to serve.
> – Henry David Thoreau, *Journal*, 1850

"There's a big difference between surface fire and crown fire," said the Pendragon Chromlis Furcifer to the L'ung assembled in the belly of the hover. "Surface fires move along the forest floor, burning through the understory." She was reading from notes that scrolled down her forearm.

"Wait, what's understory again?" asked Her Grace, Jacqueline Kristof, who was the youngest of the L'ung.

Memsen pinched the air. "You mustn't keep interrupting, Your Grace. If you have questions, query the cognisphere in slow time." She nodded at Penny. "Go ahead, Pendragon. You're doing a fine job."

"Understory is the grass, shrubs, dead leaves, fallen trees – that stuff. So anyway, a surface fire can burn fast or slow, depending. But if the flames climb into the crowns of the trees, it almost always rips right through the forest. Since the Transcendental State doesn't have the tech to stop it, Spur will have to let it burn itself out. If you look over there . . ." The group closed around her, craning to see.

Spur had been able to ignore Penny for the most part, although Cape kept scowling at the L'ung. Memsen had explained that Penny's research topic for the trip to Walden was forest fires.

The hover was not completely proof against smoke. As they skirted the roiling convection column of smoke and burning embers, the air inside the hover became tinged with the bitter stench of the burn. This impressed the L'ung. As they wandered from view to view, they would call to one another. "Here, over here. Do you smell it now? Much stronger over here!"

They had dissolved the partitions and made most of the hull transparent to observe developments in the burn. Just a single three-meter-wide band ran solid from the front of the deck to the back as a concession to Spur and Cape; the L'ung seemed totally immune from fear of heights. Spur was proud at how Cape was handling his first flight in a hover, especially since he himself felt slightly queasy whenever he looked straight down through the deck at the ridge fifteen hundred meters below.

From this vantage, Spur could see exactly what was needed to contain the burn and realized that he didn't have the resources to do it. Looking to the north, he was relieved that the burn hadn't yet crossed Lamana Ridge Road into the wilderness on the far slope. Barring an unforeseen wind change or embers lighting new spot fires, he thought he might be able to keep the burn within the Littleton valley. But he needed dozens of trained firefighters up on the ridge to defend the road as soon as possible. To the west, he saw where the flames had come close to the Sukulgunda's farmstead, but now the burn there looked to be nothing more than a surface fire that was already beginning to gutter out. Peace and the team with Engine No. 4 should have no trouble mopping up. Then he'd move them onto the ridge, not that just three people and one ancient pumper were going to be enough to beat back a wall of flame two kilometers wide.

"Where you see the darker splotches in the forest, those are evergreens, the best fuel of all," said Penny. "If they catch, you can get a blowup fire, which is what that huge column of smoke is about."

To the east and south, the prospects were grim. The burn had dropped much farther down the ridge than Spur had expected. He remembered from his training that burns were supposed to track uphill faster than down, but the spread to the north and south, upslope and down, looked about the same. As soon as the first crews responded from nearby Bode Well and Highbridge, they'd have to deploy at the base of the ridge to protect the Commons and the farmsteads beyond it.

The head of the burn was a violent crown fire racing east, beneath a chimney of malign smoke that towered kilometers above the hover. When Spur had given the Ezzats and Millisaps permission to save as much as they could from their houses, he'd thought that they'd all have more time. Now he realized that he'd miscalculated. He reached both families using the hand tell and told them to leave immediately. Bash Ezzat was weeping when she said she could already see the burn sweeping down on her. Spur tried Comfort's tell again to let her know that her farmstead was directly in the path of the burn, but still got no answer.

"DiDa," said Spur gently. He'd been dreading this moment, ever since he'd understood the true scope and direction of the burn. "I think we need to pull Livy and her people back from the creek to Blue Valley Road." He steeled himself against anger, grief and reproach. "There's no time to clear a line," he went on. "At least not one that will stop this burn."

"I think you're right," Cape said, as casually as if they were discussing which trees to prune. "It's simple, isn't it?"

Relieved but still anguished, he hugged his father. "I'm sorry, DiDa." He couldn't remember the last time they had been this close, and was not surprised that Cape did not return his embrace. "Should we send someone to the house?" he said, as he let his father go. "Have them pack some things? Papers, furniture – there's still a little time."

"No." Cape turned and cupped his hands against the transparent hull of the hover. "If I did something silly like that, the farm would burn for sure." He lowered his face into his hands as if to shade the view from glare. But the afternoon sun was a dim memory, blotted out by the seething clouds of smoke.

Spur shut his eyes then; so tight that for a moment that he could feel muscles on his temple quiver. "Memsen," he said, his voice catching in his throat, "can you put us down by the Sawatdees' house?"

Spur got more resistance from Livy than he had from his father. It took him almost ten minutes to convince her that trying to dig a firebreak along Mercy's Creek was not only futile but also dangerous. When it was over, he felt drained. As he flopped beside Cape onto one of the chairs that Memsen had caused to flow from the deck of the hover, the hand tell squawked. He groaned, anticipating that Livy was back with a new argument.

"Prosper Leung?" said a woman's voice.

"Speaking."

"I'm Commander Do Adoula, Fourth Engineers. My squad was on CR in Longwalk but we heard you have a situation there and we're on our way. We can be in Littleton in half an hour. I understand you're in a hover. What do you see?"

The handover of command was subtle but swift. Commander Adoula started by asking questions and ended by giving orders. She was coming in four light trucks with thirty-seven firefighters but no heavy equipment. She approved of Spur's decision to stop the burn at Blue Valley Road and split her force in two while they were speaking, diverting half to the ridge and half to help Livy on Blue Valley. She directed the local firefighters from Bode Well and Highbridge to dig in on the south to protect the Commons and requested that Spur stay in the hover and be her eye in the sky.

When they finished talking, Spur slumped back against his chair. He was pleased that Adoula had ratified his firefighting plans, relieved to be no longer in charge.

"The Corps?" said Cape.

"Fourth Engineers." He folded the hand tell. "They were on CR in Longwalk."

"That was lucky."

"Lucky," he agreed. He spotted the High Gregory whispering to Memsen. "How are you doing, DiDa?"

"You know, I've never visited the ocean." Cape blinked as he stared through the hull at the forest below. "Your mother wanted me to take her there, did I ever tell you that?"

"No."

"She always used to ask if we owned the farm or if the farm owned us." He made a low sound, part sigh and part whistle. "I wonder if she's still in Providence."

Spur didn't know what to say.

Cape frowned. "You haven't been in contact with her?"

"No."

"If you ever do, would you tell me?"

"Sure."

He nodded and made the whistling sound again.

"A burn this big is different from a surface fire," said Penny. "It's so hot that it makes a kind of fire weather called a convection column. Inside the column, bubbles of superheated air are surging up, only we can't see that. But on the outside, the cooler smoky edges are pouring back toward the ground."

"Yes, *yes*." The High Gregory pointed, clearly excited. "Watch at the top, to the left of the plume. It's like it's turning itself inside out."

"Awesome," said Kai Thousandfold. "Do you remember those gas sculptures we played with on Blimminey?"

"But that's going to be a problem for Spur and his firefighters," said Penny. "It's like a chimney shooting sparks and embers high into the atmosphere. They might come down anywhere and start new fires."

"Is anyone going to die?" said Senator Dowm.

"We hope not," Memsen said. "Spur is doing his best and help is on the way."

"Don't you wish she'd shut up?" muttered Cape, leaning into Spur. "This isn't some silly class. They're watching our life burn down."

"They're from the upside, DiDa. We can't judge them."

"And how does she know so much about how we fight fires? Look at her, she's just a kid."

That had been bothering Spur too, and it was getting harder and harder to put out of his mind. When had the L'ung had time to do all this research? They had arrived the day after he had first spoken to the High Gregory. Had they known ahead of time that they were coming to Walden? Was all this part of the plan?

"Memsen says they're special," he said.

"Spur." The High Gregory signed for him to come over. "Come take a look at this."

He crossed the deck to where the L'ung were gathered. The hover had descended to a thousand meters and was cruising over the Joerly farmstead.

"There," said the High Gregory, pointing to the woods they had tramped through that morning, a mix of hard and softwoods: birch and oak, hemlock and pine. In the midst of it, three tendrils of gray smoke were climbing into the sky.

"Those are spot fires," said Penny. "Caused by falling embers."

Spur didn't believe it. He'd been worried about spotting all along and had swung from side to side of the hover looking for them. But he'd decided that not enough time had passed for embers from the burn to start raining down on them. The convection column towered at least five kilometers above the valley. He stared at the plumes of smoke rising from the woods of his childhood with sickening dread. From right to left they were progressively smaller. Three fires in a series, which meant they had probably been set. What was his duty here? He was pretty sure that his scooter was still in the barn at Diligence Cottage. He could use it to get away from the burn in plenty of time. Cape could monitor the progress of the burn for Commander Adoula. Besides if someone was down there setting fires . . .

Someone.

"Memsen," he said. "I've changed my mind."

The hover glided to a stop above the unused field nearest to Diligence Cottage. Spur stepped back as guard rails flowed out of the deck around the ramp, which slowly extended like a metal tongue toward the sweet clover below. Cape, who was standing next to Spur, was smiling. What did his father think was so funny?

"We can stay here and wait for you," said Memsen. "If you have a problem, we'll come."

"Not through those trees you won't," said Spur. "No, you take Cape back up so he can report to the commander." The hover shuddered in the windstorm caused by the burn. "Besides, it's going to get rough here before too much longer. You need to protect yourselves."

"This is exciting." Her Grace, Jacqueline Kristof clapped her hands. "Are you excited, Spur?"

Memsen turned the girl around and gave her a hard shove toward the rest of the L'ung.

"DiDa?" Spur wanted to hug his father but settled for handing him the tell. "When the commander calls, just explain that I think we might have a torch and I'm on the ground looking. Then just keep track of the burn for her."

"Yes." His father was grinning broadly now. "I'm ready."

"Good. Memsen, thanks for your help."

"Go safely." She clicked her rings.

Spur held out his hand to the High Gregory but the boy dodged past it and embraced him instead. Spur was taken aback when he felt the High Gregory's kiss on his cheek. "I can see much more luck for you, friend Spur," he murmured. "Don't waste it."

The hot wind was an immediate shock after the cool interior of the hover. It blew gusty and confused, whipping Spur's hair and picking at his short sleeves. Spur paused at the bottom of the ramp to consider his next move and gather his courage. The pillar of smoke had smothered the afternoon sun, sinking the land into nightmarish and untimely gray twilight.

"Nice weather we're having," said Cape.

"DiDa, what?" He spun around, horrified. "Get back up there."

Cape snapped him a mock salute. "Since when do you give the orders on this farm, son?"

"But you have to, you can't . . ." He felt like a foolish little boy, caught by his father pretending to be a grownup. "Someone has to talk to the ground. The commander needs to know what's happening with the burn."

"I gave the tell to your know-so-much friend, Penny. She'll talk Adoula's ear off."

The ramp started to retract.

"What I have to do is too dangerous, DiDa." Spur's face was hot. "You're not coming, understand?"

"Wasn't planning to." Cape chuckled. "Never entered my mind."

Spur watched in helpless fury as the hatch closed. "Then just load whatever you want into the truck and take off. You've got maybe twenty minutes before things get hot here."

The hover rose straight up and away from the field but then paused, a dark speck in an angry sky.

"See what you've done?" Spur groaned.

"Don't worry. They'll run before too long." Cape clapped him on the back. "I don't know about you, but I have things to do."

"DiDa, are you . . . ?" Spur was uncertain whether he should leave Cape while he was in this manic mood. "Be careful."

Capability Roger Leung was not a man known for his sense of humor, but he laughed now. "Prosper, if we were being careful, we'd be up there in the sky with your strange little friends." He pointed into the woods. "Time to take some chances, son."

He turned and trotted off toward the big house without looking back.

Spur knew these woods. He and Vic and Comfort had spent hours in the cool shade pretending to be pirates or skantlings or aliens or fairies. They played queen and castle in the pukpuk ruins and pretended to be members of Morobe's original crew, exploring a strange new world for the first time. They cut paths to secret hideouts and built lean-tos from hemlock boughs and, when Vic and Spur were eleven, they even erected a ramshackle tree house with walls and a roof, although Cape made them take it down because he said it was too dangerous. Spur had been kissed for the first time in that tree house. In a contest of sibling gross out, Vic had dared his big sister to kiss his best friend. Comfort got the best of it, however, because her back dare was that Vic had to kiss Spur. As he pulled back from the kiss, Vic had punched Spur in the arm so hard it left a bruise.

The woods were dark and unnaturally quiet as he padded down the path that led past Bear Rock and the Throne of the Spruce King. Spur heard no birdsong or drone of bugs. It was as if the trees themselves were listening for the crackle of fire. When he first smelled smoke, he stopped to turn slowly and sniff, trying to estimate where it had come from. Ahead and to the north was his best guess. That meant it was time to cut off the path and bushwhack south across The Great Gosdog Swamp, which had never been very great and always dried up in the summer. His plan was to strike out in the direction of the smallest of the three fires he had seen from the hover. He knew he was getting close when it started to snow fire.

Most of what floated down was ash, but in the mix were sparks and burning embers that stung the bare skin of his arms and face. He brushed a hand through his hair and ran. Not in a panic – just to keep embers from sticking to him. To his right he could see the glow of at least one of the fires. And yes, now he could hear the distant crack and whoosh he knew all too well. The burn was working along the forest floor, he was sure of that. Crown fire sounded like a runaway train. If he were anywhere near one, he'd be deafened and then he'd be dead. Spur finally escaped the ash fall after several minutes of dodging past trees at speed. He hunched over to knead the stitch in his side, then pressed on.

The wind had picked up and now was blowing west, not east. He thought it must be an indraft. The burn that was crashing down on them had to suck air in huge gulps from every direction in order to support itself. Maybe the wind shift would work in their favor. A west wind would push these outlying spot fires back toward the burn itself. If the line of backfire was wide enough, it might actually check the advance of the burn when the two met. Of course, it would have to scorch across the best parts of the Millisap and Joerly farmsteads first.

In the gathering darkness, Spur decided to start trotting again. It was taking too long to skirt around the last fire to Mercy's Creek. And unless he saw something soon, he was turning back. He had to leave himself enough time to get away. And he wanted to make sure his father hadn't done anything crazy.

Intent on not tripping over a stone or root, Spur never saw the windblown curtain of smoke until it closed around him. He spun around, disoriented. He had been panting from running, so his nose and mouth and lungs filled immediately. It was like trying to breathe cotton. His eyes went teary and the world was reduced to a watery dissolve. Had he been out with Gold Squad, he would have been wearing goggles, a helmet and a breather. But here he was practically naked and the smoke was pervasive and smothering. He was coughing so hard he could taste the tang of blood and then his throat closed and he knew he was about to choke to death. In a panic, he hurled himself flat against the forest floor, desperately searching for the shallow layer of breathable air that they said sometimes clung to the ground. A stump poked at his side but as he laid his cheek against the mat of twigs and papery leaves, he found cooler air, rank but breathable. He tried to fill his aching lungs, coughed up mucus and blood, then tried again.

Spur didn't know exactly how long he lay there, but when he came to himself again, the haze of smoke had thinned to gauze and he knew he had taken enough chances. He had learned the hard way at Motu River that he was no hero. Why was he at it again? No more; get to the cottage, get on the scooter and get as far away from fire as possible. He pushed himself up on hands and knees, coughed and spat. His nose felt as if someone had pulled barbed wire through it. He sat back on his heels, blinking. It wasn't until he brushed at the leaf litter on his face that he realized he'd been crying. When he finally stood, he felt tottery. He grabbed a sapling to steady himself. Then he heard a twig snap and the rustle of foliage being parted. He ducked behind a beech tree that was barely wider than he was.

Comfort came trudging toward him, her face hard, eyes glassy. One look told him everything. She had changed out of the gingham dress and into a pair of baggy work pants that looked like they must have belonged to Vic. Over a smudged and dirty tee shirt, she wore a crude burlap vest to which were attached three liquid fire grenades. They bumped against her chest as she approached. She looked weary, as if she'd been carrying a weight that had pushed her to the very limit of her strength.

He had thought to leap out and overwhelm her when she passed, but she spotted him when she was still a dozen meters away and froze. He stepped from behind his tree, his hands held in front of him.

"I won't hurt you," he said.

In the instant he saw mindless animal panic in her eyes, he thought her more alien than any upsider. He had spooked her. Then she turned and sprinted away.

Spur ran after her. He wasn't thinking about the burn or his village or simplicity. He ran. He didn't have time to be either brave or afraid. He ran because he had loved this woman once and because he had watched her brother die.

As a girl, Comfort had always been the nimblest of the three of them. In an open field, Vic would have caught her, but scooting past trees and ducking under low branches, Comfort was faster than any two squirrels. After a couple of minutes of pursuit, Spur was winded. He wasn't exactly sure where they were anymore. Headed toward the creek, he guessed. If she thought she could cross over and take refuge in her own house, she truly was crazy. Suicidal.

Which made him pick up the pace, despite his fatigue. He ran so hard he thought his heart might break.

She had almost reached the creek when the chase ended abruptly. Comfort got reckless, cut a tree too close and clipped it instead. The impact knocked one of the grenades loose and spun her half around. She went to her knees and Spur leapt at her. But she kicked herself away and he skidded past and crashed into a tangle of summersweet. By the time he got to his knees she was showing him one of the grenades. He could see that she had flipped the safety and that her finger was on the igniter.

"Stop there," she said.

Spur was breathless and a little dizzy. "Comfort, don't."

"Too late." She blew a strand of dark hair off her face. "I already have."

He stood, once again holding his hands where she could see them. "What's this about, Comfort?"

"Vic," she said. "It's mostly about Vic now."

"He's gone. There's nothing you can do for him."

"We'll see." She shivered, despite the heat. "It was my fault, you know. I was the one who recruited him. But he was just supposed to pass information." Her voice shook. "They must have bullied him into becoming a torch. I killed him, Spur. I killed my brother."

"Listen to me, Comfort. He wasn't a torch. It was an accident."

The hand holding the grenade trembled slightly but then steadied. "That's not what you said this morning when you were off your head." She gave him a pitying look. "You said you tried to save him. That I believe."

He took a half step toward her. "But how does it help anyone to set fire to Littleton?" Another half step. "To our farms?"

She backed away from him. "They could stop this, you know. Your upsider friends. They could force the Cooperative to settle, put pressure on Jack Winter to do what's right. Except they don't really care about us. They come to watch, but they never get involved." Her laugh was low and scattered. "They're involved now. I hope that little brat is scared of dying."

"But they do care." He held his arms tight to his sides; otherwise he would have been waving them at her. "Memsen has a plan." Spur thought he might yet save her. "You have to believe me, Comfort. There are going to be talks with the pukpuks."

"Right." Her mouth twisted. "And you didn't see Vic torch himself."

"Besides, did you really think you could burn them up? The High Gregory is safe, Comfort. Memsen and the L'ung. Their hover came for us. That's how I got here so fast. They're in the air," he pointed backward over his shoulder, "waiting for me over the cottage."

When he saw her gaze flick up and away from him, he launched himself. He grabbed at the arm with the grenade. They twirled together in a grotesque pirouette. Then, unable to check his momentum, Spur stumbled and fell.

Comfort stepped away from him. She shook her head once. She pressed the igniter on the grenade.

It exploded into a fireball that shot out two long streams of flame in opposite directions. One soared high into the trees, the other shot down at the forest floor and gathered in a blazing puddle at her feet. She screamed as the grenade fell from her charred hand. Great tongues of flame licked up her legs. Her pants caught fire. Her singed hair curled into nothingness.

Spur screamed too. Seeing it all happen all over again was worse than any nightmare. When Vic had set the liquid fire bomb off, he had been instantly engulfed in flame. Spur had tried to knock him down, hoping to roll his friend onto the ground and put the merciless fire out. But Vic had shoved him away. With his clothes, his arms in flames, Vic had found the strength to send Spur sprawling backward.

Which saved Spur's life when the second bomb went off.

But this wasn't Motu River and Vic was dead. Comfort, his Comfort, had only grenades, designed to set backfires, not bombs designed by pukpuk terrorists. The lower half of her body had been soaked in liquid fire and was burning but he could see her face, her wild, suffering eyes, her mouth a slash of screeching pain and that last grenade still bumping against her chest.

Spur flew at her and ripped the unexploded grenade from the vest. He swept her up in his arms, taking her weight easily with a mad strength, and raced toward the creek. He had the crazy thought that if he ran fast enough, he would be able to stay ahead of the pain. He knew he was burning now but he had to save her. He had never had a chance with Vic, *take a chance*, his father had said and the High Gregory had warned him not to waste his luck. But the pain was too fast, it was catching up to him. Comfort's screams filled his head and then he was flying. He splashed down on top of her in the cool water and she didn't struggle when he forced her under, counting one, two, three, four, five, and he yanked her up and screamed at her to breathe, *breathe* and when she choked and gasped, he thrust her down again, two, three, four, five and when he pulled her up again she was limp; his poor burned Comfort had either fainted away or died in his arms but at least she wasn't on fire anymore.

Neither of them was.

XVI

The light which puts out our eyes is darkness to us.
Only that day dawns to which we are awake.
— Henry David Thoreau, *Walden*

In the dream, Spur sits in the kitchen of Diligence Cottage with Comfort, who is wearing the jade-colored pajamas. There are pies everywhere. Apple and cherry pies are stacked on the counters and across the table. Blackberry, elderberry and blueberry pies are lined up on the new oak floor against the wall with its morning glory wallpaper that Comfort ordered all the way from Providence, which is where Spur's mother lives. Maybe. He should find out. Comfort has set fiesta pear and peach surprise pies on top of the refrigerator and laid out the rhubarb pies two to a chair. Whatever else people in Littleton say about her, everyone agrees that Comfort makes the best pumpkin pies anywhere. In the dream, the pies are her idea. She has made enough pies to last him the rest of his life. He will need it if she goes. In the dream, though, it's not certain that she is leaving and he's not sure he wants her to. Besides, she certainly isn't going to catch the train back to Longwalk in those pajamas. They slide right off when you tug at them, the smooth fabric sliding lightly against her skin. In the dream she threads her way around a strawberry pie so she can kiss him. At first her kiss is like a promise. After a kiss like this, he should kick open the bedroom door and throw back the covers. But the kiss ends like a question. And the answer is no, Spur doesn't want this woman to be unhappy any more because of him. He doesn't want to dry her tears or . . .

"Enough sleeping, son." A sharp voice sliced through his dream. "Wake up and join the world."

Spur blinked, then gasped in disappointment. It wasn't fair; he didn't get to keep Comfort or the pie. The strange room he was in seemed to be a huge bay window filled with sunlight. In it was a scatter of dark shapes, one of which was moving. A cold hand pressed against his forehead.

"Thirty-eight point two degrees," said the docbot. "But then a little fever is to be expected."

"Dr. Niss?" said Spur.

"I'm never happy to see repeat customers, son." The docbot shined pinlights into Spur's eyes. "Do you know where you are? You were a little woozy when we picked you up."

He licked his lips, trying to recall. "The hospital?"

"Allworthy Memsen's hover. Open your mouth and say *ahh*." The docbot brushed its medfinger across Spur's tongue, leaving a waxy residue that tasted like motor oil.

"The hover?" There was something important that Spur couldn't quite remember. "But how did you get here?"

"I'm on call, son," said the docbot. "I can be anywhere there's a bot. Although this isn't much of an implementation. Feels two sizes too small."

Spur realized then that this docbot was different from the one at the hospital. It only had two gripper arms and its eye was set on top of its headplate. What did he mean, repeat business? Then the memory of the burn went roaring through his head. "Comfort!" Spur tried to sit up but the docbot pushed him back down. "Is she all right?"

"Still with us. We've saved her for now. But we'll talk about that after we look at your burns."

"How long have I been here? Did they stop the burn?"

The docbot reached behind Spur's neck, untied the hospital gown and pulled it to his waist. "I kept you down all last night and the better part of today to give your grafts a chance to take." The new set of burns ran in rough stripes across his chest. There was a splotch like a misshapen handprint on top of his shoulder. "You'll be on pain blockers for the next few days – they can poke holes in your memory, so don't worry if you forget how to tie your shoes." The docbot flowed warm dermslix onto the grafts. "Dermal regeneration just thirteen percent," it muttered.

"The burn, what about the burn?"

"Your people have it under control, according to that little Pendragon girl. I guess there's still some mopping up to do, but at least those kids are finally settling down. They were bouncing off the walls all last night." He pulled the gown back up. "You'll be fine son. Just stop playing with fire."

Spur was already swinging his legs off the bed as he fumbled with the ties of the gown. But when he went to stand, the deck seemed to fall away beneath his feet.

"Whoops." The docbot caught him. "Another side effect of pain blockers is that they'll tilt your sense of balance." He eased him back onto the bed. "You're going to want someone to help you get around for now." The docbot twisted off its medfinger and dropped it in the sterilizer. "I've got just the party for you. Wait here and I'll send him in."

The docbot had scarcely popped out of the room, when the High Gregory came bursting in, pushing a wheelchair. The entire bubble wall collapsed momentarily to reveal the L'ung, who started whooping and applauding for Spur. Memsen slipped in just as the wall reformed.

"You are the craziest, luckiest, bravest person I know." The High Gregory was practically squeaking with excitement. "What were you thinking when you picked her up? We were cheering so loud we thought you could probably hear us down there. I couldn't sleep all night, just thinking about it. Did you hear the L'ung just now? I taught them to clap hands for you. Here, have a seat."

Spur allowed Memsen and the High Gregory to help him into the chair, although he was certain they were going to drop him. He shut his eyes, counted to three and when he opened them again the cabin had stopped chasing its tail. "How do you know what I did?"

"We watched," said Memsen. "From the moment you stepped off the ramp, our spybugs were on you. The High Gregory is right. We were very moved."

"You watched?" He felt his cheeks flush. "I could've been killed."

"Watch is all we're supposed to do," said Memsen, "according to your covenant."

"But Memsen said we couldn't just leave you after you jumped into the water with her," said the High Gregory. "So we mowed down some forest to get to you, pulled the two of you out of the creek and QICed Dr. Niss into a bot that Betty Twosalt made." He wheeled Spur toward the hull so he could see the view. "She's good. She won a prize for her bots once."

"And Comfort is all right?" Spur glanced back over his shoulder at Memsen. "That's what Dr. Niss said."

"Saved," said Memsen, clicking her rings together. "We were able to save her."

The High Gregory parked the wheelchair as near to the hull as he could get and set the brake. He made the deck transparent too, so they could see more of the valley. "It's huge, Spur," he said, gesturing through the hull at the remains of the burn. "I've never seen anything like it."

They were passing over Mercy's Creek headed for the Joerlys, although he scarcely recognized the land beneath them as he surveyed the damage. The fires Comfort had started must have been sucked by the indraft back toward the burn as Spur had hoped, creating a backfired barrier to its progress. The backfire and the head of the burn must have met somewhere just east of the Joerlys. Comfort's house, barn and all the sheds had burned to their foundations. Farther to the west, the Millisap and Ezzat farmsteads were also obliterated. And more than half of Lamana Ridge was a wasteland of blackened spikes rising out of gray ash. Wisps of white smoke drifted across the ravaged land like the ghosts of dead trees. But dispersed through the devastation were inexplicable clumps of unscathed forest, mostly deciduous hardwood. Spur was relieved to see a blue-green crown of forest to the north along the top of the ridge, where the Corps must have beaten the burn back.

"What about the east?" said Spur. "Where did they stop it?"

But the hover was already turning and his view shifted, first south, where he could see the steeple of the communion hall on the Commons then southeast where CR22 sliced a thin line through intact forest. The High Gregory was watching him, his yellow eyes alight with anticipation.

"What?" said Spur, irked to be putting on a show for this fidgety upsider. "What are you staring at?"

"You," said the High Gregory. "There's so much luck running in your family, Spur. You know we tried to pick your father up after we got you, but he wouldn't come, even though we told him you were hurt."

"He was still there? That old idiot. Is he all right?"

"He's fine." The High Gregory patted Spur's hand. "He said he wasn't going to give his farm up without a fight. He had all your hoses out. He had this great line – I can't remember it exactly." He looked to Memsen for help. "Something about spitting?"

Memsen waited as a bench began to form from the deck. "Your father said that if the pump gave out, he'd spit at the burn until his mouth went dry."

Spur had come just out of the wheelchair, craning to see as the farm swung into view. The big house, the barns, the cottage were all untouched. But the orchards . . .

"He started his own backfire." Spur sank back onto the seat. Over half the trees were gone: the Macintosh and GoReds and Pippins were charred skeletons. But at least Cape had saved the Alumars and the Huangs and the Galas. And GiGo's trees by the cottage, all those foolish Macouns.

"The wind had changed direction." Memsen sat on the bench facing Spur. "When we arrived, he had just knocked a hole in the gas tank of your truck and said he couldn't stop to talk. He was going drive through his orchard and then set the backfire. We thought it seemed dangerous so we put spybugs on him. But he knew exactly what he was about." She showed Spur her teeth. "He's a brave man."

"Yes," mused Spur, although he wondered if that were true. Maybe his father just loved his apples more than he loved his life. Spur felt the hover accelerate then and the ground below began to race by. They shot over the Commons and headed west in the direction of Longwalk.

"We watched all night," said the High Gregory, "just like your father told us. Memsen made Penny let everyone have a turn talking to Commander Adoula on the tell. The fire was so awesome in the dark. We flew through it again and again."

The High Gregory's enthusiasm continued to annoy Spur. Three farmsteads were gone and his own orchards decimated, but this boy thought he was having an adventure. "You didn't offer to help? You could've dropped splash on the burn, maybe diverted it from the houses."

"We did offer," said Memsen. "We were told that upsiders are allowed to render assistance in the deep forest where only firefighters can see us, but not in plain sight of a village or town."

"Memsen is in trouble for landing the hover on the Commons." The High Gregory settled beside her on the bench. "We haven't even told anyone yet about what we did for you by the creek."

"So." Memsen held out her hand to him, fingers outspread. "We've been called back to Kenning to answer for our actions."

"Really?" Spur felt relieved but also vaguely disappointed. "When will you go?"

"Now, actually." Her rings glittered in the sunlight. "We asked Dr. Niss to wake you so we could say goodbye."

"But who will take Comfort and me to the hospital?"

"We'll be in Longwalk in a few moments. There's a hospital in Benevolence Park #2." Her fingers closed into a fist. "But Comfort will be coming with us."

"What?" Despite himself, Spur lurched out of the wheelchair. He tottered, the cabin spun, and the next thing he knew both Memsen and the High Gregory were easing him back down.

"Why?" He took a deep breath. "She can't."

"She can't very well stay in Littleton," said the High Gregory. "Her farm is destroyed. You're going to have to tell everyone who started the burn."

"Am I?" He considered whether he would lie to protect her. After all, he had lied for her brother. "She's told you she wants to do this? Let me talk to her."

"That's not possible." Memsen pinched the air.

"Why not?"

"Do you want to come with us, Spur?" said the High Gregory. "You could, you know."

"No." He wheeled himself backward, horrified at the idea. "Why would I want to do that? My home is in Littleton. I'm a farmer."

"Then stop asking questions," said Memsen impatiently. "As a citizen of the Transcendent State you're under a consensual cultural quarantine. We've just been reminded of that quite forcefully. There's nothing more we can say to you."

"I don't believe this," Spur heard himself shouting. "You've done something to her and you're afraid to tell me. What is it?"

Memsen hesitated, and Spur hear the low, repetitive *pa-pa-pa-ptt* that he had decided she made when she was consulting her predecessors. "If you insist, we can make it simple for you." Memsen thrust her face close to his. "Comfort died," she said harshly. "Tell that to everyone in your village. She was horribly burned and she died."

Spur recoiled from her. "But you said you saved her. Dr. Niss . . ."

"Dr. Niss can show you the body, if you care to see it." She straightened. "So."

"Goodbye, Spur," said the High Gregory. "Can we help you back onto the bed?"

Beneath them Spur could see the outskirts of Longwalk. Abruptly the hull of the hover turned opaque and the ceiling of the cabin began to glow. Spur knew from watching hovers land from the window of his hospital room that they camouflaged themselves on the final approach over a city.

"No, wait." Spur was desperate to keep the upsiders talking. "You said she was going with you. I definitely heard that. You said she was saved. Is she . . . this is like the other Memsens that you told me about, isn't it? The ones that are saved in you?"

"This is a totally inappropriate conversation." Memsen pinched the air with both hands. "We'll have to ask Dr. Niss to strike it from your memory."

"He can do that?"

"Sure," said the High Gregory. "We do it all the time. But he has to replace it with some fake memory. You'll have to tell him what you want. And if you should ever come across anything that challenges the replacement memory, you could get . . ."

Spur held up his hand to silence him. "But it's true what I just said?"

Memsen snorted in disgust and turned to leave.

"She can't admit anything." The High Gregory grasped her hand to restrain her. He held it to his chest. "But yes."

Spur was gripping the push rims of his wheelchair so hard that his hands ached. "So nobody dies on the upside?"

"No, no. Everybody dies. It's just that some of us choose to be saved to a shell afterward. Even the saved admit it's not the same as being alive. I haven't made my mind up about all that yet, but I'm only twelve standard. My birthday is next week, I wish you could be there."

"What will happen to Comfort in this shell?"

"She's going to have to adjust. She didn't expect to be saved, of course, probably didn't even know it was possible, so when they activate her, she'll be disoriented. She'll need some kind of counseling. We have some pretty good soulmasons on Kenning. And they can send for her brother, he'll want to help."

"Stop it! This is cruel." Memsen yanked his hand down. "We have to go right now."

"Why?" said the High Gregory plaintively. "He's not going to remember any of this."

"Vic was saved?" Even though he was still safe in the wheelchair, he felt as if he were falling.

"All the pukpuk martyrs were." The High Gregory tried to shake his hand loose from Memsen, but she wouldn't let him go. "That was why they agreed to sacrifice themselves."

"Enough." Memsen started to drag him from the cabin. "We're sorry, Spur. You're a decent man. Go back to your cottage and your apples and forget about us."

"Goodbye, Spur," called the High Gregory as they popped through the bulkhead. "Good luck."

As the bulkhead shivered with their passing, he felt a fierce and troubling desire burn his soul. Some part of him did want to go with them, to be with Comfort and Vic on the upside and see the wonders that Chairman Winter had forbidden the citizens of the Transcendent State. He could do it; he knew he could. After all, everyone in Littleton seemed to think he was leaving.

But then who would help Cape bring in the harvest?

Spur wasn't sure how long he sat alone in the wheelchair with a thousand thoughts buzzing in his head. The upsiders had just blown up his world and he was trying to desperately to piece it back together. Except what was the point? In a little while he wasn't going to be worrying anymore about Comfort and Vic and shells and being saved. Maybe that was for the best; it was all too complicated. Just like the Chairman had said. Spur thought he'd be happier thinking about apples and baseball and maybe kissing Melody Velez. He was ready to forget.

He realized that the hover had gone completely still. There was no vibration from the hull skimming through the air, no muffled laughter from the L'ung. He watched the hospital equipment melt into the deck. Then all the bulkheads popped and he could see the entire bay of the hover. It was empty except for his wheelchair, a gurney with Comfort's shroud-covered body and the docbot, which rolled up to him.

"So you're going to make me forget all this?" said Spur bitterly. "All the secrets of the upside?"

"If that's what you want."

Spur shivered. "I have a choice?"

"I'm just the doctor, son. I can offer treatment but you have to accept it. For example, you chose not to tell me about how you got burned that first time." The docbot rolled behind the wheelchair. "That pretty much wrecked everything I was trying to accomplish with the conciliation sim."

Spur turned around to look at it. "You knew all along?"

The docbot locked into the back of the wheelchair. "I wouldn't be much of a doctor if I couldn't tell when patients were lying to me." It started pushing Spur toward the hatch.

"But you work for the Chairman." Spur didn't know if he wanted the responsibility for making this decision.

"I take Jack Winters's money," said the docbot. "I don't take his advice when it comes to medical or spiritual practice."

"But what if I tell people that Comfort and Vic are saved and that upsiders get to go on after they die?"

"Then they'll know."

Spur tried to imagine keeping the upsiders' immortality a secret for the rest of his days. He tried to imagine what would happen to the Transcendental State if he told what he knew. His mouth went as dry as flour. He was just a farmer, he told himself; he didn't have that good an imagination. "You're saying that I don't have to have my memory of all this erased?"

"Goodness, no. Unless you'd rather forget about me."

As they passed Comfort's body, Spur said, "Stop a minute."

He reached out and touched the shroud. He expected it to be some strange upsider fabric but it was just a simple cotton sheet. "They knew that I could choose to remember, didn't they? Memsen and the High Gregory were playing me to the very end."

"Son," said Dr. Niss, "the High Gregory is just a boy and nobody in the Thousand Worlds knows what the Allworthy knows."

But Spur had stopped listening. He rubbed the shroud between his thumb and forefinger, thinking about how he and the Joerlys used to make up adventures in the ruins along Mercy's Creek when they were children. Often as not one of them would achieve some glorious death as part of the game. The explorer would boldly drink from the poisoned cup to free her comrades, the pirate captain would be run through defending his treasure, the queen of skantlings would throw down her heartstone rather than betray the castle. And then he or Vic or Comfort would stumble dramatically to the forest floor and sprawl there, cheek pressed against leaf litter, still as scattered stones. The others would pause briefly over the body and then dash into the woods, so that the fallen hero could be reincarnated and the game could go on.

"I want to go home," he said, at last.

HONOURABLE MENTIONS

2005

Brian W. Aldiss, "Pipeline," *Asimov's*, September.
Lee Allred, "East of Appomattox," *Alternate Generals III*.
Poul Anderson, "The Newcomers," *The Enchanter Completed*.
Lou Antonelli, "A Rocket for the Republic," *Asimov's*, September.
———, "The Cast-Iron Dybbuk," *Andromeda Spaceways*, June/July.
———, "Dialogue," *RevolutionSF*, November.
Catherine Asaro, "The City of Cries," *Down These Dark Space-ways*.
Neal Asher, "Acephalous Dreams," *Adventure*.
———, "Garp and Geronamid," *Interzone*, July/August.
———, "Mason's Rats," *Asimov's*, April/May.
Kage Baker, "Bad Machine," *Asimov's*, June.
———, "The Two Old Women," *Asimov's*, February.
———, "The Unfortunate Gytt," *Adventure*.
Cherith Baldry, "The Diamond Star," *Oceans of the Mind*, Fall.
Barry Baldwin, "Paris Is Burning," *Adventure*.
John Barnes, "The Diversification of Its Fancy," *Analog*, November.
Laird Barron, "The Imago Sequence," *F&SF*, May.
———, "Parallax," *SCI FICTION*, 9/7.
———, "Proboscis," *F&SF*, February.
William Barton, "Dark of the Sun," *Asimov's*, April/May.
———, "Harvest Moon," *Asimov's*, September.
Stephen Baxter, "A Signal From Earth," *Postscripts 5*.
———, "Climbing the Blue," *Analog*, July/August.
———, "Lakes of Light," *Constellations*.
———, "The Time Pit," *Analog*, October.
———, "Under Martian Ice," *Nature*, 10 February.
Peter S. Beagle, "Two Hearts," *F&SF*, October/November.
Elizabeth Bear, "And the Deep Blue Sea," *SCI FICTION*, 5/4.
———, "Botticelli," *The Agony Column*.
———, "Follow Me Light," *SCI FICTION*, 1/12.
———, "Long Cold Day," *SCI FICTION*, 9/21.
———, "One-Eyed Jack and the Suicide King," *Lenox Avenue*, March/April.
———, "Wax," *Interzone*, December.
Greg Bear, "RAM Shift Phase 2," *Nature*, 15 December.
Chris Beckett, "The Perimeter," *Asimov's*, December.

Gregory Benford, "A Life with a Semisent," *Nature*, 12 May.
——, "Beyond Pluto," *Cosmic Tales*.
——, "The Man Who Wasn't There," *Cosmos*, September.
——, "On the Brane," *Gateways*.
——, "The Pain Gun," *Analog*, July/August.
Lucy Bergman, "Damned If You Don't," *Nature*, 16 June.
Beth Bernobich, "Watercolors in the Rain," *Fictitious Force*.
Michael Bishop, "Bears Discover Smut," *SCI FICTION*, 10/26.
Terry Bisson, "Billy and the Ants," *F&SF*, October/November.
——, "Special Relativity," *Amazon Shorts*, August 19.
——, "Super 8," *SCI FICTION*, 11/24.
Leah Bobet, "Bliss," *On Spec*, Winter 04/05.
Richard Bowes, "There's a Hole in the City," *SCI FICTION*, 6/15.
Scott Bradfield, "Angry Duck," *F&SF*, July.
David Brin, "Mars Opposition," *Analog*, January/February.
Keith Brooke, "A Different Sky," *Constellations*.
Eric Brown, "A Heritage of Stars," *Constellations*.
——, "The Extraordinary Voyage of Jules Verne," *PS Publishing*.
——, "Life Beyond," *Postscripts 4*.
——, "Six Weeks in a Balloon," *New Jules Verne Adventures*.
Chris Bunch, "Gun, Not for Dinosaur," *The Enchanter Completed*.
——, "Murdering Uncle Ho," *Alternate Generals III*.
Pat Cadigan, "Is There Life After Rehab?" *SCI FICTION*.
Lillian Stewart Carl, "Over the Sea to Skye," *Alternate Generals III*.
Scott William Carter, "A Christmas in Amber," *Analog*, December.
Sally Carteret, "Nine Electric Flowers," *Polyphony 5*.
Jay Caselberg, "Sunset," *Interzone*, July/August.
Paul Chafe, "Botany Bay," *Cosmic Tales*.
Suzy McKee Charnas, "Heavy Lifting," *SCI FICTION*, 7/06.
Robert R. Chase, "Endeavor," *Analog*, July/August.
Ted Chiang, "What's Expected of Us," *Nature*, 7 July.
Brenda Clough, "Indiana Wants Me," *Future Washington*.
Deborah Coates, "Magic in a Certain Slant of Light," *Strange Horizons*, 3/21.
Michael Cobley, "The Intrigue of the Battered Box," *Nova Scotia*.
David B. Coe, "The Christmas Count," *SCI FICTION*, 7/27.
Albert E. Cowdrey, "The Amulet," *F&SF*, March.
——, "The Housewarming," *F&SF*, September.
——, "Twilight States," *F&SF*, July.
Ian Creasey, "The Lonesome Cosmogonist," *Challenging Destiny*, May.
Peter Crowther, "Cliff Rhodes and The Most Important Journey," *New Jules Verne Adventures*.
Jack Dann, "Dharma Bums," *Postscripts 4*.
——, "Dreaming with the Angels," *Postscripts 3*.
——, "Promised Land," *Amazon Shorts*, August 19.
Rjurik Davidson, "Passing of the Minotaurs," *SCI FICTION*, 4/20.
Stephen Dedman, "Static Song," *Andromeda Spaceways*, April/May.

Jack Deighton, "Dusk," *Nova Scotia*.

A. M. Dellamonica, "A Key to the Illuminated Heretic," *Alternate Generals III*.

——, "The Spear Carrier," *SCI FICTION*, 3/9.

Paul Di Filippo, "Daydream Nation," *Cosmos*, October.

——, "The Emperor of Gondwanaland," *Interzone*, January/Febuary.

——, "Harsh Oases," *Interzone*, December.

——, "The Mysterious Iowans," *New Jules Verne Adventures*.

——, "The Secret Sutras of Sally Strumpet," *F&SF*, April.

Thomas M. Disch, "The Wall of America," *F&SF*, March.

Cory Doctorow, "Human Readable," *Future Washington*.

——; "I, Robot," *Infinite Matrix*, 2/10.

Candas Jane Dorsey, "Mom and Mother Teresa," *Tesseracts Nine*.

Gardner Dozois, "When the Great Days Came," *F&SF*, December.

David Drake, "A Death in Peacetime," *Oceans of the Mind*, Spring.

L. Timmel Duchamp, "Memory Work," *Asimov's*, October/November.

——, "The Red Rose Rages (Bleeding)," *Aqueduct*.

Hal Duncan, "The Chiaroscurist," *Electric Velocipede*, Fall.

Christopher East, "Bastogne V.9," *Interzone*, May/June.

Greg Van Eekhout, "Authorwerx," *Amazing*, February.

Carol Emshwiller, "I Live in Your House," *F&SF*, March.

James Enge, "Turn Up This Crooked Way," *Black Gate*, Summer.

Steven Erikson, "The Devil Delivered," *PS Publishing*.

——, "Fishin' with Grandma Matchie," *PS Publishing*.

Gregory Feeley, "Fancy Bread," *TEL: Stories*.

Andrew C. Ferguson, "Sophie and the Sacred Fluids," *Nova Scotia*.

Charles Coleman Finlay, "Love and the Wayward Troll," *F&SF*, March.

——, "The Moon is Always Full," *Strange Horizons*, 31 October.

——, "Moons Like Great White Whales," *Strange Horizons*, 2/28.

——, "The Nursemaid's Suitor," *Black Gate*, Summer.

——, "Of Silence and the Man at Arms," *F&SF*, June.

Mark Finn, "The Bridge of Teeth," *Adventure*.

Jim Fiscus, "The Road to Endless Sleep," *Alternate Generals III*.

Karen Fishler, "Stones in Winter," *Realms of Fantasy*, June.

Michael F. Flynn, "The Ensorcelled ATM," *The Enchanter Completed*.

Jeffrey Ford, "A Man of Light," *SCI FICTION*, 1/26.

——, "Boatman's Holiday," *F&SF*, October/November.

——, "The Cosmology of the Wider World," *PS Publishing*.

——, "Holt," *Flytrap 4*.

——, "In the House of Four Seasons," *Fantasy Magazine*.

——, "The Scribble Mind," *SCI FICTION*, 5/25.

Pat Forde, "Omphalos," *Tesseracts Nine*.

Alan Dean Foster, "The Last Akialoa," *F&SF*, December.

Eugie Foster, "The Bunny of Vengeance and the Bear of Death," *Fantasy Magazine*.

Andrew Fox, "The Man Who Would Be King," *SCI FICTION*, 11/30.

Carl Frederick, "Prayer for a Dead Paramecium," *Analog*, July/August.

David Freer & Eric Flint, "Genie Out of the Bottle," *Cosmic Tales*.
Peter Friend, "The Real Deal," *Asimov's*, July.
Esther M. Friesner, "The Beau and the Beast," *F&SF*, March.
——, "The Fraud," *Asimov's*, February.
——, "Helen Remembers the Stork Club," *F&SF*, October/November.
Gregory Frost, "The Road to Recovery," *Attack of the Jazz Giants*.
——, "Upon Stepping From the Shower," *Amazon Shorts*, Aug. 19.
Neil Gaiman, "Sunbird," *Noisy Outlaws* . . .
R. Garcia y Robertson, "Oxygen Rising," *Asimov's*, February.
——, "Queen of the Balts," *F&SF*, February.
Henry Gee, "Are We Not Men?," *Nature*, 30 June.
David Gerrold, "A Quantum Bit Exists in Two States Simultaneously: Off," *F&SF*, September.
——, "A Quantum Bit Exists in Two States Simultaneously: On," *F&SF*, September.
——, "Chester," *F&SF*, June.
——, "The Diamond Sky," *Hal's Worlds*.
Craig Laurance Gidney, "The Safety of Thorns," *Say . . . 5*.
Laura Anne Gilman, "End of Day," *Aeon Four*.
D. G. K. Goldberg, "A Love for All Time," *Polyphony 5*.
Theodora Goss, "A Statement in the Case," *Realms of Fantasy*, August.
——, "The Belt," *Flytrap 4*.
——, "Death Comes for Ervina," *Polyphony 5*.
——, "Pip and the Fairies," *Strange Horizons*, 10/3.
Steven Gould & Rory Harper, "Leonardo's Hands," *RevolutionSF*, July.
Gavin J. Grant, "Heads Down, Thumbs Up," *SCI FICTION*, 4/27.
John Grant, "The Hard Stuff," *Nova Scotia*.
Dominic Green, "The Lost World," *BBC Cult site*.
Roland J. Green, "It Isn't Every Day of the Week," *Alternate Generals III*.
Colin Greenland, "Kings," *Constellations*.
Jim Grimsley, "The 120 Hours of Sodom," *Asimov's*, February.
Daniel Grotta, "RAW," *Asimov's*, July.
Joe Haldeman, "Civil Disobedience," *Future Washington*.
——, "Diminished Chord," *Renaissance Faire*.
——, "Foreclosure," *F&SF*, October/November.
——, "Heartwired," Nature, 24 March.
Peter F. Hamilton, "The Forever Kitten," *Nature*, 28 July.
Larry Hammer, "Paul Bunyan and the Photocopier," *Say . . . 5*.
Elizabeth Hand, "Calypso in Berlin," *SCI FICTION*, 7/13.
——, "Echo," *F&SF*, October/November.
John G. Hemry, "Working on Borrowed Time," *Analog*, June.
Howard V. Hendrix, "The Self-Healing Sky," *Aeon Two*.
——, "Waiting for Citizen Godel," *Aeon Five*.
David Herter, "black and green and gold," *Postscripts 3*.
Joe Hill, "Best New Horror," *Postscripts 3*.
——, "Bobby Conroy Comes Back from the Dead," *Postscripts 5*.

M. K. Hobson, "Hell Notes," *SCI FICTION*, 2/9.

James P. Hogan, "The Tree of Dreams," *Cosmic Tales*.

Nalo Hopkinson, "Men Sell Not Such in Any Town," *Nature*, 15 September.

Nick Hornby, "Small Country," *Noisy Outlaws* . . .

Robert J. Howe, "Do Neanderthals Know?" *Analog*, December.

——, "Entropy's Girlfriend," *Analog*, October.

Matthew Hughes, "The Devil You Don't," *Asimov's*, March.

——, "Finding Sajessarian," *F&SF*, April.

——, "The Gist Hunter," *F&SF*, June.

——, "Go Tell the Phoenicians," *Interzone*, May/June.

——, "Help Wonted," *F&SF*, October/November.

——, "Inner Huff," *F&SF*, February.

——, "Thwarting Jabbi Gloond," *F&SF*, August.

Gavin Inglis, "Pisces Ya Bas," *Nova Scotia*.

Alex Irvine, "The Golems of Detroit," *F&SF*, May.

——, "The Lorelei," *F&SF*, January.

Matt Jarpe, "City of Reason," *Asimov's*, January.

Michael J. Jasper & Greg van Eekhout, "California King," *Asimov's*, April/May.

Phillip C. Jennings, "Back to Moab," *Asimov's*, October/November.

——, "Invasion of the Axbeaks," *Asimov's*, January.

Daniel Kaysen, "The Jenna Set," *Strange Horizons*, 3/14.

James Patrick Kelly, "The Edge of Nowhere," *Asimov's*, June.

David Kewin, "Museum Beetles, *Abyss & Apex*, 15.

Simon Kewin, "Museum Beetles," *Abyss & Apex*, October.

Caitliln R. Kiernan, "Faces in Revolving Souls," *Outsiders*.

Damian Kilby, "Earthtime," *Asimov's*, December.

Garry Kilworth, "Murders in the White Garden," *Postscripts 3*.

Ellen Klages, "Guys Day Out," *SCI FICTION*, 4/13.

Judy Klass, "Boywave," *Tales of the Unanticipated 26*.

Ted Kosmatka, "The God Engine," *Asimov's*, October/November.

Bill Kte'pi, "The Kingfish and the Tunguska Machine," *Fortean Bureau*, June.

Michael Kurland, "Four Hundred Slaves," *Adventure*.

Marc Laidlaw, "Jane," *SCI FICTION*, 2/16.

——, "Sweetmeats," *F&SF*, June.

Douglas Lain, "A Coffee Cup/Alien Invasion Story," *Strange Horizons*, June.

Jay Lake, "Alien Dreams," *RevolutionSF*, November.

——, "Dark Flowers, Inverse Moon," *Asimov's*, October/November.

——, "Fat Jack and the Spider Clown," *Black Gate*, Summer.

——, "The Four Clowns of the Apocalypse," *Lone Star Stories*, October.

——, "Green," *Aeon Five*.

——, "The Hangman Isn't Hanging," *Lone Star Stories*, June.

——, "The Lizard of Ooze," *Flytrap 4*.

——, "Many-splendored," *Andromeda Spaceways*, June/July.

——, "Martyrs' Carnival," *Asimov's*, June.
——, & Ruth Nestvold, "The Rivers of Eden," *Futurismic*.
Alexander Lamb, "Ithrulene," *Polyphony 5*.
Geoffrey A. Landis, "Betting on Eureka," *Asimov's*, October/November.
David Langford, "New Hope for the Dead," *Nature*, 5/26.
Jaye Lawrence, "Fallen Idols," *F&SF*, October/November.
Chris Lawson, "Countless Screaming Argonauts," *Realms of Fantasy*, August.
Tanith Lee, "En Foret Noire," *Realms of Fantasy*, December.
——, "UOUS," *The Fair Folk*.
Yoon Ha Lee, "The Sun's Kiss," *Ideomancer*, September.
Edward M. Lerner, "The Day of the RFIDs," *Future Washington*.
David D. Levine, "A Book is a Journey," *Tales of the Unanticipated 26*.
——, "Circle of Compassion," *Gateways*.
——, "The Ecology of Fairie," *Realms of Fantasy*, October.
——, "Tk'tk'tk," *Asimov's*, March.
Roger Levy, "No Cure for Love," *Constellations*.
Michael Libling, "The Gospel of Hate," *F&SF*, April.
Megan Lindholm, "Grace Notes," *The Fair Folk*.
Samantha Ling, "Waking Chang-Er," *Asimov's*, July.
Kelly Link, "Magic For Beginners," *F&SF*, September.
——, "Monster," *Noisy Outlaws . . .*
James Lovegrove, "The Meteor Party," *Constellations*.
Richard A. Lovett, "A Few Good Men," *Analog*, January/February.
——, "Tomorrow's Strawberries," *Analog*, May.
—— & Mark Niemann-Russ, "Netpuppets," *Analog*, June.
Scott Mackay, "Threshold of Perception," *Interzone*, March/April.
Ken Macleod, "Undead Again," *Nature*, 17 February.
Bruce McAllister, "Hero, The Movie," *F&SF*, July.
——, "Mary," *Lady Churchill's Rosebud Wristlet*, XV.
——, "Spell," *F&SF*, August.
——, "Stu," *SCI FICTION*, 11/23.
——, "Water Angel," *Asimov's*, January.
Paul McAuley, "Meat," *Nature*, 5 May.
——, "Rats of the System," *Constellations*.
Wil McCarthy, "The Policeman's Daughter," *Analog*, June.
——, "They Will Raise You in a Box," *Asimov's*, April/May.
John G. McDaid, "Keyboard Practice, Consisting of an Aria with Diverse Variations for the Harpsichord with Two Manuals," *F&SF*, January.
Jack McDevitt, "The Big Downtown," *Down These Dark Spaceways*.
——, "Ignition," *Future Washington*.
Ian McDonald, "Written in the Stars," *Constellations*.
Sandra McDonald, "Papa and the Sea," *Andromeda Spaceways*, June/July.
A. J. McIntosh, "Not Wisely But Too Well," *Nova Scotia*.
Will McIntosh, "Soft Apocalypse," *Interzone*, October.
Vonda N. McIntyre, "A Modest Proposal . . . ," *Nature*, 3 March.

Patricia A. McKillip, "The Kelpie," *The Fair Folk*.

Elisabeth Malartre, "Looking for Mr. Goodbug," *Nature*, 9 June.

Barry N. Malzberg & Paul Di Filippo, "Beyond Mao," *Postscripts 4*.

—— & Jack Dann, "The Starry Night," *SCI FICTION*, 6/22.

Louise Marley, "Diamond Girls," *SCI FICTION*, 6/8.

Paul E. Martens, "Piper," *Tales of the Unanticipated 26*.

Steve Martinez, "Out of the Box," *Asimov's*, October/November.

John Meaney, "Lost Time," *Adventure*.

William Meikle, "Total Mental Quality, By the Way," *Nova Scotia*.

Paul Melko, "The Summer of the Seven," *Asimov's*, August.

Sean Mellican, "Gears Grind Down," *Lady Churchill's*, 16.

Paul Meloy, "Dying in the Arms of Jean Harlow," *Third Alternative*.

Anil Menon, "Archipelago," *Strange Horizons*, 4/25.

Robert A. Metzger, "Polyhedrons," *Asimov's*, February.

Eugene Mirabeli, "The Woman in Schrodinger's Wave Equation," *F&SF*, August.

Steven Mohan, Jr., "The House of the Beata Virgo," *Interzone*, July/August.

——, "Whale Falls," *Ideomancer*, December.

Nancy Jane Moore, "Dusty Wings," *Polyphony 5*.

John Morressy, "The Legend of the Whiney Man," *F&SF*, June.

James Morrow, "The Second Coming of Charles Darwin," *Amazon Shorts*, August 19.

Richard Mueller, "Age of Miracles," *F&SF*, September.

——, "Clipper's Last Ride," *Asimov's*, July.

——, "Dutch," *F&SF*, February.

Vera Nazarian, "The Clock King and the Queen of the Hourglass," *PS Publishing*.

Ruth Nestvold, "Happily Ever Awhile," *Strange Horizons*, 6/20.

——, "Rainmakers," *Asimov's*, June.

R. Neube, "Mall Warriors," *Oceans of the Mind*, Fall.

——, "Organs R Us," *Asimov's*, March.

Kim Newman, "The Gypsies in the Wood," *The Fair Folk*.

——, "The Serial Murders," *SCI FICTION*, 10/5.

Larry Niven, "Breeding Maze," *Analog*, September.

——, "Rhinemaidens," *Asimov's*, January.

——, "The Slow Ones," *Analog*, December.

—— & Brenda Cooper, "Kath and Quicksilver," *Asimov's*, August.

Claudia O'Keefe, "Black Deer," *F&SF*, April.

——, "Maze of Trees," *F&SF*, August.

John Phillip Olson, "The Company Man," *Asimov's*, September.

Jerry Oltion, "The Best-Laid Plans," *Analog*, September.

——, "Tainted," *Analog*, May.

Susan Palwick, "The Fate of Mice," *Asimov's*, January.

Richard Parks, "Empty Places," *Realms of Fantasy*, December.

——, "The Finer Points of Destruction," *Fantasy Magazine*.

——, "Foxtails," *Realms of Fantasy*, June.

——, "Lord Goji's Wedding," *Lady Churchill's Rosebud Wristlet, XV*.

Stefan Pearson, "The Bogle's Bargain," *Nova Scotia*.
Lawrence Person, "Master Lao and the Flying Horror," *Postscripts* 4.
——, "Starving Africans," *Postscripts* 3.
Ursula Pflug, "The Eyes of Horus," *The Nine Muses*.
Brian Plante, "In the Loop," *Analog*, July/August.
——, "Letters of Transit," *Analog*, April.
Frederik Pohl, "Generations," *Asimov's*, September.
Tim Pratt, "Bottom Feeding," *Asimov's*, August.
——, "The Tyrant in Love," *Fantasy Magazine*.
——, & Greg Van Eekhout, "Robots and Falling Hearts," *Realms of Fantasy*, October.
Sarah Prineas, "A Treatise on Fewmets," *Lone Star Stories*, August.
Tom Purdom, "Bank Run," *Asimov's*, October/November.
Marguerite Reed, "Bearing Witness," *Strange Horizons*, 11/14–11/21.
Robert Reed, "The Cure," *F&SF*, December.
——, "Dallas: An Essay," *Asimov's*, April/May.
——, "Finished," *Asimov's*, September.
——, "From Above," *F&SF*, February.
——, "Hidden Paradise," *SCI FICTION*, 3/16.
——, "Man for the Job," *SCI FICTION*, 11/9.
——, "The New Deity," *F&SF*, May.
——, "Poet Snow," *F&SF*, June.
——, "Pure Vision," *F&SF*, August.
——, "Think So?" *F&SF*, July.
Jessica Reisman, "Boy 12," *Interzone*, December.
Mike Resnick, "The Burning Spear at Twilight," *Alternate Generals III*.
——, "Down Memory Lane," *Asimov's*, April/May.
——, "Guardian Angel," *Down These Dark Spaceways*.
——, "Island of Annoyed Souls," *Adventure*.
——, "Me," I, *Alien*.
Alastair Reynolds, "Feeling Rejected," *Nature*, 22 September.
Carrie Richerson, "A Birth," *Asimov's*, August.
——, "A Game of Cards," *Aeon Four*.
M. Rickert, "Anyway," *SCI FICTION*, 8/31.
——, "The Harrowing," *F&SF*, April.
Chris Roberson, "Prowl Unceasing," *Adventure*.
——, "The Trouble with Superman," *Space Squid 1*.
Adam Roberts, "And Future King," *Postscripts* 4.
——, "Hector Servadac, fils," *New Jules Verne Adventures*.
——, "The Order of Things," *Constellations*.
Kim Stanley Robinson, "Primate in Forest," *Future Washington*.
——, "Prometheus Unbound," *Nature*, 11 August.
Justina Robson, "The Adventurers' League," *New Jules Verne Adventures*.
——, "Dreadnought," *Nature*, 31 March.
——, "The Little Bear," *Constellations*.
Benjamin Rosenbaum, "Falling," *Nature*, 22 September.

Mary Rosenblum, "Green Shift," *Asimov's*, March.

——, "Gypsy Tail Wind," *F&SF*, August.

——, "Hide and Seek," *Amazon Shorts*, Aug 19.

Matthew Rossi, "Ghosts of Christmas," *Adventure*.

Rudy Rucker, "Guadalupe and Hieronymus Bosch," *Interzone*, October.

——, "The Man in the Back Room at the Country Club," *Infinite Matrix*, 12/30.

Kristine Kathryn Rusch, "Boz," *SCI FICTION*, 12/21.

——, "Diving into the Wreck," *Asimov's*, December.

——, "The Injustice Collector," *I, Alien*.

——, "Killing Time," *Asimov's*, July.

——, "Scrawny Pete," *Amazon Shorts*, August 19.

——, "Worlds Enough . . . and Time," *Gateways*.

Geoff Ryman, "The Last Ten Years in the Life of Hero Kai," *F&SF*, December.

William Sanders, "Acts," *I, Alien*.

——, "Angel Kills," *Asimov's*, February.

——, "Not Fade Away," *Alternate Generals III*.

Robert J. Sawyer, "Identity Theft," *Down These Dark Spaceways*.

Eric Schaller, "Three Urban Folk Tales," *Lady Churchill's Rosebud Wristlet*, XVI.

John Schoffstall, "Adventures in Dog-Walking in Downtown Philadelphia," *Strange Horizons*, 11/7.

Ken Scholes, "The Man with Great Despair Behind His Eyes," *Talebones*, Winter.

Carter Scholz, "I Didn't Know What Time It Was," *F&SF*, September.

Mike Schultz, "Old As Books," *F&SF*, July.

David J. Schwartz, "A Whole Man," *Talebones*, Summer.

Lori Selke, "The Dodo Factory," *Asimov's*, March.

Katherine Shaffer & Jim C. Hines, "OM+," *Oceans of the Mind*, Fall.

Nisi Shawl, "Cruel Sister," *Asimov's*, October/November.

——, "Matched," *Infinite Matrix*, 5/23.

Robert Sheckley, "Reborn Again," *Infinite Matrix*, 1/8.

——, "The Two Sheckleys," *Gateways*.

Lucius Shepard, "Abimaqique," *SCI FICTION*.

——, "The Emperor," *SCI FICTION*, 12/14.

——, "The Velt," *Amazon Shorts*, August 19.

Delia Sherman, "Walpurgis Afternoon," *F&SF*, December.

Gary W. Shockley, "Late Show," *F&SF*, March.

Vandana Singh, "The Tetrahedron," InterNova.

Jack Skillingstead, "Bean There," *Asimov's*, April/May.

——, "Overlay," *Asimov's*, October/November.

——, "The Tree," *On Spec*, Fall.

Bud Sparhawk, "Bright Red Star," *Asimov's*, March.

Cat Sparks, "Macchiato Lane," *Ticonderogaonline*, September.

Norman Spinrad, "A Man of the Theatre,' *Nature*, 10 March.

Gale Sproule, "Jimmy and the Cat," *Amazing*, January.

Brian Stableford, "Jehan Thun's Quest," *New Jules Verne Adventures*.

Jason Staunchfield, "Gypsy Wings," *Aeon Five*.

Allen M. Steele, "An Incident at the Luncheon of the Boating Party," *F&SF*, December.

Bruce Sterling, "The Denial," *F&SF*, September.

——, "Ivory Tower," *Nature*, 7 April.

Renee Stern, "Fire and Ice," *Aeon Five*.

Ian Stewart, "Play It Again, Psam," *Nature*, 3 February.

S. M. Stirling, "The Apotheosis of Martin Padway," *The Enchanter Completed*.

Jason Stoddard, "Changing the Tune," *Futurismic*.

——, "Exception," *Strange Horizons*, 9/12–9/19.

——, "Panacea," *SCI FICTION*, 9/14.

——, "Saving Mars," *Interzone*, October.

——, "Winning Mars," *Interzone*, January/Febuary.

Charles Stross, "MAXO Signals," *Nature*, 25 August.

——, "Remade," *Cosmos*, August.

——, "Snowball's Chance," *Nova Scotia*.

Jerome Stueart, "Lemmings in the Third Year," *Tesseracts Nine*.

Jonathan Sullivan, "Niels Bohr and the Sleeping Dragon," *Strange Horizons*, 7/18–7/25.

Lucy Sussex, "Matricide," *SCI FICTION*, 2/2.

Michael Swanwick, "Girls and Boys, Come Out to Play," *Asimov's*, July.

Sonya Taaffe, "On the Blindside," *Flytrap 4*.

——, "White Shadows," *Say . . . 5*

Judith Tarr, "Measureless to Man," *Alternate Generals III*.

——, "Penthesilia," *The Enchanter Completed*.

John Alfred Taylor, "Striders," *Oceans of the Mind*, Summer.

E. Thomas, "Buddha's Fall," *Fortean Bureau*, Fall.

——, "Fire and Ash," *On Spec*.

——, "The Tinker's Child," *Aeon Four*.

Robert Thurston, "I.D.I.D," *F&SF*, May.

Lavie Tidhar, "The Dope Fiend," *SCI FICTION*, 12/28.

Mark W. Tiedemann, "Hard Time," *Electric Velocipede*, Fall.

Lois Tilton, "Pericles the Tyrant," *Asimov's*, October/November.

Shane Tourtellotte, "Footsteps," *Analog*, May.

Harry Turtledove, "The Haunted Bicuspid," *The Enchanter Completed*.

——, "He Woke in Darkness," *Asimov's*, August.

——, "Shock and Awe," *Alternate Generals III*.

Steven Utley, "Promised Land," *F&SF*, July.

——, "Silv'ry Moon," *F&SF*, October/November.

——, "The Wave-Function Collapse," *Asimov's*, March.

Rajnar Vajra, "Of Kings, Queens, and Angels," *Analog*, July/August.

Jeff VanderMeer, "The Farmer's Cat," *Polyphony 5*.

Mark L. Van Name, "Bring Out the Ugly," *Cosmic Tales*.

James Van Pelt, "The Ice-Cream Man," *Asimov's*, June.

——, "The Inn at Mount Either," *Analog*, May.

——, "One Day, in the Middle of the Night," *Talesbones*, Summer.

Sydney J. Van Scyoc, "Poppies by Moonlight," *F&SF*, December.

Carrie Vaughn, "Danae at Sea," *TEL*: Stories.

Edd Vick, "The Compass," *Asimov's*, July.

———, "Parachute Kid," *Asimov's*, February.

Elisabeth Vonarburg, "See Kathryn Runn," *Tesseracts Nine*.

Ray Vukcevich, "Tongues," *Polyphony 5*.

Richard Wadholm, "The Hottest Night of the Summer," *Polyphony 5*.

Howard Waldrop, "The Bravest Girl I Ever Knew," *Kong Unbound*.

———, "The Horse of a Different Color (That You Rode In On)," *SCI FICTION*, 11/2.

———, "The King of Where I Go," *SCI FICTION*, 12/7.

John Waters, "Bright Waters," *Lady Churchill's Rosebud Wristlet*, 17.

Ian Watson, "Lover of Statues," *Asimov's*, April/May.

———, "The Navigator's Children," *Constellations*.

Catherine Wells, "Point of Origin," *Asimov's*, August.

K. D. Wentworth, "Born-Again," *F&SF*, May.

Leslie What, "Dead Men on Vacation," *Asimov's*, February.

Liz Williams, "Black Thorn and Nettles," *Realms of Fantasy*, April.

———, "A Shadow on the Land," *Asimov's*, August.

———, "Ikiyoh," *Asimov's*, December.

———, "Mortegarde," *Realms of Fantasy*, December.

———, "Serpent's Tooth," *Electric Velocipede*, Spring.

———, "The Shoal," *New Jules Verne Adventures*.

Walter Jon Williams, "Solidarity," *Asimov's*, April/May.

———, "The Stickpin," *Amazon Shorts*, August 19.

Neil Williamson, "The Bunnie and the Bonobo," *Nova Scotia*.

Connie Willis, "Inside Job," *Asimov's*, January.

Robert Charles Wilson, "The Affinities," *Nature*, 28 April.

Gene Wolfe, "The Card," *Asimov's*, February.

———, "The Gunner's Mate," *F&SF*, October/November.

———, "The Vampire Kiss," *Realms of Fantasy*, April.

Jane Yolen, "A Knot of Toads," *Nova Scotia*.

———, & Midori Snyder, "Except the Queen," *The Fair Folk*.

Jim Young, "The Pitiless Stars," *F&SF*, July.